THE

WAVERLEY NOVELS

BY

SIR WALTER SCOTT, BART.

The Abbot
Woodstock

NEW YORK
THOMAS Y. CROWELL & COMPANY
PUBLISHERS

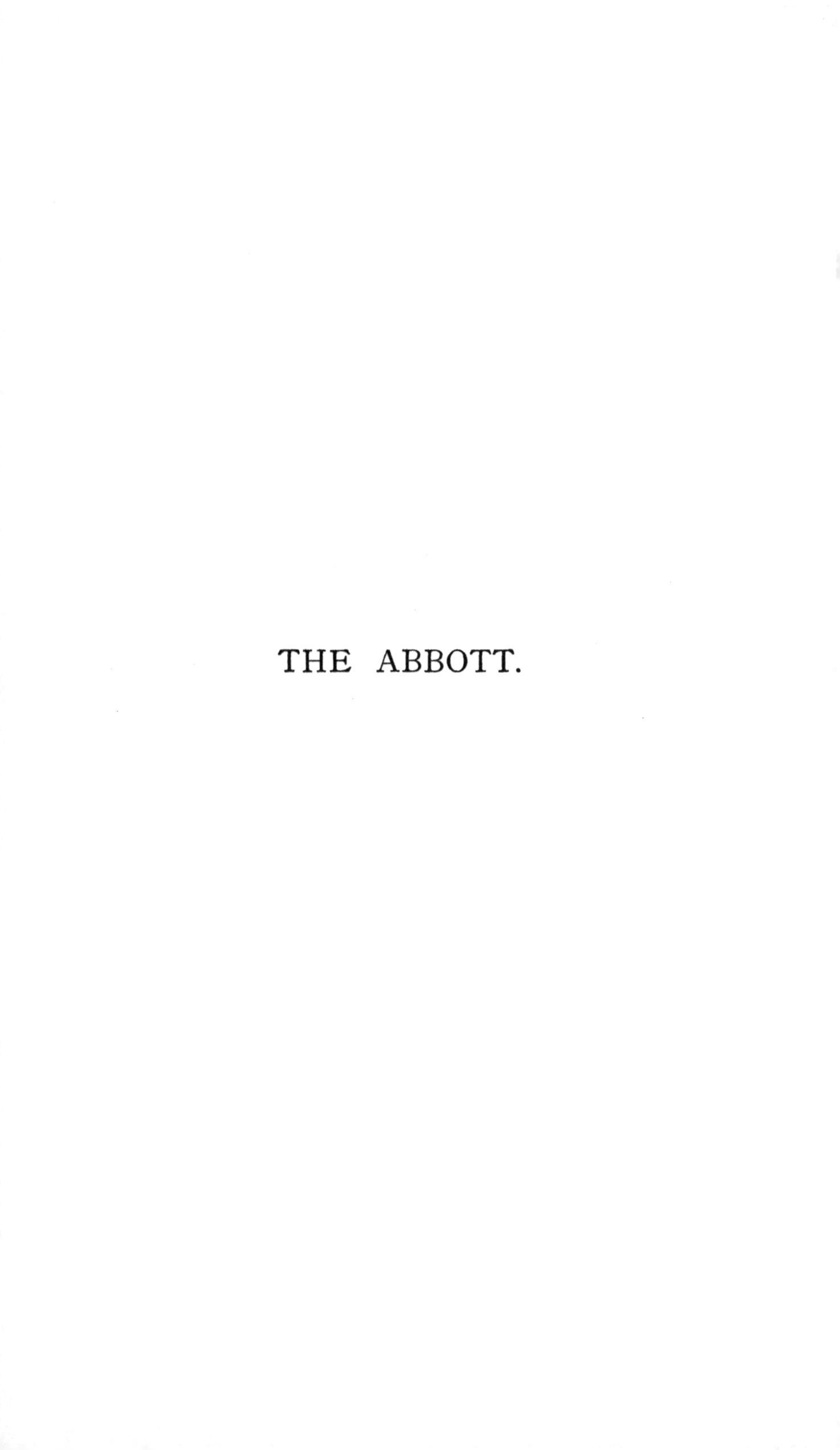

THE ABBOTT.

INTRODUCTION TO THE ABBOT

From what is said in the Introduction to the *Monastery*, it must necessarily be inferred that the Author considered that romance as something very like a failure. It is true, the booksellers did not complain of the sale, because, unless on very felicitous occasions, or on those which are equally the reverse, literary popularity is not gained or lost by a single publication. Leisure must be allowed for the tide both to flow and ebb. But I was conscious that, in my situation, not to advance was in some degree to recede, and being naturally unwilling to think that the principle of decay lay in myself, I was at least desirous to know of a certainty whether the degree of discountenance which I had incurred was now owing to an ill-managed story or an ill-chosen subject.

I was never, I confess, one of those who are willing to suppose the brains of an author to be a kind of milk, which will not stand above a single creaming, and who are eternally harping to young authors to husband their efforts, and to be chary of their reputation, lest it grow hackneyed in the eyes of men. Perhaps I was, and have always been, the more indifferent to the degree of estimation in which I might be held as an author because I did not put so high a value as many others upon what is termed literary reputation in the abstract, or at least upon the species of popularity which had fallen to my share; for though it were worse than affectation to deny that my vanity was satisfied at my success in the department in which chance had in some measure enlisted me, I was, nevertheless, far from thinking that the novelist or romance-writer stands high in the ranks of literature. But I spare the reader farther egotism on this subject, as I have expressed my opinion very fully in the Introductory Epistle to the *Fortunes of Nigel*, and, although it be composed in an imaginary character, it is as sincere and candid as if it had been written "without my gown and band."

In a word, when I considered myself as having been unsuccessful in the *Monastery*, I was tempted to try whether

I could not restore, even at the risk of totally losing my so-called reputation by a new hazard. I looked round my library, and could not but observe that, from the time of Chaucer to that of Byron, the most popular authors had been the most prolific. Even the aristarch Johnson allowed that the quality of readiness and profusion had a merit in itself, independent of the intrinsic value of the composition. Talking of Churchill, I believe, who had little merit in his prejudiced eyes, he allowed him that of fertility, with some such qualification as this—"A crab-apple can bear but crabs after all; but there is a great difference in favor of that which bears a large quantity of fruit, however indifferent, and that which produces only a few."

Looking more attentively at the patriarchs of literature, whose career was as long as it was brilliant, I thought I perceived that in the busy and prolonged course of exertion there were no doubt occasional failures, but that still those who were favorites of their age triumphed over these miscarriages. By the new efforts which they made, their errors were obliterated, they became identified with the literature of their country, and after having long received law from the critics, came in some degree to impose it. And when such a writer was at length called from the scene, his death first made the public sensible what a large share he had occupied in their attention. I recollected a passage in Grimm's *Correspondence*, that, while the unexhausted Voltaire sent forth tract after tract, to the very close of a long life, the first impression made by each as it appeared was that it was inferior to its predecessor—an opinion adopted from the general idea that the Patriarch of Ferney must at last find the point from which he was to decline. But the opinion of the public finally ranked in succession the last of Voltaire's *Essays* on the same footing with those which had formerly charmed the French nation. The inference from this and similar facts seemed to me to be that new works were often judged of by the public, not so much from their own intrinsic merit, as from extrinsic ideas which readers had previously formed with regard to them, and over which a writer might hope to triumph by patience and by exertion. There is a risk in the attempt:

If he fall in, good-night, or sink or swim.

But this is a chance incident to every literary attempt, and by which men of a sanguine temper are little moved.

I may illustrate what I mean by the feelings of most men in traveling. If we have found any stage particularly tedious or in an especial degree interesting, particularly short or much longer than we expected, our imaginations are so apt to exaggerate the original impression that, on repeating the journey, we usually find that we have considerably overrated the predominating quality, and the road appears to be duller or more pleasant, shorter or more tedious, than what we expected, and, consequently, than what is the actual case. It requires a third or fourth journey to enable us to form an accurate judgment of its beauty, its length, or its other attributes.

In the same manner, the public, judging of a new work, which it receives perhaps with little expectation, if surprised into applause, becomes very often ecstatic, gives a great deal more approbation than is due, and elevates the child of its immediate favor to a rank which, as it affects the author, it is equally difficult to keep and painful to lose. If, on this occasion, the author trembles at the height to which he is raised, and becomes afraid of the shadow of his own renown, he may indeed retire from the lottery with the prize which he has drawn, but, in future ages, his honor will be only in proportion to his labors. If, on the contrary, he rushes again into the lists, he is sure to be judged with severity proportioned to the former favor of the public. If he be daunted by a bad reception on this second occasion, he may again become a stranger to the arena. If, on the contrary, he can keep his ground, and stand the shuttlecock's fate, of being struck up and down, he will probably, at length, hold with some certainty the level in public opinion which he may be found to deserve; and he may perhaps boast of arresting the general attention, in the same manner as the Bachelor Samson Carrasco of fixing the weathercock La Giralda of Seville for weeks, months, or years, that is, for as long as the wind shall uniformly blow from one quarter. To this degree of popularity the Author had the hardihood to aspire, while, in order to attain it, he assumed the daring resolution to keep himself in the view of the public by frequent appearances before them.

It must be added, that the Author's incognito gave him the greater courage to renew his attempts to please the public, and an advantage similar to that which Jack the Giant-killer received from his coat of darkness. In sending the *Abbot* forth so soon after the *Monastery*, he had used the well-known practise recommended by Bassanio:

In my school-days, when I had lost one shaft,
I shot another of the self-same flight,
The self-same way, with more advised watch,
To find the other forth.

And, to continue the simile, his shafts, like those of the Lesser Ajax, were discharged more readily that the archer was as inaccessible to criticism, personally speaking, as the Grecian archer under his brother's sevenfold shield.

Should the reader desire to know upon what principles the *Abbot* was expected to amend the fortune of the *Monastery*, I have first to request his attention to the Introductory Epistle addressed to the imaginary Captain Clutterbuck —a mode by which, like his predecessors in this walk of fiction, the real Author makes one of his *dramatis personæ* the means of communicating his own sentiments to the public, somewhat more artificially than by a direct address to the readers. A pleasing French writer of fairy tales, Monsieur Pajon, author of the *History of Prince Soly*, has set a diverting example of the same machinery, where he introduces the presiding Genius of the land of Romance conversing with one of the personages of the tale.

In this Introductory Epistle, the Author communicates, in confidence, to Captain Clutterbuck his sense that the White Lady had not met the taste of the times, and his reason for withdrawing her from the scene. The Author did not deem it equally necessary to be candid respecting another alteration. The *Monastery* was designed, at first, to have contained some supernatural agency, arising out of the fact that Melrose had been the place of deposit of the great Robert Bruce's heart. The writer shrunk, however, from filling up, in this particular, the sketch as it was originally traced; nor did he venture to resume, in the continuation, the subject which he had left unattempted in the original work. Thus, the incident of the discovery of the heart, which occupies the greater part of the Introduction to the *Monastery*, is a mystery unnecessarily introduced, and which remains at last very imperfectly explained. In this particular, I was happy to shroud myself by the example of the author of *Caleb Williams*, who never condescends to inform us of the actual contents of that iron chest which makes such a figure in his interesting work, and gives the name to Mr. Colman's drama.

The public had some claim to inquire into this matter, but it seemed indifferent policy in the Author to give the explanation. For, whatever praise may be due to the ingenuity which brings to a general combination all the loose threads of a narrative, like the knitter at the finishing of her stocking, I am greatly deceived if in many cases a superior advantage is not attained by the air of reality which the deficiency of explanation attaches to a work written on a different system. In life itself, many things befall every mortal of which the individual never knows the real cause or origin: and were we to point out the most marked distinction between a real and a fictitious narrative, we would say, that the former, in reference to the remote causes of the events it relates, is obscure, doubtful, and mysterious; whereas, in the latter case, it is a part of the author's duty to afford satisfactory details upon the causes of the separate events he has recorded, and, in a word, to account for everything. The reader, like Mungo in the *Padlock*, will not be satisfied with hearing what he is not made fully to comprehend.

I omitted, therefore, in the Introduction to the *Abbot*, any attempt to explain the previous story or to apologize for unintelligibility.

Neither would it have been prudent to have endeavored to proclaim, in the Introduction to the *Abbot*, the real spring by which I hoped it might attract a greater degree of interest than its immediate predecessor. A taking title, or the announcement of a popular subject, is a recipe for success much in favor with booksellers, but which authors will not always find efficacious. The cause is worth a moment's examination.

There occur in every country some peculiar historical characters, which are, like a spell or a charm, sovereign to excite curiosity and attract attention, since every one in the slightest degree interested in the land which they belong to has heard much of them, and longs to hear more. A tale turning on the fortunes of Alfred or Elizabeth in England, or Wallace or Bruce in Scotland, is sure by the very announcement to excite public curiosity to a considerable degree and ensure the publisher's being relieved of the greater part of an impression, even before the contents of the work are known. This is of the last importance to the bookseller, who is at once to use a technical phrase, "brought home," all his outlay being repaid. But it is a different case with the author, since it cannot be denied that we are apt to feel least satisfied with the works of which we have been induced, by titles and laudatory advertisements, to entertain exaggerated expectation. The intention of the work has been anticipated, and misconceived or misrepresented, and although the difficulty of executing the work again reminds us of Hotspur's task of "o'erwalking a current roaring loud," yet the adventurer must look for more ridicule if he fails than applause if he executes his undertaking.

Notwithstanding a risk which should make authors pause ere they adopt a theme which, exciting general interest and curiosity, is often the preparative for disappointment, yet it would be an injudicious regulation which should deter the poet or painter from attempting to introduce historical portraits merely from the difficulty of executing the task in a satisfactory manner. Something must be trusted to the generous impulse, which often thrusts an artist upon feats of which he knows the difficulty, while he trusts courage and exertion may afford the means of surmounting it.

It is especially when he is sensible of losing ground with the public that an author may be justified in using with address such selection of subject or title as is most likely to procure a rehearing. It was with these feelings of hope and apprehension that I ventured to awaken, in a work of fiction, the memory of Queen Mary, so interesting by her wit, her beauty, her misfortunes, and the mystery which still does, and probably always will, overhang her history. In doing so, I was aware that failure would be a conclusive disaster, so that my task was something like that of an enchanter who raises a spirit over whom he is uncertain of possessing an effectual control; and I naturally paid attention to such principles of composition as I conceived were best suited to the historical novel.

Enough has been already said to explain the purpose of composing the *Abbot*. The historical references are, as usual, explained in the notes. That which relates to Queen Mary's escape from Lochleven Castle is a more minute account of that romantic adventure than is to be found in the histories of the period.

ABBOTSFORD, 1*st January*, 1831.

INTRODUCTORY EPISTLE

FROM

THE AUTHOR OF *WAVERLEY*

TO

CAPTAIN CLUTTERBUCK,

OF HIS MAJESTY'S —— REGIMENT OF INFANTRY

DEAR CAPTAIN—

I am sorry to observe, by your last favor, that you disapprove of the numerous retrenchments and alterations which I have been under the necessity of making on the Manuscript of your friend, the Benedictine, and I willingly make you the medium of apology to many who have honored me more than I deserve.

I admit that my retrenchments have been numerous, and leave gaps in the story, which, in your original manuscript, would have run well-nigh to a fourth volume, as my printer assures me. I am sensible besides, that, in consequence of the liberty of curtailment you have allowed me, some parts of the story have been huddled up without the necessary details. But, after all, it is better that the travelers should have to step over a ditch than to wade through a morass: that the reader should have to suppose what may easily be inferred than be obliged to creep through pages of dull explanation. I have struck out, for example, the whole machinery of the White Lady, and the poetry by which it is so ably-supported in the original manuscript. But you must allow that the public taste gives little encouragement to those legendary superstitions which formed alternately the delight and the terror of our predecessors. In like manner, much is omitted illustrative of the impulse of enthusiasm in favor of the ancient religion in Mother Magdalen and the abbot. But we do not feel deep sympathy at this period with what was once the most powerful and animating principle in Europe, with the exception of that of the Reformation, by which it was successfully opposed.

You rightly observe that these retrenchments have rendered the title no longer applicable to the subject, and that some other would have been more suitable to the work in its present state than that of the abbot, who made so much greater figure in the original, and for whom your friend, the Benedictine, seems to have inspired you with a sympathetic respect. I must plead guilty to this accusation, observing, at the same time, in manner of extenuation, that though the objection might have been easily removed by giving a new title to the work, yet, in doing so, I should have destroyed the necessary cohesion between the present history and its predecessor the *Monastery*, which I was unwilling to do, as the period and several of the personages were the same.

After all, my good friend, it is of little consequence what the work is called, or on what interest it turns, provided it catches the public attention; for the quality of the wine, could we but insure it, may according to the old proverb, render the bush unnecessary or of little consequence.

I congratulate you upon your having found it consistent with prudence to establish your tilbury, and approve of the color, and of your boy's livery (subdued green and pink). As you talk of completing your descriptive poem on the *Ruins of Kennaquhair, with Notes by an Antiquary*, I hope you have procured a steady horse.

I remain, with compliments to all friends, dear Captain, very much

Yours, etc. etc. etc.,

THE AUTHOR OF *WAVERLEY*.

THE ABBOT

CHAPTER I

Domum mansit, lanam fecit.
ANCIENT ROMAN EPITAPH.

She keepit close the hous, and birlit at the quhele.
GAWAIN DOUGLAS.

THE time which passes over our heads so imperceptibly makes the same gradual change in habits, manners, and character as in personal appearance. At the revolution of every five years we find ourselves another, and yet the same: there is a change of views, and no less of the light in which we regard them, a change of motives as well as of actions. Nearly twice that space had glided away over the head of Halbert Glendinning and his lady betwixt the period of our former narrative, in which they played a distinguished part, and the date at which our present tale commences.

Two circumstances only had embittered their union, which was otherwise as happy as mutual affection could render it. The first of these was indeed the common calamity of Scotland, being the distracted state of that unhappy country, where every man's sword was directed against his neighbor's bosom. Glendinning had proved what Murray expected of him, a steady friend, strong in battle and wise in council, adhering to him, from motives of gratitude, in situations where by his own unbiassed will he would either have stood neuter or have joined the opposite party. Hence, when danger was near—and it was seldom far distant—Sir Halbert Glendinning, for he now bore the rank of knighthood, was perpetually summoned to attend his patron on distant expeditions, or on perilous enterprises, or to assist him with his counsel in the doubtful intrigues of a half barbarous court. He was thus frequently, and for a long space, absent from his castle and from his lady; and to this ground of regret we must add, that their union had not been blessed with children, to occupy the attention of the Lady of Avenel while she was thus deprived of her husband's domestic society.

On such occasions she lived almost entirely secluded from the world, within the walls of her paternal mansion. Visiting amongst neighbors was a matter entirely out of the question, unless on occasions of solemn festival, and then it was chiefly confined to near kindred. Of these the Lady of Avenel had none who survived, and the dames of the neighboring barons affected to regard her less as the heiress of the house of Avenel than as the wife of a peasant, the son of a church-vassal, raised up to mushroom eminence by the capricious favor of Murray.

This pride of ancestry, which rankled in the bosom of the ancient gentry, was more openly expressed by their ladies, and was, moreover, embittered not a little by the political feuds of the time, for most of the Southron chiefs were friends to the authority of the Queen, and very jealous of the power of Murray. The Castle of Avenel was, therefore, on all these accounts, as melancholy and solitary a residence for its lady as could well be imagined. Still it had the essential recommendation of great security. The reader is already aware that the fortress was built upon an islet in a small lake, and was only accessible by a causeway, intersected by a double ditch, defended by two drawbridges, so that, without artillery, it might in those days be considered as impregnable. It was only necessary, therefore, to secure against surprise, and the service of six able men within the castle was sufficient for that purpose. If more serious danger threatened, an ample garrison was supplied by the male inhabitants of a little hamlet which, under the auspices of Halbert Glendinning, had arisen on a small piece of level ground, betwixt the lake and the hill, nearly adjoining to the spot where the causeway joined the mainland. The Lord of Avenel had found it an easy matter to procure inhabitants, as he was not only a kind and beneficent overlord, but well qualified, both by his experience in arms, his high character for wisdom and integrity, and his favor with the powerful Earl of Murray, to protect and defend those who dwelt under his banner. In leaving his castle for any length of time, he had, therefore, the consolation to reflect that this village afforded, on the slightest notice, a band of thirty stout men, which was more than sufficient for its defense; while the families of the villagers, as was usual on such occasions, fled to the recesses of the mountains, drove their cattle to the same places of shelter, and left the enemy to work their will on their miserable cottages.

One guest only resided generally, if not constantly, at

the Castle of Avenel. This was Henry Warden, who now felt himself less able for the stormy task imposed on the Reforming clergy; and having by his zeal given personal offense to many of the leading nobles and chiefs, did not consider himself as perfectly safe unless when within the walls of the strong mansion of some assured friend. He ceased not, however, to serve his cause as eagerly with his pen as he had formerly done with his tongue, and had engaged in a furious and acrimonious contest concerning the sacrifice of the mass, as it was termed, with the Abbot Eustatius, formerly the sub-prior of Kennaquhair. Answers, replies, duplies, triplies, quadruplies followed thick upon each other, and displayed, as is not unusual in controversy, fully as much zeal as Christian charity. The disputation very soon became as celebrated as that of John Knox and the Abbot of Crossraguel, raged nearly as fiercely, and, for aught I know, the publications to which it gave rise may be as precious in the eyes of bibliographers.* But the engrossing nature of his occupation rendered the theologian not the most interesting companion for a solitary female; and his grave, stern, and absorbed deportment, which seldom showed any interest except in that which concerned his religious profession, made his presence rather add to than diminish the gloom which hung over the Castle of Avenel. To superintend the tasks of numerous female domestics was the principal part of the lady's daily employment; her spindle and distaff, her Bible, and a solitary walk upon the battlements of the castle, or upon the causeway, or occasionally, but more seldom, upon the banks of the little lake, consumed the rest of the day. But so great was the insecurity of the period that, when she ventured to extend her walk beyond the hamlet, the warder on the watch-tower was directed to keep a sharp lookout in every direction, and four or five men held themselves in readiness to mount and sally forth from the castle on the slightest appearance of alarm.

Thus stood affairs at the castle, when, after an absence of several weeks, the Knight of Avenel, which was now the title most frequently given to Sir Halbert Glendinning, was daily expected to return home. Day after day, however, passed away, and he returned not. Letters in those days

* The tracts which appeared in the disputation between the Scottish Reformer and Quentin Kennedy, Abbot of Crossraguel, are among the scarcest in Scottish bibliography. See M'Crie's *Life of Knox*, p. 258.

were rarely written, and the knight must have resorted to a secretary to express his intentions in that manner; besides, intercourse of all kinds was precarious and unsafe, and no man cared to give any public intimation of the time and direction of a journey, since, if his route were publicly known, it was always likely he might, in that case meet with more enemies than friends upon the road. The precise day, therefore, of Sir Halbert's return was not fixed, but that which his lady's fond expectation had calculated upon in her own mind had long since passed, and hope delayed began to make the heart sick.

It was upon the evening of a sultry summer's day, when the sun was half-sunk behind the distant western mountains of Liddesdale, that the lady took her solitary walk on the battlements of a range of buildings, which formed the front of the castle, where a flat roof of flagstones presented a broad and convenient promenade. The level surface of the lake, undisturbed except by the occasional dipping of a teal-duck or coot, was gilded with the beams of the setting luminary, and reflected, as if in a golden mirror, the hills amongst which it lay embosomed. The scene, otherwise so lonely, was occasionally enlivened by the voices of the children in the village, which, softened by distance, reached the ear of the lady in her solitary walk, or by the distant call of the herdsman, as he guided his cattle from the glen in which they had pastured all day, to place them in greater security for the night in the immediate vicinity of the village. The deep lowing of the cows seemed to demand the attendance of the milk-maidens, who, singing shrilly and merrily, strolled forth, each with her pail on her head, to attend to the duty of the evening. The Lady of Avenel looked and listened; the sounds which she heard reminded her of former days, when her most important employment, as well as her greatest delight, was to assist Dame Glendinning and Tibb Tacket in milking the cows at Glendearg. The thought was fraught with melancholy.

"Why was I not," she said, "the peasant girl which in all men's eyes I seemed to be! Halbert and I had then spent our life peacefully in his native glen, undisturbed by the phantoms either of fear or ambition. His greatest pride had then been to show the fairest herd in the halidome; his greatest danger to repel some pilfering snatcher from the Border; and the utmost distance which would have divided us would have been the chase of some out-lying deer. But, alas! what avails the blood which Halbert has shed, and the dangers which he encounters, to support a name and rank, dear to him because he has it from me, but which we shall never transmit to our posterity? With me the name of Avenel must expire."

She sighed as these reflections arose, and, looking towards the shore of the lake, her eye was attracted by a group of children of various ages, assembled to see a little ship, constructed by some village artist, perform its first voyage on the water. It was launched amid the shouts of tiny voices and the clapping of little hands, and shot bravely forth on its voyage with a favoring wind, which promised to carry it to the other side of the lake. Some of the bigger boys ran round to receive and secure it on the farther shore, trying their speed against each other as they sprang like young fawns along the shingly verge of the lake. The rest, for whom such a journey seemed too arduous, remained watching the motions of the fairy vessel from the spot where it had been launched. The sight of their sports pressed on the mind of the childless Lady of Avenel.

"Why are none of these prattlers mine?" she continued, pursuing the tenor of her melancholy reflections. "Their parents can scarce find them the coarsest food; and I, who could nurse them in plenty—I am doomed never to hear a child call me mother!"

The thought sunk on her heart with a bitterness which resembled envy, so deeply is the desire of offspring implanted in the female breast. She pressed her hands together as if she were wringing them in the extremity of her desolate feeling, as one whom Heaven had written childless. A large staghound of the greyhound species approached at this moment, and, attracted perhaps by the gesture, licked her hands and pressed his large head against them. He obtained the desired caress in return, but still the sad impression remained.

"Wolf," she said, as if the animal could have understood her complaints, "thou art a noble and beautiful animal; but, alas! the love and affection that I long to bestow is of a quality higher than can fall to thy share, though I love thee much."

And, as if she were apologizing to Wolf for withholding from him any part of her regard, she caressed his proud head and crest, while, looking in her eyes, he seemed to ask her what she wanted, or what he could do to show his attachment. At this moment a shriek of distress was heard on the shore, from the playful group which had been lately so jovial. The lady looked, and saw the cause with great agony.

The little ship, the object of the children's delighted attention, had struck among some tufts of the plant which bears the water-lily, that marked a shoal in the lake about an arrow-flight from the shore. A hardy little boy, who had taken the lead in the race round the margin of the lake, did not hesitate a moment to strip off his "wylie-coat," plunge into the water, and swim towards the object of their common solicitude. The first movement of the lady was to call for help; but she observed that the boy swam strongly and fearlessly, and as she saw that one or two villagers, who were distant spectators of the incident, seemed to give themselves no uneasiness on his account, she supposed that he was accustomed to the exercise, and that there was no danger. But whether, in swimming, the boy had struck his breast against a sunken rock, or whether he was suddenly taken with cramp, or whether he had over-calculated his own strength, it so happened that, when he had disembarrassed the little plaything from the flags in which it was entangled and sent it forward on its course, he had scarce swam a few yards in his way to the shore, when he raised himself suddenly from the water and screamed aloud, clapping his hands at the same time with an expression of fear and pain.

The Lady of Avenel, instantly taking the alarm, called hastily to the attendants to get the boat ready. But this was an affair of some time. The only boat permitted to be used on the lake was moored within the second cut which intersected the canal, and it was several minutes ere it could be unmoored and got under way. Meantime, the Lady of Avenel, with agonizing anxiety, saw that the efforts which the poor boy made to keep himself afloat were now exchanged for a faint struggling, which would soon have been over, but for aid equally prompt and unhoped-for. Wolf, who, like some of that large species of greyhound, was a practised water-dog, had marked the object of her anxiety, and, quitting his mistress's side, had sought the nearest point from which he could with safety plunge into the lake. With the wonderful instinct which these noble animals have so often displayed in the like circumstances, he swam straight to the spot where his assistance was so much wanted, and seizing the child's under-dress in his mouth, he not only kept him afloat, but towed him towards the causeway. The boat, having put off with a couple of men, met the dog half-way, and relieved him of his burden. They landed on the causeway, close by the gate of the castle, with their yet lifeless charge, and were there met by the Lady of Avenel, attended by one or two of her maidens, eagerly waiting to administer assistance to the sufferer.

He was borne into the castle, deposited upon a bed, and every mode of recovery resorted to which the knowledge of the times, and the skill of Henry Warden, who professed some medical science, could dictate. For some time it was all in vain, and the lady watched with unspeakable earnestness the pallid countenance of the beautiful child. He seemed about ten years old. His dress was of the meanest sort; but his long curled hair, and the noble cast of his features, partook not of that poverty of appearance. The proudest noble in Scotland might have been yet prouder could he have called that child his heir. While, with breathless anxiety, the Lady of Avenel gazed on his well-formed and expressive features, a slight shade of color returned gradually to the cheek; suspended animation became restored by degrees, the child sighed deeply, opened his eyes, which to the human countenance produces the effect of light upon the natural landscape, stretched his arms toward the lady, and muttered the word "Mother"—that epithet of all others which is dearest to the female ear.

"God, madam," said the preacher, "has restored the child to your wishes; it must be yours so to bring him up that he may not one day wish that he had perished in his innocence."

"It shall be my charge," said the lady; and again throwing her arms around the boy, she overwhelmed him with kisses and caresses, so much was she agitated by the terror arising from the danger in which he had been just placed, and by joy at his unexpected deliverance.

"But you are not my mother," said the boy, recovering his recollection, and endeavoring, though faintly, to escape from the caresses of the Lady of Avenel—"you are not my mother. Alas! I have no mother—only I have dreamed that I have one."

"I will read the dream for you, my love," answered the Lady of Avenel; "and I will be myself your mother. Surely God has heard my wishes, and in his own marvelous manner hath sent me an object on which my affections may expand themselves." She looked toward Warden as she spoke. The preacher hesitated what he should reply to a burst of passionate feeling which, perhaps, seemed to him more enthusiastic than the occasion demanded. In the mean while, the large staghound, Wolf, which, dripping wet as he was, had followed his mistress into the apartment, and had sate by the bedside, a patient and quiet spectator of all the means used for resuscitation of the being whom he had preserved, now became impatient of remaining any longer unnoticed, and began to, whine and fawn upon the lady with his great rough paws.

"Yes," she said, "good Wolf, and you shall be remembered also for your day's work; and I will think the more of you for having preserved the life of a creature so beautiful."

But Wolf was not quite satisfied with the share of attention which he thus attracted: he persisted in whining and pawing upon his mistress, his caresses rendered still more troublesome by his long shaggy hair being so much and thoroughly wetted, till she desired one of the domestics with whom he was familiar, to call the animal out of the apartment. Wolf resisted every invitation to this purpose, until his mistress positively commanded him to begone in an angry tone; when turning towards the bed on which the boy still lay, half-awake to sensation, half-drowned in the meanders of a fluctuating delirum, he uttered a deep and savage growl, curled up his nose and lips, showing his full range of white and sharpened teeth, which might have matched those of an actual wolf, and then, turning round, sullenly followed the domestic out of the apartment.

"It is singular," said the lady, addressing Warden; "the animal is not only so good-natured to all, but so particularly fond of children. What can ail him at the little fellow whose life he has saved?"

"Dogs," replied the preacher, "are but too like the human race in their foibles, though their instinct be less erring than the reason of poor mortal man when relying upon his own unassisted powers. Jealousy, my good lady, is a passion not unknown to them, and they often evince it, not only with respect to the preferences which they see given by their masters to individuals of their own species, but even when their rivals are children. You have caressed that child much and eagerly, and the dog considers himself as a discarded favorite."

"It is a strange instinct," said the lady; "and from the gravity with which you mention it, my reverend friend, I would almost say that you supposed this singular jealousy of my favorite, Wolf, was not only well founded but justifiable. But perhaps you speak in jest?"

"I seldom jest," answered the preacher; "life was not lent to us to be expended in that idle mirth which resembles the crackling of thorns under the pot. I would only have you derive, if it so please you, this lesson from what I have said, that the best of our feelings, when indulged to excess, may give pain to others. There is but one in which we may indulge to the utmost limit of vehemence of which our bosom is capable, secure that excess cannot exist in the greatest intensity to which it can be excited: I mean the love of our Maker."

"Surely," said the Lady of Avenel, "we are commanded by the same authority to love our neighbor?"

"Ay, madam," said Warden, "but our love to God is to be unbounded; we are to love Him with our whole heart, our whole soul, and our whole strength. The love which the precept commands us to bear to our neighbor has affixed to it a direct limit and qualification: we are to love our neighbor as ourself; as it is elsewhere explained by the great commandment, that we must do unto him as we would that he should do unto us. Here there is a limit and a bound even to the most praiseworthy of our affections, so far as they are turned upon sublunary and terrestrial objects. We are to render to our neighbor, whatever be his rank or degree, that corresponding portion of affection with which we could rationally expect we should ourselves be regarded by those standing in the same relation to us. Hence, neither husband nor wife, neither son nor daughter, neither friend nor relation, are lawfully to be made the objects of our idolatry. The Lord our God is a jealous God, and will not endure that we bestow on the creature that extremity of devotion which He who made us demands as His own share. I say to you, lady, that even in the fairest and purest and most honorable feelings of our nature there is that original taint of sin which ought to make us pause and hesitate ere we indulge them to excess."

"I understand not this, reverend sir," said the lady; "nor do I guess what I can have now said or done to draw down on me an admonition which has something a taste of reproof."

"Lady," said Warden, "I crave your pardon if I have urged aught beyond the limits of my duty. But consider whether, in the sacred promise to be not only a protectress but a mother to this poor child, your purpose may meet the wishes of the noble knight your husband. The fondness which you have lavished on the unfortunate, and, I own, most lovely, child has met something like a reproof in the bearing of your household dog. Displease not your noble husband. Men, as well as animals, are jealous of the affections of those they love."

"This is too much, reverend sir," said the Lady of Avenel, greatly offended. "You have been long our guest, and have received from the Knight of Avenel and myself that honor and regard which your character and profession so justly demand. But I am yet to learn that we have at any time authorized your interference in our family arrangements, or placed you as a judge of our conduct towards each other. I pray this may be forborne in future."

"Lady," replied the preacher, with the boldness peculiar to the clergy of his persuasion at that time, "when you weary of my admonitions, when I see that my services are no longer acceptable to you and the noble knight your husband, I shall know that my Master wills me no longer to abide here; and, praying for a continuance of His best blessings on your family, I will then, were the season the depth of winter, and the hour midnight, walk out on yonder waste, and travel forth through these wild mountains, as lonely and unaided, though far more helpless, than when I first met your husband in the valley of Glendearg. But while I remain here, I will not see you err from the true path, no, not a hair's-breadth, without making the old man's voice and remonstrance heard."

"Nay, but," said the lady, who both loved and respected the good man, though sometimes a little offended at what she conceived to be an exuberant degree of zeal, "we will not part this way, my good friend. Women are quick and hasty in their feelings; but, believe me, my wishes and my purposes towards this child are such as both my husband and you will approve of."

The clergyman bowed, and retreated to his own apartment.

CHAPTER II

How steadfastly he fix'd his eyes on me—
His dark eyes shining through forgotten tears—
Then stretch'd his little arms, and call'd me mother!
What could I do? I took the bantling home;
I could not tell the imp he had no mother.

Count Basil.

WHEN Warden had left the apartment, the Lady of Avenel gave way to the feelings of tenderness which the sight of the boy, his sudden danger, and his recent escape had inspired; and no longer awed by the sternness, as she deemed it, of the preacher, heaped with caresses the lovely and interesting child. He was now in some measure recovered from the consequences of his accident, and received passively, though not without wonder, the tokens of kindness with which he was thus loaded. The face of the lady was strange to him, and her dress different and far more sumptuous than any he remembered. But the boy was naturally of an undaunted temper; and indeed children are generally acute physiognomists, and not only pleased by that which is beautiful in itself, but peculiarly quick in distinguishing and replying to the attentions of those who really love them. If they see a person in company, though a perfect stranger, who is by nature fond of children, the little imps seem to discover it by a sort of freemasonry, while the awkward attempts of those who make advances to them for the purpose of recommending themselves to the parents usually fail in attracting their reciprocal attention The little, boy therefore, appeared in some degree sensible of the lady's caresses, and it was with difficulty she withdrew herself from his pillow to afford him leisure for necessary repose.

"To whom belongs our little rescued varlet?" was the first question which the Lady of Avenel put to her handmaiden Lilias, when they had retired to the hall.

"To an old woman in the hamlet," said Lilias, "who is even now come so far as the porter's lodge to inquire concerning his safety. Is it your pleasure that she be admitted?"

"Is it my pleasure!" said the Lady of Avenel, echoing the question with a strong accent of displeasure and surprise; "can you make any doubt of it? What woman but must pity the agony of the mother whose heart is throbbig for the safety of a child so lovely!"

"Nay, but, madam," said Lilias, "this woman is too old to be the mother of the child; I rather think she must be his grandmother, or some more distant relation."

"Be she who she will, Lilias," replied the lady, "she must have an aching heart while the safety of a creature so lovely is uncertain. Go instantly and bring her hither. Besides, I would willingly learn something concerning his birth."

Lilias left the hall, and presently afterwards returned, ushering in a tall female very poorly dressed, yet with more pretension to decency and cleanliness than was usually combined with such coarse garments. The Lady of Avenel knew her figure the instant she presented herself. It was the fashion of the family that, upon every Sabbath, and on two evenings in the week besides, Henry Warden preached or lectured in the chapel at the castle. The extension of the Protestant faith was, upon principle, as well as in good policy, a primary object with the Knight of Avenel. The inhabitants of the village were therefore invited to attend upon the instructions of Henry Warden, and many of them were speedily won to the doctrine which their master and protector approved. These sermons, homilies, and lectures had made a great impression on the mind of the Abbot Eustace, or Eustatius, and were a sufficient spur to the severity and sharpness of his controversy with his old fellow-collegiate; and, ere Queen Mary was dethroned, and while the Catholics still had considerable authority in the Border provinces, he more than once threatened to levy his vassals, and assail and level with the earth that stronghold of heresy, the Castle of Avenel. But notwithstanding the abbot's impotent resentment, and notwithstanding also the disinclination of the country to favor the new religion, Henry Warden proceeded without remission in his labors, and made weekly converts from the faith of Rome to that of the Reformed church. Amongst those who gave most earnest and constant attendance on his ministry was the aged woman, whose form, tall, and otherwise too remarkable to be forgotten, the lady had of late observed frequently as being conspicuous amongst the little audience. She had indeed more than once desired to know who that stately-looking woman was, whose appearance was so much above the poverty of her vestments. But the reply had always been that she was an Englishwoman, who was tarrying for a season at the hamlet, and that no one knew more concerning her. She now asked her after her name and birth.

"Magdalen Græme is my name," said the woman; "I come of the Græmes of Heathergill, in Nicol Forest, a people of ancient blood."

"And what make you," continued the lady, "so far distant from your home?"

"I have no home," said Magdalen Græme: "it was burned by your Border riders; my husband and my son were slain; there is not a drop's blood left in the veins of any one which is of kin to mine."

"That is no uncommon fate in these wild times, and in this unsettled land," said the lady; "the English hands have been as deeply dyed in our blood as ever those of Scotsmen have been in yours."

"You have right to say it, lady," answered Magdalen Græme; "for men tell of a time when this castle was not strong enough to save your father's life, or to afford your mother and her infant a place of refuge. And why ask ye me, then, wherefore I dwell not in mine own home, and with mine own people?"

"It was indeed an idle question," answered the lady, "where misery so often makes wanderers; but wherefore take refuge in a hostile country?"

"My neighbors were Popish and mass-mongers," said the old woman; "it has pleased Heaven to give me a clearer sight of the Gospel, and I have tarried here to enjoy the ministry of that worthy man Henry Warden, who, to the praise and comfort of many, teacheth the Evangel in truth and in sincerity."

"Are you poor?" again demanded the Lady of Avenel.

"You hear me ask alms of no one," answered the Englishwoman.

Here there was a pause. The manner of the woman was if not disrespectful, at least much less than gracious; and she appeared to give no encouragement to farther communication. The Lady of Avenel renewed the conversation on a different topic.

"You have heard of the danger in which your boy has been placed?"

"I have, lady, and how by an especial providence he was

rescued from death. May Heaven make him thankful, and me!"

"What relation do you bear to him?"

"I am his grandmother, lady, if it so please you; the only relation he hath left upon earth to take charge of him."

"The burden of his maintenance must necessarily be grievous to you in your deserted situation?" pursued the lady.

"I have complained of it to no one," said Magdalen Græme, with the same unmoved, dry, and unconcerned tone of voice in which she had answered all the former questions.

"If," said the Lady of Avenel, "your grandchild could be received into a noble family, would it not advantage both him and you?"

"Received into a noble family!" said the old woman, drawing herself up, and bending her brows until her forehead was wrinkled into a frown of unusual severity; "and for what purpose, I pray you?—to be my lady's page, or my lord's jack-man, to eat broken victuals, and contend with other menials for the remnants of the master's meal? Would you have him to fan the flies from my lady's face while she sleeps, to carry her train while she walks, to hand her trencher when she feeds, to ride before her on horseback, to walk after her on foot, to sing when she lists, and to be silent when she bids?—a very weathercock, which though furnished in appearance with wings and plumage, cannot soar into the air—cannot fly from the spot where it is perched, but receives all its impulses, and performs all its revolutions, obedient to the changeful breath of a vain woman? When the eagle of Helvellyn perches on the tower of Lanercost, and turns and changes his place to show how the wind sits, Roland Græme shall be what you would make him."

The woman spoke with a rapidity and vehemence which seemed to have in it a touch of insanity; and a sudden sense of the danger to which the child must necessarily be exposed in the charge of such a keeper increased the lady's desire to keep him in the castle, if possible.

"You mistake me, dame," she said, addressing the old woman in a soothing manner; "I do not wish your boy to be in attendance on myself, but upon the good knight, my husband. Were he himself the son of a belted earl, he could not better be trained to arms, and all that befits a gentleman, than by the instructions and discipline of Sir Halbert Glendinning."

"Ay," answered the old woman, in the same style of bitter irony, "I know the wages of that service—a curse when the corselet is not sufficiently brightened, a blow when the girth is not tightly drawn; to be beaten because the hounds are at fault; to be reviled because the foray is unsuccessful; to stain his hands for the master's bidding in the blood alike of beast and of man; to be a butcher of harmless deer, a murderer and defacer of God's own image, not at his own pleasure, but at that of his lord; to live a brawling ruffian, and a common stabber—exposed to heat, to cold, to want of food, to all the privations of an anchoret, not for the love of God, but for the service of Satan; to die by the gibbet, or in some obscure skirmish; to sleep out his brief life in carnal security, and to awake in the eternal fire which is never quenched."

"Nay," said the Lady of Avenel, "but to such unhallowed course of life your grandson will not be here exposed. My husband is just and kind to those who live under his banner; and you yourself well know that youth have here a strict as well as a good preceptor in the person of our chaplain."

The old woman appeared to pause.

"You have named," she said, "the only circumstance which can move me. I must soon onward, the vision has said it: I must not tarry in the same spot—I must on—I must on, it is my weird. Swear, then, that you will protect the boy as if he were your own, until I return hither and claim him, and I will consent for a space to part with him. But especially swear, he shall not lack the instruction of the godly man who hath placed the Gospel truth high above those idolatrous shavelings, the monks and friars."

"Be satisfied, dame," said the Lady of Avenel; "the boy shall have as much care as if he were born of my own blood. Will you see him now?"

"No," answered the old woman, sternly; "to part is enough. I go forth on my own mission. I will not soften my heart by useless tears and wailings, as one that is not called to a duty."

"Will you not accept of something to aid you in your pilgrimage?" said the Lady of Avenel, putting into her hand two crowns of the sun. The old woman flung them down on the table.

"Am I of the race of Cain," she said, "proud lady, that you offer me gold in exchange for my own flesh and blood?"

"I had no such meaning," said the lady, gently; "nor am I the proud woman you term me. Alas! my own fortunes might have taught me humility, even had it not been born with me."

The old woman seemed somewhat to relax her tone of severity.

"You are of gentle blood," she said, "else we had not parleyed thus long together. You are of gentle blood, and to such," she added, drawing up her tall form as she spoke, "pride is as graceful as is the plume upon the bonnet. But for these pieces of gold, lady, you must needs resume them. I need not money. I am well provided; and I may not care for myself, nor think how, or by whom, I shall be sustained. Farewell, and keep your word. Cause your gates to be opened and your bridges to be lowered. I will set forward this very night. When I come again I will demand from you a strict account, for I have left with you the jewel of my life! Sleep will visit me but in snatches, food will not refresh me, rest will not restore my strength, until I see Roland Græme. Once more, farewell."

"Make your obeisance, dame," said Lilias to Magdalen Græme, as she retired—"make your obeisance to her ladyship, and thank her for her goodness, as is but fitting and right."

The old woman turned short round on the officious waiting-maid. "Let her make her obeisance to me then, and I will return it. Why should I bend to her?—is it because her kirtle is of silk, and mine of blue lockeram? Go to, my lady's waiting-woman. Know that the rank of the man rates that of the wife, and that she who marries a churl's son, were she a king's daughter, is but a peasant's bride."

Lilias was about to reply in great indignation, but her mistress imposed silence on her, and commanded that the old woman should be safely conducted to the mainland.

"Conduct her safe!" exclaimed the incensed waiting-woman, while Magdalen Græme left the apartment; "I say, duck her in the loch, and then we will see whether she is witch or not, as everybody in the village of Lochside will say and swear. I marvel your ladyship could bear so long with her insolence."

But the commands of the lady were obeyed, and the old dame dismissed from the castle, was committed to her fortune. She kept her word, and did not long abide in that place, leaving the hamlet on the very night succeeding the interview, and wandering no one asked whither. The Lady of Avenel inquired under what circumstances she had appeared among them, but could only learn that she was believed to be the widow of some man of consequence among the Græmes who then inhabited the Debateable Land, a name given to a certain portion of territory which was the frequent subject of dispute betwixt Scotland and England; that she had suffered great wrong in some of the frequent forays by which that unfortunate district was wasted, and had been driven from her dwelling-place. She had arrived in the hamlet no one knew for what purpose, and was held by some to be a witch, by others a zealous Protestant, and by others again a Catholic devotee. Her language was mysterious, and her manners repulsive; and all that could be collected from her conversation seemed to imply that she was under the influence either of a spell or of a vow—there was no saying which, since she talked as one who acted under a powerful and external agency.

Such were the particulars which the lady's inquiries were able to collect concerning Magdalen Græme, being far too meager and contradictory to authorize any satisfactory deduction. In truth, the miseries of the time, and the various turns of fate incidental to a frontier country, were perpetually chasing from their habitations those who had not the means of defense or protection. These wanderers in the land were too often seen to excite much attention or sympathy. They received the cold relief which was extorted by general feelings of humanity; a little excited in some breasts, and perhaps rather chilled in others, by the recollection that they who gave the charity to-day might themselves want it to-morrow. Magdalen Græme, therefore, came and departed like a shadow from the neighborhood of Avenel Castle.

The boy whom Providence, as she thought, had thus strangely placed under her care, was at once established a favorite with the lady of the castle. How could it be otherwise? He became the object of those affectionate feelings which, finding formerly no object on which to expand themselves, had increased the gloom of the castle, and embittered the solitude of its mistress. To teach him reading and writing as far as her skill went, to attend to his childish comforts, to watch his boyish sports, became the lady's favorite amusement. In her circumstances, where the ear only heard the lowing of the cattle from the distant hills, or the heavy step of the warder as he walked upon his post, or the half-envied laugh of her maiden as she turned her wheel, the appearance of the blooming and beautiful boy gave an interest which can hardly be conceived by those who live amid gayer or busier scenes. Young Roland was to the Lady of Avenel what the flower which occupies the window of some solitary captive is to the poor wight by whom it is nursed and cultivated—something which at once excited and repaid her care ; and in giving the boy her affection, she felt, as it were, grateful to him for releasing her from the state of dull apathy in which she had usually found herself during the absence of Sir Halbert Glendinning.

But even the charms of this blooming favorite were unable to chase the recurring apprehensions which arose from her husband's procrastinated return. Soon after Roland Græme became a resident at the castle, a groom, despatched by Sir Halbert, brought tidings that business of importance still delayed the knight at the court of Holyrood. The more distant period which the messenger had assigned for his master's arrival at length glided away, summer melted into autumn, and autumn was about to give place to winter, and yet he came not.

CHAPTER III

The waning harvest-moon shone broad and bright,
The warder's horn was heard at dead of night,
And while the folding portals wide were flung,
With trampling hoofs the rocky pavement rung.
LEYDEN.

"AND you, too, would be a soldier, Roland?" said the Lady of Avenel to her young charge, while, seated on a stone chair at one end of the battlements, she saw the boy attempt with a long stick to mimic the motions of the warder as he alternately shouldered, or ported, or sloped pike.

"Yes, lady," said the boy, for he was now familiar, and replied to her questions with readiness and alacrity—"a soldier will I be; for there ne'er was gentleman but who belted him with brand."

"Thou a gentleman!" said Lilias, who, as usual, was in attendance; "such a gentleman as I would make of a bean-cod with a rusty knife."

"Nay, chide him not, Lilias," said the Lady of Avenel, "for, beshrew me, but I think he comes of gentle blood; see how it musters in his face at your injurious reproof."

"Had I my will, madam," answered Lilias, "a good birchen wand should make his color muster to better purpose still."

"On my word, Lilias," said the lady, "one would think you had received harm from the poor boy; or is he so far on the frosty side of your favor because he enjoys the sunny side of mine?"

"Over Heaven's forbode, my lady!" answered Lilias; "I have lived too long with gentles, I praise my star for it, to fight with either follies or fantasies, whether they relate to beast, bird, or boy."

Lilias was a favorite in her own class, a spoiled domestic, and often accustomed to take more license than her mistress was at all times willing to encourage. But what did not please the Lady of Avenel she did not choose to hear, and thus it was on the present occasion. She resolved to look more close and sharply after the boy, who had hitherto been committed chiefly to the management of Lilias. He must, she thought be born of gentle blood; it were shame to think otherwise of a form so noble and features so fair; the very wildness in which he occasionally indulged, his contempt of danger and impatience of restraint, had in them something noble: assuredly the child was born of high rank. Such was her conclusion, and she acted upon it accordingly. The domestics around her, less jealous or less scrupulous than Lilias, acted as servants usually do, following the bias, and flattering for their own purposes, the humor of the lady; and the boy soon took on him those airs of superiority which the sight of habitual deference seldom fails to inspire. It seemed, in truth, as if to command were his natural sphere, so easily did he use himself to exact and receive compliance with his humors. The chaplain, indeed, might have interposed to check the air of assumption which Roland Græme so readily indulged, and most probably would have willingly rendered him that favor; but the necessity of adjusting with his brethren some disputed points of church discipline had withdrawn him for some time from the castle, and detained him in a distant part of the kingdom.

Matters stood thus in the Castle of Avenel, when a winded bugle sent its shrill and prolonged notes from the shore of the lake, and was replied to cheerily by the signal of the warder. The Lady of Avenel knew the sounds of her husband, and rushed to the window of the apartment in which she was sitting. A band of about thirty spearmen, with a pennon displayed before them, winded along the indented shores of the lake, and approached the causeway. A single horseman rode at the head of the party, his bright arms catching a glance of the October sun as he moved steadily along. Even at that distance, the lady recognized the lofty plume, bearing the mingled colors of her own liveries and those of Glendonwyne, blended with the holly-branch; and the firm seat and dignified demeanor of the rider, joined to the stately motion of the dark brown steed, sufficiently announced Halbert Glendinning.

The lady's first thought was that of rapturous joy at her husband's return: her second was connected with a fear which had sometimes intruded itself, that he might not altogether approve the peculiar distinction with which she had treated her orphan ward. In this fear there was implied a consciousness that the favor she had shown him was excessive; for Halbert Glendinning was at least as gentle and indulgent as he was firm and rational in the intercourse

of his household ; and to her, in particular, his conduct had ever been most affectionately tender.

Yet she did fear that, on the present occasion, her conduct might incur Sir Halbert's censure ; and hastily resolving that she would not mention the anecdote of the boy until the next day, she ordered him to be withdrawn from the apartment by Lilias.

"I will not go with Lilias, madam," answered the spoiled child, who had more than once carried his point by perseverance, and who, like his betters, delighted in the exercise of such authority—"I will not go to Lilias's gousty room ; I will stay and see that brave warrior who comes riding so gallantly along the drawbridge,"

"You must not stay, Roland," said the lady, more positively than she usually spoke to her little favorite.

"I will," reiterated the boy, who had already felt his consequence, and the probable chance of success.

"You *will*, Roland !" answered the lady ; "what manner of word is that ? I tell you, you must go."

"'Will,'" answered the forward boy, "is a word for a man, and 'must' is no word for a lady."

"You are saucy, sirrah," said the lady. "Lilias, take him with you instantly."

"I always thought," said Lilias, smiling, as she seized the reluctant boy by the arm, "that my young master must give place to my old one."

"And you too are malapert, mistress," said the lady. "Hath the moon changed, that ye all of you thus forget yourselves ?"

Lilias made no reply, but led off the boy, who too proud to offer unavailing resistance, darted at his benefactress a glance which intimated plainly how willingly he would have defied her authority had he possessed the power to make good his point.

The Lady of Avenel was vexed to find how much this trifling circumstance had discomposed her at the moment when she ought naturally to have been entirely engrossed by her husband's return. But we do not recover composure by the mere feeling that agitation is mistimed. The glow of displeasure had not left the lady's cheek, her ruffled deportment was not yet entirely composed, when her husband, unhelmeted, but still wearing the rest of his arms, entered the apartment. His appearance banished the thoughts of everything else ; she rushed to him, clasped his iron-sheathed frame in her arms, and kissed his martial and manly face with an affection which was at once evident and sincere. The warrior returned her embrace and her caress with the same fondness; for the time which had passed since their union had diminished its romantic ardor, perhaps, but it had rather increased its rational tenderness, and Sir Halbert Glendinning's long and frequent absences from his castle had prevented affection from degenerating by habit into indifference.

When the first eager greetings were paid and received, the lady gazed fondly on her husband's face as she remarked—"You are altered, Halbert: you have ridden hard and far to-day, or you have been ill?"

"I have been well, Mary," answered the knight—"passing well have I been; and a long ride is to me, thou well knowest, but a thing of constant custom. Those who are born noble may slumber out their lives within the walls of their castles and manor-houses; but he who hath achieved nobility by his own deeds must ever be in the saddle, to show that he merits his advancement."

While he spoke thus, the lady gazed fondly on him, as if endeavoring to read his inmost soul; for the tone in which he spoke was that of melancholy depression."

Sir Halbert Glendinning was the same, yet a different person from what he had appeared in his early years. The fiery freedom of the aspiring youth had given place to the steady and stern composure of the approved soldier and skilful politician. There were deep traces of care on those noble features, over which each emotion used formerly to pass like light clouds across a summer sky. That sky was now, not perhaps clouded, but still and grave, like that of the sober autumn evening. The forehead was higher and more bare than in early youth, and the locks which still clustered thick and dark on the warrior's head were worn away at the temples, not by age, but by the constant pressure of the steel cap, or helmet. His beard, according to the fashion of the times, grew short and thick, and was turned into mustachois on the upper lip, and peaked at the extremity. The cheek, weatherbeaten and embrowned, had lost the glow of youth, but showed the vigorous complexion of active and confirmed manhood. Halbert Glendinning was, in a word, a knight to ride at a king's right hand, to bear his banner in war, to be his counselor in time of peace; for his looks expressed the considerate firmness which can resolve wisely and dare boldly. Still, over these noble features there now spread an air of dejection, of which, perhaps, the owner was not conscious, but which did not escape the observation of his anxious and affectionate partner.

"Something has happened, or is about to happen," said the Lady of Avenel; "this sadness sits not on your brow without cause—misfortune, national or particular must needs be at hand."

"There is nothing new that I wot of," said Halbert Glendining; "but there is little of evil which can befall a kingdom that may not be apprehended in this unhappy and divided realm."

"Nay, then," said the lady, "I see there has really been some fatal work on foot. My Lord of Murray has not so long detained you at Holyrood, save that he wanted your help in some weighty purpose."

"I have not been at Holyrood, Mary," answered the knight; "I have been several weeks abroad."

"Abroad! and sent me no word!" replied the lady.

"What would the knowledge have availed, but to have rendered you unhappy, my love?" replied the knight; "your thoughts would have converted the slightest breeze that curled your own lake into a tempest raging in the German Ocean."

"And have you then really crossed the sea?" said the lady, to whom the very idea of an element which she had never seen conveyed notions of terror and of wonder—"really left your own native land and trodden distant shores, where the Scottish tongue is unheard and unknown?"

"Really, and really," said the knight, taking her hand in affectionate playfulness, "I have done this marvelous deed—have rolled on the ocean for three days and three nights, with the deep green waves dashing by the side of my pillow, and but a thin plank to divide me from it."

"Indeed, my Halbert," said the lady, "that was a tempting of Divine Providence. I never bade you unbuckle the sword from your side, or lay the lance from your hand; I never bade you sit still when your honor called you to rise and ride; but are not blade and spear dangers enough for one man's life, and why would you trust rough winds and raging seas?"

"We have in Germany and in the Low Countries, as they are called," answered Glendenning, "men who are united with us in faith, and with whom it is fitting we should unite in alliance. To some of these I was despatched on business as important as it was secret. I went in safety, and I returned in security: there is more danger to a man's life betwixt this and Holyrood than in all the seas that wash the lowlands of Holland."

"And the country, my Halbert, and the people," said the lady, "are they like our kindly Scots? or what bearing have they to strangers?"

"They are a people, Mary, strong in their wealth, which renders all other nations weak, and weak in those arts of war by which other nations are strong."

"I do not understand you," said the lady.

"The Hollander and the Fleming, Mary, pour forth their spirit in trade, and not in war; their wealth purchases them the arms of foreign soldiers, by whose aid they defend it. They erect dikes on the sea-shore to protect the land which they have won, and they levy regiments of the stubborn Switzers and hardy Germans to protect the treasures which they have amassed. And thus they are strong in their weakness; for the very wealth which tempts their masters to destroy them arms strangers in their behalf."

"The slothful hinds!" exclaimed Mary, thinking and feeling like a Scotswoman of the period; "have they hands, and fight not for the land which bore them? They should be notched off at the elbow."

"Nay, that were but hard justice," answered her husband; "for their hands serve their country, though not in battle, like ours. Look at these barren hills, Mary, and at that deep winding vale by which the cattle are even now returning from their scanty browse. The hand of the industrions Fleming would cover these mountains with wood, and raise corn where we now see a starved and scanty sward of heath and ling. It grieves me, Mary, when I look on that land, and think what benefit it might receive from such men as I have lately seen—men who seek not the idle fame derived from dead ancestors, or the bloody renown won in modern broils, but tread along the land as preservers and improvers, not as tyrants and destroyers."

"These amendments would here be but a vain fancy, my Halbert," answered the Lady of Avenel: "the trees would be burned by the English foeman ere they ceased to be shrubs, and the grain that you raised would be gathered in by the first neighbor that possessed more riders than follow your train. Why should you repine at this? The fate that made you Scotsman by birth, gave you head, and heart, and hand to uphold the name as it must needs be upheld."

"It gave *me* no name to uphold," said Halbert, pacing the floor slowly; "my arm has been foremost in every strife, my voice has been heard in every council, nor have the wisest rebuked me. The crafty Lethington, the deep and dark Morton, have held secret council with me, and Grange and Lindesay have owned that in the field I did the devoir of a gallant knight; but let the emergence be passed when they need my head and hand, and they only know me as son of the obscure portioner of Glendearg."

This was a theme which the lady always dreaded; for the rank conferred on her husband, the favor in which he was held by the powerful Earl of Murray, and the high talents by which he vindicated his right to that rank and that favor, were qualities which rather increased than diminished the envy which was harbored against Sir Halbert Glendinning among a proud aristocracy, as a person originally of inferior and obscure birth, who had risen to his present eminence solely by his personal merit. The natural firmness of his mind did not enable him to despise the ideal advantages of a higher pedigree, which were held in such universal esteem by all with whom he conversed; and so open are the noblest minds to jealous inconsistencies, that there were moments in which he felt mortified that his lady should possess those advantages of birth and high descent which he himself did not enjoy, and regretted that his importance as the proprietor of Avenel was qualified by his possessing it only as the husband of the heiress. He was not so unjust as to permit any unworthy feelings to retain permanent possession of his mind, but yet they recurred from time to time, and did not escape his lady's anxious observation.

"Had we been blessed with children," she was wont on such occasions to say to herself—"had our blood been united in a son who might have joined my advantages of descent with my husband's personal worth, these painful and irksome reflections had not disturbed our union even for a moment. But the existence of such an heir, in whom our affections, as well as our pretensions, might have centered, has been denied to us."

With such mutual feelings, it cannot be wondered that it gave the lady pain to hear her husband verging towards this topic of mutual discontent. On the present, as on other similar occasions, she endeavored to divert the knight's thoughts from this painful channel.

"How can you," she said, "suffer yourself to dwell upon things which profit nothing? Have you indeed no name to uphold? You the good and the brave, the wise in council and the strong in battle, have you not to support the reputation your own deeds have won—a reputation more honorable than mere ancestry can supply? Good men love and honor you, the wicked fear and the turbulent obey you; and is it not necessary you should exert yourself to ensure the endurance of that love, that honor, that wholesome fear, and that necessary obedience?"

As she thus spoke, the eye of her husband caught from hers courage and comfort, and it lightened as he took her hand and replied, "It is most true, my Mary, and I deserve thy rebuke, who forget what I am, in repining because I am not what I cannot be. I am now what the most famed ancestors of those I envy were, the mean man raised into eminence by his own exertions; and sure it is a boast as honorable to have those capacities which are necessary to the foundation of a family as to be descended from one who possessed them some centuries before. The Hay of Luncarty who bequeathed his bloody yoke to his lineage, the "dark gray man" who first founded the house of Douglas, had yet less of ancestry to boast than I have. For thou knowest, Mary, that my name derives itself from a line of ancient warriors, although my immediate forefathers preferred the humble station in which thou didst first find them; and war and counsel are not less proper to the house of Glendonwyne,* even in its most remote descendants, than to the proudest of their baronage."

He strode across the hall as he spoke; and the lady smiled internally to observe how much his mind dwelt upon the prerogatives of birth, and endeavored to establish his claims, however remote, to a share in them, at the very moment when he affected to hold them in contempt. It will easily be guessed, however, that she permitted no symptom to escape her that could show she was sensible of the weakness of her husband—a perspicacity which perhaps his proud spirit could not very easily have brooked.

As he returned from the extremity of the hall, to which he had stalked while in the act of vindicating the title of the house of Glendonwyne in its most remote branches to the full privileges of aristocracy, "Where," he said, "is Wolf? I have not seen him since my return, and he was usually the first to welcome my home-coming."

"Wolf," said the lady, with a slight degree of embarrassment, for which, perhaps, she would have found it difficult to assign any reason even to herself—"Wolf is chained up for the present. He hath been surly to my page."

* See Note 1.

"Wolf chained up—and Wolf surly to your page!" answered Sir Albert Glendinning. "Wolf never was surly to any one; and the chain will either break his spirit or render him savage. So ho, there—set Wolf free directly."

He was obeyed; and the huge dog rushed into the hall, disturbing by his unwieldy and boisterous gambols the whole economy of reels, rocks, and distaffs with which the maidens of the household were employed, when the arrival of their lord was a signal to them to withdraw, and extracting from Lilias, who was summoned to put them again in order, the natural observation, "That the laird's pet was as troublesome as the lady's page."

"And who is this page, Mary?" said the knight, his attention again called to the subject by the observation of the waiting-woman—"who is this page, whom every one seems to weigh in the balance with my old friend and favorite, Wolf? When did you aspire to the dignity of keeping a page, or who is the boy?"

"I trust, my Halbert," said the lady, not without a blush, "you will not think your wife entitled to less attendance than other ladies of her quality."

"Nay, Dame Mary," answered the knight, "it is enough you desire such an attendant. Yet I have never loved to nurse such useless menials. A lady's page—it may well suit the proud English dames to have a slender youth to bear their trains from bower to hall, fan them when they slumber, and touch the lute for them when they please to listen; but our Scottish matrons were wont to be above such vanities, and our Scottish youth ought to be bred to the spear and the stirrup."

"Nay, but, my husband," said the lady, "I did but jest when I called this boy my page; he is in sooth a little orphan whom we saved from perishing in the lake, and whom I have since kept in the castle out of charity. Lilias, bring little Roland hither."

Roland entered accordingly, and, flying to the lady's side, took hold of the plaits of her gown, and then turned round and gazed with an attention, not unmingled with fear, upon the stately form of the knight. "Roland," said the lady, "go kiss the hand of the noble knight, and ask him to be thy protector." But Roland obeyed not, and, keeping his station, continued to gàze fixedly and timidly on Sir Halbert Glendinning. "Go to the knight, boy," said the lady; "what dost thou fear, child? Go kiss Sir Halbert's hand."

"I will kiss no hand save yours, lady," answered the boy.

"Nay, but do as you are commanded, child," replied the lady. "He is dashed by your presence," she said, apologizing to her husband; "but is he not a handsome boy?"

"And so is Wolf," said Sir Halbert, as he patted his huge four-footed favorite, "a handsome dog; but he has this double advantage over your new favorite, that he does what he is commanded, and hears not when he is praised."

"Nay, now you are displeased with me," replied the lady; "and yet why should you be so? There is nothing wrong in relieving the distressed orphan, or in loving that which is in itself lovely and deserving of affection. But you have seen Mr. Warden at Edinburgh, and he has set you against the poor boy."

"My dear Mary," answered her husband, "Mr. Warden better knows his place than to presume to interfere either in your affairs or in mine. I neither blame your relieving this boy nor your kindness for him. But I think, considering his birth and prospects, you ought not to treat him with injudicious fondness, which can only end in rendering him unfit for the humble situation to which Heaven has designed him."

"Nay, but, my Halbert, do but look at the boy," said the lady, "and see whether he has not the air of being intended by Heaven for something nobler than a mere peasant. May he not be designed, as others have been, to rise out of a humble situation into honor and eminence?"

Thus far had she proceeded, when the consciousness that she was treading upon delicate ground at once occurred to her, and induced her to take the most natural but the worst of all courses on such occasions, whether in conversation or in an actual bog, namely, that of stopping suddenly short in the illustration which she had commenced. Her brow crimsoned, and that of Sir Halbert Glendinning was slightly overcast. But it was only for an instant; for he was incapable of mistaking his lady's meaning or supposing that she meant intentional disrespect to him.

"Be it as you please, my love," he replied; "I owe you too much to contradict you in aught which may render your solitary mode of life more endurable. Make of this youth what you will, and you have my full authority for doing so; but remember he is your charge, not mine. Remember he hath limbs to do man's service, a soul and a tongue to worship God; breed him, therefore, to be true to his country and to Heaven; and for the rest, dispose of him as you list. It is, and shall rest, your own matter."

This conversation decided the fate of Roland Græme, who from thenceforward was little noticed by the master of the mansion of Avenel, but indulged and favored by its mistress.

This situation led to many important consequences, and, in truth, tended to bring forth the character of the youth in all its broad lights and deep shadows. As the knight himself seemed tacitly to disclaim alike interest and control over the immediate favorite of his lady, young Roland was, by circumstances, exempted from the strict discipline to which, as the retainer of a Scottish man of rank, he would otherwise have been subjected, according to all the rigor of the age. But the steward, or master of the household—such was the proud title assumed by the head domestic of each petty baron—deemed it not advisable to interfere with the favorite of the lady, and especially since she had brought the estate into the present family. Master Jasper Wingate was a man experienced, as he often boasted, in the ways of great families, and knew how to keep the steerage even, when wind and tide chanced to be in contradiction.

This prudent personage winked at much, and avoided giving opportunity for further offense, by requesting little of Roland Græme beyond the degree of attention which he was himself disposed to pay; rightly conjecturing that, however lowly the place which the youth might hold in the favor of the Knight of Avenel, still to make an evil report of him would make an enemy of the lady, without securing the favor of her husband. With these prudential considerations, and doubtless not without an eye to his own ease and convenience, he taught the boy as much, and only as much, as he chose to learn, readily admitting whatever apology it pleased his pupil to allege in excuse for idleness or negligence. As the other persons in the castle to whom such tasks were delegated readily imitated the prudential conduct of the major-domo, there was little control used towards Roland Græme, who, of course, learned no more than what a very active mind, and a total impatience of absolute idleness, led him to acquire upon his own account, and by dint of his own exertions. The latter were especially earnest when the lady herself condescended to be his tutoress or to examine his progress.

It followed also, from his quality as my lady's favorite, that Roland was viewed with no peculiar good-will by the followers of the knight, many of whom, of the same age, and apparently similar origin, with the fortunate page, were subjected to severe observance of the ancient and rigorous discipline of a feudal retainer. To these, Roland Græme was, of course, an object of envy, and, in consequence, of dislike and detraction; but the youth possessed qualities which it was impossible to depreciate. Pride and a sense of early ambition did for him what severity and constant instruction did for others. In truth, the youthful Roland displayed that early flexibility both of body and mind which renders exercise, either mental or bodily, rather matter of sport than of study; and it seemed as if he acquired accidentally, and by starts, those accomplishments which earnest and constant instruction, enforced by frequent reproof and occasional chastisement, had taught to others. Such military exercises, such lessons of the period, as he found it agreeable or convenient to apply to, he learned so perfectly as to confound those who were ignorant how often the want of constant application is compensated by vivacity of talent and ardent enthusiasm. The lads, therefore, who were more regularly trained to arms, to horsemanship, and to other necessary exercises of the period, while they envied Roland Græme the indulgence or negligence with which he seemed to be treated, had little reason to boast of their own superior acquirements: a few hours, with the powerful exertion of the most energetic will, seemed to do for him more than the regular instruction of weeks could accomplish for others.

Under these advantages, if, indeed, they were to be termed such, the character of young Roland began to develop itself. It was bold, peremptory, decisive, and overbearing; generous if neither withstood nor contradicted; vehement and passionate if censured or opposed. He seemed to consider himself as attached to no one, and responsible to no one, except his mistress; and even over her mind he had gradually acquired that species of ascendency which indulgence is so apt to occasion. And although the immediate followers and dependants of Sir Halbert Glendinning saw his ascendency with jealousy, and often took occasion to mortify his vanity, there wanted not those who were willing to acquire the favor of the Lady of Avenel by humoring and taking part with the youth whom she protected; for although a favorite, as the poet assures us, has no friend, he seldom fails to have both followers and flatterers.

The partisans of Roland Græme were chiefly to be found amongst the inhabitants of the little hamlet on the shore of the lake. These villagers, who were sometimes tempted to compare their own situation with that of the immediate and constant followers of the knight, who attended him on his frequent journeys to Edinburgh and elsewhere, delighted in considering and representing themselves as more properly the subjects of the Lady of Avenel than of her husband. It is true, her wisdom and affection on all occasions discountenanced the distinction which was here implied; but the villagers persisted in thinking it must be agreeable to her to enjoy their peculiar and undivided homage, or at least in acting as if they thought so; and one chief mode by which they evinced their sentiments was by the respect they paid to young Roland Græme, the favorite attendant of the descendant of their ancient lords. This was a mode of flattery too pleasing to encounter rebuke or censure; and the opportunity which it afforded the youth to form, as it were, a party of his own within the limits of the ancient barony of Avenel, added not a little to the audacity and decisive tone of a character which was by nature bold, impetuous, and incontrollable.

Of the two members of the household who had manifested an early jealously of Roland Græme, the prejudices of Wolf were easily overcome; and in process of time the noble dog slept with Bran, Luath, and the celebrated hounds of ancient days. But Mr. Warden, the chaplain, lived, and retained his dislike to youth. That good man, single-minded and benevolent as he really was, entertained rather more than a reasonable idea of the respect due to him as a minister, and exacted from the inhabitants of the castle more deference than the haughty young page, proud of his mistress's favor, and petulant from youth and situation, was at all times willing to pay. His bold and free demeanor, his attachment to rich dress and decoration, his inaptitude to receive instruction, and his hardening himself against rebuke, were circumstances which induced the good old man, with more haste than charity, to set the forward page down as a vessel of wrath, and to presage that the youth nursed that pride and haughtiness of spirit which goes before ruin and destruction. On the other hand, Roland evinced at times a marked dislike, and even something like contempt, of the chaplain. Most of the attendants and followers of Sir Halbert Glendinning entertained the same charitable thoughts as the reverend Mr. Warden; but while Roland was favored by their lady, and endured by their lord, they saw no policy in making their opinions public.

Roland Græme was sufficiently sensible of the unpleasant situation in which he stood; but in the haughtiness of his heart he retorted upon the other domestics the distant, cold, and sarcastic manner in which they treated him, assumed an air of superiority which compelled the most obstinate to obedience, and had the satisfaction at least to be dreaded, if he was heartily hated.

The chaplain's marked dislike had the effect of recommending him to the attention of Sir Halbert's brother, Edward, who now, under the conventional appellation of Father Ambrose, continued to be one of the few monks who, with the Abbot Eustatius, had, notwithstanding the nearly total downfall of their faith under the regency of Murray, been still permitted to linger in the cloisters at Kennaquhair. Respect to Sir Halbert had prevented their being altogether driven out of the abbey, though their order was now in a great measure suppressed, and they were interdicted the public exercise of their ritual, and only allowed for their support a small pension out of their once splendid revenues. Father Ambrose, thus situated, was an occasional, though very rare, visitant at the Castle of Avenel, and was at such times observed to pay particular attention to Roland Græme, who seemed to return it with more depth of feeling than consisted with his usual habits.

Thus situated, years glided on, during which the knight of Avenel continued to act a frequent and important part in the convulsions of his distracted country; while young Græme anticipated, both in wishes and personal accomplishments, the age which should enable him to emerge from the obscurity of his present situation.

CHAPTER IV

> Amid their cups that freely flow'd,
> Their revelry and mirth,
> A youthful lord tax'd Valentine
> With base and doubtful birth.
> *Valentine and Orson.*

WHEN Roland Græme was a youth about seventeen years of age, he chanced one summer morning to descend to the mew in which Sir Halbert Glendinning kept his hawks, in order to superintend the training of an eyas, or young hawk, which he himself, at the imminent risk of neck and limbs, had taken from a celebrated eyrie in the neighborhood, called Gledscraig. As he was by no means satisfied with the attention which had been bestowed on his favorite bird, he was not slack in testifying his displeasure to the falconer's lad, whose duty it was to have attended upon it.

"What, ho! sir knave," exclaimed Roland, "is it thus you feed the eyas with unwashed meat as if you were gorging the foul brancher of a worthless hoodie-crow? By the mass, and thou hast neglected its castings also for these two days! Think'st thou I ventured my neck to bring the bird down from the crag that thou shouldst spoil her by thy neglect?" And to add force to his remonstrances, he conferred a cuff or two on the negligent attendant of the hawks, who, shouting rather louder than was necessary under all the circumstances, brought the master falconer to his assistance.

Adam Woodcock, the falconer of Avenel, was an Englishman by birth, but so long in the service of Glendinning that he had lost much of his national attachment in that which he had formed to his master. He was a favorite in his department, jealous and conceited of his skill, as masters of the game usually are; for the rest of his character, he was a jester and a parcel poet (qualities which by no means abated his natural conceit), a jolly fellow, who, though a sound Protestant, loved a flagon of ale better than a long sermon, a stout man of his hands when need required, true to his master, and a little presuming on his interest with him.

Adam Woodcock, such as we have described him, by no means relished the freedom used by young Græme in chastising his assistant. "Hey, hey, my lady's page," said he, stepping between his own boy and Roland, "fair and softly, an it like your gilt jacket—hands off is fair play—if my boy has done amiss, I can beat him myself, and then you may keep your hands soft."

"I will beat him and thee too," answered Roland, without hesitation, "an ye look not better after your business. See how the bird is cast away between you. I found the careless lurdane feeding her with unwashed flesh, and she an eyas."*

"Go to," said the falconer, "thou art but an eyas thyself, child Roland. What knowest thou of feeding? I say that the eyas should have her meat unwashed until she becomes a brancher: 'twere the ready way to give her the frounce, to wash her meat sooner, and so knows every one who knows a gled from a falcon."

"It is thine own laziness, thou false English blood, that dost nothing but drink and sleep," retorted the page, "and leaves that lither lad to do the work, which he minds as little as thou."

"And am I so idle then," said the falconer, "that have three cast of hawks to look after, at perch and mew, and to fly them in the field to boot?—and is my lady's page so busy a man that he must take me up short?—and am I of false English blood? I marvel what blood thou art—neither Englander nor Scot—fish nor flesh—a bastard from the Debateable Land, without either kith, kin, or ally! Marry, out upon thee, foul kite, that would fain be a tercel gentle!"

The reply to this sarcasm was a box on the ear, so well applied that it overthrew the falconer into the cistern in which water was kept for the benefit of the hawks. Up started Adam Woodcock, his wrath nowise appeased by the cold immersion, and seizing on a truncheon which stood by, would have soon requited the injury he had received, had not Roland laid his hand on his poniard, and sworn by all that was sacred that, if he offered a stroke towards him, he would sheath the blade in his bowels. The noise was now so great that more than one of the household came in, and amongst others the major-domo, a grave personage, already

* There is a difference amongst authorities how long the nestling hawk should be fed with flesh which has previously been washed.

mentioned, whose gold chain and white wand intimated his authority. At the appearance of this dignitary, the strife was for the present appeased. He embraced, however, so favorable an opportunity to read Roland Græme a shrewd lecture on the impropriety of his deportment to his fellow-menials, and to assure him that, should he communicate this fray to his master (who, though now on one of his frequent expeditions, was speedily expected to return), which but for respect to his lady he would most certainly do, the residence of the culprit in the Castle of Avenel would be but of brief duration. "But, however," added the prudent master of the household, "I will report the matter first to my lady."

"Very just—very right, Master Wingate," exclaimed several voices together; "my lady will consider if daggers are to be drawn on us for every idle word, and whether we are to live in a well-ordered household, where there is the fear of God, or amongst drawn dirks and sharp knives."

The object of this general resentment darted an angry glance around him, and suppressing with difficulty the desire which urged him, to reply in furious or in contemptuous language, returned his dagger into the scabbard, looked disdainfully around upon the assembled menials, turned short upon his heel, and pushing aside those who stood betwixt him and the door, left the apartment.

"This will be no tree for my nest," said the falconer, "if this cock-sparrow is to crow over us as he seems to do."

"He struck me with his switch yesterday," said one of the grooms, "because the tail of his worship's gelding was not trimmed altogether so as suited his humor."

"And I promise you," said the laundress, "my young master will stick nothing to call an honest woman 'slut' and 'quean' if there be but a speck of shoot upon his band-collar."

"If Master Wingate do not his errand to my lady," was the general result, "there will be no tarrying in the same house with Roland Græme."

The master of the household heard them all for some time, and then, motioning for universal silence, he addressed them with all the dignity of Malvolio himself.—"My masters—not forgetting you, my mistresses—do not think the worse of me that I proceed with as much care as haste in this matter. Our master is a gallant knight, and will have his sway at home and abroad, in wood and field, in hall and bower, as the saying is. Our lady, my benison upon her! is also a noble person of long descent, and rightful heir of this place and barony, and she also loves her will; as for that matter, show me the woman who doth not. Now, she hath favored, doth favor, and will favor this jackanapes, for what good part about him I know not, save that as one noble lady will love a messan dog, and another a screaming popinjay, and a third a barbary ape, so doth it please our noble dame to set her affections upon this stray elf of a page, for nought that I can think of, save that she was the cause of his being saved—the more's the pity—from drowning." And here Master Wingate made a pause.

"I would have been his caution for a gray groat, against salt water or fresh," said Roland's adversary, the falconer; "marry, if he crack not a rope for stabbing or for snatching, I will be content never to hood hawk again."

"Peace, Adam Woodcock," said Wingate, waving his hand —"I prithee, peace, man. Now, my lady, liking this springald, as aforesaid, differs therein from my lord, who loves never a bone in his skin. Now, is it for me to stir up strife betwixt them, and put as 'twere my finger betwixt the bark and the tree, on account of a pragmatical youngster, whom, nevertheless, I would willingly see whipped forth of the barony? Have patience, and this boil will break without our meddling. I have been in service since I wore a beard on my chin, till now that that beard is turned gray, and I have seldom known any one better themselves even by taking the lady's part against the lord's; but never one who did not dirk himself if he took the lord's against the lady's."

"And so," said Lilias, "we are to be crowed over, every one of us, men and women, cock and hen, by this little upstart? I will try titles with him first, I promise you. I fancy, Master Wingate, for as wise as you look, you will be pleased to tell what you have seen to-day, if my lady commands you?"

"To speak the truth when my lady commands me," answered the prudential major-domo, "is in some measure my duty, Mistress Lilias; always providing for and excepting those cases in which it cannot be spoken without breeding mischief and inconvenience to myself or my fellow-servants; for the tongue of a tale-bearer breaketh bones as well as a Jeddart staff."

"But this imp of Satan is none of your friends or fellow-servants," said Lilias; "and I trust you mean not to stand up for him against the whole family besides?"

"Credit me, Mrs. Lilias," replied the senior, "should I

see the time fitting, I would with right good-will give him a lick with the rough side of my tongue."

"Enough said, Master Wingate," answered Lilias; "then trust me, his song shall soon be laid. If my mistress does not ask me what is the matter below stairs before she be ten minutes of time older, she is no born woman, and my name is not Lilias Bradbourne."

In pursuance of her plan, Mistress Lilias failed not to present herself before her mistress with all the exterior of one who is possessed of an important secret—that is, she had the corners of her mouth turned down, her eyes raised up, her lips pressed as fast together as if they had been sewed up, to prevent her blabbing, and an air of prim mystical importance diffused over her whole person and demeanor, which seemed to intimate, "I know something which I am resolved not to tell you!"

Lilias had rightly read her mistress's temper, who, wise and good as she was, was yet a daughter of grandame Eve, and could not witness this mysterious bearing on the part of her waiting-woman without longing to ascertain the secret cause. For a space, Mrs. Lilias was obdurate to all inquiries, sighed, turned her eyes up higher yet to Heaven, hoped for the best, but had nothing particular to communicate. All this, as was most natural and proper, only stimulated the lady's curiosity; neither was her importunity to be parried with—"Thank God, I am no makebate—no tale-bearer—thank God, I never envied any one's favor, or was anxious to propale their misdemeanor—only, thank God, there has been no bloodshed and murder in the house—that is all."

"Bloodshed and murder!" exclaimed the lady, "what does the quean mean? If you speak not plain out, you shall have something you will scarce be thankful for."

"Nay, my lady," answered Lilias, eager to disburden her mind, or, in Chaucer's phrase, to "unbuckle her mail," "if you bid me speak out the truth, you must not be moved with what might displease you: Roland Græme has dirked Adam Woodcock—that is all."

"Good Heaven!" said the lady, turning pale as ashes, "is the man slain?"

"No, madam," replied Lilias, "but slain he would have been if there had not been ready help; but maybe it is your lady ship's pleasure that this young esquire shall poniard the servants, as well as switch and baton them?"

"Go to, minion," said the lady, "you are saucy; tell the master of the household to attend me instantly."

Lilias hastened to seek out Mr. Wingate, and hurry him to his lady's presence, speaking as a word in season to him on the way, "I have set the stone a-trowling, look that you do not let it stand still."

The steward, too prudential a person to commit himself otherwise, answered by a sly look and a nod of intelligence, and presently after stood in the presence of the Lady of Avenel, with a look of great respect for his lady, partly real, partly affected, and an air of great sagacity, which inferred no ordinary conceit of himself.

"How is this, Wingate," said the lady, "and what rule do you keep in the castle, that the domestics of Sir Halbert Glendinning draw the dagger on each other as in a cavern of thieves and murderers? Is the wounded man much hurt? and what—what hath become of the unhappy boy?"

"There is no one wounded as yet, madam," replied he of the golden chain; "it passes my poor skill to say how many may be wounded before Pasche, if some rule be not taken with this youth; not but the youth is a fair youth," he added, correcting himself, "and able at his exercise; but somewhat too ready with the ends of his fingers, the butt of his riding-switch, and the point of his dagger."

"And whose fault is that," said the lady, "but yours, who should have taught him better discipline than to brawl or to draw his dagger?"

"If it please your ladyship so to impose the blame on me," answered the steward, "it is my part, doubtless, to bear it; only I submit to your consideration that, unless I nailed his weapon to the scabbard, I could no more keep it still than I could fix quicksilver, which defied even the skill of Raymond Lullius."

"Tell me not of Raymond Lullius," said the lady, losing patience, "but send me the chaplain hither. You grow all of you too wise for me during your lord's long and repeated absence. I would to God his affairs would permit him to remain at home and rule his own household, for it passes my wit and skill!"

"God forbid, my lady!" said the old domestic, "that you should sincerely think what you are now pleased to say: your old servants might well hope that, after so many years' duty, you would do their service more justice than to distrust their gray hairs, because they cannot rule the peevish humor of a green head, which the owner carries, it may be, a brace of inches higher than becomes him."

"Leave me," said the lady; "Sir Halbert's return must

now be expected daily, and he will look into these matters himself—leave me, I say, Wingate, without saying more of it. I know you are honest, and I believe the boy is petulant; and yet I think it is my favor which hath set all of you against him."

The steward bowed and retired, after having been silenced in a second attempt to explain the motives on which he acted.

The chaplain arrived; but neither from him did the lady receive much comfort. On the contrary, she found him disposed, in plain terms, to lay to the door of her indulgence all the disturbances which the fiery temper of Roland Græme had already occasioned, or might hereafter occasion, in the family. "I would," he said, "honored lady, that you had deigned to be ruled by me in the outset of this matter, sith it is easy to stem evil in the fountain, but hard to struggle against it in the stream. You honored madam—a word which I do not use according to the vain forms of this world, but because I have ever loved and honored you as an honorable and an elect lady—you, I say, madam, have been pleased, contrary to my poor but earnest counsel, to raise this boy from his station into one approaching to your own."

"What mean you, reverend sir?" said the lady. "I have made this youth a page; is there aught in my doing so that does not become my character and quality?"

"I dispute not, madam," said the pertinacious preacher, "your benevolent purpose in taking charge of this youth, or your title to give him this idle character of page, if such was your pleasure; though what the education of a boy in the train of a female can tend to, save to ingraft foppery and effeminacy on conceit and arrogance, it passes my knowledge to discover. But I blame you more directly for having taken little care to guard him against the perils of his condition, or to tame and humble a spirit naturally haughty, overbearing, and impatient. You have brought into your bower a lion's cub; delighted with the beauty of his fur, and the grace of his gambols, you have bound him with no fetters befitting the fierceness of his disposition. You have let him grow up as unawed as if he had been still a tenant of the forest, and now you are surprised, and call out for assistance, when he begins to ramp, rend, and tear, according to his proper nature."

"Mr. Warden," said the lady, considerably offended, "you are my husband's ancient friend, and I believe your love sincere to him and to his household. Yet let me say, that when I asked you for counsel, I expected not this asperity of rebuke.

If I have done wrong in loving this poor orphan lad more than others of his class, I scarce think the error merited such severe censure ; and if stricter discipline were required to keep his fiery temper in order, it ought, I think, to be considered that I am a woman, and that, if I have erred in this matter, it becomes a friend's part rather to aid than to rebuke me. I would these evils were taken order with before my lord's return. He loves not domestic discord or domestic brawls ; and I would not willingly that he thought such could arise from one whom I have favored. What do you counsel me to do ?"

"Dismiss this youth from your service, madam," replied the preacher.

"You cannot bid me do so," said the lady—"you cannot, as a Christian and a man of humanity, bid me turn away an unprotected creature against whom my favor—my injudicious favor, if you will—has reared up so many enemies."

"It is not necessary you should altogether abandon him, though you dismiss him to another service, or to a calling better suiting his station and character," said the preacher ; "elsewhere he may be an useful and profitable member of the common-weal ; here he is but a makebate and a stumbling-block of offense. The youth has snatches of sense and of intelligence, though he lacks industry. I will myself give him letters commendatory to Olearius Schinderhausen, a learned professor at the famous university of Leyden, where they lack an under-janitor ; where, besides gratis instruction, if God give him the grace to seek it, he will enjoy five marks by the year, and the professor's cast-off suit, which he disparts with biennially."

"This will never do, good Mr. Warden," said the lady, scarce able to suppress a smile ; "we will think more at large upon this matter. In the meanwhile, I trust to your remonstrances with this wild boy and with the family for restraining these violent and unseemly jealousies and bursts of passion ; and I entreat you to press on him and them their duty in this respect towards God and towards their master."

"You shall be obeyed, madam," said Warden. "On the next Thursday I exhort the family, and will, with God's blessing, so wrestle with the demon of wrath and violence which hath entered into my little flock that I trust to hound the wolf out of the fold, as if he were chased away with bandogs."

This was the part of the conference from which Mr. Warden derived the greatest pleasure. The pulpit was at that time the same powerful engine for affecting popular feeling which the press has since become, and he had been no unsuccessful preacher, as we have already seen. It followed as a natural consequence that he rather over-estimated the powers of his own oratory, and, like some of his brethren about the period, was glad of an opportunity to handle any matters of importance, whether public and private, the discussion of which could be dragged into his discourse. In that rude age the delicacy was unknown which prescribed time and place to personal exhortations; and as the court preacher often addressed the king individually, and dictated to him the conduct he ought to observe in matters of state, so the nobleman himself, or any of his retainers, were in the chapel of the feudal castle, often incensed or appalled, as the case might be, by the discussion of their private faults in the evening exercise, and by spiritual censures directed against them specifically, personally, and by name.

The sermon by means of which Henry Warden proposed to restore concord and good order to the Castle of Avenel bore for text the well-known words, "He who striketh with the sword shall perish by the sword," and was a singular mixture of good sense and powerful oratory with pedantry and bad taste. He enlarged a good deal on the word "striketh," which he assured his hearers comprehended blows given with the point as well as with the edge, and more generally shooting with hand-gun, cross-bow or long-bow, thrusting with a lance, or doing anything whatever by which death might be occasioned to the adversary. In the same manner, he proved satisfactorily that the word "sword" comprehended all descriptions, whether backsword or basket-hilt, cut-and-thrust or rapier, falchion or scimitar. "But if," he continued, with still greater animation, "the text includeth in its anathema those who strike with any of those weapons which man hath devised for the exercise of his open hostility, still more doth it comprehend such as from their form and size are devised rather for the gratification of privy malice by treachery than for the destruction of an enemy prepared and standing upon his defense. Such," he proceeded, looking sternly at the place where the page was seated on a cushion at the feet of his mistress, and wearing in his crimson belt a gay dagger with a gilded hilt —"such, more especially, I hold to be those implements of death which, in our modern and fantastic times, are worn not only by thieves and cut-throats, to whom they most properly belong, but even by those who attend upon women, and wait in the chambers of honorable ladies. Yes, my friends, every species of this unhappy weapon, framed for all evil and for no good, is comprehended under this deadly denunciation : whether it be a stilet, which we have borrowed from the treacherous Italian, or a dirk, which is borne by the savage Highlandmen, or a whinger, which is carried by our own Border thieves and cut-throats, or a dudgeon-dagger, all are alike engines invented by the devil himself, for ready implements of deadly wrath, sudden to execute, and difficult to be parried. Even the common sword-and-buckler brawler despises the use of such a treacherous and malignant instrument, which is therefore fit to be used, not by men or soldiers, but by those who, trained under female discipline, become themselves effeminate hermaphrodites, having female spite and female cowardice added to the infirmities and evil passions of their masculine nature."

The effect which this oration produced upon the assembled congregation of Avenel cannot very easily be described. The lady seemed at once embarrassed and offended ; the menials could hardly contain, under an affectation of deep attention, the joy with which they heard the chaplain launch his thunders at the head of the unpopular favorite, and the weapon which they considered as a badge of affectation and finery. Mrs. Lilias crested and drew up her head with all the deep-felt pride of gratified resentment ; while the steward, observing a strict neutrality of aspect, fixed his eyes upon an old scutcheon on the opposite side of the wall, which he seemed to examine with the utmost accuracy, more willing, perhaps, to incur the censure of being inattentive to the sermon than that of seeming to listen with marked approbation to what appeared so distasteful to his mistress.

The unfortunate subject of the harangue, whom nature had endowed with passions which had hitherto found no effectual restraint, could not disguise the resentment which he felt at being thus directly held up to the scorn, as well as the censure, of the assembled inhabitants of the little world in which he lived. His brow grew red—his lip grew pale—he set his teeth—he clenched his hand, and then with mechanical readiness grasped the weapon of which the clergyman had given so hideous a character ; and at length, as the preacher heightened the coloring of his invective, he felt his rage become so ungovernable that, fearful of being hurried into some deed of desperate violence, he rose up, traversed the chapel with hasty steps, and left the congregation.

The preacher was surprised into a sudden pause, while the fiery youth shot across him like a flash of lightning, regarding him as he passed, as if he had wished to dart from his eyes the same power of blighting and of consuming. But no sooner had he crossed the chapel, and shut with violence behind him the door of the vaulted entrance by which it communicated with the castle, than the impropriety of his conduct supplied Warden with one of those happier subjects for eloquence, of which he knew how to take advantage for making a suitable impression on his hearers. He paused for an instant, and then pronounced, in slow and solemn voice, the deep anathema: "He hath gone out from us because he was not of us: the sick man hath been offended at the wholesome bitter of the medicine—the wounded patient hath flinched from the friendly knife of the surgeon—the sheep hath fled from the sheepfold and delivered himself to the wolf, because he could not assume the quiet and humble conduct demanded of us by the great Shepherd. Ah! my brethren, beware of wrath—beware of pride—beware of the deadly and destroying sin which so often shows itself to our frail eyes in the garments of light! What is our earthly honor? Pride, and pride only. What our earthly gifts and graces? Pride and vanity. Voyagers speak of Indian men who deck themselves with shells, and anoint themselves with pigments, and boast of their attire as we do of our miserable carnal advantages. Pride could draw down the morning-star from Heaven even to the verge of the pit. Pride and self-opinion kindled the flaming sword which waves us off from Paradise. Pride made Adam mortal, and a weary wanderer on the face of the earth which he had else been at this day the immortal lord of. Pride brought amongst us sin, and doubles every sin it has brought. It is the outpost which the devil and the flesh most stubbornly maintain against the assaults of grace; and until it be subdued, and its barriers leveled with the very earth, there is more hope of a fool than of the sinner. Rend then, from your bosoms this accursed shoot of the fatal apple: tear it up by the roots, though it be twisted with the chords of your life. Profit by the example of the miserable sinner that has passed from us, and embrace the means of grace while it is called to-day—ere your conscience is seared as with a firebrand, and your ears deafened like those of the adder, and your heart hardened like the nether millstone. Up, then, and be doing: wrestle and overcome; resist, and the enemy shall flee from you. Watch and pray, lest ye fall into temptation, and let the stumbling of others be your warning and your example. Above all, rely not on yourselves, for such self-confidence is even the worst symptom of the disorder itself. The Pharisee perhaps deemed himself humble while he stooped in the Temple, and thanked God that he was not as other men, and even as the publican. But while his knees touched the marble pavement, his head was as high as the topmost pinnacle of the Temple. Do not therefore deceive yourselves, and offer false coin, where the purest you can present is but as dross: think not that such will pass the assay of Omnipotent Wisdom. Yet shrink not from the task because, as is my bounden duty, I do not disguise from you its difficulties. Self-searching can do much—meditation can do much—grace can do all."

And he concluded with a touching and animating exhortation to his hearers to seek Divine grace, which is perfected in human weakness.

The audience did not listen to this address without being considerably affected; though it might be doubted whether the feelings of triumph excited by the disgraceful retreat of the favorite page did not greatly qualify in the minds of many the exhortations of the preacher to charity and to humility. And, in fact, the expression of their countenances much resembled the satisfied, triumphant air of a set of children, who, having just seen a companion punished for a fault in which they had no share, con their task with double glee, both because they themselves are out of the scrape and because the culprit is in it.

With very different feelings did the Lady of Avenel seek her own apartment. She felt angry at Warden having made a domestic matter, in which she took a personal interest, the subject of such public discussion. But this she knew the good man claimed as a branch of his Christian liberty as a preacher, and also that it was vindicated by the universal custom of his brethren. But the self-willed conduct of her *protége* afforded her yet deeper concern. That he had broken through, in so remarkable a degree, not only the respect due to her presence, but that which was paid to religious admonition in those days with such peculiar reverence, argued a spirit as untameable as his enemies had represented him to possess. And yet, so far as he had been under her own eye, she had seen no more of that fiery spirit than appeared to her to become his years and his vivacity. This opinion might be founded in some degree on partiality; in some degree, too, it might be owing to the kindness and indulgence which she had always extended to him; but still she thought it impossible that she could be totally mistaken in the estimate she had formed of his character. The extreme of violence is scarce consistent with a course of continued hypocrisy (although Lilias charitably hinted that in some instances they were happily united), and therefore she could not exactly trust the report of others against her own experience and observation. The thoughts of this orphan boy clung to her heartstrings with a fondness for which she herself was unable to account. He had seemed to have been sent to her by Heaven to fill up those intervals of languor and vacuity which deprived her of much enjoyment. Perhaps he was not less dear to her because she well saw that he was a favorite with no one else, and because she felt that to give him up was to afford the judgment of her husband and others a triumph over her own—a circumstance not quite indifferent to the best of spouses of either sex.

In short, the Lady of Avenel formed the internal resolution that she would not desert her page while her page could be rationally protected; and, with the view of ascertaining how far this might be done, she caused him to be summoned to her presence.

CHAPTER V

In the wild storm,
The seaman hews his mast down, and the merchant
Heaves to the billows wares he once deem'd precious;
So prince and peer' 'mid popular contentions,
Cast off their favorites.

Old Play.

It was some time ere Roland Græme appeared. The messenger (his old friend Lilias) had at first attempted to open the door of his little apartment, with the charitable purpose, doubtless, of enjoying the confusion, and marking the demeanor, of the culprit. But an oblong bit of iron, yclept a bolt, was passed across the door on the inside, and prevented her benign intentions. Lilias knocked, and called at intervals, "Roland—Roland Græme—*Master* Roland Græme (an emphasis on the word "Master"), will you be pleased to undo the door? What ails you?—are you at your prayers in private, to complete the devotion which you left unfinished in public? Surely we must have a screened seat for you in the chapel, that your gentility may be free from the eyes of common folks!" Still no whisper was heard in reply. "Well, Master Roland," said the waiting-maid, "I must tell my mistress that, if she would have an answer, she must either come herself or send those on errand to you who can beat the door down."

"What says your lady?" inquired the page from within.

"Marry, open the door and you shall hear," answered the waiting-maid. "I trow it becomes my lady's message to be listened to face to face; and I will not, for your idle pleasure, whistle it through a keyhole."

"Your mistress's name," said the page, opening the door, "is too fair a cover for your impertinence. What says my lady?"

"That you will be pleased to come to her directly, in the withdrawing-room," answered Lilias. "I presume she has some directions for you concerning the forms to be observed in leaving chapel in future."

"Say to my lady that I will directly wait on her," said

the page; and, returning into his own apartment, he once more locked the door in the face of the waiting-maid.

"Rare courtesy!" muttered Lilias; and, returning to her mistress, acquainted her that Roland Græme would wait on her when it suited his convenience.

"What! is that his phrase or your own addition, Lilias?" said the lady, coolly.

"Nay, madam," replied the attendant, not directly answering the question, "he looked as if he could have said much more impertinent things than that, if I had been willing to hear them. But here he comes to answer for himself."

Roland Græme entered the apartment with a loftier mien and somewhat a higher color than his wont; there was embarrassment in his manner, but it was neither that of fear nor of penitence.

"Young man," said the lady, "what trow you am I to think of your conduct this day?"

"If it has offended you, madam, I am deeply grieved," said the youth.

"To have offended me alone," said the lady, "were but little. You have been guilty of conduct which will highly offend your master—of violence to your fellow-servants, and of disrespect to God Himself, in the person of His ambassador."

"Permit me again to reply," said the page, "that, if I have offended my only mistress, friend, and benefactress, it includes the sum of my guilt, and deserves the sum of my penitence. Sir Halbert Glendinning calls me not servant, nor do I call him master: he is not entitled to blame me for chastising an insolent groom; nor do I fear the wrath of Heaven for treating with scorn the uuauthorized interference of a meddling preacher."

The Lady of Avenel had before this seen symptoms in her favorite of boyish petulance and of impatience of censure or reproof. But his present demeanor was of a graver and more determined character, and she was for a moment at a loss how she should treat the youth, who seemed to have at once assumed the character not only of a man, but of a bold and determined one. She paused an instant, and then assuming the dignity which was natural to her, she said, "Is it to me, Roland, that you hold this language? Is it for the purpose of making me repent the favor I have shown you that you declare yourself independent both of an earthly and a Heavenly master? Have you forgotten what you were, and to what the loss of my protection would speedily again reduce you?"

"Lady," said the page, "I have forgot nothing: I remember but too much. I know that, but for you, I should have perished in yon blue waves," pointing, as he spoke, to the lake, which was seen through the window, agitated by the western wind. "Your goodness has gone farther, madam: you have protected me against the malice of others, and against my own folly. You are free, if you are willing, to abandon the orphan you have reared. You have left nothing undone by him, and he complains of nothing. And yet, lady, do not think I have been ungrateful: I have endured something on my part, which I would have borne for the sake of no one but my benefactress."

"For my sake!" said the lady; "and what is it that I can have subjected you to endure, which can be remembered with other feelings than those of thanks and gratitude?"

"You are too just, madam, to require me to be thankful for the cold neglect with which your husband has uniformly treated me—neglect not unmingled with fixed aversion. You are too just, madam, to require me to be grateful for the constant and unceasing marks of scorn and malevolence with which I have been treated by others, or for such a homily as that with which your reverend chaplain has, at my expense, this very day regaled the assembled household."

"Heard mortal ears the like of this!" said the waiting-maid, with her hands expanded, and her eyes turned up to Heaven; "he speaks as if he were son of an earl, or of a belted knight the least penny!"

The page glanced on her a look of supreme contempt, but vouchsafed no other answer. His mistress, who began to feel herself seriously offended, and yet sorry for the youth's folly, took up the same tone.

"Indeed, Roland, you forget yourself so strangely," said she, "that you will tempt me to take serious measures to lower you in your own opinion by reducing you to your proper station in society."

"And that," added Lilias, "would be best done by turning him out the same beggar's brat that your ladyship took him in."

"Lilias speaks too rudely," continued the lady, "but she has spoken the truth, young man; nor do I think I ought to spare that pride which hath so completely turned your head. You have been tricked up with fine garments, and treated like the son of a gentleman, until you have forgot the fountain of your churlish blood."

"Craving your pardon, most honorable madam, Lilias hath *not* spoken truth, nor does your ladyship know aught of my descent which should entitle you to treat it with such decided scorn. I am no beggar's brat: my grandmother begged from no one, here nor elsewhere; she would have perished sooner on the bare moor. We were harried out and driven from our home—a chance which has happed elsewhere, and to others. Avenel Castle, with its lake and its towers, was not at all times able to protect its inhabitants from want and desolation."

"Hear but his assurance!" said Lilias; "he upbraids my lady with the distresses of her family!"

"It had indeed been a theme more gratefully spared," said the lady, affected nevertheless with the allusion.

"It was necessary, madam, for my vindication," said the page, "or I had not even hinted at a word that might give you pain. But believe, honored lady, I am of no churl's blood. My proper descent I know not; but my only relation has said, and my heart has echoed it back and attested the truth, that I am sprung of gentle blood, and deserve gentle usage."

"And upon an assurance so vague as this," said the lady, "do you propose to expect all the regard, all the privileges, befitting high rank and distinguished birth, and become a contender for concessions which are only due to the noble? Go to, sir, know yourself, or the master of the household shall make you know you are liable to the scourge as a malapert boy. You have tasted too little the discipline fit for your age and station."

"The master of the household shall taste of my dagger ere I taste of his discipline," said the page, giving way to his restrained passion. "Lady, I have been too long the vassal of a pantoufle, and the slave of a silver whistle. You must henceforth find some other to answer your call; and let him be of birth and spirit mean enough to brook the scorn of your menials and to call a church vassal his master."

"I have deserved this insult," said the lady, coloring deeply, "for so long enduring and fostering your petulance. Begone, sir. Leave this castle to-night. I will send you the means of subsistence till you find some honest mode of support, though I fear your imaginary grandeur will be above all others save those of rapine and violence. Begone, sir, and see my face no more."

4

The page threw himself at her feet in an agony of sorrow. "My dear and honored mistress——" he said, but was unable to bring out another syllable.

"Arise, sir," said the lady, "and let go my mantle: hypocrisy is a poor cloak for ingratitude."

"I am incapable of either, madam," said the page, springing up with the hasty start of passion which belonged to his rapid and impetuous temper. "Think not I meant to implore permission to reside here; it has been long my determination to leave Avenel, and I will never forgive myself for having permitted you to say the word 'begone' ere I said, 'I leave you.' I did but kneel to ask your forgiveness for an ill-considered word used in the height of displeasure, but which ill-became my mouth as addressed to you. Other grace I asked not; you have done much for me, but I repeat, that you better know what you yourself have done than what I have suffered."

"Roland," said the lady, somewhat appeased, and relenting towards her favorite, "you had me to appeal to when you were aggrieved. You were neither called upon to suffer wrong nor entitled to resent it when you were under my protection."

"And what," said the youth, "if I sustained wrong from those you loved and favored, was I to disturb your peace with idle tale-bearings and eternal complaints? No, madam; I have borne my own burden in silence, and without disturbing you with murmurs; and the respect which you accuse me of wanting furnishes the only reason why I have neither appealed to you nor taken vengeance at my own hand in a manner far more effectual. It is well, however, that we part. I was not born to be a stipendiary, favored by his mistress until ruined by the calumnies of others. May Heaven multiply its choicest blessings on your honored head; and, for your sake, upon all that are dear to you!"

He was about to leave the apartment, when the lady called upon him to return. He stood still, while she thus addressed him: "It was not my intention, nor would it be just, even in the height of my displeasure, to dismiss you without the means of support: take this purse of gold."

"Forgive me, lady," said the boy, "and let me go hence with the consciousness that I have not been degraded to the point of accepting alms. If my poor services can be placed against the expense of my apparel and my maintenance, I only remain debtor to you for my life, and that alone is a debt which I can never repay; put up then that purse, and only say instead that you do not part from me in anger."

"No, not in anger," said the lady, "in sorrow rather for your wilfulness; but take the gold—you cannot but need it,"

"May God evermore bless you for the kind tone and the kind word, but the gold I cannot take. I am able of body, and do not lack friends so wholly as you may think; for the time may come that I may yet show myself more thankful than by mere words." He threw himself on his knees, kissed the hand which she did not withdraw, and then hastily left the apartment.

Lilias for a moment or two kept her eye fixed on her mistress, who looked so unusually pale that she seemed about to faint; but the lady instantly recovered herself, and declining the assistance which her attendant offered her, walked to her own apartment.

CHAPTER VI

> Thou hast each secret of the household, Francis.
> I dare be sworn thou hast been in the buttery
> Steeping thy curious humor in fat ale
> And in the butler's tattle—ay, or chatting
> With the glib waiting-woman o'er her comfits—
> These bear the key to each domestic mystery
>
> *Old Play*

UPON the morrow succeeding the scene we have described, the disgraced favorite left the castle ; and at breakfast-time the cautious old steward and Mrs. Lilias sat in the apartment of the latter personage, holding grave converse on the important event of the day, sweetened by a small treat of comfits, to which the providence of Mr. Wingate had added a little flask of racy canary.

"He is gone at last," said the abigail, sipping her glass ; "and here is to his good journey."

"Amen," answered the steward, gravely ; "I wish the poor deserted lad no ill."

"And he is gone like a wild duck, as he came," continued Mrs. Lilias ; "no lowering of drawbridges or pacing along causeways for him. My master has pushed off in the boat which they call the 'Little Herod' (more shame to them for giving the name of a Christian to wood and iron), and has rowed himself by himself to the further side of the loch, and off and away with himself, and left all his finery strewed about his room. I wonder who is to clean his trumpery out after him—though the things are worth lifting too."

"Doubtless, Mrs. Lilias," answered the master of the household ; "in the which case I am free to think they will not long cumber the floor."

"And now tell me, Mr. Wingate," continued the damsel, "do not the very cockles of your heart rejoice at the house being rid of this upstart whelp, that flung us all into shadow ?"

"Why, Mrs. Lilias," replied Wingate, "as to rejoicing—those who have lived as long in great families as has been my lot will be in no hurry to rejoice at anything. And for Roland Græme, though he may be a good riddance in the main, yet what says the very sooth proverb, 'Seldom comes a better.'"

"Seldom comes a better, indeed!" echoed Mrs. Lilias. "I say, never can come a worse, or one half so bad. He might have been the ruin of our poor dear mietress (here she used her kerchief), body and soul, and estate too; for she spent more coin on his apparel than on any four servants about the house."

"Mrs. Lilias," said the sage steward, "I do opine that our mistress requireth not this pity at our hands, being in all respects competent to take care of her own body, soul, and estate into the bargain."

"You would not mayhap have said so," answered the waiting-woman, "had you seen how like Lot's wife she looked when young master took his leave. My mistress is a good lady, and a virtuous, and a well-doing lady, and a well-spoken of—but I would not Sir Halbert had seen her last evening for two and a plack."

"Oh, foy! foy! foy!" reiterated the steward; "servants should hear and see, and say nothing. Besides that, my lady is utterly devoted to Sir Halbert, as well she may, being, as he is, the most renowned knight in these parts."

"Well—well," said the abigail, "I mean no more harm; but they that seek least renown abroad are most apt to find quiet at home, that's all; and my lady's lonesome situation is to be considered, that made her fain to take up with the first beggar's brat that a dog brought her out of the loch."

"And, therefore," said the steward, "I say, rejoice not too much or too hastily, Mrs. Lilias; for if your lady wished a favorite to pass away the time, depend upon it, the time will not pass lighter now that he is gone. So she will have another favorite to choose for herself, and be assured, if she wishes such a toy, she will not lack one."

"And where should she choose one, but among her own tried and faithful servants," said Mrs. Lilias, "who have broken her bread and drank her drink for so many years? I have known many a lady as high as she that never thought either of a friend or favorite beyond their own waiting-woman—always having a proper respect, at the same time, for their old and faithful master of the household, Mr. Wingate."

"Truly, Mrs. Lilias," replied the steward, "I do partly see the mark at which you shoot, but I doubt your bolt will fall short. Matters being with our lady as it likes you to suppose it will neither be your crimped pinners, Mrs. Lilias

—speaking of them with due respect—nor my silver hair or golden chain, that will fill up the void which Roland Græme must needs leave in our lady's leisure. There will be a learned young divine with some new doctrine; a learned leech with some new drug; a bold cavalier, who will not be refused the favor of wearing her colors at a running at the ring; a cunning harper that could harp the heart out of a woman's breast, as they say Signor David Rizzio did to our poor Queen—these are the sort of folk who supply the loss of a well-favored favorite, and not an old steward or a middle-aged waiting-woman."

"Well," replied Lilias, "you have experience, Master Wingate, and truly I would my master would leave off his pricking hither and thither, and look better after the affairs of his household. There will be a Papistrie among us next, for what should I see among master's clothes but a string of gold beads? I promise you, aves and credos both! I seized on them like a falcon."

"I doubt it not,—I doubt it not," said the steward, sagaciously nodding his head; "I have often noticed that the boy had strange observances which savored of Popery, and that he was very jealous to conceal them. But you will find the Catholic under the Presbyterian cloak as often as the knave under the friar's hood—what then? we are all mortal. Right proper beads they are," he added, looking attentively at them, "and may weigh four ounces of fine gold."

"And I will have them melted down presently," she said, "before they be the misguiding of some poor blinded soul."

"Very cautious, indeed, Mrs. Lilias," said the steward, nodding his head in assent.

"I will have them made," said Mrs. Lilias, "into a pair of shoe-buckles; I would not wear the Pope's trinkets, or whatever has once borne the shape of them, one inch above my instep, were they diamonds instead of gold. But this is what has come of Father Ambrose coming about the castle, as demure as a cat that is about to steal cream."

"Father Ambrose is our master's brother," said the steward, gravely.

"Very true, Master Wingate," replied the dame; "but is that a good reason why he should pervert the king's liege subjects to Papistrie?"

"Heaven forbid, Mrs. Lilias," answered the sententious major-domo; "but yet there are worse folk than the Papists."

"I wonder where they are to be found," said the waiting-woman, with some asperity; "but I believe, Master Wingate, if one were to speak to you about the devil himself, you would say there were worse people than Satan."

"Assuredly I might say so," replied the steward, "supposing that I saw Satan standing at my elbow."

The waiting-woman started, and having exclaimed, "God bless us!" added, "I wonder, Mr. Wingate, you can take pleasure in frightening one thus."

"Nay, Mrs. Lilias, I had no such purpose," was the reply; "but look you here—the Papists are put down for the present, but who knows how long this word 'present' will last? There are two great Popish earls in the north of England that abominate the very word 'Reformation:' I mean the Northumberland and Westmoreland earls, men of power enough to shake any throne in Christendom. Then, though our Scottish King be, God bless him, a true Protestant, yet he is but a boy; and here is his mother that was our Queen—I trust there is no harm to say God bless her too—and she is a Catholic; and many begin to think she has had but hard measure, such as the Hamiltons in the west, and some of our Border clans here, and the Gordons in the north, who are all wishing to see a new world; and if such a new world should chance to come up, it is like that the Queen will take back her own crown, and that the mass and the cross will come up, and then down go pulpits, Genava gowns, and black silk skull-caps."

"And have you, Mr. Jasper Wingate, who have heard the Word, and listened unto pure and precious Mr. Henry Warden—have you, I say, the patience to speak, or but to think, of Popery coming down on us like a storm, or of the woman Mary again making the royal seat of Scotland a throne of abomination? No marvel that you are so civil to the cowled monk, Father Ambrose, when he comes hither with his downcast eyes that he never raises to my lady's face, and with his low sweet-toned voice, and his *benedicites*, and his benisons; and who so ready to take them kindly as Mr. Wingate?"

"Mrs. Lilias," replied the butler, with an air which was intended to close the debate, "there are reasons for all things. If I received Father Ambrose debonairly, and suffered him to steal a word now and then with this same Roland Græme, it was not that I cared a brass boddle for his benison or malison either, but only because I respected my master's blood. And who can answer, if Mary come in again, whether he may not be as stout a tree to lean to as ever his brother hath proved to us? For down goes the Earl of Murray when the Queen comes by her own again; and good is his luck if he can keep the head on his own shoulders. And down goes our knight with the Earl, his patron; and who so like to mount into his empty saddle as this same Father Ambrose? The Pope of Rome can soon dispense with his vows, and then we should have Sir Edward the soldier, instead of Ambrose the priest."

Anger and astonishment kept Mrs. Lilias silent, while her old friend, in his self-complacent manner, was making known to her his political speculations. At length her resentment found utterance in words of great ire and scorn. "What, Master Wingate! have you eaten my mistress's bread, to say nothing of my master's, so many years, that you could live to think of her being dispossessed of her own Castle of Avenel by a wretched monk who is not a drop's blood to her in the way of relation? I, that am but a woman, would try first whether my rock or his cowl were the better metal. Shame on you, Master Wingate! If I had not held you as so old an acquaintance, this should have gone to my lady's ears, though I had been called pickthank and tale-pyet for my pains, as when I told of Roland Græme shooting the wild swan."

Master Wingate was somewhat dismayed at perceiving that the details which he had given of his far-sighted political views had produced on his hearer rather suspicion of his fidelity than admiration of his wisdom, and endeavored as hastily as possible to apoligize and to explain, although internally extremely offended at the unreasonable view, as he deemed it. which it had pleased Mistress Lilias Bradbourne to take of his expressions; and mentally convinced that her disapprobation of his sentiments arose solely out of the consideration that, though Father Ambrose, supposing him to become the master of the castle, would certainly require the services of a steward, yet those of a waiting-woman would, in the supposed circumstances, be altogether superfluous.

After this explanation had been received as explanations usually are, the two friends separated; Lilias to attend the silver whistle which called her to her mistress's chamber, and the sapient major-domo to the duties of his own department. They parted with less than their usual degree of reverence and regard; for the steward felt that his worldly wisdom was rebuked by the more disinterested attachment of the waiting-woman, and Mistress Lilias Bradbourne was compelled to consider her old friend as something little better than a time-saver.

CHAPTER VII

When I hae a saxpence under my thumb,
Then I get credit in ilka town;
But when I am poor, they bid me gaè by.
O poverty parts good company!

Old Song.

While the departure of the page afforded subject for the conversation which we have detailed in our last chapter, the late favorite was far advanced on his solitary journey, without well knowing what was its object, or what was likely to be its end. He had rowed the skiff in which he left the castle to the side of the lake most distant from the village, with the desire of escaping from the notice of the inhabitants. His pride whispered that he would be, in his discarded state, only the subject of their wonder and compassion; and his generosity told him that any mark of sympathy which his situation should excite might be unfavorably reported at the castle. A trifling incident convinced him he had little to fear for his friends on the latter score. He was met by a young man some years older than himself, who had on former occasions been but too happy to be permitted to share in his sports in the subordinate character of his assistant. Ralph Fisher approached to greet him with all the alacrity of an humble friend.

"What, Master Roland, abroad on this side, and without either hawk or hound?"

"Hawk or hound," said Roland, "I will never perhaps halloo to again. I have been dismissed—that is, I have left the castle."

Ralph was surprised. "What! you are to pass into the knight's service, and take the black-jack and the lance?"

"Indeed," replied Roland Græme, "I am not; I am now leaving the service of Avenel forever."

"And whither are you going then?" said the yonng peasant.

"Nay, that is a question which it craves time to answer: I have that matter to determine yet," replied the disgraced favorite.

"Nay, nay," said Ralph, "I warrant you it is the same to

you which way you go: my lady would not dismiss you till she had put some lining into the pouches of your doublet."

"Sordid slave!" said Roland Græme, "dost thou think I would have accepted a boon from one who was giving me over a prey to detraction and to ruin, at the instigation of a canting priest and a meddling serving-woman? The bread that I had bought with such an alms would have choked me at the first mouthful."

Ralph looked at his quondam friend with an air of wonder not unmixed with contempt. "Well," he said at length, "no occasion for passion—each man knows his own stomach best; but, were I on a black moor at this time of day, not knowing whither I was going, I should be glad to have a broad piece or two in my pouch, come by them as I could. But perhaps you will go with me to my father's—that is, for a night, for to-morrow we expect my uncle Menelaus and all his folk; but, as I said, for one night——"

The cold-blooded limitation of the offered shelter to one night only, and that tendered most unwillingly, offended the pride of the discarded favorite.

"I would rather sleep on the fresh heather, as I have done many a night on less occasion," said Roland Græme, "than in the smoky garret of your father, that smells of peat-smoke and usquebaugh like a Highlander's plaid."

"You may choose, my master, if you are so nice," replied Ralph Fisher; "you may be glad to smell a peat-fire, and usquebaugh too, if you journey long in the fashion you propose. You might have said 'God-a-mercy for your proffer,' though; it is not every one will put themselves in the way of ill-will by harboring a discarded serving-man."

"Ralph," said Roland Græme, "I would pray you to remember that I have switched you before now, and this is the same riding-wand which you have tasted."

Ralph, who was a thickset clownish figure, arrived at his full strength, and conscious of the most complete personal superiority, laughed contemptuously at the threats of the slight-made stripling.

"It may be the same wand," he said, "but not the same hand; and that is as good rhyme as if it were in a ballad. Look you, my lady's page that was, when your switch was up, it was no fear of you, but of your betters, that kept mine down; and I wot not what hinders me from clearing old scores with this hazel rung, and showing you it was your lady's livery-coat which I spared, and not your flesh and blood, Master Roland."

In the midst of his rage, Roland Græme was just wise enough to see that, by continuing this altercation, he would subject himself to very rude treatment from the boor, who was so much older and stronger than himself; and while his antagonist, with a sort of jeering laugh of defiance, seemed to provoke the contest, he felt the full bitterness of his own degraded condition, and burst into a passion of tears, which he in vain endeavored to conceal with both his hands.

Even the rough churl was moved with the distress of his quondam companion.

"Nay, Master Roland," he said, "I did but as 'twere jest with thee; I would not harm thee, man, were it but for old acquaintance sake. But ever look to a man's inches ere you talk of switching; why, thine arm, man, is but like a spindle compared to mine. But hark, I hear old Adam Woodcock hallooing to his hawk. Come along, man, we will have a merry afternoon, and go jollily to my father's, in spite of the peat-smoke and usquebaugh to boot. Maybe we may put you into some honest way of winning your bread, though it's hard to come by in these broken times."

The unfortunate page made no answer, nor did he withdraw his hands from his face, and Fisher continued in what he imagined a suitable tone of comfort.

"Why, man, when you were my lady's minion, men held you proud, and some thought you a Papist, and I wot not what; and so, now that you have no one to bear you out, you must be companionable and hearty, and wait on the minister's examinations, and put these things out of folks' heads; and if he says you are in fault, you must jouk your head to the stream; and if a gentleman, or a gentleman's gentleman, gives you a rough word, or a light blow, you must only say, 'Thank you for dusting my doublet,' or the like, as I have done by you. But hark to Woodcock's whistle again. Come, and I will teach you all the trick on't as we go on."

"I thank you," said Roland Græme, endeavoring to assume an air of indifference and of superiority; "but I have another path before me, and were it otherwise, I could not tread in yours."

"Very true, Master Roland," replied the clown; "and every man knows his own matters best, and so I will not keep you from the path, as you say. Give us a grip of your hand, man, for auld lang syne. What! not clap palms ere we part?—well, so be it—a wilful man will have his way, and so farewell, and the blessing of the morning to you."

"Good-morrow—good-morrow," said Roland, hastily; and the clown walked lightly off, whistling as he went, and glad, apparently, to be rid of an acquaintance whose claims might be troublesome, and who had no longer the means to be serviceable to him.

Roland Græme compelled himself to walk on while they were within sight of each other, that his former intimate might not augur any vacillation of purpose, or uncertainty of object, from his remaining on the same spot; but the effort was a painful one. He seemed stunned, as it were and giddy; the earth on which he stood felt as if unsound, and quaking under his feet like the surface of a bog; and he had once or twice nearly fallen, though the path he trode was of firm greensward. He kept resolutely moving forward, in spite of the internal agitation to which these symptoms belonged, until the distant form of his acquaintance disappeared behind the slope of a hill, when his heart failed at once; and, sitting down on the turf, remote from human ken, he gave way to the natural expressions of wounded pride, grief, and fear, and wept with unrestrained profusion and unqualified bitterness.

When the first violent paroxysm of his feelings had subsided, the deserted and friendless youth felt that mental relief which usually follows such discharges of sorrow. The tears continued to chase each other down his cheeks, but they were no longer accompanied by the same sense of desolation: an afflicting yet milder sentiment was awakened in his mind by the recollection of his benefactress, of the unwearied kindness which had attached her to him, in spite of many acts of provoking petulance, now recollected as offenses of a deep dye, which had protected him against the machinations of others, as well as against the consequences of his own folly, and would have continued to do so, had not the excess of his presumption compelled her to withdraw her protection.

"Whatever indignity I have borne," he said, "has been the just reward of my own ingratitude. And have I done well to accept the hospitality, the more than maternal kindness, of my protectress, yet to detain from her the knowledge of my religion? But she shall know that a Catholic has as much gratitude as a Puritan; that I have been thoughtless, but not wicked; that in my wildest moments I have loved, respected, and honored her; and that the orphan boy might indeed be heedless, but was never ungrateful!"

He turned, as these thoughts passed through his mind,

and began hastily to retread his footsteps towards the castle. But he checked the first eagerness of his repentant haste when he reflected on the scorn and contempt with which the family were likely to see the return of the fugitive, humbled, as they must necessarily suppose him, into a supplicant, who requested pardon for his fault, and permission to return to his service. He slackened his pace, but he stood not still.

"I care not," he resolutely determined; "let them wink, point, nod, sneer, speak of the conceit which is humbled, of the pride which has had a fall—I care not; it is a penance due to my folly, and I will endure it with patience. But if she also, my benefactress—if she also should think me sordid and weak-spirited enough to beg, not for her pardon alone, but for a renewal of the advantages which I derived from her favor—*her* suspicion of my meanness I cannot—I will not brook."

He stood still, and his pride, rallying with constitutional obstinacy against his more just feeling, urged that he would incur the scorn of the Lady of Avenel rather than obtain her favor by following the course which the first ardor of his repentant feelings had dictated to him.

"If I had but some plausible pretext," he thought—"some ostensible reason for my return, some excuse to allege which might show I came not as a degraded supplicant or a discarded menial, I might go thither; but as I am, I cannot: my heart would leap from its place and burst."

As these thoughts swept through his mind, something passed in the air so near him as to dazzle his eyes, and almost to brush the plume in his cap. He looked up—it was the favorite falcon of Sir Halbert, which, flying around his head, seemed to claim his attention, as that of a well-known friend. Roland extended his arm, and gave the accustomed whoop, and the falcon instantly settled on his wrist, and began to prune itself, glancing at the youth from time to time an acute and brilliant beam of its hazel eye, which seemed to ask why he caressed it not with his usual fondness.

"Ah, Diamond!" he said, as if the bird understood him, "thou and I must be strangers henceforward. Many a gallant stoop have I seen thee make, and many a brave heron strike down; but that is all gone and over, and there is no hawking more for me!"

"And why not, Master Roland," said Adam Woodcock, the falconer, who came at that instant from behind a few alder bushes which had concealed him from view—"why should there be no more hawking for you? Why, man, what were our life without our sports? Thou know'st the jolly old song—

And rather would Allan in dungeon lie,
Than live at large where the falcon cannot fly;
And Allan would rather lie in sexton's pound,
Than live where he follow'd not the merry hawk and hound."

The voice of the falconer was hearty and friendly, and the tone in which he half-sung, half-recited his rude ballad implied honest frankness and cordiality. But remembrance of their quarrel, and its consequences, embarrassed Roland, and prevented his reply. The falconer saw his hesitation, and guessed the cause.

"What now," said he, "Master Roland? do you, who are half an Englishman, think that I, who am a whole one, would keep up anger against you, and you in distress? That were like some of the Scots—my master's reverence always excepted—who can be fair and false, and wait their time, and keep their mind, as they say, to themselves, and touch pot and flagon with you, and hunt and hawk with you, and, after all, when time serves, pay off some old feud with the point of the dagger. Canny Yorkshire has no memory for such old sores. Why, man, an you had hit me a rough blow, maybe I would rather have taken it from you than a rough word from another; for you have a good notion of falconry, though you stand up for washing the meat for the eyases. So give us your hand, man, and bear no malice."

Roland, though he felt his proud blood rebel at the familiarity of honest Adam's address, could not resist its downright frankness. Covering his face with the one hand, he held out the other to the falconer, and returned with readiness his friendly grasp.

"Why, this is hearty now," said Woodcock; "I always said you had a kind heart, though you have a spice of the devil in your disposition, that is certain. I came this way with the falcon on purpose to find you, and yon half-bred lubbard told me which way you took flight. You ever thought too much of that kestril-kite, Master Roland, and he knows naught of sport, after all, but what he caught from you. I saw how it had been betwixt you, and I sent him out of my company with a wanion; I would rather have a rifler on my perch than a false knave at my elbow. And now, Master Roland, tell me what way wing ye?"

"That is as God pleases," replied the page, with a sigh which he could not suppress.

"Nay, man, never droop a feather for being cast off," said the falconer; "who knows but you may soar the better and fairer flight for all this yet? Look at Diamond there; 'tis a noble bird, and shows gallantly with his hood and bells and jesses; but there is many a wild falcon in Norway that would not change properties with him. And that is what I would say of you. You are no longer my lady's page, and you will not clothe so fair, or feed so well, or sleep so soft, or show so gallant. What of all that? if you are not her page, you are your own man, and may go where you will, without minding whoop or whistle. The worst is the loss of the sport, but who knows what you may come to? They say that Sir Halbert himself—I speak with reverence—was once glad to be the abbot's forester, and now he has hounds and hawks of his own, and Adam Woodcock for a falconer to the boot."

"You are right, and say well, Adam," answered the youth, the blood mantling in his cheeks: "the falcon will soar higher without his bells than with them, though the bells be made of silver."

"That is cheerily spoken," replied the falconer; "and whither now?"

"I thought of going to the Abbey of Kennaquhair," answered Roland Græme, "to ask the counsel of Father Ambrose."

"And joy go with you," said the falconer, "though it is likely you may find the old monks in some sorrow: they say the commons are threatening to turn them out of their cells, and make a devil's mass of it in the old church, thinking they have forborne that sport too long; and troth I am clear of the same opinion."

"Then will Father Ambrose be the better of having a friend beside him!" said the page, manfully.

"Ay, but, my young fearnaught," replied a falconer, "the friend will scarce be the better of being beside Father Ambrose: he may come by the redder's lick, and that is ever the worst of the battle."

"I care not for that," said the page; "the dread of a lick should not hold me back; but I fear I may bring trouble between the brothers by visiting Father Ambrose. I will tarry to-night at St. Cuthbert's cell, where the old priest will give me a night's shelter; and I will send to Father Ambrose to ask his advice before I go down to the convent."

"By Our Lady," said the falconer, "and that is a likely plan! And now," he continued, changing his frankness of manner for a sort of awkward embarrassment, as if he had somewhat to say that he had no ready means to bring out—"and now, you wot well that I wear a pouch for my hawks' meat,* and so forth, but wot ye what it is lined with, Master Roland?"

"With leather, to be sure," replied Roland, somewhat surprised at the hesitation with which Adam Woodcock asked a question apparently so simple.

"With leather, lad?" said Woodcock; "ay, and with silver to the boot of that. See here," he said, showing a secret slit in the lining of his bag of office—"here they are, thirty good Harry groats as ever were struck in bluff old Hal's time, and ten of them are right heartily at your service; and now the murder is out."

Roland's first idea was to refuse this assistance; but he recollected the vows of humility which he had just taken upon him, and it occurred that this was the opportunity to put his new-formed resolution to the test. Assuming a strong command of himself, he answered Adam Woodcock with as much frankness as his nature permitted him to wear, in doing what was so contrary to his inclinations, that he accepted thankfully of his kind offer, while to soothe his own reviving pride, he could not help adding, "He hoped soon to requite the obligation."

"That as you list—that as you list, young man," said the falconer, with glee, counting out and delivering to his young friend the supply he had so generously offered, and then adding with great cheerfulness—"Now you may go through the world; for he that can back a horse, wind a horn, halloo a greyhound, fly a hawk, and play at sword and buckler, with a whole pair of shoes, a green jacket, and ten lily-white groats in his pouch, may bid Father Care hang himself in his own jesses. Farewell, and God be with you!"

So saying, and as if desirous to avoid the thanks of his companion, he turned hastily round, and left Roland Græme to pursue his journey alone.

* See Bag for Hawks' Meat. Note 2.

CHAPTER VIII

The sacred tapers' lights are gone,
Gray moss has clad the altar stone,
The holy image is o'erthrown,
  The bell has ceased to toll.
The long ribb'd aisles are burst and shrunk,
The holy shrines to ruin sunk,
Departed is the pious monk,
  God's blessing on his soul!

Rediviva.

THE cell of St. Cuthbert, as it was called, marked, or was supposed to mark, one of those resting-places which that venerable saint was pleased to assign to his monks, when his convent, being driven from Lindisfern by the Danes, became a peripatetic society of religionists, and, bearing their patron's body on their shoulders, transported him from place to place through Scotland and the borders of England, until he was pleased at length to spare them the pain of carrying him farther, and to choose his ultimate place of rest in the lordly towers of Durham. The odor of his sanctity remained behind him at each place where he had granted the monks a transient respite from their labors; and proud were those who could assign as his temporary resting-place any spot within their vicinity. There were few cells more celebrated and honored than that of St. Cuthbert, to which Roland Græme now bent his way, situated considerably to the northwest of the great Abbey of Kennaquhair, on which it was dependent. In the neighborhood were some of those recommendations which weighed with the experienced priesthood of Rome in choosing their sites for places of religion.

There was a well, possessed of some medicinal qualities, which, of course, claimed the saint for its guardian and patron, and occasionally produced some advantage to the recluse who inhabited his cell, since none could reasonably expect to benefit by the fountain who did not extend their bounty to the saint's chaplain. A few roods of fertile land afforded the monk his plot of garden ground; an eminence well clothed with trees rose behind the cell, and sheltered it from the north and the east, while the front, opening to the southwest, looked up a wild but pleasant valley, down which wandered a lively brook, which battled with every stone that interrupted its passage.

The cell itself was rather plainly than rudely constructed —a low Gothic building with two small apartments, one of which served the priest for his dwelling-place, the other for his chapel. As there were few of the secular clergy who durst venture to reside so near the Border, the assistance of this monk in spiritual affairs had not been useless to the community while the Catholic religion retained the ascendency, as he could marry, christen, and administer the other sacraments of the Roman Church. Of late, however, as the Protestant doctrines gained ground, he had found it convenient to live in close retirement, and to avoid, as much as possible, drawing upon himself observation or animadversion. The appearance of his habitation, however, when Roland Græme came before it in the close of the evening, plainly showed that his caution had been finally ineffectual.

The page's first movement was to knock at the door, when he observed, to his surprise, that it was open, not from being left unlatched, but because, beat off its upper hinge, it was only fastened to the door-post by the lower, and could therefore no longer perform its functions. Somewhat alarmed at this, and receiving no answer when he knocked and called, Roland began to look more at leisure upon the exterior of the little dwelling, before he ventured to enter it. The flowers, which had been trained with care against the walls, seemed to have been recently torn down, and trailed their dishonored garlands on the earth; the latticed window was broken and dashed in. The garden, which the monk had maintained by his constant labor in the highest order and beauty, bore marks of having been lately trod down and destroyed by the hoofs of animals and the feet of men.

The sainted spring had not escaped. It was wont to rise beneath a canopy of ribbed arches, with which the devotion of elder times had secured and protected its healing waters. These arches were now almost entirely demolished, and the stones of which they were built were tumbled into the well, as if for the purpose of choking up and destroying the fountain, which, as it had shared in other days the honor of the saint, was, in the present, doomed to partake his unpopularity. Part of the roof had been pulled down from the house itself, and an attempt had been made with crows and levers upon one of the angles, by which several large corner-stones had been forced out of their place; but the solidity of ancient masonwork had proved too great for the time or patience of the assailants, and they had relinquished their task of destruction. Such dilapidated buildings, after the lapse of years, during which nature has gradually covered the effects of violence with creeping plants and with weather-stains, exhibit, amid their decay, a melancholy beauty. But when the visible effects of violence appear raw and recent there is no feeling to mitigate the sense of devastation with which they impress the spectators; and such was now the scene on which the youthful page gazed, with the painful feelings it was qualified to excite.

When his first momentary surprise was over, Roland Græme was at no loss to conjecture the cause of these ravages. The destruction of the Popish edifices did not take place at once throughout Scotland, but at different times, and according to the spirit which actuated the Reformed clergy, some of whom instigated their hearers to these acts of demolition, and others, with better taste and feelings, endeavored to protect the ancient shrines, while they desired to see them purified from the objects which had attracted idolatrous devotion. From time to time, therefore, the populace of the Scottish towns and villages, when instigated either by their own feelings of abhorrence for Popish superstition or by the doctrines of the more zealous preachers, resumed the work of destruction, and exercised it upon some sequestered church, chapel, or cell, which had escaped the first burst of their indignation against the religion of Rome. In many places, the vices of the Catholic clergy, arising out of the wealth and the corruption of that tremendous hierarchy, furnished too good an apology for wreaking vengeance upon the splendid edifices which they inhabited; and of this an old Scottish historian gives a remarkable instance.

"Why mourn ye," said an aged matron, seeing the discontent of some of the citizens while a stately convent was burnt by the multitude—"why mourn ye for its destruction? If you knew half the flagitious wickedness which had been perpetrated within that house, you would rather bless the Divine judgment which permits not even the senseless walls that screened such profligacy any longer to cumber Christian ground!"

But although, in many instances, the destruction of the Roman Catholic buildings might be, in the matron's way of judging, an act of justice, and in others an act of policy, there is no doubt that the humor of demolishing monuments of ancient piety and munificence, and that in a poor country like Scotland, where there was no chance of their being replaced, was both useless, mischievous, and barbarous.

In the presence instance, the unpretending and quiet seclusion of the monk of St Cuthbert's had hitherto saved him from the general wreck; but it would seem ruin had now at length reached him. Anxious to discover if he had at least escaped personal harm, Roland Græme entered the half-ruined cell.

The interior of the building was in a state which fully justified the opinion he had formed from its external injuries. The few rude utensils of the solitary's hut were broken down, and lay scattered on the floor, where it seemed as if a fire had been made with some of the fragments to destroy the rest of his property, and to consume, in particular, the rude old image of St. Cuthbert, in its episcopal habit, which lay on the hearth, like Dagon of yore, shattered with the ax and scorched with the flames, but only partially destroyed. In the little apartment which served as a chapel, the altar was overthrown, and the four huge stones of which it had been once composed lay scattered around the floor. The large stone crucifix which occupied the niche behind the altar, and fronted the supplicant while he paid his devotion there, had been pulled down, and dashed by its own weight into three fragments. There were marks of sledge-hammers on each of these; yet the image had been saved from utter demolition by the size and strength of the remaining fragments, which, though much injured, retained enough of the original sculpture to show what it had been intended to represent.*

Roland Græme, secretly nursed in the tenets of Rome, saw with horror the profanation of the most sacred emblem, according to his creed, of our holy religion.

"It is the badge of our redemption," he said, "which the felons have dared to violate; would to God my weak strength were able to replace it—my humble reverence to atone for the sacrilege!"

He stooped to the task he first meditated, and with a sudden, and to himself almost an incredible, exertion of power he lifted up the one extremity of the lower shaft of the cross, and rested it upon the edge of the large stone which served for its pedestal. Encouraged by this success, he applied his

* See Cell of St. Cuthbert. Note 3.

"'Well done, thou good and faithful servant!'"

force to the other extremity, and, to his own astonishment, succeeded so far as to erect the lower end of the limb into the socket, out of which it had been forced, and to place this fragment of the image upright.

While he was employed in this labor, or rather at the very moment when he had accomplished the elevation of the fragment, a voice, in thrilling and well-known accents, spoke behind him these words: "Well done, thou good and faithful servant! Thus would I again meet the child of my love—the hope of my aged eyes."

Roland turned round in astonishment, and the tall commanding form of Magdalen Græme stood beside him. She was arrayed in a sort of loose habit, in form like that worn by penitents in Catholic countries, but black in color, and approaching as near to a pilgrim's cloak as it was safe to wear in a country where the suspicion of Catholic devotion in many places endangered the safety of those who were suspected of attachment io the ancient faith. Roland Græme threw himself at her feet. She raised and embraced him, with affection indeed, but not unmixed with gravity which amounted almost to sternness.

"Thou has kept well," she said, "the bird in thy bosom.* As a boy, as a youth, thou hast held fast thy faith amongst heretics: thou hast kept thy secret and mine own amongst thine enemies. I wept when I parted from you—I, who seldom weep, then shed tears, less for thy death than for thy spiritual danger. I dared not even see thee to bid thee a last farewell; my grief—my swelling grief had betrayed me to these heretics. But thou hast been faithful; down—down on thy knees before the holy sign, which evil men injure and blaspheme—down and praise saints and angels for the grace they have done thee, in preserving thee from the leprous plague which cleaves to the house in which thou wert nurtured!"

"If, my mother—so I must ever call you," replied Græme—"if I am returned such as thou wouldst wish me, thou must thank the care of the pious Father Ambrose, whose instructions confirmed your early precepts, and taught me at once to be faithful and to be silent."

"Be he blessed for it!" said she—"blessed in the cell and in the field, in the pulpit and at the altar! The saints rain blessings on him! They are just, and employ his pious care

* An expression used by Sir Ralph Percy, slain in the battle of Hedgely Moor in 1464, when dying, to express his having preserved unstained his fidelity to the house of Lancaster.

to counteract the evils which his detested brother works against the realm and the church. But he knew not of thy lineage?"

"I could not myself tell him that," answered Roland. "I knew but darkly from your words that Sir Halbert Glendinning holds mine inheritance, and that I am of blood as noble as runs in the veins of any Scottish baron; these are things not to be forgotten, but for the explanation I must now look to you."

"And when time suits thou shalt not ask for it in vain. But men say, my son, that thou art bold and sudden; and those who bear such tempers are not lightly to be trusted with what will strongly move them."

"Say rather, my mother," returned Roland Græme, "that I am laggard and cold-blooded; what patience or endurance can you require of which *he* is not capable who for years has heard his religion ridiculed and insulted, yet failed to plunge his dagger into the blasphemer's bosom!"

"Be contented, my child," replied Magdalen Græme; "the time which then and even now demands patience, will soon ripen to that of effort and action; great events are on the wing, and thou—thou shalt have thy share in advancing them. Thou hast relinquished the service of the Lady of Avenel?"

"I have been dismissed from it, my mother—I have lived to be dismissed, as if I were the meanest of the train."

"It is the better, my child," replied she; "thy mind will be the more hardened to undertake that which must be performed."

"Let it be nothing, then, against the Lady of Avenel," said the page, "as thy look and words seem to imply. I have eaten her bread—I have experienced her favor; I will neither injure nor betray her."

"Of that hereafter, my son," said she; "but learn this, that it is not for thee to capitulate in thy duty, and to say this will I do, and that will I leave undone. No, Roland! God and man will no longer abide the wickedness of this generation. Seest thou these fragments—knowest thou what they represent?—and canst thou think it is for thee to make distinctions amongst a race so accursed by Heaven that they renounce, violate, blaspheme, and destroy whatsoever we are commanded to believe in, whatsoever we are commanded to reverence?"

As she spoke, she bent her head towards the broken image, with a countenance in which strong resentment and zeal were mingled with an expression of ecstatic devotion; she raised her left hand aloft as in the act of making a vow, and thus proceeded: "Bear witness for me, blessed symbol of our salvation—bear witness, holy saint, within whose violated temple we stand, that as it is not for vengeance of my own that my hate pursues these people, so neither, for any favor or earthly affection towards any amongst them, will I withdraw my hand from the plow, when it shall pass through the devoted furrow! Bear witness, holy saint, once thyself a wanderer and a fugitive as we are now—bear witness, Mother of Mercy, Queen of Heaven—bear witness, saints and angels!"

In this high strain of enthusiasm she stood, raising her eyes through the fractured roof of the vault to the stars which now began to twinkle through the pale twilight, while the long gray tresses which hung down over her shoulders waved in the night-breeze, which the chasm and fractured windows admitted freely.

Roland Græme was too much awed by early habits, as well as by the mysterious import of her words, to ask for further explanation of the purpose she obscurely hinted at. Nor did she farther press him on the subject; for, having concluded her prayer or obtestation, by clasping her hands together with solemnity, and then signing herself with the cross, she again addressed her grandson, in a tone more adapted to the ordinary business of life.

"Thou must hence," she said, "Roland—thou must hence, but not till morning. And now, how wilt thou shift for thy night's quarters? Thou hast been more softly bred than when we were companions in the misty hills of Cumberland and Liddesdale."

"I have at least preserved, my good mother, the habits which I then learned—can lie hard, feed sparingly, and think it no hardship. Since I was a wanderer with thee on the hills, I have been a hunter, and fisher, and fowler, and each of these is accustomed to sleep freely in a worse shelter than sacrilege has left us here."

"Than sacrilege has left us here!" said the matron, repeating his words, and pausing on them. "Most true, my son; and God's faithful children are now worst sheltered when they lodge in God's own house and the demesne of His blessed saints. We shall sleep cold here under the night-wind, which whistles through the breaches that heresy has made. They shall lie warmer who made them—ay, and through a long hereafter!'

Notwithstanding the wild and singular expression of this

female, she appeared to retain towards Roland Græme, in a strong degree, that affectionate and sedulous love which women bear to their nurslings, and the children dependent on their care. It seemed as if she would not permit him to do aught for himself which in former days her attention had been used to do for him, and that she considered the tall stripling before her as being equally dependent on her careful attention as when he was the orphan child who had owed all to her affectionate solicitude

"What hast thou to eat now?" she said, as, leaving the chapel, they went into the deserted habitation of the priest; "or what means of kindling a fire, to defend thee from this raw and inclement air? Poor child! thou hast made slight provision for a long journey; nor hast thou skill to help thyself by wit when means are scanty. But Our Lady has placed by thy side one to whom want, in all its forms, is as familiar as plenty and splendor have formerly been. And with want, Roland, come the arts of which she is the inventor."

With an active and officious diligence, which strangely contrasted with her late abstracted and high tone of Catholic devotion, she set about her domestic arrangements for the evening. A pouch, which was hidden under her garment, produced a flint and steel, and from the scattered fragments around (those pertaining to the image of St. Cuthbert scrupulously excepted) she obtained splinters sufficient to raise a sparkling and cheerful fire on the hearth of the deserted cell.

"And now," she said, "for needful food."

"Think not of it, mother," said Roland, "unless you yourself feel hunger. It is a little thing for me to endure a night's abstinence, and a small atonement for the necessary transgression of the rules of the church upon which I was compelled during my stay in the castle."

"Hunger for myself!" answered the matron. "Know, youth, that a mother knows not hunger till that of her child is satisfied." And with affectionate inconsistency, totally different from her usual manner, she added, "Roland, you must not fast; you have dispensation; you are young, and to youth food and sleep are necessaries not to be dispensed with. Husband your strength, my child; your sovereign, your religion, your country require it. Let age macerate by fast and vigil a body which can only suffer; let youth, in these active times, nourish the limbs and the strength which action requires."

While she thus spoke, the scrip, which had produced the means of striking fire, furnished provisions for a meal; of which she herself scarce partook, but anxiously watched her charge, taking a pleasure, resembling that of an epicure, in each morsel which he swallowed, with a youthful appetite which abstinence had rendered unusually sharp. Roland readily obeyed her recommendations, and ate the food which she so affectionately and earnestly placed before him. But she shook her head when invited by him in return to partake of the refreshment her own cares had furnished; and when his solicitude became more pressing, she refused him in a loftier tone of rejection.

"Young man," she said, "you know not to whom, or of what, you speak. They to whom Heaven declares its purpose must merit its communication by mortifying the senses; they have that within which requires not the superfluity of earthly nutriment, which is necessary to those who are without the sphere of the Vision. To them the watch spent in prayer is a refreshing slumber, and the sense of doing the will of Heaven is a richer banquet than the tables of monarchs can spread before them! But do thou sleep soft, my son," she said, relapsing from the tone of fanaticism into that of maternal affection and tenderness—"do thou sleep sound while life is but young with thee, and the cares of the day can be drowned in the slumbers of the evening. Different is thy duty and mine, and as different the means by which we must qualify and strengthen ourselves to perform it. From thee is demanded strength of body—from me strength of soul."

When she thus spoke, she prepared with ready address a pallet-couch, composed partly of the dried leaves which had once furnished a bed to the solitary, and the guests who occasionally received his hospitality, and which, neglected by the destroyers of his humble cell, had remained little disturbed in the corner allotted for them. To these her care added some of the vestures which lay torn and scattered on the floor. With a zealous hand she selected all such as appeared to have made any part of the sacerdotal vestments, laying them aside as sacred from ordinary purposes, and with the rest she made, with dexterous promptness, such a bed as a weary man might willingly stretch himself on; and during the time she was preparing it, rejected, even with acrimony, any attempt which the youth made to assist her, or any entreaty which he urged that she should accept of the place of rest for her own use. "Sleep thou," said she,

"Roland Græme—sleep thou—the persecuted, the disinherited orphan—the son of an ill-fated mother—sleep thou! I go to pray in the chapel beside thee."

The manner was too enthusiastically earnest, too obstinately firm, to permit Roland Græme to dispute her will any farther. Yet he felt some shame in giving way to it. It seemed as if she had forgotten the years that had passed away since their parting; and expected to meet, in the tall, indulged, and wilful youth whom she had recovered, the passive obedience of the child whom she had left in the Castle of Avenel. This did not fail to hurt her grandson's characteristic and constitutional pride. He obeyed, indeed, awed into submission by the sudden recurrence of former subordination, and by feelings of affection and gratitude. Still, however, he felt the yoke.

"Have I relinquished the hawk and the hound," he said, "to become the pupil of her pleasure, as if I were still a child? I, whom even my envious mates allowed to be superior in those exercises which they took most pains to acquire, and which came to me naturally, as if a knowledge of them had been my birthright? This may not, and must not be. I will be no reclaimed sparrow-hawk, who is carried hooded on a woman's wrist, and has his quarry only shown to him when his eyes are uncovered for his flight. I will know her purpose ere it is proposed to me to aid it."

These and other thoughts streamed through the mind of Roland Græme; and, although wearied with the fatigues of the day, it was long ere he could compose himself to rest.

CHAPTER IX

Kneel with me—swear it—'tis not in words I trust,
Save when they're fenced with an appeal to Heaven.
Old Play.

AFTER passing the night in that sound sleep for which agitation and fatigue had prepared him, Roland was awakened by the fresh morning air, and by the beams of the rising sun. His first feeling was that of surprise ; for, instead of looking forth from a turret window on the waters of the lake of Avenel, which was the prospect his former apartment afforded, an unlatticed aperture gave him the view of the demolished garden of the banished anchorite. He sate up on his couch of leaves, and arranged in his memory, not without wonder, the singular events of the preceding day, which appeared the more surprising the more he considered them. He had lost the protectress of his youth, and, in the same day, he had recovered the guide and guardian of his childhood. The former deprivation he felt ought to be matter of unceasing regret, and it seemed as if the latter could hardly be the subject of unmixed self-congratulation. He remembered this person, who had stood to him in the relation of a mother, as equally affectionate in her attention and absolute in her authority. A singular mixture of love and fear attended upon his early remembrances as they were connected with her ; and the fear that she might desire to resume the same absolute control over his motions—a fear which her conduct of yesterday did not tend much to dissipate—weighed heavily against the joy of this second meeting.

"She cannot mean," said his rising pride, "to lead and direct me as a pupil, when I am at the age of judging of my own actions ?—this she cannot mean, or meaning it, will feel herself strangely deceived."

A sense of gratitude towards the person against whom his heart thus rebelled checked this course of feeling. He resisted the thoughts which involuntarily arose in his mind, as he would have resisted an actual instigation of the foul fiend ; and to aid him in his struggle, he felt for his beads.

But, in his hasty departure from the Castle of Avenel, he had forgotten and left them behind him.

"This is yet worse," he said; "but two things I learned of her under the most deadly charge of secrecy—to tell my beads, and to conceal that I did so; and I have kept my word till now; and when she shall ask me for the rosary, I must say I have forgotten it! Do I deserve she should believe me when I say I have kept the secret of my faith, when I set so light by its symbol?"

He paced the floor in anxious agitation. In fact, his attachment to his faith was of a nature very different from that which animated the enthusiastic matron, but which, notwithstanding, it would have been his last thought to relinquish.

The early charges impressed on him by his grandmother had been instilled into a mind and memory of a character peculiarly tenacious. Child as he was, he was proud of the confidence reposed in his discretion, and resolved to show that it had not been rashly entrusted to him. At the same time, his resolution was no more than that of a child, and must, necessarily, have gradually faded away under the operation both of precept and example, during his residence at the Castle of Avenel, but for the exhortations of Father Ambrose, who, in his late estate, had been called Edward Glendinning. This zealous monk had been apprised, by an unsigned letter placed in his hand by a pilgrim, that a child educated in the Catholic faith was now in the Castle of Avenel, perilously situated (so was the scroll expressed) as ever the three children who were cast into the fiery furnace of persecution. The letter threw upon Father Ambrose the fault should this solitary lamb, unwillingly left within the demesnes of the prowling wolf, become his final prey. There needed no farther exhortation to the monk than the idea that a soul might be endangered, and that a Catholic might become an apostate; and he made his visits more frequent than usual to the Castle of Avenel, lest, through want of the private encouragement and instruction which he always found some opportunity of dispensing, the church should lose a proselyte, and, according to the Romish creed, the devil acquire a soul.

Still these interviews were rare; and though they encouraged the solitary boy to keep his secret and hold fast his religion, they were neither frequent nor long enough to inspire him with anything beyond a blind attachment to the observances which the priest recommended. He adhered to the forms of his religion, rather because he felt it would be dishonorable to change that of his fathers than from any rational conviction or sincere belief of its mysterious doctrines. It was a principal part of the distinction which, in his own opinion, singled him out from those with whom he lived, and gave him an additional, though an internal and concealed, reason for contemning those of the household who showed an undisguised dislike of him, and for hardening himself against the instructions of the chaplain, Henry Warden.

"The fanatic preacher," he thought within himself, during some one of the chaplain's frequent discourses against the Church of Rome, "he little knows whose ears are receiving his profane doctrine, and with what contempt and abhorrence they hear his blasphemies against the holy religion by which kings have been crowned and for which martyrs have died!"

But in such proud feelings of defiance of heresy, as it was termed, and of its professors, which associated the Catholic religion with a sense of generous independence, and that of the Protestants with the subjugation of his mind and temper to the direction of Mr. Warden, began and ended the faith of Roland Græme, who, independently of the pride of singularity, sought not to understand, and had no one to expound to him, the peculiarities of the tenets which he professed. His regret, therefore, at missing the rosary which had been conveyed to him through the hands of Father Ambrose was rather the shame of a soldier who has dropped his cockade, or badge of service, than that of a zealous votary who had forgotten a visible symbol of his religion.

His thoughts on the subject, however, were mortifying, and the more so from apprehension that his negligence must reach the ears of his relative. He felt it could be no one but her who had secretly transmitted these beads to Father Ambrose for his use, and that his carelessness was but an indifferent requital of her kindness.

"Nor will she omit to ask me about them," said he to himself; "for hers is a zeal which age cannot quell; and if she has not quitted her wont, my answer will not fail to incense her."

While he thus communed with himself, Magdalen Græme entered the apartment. "The blessing of the morning on your youthful head, my son," she said, with a solemnity of expression which thrilled the youth to the heart, so sad and earnest did the benediction flow from her lips, in a tone where devotion was blended with affection. "And thou hast started thus early from thy couch to catch the first breath of the dawn? But it is not well, my Roland. Enjoy slumber while thou canst; the time is not far behind when the waking eye must be thy portion as well as mine."

She uttered these words with an affectionate and anxious tone, which showed that, devotional as were the habitual exercises of her mind, the thoughts of her nursling yet bound her to earth with the cords of human affection and passion.

But she abode not long in a mood which she probably regarded as a momentary dereliction of her imaginary high calling. "Come," she said, "youth, up and be doing. It is time that we leave this place."

"And whither do we go?" said the young man; "or what is the object of our journey?"

The matron stepped back, and gazed on him with surprise, not unmingled with displeasure.

"To what purpose such a question?" she said; "is it not enough that I lead the way? Hast thou lived with heretics till thou hast learned to instal the vanity of thine own private judgment in the place of due honor and obedience?"

"The time," thought Roland Græme within himself, "is already come when I must establish my freedom or be a willing thrall forever. I feel that I must speedily look to it."

She instantly fulfilled his foreboding, by recurring to the theme by which her thoughts seemed most constantly engrossed, although, when she pleased, no one could so perfectly disguise her religion.

"Thy beads, my son—hast thou told thy beads?"

Roland Græme colored high; he felt the storm was approaching, but scorned to avert it by a falsehood.

"I have forgotten my rosary," he said, "at the Castle of Avenel."

"Forgotten thy rosary!" she exclaimed; "false both to religion and to natural duty, hast thou lost what was sent so far, and at such a risk, a token of the truest affection, that should have been, every bead of it, as dear to thee as thine eyeballs?"

"I am grieved it should have so chanced, mother," replied the youth, "and much did I value the token, as coming from you. For what remains, I trust to win gold enough, when I push my way in the world; and till then beads of black oak, or a rosary of nuts, must serve the turn."

"Hear him!" said his grandmother; "young as he is, he

hath learned already the lessons of the devil's school! The rosary consecrated by the Holy Father himself, and sanctified by his blessings, is but a few knobs of gold, whose value may be replaced by the wages of his profane labor, and whose virtue may be supplied by a string of hazel nuts! This is heresy. Sir Henry Warden, the wolf who ravages the flock of the Shepherd, hath taught thee to speak and to think."

"Mother," said Roland Græme, "I am no heretic: I believe and I pray according to the rules of our church. This misfortune I regret, but I cannot amend it."

"Thou canst repent it, though," replied his spiritual directress—"repent it in dust and ashes, atone for it by fasting, prayer, and penance, instead of looking on me with a countenance as light as if thou hadst lost but a button from thy cap."

"Mother," said Roland, "be appeased; I will remember my fault in the next confession which I have space and opportunity to make, and will do whatever the priest may require of me in atonement. For the heaviest fault I can do no more. But, mother," he added, after a moment's pause, "let me not incur your farther displeasure, if I ask whither our journey is bound, and what is its object. I am no longer a child, but a man, and at my own disposal, with down upon my chin and a sword by my side; I will go to the end of the world with you to do your pleasure, but I owe it to myself to inquire the purpose and direction of our travels."

"You owe it to yourself, ungrateful boy!" replied his relative, passion rapidly supplying the color which age had long chased from her features. "To yourself you owe nothing—you can owe nothing; to me you owe everything—your life when an infant—your support when a child—the means of instruction and the hopes of honor; and, sooner than thou shouldst abandon the noble cause to which I have devoted thee, would I see thee lie a corpse at my feet!"

Roland was alarmed at the vehement agitation with which she spoke, and which threatened to overpower her aged frame; and he hastened to reply—"I forget nothing of what I owe to you, my dearest mother; show me how my blood can testify my gratitude, and you shall judge if I spare it. But blindfold obedience has in it as little merit as reason."

"Saints and angels!" replied Magdalen, "and do I hear these words from the child of my hopes, the nursling by whose bed I have kneeled, and for whose weal I have wearied every saint in Heaven with prayers? Roland, by obedience only canst thou show thy affection and thy gratitude. What avails it that you might perchance adopt the course I propose to thee, were it to be fully explained? Thou wouldst not then follow my command, but thine own judgment; thou wouldst not do the will of Heaven, communicated through thy best friend, to whom thy owest thine all; but thou wouldst observe the blinded dictates of thine own imperfect reason. Hear me, Roland! a lot calls thee—solicits thee—demands thee—the proudest to which man can be destined, and it uses the voice of thine earliest—thy best—thine only friend. Wilt thou resist it? Then go thy way—leave me here; my hopes on earth are gone and withered. I will kneel me down before yonder profaned altar, and when the raging heretics return, they shall dye it with the blood of a martyr!"

"But, my dearest mother," said Roland Græme, whose early recollections of her violence were formidably renewed by these wild expressions of reckless passion, "I will not forsake you—I will abide with you: worlds shall not force me from your side. I will protect—I will defend you; I will live with you, and die for you!"

"One word, my son, were worth all these; say only, 'I will obey you.'"

"Doubt it not, mother," replied the youth, "I will, and that with all my heart; only——"

"Nay, I receive no qualifications of thy promise," said Magdalen Græme, catching at the word, "the obedience which I require is absolute; and a blessing on thee, thou darling memory of my beloved child, that thou hast power to make a promise so hard to human pride! Trust me well, that in the design in which thou dost embark thou hast for thy partners the mighty and the valiant, the power of the church, and the pride of the noble. Succeed or fail, live or die, thy name shall be among those with whom success or failure is alike glorious, death or life alike desirable. Forward then—forward! life is short, and our plan is laborious. Angels, saints, and the whole blessed host of Heaven have their eyes even now on this barren and blighted land of Scotland. What say I? On Scotland? Their eye is on *us*, Roland—on the frail woman, on the inexperienced youth, who, amidst the ruins which sacrilege hath made in the holy place, devote themselves to God's cause, and that of their lawful sovereign. Amen, so be it! The blessed eyes of saints and martyrs, which see our resolve, shall witness the execution; or their ears, which hear our vow, shall hear our death-groan drawn in the sacred cause!"

While thus speaking, she held Ronald Græme firmly with one hand, while she pointed upward with the other, to leave him, as it were, no means of protest against the obtestation to which he was thus made a party. When she had finished her appeal to Heaven, she left him no leisure for farther hesitation, or for asking any explanation of her purpose; but, passing with the same ready transition as formerly to the solicitous attentions of an anxious parent, overwhelmed him with questions concerning his residence in the Castle of Avenel, and the qualities and accomplishments he had acquired.

"It is well," she said, when she had exhausted her inquiries: "my gay goss-hawk* hath been well trained, and will soar high; but those who bred him will have cause to fear as well as to wonder at his flight. Let us now," she said, "to our morning meal, and care not though it be a scanty one. A few hours' walk will bring us to more friendly quarters."

They broke their fast accordingly on such fragments as remained of their yesterday's provision, and immediately set out on their farther journey. Magdalen Græme led the way, with a firm and active step much beyond her years, and Roland Græme followed, pensive and anxious, and far from satisfied with the state of dependence to which he seemed again to be reduced.

"Am I forever," he said to himself, "to be devoured with the desire of independence and free agency, and yet to be forever led on by circumstances to follow the will of others?"

*See Note 4.

CHAPTER X

She dwelt unnoticed and alone,
  Beside the springs of Dove—
A maid whom there was none to praise,
  And very few to love.

WORDSWORTH.

IN the course of their journey the travelers spoke little to each other. Magdalen Græme chanted, from time to time, in a low voice, a part of some one of those beautiful old Latin hymns which belong to the Catholic service, muttered an ave or a credo, and so passed on, lost in devotional contemplation. The meditations of her grandson were more bent on mundane matters ; and many a time, as a moorfowl arose from the heath and shot along the moor, uttering his bold crow of defiance, he thought of the jolly Adam Woodcock and his trusty gross-hawk ; or, as they passed a thicket where the low trees and bushes were intermingled with tall fern, furze, and broom, so as to form a thick and intricate cover, his dreams were of a roebuck and a brace of gazehounds. But frequently his mind returned to the benevolent and kind mistress whom he had left behind him offended justly, and unreconciled by any effort of his.

"My step would be lighter," he thought, "and so would my heart, could I but have returned to see her for one instant, and to say, 'Lady, the orphan boy was wild, but not ungrateful!'"

Traveling in these divers moods, about the hour of noon they reached a small straggling village, in which, as usual, were seen one or two of those predominating towers, or peel-houses, which, for reasons of defense elsewhere detailed, were at that time to be found in every Border hamlet. A brook flowed beside the village, and watered the valley in which it stood. There was also a mansion at the end of the village and a little way separated from it, much dilapidated and in very bad order, but appearing to have been the abode of persons of some consideration. The situation was agreeable, being an angle formed by the stream, bearing three or four large sycamore-trees, which were in full leaf, and served to relieve the dark appearance of the mansion, which was built of a deep-red stone. The house itself was a large one, but was now obviously too big for the inmates; several windows were built up, especially those which opened from the lower story; others were blockaded in a less substantial manner. The court before the door, which had once been defended with a species of low outer wall, now ruinous, was paved, but the stones were completely covered with long gray nettles, thistles, and other weeds, which, shooting up betwixt the flags, had displaced many of them from their level. Even matters demanding more peremptory attention had been left neglected, in a manner which argued sloth or poverty in the extreme. The stream, undermining a part of the bank near an angle of the ruinous wall, had brought it down, with a corner turret, the ruins of which lay in the bed of the river. The current, iuterrupted by the ruins which it had overthrown, and turned yet nearer to the site of the tower, had greatly enlarged the breach it had made, aud was in the process of undermining the ground on which the house itself stood, unless it were speedily protected by sufficient bulwarks.

All this attracted Roland Græme's observation, as they approached the dwelling by a winding path, which gave them, at intervals, a view of it from different points.

"If we go to yonder house," he said to his [grand-] mother, "I trust it is but for a short visit. It looks as if two rainy days from the northwest would send the whole into the brook."

"You see but with the eyes of the body," said the old woman; "God will defend His own, though it be forsaken and despised of men. Better to dwell on the sand, under His law, than fly to the rock of human trust."

As she thus spoke, they entered the court before the old mansion, and Roland could observe that the front of it had formerly been considerably ornamented with carved work, in the same dark-colored freestone of which it was built. But all these ornaments had been broken down and destroyed, and only the shattered vestiges of niches and entablatures now strewed the place which they had once occupied. The larger entrance in front was walled up, but a little footpath, which, from its appearance, seemed to be rarely trodden, led to a small wicket, defended by a door well clenched with iron-headed nails, at which Magdalen Græme knocked three times, pausing betwixt each knock, until she heard an answering tap from within. At the last knock, the wicket was opened by a pale thin female, who said, '*Benedicti qui veniunt in nomine Domini.*' They entered, and the portress hastily shut behind them the wicket, and made fast the massive fastenings by which it was secured.

The female led the way through a narrow entrance, into a vestibule of some extent, paved with stone, and having benches of the same solid material ranged around. At the upper end was an oriel window, but some of the intervals formed by the stone shafts and mullions were blocked up, so that the apartment was very gloomy.

Here they stopped, and the mistress of the mansion, for such she was, embraced Magdalen Græme, and greeting her by the title of sister, kissed her, with much solemnity, on either side of the face.

"The blessing of Our Lady be upon you, my sister," were her next words ; and they left no doubt upon Roland's mind respecting the religion of their hostess, even if he could have suspected his venerable and zealous guide of resting elsewhere than in the habitation of an orthodox Catholic. They spoke together a few words in private, during which he had leisure to remark more particularly the appearance of his grandmother's friend.

Her age might be betwixt fifty and sixty ; her looks had a mixture of melancholy and unhappiness that bordered on discontent, and obscured the remains of beauty which age had still left on her features. Her dress was of the plainest and most ordinary description, of a dark color, and, like Magdalen Græme's, something approaching to a religious habit. Strict neatness and cleanliness of person seemed to intimate that, if poor, she was not reduced to squalid or heart-broken distress, and that she was still sufficiently attached to life to retain a taste for its decencies, if not its elegancies. Her manner, as well as her features and appearance, argued an original condition and education far above the meanness of her present appearance. In short, the whole figure was such as to excite the idea, "That female must have had a history worth knowing." While Roland Græme was making this very reflection, the whispers of the two females ceased, and the mistress of the mansion, approaching him, looked on his face and person with much attention, and, as it seemed, some interest.

"This, then," she said, addressing his relative, "is the child of thine unhappy daughter, Sister Magdalen ; and him, the only shoot from your ancient tree, you are willing to devote to the good cause ?"

"Yes, by the rood," answered Magdalen Græme, in her

usual tone of resolved determination, "to the good cause I devote him, flesh and fell, sinew and limb, body and soul!"

"Thou art a happy woman, Sister Magdalen," answered her companion, "that, lifted so high above human affection and human feeling, thou canst bind such a victim to the horns of the altar. Had I been called to make such sacrifice —to plunge a youth so young and fair into the plots and bloodthirsty dealings of the time, not the patriarch Abraham, when he led Isaac up the mountain, would have rendered more melancholy obedience."

She then continued to look at Roland with a mournful aspect of compassion, until the intentness of her gaze occasioned his color to rise, and he was about to move out of its influence, when he was stopped by his grandmother with one hand, while with the other she divided the hair upon his forehead, which was now crimson with bashfulness, while she added, with a mixture of proud affection and firm resolution— "Ay, look at him well, my sister, for on a fairer face thine eye never rested. I too, when first I saw him, after a long separation, felt as the worldly feel, and was half shaken in my purpose. But no wind can tear a leaf from the withered tree which has long been stripped of its foliage, and no mere human casualty can awaken the mortal feelings which have long slept in the calm of devotion."

While the old woman thus spoke, her manner gave the lie to her assertions, for the tears rose to her eyes while she added, "But the fairer and the more spotless the victim, is it not, my sister, the more worthy of acceptance?" She seemed glad to escape from the sensations which agitated her, and instantly added, "He will escape, my sister: there will be a ram caught in the thicket, and the hand of our revolted brethren shall not be on the youthful Joseph. Heaven can defend its own rights, even by means of babes and sucklings, of women and beardless boys."

"Heaven hath left us," said the other female: "for our sins and our father's the succors of the blessed saints have abandoned this accursed land. We may win the crown of martyrdom, but not that of earthly triumph. One, too, whose prudence was at this deep crisis so indispensable, has been called to a better world. The Abbot Eustatius is no more."

"May his soul have mercy!" said Magdalen Græme, "and may Heaven, too, have mercy upon us, who linger behind in this bloody land! His loss is indeed a perilous blow to our enterprise; for who remains behind possessing his far-fetched experience, his self-devoted zeal, his consummate wisdom, and his undaunted courage! He hath fallen with the church's standard in his hand, but God will raise up another to lift the blessed banner. Whom have the chapter elected in his room?"

"It is rumored no one of the few remaining brethren dare accept the office. The heretics have sworn that they will permit no future election, and will heavily punish any attempt to create a new abbot of St. Mary's. *Conjuraverunt inter se principes, dicentes, Projiciamus laqueos ejus.*"

"*Quousque, Domine?*" ejaculated Magdalen. "This, my sister, were indeed a perilous and fatal breach in our band; but I am firm in my belief that another will arise in the place of him so untimely removed. Where is thy daughter Catherine?"

"In the parlor," answered the matron, "but——" She looked at Roland Græme, and muttered something in the ear of her friend.

"Fear it not," answered Magdalen Græme, "it is both lawful and necessary; fear nothing from him: I would he were as well grounded in the faith by which alone comes safety as he is free from thought, deed, or speech of villainy. Therein is the heretics' discipline to be commended, my sister, that they train up their youth in strong morality, and choke up every inlet to youthful folly."

"It is but a cleansing of the outside of the cup," answered her friend—"a whitening of the sepulcher; but he shall see Catherine, since you, sister, judge it safe and meet. Follow us, youth," she added, and led the way from the apartment with her friend. These were the only words which the matron had addressed to Roland Græme, who obeyed them in silence. As they paced through several winding passages and waste apartments with a very slow step, the young page had leisure to make some reflection on his situation—reflections of a nature which his ardent temper considered as specially disagreeable. It seemed he had now got two mistresses, or tutoresses instead of one, both elderly women, and both, it would seem, in league to direct his motions according to their own pleasure, and for the accomplishment of plans to which he was no party. This, he thought was too much; arguing, reasonably enough, that whatever right his grandmother and benefactress had to guide his motions, she was neither entitled to transfer her authority or to divide it with another, who seemed to assume, without ceremony, the same tone of absolute command over him.

"But it shall not long continue thus," thought Roland;

"I will not be all my life the slave of a woman's whistle, to go when she bids, and come when she calls. No, by St. Andrew! the hand that can hold the lance is above the control of the distaff. I will leave them the slipped collar in their hands on the first opportunity, and let them execute their own devices by their own proper force. It may save them both from peril, for I guess what they meditate is not likely to prove either safe or easy: the Earl of Murray, and his heresy are too well rooted to be grubbed up by two old women."

As he thus resolved, they entered a low room, in which a third female was seated. This apartment was the first he had observed in the mansion which was furnished with moveable seats, and with a wooden table, over which was laid a piece of tapestry. A carpet was spread on the floor, there was a grate in the chimney, and, in brief, the apartment had the air of being habitable and inhabited.

But Roland's eyes found better employment than to make observations on the accommodations of the chamber; for this second female inhabitant of the mansion seemed something very different from anything he had yet seen there. At his first entry she had greeted with a silent and low obeisance the two aged matrons, then glancing her eyes towards Roland, she adjusted a veil which hung back over her shoulders so as to bring it over her face—an operation which she performed with much modesty, but without either affected haste or embarrassed timidity.

During this maneuver, Roland had time to observe that the face was that of a girl apparently not much past sixteen, and that the eyes were at once soft and brilliant. To these very favorable observations was added the certainty that the fair object to whom they referred possessed an excellent shape bordering perhaps on *embonpoint*, and therefore rather that of a Hebe than of a sylph, but beautifully formed, and shown to great advantage by the close jacket and petticoat which she wore after a foreign fashion, the last not quite long enough absolutely to conceal a very pretty foot, which rested on a bar of the table at which she sate; her round arms and taper fingers very busily employed in repairing the piece of tapestry which was spread on it, which exhibited several deplorable fissures, enough to demand the utmost skill of the most expert seamstress.

It is to be remarked, that it was by stolen glances that Roland Græme contrived to ascertain these interesting particulars; and he thought he could once or twice, notwithstanding the texture of the veil, detect the damsel in the act of taking similar cognizance of his own person. The matrons in the meanwhile continued their separate conversation, eyeing from time to time the young people, in a manner which left Roland in no doubt that they were the subject of their conversation. At length he distinctly heard Magdalen Græme say these words—"Nay, my sister, we must give them opportunity to speak together, and to become acquainted; they must be personally known to each other, or how shall they be able to execute what they are entrusted with?"

It seemed as if the matron, not fully satisfied with her friend's reasoning, continued to offer some objections; but they were borne down by her more dictatorial friend.

"It must be so," she said, "my dear sister; let us therefore go forth on the balcony to finish our conversation. And do you," she added, addressing Roland and the girl, "become acquainted with each other."

With this she stepped up to the young woman, and raising her veil, discovered features which, whatever might be their ordinary complexion, were now covered with a universal blush.

"*Licitum sit,*" said Magdalen, looking at the other matron.

"*Vix licitum,*" replied the other, with reluctant and hesitating acquiescence; and again adjusting the veil of the blushing girl, she dropped it so as to shade, though not to conceal, her countenance, and whispered to her, in a tone loud enough for the page to hear, "Remember, Catherine, who thou art, and for what destined."

The matron then retreated with Magdalen Græme through one of the casements of the apartment, that opened on a large broad balcony, which, with its ponderous balustrade, had once run along the whole south front of the building which faced the brook, and formed a pleasant and commodious walk in the open air. It was now in some places deprived of the balustrade, in others broken and narrowed; but, ruinous as it was, could still be used as a pleasant promenade. Here then walked the two ancient dames, busied in their private conversation; yet not so much so but that Roland could observe the matrons, as their thin forms darkened the casement in passing or repassing before it dart a glance into the apartment, to see how matters were going on there.

CHAPTER XI

> Life hath its May, and it is mirthful then:
> The woods are vocal, and the flowers all odor;
> Its very blast has mirth in't—and the maidens,
> The while they don their cloaks to skreen their kirtles,
> Laugh at the rain that wets them.
>
> *Old Play.*

CATHERINE was at the happy age of innocence and buoyancy of spirit when, after the first moment of embarrassment was over, a situation of awkwardness like that in which she was suddenly left to make acquaintance with a handsome youth, not even known to her by name, struck her, in spite of herself, in a ludicrous point of view. She bent her beautiful eyes upon the work with which she was busied, and with infinite gravity sate out the two first turns of the matrons upon the balcony; but then glancing her deep blue eyes a little towards Roland, and observing the embarrassment under which he labored, now shifting on his chair, and now dangling his cap, the whole man evincing that he was perfectly at a loss how to open the conversation, she could keep her composure no longer, but, after a vain struggle, broke out into a sincere, though a very involuntary, fit of laughing, so richly accompanied by the laughter of her merry eyes, which actually glanced through the tears which the effort filled them with, and by the waving of her rich tresses, that the goddess of smiles herself never looked more lovely than Catherine at that moment. A court page would not have left her long alone in her mirth; but Roland was country-bred, and, besides, having some jealousy, as well as bashfulness, he took it into his head that he was himself the object of her inextinguishable laughter. His endeavors to sympathize with Catherine, therefore, could carry him no farther than a forced giggle, which had more of displeasure than of mirth in it, and which so much enhanced that of the girl that it seemed to render it impossible for her ever to bring her laughter to an end, with whatever anxious pains she labored to do so. For every one has felt that when a paroxysm of laughter has seized him, at a misbecoming time and place, the efforts which he makes to suppress it, nay, the very sense of the impropriety of giving way to it, tend only to augment and prolong the irresistible impulse.

It was undoubtedly lucky for Catherine, as well as for Roland, that the latter did not share in the excessive mirth of the former. For seated as she was, with her back to the casement, Catherine could easily escape the observation of the two matrons during the course of their promenade; whereas Græme was so placed, with his side to the window, that his mirth, had he shared that of his companion, would have been instantly visible, and could not have failed to give offense to the personages in question. He sate, however, with some impatience, until Catherine had exhausted either her power or her desire of laughing, and was returning with good grace to the exercise of her needle, and then he observed with some dryness, that "There seemed no great occasion to recommend to them to improve their acquaintance, as it seemed that they were already tolerably familiar."

Catherine had an extreme desire to set off upon a fresh score, but she repressed it strongly, and fixing her eyes on her work, replied by asking his pardon, and promising to avoid future offense.

Roland had sense enough to feel that an air of offended dignity was very much misplaced, and that it was with a very different bearing he ought to meet the deep blue eyes which had borne such a hearty burden in the laughing scene. He tried, therefore, to extricate himself as well as he could from his blunder, by assuming a tone of corresponding gaiety, and requesting to know of the nymph, "How it was, her pleasure that they should proceed in improving the acquaintance which had commenced so merrily."

"That," she said, "you must yourself discover; perhaps I have gone a step too far in opening our interview."

"Suppose," said Roland Græme, "we should begin as in a tale-book, by asking each other's names and histories."

"It is right well imagined," said Catherine, "and shows an argute judgment. Do you begin, and I will listen, and only put in a question or two at the dark parts of the story. Come, unfold then your name and history, my new acquaintance."

"I am called Roland Græme, and that tall old woman is my grandmother."

"And your tutoress? Good. Who are your parents?"

"They are both dead," replied Roland.

"Ay, but who were they? You *had* parents, I presume?"

"I suppose so," said Roland, "but I have never been able to learn much of their history. My father was a Scottish knight, who died gallantly in his stirrups; my mother was a Græme of Heathergill in the Debateable Land; most of her family were killed when the Debateable country was burned by the Lord Maxwell and Herries of Caerlaverock."

"Is it long ago?" said the damsel.

"Before I was born," answered the page.

"That must be a great while since," said she, shaking her head gravely; "look you, I cannot weep for them."

"It needs not," said the youth, "they fell with honor."

"So much for your lineage, fair sir," replied his companion, "of whom I like the living specimen (a glance at the casement) far less than those that are dead. Your much honored grandmother looks as if she could make one weep in sad earnest. And now, fair sir, for your own person; if you tell not the tale faster, it will be cut short in the middle: Mother Bridget pauses longer and longer every time she passes the window, and with her there is as little mirth as in the grave of your ancestors."

"My tale is soon told. I was introduced into the Castle of Avenel to be page to the lady of the mansion."

"She is a strict Huguenot, is she not?" said the maiden.

"As strict as Calvin himself. But my grandmother can play the Puritan when it suits her purpose, and she had some plan of her own for quartering me in the castle; it would have failed, however, after we had remained several weeks at the hamlet, but for an unexpected master of ceremonies——"

"And who was that?" said the girl.

"A large black dog, Wolf by name, who brought me into the castle one day in his mouth like a hurt wild duck, and presented me to the lady."

"A most respectable introduction, truly," said Catherine; "and what might you learn at this same castle? I love dearly to know what my acquaintances can do at need."

"To fly a hawk, halloo to a hound, back a horse, and wield lance, bow, and brand."

"And to boast of all this when you have learned it," said Catherine, "which, in France at least, is the surest accomplishment of a page. But proceed, fair sir; how came your Huguenot lord and your no less Huguenot lady to receive and keep in the family so perilous a person as a Catholic page?"

"Because they knew not that part of my history, which from infancy I had been taught to keep secret; and because my grand-dame's former zealous attendance on their heretic chaplain had laid all this suspicion to sleep, most fair Calipolis," said the page, and in so saying he edged his chair towards the seat of the fair querist.

"Nay, but keep your distance, most gallant sir," answered the blue-eyed maiden, "for, unless I greatly mistake, these reverend ladies will soon interrupt our amicable conference if the acquaintance they recommend shall seem to proceed beyond a certain point; so, fair sir, be pleased to abide by your station, and reply to my questions. By what achievements did you prove the qualities of a page, which you had thus happily acquired?"

Roland, who began to enter into the tone and spirit of the damsel's conversation, replied to her with becoming spirit.

"In no feat, fair gentlewoman, was I found inexpert, wherein there was mischief implied. I shot swans, hunted cats, frightened serving-women, chased the deer, and robbed the orchard. I say nothing of tormenting the chaplain in various ways, for that was my duty as a good Catholic."

"Now, as I am a gentlewoman," said Catherine, "I think these heretics have done Catholic penance in entertaining so all-accomplished a serving-man! And what, fair sir, might have been the unhappy event which deprived them of an inmate altogether so estimable?"

"Truly, fair gentlewoman," answered the youth, "your real proverb says that the longest lane will have a turning, and mine was more—it was, in fine, a turning off."

"Good!" said the merry young maiden, "it is an apt play on the word. And what occasion was taken for so important a catastrophe? Nay, start not for my learning, I do know the schools—in plain phrase, why were you sent from service?"

The page shrugged his shoulders while he replied, "A short tale is soon told, and a short horse soon curried. I made the falconer's boy taste of my switch; the falconer threatened to make me brook his cudgel. He is a kindly clown as well as a stout, and I would rather have been cudgelled by him than any man in Christendom to choose; but I knew not his qualities at that time, so I threatened to make him brook the stab, and my lady made me brook the 'Begone'; so adieu to the page's office and the fair Castle of Avenel. I had not traveled far before I met my venerable parent. And so tell your tale, fair gentlewoman, for mine is done."

"A happy grandmother," said the maiden, "who had the luck to find the stray page just when his mistress had slipped his leash, and a most lucky page that has jumped at once from a page to an old lady's gentleman-usher!"

"All this is nothing of your history," answered Roland Græme, who began to be much interested in the congenial vivacity of this facetious young gentlewoman—"tale for tale is fellow-travelers' justice."

"Wait till we are fellow-travelers, then," replied Catherine.

"Nay, you escape me not so," said the page; "if you deal not justly by me, I will call out to Dame Bridget, or whatever your dame be called, and proclaim you for a cheat."

"You shall not need," answered the maiden. "My history is the counterpart of your own; the same words might almost serve, change but dress and name. I am called Catherine Seyton, and I also am an orphan."

"Have your parents been long dead?"

"That is the only question," said she, throwing down her fine eyes with a sudden expression of sorrow—"that is the only question I cannot laugh at."

"And Dame Bridget is your grandmother?"

The sudden cloud passed away like that which crosses for an instant the summer sun, and she answered, with her usual lively expression, "Worse by twenty degrees—Dame Bridget is my maiden aunt."

"Over God's forbode!" said Roland. "Alas! that you have such a tale to tell! And what horror comes next?"

"Your own history, exactly. I was taken upon trial for service——"

"And turned off for pinching the duenna, or affronting my lady's waiting-woman?"

"Nay, our history varies there," said the damsel. "Our mistress broke up house, or had her house broke up, which is the same thing, and I am a free woman of the forest."

"And I am as glad of it as if any one had lined my doublet with cloth of gold," said the youth.

"I thank you for your mirth," said she, "but the matter is not likely to concern you."

"Nay, but go on," said the page, "for you will be presently interrupted; the two good dames have been soaring yonder on the balcony, like two old hooded crows, and their croak grows hoarser as night comes on; they will wing to roost presently. This mistress of yours, fair gentlewoman, who was she, in God's name?"

"O, she has a fair name in the world," replied Catherine Seyton. "Few ladies kept a fairer house, or held more gentlewomen in her household; my aunt Bridget was one of her housekeepers. We never saw our mistress's blessed face, to be sure, but we heard enough of her; were up early and down late, and were kept to long prayers and light food."

"Out upon the penurious old beldam!" said the page.

"For Heaven's sake, blaspheme not!" said the girl, with an expression of fear. "God pardon us both! I mean no harm. I speak of our blessed St. Catherine of Sienna!—may God forgive me that I spoke so lightly, and made you do a great sin and a great blasphemy! This was her nunnery, in which there were twelve nuns and an abbess. My aunt was the abbess, till the heretics turned all adrift."

"And where are your companions?" asked the youth.

"With the last year's snow," answered the maiden—"east, north, south, and west: some to France, some to Flanders, some, I fear, into the world and its pleasures. We have got permission to remain, or rather our remaining has been connived at, for my aunt has great relations among the Kerrs, and they have threatened a death-feud if any one touches us; and bow and spear are the best warrants in these times."

"Nay, then, you sit under a sure shadow," said the youth; "and I suppose you wept yourself blind when St. Catherine broke up housekeeping before you had taken arles in her service?"

"Hush! for Heaven's sake," said the damsel, crossing herself, "no more of that! But I have not quite cried my eyes out," said she, turning them upon him, and instantly again bending them upon her work. It was one of those glances which would require the threefold plate of brass around the heart, more than it is needed by the mariners of whom Horace recommends it. Our youthful page had no defense whatever to offer.

"What say you, Catherine," he said, "if we two, thus strangely turned out of service at the same time, should give our two most venerable duennas the torch to hold, while we walk a merry measure with each other over the floor of this weary world?"

"A goodly proposal, truly," said Catherine, "and worthy the madcap brain of a discarded page! And what shifts does your worship propose we should live by?—by singing ballads, cutting purses, or swaggering on the highway? for there, I think, you will find your most productive exchequer."

"Choose, you proud peat!" said the page, drawing off in huge disdain at the calm and unembarrassed ridicule with which his wild proposal was received. And as he spoke the words, the casement was again darkened by the forms of the matrons; it opened, and admitted Magdalen Græme and the mother abbess, so we must now style her, into the apartment.

CHAPTER XII

> Nay, hear me, brother; I am elder, wiser,
> And holier than thou. And age, and wisdom,
> And holiness, have peremptory claims,
> And will be listen'd to.
>
> *Old Play.*

When the matrons re-entered, and put an end to the conversation which we have detailed in the last chapter, Dame Magdalen Græme thus addressed her grandson and his pretty companion: "Have you spoke together, my children. Have you become known to each other as fellow-travelers on the same dark and dubious road, whom chance hath brought together, and who study to learn the tempers and dispositions of those by whom their perils are to be shared?"

It was seldom the light-hearted Catherine could suppress a jest, so that she often spoke when she would have acted more wisely in holding her peace.

"Your grandson admires the journey which you propose so very greatly that he was even now preparing for setting out upon it instantly."

"This is to be too forward, Roland," said the dame, addressing him, "as yesterday you were over slack; the just mean lies in obedience, which both waits for the signal to start and obeys it when given. But once again, my children, have you so perused each other's countenances that, when you meet, in whatever disguise the times may impose upon you, you may recognize each in the other the secret agent of the mighty work in which you are to be leagued? Look at each other, know each line and lineament of each other's countenance. Learn to distinguish by the step, by the sound of the voice, by the motion of the hand, by the glance of the eye, the partner whom Heaven hath sent to aid in working its will. Wilt thou know that maiden, whensoever or wheresoever you shall again meet her, my Roland Græme?"

As readily as truly did Roland answer in the affirmative.

"And thou, my daughter, wilt thou again remember the features of this youth?"

"Truly, mother," replied Catherine Seyton, "I have not seen so many men of late that I should immediately forget your grandson, though I mark not much about him that is deserving of special remembrance."

"Join hands, then, my children," said Magdalen Græme; but, in saying so, was interrupted by her companion, whose conventual prejudices had been gradually giving her more and more uneasiness, and who could remain acquiescent no longer.

"Nay, my good sister, you forget," said she to Magdalen, "Catherine is the betrothed bride of Heaven; these intimacies cannot be."

"It is in the cause of Heaven that I command them to embrace," said Magdalen, with the full force of her powerful voice; "the end, sister, sanctifies the means we must use."

"They call me lady abbess, or mother at the least, who address me," said Dame Bridget, drawing herself up, as if offended at her friend's authoritative manner; "the Lady of Heathergill forgets that she speaks to the abbess of St. Catherine."

"When I was what you call me," said Magdalen, "you indeed were the abbess of St. Catherine; but both names are now gone, with all the rank that the world and that the church gave to them; and we are now, to the eye of human judgment, two poor, despised, oppressed women, dragging our dishonored old age to a humble grave. But what are we in the eye of Heaven? Ministers, sent forth to work His will, in whose weakness the strength of the church shall be manifested, before whom shall be humbled the wisdom of Murray and the dark strength of Morton. And to such wouldst thou apply the narrow rules of thy cloistered seclusion? or hast thou forgotten the order which I showed thee from thy superior, subjecting thee to me in these matters?"

"On thy head, then, be the scandal and the sin," said the abbess, sullenly.

"On mine be they both," said Magdalen. "I say, embrace each other, my children."

But Catherine, aware, perhaps, how the dispute was likely to terminate, had escaped from the apartment, and so disappointed the grandson at least as much as the old matron.

"She is gone," said the abbess, "to provide some little refreshment. But it will have little savor to those who dwell in the world; for I, at least, cannot dispense with the rules to which I am vowed, because it is the will of wicked men to break down the sanctuary in which they wont to be observed."

"It is well, my sister," replied Magdalen, "to pay each even the smallest tithes of mint and cummin which the church demands, and I blame not thy scrupulous observance of the rules of thine order. But they were established by the church, and for the church's benefit; and reason it is that they should give way when the salvation of the church herself is at stake."

The abbess made no reply.

One more acquainted with human nature than the inexperienced page might have found amusement in comparing the different kinds of fanaticism which these two females exhibited. The abbess, timid, narrow-minded, and discontended, clung to ancient usages and pretensions which were ended by the Reformation, and was in adversity, as she had been in prosperity, scrupulous, weak-spirited, and bigoted; while the fiery and more lofty spirit of her companion suggested a wider field of effort, and would not be limited by ordinary rules in the extraordinary schemes which were suggested by her bold and irregular imagination. But Roland Græme, instead of tracing these peculiarities of character in the two old dames, only waited with great anxiety for the return of Catherine, expecting probably that the proposal of the fraternal embrace would be renewed, as his grandmother seemed disposed to carry matters with a high hand.

His expectations, or hopes, if we may call them so, were, however, disappointed; for, when Catherine re-entered on the summons of the abbess, and placed on the table an earthen pitcher of water, and four wooden platters, with cups of the same materials, the Dame of Heathergill, satisfied with the arbitrary mode in which she had borne down the opposition of the abbess, pursued her victory no farther—a moderation for which her grandson, in his heart, returned her but slender thanks.

In the mean while, Catherine continued to place upon the table the slender preparations for the meal of a recluse, which consisted almost entirely of colewort, boiled, and served up in a wooden platter, having no better seasoning than a little salt, and no better accompaniment than some coarse barley-bread in very moderate quantity. The water-pitcher already mentioned furnished the only beverage. After a Latin grace, delivered by the abbess, the guests sat down to their spare entertainment. The simplicity of the fare appeared to produce no distaste in the females, who ate of it moderately, but with the usual appearance of appetite. But Roland Græme had been used to better cheer. Sir Halbert Glendinning, who affected even an unusual degree of nobleness in his housekeeping, maintained it in a style of genial hospitality which rivaled that of the northern barons of England. He might think, perhaps, that by doing so he acted yet more completely the part for which he was born—that of a great baron and a leader. Two bullocks and six sheep weekly were the allowance when the baron was at home, and the number was not greatly diminished during his absence. A boll of malt was weekly brewed into ale, which was used by the household at discretion. Bread was baked in proportion for the consumption of his domestics and retainers; and in this scene of plenty had Roland Græme now lived for several years. It formed a bad introduction to lukewarm greens and spring water; and probably his countenance indicated some sense of the difference, for the abbess observed, "It would seem, my son, that the tables of the heretic baron, whom you have so long followed, are more daintily furnished than those of the suffering daughters of the church; and yet, not upon the most solemn nights of festival, when the nuns were permitted to eat their portion at mine own table, did I consider the cates which were then served up as half so delicious as these vegetables and this water, on which I prefer to feed, rather than do aught which may derogate from the strictness of my vow. It shall never be said that the mistress of this house made it a house of feasting when days of darkness and of affliction were hanging over the Holy Church, of which I am an unworthy member."

"Well hast thou said, my sister," replied Magdalen Græme; "but now it is not only time to suffer in the good cause, but to act in it. And since our pilgrim's meal is finished, let us go apart to prepare for our journey of to-morrow, and to advise on the manner in which these children shall be employed, and what measures we can adopt to supply their thoughtlessness and lack of discretion."

Notwithstanding his indifferent cheer, the heart of Roland Græme bounded high at this proposal, which he doubted not would lead to another *tête-á-tête* betwixt him and the pretty novice. But he was mistaken. Catherine, it would seem, had no mind so far to indulge him; for, moved either by delicacy or caprice, or some of those indescribable shades betwixt the one or the other with which women love to tease, and at the same time to captivate, the ruder sex, she reminded the abbess that it was necessary she should retire for an hour before vespers; and, receiving the ready and approving nod of her superior, she arose to withdraw. But, before leaving the apartment, she made obeisance to the matrons, bending herself till her hands touched her knees, and then made a lesser reverence to Roland, which consisted in a slight bend of the body and gentle depression of the head. This she performed very demurely; but the party on whom the salutation was conferred thought he could discern in her manner an arch and mischievous exultation over his secret disappointment. "The devil take the saucy girl," he thought in his heart, though the presence of the abbess should have repressed all such profane imaginations, "she is as hard-hearted as the laughing hyæna that the story-books tell of; she has a mind that I shall not forget her this night at least."

The matrons now retired also, giving the page to understand that he was on no account to stir from the convent, or to show himself at the windows, the abbess assigning as a reason the readiness with which the rude heretics caught at every occasion of scandalizing the religious orders.

"This is worse than the rigor of Mr. Henry Warden himself," said the page, when he was left alone; "for, to do him justice, however strict in requiring the most rigid attention during the time of his homilies, he left us to the freedom of our own wills afterwards; ay, and would take a share in our pastimes, too, if he thought them entirely innocent. But these old women are utterly wrapt up in gloom, mystery, and self-denial. Well, then, if I must neither stir out of the gate nor look out at window, I will at least see what the inside of the house contains that may help to pass away one's time; peradventure I may light on that blue-eyed laugher in some corner or other."

Going, therefore, out of the chamber by the entrance opposite to that through which the two matrons had departed (for it may be readily supposed that he had no desire to intrude on *their* privacy), he wandered from one chamber to another, through the deserted edifice, seeking with boyish eagerness some source of interest or amusement. Here he passed through a long gallery, opening on either hand into the little cells of the nuns, all deserted, and deprived of the few trifling articles of furniture which the rules of the order admitted.

"The birds are flown," thought the page; "but whether they will find themselves worse off in the open air than in these damp narrow cages, I leave my lady abbess and my venerable relative to settle betwixt them. I think the wild young lark whom they have left behind them would like best to sing under God's free sky."

A winding stair, strait and narrow, as if to remind the nuns of their duties of fast and maceration, led down to a lower suite of apartments, which occupied the ground story of the house. These rooms were even more ruinous than those which he had left; for, having encountered the first fury of the assailants by whom the nunnery had been wasted, the windows had been dashed in, the doors broken down, and even the partitions betwixt the apartments in some places destroyed. As he thus stalked from desolation to desolation, and began to think of returning from so uninteresting a research to the chamber which he had left, he was surprised to hear the low of a cow very close to him. The sound was so unexpected at the time and place that Roland Græme started as if it had been the voice of a lion, and laid his hand on his dagger, while at the same moment the light and lovely form of Catherine Seyton presented itself at the door of the apartment from which the sound had issued.

"Good even to you, valiant champion!" said she; "since the days of Guy of Warwick, never was one more worthy to encounter a dun cow."

"Cow!" said Roland Græme, "by my faith, I thought it had been the devil that roared so near me. Who ever heard of a convent containing a cow-house?"

"Cow and calf may come hither now," answered Catherine, "for we have no means to keep out either. But I advise you, kind sir, to return to the place from whence you came."

"Not till I see your charge, fair sister," answered Ronald, and made his way into the apartment, in spite of the half-serious, half-laughing remonstrances of the girl.

The poor solitary cow, now the only severe recluse within the nunnery, was quartered in a spacious chamber, which had once been the refectory of the convent. The roof was graced with groined arches, and the wall with niches, from which the images had been pulled down. These remnants of architectural ornaments were strangely contrasted with the rude crib constructed for the cow in one corner of the apartment, and the stack of fodder which was piled beside it for her food.*

"By my faith," said the page, "Crombie is more lordly lodged than any one here!"

"You had best remain with her," said Catherine, "and supply by your filial attentions the offspring she has had the ill-luck to lose."

*See Nunnery of St. Bridget. Note 5.

"I will remain, at least, to help you to prepare her night's lair, pretty Catherine," said Ronald, seizing upon a pitchfork.

"By no means," said Catherine; "for, besides that you know not in the least how to do her that service, you will bring a chiding my way, and I get enough of that in the regular course of things."

"What! for accepting my assistance?" said the page—"for accepting *my* assistance, who am to be your confederate in some deep matter of import? That were altogether unreasonable; and, now I think on it, tell me, if you can, what is this mighty emprise to which I am destined?"

"Robbing a bird's nest, I should suppose," said Catherine, "considering the champion whom they have selected."

"By my faith," said the youth, "and he that has taken a falcon's nest in the scaurs of Polmoodie has done something to brag of, my fair sister. But that is all over now: a murrain on the nest, and the eyases and their food, washed or unwashed, for it was all anon of cramming these worthless kites that I was sent upon my present travels. Save that I have met with you, pretty sister, I could eat my dagger-hilt for vexation at my own folly. But, as we are to be fellow-travelers——"

"Fellow-laborers, not fellow-travelers," answered the girl; "for to your comfort be it known, that the lady abbess and I set out earlier than you and your respected relative to-morrow, and that I partly endure your company at present because it may be long ere we meet again."

"By St. Andrew, but it shall not, though," answered Roland; "I will not hunt at all unless we are to hunt in couples."

"I suspect, in that and in other points, we must do as we are bid," replied the young lady. "But hark! I hear my aunt's voice."

The old lady entered in good earnest, and darted a severe glance at her niece, while Roland had the ready wit to busy himself about the halter of the cow.

"The young gentleman," said Catherine, gravely, "is helping me to tie the cow up faster to her stake, for I find that last night, when she put her head out of window and lowed, she alarmed the whole village; and we shall be suspected of sorcery among the heretics if they do not discover the cause of the apparition, or lose our cow if they do."

"Relieve yourself of that fear," said the abbess, somewhat ironically; "the person to whom she is now sold comes for the animal presently."

"Good night, then, my poor companion," said Catherine, patting the animal's shoulders; "I hope thou hast fallen into kind hands, for my happiest hours of late have been spent in tending thee. I would I had been born to no better task!"

"Now, out upon thee, mean-spirited wench!" said the abbess; "is that a speech worthy of the name of Seyton, or of the mouth of a sister of this house, treading the path of election; and to be spoken before a stranger youth, too! Go to my oratory, minion; there read your *Hours* till I come thither, when I will read you such a lecture as shall make you prize the blessings which you possess."

Catherine was about to withdraw in silence, casting a half-sorrowful, half-comic glance at Roland Græme, which seemed to say, "You see to what your untimely visit has exposed me," when, suddenly changing her mind, she came forward to the page, and extended her hand as she bid him good evening. Their palms had pressed each other ere the astonished matron could interfere, and Catherine had time to say, "Forgive me, mother; it is long since we have seen a face that looked with kindness on us. Since these disorders have broken up our peaceful retreat all has been gloom and malignity. I bid this youth kindly farewell, because he has come hither in kindness, and because the odds are great that we may never again meet in this world. I guess better than he that the schemes on which you are rushing are too mighty for your management, and that you are now setting the stone a-rolling which must surely crush you in its descent. I bid farewell," she added, "to my fellow-victim!"

This was spoken with a tone of deep and serious feeling, altogether different from the usual levity of Catherine's manner, and plainly showed that, beneath the giddiness of extreme youth and total inexperience, there lurked in her bosom a deeper power of sense and feeling than her conduct had hitherto expressed.

The abbess remained a moment silent after she had left the room. The proposed rebuke died on her tongue, and she appeared struck with the deep and foreboding tone in which her niece had spoken her good even. She led the way in silence to the apartment which they had formerly occupied, and where there was prepared a small refection, as the abbess termed it, consisting of milk and barley-bread. Magdalen Græme, summoned to take share in this collation, appeared from an adjoining apartment; but Catherine was seen no more. There was little said during the hasty meal, and after it was finished Roland Græme was dismissed to the nearest cell, where some preparations had been made for his repose.

The strange circumstances in which he found himself had their usual effect in preventing slumber from hastily descending on him, and he could distinctly hear, by a low but earnest murmuring in the apartment which he had left, that the matrons continued in deep consultation to a late hour. As they separated, he heard the abbess distinctly express herself thus: "In a word, my sister, I venerate your character and the authority with which my superiors have invested you; yet it seems to me that, ere entering on this perilous course, we should consult some of the fathers of the church."

"And how and where are we to find a faithful bishop or abbot at whom to ask counsel? The faithful Eustatius is no more: he is withdrawn from a world of evil, and from the tyranny of heretics. May Heaven and Our Lady assoilzie him of his sins, and abridge the penance of his mortal infirmities! Where shall we find another with whom to take counsel?"

"Heaven will provide for the church," said the abbess; "and the faithful fathers who yet are suffered to remain in the house of Kennaquhair will proceed to elect an abbot. They will not suffer the staff to fall down, or the miter to be unfilled, for the threats of heresy."

"That will I learn to-morrow," said Magdalen Græme; "yet who now takes the office of an hour, save to partake with the spoilers in their work of plunder? To-morrow will tell us if one of the thousand saints who are sprung from the house of St. Mary's continues to look down on it in its misery. Farewell, my sister, we meet at Edinburgh."

"*Benedicite!*" answered the abbess, and they parted.

"To Kennaquhair and to Edinburgh we bend our way," thought Roland Græme. "That information have I purchased by a sleepless hour: it suits well with my purpose. At Kennaquhair I shall see Father Ambrose; at Edinburgh I shall find the means of shaping my own course through this bustling world, without burdening my affectionate relation; at Edinburgh, too, I shall see again the witching novice, with her blue eyes and her provoking smile." He fell asleep, and it was to dream of Catherine Seyton.

CHAPTER XIII

What, Dagon up again! I thought we had hurl'd him
Down on the threshold never more to rise.
Bring wedge and ax; and, neighbors, lend your hands,
And rive the idol into winter fagots!
Athelstane, or the Converted Dane.

ROLAND GRÆME slept long and sound, and the sun was high over the horizon when the voice of his companion summoned him to resume their pilgrimage; and when, hastily arranging his dress, he went to attend her call, the enthusiastic matron stood already at the threshold, prepared for her journey. There was in all the deportment of this remarkable woman a promptitude of execution, and a sternness of perseverance, founded on the fanaticism which she nursed so deeply, and which seemed to absorb all the ordinary purposes and feelings of mortality. One only human affection gleamed through her enthusiastic energies, like the broken glimpses of the sun through the rising clouds of a storm. It was her maternal fondness for her grandson—a fondness carried almost to the verge of dotage in circumstances where the Catholic religion was not concerned, but which gave way instantly when it chanced either to thwart or come in contact with the more settled purpose of her soul, and the more devoted duty of her life. Her life she would willingly have laid down to save the earthly object of her affection; but that object itself she was ready to hazard, and would have been willing to sacrifice, could the restoration of the Church of Rome have been purchased with his blood. Her discourse by the way, excepting on the few occasions in which her extreme love of her grandson found opportunity to display itself in anxiety for his health and accommodation, turned entirely on the duty of raising up the fallen honors of the church, and replacing a Catholic sovereign on the throne. There were times at which she hinted, though very obscurely and distantly, that she herself was foredoomed by Heaven to perform a part in this important task; and that she had more than mere human warranty for the zeal with which she engaged in it. But on this subject she expressed herself in such general language that it was not easy to decide whether she made any actual pretensions to a direct and supernatural call, like the celebrated Elizabeth Barton, commonly called the Nun of Kent;* or whether she only dwelt upon the general duty which was incumbent on all Catholics of the time, and the pressure of which she felt in an extraordinary degree.

Yet, though Magdalen Græme gave no direct intimation of her pretensions to be considered as something beyond the ordinary class of mortals, the demeanor of one or two persons amongst the travelers whom they occasionally met, as they entered the more fertile and populous part of the valley, seemed to indicate their belief in her superior attributes. It is true that two clowns, who drove before them a herd of cattle; one or two village wenches, who seemed bound for some merry-making; a strolling soldier, in a rusted morion; and a wandering student, as his threadbare black cloak and his satchel of books proclaimed him, passed our travelers without observation, or with a look of contempt; and, moreover, that two or three children, attracted by the appearance of a dress so nearly resembling that of a pilgrim, joined in hooting and calling, "Out upon the old mass-monger!" But one or two, who nourished in their bosoms respect for the downfallen hierarchy, casting first a timorous glance around, to see that no one observed them, hastily crossed themselves, bent their knee to Sister Magdalen, by which name they saluted her, kissed her hand, or even the hem of her dalmatique, received with humility the *benedicite* with which she repaid their obeisance; and then, starting up, and again looking timidly round to see that they had been unobserved, hastily resumed their journey. Even while within sight of persons of the prevailing faith, there were individuals bold enough, by folding their arms and bending their head, to give distant and silent intimation that they recognized Sister Magdalen, and honored alike her person and her purpose.

She failed not to notice to her grandson these marks of honor and respect which from time to time she received. "You see," she said, "my son, that the enemies have been unable altogether to suppress the good spirit, or to root out the true seed. Amid heretics and schismatics, spoilers of the church's lands, and scoffers at sacraments, there is left a remnant."

"It is true, my mother," said Roland Græme; "but methinks they are of a quality which can help us but little.

* See Note 6.

See you not all those who wear steel at their side, and bear marks of better quality, ruffle past us as they would pass the meanest beggars? for those who give us any marks of sympathy are the poorest of the poor, and most outcast of the needy, who have neither bread to share with us, nor swords to defend us, nor skill to use them if they had. That poor wretch that last kneeled to you with such deep devotion, and who seemed emaciated by the touch of some wasting disease within, and the grasp of poverty without—that pale, shivering, miserable caitiff, how can he aid the great schemes you meditate?"

"Much, my son," said the matron, with more mildness than the page perhaps expected. "When that pious son of the church returns from the shrine of St. Ringan, whither he now travels by my counsel, and by the aid of good Catholics—when he returns healed of his wasting malady, high in health and strong in limb, will not the glory of his faithfulness, and its miraculous reward, speak louder in the ears of this besotted people of Scotland than the din which is weekly made in a thousand heretical pulpits?"

"Ay, but, mother, I fear the saint's hand is out. It is long since we have heard of a miracle performed at St. Ringan's."

The matron made a dead pause, and, with a voice tremulous with emotion, asked, "Art thou so unhappy as to doubt the power of the blessed saint?"

"Nay, mother," the youth hastened to reply, "I believe as the Holy Church commands, and doubt not St. Ringan's power of healing; but, be it said with reverence, he hath not of late showed the inclination."

"And has this land deserved it?" said the Catholic matron, advancing hastily while she spoke, until she attained the summit of a rising ground, over which the path led, and then standing again still. "Here," she said, "stood the cross, the limits of the halidome of St. Mary's—here, on this eminence, from which the eye of the holy pilgrim might first catch a view of that ancient monastery, the light of the land, the abode of saints, and the grave of monarchs. Where is now that emblem of our faith? It lies on the earth a shapeless block, from which the broken fragments have been carried off, for the meanest uses, till now no semblance of its original form remains. Look towards the east, my son, where the sun was wont to glitter on stately spires, from which crosses and bells have now been hurled, as if the land had been invaded once more by barbarous heathens—look at yonder battlements, of which we can, even at this distance, descry the partial demolition; and ask if this land can expect from the blessed saints, whose shrines and whose images have been profaned, any other miracles but those of vengeance? How long," she exclaimed, looking upward—"how long shall it be delayed?" She paused, and then resumed with enthusiastic rapidity, "Yes, my son, all on earth is but for a period: joy and grief, triumph and desolation, succeed each other like cloud and sunshine; the vineyard shall not be forever trodden down, the gaps shall be amended, and the fruitful branches once more dressed and trimmed. Even this day—ay, even this hour, I trust to hear news of importance. Dally not—let us on; time is brief, and judgment is certain."

She resumed the path which led to the abbey—a path which, in ancient times, was carefully marked out by posts and rails, to assist the pilgrim in his journey; these were now torn up and destroyed. An half-hour's walk placed them in front of the once splendid monastery, which, although the church was as yet entire, had not escaped the fury of the times. The long range of cells and of apartments for the use of the brethren, which occupied two sides of the great square, were almost entirely ruinous, the interior having been consumed by fire, which only the massive architecture of the outward walls had enabled them to resist. The abbot's house, which formed the third side of the square, was, though injured, still inhabited, and afforded refuge to the few brethren who yet, rather by connivance than by actual authority, were permitted to remain at Kennaquhair. Their stately offices, their pleasant gardens, the magnificent cloisters constructed for their recreation, were all dilapidated and ruinous; and some of the building materials had apparently been put into requisition by persons in the village and in the vicinity, who, formerly vassals of the monastery, had not hesitated to appropriate to themselves a part of the spoils. Roland saw fragments of Gothic pillars, richly carved, occupying the place of door-posts to the meanest huts; and here and there a mutilated statue, inverted or laid on its side, made the door-post or threshold of a wretched cow-house. The church itself was less injured than the other buildings of the monastery. But the images which had been placed in the numerous niches of its columns and buttresses, having all fallen under the charge of idolatry, to which the superstitious devotion of the Papists had justly exposed them, had been broken and thrown down, without much regard to the preservation of the rich and airy canopies and pedestals on which they were placed ; nor, if the devastation had stopped short at this point, could we have considered the preservation of these monuments of antiquity as an object to be put in the balance with the introduction of the Reformed worship.

Our pilgrims saw the demolition of these sacred and venerable representations of saints and angels—for as sacred and venerable they had been taught to consider them—with very different feelings. The antiquary may be permitted to regret the necessity of the action, but to Magdalen Græme it seemed a deed of impiety, deserving the instant vengeance of Heaven —a sentiment in which her relative joined for the moment as cordially as herself. Neither, however, gave vent to their feelings in words, and uplifted hands and eyes formed their only mode of expressing them. The page was about to approach the great eastern gate of the church, but was prevented by his guide. "That gate," she said, "has long been blockaded, that the heretical rabble may not know there still exist among the brethren of St. Mary's men who dare worship where their predecessors prayed while alive, and were interred when dead ; follow me this way, my son."

Roland Græme followed accordingly ; and Magdalen, casting a hasty glance to see whether they were observed (for she had learned caution from the danger of the times), commanded her grandson to knock at a little wicket which she pointed out to him. "But knock gently," she added, with a motion expressive of caution. After a little space, during which no answer was returned, she signed to Roland to repeat his summons for admission ; and the door at length partially opening, discovered a glimpse of the thin and timid porter, by whom the duty was performed, skulking from the observation of those who stood without, but endeavoring at the same time to gain a sight of them without being himself seen. How different from the proud consciousness of dignity with which the porter of ancient days offered his important brow and his goodly person to the pilgrims who repaired to Kennaquhair ! His solemn "*Intrate, mei filii,*" was exchanged for a tremulous "You cannot enter now : the brethren are in their chambers." But when Magdalen Græme asked, in an under tone of voice, "Hast thou forgotten me, my brother ?" he changed his apologetic refusal to "Enter, my honored sister—enter speedily, for evil eyes are upon us."

They entered accordingly, and having waited until the porter had, with jealous haste, barred and bolted the wicket were conducted by him through several dark and winding passages. As they walked slowly on, he spoke to the matron in a subdued voice, as if he feared to trust the very walls with the avowal which he communicated.

"Our fathers are assembled in the chapter-house, worthy sister—yes, in the chapter-house—for the election of an abbot. Ah, *benedicite!* there must be no ringing of bells—no high mass—no opening of the great gates now, that the people might see and venerate their spiritual father! Our fathers must hide themselves rather like robbers who choose a leader than godly priests who elect a mitered abbot."

"Regard not that, my brother," answered Magdalen Græme; "the first successors of St. Peter himself were elected, not in sunshine, but in tempest; not in the halls of the Vatican, but in the subterranean vaults and dungeons of heathen Rome; they were not gratulated with shouts and salvos of cannon-shot and of musketry, and the display of artificial fire—no, my brother, but by the hoarse summons of lictors and prætors, who came to drag the fathers of the church to martyrdom. From such adversity was the church once raised, and by such will it now be purified. And mark me, brother! not in the proudest days of the mitered abbey was a superior ever chosen whom his office shall so much honor as *he* shall be honored who now takes it upon him in these days of tribulation. On whom, my brother, will the choice fall?"

"On whom can it fall—or, alas! who would dare to reply to the call—save the worthy pupil of the sainted Eustatius, the good and valiant Father Ambrose?"

"I know it," said Magdalen; "my heart told me, long ere your lips had uttered his name. Stand forth, courageous champion, and man the fatal breach! Rise, bold and experienced pilot, and seize the helm while the tempest rages! Turn back the battle, brave raiser of the fallen standard! Wield crook and sling, noble shepherd of a scattered flock."

"I pray you, hush, my sister!" said the porter, opening a door which led into the great church, "the brethren will be presently here to celebrate their election with a solemn mass; I must marshal them the way to the high altar: all the offices of this venerable house have now devolved on one poor decrepit old man."

He left the church, and Magdalen and Roland remained

alone in that great vaulted space, whose style of rich yet chaste architecture referred its origin to the early part of the 14th century, the best period of Gothic building. But the niches were stripped of their images in the inside as well as the outside of the church; and in the pell-mell havoc the tombs of warriors and of princes had been included in the demolition of the idolatrous shrines. Lances and swords of antique size, which had hung over the tombs of mighty warriors of former days, lay now strewn among relics with which the devotion of pilgrims had graced those of their peculiar saints; and the fragments of the knights and dames, which had once lain recumbent, or kneeled in an attitude of devotion, where their mortal relics were reposed, were mingled with those of the saints and angels of the Gothic chisel which the hand of violence had sent headlong from their stations.

The most fatal symptom of the whole appeared to be that, though this violence had now been committed for many months, the fathers had lost so totally all heart and resolution that they had not adventured even upon clearing away the rubbish, or restoring the church to some decent degree of order. This might have been done without much labor. But terror had overpowered the scanty remains of a body once so powerful, and, sensible they were only suffered to remain in this ancient seat by connivance and from compassion, they did not venture upon taking any step which might be construed into an assertion of their ancient rights, contenting themselves with the secret and obscure exercise of their religious ceremonial, in as unostentatious a manner as was possible.

Two or three of the more aged brethren had sunk under the pressure of the times, and the ruins had been partly cleared away to permit their interment. One stone had been laid over Father Nicolas, which recorded of him in special that he had taken the vows during the incumbency of Abbot Ingelram, the period to which his memory so frequently recurred. Another flagstone, yet more recently deposited, covered the body of Philip the sacristan, eminent for his aquatic excursion with the phantom of Avenel; and a third, the most recent of all, bore the outline of a miter, and the words *Hic jacet Eustatius Abbas;* for no one dared to add a word of commendation in favor of his learning and strenuous zeal for the Roman Catholic faith.

Magdalen Græme looked at and perused the brief records of these monuments successively, and paused over that of

Father Eustace. "In a good hour for thyself," she said, "but oh! in an evil hour for the church, wert thou called from us. Let thy spirit be with us, holy man; encourage thy successor to tread in thy footsteps; give him thy bold and inventive capacity, thy zeal, and thy discretion; even *thy* piety exceeds not his." As she spoke, a side door, which closed a passage from the abbot's house into the church, was thrown open, that the fathers might enter the choir, and conduct to the high altar the superior whom they had elected.

In former times, this was one of the most splendid of the many pageants which the hierarchy of Rome had devised to attract the veneration of the faithful. The period during which the abbacy remained vacant was a state of mourning, or, as their emblematical phrase expressed it, of widowhood—a melancholy term, which was changed into rejoicing and triumph when a new superior was chosen. When the folding doors were on such solemn occasions thrown open, and the new abbot appeared on the threshold in full-blown dignity, with ring and miter, and dalmatique and crosier, his hoary standard-bearers and his juvenile dispensers of incense-preceding him, and the venerable train of monks behind him, with all besides which could announce the supreme authority to which he was now raised, his appearance was a signal for the magnificent *Jubilate* to rise from the organ and music-loft, and to be joined by the corresponding bursts of *Alleluiah* from the whole assembled congregation. Now all was changed. In the midst of rubbish and desolation, seven or eight old men, bent and shaken, as much by grief and fear as by age, shrouded hastily in the proscribed dress of their order, wandered like a procession of specters from the door which had been thrown open, up through the encumbered passage to the high altar, there to install their elected superior a chief of ruins. It was like a band of bewildered travelers choosing a chief in the wilderness of Arabia; or a shipwrecked crew electing a captain upon the barren island on which fate has thrown them.

They who, in peaceful times, are most ambitious of authority among others, shrink from the competition at such eventful periods, when neither ease nor parade attend the possession of it, and when it gives only a painful preeminence both in danger and in labor, and exposes the ill-fated chieftain to the murmurs of his discontented associates, as well as to the first assault of the common enemy. But he on whom the offices of the Abbot of St. Mary's was now conferred had a mind fitted for the situation to which he was called. Bold and enthusiastic, yet generous and forgiving; wise and skilful, yet zealous and prompt, he wanted but a better cause than the support of a decaying superstition to have raised him to the rank of a truly great man. But as the end crowns the work, it also forms the rule by which it must be ultimately judged; and those who, with sincerity and generosity, fight and fall in an evil cause, posterity can only compassionate as victims of a generous but fatal error. Amongst these we must rank Ambrosius, the last abbot of Kennaquhair, whose designs must be condemned, as their success would have riveted on Scotland the chains of antiquated superstition and spiritual tyranny; but whose talents commanded respect, and whose virtues, even from the enemies of his faith, extorted esteem.

The bearing of the new abbot served of itself to dignify a ceremonial which was deprived of all other attributes of grandeur. Conscious of the peril in which they stood, and recalling, doubtless, the better days they had seen, there hung over his brethren an appearance of mingled terror, and grief, and shame, which induced them to hurry over the office in which they were engaged, as something at once degrading and dangerous.

But not so Father Ambrose. His features, indeed, expressed a deep melancholy, as he walked up the center aisle, amid the ruin of things which he considered as holy, but his brow was undejected, and his step firm and solemn. He seemed to think that the dominion which he was about to receive depended in no sort upon the external circumstances under which it was conferred; and if a mind so firm was accessible to sorrow or fear, it was not on his own account, but on that of the church to which he had devoted himself.

At length he stood on the broken steps of the high altar, barefooted, as was the rule, and holding in his hand his pastoral staff, for the gemmed ring and jeweled miter had become secular spoils. No obedient vassals came, man after man, to make their homage and to offer the tribute which should provide their spiritual superior with palfrey and trappings. No bishop assisted at the solemnity, to receive into the higher ranks of the church nobility a dignitary whose voice in the legislature was as potential as his own. With hasty and maimed rites, the few remaining brethren stepped forward alternately to give their new abbot the kiss of peace, in token of fraternal affection and spiritual homage. Mass was then hastily performed, but in such precipitation as if it had been hurried over rather to satisfy the scruples of a few youths, who were impatient to set out on a hunting party,* than as if it made the most solemn part of a solemn ordination. The officiating priest faltered as he spoke the service, and often looked around, as if he expected to be interrupted in the midst of his office; and the brethren listened as to that which, short as it was, they wished yet more abridged.

These symptoms of alarm increased as the ceremony proceeded, and, as it seemed, were not caused by mere apprehension alone; for, amid the pauses of the hymn, there were heard without sounds of a very different sort, beginning faintly and at a distance, but at length approaching close to the exterior of the church, and stunning with dissonant clamor those engaged in the service. The winding of horns, blown with no regard to harmony or concert; the jangling of bells, the thumping of drums, the squeaking of bagpipes, and the clash of cymbals; the shouts of a multitude, now as in laughter, now as in anger; the shrill tones of female voices, and of those of children, mingling with the deeper clamors of men, formed a Babel of sounds, which first drowned, and then awed into utter silence, the official hymns of the convent. The cause and result of this extraordinary interruption will be explained in the next chapter.

*See Hunting Mass. Note 7.

CHAPTER XIV

> Not the wild billow, when it breaks its barrier,
> Not the wild wind, escaping from its cavern,
> Not the wild fiend, that mingles both together,
> And pours their rage upon the ripening harvest,
> Can match the wild freaks of this mirthful meeting—
> Comic, yet fearful; droll, and yet destructive.
>
> *The Csnspiracy.*

THE monks ceased their song, which, like that of the choristers in the legend of the Witch of Berkley, died away in a quaver of consternation; and like a flock of chickens disturbed by the presence of the kite, they at first made a movement to disperse and fly in different directions, and then, with despair rather than hope, huddled themselves around their new abbot; who, retaining the lofty and undismayed look which had dignified him through the whole ceremony, stood on the higher step of the altar, as if desirous to be the most conspicuous mark on which danger might discharge itself, and to save his companions by his self-devotion, since he could afford them no other protection.

Involuntarily, as it were, Magdalen Græme and the page stepped from the station which hitherto they had occupied unnoticed, and approached to the altar, as desirous of sharing the fate which approached the monks, whatever that might be. Both bowed reverently low to the abbot; and while Magdalen seemed about to speak, the youth, looking towards the main entrance, at which the noise now roared most loudly, and which was at the same time assailed with much knocking, laid his hand upon his dagger.

The abbot motioned to both to forbear. "Peace, my sister," he said, in a low tone, but which, being in a different key from the tumultuary sounds without, could be distinctly heard even amidst the tumult—"peace," he said, "my sister; let the new superior of St. Mary's himself receive and reply to the grateful acclamations of the vassals who come to celebrate his installation. And thou, my son, forbear, I charge thee, to touch thy earthly weapon; if it is the pleasure of our protectress that her shrine be this day desecrated by deeds of violence, and polluted by blood-shedding, let it not, I charge thee, happen through the deed of a Catholic son of the church."

The noise and knocking at the outer gate became now every moment louder, and voices were heard impatiently demanding admittance. The abbot, with dignity, and with a step which even the emergency of danger rendered neither faltering nor precipitate, moved towards the portal, and demanded to know, in a tone of authority, who it was that disturbed their worship, and what they desired."

There was a moment's silence, and then a loud laugh from without. At length a voice replied, "We desire entrance into the church; and when the door is opened you will soon see who we are."

"By whose authority do you require entrance?" said the father.

"By authority of the right reverend Lord Abbot of Unreason," * replied the voice from without; and, from the laugh which followed, it seemed as if there was something highly ludicrous crouched under this reply.

"I know not, and seek not to know, your meaning," replied the abbot, "since it is probably a rude one. But begone, in the name of God, and leave His servants in peace. I speak this as having lawful authority to command here."

"Open the door," said another rude voice, "and we will try titles with you, sir monk, and show you a superior we must all obey."

"Break open the doors if he dallies any longer," said a third, "and down with the carrion monks who would bar us of our privilege! A general shout followed. Ay, ay, our privilege!—our privilege! Down with the doors, and with the lurdane monks if they make opposition!"

The knocking was now exchanged for blows with great hammers, to which the doors, strong as they were, must soon have given way. But the abbot, who saw resistance would be vain, and who did not wish to incense the assailants by an attempt at offering it, besought silence earnestly, and with difficulty obtained a hearing. "My children," said he, "I will save you from committing a great sin. The porter will presently undo the gate—he is gone to fetch the keys; meantime I pray you to consider with yourselves if you are in a state of mind to cross the holy threshold."

"Tillyvalley for your Papistry!" was answered from with-

* See Note 8.

out; "we are in the mood of the monks when they are merriest, and that is when they sup beef-brewis for lenten-kail. So, if your porter hath not the gout, let him come speedily, or we heave away readily. Said I well, comrades?"

"Bravely said, and it shall be as bravely done," said the multitude; and had not the keys arrived at that moment, and the porter in hasty terror performed his office, throwing open the great door, the populace would have saved him the trouble. The instant he had done so, the affrighted janitor fled, like one who has drawn the bolts of a flood-gate, and expects to be overwhelmed by the rushing inundation. The monks, with one consent, had withdrawn themselves behind the abbot, who alone kept his station, about three yards from the entrance, showing no signs of fear or perturbation. His brethren, partly encouraged by his devotion, partly ashamed to desert him, and partly animated by a sense of duty, remained huddled close together at the back of their superior. There was a loud laugh and huzza when the doors were opened; but, contrary to what might have been expected, no crowd of enraged assailants rushed into the church. On the contrary, there was a cry of "A halt!—a halt! to order, my masters! and let the two reverend fathers greet each other, as beseems them."

The appearance of the crowd who were thus called to order was grotesque in the extreme. It was composed of men, women, and children, ludicrously disguised in various habits, and presenting groups equally diversified and grotesque. Here one fellow with a horse's head painted before him, and a tail behind, and the whole covered with a long foot-cloth, which was supposed to hide the body of the animal, ambled, caracoled, pranced, and plunged, as he performed the celebrated part of the hobby-horse,* so often alluded to in our ancient drama, and which still flourishes on the stage in the battle that concludes Bayes's tragedy. To rival the address and agility displayed by this character, another personage advanced, in the more formidable character of a huge dragon, with gilded wings, open jaws, and a scarlet tongue, cloven at the end, which made various efforts to overtake and devour a lad, dressed as the lovely Sabæa, daughter of the King of Egypt, who fled before him; while a martial St. George, grotesquely armed with a goblet for a helmet and a spit for a lance, ever and anon interfered, and compelled the monster to relinquish his prey. A bear, a wolf, and one or two other wild animals, played their parts with the discretion of

* See Note 9.

Snug the joiner; for the decided preference which they gave to the use of their hind legs was sufficient, without any formal annunciation, to assure the most timorous spectators that they had to do with habitual bipeds. There was a group of outlaws, with Robin Hood and Little John at their head* —the best representation exhibited at the time; and no great wonder, since most of the actors were, by profession, the banished men and thieves whom they presented. Other masqueraders there were, of a less marked description. Men were disguised as women, and women as men; children wore the dress of aged people, and tottered with crutch-sticks in their hands, furred gowns on their little backs, and caps on their round heads; while grandsires assumed the infantine tone as well as the dress of children. Besides these, many had their faces painted, and wore their shirts over the rest of their dress; while colored pasteboard and ribbons furnished out decorations for others. Those who wanted all these properties, blacked their faces, and turned their jackets inside out; and thus the transmutation of the whole assembly into a set of mad grotesque mummers was at once completed.

The pause which the masqueraders made, waiting apparently for some person of the highest authority amongst them, gave those within the abbey church full time to observe all these absurdities. They were at no loss to comprehend their purpose and meaning.

Few readers can be ignorant that, at an early period, and during the plenitude of her power, the Church of Rome not only connived at, but even encouraged, such saturnalian licenses as the inhabitants of Kennaquhair and the neighborhood had now in hand, and that the vulgar, on such occasions, were not only permitted but encouraged, by a number of gambols, sometimes puerile and ludicrous, sometimes immoral and profane, to indemnify themselves for the privations and penances imposed on them at other seasons. But, of all other topics for burlesque and ridicule, the rites and ceremonial of the church itself were most frequently resorted to; and, strange to say, with the approbation of the clergy themselves.

While the hierarchy flourished in full glory, they do not appear to have dreaded the consequences of suffering the people to become so irreverently familiar with things sacred: they then imagined the laity to be much in the condition of a laborer's horse, which does not submit to the bridle and

* See Note 10.

the whip with greater reluctance because, at rare intervals, he is allowed to frolic at large in his pasture, and fling out his heels in clumsy gambols at the master who usually drives him. But, when times changed—when doubt of the Roman Catholic doctrine, and hatred of their priesthood, had possessed the Reformed party—the clergy discovered, too late, that no small inconvenience arose from the established practise of games and merry-makings, in which they themselves, and all they held most sacred, were made the subject of ridicule. It then became obvious to duller politicians than the Romish churchmen, that the same actions have a very different tendency when done in the spirit of sarcastic insolence and hatred, than when acted merely in exuberance of rude and uncontrollable spirits. They, therefore, though of the latest, endeavored, where they had any remaining influence, to discourage the renewal of these indecorous festivities. In this particular, the Catholic clergy were joined by most of the Reformed preachers, who were more shocked at the profanity and immorality of many of these exhibitions than disposed to profit by the ridiculous light in which they placed the Church of Rome and her observances. But it was long ere these scandalous and immoral sports could be abrogated; the rude multitude continued attached to their favorite pastimes; and, both in England and Scotland, the miter of the Catholic, the rocket of the Reformed bishop, and the cloak and band of the Calvinistic divine, were, in turn, compelled to give place to those jocular personages, the Pope of Fools, the Boy Bishop, and the Abbot of Unreason.*

It was the latter personage who now, in full costume, made his approach to the great door of the church of St. Mary's, accoutered in such a manner as to form a caricature, or practical parody, on the costume and attendants of the real superior, whom he came to beard on the very day of his installation, in the presence of his clergy, and in the chancel of his church. The mock dignitary was a stout-made, under-sized fellow, whose thick squab form had been rendered grotesque by a supplemental paunch, well stuffed. He wore a miter of leather, with the front like a grenadier's cap, adorned with mock embroidery and trinkets of tin. This surmounted a visage the nose of which was the most prominent feature, being of unusual size, and at least as richly gemmed as his head-gear. His robe was of buckram, and his cope of canvas, curiously painted, and cut into open

* From the interesting novel entitled *Anastasius*, it seems the same burlesque ceremonies were practised in the Greek Church.

work. On one shoulder was fixed the painted figure of an owl; and he bore in the right hand his pastoral staff, and in the left a small mirror having a handle to it, thus resembling a celebrated jester, whose adventures, translated into English, were whilom extremely popular, and which may still be procured in black letter for about one sterling pound per leaf.

The attendants of this mock dignitary had their proper dresses and equipage, bearing the same burlesque resemblance to the officers of the convent which their leader did to the superior. They followed their leader in regular procession, and the motley characters, which had waited his arrival, now crowded into the church in his train, shouting as they came —"A hall—a hall! for the venerable Father Howleglas, the learned Monk of Misrule, and the Right Reverend Abbot of Unreason!"

The discordant minstrelsy of every kind renewed its din: the boys shrieked and howled, and the men laughed and hallooed, and the women giggled and screamed, and the beasts roared, and the dragon walloped and hissed, and the hobby-horse neighed, pranced, and capered, and the rest frisked and frolicked, clashing their hobnailed shoes against the pavement, till it sparkled with the marks of their energetic caprioles.

It was, in fine, a scene of ridiculous confusion, that deafened the ear, made the eyes giddy, and must have altogether stunned any indifferent spectator; the monks, whom personal apprehension and a consciousness that much of the popular enjoyment arose from the ridicule being directed against them, were, moreover, little comforted by the reflection that, bold in their disguise, the mummers who whooped and capered around them might, on slight provocation, turn their jest into earnest, or at least proceed to those practical pleasantries which at all times arise so naturally out of the frolicsome and mischievous disposition of the populace. They looked to their abbot amid the tumult, with such looks as landsmen cast upon the pilot when the storm is at the highest—looks which express that they are devoid of all hope arising from their own exertions, and not very confident in any success likely to attend those of their Palinurus.

The abbot himself seemed at a stand; he felt no fear, but he was sensible of the danger of expressing his rising indignation, which he was scarcely able to suppress. He made a gesture with his hand as if commanding silence, which was at first only replied to by redoubled shouts, and peals of wild

"The appearance of the crowd was grotesque in the extreme."

laughter. When, however, the same motion, and as nearly in the same manner, had been made by Howleglas, it was immediately obeyed by his riotous companions, who expected fresh food for mirth in the conversation betwixt the real and mock abbot, having no small confidence in the vulgar wit and impudence of their leader. Accordingly, they began to shout, "To it, fathers—to it!" "Fight monk, fight madcap: abbot against abbot is fair play, and so is reason against unreason, and malice against monkery!"

"Silence, my mates!" said Howleglas; "cannot two learned fathers of the church hold communing together, but you must come here with your beer-garden whoop and halloo, as if you were hounding forth a mastiff upon a mad bull? I say, silence! and let this learned father and me confer touching matters affecting our mutual state and authority."

"My children——" said Father Ambrose.

"*My* children too—and happy children they are!" said his burlesque counterpart; "many a wise child knows not its own father, and it is well they have two to choose betwixt."

"If thou hast aught in thee, save scoffing and ribaldry," said the real abbot, "permit me, for thine own soul's sake, to speak a few words to these misguided men."

"Aught in me but scoffiing, say'st thou?" retorted the Abbot of Unreason; "why, reverend brother, I have all that becomes mine office at this time a-day: I have beef, ale, and brandy-wine, with other condiments not worth mentioning; and for speaking, man—why, speak away, and we will have turn about, like honest fellows."

During this discussion the wrath of Magdalen Græme had risen to the uttermost; she approached the abbot, and, placing herself by his side, said in a low and yet distinct tone—"Wake and arouse thee, father; the sword of St. Peter is in thy hand—strike and avenge St. Peter's patrimony! Bind them in the chains, which, being riveted by the church on earth, are riveted in Heaven——"

"Peace, sister!" said the abbot; "let not their madness destroy our discretion—I pray thee, peace, and let me do mine office. It is the first, peradventure it may be the last, time I shall be called on to discharge it."

"Nay, my holy brother!" said Howleglas, "I rede you, take the holy sister's advice: never throve convent without woman's counsel."

"Peace, vain man!" said the abbot; "and you, my brethren——"

"Nay, nay!" said the Abbot of Unreason, "no speaking

to the lay people until you have conferred with your brother of the cowl. I swear by bell, book, and candle that not one of my congregation shall listen to one word you have to say; so you had as well address yourself to me who will."

To escape a conference so ludicrous, the abbot again attempted an appeal to what respectful feelings might yet remain amongst the inhabitants of the halidome, once so devoted to their spiritual superiors. Alas! the Abbot of Unreason had only to flourish his mock crosier, and the whooping, the hallooing, and the dancing were renewed with a vehemence which would have defied the lungs of Stentor.

"And now, my mates," said the Abbot of Unreason, "once again dight your gabs and be hushed; let us see if the cock of Kennaquhair will fight or flee the pit."

There was again a dead silence of expectation, of which Father Ambrose availed himself to address his antagonist, seeing plainly that he could gain an audience on no other terms. "Wretched man!" said he, "hast thou no better employment for thy carnal wit than to employ it in leading these blind and helpless creatures into the pit of utter darkness?"

"Truly, my brother," replied Howleglas, "I can see little difference betwixt your employment and mine, save that you make a sermon of a jest and I make a jest of a sermon."

"Unhappy being," said the abbot, "who hast no better subject of pleasantry than that which should make thee tremble, no sounder jest than thine own sins, and no better objects for laughter than those who can absolve thee from the guilt of them!"

"Verily, my reverend brother," said the mock abbot, "what you say might be true, if, in laughing at hypocrites, I meant to laugh at religion. O, it is a precious thing to wear a long dress, with a girdle and a cowl: we become a holy pillar of Mother Church, and a boy must not play at ball against the walls for fear of breaking a painted window!"

"And will you, my friends," said the abbot, looking round and speaking with a vehemence which secured him a tranquil audience for some time—"will you suffer a profane buffoon, within the very church of God, to insult His ministers? Many of you—all of you, perhaps—have lived under my holy predecessors, who were called upon to rule in this church where I am called upon to suffer. If you have worldly goods, they are their gift; and, when you scorned not to accept better gifts—the mercy and forgiveness of the church—were they not ever at your command? —did we not pray while you were jovial, wake while you slept?"

"Some of the good wives of the halidome were wont to say so," said the Abbot of Unreason; but his jest met in this instance but slight applause, and Father Ambrose, having gained a moment's attention, hastened to improve it.

"What!" said he; "and is this grateful—is it seemly—is it honest—to assail with scorn a few old men, from whose predecessors you hold all, and whose only wish is to die in peace among these fragments of what was once the light of the land, and whose daily prayer is, that they may be removed ere that hour comes when the last spark shall be extinguished, and the land left in the darkness which it has chosen rather than light? We have not turned against you the edge of the spiritual sword, to revenge our temporal persecution; the tempest of your wrath hath despoiled us of land, and deprived us almost of our daily food, but we have not repaid it with the thunders of excommunication; we only pray your leave to live and die within the church which is our own, invoking God, Our Lady, and the holy saints to pardon your sins, and our own, undisturbed by scurril buffoonery and blasphemy."

This speech, so different in tone and termination from that which the crowd had expected, produced an effect upon their feelings unfavorable to the prosecution of their frolic. The morrice-dancers stood still, the hobby-horse surceased his capering, pipe and tabor were mute, and "silence, like a heavy cloud," seemed to descend on the late noisy rabble. Several of the beasts were obviously moved to compunction: the bear could not restrain his sobs, and a huge fox was observed to wipe his eyes with his tail. Bnt in especial the dragon, lately so formidably rampant, now relaxed the terror of his claws, uncoiled his tremendous rings, and grumbled out of his fiery throat in a repentant tone, "By the mass, I thought no harm in exercising our old pastime, but an I had thought the good father would have taken it so to heart I would as soon have played your devil as your dragon."

In this momentary pause, the abbot stood amongst the miscellaneous and grotesque forms by which he was surrounded, triumphant as St. Anthony, in Callot's Temptations; but Howleglas would not so resign his purpose.

"And how now, my masters!" said he; "is this fair play or no? Have you not chosen me Abbot of Unreason, and is it lawful for any of you to listen to common-sense to-day?

Was I not formally elected by you in solemn chapter, held in Luckie Martin's change-house, and will you now desert me, and give up your old pastime and privilege? Play out the play; and he that speaks the next word of sense or reason, or bids us think or consider, or the like of that, which befits not the day, I will have him solemnly ducked in the mill-dam!"

The rabble, mutable as usual, huzzaed, the pipe and tabor struck up, the hobby-horse pranced, the beasts roared, and even the repentant dragon began again to coil up his spires and prepare himself for fresh gambols. But the abbot might have still overcome, by his eloquence and his entreaties, the malicious designs of the revelers, had not Dame Magdalen Græme given loose to the indignation which she had long suppressed.

"Scoffers," she said, "and men of Belial—blasphemous heretics and truculent tyrants——"

"Your patience, my sister, I entreat and I command you!" said the abbot; "let me do my duty: disturb me not in mine office."

But Dame Magdalen continued to thunder forth her threats in the name of popes and councils, and in the name of every saint from St. Michael downward.

"My comrades!" said the Abbot of Unreason, "this good dame hath not spoke a single word of reason, and therein may esteem herself free from the law. But what she spoke was meant for reason, and, therefore, unless she confesses and avouches all which she has said to be nonsense, it shall pass for such, so far as to incur the penalty of our statutes. Wherefore, holy dame, pilgrim, or abbess, or whatever thou art, be mute with thy mummery or beware the mill-dam. We will have neither spiritual nor temporal scolds in our diocese of Unreason!"

As he spoke thus, he extended his hand towards the old woman, while his followers shouted, "A doom—a doom!" and prepared to second his purpose, when lo! it was suddenly frustrated. Roland Græme had witnessed with indignation the insults offered to his old spiritual perceptor, but yet had wit enough to reflect he could render him no assistance, but might well, by ineffective interference, make matters worse. But when he saw his aged relative in danger of personal violence, he gave way to the natural impetuosity of his temper, and, stepping forward, struck his poniard into the body of the Abbot of Unreason, whom the blow instantly prostrated on the pavement.

CHAPTER XV

As when in tumults rise the ignoble crowd,
Mad are their motions, and their tongues are loud,
And stones and brands in rattling furies fly,
And all the rustic arms which fury can supply—
Then if some grave and pious man appear,
They hush their noise, and lend a listening ear.
DRYDEN'S *Virgil.*

A DREADFUL shout of vengeance was raised by the revelers, whose sport was thus so fearfully interrupted; but, for an instant, the want of weapons amongst the multitude, as well as the inflamed features and brandished poniard of Roland Græme, kept them at bay, while the abbot, horror-struck at the violence, implored, with uplifted hands, pardon for bloodshed committed within the sanctuary. Magdalene Græme alone expressed triumph in the blow her descendant had dealt to the scoffer, mixed, however, with a wild and anxious expression of terror for her grandson's safety. "Let him perish," she said, "in his blasphemy—let him die on the holy pavement which he has insulted!"

But the rage of the multitude, the grief of the abbot, the exultation of the enthusiastic Magdalen, were all mistimed and unnecessary. Howleglas, mortally wounded as he was supposed to be, sprung alertly up from the floor, calling aloud, "A miracle—a miracle, my masters! as brave a miracle as ever was wrought in the kirk of Kennaquhair. And I charge you, my masters, as your lawfully chosen abbot, that you touch no one without my command. You, wolf and bear, will guard this pragmatic youth, but without hurting him. And you reverend brother, will, with your comrades, withdraw to your cells; for our conference has ended like all conferences, leaving each of his own mind, as before; and if we fight, both you, and your brethren, and the kirk, will have the worst on't. Wherefore, pack up your pipes and begone."

The hubbub was beginning again to awaken, but still Father Ambrose hesitated, as uncertain to what path his duty called him, whether to face out the present storm or to reserve himself for a better moment. His brother of Unreason observed his difficulty, and said, in a tone more natural and less affected than that with which he had hitherto sustained his character. "We came hither, my good sir, more in mirth than in mischief: our bark is worse than our bite; and, especially, we mean you no personal harm; wherefore, draw off while the play is good; for it is ill whistling for a hawk when she is once on the soar, and worse to snatch the quarry from the ban-dog. Let these fellows once begin their brawl, and it will be too much for madness itself, let alone the Abbot of Unreason, to bring them back to the lure."

The brethren crowded around Father Ambrosius, and joined in urging him to give place to the torrent. The present revel was, they said, an ancient custom which his predecessors had permitted, and old Father Nicolas himself had played the dragon in the days of the Abbot Ingelram.

"And we now reap the fruit of the seed which they have so unadvisedly sown," said Ambrosius: "they taught men to make a mock of what is holy, what wonder that the descendants of scoffers become robbers and plunderers? But be it as you list, my brethren—move towards the dortour. And you, dame, I command you, by the authority which I have over you, and by your respect for that youth's safety, that you go with us without farther speech. Yet, stay—what are your intentions towards that youth whom you detain prisoner? Wot ye," he continued, addressing Howleglas in a stern tone of voice, "that he bears the livery of the house of Avenel? They who fear not the anger of Heaven may at least dread the wrath of man."

"Cumber not yourself concerning him," answered Howleglas, "we know right well who and what he is."

"Let me pray," said the abbot, in a tone of entreaty, "that you do him no wrong for the rash deed which he attempted in his imprudent zeal."

"I say, trouble not yourself about it, father," answered Howleglas; "but move off with your train, male and female, or I will not undertake to save yonder she-saint from the ducking-stool. And as for bearing of malice, my stomach has no room for it; it is," he added, clapping his hand on his portly belly, "too well bumbasted out with straw and buckram; gramercy to them both—they kept out that madcap's dagger as well as a Milan corslet could have done."

In fact, the home-driven poniard of Roland Græme had lighted upon the stuffing of the fictitious paunch, which the Abbot of Unreason wore as a part of his characteristic dress, and it was only the force of the blow which had prostrated that reverend person on the ground for a moment.

Satisfied in some degree by this man's assurance, and compelled to give way to superior force, the Abbot Ambrosius retired from the church at the head of the monks, and left the court free for the revelers to work their will. But wild and wilful as these rioters were, they accompanied the retreat of the religionists with none of those shouts of contempt and derision with which they had at first hailed them. The abbot's discourse had affected some of them with remorse, others with shame, and all with a transient degree of respect. They remained silent until the last monk had disappeared through the side-door which communicated with their dwelling-place, and even then it cost some exhortations on the part of Howleglas, some caprioles of the hobby-horse, and some wallops of the dragon, to rouse once more the rebuked spirit of revelry.

"And how now, my masters?" said the Abbot of Unreason; "and wherefore look on me with such blank Jack-a-Lent visages? Will you lose your old pastime for an old wife's tale of saints and purgatory? Why, I thought you would have made all split long since. Come, strike up, tabor and harp—strike up, fiddle and rebeck; dance and be merry to-day, and let care come to-morrow! Bear and wolf, look to your prisoner; prance hobby; hiss dragon, and halloo, boys; we grow older every moment we stand idle, and life is too short to be spent in playing mumchance."

This pithy exhortation was attended with the effect desired. They fumigated the church with burnt wood and feathers instead of incense, put foul water into the holy-water basins, and celebrated a parody on the church service, the mock abbot officiating at the altar; they sang ludicrous and indecent parodies to the tunes of church hymns; they violated whatever vestments or vessels belonging to the abbey they could lay their hands upon; and, playing every freak which the whim of the moment could suggest to their wild caprice, at length they fell to more lasting deeds of demolition, pulled down and destroyed some carved woodwork, dashed out the painted windows which had escaped former violence, and, in their rigorous search after sculpture dedicated to idolatory, began to destroy what ornaments yet remained entire upon the tombs and around the cornices of the pillars.

The spirit of demolition, like other tastes, increases by indulgence: from these lighter attempts at mischief, the more tumultuous part of the meeting began to meditate destruction on a more extended scale. "Let us heave it down altogether, the old crow's nest," became a general cry among among them; "it has served the Pope and his rooks too long"; and up they struck a ballad which was then popular among the lower classes:

"The Paip, that pagan full of pride,
Hath blinded us ower lang,
For where the blind the blind doth lead,
No marvel baith gae wrang.
Like prince and king,
He led the ring
Of all iniquity.
Sing hay trix, trim-go-trix,
Under the greenwood tree.

The bishop rich, he could not preach
For sporting with the lasses;
The silly friar behoved to fleech
For awmous as he passes;
The curate his creed
He could not read—
Shame fa' the company!
Sing hay trix, trim-go-trix,
Under the greenwood tree."*

Thundering out this chorus of a notable hunting song, which had been pressed into the service of some polemical poet, the followers of the Abbot of Unreason were turning every moment more tumultuous, and getting beyond the management of even that reverend prelate himself, when a knight in full armor, followed by two or three men-at-arms, entered the church and in a stern voice commanded them to forbear their riotous mummery.

His visor was up, but, if it had been lowered, the cognizance of the holly-branch sufficiently distinguished Sir Halbert Glendinning, who, on his homeward road, was passing through the village of Kennaquhair; and, moved perhaps by anxiety for his brother's safety, had come directly to the church on hearing of the uproar.

"What is the meaning of this," he said, "my masters? Are ye Christian men, and the king's subjects, and yet waste and destroy church and chancel like so many heathens?"

All stood silent, though doubtless there were several disappointed and surprised at receiving chiding instead of thanks from so zealous a Protestant.

The dragon, indeed, did at length take upon him to be

* See "The Paip, that Pagan." Note 11.

spokesman, and growled from the depth of his painted maw, that they did but sweep Popery out of the church with the besom of destruction.

"What! my friends," replied Sir Halbert Glendinning, "think you this mumming and masquing has not more of Popery in it than have these stone walls? Take the leprosy out of your flesh before you speak of purifying stone walls: abate your insolent license, which leads but to idle vanity and sinful excess; and know, that what you now practise is one of the profane and unseemly sports introduced by the priests of Rome themselves, to mislead and to brutify the souls which fell into their net."

"Marry come up—are you there with your bears?" muttered the dragon, with a draconic sullenness which was in good keeping with his character; "we had as good have been Romans still, if we are to have no freedom in our pastimes!"

"Dost thou reply to me so?" said Sir Halbert Glendinning; "or is there any pastime in groveling on the ground there like a gigantic kail-worm? Get out of thy painted case, or, by my knighthood, I will treat you like the beast and reptile you have made yourself."

"Beast and reptile!" retorted the offended dragon; "setting aside your knighthood, I hold myself as well a born man as thyself."

The knight made no answer in words, but bestowed two such blows with the butt of his lance on the petulant dragon, that, had not the hoops which constituted the ribs of the machine been pretty strong, they would hardly have saved those of the actor from being broken. In all haste the masquer crept out of his disguise, unwilling to abide a third buffet from the lance of the enraged knight. And when the ex-dragon stood on the floor of the church, he presented to Halbert Glendinning the well-known countenance of Dan of the Howlethirst, an ancient comrade of his own, ere fate had raised him so high above the rank to which he was born. The clown looked sulkily upon the knight, as if to upbraid him for his violence towards an old acquaintance, and Glendinning's own good-nature reproached him for the violence he had acted upon him.

"I did wrong to strike thee, Dan," he said; "but in truth I knew thee not: thou wert ever a mad fellow. Come to Avenel Castle, and we shall see how my hawks fly."

"And if we show him not falcons that will mount as merrily as rockets," said the abbot of Unreason, "I would your honor laid as hard on my bones as you did on his even now."

"How now, sir knave," said the knight, "and what has brought you hither?"

The abbot, hastily ridding himself of the false nose which mystified his physiognomy, and the supplementary belly which made up his disguise, stood before his master in his real character of Adam Woodcock, the falconer of Avenel.

"How, varlet!" said the knight; "hast thou dared to come here, and disturb the very house my brother was dwelling in?"

"And it was even for that reason, craving your honor's pardon, that I came hither; for I heard the country was to be up to choose an Abbot of Unreason, and 'Sure,' thought I. 'I that can sing, dance, leap backwards over a broadsword, and am as good a fool as ever sought promotion, have all chance of carrying the office; and if I gain my election, I may stand his honor's brother in some stead, supposing things fall roughly out at the kirk of St. Mary's.'"

"Thou art but a cogging knave," said Sir Halbert, "and well I wot that love of ale and brandy, besides the humor of riot and frolic, would draw thee a mile, when love of my house would not bring thee a yard. But, go to—carry thy roisterers elsewhere—to the alehouse if they list, and there are crowns to pay your charges; make out the day's madness without doing more mischief, and be wise men to-morrow; and hereafter learn to serve a good cause better than by acting like buffoons or ruffians."

Obedient to his master's mandate, the falconer was collecting his discouraged followers, and whispering into their ears —"Away, away—*tace* is Latin for a candle. Never mind the good knight's Puritanism—we will play the frolic out over a stand of double ale in Dame Martin the brewster's barn-yard. Draw off, harp and tabor, bagpipe and drum, num till you are out of the churchyard, then let the welkin ring again; move on, wolf and bear—keep the hind legs till you cross the kirk-stile, and then show yourselves beasts of mettle; what devil sent him here to spoil our holiday! But anger him not, my hearts; his lance is no goose-feather, as Dan's ribs can tell."

"By my soul," said Dan, "had it been another than my ancient comrade, I would have made my father's old fox fly about his ears!"

"Hush!—hush! man," replied Adam Woodcock, "not a word that way, as you value the safety of your bones; what, man! we must take a clink as it passes, so it is not bestowed in downright ill-will."

"But I will take no such thing," said Dan of the Howlet-hirst, sullenly resisting the efforts of Woodcock, who was dragging him out of the church; when, the quick military eye of Sir Halbert Glendinning detecting Roland Græme betwixt his two guards, the knight exclaimed, "So ho! falconer—Woodcock—knave, hast thou brought my lady's page in mine own livery to assist at this hopeful revel of thine, with your wolves and bears? Since you were at such mummings, you might, if you would, have at least saved the credit of my household by dressing him up as a jackanapes. Bring him hither, fellows!"

Adam Woodcock was too honest and downright to permit blame to light upon the youth when it was undeserved. "I swear," he said, "by St. Martin of Bullions——"

"And what hast thou to do with St. Martin?"

"Nay, little enough, sir, unless when he sends such rainy days that we cannot fly a hawk; but I say to your worshipful knighthood that, as I am a true man——"

"As you are a false varlet, had been the better obtestation."

"Nay, if your knighthood allows me not to speak," said Adam, "I can hold my tongue; but the boy came not hither by my bidding, for all that."

"But to gratify his own malapert pleasure, I warrant me," said Sir Halbert Glendinning. "Come hither, young springald, and tell me whether you have your mistress's license to be so far absent from the castle, or to dishonor my livery by mingling in such a May-game?"

"Sir Halbert Glendinning," answered Roland Græme, with steadiness, "I have obtained the permission, or rather the commands, of your lady to dispose of my time hereafter according to my own pleasure. I have been a most unwilling spectator of this May-game, since it is your pleasure so to call it; and I only wear your livery until I can obtain clothes which bear no such badge of servitude."

"How am I to understand this, young man?" said Sir Halbert Glendinning; "speak plainly, for I am no reader of riddles. That my lady favored thee, I know. What hast thou done to disoblige her, and occasion thy dismissal?"

"Nothing to speak of," said Adam Woodcock, answering for the boy; "a foolish quarrel with me, which was more foolishly told over again to my honored lady, cost the poor boy his place. For my part, I will say freely that I was wrong from beginning to end, except about the washing of the eyas's meat. There I stand to it that I was right."

With that, the good-natured falconer repeated to his master the whole history of the squabble which had brought Roland Græme into disgrace with his mistress, but in a manner so favorable for the page that Sir Halbert could not but suspect his generous motive."

"Thou art a good-natured fellow," he said, "Adam Woodcock."

"As ever had falcon upon fist," said Adam; "and, for that matter, so is Master Roland; but, being half a gentleman by his office, his blood is soon up, and so is mine."

"Well," said Sir Halbert, "be it as it will, my lady has acted hastily, for this was no great matter of offense to discard the lad whom she had trained up for years; but he, I doubt not, made it worse by his prating; it jumps well with a purpose, however, which I had in my mind. Draw off these people, Woodcock; and you, Roland Græme, attend me."

The page followed him in silence into the abbot's house, where, stepping into the first apartment which he found open, he commanded one of his attendants to let his brother, Master Edward Glendinning, know that he desired to speak with him. The men-at-arms went gladly off to join their comrade, Adam Woodcock, and the jolly crew whom he had assembled at Dame Martin's, the hostler's wife, and the page and knight were left alone in the apartment. Sir Halbert Glendinning paced the floor for a moment in silence, and then thus addressed his attendant:

"Thou mayest have remarked, stripling, that I have but seldom distinguished thee by much notice—I see thy color rises, but do not speak till thou hearest me out. I say, I have never much distinguished thee, not because I did not see that in thee which I might well have praised, but because I saw something blamable, which such praises might have made worse. Thy mistress, dealing according to her pleasure in her own household, as no one hath better reason or title, had picked thee from the rest, and treated thee more like a relation than a domestic; and if thou didst show some vanity and petulance under such distinction, it were injustice not to say that thou hast profited both in thy exercises and in thy breeding, and hast shown many sparkles of a gentle and manly spirit. Moreover, it were ungenerous, having bred thee up freakish and fiery, to dismiss thee to want or wandering for showing that very peevishness and impatience of discipline which arose from thy too delicate nurture. Therefore, and for the credit of my own household, I am determined to retain thee in my train, until I can honorably dispose of thee elsewhere, with a fair prospect of thy going through the world with credit to the house that brought thee up."

If there was something in Sir Halbert Glendinning's speech which flattered Roland's pride, there was also much that, according to his mode of thinking, was an alloy to the compliment. And yet his conscience instantly told him that he ought to accept, with grateful deference, the offer which was made him by the husband of his kind protectress ; and his prudence, however slender, could not but admit he should enter the world under very different auspices as a retainer of Sir Halbert Glendinning, so famed for wisdom, courage, and influence, from those under which he might partake the wanderings, and become an agent in the visionary schemes —for such they appeared to him—of Magdalen, his relative. Still, a strong reluctance to re-enter a service from which he had been dismissed with contempt almost counterbalanced these considerations.

Sir Halbert looked on the youth with surprise, and resumed : "You seem to hesitate, young man. Are your own prospects so inviting that you should pause ere you accept those which I offer to you ? or must I remind you that, although you have offended your benefactress, even to the point of her dismissing you, yet I am convinced, the knowledge that you have gone unguided on your own wild way, into a world so disturbed as ours of Scotland, cannot, in the upshot, but give her sorrow and pain ; from which it is, in gratitude, your duty to preserve her, no less than it is in common wisdom your duty to accept my offered protection, for your own sake, where body and soul are alike endangered should you refuse it."

Roland Græme replied in a respectful tone, but at the same time with some spirit, "I am not ungrateful for such countenance as has been afforded me by the Lord of Avenel, and I am glad to learn, for the first time, that I have not had the misfortune to be utterly beneath his observation, as I had thought. And it is only needful to show me how I can testify my duty and my gratitude towards my early and constant benefactress with my life's hazard, and I will gladly peril it." He stopped.

"These are but words, young man," answered Glendinning; "large protestations are often used to supply the place of effectual service. I know nothing in which the peril of your life can serve the Lady of Avenel ; I can only say, she will be pleased to learn you have adopted some course which may ensure the safety of your person and the weal of your soul. What ails you, that you accept not that safety when it is offered you ?"

"My only relative who is alive," answered Roland—"at least the only relative whom I have ever seen, has rejoined me since I was dismissed from the Castle of Avenel, and I must consult with her whether I can adopt the line to which you now call me, or whether her increasing infirmities, or the authority which she is entitled to exercise over me, may not require me to abide with her."

"Where is this relation ?" said Sir Halbert Glendinning.

"In this house," answered the page.

"Go, then, and seek her out," said the Knight of Avenel ; "more than meet it is that thou shouldst have her approbation, yet worse than foolish would she show herself in denying it."

Roland left the apartment to seek for his grandmother, and as he retreated the abbot entered.

The two brothers met as brothers who love each other fondly, yet meet rarely together. Such indeed was the case. Their mutual affection attached them to each other ; but in every pursuit, habit, or sentiment connected with the discords of the times the friend and counselor of Murray stood opposed to the Roman Catholic priest ; nor, indeed, could they have held very much society together without giving cause of offense and suspicion to their confederates on each side. After a close embrace on the part of both, and a welcome on that of the abbot, Sir Halbert Glendinning expressed his satisfaction that he had come in time to appease the riot raised by Howleglas and his tumultuous followers.

"And yet," he said, "when I look on your garments, brother Edward, I cannot help thinking there still remains an Abbot of Unreason within the bounds of the monastery."

"And wherefore carp at my garments, brother Halbert ?" said the abbot, "it is the spiritual armor of my calling, and, as such, beseems me as well as breastplate and baldric become your own bosom."

"Ay, but there were small wisdom, methinks, in putting on armor where we have no power to fight : it is but a dangerous temerity to defy the foe whom we cannot resist."

"For that, my brother, no one can answer," said the

abbot, "until the battle be fought; and, were it even as you say, methinks a brave man, though desperate of victory, would rather desire to fight and fall than to resign sword and shield on some mean and dishonorable composition with his insulting antagonist. But let us not, dear Halbert, make discord of a theme on which we cannot agree, but rather stay and partake, though a heretic, of my admission feast. You need not fear, my brother, that your zeal for restoring the primitive discipline of the church will on this occasion, be offended with the rich profusion of a conventual banquet. The days of our old friend Abbot Boniface are over; and the superior of St. Mary's has neither forests nor fishings, woods nor pastures, nor cornfields; neither flocks nor herds, bucks nor wild-fowl, granaries of wheat nor storehouses of oil and wine, of ale and of mead. The refectioner's office is ended; and such a meal as a hermit in romance can offer to a wandering knight is all we have to set before you. But, if you will share it with us, we shall eat it with a cheerful heart, and thank you, my brother, for your timely protection against these rude scoffers."

"My dearest Edward," said the knight, "it grieves me deeply I cannot abide with you; but it would sound ill for us both were one of the Reformed congregation to sit down at your admission feast; and, if I can ever have the satisfaction of affording you effectual protection, it will be much owing to my remaining unsuspected of countenancing or approving your religious rites and ceremonies. It will demand whatever consideration I can acquire among my own friends to shelter the bold man who, contrary to law and the edicts of parliament, has dared to take up the office of abbot of St. Mary's."

"Trouble not yourself with the task, my brother," replied Father Ambrosius. "I would lay down my dearest blood to know that you defended the church for the church's sake; but, while you remain unhappily her enemy, I would not that you endangered your own safety, or diminished your own comfort, for the sake of my individual protection. But who comes hither to disturb the few minutes of fraternal communication which our evil fate allows us?"

"The door of the apartment opened as the abbot spoke, and Dame Magdalen entered.

"Who is this woman?" said Sir Halbert Glendinning, somewhat sternly, "and what does she want?"

"That you know me not," said the matron, "signifies little; I come by your own order, to give my free consent that the stripling, Roland Græme, return to your service; and, having said so, I cumber you no longer with my presence. Peace be with you!" She turned to go away, but was stopped by the inquiries of Sir Halbert Glendinning.

"Who are you?—what are you?—and why do you not await to make me answer?"

"I was," she replied, "while yet I belonged to the world, a matron of no vulgar name; now I am Magdalen, a poor pilgrimer, for the sake of Holy Kirk."

"Yea," said Sir Halbert, "art thou a Catholic? I thought my dame said that Roland Græme came of Reformed kin."

"His father," said the matron, "was a heretic, or rather one regarded neither orthodoxy nor heresy—neither the temple of the church or of antichrist. I, too—for the sins of the times make sinners—have seemed to conform to your unhallowed rites; but I had my dispensation and my absolution."

"You see, brother," said Sir Halbert, with a smile of meaning towards the abbot, "that we accuse you not altogether without grounds of mental equivocation."

"My brother, you do us injustice," replied the abbot; "this woman, as her bearing may of itself warrant you, is not in her perfect mind. Thanks, I must needs say, to the persecution of your marauding barons and of your latitudinarian clergy."

"I will not dispute the point," said Sir Halbert; "the evils of the time are unhappily so numerous that both churches may divide them and have enow to spare." So saying, he leaned from the window of the apartment and winded his bugle.

"Why do you sound your horn, my brother?" said the abbot; "we have spent but few minutes together."

"Alas!" said the elder brother, "and even these few have been sullied by disagreement. I sound to horse, my brother, the rather that, to avert the consequences of this day's rashness on your part requires hasty efforts on mine. Dame, you will oblige me by letting your young relative know that we mount instantly. I intend not that he shall return to Avenel with me; it would lead to new quarrels betwixt him and my household; at least, to taunts which his proud heart could ill brook, and my wish is to do him kindness. He shall, therefore, go forward to Edinburgh with one of my retinue, whom I shall send back to say what has chanced here. You seem rejoiced at this?" he added, fixing his eyes keenly on Magdalen Græme, who returned his gaze with calm indifference.

"I would rather," she said, "that Roland, a poor and friendless orphan, were the jest of the world at large than of the menials at Avenel."

"Fear not, dame, he shall be scorned by neither," answered the knight.

"It may be," she replied—"it may well be; but I will trust more to his own bearing than to your countenance." She left the room as she spoke.

The knight looked after her as she departed, but turned instantly to his brother, and expressing, in the most affectionate terms, his wishes for his welfare and happiness, craved his leave to depart. "My knaves," he said, "are too busy at the ale-stand to leave their revelry for the empty breath of a bugle-horn."

"You have freed them from higher restraint, Halbert," answered the abbot, "and therein taught them to rebel against your own."

"Fear not that, Edward," exclaimed Halbert, who never gave his brother his monastic name of Ambrosius; "none obey the command of real duty so well as those who are free from the observance of slavish bondage."

He was turning to depart, when the abbot said, "Let us not yet part, my brother; here comes some light refreshment. Leave not the house which I must now call mine, till force expel me from it, until you have at least broken bread with me."

The poor lay brother, the same who acted as porter, now entered the apartment, bearing some simple refreshment and a flask of wine. "He had found it," he said with officious humility, "by rummaging through every nook of the cellar."

The knight filled a small silver cup, and, quaffing it off, asked his brother to pledge him, observing, the wine was Bacharac, of the first vintage, and great age.

"Ay," said the poor lay brother, "it came out of the nook which old Brother Nicolas—may his soul be happy!—was wont to call Abbot Ingelram's corner; and Abbot Ingelram was bred at the convent of Würtzburg, which I understand to be near where that choice wine grows."

"True, my reverend sir," said Sir Halbert; "and therefore I entreat my brother, and you to pledge me in a cup of this orthodox vintage."

The thin old porter looked with a wishful glance towards the abbot. "*Do veniam*," said his superior; and the old man seized, with a trembling hand, a beverage to which he had been long unaccustomed, drained the cup with protracted delight, as if dwelling on the flavor and perfume, and set it down with a melancholy smile and shake of the head, as if bidding adieu in future to such delicious potations. The brothers smiled. But when Sir Halbert motioned to the abbot to take up his cup and do him reason, the abbot, in turn, shook his head, and replied, "This is no day for the abbot of St. Mary's to eat the fat and drink the sweet. In water from Our Lady's well," he added, filling a cup with the limpid element, "I wish you, my brother, all happiness, and, above all, a true sight of your spiritual errors."

"And to you, my beloved Edward," replied Glendinning, "I wish the free exercise of your own free reason, and the discharge of more important duties than are connected with the idle name which you have so rashly assumed."

The brothers parted with deep regret; and yet each, confident in his opinion, felt somewhat relieved by the absence of one whom he respected so much, and with whom he could agree so little.

Soon afterwards the sound of the Knight of Avenel's trumpets was heard, and the abbot went to the top of a tower, from whose dismantled battlements he could soon see the horsemen ascending the rising ground in the direction of the drawbridge. As he gazed, Magdalen Græme came to his side.

"Thou art come," he said, "to catch the last glimpse of thy grandson, my sister. Yonder he wends, under the charge of the best knight in Scotland, his faith ever excepted."

"Thou canst bear witness, my father, that it was no wish either of mine or of Roland's," replied the matron, "which induced the Knight of Avenel, as he is called, again to entertain my grandson in his household. Heaven, which confounds the wise with their own wisdom, and the wicked with their own policy, hath placed him where, for the service of the church, I would most wish him to be."

"I know not what you mean, my sister," said the abbot.

"Reverend father," replied Magdalen, "hast thou never heard that there are spirits powerful to rend the walls of a castle asunder when once admitted, which yet cannot enter the house unless they are invited, nay, dragged over the threshold?* Twice hath Roland Græme been thus drawn into the household of Avenel by those who now hold the title. Let them look to the issue."

So saying, she left the turret; and the abbot, after pausing a moment on her words, which he imputed to the unsettled state of her mind, followed down the winding stair to celebrate his admission to his high office by fast and prayer, instead of reveling and thanksgiving.

*See Inability of Evil Sprits to enter a House uninvited. Note 12.

CHAPTER XVI

Youth! thou wear'st to manhood now.
Darker lip and darker brow,
Statelier step, more pensive mien,
In thy face and gait are seen:
Thou must now brook midnight watches,
Take thy food and sport by snatches!
For the gambol and the jest,
Thou wert wont to love the best,
Graver follies must thou follow,
But as senseless, false, and hollow.

Life, a Poem.

YOUNG Roland Græme now trotted gaily forward in the train of Sir Halbert Glendinning. He was relieved from his most galling apprehension—the encounter of the scorn and taunt which might possibly hail his immediate return to the Castle of Avenel. "There will be a change ere they see me again," he thought to himself; "I shall wear the coat of plate, instead of the green jerkin, and the steel morion for the bonnet and feather. They will be bold that may venture to break a gibe on the man-at-arms for the follies of the page; and I trust that, ere we return, I shall have done something more worthy of note than hallooing a hound after a deer, or scrambling a crag for a kite's nest." He could not, indeed, help marveling that his grandmother, with all her religious prejudices leaning, it would seem, to the other side, had consented so readily to his re-entering the service of the house of Avenel; and yet more at the mysterious joy with which she took leave of him at the abbey.

"Heaven," said the dame, as she kissed her young relation, and bade him farewell, "works its own work, even by the hands of those of our enemies who think themselves the strongest and the wisest. Thou, my child, be ready to act upon the call of thy religion and country; and remember, each earthly bond which thou canst form is, compared to the ties which bind thee to them, like the loose flax to the twisted cable. Thou hast not forgot the face or form of the damsel Catherine Seyton?"

Roland would have replied in the negative, but the word

seemed to stick in his throat, and Magdalen continued her exhortations.

"Thou must not forget her, my son ; and here I entrust thee with a token, which I trust thou wilt speedily find an opportunity of delivering with care and secrecy into her own hand."

She put here into Roland's hand a very small packet, of which she again enjoined him to take the strictest care, and to suffer it to be seen by no one save Catherine Seyton, who, she again (very unneccessarily) reminded him, was the young maiden he had met on the preceding day. She then bestowed on him her solemn benediction, and bade God speed him.

There was something in her manner and her conduct which implied mystery ; but Roland Græme was not of an age or temper to waste much time in endeavoring to decipher her meaning. All that was obvious to his perception in the present journey promised pleasure and novelty. He rejoiced that he was traveling towards Edinburgh, in order to assume the character of a man, and lay aside that of a boy. He was delighted to think that he would have an opportunity of rejoining Catherine Seyton, whose bright eyes and lively manners had made so favorable an impression on his imagination ; and, as an inexperienced yet high-spirited youth, entering for the first time upon active life, his heart bounded at the thought that he was about to see all those scenes of courtly splendor and warlike adventures of which the followers of Sir Halbert used to boast on their occasional visits to Avenel, to the wonderment and envy of those who, like Roland, knew courts and camps only by hearsay, and were condemned to the solitary sports and almost monastic seclusion of Avenel, surrounded by its lonely lake, and embosomed among its pathless mountains. "They shall mention my name," he said to himself, "if the risk of my life can purchase me opportunities of distinction, and Catherine Seyton's saucy eye shall rest with more respect on the distinguished soldier than that with which she laughed to scorn the raw and inexperienced page." There was wanting but one accessary to complete the sense of rapturous excitation, and he possessed it by being once more mounted on the back of a fiery and active horse, instead of plodding along on foot, as had been the case during the preceding days.

Impelled by the liveliness of his own spirits, which so many circumstances tendered naturally to exalt, Roland Græme's voice and his laughter were soon distinguished amid the trampling of the horses of the retinue, and more than once attracted the attention of their leader, who remarked with satisfaction that the youth replied with good-humored raillery to such of the train as jested with him on his dismissal and return to the service of the house of Avenel.

"I thought the holly-branch in your bonnet had been blighted, Master Roland?" said one of the men-at-arms.

"Only pinched with half an hour's frost; you see it flourishes as green as ever."

"It is too grave a plant to flourish on so hot a soil as that head-piece of thine, Master Roland Græme," retorted the other, who was an old equerry of Sir Halbert Glendinning.

"If it will not flourish alone," said Roland, "I will mix it with the laurel and the myrtle; and I will carry them so near the sky that it shall make amends for their stinted growth."

Thus speaking, he dashed his spurs into his horse's sides, and, checking him at the same time, compelled him to execute a lofty caracole. Sir Halbert Glendinning looked at the demeanor of his new attendant with that sort of melancholy pleasure with which those who have long followed the pursuits of life, and are sensible of their vanity, regard the gay, young, and buoyant spirits to whom existence as yet is only hope and promise.

In the mean while, Adam Woodcock, the falconer, stripped of his masquing habit, and attired, according to his rank and calling, in the green jerkin, with a hawking-bag on the one side and a short hanger on the other, a glove on his left hand which reached half-way up his arm, and a bonnet and feather upon his head, came after the party as fast as his active little Galloway nag could trot, and immediately entered into parley with Roland Græme.

"So, my youngster, you are once more under shadow of the holly-branch?"

"And in case to repay you, my good friend," answered Roland, "your ten groats of silver."

"Which, but an hour since," said the falconer, "you had nearly paid me with ten inches of steel. On my faith, it is written in the book of our destiny that I must brook your dagger, after all."

"Nay, speak not of that, my good friend," said the youth, "I would rather have broached my own bosom than yours; but who could have known you in the mumming dress you wore?"

"Yes," the falconer resumed, for both as a poet and actor he had his own professional share of self-conceit, "I think I was as good an Howleglas as ever played part at a Shrovetide revelry, and not a much worse Abbot of Unreason. I defy the Old Enemy to unmasque me when I choose to keep my vizard on. What the devil brought the knight on us before we had the game out? You would have heard me halloo my own new ballad with a voice should have reached to Berwick. But I pray you, Master Roland, be less free of cold steel on slight occasions; since, but for the stuffing of my reverend doublet, I had only left the kirk to take my place in the kirkyard."

"Nay, spare me that feud," said Roland Græme, "we shall have no time to fight it out; for, by our lord's command, I am bound for Edinburgh."

"I know it," said Adam Woodcock, "and even therefore we shall have time to solder up this rent by the way, for Sir Halbert has appointed me your companion and guide."

"Ay? and with what purpose?" said the page.

"That," said the falconer, "is a question I cannot answer; but I know that, be the food of the eyases washed or unwashed, and, indeed, whatever becomes of perch and mew, I am to go with you to Edinburgh, and see you safely delivered to the Regent at Holyrood."

"How, to the Regent?" said Roland, in surprise.

"Ay, by my faith, to the Regent," replied Woodcock; "I promise you that, if you are not to enter his service, at least you are to wait upon him in the character of a retainer of our Knight of Avenel."

"I know no right," said the youth, "which the Knight of Avenel hath to transfer my service, supposing that I owe it to himself."

"Hush—hush!" said the falconer; "that is a question I advise no one to stir in until he has the mountain or the lake, or the march of another kingdom, which is better than either, betwixt him and his feudal superior."

"But Sir Halbert Glendinning," said the youth, "is not my feudal superior; nor has he aught of authority——"

"I pray you, my son, to rein your tongue," answered Adam Woodcock; "my lord's displeasure, if you provoke it, will be worse to appease than my lady's. The touch of his least finger were heavier than her hardest blow. And, by my faith, he is a man of steel, as true and as pure, but as hard and as pitiless. You remember the Cock of Capperlaw, whom he hanged over his gate for a mere mistake—

a poor yoke of oxen taken in Scotland, when he thought he was taking them in English land? I loved the Cock of Capperlaw; the Kerrs had not an honester man in their clan, and they have had men that might have been a pattern to the Border—men that would not have lifted under twenty cows at once, and would have held themselves dishonored if they had taken a drift of sheep or the like, but always managed their raids in full credit and honor. But see, his worship halts, and we are close by the bridge. Ride up—ride up; we must have his last instructions."

It was as Adam Woodcock said. In the hollow way descending towards the bridge, which was still in the guardianship of Peter Bridge-Ward, as he was called, though he was now very old, Sir Halbert Glendinning halted his retinue, and beckoned to Woodcock and Græme to advance to the head of the train.

"Woodcock," said he, "thou knowest to whom thou art to conduct this youth. And thou, young man, obey discreetly and with diligence the orders that shall be given thee. Curb thy vain and peevish temper. Be just, true, and faithful; and there is in thee that which may raise thee many a degree above thy present station. Neither shalt thou—always supposing thine efforts to be fair and honest—want the protection and countenance of Avenel."

Leaving them in front of the bridge, the center tower of which now began to cast a prolonged shade upon the river, the Knight of Avenel turned to the left, without crossing the river, and pursued his way towards the chain of hills within whose recesses are situated the Lake and Castle of Avenel. There remained behind, the falconer, Roland Græme, and a domestic of the knight, of inferior rank, who was left with them to look after their horses while on the road, to carry their baggage, and to attend to their convenience.

So soon as the more numerous body of riders had turned off to pursue their journey westward, those whose route lay across the river, and was directed towards the north, summoned the bridge-ward, and demanded a free passage.

"I will not lower the bridge," answered Peter, in a voice querulous with age and ill-humor. "Come Papist, come Protestant, ye are all the same. The Papists threatened us with purgatory, and fleeched us with pardons; the Protestant mints at us with the sword, and cuittles us with the liberty of conscience; but never a one of either says, 'Peter, there is your penny.' I am well tired of all this, and for no man shall the bridge fall that pays me not ready money; and I would have you know I care as little for Geneva as for Rome, as little for homilies as for pardons; and the silver pennies are the only passports I will hear of."

"Here is a proper old chuff!" said Woodcock to his companion; then raising his voice, he exclaimed, "Hark thee, dog—bridge-ward—villain, dost thou think we have refused thy namesake Peter's pence to Rome, to pay thine at the bridge of Kennaquhair? Let thy bridge down instantly to the followers of the house of Avenel, or by the hand of my father, and that handled many a bridle rein, for he was a bluff Yorkshireman—I say, by my father's hand, our knight will blow thee out of thy solan-goose's nest there in the middle of the water, with the light falconet which we are bringing southward from Edinburgh to-morrow."

The bridge-ward heard, and muttered, "A plague on falcon and falconet, on cannon and demi-cannon, and all the barking bull-dogs whom they halloo against stone and lime in these our days! It was a merry time when there was little besides handy blows, and it may be a flight of arrows that harmed an ashler wall as little as so many hailstones. But we must jouk and let the jaw gang by." Comforting himself in his state of disminished consequence with this pithy old proverb, Peter Bridge-Ward lowered the drawbridge, and permitted them to pass over. At the sight of his white hair, albeit it discovered a visage equally peevish through age and misfortune, Roland was inclined to give him an alms, but Adam Woodcock prevented him. "E'en let him pay the penalty of his former churlishness and greed," he said; "the wolf, when he has lost his teeth, should be treated no better than a cur."

Leaving the bridge-ward to lament the alteration of times which sent domineering soldiers and feudal retainers to his place of passage, instead of peaceful pilgrims, and reduced him to become the oppressed, instead of playing the extortioner, the travelers turned them northward; and Adam Woodcock, well acquainted with that part of the country, proposed to cut short a considerable portion of the road by traversing the little vale of Glendearg, so famous for the adventures which befell therein during the earlier part of the Benedictine's Manuscript. With these, and with the thousand commentaries, representations and misrepresentations to which they had given rise, Roland Græme was, of course, well acquainted; for in the Castle of Avenel, as well as in other great establishments, the inmates talked of nothing so often, or with such pleasure, as of the private affairs of their lord and lady. But while Roland was viewing with interest these haunted scenes, in which things were said to have passed beyond the ordinary laws of nature, Adam Woodcock was still regretting in his secret soul the unfinished revel and the unsung ballad, and kept every now and then breaking out with some such verses as these:

"The friars of Fail drank berry-brown ale,
The best that e'er was tasted;
The monks of Melrose made gude kale
On Fridays, when they fasted.
St. Monance' sister,
The gray priest kist her—
Friend save the company!
Sing hay trix, trim-go-trix,
Under the greenwood tree!"

"By my hand, friend Woodcock," said the page, "though I know you for a hardy Gospeller, that fear neither saint nor devil, yet, if I were you, I would not sing your profane songs in this valley of Glendearg, considering what has happened here before our time."

"A straw for your wandering spirits!" said Adam Woodcock; "I mind them no more than an earn cares for a string of wild geese; they have all fled since the pulpits were filled with honest men, and the people's ears with sound doctrine. Nay, I have a touch at them in my ballad, an I had but had the good luck to have sung it to end; and again he set off in the same key:

"From haunted spring and grassy ring
Troop goblin, elf, and fairy;
And the kelpie must flit from the black bog-pit
And the brownie must not tarry;
To Limbo lake
Their way they take,
With scarce the pith to flee
Sing hay trix, trim-go-trix,
Under the greenwood tree!

I think," he added, "that, could Sir. Halbert's patience have stretched till we came that length, he would have had a hearty laugh, and that is what he seldom enjoys."

"If it be all true that men tell of his early life," said Roland, "he has less right to laugh at goblins than most men."

"Ay, *if* it be all true," answered Adam Woodcock; "but who can ensure us of that? Moreover, these were but tales the monks used to gull us simple laymen withal; they knew that fairies and hobgoblins brought aves and paternosters into repute; but now we have given up worship of images in wood and stone, methinks it were no time to be afraid of bubbles in the water or shadows in the air."

"However," said Roland Græme, "as the Catholics say they do not worship wood or stone, but only as emblems of the holy saints, and not as things holy in themselves——"

"Pshaw! pshaw!" answered the falconer; "a rush for their prating. They told us another story when these baptized idols of theirs brought pike-staves and sandaled shoon from all the four winds, and whillied the old women out of their corn and their candle-ends, and their butter, bacon, wool, and cheese, and when not so much as a gray groat escaped tithing."

Roland Græme had been long taught, by necessity, to consider his form of religion as a profound secret, and to say nothing whatever in its defense when assailed, lest he should draw on himself the suspicion of belonging to the unpopular and exploded church. He therefore suffered Adam Woodcock to triumph without farther opposition, marveling in his own mind whether any of the goblins, formerly such active agents, would avenge his rude raillery before they left the valley of Glendearg. But no such consequences followed. They passed the night quietly in a cottage in the glen, and the next day resumed their route to Edinburgh.

CHAPTER XVII

> Edina! Scotia's darling seat,
> All hail thy palaces and towers,
> Where once, beneath a monarch's feet,
> Sate legislation's sovereign powers!
>
> BURNS.

"THIS, then, is Edinburgh?" said the youth, as the fellow-travelers arrived at one of the heights to the southward, which commanded a view of the great northern capital—"this is that Edinburgh of which we have heard so much?"

"Even so," said the falconer; "yonder stands Auld Reekie; you may see the smoke hover over her at twenty miles' distance, as the goss-hawk hangs over a plump of young wild ducks; ay, yonder is the heart of Scotland, and each throb that she gives is felt from the edge of Solway to Duncansby Head. See, yonder is the old Castle; and see to the right, on yon rising ground, that is the Castle of Craigmillar, which I have known a merry place in my time."

"Was it not there," said the page in a low voice, "that the Queen held her court?"

"Ay, ay," replied the falconer—"Queen she was then, though you must not call her so now. Well, they may say what they will—many a true heart will be sad for Mary Stuart, e'en if all be true men say of her; for look you, Master Roland, she was the loveliest creature to look upon that I ever saw with eye, and no lady in the land liked better the fair flight of a falcon. I was at the great match on Roslin Moor betwixt Bothwell—he was a black sight to her that Bothwell—and the Baron of Roslin, who could judge a hawk's flight as well as any man in Scotland: a butt of Rhenish and a ring of gold was the wager, and it was flown as fairly for as ever was red gold and bright wine. And to see her there on her white palfrey, that flew as if it scorned to touch more than the heather blossom; and to hear her voice, as clear and sweet as the mavis's whistle, mix among our jolly whooping and whistling; and to mark all the nobles dashing round her—happiest he who got a word or a look—tearing through moss and hag, and venturing neck and limb to gain the praise of a bold rider, and the blink of a bonny queen's bright eye! She will see little hawking where she lies now; ay, ay, pomp and pleasure pass away as speedily as the wap of a falcon's wing."

"And where is this poor queen now confined?" said Roland Græme, interested in the fate of a woman whose beauty and grace had made so strong an impression even on the blunt and careless character of Adam Woodcock.

"Where is she now imprisoned?" said honest Adam; "why, in some castle in the north, they say. I know not where, for my part, nor is it worth while to vex one's self anent what cannot be mended. An she had guided her power well whilst she had it she had not come to so evil a pass. Men say she must resign her crown to this little baby of a prince, for that they will trust her with it no longer. Our master has been as busy as his neighbors in all this work. If the Queen should come to her own again, Avenal Castle is like to smoke for it, unless he makes his bargain all the better."

"In a castle in the north Queen Mary is confined?" said the page.

"Why, ay—they say so, at least. In a castle beyond that great river which comes down yonder, and looks like a river; but it is a branch of the sea, and as bitter as brine."

"And amongst all her subjects," said the page, with some emotion, "is there none that will adventure anything for her relief?"

"That is a kittle question," said the falconer; "and if you ask it often, Master Roland, I am fain to tell you that you will be mewed up yourself in some of those castles, if they do not prefer twisting your head off, to save farther trouble with you. Adventure anything! Lord, why, Murray has the wind in his poop now, man, and flies so high and strong that the devil a wing of them can match him. No, no; there she is, and there she must lie, till Heaven send her deliverance, or till her son has the management of all. But Murray will never let her loose again, he knows her too well. And hark thee, we are now bound for Holyrood, where thou will find plenty of news and of courtiers to tell it. But, take my counsel, and keep a calm sough, as the Scots say: hear every man's counsel, and keep your own. And if you hap to learn any news you like, leap not up as if you were to put on armor direct in the cause. Our old Mr. Wingate says—and he knows court cattle well—that if you are told old King

Coul is come alive again, you should turn it off with, 'And is he, in truth? I heard not of it,' and should seem no more moved than if one told you, by way of novelty, that old King Coul was dead and buried. Wherefore, look well to your bearing, Master Roland, for I promise you, you come among a generation that are keen as a hungry hawk. And never be dagger out of sheath at every wry word you hear spoken; for you will find as hot blades as yourself, and then will be letting of blood without advice either of leach or almanack."

"You shall see how staid I will be, and how cautious, my good friend," said Græme; "but, blessed Lady, what goodly house is that which is lying all in ruins so close to the city? Have they been playing at the Abbot of Unreason here, and ended the gambol by burning the church?"

"There again now," replied his companion, "you go down the wind like a wild haggard, that minds neither lure nor beck; that is a question you should have asked in as low a tone as I shall answer it."

"If I stay here long," said Roland Græme, "it is like I shall lose the natural use of my voice; but what are the ruins then?"

"The Kirk of Field", said the falconer, in a low and impressive whisper, laying at the same time his finger on his lip; "ask no more about it; somebody got foul play, and somebody got the blame of it; and the game began there which perhaps may not be played out in our time. Poor Henry Darnley! to be an ass, he understood somewhat of a hawk! but they sent him on the wing through the air himself one bright moonlight night."

The memory of this catastrophe was so recent that the page averted his eyes with horror from the scathed ruins in which it had taken place; and the accusations against the Queen, to which it had given rise, came over his mind with such strength as to balance the compassion he had begun to entertain for her present forlorn situation.

It was, indeed, with that agitating state of mind which arises partly from horror, but more from anxious interest and curiosity, that young Græme found himself actually traversing the scene of those tremendous events the report of which had disturbed the most distant solitudes in Scotland, like the echoes of distant thunder rolling among the mountains.

"Now," he thought—"now or never shall I become a man, and bear my part in those deeds which the simple inhabitants of our hamlets repeat to each other as if they were wrought by beings of a superior order to their own! I will know now wherefore the Knight of Avenel carries his crest so much above those of the neighboring baronage, and how it is that men, by valor and wisdom, work their way from the hodden-gray coat to the cloak of scarlet and gold. Men say I have not much wisdom to recommend me; and if that be true, courage must do it; for I will be a man amongst living men, or a dead corpse amongst the dead."

From these dreams of ambition he turned his thoughts to those of pleasure, and began to form many conjectures when and where he should see Catherine Seyton, and in what manner their acquaintance was to be renewed. With such conjectures he was amusing himself, when he found that they had entered the city, and all other feelings were suspended in the sensation of giddy astonishment with which an inhabitant of the country is affected when, for the first time, he finds himself in the streets of a large and populous city, an unit in the midst of thousands.

The principal street of Edinburgh was then, as now, one of the most spacious in Europe. The extreme height of the houses, and the variety of Gothic gables, and battlements, and balconies, by which the sky-line on each side was crowned and terminated, together with the width of the street itself, might have struck with surprise a more practised eye than that of young Græme. The population, close packed within the walls of the city, and at this time increased by the number of the lords of the King's party who had thronged to Edinburgh to wait upon the Regent Murray, absolutely swarmed like bees on the wide and stately street. Instead of the shop-windows, which are now calculated for the display of goods, the traders had their open booths projecting on the street, in which, as in the fashion of the modern bazars, all was exposed which they had upon sale. And though the commodities were not of the richest kinds, yet Græme thought he beheld the wealth of the whole world in the various bales of Flanders cloths and the specimens of tapestry; and at other places the display of domestic utensils and pieces of plate struck him with wonder. The sight of cutlers' booths, furnished with swords and poniards, which were manufactured in Scotland, and with pieces of defensive armor, imported from Flanders, added to his surprise; and at every step he found so much to admire and to gaze upon that Adam Woodcock had no little difficulty in prevailing on him to advance through such a scene of enchantment.

The sight of the crowds which filled the streets was equally a subject of wonder. Here a gay lady, in her muffler, or silken veil, traced her way delicately, a gentleman-usher making way for her, a page bearing up her train, and a waiting gentlewoman carrying her Bible, thus intimating that her purpose was towards the church. There he might see a group of citizens bending the same way, with their short Flemish cloaks, wide trousers, and high-caped doublets—a fashion to which, as well as to their bonnet and feather, the Scots were long faithful. Then, again, came the clergyman himself, in his black Geneva cloak and band, lending a grave and attentive ear to the discourse of several persons who accompanied him, and who were doubtless holding serious converse on the religious subject he was about to treat of. Nor did there lack passengers of a different class and appearance.

At every turn, Roland Græme might see a gallant ruffle along in the newer or French mode, his doublet slashed, and his points of the same colors with the lining, his long sword on one side, and his poniard on the other, behind him a body of stout serving-men, proportioned to his estate and quality, all of whom walked with the air of military retainers, and were armed with sword and buckler, the latter being a small round shield, not unlike the Highland target, having a steel spike in the center. Two of these parties, each headed by a person of importance, chanced to meet in the very center of the street, or, as it was called, "the crown of the causeway"—a post of honor as tenaciously asserted in Scotland as that of giving or taking the wall used to be in the more southern part of the island. The two leaders being of equal rank, and, most probably, either animated by political dislike or by recollection of some feudal enmity, marched close up to each other, without yielding an inch to the right or the left; and neither showing the least purpose of giving way, they stopped for an instant, and then drew their swords. Their followers imitated their example; about a score of weapons at once flashed in the sun, and there was an immediate clatter of swords and bucklers, while the followers on either side cried their master's name: the one shouting, "Help, a Leslie!—a Leslie!" while the others answered with shouts of "Seyton!—Seyton!" with the additional punning slogan, "Set on—set on; bear the knaves to the ground!"

If the falconer found difficulty in getting the page to go forward before, it was now perfectly impossible. He reined up his horse, clapped his hands, and, delighted with the fray, cried and shouted as fast as any of those who were actually engaged in it.

The noise and cries thus arising on the Highgate, as it was called, drew into the quarrel two or three other parties of gentlemen and their servants, besides some single passengers, who, hearing a fray betwixt these two distinguished names, took part in it, either for love or hatred.

The combat became now very sharp, and although the sword-and-buckler men made more clatter and noise than they did real damage, yet several good cuts were dealt among them; and those who wore rapiers—a more formidable weapon than the ordinary Scottish sword—gave and received dangerous wounds. Two men were already stretched on the causeway, and the party of Seyton began to give ground, being much inferior in number to the other, with which several of the citizens had united themselves, when young Roland Græme, beholding their leader, a noble gentleman, fighting bravely, and hard pressed with numbers, could withhold no longer. "Adam Woodcock," he said, "an you be a man, draw, and let us take part with the Seyton." And without waiting a reply, or listening to the falconer's earnest entreaty that he would leave alone a strife in which he had no concern, the fiery youth sprung from his horse, drew his short sword, and shouting like the rest, "A Seyton!—a Seyton! Set on!—set on!" thrust forward into the throng, and struck down one of those who was pressing hardest upon the gentleman whose cause he espoused. This sudden reinforcement gave spirit to the weaker party, who began to renew the combat with much alacrity, when four of the magistrates of the city, distinguished by their velvet cloaks and gold chains, came up with a guard of halberdiers and citizens, armed with long weapons, and well accustomed to such service, thrust boldly forward, and compelled the swordsmen to separate, who immediately retreated in different directions, leaving such of the wounded on both sides as had been disabled in the fray lying on the street.

The falconer, who had been tearing his beard for anger at his comrade's rashness, now rode up to him with the horse, which he had caught by the bridle, and accosted him with "Master Roland—master goose—master madcap—will it please you to get on horse, and budge? or will you remain here to be carried to prison, and made to answer for this pretty day's work?"

The page, who had begun his retreat along with the Seytons, just as if he had been one of their natural allies, was by this unceremonious application made sensible that he was acting a foolish part; and, obeying Adam Woodcock, with some sense of shame, he sprung actively on horseback, and upsetting with the shoulder of the animal a city-officer who was making towards him, he began to ride smartly down the street, along with his companion, and was quickly out of the reach of the hue and cry. In fact, rencounters of the kind were so common in Edinburgh at that period that the disturbance seldom excited much attention after the affray was over, unless some person of consequence chanced to have fallen, an incident which imposed on his friends the duty of avenging his death on the first convenient opportunity. So feeble, indeed, was the arm of the police, that it was not unusual for such skirmishes to last for hours, where the parties were numerous and well matched. But at this time the Regent, a man of great strength of character, aware of the mischief which usually arose from such acts of violence, had prevailed with the magistrates to keep a constant guard on foot, for preventing or separating such affrays as had happened in the present case.

The falconer and his young companion were now riding down the Canongate, and had slackened their pace to avoid attracting attention, the rather that there seemed to be no appearance of pursuit. Roland hung his head as one who was conscious his conduct had been none of the wisest, while his companion thus addressed him:

"Will you be pleased to tell me one thing, Master Roland Græme, and that is, whether there be a devil incarnate in you or no?"

"Truly, Master Adam Woodcock," answered the page, "I would fain hope there is not."

"Then," said Adam, "I would fain know by what other influence or instigation you are perpetually at one end or the other of some bloody brawl? What, I pray, had you to do with these Seytons and Leslies, that you had never heard the names of in your life before?"

"You are out there, my friend," said Roland Græme, "I have my own reasons for being a friend to the Seytons."

"They must have been very secret reasons, then," answered Adam Woodcock, "for I think I could have wagered you had never known one of the name; and I am apt to believe still that it was your unhallowed passion for that clashing of cold iron, which has as much charm for you as the clatter of a brass pan hath for a hive of bees, rather than any care either for Seyton or for Leslie, that persuaded you to thrust your fool's head into a quarrel that nowise concerned you. But take this for a warning, my young master, that if you are to draw sword with every man who draws swords on the Highgate here, it will be scarce worth your while to sheath bilbo again for the rest of your life, since, if I guess rightly, it will scarce endure on such terms for many hours —all which I leave to your serious consideration."

"By my word, Adam, I honor your advice; and I promise you that I will practise by it as faithfully as if I were sworn apprentice to you, to the trade and mystery of bearing myself with all wisdom and safety through the new paths of life that I am about to be engaged in."

"And therein you will do well," said the falconer, "and I do not quarrel with you, Master Roland, for having a grain over much spirit, because I know one may bring to the hand a wild hawk, which one never can a dunghill hen; and so betwixt two faults you have the best side on't. But, besides your peculiar genius for quarreling and lugging out your side companion, my dear Master Roland, you have also the gift of peering under every woman's muffler and screen, as if you expected to find an old acquaintance. Though, were you to spy one, I should be as much surprised at it, well wotting how few you have seen of these same wild-fowl, as I was at your taking so deep an interest even now in the Seyton."

"Tush, man! nonsense and folly," answered Roland Græme; "I but sought to see what eyes these gentle hawks have got under their hood."

"Ay, but it's a dangerous subject of inquiry," said the falconer; "you had better hold out your bare wrist for an eagle to perch upon. Look you, Master Roland, these pretty wild geese cannot be hawked at without risk: they have as many divings, boltings, and volleyings as the most gamesome quarry that falcon ever flew at. And besides, every woman of them is manned with her husband, or her kind friend, or her brother, or her cousin, or her sworn servant at the least. But you heed me not, Master Roland, though I know the game so well: your eye is all on that pretty damsel who trips down the gate before us; by my certes, I will warrant her a blythe dancer either in reel or revel—a pair of silver morisco bells would become these pretty ankles as well as the jesses would suit the fairest Norway hawk."

"Thou art a fool, Adam," said the page, "and I care not a button about the girl or her ankles. But, what the foul fiend, one must look at something!"

"Very true, Master Roland Græme," said his guide, "but let me pray you to choose your objects better. Look you. there is scarce a woman walks this Highgate with a silk screen or a pearlin muffler, but, as I said before, she has either gentleman-usher before her, or kinsman, or lover, or husband, at her elbow, or it may be a brace of stout fellows with sword and buckler, not so far behind but what they can follow close. But you heed me no more than a goss-hawk minds a yellow yoldring."

"O yes, I do—I do mind you indeed," said Roland Græme; "but hold my nag a bit—I will be with you in the exchange of a whistle." So saying, and ere Adam Woodcock could finish the sermon which was dying on his tongue, Roland Græme, to the falconer's utter astonishment, threw him the bridle of his jennet, jumped off horseback, and pursued down one of the closes or narrow lanes, which opening under a vault, terminate upon the main street, the very maiden to whom his friend had accused him of showing so much attention, and who had turned down the pass in question.

"St. Mary—St. Magdalen—St. Benedict—St. Barnabas!" cried the poor falconer, when he found himself thus suddenly brought to a pause in the midst of the Canongate, and saw his young charge start off like a madman in quest of a damsel whom he had never, as Adam supposed, seen in his life before—"St. Satan and St. Beelzebub—for this would make one swear saint and devil—what can have come over the lad with a wanion! And what shall I do the whilst? He will have his throat cut, the poor lad, as sure as I was born at the foot of Roseberry Topping. Could I find some one to hold the horses! But they are as sharp here north-way as in canny Yorkshire herself, and quit bridle, quit titt, as we say. An I could but see one of our folks now, a holly-sprig were worth a gold tassel; or could I but see one of the Regent's men; but to leave the horses to a stranger, that I cannot; and to leave the place while the lad is in jeopardy, that I wonot."

We must leave the falconer, however, in the midst of his distress, and follow the hot-headed youth who was the cause of his perplexity.

The latter part of Adam Woodcock's sage remonstrance had been in a great measure lost upon Roland, for whose benefit it was intended; because, in one of the female forms which tripped along the streets, muffled in a veil of striped silk, like the women of Brussels at this day, his eye had discerned something which closely resembled the exquisite shape and spirited bearing of Catherine Seyton. During all the grave advice which the falconer was dinning into his ear, his eye continued intent upon so interesting an object of observation; and at length, as the damsel, just about to dive under one of the arched passages which afforded an outlet to the Canongate from the houses beneath (a passage graced by a projecting shield of arms, supported by two hugh foxes of stone), had lifted her veil for the purpose perhaps of descrying who the horseman was who for some time had eyed her so closely, young Roland saw, under the shade of the silken plaid, enough of the bright azure eyes, fair locks, and blythe features to induce him, like an inexperienced and rash madcap, whose wilful ways had never been traversed by contradiction, nor much subjected to consideration, to throw the bridle of his horse into Adam Woodcock's hand, and leave him to play the waiting gentleman, while he dashed down the paved court after Catherine Seyton—all as aforesaid.

Women's wits are proverbially quick, but apparently those of Catherine suggested no better expedient than fairly to betake herself to speed of foot, in hopes of baffling the page's vivacity, by getting safely lodged before he could discover where. But a youth of eighteen, in pursuit of a mistress, is not so easily outstripped. Catherine fled across a paved court, decorated with large formal vases of stone, in which yews, cypresses, and other evergreens vegetated in somber sullenness, and gave a correspondent degree of solemnity to the high and heavy building in front of which they were placed as ornaments, aspiring towards a square portion of the blue hemisphere, corresponding exactly in extent to the quadrangle in which they were stationed, and all around which rose huge black walls, exhibiting windows in rows of five stories, with heavy architraves over each, bearing armorial and religious devices.

Through this court Catherine Seyton flashed like a hunted doe, making the best use of those pretty legs which had attracted the commendation even of the reflective and cautious Adam Woodcock. She hastened towards a large door in the center of the lower front of the court, pulled the bobbin till the latch flew up, and esconced herself in the ancient mansion. But, if she fled like a doe, Roland Græme followed with the speed and ardor of a youthful staghound, loosed for the first time on his prey. He kept her in view in spite of her efforts; for it is remarkable what an advantage in such a race the gallant who desires to see possesses over the maiden who wishes not to be seen—an advantage which I have known counterbalance a great start in point of distance. In short, he saw the waving of her screen, or veil, at one corner, heard the tap of her foot, light as that was, as it crossed the court, and caught a glimpse of her figure just as she entered the door of the mansion.

Roland Græme, inconsiderate and headlong as we have described him, having no knowledge of real life but from the romances which he had read, and not an idea of checking himself in the midst of an eager impulse, possessed, besides, of much courage and readiness, never hesitated for a moment to approach the door through which the object of his search had disappeared. He too pulled the bobbin, and the latch, though heavy and massive, answered to the summons, and rose. The page entered with the same precipation which had marked his whole proceeding, and found himself in a large gloomy hall, or vestibule, dimly enlightened by latticed casements of painted glass, and rendered yet dimmer through the exclusion of the sunbeams, owing to the height of the walls of those buildings by which the courtyard was inclosed. The walls of the hall were surrounded with suits of ancient and rusted armor, interchanged with huge and massive stone scutcheons, bearing double tressures, fleured and counter-fleured, wheat-sheaves, coronets, and so forth—things which Roland Græme gave not a moment's attention.

In fact, he only deigned to observe the figure of Catherine Seyton, who, deeming herself safe in the hall, had stopped to take breath after her course, and was reposing herself for a moment on a large oaken settle which stood at the upper end of the hall. The noise of Roland's entrance at once disturbed her; she startled up with a faint scream of surprise, and escaped through one of the several folding-doors which opened into this apartment as a common center. This door, which Roland Græme instantly approached, opened on a large and well-lighted gallery, at the upper end of which he could hear several voices and the noise of hasty steps approaching towards the hall, or vestibule. A little recalled to sober thought by an appearance of serious danger, he was deliberating whether he should stand fast or retire, when Catherine Seyton re-entered from a side door, running towards him with as much speed as a few minutes since she had fled from him.

"O, what mischief brought you hither?" she said. "Fly—fly, or you are a dead man; or stay—they come—flight is impossible; say you came to ask for Lord Seyton."

She sprung from him and disappeared through the door by which she had made her second appearance ; and, at the same instant, a pair of large folding-doors at the upper end of the gallery flew open with vehemence, and six or seven young gentlemen, richly dressed, pressed forward into the apartment, having for the greater part, their swords drawn.

"Who is it," said one, "dare intrude on us in our own mansion?"

"Cut him to pieces," said another; "let him pay for this day's insolence and violence; he is some follower of the Rothes."

"No, by St. Mary," said another; "he is a follower of the arch-fiend and ennobled clown, Halbert Glendinning, who takes the style of Avenel—once a church-vassal, now a pilager of the church."

"It is so," said a fourth; "I know him by the holly-sprig, which is their cognizance. Secure the door; he must answer for this insolence."

Two of the gallants, hastily drawing their weapons, passed on to the door by which Roland had entered the hall, and stationed themselves there as if to prevent his escape. The others advanced on Græme, who had just sense enough to perceive that any attempt at resistance would be alike fruitless and imprudent. At once, and by various voices, none of which sounded amicably, the page was required to say who he was, whence he came, his name, his errand, and who sent him hither. The number of the questions demanded of him at once afforded a momentary apology for his remaining silent, and ere that brief truce had elapsed a personage entered the hall, at whose appearance those who had gathered fiercely around Roland fell back with respect.

This was a tall man, whose dark hair was already grizzled, though his eye and haughty features retained all the animation of youth. The upper part of his person was undressed to his Holland shirt whose ample folds were stained with blood. But he wore a mantle of crimson, lined with rich fur, cast around him, which supplied the deficiency of his dress. On his head he had a crimson velvet bonnet, looped up on one side with a small golden chain of many links, which, going thrice round the hat, was fastened by a medal, agreeable to the fashion amongst the grandees of the time.

"Whom have you here, sons and kinsmen," said he, "around whom you crowd thus roughly? Know you not that the shelter of this roof should secure every one fair treatment who shall come hither either in fair peace or in open and manly hostility?"

"But here, my lord," answered one of the youths, "is a knave who comes on treacherous espial!"

"I deny the charge," said Roland Græme, boldly; "I came to inquire after my Lord Seyton."

"A likely tale," answered his accusers, "in the mouth of a follower of Glendinning."

"Stay young man," said the Lord Seyton, for it was that nobleman himself, "let me look at this youth. By Heaven, it is the very same who came so boldly to my side not very many minutes since, when some of my own knaves bore themselves with more respect to their own worshipful safety than to mine! Stand back from him, for he well deserves honor and a friendly welcome at your hands, instead of this rough treatment."

They fell back on all sides, obedient to Lord Seyton's commands, who, taking Roland Græme by the hand, thanked him for his prompt and gallant assistance, adding, that he nothing doubted "the same interest which he had taken in his cause in the affray brought him hither to inquire after his hurt."

Roland bowed low in acquiescence.

"Or is there anything in which I can serve you, to show my sense of your ready gallantry?"

But the page, thinking it best to abide by the apology for his visit which the Lord Seyton had so aptly himself suggested replied, "That to be assured of his lordship's safety had been the only cause of his intrusion. He judged," he added, "he had seen him receive some hurt in the affray."

"A trifle," said Lord Seyton; "I had but stripped my doublet, that the chirurgeon might put some dressing on the paltry scratch, when these rash boys interrupted us with their clamor."

Roland Græme, making a low obeisance, was now about to depart, for, relieved from the danger of being treated as a spy, he began next to fear that his companion, Adam Woodcock, whom he had so unceremoniously quitted, would either bring him into some farther dilemma by venturing into the hotel in quest of him, or ride off and leave him behind altogether. But Lord Seyton did not permit him to escape so easily. "Tarry," he said, "young man, and let me know thy rank and name. The Seyton has of late been more wont to see friends and followers shrink from his side than to receive aid from strangers; but a new world may come round, in which he may have the chance of rewarding his well-wishers."

"My name is Roland Græme, my lord," answered the youth, "a page, who for the present is in the service of Sir Halbert Glendinning."

"I said so from the first," said one of the young men; "my life I will wager that this is a shaft out of the heretic's quiver—a stratagem from first to last, to injeer into your confidence some espial of his own. They know how to teach both boys and women to play the intelligencers."

"That is false, if it be spoken of me," said Roland; "no man in Scotland should teach me such a foul part!"

"I believe thee, boy," said Lord Seyton, "for thy strokes were too fair to be dealt upon an understanding with those that were to receive them. Credit me, however, I little expected to have help at need from one of your master's household; and I would know what moved thee in my quarrel, to thine own endangering?"

"So please you, my lord," said Ronald, "I think my master himself would not have stood by and seen an honorable man borne to earth by odds, if his single arm could help him. Such at least is the lesson we were taught in chivalry at the Castle of Avenel."

"The good seed hath fallen into good ground, young man," said Seyton; "but, alas! if thou practise such honorable war in these dishonorable days, when right is everywhere borne down by mastery, thy life, my poor boy, will be but a short one."

"Let it be short, so it be honorable," said Roland Græme; "and permit me now, my lord, to commend me to your grace, and to take my leave. A comrade waits with my horse in the street."

"Take this, however, young man," said Lord Seyton,* undoing from his bonnet the golden chain and medal, "and wear it for my sake."

With no little pride Ronald Græme accepted the gift, which he hastily fastened around his bonnet, as he had seen gallants wear such an ornament, and, renewing his obeisance to the baron, left the hall, traversed the court, and appeared in the street, just as Adam Woodcock, vexed and anxious at his delay, had determined to leave the horses to their fate and go in quest of his youthful comrade. "Whose barn hast thou broken next?" he exclaimed, greatly relieved by

* See Note 13.

his appearance, although his countenance indicated that he had passed through an agitating scene.

"Ask me no questions," said Ronald, leaping gaily on his horse; "but see how short time it takes to win a chain of gold," pointing to that which he now wore.

"Now, God forbid that thou hast either stolen it or reft it by violence," said the falconer; "for, otherwise, I wot not how the devil thou couldst compass it. I have been often here, ay, for months at an end, and no one gave me either chain or medal."

"Thou seest I have got one on shorter acquaintance with the city," answered the page; "but set thine honest heart at rest: that which is fairly won and freely given is neither reft nor stolen."

"Marry, hang thee, with thy fanfarona * about thy neck!" said the falconer; "I think water will not drown nor hemp strangle thee. Thou hast been discarded as my lady's page, to come in again as my lord's squire; and, for following a noble young damsel into some great household, thou getst a chain and medal, where another would have had the baton across his shoulders, if he missed having the dirk in his body. But here we come in front of the old abbey. Bear thy good luck with you when you cross these paved stones, and, by Our Lady, you may brag Scotland."

As he spoke, they checked their horses, where the huge old vaulted entrance to the Abbey or Palace of Holyrood crossed the termination of the street down which they had proceeded. The courtyard of the palace opened within this gloomy porch, showing the front of an irregular pile of monastic buildings, one wing of which is still extant, forming a part of the modern palace, erected in the days of Charles I.

At the gate of the porch the falconer and page resigned their horses to the serving-man in attendance; the falconer commanding him, with an air of authority, to carry them safely to the stables. "We follow," he said, "the Knight of Avenel. We must bear ourselves for what we are here," said he in a whisper to Ronald, "for every one here is looked on as they demean themselves; and he that is too modest must to the wall, as the proverb says; therefore, cock thy bonnet, man, and let us brook the causeway bravely."

Assuming, therefore, an air of consequence corresponding to what he supposed to be his master's importance and quality, Adam Woodcock led the way into the courtyard of the Palace of Holyrood.

* See Note 14.

CHAPTER XVIII

> The sky is clouded, Gaspard,
> And the vex'd ocean sleeps a troubled sleep,
> Beneath a lurid gleam of parting sunshine.
> Such slumber hangs o'er discontented lands,
> While factions doubt, as yet, if they have strength
> To front the open battle.
>
> *Albion, a Poem.*

THE youthful page paused on the entrance of the court-yard, and implored his guide to give him a moment's breathing-space. "Let me but look around me, man," said he; "you consider not I have never seen such a scene as this before. And this is Holyrood—the resort of the gallant and gay, and the fair, and the wise, and the powerful!"

"Ay, marry, is it!" said Woodcock; "but I wish I could hood thee as they do the hawks, for thou startest as wildly as if you sought another fray or another Sanfarona. I would I had thee safely housed, for thou lookest wild as a goss-hawk."

It was indeed no common sight to Roland, the vestibule of a palace, traversed by its various groups—some radiant with gaiety, some pensive, and apparently weighed down by affairs concerning the state or concerning themselves. Here the hoary statesman, with his cautious yet commanding look, his furred cloak and sable pantoufles; there the soldier, in buff and steel, his long sword jarring against the pavement, and his whiskered upper lip and frowning brow looking a habitual defiance of danger which perhaps was not always made good; there again passed my lord's serving-man, high of heart and bloody of hand, humble to his master and his master's equals, insolent to all others. To these might be added, the poor suitor, with his anxious look and depressed mien; the officer, full of his brief authority, elbowing his betters, and possibly his benefactors, out of the road; the proud priest, who sought a better benefice; the proud baron, who sought a grant of church lands; the robber chief, who came to solicit a pardon for the injuries he had inflicted on his neighbors; the plundered franklin, who came to seek vengeance for that which he had himself received. Besides, there was the mustering and disposition of guards and soldiers; the despatching of messengers, and the receiving them; the trampling and neighing of horses without the gate; the flashing of arms, and rustling of plumes, and jingling of spurs, within it. In short, it was that gay and splendid confusion in which the eye of youth sees all that is brave and brilliant, and that of experience much that is doubtful, deceitful, false, and hollow—hopes that will never be gratified, promises which will never be fulfilled, pride in the disguise of humility, and insolence in that of frank and generous bounty.

As, tired of the eager and enraptured attention which the page gave to a scene so new to him, Adam Woodcock endeavored to get him to move forward, before his exuberance of astonishment should attract the observation of the sharp-witted denizens of the court, the falconer himself became an object of attention to a gay menial in a dark-green bonnet and feather, with a cloak of a corresponding color, laid down, as the phrase then went, by six broad bars of silver lace, and welted with violet and silver. The words of recognition burst from both at once. "What! Adam Woodcock at court!" and "What! Michael Wing-the-Wind—and how runs the hackit greyhound bitch now?"

"The waur for the wear, like ourselves, Adam,—eight years this grass—no four legs will carry a dog forever; but we keep her for the breed, and so she 'scapes Border doom. But why stand you gazing there? I promise you, my lord has wished for you and asked for you."

"My Lord of Murray asked for me, and he Regent of the kingdom too!" said Adam. "I hunger and thirst to pay my duty to my good lord; but I fancy his good lordship remembers the day's sport on Carnwath Moor; and my Drummelzier falcon, that beat the hawks from the Isle of Man, and won his lordship a hundred crowns from the Southern baron whom they called Stanley."

"Nay, not to flatter thee, Adam," said his court friend, "he remembers nought of thee, or of thy falcon either. He hath flown many a higher flight since that, and struck his quarry too. But come—come hither away; I trust we are to be good comrades on the old score."

"What!" said Adam, "you would have me crush a pot with you? but I must first dispose of my eyas, where he will neither have girl to chase nor lad to draw sword upon."

"Is the youngster such a one?" said Michael.

"Ay, by my hood, he flies at all game," replied Woodcock.

"Then had he better come with us," said Michael Wing-the-Wind; "for we cannot have a proper carouse just now, only I would wet my lips, and so must you. I want to hear the news from St. Mary's before you see my lord, and I will let you know how the wind sits up yonder."

While he thus spoke, he led the way to a side door which opened into the court; and threading several dark passages with the air of one who knew the most secret recesses of the palace, conducted them to a small matted chamber, where he placed bread and cheese and a foaming flagon of ale before the falconer and his young companion, who immediately did justice to the latter in a hearty draught, which nearly emptied the measure. Having drawn his breath, and dashed the froth from his whiskers, he observed, that his anxiety for the boy had made him deadly dry.

"Mend your draught," said his hospitable friend, again supplying the flagon from a pitcher which stood beside. "I know the way to the buttery-bar. And now, mind what I say. This morning the Earl of Morton came to my lord in a mighty chafe."

"What! they keep the old friendship, then?" said Woodcock.

"Ay, ay, man, what else?" said Michael; "one hand must scratch the other. But in a mighty chafe was my Lord of Morton, who, to say truth, looketh on such occasions altogether uncanny, and, as it were, fiendish; and he says to my lord—for I was in the chamber taking orders about a cast of hawks that are to be fetched from Darnaway; they match your long-winged falcons, friend Adam."

"I will believe that when I see them fly as high a pitch," replied Woodcock, this professional observation forming a sort of parenthesis.

"However," said Michael, pursuing his tale, "my Lord of Morton, in a mighty chafe, asked my Lord Regent whether he was well dealt with—'For my brother,' said he, 'should have had a gift to be commendator of Kennaquhair, and to have all the temporalities erected into a lordship of regality for his benefit; and here,' said he, 'the false monks have had the insolence to choose a new abbot to put his claim in my brother's way; and, moreover, the rascality of the neighborhood have burned and plundered all that was left in the abbey, so that my brother will not have a house to dwell in when he hath ousted the lazy hounds of priests.' And my lord, seeing him chafed, said mildly to him, 'These are shrewd tidings, Douglas, but I trust they be not true; for

Halbert Glendinning went southward yesterday with a band of spears, and assuredly, had either of these chances happened, that the monks had presumed to choose an abbot, or that the abbey had been burnt, as you say, he had taken order on the spot for the punishment of such insolence, and had despatched us a messenger.' And the Earl of Morton replied—— Now I pray you, Adam, to notice that I say this out of love to you and your lord, and also for old comradeship; and also because Sir Halbert hath done me good, and may again; and also because I love not the Earl of Morton, as indeed more fear than like him—so then it were a foul deed in you to betray me.—'But,' said the Earl to the Regent, 'take heed, my lord, you trust not this Glendinning too far: he comes of churl's blood, which was never true to the nobles.' By St. Andrew, these were his very words. 'And besides,' he said, 'he hath a brother a monk in St. Mary's, and walks all by his guidance, and is making friends on the Border with Buccleuch and with Ferniehers,* and will join hand with them, were there likelihood of a new world.' And my lord answered like a free noble lord as he is: 'Tush! my Lord of Morton, I will be warrant for Glendinning's faith; and for his brother, he is a dreamer, that thinks of naught but book and breviary; and if such hap have chanced as you tell of, I look to receive from Glendinning the cowl of a hanged monk, and the head of a riotous churl, by way of sharp and sudden justice.' And my Lord of Morton left the place, and, as it seemed to me, somewhat malcontent. But since that time my lord has asked me more than once whether there has arrived no messenger from the Knight of Avenel. And all this I have told you, that you may frame your discourse to the best purpose, for it seems to me that my lord will not be well pleased if aught has happened like what my Lord of Morton said, and if your lord hath not ta'en strict orders with it."

There was something in this communication which fairly blanked the bold visage of Adam Woodcock, in spite of the reinforcement which his natural hardihood had received from the berry-brown ale of Holyrood.

"What was it he said about a churl's head, that grim Lord of Morton?" said the disconcerted falconer to his friend.

"Nay, it was my Lord Regent, who said that he expected, if the abbey was injured, your knight would send him the head of the ringleader among the rioters."

* Both these Border chieftains were great friends of Queen Mary.

"Nay, but is this done like a good Protestant," said Adam Woodcock, "or a true Lord of the Congregation? We used to be their white-boys and darlings when we pulled down the convents in Fife and Perthshire."

"Ay, but that," said Michael, "was when old mother Rome held her own, and her [the] great folks were determined she should have no shelter for her head in Scotland. But, now that the priests are fled in all quarters, and their houses and lands are given to our grandees, they cannot see that we are working the work of reformation in destroying the palaces of zealous Protestants."

"But I tell you St. Mary's is not destroyed!" said Woodcock, in increasing agitation; "some trash of painted windows there were broken—things that no nobleman could have brooked in his house; some stone saints were brought on their marrow-bones, like old Widdrington at Chevy Chase; but as for fire-raising, there was not so much as a lighted lunt amongst us, save the match which the dragon had to light the burning tow withal, which he was to spit against St. George; nay, I had caution of that."

"How! Adam Woodcock," said his comrade, "I trust thou hadst no hand in such a fair work? Look you, Adam, I were loth to terrify you, and you just come from a journey; but I promise you, Earl Morton hath brought you down a 'maiden' from Halifax, you never saw the like of her; and she'll clasp you round the neck, and your head will remain in her arms."

"Pshaw!" answered Adam, "I am too old to have my head turned by any maiden of them all. I know my Lord of Morton will go as far for a buxom lass as any one; but what the devil took him to Halifax all the way? and if he has got a gamester there, what hath she to do with my head?"

"Much—much!" answered Michael. "Herod's daughter, who did such execution with her foot and ankle, danced not men's heads off more cleanly than this maiden of Morton.* 'Tis an ax, man—an ax which falls of itself like a sash window, and never gives the headsman the trouble to wield it."

"By my faith, a shrewd device," said Woodcock; "Heaven keep us free on't!"

The page, seeing no end to the conversation between these two old comrades, and anxious, from what he had heard, concerning the fate of the abbot, now interrupted their conference.

* See Note 15.

"Methinks," he said, "Adam Woodcock, thou hadst better deliver thy master's letter to the Regent; questionless he hath therein stated what has chanced at Kennaquhair, in the way most advantageous for all concerned."

"The boy is right," said Michael Wing-the-Wind, "my lord will be very impatient."

"The child hath wit enough to keep himself warm," said Adam Woodcock, producing from his hawking-bag his lord's letter, addressed to the Earl of Murray, "and for that matter so have I. So, Master Roland, you will e'en please to present this yourself to the Lord Regent; his presence will be better graced by a young page than by an old falconer."

"Well said, canny Yorkshire!" replied his friend; "and but now you were so earnest to see our good lord! Why, wouldst thou put the lad into the noose that thou mayst slip tether thyself? or dost thou think the maiden will clasp his fair young neck more willingly than thy old sunburnt weasand?"

"Go to," answered the falconer; "thy wit towers high an it could strike the quarry. I tell thee, the youth has naught to fear: he had nothing to do with the gambol. A rare gambol it was, Michael, as madcaps ever played; and I had made as rare a ballad, if we had had the luck to get it sung to an end. But mum for that—*tace*, as I said before, is Latin for a candle. Carry the youth to the presence, and I will remain here, with bridle in hand, ready to strike the spurs up to the rowel-heads, in case the hawk flies my way. I will soon put Soltra Edge, I trow, betwixt the Regent and me, if he means me less than fair play."

"Come on then, my lad," said Michael, "since thou must needs take the spring before canny Yorkshire." So saying, he led the way through winding passages, closely followed by Roland Græme, until they arrived at a large winding stone stair, the steps of which were so long and broad, and at the same time so low, as to render the ascent uncommonly easy. When they had ascended about the height of one story, the guide stepped aside, and pushed open the door of a dark and gloomy ante-chamber; so dark, indeed, that his youthful companion stumbled, and nearly fell down upon a low step, which was awkwardly placed on the very threshold.

"Take heed," said Michael Wing-the-Wind, in a very low tone of voice, and first glancing cautiously round to see if any one listened—"take heed, my young friend, for those who fall on these boards seldom rise again. Seest thou that," he added, in a still lower voice, pointing to some dark crimson stains on the floor, on which a ray of light, shot through a small aperture, and traversing the general gloom of the apartment, fell with mottled radiance—" seest thou that, youth? Walk warily, for men have fallen here before you."

"What mean you?" said the page, his flesh creeping, though he scarce knew why. "Is it blood?"

"Ay, ay," said the domestic, in the same whispering tone, and dragging the youth on by the arm. "Blood it is—but this is no time to question, or even to look at it. "Blood it is, foully and fearfully shed, as foully and fearfully avenged. The blood," he added, in a still more cautious tone, "of Seignor David."

Roland Græme's heart throbbed when he found himself so unexpectedly in the scene of Rizzio's slaughter—a catastrophe which had chilled with horror all even in that rude age, which had been the theme of wonder and pity through every cottage and castle in Scotland, and had not escaped that of Avenel. But his guide hurried him forward, permitting no further question, and with the manner of one who has already tampered too much with a dangerous subject. A tap which he made at a low door at one end of the vestibule was answered by a huissier, or usher, who, opening it cautiously, received Michael's intimation that a page waited the Regent's leisure, who brought letters from the Knight of Avenel.

"The council is breaking up," said the usher; "but give me the packet; his Grace the Regent will presently see the messenger."

"The packet," replied the page, "must be delivered into the Regent's own hands; such were the orders of my master."

The usher looked at him from head to foot, as if surprised at his boldness, and then replied, with some asperity, "Say you so, my young master? Thou crowest loudly to be but a chicken, and from a country barnyard too."

"Were it a time or place," said Roland, "thou shouldst see I can do more than crow; but do your duty, and let the Regent know I wait his pleasure."

"Thou art but a pert knave to tell me of my duty," said the courtier in office; "but I will find a time to show you you are out of yours; meanwhile, wait there till you are wanted." So saying, he shut the door in Roland's face.

Michael Wing-the-Wind, who had shrunk from his youthful companion during this altercation, according to the established maxim of courtiers of all ranks, and in all ages, now transgressed their prudential line of conduct so far as to come up to him once more. "Thou art a hopeful young springald," said he, "and I see right well old Yorkshire had reason in his caution. Thou hast been five minutes in the court, and hast employed thy time so well as to make a powerful and a mortal enemy of the usher of the council-chamber. Why, man, you might almost as well have offended the deputy butler!"

"I care not what he is," said Roland Græme; "I will teach whomever I speak with to speak civilly to me in return. I did not come from Avenel to be browbeaten in Holyrood."

"Bravo, my lad!" said Michael; "it is a fine spirit if you can hold it; but see, the door opens."

The usher appeared, and, in a more civil tone of voice and manner, said that his Grace the Regent would receive the Knight of Avenel's message; and accordingly marshaled Roland Græme the way into the apartment, from which the council had been just dismissed, after finishing their consultations. There was in the room a long oaken table, surrounded by stools of the same wood, with a large elbow-chair, covered with crimson velvet at the head. Writing materials and papers were lying there in apparent disorder; and one or two of the privy-councilors who had lingered behind, assuming their cloaks, bonnets, and swords, and bidding farewell to the Regent, were departing slowly by a large door, on the opposite side to that through which the page entered. Apparently the Earl of Murray had made some jest, for the smiling countenances of the statesmen expressed that sort of cordial reception which is paid by courtiers to the condescending pleasantries of a prince.

The Regent himself was laughing heartily as he said, "Farewell, my lords, and hold me remembered to the Cock of the North."

He then turned slowly round towards Roland Græme, and the marks of gaiety, real or assumed, disappeared from his countenance as completely as the passing bubbles leave the dark mirror of a still profound lake into which a traveler has cast a stone; in the course of a minute his noble features had assumed their natural expression of deep and even melancholy gravity.

This distinguished statesman, for as such his worst enemies acknowledged him, possessed all the external dignity, as well as almost all the noble qualities, which could grace the power that he enjoyed; and had he succeeded to the throne as his legitimate inheritance, it is probable he would have been recorded as one of Scotland's wisest and greatest kings. But that he held his authority by the deposition and imprisonment of his sister and benefactress was a crime which those only can excuse who think ambition an apology for ingratitude. He was dressed plainly in black velvet, after the Flemish fashion, and wore in his high-crowned hat a jeweled clasp, which looped up on one side, and formed the only ornament of his apparel. He had his poniard by his side, and his sword lay on the council table.

Such was the personage before whom Roland Græme now presented himself, with a feeling of breathless awe, very different from the usual boldness and vicacity of his temper. In fact, he was, from education and nature, forward, but not impudent, and was much more easily controlled by the moral superiority, arising from the elevated talents and renown of those with whom he conversed, than by pretensions founded only on rank or external show. He might have braved with indifference the presence of an earl, merely distinguished by his belt and coronet; but he felt overawed in that of the eminent soldier and statesman, the wielder of a nation's power, and the leader of her armies. The greatest and wisest are flattered by the deference of youth, so graceful and becoming in itself; and Murray took, with much corrtesy, the letter from the hands of the abashed and blushing page, and answered with complaisance to the imperfect and half-muttered greeting which he endeavored to deliver to him on the part of Sir Halbert of Avenel. He even paused a moment ere he broke the silk with which the letter was secured, to ask the page his name, so much he was struck with his very handsome features and form.

"Roland Graham," he said, repeating the words after the hesitating page, "what, of the Grahams of Lennox?"

"No, my lords," replied Roland; "my parents dwelt in the Debateable Land."

Murray made no farther inquiry; but proceeded to read his despatches, during the perusal of which his brow began to assume a stern expression of displeasure, as that of one who found something which at once surprised and disturbed him. He sate down on the nearest seat, frowned till his eyebrows almost met together, read the letter twice over, and was then silent for several minutes. At length, raising his head, his eye encountered that of the usher, who in vain endeavored to exchange the look of eager and curious observation with which he had been perusing the Regent's features for that open and unnoticing expression of countenance which, in looking at all, seems as if it saw and marked nothing—a cast of look which may be practised with advantage by all those, of whatever degree, who are admitted to witness the familiar and unguarded hours of their superiors. Great men are as jealous of their thoughts as the wife of King Candaules was of her charms, and will as readily punish those who have, however involuntarily, beheld them in mental dishabille and exposure.

"Leave the apartment, Hyndman," said the Regent, sternly, "and carry your observation elsewhere. You are too knowing, sir, for your post, which, by special order, is destined for men of blunter capacity. So! now you look more like a fool than you did (for Hyndman, as may easily be supposed, was not a little disconcerted by this rebuke); keep that confused stare, and it may keep your office. Begone, sir!"

The usher departed in dismay, not forgetting to register, amongst his other causes of dislike to Roland Græme, that he had been the witness of this disgraceful chiding. When he had left the apartment, the Regent again addressed the page.

"Your name you say is Armstrong?"

"No," replied Roland, "my name is Græme, so please you—Roland Græme, whose forbears were designated of Heathergill, in the Debateable Land."

"Ay, I knew it was a name from the Debateable Land. Hast thou any aquaintances here in Edinburgh?"

"My lord," replied Roland, willing rather to evade this question than to answer it directly, for the prudence of being silent with respect to Lord Seyton's adventure immediately struck him, "I have been in Edinburgh scarce an hour, and that for the first time in my life."

"What! and thou Sir Halbert Glendinning's page?" said the Regent.

"I was brought up as my lady's page," said the youth, "and left Avenel Castle for the first time in my life—at least since my childhood—only three days since."

"My lady's page!" repeated the Earl of Murray, as if speaking to himself; "it was strange to send his lady's page on a matter of such deep concernment. Morton will say it is of a piece with the nomination of his brother to be abbot; and yet in some sort an inexperienced youth will best serve the turn. What hast thou been taught, young man, in thy doughty apprenticeship!"

"To hunt, my lord, and to hawk," said Roland Gæme.

"To hunt coneys, and to hawk at ouzels ? said the Regent, smiling; "for such are the sports of ladies and their followers."

Græme's cheek reddened deeply as he replied, not without some emphasis, "To hunt red-deer of the first head, and to strike down herons of the highest soar, my lord, which, in Lothian speech, may be termed, for aught I know, coneys and ouzels; also, I can wield a brand and couch a lance, according to our Border meaning; in inland speech these may be termed water-flags and bulrushes."

"Thy speech rings like metal," said the Regent, "and I pardon the sharpness of it for the truth. Thou knowest, then, what belongs to the duty of a man-at-arms ?"

"So far as exercise can teach it, without real service in the field," answered Roland Græme; "but our knight permitted none of his household to make raids, and I never had the good fortune to see a stricken field."

"The good fortune !" repeated the Regent, smiling somewhat sorrowfully; "take my word, young man, war is the only game from which both parties rise losers."

"Not always, my lord," answered the page, with his characteristic audacity, "if fame speaks truth."

"How, sir ?" said the Regent, coloring in his turn, and perhaps suspecting an indiscreet allusion to the height which he himself had attained by the hap of civil war.

"Because, my lord," said Roland Græme, without change of tone, "he who fights well must have fame in life or honor in death; and so war is a game from which no one can rise a loser."

The Regent smiled and shook his head, when at that moment the door opened, and the Earl of Morton presented himself.

"I come somewhat hastily," he said, "and I enter unannounced, because my news are of weight. It is as I said: Edward Glendinning is named abbot, and——"

"Hush, my lord !" said the Regent, "I know it, but——"

"And perhaps you knew it before I did, my Lord of Murray," answered Morton, his dark red brow growing darker and redder as he spoke.

"Morton," said Murray, "suspect me not—touch not mine honor; I have to suffer enough from the calumnies of foes, let me not have to contend with the unjust suspicions of my friends. We are not alone," said he, recollecting himself "or I could tell thee more."

He led Morton into one of the deep embrasures which the windows formed in the massive wall, and which afforded a retiring-place for their conversing apart. In this recess, Roland observed them speak together with much earnestness, Murray appearing to be grave and earnest, and Morton having a jealous and offended air, which seemed gradually to give way to the assurances of the Regent.

As their conversation grew more earnest, they became gradually louder in speech, having perhaps forgotten the presence of the page, the more readily as his position in the apartment placed him out of sight, so that he found himself unwillingly privy to more of their discourse than he cared to hear. For, page though he was, a mean curiosity after the secrets of others had never been numbered amongst Roland's failings ; and, moreover, with all his natural rashness, he could not but doubt the safety of becoming privy to the secret discourse of these powerful and dreaded men. Still, he could neither stop his ears nor with propriety leave the apartment ; and while he thought of some means of signifying his presence, he had already heard so much that to have produced himself suddenly would have been as awkward, and perhaps as dangerous, as in quiet to abide the end of their conference. What he overheard, however, was but an imperfect part of their communication ; and although a more expert politician, acquainted with the circumstances of the times, would have had little difficulty in tracing the meaning, yet Ronald Græme could only form very general and vague conjectures as to the import of their discourse.

"All is prepared," said Murray, "and Lindesay is setting forward. She must hesitate no longer ; thou seest I act by thy counsel, and harden myself against softer considerations."

"True, my lord," replied Morton, "in what is necessary to gain power you do not hesitate, but go boldly to the mark. But are you as careful to defend and preserve what you have won ? Why this establishment of domestics around her ? Has not your sister men and maidens enough to tend her, but you must consent to this superfluous and dangerous retinue ?"

"For shame, Morton ! a princess, and my sister, could I do less than allow her due tendance ?"

"Ay," replied Morton, "even thus fly all your shafts—smartly enough loosened from the bow, and not unskilfully aimed, but a breath of foolish affection ever crosses in the mid volley, and sways the arrow from the mark."

"Say not so, Morton !" replied Murray ; "I have both dared and done——"

"Yes, enough to gain, but not enough to keep; reckon not that she will think and act thus. You have wounded her deeply both in pride and in power; it signifies nought that you would tent now the wound with unavailing salves: as matters stand with you, you must forfeit the title of an affectionate brother, to hold that of a bold and determined statesman."

"Morton!" said Murray, with some impatience, "I brook not these taunts; what I have done I have done; what I must farther do, I must and will; but I am not made of iron like thee, and I cannot but remember. Enough of this—my purpose holds."

"And I warrant me," said Morton, "the choice of these domestic consolations will rest with——"

Here he whispered names which escaped Roland Græme's ear. Murray replied in a similar tone, but so much raised towards the conclusion of the sentence that the page heard these words—"And of him I hold myself secure, by Glendinning's recommendation."

"Ay, which may be as much trustworthy as his late conduct at the Abbey of St. Mary's: you have heard that his brother's election has taken place. Your favorite Sir Halbert, my Lord of Murray, has as much fraternal affection as yourself."

"By Heaven, Morton, that taunt demanded an unfriendly answer, but I pardon it, for your brother also is concerned; but this election shall be annulled. I tell you, Earl of Morton, while I hold the sword of state in my royal nephew's name, neither lord nor knight in Scotland shall dispute my authority; and if I bear with insults from my friends, it is only while I know them to be such, and forgive their follies for their faithfulness."

Morton muttered what seemed to be some excuse, and the Regent answered him in a milder tone, and then subjoined, "Besides, I have another pledge than Glendinning's recommendation for this youth's fidelity: his nearest relative has placed herself in my hands as his security, to be dealt withal as his doings shall deserve."

"That is something," replied Morton: "but yet, in fair love and good-will, I must still pray you to keep on your guard. The foes are stirring again, as horse-flies and hornets become busy so soon as the storm-blast is over. George of Seyton was crossing the causeway this morning with a score of men at his back, and had a ruffle with my friends of the house of Leslie; they met at the Tron, and were fighting hard, when the provost, with his guard of partizans, came in thirdsman, and staved them asunder with their halberds, as men part dog and bear."

"He hath my order for such interference," said the Regent. "Has any one been hurt?"

"George of Seyton himself, by black Ralph Leslie; the devil take the rapier that ran not through from side to side! Ralph has a bloody coxcomb, by a blow from a messan page whom nobody knew; Dick Seyton of Windygowl is run through the arm; and two gallants of the Leslies have suffered phlebotomy. This is all the gentle blood which has been spilled in the revel; but a yeoman or two on both sides have had bones broken and ears cropped. The hostler-wives, who are like to be the only losers by their miscarriage, have dragged the knaves off the street, and are crying a drunken coronach over them."

"You take it lightly, Douglas," said the Regent; "these broils and feuds would shame the capital of the Great Turk, let alone that of a Christian and Reformed state. But, if I live, this gear shall be amended; and men shall say, when they read my story, that if it were my cruel hap to rise to power by the dethronement of a sister, I employed it, when gained, for the benefit of the commonweal."

"And of your friends," replied Morton; "wherefore I trust for your instant order annulling the election of this lurdane abbot, Edward Glendinning."

"You shall be presently satisfied," said the Regent, and, stepping forward, he began to call, "So ho, Hyndman!" when suddenly his eye lighted on Roland Græme. "By my faith, Douglas," said he, turning to his friend, "here have been three at counsel!"

"Ay, but only two can keep counsel," said Morton; "the galliard must be disposed of."

"For shame, Morton—an orphan boy! Hearken thee, my child. Thou hast told me some of thy accomplishments—canst thou speak truth?"

"Ay, my lord, when it serves my turn," replied Græme.

"It shall serve thy turn now," said the Regent; "and falsehood shall be thy destruction. How much hast thou heard or understood of what we two have spoken together?"

"But little, my lord," replied Roland Græme, boldly, "which met my apprehension, saving that it seemed to me as if in something you doubted the faith of the Knight of Avenel, under whose roof I was nurtured."

"And what hast thou to say on that point, young man?"

continued the Regent, bending his eyes upon him with a keen and strong expression of observation.

"That," said the page, "depends on the quality of those who speak against his honor whose bread I have long eaten. If they be my inferiors, I say they lie, and will maintain what I say with my baton; if my equals, still I say they lie, and will do battle in the quarrel, if they list, with my sword; if my superiors——" he paused.

"Proceed boldly," said the Regent. "What if thy superiors said aught that nearly touched your master's honor?"

"I would say," replied Græme, "that he did ill to slander the absent, and that my master was a man who could render an account of his actions to any one who should manfully demand it of him to his face."

"And it were manfully said," replied the Regent. "What thinkest thou, my Lord of Morton?"

"I think," replied Morton, "that if the young galliard resemble a certain ancient friend of ours as much in the craft of his disposition as he does in eye and in brow, there may be a wide difference betwixt what he means and what he speaks."

"And whom meanest thou that he resembles so closely?" said Murray.

"Even the true and trusty Julian Avenel," replied Morton.

"But this youth belongs to the Debateable Land," said Murray.

"It may be so; but Julian was an outlying striker of venison, and made many a far cast when he had a fair doe in chase."

"Pshaw!" said the Regent, "this is but idle talk. Here, thou Hyndman—thou curiosity," calling to the usher, who now entered, "conduct this youth to his companion. You will both," he said to Græme, "keep yourselves in readiness to travel on short notice." And then motioning to him courteously to withdraw, he broke up the interview.

CHAPTER XIX

It is and is not—'tis the thing I sought for.
Have kneel'd for, pray'd for, risk'd my fame and life for,
And yet it is not—no more than the shadow
Upon the hard, cold, flat, and polish'd mirror
Is the warm, graceful, rounded, living substance
Which it presents in form and lineament.

Old Play.

THE usher, with gravity which ill concealed a jealous scowl, conducted Roland Græme to a lower apartment, where he found his comrade, the falconer. The man of office then briefly acquainted them that this would be their residence till his Grace's further orders; that they were to go to the pantry, to the buttery, to the cellar, and to the kitchen, at the usual hours, to receive the allowances becoming their station—instructions which Adam Woodcock's old familiarity with the court made him perfectly understand. "For your beds," he said, "you must go to the hostelry of St. Michael's, in respect the palace is now full of the domestics of the greater nobles."

No sooner was the usher's back turned than Adam exclaimed, with all the glee of eager curiosity, "And now, Master Roland, the news—the news; come, unbutton thy pouch and give us thy tidings. What says the Regent? Asks he for Adam Woodcock? And is all soldered up, or must the Abbot of Unreason strap for it?"

"All is well in that quarter," said the page; "and for the rest—— But, hey-day, what! have you taken the chain and medal off from my bonnet?"

"And meet time it was, when yon usher, vinegar-faced rogue that he is, began to inquire what Popish trangam you were wearing. By the mass, the metal would have been confiscated for conscience, sake, like your other rattle-trap yonder at Avenel, which Mrs. Lilias bears about on her shoes in the guise of a pair of shoe-buckles. This comes of carrying Popish nicknackets about you."

"The jade!" exclaimed Roland Græme, "has she melted down my rosary into buckles for her clumsy hoofs, which will set off such a garnish nearly as well as a cow's might?

But, hang her, let her keep them; many a dog's trick have I played old Lilias, for want of having something better to do, and the buckles will serve for a remembrance. Do you remember the verjuice I put into the comfits, when old Wingate and she were to breakfast together on Easter morning?"

"In troth do I, Master Roland; the major-domo's mouth was as crooked as a hawk's beak for the whole morning afterwards, and any other page in your room would have tasted the discipline of the porter's lodge for it. But my lady's favor stood between your skin and many a jerking. Lord send you may be the better for her protection in such matters!"

"I am at least grateful for it, Adam; and I am glad you put me in mind of it."

"Well, but the news, my young master," said Woodcock—"spell me the tidings; what are we to fly at next? What did the Regent say to you?"

"Nothing that I am to repeat again," said Roland Græme, shaking his head.

"Why, hey-day," said Adam, "how prudent we are become all of a sudden! You have advanced rarely in brief space, Master Roland. You have wellnigh had your head broken, and you have gained your gold chain, and you have made an enemy, Master Usher to wit, with his two legs like hawks' perches, and you have had audience of the first man in the realm, and bear as much mystery in your brow as if you had flown in the court-sky ever since you were hatched. I believe in my soul you would run with a piece of egg-shell on your head like the curlews, which—I would we were after them again—we used to call whaups in the halidome and its neighborhood. But sit thee down, boy; Adam Woodcock was never the lad to seek to enter into forbidden secrets—sit thee down, and I will go fetch the vivers; I know the butler and the pantler of old."

The good-natured falconer set forth upon his errand, busying himself about procuring their refreshment; and during his absence Roland Græme abandoned himself to the strange, complicated, and yet heart-stirring reflections to which the events of the morning had given rise. Yesterday he was of neither mark nor likelihood, a vagrant boy, the attendant on a relative of whose sane judgment he himself had not the highest opinion; but now he had become, he knew not why, or wherefore, or to what extent, the custodier, as the Scottish phrase went, of some important state secret, in the safe keeping of which the Regent himself was concerned. It did not diminish from, but rather added to, the interest of a situation so unexpected that Roland himself did not perfectly understand wherein he stood committed by the state secrets in which he had unwittingly become participator. On the contrary, he felt like one who looks on a romantic landscape, of which he sees the features for the first time, and then obscured with mist and driving tempest. The imperfect glimpse which the eye catches of rocks, trees, and other objects around him adds double dignity to these shrouded mountains and darkened abysses, of which the height, depth, and extent are left to imagination.

But mortals, especially at the well-appetized age which precedes twenty years, are seldom so much engaged either by real or conjectural subjects of speculation but that their earthly wants claim their hour of attention. And with many a smile did our hero, so the reader may term him if he will, hail the reappearance of his friend Adam Woodcock, bearing on one wooden platter a tremendous portion of boiled beef, and on another a plentiful allowance of greens, or rather what the Scotch call lang-kale. A groom followed with bread, salt, and the other means of setting forth a meal; and when they had both placed on the oaken table what they bore in their hands, the falconer observed that, since he knew the court, it had got harder and harder every day to the poor gentlemen and yeomen retainers, but that now it was an absolute flaying of a flea for the hide and tallow. Such thronging to the wicket, and such churlish answers, and such bare beef-bones, such a shouldering at the buttery-hatch, and cellarage, and nought to be gained beyond small insufficient single ale, or at best with a single "straike" of malt to counterbalance a double allowance of water. "By the mass, though, my young friend," said he, while he saw the food disappearing fast under Roland's active exertions, "it is not so well to lament for former times as to take the advantage of the present, else we are like to lose on both sides."

So saying, Adam Woodcook drew his chair towards the table, unsheathed his knife (for every one carried that minister of festive distribution for himself), and imitated his young companion's example, who for the moment had lost his anxiety for the future in the eager satisfaction of an appetite sharpened by youth and abstinence.

In truth, they made, though the materials were sufficiently simple, a very respectable meal at the expense of the royal allowance; and Adam Woodcock, notwithstanding the deliberate censure which he had passed on the household beer of the palace, had taken the fourth deep draught of the black-jack ere he remembered him that he had spoken in its dispraise. Then, flinging himself jollily and luxuriously back in an old Danske elbow-chair, and looking with careless glee towards the page, extending at the same time his right leg, and stretching the other easily over it, he reminded his companion that he had not yet heard the ballad which he had made for the Abbot of Unreason's revel. And accordingly he struck merrily up with

> "The Pope, that pagan full of pride,
> Has blinded us full lang——"

Roland Græme, who felt no great delight, as may be supposed, in the falconer's satire, considering its subject, began to snatch up his mantle and fling it around his shoulders, an action which instantly interrupted the ditty of Adam Woodcock.

"Where the vengeance are you going now," he said, "thou restless boy? Thou hast quicksilver in the veins of thee to a certainty, and canst no more abide any douce and sensible communing than a hoodless hawk would keep perched on my wrist!"

"Why, Adam," replied the page, "if you must needs know, I am about to take a walk and look at this fair city. One may as well be still mewed up in the old castle of the lake, if one is to sit the livelong night between four walls, and hearken to old ballads."

"It is a new ballad, the Lord help thee!" replied Adam, "and that one of the best that ever was matched with a rousing chorus."

"Be it so," said the page, "I will hear it another day, when the rain is dashing against the windows, and there is neither steed stamping, nor spur jingling, nor feather waving in the neighborhood, to mar my marking it well. But, even now, I want to be in the world, and to look about me."

"But the never a stride shall you go without me," said the falconer, "until the Regent shall take you whole and sound off my hand; and so, if you will, we may go the hostelry of St. Michael's, and there you will see company enough, but through the casement, mark you me; for as to rambling through the street to seek Seytons and Leslies, and having a dozen holes rifted in your new jacket with rapier and poniard, I will yield no way to it."

"To the hostelry of St. Michael's, then, with all my heart," said the page; and they left the palace accordingly, rendered to the sentinels at the gate, who had now taken their posts for the evening, a strict account of their names and business, were dismissed through a small wicket of the close-barred portal, and soon reached the inn or hostelry of St. Michael, which stood in a large courtyard, off the main street, close under the descent of the Calton Hill. The place, wide, waste, and uncomfortable, resembled rather an Eastern caravansary, where men found shelter indeed, but were obliged to supply themselves with everything else, than one of our modern inns—

> Where not one comfort shall to those be lost,
> Who never ask, or never feel, the cost.

But still, to the inexperienced eye of Roland Græme, the bustle and confusion of this place of public resort furnished excitement and amusement. In the large room, into which they had rather found their own way than been ushered by mine host, travelers and natives of the city entered and departed, met and greeted, gamed or drank together, forming the strongest contrast to the stern and monotonous order and silence with which matters were conducted in the well-ordered household of the Knight of Avenel. Altercation of every kind, from brawling to jesting, was going on among the groups around them, and yet the noise and mingled voices seemed to disturb no one, and indeed to be noticed by no others than by those who composed the group to which the speaker belonged.

The falconer passed through the apartment to a projecting latticed window, which formed a sort of recess from the room itself; and having here esconced himself and his companion, he called for some refreshments; and a tapster, after he had shouted for the twentieth time, accommodated him with the remains of a cold capon and a neat's tongue, together with a pewter stoup of weak French *vin-de-pays*. "Fetch a stoup of brandy-wine, thou knave. We will be jolly to-night, Master Roland," said he, when he saw himself thus accommodated, "and let care come to-morrow."

But Roland had eaten too lately to enjoy the good cheer; and feeling his curiosity much sharper than his appetite, he made it his choice to look out of the lattice, which overhung a large yard surrounded by the stables of the hostelry, and fed his eyes on the busy sight beneath; while Adam Woodcock, after he had compared his companion to the Laird of MacFarlane's geese, who liked their play better than their meat,* disposed of his time with the aid of cup and trencher, occasionally humming the burden of his birth-strangled ballad, and beating time to it with his fingers on the little round table. In this exercise he was frequently interrupted by the exclamations of his companion, as he saw something new in the yard beneath to attract and interest him.

It was a busy scene, for the number of gentlemen and nobles who were now crowded into the city had filled all spare stables and places of public reception with their horses and military attendants. There were some score of yeomen dressing their own or their masters' horses in the yard—whistling, singing, laughing, and upbraiding each other, in a style of wit which the good order of Avenel Castle rendered strange to Roland Græme's ears. Others were busy repairing their own arms, or cleaning those of their masters. One fellow, having just bought a bundle of twenty spears, was sitting in a corner, employed in painting the white staves of the weapons with yellow and vermilion. Other lackeys led large staghounds, or wolf-dogs, of noble race, carefully muzzled to prevent accidents to passengers. All came and went, mixed together and separated, under the delighted eye of the page, whose imagination had not even conceived a scene so gaily diversified with the objects he had most pleasure in beholding; so that he was perpetually breaking the quiet reverie of honest Woodcock, and the mental progress which he was making in his ditty, by exclaiming, "Look here, Adam—look at the bonny bay horse; St. Anthony, what a gallant forehand he hath got! And see the goodly gray, which yonder fellow in the frieze jacket is dressing as awkwardly as if he had never touched aught but a cow; I would I were nigh him to teach him his trade! And lo you, Adam, the gay Milan armor that the yeoman is scouring, all steel and silver, like our knight's prime suit, of which old Wingate makes such account. And see to yonder pretty wench, Adam, who comes tripping through them all with her milk-pail; I warrant me she has had a long walk from the loaning; she has a stammel waistcoat, like your favorite Cicely Sunderland, Master Adam!"

"By my hood, lad," answered the falconer, "it is well for thee thou wert brought up where grace grew. Even in the Castle of Avenel thou wert a wild-blood enough; but hadst thou been nurtured here, within a flight-shot of the court,

* [See *The Monastery*. Note 10, p. 441].

thou hadst been the veriest crack-hemp of a page that ever wore feather in thy bonnet or steel by thy side; truly, I wish it may end well with thee."

"Nay, but leave thy senseless humming and drumming, old Adam, and come to the window ere thou hast drenched thy senses in the pint-pot there. See, here comes a merry minstrel with his crowd, and a wench with him, that dances with bells at her ankles; and see, the yeomen and pages leave their horses and the armor they were cleaning, and gather round, as is very natural, to hear the music. Come, old Adam, we will thither too."

"You shall call me 'cut' if I do go down," said Adam; "you are near as good minstrelsy as the stroller can make, if you had but the grace to listen to it."

"But the wench in the stammel waistcoat is stopping too, Adam; by Heaven, they are going to dance! Frieze jacket wants to dance with stammel waistcoat, but she is coy and recusant."

Then suddenly changing his tone of levity into one of deep interest and surprise, he exclaimed, "Queen of Heaven! what is it that I see?" and then remained silent.

The sage Adam Woodcock, who was in a sort of languid degree amused with the page's exclamations, even while he professed to despise them, became at length rather desirous to set his tongue once more a-going, that he might enjoy the superiority afforded by his own intimate familiarity with all the circumstances which excited in his young companion's mind so much wonderment.

"Well, then," he said at last, "what is it you do see, Master Roland, that you have become mute all of a sudden?"

Roland returned no answer.

"I say, Master Roland Græme," said the falconer, "it is manners in my country for a man to speak when he is spoken to."

Roland Græme remained silent.

"The murrain is in the boy," said Adam Woodcock, "he has stared out his eyes and talked his tongue to pieces, I think!"

The falconer hastily drank off his can of wine, and came to Roland, who stood like a statue, with his eyes eagerly bent on the courtyard, though Adam Woodcock was unable to detect amongst the joyous scene which it exhibited aught that could deserve such devoted attention.

"The lad is mazed!" said the falconer to himself.

But Roland Græme had good reasons for his surprise,

though they were not such as he could communicate to his companion.

The touch of the old minstrel's instrument, for he had already begun to play, had drawn in several auditors from the street, when one entered the gate of the yard whose appearance exclusively arrested the attention of Roland Græme. He was of his own age, or a good deal younger, and from his dress and bearing might be of the same rank and calling, having all the air of coxcombry and pretension which accorded with a handsome, though slight and low, figure and an elegant dress, in part hid by a large purple cloak. As he entered, he cast a glance up towards the windows, and, to his extreme astonishment, under the purple velvet bonnet and white feather, Roland recognized the features so deeply impressed on his memory, the bright and clustered tresses, the laughing full blue eyes, the well-formed eyebrows, the nose with the slightest possible inclination to be aquiline, the ruby lip, of which an arch and half-suppressed smile seemed the habitual expression—in short, the form and face of Catherine Seyton ; in man's attire, however, and mimicking, as it seemed not unsuccessfully, the bearing of a youthful but forward page.

"St. George and St. Andrew !" exclaimed the mazed Roland Græme to himself, "was there ever such an audacious quean ! She seems a little ashamed of her mummery too, for she holds the lap of her cloak to her face, and her color is heightened; but, Sancta Maria, how she threads the throng, with as firm and bold a step as if she had never tied petticoat round her waist ! Holy saints ! she holds up her riding-rod as if she would lay it about some of their ears that stand most in her way ; by the hand of my father ! she bears herself like the very model of pagehood. Hey ! what ! sure she will not strike frieze jacket in earnest ?" But he was not long left in doubt ; for the lout whom he had before repeatedly noticed, standing in the way of the bustling page, and maintaining his place with clownish obstinacy or stupidity, the advanced riding-rod was, without a moment's hesitation, sharply applied to his shoulders, in a manner which made him spring aside, rubbing the part of the body which had received so unceremonious a hint that it was in the way of his betters. The party injured growled forth an oath or two of indignation, and Roland Græme began to think of flying downstairs to the assistance of the translated Catherine ; but the laugh of the yard was against frieze jacket, which indeed had, in those days, small chance of fair play in a quarrel with velvet and embroidery; so that the fellow, who was a menial in the inn, slunk back to finish his task of dressing the bonny gray, laughed at by all, but most by the wench in the stammel waistcoat, his fellow-servant, who, to crown his disgrace, had the cruelty to cast an applauding smile upon the author of the injury, while, with a freedom more like the milkmaid of the town than she of the plains, she accosted him with—"Is there any one you want here, my pretty gentleman, that you seem in such haste?"

"I seek a slip of a lad," said the seeming gallant, "with a sprig of holly in his cap, black hair and black eyes, green jacket, and the air of a country coxcomb; I have sought him through every close and alley in the Canongate—the fiend gore him!"

"Why, God-a-mercy, nun!" muttered Roland Græme, much bewildered.

"I will inquire him presently out for your fair young worship," said the wench of the inn.

"Do," said the gallant squire, "and if you bring me to him you shall have a groat to-night, and a kiss on Sunday when you have on a cleaner kirtle."

"Why, God-a-mercy, nun!" again muttered Roland, "this is a note above E La."

In a moment after the servant entered the room, and ushered in the object of his surprise.

While the disguised vestal looked with unabashed brow, and bold and rapid glance of her eye, through the various parties in the large old room, Roland Græme, who felt an internal awkward sense of bashful confusion, which he deemed altogether unworthy of the bold and dashing character to which he aspired, determined not to be browbeaten and put down by this singular female, but to meet her with a glance of recognition so sly, so penetrating, so expressively humorous, as should show her at once he was in possession of her secret and master of her fate, and should compel her to humble herself towards him, at least into the look and manner of respectful and deprecating observance.

This was extremely well planned; but, just as Roland had called up the knowing glance, the suppressed smile, the shrewd intelligent look which was to insure his triumph, he encountered the bold, firm, and steady gaze of his brother or sister page, who, casting on him a falcon glance, and recognizing him at once as the object of his search, walked up with the most unconcerned look, the most free and undaunted composure, and hailed him with, "You, sir holly-top, I would speak with you."

The steady coolness and assurance with which these words were uttered, although the voice was the very voice he had heard at the old convent, and although the features more nearly resembled those of Catherine when seen close than when viewed from a distance, produced, nevertheless, such a confusion in Roland's mind that he became uncertain whether he was not still under a mistake from the beginning; the knowing shrewdness which should have animated his visage faded into a sheepish bashfulness, and the half-suppressed but most intelligible smile became the senseless giggle of one who laughs to cover his own disorder of ideas.

"Do they understand a Scotch tongue in thy country, holly-top?" said this marvelous specimen of metamorphosis. "I said I would speak with thee."

"What is your business with my comrade, my young chick of the game?" said Adam Woodcock, willing to step in to his companion's assistance, though totally at a loss to account for the sudden disappearance of all Roland's usual smartness and presence of mind.

"Nothing to you, my old cock of the perch," replied the gallant; "go mind your hawk's castings. I guess by your bag and your gauntlet that you are squire of the body to a sort of kites."

He laughed as he spoke, and the laugh reminded Roland so irresistibly of the hearty fit of risibility in which Catherine had indulged at his expense when they first met in the old nunnery, that he could scarce help exclaiming, "Catherine Seyton, by Heavens!" He checked the exclamation, however, and only said, "I think, sir, we two are not totally strangers to each other."

"We must have met in our dreams, then," said the youth; "and my days are too busy to remember what I think on at nights."

"Or apparently to remember upon one day those whom you may have seen on the preceding eve," said Roland Græme.

The youth in his turn cast on him a look of some surprise, as he replied, "I know no more of what you mean than does the horse I ride on; if there be offense in your words, you shall find me as ready to take it as any lad in Lothian."

"You know well," said Roland, "though it pleases you to use the language of a stranger, that with you I can have no purpose to quarrel."

"Let me do mine errand, then, and be rid of you," said the page. "Step hither this way, out of that old leathern fist's hearing."

They walked into the recess of the window, which Roland had left upon the youth's entrance into the apartment. The messenger then turned his back on the company, after casting a hasty and sharp glance around to see if they were observed. Roland did the same, and the page in the purple mantle thus addressed him, taking at the same time from under his cloak a short, but beautifully-wrought sword, with the hilt and ornaments upon the sheath of silver, massively chased and over-gilded: "I bring you this weapon from a friend, who gives it you under the solemn condition that you will not unsheathe it until you are commanded by your rightful sovereign. For your warmth of temper is known, and the presumption with which you intrude yourself into the quarrels of others; and, therefore, this is laid upon you as a penance by those who wish you well, and whose hand will influence your destiny for good or for evil. This is what I was charged to tell you. So if you will give a fair word for a fair sword, and pledge your promise, with hand and glove, good and well; and if not, I will carry back Caliburn to those who sent it."

"And may I not ask who these are?" said Roland Græme, admiring at the same time the beauty of the weapon thus offered him.

"My commission in no way leads me to answer such a question," said he of the purple mantle.

"But if I am offended," said Roland, "may I not draw to defend myself?"

"Not *this* weapon," answered the sword-bearer; "but you have your own at command, and, besides, for what do you wear your poniard?"

"For no good," said Adam Woodcock, who had now approached close to them, "and that I can witness as well as any one."

"Stand back, fellow," said the messenger; "thou hast an intrusive, curious face, that will come by a buffet if it is found where it has no concern."

"A buffet, my young Master Malapert?" said Adam, drawing back, however; "best keep down fist, or, by Our Lady, buffet will beget buffet!"

"Be patient, Adam Woodcock," said Roland Græme; "and let me pray you, fair sir, since by such addition you choose for the present to be addressed, may I not barely unsheathe this weapon, in pure simplicity of desire to know whether so fair a hilt and scabbard are matched with a befitting blade ?"

"By no manner of means," said the messenger; "at a word, you must take it under the promise that you never draw it until you receive the commands of your lawful sovereign, or you must leave it alone."

"Under that condition, and coming from your friendly hand, I accept of the sword," said Roland, taking it from his hand; "but credit me, that if we are to work together in any weighty emprise, as I am induced to believe, some confidence and openness on your part will be necessary to give the right impulse to my zeal. I press for no more at present, it is enough that you understand me."

"I understand you!" said the page, exhibiting the appearance of unfeigned surprise in his turn. "Renounce me if I do! Here you stand jiggling, and sniggling, and looking cunning, as if there were some mighty matter of intrigue and common understanding betwixt you and me, whom you never set your eyes on before!"

"What!" said Roland Græme, "will you deny that we have met before?"

"Marry that I will, in any Christian court," said the other page.

"And will you also deny," said Roland, "that it was recommended to us to study each other's features well, that, in whatever disguise the time might impose upon us, each should recognize in the other the secret agent of a mighty work? Do not you remember that Sisters Magdalen and Dame Bridget——"

The messenger here interrupted him, shrugging up his shoulders with a look of compassion—"Bridget and Magdalen! why, this is madness and dreaming! Hark ye, Master Hollytop, your wits are gone on wool-gathering; comfort yourself with a caudle, thatch your brain-sick noddle with a woolen nightcap, and so God be with you!"

As he concluded this polite parting address, Adam Woodcock, who was again seated by the table on which stood the now empty can, said to him, "Will you drink a cup, young man, in the way of courtesy, now you have done your errand, and listen to a good song?" and without waiting for an answer, he commenced his ditty—

> "The Pope, that pagan full of pride
> Hath blinded us full long——"

It is probable that the good wine had made some innovation in the falconer's brain, otherwise he would have recollected the danger of introducing anything like political or polemical pleasantry into a public assemblage, at a time when men's minds were in a state of great irritability. To do him justice, he perceived his error, and stopped short so soon as he saw that the word "Pope" had at once interrupted the separate conversations of the various parties which were assembled in the apartment; and that many began to draw themselves up, bridle, look big, and prepare to take part in the impending brawl; while others, more decent and cautious persons, hastily paid down their lawing, and prepared to leave the place ere bad should come to worse.

And to worse it was soon likely to come; for no sooner did Woodcock's ditty reach the ear of the stranger page, than, uplifting his riding-rod, he exclaimed, "He who speaks irreverently of the Holy Father of the church in my presence is the cub of a heretic wolf-bitch, and I will switch him as I would a mongrel cur!"

"And I will break thy young pate," said Adam, "if thou darest to lift a finger to me." And then, in defiance of the young Drawcansir's threats, with a stout heart and dauntless accent, he again uplifted the stave,

"The Pope, that pagan full of pride,
Hath blinded——"

But Adam was able to proceed farther, being himself unfortunately blinded by a stroke of the impatient youth's switch across his eyes. Enraged at once by the smart and the indignity, the falconer started up, and darkling as he was—for his eyes watered too fast to permit his seeing anything—he would soon have been at close grips with his insolent adversary, had not Roland Græme, contrary to his nature, played for once the prudent man and the peacemaker, and thrown himself betwixt them, imploring Woodcock's patience "You know not," he said, "with whom you have to do. And thou," addressing the messenger, who stood scornfully laughing at Adam's rage, "get thee gone, whoever thou art; if thou be'st what I guess thee, thou well knowest there are earnest reasons why thou shouldst."

"Thou hast hit it right for once, holly-top," said the gallant, "though I guess you drew your bow at a venture. Here, host, let this yeoman have a bottle of wine to wash the smart out of his eyes, and there is a French crown for him."

So saying, he threw the piece of money on the table, and left the apartment with a quick but steady pace, looking firmly at right and left, as if to defy interruption, and snapping his fingers at two or three respectable burghers, who, declaring it was a shame that any one should be suffered to rant and ruffle in defense of the Pope, were laboring to find the hilts of their swords, which had got for the present unhappily entangled in the folds of their cloaks. But, as the adversary was gone ere any of them had reached his weapon, they did not think it necessary to unsheathe cold iron, but merely observed to each other, "This is more than masterful violence, to see a poor man stricken in the face just for singing a ballad against the Whore of Babylon! If the Pope's champions are to be bangsters in our very change-houses, we shall soon have the old shavelings back again."

"The provost should look to it," said another, "and have some five or six armed with partisans, to come in upon the first whistle, to teach these gallants their lesson. For, look you, neighbor Lugleather, it is not for decent householders like ourselves to be brawling with the godless grooms and pert pages of the nobles, that are bred up to little else save bloodshed and blasphemy."

"For all that, neighbor," said Lugleather, "I would have curried that youngster as properly as ever I curried a lamb's hide, had not the hilt of my bilbo been for the instant beyond my grasp; and before I could turn my girdle, gone was my master!"

"Ay," said the others, "the devil go with him, and peace abide with us; I give my rede, neighbors, that we pay the lawing, and be stepping homeward, like brother and brother; for old St. Giles's is tolling curfew, and the street grows dangerous at night."

With that the good burghers adjusted their cloaks and prepared for their departure, while he that seemed the briskest of the three, laying his hand on his Andrea Ferrara, observed, "That they that spoke in praise of the Pope on the Highgate of Edinburgh had best bring the sword of St. Peter to defend them."

While the ill humor excited by the insolence of the young aristocrat was thus evaporating in empty menace, Roland Græme had to control the far more serious indignation of Adam Woodcock. "Why man, it was but a switch across the mazzard; blow your nose, dry your eyes, and you will see all the better for it."

"By this light, which I cannot see," said Adam Woodcock,

"thou hast been a false friend to me, young man, neither taking up my rightful quarrel nor letting me fight it out myself."

"Fy, for shame, Adam Woodcock," replied the youth, determined to turn the tables on him, and become in turn the counselor of good order and peaceable demeanor—"I say, fy for shame! Alas, that you will speak thus! Here are you sent with me, to prevent an innocent youth getting into snares——"

"I wish your innocent youth were cut short with a halter, with all my heart!" said Adam, who began to see which way the admonition tended.

—"And instead of setting before me," continued Roland, "an example of patience and sobriety becoming the falconer of Sir Halbert Glendenning, you quaff me off I know not how many flagons of ale, besides a gallon of wine, and a full measure of strong waters!"

"It was but one small pottle," said poor Adam, whom consciousness of his own indiscretion now reduced to a merely defensive warfare.

"It was enough to pottle you handsomely, however," said the page. "And then instead of going to bed to sleep off your liquor, you must sit singing your roisterous songs about popes and pagans, till you have got your eyes almost switched out of your head; and but for my interference, whom your drunken ingratitude accuses of deserting you, yon galliard would have cut your throat, for he was whipping out a whinger as broad as my hand and as sharp as a razor. And these are lessons for an inexperienced youth! Oh, Adam! out upon you!—out upon you!"

"Marry, amen, and with all my heart," said Adam; "out upon my folly for expecting anything but impertinent raillery from a page like thee, that, if he saw his father in a scrape, would laugh at him, instead of lending him aid!"

"Nay, but I will lend you aid," said the page, still laughing; "that is, I will lend thee aid to thy chamber, good Adam, where thou shalt sleep off wine and ale, ire and indignation, and awake the next morning with as much fair wit as nature has blessed thee withal. Only one thing I will warn thee, good Adam, that henceforth and forever, when thou railest at me for being somewhat hot at hand, and rather too prompt to out with poniard or so, thy admonition shall serve as a prologue to the memorable adventure of the switching of St. Michael's."

With such condoling expressions he got the crestfallen

falconer to his bed, and then retired to his own pallet, where it was some time ere he could fall asleep. If the messenger whom he had seen were really Catherine Seyton, what a masculine virago and termagant must she be! and stored with what an inimitable command of insolence and assurance! The brass on her brow would furbish the front of twenty pages; "and I should know," thought Roland, "what that amounts to. And yet, her features, her look, her light gait, her laughing eye, the art with which she disposed the mantle to show no more of her limbs than needs must be seen—I am glad she had at least that grace left—the voice, the smile—it must have been Catherine Seyton, or the devil in her likeness! One thing is good, I have silenced the eternal predictions of that ass, Adam Woodcock, who has set up for being a preacher and a governor over me, so soon as he has left the hawk's mew behind him."

And with this comfortable reflection, joined to the happy indifference which youth hath for the events of the morrow, Roland Græme fell fast asleep.

CHAPTER XX

Now have you reft me from my staff, my guide,
Who taught my youth, as men teach untamed falcons,
To use my strength discreetly—I am reft
Of comrade and of counsel!

Old Play.

In the gray of the next morning's dawn there was a loud knocking at the gate of the hostelry, and those without, proclaiming that they came in the name of the Regent were instantly admitted. A moment or two afterwards, Michael Wing-the-Wind stood by the bedside of our travelers.

"Up!—up!" he said, "there is no slumber where Murray hath work ado."

Both sleepers sprung up, and began to dress themselves.

"You, old friend," said Wing-the-Wind to Adam Woodcock, "must to horse instantly, with this packet to the monks of Kennaquhair, and with this," delivering them as he spoke, "to the Knight of Avenel."

"As much as commanding the monks to annul their election, I'll warrant me, of an abbot," quoth Adam Woodcock, as he put the packets into his bag, "and charging my master to see it done. To hawk at one brother with another is less than fair play, methinks."

"Fash not thy beard about it, old boy," said Michael, "but betake thee to the saddle presently; for if these orders are not obeyed there will be bare walls at the kirk of St. Mary's, and it may be at the Castle of Avenel to boot; for I heard my Lord of Morton loud with the Regent, and we are at a pass that we cannot stand with him anent trifles."

"But," said Adam, "touching the Abbot of Unreason—what say they to that outbreak? An they be shrewishly disposed, I were better pitch the packets to Satan, and take the other side of the Border for my bield."

"O, that was passed over as a jest, since there was little harm done. But hark thee, Adam," continued his comrade, "if there were a dozen vacant abbacies in your road, whether of jest or earnest, reason or unreason, draw thou never one of their miters over thy brows. The time is not fitting, man; besides, our maiden longs to clip the neck of a fat churchman."

"She shall never sheer mine in that capacity," said the falconer, while he knotted the kerchief in two or three double folds around his sunburnt bull-neck, calling out at the same time, "Master Roland—Master Roland, make haste! we must back to perch and mew, and, thank Heaven more than our own wit, with our bones whole, and without a stab in the stomach."

"Nay, but," said Wing-the-Wind, "the page goes not back with you: the Regent has other employment for him."

"Saints and sorrows!" exclaimed the falconer. "Master Roland Græme to remain here, and I to return to Avenel! Why, it cannot be: the child cannot manage himself in this wide world without me, and I question if he will stoop to any other whistle than mine own; there are times I myself can hardly bring him to my lure."

It was at Roland's tongue's end to say something concerning the occasion they had for using mutually each other's prudence; but the real anxiety which Adam evinced at parting with him took away his disposition to such ungracious raillery. The falconer did not altogether escape, however, for, in turning his face towards the lattice, his friend Michael caught a glimpse of it, and exclaimed, "I prithee, Adam Woodcock, what hast thou been doing with these eyes of thine? They are swelled to the starting from the socket!"

"Nought in the world," said he, after casting a deprecating glace at Roland Græme, "but the effect of sleeping in this d——d truckle without a pillow."

"Why, Adam Woodcock, thou must be grown strangely dainty," said his old companion; "I have known thee sleep all night with no better pillow than a bush of ling, and start up with the sun as gleg as a falcon; and now thine eyes resemble——"

"Tush man, what signifies how mine eyes look now?" said Adam. "Let us but roast a crab-apple, pour a pottle of ale on it, and bathe our throats withal, thou shalt see a change in me."

"And thou wilt be in heart to sing thy jolly ballad about the Pope?" said his comrade.

"Ay, that I will," replied the falconer, "that is, when we have left this quiet town five miles behind us, if you will take your hobby and ride so far on my way."

"Nay, that I may not," said Michael; "I can but stop

to partake your morning's draught, and see you fairly to horse; I will see that they saddle them, and toast the crab for thee, without loss of time."

During his absence the falconer took the page by the hand. "May I never hood hawk again," said the good-natured fellow, "if I am not as sorry to part with you as if you were a child of mine own, craving pardon for the freedom; I cannot tell what makes me love you so much, unless it be for the reason that I loved the vicious devil of a brown Galloway nag, whom my master the knight called Satan, till Master Warden changed his name to Seyton; for he said it was over boldness to call a beast after the King of Darkness——"

"And," said the page, "it was over boldness in him, I trow, to call a vicious brute after a noble family."

"Well," proceeded Adam, "Seyton or Satan, I loved that nag over every other horse in the stable. There was no sleeping on his back: he was forever fidgeting, bolting, rearing, biting, kicking, and giving you work to do, and maybe the measure of your back on the heather to the boot of it all. And I think I love you better than any lad in the castle for the self-same qualities."

"Thanks—thanks, kind Adam. I regard myself bound to you for the good estimation in which you hold me."

"Nay, interrupt me not," said the falconer; "Satan was a good nag. But, I say, I think I shall call the two eyases after you—the one Roland and the other Græme; and, while Adam Woodcock lives, be sure you have a friend. Here is to thee, my dear son."

Roland most heartily returned the grasp of the hand, and Woodcock, having taken a deep draught, continued his farewell speech.

"There are three things I warn you against, Roland, now that you are to tread this weary world without my experience to assist you. In the first place, never draw dagger on slight occasion: every man's doublet is not so well stuffed as a certain abbot's that you wot of. Secondly, fly not at every pretty girl, like a merlin at a thrush; you will not always win a gold chain for your labor; and, by the way, here I return to you your fanfarona; keep it close, it is weighty, and may benefit you at a pinch more ways than one. Thirdly, and to conclude, as our worthy preacher says, beware of the pottle-pot: it has drenched the judgment of wiser men than you. I could bring some instances of it, but I daresay it needeth not; for if you should forget your own mishaps, you will scarce fail to remember mine. And so farewell, my dear son."

Roland returned his good wishes, and failed not to send his humble duty to his kind lady, charging the falconer at the same time to express his regret that he should have offended her, and his determination so to bear him in the world that she would not be ashamed of the generous protection she had afforded him.

The falconer embraced his young friend, mounted his stout, round-made, trotting nag, which the serving-man who had attended him held ready at the door, and took the road to the southward. A sullen and heavy sound echoed from the horse's feet, as if indicating the sorrow of the good-natured rider. Every hoof-tread seemed to tap upon Roland's heart as he heard his comrade withdraw with so little of his usual alert activity, and felt that he was once more alone in the world.

He was roused from his reverie by Michael Wing-the-Wind, who reminded him that it was necessary they should instantly return to the palace, as my Lord Regent went to the sessions early in the morning. They went thither accordingly, and Wing-the-Wind, a favorite old domestic, who was admitted nearer to the Regent's person and privacy than many whose posts were more ostensible, soon introduced Græme into a small matted chamber, where he had an audience of the present head of the troubled state of Scotland. The Earl of Murray was clad in a sad-colored morning-gown, with a cap and slippers of the same cloth; but, even in this easy dishabille, held his sheathed rapier in his hand—a precaution which he adopted when receiving strangers, rather in compliance with the earnest remonstrances of his friends and partizans than from any personal apprehensions of his own. He answered with a silent nod the respectful obeisance of the page, and took one or two turns through the small apartment in silence, fixing his keen eye on Roland, as if he wished to penetrate into his very soul. At length he broke silence.

"Your name is, I think, Julian Græme?"

"Roland Græme, my lord—not Julian," replied the page.

"Right—I was misled by some trick of my memory. Roland Græme, from the Debateable Land. Roland, thou knowest the duties which belong to a lady's service?"

"I should know them, my lord," replied Roland, "having been bred so near the person of my Lady of Avenel; but

I trust never more to practise them, as the knight hath promised——"

"Be silent, young man," said the Regent; "I am to speak, and you to hear and obey. It is necessary that, for some space at least, you shall again enter into the service of a lady, who in rank hath no equal in Scotland; and this service accomplished, I give thee my word as knight and prince that it shall open to you a course of ambition such as may well gratify the aspiring wishes of one whom circumstances entitle to entertain much higher views than thou. I will take thee into my household and near to my person, or at your own choice, I will give you the command of a foot-company; either is a preferment which the proudest laird in the land might be glad to insure for a second son."

"May I presume to ask, my lord," said Roland, observing the Earl paused for a reply, "to whom my poor services are in the first place destined?"

"You will be told hereafter," said the Regent; and then, as if overcoming some internal reluctance to speak further himself, he added, "or why should I not myself tell you that you are about to enter into the service of a most illustrious—most unhappy, lady—into the service of Mary of Scotland."

"Of the Queen, my lord?" said the page, unable to repress his surprise.

"Of her who was the Queen!" said Murray, with a singular mixture of displeasure and embarrassment in his tone of voice. "You must be aware, young man, that her son reigns in her stead."

He sighed from an emotion partly natural, perhaps, and partly assumed.

"And am I to attend upon her Grace in her place of imprisonment, my lord?" again demanded the page, with a straightforward and hardy simplicity which somewhat disconcerted the sage and powerful statesman.

"She is not imprisoned," answered Murray, angrily, "God forbid she should: she is only sequestrated from state affairs, and from the business of the public, until the world be so effectually settled that she may enjoy her natural and uncontrolled freedom, without her royal disposition being exposed to the practises of wicked and designing men. It is for this purpose," he added, "that, while she is to be furnished, as right is, with such attendance as may befit her present secluded state, it becomes necessary that those placed around her are persons on whose prudence I can have reliance.

You see, therefore, you are at once called on to discharge an office most honorable in itself, and so to discharge it that you may make a friend of the Regent of Scotland. Thou art, I have been told, a singularly apprehensive youth ; and I perceive by thy look that thou dost already understand what I would say on this matter. In this schedule your particular points of duty are set down at length ; but the sum required of you is fidelity—I mean fidelity to myself and to the state. You are, therefore, to watch every attempt which is made, or inclination displayed, to open any communication with any of the lords who have become banders in the west—with Hamilton, Seyton, with Fleming, or the like. It is true that my gracious sister, reflecting upon the ill chances that have happed to the state of this poor kingdom, from evil counselors who have abused her royal nature in time past, hath determined to sequestrate herself from state affairs in future. But it is our duty, as acting for and in the name of our infant nephew, to guard against the evils which may arise from any mutation or vacillation in her royal resolutions. Wherefore, it will be thy duty to watch, and report to our lady mother, whose guest our sister is for the present, whatever may infer a disposition to withdraw her person from the place of security in which she is lodged, or to open communication with those without. If, however, your observation should detect anything of weight, and which may exceed mere suspicion, fail not to send notice by an especial messenger to me directly, and this ring shall be thy warrant to order horse and man on such service. And now begone. If there be half the wit in thy head that there is apprehension in thy look, thou fully comprehendest all that I would say. Serve me faithfully, and sure as I am belted earl thy reward shall be great."

Roland Græme made an obeisance, and was about to depart.

The Earl signed to him to remain. "I have trusted thee deeply," he said, "young man, for thou art the only one of her suite who has been sent to her by my own recommendation. Her gentlewomen are of her own nomination : it were too hard to have barred her that privilege, though some there were who reckoned it inconsistent with sure policy. Thou art young and handsome. Mingle in their follies, and see they cover not deeper designs under the appearance of female levity ; if they do mine, do thou countermine. For the rest, bear all decorum and respect to the person of thy mistress : she is a princess, though a most unhappy one, and hath been a queen, though now, alas! no longer such. Pay, therefore, to her all honor and respect consistent with thy fidelity to the King and me. And now, farewell! Yet stay—you travel with Lord Lindesay, a man of the old world, rough and honest, though untaught; see that thou offend him not, for he is not patient of raillery, and thou, I have heard, art a crack-halter." This he said with a smile; then added, "I could have wished the Lord Lindesay's mission had been entrusted to some other and more gentle noble."

"And wherefore should you wish that, my lord?" said Morton, who even then entered the apartment; "the council have decided for the best; we have had but too many proofs of this lady's stubbornness of mind, and the oak that resists the sharp steel ax must be riven with the rugged iron wedge. And this is to be her page? My Lord Regent hath doubtless instructed you, young man, how you shall guide yourself in these matters; I will add but a little hint on my part. You are going to the castle of a Douglas, where treachery never thrives: the first moment of suspicion will be the last of your life. My kinsman, William Douglas, understands no raillery, and if he once have cause to think you false, you will waver in the wind from the castle battlements ere the sun set upon his anger. And is the lady to have an almoner withal?"

"Occasionally, Douglas," said the R gent; "it were hard to deny the spiritual consolation which she thinks essential to her salvation."

"You are ever too soft-hearted, my lord. What! a false priest to communicate her lamentations, not only to our unfriends in Scotland, but to the Guises, to Rome, to Spain, and I know not where!"

"Fear not," said the Regent, "we will take such order that no treachery shall happen."

"Look to it, then," said Morton; "you know my mind respecting the wench you have consented she shall receive as a waiting-woman—one of a family which, of all others, has ever been devoted to her and inimical to us. Had we not been wary, she would have been purveyed of a page as much to her purpose as her waiting-damsel. I hear a rumor that an old mad Romish pilgrimer, who passes for at least half a saint among them, was employed to find a fit subject."

"We have escaped that danger at least," said Murray, "and converted it into a point of advantage by sending this boy of Glendinning's; and for her waiting-damsel, you cannot grudge her one poor maiden instead of her four noble Maries and all their silken train?"

"I care not so much for the waiting-maiden," said Morton, "but I cannot brook the almoner: I think priests of all persuasions are much like each other. Here is John Knox, who made such a noble puller-down, is ambitious of becoming a setter-up, and a founder of schools and colleges out of the abbey lands, and bishops' rents, and other spoils of Rome, which the nobility of Scotland have won with their sword and bow, and with which he would now endow new hives to sing the old drone."

"John is a man of God," said the Regent, "and his scheme is a devout imagination."

The sedate smile with which this was spoken left it impossible to conjecture whether the words were meant in approbation or in derision of the plan of the Scottish Reformer. Turning then to Roland Græme, as if he thought he had been long enough a witness of this conversation, he bade him get him presently to horse, since my Lord of Lindesay was already mounted. The page made his reverence, and left the apartment.

Guided by Michael Wing-the-Wind, he found his horse ready saddled and prepared for the journey in front of the palace porch, where hovered about a score of men-at-arms, whose leader showed no small symptoms of surly impatience.

"Is this the jackanape page for whom we have waited thus long?" said he to Wing-the-Wind. "And my Lord Ruthven will reach the castle long before us!"

Michael assented, and added that the boy had been detained by the Regent to receive some parting instructions. The leader made an inarticulate sound in his throat, expressive of sullen acquiescence, and calling to one of his domestic attendants, "Edward," said he, "take the gallant into your charge, and let him speak with no one else."

He then addressed, by the title of Sir Robert, an elderly and respectable-looking gentleman, the only one of the party who seemed above the rank of a retainer or domestic, and observed that they must get to horse with all speed.

During this discourse, and while they were riding slowly along the street of the suburb, Roland had time to examine more accurately the looks and figure of the baron who was at their head.

Lord Lindesay of the Byres was rather touched than stricken with years. His upright stature and strong limbs still showed him fully equal to all the exertions and fatigues of war. His thick eyebrows, now partially grizzled, lowered over large eyes full of dark fire, which seemed yet darker from the uncommon depth at which they were set in his head. His features, naturally strong and harsh, had their sternness exaggerated by one or two scars received in battle. These features, naturally calculated to express the harsher passions, were shaded by an open steel cap, with a projecting front, but having no visor, over the gorget of which fell the black and grizzled beard of the grim old baron, and totally hid the lower part of his face. The rest of his dress was a loose buff-coat, which had once been lined with silk and adorned with embroidery, but which seemed much stained with travel and damaged with cuts, received probably in battle. It covered a corslet which had once been of polished steel, fairly gilded, but was now somewhat injured with rust. A sword of antique make and uncommon size, framed to be wielded with both hands, a kind of weapon which was then beginning to go out of use, hung from his neck in a baldric, and was so disposed as to traverse his whole person, the huge hilt appearing over his left shoulder, and the point reaching well-nigh to the right heel, and jarring against his spur as he walked. This unwieldy weapon could only be unsheathed by pulling the handle over the left shoulder, for no human arm was long enough to draw it in the usual manner. The whole equipment was that of a rude warrior, negligent of his exterior even to misanthropical sullenness; and the short, harsh, haughty tone which he used towards his attendants belonged to the same unpolished character.

The personage who rode with Lord Lindesay at the head of the party was an absolute contrast to him in manner, form, and features. His thin and silky hair was already white, though he seemed not above forty-five or fifty years old. His tone of voice was soft and insinuating; his form thin, spare, and bent by an habitual stoop; his pale cheek was expressive of shrewdness and intelligence; his eye was quick though placid, and his whole demeanor mild and conciliatory. He rode an ambling nag, such as were used by ladies, clergymen, or others of peaceful professions; wore a riding habit of black velvet, with a cap and feather of the same hue, fastened up by a golden medal; and for show, and as a mark of rank rather than for use, carried a walking sword (as the short light rapiers were called), without any other arms, offensive or defensive.

The party had now quitted the town, and proceeded, at

a steady trot, towards the west. As they prosecuted their journey, Roland Græme would gladly have learned something of its purpose and tendency, but the countenance of the personage next to whom he had been placed in the train discouraged all approach to familiarity. The baron himself did not look more grim and inaccessible than his feudal retainer, whose grisly beard fell over his mouth like the portcullis before the gate of the castle, as if for the purpose of preventing the escape of any word of which absolute necessity did not demand the utterance. The rest of the train seemed under the same taciturn influence, and journeyed on without a word being exchanged amongst them, more like a troop of Carthusian friars than a party of military retainers. Roland Græme was surprised at this extremity of discipline; for even in the household of the Knight of Avenel, though somewhat distinguished for the accuracy with which decorum was enforced, a journey was a period of license, during which jest and song, and everything within the limits of becoming mirth and pastime, was freely permitted. This unusual silence was, however, so far acceptable that it gave him time to bring any shadow of judgment which he possessed to council on his own situation and prospects, which would have appeared to any reasonable person in the highest degree dangerous and perplexing.

It was quite evident that he had, through various circumstances not under his own control, formed contradictory connections with both the contending factions by whose strife the kingdom was distracted, without being properly an adherent of either. It seemed also clear that the same situation in the household of the deposed Queen, to which he was now promoted by the influence of the Regent, had been destined to him by his enthusiastic grandmother, Magdalen Græme; for on this subject the words which Morton had dropped had been a ray of light; yet it was no less clear that these two persons, the one the declared enemy, the other the enthusiastic votary, of the Catholic religion; the one at the head of the King's new government, the other, who regarded that government as a criminal usurpation, must have required and expected very different services from the individual whom they had thus united in recommending. It required very little reflection to foresee that these contradictory claims on his service might speedily place him in a situation where his honor as well as his life might be endangered. But it was not in Roland Græme's nature to anticipate evil before it came, or to prepare to combat difficulties before they arrived. "I will see this beautiful and unfortunate Mary Stuart," he said, "of whom we have heard so much, and then there will be time enough to determine whether I will be kingsman or queensman. None of them can say I have given word or promise to either of their factions; for they have led me up and down like a blind Billy, without giving me any light into what I was to do. But it was lucky that grim Douglas came into the Regent's closet this morning, otherwise I had never got free of him without plighting my troth to do all the Earl would have me, which seemed, after all, but foul play to the poor imprisoned lady, to place her page as an espial on her."

Skipping thus lightly over a matter of such consequence, the thoughts of the hare-brained boy went a-wool-gathering after more agreeable topics. Now he admired the Gothic towers of Barnbougle, rising from the sea-beaten rock, and overlooking one of the most glorious landscapes in Scotland; and now he began to consider what notable sport for the hounds and the hawks must be afforded by the variegated ground over which they travelled; and now he compared the steady and dull trot at which they were then prosecuting their journey with the delight of sweeping over hill and dale in pursuit of his favorite sports. As, under the influence of these joyous recollections, he gave his horse the spur, and made him execute a gambade, he instantly incurred the censure of his grave neighbor, who hinted to him to keep the pace, and move quietly and in order, unless he wished such notice to be taken of his eccentric movements as was likely to be very displeasing to him.

The rebuke and the restraint under which the youth now, found himself brought back to his recollection his late good-humored and accommodating associate and guide, Adam Woodcock; and from that topic his imagination made a short flight to Avenel Castle, to the quiet and unconfined life of its inhabitants, the goodness of his early protectress, not forgetting the denizens of its stables, kennels, and hawk-mews. In a brief space, all these subjects of meditation gave way to the remembrance of that riddle of womankind, Catherine Seyton, who appeared before the eye of his mind now in her female form, now in her male attire, now in both at once, like some strange dream, which presents to us the same individual under two different characters at the same instant. Her mysterious present also recurred to his recollection—the sword which he now wore at his side, and which he was not to draw, save by command of his legitimate sovereign! But the key of this mystery he judged he was likely to find in the issue of his present journey.

With such thoughts passing through his mind, Roland Græme accompanied the party of Lord Lindesay to the Queen's Ferry, which they passed in vessels that lay in readiness for them. They encountered no adventure whatever in their passage, excepting one horse being lamed in getting into the boat—an incident very common on such occasions, until a few years ago, when the ferry was completely regulated. What was more peculiarly characteristic of the olden age was the discharge of a culverin at the party from the battlements of the old castle of Rosythe, on the north side of the ferry, the lord of which happened to have some public or private quarrel with the Lord Lindesay, and took this mode of expressing his resentment. The insult, however, as it was harmless, remained unnoticed and unavenged, nor did anything else occur worth notice until the band had come where Lochleven spread its magnificent sheet of waters to the beams of a bright summer sun.

The ancient castle, which occupies an island nearly in the center of the lake, recalled to the page that of Avenel, in which he had been nurtured. But the lake was much larger, and adorned with several islets besides that on which the fortress was situated; and instead of being embosomed in hills like that of Avenel, had upon the southern side only a splendid mountainous screen, being the descent of one of the Lomond hills and on the other was surrounded by the extensive and fertile plain of Kinross. Roland Græme looked with some degree of dismay on the water-girdled fortress, which then, as now, consisted only of one large donjon-keep, surrounded with a courtyard, with two round flanking towers at the angles, which contained within its circuit some other buildings of inferior importance. A few old trees, clustered together near the castle, gave some relief to the air of desolate seclusion; but yet the page, while he gazed upon a building so sequestrated, could not but feel for the situation of a captive princess doomed to dwell there, as well as for his own. "I must have been born," he thought, "under the star that presides over ladies and lakes of water, for I cannot by any means escape from the service of the one or from dwelling in the other. But if they allow me not the fair freedom of my sport and exercise, they shall find it as hard to confine a wild drake as a youth who can swim like one."

The band had now reached the edge of the water, and one

of the party advancing displayed Lord Lindesay's pennon, waving it repeatedly to and fro, while that baron himself blew a clamorous blast on his bugle. A banner was presently displayed from the roof of the castle in reply to these signals, and one or two figures were seen busied as if unmooring a boat which lay close to the islet.

"It will be some time ere they can reach us with the boat," said the companion of the Lord Lindesay; "should we not do well to proceed to the town, and array ourselves in some better order, ere we appear before——"

"You may do as you list, Sir Robert," replied Lindesay, "I have neither time nor temper to waste on such vanities. She has cost me many a hard ride, and must not now take offense at the threadbare cloak and soiled doublet that I am arrayed in. It is the livery to which she has brought all Scotland."

"Do not speak so harshly," said Sir Robert; "if she hath done wrong, she hath dearly abeyed it; and in losing all real power, one would not deprive her of the little external homage due at once to a lady and a princess."

"I say to you once more, Sir Robert Melville," replied Lindesay, "do as you will; for me, I am now too old to dink myself as a gallant to grace the bower of dames."

"The bower of dames, my lord!" said Melville, looking at the rude old tower: "is it yon dark and grated castle, the prison of a captive queen, to which you give so gay a name?"

"Name it as you list," replied Lindesay; "had the Regent desired to send an envoy capable to speak to a captive queen, there are many gallants in his court who would have courted the occasion to make speeches out of *Amadis of Gaul* or the *Mirror of Knighthood*. But when he sent blunt old Lindesay, he knew he would speak to a misguided woman, as her former misdoings and her present state render necessary. I sought not this employment: it has been thrust upon me; and I will not cumber myself with more form in the discharge of it than needs must be tacked to such an occupation."

So saying, Lord Lindesay threw himself from horseback, and, wrapping his riding-cloak around him, lay down at lazy length upon the sward, to await the arrival of the boat, which was now seen rowing from the castle towards the shore. Sir Robert Melville, who had also dismounted, walked at short turns to and fro upon the bank, his arms crossed on his breast, often looking to the castle, and displaying in his countenance a mixture of sorrow and of anxiety. The rest of the party sate like statues on horseback, without moving so much as the points of their lances, which they held upright in the air.

As soon as the boat approached a rude quay or landing-place near to which they had stationed themselves, Lord Lindesay started up from his recumbent posture, and asked the person who steered why he had not brought a larger boat with him to transport his retinue.

"So please you," replied the boatman, "because it is the order of our lady that we bring not to the castle more than four persons."

"Thy lady is a wise woman," said Lindesay, "to suspect me of treachery! Or, had I intended it, what is to hinder us from throwing you and your comrades into the lake and filling the boat with my own fellows?"

The steersman, on hearing this, made a hasty signal to his men to back their oars, and hold off from the shore which they were approaching.

"Why, thou ass," said Lindesay, "thou didst not think that I meant thy fool's head serious harm? Hark thee, friend, with fewer than three servants I will go no whither; Sir Robert Melville will require at least the attendance of one domestic; and it will be at your peril and your lady's to refuse us admission, come hither as we are on matters of great national concern."

The steersman answered with firmness, but with great civility of expression, that his orders were positive to bring no more than four into the island, but he offered to row back to obtain a revisal of his instructions.

"Do so, my friend," said Sir Robert Melville, after he had in vain endeavored to persuade his stubborn companion to consent to a temporary abatement of his train: "row back to the castle, sith it will be no better, and obtain thy lady's orders to transport the Lord Lindesay, myself, and our retinue thither."

"And hearken," said Lord Lindesay, "take with you this page, who comes as an attendant on your lady's guest. Dismount, sirrah," said he, addressing Roland, "and embark with them in that boat."

"And what is to become of my horse?" said Græme; "I am answerable for him to my master."

"I will relieve you of the charge," said Lindesay; "thou wilt have little enow to do with horse, saddle, or bridle for ten years to come. Thou mayst take the halter an thou wilt: it may stand thee in a turn."

"If I thought so," said Roland——

But he was interrupted by Sir Robert Melville, who said to him, good-humoredly, "Dispute it not, young friend: resistance can do no good, but may well run thee into danger."

Roland Græme felt the justice of what he said, and, though neither delighted with the matter nor manner of Lindesay's address, deemed it best to submit to necessity, and to embark without further remonstrance. The men plied their oars. The quay, with the party of horse stationed near it, receded from the page's eyes, the castle and the islet seemed to draw near in the same proportion, and in a brief space he landed under the shadow of a huge old tree which overhung the landing-place. The steersman and Græme leaped ashore; the boatmen remained lying on their oars ready for further service.

CHAPTER XXI

Could valor aught avail or people's love,
  France had not wept Navarre's brave Henry slain;
If wit or beauty could compassion move,
  The Rose of Scotland had not wept in vain.
        LEWIS, *Elegy in a Royal Mausoleum.*

AT the gate of the courtyard of Lochleven appeared the stately form of the Lady of Lochleven, a female whose early charms had captivated James V., by whom she became mother of the celebrated Regent Murray. As she was of noble birth, being a daughter of the house of Mar, and of great beauty, her intimacy with James did not prevent her being afterwards sought in honorable marriage by many gallants of the time, among whom she had preferred Sir William Douglas of Lochleven. But well has it been said,—

Our pleasant vices
Are made the whips to scourge us.

The station which the Lady of Lochleven now held as the wife of a man of high rank and interest, and the mother of a lawful family, did not prevent her nourishing a painful sense of degradation, even while she was proud of the talents, the power, and the station of her son, now prime ruler of the state, but still a pledge of her illicit intercourse. "Had James done to her," she said in her secret heart, "the justice he owed her, she had seen in her son, as a source of unmixed delight and of unchastened pride, the lawful monarch of Scotland, and one of the ablest who ever swayed the scepter. The house of Mar, not inferior in antiquity or grandeur to that of Drummond, would then have also boasted a queen among its daughters, and escaped the stain attached to female frailty, even when it has a royal lover for its apology." While such feelings preyed on a bosom naturally proud and severe, they had a corresponding effect on her countenance, where with the remains of great beauty, were mingled traits indicative of inward discontent and peevish melancholy. It perhaps contributed to increase this habitual temperament, that the Lady Lochleven had adopted uncommonly rigid and severe views of religion, imitating in her ideas of Reformed faith the very worst errors of the Catholics, in limiting the benefit of the Gospel to those who profess their own speculative tenets.

In every respect, the unfortunate Queen Mary, now the compulsory guest, or rather prisoner, of this sullen lady, was obnoxious to her hostess. Lady Lochleven disliked her as the daughter of Mary of Guise, the legal possessor of those rights over James's heart and hand of which she conceived herself to have been injuriously deprived; and yet more so as the professor of a religion which she detested worse than paganism.

Such was the dame who, with stately mien, and sharp yet handsome features, shrouded by her black velvet coif, interrogated the domestic who steered her barge to the shore, what had become of Lindesay and Sir Robert Melville. The man related what had passed, and she smiled scornfully as she replied, "Fools must be flattered, not foughten with Row back—make thy excuse as thou canst—say Lord Ruthven hath already reached this castle, and that he is impatient for Lord Lindesay's presence. Away with thee, Randal—yet stay, what galopin is that thou hast brought hither?"

"So please you, my lady, he is the page who is to wait upon——"

"Ay, the new male minion," said the Lady Lochleven; "the female attendant arrived yesterday. I shall have a well-ordered house with this lady and her retinue; but I trust they will soon find some others to undertake such a charge. Begone, Randal; and you (to Roland Græme), follow me to the garden."

She led the way with a slow and stately step to the small garden, which, inclosed by a stone wall ornamented with statues, and an artificial fountain in the center, extented its dull parterres on the side of the courtyard, with which it communicated by a low and arched portal. Within the narrow circuit of its formal and limited walks, Mary Stuart was now learning to perform the weary part of a prisoner, which, with little interval, she was doomed to sustain during the remainder of her life. She was followed in her slow and melancholy exercise by two female attendants; but in the first glance which Roland Græme bestowed upon one so illustrious by birth, so distinguished by her beauty, accomplishments, and misfortunes, he was sensible of the presence of no other than the unhappy Queen of Scotland.

Her face, her form, have been so deeply impressed upon the imagination that, even at the distance of nearly three centuries, it is unnecessary to remind the most ignorant and uninformed reader of the striking traits which characterize that remarkable countenance, which seems at once to combine our idea of the majestic, the pleasing, and the brilliant, leaving us to doubt whether they express most happily the queen, the beauty, or the accomplished woman. Who is there that, at the very mention of Mary Stuart's name, has not her countenance before him, familiar as that of the mistress of his youth, or the favorite daughter of his advanced age? Even those who feel themselves compelled to believe all, or much, of what her enemies laid to her charge, cannot think without a sigh upon a countenance expressive of anything rather than the foul crimes with which she was charged when living, and which still continue to shade, if not to blacken, her memory. That brow, so truly open and regal; those eyebrows, so regularly graceful, which yet were saved from the charge of regular insipidity by the beautiful effect of the hazel eyes which they overarched, and which seem to utter a thousand histories; the nose, with all its Grecian precision of outline; the mouth, so well-proportioned, so sweetly formed as if designed to speak nothing but what was delightful to hear; the dimpled chin; the stately, swan-like neck—form a countenance the like of which we know not to have existed in any other character moving in that high class of life where the actresses as well as the actors command general and undivided attention. It is in vain to say that the portraits which exist of this remarkable woman are not like each other; for, amidst their discrepancy, each possesses general features which the eye at once acknowledges as peculiar to the vision which our imagination has raised while we read her history for the first time, and which has been impressed upon it by the numerous prints and pictures which we have seen. Indeed, we cannot look on the worst of them, however deficient in point of execution, without saying that it is meant for Queen Mary; and no small instance it is of the power of beauty, that her charms should have remained the subject not merely of admiration, but of warm and chivalrous interest, after the lapse of such a length of time. We know that by far the most acute of those who, in latter days, have adopted the unfavorable view of Mary's character, longed, like the executioner before his dreadful task was performed, to kiss the fair hand of her on whom he was about to perform so horrible a duty.

Dressed, then, in a deep mourning robe, and with all those charms of face, shape, and manner with which faithful tradition has made each reader familiar, Mary Stewart advanced to meet the Lady of Lochleven, who, on her part, endeavored to conceal dislike and apprehension under the appearance of respectful indifference. The truth was, that she had experienced repeatedly the Queen's superiority in that species of disguised yet cutting sarcasm with which women can successfully avenge themselves for real and substantial injuries. It may be well doubted whether this talent was not as fatal to its possessor as the many others enjoyed by that highly gifted, but most unhappy, female; for, while it often afforded her a momentary triumph over her keepers, it failed not to exasperate their resentment; and the satire and sarcasm in which she had indulged were frequently retaliated by the deep and bitter hardships which they had the power of inflicting. It is well known that her death was at length hastened by a letter which she wrote to Queen Elizabeth, in which she treated her jealous rival and the Countess of Shrewsbury with the keenest irony and ridicule.

As the ladies met together, the Queen said, bending her head at the same time in return to the obeisance of the Lady Lochleven—"We are this day fortunate: we enjoy the company of our amiable hostess at an unusual hour, and during a period which we have hitherto been permitted to give to our private exercise. But our good hostess knows well she has at all times access to our presence, and need not observe the useless ceremony of requiring our permission."

"I am sorry my presence is deemed an intrusion by your Grace," said the Lady of Lochleven. "I came but to announce the arrival of an addition to your train," motioning with her hand towards Roland Græme, "a circumstance to which ladies are seldom indifferent."

"O! I crave your ladyship's pardon; and am bent to the earth with obligations for the kindness of my nobles—or my sovereigns, shall I call them?—who have permitted me such a respectable addition to my personal retinue."

"They have indeed studied, madam," said the Lady of Locheven, "to show their kindness toward your Grace something at the risk perhaps of sound policy, and I trust their doings will not be misconstrued."

"Impossible!" said the Queen; "the bounty which permits the daughter of so many kings, and who yet is queen of the realm, the attendance of two waiting-women and a boy, is a grace which Mary Stuart can never sufficiently acknowledge. Why! my train will be equal to that of any country dame in this your kingdom of Fife, saving but the lack of a gentleman-usher and a pair or two of blue-coated serving-men. But I must not forget, in my selfish joy, the additional trouble and charges to which this magnificent augumentation of our train will put our kind hostess and the whole house of Lochleven. It is this prudent anxiety, I am aware, which clouds your brows, my worthy lady. But be of good cheer: the crown of Scotland has many a fair manor, and your affectionate son, and my no less affectionate brother, will endow the good knight your husband with the best of them, ere Mary should be dismissed from this hospitable castle from your ladyship's lack of means to support the charges."

"The Douglasses of Lochleven, madam," answered the lady, "have known for ages how to discharge their duty to the state, without looking for reward, even when the task was both irksome and dangerous."

"Nay! but, my dear Lochleven," said the Queen, "you are over-scrupulous; I pray you accept of a goodly manor; what should support the Queen of Scotland, in this her princely court, saving her own crown-lands; and who should minister to the wants of a mother, save an affectionate son like the Earl of Murray, who possesses so wonderfully both the power and inclination? Or said you it was the danger of the task which clouded your smooth and hospitable brow? No doubt, a page is a formidable addition to my body-guard of females; and I bethink me it must have been for that reason that my Lord of Lindesay refused even now to venture within the reach of a foree so formidable, without being attended by a competent retinue."

The Lady Lochleven started, and looked something surprised; and Mary, suddenly changing her manner from the smooth, ironical affectation of mildness to an accent of austere command, and drawing up at the same time her fine person, said, with the full majesty of her rank, "Yes! Lady of Lochleven, I know that Ruthven is already in the castle, and that Lindesay waits on the bank the return of your barge to bring him hither along with Sir Robert Melville. For what purpose do these nobles come? and why am I not in ordinary decency apprised of their arrival?"

"Their purpose, madam," replied the Lady of Lochleven, "they must themselves explain; but a formal annunication were needless, where your Grace hath attendants who can play the espial so well."

"Alas! poor Fleming," said the Queen, turning to the elder of the female attendants, "thou wilt be tried, condemned, and gibbeted for a spy in the garrison, because thou didst chance to cross the great hall while my good Lady of Lochleven was parleying at the full pitch of her voice with her pilot Randal. Put black wool in thy ears, girl, as you value the wearing of them longer. Remember, in the Castle of Lochleven, ears and tongues are matters not of use, but for show merely. Our good hostess can hear, as well as speak for us all. We excuse your further attendance, my lady hostess," she said, once more addressing the object of her resentment, "and retire to prepare for an interview with our rebel lords. We will use the ante-chamber of our sleeping apartment as our hall of audience. You, young man," she proceeded, addressing Roland Græme, and at once softening the ironical sharpness of her manner into good-humored raillery—"you, who are all our male attendance, from our Lord High Chamberlain down to our least galopin, follow us to prepare our court."

She turned, and walked slowly towards the castle. The Lady of Lochleven folded her arms, and smiled in bitter resentment, as she watched her retiring steps.

"Thy whole male attendance!" she muttered, repeating the Queen's last words, "and well for thee had it been had thy train never been larger;" then turning to Roland, in whose way she had stood while making this pause, she made room for him to pass, saying at the same time, "Art thou already eavesdropping? follow thy mistress, minion, and, if thou wilt, tell her what I have now said."

Roland Græme hastened after his royal mistress and her attendants, who had just entered a postern gate communicating betwixt the castle and the small garden. They ascended a winding stair as high as the second story, which was in a great measure occupied by a suite of three rooms, opening into each other, and assigned as the dwelling of the captive princess. The outermost was a small hall or anteroom, within which opened a large parlor, and from that again the Queen's bedroom. Another small apartment, which opened into the same parlor, contained the beds of the gentlewomen in waiting.

Roland Græme stopped, as became his station, in the outermost of these apartments, there to await such orders as might be communicated to him. From the grated window of the room he saw Lindesay, Melville, and their followers disembark; and observed that they were met at the castle gate by a third noble, to whom Lindesay exclaimed, in his loud harsh voice, "My Lord of Ruthven, you have the start of us!"

At this instant the page's attention was called to a burst of hysterical sobs from the inner apartment, and to the hurried ejaculations of the terrified females, which led him almost instantly to hasten to their assistance. When he entered, he saw that the Queen had thrown herself into the large chair which stood nearest the door, and was sobbing for breath in a strong fit of hysterical affection. The elder female supported her in her arms, while the younger bathed her face with water and with tears alternately.

"Hasten, young man!" said the elder lady, in alarm—"fly—call in assistance; she is swooning!"

But the Queen ejaculated in a faint and broken voice, "Stir not, I charge you!—call no one to witness; I am better—I shall recover instantly." And, indeed, with an effort which seemed like that of one struggling for life, she sate up in her chair and endeavored to resume her composure, while her features yet trembled with the violent emotion of body and mind which she had undergone. "I am ashamed of my weakness, girls," she said, taking the hands of her attendants; "but it is over—and I am Mary Stuart once more. The savage tone of that man's voice—my knowledge of his insolence—the name which he named—the purpose for which they come, may excuse a moment's weakness, and it shall be a moment's only." She snatched from her head the curch, or cap, which had been disordered during her hysterical agony; shook down the thick clustered tresses of dark brown which had been before veiled under it; and, drawing her slender fingers across the labyrinth which they formed, she arose from the chair, and stood like the inspired image of a Grecian prophetess, in a mood which partook at once of sorrow and pride, of smiles and of tears. "We are ill appointed," she said, "to meet our rebel subjects; but, as far as we may, we will strive to present ourselves as becomes their queen. Follow me, my maidens," she said; "what says thy favorite song, my Fleming?—

> My maids, come to my dressing-bower,
> And deck my nut-brown hair;
> Where'er ye laid a plait before,
> Look ye lay ten times mair.

Alas!" she added, when she had repeated with a smile these lines of an old ballad, "violence has already robbed me of the ordinary decorations of my rank; and the few that nature gave me have been destroyed by sorrow and by fear." Yet, while she spoke thus, she again let her slender fingers stray through the wilderness of the beautiful tresses which veiled her kingly neck and swelling bosom, as if, in her agony of mind, she had not altogether lost the consciousness of her unrivaled charms. Roland Græme, on whose youth, inexperience, and ardent sense of what was dignified and lovely, the demeanor of so fair and high-born a lady wrought like the charm of a magician, stood rooted to the spot with surprise and interest, longing to hazard his life in a quarrel so fair as that which Mary Stuart's must needs be. She had been bred in France—she was possessed of the most distinguished beauty—she had reigned a queen, and a Scottish queen, to whom knowledge of character was as essential as the use of vital air. In all these capacities Mary was, of all women on the earth, most alert at perceiving and using the advantages which her charms gave her over almost all who came within the sphere of their influence. She cast on Roland a glance which might have melted a heart of stone. "My poor boy," she said, with a feeling partly real, partly politic, "thou art a stranger to us, sent to this doleful captivity from the society of some tender mother, or sister, or maiden, with whom you had freedom to tread a gay measure round the Maypole. I grieve for you; but you are the only male in my limited household—wilt thou obey my orders?"

"To the death, madam," said Græme, in a determined tone.

"Then keep the door of mine apartment," said the Queen—"keep it till they offer actual violence, or till we shall be fitly arrayed to receive the intrusive visitors."

"I will defend it till they pass over my body," said Roland Græme, any hesitation which he had felt concerning the line of conduct he ought to pursue being completely swept away by the impulse of the moment.

"Not so, my good youth," answered Mary—"not so, I command thee. If I have one faithful subject beside me, much need, God wot, I have to care for his safety. Resist them but till they are put to the shame of using actual violence, and then give way, I charge you. Remember my commands." And, with a smile expressive at once of favor and of authority, she turned from him, and, followed by her attendants, entered the bedroom.

The youngest paused for half a second ere she followed her companion, and made a signal to Roland Græme with her hand. He had been already long aware that this was Catherine Seyton—a circumstance which could not much surprise a youth of quick intellect, who recollected the sort of mysterious discourse which had passed betwixt the two matrons at the deserted nunnery, and on which his meeting with Catherine in this place seemed to cast so much light. Yet, such was the engrossing effect of Mary's presence, that it surmounted for the moment even the feelings of a youthful lover; and it was not until Catherine Seyton had disappeared that Roland began to consider in what relation they were to stand to each other. "She held up her hand to me in a commanding manner," he thought; "perhaps she wanted to confirm my purpose for the execution of the Queen's commands; for I think she could scarce purpose to scare me with the sort of discipline which she administered to the groom in the frieze jacket and to poor Adam Woodcock. But we will see to that anon; meantime, let us do justice to the trust reposed in us by this unhappy Queen. I think my Lord of Murray will himself own that it is the duty of a faithful page to defend his lady against intrusion on her privacy."

Accordingly, he stepped to the little vestibule, made fast, with lock and bar, the door which opened from thence to the large staircase, and then sat himself down to attend the result. He had not long to wait: a rude and strong hand first essayed to lift the latch, then pushed and shook the door with violence, and, when it resisted his attempt to open it, exclaimed, "Undo the door there, you within!"

"Why, and at whose command," said the page, "am I to undo the door of the apartments of the Queen of Scotland?"

Another vain attempt, which made hinge and bolts jingle, showed that the impatient applicant without would willingly have entered altogether regardless of his challenge; but at length an answer was returned.

"Undo the door, on your peril: the Lord Lindesay comes to speak with the Lady Mary of Scotland."

"The Lord Lindesay, as a Scottish noble," answered the page, "must await his sovereign's leisure."

An earnest altercation ensued amongst those without, in which Roland distinguished the remarkably harsh voice of Lindesay in reply to Sir Robert Melville, who appeared to have been using some soothing language—"No! no! no! I tell thee no! I will place a petard against the door rather than be baulked by a profligate woman, and bearded by an insolent footboy."

"Yet, at least," said Melville, "let me try fair means in the first instance. Violence to a lady would stain your scutcheon forever. Or await till my Lord Ruthven comes."

"I will await no longer," said Lindesay; "it is high time the business were done, and we on our return to the council. But thou mayst try thy fair play, as thou callest it, while I cause my train to prepare the petard. I came hither provided with as good gunpowder as blew up the Kirk of Field."

"For God's sake, be patient," said Melville; and, approaching the door, he said, as speaking to those within, "Let the Queen know that I, her faithful servant, Robert Melville, do entreat her, for her own sake, and to prevent worse consequences, that she will undo the door, and admit Lord Lindesay, who brings a mission from the council of state."

"I will do your errand to the Queen," said the page, "and report to you her answer."

He went to the door of the bedchamber, and, tapping against it gently, it was opened by the elder lady to whom he communicated his errand, and returned with directions from the Queen to admit Sir Robert Melville and Lord Lindesay. Roland Græme returned to the vestibule, and opened the door accordingly, into which the Lord Lindesay strode, with the air of a soldier who has fought his way into a conquered fortress; while Melville, deeply dejected, followed him more slowly.

"I draw you to witness and to record," said the page to this last, "that, save for the especial commands of the Queen, I would have made good the entrance, with my best strength and my best blood, against all Scotland."

"Be silent, young man," said Melville, in a tone of grave rebuke: "add not brands to fire; this is no time to make a flourish of thy boyish chivalry."

"She has not appeared even yet," said Lindesay, who had now reached the midst of the parlor or audience-room; "how call you this trifling?"

"Patience, my lord," replied Sir Robert, "time presses not; and Lord Ruthven hath not as yet descended."

At this moment the door of the inner apartment opened, and Queen Mary presented herself, advancing with an air of peculiar grace and majesty, and seeming totally unruffled, either by the visit or by the rude manner in which it had been enforced. Her dress was a robe of black velvet; a small ruff, open in front, gave a full view of her beautifully formed chin and neck, but veiled the bosom. On her head she wore a small cap of lace, and a transparent white veil hung from her shoulders over the long black robe, in large loose folds, so that it could be drawn at pleasure over the face and person. She wore a cross of gold around her neck, and had her rosary of gold and ebony hanging from her girdle. She was closely followed by her two ladies, who remained standing behind her during the conference. Even Lord Lindesay, though the rudest noble of that rude age, was surprised into something like respect by the unconcerned and majestic mien of her whom he had expected to find frantic with impotent passion, or dissolved in useless and vain sorrow, or overwhelmed with the fears likely in such a situation to assail fallen royalty.

"We fear we have detained you, my Lord of Lindesay," said the Queen, while she courtesied with dignity in answer to his reluctant obeisance; "but a female does not willingly receive her visitors without some minutes spent at the toilet. Men, my lord, are less dependent on such ceremonies."

Lord Lindesay, casting his eye down on his own travel-stained and disordered dress, muttered something of a hasty journey, and the Queen paid her greeting to Sir Robert Melville with courtesy, and even, as it seemed, with kindness. There was then a dead pause, during which Lindesay looked towards the door, as if expecting with impatience the colleague of their embassy. The Queen alone was entirely unembarrassed, and, as if to break the silence, she addressed Lord Lindesay, with a glance at the large and cumbrous sword which he wore, as already mentioned, hanging from his neck.

"You have there a trusty and a weighty traveling companion, my lord. I trust you expected to meet with no enemy here, against whom such a formidable weapon could be necessary? It is, methinks, somewhat a singular ornament for a court, though I am, as I was need to be, too much of a Stuart to fear a sword."

"It is not the first time, madam," replied Lindesay, bringing around the weapon so as to rest its point on the ground, and leaning one hand on the huge cross-handle—"it is not the first time that this weapon has intruded itself into the presence of the house of Stuart."

"Possibly, my lord," replied the Queen, "it may have done service to my ancestors. Your ancestors were men of loyalty."

"Ay, madam," replied he, "service it hath done; but such as kings love neither to acknowledge nor to reward. It was the service which the knife renders to the tree when trimming it to the quick, and depriving it of the superfluous growth of rank and unfruitful suckers, which rob it of nourishment."

"You talk riddles, my lord," said Mary; "I will hope the explanation carries nothing insulting with it."

"You shall judge, madam," answered Lindesay. "With this good sword was Archibald Douglas, Earl of Angus, girded on the memorable day when he acquired the name of Bell-the-Cat, for dragging from the presence of your great-grandfather, the third James of the race, a crew of minions, flatterers, and favorites, whom he hanged over the bridge of Lauder, as a warning to such reptiles how they approach a Scottish throne. With this same weapon, the same inflexible champion of Scottish honor and nobility slew at one blow Spens of Kilspindie, a courtier of your grandfather, James the Fourth, who had dared to speak lightly of him in the royal presence. They fought near the brook of Fala; and Bell-the-Cat, with this blade, sheared through the thigh of his opponent, and lopped the limb as easily as a shepherd's boy slices a twig from a sapling."

"My lord," replied the Queen, reddening, "my nerves are too good to be alarmed even by this terrible history. May I ask how a blade so illustrious passed from the house of Douglas to that of Lindesay? Methinks it should have been preserved as a consecrated relic by a family who have held all that they could do against their king to be done in favor of their country."

"Nay, madam," said Melville, anxiously interfering, "ask not that question of Lord Lindesay. And you, my lord, for shame—for decency, forbear to reply to it."

"It is time that this lady should hear the truth," replied Lindesay.

"And be assured," said the Queen, "that she will be moved to anger by none that you can tell her, my lord. There are cases in which just scorn has always the mastery over just anger."

"Then know," said Lindesay, "that upon the field of Carberry Hill, when that false and infamous traitor and murderer, James, sometime Earl of Bothwell, and nicknamed Duke of Orkney, offered to do personal battle with any of the associated nobles who came to drag him to justice, I accepted his challenge, and was by the noble Earl of

Morton gifted with his good sword that I might therewith fight it out. Ah! so help me Heaven, had his presumption been one grain more, or his cowardice one grain less, I should have done such work with this good steel on his traitorous corpse that the hounds and carrion-crows should have found their morsels daintily carved to their use!"

The Queen's courage wellnigh gave way at the mention of Bothwell's name—a name connected with such a train of guilt, shame, and disaster. But the prolonged boast of Lindesay gave her time to rally herself, and to answer with an appearance of cold contempt—"It is easy to slay an enemy who enters not the lists. But had Mary Stuart inherited her father's sword as well as his scepter, the boldest of her rebels should not upon that day have complained that they had no one to cope withal. Your lordship will forgive me if I abridge this conference. A brief description of a bloody fight is long enough to satisfy a lady's curiosity; and unless my Lord of Lindesay has something more important to tell us than of the deeds which old Bell-the-Cat achieved, and how he would himself have emulated them, had time and tide permitted, we will retire to our private apartment; and you, Fleming, shall finish reading to us yonder little treatise *Des Rodomontades Espagnolles.*"

"Tarry, madam," said Lindesay, his complexion reddening in his turn; "I know your quick wit too well of old to have sought an interview that you might sharpen its edge at the expense of my honor. Lord Ruthven and myself, with Sir Robert Melville as a concurrent, come to your Grace on the part of the secret council, to tender to you what much concerns the safety of your own life and the welfare of the state."

"The secret council!" said the Queen. "By what powers can it subsist or act, while I, from whom it holds its character, am here detained under unjust restraint? But it matters not: what concerns the welfare of Scotland shall be acceptable to Mary Stuart, come from whatever quarter it will; and for what concerns her own life, she has lived long enough to be weary of it, even at the age of twenty-five. Where is your colleague, my lord; why tarries he?"

"He comes, madam," said Melville, and Lord Ruthven entered at the instant, holding in his hand a packet. As the Queen returned his salutation, she became deadly pale, bnt instantly recovered herself by dint of strong and sudden resolution, just as the noble, whose appearance seemed to excite such emotions in her bosom, entered the apartment in company with George Douglas, the youngest son of the Knight of Lochleven, who, during the absence of his father and brethren, acted as seneschal of the castle, under the direction of the elder Lady Lochleven, his father's mother.

CHAPTER XXII

I give this heavy weight from off my head,
And this unwieldy scepter from my hand;
With mine own tears I wash away my balm,
With my own hand I give away my crown,
With mine own tongue deny my sacred state,
With mine own breath release all duteous oaths.
Richard II.

Lord Ruthven had the look and bearing which became a soldier and a statesman, and the martial cast of his form and features procured him the popular epithet of Greystil, by which he was distinguished by his intimates, after the hero of a metrical romance then generally known. His dress, which was a buff coat embroidered, had a half-military character, but exhibited nothing of the sordid negligence which distinguished that of Lindesay. But the son of an ill-fated sire, and the father of a yet more unfortunate family, bore in his look that cast of inauspicious melancholy by which the physiognomists of that time pretended to distinguish those who were predestined to a violent and unhappy death.

The terror which the presence of this nobleman impressed on the Queen's mind arose from the active share he had borne in the slaughter of David Rizzio; his father having presided at the perpetration of that abominable crime, although so weak from long and wasting illness that he could not endure the weight of his armor, having arisen from a sick-bed to commit a murder in the presence of his sovereign. On that occasion his son also had attended and taken an active part. It was little to be wondered at that the Queen, considering her condition when such a deed of horror was acted in her presence, should retain an instinctive terror for the principal actors in the murder. She returned, however, with grace the salutation of Lord Ruthven, and extended her hand to George Douglas, who kneeled and kissed it with respect—the first mark of a subject's homage which Roland Græme had seen any of them render to the captive sovereign. She returned his greeting in silence, and there was a brief pause, during which the steward of the castle, a man of a sad brow and a severe eye, placed, under George Douglas's directions, a table and writing materials; and the page, obedient to his mistress's dumb signal, advanced a large chair to the side on which the Queen stood, the table thus forming a sort of bar which divided the Queen and her personal followers from her unwelcome visitors. The steward then withdrew, after a low reverence. When he had closed the door behind him, the Queen broke silence. "With favor, my lords, I will sit; my walks are not indeed extensive enough at present to fatigue me greatly, yet I find repose something more necessary than usual."

She sat down accordingly, and, shading her cheek with her beautiful hand, looked keenly and impressively at each of the nobles in turn. Mary Fleming applied her kerchief to her eyes, and Catherine Seyton and Roland Græme exchanged a glance, which showed that both were too deeply engrossed with sentiments of interest and commiseration for their royal mistress to think of anything which regarded themselves.

"I wait the purpose of your mission, my lords," said the Queen, after she had been seated for about a minute without a word being spoken—"I wait your message from those you call the secret council. I trust it is a petition of pardon, and a desire that I will resume my rightful throne, without using with due severity my right of punishing those who have dispossessed me of it?"

"Madam," replied Ruthven, "it is painful for us to speak harsh truths to a princess who has long ruled us. But we come to offer, not to implore, pardon. In a word, madam, we have to propose to you, on the part of the secret council, that you sign these deeds, which will contribute greatly to the pacification of the state, the advancement of God's Word, and the welfare of your own future life."

"Am I expected to take these fair words on trust, my lord? or may I hear the contents of these reconciling papers ere I am asked to sign them?"

"Unquestionably, madam; it is our purpose and wish you should read what you are required to sign," replied Ruthven.

"Required?" replied the Queen, with some emphasis; "but the phrase suits well the matter. Read, my lord."

The Lord Ruthven proceeded to read a formal instrument running in the Queen's name, and setting forth that she had been called, at an early age, to the administration of the crown and realm of Scotland, and had toiled diligently therein, until she was in body and spirit so wearied out and disgusted that she was unable any longer to endure the travail and pain of state affairs; and that, since God had blessed her with a fair and hopeful son, she was desirous to ensure to him, even while she yet lived, his succession to the crown, which was his by right of hereditary descent. "Wherefore," the instrument proceeded, "we, of the motherly affection we bear to our said son, have renounced and demitted, and, by these our letters of free good-will, renounce and demit, the crown, government, and guiding of the realm of Scotland, in favor of our said son, that he may succeed to us as native prince thereof, as much as if we had been removed by disease, and not by our own proper act. And that this dismission of our royal authority may have the more full and solemn effect, and none pretend ignorance, we give, grant, and commit full and free and plain power to our trusty cousins, Lord Lindesay of the Byres and William Lord Ruthven, to appear in our name before as many of the nobility, clergy, and burgesses as may be assembled at Stirling, and there, in our name and behalf, publicly, and in their presence, to renounce the crown, guidance, and government of this our kingdom of Scotland."

The Queen here broke in with an air of extreme surprise. "How is this, my lords?" she said. "Are my ears turned rebels, that they deceive me with sounds so extraordinary? And yet it is no wonder that, having conversed so long with rebelion, they should now force its language upon my understanding. Say I am mistaken, my lords—say, for the honor of yourselves and the Scottish nobility, that my right trusty cousins of Lindesay and Ruthven, two barons of warlike fame and ancient line, have not sought the prison-house of their kind mistress for such a purpose as these words seem to imply. Say, for the sake of honor and loyalty, that my ears have deceived me."

"No, madam," said Ruthven, gravely, "your ears do *not* deceive you; they deceived you when they were closed against the preachers of the Evangel, and the honest advice of your faithful subjects; and when they were ever open to flattery of pickthanks and traitors, foreign cubiculars and domestic minions. The land may no longer brook the rule of one who cannot rule herself; wherefore I pray you to comply with the last remaining wish of your subjects and counselors, and spare yourself and us the further agitation of matters so painful."

"And is this *all* my loving subjects require of me, my lord?" said Mary, in a tone of bitter irony. "Do they really stint themselves to the easy boon that I should yield up the crown, which is mine by birthright, to an infant which is scarcely more than a year old; fling down my scepter, and take up a distaff? O no! it is too little for them to ask. That other roll of parchment contains something harder to be compiled with, and which may more highly tax my readiness to comply with the petitions of my lieges."

"This parchment," answered Ruthven, in the same tone of inflexible gravity, and unfolding the instrument as he spoke, "is one by which your Grace constitutes your nearest in blood, and the most honorable and trustworthy of your subjects, James Earl of Murray, regent of the kingdom during the minority of the young King. He already holds the appointment from the secret council."

The Queen gave a sort of shriek, and clapping her hands together, exclaimed, "Comes the arrow out of his quiver?—out of my brother's bow? Alas! I looked for his return from France as my sole, at least my readiest, chance of deliverance. And yet, when I heard that he had assumed the government, I guessed he would shame to wield it in my name."

"I must pray your answer, madam," said Lord Ruthven, "to the demand of the council."

"The demand of the council!" said the Queen; "say rather the demand of a set of robbers, impatient to divide the spoil they have seized. To such a demand, and sent by the mouth of a traitor, whose scalp, but for my womanish mercy, should long since have stood on the city gates, Mary of Scotland has no answer."

"I trust, madam," said Lord Ruthven, "my being unacceptable to your presence will not add to your obduracy of resolution. It may become you to remember that the death of the minion, Rizzio, cost the house of Ruthven its head and leader. My father, more worthy than a whole province of such vile sycophants, died in exile, and broken-hearted."

The Queen clasped her hands on her face, and, resting her arms on the table, stooped down her head and wept so bitterly that the tears were seen to find their way in streams between the white and slender fingers with which she endeavored to conceal them.

"My lords," said Sir Robert Melville, "this is too much rigor. Under your lordships' favor, we came hither, not to revive old griefs, but to find the mode of avoiding new ones."

"Sir Robert Melville," said Ruthven, "we best know for what purpose we were delegated hither, and wherefore you were somewhat unnecessarily sent to attend us."

"Nay, by my hand," said Lord Lindesay, "I know not why we were cumbered with the good knight, unless he comes in place of the lump of sugar which pothicars put into their wholesome but bitter medicaments, to please a froward child—a needless labor, methinks, where men have the means to make them swallow the physic otherwise."

"Nay, my lords," said Melville, "ye best know your own secret instructions. I conceive I shall best obey mine in striving to mediate between her Grace and you."

"Be silent, Sir Robert Melville," said the Queen, arising, and her face still glowing with agitation as she spoke. "My kerchief, Fleming; I shame that traitors should have power to move me thus. Tell me, proud lords," she added, wiping away the tears as she spoke, "by what earthly warrant can liege subjects pretend to challenge the rights of an anointed sovereign, to throw off the allegiance they have vowed, and to take away the crown from the head on which Divine warrant had placed it?"

"Madam," said Ruthven, "I will deal plainly with you. Your reign, from the dismal field of Pinkie Cleuch, when you were a babe in the cradle, till now that ye stand a grown dame before us, hath been such a tragedy of losses, disasters, civil dissensions, and foreign wars that the like is not to be found in our chronicles. The French and English have, with one consent, made Scotland the battlefield on which to fight out their own ancient quarrel. For ourselves, every man's hand hath been against his brother, nor hath a year passed over without rebellion and slaughter, exile of nobles, and oppressing of the commons. We may endure it no longer; and, therefore, as a prince to whom God hath refused the gift of hearkening to wise counsel, and on whose dealings and projects no blessing hath ever descended, we pray you to give way to other rule and governance of the land, that a remnant may yet be saved to this distracted realm."

"My lord," said Mary, "it seems to me that you fling on my unhappy and devoted head those evils which, with far more justice, I may impute to your own turbulent, wild, and untamable dispositions: the frantic violence with which you, the magnates of Scotland, enter into feuds against each other, sticking at no cruelty to gratify your wrath, taking deep revenge for the slightest offenses, and setting at defiance those wise laws which your ancestors made for stanching of such cruelty, rebelling against the lawful authority, and bearing yourselves as if there were no king in the land, or rather as if each were king in his own premises. And now you throw the blame on me—on me, whose life has been embittered—whose sleep has been broken—whose happiness has been wrecked, by your dissensions. Have I not myself been obliged to traverse wilds and mountains, at the head of a few faithful followers, to maintain peace and to put down oppression? Have I not worn harness on my person, and carried pistols at my saddle; fain to lay aside the softness of a woman, and the dignity of a queen, that I might show an example to my followers?"

"We grant, madam," said Lindesay, "that the affrays occasioned by your misgovernment may sometimes have startled you in the midst of a masque or galliard; or it may be that such may have interrupted the idolatry of the mass, or the Jesuitical counsels of some French ambassador. But the longest and severest journey which your Grace has taken in my memory was from Hawick to Hermitage Castle; and whether it was for the weal of the state, or for your own honor, rests with your Grace's conscience."

The Queen turned to him with inexpressible sweetness of tone and manner, and that engaging look which Heaven had assigned her, as if to show that the choicest arts to win men's affections may be given in vain. "Lindesay," she said, "you spoke not to me in this stern tone, and with such scurril taunt, yon fair summer evening, when you and I shot at the butts against the Earl of Mar and Mary Livingstone, and won of them the evening's collation, in the privy garden of St. Andrews. The Master of Lindesay was then my friend, and vowed to be my soldier. How I have offended the Lord of Lindesay I know not, unless honors have changed manners."

Hard-hearted as he was, Lindesay seemed struck with this unexpected appeal, but almost instantly replied, "Madam, it is well known that your Grace could in those days make fools of whomever approached you. I pretend not to have been wiser than others. But gayer men and better courtiers soon jostled aside my rude homage, and I think your Grace cannot but remember times when my awkward attempts to take the manners that pleased you were the sport of the court popinjays, the Maries and the Frenchwomen."

"My lord, I grieve if I have offended you through idle gaiety," said the Queen, "and can but say it was most unwittingly done. You are fully revenged; for through gaiety," she said with a sigh, "will I never offend any one more."

"Our time is wasting, madam," said Lord Ruthven; "I must pray your decision on this weighty matter which I have submitted to you."

"What, my lord!" said the Queen, "upon the instant, and without a moment's time to deliberate? Can the council, as they term themselves, expect this of me?"

"Madam," replied Ruthven, "the council hold the opinion that, since the fatal term which passed betwixt the night of King Henry's murder and the day of Carberry Hill, your Grace should have held you prepared for the measure now proposed, as the easiest escape from your numerous dangers and difficulties."

"Great God!" exclaimed the Queen; "and is it as a boon that you propose to me, what every Christian king ought to regard as a loss of honor equal to the loss of life! You take from me my crown, my power, my subjects, my wealth, my state. What, in the name of every saint, can you offer, or do you offer, in requital of my compliance?"

"We give you pardon," answered Ruthven, sternly; "we give you space and means to spend your remaining life in penitence and seclusion; we give you time to make your peace with Heaven, and to receive the pure Gospel, which you have ever rejected and persecuted."

The Queen turned pale at the menace which this speech, as well as the rough and inflexible tones of the speaker, seemed distinctly to infer. "And if I do not comply with your request so fiercely urged, my lord, what then follows?"

She said this in a voice in which female and natural fear was contending with the feelings of insulted dignity. There was a pause, as if no one cared to return to the question a distinct answer. At length Ruthven spoke. "There is little need to tell to your Grace, who are well read both in the laws and in the chronicles of the realm, that murder and adultery are crimes for which ere now queens themselves have suffered death."

"And where, my lord, or how, found you an accusation so horrible against her who stands before you?" said Queen Mary. "The foul and odious calumnies which have poisoned the general mind of Scotland, and have placed me a helpless prisoner in your hands, are surely no proof of guilt?"

"We need look for no further proof," replied the stern Lord Ruthven, "than the shameless marriage betwixt the widow of the murdered and the leader of the band of murderers! They that joined hands in the fated month of May had already united hearts and counsel in the deed which preceeded that marriage but a few brief weeks."

"My lord—my lord," said the Queen, eagerly, "remember well there were more consents than mine to that fatal union—that most unhappy act of a most unhappy life. The evil steps adonted by sovereigns are often the suggestion of bad counselors; but these counselors are worse than fiends who tempt and betray, if they themselves are the first to call their unfortunate princes to answer for the consequences of their own advice. Heard ye never of a bond by the nobles, my lords, recommending that ill-fated union to the ill-fated Mary? Methinks, were it carefully examined, we should see that the names of Morton, and of Lindesay, and of Ruthven may be found in that bond, which pressed me to marry that unhappy man. Ah! stout and loyal Lord Herries, who never knew guile or dishonor, you bent your noble knee to me in vain, to warn me of my danger, and wert yet the first to draw thy good sword in my cause when I suffered for neglecting thy counsel! Faithful knight and true noble, what a difference betwixt thee and those counselors of evil who now threaten my life for having fallen into the snares they spread for me!"

"Madam," said Ruthven, "we know that you are an orator; and perhaps for that reason the council has sent hither men whose converse hath been more with the wars than with the language of the schools or the cabals of state. We but desire to know if, on assurance of life and honor, ye will demit the rule of this kingdom of Scotland?"

"And what warrant have I," said the Queen, "that ye will keep that treaty with me, if I should barter my kingly estate for seclusion and leave to weep in secret?"

"Our honor and our word, madam," answered Ruthven.

"They are too slight and unsolid pledges, my lord," said the Queen; "add at least a handful of thistle-down to give them weight in the balance."

"Away, Ruthven," said Lindesay; "she was ever deaf to counsel, save of slaves and sycophants: let her remain by her refusal, and abide by it!"

"Stay, my lord," said Sir Robert Melville, "or rather permit me to have but a few minutes' private audience with her Grace. If my presence with you could avail aught, it must be as a mediator; do not, I conjure you, leave the castle, or break off the conference, until I bring you word how her Grace shall finally stand disposed."

"We will remain in the hall," said Lindesay, "for half an hour's space; but in despising our words and our pledge of honor, she has touched the honor of my name: let her look herself to the course she has to pursue. If the half-hour should pass away without her determining to comply with the demands of the nation, her career will be brief enough."

With little ceremony the two nobles left the apartment, traversed the vestibule, and descended the winding stairs, the clash of Lindesay's huge sword being heard as it rang against each step in his descent. George Douglas followed them, after exchanging with Melville a gesture of surprise and sympathy.

As soon as they were gone, the Queen, giving way to grief, fear, and agitation, threw herself into the seat, wrung her hands, and seemed to abandon herself to despair. Her female attendants, weeping themselves, endeavored yet to pray her to be composed, and Sir Robert Melville, kneeling at her feet, made the same entreaty. After giving way to a passionate burst of sorrow, she at length said to Melville, "Kneel not to me, Melville—mock me not with the homage of the person, when the heart is far away. Why stay you behind with the deposed—the condemned?—her who has but few hours perchance to live? You have been favored as well as the rest; why do you continue the empty show of gratitude and thankfulness any longer than they?"

"Madam," said Sir Robert Melville, "so help me Heaven at my need, my heart is as true to you as when you were in your highest place."

"True to me!—true to me!" repeated the Queen, with some scorn; "tush, Melville, what signifies the truth which walks hand in hand with my enemies' falsehood? Thy hand and thy sword have never been so well acquainted that I can trust thee in aught where manhood is required. O, Seyton, for thy bold father, who is both wise, true, and valiant!"

Roland Græme could withstand no longer his earnest desire to offer his services to a princess so distressed and so beautiful. "If one sword," he said, "madam, can do anything to back the wisdom of this grave counselor, or to defend your rightful cause, here is my weapon, and here is my hand ready to draw and use it." And raising his sword with one hand, he laid the other upon the hilt.

As he thus held up the weapon, Catherine Seyton exclaimed, "Methinks I see a token from my father, madam;"

and immediately crossing the apartment, she took Roland Græme by the skirt of the cloak, and asked him earnestly whence he had that sword.

"The page answered with surprise, "Methinks this is no presence in which to jest. Surely, damsel, you yourself best know whence and how I obtained the weapon."

"Is this a time for folly ?" said Catherine Seyton. "Unsheathe the sword instantly !"

"If the Queen commands me," said the youth, looking towards his royal mistress.

"For shame, maiden !" said the Queen ; "wouldst thou instigate the poor boy to enter into useless strife with the two most approved soldiers in Scotland ?"

"In your Grace's cause," replied the page, "I will venture my life upon them !" And as he spoke he drew his weapon partly from the sheath, and a piece of parchment, rolled around the blade, fell out and dropped on the floor.

Catherine Seyton caught it up with eager haste. "It is my father's handwriting," she said, "and doubtless conveys his best duteous advice to your Majesty ; I knew that it was prepared to be sent in this weapon, but I expected another messenger."

"By my faith, fair one," thought Roland, "and if you knew not that I had such a secret missive about me, I was yet more ignorant."

The Queen cast her eye upon the scroll, and remained a few minutes wrapped in deep thought. "Sir Robert Melville," she at length said, "this scroll advises me to submit myself to necessity, and to subscribe the deeds these hard men have brought with them, as one who gives way to the natural fear inspired by the threats of rebels and murderers. You, Sir Robert, are a wise man, and Seyton is both sagacious and brave. Neither, I think, would mislead me in this matter."

"Madam," said Melville, "if I have not the strength of body of the Lords Herries or Seyton, I will yield to neither in zeal for your Majesty's service. I cannot fight for you like these lords, but neither of them is more willing to die for your service."

"I believe it, my old and faithful counselor," said the Queen, "and believe me, Melville, I did thee but a moment's injustice. Read what my Lord Seyton hath written to us, and give us thy best counsel."

He glanced over the parchment, and instantly replied, "O ! my dear and royal mistress, only treason itself could give you other advice than Lord Seyton has here expressed. He, Herries, Huntly, the English ambassador Throgmorton, and others, your friends, are all alike of opinion that whatever deeds or instruments you execute within these walls must lose all force and effect, as extorted from your Grace by duress, by sufferance of present evil, and fear of men, and harm to ensue on your refusal. Yield, therefore, to the tide, and be assured that, in subscribing what parchments they present to you, you bind yourself to nothing, since your act of signature wants that which alone can make it valid, the free will of the grantor."

"Ay, so says my Lord Seyton," replied Mary; "yet methinks, for the daughter of so long a line of sovereigns to resign her birthright, because rebels press upon her with threats, argues little of royalty, and will read ill for the fame of Mary in future chronicles. Tush! Sir Robert Melville, the traitors may use black threats and bold words, but they will not dare to put their hands forth on our person?"

"Alas! madam, they have already dared so far, and incurred such peril by the lengths which they have gone, that they are but one step from the worst and uttermost."

"Surely," said the Queen, her fears again predominating, "Scottish nobles would not lend themselves to assassinate a helpless woman?"

"Bethink you, madam," he replied, "what horrid spectacles have been seen in our day; and what act is so dark that some Scottish hand has not been found to dare it? Lord Lindesay, besides his natural sullenness and hardness of temper, is the near kinsman of Henry Darnley, and Ruthven has his own deep and dangerous plans. The council, besides, speak of proofs by writ and word, of a casket with letters—of I know not what."

"Ah! good Melville," answered the Queen, "were I as sure of the even-handed integrity of my judges as of my own innocence—and yet——"

"Oh! pause, madam," said Melville; "even innocence must sometimes for a season stoop to injurious blame. Besides, you are here——"

He looked round and paused.

"Speak out, Melville," said the Queen, "never one approached my person who wished to work me evil; and even this poor page, whom I have to-day seen for the first time in my life, I can trust safely with your communication."

"Nay, madam," answered Melville, "in such emergence, and he being the bearer of Lord Seyton's message, I will venture to say before him and these fair ladies, whose truth and fidelity I dispute not—I say, I will venture to say, that there are other modes besides that of open trial by which deposed sovereigns often die; and that, as Machiavel saith, there is but one step betwixt a king's prison and his grave."

"Oh! were it but swift and easy for the body," said the unfortunate princess, "were it but a safe and happy change for the soul, the woman lives not that would take the step so soon as I! But, alas! Melville, when we think of death, a thousand sins, which we have trod as worms beneath our feet, rise up against us as flaming serpents. Most injuriously do they accuse me of aiding Darnley's death; yet, blessed Lady! I afforded too open occasion for the suspicion; I espoused Bothwell."

"Think not of that now, madam," said Melville, "think rather of the immediate mode of saving yourself and son. Comply with the present unreasonable demands, and trust that better times will shortly arrive."

"Madam," said Roland Græme, "if it pleases you that I should do so, I will presently swim through the lake, if they refuse me other conveyance to the shore; I will go to the courts successively of England, France, and Spain, and will show you have subscribed these vile instruments from no stronger impulse than the fear of death, and I will do battle against them that say otherwise."

The Queen turned her round, and with one of those sweet smiles which, during the era of life's romance, overpay every risk, held her hand towards Roland, but without speaking a word. He kneeled reverently and kissed it, and Melville again resumed his plea.

"Madam," he said, "time presses, and you must not let those boats, which I see they are even now preparing, put forth on the lake. Here are enough of witnesses—your ladies—this bold youth—myself, when it can serve your cause effectually, for I would not hastily stand committed in this matter; but even without me here is evidence enough to show that you have yielded to the demands of the council through force and fear, but from no sincere and unconstrained assent. Their boats are already manned for their return; oh! permit your old servant to recall them!"

"Melville," said the Queen, "thou art an ancient courtier; when didst thou ever know a sovereign prince recall to his presence subjects who had parted from him on such terms as those on which these envoys of the council left us, and who yet were recalled without submission or apology? Let it cost me both life and crown, I will not again command them to my presence."

"Alas! madam, that empty form should make a barrier! If I rightly understand, you are not unwilling to listen to real and advantageous counsel; but your scruple is saved, I hear them returning to ask your final resolution. O! take the advice of the noble Seyton, and you may once more command those who now usurp a triumph over you. But hush! I hear them in the vestibule."

As he concluded speaking, George Douglas opened the door of the apartment, and marshaled in the two noble envoys.

"We come, madam," said the Lord Ruthven, "to request your answer to the proposal of the council."

"Your final answer," said Lord Lindesay; "for with a refusal you must couple the certainty that you have precipitated your fate, and renounced the last opportunity of making peace with God, and ensuring your longer abode in the world."

"My lords," said Mary, with inexpressible grace and dignity, "the evils we cannot resist we must submit to: I will subscribe these parchments with such liberty of choice as my condition permits me. Were I on yonder shore, with a fleet jennet and ten good and loyal knights around me, I would subscribe my sentence of eternal condemnation as soon as the resignation of my throne. But here, in the Castle of Lochleven, with deep water around me, and you, my lords, beside me, I have no freedom of choice. Give me the pen, Melville, and bear witness to what I do, and why I do it."

"It is our hope your Grace will not suppose yourself compelled, by any apprehensions from us," said the Lord Ruthven, "to execute what must be your own voluntary deed."

The Queen had already stooped towards the table, and placed the parchment before her, with the pen between her fingers, ready for the important act of signature. But when Lord Ruthven had done speaking, she looked up, stopped short, and threw down the pen. "If," she said, "I am expected to declare I give away my crown of free will, or otherwise than because I am compelled to renounce it by the threat of worse evils to myself and my subjects, I will not put my name to such an untruth—not to gain full possession of England, France, and Scotland! all once my own, in possession, or by right."

"Beware, madam," said Lindesay, and, snatching hold of the Queen's arm with his own gauntleted hand, he pressed it, in the rudeness of his passion, more closely, perhaps, than he was himself aware of—"beware how you contend with those who are the stronger, and have the mastery of your fate!"

He held his grasp on her arm, bending his eyes on her with a stern and intimidating look, till both Ruthven and Melville cried "Shame!" and Douglas, who had hitherto remained in a state of apparent apathy, had made a stride from the door, as if to interfere. The rude baron then quitted his hold, disguising the confusion which he really felt at having indulged his passion to such an extent under a sullen and contemptuous smile.

The Queen immediately began, with an expression of pain, to bare the arm which he had grasped, by drawing up the sleeve of her gown, and it appeared that his gripe had left the purple marks of his iron fingers upon her flesh. "My lord," she said, "as a knight and a gentleman, you might have spared my frail arm so severe a proof that you have the greater strength on your side, and are resolved to use it. But I thank you for it—it is the most decisive token of the terms on which this day's business is to rest. I draw you to witness, both lords and ladies," she said, showing the marks of the grasp on her arm, "that I subscribe these instruments in obedience to the sign-manual of my Lord of Lindesay, which you may see imprinted on mine arm." *

Lindesay would have spoken, but was restrained by his colleague Ruthven, who said to him, "Peace, my Lord. Let the Lady Mary of Scotland ascribe her signature to what she will, it is our business to procure it, and carry it to the council. Should there be debate hereafter on the manner in which it was adhibited, there will be time enough for it."

Lindesay was silent accordingly, only muttering within his beard. "I meant not to hurt her; but I think women's flesh be as tender as new-fallen snow."

The Queen meanwhile subscribed the rolls of parchment with a hasty indifference, as if they had been matters of slight consequence, or of mere formality. When she had performed this painful task, she arose, and, having courtesied to the lords, was about to withdraw to her chamber. Ruthven and Sir Robert Melville made, the first a formal reverence, the second an obeisance, in which his desire to acknowledge his sympathy was obviously checked by the fear of appearing in the eyes of his colleagues too partial to his former mistress. But Lindesay stood motionless, even when they were preparing to withdraw. At length, as if moved by a sudden im-

* See The Resignation of Queen Mary. Note 16.

"'Beware, Madam!' said Lindesay, snatching hold of the Queen's arm."

pulse, he walked round the table which had hitherto been betwixt them and the Queen, kneeled on one knee, took her hand, kissed it, let it fall, and arose. "Lady," he said, "thou art a noble creature, even though thou hast abused God's choicest gifts. I pay that devotion to thy manliness of spirit which I would not have paid to the power thou hast long undeservedly wielded: I kneel to Mary Stuart, not to the Queen."

"The Queen and Mary Stuart pity thee alike, Lindesay," said Mary—"alike they pity, and they forgive thee. An honored soldier hadst thou been by a king's side; leagued with rebels, what art thou but a good blade in the hands of a ruffian? Farewell, my Lord Ruthven, the smoother but the deeper traitor. Farewell, Melville. Mayst thou find masters that can understand state policy better, and have the means to reward it more richly, than Mary Stuart! Farewell, George of Douglas; make your respected grand-dame comprehend that we would be alone for the remainder of the day, God wot, we have need to collect our thoughts."

All bowed and withdrew; but scarce had they entered the vestibule ere Ruthven and Lindesay were at variance. "Chide not with me, Ruthven," Lindesay was heard to say in answer to something more indistinctly urged by his colleague—"chide not with me, for I will not brook it! You put the hangman's office on me in this matter, and even the very hangman hath leave to ask some pardon of those on whom he does his office. I would I had as deep cause to be this lady's friend as I have to be her enemy: thou shouldst see if I spared limb and life in her quarrel."

"Thou art a sweet minion," said Ruthven, "to fight a lady's quarrel, and all for a brent brow and a tear in the eye! Such toys have been out of thy thoughts this many a year."

"Do me right, Ruthven," said Lindesay. "You are like a polished corslet of steel: it shines more gaudily, but it is not a whit softer—nay, it is five times harder—than a Glasgow breast-plate of hammered iron. Enough. We know each other."

They descended the stairs, were heard to summon their boats, and the Queen signed to Roland Græme to retire to the vestibule, and leave her with her female attendants.

CHAPTER XXIII

> Give me a morsel on the greensward rather,
> Coarse as you will the cooking. Let the fresh spring
> Bubble beside my napkin, and the free birds,
> Twittering and chirping, hop from bough to bough,
> To claim the crumbs I leave for perquisites;
> Your prison-feasts I like not.
>
> *The Woodsman, a Drama.*

A RECESS in the vestibule was enlightened by a small window, at which Roland Græme stationed himself to mark the departure of the lords. He could see their followers mustering on horseback under their respective banners, the western sun glancing on their corslets and steel caps as they moved to and fro, mounted or dismounted, at intervals. On the narrow space betwixt the castle and the water, the Lords Ruthven and Lindesay were already moving slowly to their boats, accompanied by the Lady of Lochleven, her grandson, and their principal attendants. They took a ceremonious leave of each other, as Roland could discern by their gestures, and the boats put off from their landing-place; the boatmen stretched to their oars, and they speedily diminished upon the eye of the idle gazer, who had no better employment than to watch their motions. Such seemed also the occupation of the Lady Lochleven and George Douglas, who, returning from the landing-place, looked frequently back to the boats, and at length stopped, as if to observe their progress, under the window at which Roland Græme was stationed. As they gazed on the lake, he could hear the lady distinctly say, "And she has bent her mind to save her life at the expense of her kingdom?"

"Her life, madam!" replied her son; "I know not who would dare to attempt it in the castle of my father. Had I dreamt that it was with such purpose that Lindesay insisted on bringing his followers hither, neither he nor they should have passed the iron gate of Lochleven Castle."

"I speak not of private slaughter, my son, but of open trial, condemnation, and execution; for with such she has been threatened, and to such threats she has given way. Had she not more of the false Guisian blood than of the royal race of Scotland in her veins, she had bidden them defiance to their teeth. But it is all of the same complexion, and meanness is the natural companion of profligacy. I am discharged, forsooth, from intruding on her gracious presence this evening. Go thou, my son, and render the usual service of the meal to this unqueened queen."

"So please you, lady mother," said Douglas, "I care not greatly to approach her presence."

"Thou art right, my son; and therefore I trust thy prudence, even because I have noted thy caution. She is like an isle on the ocean, surrounded with shelves and quicksands: its verdure fair and inviting to the eye, but the wreck of many a goodly vessel which had approached it too rashly. But for thee, my son, I fear nought; and we may not, with our honor, suffer her to eat without the attendance of one of us. She may die by the judgment of Heaven, or the fiend may have power over her in her despair; and then we would be touched in honor to show that, in our house, and at our table, she had had all fair play and fitting usage."

Here Roland was interrupted by a smart tap on the shoulders reminding him sharply of Adam Woodcock's adventure of the preceding evening. He turned round, almost expecting to see the page of St. Michael's hostelry. He saw, indeed, Catherine Seyton; but she was in female attire, differing, no doubt, a great deal in shape and materials from that which she had worn when they first met, and becoming her birth as the daughter of a great baron, and her rank as the attendant on a princess. "So, fair page," said she, "eavesdropping is one of your page-like qualities, I presume?"

"Fair sister," answered Roland, in the same tone, "if some friends of mine be as well acquainted with the rest of our mystery as they are with the arts of swearing, swaggering, and switching, they need ask no page in Christendom for further insight into his vocation."

"Unless that pretty speech infer that you have yourself had the discipline of the switch since we last met, the probability whereof I nothing doubt, I profess, fair page, I am at a loss to conjecture your meaning. But there is no time to debate it now—they come with the evening meal. Be pleased, sir page, to do your duty."

Four servants entered bearing dishes, preceded by the same stern old steward whom Roland had already seen, and followed by George Douglas, already mentioned as the grandson of the Lady of Lochleven, and who, acting as seneschal, represented upon this occasion his father, the lord of the castle.

He entered with his arms folded on his bosom, and his looks bent on the ground. With the assistance of Roland Græme, a table was suitably covered in the next or middle apartment, on which the domestics placed their burdens with great reverence, the steward and Douglas bending low when they had seen the table properly adorned, as if their royal prisoner had sat at the board in question. The door opened, and Douglas, raising his eyes hastily, cast them again on the earth, when he perceived it was only the Lady Mary Fleming who entered.

"Her Grace," she said, "will not eat to-night."

"Let us hope she may be otherwise persuaded," said Douglas; "meanwhile, madam, please to see our duty performed."

A servant presented bread and salt on a silver plate, and the old steward carved for Douglas a small morsel in succession from each of the dishes presented, which he tasted, as was then the custom at the tables of princes, to which death was often suspected to find its way in the disguise of food.

"The Queen will not then come forth to-night?" said Douglas.

"She has so determined," replied the lady.

"Our further attendance then is unnecessary: we leave you to your supper, fair ladies, and wish you good even."

He retired slowly as he came, and with the same air of deep dejection, and was followed by the attendants belonging to the castle. The two ladies sate down to their meal, and Roland Græme, with ready alacrity, prepared to wait upon them. Catherine Seyton whispered to her companion, who replied with the question, spoken in a low tone, but looking at the page—"Is he of gentle blood and well nurtured?"

The answer which she received seemed satisfactory, for she said to Roland, "Sit down, young gentleman, and eat with your sisters in captivity."

"Permit me rather to perform my duty in attending them," said Roland, anxious to show he was possessed of the high tone of deference prescribed by the rules of chivalry towards the fair sex, and especially to dames and maidens of quality.

"You will find, sir page," said Catherine, "you will have little time allowed you for your meal; waste it not in ceremony, or you may rue your politeness ere to-morrow morning."

"Your speech is too free, maiden," said the elder lady; "the modesty of the youth may teach you more fitting fashions towards one whom to-day you have seen for the first time."

Catherine Seyton cast down her eyes, but not till she had given a single glance of inexpressible archness towards Roland, whom her more grave companion now addressed in a tone of protection.

"Regard her not, young gentleman; she knows little of the world, save the forms of a country nunnery; take thy place at the board-end, and refresh thyself after thy journey."

Roland Græme obeyed willingly, as it was the first food he had that day tasted; for Lindesay and his followers seemed regardless of human wants. Yet, notwithstanding the sharpness of his appetite, a natural gallantry of disposition, the desire of showing himself a well-nurtured gentleman in all courtesies towards the fair sex, and, for aught I know, the pleasure of assisting Catherine Seyton, kept his attention awake, during the meal, to all those nameless acts of duty and service which gallants of that age were accustomed to render. He carved with neatness and decorum, and selected duly whatever was most delicate to place before the ladies. Ere they could form a wish, he sprung from the table ready to comply with it—poured wine—tempered it with water—removed and exchanged trenchers, and performed the whole honors of the table, with an air at once of cheerful diligence, profound respect, and graceful promptitude.

When he observed that they had finished eating, he hastened to offer to the elder lady the silver ewer, basin, and napkin, with the ceremony and gravity which he would have used towards Mary herself. He next, with the same decorum, having supplied the basin with fair water, presented it to Catherine Seyton. Apparently she was determined to disturb his self-possession if possible; for, while in the act of bathing her hands, she contrived, as it were by accident, to flirt some drops of water upon the face of the assiduous assistant. But if such was her mischievous purpose she was completely disappointed; for Roland Græme, internally piquing himself on his self-command, neither laughed nor was discomposed; and all that the maiden gained by her frolic was a severe rebuke from her companion, taxing her with mal-address and indecorum. Catherine replied not, but sat pouting, something in the humor of a spoilt child, who watches the opportunity of wreaking upon some one or other its resentment for a deserved reprimand.

The Lady Mary Fleming, in the meanwhile, was naturally well pleased with the exact and reverent observance of the page, and said to Catherine, after a favorable glance at Roland Græme, "You might well say, Catherine, our companion in captivity was well born and gently nurtured. I would not make him vain by my praise, but his services enable us to dispense with those which George Douglas condescends not to afford us, save when the Queen is herself in presence."

"Umph! I think hardly," answered Catherine. "George Douglas is one of the most handsome gallants in Scotland, and 'tis pleasure to see him even still, when the gloom of Lochleven Castle has shed the same melancholy over him that it has done over everything else. When he was at Holyrood, who would have said the young sprightly George Douglas would have been contented to play the locksman here in Lochleven, with no gayer amusement than that of turning the key on two or three helpless women? A strange office for a knight of the bleeding heart; why does he not leave it to his father or his brothers?"

"Perhaps, like us, he has no choice," answered the Lady Fleming. "But, Catherine, thou hast used thy brief space at court well, to remember what George Douglas was then."

"I used mine eyes, which I suppose was what I was designed to do, and they were worth using there. When I was at the nunnery, they were very useless appurtenances; and now I am at Lochleven, they are good for nothing, save to look over that eternal work of embroidery."

"You speak thus, when you have been but a few brief hours amongst us: was this the maiden who would live and die in a dungeon, might she but have permission to wait on her gracious queen?"

"Nay, if you chide in earnest, my jest is ended," said Catherine Seyton. "I would not yield in attachment to my poor godmother to the gravest dame that ever had wise saws upon her tongue, and a double-starched ruff around her throat—you know I would not, Dame Mary Fleming, and it is putting shame on me to say otherwise."

"She will challenge the other court lady," thought Roland Græme—"she will to a certainty fling down her glove, and if Dame Mary Fleming hath but the soul to lift it, we may have a combat in the lists!" But the answer of Lady Mary Fleming was such as turns away wrath.

"Thou art a good child," she said, "my Catherine, and a faithful; but Heaven pity him who shall have one day a creature so beautiful to delight him, and a thing so mischievous to torment him: thou art fit to drive twenty husbands stark mad."

"Nay," said Catherine, resuming the full career of her careless good-humor, "he must be half-witted beforehand that gives me such an opportunity. But I am glad you are not angry with me in sincerity," casting herself as she spoke into the arms of her friend, and continuing, with a tone of apologetic fondness, while she kissed her on either side of the face—"You know, my dear Fleming, that I have to contend with both my father's lofty pride and with my mother's high spirit. God bless them! they have left me these good qualities, having small portion to give besides, as times go; and so I am wilful and saucy; but let me remain only a week in this castle, and O, my dear Fleming, my spirit will be as chastised and as humble as thine own."

Dame Mary Fleming's sense of dignity, and love of form, could not resist this affectionate appeal. She kissed Catherine Seyton in her turn affectionately; while, answering the last part of her speech, she said, "Now, Our Lady forbid, dear Catherine, that you should lose aught that is beseeming of what becomes so well your light heart and lively humor. Keep but your sharp wit on this side of madness, and it cannot but be a blessing to us. But let me go, mad wench—I hear her Grace touch her silver call." And, extricating herself from Catherine's grasp, she went towards the door of Queen Mary's apartment, from which was heard the low tone of a silver whistle, which, now only used by the boatswains in the navy, was then, for want of bells, the ordinary mode by which ladies, even of the very highest rank, summoned their domestics. When she had made two or three steps towards the door, however, she turned back, and advancing to the young couple whom she left together, she said, in a very serious though a low tone, "I trust it is impossible that we can, any of us, or in any circumstances, forget that, few as we are, we form the household of the Queen of Scotland; and that, in her calamity, all boyish mirth and childish jesting can only serve to give a great triumph to her enemies, who have already found their account in objecting to her the lightness of every idle folly that the young and the gay practised in her court." So saying, she left the apartment.

Catherine Seyton seemed much struck with this remonstrance. She suffered herself to drop into the seat which she had quitted when she went to embrace Dame Mary Fleming, and for some time rested her brow upon her hands;

while Roland Græme looked at her earnestly, with a mixture of emotions which perhaps he himself could neither have analyzed nor explained. As she raised her face slowly from the posture to which a momentary feeling of self-rebuke had depressed it, her eyes encountered those of Roland, and became gradually animated with their usual spirit of malicious drollery, which not unnaturally excited a similar expression in those of the equally volatile page. They sat for the space of two minutes, each looking at the other with great seriousness on their features, and much mirth in their eyes, until at length Catherine was the first to break silence.

"May I pray you, fair sir," she began, very demurely, "to tell me what you see in my face to arouse looks so extremely sagacious and knowing as those with which it is your worship's pleasure to honor me? It would seem as there were some wonderful confidence and intimacy betwixt us, fair sir, if one is to judge from your extremely cunning looks; and so help me, Our Lady, as I never saw you but twice in my life before."

"And where were those happy occasions," said Roland, "if I may be bold enough to ask the question?"

"At the nunnery of St. Catherine's," said the damsel, "in the first instance; and, in the second, during five minutes of a certain raid or foray which it was your pleasure to make into the lodging of my lord and father, Lord Seyton, from which, to my surprise, as probably to your own, you returned with a token of friendship and favor instead of broken bones, which were the more probable reward of your intrusion, considering the prompt ire of the house of Seyton. I am deeply mortified," she added, ironically, "that your recollection should require refreshment on a subject so important; and that my memory should be stronger than yours on such an occasion is truly humiliating."

"Your own memory is not so exactly correct, fair mistress," answered the page, "seeing you have forgotten meeting the third, in the hostelry of St. Michael's when it pleased you to lay your switch across the face of my comrade, in order, I warrant, to show that, in the house of Seyton, neither the prompt ire of its descendants, nor the use of the doublet and hose, are subject to Salique law, or confined to the use of the males."

"Fair sir," answered Catherine, looking at him with great steadiness and some surprise, "unless your fair wits have forsaken you, I am at a loss what to conjecture of your meaning."

"By my troth, fair mistress," answered Roland, "and were I as wise a warlock as Michael Scott, I could scarce riddle the dream you read me. Did I not see you last night in the hostelry of St. Michael's? Did you not bring me this sword, with command not to draw it save at the command of my native and rightful sovereign? And have I not done as you required me? Or is the sword a piece of lath, my word a bulrush, my memory a dream, and my eyes good for nought—espials which corbies might pick out of my head?"

"And if your eyes serve you not more truly on other occasions than in your vision of St. Michael," said Catherine, "I know not, the pain apart, that the corbies would do you any great injury in the deprivation. But hark, the bell; hush, for God's sake, we are interrupted——"

The damsel was right; for no sooner had the dull toll of the castle bell begun to resound through the vaulted apartment than the door of the vestibule flew open, and the steward with his severe countenance, his gold chain, and his white rod, entered the apartment, followed by the same train of domestics who had placed the dinner on the table, and who now, with the same ceremonious formality began to remove it.

The steward remained motionless as some old picture, while the domestics did their office; and when it was accomplished, everything removed from the table, and the board itself taken from its tressels and disposed against the wall, he said aloud, without addressing any one in particular, and somewhat in the tone of a herald reading a proclamation, "My noble lady, Dame Margaret Erskine, by marriage Douglas, lets the Lady Mary of Scotland and her attendants to wit, that a servant of the true Evangel, her reverend chaplain, will to-night, as usual, expound, lecture, and catechise, according to the forms of the congregation of Gospellers."

"Hark you, my friend, Mr. Dryfesdale," said Catherine, "I understand this announcement is a nightly form of yours. Now, I pray you to remark, that the Lady of Fleming and I—for I trust your insolent invitation concerns us only—have chosen St. Peter's pathway to Heaven; so I see no one whom your godly exhortation, catechise, or lecture can benefit, excepting this poor page, who, being in Satan's hand as well as yourself, had better worship with you than remain to cumber our better advised devotions."

The page was wellnigh giving a round denial to the assertions which this speech implied, when, remembering what had passed betwixt him and the Regent, and seeing Catherine's finger raised in a monitory fashion, he felt himself, as on former occasions at the Castle of Avenel, obliged to submit to the task of dissimulation, and followed Dryfesdale down to the castle chapel, where he assisted in the devotions of the evening.

The chaplain was named Elias Henderson. He was a man in the prime of life, and possessed of good natural parts, carefully improved by the best education which those times afforded. To these qualities were added a faculty of close and terse reasoning, and, at intervals, a flow of happy illustration and natural eloquence. The religious faith of Roland Græme, as we have already had opportunity to observe, rested on no secure basis, but was entertained rather in obedience to his grandmother's behests, and his secret desire to contradict the chaplain of Avenel Castle, than from any fixed or steady reliance which he placed on the Romish creed. His ideas had been of late considerably enlarged by the scenes he had passed through; and feeling that there was shame in not understanding something of those political disputes betwixt the professors of the ancient and of the Reformed faith, he listened, with more attention than it had hitherto been in his nature to yield on such occasions, to an animated discussion of some of the principal points of difference betwixt the churches.

So passed away the first day in the Castle of Lochleven; and those which followed it were, for some time, of a very monotonous and uniform tenor.

CHAPTER XXIV

'Tis a weary life this . . . .
Vaults overhead, and grates and bars around me,
And my sad hours spent with as sad companions,
Whose thoughts are brooding o'er their own mischances,
Far, far too deeply to take part in mine.

The Woodsman.

THE course of life to which Mary and her little retinue were doomed was in the last degree secluded and lonely, varied only as the weather permitted or rendered impossible the Queen's usual walk in the garden or on the battlements. The greater part of the morning she wrought with her ladies at those pieces of needlework many of which still remain, proofs of her indefatigable application. At such hours the page was permitted the freedom of the castle and islet; nay, he was sometimes invited to attend George Douglas when he went a-sporting upon the lake or on its margin—opportunities of diversion which were only clouded by the remarkable melancholy which always seemed to brood on that gentleman's brow, and to mark his whole demeanor—a sadness so profound that Roland never observed him to smile, or to speak any word unconnected with the immediate object of their exercise.

The most pleasant part of Roland's day was the occasional space which he was permitted to pass in personal attendance on the Queen and her ladies, together with the regular dinner-time, which he always spent with Dame Mary Fleming and Catherine Seyton. At these periods, he had frequent occasion to admire the lively spirit and inventive imagination of the latter damsel, who was unwearied in her contrivances to amuse her mistress, and to banish, for a time at least, the melancholy which preyed on her bosom. She danced, she sung, she recited tales of ancient and modern times, with that heartfelt exertion of talent of which the pleasure lies not in the vanity of displaying it to others, but in the enthusiastic consciousness that we possess it ourselves. And yet these high accomplishments were mixed with an air of rusticity and hare-brained vivacity which seemed rather to belong to some village maid, the coquette of the ring around the Maypole, than to the high-bred descendant of an ancient baron. A touch of audacity, altogether short of effrontery, and far less approaching to vulgarity, gave, as it were, a wildness to all that she did; and Mary, while defending her from some of the occasional censures of her grave companion, compared her to a trained singing-bird escaped from a cage, which practises in all the luxuriance of freedom, and in full possession of the greenwood bough, the airs which it had learned during its earlier captivity.

The moments which the page was permitted to pass in the presence of this fascinating creature danced so rapidly away that, brief as they were, they compensated the weary dulness of all the rest of the day. The space of indulgence, however, was always brief, nor were any private interviews betwixt him and Catherine permitted, or even possible. Whether it were some special precaution respecting the Queen's household, or whether it were her general ideas of propriety, Dame Fleming seemed particularly attentive to prevent the young people from holding any separate correspondence together, and bestowed, for Catherine's sole benefit in this matter, the full stock of prudence and experience which she had acquired when mother of the Queen's maidens of honor, and by which she had gained their hearty hatred. Casual meetings, however, could not be prevented, unless Catherine had been more desirous of shunning, or Roland Græme less anxious in watching for them. A smile, a gibe, a sarcasm, disarmed of its severity by the arch look with which it was accompanied, was all that time permitted to pass between them on such occasions. But such passing interviews neither afforded means nor opportunity to renew the discussion of the circumstances attending their earlier acquaintance, nor to permit Roland to investigate more accurately the mysterious apparition of the page in the purple velvet cloak at the hostelry of St. Michael's.

The winter months slipped heavily away, and spring was already advanced, when Roland Græme observed a gradual change in the manners of his fellow-prisoners. Having no business of his own to attend to, and being, like those of his age, education, and degree, sufficiently curious concerning what passed around, he began by degrees to suspect, and finally to be convinced, that there was something in agitation among his companions in captivity to which they did not desire that he should be privy. Nay, he became almost certain that, by some means unintelligible to him, Queen Mary held correspondence beyond the walls and waters which surrounded her prison-house, and that she nourished some secret hope of deliverance or escape. In the conversations betwixt her and her attendants at which he was necessarily present, the Queen could not always avoid showing that she was acquainted with the events which were passing abroad in the world, and which he only heard through her report. He observed that she wrote more and worked less than had been her former custom, and that, as if desirous to lull suspicion asleep, she changed her manner towards the Lady Lochleven into one more gracious, and which seemed to express a resigned submission to her lot. "They think I am blind," he said to himself, "and that I am unfit to be trusted because I am so young, or it may be because I was sent hither by the Regent. Well! be it so; they may be glad to confide in me in the long run; and Catherine Seyton, for as saucy as she is, may find me as safe a confidant as that sullen Douglas, whom she is always running after. It may be they are angry with me for listening to Master Elias Henderson, but it was their own fault for sending me there; and if the man speaks truth and good sense, and preaches only the Word of God, he is as likely to be right as either Pope or councils."

It is probable that in this last conjecture Roland Græme had hit upon the real cause why the ladies had not entrusted him with their counsels. He had of late had several conferences with Henderson on the subject of religion, and had given him to understand that he stood in need of his instructions, although he had not thought there was either prudence or necessity for confessing that hitherto he had held the tenets of the Church of Rome.

Elias Henderson, a keen propagator of the Reformed faith, had sought the seclusion of Lochleven Castle with the express purpose and expectation of making converts from Rome amongst the domestics of the dethroned Queen, and confirming the faith of those who already held the Protestant doctrines. Perhaps his hopes soared a little higher, and he might nourish some expectation of a proselyte more distinguished, in the person of the deposed Queen. But the pertinacity with which she and her female attendants refused to see or listen to him rendered such hope, if he nourished it, altogether abortive.

The opportunity, therefore, of enlarging the religious information of Roland Græme, and bringing him to a more due sense of his duties to Heaven, was hailed by the good man as a door opened by Providence for the salvation of a sinner.

He dreamed not, indeed, that he was converting a Papist, but such was the ignorance which Roland displayed upon some material points of the Reformed doctrine, that Master Henderson, while praising his docility to the Lady Lochleven and her grandson, seldom failed to add, that his venerable brother, Henry Warden, must be now decayed in strength and in mind, since he found a catechumen of his flock so ill-grounded in the principles of his belief. For this, indeed, Roland Græme thought it was unnecessary to assign the true reason, which was his having made it a point of honor to forget all that Henry Warden taught him, as soon as he was no longer compelled to repeat it over as a lesson acquired by rote. The lessons of his new instructor, if not more impressively delivered, were received by a more willing ear and a more awakened understanding, and the solitude of Lochleven Castle was favorable to graver thoughts than the page had hitherto entertained. He wavered yet, indeed, as one who was almost persuaded; but his attention to the chaplain's instructions procured him favor even with the stern old dame herself; and he was once or twice, but under great precaution, permitted to go to the neighboring village of Kinross, situated on the mainland, to execute some ordinary commission of his unfortunate mistress.

For some time Roland Græme might be considered as standing neuter betwixt the two parties who inhabited the water-girdled Tower of Lochleven; but, as he rose in the opinion of the lady of the castle and her chaplain, he perceived, with great grief, that he lost ground in that of Mary and her female allies.

He came gradually to be sensible that he was regarded as a spy upon their discourse, and that, instead of the ease with which they had formerly conversed in his presence, without suppressing any of the natural feelings of anger, of sorrow, or mirth which the chance topic of the moment happened to call forth, their talk was now guardedly restricted to the most indifferent subjects, and a studied reserve observed even in the mode of treating these. This obvious want of confidence was accompanied with a correspondent change in their personal demeanor towards the unfortunate page. The Queen, who had at first treated him with marked courtesy, now scarce spoke to him, save to convey some necessary command for her service. The Lady Fleming restricted her notice to the most dry and distant expressions of civility; and Catherine Seyton became bitter in her pleasantries, and shy, cross, and pettish in any intercourse they had together. What was yet more provoking, he saw, or thought he saw, marks of intelligence betwixt George Douglas and the beautiful Catherine Seyton; and, sharpened by jealousy, he wrought himself almost into a certainty that the looks which they exchanged conveyed matters of deep and serious import. "No wonder," he thought, "if, courted by the son of a proud and powerful baron, she can no longer spare a word or look to the poor fortuneless page."

In a word, Roland Græme's situation became truly disagreeable, and his heart naturally enough rebelled against the injustice of this treatment, which deprived him of the only comfort which he had received for submitting to a confinement in other respects irksome. He accused Queen Mary and Catherine Seyton (for concerning the opinion of Dame Fleming he was indifferent) of inconsistency in being displeased with him on account of the natural consequences of an order of their own. Why did they send him to hear this overpowering preacher? The Abbot Ambrosius, he recollected, understood the weakness of their Popish cause better, when he enjoined him to repeat within his own mind aves, and credos, and paters all the while old Henry Warden preached or lectured, that so he might secure himself against lending even a momentary ear to his heretical doctrine. "But I will endure this life no longer," said he to himself, manfully; "do they suppose I would betray my mistress, because I see cause to doubt of her religion? That would be a serving, as they say, the devil for God's sake. I will forth into the world; he that serves fair ladies may at least expect kind looks and kind words; and I bear not the mind of a gentleman, to submit to cold treatment and suspicion, and a life-long captivity besides. I will speak to George Douglas to-morrow when we go out a-fishing."

A sleepless night was spent in agitating this magnanimous resolution, and he arose in the morning not perfectly decided in his own mind whether he should abide by it or not. It happened that he was summoned by the Queen at an unusual hour, and just as he was about to go out with George Douglas. He went to attend her commands in the garden; but, as he had his angling-rod in his hand, the circumstance announced his previous intention, and the Queen, turning to the Lady Fleming, said, "Catherine must devise some other amusement for us, *ma bonne amie:* our discreet page has already made his party for the day's pleasure."

"I said from the beginning," answered the Lady Fleming, "that your Grace ought not to rely on being favored with the company of a youth who has so many Huguenot acquaintances, and has the means of amusing himself far more agreeably than with us."

"I wish," said Catherine, her animated features reddenning with mortification, "that his friends would sail away with him for good, and bring us in return a page—if such a thing can be found—faithful to his Queen and to his religion."

"One part of your wishes may be granted, madam," said Roland Græme, unable any longer to restrain his sense of the treatment which he received on all sides; and he was about to add, "I heartily wish you a companion in my room, if such can be found, who is capable of enduring women's caprices without going distracted." Luckily, he recollected the remorse which he had felt at having given way to the vivacity of his temper upon a similar occasion; and closing his lips, imprisoned, until it died on his tongue, a reproach so misbecoming the presence of majesty.

"Why do you remain there," said the Queen, "as if you were rooted to the parterre?"

"I but attend your Grace's commands," said the page.

"I have none to give you. Begone, sir!"

As he left the garden to go to the boat, he distinctly heard Mary upbraid one of her attendants in these words: "You see to what you have exposed us!"

This brief scene at once determined Roland Græme's resolution to quit the castle, if it were possible, and to impart his resolution to George Douglas without loss of time. That gentleman, in his usual mood of silence, sate in the stern of the little skiff which they used on such occasions, trimming his fishing-tackle, and, from time to time, indicating by signs to Græme, who pulled the oars, which way he should row. When they were a furlong or two from the castle, Roland rested on the oars, and addressed his companion somewhat abruptly—"I have something of importance to say to you, under your pleasure, fair sir."

The pensive melancholy of Douglas's countenance at once gave way to the eager, keen, and startled look of one who expects to hear something of deep and alarming import.

"I am wearied to the very death of this Castle of Lochleven," continued Roland.

"Is that all?" said Douglas; "I know none of its inhabitants who are much better pleased with it."

"Ay—but I am neither a native of the house nor a prisoner in it, and so I may reasonably desire to leave it."

"You might desire to quit it with equal reason," answered Douglas, "if you were both the one and the other."

"But," said Roland Græme, "I am not only tired of living in Lochleven Castle, but I am determined to quit it."

"That is a resolution more easily taken than executed," replied Douglas.

"Not if yourself, sir, and your lady [grand-] mother choose to consent," answered the page.

"You mistake the matter, Roland," said Douglas: "you will find that the consent of two other persons is equally essential—that of the Lady Mary, your mistress, and that of my uncle the Regent, who placed you about her person, and who will not think it proper that she should change her attendants so soon."

"And must I then remain whether I will or no?" demanded the page, somewhat appalled at a view of the subject which would have occurred sooner to a person of more experience.

"At least," said George Douglas, "you must will to remain till my uncle consents to dismiss you."

"Frankly," said the page, "and speaking to you as a gentleman who is incapable of betraying me, I will confess that, if I thought myself a prisoner here, neither walls nor water should confine me long."

"Frankly," said Douglas, "I could not much blame you for the attempt; yet, for all that, my father, or uncle, or the earl, or any of my brothers, or, in short, any of the King's lords into whose hand you fell, would in such a case hang you like a dog, or like a sentinel who deserts his post; and I promise you that you will hardly escape them. But row towards St. Serf's Island: there is a breeze from the west, and we shall have sport, keeping to windward of the isle, where the ripple is strongest. We will speak more of what you have mentioned when we have had an hour's sport."

Their fishing was successful, though never did two anglers pursue even that silent and unsocial pleasure with less of verbal intercourse.

When their time was expired, Douglas took the oars in his turn, and by his order Roland Græme steered the boat, directing her course upon the landing-place at the castle. But he also stopped in the midst of his course, and, looking around him, said to Græme. "There is a thing which I could mention to thee; but it is so deep a secret that even here, surrounded as we are by waves and sky, without the possibility of a listener, I cannot prevail on myself to speak it out."

"Better leave it unspoken, sir," answered Roland Græme, "if you doubt the honor of him who alone can hear it."

"I doubt not your honor," replied George Douglas; "but you are young, imprudent, and changeful."

"Young," said Roland, "I am, and it may be imprudent. but who hath informed you that I am changeful?"

"One that knows you, perhaps, better than you know yourself," replied Douglas.

"I suppose you mean Catherine Seyton," said the page, his heart rising as he spoke; "but she is herself fifty times more variable in her humor than the very water which we are floating upon."

"My young acquaintance," said Douglas, "I pray you to remember that Catherine Seyton is a lady of blood and birth, and must not be lightly spoken of."

"Master George of Douglas," said Græme, "as that speech seemed to be made under the warrant of something like a threat, I pray you to observe that I value not the threat at the estimation of a fin of one of these dead trouts; and, moreover, I would have you to know that the champion who undertakes the defense of every lady of blood and birth whom men accuse of change of faith and of fashion is like to have enough of work on his hands."

"Go to," said the seneschal, but in a tone of good-humor, "thou art a foolish boy, unfit to deal with any matter more serious than the casting of a net or the flying of a hawk."

"If your secret concerns Catherine Seyton," said the page, "I care not for it, and so you may tell her if you will. I wot she can shape you opportunity to speak with her, as she has ere now."

The flush which passed over Douglas's face made the page aware that he had lighted on a truth when he was, in fact, speaking at random; and the feeling that he had done so was like striking a dagger into his own heart. His companion, without further answer, resumed the oars, and pulled lustily till they arrived at the island and the castle. The servants received the product of their sport, and the two fishers, turning from each other in silence, went each to his several apartment.

Roland Græme had spent about an hour in grumbling against Catherine Seyton, the Queen, the Regent, and the whole house of Lochleven, with George Douglas at the head of it, when the time approached that his duty called him to attend the meal of Queen Mary. As he arranged his dress for this purpose, he grudged the trouble, which on similar occasions he used, with boyish foppery, to consider as one of the most important duties of his day; and when he went to take his place behind the chair of the Queen, it was with an air of offended dignity which could not escape her observation, and probably appeared to her ridiculous enough, for she whispered something in French to her ladies, at which the Lady Fleming laughed, and Catherine appeared half diverted and half disconcerted. This pleasantry, of which the subject was concealed from him, the unfortunate page received, of course, as a new offense, and called an additional degree of sullen dignity into his mien, which might have exposed him to farther raillery, but that Mary appeared disposed to make allowance for and compassionate his feelings.

With the peculiar tact and delicacy which no woman possessed in greater perfection, she began to soothe by degrees the vexed spirit of her magnanimous attendant. The excellence of the fish which he had taken in his expedition, the high flavor and beautiful red color of the trouts, which have long given distinction to the lake, led her first to express her thanks to her attendant for so agreeable an addition to her table, especially upon a *jour de jeune;* and then brought on inquiries into the place where the fish had been taken, their size, their peculiarities, the times when they were in season, and a comparison between the Lochleven trouts and those which are found in the lakes and rivers of the south of Scotland. The ill-humor of Roland Græme was never of an obstinate character. It rolled away like mist before the sun, and he was easily engaged in a keen and animated dissertation about Lochleven trout, and sea trout, and river trout, and bull trout, and char, which never rise to a fly, and par which some suppose infant salmon, and "herlings," which frequent the Nith and "vendisses," which are only found in the Castle Loch of Lochmaben; and he was hurrying on with the eager impetuosity and enthusiasm of a young sportsman, when he observed that the smile with which the Queen at first listened to him died languidly away, and that, in spite of her efforts to suppress them, tears rose to her eyes. He stopped suddenly short, and, distressed in his turn, asked, "If he had had the misfortune unwittingly to give displeasure to her Grace?"

"No, my poor boy," replied the Queen; "but, as you numbered up the lakes and rivers of my kingdom, imagination cheated me, as it will do, and snatched me from these dreary walls away to the romantic streams of Nithsdale and the royal towers of Lochmaben. O land, which my fathers have so long ruled! of the pleasures which you extend so freely your Queen is now deprived, and the poorest beggar, who may wander free from one landward town to another, would scorn to change fates with Mary of Scotland!"

"Your Highness," said the Lady Fleming, "will do well to withdraw."

"Come with me then, Fleming," said the Queen: "I would not burden hearts so young as these are with the sight of my sorrows."

She accompanied these words with a look of melancholy compassion towards Roland and Catherine, who were now left alone together in the apartment.

The page found his situation not a little embarrassing; for as every reader has experienced who may have chanced to be in such a situation, it is extremely difficult to maintain the full dignity of an offended person in the presence of a beautiful girl, whatever reason we may have for being angry with her. Catherine Seyton, on her part, sat still like a lingering ghost, which, conscious of the awe which its presence imposes, is charitably disposed to give the poor confused mortal whom it visits time to recover his senses, and comply with the grand rule of demonology by speaking first. But as Roland seemed in no hurry to avail himself of her condescension, she carried it a step farther, and herself opened the conversation.

"I pray you, fair sir, if it may be permitted me to disturb your august reverie by a question so simple, what may have become of your rosary?"

"It is lost, madam—lost some time since," said Roland, partly embarrassed and partly indignant.

"And may I ask farther, sir," said Catherine, "why you have not replaced it with another? I have half a mind," she said, taking from her pocket a string of ebony beads adorned with gold, "to bestow one upon you, to keep for my sake, just to remind you of former acquaintance."

There was a little tremulous accent in the tone with which these words were delivered, which at once put to flight Roland Græme's resentment, and brought him to Catherine's side; but she instantly resumed the bold and firm accent which was more familiar to her. "I did not bid you," she said, "come and sit so close by me; for the acquaintance that I spoke of has been stiff and cold, dead and buried, for this many a day."

"Now Heaven forbid!" said the page, "it has only

slept; and now that you desire it should awake, fair Catherine, believe me that a pledge of your returning favor——"

"Nay, nay," said Catherine, withholding the rosary, towards which, as he spoke, he extended his hand, "I have changed my mind on better reflection. What should a heretic do with these holy beads, that have been blessed by the Father of the church himself?"

Roland winced grievously, for he saw plainly which way the discourse was now likely to tend, and felt that it must at all events be embarrassing. "Nay, but," he said, "it was as a token of your own regard that you offered them."

"Ay, fair sir, but that regard attended the faithful subject, the loyal and pious Catholic, the individual who was so solemnly devoted at the same time with myself to the same grand duty; which, you must now understand, was to serve the church and Queen. To such a person, if you ever heard of him, was my regard due, and not to him who associates with heretics, and is about to become a renegado."

"I should scarce believe, fair mistress," said Roland, indignantly, "that the vane of your favor turned only to a Catholic wind, considering that it points so plainly to George Douglas, who, I think, is both kingsman and Protestant."

"Think better of George Douglas," said Catherine, "than to believe——" and then checking herself, as if she had spoken too much, she went on, "I assure you, fair Master Roland, that all who wish you well are sorry for you."

"Their number is very few, I believe," answered Roland, "and their sorrow, if they feel any, not deeper than ten minutes' time will cure."

"They are more numerous, and think more deeply concerning you, than you seem to be aware," answered Catherine. "But perhaps they think wrong. You are the best judge in your own affairs; and if you prefer gold and church lands to honor and loyalty, and the faith of your fathers, why should you be hampered in conscience more than others?"

"May Heaven bear witness for me," said Roland, "that if I entertain any difference of opinion—that is, if I nourish any doubts in point of religion, they have been adopted on the conviction of my own mind, and the suggestion of my own conscience!"

"Ay, ay, your conscience—your conscience!" repeated she with satiric emphasis—"your conscience is the scapegoat; I warrant it an able one: it will bear the burden of one of the best manors of the Abbey of St. Mary of Kennaquhair, lately forfeited to our noble Lord the King by the abbot and community thereof, for the high crime of fidelity to their religious vows, and now to be granted by the High and Mighty Traitor, and so forth, James Earl of Murray, to the good squire of dames, Roland Græme, for his loyal and faithful service as under-espial and deputy-turnkey for securing the person of his lawful sovereign, Queen Mary."

"You misconstrue me cruelly," said the page—"yes, Catherine, most cruelly. God knows I would protect this poor lady at the risk of my life, or with my life; but what can I do—what can any one do for her?"

"Much may be done—enough may be done—all may be done—if men will be but true and honorable, as Scottish men were in the days of Bruce and Wallace. O, Roland, from what an enterprise you are now withdrawing your heart and hand, through mere fickleness and coldness of spirit!"

"How can I withdraw," said Roland, "from an enterprise which has never been communicated to me? Has the Queen, or have you, or has any one, communicated with me upon anything for her service which I have refused? Or have you not, all of you, held me at such a distance from your counsels as if I were the most faithless spy since the days of Ganelon?" *

"And who," said Catherine Seyton, "would trust the sworn friend, and pupil, and companion of the heretic preacher Henderson? Ay, a proper tutor you have chosen, instead of the excellent Ambrosius, who is now turned out of house and homestead, if indeed he is not languishing in a dungeon, for withstanding the tyranny of Morton, to whose brother the temporalities of that noble house of God have been gifted away by the Regent."

"Is it possible?" said the page; "and is the excellent Father Ambrose in such distress?"

"He would account the news of your falling away from the faith of your fathers," answered Catherine, "a worse mishap than aught that tyranny can inflict on himself."

"But why," said Roland, very much moved—"why should you suppose that—that—that it is with me as you say?"

"Do you yourself deny it?" replied Catherine; "do you not admit that you have drunk the poison which you should have dashed from your lips? Do you deny that it now ferments in your veins, if it has not altogether corrupted the springs of life? Do you deny that you have your doubts, as you proudly term them, respecting what popes and coun-

*See Note 17.

cils have declared it unlawful to doubt of? Is not your faith wavering, if not overthrown? Does not the heretic preacher boast his conquest? Does not the heretic woman of this prison-house hold up thy example to others? Do not the Queen and the Lady Fleming believe in thy falling away? And is there any except one—yes, I will speak it out, and think as lightly as you please of my good-will—is there one except myself that holds even a lingering hope that you may yet prove what we once all believed of you?"

"I know not," said our poor page, much embarrassed by the view which was thus presented to him of the conduct he was expected to pursue, and by a person in whom he was not the less interested that so long a residence in Lochleven Castle, with no object so likely to attract his undivided attention, had taken place since they had first met—"I know not what you expect of me, or fear from me. I was sent hither to attend Queen Mary, and to her I acknowledge the duty of a servant through life and death. If any one had expected service of another kind, I was not the party to render it. I neither avow nor disclaim the doctrines of the Reformed Church. Will you have truth? It seems to me that the profligacy of the Catholic clergy has brought this judgment on their own heads. and, for aught I know, it may be for their reformation. But, for betraying this unhappy Queen, God knows I am guiltless of the thought. Did I even believe worse of her than as her servant I wish—as her subject I dare—to do, I would not betray her; far from it—I would aid her in aught which could tend to a fair trial of her cause."

"Enough!—enough!" answered Catherine, clasping her hands together; "then thou wilt not desert us if any means are presented by which, placing our royal mistress at freedom, this case may be honestly tried betwixt her and her rebellious subjects?"

"Nay, but, fair Catherine," replied the page, "hear but what the Lord of Murray said when he sent me hither——"

"Hear but what the devil said," replied the maiden, "rather than what a false subject, a false brother, a false counselor, a false friend said! A man raised from a petty pensioner on the crown's bounty to be the counselor of majesty, and the prime distributor of the bounties of the state; one with whom rank, fortune, title, consequence, and power all grew up like a mushroom by the mere warm good-will of the sister whom, in requital, he hath mewed up in this place of melancholy seclusion; whom, in further requital, he has deposed; and whom, if he dared, he would murder!"

"I think not so ill of the Earl of Murray," said Roland Græme; "and sooth to speak," he added, with a smile, "it would require some bribe to make me embrace, with firm and deperate resolution, either one side or the other."

"Nay, if that is all," replied Catherine Seyton, in a tone of enthusiasm, "you shall be guerdoned with prayers from oppressed subjects—from dispossessed clergy—from insulted nobles—with immortal praise by future ages—with eager gratitude by the present—with fame on earth and with felicity in Heaven! Your country will thank you—your Queen will be debtor to you—you will achieve at once the highest from the lowest degree in chivalry—all men will honor, all women will love you—and I, sworn with you so early to the accomplishment of Queen Mary's freedom, will—yes, I will love you better than—ever sister loved brother!"

"Say on—say on!" whispered Roland, kneeling on one knee, and taking her hand, which, in the warmth of exhortation, Catherine held towards him.

"Nay," said she, pausing, "I have already said too much—far too much if I prevail not with you, far too little if I do. But I prevail," she continued, seeing that the countenance of the youth she addressed returned the enthusiasm of her own—"I prevail; or rather the good cause prevails through its own strength—thus I devote thee to it." And as she spoke she approached her finger to the brow of the astonished youth, and, without touching it, signed the cross over his forehead; stooped her face towards him, and seemed to kiss the empty space in which she had traced the symbol; then starting up, and extricating herself from his grasp, darted into the Queen's apartment.

Roland Græme remained as the enthusiastic maiden had left him, kneeling on one knee, with breath withheld, and with eyes fixed upon the space which the fairy form of Catherine Seyton had so lately occupied. If his thoughts were not of unmixed delight, they at least partook of that thrilling and intoxicating, though mingled, sense of pain and pleasure, the most overpowering which life offers in its blended cup. He rose and retired slowly; and although the chaplain, Mr. Henderson, preached on that evening his best sermon against the errors of Popery, I would not engage that he was followed accurately through the train of his reasoning by the young proselyte, with a view to whose especial benefit he had handled the subject.

CHAPTER XXV

And when Love's torch hath set the heart in flame,
Comes Seignor Reason, with his saws and cautions,
Giving such aid as the old gray-beard sexton,
Who from the church-vault drags his crazy engine,
To ply its dribbling ineffectual streamlet
Against a conflagration.

Old Play.

IN a musing mood, Roland Græme upon the ensuing morning betook himself to the battlements of the castle, as a spot where he might indulge the course of his thick-coming fancies with least chance of interruption. But his place of retirement was in the present case ill chosen, for he was presently joined by Mr. Elias Henderson.

"I sought you young man," said the preacher, "having to speak of something which concerns you nearly."

The page had no pretense for avoiding the conference which the chaplain thus offered, though he felt that it might prove an embarrassing one.

"In teaching thee, as far as my feeble knowledge hath permitted, thy duty towards God," said the chaplain, "there are particulars of your duty towards man upon which I was unwilling long or much to insist. You are here in the service of a lady, honorable as touching her birth, deserving of all compassion as respects her misfortunes, and garnished with even but too many of those outward qualities which win men's regard and affection. Have you ever considered your regard to this Lady Mary of Scotland in its true light and bearing?"

"I trust, reverend sir," replied Roland Græme, "that I am well aware of the duties a servant in my condition owes to his royal mistress, especially in her lowly and distressed state."

"True," answered the preacher; "but it is even that honest feeling which may, in the Lady Mary's case, carry thee into great crime and treachery."

"How so, reverend sir?" replied the page; "I profess I understand you not."

"I speak to you not of the crimes of this ill-advised lady," said the preacher; "they are not subjects for the ears of her sworn servant. But it is enough to say that this unhappy person hath rejected more offers of grace, more hopes of glory, than ever were held out to earthly princes; and that she is now, her day of favor being passed, sequestered in this lonely castle, for the commonweal of the people of Scotland, and it may be for the benefit of her own soul."

"Reverend sir," said Roland, somewhat impatiently, "I am but too well aware that my unfortunate mistress is imprisoned, since I have the misfortune to share in her restraint myself, of which, to speak sooth, I am heartily weary."

"It is even of that which I am about to speak," said the chaplain, mildly; "but first, my good Roland, look forth on the pleasant prospect of yonder cultivated plain. You see, where the smoke arises, yonder village standing half-hidden by the trees, and you know it to be the dwelling-place of peace and industry. From space to space, each by the side of its own stream, you see the gray towers of barons, with cottages interspersed; and you know that they also, with their household, are now living in unity—the lance hung upon the wall and the sword resting in its sheath. You see, too, more than one fair church where the pure waters of life are offered to the thirsty' and where the hungry are refreshed with spiritual food. What would he deserve who should bring fire and slaughter into so fair and happy a scene—who should bear the swords of the gentry and turn them against each other—who should give tower and cottage to the flames, and slake the embers with the blood of the indwellers? What would he deserve who should lift up again that ancient Dagon of superstition whom the worthies of the time have beaten down, and who should once more make the churches of God the high places of Baal?"

"You have limned a frightful picture, reverend sir," said Roland Græme; "yet I guess not whom you would charge with the purpose of effecting a change so horrible."

"God forbid," replied the preacher, "that I should say to thee, thou art the man. Yet beware, Roland Græme, that thou, in serving thy mistress, hold fast the still higher service which thou owest to the peace of thy country and the prosperity of her inhabitants; else, Roland Græme, thou mayst be the very man upon whose head will fall the curses and assured punishment due to such work. If thou art won by the song of these sirens to aid that unhappy lady's escape from this place of penitence and security, it is over with the peace of Scotland's cottages and with the prosperity of her palaces; and the babe unborn shall curse the name of the man who gave inlet to the disorder which will follow the war betwixt the mother and the son."

"I know of no such plan, reverend sir," answered the page, "and therefore can aid none such. My duty towards the Queen has been simply that of an attendant; it is a task of which, at times, I would willingly have been freed; nevertheless——"

"It is to prepare thee for the enjoyment of something more of liberty," said the preacher, "that I have endeavored to impress upon you the deep responsibility under which your office must be discharged. George Douglas hath told the Lady Lochleven that you are weary of this service, and my intercession hath partly determined her good ladyship that, as your discharge cannot be granted, you shall, instead, be employed in certain commissions on the mainland, which have hitherto been discharged by other persons of confidence. Wherefore, come with me to the lady, for even to-day such duty will be imposed on you."

"I trust you will hold me excused, reverend sir," said the page, who felt that an increase of confidence on the part of the lady of the castle and her family would render his situation in a moral view doubly embarrassing, "one cannot serve two masters; and I much fear that my mistress will not hold me excused for taking employment under another."

"Fear not that," said the preacher; "her consent shall be asked and obtained. I fear she will yield it but too easily, as hoping to avail herself of your agency to maintain correspondence with her friends, as those falsely call themselves who would make her name the watchward for civil war."

"And thus," said the page, "I shall be exposed to suspicion on all sides; for my mistress will consider me as a spy placed on her by her enemies, seeing me so far trusted by them; and the Lady Lochleven will never cease to suspect the possibility of my betraying her, because circumstances put it into my power to do so; I would rather remain as I am."

There followed a pause of one or two minutes, during which Henderson looked steadily in Roland's countenance, as if desirous to ascertain whether there was not more in the answer than the precise words seemed to imply. He failed in this point, however; for Roland, bred a page from childhood, knew how to assume a sullen, pettish cast of countenance, well enough calculated to hide all internal emotions.

"I understand thee not, Roland," said the preacher, "or rather thou thinkst on this matter more deeply than I apprehended to be in thy nature. Methought the delight of going on shore with thy bow, or thy gun, or thy angling-rod, would have borne away all other feelings."

"And so it would," replied Roland, who perceived the danger of suffering Henderson's half-raised suspicions to become fully awake—"I would have thought of nothing but the gun and the oar, and the wild water-fowl that tempt me by sailing among the sedges yonder so far out of flight-shot, had you not spoken of my going on shore as what was to occasion burning of town and tower, the downfall of the Evangel, and the upsetting of the mass."

"Follow me, then," said Henderson, "and we will seek the Lady Lochleven."

They found her at breakfast with her grandson George Douglas. "Peace be with your ladyship!" said the preacher, bowing to his patroness; "Ronald Græme awaits your order."

"Young man," said the lady, "our chaplain hath warranted for thy fidelity, and we are determined to give you certain errands to do for us in our town of Kinross."

"Not by my advice," said Douglas, coldly.

"I said not that it was," answered the lady, something sharply. "The mother of thy father may, I should think, be old enough to judge for herself in a matter so simple. Thou wilt take the skiff, Roland, and two of my people, whom Dryfesdale or Randal will order out, and fetch off certain stuff of plate and hangings which should last night be lodged at Kinross by the wains from Edinburgh."

"And give this packet," said George Douglas, "to a servant of ours, whom you will find in waiting there. It is the report to my father," he added, looking towards his grandmother, who acquiesced by bending her head.

"I have already mentioned to Master Henderson," said Roland Græme, "that, as my duty requires my attendance on the Queen, her Grace's permission for my journey ought to be obtained before I can undertake your commission."

"Look to it, my son," said the old lady, "the scruple of the youth is honorable."

"Craving your pardon, madam, I have no wish to force myself on her presence thus early," said Douglas in an indifferent tone; "it might displease her, and were no way agreeable to me."

"And I," said the Lady Lochleven, "although her temper

hath been more gentle of late, have no will to undergo, without necessity, the rancor of her wit."

"Under your permission, madam," said the chaplain, "I will myself render your request to the Queen. During my long residence in this house she hath not deigned to see me in private, or to hear my doctrine; yet so may Heaven prosper my labors, as love for her soul, and desire to bring her into the right path, was my chief motive for coming hither."

"Take care, Master Henderson," said Douglas, in a tone which seemed almost sarcastic, "lest you rush hastily on an adventure to which you have no vocation; you are learned, and know the adage, *Ne accesseris in consilium nisi vocatus.* Who hath required this at your hand?"

"The Master to whose service I am called," answered the preacher, looking upward—"He who hath commanded me to be earnest in season and out of season."

"Your acquaintance hath not been much, I think, with courts or princes," continued the young esquire.

"No, sir," replied Henderson, "but, like my master Knox, I see nothing frightful in the fair face of a pretty lady."

"My son," said the Lady of Lochleven, "quench not the good man's zeal: let him do the errand to this unhappy princess."

"With more willingness than I would do it myself," said George Douglas. Yet something in his manner appeared to contradict his words.

The minister went accordingly, followed by Roland Græme, and, demanding an audience of the imprisoned princess, was admitted. He found her with her ladies engaged in the daily task of embroidery. The Queen received him with that courtesy which, in ordinary cases, she used towards all who approached her, and the clergyman, in opening his commission, was obviously somewhat more embarrassed than he had expected to be. "The good Lady of Lochleven, may it please your Grace——"

He made a short pause, during which Mary said, with a smile, "My Grace would, in truth, be well pleased were the Lady of Lochleven our *good* lady; but go on—what is the will of the good Lady of Lochleven?"

"She desires, madam," said the chaplain, "that your Grace will permit this young gentleman, your page, Roland Græme, to pass to Kinross, to look after some household stuff and hangings sent hither for the better furnishing of your Grace's apartments."

"The Lady of Lochleven," said the Queen, "uses needless ceremony, in requesting our permission for that which stands within her own pleasure. We well know that this young gentleman's attendance on us had not been so long permitted were he not thought to be more at the command of that good lady than at ours. But we cheerfully yield consent that he shall go on her errand; with our will we would doom no living creature to the captivity which we ourselves must suffer."

"Ay, madam," answered the preacher, "and it is doubtless natural for humanity to quarrel with its prison-house. Yet there have been those who have found that time spent in the house of temporal captivity may be so employed as to redeem us from spiritual slavery."

"I apprehend your meaning, sir," replied the Queen, "but I have heard your apostle—I have heard Master John Knox; and were I to be perverted, I would willingly resign to the ablest and most powerful of heresiarchs the poor honor he might acquire by overcoming my faith and my hope."

"Madam," said the preacher, "it is not to the talents or skill of the husbandman that God gives the increase: the words which were offered in vain by him whom you justly call our apostle, during the bustle and gaiety of a court, may yet find better acceptance during the leisure for reflection which this place affords. God knows, lady, that I speak in singleness of heart, as one who would as soon compare himself to the immortal angels as to the holy man whom you have named. Yet would you but condescend to apply to their noblest use those talents and that learning which all allow you to be possessed of—would you afford us but the slightest hope that you would hear and regard what can be urged against the blinded superstition and idolatry in which you were brought up, sure am I, that the most powerfully gifted of my brethren, that even John Knox himself, would hasten hither, and account the rescue of your single soul from the nets of Romish error——"

"I am obliged to you and to them for their charity," said Mary; "but as I have at present but one presence-chamber, I would reluctantly see it converted into a Huguenot synod."

"At least, madam, be not thus obstinately blinded in your errors! Hear one who has hungered and thirsted, watched and prayed, to undertake the good work of your conversion, and who would be content to die the instant that a work so advantageous for yourself and so beneficial to Scotland were accomplished. Yes, lady, could I but shake the remaining pillar of the heathen temple in this land—and that permit me to term your faith in the delusions of Rome—I could be content to die overwhelmed in the ruins!"

"I will not insult your zeal, sir," replied Mary, "by saying you are more likely to make sport for the Philistines than to overwhelm them: your charity claims my thanks, for it is warmly expressed, and may be truly purposed. But believe as well of me as I am willing to do of you, and think that I may be as anxious to recall you to the ancient and only road as you are to teach me your new bye-ways to Paradise."

"Then, madam, if such be your generous purpose," said Henderson, eagerly, "what hinders that we should dedicate some part of that time unhappily now too much at your Grace's disposal to discuss a question so weighty? You by report of all men are both learned and witty; and I, though without such advantages, am strong in my cause as in a tower of defense. Why should we not spend some space in endeavoring to discover which of us hath the wrong side in this important matter?"

"Nay," said Queen Mary, "I never alleged my force was strong enough to accept of a combat *en champ clos* with a scholar and a polemic. Besides, the match is not equal. You, sir, might retire when you felt the battle go against you, while I am tied to the stake, and have no permission to say the debate wearies me. I would be alone."

She courtesied low to him as she uttered these words; and Henderson, whose zeal was indeed ardent, but did not extend to the neglect of delicacy, bowed in return, and prepared to withdraw.

"I would," he said, "that my earnest wish, my most zealous prayer, could procure to your Grace any blessing or comfort, but especially that in which alone blessing or comfort is, as easily as the slightest intimation of your wish will remove me from your presence."

He was in the act of departing, when Mary said to him with much courtesy, "Do me no injury in your thoughts, good sir; it may be, that if my time here be protracted longer—as surely I hope it will not, trusting that either my rebel subjects will repent of their disloyalty, or that my faithful lieges will obtain the upper hand—but if my time be here protracted, it may be I shall have no displeasure in hearing one who seems so reasonable and compassionate as yourself, and I may hazard your contempt by endeavoring to recollect and repeat the reasons which schoolmen and councils give for the faith that is in me, although I fear that, God help me! my Latin has deserted me with my other possessions. This must, however, be for another day. Meanwhile, sir, let the Lady of Lochleven employ my page as she lists; I will not afford suspicion by speaking a word to him before he goes. Roland Græme, my friend, lose not an opportunity of amusing thyself: dance, sing, run, and leap—all may be done merrily on the mainland; but he must have more than quicksilver in his veins who would frolic here."

"Alas! madam," said the preacher, "to what is it you exhort the youth, while time passes and eternity summons! Can our salvation be insured by idle mirth, or our good work wrought out without fear and trembling?"

"I cannot fear or tremble," replied the Queen: "to Mary Stuart such emotions are unknown. But, if weeping and sorrow on my part will atone for the boy's enjoying an hour of boyish pleasure, be assured the penance shall be duly paid."

"Nay, but, gracious lady," said the preacher, "in this you greatly err: our tears and our sorrows are all too little for our own faults and follies, nor can we transfer them, as your church falsely teaches, to the benefit of others."

"May I pray you, sir," answered the Queen, "with as little offense as such a prayer may import, to transfer yourself elsewhere? We are sick at heart, and may not now be disturbed with further controversy; and thou, Roland, take this little purse"—then turning to the divine, she said, showing its contents,—"Look, reverend sir, it contains only these two or three gold testoons—a coin which, though bearing my own poor features, I have ever found more active against me than on my side, just as my subjects take arms against me, with my own name for their summons and signal. Take this purse that thou mayst want no means of amusement. Fail not—fail not to bring me back news from Kinross; only let it be such as, without suspicion or offense, may be told in the presence of this reverend gentleman, or of the good Lady Lochleven herself."

The last hint was too irresistible to be withstood; and Henderson withdrew, half-mortified, half-pleased with his reception; for Mary, from long habit and the address which was natural to her, had learned, in an extraordinary degree, the art of evading discourse which was disagreeable to her feelings or prejudices, without affronting those by whom it was proffered.

Roland Græme retired with the chaplain at a signal from his lady ; but it did not escape him that, as he left the room, stepping backwards and making the deep obeisance due to royalty, Catherine Seyton held up her slender forefinger, with a gesture which he alone could witness, and which seemed to say, " Remember what has passed betwixt us."

The young page had now his last charge from the Lady of Lochleven. "There are revels," she said, "this day at the village. My son's authority is, as yet, unable to prevent these continued workings of the ancient leaven of folly which the Romish priests have kneaded into the very souls of the Scottish peasantry. I do not command thee to abstain from them—that would be only to lay a snare for thy folly, or to teach thee falsehood ; but enjoy these vanities with moderation, and mark them as something thou must soon learn to renounce and contemn. Our chamberlain at Kinross, Luke Lundin—Doctor, as he foolishly calleth himself—will acquaint thee what is to be done in the matter about which thou goest. Remember thou art trusted ; show thyself, therefore, worthy of trust."

When we recollect that Roland Græme was not yet nineteen, and that he had spent his whole life in the solitary Castle of Avenel, excepting the few hours he had passed in Edinburgh, and his late residence at Lochleven, the latter period having very little served to enlarge his acquaintance with the gay world, we cannot wonder that his heart beat high with hope and curiosity at the prospect of partaking the sport even of a country wake. He hastened to his little cabin, and turned over the wardrobe with which, in every respect becoming his station, he had been supplied from Edinburgh, probably by order of the Earl of Murray. By the Queen's command he had hitherto waited upon her in mourning, or at least in sad-colored raiment. Her condition, she said, admitted of nothing more gay. But now he selected the gayest dress his wardrobe afforded, composed of scarlet, slashed with black satin—the royal colors of Scotland ; combed his long curled hair ; disposed his chain and medal round a beaver hat of the newest block ; and with the gay falchion which had reached him in so mysterious a manner hung by his side in an embroidered belt, his apparel, added to his natural frank mien and handsome figure, formed a most commendable and pleasing specimen of the young gallant of the period. He sought to make his parting reverence to the Queen and her ladies, but old Dryfesdale hurried him to the boat.

"We will have no private audiences," he said, "my master; since you are to be trusted with somewhat, we will try at least to save thee from the temptation of opportunity. God help thee, child," he added, with a glance of contempt at his gay clothes, "an the bear-ward be yonder from St. Andrews, have a care thou go not near him."

"And wherefore, I pray you?" said Roland.

"Lest he take thee for one of his runaway jackanapes," answered the steward, smiling sourly.

"I wear not my clothes at thy cost," said Roland, indignantly.

"Nor at thine own either, my son," replied the steward, "else would thy garb more nearly resemble thy merit and thy station."

Roland Græme suppressed with difficulty the repartee which arose to his lips, and, wrapping his scarlet mantle around him, threw himself into the boat, which two rowers, themselves urged by curiosity to see the revels, pulled stoutly towards the west end of the lake. As they put off, Roland thought he could discover the face of Catherine Seyton, though carefully withdrawn from observation, peeping from a loophole to view his departure. He pulled off his hat, and held it up as a token that he saw and wished her adieu. A white kerchief waved for a second across the window, and for the rest of the little voyage the thoughts of Catherine Seyton disputed ground in his breast with the expectations excited by the approaching revel. As they drew nearer and nearer the shore, the sounds of mirth and music, the laugh, the halloo, and the shout came thicker upon the ear, and in a trice the boat was moored, and Roland Græme hastened in quest of the chamberlain, that, being informed what time he had at his own disposal, he might lay it out to the best advantage.

CHAPTER XXVI

Room for the master of the ring, ye swains,
Divide your crowded ranks; before him march
The rural minstrelsy, the rattling drum,
The clamorous war-pipe, and far-echoing horn.
SOMERVILLE, *Rural Sports.*

No long space intervened ere Roland Græme was able to discover among the crowd of revelers, who gamboled upon the open space which extends betwixt the village and the lake, a person of so great importance as Doctor Luke Lundin upon whom devolved officially the charge of representing the lord of the land, and who was attended for support of his authority by a piper, a drummer, and four sturdy clowns armed with rusty halberds, garnished with parti-colored ribbons—myrmidons who, early as the day was, had already broken more than one head in the awful names of the Laird of Lochleven and his chamberlain.*

As soon as this dignitary was informed that the castle skiff had arrived, with a gallant, dressed like a lord's son at the least, who desired presently to speak to him, he adjusted his ruff and his black coat, turned round his girdle till the garnished hilt of his long rapier became visible, and walked with due solemnity towards the beach. Solemn indeed he was entitled to be, even on less important occasions, for he had been bred to the venerable study of medicine, as those acquainted with the science very soon discovered from the aphorisms which ornamented his discourse. His success had not been equal to his pretensions; but as he was a native of the neighboring kingdom of Fife, and bore distant relation to, or dependence upon, the ancient family of Lundin of that ilk, who were bound in close friendship with the house of Lochleven, he had, through their interest, got planted comfortably enough in his present station upon the banks of that beautiful lake. The profits of his chamberlainship being moderate, especially in those unsettled times, he had eked it out a little with some practise in his original profession; and it was said that the inhabitants of the vil-

* See Scottish Fairs. Note 18.

lage and barony of Kinross were not more effectually thirled (which may be translated enthralled) to the baron's mill than they were to the medical monopoly of the chamberlain. Wo betide the family of the rich boor who presumed to depart this life without a passport from Dr. Luke Lundin! for if his representatives had aught to settle with the baron, as it seldom happened otherwise, they were sure to find a cold friend in the chamberlain. He was considered enough, however, gratuitously to help the poor out of their ailments, and sometimes out of all their other distresses at the same time.

Formal, in a double proportion, both as a physician and as a person in office, and proud of the scraps of learning which rendered his language almost universally unintelligible, Dr. Luke Lundin approached the beach, and hailed the page as he advanced towards him. "The freshness of the morning to you, fair sir. You are sent, I warrant me, to see if we observe here the regimen which her good ladyship hath prescribed, for eschewing all superstitious ceremonies and idle anilities in these our revels. I am aware that her good ladyship would willingly have altogether abolished and abrogated them. But as I had the honor to quote to her from the works of the learned Hercules of Saxony, *omnis curatio est vel canonica vel coacta*—that is, fair sir—for silk and velvet have seldom their Latin *ad unguem*—every cure must be wrought either by art and induction of rule or by constraint; and the wise physician chooseth the former. Which argument her ladyship being pleased to allow well of, I have made it my business so to blend instruction and caution with delight—*fiat mixtio*, as we say—that I can answer that the vulgar mind will be defecated and purged of anile and Popish fooleries by the medicament adhibited, so that the *primæ viæ* being cleansed, Master Henderson, or any other able pastor, may at will throw in tonics, and effectuate a perfect moral cure, *tuto, cito, jucunde*."

"I have no charge, Doctor Lundin," replied the page——

"Call me not doctor," said the chamberlain, "since I have laid aside my furred gown and bonnet, and retired me into this temporality of chamberlainship."

"O, sir," said the page, who was no stranger by report to the character of this original, "the cowl makes not the monk, neither the cord the friar: we have all heard of the cures wrought by Doctor Lundin."

"Toys, young sir—trifles," answered the leech with grave disclamation of superior skill; "the hit-or-miss practise of a poor retired gentleman, in a short cloak and doublet. Marry, Heaven sent its blessing; and this I must say, better fashioned mediciners have brought fewer patients through—*lunga roba cortá scienzia,* saith the Italian—ha, fair sir, you have the language?"

Roland Græme did not think it necessary to expound to this learned Theban whether he understood him or no; but, leaving that matter uncertain, he told him he came in quest of certain packages which should have arrived at Kinross and been placed under the chamberlain's charge the evening before.

"Body o' me!" said Doctor Lundin, "I fear our common carrier, John Auchtermuchty, hath met with some mischance, that he came not up last night with his wains: bad land this to journey in, my master; and the fool will travel by night too, although—besides all maladies, from your *tussis* to your *pestis,* which walk abroad in the night air—he may well fall in with half a dozen swashbucklers, who will ease him at once of his baggage and his earthly complaints. I must send forth to inquire after him, since he hath stuff of the honorable household on hand; and, by Our Lady, he hath stuff of mine too—certain drugs sent me from the city for composition of my alexipharmics; this gear must be looked to. Hodge," said he, addressing one of redoubted bodyguard, "do thou and Toby Telford take the mickle brown aver and the black cut-tailed mare, and make out towards the Keiry Craigs,* and see what tidings you can have of Auchtermuchty and his wains; I trust it is only the medicine of the pottle-pot—being the only *medicamentum* which the beast useth—which has caused him to tarry on the road. Take the ribbons from your halberds, ye knaves, and get on your jacks, plate-sleeves, and knapsculls, that your presence may work some terror if you meet with opposers." He then added, turning to Roland Græme, "I warrant me we shall have news of the wains in brief season. Meantime it will please you to look upon the sports; but first to enter my poor lodging and take your morning's cup. For what saith the school of Salerno—

Poculum, name haustum,
Resturat naturam exhaustam?"

"Your learning is too profound for me," replied the page; "and so would your draught be likewise, I fear."

"Not a whit, fair sir: a cordial cup of sack, impregnated

* See Note 19.

with wormwood, is the best anti-pestilential draught; and, to speak truth, the pestilential miasmata are now very rife in the atmosphere. We live in a happy time, young man," continued he, in a tone of grave irony, "and have many blessings unknown to our fathers. Here are two sovereigns in the land, a regnant and a claimant; that is enough of one good thing, but, if any one wants more, he may find a king in every peel-house in the country; so, if we lack government, it is not for want of governors. Then have we a civil war to phlebotomize us every year, and to prevent our population from starving for want of food; and for the same purpose we have the plague proposing us a visit, the best of all recipes for thinning a land, and converting younger brothers into elder ones. Well, each man in his vocation. You young fellows of the sword desire to wrestle, fence, or so forth with some expert adversary; and for my part, I love to match myself for life or death against that same plague."

As they proceeded up the street of the little village towards the doctor's lodgings, his attention was successively occupied by the various personages whom he met, and pointed out to the notice of his companion.

"Do you see that fellow with the red bonnet, the blue jerkin, and the great rough baton in his hand? I believe that clown hath the strength of a tower: he has lived fifty years in the world, and never encouraged the liberal sciences by buying one pennyworth of medicaments. But see you that man with the *facies Hippocratica?*" said he, pointing out to a thin peasant, with swelled legs, and a most cadaverous countenance; "that I call one of the worthiest men in the barony: he breakfasts, luncheons, dines, and sups by my advice, and not without my medicine; and, for his own single part, will go farther to clear out a moderate stock of pharmaceutics than half the country besides. How do you, my honest friend?" said he to the party in question, with a tone of condolence.

"Very weakly, sir, since I took the electuary," answered the patient; "it neighbored ill with the two spoonfuls of pease-porridge and the kirn-milk."

"Pease-porridge and kirn-milk! Have you been under medicine these ten years, and keep your diet so ill? The next morning take the electuary by itself, and touch nothing for six hours." The poor object bowed and limped off.

The next whom the doctor deigned to take notice of was

a lame fellow, by whom the honor was altogether undeserved, for at sight of the mediciner he began to shuffle away in the crowd as fast as his infirmities would permit.

"There is an ungrateful hound for you," said Doctor Lundin: "I cured him of the gout in his feet, and now he talks of the chargeableness of medicine, and makes the first use of his restored legs to fly from his physician. His *podagra* hath become a *chiragra,* as honest Martial hath it: the gout has got into his fingers, and he cannot draw his purse. Old saying and true—

Præmia cum poscit medicus, Sathan est.

We are angels when we come to cure, devils when we ask payment; but I will administer a purgation to his purse, I warrant him. There is his brother too, a sordid chuff. So ho, there! Saunders Dartlet! you have been ill, I hear?"

"Just got the turn, as I was thinking to send to your honor, and I am brawly now again; it was nae great thing that ailed me."

"Hark you, sirrah," said the doctor, "I trust you remember your owing to the laird four stones of barley-meal and a bow of oats; and I would have you send no more such kain-fowls as you sent last season, that looked as wretchedly as patients just dismissed from a plague-hospital; and there is hard money owing besides."

"I was thinking, sir," said the man, *more Scotico,* that is, returning no direct answer on the subject on which he was addressed, "my best way would be to come down to your honor, and take your advice yet, in case my trouble should come back."

"Do so then, knave," replied Lundin, "and remember what Ecclesiasticus saith—'Give place to the physician: let him not go from thee, for thou hast need of him.'"

His exhortation was interrupted by an apparition which seemed to strike the doctor with as much horror and surprise as his own visage inflicted upon sundry of those persons whom he had addressed.

The figure which produced this effect on the Esculapius of the village was that of a tall old woman, who wore a high-crowned hat and muffler. The first of these habiliments added apparently to her stature, and the other served to conceal the lower part of her face, and as the hat itself was slouched, little could be seen besides two brown cheek-bones, and the eyes of swarthy fire, that gleamed from under two shaggy gray eyebrows. She was dressed in a long dark-colored robe of unusual fashion, bordered at the skirts and on the stomacher with a sort of white trimming resembling the Jewish phylacteries, on which was wrought the characters of some unknown language. She held in her hand a walking-staff of black ebony.

"By the soul of Celsus," said Doctor Luke Lundin, "it is old Mother Nicneven herself; she hath come to beard me within mine own bounds, and in the very execution of mine office! 'Have at thy coat, old woman,' as the song says. Hob Anster, let her presently be seized and committed to the tolbooth; and if there are any zealous brethren here who would give the hag her deserts, and duck her, as a witch, in the loch, I pray let them in no way be hindered."

But the myrmidons of Doctor Lundin showed in this case no alacrity to do his bidding. Hob Anster even ventured to remonstrate in the name of himself and his brethren. "To be sure he was to do his honor's bidding; and for a' that folk said about the skill and witcheries of Mother Nicneven, he would put his trust in God, and his hand on her collar, without dreadour. But she was no common spae-wife, this Mother Nicneven, like Jean Jopp that lived in the Brierie Baulk. She had lords and lairds that would ruffle for her. There was Moncrieff of Tippermalloch, that was Popish, and the laird of Carslogie, a kenn'd queensman, were in the fair, with wha kenn'd how mony swords and bucklers at their back; and they would be sure to make a break-out if the officers meddled with the auld Popish witch-wife, who was sae weel friended; mair especially as the laird's best men, such as were not in the castle, were in Edinburgh with him, and he doubted his honor the doctor would find ower few to make a good backing if blades were bare."

The doctor listened unwillingly to this prudential counsel, and was only comforted by the faithful promise of his satellite that "The old woman should," as he expressed it, "be ta'en canny the next time she trespassed on the bounds."

"And in that event," said the doctor to his companion, "fire and fagot shall be the best of her welcome."

This he spoke in hearing of the dame herself, who even then, and in passing the doctor, shot towards him from under her gray eyebrows a look of the most insulting and contemptuous superiority.

"This way," continued the physician—"this way," marshaling his guest into his lodging; "take care you stumble not over a retort, for it is hazardous for the ignorant to walk in the ways of art."

The page found all reason for the caution; for, besides stuffed birds, and lizards, and bottled snakes, and bundles of simples made up, and other parcels spread out to dry, and all the confusion, not to mention the mingled and sickening smells, incidental to a druggist's stock-in-trade, he had also to avoid heaps of charcoal, crucibles, bolt-heads, stoves, and the other furniture of a chemical laboratory.

Amongst his other philosophical qualities, Doctor Lundin failed not to be a confused sloven, and his old housekeeper, whose life, as she said, was spent in "redding him up," had trotted off to the mart of gaiety with other and younger folks. Much clattering and jangling therefore there was among jars, and bottles, and phials, ere the doctor produced the salutiferous potion which he recommended so strongly, and a search equally long and noisy followed among broken cans and cracked pipkins ere he could bring forth a cup out of which to drink it. Both matters being at length achieved, the doctor set the example to his guest, by quaffing off a cup of the cordial, and smacking his lips with approbation as it descended his gullet. Roland, in turn, submitted to swallow the potion which his host so earnestly recommended, but which he found so insufferably bitter that he became eager to escape from the laboratory in search of a draught of fair water to expel the taste. In spite of his efforts, he was nevertheless detained by the garrulity of his host, till he gave him some account of Mother Nicneven.

"I care not to speak of her," said the doctor, "in the open air, and among the throng of people: not for fright, like yon cowardly dog, Anster, but because I would give no occasion for a fray, having no leisure to look to stabs, slashes, and broken bones. Men call the old hag a prophetess; I do scarce believe she could foretell when a brood of chickens will chip the shell. Men say she reads the heavens; my black bitch knows as much of them when she sits baying the moon. Men pretend the ancient wretch is a sorceress, a witch, and what not; *inter nos*, I will never contradict a rumor which may bring her to the stake which she so richly deserves, but neither will I believe that the tales of witches which they din into our ears are aught but knavery, cozenage, and old women's fables."

"In the name of Heaven, what is she then," said the page, "that you make such a stir about her?"

"She is one of those cursed old women," replied the

doctor, "who take currently and impudently upon themselves to act as advisers and curers of the sick, on the strength of some trash of herbs, some rhyme of spells, some julep or diet, drink or cordial."

"Nay, go no farther," said the page; "if they brew cordials, evil be their lot and all their partakers!"

"You say well, young man," said Doctor Lundin; "for mine own part, I know no such pests to the commonwealth as these old incarnate devils, who haunt the chambers of the brain-sick patients, that are mad enough to suffer them to interfere with, disturb, and let the regular progress of a learned and artificial cure, with their syrups, and their juleps, and diascordium, and mithridate, and my Lady What-shall-call'um's powder, and worthy Dame Trashem's pill; and thus make widows and orphans, and cheat the regular and well-studied physician, in order to get the name of wise women and skeely neighbors, and so forth. But no more on't. Mother Nicneven * and I will meet one day, and she shall know there is danger in dealing with the doctor."

"It is a true word, and many have found it," said the page; "but, under your favor, I would fain walk abroad for a little and see these sports."

"It is well moved," said the doctor, "and I too should be showing myself abroad. Moreover, the play waits us, young man; to-day, *totus mundus agit histrionem.*" And they sallied forth accordingly into the mirthful scene.

* See Note 20.

CHAPTER XXVII

> See on yon verdant lawn, the gathering crowd
> Thickens amain; the buxom nymphs advance,
> Usher'd by jolly clowns; distinctions cease,
> Lost in the common joy, and the bold slave
> Leans on his wealthy master unreproved.
>
> SOMERVILLE, *Rural Sports*.

THE reappearance of the dignified chamberlain on the street of the village was eagerly hailed by the revelers, as a pledge that the play, or dramatic representation, which had been postponed owing to his absence, was now full surely to commence. Anything like an approach to this most interesting of all amusements was of recent origin in Scotland, and engaged public attention in proportion. All other sports were discontinued. The dance around the Maypole was arrested, the ring broken up and dispersed, while the dancers, each leading his partner by the hand, tripped off to the sylvan theater. A truce was in like manner achieved betwixt a huge brown bear and certain mastiffs, who were tugging and pulling at his shaggy coat, under the mediation of the bear-ward and half a dozen butchers and yeomen, who, by dint of "staving and tailing," as it was technically termed, separated the unfortunate animals, whose fury had for an hour past been their chief amusement. The itinerant minstrel found himself deserted by the audience he had collected, even in the most interesting passage of the romance which he recited, and just as he was sending about his boy, with bonnet in hand, to collect their oblations. He indignantly stopped short in the midst of *Rosewal and Lilian*, and, replacing his three-stringed fiddle, or rebeck, in its leathern case, followed the crowd, with no good-will, to the exhibition which had superseded his own. The juggler had ceased his exertions of emitting flame and smoke, and was content to respire in the manner of ordinary mortals rather than to play gratuitously the part of a fiery dragon. In short, all other sports were suspended, so eagerly did the revelers throng towards the place of representation.

They would err greatly who should regulate their ideas of this dramatic exhibition upon those derived from a modern theater ; for the rude shows of Thespis were far less different from those exhibited by Euripides on the stage of Athens, with all its magnificent decorations and pomp of dresses and of scenery. In the present case there were no scenes, no stage, no machinery, no pit, box, and gallery, no box-lobby ; and, what might in poor Scotland be some consolation for other negations, there was no taking of money at the door. As in the devices of the magnanimous Bottom, the actors had a greensward plot for a stage, and a hawthorn bush for a greenroom and tiring-house ; the spectators being accommodated with seats on the artificial bank which had been raised around three-fourths of the playground, the remainder being left open for the entrance and exit of the performers. Here sate the uncritical audience, the chamberlain in the center, as the person highest in office—all alive to enjoyment and admiration, and all therefore dead to criticism.

The characters which appeared and disappeared before the amused and interested audience were those which fill the earlier stage in all nations—old men, cheated by their wives and daughters, pillaged by their sons, and imposed on by their domestics, a braggadocio captain, a knavish pardoner or quæstionary, a country bumpkin, and a wanton city dame. Amid all these, and more acceptable than almost the whole put together, was the all-licensed fool, the Gracioso of the Spanish drama, who, with his cap fashioned into the resemblance of a coxcomb, and his bauble, a truncheon terminated by a carved figure, wearing a fool's cap, in his hand, went, came, and returned, mingling in every scene of the piece, and interrupting the business, without having any share himself in the action, and ever and anon transfering his gibes from the actors on the stage to the audience who sat around, prompt to applaud the whole.

The wit of the piece, which was not of the most polished kind, was chiefly directed against the superstitious practises of the Catholic religion ; and the stage artillery had on this occasion been leveled by no less a person than Doctor Lundin, who had not only commanded the manager of the entertainment to select one of the numerous satires which had been written against the Papists (several of which were cast in a dramatic form), but had even, like the Prince of Denmark, caused them to insert, or, according to his own phrase, to infuse, here and there, a few pleasantries of his own penning, on the same inexhaustible subject, hoping thereby to mollify the rigor of the Lady of Lochleven towards pastimes of this description. He failed not to jog Roland's elbow, who was sitting in state behind him, and recommend to his particular attention those favorite passages. As for the page, to whom the very idea of such an exhibition, simple as it was, was entirely new, he beheld it with the undiminished and ecstatic delight with which men of all ranks look for the first time on dramatic representation, and laughed, shouted, and clapped his hands as the performance proceeded. An incident at length took place which effectually broke off his interest in the business of the scene.

One of the principal personages in the comic part of the drama was, as we have already said, a quæstionary or pardoner, one of those itinerants who hawked about from place to place relics, real or pretended, with which he excited the devotion at once and the charity of the populace, and generally deceived both the one and the other. The hypocrisy, impudence, and profligacy of these clerical wanderers had made them the subject of satire from the time of Chaucer down to that of Heywood. Their present representative failed not to follow the same line of humor, exhibiting pig's bones for relics, and boasting the virtues of small tin crosses, which had been shaken in the holy porringer at Loretto, and of cockle-shells, which had been brought from the shrine of St. James of Compostella, all which he disposed of to the devout Catholics at nearly as high a price as antiquaries are now willing to pay for the baubles of similar intrinsic value. A length the pardoner pulled from his scrip a small phial of clear water, of which he vaunted the quality in the following verses :—

" Listneth, gode people, everiche one,
For in the londe of Babylone,
Far eastward I wot it lyeth,
And is the first londe the sonne espieth,
Ther, as he cometh fro out the sé ;
In this ilk londe, as thinketh me,
Right as holie legendes tell,
Snottreth from a roke a well,
And falleth into ane bath of ston,
Wher chast Susanne, in times long gon
Was wont to wash her bodie and lim.
Mickle virtue hath that streme,
As ye shall se er that ye pas,
Ensample by this little glas.
Through nightés cold and dayés hote,
Hiderward I have it brought ;
Hath a wife made slip or slide,
Or a maiden stepp'd aside,
Putteth this water under her nese,
Wold she nold she, she shall snese."

The jest, as the reader skilful in the antique language of the drama must at once perceive, turned on the same pivot as in the old minstrel tales of the *Drinking-Horn of King Arthur* and the *Mantle made Amiss.* But the audience were neither learned nor critical enough to challenge its want of originality. The potent relic was, after such grimace and buffoonery as befitted the subject, presented successively to each of the female personages of the drama, not one of whom sustained the supposed test of discretion ; but, to the infinite delight of the audience, sneezed much louder and longer than perhaps they themselves had counted on. The jest seemed at last worn threadbare, and the pardoner was passing on to some new pleasantry, when the jester or clown of the drama, possessing himself secretly of the phial which contained the wondrous liquor, applied it suddenly to the nose of a young woman, who, with her black silk muffler, or screen, drawn over her face, was sitting in the foremost rank of the spectators, intent apparently upon the business of the stage. The contents of the phial, well calculated to sustain the credit of the pardoner's legend, set the damsel a-sneezing violently, an admission of frailty which was received with shouts of rapture by the audience. These were soon, however, renewed at the expense of the jester himself, when the insulted maiden extricated, ere the paroxysm was well over, one hand from the folds of her mantle, and bestowed on the wag a buffet, which made him reel fully his own length from the pardoner, and then acknowledge the favor by instant prostration.

No one pities a jester overcome in his vocation, and the clown met with little sympathy when, rising from the ground and whimpering forth his complaints of harsh treatment, he invoked the assistance and sympathy of the audience. But the chamberlain, feeling his own dignity insulted, ordered two of his halberdiers to bring the culprit before him. When these official persons first approached the virago, she threw herself into an attitude of firm defiance, as if determined to resist their authority ; and from the sample of strength and spirit which she had already displayed, they showed no alacrity at executing their commission. But on half a minute's reflection, the damsel changed totally her attitude and manner, folded her cloak around her arms in modest and maiden-like fashion, and walked of her own accord to the presence of the great man, followed and guarded by the two manful satellites. As she moved across the vacant space, and more especially as she stood at the footstool of the doctor's judgment-seat, the maiden discovered that lightness and elasticity of step, and natural grace of manner, which connoisseurs in female beauty know to be seldom divided from it. Moreover, her neat russet-colored jacket, and short petticoat of the same color, displayed a handsome form and a pretty leg. Her features were concealed by the screen; but the doctor, whose gravity did not prevent his pretensions to be a connoisseur of the school we have hinted at, saw enough to judge favorably of the piece by the sample.

He began, however, with considerable austerity of manner. "And how now, saucy quean!" said the medical man of office; "what have you to say why I should not order you to be ducked in the loch for lifting your hand to the man in my presence?"

"Marry," replied the culprit, "because I judge that your honor will not think the cold bath necessary for my complaints."

"A pestilent jade," said the doctor, whispering to Roland Græme, "and I'll warrant her a good one: her voice is as sweet as sirup. But, my pretty maiden," said he, "you show us wonderful little of that countenance of yours; be pleased to throw aside your muffler."

"I trust your honor will excuse me till we are more private," answered the maiden; "for I have acquaintance, and I should like ill to be known in the country as the poor girl whom that scurvy knave put his jest upon."

"Fear nothing for thy good name, my sweet little modicum of candied manna!" replied the doctor; "for I protest to you, as I am chamberlain of Lochleven, Kinross, and so forth, that the chaste Susanna herself could not have snuffed that elixir without sternutation, being in truth a curious distillation of rectified *acetum*, or vinegar of the sun, prepared by mine own hands. Wherefore, as thou sayest thou wilt come to me in private, and express thy contrition for the offense whereof thou hast been guilty, I command that all for the present go forward as if no such interruption of the prescribed course had taken place."

The damsel courtesied and tripped back to her place. The play proceeded, but it no longer attracted the attention of Roland Græme.

The voice, the figure, and what the veil permitted to be seen of the neck and tresses, of the village damsel bore so strong a resemblance to those of Catherine Seyton that he felt like one bewildered in the mazes of a changeful and stupifying dream. The memorable scene of the hostelry rushed on his recollection, with all its doubtful and marvelous circumstances. Were the tales of enchantment which he had read in romances realized in this extraordinary girl? Could she transport herself from the walled and guarded Castle of Lochleven, moated with its broad lake (towards which he cast back a look as if to ascertain it was still in existence), and watched with such scrupulous care as the safety of a nation demanded. Could she surmount all these obstacles, and make such careless and dangerous use of her liberty as to engage herself publicly in a quarrel in a village fair? Roland was unable to determine whether the exertions which it must have cost her to gain her freedom or the use to which she had put it rendered her the most unaccountable creature.

Lost in these meditations, he kept his gaze fixed on the subject of them; and in every casual motion discovered, or thought he discovered, something which reminded him still more strongly of Catherine Seyton. It occurred to him more than once, indeed, that he might be deceiving himself by exaggerating some casual likeness into absolute identity. But then the meeting at the hostelry of St. Michael's returned to his mind, and it seemed in the highest degree improbable that, under such various circumstances, mere imagination should twice have found opportunity to play him the self-same trick. This time, however, he determined to have his doubts resolved, and for this purpose he sate during the rest of the play like a greyhound in the slip, ready to spring upon the hare the instant that she was started. The damsel, whom he watched attentively lest she should escape in the crowd when the spectacle was closed, sate as if perfectly unconscious that she was observed. But the worthy doctor marked the direction of his eyes, and magnanimously suppressed his own inclination to become the Theseus to this Hippolyta, in deference to the rights of hospitality, which enjoined him to forbear interference with the pleasurable pursuits of his young friend. He passed one or two formal gibes upon the fixed attention which the page paid to the unknown, and upon his own jealousy; adding, however, that if both were to be presented to the patient at once, he had little doubt she would think the younger man the sounder prescription. "I fear me," he added, "we shall have no news of the knave Auchtermuchty for some time, since the vermin whom I sent after him seem to have proved corbie-messengers. So you have an hour or two on your hands, Master Page; and as the minstrels are beginning to strike up, now that the play is ended, why, an you incline for a dance, yonder is the green, and there sits your partner. I trust you will hold me perfect in my diagnostics, since I see with half an eye what disease you are sick of, and have administered a pleasing remedy.

Discernit sapiens res (as Chambers hath it) quas confundit asellus."

The page hardly heard the end of the learned adage, or the charge which the chamberlain gave him to be within reach, in case of the wains arriving suddenly, and sooner than expected, so eager was he at once to shake himself free of his learned associate and to satisfy his curiosity regarding the unknown damsel. Yet, in the haste which he made towards her, he found time to reflect that, in order to secure an opportunity of conversing with her in private, he must not alarm her at first accosting her. He therefore composed his manner and gait, and advancing with becoming self-confidence before three or four country-fellows who were intent on the same design, but knew not so well how to put their request into shape, he acquainted her that he, as the deputy of the venerable chamberlain, requested the honor of her hand as a partner.

"The venerable chamberlain," said the damsel, frankly, reaching the page her hand, "does very well to exercise this part of his privilege by deputy; and I suppose the laws of the revels leave me no choice but to accept of his faithful delegate."

"Provided, fair damsel," said the page, "his choice of a delegate is not altogether distasteful to you."

"Of that, fair sir," replied the maiden, "I will tell you more when we have danced the first measure."

Catherine Seyton had admirable skill in gestic lore, and was sometimes called on to dance for the amusement of her royal mistress. Roland Græme had often been a spectator of her skill, and sometimes, at the Queen's command, Catherine's partner on such occasions. He was, therefore, perfectly acquainted with Catherine's mode of dancing; and observed that his present partner, in grace, in agility, in quickness of ear, and precision of execution, exactly ressembled her, save that the Scottish jig which he now danced with her required a more violent and rapid motion, and more rustic agility, than the stately pavens, lavoltas, and courantoes which he had seen her execute in the chamber of Queen Mary. The active duties of the dance left him little time for reflection, ard none for conversation; but when their *pas de deux* was finished, amidst the acclamations of the villagers, who had seldom witnessed such an exhibition, he took an opportunity, when they yielded up the green to another couple, to use the privilege of a partner, and enter into conversation with the mysterious maiden whom he still held by the hand.

"Fair partner, may I not crave the name of her who has graced me thus far?"

"You may," said the maiden; "but it is a question whether I shall answer you."

"And why?" asked Roland.

"Because nobody gives anything for nothing, and you can tell me nothing in return which I care to hear."

"Could I not tell you my name and lineage, in exchange for yours?" returned Roland.

"No!" answered the maiden, "for you know little of either."

"How?" said the page, somewhat angrily.

"Wrath you not for the matter," said the damsel; "I will show you in an instant that I know more of you than you do of yourself."

"Indeed!" answered Græme; "for whom then do you take me?"

"For the wild falcon," answered she, "whom a dog brought in his mouth to a certain castle, when he was but an unfledged eyas; for the hawk whom men dare not let fly, lest he should check at game and pounce on carrion; whom folk must keep hooded till he has the proper light of his eyes, and can discover good from evil."

"Well—be it so," replied Roland Græme; "I guess at a part of your parable, fair mistress mine; and perhaps I know as much of you as you do of me, and can well dispense with the information which you are so niggard in giving."

"Prove that," said the maiden, "and I will give you credit for more penetration than I judged you to be gifted withal."

"It shall be proved instantly," said Roland Græme. "The first letter of your name is S and the last N."

"Admirable!" said his partner; "guess on."

"It pleases you to-day," continued Roland, "to wear the snood and kirtle, and perhaps you may be seen to-morrow in hat and feather, hose and doublet."

"In the clout!—in the clout! you have hit the very white," said the damsel, suppressing a great inclination to laugh.

"You can switch men's eyes out of their heads, as well as the hearts out of their bosoms."

These last words were uttered in a low and tender tone, which, to Roland's great mortification, and somewhat to his displeasure, was so far from allaying that it greatly increased, his partner's disposition to laughter. She could scarce compose herself while she replied, "If you had thought my hand so formidable," extricating it from his hold, "you would not have grasped it so hard; but I perceive you know me so fully that there is no occasion to show you my face."

"Fair Catherine," said the page, "he were unworthy ever to have seen you, far less to have dwelt so long in the same service, and under the same roof with you, who could mistake your air, your gesture, your step in walking or in dancing, the turn of your neck, the symmetry of your form: none could be so dull as not to recognize you by so many proofs; but for me, I could swear even to that tress of hair that escapes from under your muffler."

"And to the face, of course, which that muffler covers," said the maiden, removing her veil, and in an instant endeavoring to replace it. She showed the features of Catherine; but an unusual degree of petulant impatience inflamed them when, from some awkwardness in her management of the muffler, she was unable again to adjust it with that dexterity which was a principal accomplishment of the coquettes of the time.

"The fiend rive the rag to tatters!" said the damsel, as the veil fluttered about her shoulders, with an accent so earnest and decided that it made the page start. He looked again at the damsel's face, but the information which his eyes received was to the same purport as before. He assisted her to adjust her muffler, and both were for an instant silent. The damsel spoke first, for Roland Græme was overwhelmed with surprise at the contrarieties which Catherine Seyton seemed to include in her person and character.

"You are surprised," said the damsel to him, "at what you see and hear. But the times which make females men are least of all fitted for men to become women; yet you yourself are in danger of such a change."

"I in danger of becoming effeminate!" said the page.

"Yes, you for all the boldness of your reply," said the damsel. "When you should hold fast your religion, because it is assailed on all sides by rebels, traitors, and heretics, you let it glide out of your breast like water grasped in the hand. If you are driven from the faith of your fathers from fear of a traitor, is not that womanish? If you are cajoled by the cunning arguments of a trumpeter of heresy, or the praises of a Puritanic old woman, is not that womanish? If you are bribed by the hope of spoil and preferment, is not that womanish? And when you wonder at my venting a threat or an execration, should you not wonder at yourself, who, pretending to a gentle name, and aspiring to knighthood, can be at the same time cowardly, silly, and self-interested?"

"I would that a man would bring such a charge!" said the page; "he should see, ere his life was a minute older, whether he had cause to term me coward or no."

"Beware of such big words," answered the maiden; "you said but anon that I sometimes wear hose and doublet."

"But remain still Catherine Seyton, wear what you list," said the page, endeavoring again to possess himself of her hand.

"You indeed are pleased to call me so," replied the maiden, evading his intention, "but I have many other names besides."

"And will you not reply to that," said the page, "by which you are distinguished beyond every other maiden in Scotland?"

The damsel, unallured by his praises, still kept aloof, and sung with a gaiety a verse from an old ballad—

"O some do call me Jack, sweet love,
And some do call me Gill;
But when I ride to Holyrood,
My name is Wilful Will."

"Wilful Will!" exclaimed the page, impatiently; "say rather Will o' the Wisp—Jack with the Lantern, for never was such a deceitful or wandering meteor!"

"If I be such," replied the maiden, "I ask no fools to follow me. If they do so, it is at their own pleasure, and must be on their own proper peril."

"Nay, but, dearest Catherine," said Roland Græme, "be for one instant serious."

"If you will call me your dearest Catherine, when I have given you so many names to choose upon," replied the damsel, "I would ask you how, supposing me for two or three hours of my life escaped from yonder tower, you have the cruelty to ask me to be serious during the only merry moments I have seen perhaps for months?"

"Ay, but, fair Catherine, there are moments of deep and true feeling which are worth ten thousand years of the liveliest mirth; and such was that of yesterday, when you so nearly——"

"So nearly what?" demanded the damsel, hastily.

"When you approached your lips so near to the sign you had traced on my ferehead."

"Mother of Heaven!" exclaimed she, in a yet fiercer tone, and with a more masculine manner than she had yet exhibited. "Catherine Seyton approached her lips to a man's brow, and thou that man! Vassal, thou liest!"

The page stood astonished; but, conceiving he had alarmed the damsel's delicacy by alluding to the enthusiasm of a moment, and the manner in which she had expressed it, he endeavored to falter forth an apology. His excuses, though he was unable to give them any regular shape, were accepted by his companion, who had indeed suppressed her indignation after its first explosion. "Speak no more on't," she said. "And now let us part; our conversation may attract more notice than is convenient for either of us."

"Nay, but allow me at least to follow you to some sequestered place."

"You dare not," replied the maiden.

"How," said the youth, "dare not? where is it you dare go, where I dare not follow?"

"You fear a will o' the wisp," said the damsel; "how would you face a fiery dragon, with an enchantress mounted on its back?"

"Like Sir Eger, Sir Grime, or Sir Greysteil," said the page; "but be there such toys to be seen here?"

"I go to Mother Nicneven's," answered the maid; "and she is witch enough to rein the horned devil, with a red silk thread for a bridle, and a rowan-tree switch for a whip."

"I will follow you," said the page.

"Let it be at some distance," said the maiden.

And wrapping her mantle round her with more success than on her former attempt, she mingled with the throng, and walked towards the village, heedfully followed by Roland Græme at some distance, and under every precaution which he could use to prevent his purpose from being observed.

CHAPTER XXVIII

Yes, it is she whose eyes look'd on thy childhood,
And watch'd with trembling hope thy dawn of youth,
That now, with these same eyeballs dimm'd with age,
And dimmer yet with tears, see thy dishonor.

Old Play.

At the entrance of the principal, or indeed, so to speak, the only, street in Kinross the damsel, whose steps were pursued by Roland Græme, cast a glance behind her, as if to be certain he had not lost trace of her, and then plunged down a very narrow lane which ran betwixt two rows of poor and ruinous cottages. She paused for a second at the door of one of those miserable tenements, again cast her eye up the lane towards Roland, then lifted the latch, opened the door, and disappeared from his view.

With whatever haste the page followed her example, the difficulty which he found in discovering the trick of the latch, which did not work quite in the usual manner, and in pushing open the door, which did not yield to his first effort, delayed for a minute or two his entrance into the cottage. A dark and smoky passage led, as usual, betwixt the exterior wall of the house and the "hallan," or clay wall, which served as a partition betwixt it and the interior. At the end of this passage, and through the partition, was a door leading into the "ben," or inner chamber of the cottage, and when Roland Græme's hand was upon the latch of this door, a female voice pronounced, "*Benedictus qui veniat in nomine Domini, damnandus qui in nomine inimici.*" On entering the apartment, he perceived the figure which the chamberlain had pointed out to him as Mother Nicneven, seated beside the lowly hearth. But there was no other person in the room. Roland Græme gazed around in surprise at the disappearance of Catherine Seyton, without paying much regard to the supposed sorceress, until she attracted and riveted his regard by the tone in which she asked him—"What seekest thou here?"

"I seek," said the page, with much embarrassment—"I seek——"

But his answer was cut short when the old woman, drawing her huge gray eyebrows sternly together, with a frown which knitted her brow into a thousand wrinkles, arose, and erecting herself up to her full natural size, tore the kerchief from her head, and seizing Roland by the arm, made two strides across the floor of the apartment to a small window through which the light fell full on her face, and showed the astonished youth the countenance of Magdalen Græme.

"Yes, Roland," she said, "thine eyes deceive thee not: they show thee truly the features of her whom thou hast thyself deceived, whose wine thou hast turned into gall, her bread of joyfulness into bitter poison, her hope into the blackest despair. It is she who now demands of thee, what seekest thou here?—she whose heaviest sin towards Heaven hath been, that she loved thee even better than the weal of the whole church, and could not without reluctance surrender thee even in the cause of God—she now asks you, what seekest thou here?"

While she spoke, she kept her broad black eye riveted on the youth's face, with the expression with which the eagle regards his prey ere he tears it to pieces. Roland felt himself at the moment incapable either of reply or evasion. This extraordinary enthusiast had preserved over him in some measure the ascendency which she had acquired during his childhood; and, besides, he knew the violence of her passions and her impatience of contradiction, and was sensible that almost any reply which he could make was likely to throw her into an ecstasy of rage. He was therefore silent; and Magdalen Græme proceeded with increasing enthusiasm in her apostrophe—"Once more, what seek'st thou, false boy?—seek'st thou the honor thou hast renounced, the faith thou hast abandoned, the hopes thou hast destroyed? Or didst thou seek me, the sole protectress of thy youth, the only parent whom thou hast known, that thou mayest trample on my gray hairs, even as thou hast already trampled on the best wishes of my heart?"

"Pardon me, mother," said Roland Græme; "but, in truth and reason, I deserve not your blame. I have been treated amongst you—even by yourself, my revered parent, as well as by others—as one who lacked the common attributes of freewill and human reason, or was at least deemed unfit to exercise them. A land of enchantment have I been led into, and spells have been cast around me—every one has met me in disguise—every one has spoken to me in parables—I have been like one who walks in a weary and bewildering dream; and now you blame me that I have not the sense, and judgment, and steadiness of a waking, and a disenchanted, and a reasonable man, who knows what he is doing, and wherefore he does it! If one must walk with masks and specters, who waft themselves from place to place as it were in vision rather than reality, it might shake the soundest faith and turn the wisest head. I sought, since I must needs avow my folly, the same Catherine Seyton with whom you made me first acquainted, and whom I most strangely find in this village of Kinross, gayest among the revelers, when I had but just left her in the well-guarded Castle of Lochleven, the sad attendant of an imprisoned Queen. I sought her, and in her place I find you, my mother, more strangely disguised than even she is."

"And what hadst thou to do with Catherine Seyton?" said the matron, sternly; "is this a time or a world to follow maidens, or to dance around a Maypole? When the trumpet summons every true-hearted Scotsman around the standard of the true sovereign, shalt thou be found loitering in a lady's bower?"

"No, by Heaven, nor imprisoned in the rugged walls of an island castle!" answered Roland Græme. "I would the blast were to sound even now, for I fear that nothing less loud will dispel the chimerical visions by which I am surrounded."

"Doubt not that it will be winded," said the matron, "and that so fearfully loud, that Scotland will never hear the like until the last and loudest blast of all shall announce to mountain and to valley that time is no more. Meanwhile, be thou but brave and constant. Serve God, and honor thy sovereign. Abide by thy religion. I cannot—I will not—I dare not ask thee the truth of the terrible surmises I have heard touching thy falling away—perfect not that accursed sacrifice; and yet, even at this late hour, thou mayst be what I have hoped for, the son of my dearest hope. What say I? The son of *my* hope? Thou shalt be the hope of Scotland, her boast and her honor! Even thy wildest and most foolish wishes may perchance be fulfilled. I might blush to mingle meaner motives with the noble guerdon I hold out to thee. It shames me, being such as I am, to mention the idle passions of youth, save with contempt and the purpose of censure. But we must bribe children to wholesome medicine by the offer of cates, and youth to honorable achievement with the promise of pleasure. Mark me, therefore, Roland. The love of Catherine Seyton will follow him only who shall achieve the freedom of her mistress : and believe, it may be one day in thine own power to be that happy lover. Cast, therefore, away doubt and fear, and prepare to do what religion calls for, what thy country demands of thee, what thy duty as a subject and as a servant alike require at your hand; and be assured, even the idlest or wildest wishes of thy heart will be most readily attained by following the call of thy duty."

As she ceased speaking, a double knock was heard against the inner door. The matron, hastily adjusting her muffler and resuming her chair by the hearth, demanded who was there.

"*Salve in nomine sancto,*" was answered from without.

"*Salvete et vos,*" answered Magdalen Græme.

And a man entered in the ordinary dress of a nobleman's retainer, wearing at his girdle a sword and buckler. "I sought you," said he, "my mother, and him whom I see with you." Then addressing himself to Roland Græme, he said to him, "Hast thou not a packet from George Douglas?"

"I have," said the page, suddenly recollecting that which had been committed to his charge in the morning, "but I may not deliver it to any one without some token that they have a right to ask it."

"You say well," replied the serving-man, and whispered into his ear, "The packet which I ask is the report to his father, will this token suffice?"

"It will," replied the page, and taking the packet from his bosom, gave it to the man.

"I will return presently," said the serving-man, and left the cottage.

Roland had now sufficiently recovered his surprise to accost his relative in turn, and request to know the reason why he found her in so precarious a disguise, and a place so dangerous. "You cannot be ignorant," he said, "of the hatred that the Lady of Lochleven bears to those of your—that is of our religion; your present disguise lays you open to suspicions of a different kind, but inferring no less hazard; and whether as a Catholic, or as a sorceress, or as a friend to the unfortunate Queen, you are in equal danger, if apprehended within the bounds of the Douglas; and in the chamberlain who administers their authority you have, for his own reasons, an enemy, and a bitter one."

"I know it," said the matron, her eyes kindling with triumph; "I know that, vain of his schoolcraft and carnal wisdom, Luke Lundin views with jealousy and hatred the blessings which the saints have conferred on my prayers, and on the holy relics, before the touch, nay, before the bare presence, of which disease and death have so often been known to retreat. I know he would rend and tear me: but there is a chain and a muzzle on the ban-dog that shall restrain his fury, and the Master's servant shall not be offended by him until the Master's work is wrought. When that hour comes, let the shadows of the evening descend on me in thunder and in tempest: the time shall be welcome that relieves my eyes from seeing guilt, and my ears from listening to blasphemy. Do thou but be constant; play thy part as I have played and will play mine; and my release shall be like that of a blessed martyr whose ascent to Heaven angels hail with psalm and song, while earth pursues him with hiss and with execration."

As she concluded, the serving-man again entered the cottage, and said, "All is well! the time holds for to-morrow night."

"What time? what holds?" exclaimed Roland Græme. "I trust I have given the Douglas's packet to no wrong——"

"Content yourself, young man," answered the serving-man; "thou hast my word and token."

"I know not if the token be right," said the page; "and I care not much for the word of a stranger."

"What," said the matron, "although thou mayst have given a packet delivered to thy charge by one of the Queen's rebels into the hand of a loyal subject—there were no great mistake in that, thou hot-brained boy!"

"By St. Andrew, there were foul mistake, though," answered the page; "it is the very spirit of my duty, in this first stage of chivalry, to be faithful to my trust; and had the devil given me a message to discharge, I would not—so I had plighted my faith to the contrary—betray his counsel to an angel of light."

"Now, by the love I once bore thee," said the matron, "I could slay thee with mine own hand, when I hear thee talk of a dearer faith being due to rebels and heretics than thou owest to thy church and thy prince!"

"Be patient, my good sister," said the serving-man; "I will give him such reasons as shall counterbalance the scruples which beset him: the spirit is honorable, though now it may be mistimed and misplaced. Follow me, young man."

"Ere I go to call this stranger to a reckoning," said the page to the matron, "is there nothing I can do for your comfort and safety?"

"Nothing," she replied—"nothing, save what will lead more to thy own honor: the saints who have protected me thus far will lend me succor as I need it. Tread the path of glory that is before thee, and only think of me as the creature on earth who will be most delighted to hear of thy fame. Follow the stranger; he hath tidings for you that you little expect."

That stranger remained on the threshold as if waiting for Roland, and as soon as he saw him put himself in motion he moved on before at a quick pace. Diving still deeper down the lane, Roland perceived that it was now bordered by buildings upon the one side only, and that the other was fenced by a high old wall, over which some trees extended their branches. Descending a good way farther, they came to a small door in the wall. Roland's guide paused, looked around for an instant to see if any one were within sight, then taking a key from his pocket, opened the door and entered, making a sign to Roland Græme to follow him. He did so, and the stranger locked the door carefully on the inside. During this operation the page had a moment to look around, and perceived that he was in a small orchard very trimly kept.

The stranger led him through an alley or two, shaded by trees loaded with summer-fruit, into a pleached arbor, where, taking the turf-seat which was on the one side, he motioned to Roland to occupy that which was opposite to him, and, after a momentary silence, opened the conversation as follows: "You have asked a better warrant than the word of a mere stranger to satisfy you that I have the authority of George of Douglas for possessing myself of the packet entrusted to your charge?"

"It is precisely the point on which I demand reckoning of you," said Roland. "I fear I have acted hastily; if so, I must redeem my error as I best may."

"You hold me then as a perfect stranger?" said the man. "Look at my face more attentively, and see if the features do not resemble those of a man much known to you formerly."

Roland gazed attentively; but the ideas recalled to his mind were so inconsistent with the mean and servile dress of the person before him that he did not venture to express the opinion which he was irresistibly induced to form.

"Yes, my son," said the stranger, observing his embarrassment, "you do indeed see before you the unfortunate Father Ambrosius, who once accounted his ministry crowned in your preservation from the snares of heresy, but who is now condemned to lament thee as a castaway!"

Roland Græme's kindness of heart was at least equal to his vivacity of temper: he could not bear to see his ancient and honored master and spiritual guide in a situation which inferred a change of fortune so melancholy, but, throwing himself at his feet, grasped his knees and wept aloud.

"What mean these tears, my son?" said the abbot; "if they are shed for your own sins and follies, surely they are gracious showers, and may avail thee much; but weep not, if they fall on my account. You indeed see the superior of the community of St. Mary's in the dress of a poor sworder, who gives his master the use of his blade and buckler, and, if needful, of his life, for a coarse livery coat, and four marks by the year. But such a garb suits the time, and, in the period of the church militant, as well becomes her prelates as staff, miter, and crosier in the days of the church's triumph."

"By what fate," said the page—"and yet why," added he, checking himself, "need I ask? Catherine Seyton in some sort prepared me for this. But that the change should be so absolute, the destruction so complete!"

"Yes, my son," said the Abbot Ambrosius, "thine own eyes beheld, in my unworthy elevation to the abbot's stall, the last especial act of holy solemnity which shall be seen in the church of St. Mary's, until it shall please Heaven to turn back the captivity of the church. For the present, the shepherd is smitten—ay, wellnigh to the earth, the flocks are scattered, and the shrines of saints and martyrs, and pious benefactors to church, are given to the owls of night and the satyrs of the desert."

"And your brother, the Knight of Avenel—could he do nothing for your protection?"

"He himself hath fallen under the suspicion of the ruling powers," said the abbot, "who are as unjust to their friends as they are cruel to their enemies. I could not grieve at it, did I hope it might estrange him from his course; but I know the soul of Halbert, and I rather fear it will drive him to prove his fidelity to their unhappy cause by some deed which may be yet more destructive to the church, and more offensive to Heaven. Enough of this; and now to the business of our meeting. I trust you will hold it sufficient if I pass my word to you, that the packet of which you were lately the bearer was designed for my hands by George of Douglas?"

"Then," said the page, "is George of Douglas——"

"A true friend to his Queen, Roland; and will soon, I trust, have his eyes opened to the errors of his—miscalled—church."

"But what is he to his father, and what to the Lady of Lochleven, who has been as a mother to him?" said the page, impatiently.

"The best friend to both, in time and through eternity," said the abbot, "if he shall prove the happy instrument for redeeming the evil they have wrought, and are still working."

"Still," said the page, "I like not that good service which begins in breach of trust."

"I blame not thy scruples, my son," said the abbot; "but the time which has wrenched asunder the allegiance of Christians to the church, and of subjects of their king, has dissolved all the lesser bonds of society; and, in such days, mere human ties must no more restrain our progress than the brambles and briers, which catch hold of his garments, should delay the path of a pilgrim who travels to pay his vows."

"But, my father——" said the youth, and then stopped short in a hesitating manner.

"Speak on, my son," said the abbot—"speak without fear."

"Let me not offend you, then," said Roland, "when I answer, that it is even this which our adversaries charge against us, when they say that, shaping the means according to the end, we are willing to commit great moral evil in order that we may work out eventual good."

"The heretics have played their usual arts on you, my son," said the abbot; "they would willingly deprive us of the power of acting wisely and secretly, though their possession of superior force forbids our contending with them on the terms of equality. They have reduced us to a state of exhausted weakness, and now would fain proscribe the means by which weakness, through all the range of nature, supplies the lack of strength, and defends itself against its potent enemies. As well might the hound say to the hare, 'Use not these wily turns to escape me, but contend with me in pitched battle,' as the armed and powerful heretic demand of the down-trodden and oppressed Catholic to lay aside the wisdom of the serpent, by which alone they may again hope to raise up the Jerusalem over which they weep, and which it is their duty to rebuild. But more of this hereafter. And now, my son, I command thee on thy faith to tell me truly and particularly what has chanced to thee since we parted, and what is the present state of thy conscience. Thy relation, our sister Magdalen, is a woman of excellent gifts, blessed with a zeal which neither doubt nor danger can quench; but yet it is not a zeal altogether according to knowledge; wherefore, my son, I would willingly be myself thy interrogator and the counselor in these days of darkness and stratagem."

With the respect which he owed to his first instructor, Roland Græme went rapidly through the events which the reader is acquainted with; and while he disguised not from the prelate the impression which had been made on his mind by the arguments of the preacher Henderson, he accidentally, and almost involuntarily, gave his father confessor to understand the influence which Catherine Seyton had acquired over him.

"It is with joy I discover, my dearest son," replied the abbot, "that I have arrived in time to arrest thee on the verge of the precipice to which thou wert approaching. These doubts of which you complain are the weeds which naturally grow up in a strong soil, and require the careful hand of the husbandman to eradicate them. Thou must study a little volume, which I will impart to thee in fitting time, in which, by Our Lady's grace, I have placed in somewhat a clearer light than heretofore the points debated betwixt us and these heretics, who sow among the wheat the same tares which were formerly privily mingled with the good seed by the Albigenses and the Lollards. But it is not by reason alone that you must hope to conquer these insinuations of the enemy. It is sometimes by timely resistance, but oftener by timely flight. You must shut your ears against the arguments of the heresiarch, when circumstances permit you not to withdraw the foot from his company. Anchor your thoughts upon the service of Our Lady, while he is expending in vain his heretical sophistry. Are you unable to maintain your attention on Heavenly objects, think rather on thine own earthly pleasures than tempt Providence and the saints by giving an attentive ear to the erring doctrine: think of thy hawk, thy hound, thine angling-rod, thy sword and buckler—think even of Catherine Seyton, rather than give thy soul to the lessons of the tempter. Alas! my son, believe not that, worn out with woes, and bent more by affliction than by years, I have forgotten the effect of beauty over the heart of youth. Even in the watches of the night, broken by thoughts of an imprisoned queen, a distracted kingdom, a church laid waste and ruinous, come other thoughts than these suggest, and feelings which belonged to an earlier and happier course of life. Be it so—we must bear our load as we may; and not in vain are these passions implanted in our breast, since, as now in thy case, they may come in aid of resolutions founded upon higher grounds. Yet beware, my son—this Catherine Seyton is the daughter of one of Scotland's proudest, as well as most worthy barons; and thy state may not suffer thee, as yet, to aspire so high. But thus it is—Heaven works its purposes through human folly; and Douglas's ambitious affection as well as thine shall contribute alike to the desired end."

"How, my father," said the page, "my suspicions are then true! Douglas loves——"

"He does; and with a love as much misplaced as thine own; but beware of him—cross him not—thwart him not."

"Let him not cross or thwart me," said the page; "for I will not yield him an inch of way, had he in his body the soul of every Douglas that has lived since the time of the Dark Gray Man."*

"Nay, have patience, idle boy, and reflect that your suit can never interfere with his. But a truce with these vanities, and let us better employ the little space which still remains to us to spend together. To thy knees, my son, and resume the long-interrupted duty of confession, that, happen what may, the hour may find in thee a faithful Catholic, relieved from the guilt of his sins by authority of the Holy Church. Could I but tell thee, Roland, the joy with which I see thee once more put thy knee to its best and fittest use! *Quid dicis, mi fili?*"

"*Culpas meas,*" answered the youth; and, according to the ritual of the Catholic Church, he confessed and received absolution, to which was annexed the condition of performing certain enjoined penances.

When this religious ceremony was ended, an old man, in the dress of a peasant of the better order, approached the arbor and greeted the abbot. "I have waited the conclusion of your devotions," he said, "to tell you the youth is sought after by the chamberlain, and it were well he should

*See Note 21.

appear without delay. Holy St. Francis, if the halberdiers were to seek him here, they might sorely wrong my garden-plot: they are in office, and reck not where they tread, were each step on jessamine and clove-gillyflowers."

"We will speed him forth, my brother," said the abbot; "but, alas! is it possible that such trifles should live in your mind at a crisis so awful as that which is now impending?"

"Reverend father," answered the proprietor of the garden, for such he was, "how oft shall I pray you to keep your high counsel for high minds like your own? What have you required of me, that I have not granted unresistingly, though with an aching heart?"

"I would require of you to be yourself, my brother," said the Abbot Ambrosius: "to remember what you were, and to what your early vows have bound you."

"I tell thee, Father Ambrosius," replied the gardener, "the patience of the best saint that ever said paternoster would be exhausted by the trials to which you have put mine. What I have been, it skills not to speak at present: no one knows better than yourself, father, what I renounced, in hopes to find ease and quiet during the remainder of my days; and no one better knows how my retreat has been invaded, my fruit-trees broken, my flower-beds trodden down, my quiet frightened away, and my very sleep driven from my bed, since ever this poor Queen, God bless her! hath been sent to Lochleven. I blame her not: being a prisoner, it is natural she should wish to get out from so vile a hold, where there is scarcely any place even for a tolerable garden, and where the water-mists, as I am told, blight all the early blossoms—I say, I cannot blame her for endeavoring for her freedom; but why I should be drawn into the scheme; why my harmless arbors, that I planted with my own hands, should become places of privy conspiracy; why my little quay, which I built for my own fishing-boat, should have become a haven for secret embarkations; in short, why I should be dragged into matters where both heading and hanging are like to be the issue, I profess to you, reverend father, I am totally ignorant."

"My brother," answered the abbot, "you are wise, and ought to know——"

"I am not—I am not—I am not wise," replied the horticulturist, pettishly, and stopping his ears with his fingers; "I was never called wise, but when men wanted to engage me in some action of notorious folly.

"But, my good brother," said the abbot——

"I am not good, neither," said the peevish gardener—"I am neither good nor wise. Had I been wise, you would not have been admitted here; and were I good, methinks I should send you elsewhere to hatch plots for destroying the quiet of the country. What signifies disputing about queen or king, when men may sit at peace *sub umbra vitis sui?* And so would I do, after the precept of Holy Writ, were I, as you term me, wise or good. But such as I am, my neck is in the yoke, and you make me draw what weight you list. Follow me, youngster. This reverend father, who makes in his jackman's dress nearly as reverend a figure as I myself, will agree with me in one thing at least, and that is, that you have been long enough here."

"Follow the good father, Roland," said the abbot, "and remember my words—a day is approaching that will try the temper of all true Scotsmen; may thy heart prove faithful as the steel of thy blade!"

The page bowed in silence, and they parted; the gardener, notwithstanding his advanced age, walking on before him very briskly, and muttering as he went, partly to himself, partly to his companion, after the manner of old men of weakened intellects. "When I was great," thus ran his maundering, "and had my mule and my ambling palfrey at command, I warrant you I could have as well flown through the air as have walked at this pace. I had my gout and my rheumatics, and an hundred things besides, that hung fetters on my heels; and now, thanks to Our Lady and honest labor, I can walk with any good man of my age in the kingdom of Fife. Fy upon it, that experience should be so long in coming!"

As he was thus muttering, his eye fell upon the branch of a pear-tree which drooped down for want of support, and at once forgetting his haste, the old man stopped and set seriously about binding it up. Roland Græme hath both readiness, neatness of hand, and good-nature in abundance: he immediately lent his aid, and in a minute or two the bough was supported, and tied up in a way perfectly satisfactory to the old man, who looked at it with a great complaisance. "They are bergamots," he said, "and if you will come ashore in autumn, you shall taste of them; the like are not in Lochleven Castle. The garden there is a poor pinfold, and the gardener, Hugh Houkham, hath little skill of his craft: so come ashore, Master Page, in autumn, when you would eat pears. But what am I thinking of? ere that time come, they may have given thee sour pears for plums. Take an old man's advice, youth, one who hath seen many days, and sat in higher places than thou canst hope for : bend thy sword into a pruning-hook, and make a dibble of thy dagger —thy days should be the longer, and thy health the better for it—and come to aid me in my garden, and I will teach thee the real French fashion of 'imping,' which the Southron call graffing. Do this, and do it without loss of time, for there is a whirlwind coming over the land, and only those shall escape who lie too much beneath the storm to have their boughs broken by it."

So saying, he dismissed Roland Græme through a different door from that by which he had entered, signed a cross and pronounced a *benedicite* as they parted, and then, still muttering to himself, retired into the garden, and locked the door on the inside.

CHAPTER XXIX

Pray God she prove not masculine ere long!
King Henry IV.

Dismissed from the old man's garden, Roland Græme found that a grassy paddock, in which sauntered two cows, the property of the gardener, still separated him from the village. He paced through it, lost in meditation upon the words of the abbot. Father Ambrosius had, with success enough, exerted over him that powerful influence which the guardians and instructors of our childhood possess over our more mature youth. And yet, when Roland looked back upon what the father had said, he could not but suspect that he had rather sought to evade entering into the controversy betwixt the churches than to repel the objections and satisfy the doubts which the lectures of Henderson had excited. "For this he had no time," said the page to himself, "neither have I now calmness and learning sufficient to judge upon points of such magnitude. Besides, it were base to quit my faith while the wind of fortune sets against it, unless I were so placed that my conversion, should it take place, were free as light from the imputation of self-interest. I was bred a Catholic—bred in the faith of Bruce and Wallace—I will hold that faith till time and reason shall convince me that it errs. I will serve this poor Queen as a subject should serve an imprisoned and wronged sovereign. They who placed me in her service have to blame themselves: they sent me hither, a gentleman trained in the paths of loyalty and honor, when they should have sought out some truckling, cogging, double-dealing knave, who would have been at once the observant page of the Queen and the obsequious spy of her enemies. Since I must choose betwixt aiding and betraying her, I will decide as becomes her servant and her subject; but Catherine Seyton—Catherine Seyton, beloved by Douglas, and holding me on or off as the intervals of her leisure or caprice will permit—how shall I deal with the coquette? By Heaven, when I next have an opportunity, she shall render me some reason for her conduct, or I will break with her forever!"

As he formed this doughty resolution, he crossed the stile which led out of the little inclosure, and was almost immediately greeted by Dr. Luke Lundin.

"Ha! my most excellent young friend," said the doctor, "from whence come you?—but I note the place. Yes, neighbor Blinkhoolie's garden is a pleasant rendezvous, and you are of the age when lads look after a bonny lass with one eye and a dainty plum with another. But hey! you look subtriste and melancholic: I fear the maiden has proved cruel, or the plums unripe; and surely, I think neighbor Blinkhoolie's damsons can scarcely have been well preserved throughout the winter—he spares the saccharine juice on his confects. But courage, man, there are more Kates in Kinross; and for the immature fruit, a glass of my double distilled *aqua mirabilis! probatum est.*"

The page darted an ireful glance at the facetious physician; but presently recollecting that the name "Kate," which had provoked his displeasure, was probably but introduced for the sake of alliteration, he suppressed his wrath, and only asked if the wains had been heard of.

"Why, I have been seeking for you this hour, to tell you that the stuff is in your boat, and that the boat waits your pleasure. Auchtermuchty had only fallen into company with an idle knave like himself, and a stoup of aquavitæ between them. Your boatmen lie on their oars, and there have already been made two wefts from the warder's turret, to intimate that those in the castle are impatient for your return. Yet there is time for you to take a slight repast; and, as your friend and physician, I hold it unfit you should face the water-breeze with an empty stomach."

Roland Græme had nothing for it but to return, with such cheer as he might, to the place where his boat was moored on the beach, and resisted all offer of refreshment, although the doctor promised that he should prelude the collation with a gentle appetizer—a decoction of herbs, gathered and distilled by himself. Indeed, as Roland had not forgotten the contents of his morning cup, it is possible that the recollection induced him to stand firm in his refusal of all food to which such an unpalatable preface was the preliminary. As they passed towards the boat (for the ceremonious politeness of the worthy chamberlain would not permit the page to go thither without attendance), Roland Græme, amidst a group who seemed to be assembled around a party of wandering musicians, distinguished, as he thought, the dress of Catherine Seyton. He shook himself clear from his attendant, and at one spring was in the midst of the crowd, and at the side of the damsel. "Catherine," he whispered, "is it well for you to be still here?—will you not return to the castle?"

"To the devil with your Catherines and your castles!" answered the maiden, snappishly; "have you not had time enough already to get rid of your follies? Begone! I desire not your farther company, and there will be danger in thrusting it upon me."

"Nay, but if there be danger, fairest Catherine," replied Roland, "why will you not allow me to stay and share it with you?"

"Intruding fool," said the maiden, "the danger is all on thine own side: the risk is, in plain terms, that I strike thee on the mouth with the hilt of my dagger." So saying, she turned haughtily from him, and moved through the crowd, who gave way in some astonishment at the masculine activity with which she forced her way among them.

As Roland, though much irritated, prepared to follow, he was grappled on the other side by Doctor Luke Lundin, who reminded him of the loaded boat, of the two wefts, or signals with the flag, which had been made from the tower, of the danger of the cold breeze to an empty stomach, and of the vanity of spending more time upon coy wenches and sour plums. Roland was thus, in a manner, dragged back to his boat, and obliged to launch her forth upon his return to Lochleven Castle.

That little voyage was speedily accomplished, and the page was greeted at the landing-place by the severe and caustic welcome of old Dryfesdale. "So, young gallant, you are come at last, after a delay of six hours, and after two signals from the castle? But, I warrant, some idle junketing had occupied you too deeply to think of your service or your duty. Where is the note of the plate and household stuff? Pray Heaven it hath not been diminished under the sleeveless care of so heedless a gadabout!"

"Diminished under my care, sir steward?" retorted the page, angrily; "say so in earnest, and by Heaven your gray hair shall hardly protect your saucy tongue!"

"A truce with your swaggering, young esquire," returned the steward; "we have bolts and dungeons for brawlers. Go to my lady and swagger before her, if thou darest; she will give thee proper cause of offense, for she has waited for thee long and impatiently."

"And where then is the Lady of Lochleven?" said the page; "for I conceive it is of her thou speakest."

"Ay, of whom else?" replied Dryfesdale; "or who besides the Lady of Lochleven hath a right to command in this castle!"

"The Lady of Lochleven is thy mistress," said Roland Græme; "but mine is the Queen of Scotland."

The steward looked at him fixedly for a moment, with an air in which suspicion and dislike were ill concealed by an affectation of contempt. "The bragging cock-chicken," he said, "will betray himself by his rash crowing. I have marked thy altered manner in the chapel of late—ay, and your changing of glances at meal-time with a certain idle damsel, who, like thyself, laughs at all gravity and goodness. There is something about you, my master, which should be looked to. But, if you would know whether the Lady of Lochleven or that other lady hath right to command thy service, thou wilt find them together in the Lady Mary's ante-room."

Roland hastened thither, not unwilling to escape from the ill-natured penetration of the old man, and marveling at the same time what peculiarity could have occasioned the Lady of Lochleven's being in the Queen's apartment at this time of the afternoon, so much contrary to her usual wont. His acuteness instantly penetrated the meaning. "She wishes," he concluded, "to see the meeting betwixt the Queen and me on my return, that she may form a guess whether there is any private intelligence or understanding betwixt us. I must be guarded."

With this resolution he entered the parlor, where the Queen, seated in her chair, with the Lady Fleming leaning upon the back of it, had already kept the Lady of Lochleven standing in her presence for the space of nearly an hour, to the manifest increase of her very visible bad-humor. Roland Græme, on entering the apartment, made a deep obeisance to the Queen, and another to the lady, and then stood still as if to await their further question. Speaking almost together, the Lady of Lochleven said, "So, young man, you are returned at length?" And then stopped indignantly short, while the Queen went on without regarding her—"Roland, you are welcome home to us; you have proved the true dove and not the raven. Yet I am sure I could have forgiven you if, once dismissed from this water-circled ark of ours, you had never again returned to us. I trust you have brought back an olive branch, for our kind and worthy hostess has chafed herself much on account of your long absence, and we never needed more some symbol of peace and reconciliation."

"I grieve I should have been detained, madam," answered the page; "but, from the delay of the person entrusted with the matters for which I was sent, I did not receive them till late in the day."

"See you there now," said the Queen to the Lady Lochleven; "we could not persuade you, our dearest hostess, that your household goods were in all safe keeping and surety. True it is, that we can excuse your anxiety, considering that these august apartments are so scantily furnished that we have not been able to offer you even the relief of a stool during the long time you have afforded us the pleasure of your society."

"The will, madam," said the lady—"the will to offer such accommodation was more wanting than the means."

"What!" said the Queen, looking round, and affecting surprise, "there are then stools in this apartment—one, two—no less than four, including the broken one—a royal garniture! We observed them not; will it please your ladyship to sit?"

"No, madam, I will soon relieve you of my presence," replied the Lady Lochleven; "and, while with you, my aged limbs can still better brook fatigue than my mind stoop to accept of constrained courtesy."

"Nay, Lady of Lochleven, if you take it so deeply," said the Queen, rising and motioning to her own vacant chair, "I would rather you assumed my seat; you are not the first of your family who has done so."

The Lady of Lochleven courtesied a negative, but seemed with much difficulty to suppress the angry answer which rose to her lips.

During this sharp conversation, the page's attention had been almost entirely occupied by the entrance of Catherine Seyton, who came from the inner apartment, in the usual dress in which she attended upon the Queen, and with nothing in her manner which marked either the hurry or confusion incident to a hasty change of disguise or the conscious fear of detection in a perilous enterprise. Roland Græme ventured to make her an obeisance as she entered, but she returned it with an air of the utmost indifference, which, in his opinion, was extremely inconsistent with the circumstances in which they stood towards each other. "Surely," he thought, "she cannot in reason expect to bully me out of the belief due to mine own eyes, as she tried to do concerning the apparition in the hostelry of St. Michael's. I will try if I cannot make her feel that this will be but a vain task, and that confidence in me is the wiser and safer course to pursue."

These thoughts had passed rapidly through his mind, when the Queen, having finished her altercation with the lady of the castle, again addressed him—"What of the revels at Kinross, Roland Græme? Methought they were gay, if I may judge from some faint sounds of mirth and distant music which found their way so far as these grated windows, and died when they entered them, as all that is mirthful must. But thou lookest as sad as if thou hadst come from a conventicle of the Huguenots!"

"And so perchance he hath, madam," replied the Lady of Lochleven, at whom this side-shaft was launched. "I trust, amid yonder idle fooleries, there wanted not some pouring forth of doctrine to a better purpose than that vain mirth which, blazing and vanishing like the crackling of dry thorns, leaves to the fools who love it nothing but dust and ashes."

"Mary Fleming," said the Queen, turning round and drawing her mantle about her, "I would that we had the chimney-grate supplied with a fagot or two of these same thorns which the Lady of Lochleven describes so well. Methinks the damp air from the lake, which stagnates in these vaulted rooms, renders them deadly cold."

"Your Grace's pleasure shall be obeyed," said the Lady of Lochleven; "yet may I presume to remind you that we are now in summer?"

"I thank you for the information, my good lady," said the Queen; "for prisoners better learn their calendar from the mouth of their jailer than from any change they themselves feel in the seasons. Once more, Roland Græme, what of the revels?"

"They were gay, madam," said the page, "but of the usual sort, and little worth your Highness's ear."

"O, you know not," said the Queen, "how very indulgent my ear has become to all that speaks of freedom and the pleasures of the free. Methinks I would rather have seen the gay villagers dance their ring round the Maypole than have witnessed the most stately masques within the precincts of a palace. The absence of stone walls, the sense that the green turf is under the foot which may tread it free and unrestrained, is worth all that art or splendor can add to more courtly revels."

"I trust," said the Lady Lochleven, addressing the page in her turn, "there were amongst these follies none of the riots or disturbances to which they so naturally lead?"

Roland gave a slight glance to Catherine Seyton, as if to bespeak her attention, as he replied, "I witnessed no offense, madam, worthy of marking—none indeed of any kind, save that a bold damsel made her hand somewhat too familiar with the cheek of a player-man, and ran some risk of being ducked in the lake."

As he uttered these words he cast a hasty glance at Catherine; but she sustained, with the utmost serenity of manner and countenance, the hint which he had deemed could not have been thrown out before her without exciting some fear and confusion.

"I will cumber your Grace no longer with my presence," said the Lady of Lochleven, "unless you have aught to command me."

"Nought, our good hostess," answered the Queen, "unless it be to pray you, that on another occasion you deem it not needful to postpone your better employment to wait so long upon us."

"May it please you," added the Lady Lochleven, "to command this your gentleman to attend us, that I may receive some account of these matters which have been sent hither for your Grace's use?"

"We may not refuse what you are pleased to require, madam," answered the Queen. "Go with the lady, Roland, if our commands be indeed necessary to thy doing so. We will hear to-morrow the history of thy Kinross pleasures. For this night we dismiss thy attendance."

Roland Græme went with the Lady of Lochleven, who failed not to ask him many questions concerning what had passed at the sports, to which he rendered such answers as were most likely to lull asleep any suspicions which she might entertain of his disposition to favor Queen Mary, taking especial care to avoid all allusion to the apparition of Magdalen Græme and of the Abbot Ambrosius. At length, after undergoing a long and somewhat close examination, he was dismissed with such expressions as, coming from the reserved and stern Lady of Lochleven, might seem to express a degree of favor and countenance.

His first care was to obtain some refreshment, which was more cheerfully afforded him by a good-natured pantler than by Dryfesdale, who was, on this occasion, much disposed to abide by the fashion of Pudding-burn House, where

They who came not the first call
Gat no more meat till the next meal.

When Roland Græme had finished his repast, having his dismissal from the Queen for the evening, and being little inclined for such society as the castle afforded, he stole into the garden, in which he had permission to spend his leisure time, when it pleased him. In this place, the ingenuity of the contriver and disposer of the walks had exerted itself to make the most of little space, and by screens, both of stone ornamented with rude sculpture and hedges of living green, had endeavored to give as much intricacy and variety as the confined limits of the garden would admit.

Here the young man walked sadly, considering the events of the day, and comparing what had dropped from the abbot with what he had himself noticed of the demeanor of George Douglas. "It must be so," was the painful but inevitable conclusion at which he arrived—"it must be by his aid that she is thus enabled, like a phantom, to transport herself from place to place, and to appear at pleasure on the mainland or on the islet. It must be so," he repeated once more; "with him she holds a close, secret, and intimate correspondence, altogether inconsistent with the eye of favor which she has sometimes cast upon me, and destructive to the hopes which she must have known these glances have necessarily inspired." And yet (for love will hope where reason despairs) the thought rushed on his mind that it was possible she only encouraged Douglas's passion so far as might serve her mistress's interest, and that she was of too frank, noble, and candid a nature to hold out to himself hopes which she meant not to fulfil. Lost in these various conjectures, he seated himself upon a bank of turf, which commanded a view of the lake on the one side, and on the other of that front of the castle along which the Queen's apartments were situated.

The sun had now for some time set, and the twilight of May was rapidly fading into a serene night. On the lake, the expanded water rose and fell, with the slightest and softest influence of a southern breeze, which scarcely dimpled the surface over which it passed. In the distance was still seen the dim outline of the island of St. Serf, once visited by many a sandaled pilgrim, as the blessed spot trodden by a man of God; now neglected or violated, as the refuge of lazy priests, who had with justice been compelled to give place to the sheep and the heifers of a Protestant baron.

As Roland gazed on the dark speck, amid the lighter blue

of the waters which surrounded it, the mazes of polemical discussion again stretched themselves before the eye of his mind. Had these men justly suffered their exile as licentious drones, the robbers, at once, and disgrace of the busy hive; or had the hand of avarice and rapine expelled from the temple not the ribalds who polluted, but the faithful priests who served, the shrine in honor and fidelity? The arguments of Henderson, in this contemplative hour, rose with double force before him, and could scarcely be parried by the appeal which the Abbot Ambrosius had made from his understanding to his feelings—an appeal which he had felt more forcibly amid the bustle of stirring life than now when his reflections were more undisturbed. It required an effort to divert his mind from this embarrassing topic; and he found that he best succeeded by turning his eyes to the front of the tower, watching where a twinkling light still streamed from the casement of Catherine Seyton's apartment, obscured by times for a moment, as the shadow of the fair inhabitant passed betwixt the taper and the window. At length the light was removed or extinguished, and that object of speculation was also withdrawn from the eyes of the meditative lover. Dare I confess the fact, without injuring his character forever as a hero of romance? These eyes gradually became heavy; speculative doubts on the subject of religious controversy, and anxious conjectures concerning the state of his mistress's affections, became confusedly blended together in his musings; the fatigues of a busy day prevailed over the harassing subjects of contemplation which occupied his mind, and he fell fast asleep.

Sound were his slumbers, until they were suddenly dispelled by the iron tongue of the castle bell, which sent its deep and sullen sounds wide over the bosom of the lake, and awakened the echoes of Bennarty, the hill which descends steeply on its southern bank. Roland started up, for this bell was always tolled at ten o'clock, as the signal for locking the castle gates, and placing the keys under the charge of the seneschal. He therefore hastened to the wicket by which the garden communicated with the building, and had the mortification, just as he reached it, to hear the bolt leave its sheath with a discordant crash, and enter the stone groove of the door-lintel.

"Hold—hold," cried the page, "and let me in ere you lock the wicket."

The voice of Dryfesdale replied from within, in his usual tone of imbittered sullenness, "The hour is past, fair master; you like not the inside of these walls; even make it a complete holiday, and spend the night as well as the day out of bounds."

"Open the door," exclaimed the indignant page, "or by St. Giles I will make thy gold chain smoke for it!"

"Make no alarm here," retorted the inpenetrable Dryfesdale, "but keep thy sinful oaths and silly threats for those that regard them. I do mine office, and carry the keys to the seneschal. Adieu, my young master! the cool night air will advantage your hot blood."

The steward was right in what he said; for the cooling breeze was very necessary to appease the feverish fit of anger which Roland experienced, nor did the remedy succeed for some time. At length, after some hasty turns made through the garden, exhausting his passion in vain vows of vengeance, Roland Græme began to be sensible that his situation ought rather to be held as matter of laughter than of serious resentment. To one bred a sportsman, a night spent in the open air had in it little of hardship, and the poor malice of the steward seemed more worthy of his contempt than his anger. "I would to God," he said, "that the grim old man may always have contented himself with such sportive revenge. He often looks as he were capable of doing us a darker turn." Returning, therefore, to the turf-seat which he had formerly occupied, and which was partially sheltered by a trim fence of green holly, he drew his mantle around him, stretched himself at length on the verdant settle, and endeavored to resume that sleep which the castle bell had interrupted to so little purpose.

Sleep, like other earthly blessings, is niggard of its favors when most courted. The more Roland invoked her aid, the further she fled from his eyelids. He had been completely awakened, first by the sounds of the bell, and then by his own aroused vivacity of temper, and he found it difficult again to compose himself to slumber. At length, when his mind was wearied out with a maze of unpleasing meditation, he succeeded in coaxing himself into a broken repose. This was again dispelled by the voices of two persons who were walking in the garden, the sound of whose conversation, after mingling for some time in the page's dreams, at length succeeded in awaking him thoroughly. He raised himself from his reclining posture in the utmost astonishment, which the circumstance of hearing two persons at that late hour conversing on the outside of the watchfully guarded Castle of Lochleven was so well calculated to excite. His first thought was of supernatural beings; his next, upon some attempt on the part of Queen Mary's friends and followers; his last was that George of Douglas, possessed of the keys, aud having the means of ingress and egress at pleasure, was availing himself of his office to hold a rendezvous with Catherine Seyton in the castle garden. He was confirmed in this opinion by the tone of the voice which asked in a low whisper "Whether all was ready?"

CHAPTER XXX

> **In some breasts passion lies conceal'd and silent,**
> Like war's swart powder in a castle vault,
> Until occasion, like the linstock, lights it;
> Then comes at once the lightning and the thunder,
> And distant echoes tell that all is rent asunder.
>
> *Old Play.*

ROLAND GRÆME, availing himself of a breach in the holly screen, and of the assistance of the full moon, which was now arisen, had a perfect opportunity, himself unobserved, to reconnoiter the persons and the motions of those by whom his rest had been thus unexpectedly disturbed; and his observations confirmed his jealous apprehensions. They stood together in close and earnest conversation within four yards of the place of his retreat, and he could easily recognize the tall form and deep voice of Douglas, and the no less remarkable dress and tone of the page at the hostelry of St. Michael's.

"I have been at the door of the page's apartment," said Douglas, "but he is not there, or he will not answer. It is fast bolted on the inside, as is the custom, and we cannot pass through it; and what his silence may bode I know not."

"You have trusted him too far," said the other—"a feather-headed coxcomb, upon whose changeable mind and hot brain there is no making an abiding impression."

"It was not I who was willing to trust him," said Douglas; "but I was assured he would prove friendly when called upon, for——" Here he spoke so low that Roland lost the tenor of his words, which was the more provoking as he was fully aware that he was himself the subject of their conversation.

"Nay," replied the stranger, more aloud, "I have on my side put him off with fair words, which make fools fain; but now, if you distrust him at the push, deal with him with your dagger, and so make open passage."

"That was too rash," said Douglas; "and besides, as I told you, the door of his apartment is shut and bolted. I will essay again to waken him."

Græme instantly comprehended that the ladies, having been somehow made aware of his being in the garden, had secured the door of the outer room in which he usually slept, as a sort of sentinel upon that only access to the Queen's apartments. But then, how came Catherine Seyton to be abroad, if the Queen and the other lady were still within their chambers, and the access to them locked and bolted? "I will be instantly at the bottom of these mysteries," he said, "and then thank Mrs. Catherine, if this be really she, for the kind use which she exhorted Douglas to make of his dagger; they seek me, as I comprehend, and they shall not seek me in vain."

Douglas had by this time re-entered the castle by the wicket, which was now open. The stranger stood alone in the garden walk, his arms folded on his breast, and his eyes cast impatiently up to the moon, as if accusing her of betraying him by the magnificence of her luster. In a moment Roland Græme stood before him. "A goodly night," he said, "Mrs. Catherine, for a young lady to stray forth in disguise, and to meet with men in an orchard!"

"Hush!" said the stranger page—"hush, thou foolish patch, and tell us in a word if thou art friend or foe."

"How should I be friend to one who deceives me by fair words, and who would have Douglas deal with me with his poniard?" replied Roland.

"The fiend receive George of Douglas and thee too, thou born madcap and sworn marplot!" said the other; "we shall be discovered, and then death is the word."

"Catherine," said the page, "you have dealt falsely and cruelly with me, and the moment of explanation is now come; neither it nor you shall escape me."

"Madman!" said the stranger, "I am neither Kate nor Catherine: the moon shines bright enough surely to know the hart from the hind."

"That shift shall not serve you, fair mistress," said the page, laying hold on the lap of the stranger's cloak; "this time, at least, I will know with whom I deal."

"Unhand me," said she, endeavoring to extricate herself from his grasp; and in a tone where anger seemed to contend with a desire to laugh, "Use you so little discretion towards a daughter of Seyton?"

But as Roland, encouraged perhaps by her risibility to suppose his violence was not unpardonably offensive, kept hold on her mantle, she said, in a sterner tone of unmixed resentment, "Madman, let me go! there is life and death in this moment. I would not willingly hurt thee, and yet beware!"

As she spoke, she made a sudden effort to escape, and in

doing so a pistol which she carried in her hands or about her person went off.

This warlike sound instantly awakened the well-warded castle. The warder blew his horn, and began to toll the castle bell, crying out at the same time, "Fy, treason! treason! cry all!—cry all!"

The apparition of Catherine Seyton, which the page had let loose in the first moment of astonishment, vanished in darkness, but the plash of oars was heard, and in a second or two five or six harquebusses and a falconet were fired from the battlements of the castle successively, as if leveled at some object on the water. Confounded with these incidents, no way for Catherine's protection (supposing her to be in the boat which he had heard put from the shore) occurred to Roland, save to have recourse to George of Douglas. He hastened for this purpose towards the apartment of the Queen, whence he heard loud voices and much trampling of feet. When he entered, he found himself added to a confused and astonished group, which, assembled in that apartment, stood gazing upon each other. At the upper end of the room stood the Queen, equipped as for a journey, and attended not only by the Lady Fleming, but by the omnipresent Catherine Seyton, dressed in the habit of her own sex, and bearing in her hand the casket, in which Mary kept such jewels as she had been permitted to retain. At the other end of the hall was the Lady of Lochleven, hastily dressed, as one startled from slumber by the sudden alarm, and surrounded by domestics, some bearing torches, others, holding naked swords, partizans, pistols, or such other weapons as they had caught up in the hurry of a night alarm. Betwixt these two parties stood George of Douglas, his arms folded on his breast, his eyes bent on the ground, like a criminal whc knows not how to deny, yet continues unwilling to avow, the guilt in which he had been detected.

"Speak George of Douglas," said the Lady of Lochleven—"speak, and clear the horrid suspicion which rests on thy name. Say, 'A Douglas was never faithless to his trust, and I am a Douglas.' Say this, my dearest son, and it is all I ask thee to say to clear thy name, even under such a foul charge. Say it was but the wile of these unhappy women and this false boy which plotted an escape so fatal to Scotland, so destructive to thy father's house."

"Madam," said old Dryfesdale, the steward, "this much do I say for this silly page, that he could not be accessary to unlocking the doors, since I myself this night bolted him out of the castle. Whoever limned this night-piece, the lad's share in it seems to have been small."

"Thou liest, Dryfesdale," said the lady, "and wouldst throw the blame on thy master's house, to save the worthless life of a gipsy boy."

"His death were more desirable to me than his life," answered the steward, sullenly; "but the truth is the truth."

At these words, Douglas raised his head, drew up his figure to its full height, and spoke boldly and sedately, as one whose resolution was taken. "Let no life be endangered for me. I alone——"

"Douglas," said the Queen, interrupting him, "art thou mad? Speak not, I charge you."

"Madam," he replied, bowing with the deepest respect, "gladly would I obey your commands, but they must have a victim, and let it be the true one. Yes, madam," he continued, addressing the Lady of Lochleven, "I alone am guilty in this matter. If the word of a Douglas has yet any weight with you, believe me that this boy is innocent; and on your conscience I charge you, do him no wrong; nor let the Queen suffer hardship for embracing the opportunity of freedom which sincere loyalty—which a sentiment yet deeper—offered to her acceptance.—Yes! I had planned the escape of the most beautiful, the most persecuted of women; and far from regretting that I, for a while, deceived the malice of her enemies, I glory in it, and am most willing to yield up life itself in her cause."

"Now, may God have compassion on my age," said the Lady of Lochleven, "and enable me to bear their load of affliction! O Princess! born in a luckless hour, when will you cease to be the instrument of seduction and of ruin to all who approach you? O ancient house of Lochleven, famed so long for birth and honor, evil was the hour which brought the deceiver under thy roof!"

"Say not so, madam," replied her grandson; "the old honors of the Douglas line will be outshone when one of its descendants dies for the most injured of queens—for the most lovely of women."

"Douglas," said the Queen, "must I at this moment—ay, even at this moment, when I may lose a faithful subject forever—chide thee for forgetting what is due to me as thy queen?"

"Wretched boy," said the distracted Lady of Lochleven, "hast thou fallen even thus far into the snare of this Moabitish woman ?—hast thou bartered thy name, thy allegiance, thy knightly oath, thy duty to thy parents, thy country, and thy God, for a feigned tear, or a sickly smile, from lips which flattered the infirm Francis—lured to death the idiot Darnley—read luscious poetry with the minion Chastelar—mingled in the lays of love which were sung by the beggar Rizzio—and which were joined in rapture to those of the foul and licentious Bothwell ?"

"Blaspheme not, madam!" said Douglas; "nor you, fair Queen, and virtuous as fair, chide at this moment the presumption of thy vassal! Think not that the mere devotion of a subject could have moved me to the part I have been performing. Well you deserve that each of your lieges should die for you; but I have done more—have done that to which love alone could compel a Douglas: I have dissembled. Farewell, then, queen of all hearts, and empress of that of Douglas! When you are freed from this vile bondage—as freed you shall be, if justice remains in Heaven—and when you load with honors and titles the happy man who shall deliver you, cast one thought on him whose heart would have despised every reward for a kiss of your hand—cast one thought on his fidelity, and drop one tear on his grave." And throwing himself at her feet, he seized her hand, and pressed it to his lips.

"This before my face!" exclaimed the Lady of Lochleven—"wilt thou court thy adulterous paramour before the eyes of a parent? Tear them asunder, and put him under strict ward! Seize him, upon your lives!" she added, seeing that her attendants looked on each other with hesitation.

"They are doubtful," said Mary. "Save thyself, Douglas, I command thee!"

He started up from the floor, and only exclaiming, "My life or death are yours, and at your disposal!" drew his sword, and broke through those who stood betwixt him and the door. The enthusiasm of his onset was too sudden and too lively to have been resisted by anything short of the most decided opposition; and as he was both loved and feared by his father's vassals, none of them would offer him any actual injury.

The Lady of Lochleven stood astonished at his sudden escape. "Am I surrounded," she said, "by traitors? Upon him, villains!—pursue, stab, cut him down!"

"He cannot leave the island, madam," said Dryfesdale, interfering: "I have the key of the boat-chain."

But two or three voices of those who pursued from curiosity

or command of their mistress exclaimed from below, that he had cast himself into the lake.

"Brave Douglas still!" exclaimed the Queen. "O, true and noble heart, that prefers death to imprisonment!"

"Fire upon him!" said the Lady of Lochleven: "if there be here a true servant of his father, let him shoot the runagate dead, and let the lake cover our shame!"

The report of a gun or two was heard, but they were probably shot rather to obey the lady than with any purpose of hitting the mark; and Randal immediately entering, said that Master George had been taken up by a boat from the castle, which lay at a little distance.

"Man a barge and pursue them!" said the lady.

"It were quite vain," said Randal; "by this time they are half-way to shore, and a cloud has come over the moon."

"And has the traitor then escaped?" said the lady, pressing her hands against her forehead with a gesture of despair; "the honor of our house is forever gone, and all will be deemed accomplices in this base treachery!"

"Lady of Lochleven," said Mary, advancing towards her, "you have this night cut off my fairest hopes: you have turned my expected freedom into bondage, and dashed away the cup of joy in the very instant I was advancing it to my lips; and yet I feel for your sorrow the pity that you deny to mine. Gladly would I comfort you if I might; but as I may not, I would at least part from you in charity."

"Away, proud woman!" said the lady; "who ever knew so well as thou to deal the deepest wounds under the pretense of kindness and courtesy? Who, since the great traitor, could ever so betray with a kiss?"

"Lady Douglas of Lochleven," said the Queen, "in this moment thou canst not offend me—no, not even by thy coarse and unwomanly language, held to me in the presence of menials and armed retainers. I have this night owed so much to one member of the house of Lochleven as to cancel whatever its mistress can do or say in the wildness of her passion."

"We are bounden to you, Princess," said Lady Lochleven, putting a strong constraint on herself, and passing from her tone of violence to that of bitter irony; "our poor house hath been but seldom graced with royal smiles, and will hardly, with my choice, exchange their rough honesty for such court honor as Mary of Scotland has now to bestow."

"They," replied Mary, "who knew so well how to take

may think themselves excused from the obligation implied in receiving. And that I have now little to offer is the fault of the Douglasses and their allies."

"Fear nothing, madam," replied the Lady of Lochleven, in the same bitter tone, "you retain an exchequer which neither your own prodigality can drain nor your offended country deprive you of. While you have fair words and delusive smiles at command, you need no other bribes to lure youth to folly."

The Queen cast a not ungratified glance on a large mirror, which, hanging on one side of the apartment, and illuminated by the torch-light, reflected her beautiful face and person. "Our hostess grows complaisant," she said, "my Fleming; we had not thought that grief and captivity had left us so well stored with that sort of wealth which ladies prize most dearly."

"Your Grace will drive this severe woman frantic," said Fleming, in a low tone. "On my knees I implore you to remember she is already dreadfully offended, and that we are in her power."

"I will not spare her, Fleming," answered the Queen; "it is against my nature. She returned my honest sympathy with insult and abuse, and I will gall her in return. If her words are too blunt for answer, let her use her poniard if she dare!"

"The Lady Lochleven," said the Lady Fleming aloud, "would surely do well now to withdraw and to leave her Grace to repose."

"Ay," replied the lady, "or to leave her Grace and her Grace's minions to think what silly fly they may next wrap their meshes about. My eldest son is a widower—were he not more worthy the flattering hopes with which you have seduced his brother [son]? True, the yoke of marriage has been already thrice fitted on; but the Church of Rome calls it a sacrament, and its votaries may deem it one in which they cannot too often participate."

"And the votaries of the Church of Geneva," replied Mary, coloring with indignation, "as they deem marriage *no* sacrament, are said at times to dispense with the holy ceremony." Then, as if afraid of the consequences of this home allusion to the errors of Lady Lochleven's early life, the Queen added, "Come, my Fleming, we grace her too much by this altercation: we will to our sleeping-apartment. If she would disturb us again to-night, she must cause the door to be forced." So saying, she retired to her bedroom, followed by her two women. Lady Lochleven, stunned as it were by this last sarcasm, and not the less deeply incensed that she had drawn it upon herself, remained like a statue on the spot which she had occupied when she received an affront so flagrant. Dryfesdale and Randal endeavored to rouse her to recollection by questions.

"What is your honorable ladyship's pleasure in the premises?"

"Shall we not double the sentinels, and place one upon the boats and another in the garden?" said Randal.

"Would you that despatches were sent to Sir William at Edinburgh, to acquaint him with what has happened?" demanded Dryfesdale; "and ought not the place of Kinross to be alarmed, lest there be force upon the shores of the lake?"

"Do all as thou wilt," said the lady, collecting herself, and about to depart. "Thou hast the name of a good soldier, Dryfesdale, take all precautions. Sacred Heaven! that I should be thus openly insulted!"

"Would it be your pleasure," said Dryfesdale, hesitating, "that this person—this lady—be more severely restrained?"

"No, vassal!" answered the lady, indignantly, "my revenge stoops not to so low a gratification. But I will have more worthy vengeance, or the tomb of my ancestors shall cover my shame!"

"And you shall have it, madam," replied Dryfesdale. "Ere two suns go down, you shall term yourself amply revenged."

The lady made no answer, perhaps did not hear his words, as she presently left the apartment. By the command of Dryfesdale, the rest of the attendants were dismissed, some to do the duty of guard, others to their repose. The steward himself remained after they had all departed; and Roland Græme, who was alone in the apartment, was surprised to see the old soldier advance towards him with an air of greater cordiality than he had ever before assumed to him, but which sat ill on his scowling features.

"Youth," he said, "I have done thee some wrong: it is thine own fault, for thy behavior hath seemed as light to me as the feather thou wearest in thy hat; and surely thy fantastic apparel, and idle humor of mirth and folly, have made me construe thee something harshly. But I saw this night from my casement, as I looked out to see how thou hadst disposed of thyself in the garden—I saw, I say, the true efforts which thou didst make to detain the companion of the perfidy of him who is no longer worthy to be called by his father's name, but must be cut off from his house like a rotten branch. I was just about to come to thy assistance when the pistol went off; and the warder—a false knave, whom I suspect to be bribed for the nonce—was himself forced to give the alarm, which, perchance, till then he had wilfully withheld. To atone, therefore, for my injustice towards you, I would willingly render you a courtesy, if you would accept of it from my hands."

"May I first crave to know what it is?" replied the page.

"Simply to carry the news of this discovery to Holyrood, where thou mayst do thyself much grace, as well with the Earl of Morton and the Regent himself as with Sir William Douglas, seeing thou hast seen the matter from end to end, and borne faithful part therein. The making thine own fortune will be thus lodged in thine own hand, when I trust thou wilt estrange thyself from foolish vanities, and learn to walk in this world as one who thinks upon the next."

"Sir steward," said Roland Græme, "I thank you for your courtesy, but I may not do your errand. I pass that I am the Queen's sworn servant, and may not be of counsel against her. But, setting this apart, methinks it were a bad road to Sir William of Lochleven's favor to be the first to tell him of his son's defection; neither would the Regent be over well pleased to hear the infidelity of his vassal, nor Morton to learn the falsehood of his kinsman."

"Um!" said the steward, making that inarticulate sound which expresses surprise mingled with displeasure. "Nay, then, even fly where ye list; for, giddy-pated as ye may be, you know how to bear you in the world."

"I will show you my system is less selfish than ye think for," said the page; "for I hold truth and mirth to be better than gravity and cunning—ay, and in the end to be a match for them. You never loved me less, sir steward, than you do at this moment. I know you will give me no real confidence, and I am resolved to accept no false protestations as current coin. Resume your old course: suspect me is much and watch me as closely as you will, I bid you defiance. You have met with your match."

"By Heaven, young man," said the steward, with a look of bitter malignity, "if thou darest to attempt any treachery towards the house of Lochleven, thy head shall blacken in the sun from the warder's turret!"

"He cannot commit treachery who refuses trust," said the

page; " and for my head, it stands as securely on mine own shoulders as on any turret that ever mason built."

" Farewell, thou prating and speckled pie," said Dryfesdale, " thou art so vain of thine idle tongue and variegated coat! Beware trap and lime-twig."

" And fare thee well, thou hoarse old raven," answered the page; " thy solemn flight, sable hue, and deep croak are no charms against bird-bolt or hail-shot, and that thou mayst find. It is open war betwixt us, each for the cause of our mistress, and God show the right!"

" Amen, and defend His own people!" said the steward. " I will let my mistress know what addition thou hast made to this mess of traitors. Good night, Monsieur Featherpate."

" Good night, Seignior Sowersby," replied the page; and when the old man departed, he betook himself to rest.

CHAPTER XXXI

Poison'd—ill fare! dead, forsook, cast off!
King John.

HOWEVER weary Roland Græme might be of the Castle of Lochleven, however much he might wish that the plan for Mary's escape had been perfected, I question if he ever awoke with more pleasing feelings than on the morning after George Douglas's plan for accomplishing her deliverance had been frustrated. In the first place, he had the clearest conviction that he had misunderstood the innuendo of the abbot, and that the affections of Douglas were fixed, not on Catherine Seyton, but on the Queen; and in the second place from the sort of explanation which had taken place betwixt the steward and him, he felt himself at liberty, without any breach of honor towards the family of Lochleven, to contribute his best aid to any scheme which should in future be formed for the Queen's escape; and, independently of the good-will which he himself had to the enterprise, he knew he could find no surer road to the favor of Catherine Seyton. He now sought but an opportunity to inform her that he had dedicated himself to this task, and fortune was propitious in affording him one which was unusually favorable.

At the ordinary hour of breakfast, it was introduced by the steward with his usual forms, who, as soon as it was placed on the board in the inner apartment, said to Roland Græme, with a glance of sarcastic import, "I leave you, my young sir, to do the office of sewer; it has been too long rendered to the Lady Mary by one belonging to the house of Douglas."

"Were it the prime and principal who ever bore the name," said Roland, "the office were an honor to him."

The steward departed without replying to this bravade, otherwise than by a dark look of scorn. Græme, thus left alone, busied himself, as one engaged in a labor of love, to imitate, as well as he could, the grace and courtesy with which George of Douglas was wont to render his ceremonial service at meals to the Queen of Scotland. There was more than youthful vanity, there was a generous devotion, in the feeling with which he took up the task, as a brave soldier assumes the place of a comrade who has fallen in the front of battle. "I am now," he said, "their only champion; and, come weal, come wo, I will be, to the best of my skill and power, as faithful, as trustworthy, as brave, as any Douglas of them all could have been."

At this moment Catherine Seyton entered alone, contrary to her custom; and not less contrary to her custom, she entered with her kerchief at her eyes. Roland Græme approached her with beating heart and with downcast eyes, and asked her in a low and hesitating voice whether the Queen were well.

"Can you suppose it?" said Catherine; "think you her heart and body are framed of steel and iron, to endure the cruel disappointment of yestereven, and the infamous taunts of yonder Puritanic hag? Would to God that I were a man, to aid her more effectually!"

"If those who carry pistols, and batous, and poniards," said the page, "are not men, they are at least Amazons, and that is as formidable."

"You are welcome to the flash of your wit, sir," replied the damsel; "I am neither in spirits to enjoy or to reply to it."

"Well, then," said the page, "list to me in all serious truth. And, first, let me say, that the gear last night had been smoother had you taken me into your counsels."

"And so we meant; but who could have guessed that Master Page should choose to pass all night in the garden, like some moon-stricken knight in a Spanish romance, instead of being in his bedroom, when Douglas came to hold communication with him on our project?"

"And why," said the page, "defer to so late a moment so important a confidence?"

"Because your communications with Henderson, and—with pardon—the natural impetuosity and fickleness of your disposition, made us dread to entrust you with a secret of such consequence till the last moment?"

"And why at the last moment?" said the page, offended at this frank avowal—"why at that or any other moment, since I had the misfortune to incur so much suspicion?"

"Nay, now you are angry again," said Catherine; "and to serve you aright I should break off this talk; but I will be magnanimous, and answer your question. Know, then, our reason for trusting you was twofold. In the first place, we could scarce avoid it, since you slept in the room through which we had to pass. In the second place——"

"Nay," said the page, "you may dispense with a second reason, when the first makes your confidence in me a case of necessity."

"Good now, hold thy peace," said Catherine. "In the second place, as I said before, there is one foolish person among us who believes that Roland Græme's heart is warm, though his head is giddy; that his blood is pure, though it boils too hastily; and that his faith and honor are true as the loadstar, though his tongue sometimes is far less than discreet."

This avowal Catherine repeated in a low tone, with her eyes fixed on the floor, as if she shunned the glance of Roland while she suffered it to escape her lips. "And this single friend," exclaimed the youth in rapture—"this only one who would do justice to the poor Roland Græme, and whose own generous heart taught her to distinguish between follies of the brain and faults of the heart—will you not tell me, dearest Catherine, to whom I owe my most grateful, my most heartfelt thanks?"

"Nay," said Catherine, with her eyes still fixed on the ground, "if your own heart tell you not——"

"Dearest Catherine!" said the page, seizing upon her hand, and kneeling on one knee.

"If your own heart, I say, tell you not," said Catherine, gently disengaging her hand, "it is very ungrateful; for since the maternal kindness of the Lady Fleming——"

The page started on his feet. "By Heaven, Catherine, your tongue wears as many disguises as your person! But you only mock me, cruel girl. You know the Lady Fleming has no more regard for any one than hath the forlorn princess who is wrought into yonder piece of old figured court-tapestry."

"It may be so," said Catherine Seyton, "but you should not speak so loud."

"Pshaw!" answered the page, but at the same time lowering his voice, "she cares for no one but herself and the Queen. And you know, besides, there is no one of you whose opinion I value, if I have not your own. No—not that of Queen Mary herself."

"The more shame for you, if it be so," said Catherine, with great composure.

"Nay, but, fair Catherine," said the page, "why will you thus damp my ardor, when I am devoting myself, body and soul, to the cause of your mistress?"

"It is because in doing so," said Catherine, "you debase

a cause so noble by naming along with it any lower or more selfish motive. Believe me," she said, with kindling eyes, and while the blood mantled on her cheek, "they think vilely and falsely of women—I mean of those who deserve the name—who deem that they love the gratification of their vanity, or the mean purpose of engrossing a lover's admiration and affection better than they love the virtue and honor of the man they may be brought to prefer. He that serves his religion, his prince, and his country with ardor and devotion need not plead his cause with the commonplace rant of romantic passion: the woman whom he honors with his love becomes his debtor, and her corresponding affection is engaged to repay his glorious toil."

"You hold a glorious prize for such toil," said the youth, bending his eyes on her with enthusiasm.

"Only a heart which knows how to value it," said Catherine. "He that should free this injured princess from these dungeons, and set her at liberty among her loyal and warlike nobles, whose hearts are burning to welcome her—where is the maiden in Scotland whom the love of such a hero would not honor, were she sprung from the blood royal of the land, and he the offspring of the poorest cottager that ever held a plow!"

"I am determined," said Roland, "to take the adventure. Tell me first, however, fair Catherine, and speak it as if you were confessing to the priest—this poor Queen, I know she is unhappy—but, Catherine, do you hold her innocent? She is accused of murder."

"Do I hold the lamb guilty, because it is assailed by the wolf?" answered Catherine. "Do I hold yonder sun polluted, because an earth-damp sullies his beams?"

The page sighed and looked down. "Would my conviction were as deep as thine! But one thing is clear, that in this captivity she hath wrong. She rendered herself up on a capitulation, and the terms have been refused her. I will embrace her quarrel to the death!"

"Will you—will you, indeed?" said Catherine, taking his hand in her turn. "O be but firm in mind, as thou art bold in deed and quick in resolution; keep but thy plighted faith, and after ages shall honor thee as the saviour of Scotland!"

"But when I have toiled successfully to win that Leah, honor, thou wilt not, my Catherine," said the page, "condemn me to a new term of service for that Rachel, love?"

"Of that," said Catherine, again extricating her hand from

his grasp, "we shall have full time to speak; but honor is the elder sister, and must be won the first."

"I may not win her," answered the page; "but I will venture fairly for her, and man can do no more. And know, fair Catherine—for you shall see the very secret thought of my heart—that not honor only, not only that other and fairer sister, whom you frown on me for so much as mentioning, but the stern commands of duty also, compel me to aid the Queen's deliverance."

"Indeed!" said Catherine; "you were wont to have doubts on that matter."

"Ay, but her life was not then threatened," replied Roland.

"And is it now more endangered than heretofore?" asked Catherine Seyton, in anxious terror.

"Be not alarmed," said the page; "but you heard the terms on which your royal mistress parted with the Lady of Lochleven?"

"Too well—but too well," said Catherine; "alas! that she cannot rule her princely resentment, and refrain from encounters like these!"

"That hath passed betwixt them," said Roland, "for which woman never forgives woman. I saw the lady's brow turn pale, and then black, when, before all the menzie, and in her moment of power, the Queen humbled her to the dust by taxing her with her shame. And I heard the oath of deadly resentment and revenge which she muttered in the ear of one who, by his answer, will, I judge, be but too ready an executioner of her will."

"You terrify me," said Catherine.

"Do not so take it up; call up the masculine part of your spirit; we will counteract and defeat her plans, be they dangerous as they may. Why do you look upon me thus, and weep?"

"Alas!" said Catherine, "because you stand there before me a living and breathing man, in all the adventurous glow and enterprise of youth, yet still possessing the frolic spirits of childhood—there you stand, full alike of generous enterprise and childish recklessness; and if to-day, to-morrow, or some such brief space, you lie a mangled and lifeless corpse upon the floor of these hateful dungeons, who but Catherine Seyton will be the cause of your brave and gay career being broken short as you start from the goal? Alas! she whom you have chosen to twine your wreath may too probably have to work your shroud!"

"And be it so, Catherine," said the page, in the full glow

of youthful enthusiasm; "and *do* thou work my shroud! and if thou grace it with such tears as fall now at the thought, it will honor my remains more than an earl's mantle would my living body. But shame on this faintness of heart! the time craves a firmer mood. Be a woman, Catherine, or rather be a man; thou canst be a man if thou wilt."

Catherine dried her tears, and endeavored to smile.

"You must not ask me," she said, "about that which so much disturbs your mind; you shall know all in time—nay, you should know all now, but that—— Hush! here comes the Queen."

Mary entered from her apartment, paler than usual, and apparently exhausted by a sleepless night, and by the painful thoughts which had ill supplied the place of repose; yet the languor of her looks was so far from impairing her beauty that it only substituted the frail delicacy of the lovely woman for the majestic grace of the Queen. Contrary to her wont, her toilette had been very hastily despatched, and her hair, which was usually dressed by Lady Fleming with great care, escaping from beneath the head-tire, which had been hastily adjusted, fell, in long and luxuriant tresses of nature's own curling, over a neck and bosom which were somewhat less carefully veiled than usual.

As she stepped over the threshold of her apartment, Catherine, hastily drying her tears, ran to meet her royal mistress, and having first kneeled at her feet and kissed her hand, instantly rose, and placing herself on the other side of the Queen, seemed anxious to divide with the Lady Fleming the honor of supporting and assisting her. The page, on his part, advanced and put in order the chair of state, which she usually occupied, and having placed the cushion and footstool for her accommodation, stepped back, and stood ready for service in the place usually occupied by his predecessor, the young seneschal. Mary's eye rested an instant on him, and could not but remark the change of persons. Hers was not the female heart which could refuse compassion, at least, to a gallant youth who had suffered in her cause, although he had been guided in his enterprise by a too presumptuous passion, and the words "Poor Douglas!" escaped from her lips, perhaps unconsciously, as she leant herself back in her chair, and put the kerchief to her eyes.

"Yes, gracious madam," said Catherine, assuming a cheerful manner, in order to cheer her sovereign, "our gallant knight is indeed banished—the adventure was not reserved for him; but he has left behind him a youthful esquire as much devoted to your Grace's service, and who, by me, makes you tender of his hand and sword."

"If they may in aught avail your Grace," said Roland Græme, bowing profoundly.

"Alas!" said the Queen, "what needs this, Catherine? —why prepare new victims to be involved in, and overwhelmed by, my cruel fortune? Were we not better cease to struggle, and ourselves sink in the tide without further resistance, than thus drag into destruction with us every generous heart which makes an effort in our favor? I have had but too much of plot and intrigue around me, since I was stretched an orphan child in my very cradle, while contending nobles strove which should rule in the name of the unconscious innocent. Surely time it were that all this busy and most dangerous coil should end. Let me call my prison a convent, and my seclusion a voluntary sequestration of myself from the world and its ways!"

"Speak not thus, madam, before your faithful servants," said Catherine, "to discourage their zeal at once and to break their hearts. Daughter of kings, be not in this hour so unkingly. Come, Roland, and let us, the youngest of her followers, show ourselves worthy of her cause: let us kneel before her footstool, and implore her to be her own magnanimous self." And leading Roland Græme to the Queen's seat, they both kneeled down before her. Mary raised herself in her chair, and sat erect, while, extending one hand to be kissed by the page, she arranged with the other the clustering locks which shaded the bold yet lovely brow of the high-spirited Catherine.

"Alas! *ma mignonne*," she said, for so in fondness she often called her young attendant, "that you should thus desperately mix with my unhappy fate the fortune of your young lives! Are they not a lovely couple, my Fleming? and is it not heart-rending to think that I must be their ruin?"

"Not so," said Roland Græme; "it is we, gracious sovereign, who will be your deliverers."

"*Ex oribus parvulorum!*" said the Queen, looking upward; "if it is by the mouth of these children that Heaven calls me to resume the stately thoughts which become my birth and my rights, Thou wilt grant them Thy protection, and to me the power of rewarding their zeal!" Then turning to Fleming, she instantly added, "Thou knowest, my friend, whether to make those who have served me happy was not ever Mary's favorite pastime. When I have been rebuked by the stern preachers of the Calvinistic heresy, when I have seen the fierce countenances of my nobles averted from me, has it not been because I mixed in the harmless pleasures of the young and gay, and, rather for the sake of their happiness than my own, have mingled in the masque, the song, or the dance, with the youth of my household? Well, I repent not of it, though Knox termed it sin, and Morton degradation. I was happy, because I saw happiness around me; and woe betide the wretched jealousy that can extract guilt out of the overflowings of an unguarded gaiety! Fleming, if we are restored to our throne, shall we not have one blythesome day at a blythesome bridal, of which we must now name neither the bride nor the bridegroom? But that bridegroom shall have the barony of Blairgowrie, a fair gift even for a queen to give, and that bride's chaplet shall be twined with the fairest pearls that ever were found in the depths of Loch Lomond; and thou thyself, Mary Fleming, the best dresser of tires that ever busked the tresses of a queen, and who would scorn to touch those of any women of lower rank—thou thyself shalt, for my love, twine them into the bride's tresses. Look my Fleming, suppose them such clustered locks as those of our Catherine, they would not put shame upon thy skill."

So saying, she passed her hand fondly over the head of her youthful favorite, while her more aged attendant replied despondently, "Alas! madam, your thoughts stray far from home."

"They do, my Fleming," said the Queen; "but is it well or kind in you to call them back? God knows, they have kept the perch this night but too closely. Come, I will recall the gay vision, were it but to punish them. Yes, at that blythesome bridal Mary herself shall forget the weight of sorrows and the toil of state, and herself once more lead a measure. At whose wedding was it that we last danced, my Fleming? I think care has troubled my memory—yet something of it I should remember; canst thou not aid me? I know thou canst."

"Alas! madam," replied the lady——

"What!" said Mary, "wilt thou not help us so far? This is a peevish adherence to thine own graver opinion, which holds our talk as folly. But thou art court-bred, and wilt well understand me when I say, the Queen *commands* Lady Fleming to tell her where she led the last "branle.""

With a face deadly pale, and a mien as if she were about to sink into the earth, the court-bred dame, no longer daring to refuse obedience, faltered out—"Gracious lady—if my memory err not—it was at a masque in Holyrood—at the marriage of Sebastian."

The unhappy Queen, who had hitherto listened with a melancholy smile, provoked by the reluctance with which the Lady Fleming brought out her story, at this ill-fated word interrupted her with a shriek so wild and loud that the vaulted apartment rang, and both Roland and Catherine sprang to their feet in the utmost terror and alarm. Meantime, Mary seemed, by the train of horrible ideas thus suddenly excited, surprised not only beyond self-command, but for the moment beyond the verge of reason.

"Traitress," she said to the Lady Fleming, "thou wouldst slay thy sovereign. Call my French guards—*à moi!-à moi! mes Français*! I am beset with traitors in mine own palace—they have murdered my husband. Rescue!—rescue! for the Queen of Scotland!" She started up from her chair; her features, late so exquisitely lovely in their paleness, now inflamed with the fury of frenzy, and resembling those of a Bellona. "We will take the field ourself," she said; "warn the city—warn Lothian and Fife—saddle our Spanish barb and bid French Paris see our petronel be charged! Better to die at the head of our brave Scotsmen, like our grandfather at Floddan, than of a broken heart like our ill-starred father."

"Be patient—be composed, dearest sovereign!" said Catherine; and then addressing Lady Fleming angrily, she added, "How can you say aught that reminded her of her husband?"

The word reached the ear of the unhappy princess, who caught it up, speaking with great rapidity. "Husband!—What husband? Not his most Christian Majesty; he is ill at ease—he cannot mount on horseback. Not him of the Lennox; bnt it was the Duke of Orkney thou wouldst say."

"For God's love, madam, be patient!" said the Lady Fleming.

"But the Queen's excited imagination could by no entreaty be diverted from its course. "Bid him come hither to our aid," she said, "and bring with him his lambs, as he calls them—Bowton, Hay of Talla, Black Ormiston, and his kinsman Hob. Fie! how swart they are, and how they smell of sulphur! What! closeted with Morton? Nay, if the Douglas and the Hepburn hatch the complot together, the bird, when it breaks the shell, will scare Scotland. Will it not, my Fleming?"

" Mary seemed surprised by the train of horrible ideas . . . beyond the the verge of reason."

"She grows wilder and wilder," said Fleming; "we have too many hearers for these strange words."

"Roland," said Catherine, "in the name of God begone! You cannot aid us here. Leave us to deal with her alone. away—away!"

She thrust him to the door of the ante-room; yet even when he had entered that apartment and shut the door, he could still hear the Queen talk in a loud and determined tone, as if giving forth orders, until at length the voice died away in a feeble and continued lamentation.

At this crisis Catherine entered the ante-room. "Be not too anxious," she said, "the crisis is now over; but keep the door fast—let no one enter until she is more composed."

"In the name of God, what does this mean?" said the page; "or what was there in the Lady Fleming's words to excite so wild a transport?"

"O, the Lady Fleming—the Lady Fleming," said Catherine, repeating the words impatiently—the Lady Fleming is a fool: she loves her mistress, yet knows so little how to express her love that, were the Queen to ask her for very poison, she would deem it a point of duty not to resist her commands. I could have torn her starched head-tire from her formal head. The Queen should have as soon had the heart out of my body as the word 'Sebastian' out of my lips. That that piece of weaved tapestry should be a woman, and yet not have wit enough to tell a lie!"

"And what was this story of Sebastian?" said the page. "By Heaven, Catherine, you are all riddles alike."

"You are as great a fool as Fleming," returned the impatient maiden. "Know ye not, that on the night of Henry Darnley's murder, and at the blowing up of the Kirk of Field, the Queen's absence was owing to her attending on a masque at Holyrood, given by her to grace the marriage of this same Sebastian, who, himself a favored servant, married one of her female attendants, who was near to her person?"

"By St. Giles," said the page, "I wonder not at her passion, but only marvel by what forgetfulness it was that she could urge the Lady Fleming with such a question."

"I cannot account for it," said Catherine; "but it seems as if great and violent grief or horror sometimes obscure the memory, and spread a cloud, like that of an exploding cannon, over the circumstances with which they are accompanied. But I may not stay here, where I came not to moralize with your wisdom, but simply to cool my resentment against that unwise Lady Fleming, which I think hath now somewhat abated, so that I shall endure her presence without any desire to damage either her curch or vasquine. Meanwhile, keep fast that door: I would not for my life that any of these heretics saw her in the unhappy state which, brought on her as it has been by the success of their own diabolical plotting, they would not stick to call, in their snuffling cant, the judgment of Providence."

She left the apartment just as the latch of the outward door was raised from without. But the bolt, which Roland had drawn on the inside, resisted the efforts of the person desirous to enter.

"Who is there?" said Græme aloud.

"It is I," replied the harsh and yet low voice of the steward Dryfesdale.

"You cannot enter now," returned the youth.

"And wherefore?" demanded Dryfesdale, "seeing I come but to do my duty, and inquire what mean the shrieks from the apartment of the Moabitish woman. Wherefore, I say, since such is mine errand, can I not enter?"

"Simply," replied the youth, "because the bolt is drawn, and I have no fancy to undo it. I have the right side of the door to-day, as you had last night."

"Thou art ill-advised, thou malapert boy," replied the steward, "to speak to me in such a fashion; but I shall inform my lady of thine insolence."

"The insolence," said the page, "is meant for thee only, in fair guerdon of thy discourtesy to me. For thy lady's information, I have answer more courteous: you may say that the Queen is ill at ease, and desires to be disturbed neither by visits nor messages."

"I conjure you, in the name of God," said the old man, with more solemnity in his tone than he had hitherto used, "to let me know if her malady really gains power on her!"

"She will have no aid at your hand or at your lady's; wherefore, begone, and trouble us no more: we neither want, nor will accept of, aid at your hands."

With this positive reply, the steward, grumbling and dissatisfied, returned downstairs.

CHAPTER XXXII

> It is the curse of kings to be attended
> By slaves, who take their humors for a warrant
> To break into the bloody house of life,
> And on the winking of authority
> To understand a law.
>
> *King John.*

THE Lady of Lochleven sat alone in her chamber, endeavoring with sincere but imperfect zeal to fix her eyes and her attention on the black-letter Bible which lay before her, bound in velvet and embroidery, and adorned with massive silver clasps and knosps. But she found her utmost efforts unable to withdraw her mind from the resentful recollection of what had last night passed betwixt her and the Queen, in which the latter had with such bitter taunt reminded her of her early and long-repented transgression.

"Why," she said, "should I resent so deeply that another reproaches me with that which I have never ceased to make matter of blushing to myself? And yet, why should this woman, who reaps—at least, has reaped—the fruits of my folly, and has jostled my son aside from the throne—why should she, in the face of all my domestics and of her own, dare to upbraid me with my shame? Is she not in my power? Does she not fear me? Ha! wily tempter, I will wrestle with thee strongly, and with better suggestions than my own evil heart can supply!"

She again took up the sacred volume, and was endeavoring to fix her attention on its contents, when she was disturbed by a tap at the door of her room. It opened at her command, and the steward Dryfesdale entered, and stood before her with a gloomy and perturbed expression on his brow.

"What has chanced, Dryfesdale, that thou lookest thus?" said his mistress. "Have there been evil tidings of my son or of my grandchildren?"

"No, lady," replied Dryfesdale, "but you were deeply insulted last night, and I fear me thou art as deeply avenged this morning. Where is the chaplain?"

"What mean you by hints so dark, and a question so

sudden? The chaplain, as you well know, is absent at Perth upon an assembly of the brethren."

"I care not," answered the steward; "he is but a priest of Baal."

"Dryfesdale," said the lady, sternly, "what meanest thou? I have ever heard that in the Low Countries thou didst herd with the Anabaptist preachers—those boars which tear up the vintage. But the ministry which suits me and my house must content my retainers."

"I would I had good ghostly counsel, though," replied the steward, not attending to his mistress's rebuke, and seeming to speak to himself. "This woman of Moab——"

"Speak of her with reverence," said the lady: "she is a king's daughter."

"Be it so," replied Dryfesdale; "she goes where there is little difference betwixt her and a beggar's child. Mary of Scotland is dying."

"Dying, and in my castle!" said the lady, starting up in alarm; "of what disease, or by what accident?"

"Bear patience, lady. The ministry was mine."

"Thine, villain and traitor! how didst thou dare——"

"I heard you insulted, lady—I heard you demand vengeance; I promised you should have it, and I promised you should have it, and I now bring tidings of it."

"Dryfesdale, I trust thou ravest?" said the lady.

"I rave not," replied the steward. "That which was written of me a million of years ere I saw the light must be executed by me. She hath that in her veins that, I fear me, will soon stop the springs of life."

"Cruel villain," exclaimed the lady, "thou hast not poisoned her?"

"And if I had," said Dryfesdale, "what does it so greatly merit? Men bane vermin; why not rid them of their enemies so? In Italy they will do it for a cruizuedor."

"Cowardly ruffian, begone from my sight!"

"Think better of my zeal, lady," said the steward, "and judge not without looking around you. Lindesay, Ruthven, and your kinsmen Morton poniarded Rizzio, and yet you now see no blood on their embroidery; the Lord Semple stabbed the Lord of Sanquhar—does his bonnet sit a jot more awry on his brow? What noble lives in Scotland who has not had a share, for policy or revenge, in some such dealing? And who imputes it to them? Be not cheated with names: a dagger or a draught work to the same end, and are little unlike—a glass phial imprisons the one, and a leathern sheath the other; one deals with the brain, the other sluices the blood. Yet, I say not I gave aught to this lady."

"What dost thou mean by thus dallying with me?" said the lady; "as thou wouldst save thy neck from the rope it merits, tell me the whole truth of this story; thou hast long been known a dangerous man."

"Ay, in my master's service I can be cold and sharp as my sword. Be it known to you that, when last on shore, I consulted with a woman of skill and power, called Nicneven, of whom the country has rung for some brief time past. Fools asked for her charms to make them beloved, misers for means to increase their store; some demanded to know the future—an idle wish, since it cannot be altered; others would have an explanation of the past—idler still, since it cannot be recalled. I heard their queries with scorn, and demanded the means of avenging myself of a deadly enemy, for I grow old, and may trust no longer to Bilboa blade. She gave me a packet. 'Mix that,' said she, 'with any liquid, and thy vengeance is complete.'"

"Villain! and you mixed it with the food of this imprisoned lady, to the dishonor of thy master's house?"

"To redeem the insulted honor of my master's house, I mixed the contents of the packet with the jar of succory water. They seldom fail to drain it, and the woman loves it over all."

"It was a work of hell," said the Lady Lochleven, "both the asking and the granting. "Away, wretched man let us see if aid be yet too late!"

"They will not admit us, madam, save we enter by force. I have been twice at the door, but can obtain no entrance."

"We will beat it level with the ground, if needful. And hold—summon Randal hither instantly. Randal, here is a foul and evil chance befallen; send off a boat instantly to Kinross—the chamberlain Luke Lundin is said to have skill. Fetch off, too, that foul witch Nicneven; she shall first counteract her own spell, and then be burned to ashes in in the island of St. Serf. Away—away. Tell them to hoist sail and ply oar, as ever they would have good of the Douglas's hand!"

"Mother Nicneven will not be lightly found, or fetched hither on these conditions," answered Dryfesdale.

"Then grant her full assurance of safety. Look to it, for thine own life must answer for this lady's recovery."

"I might have guessed that," said Dryfesdale, sullenly; "but it is my comfort I have avenged mine own cause as well as yours. She hath scoffed and scripped at me, and encouraged her saucy minion of a page to ridicule my stiff gait and slow speech. I felt it borne in upon me that I was to be avenged on them."

"Go to the western turret," said the lady, "and remain there in ward until we see how this gear will terminate. I know thy resolved disposition : thou wilt not attempt escape."

"Not were the walls of the turret of egg-shells, and the lake sheeted with ice," said Dryfesdale. "I am well taught, and strong in belief that man does nought of himself; he is but the foam on the billow, which rises, bubbles, and bursts, not by its own effort, but by the mightier impulse of fate which urges him. Yet, lady, if I may advise, amid this zeal for the life of the Jezebel of Scotland, forget not what is due to thine own honor, and keep the matter secret as you may."

So saying, the gloomy fatalist turned from her, and stalked off with sullen composure to the place of confinement allotted to him.

His lady caught at his last hint, and only expressed her fear that the prisoner had partaken of some unwholesome food, and was dangerously ill. The castle was soon alarmed and in confusion. Randal was despatched to the shore to fetch off Lundin, with such remedies as could counteract poison; and with farther instructions to bring Mother Nicneven, if she could be found, with full power to pledge the Lady of Lochleven's word for her safety.

Meanwhile, the Lady of Lochleven herself held parley at the door of the Queen's apartment, and in vain urged the page to undo it.

"Foolish boy!" she said, "thine own life and thy lady's are at stake. Open, I say, or we will cause the door to be broken down."

"I may not open the door without my royal mistress's orders," answered Roland. "She has been very ill, and now she slumbers; if you wake her by using violence, let the consequence be on you and your followers."

"Was ever woman in a strait so fearful!" exclaimed the Lady of Lochleven. "At least, thou rash boy, beware that no one tastes the food, but especially the jar of succory water."

She then hastened to the turret, where Dryfesdale had composedly resigned himself to imprisonment. She found him reading, and demanded of him, "Was thy fell potion of speedy operation?"

"Slow," answered the steward. "The hag asked me which I chose; I told her I loved a slow and sure revenge.

'Revenge,' said I, 'is the highest-flavor draught which man tastes upon earth, and he should sip it by little and little, not drain it up greedily at once.'"

"Against whom, unhappy man, couldst thou nourish so fell a revenge?"

"I had many objects, but the chief was that insolent page."

"The boy! thou inhuman man," exclaimed the lady; "what could he do to deserve thy malice?"

"He rose in your favor, and you graced him with your commissions—that was one thing. He rose in that of George Douglas also—that was another. He was the favorite of the Calvinistic Henderson, who hated me because my spirits disowns a separate priesthood. The Moabitish Queen held him dear—winds from each opposing point blew in his favor; the old servitor of your house was held lightly among ye; above all, from the first time I saw his face, I longed to destroy him."

"What fiend have I nurtured in my house!" replied the lady. "May God forgive me the sin of having given thee food and raiment!"

"You might not choose, lady," answered the steward. "Long ere this castle was builded—ay, long ere the islet which sustains it reared its head above the blue water—I was destined to be your faithful slave, and you to be my ungrateful mistress. Remember you not when I plunged amid the victorious French, in the time of this lady's mother, and brought off your husband, when those who had hung at the same breasts with him dared not attempt the rescue? Remember how I plunged into the lake when your grandson's skiff was overtaken by the tempest, boarded, and steered her safe to the land. Lady, the servant of a Scottish baron is he who regards not his own life or that of any other, save his master. And, for the death of the woman, I had tried the potion on her sooner, had not Master George been her taster. Her death—would it not be the happiest news that Scotland ever heard? Is she not of the bloody Guisian stock, whose sword was so often red with the blood of God's saints? Is she not the daughter of the wretched tyrant James, whom Heaven cast down from his kingdom and his pride, even as the king of Babylon was smitten?"

"Peace, villain!" said the lady, a thousand varied recollections thronging on her mind at the mention of her royal lover's name—"peace, and disturb not the ashes of the dead—of the royal, of the unhappy dead. Read thy Bible; and may God grant thee to avail thyself better of its contents than thou hast yet done!" She departed hastily, and as she reached the next apartment, the tears rose to her eyes so hastily that she was compelled to stop and use her kerchief to dry them. "I expected not this," she said, "no more than to have drawn water from the hard flint, or sap from a withered tree. I saw with a dry eye the apostacy and shame of George Douglas—the hope of my son's house, the child of my love; and yet I now weep for him who has so long lain in his grave—for him to whom I owe it that his daughter can make a scoffing and a jest of my name! But she is *his* daughter; my heart, hardened against her for so many causes, relents when a glance of her eye places her father unexpectedly before me; and as often her likeness to that true daughter of the house of Guise, her detested mother, has again confirmed my resolution. But she must not—must not die in my house, and by so foul a practise. Thank God, the operation of the potion is slow, and may be counteracted! I will to her apartment once more. But O! that hardened villain, whose fidelity we held in such esteem, and had such high proofs of! What miracle can unite so much wickedness and so much truth in one bosom!"

The Lady of Lochleven was not aware how far minds of a certain gloomy and determined cast by nature may be warped by a keen sense of petty injuries and insults, combining with the love of gain, and sense of self-interest, and amalgamated with the crude, wild, and indigested fanatical opinions which this man had gathered among the crazy sectaries of Germany; or how far the doctrines of fatalism, which he had embraced so decidedly, sear the human conscience, by representing our actions as the result of inevitable necessity.

During her visit to the prisoner, Roland had communicated to Catherine the tenor of the conversation he had had with her at the door of the apartment. The quick intelligence of that lively maiden instantly comprehended the outline of what was believed to have happened, but her prejudices hurried her beyond the truth.

"They meant to have poisoned us," she exclaimed in horror, "and there stands the fatal liquor which should have done the deed! Ay, as soon as Douglas ceased to be our taster, our food was likely to be fatally seasoned. Thou, Roland, who should have made the essay, wert readily doomed to die with us. O, dearest Lady Fleming, pardon—pardon for the injuries I said to you in my anger: your words were prompted by Heaven to save our lives, and especially that of the injured Queen. But what have we now to do? That old crocodile of the lake will be presently back to shed her hypocritical tears over our dying agonies. Lady Fleming, what shall we do?"

"Our Lady help us in our need!" she replied; "how should I tell, unless we were to make our plaint to the Regent?"

"Make our plaint to the devil," said Catherine, impatiently, "and accuse his dam at the foot of his burning throne! The Queen still sleeps; we must gain time. The poisoning hag must not know her scheme has miscarried; the old envenomed spider has but too many ways of mending her broken web. The jar of succory water," said she—"Roland, if thou be'st a man, help me: empty the jar on the chimney or from the window; make such waste among the viands as if we had made our usual meal, and leave the fragments on cup and porringer, but taste nothing as thou lovest thy life. I will sit by the Queen, and tell her, at her waking, in what a fearful pass we stand. Her sharp wit and ready spirit will teach us what is best to be done. Meanwhile, till farther notice, observe, Roland, that the Queen is in a state of torpor; that Lady Fleming is indisposed—that character (speaking in a lower tone) will suit her best, and save her wits some labor in vain. I am not so much indisposed, thou understandest."

"And I," said the page.

"You!" replied Catherine, "you are quite well; who thinks it worth while to poison puppy-dogs or pages?"

"Does this levity become the time?" asked the page.

"It does—it does," answered Catherine Seyton. "If the Queen approves, I see plainly how this disconcerted attempt may do us good service."

She went to work while she spoke, eagerly assisted by Roland. The breakfast-table soon displayed the appearance as if the meal had been eaten as usual; and the ladies retired as softly as possible into the Queen's sleeping-apartment. At a new summons of the Lady Lochleven, the page undid the door, and admitted her into the ante-room, asking her pardon for having withstood her, alleging in excuse that the Queen had fallen into a heavy slumber since she had broken her fast.

"She has eaten and drunken, then?" said the Lady of Lochleven.

"Surely," replied the page, "according to her grace's ordinary custom, unless upon the fasts of the church."

"The jar," she said, hastily examining it, "it is empty; drank the Lady Mary the whole of this water?"

"A large part, madam; and I heard the Lady Catherine Seyton jestingly upbraid the Lady Mary Fleming with having taken more than a just share of what remained, so that but little fell to her own lot."

"And are they well in health?" said the Lady of Lochleven.

"Lady Fleming," said the page, "complains of lethargy, and looks duller than usual; and the Lady Catherine of Seyton feels her head somewhat more giddy than is her wont."

He raised his voice a little as he said these words, to apprise the ladies of the part assigned to each of them, and not, perhaps, without the wish of conveying to the ears of Catherine the page-like jest which lurked in the allotment.

"I will enter the Queen's chamber," said the Lady Lochleven; "my business is express."

As she advanced to the door, the voice of Catherine Seyton was heard from within. "No one can enter here; the Queen sleeps."

"I will not be controled, young lady," replied the Lady of Lochleven; "there is, I wot, no inner bar, and I will enter in your despite."

"There is, indeed, no inner bar," answered Catherine, firmly, "but there are the staples where that bar should be; and into those staples have I thrust mine arm, like an ancestress of your own, when, better employed than the Douglasses of our days, she thus defended the bedchamber of her sovereign against murderers. Try your force, then, and see whether a Seyton cannot rival in courage a maiden of the house of Douglas."

"I dare not attempt the pass at such risk," said the Lady of Lochleven. "Strange, that this princess, with all that justly attaches to her as blameworthy, should preserve such empire over the minds of her attendants! Damsel, I give thee my honor that I come for the Queen's safety and advantage. Awake her, if thou lovest her, and pray her leave that I may enter. I will retire from the door the whilst."

"Thou wilt not awaken the Queen?" said the Lady Fleming.

"What choice have we?" said the ready-witted maiden, "unless you deem it better to wait till the Lady Lochleven herself plays lady of the bedchamber. Her fit of patience will not last long, and the Queen must be prepared to meet her."

"But thou wilt bring back her Grace's fit by thus disturbing her."

"Heaven forbid!" replied Catherine; "but if so, it must pass for an effect of the poison. I hope better things, and that the Queen will be able when she wakes to form her own judgment in this terrible crisis. Meanwhile, do thou, dear Lady Fleming, practise to look as dull and heavy as the alertness of thy spirit will permit."

Catherine kneeled by the side of the Queen's bed, and, kissing her hand repeatedly, succeeded at last in awakening without alarming her. She seemed surprised to find that she was ready dressed, but sate up in her bed, and appeared so perfectly composed that Catherine Seyton, without farther preamble, judged it safe to inform her of the predicament in which they were placed. Mary turned pale, and crossed herself again and again, when she heard the imminent danger in which she had stood. But, like the Ulysses of Homer—

> Hardly waking yet,
> Sprung in her mind the momentary wit,

and she at once understood her situation, with the dangers and advantages that attended it.

"We cannot do better," she said, after her hasty conference with Catherine, pressing her at the same time to her bosom, and kissing her forehead—"we cannot do better than to follow the scheme so happily devised by thy quick wit and bold affection. Undo the door to the Lady Lochleven. She shall meet her match in art, though not in perfidy. Fleming, draw close the curtain, and get thee behind it—thou art a better tire-woman than an actress; do but breathe heavily, and, if thou wilt, groan slightly, and it will top thy part. Hark! they come. Now, Catherine of Medicis, may thy spirit inspire me, for a cold northern brain is too blunt for this scene!"

Ushered by Catherine Seyton, and stepping as light as she could, the Lady Lochleven was shown into the twilight apartment, and conducted to the side of the couch, where Mary, pallid and exhausted from a sleepless night and the subsequent agitation of the morning, lay extended so listlessly as might well confirm the worst fears of her hostess.

"Now, God forgive us our sins!" said the Lady of Lochleven, forgetting her pride, and throwing herself on her knees by the side of her bed; "it is too true—she is murdered!"

"Who is in the chamber?" said Mary, as if awaking from

a heavy sleep. "Seyton, Fleming, where are you? I heard a strange voice. Who waits? Call Courcelles."

"Alas! her memory is at Holyrood, though her body is at Lochleven. Forgive, madam," continued the lady, "if I call your attention to me. I am Margaret Erskine, of the house of Mar, by marriage Lady Douglas of Lochleven."

"O, our gentle hostess," answered the Queen, "who hath such care of our lodgings and of our diet. We cumber you too much and too long, good Lady of Lochleven; but we now trust your task of hospitality is wellnigh ended."

"Her words go like a knife through my heart," said the Lady of Lochleven. "With a breaking heart, I pray your Grace to tell me what is your ailment, that aid may be had, if there be yet time?"

"Nay, my ailment," replied the Queen, "is nothing worth telling, or worth a leech's notice: my limbs feel heavy—my heart feels cold—a prisoner's limbs and heart are rarely otherwise. Fresh air, methinks, and freedom would soon revive me; but as the estates have ordered it, death alone can break my prison doors."

"Were it possible, madam," said the lady, "that your liberty could restore your perfect health, I would myself encounter the resentment of the Regent—of my son, Sir William—of my whole friends, rather than you should meet your fate in this castle!"

"Alas! madam," said the Lady Fleming, who conceived the time propitious to show that her own address had been held too lightly of; "it is but trying what good freedom may work upon us; for myself, I think a free walk on the greensward would do me much good at heart."

The Lady of Lochleven rose from the bedside, and darted a penetrating look at the elder valetudinary. "Are you so evil-disposed, Lady Fleming?"

"Evil-disposed indeed, madam," replied the court dame, "and more especially since breakfast."

"Help!—help!" exclaimed Catherine, anxious to break off a conversation which boded her schemes no good—"help! I say—help! the Queen is about to pass away. Aid her, Lady Lochleven, if you be a woman!"

The lady hastened to support the Queen's head, who, turning her eyes towards her with an air of great languor, exclaimed, "Thanks, my dearest Lady of Lochleven; notwithstanding some passages of late, I have never misconstrued or misdoubted your affection to our house. It was proved, as I have heard, before I was born."

The Lady Lochleven sprung from the floor, on which she had again knelt, and having paced the apartment in great disorder, flung open the lattice, as if to get air.

"Now, Our Lady forgives me!" said Catherine to herself; "how deep must the love of sarcasm be implanted in the breasts of us women, since the Queen, with all her sense, will risk ruin rather then rein in her wit!" She then adventured, stooping over the Queen's person, to press her arm with her hand, saying, at the same time, "For God's sake, madam, restrain yourself!"

"Thou art too forward, maiden," said the Queen; but immediately added, in a low whisper, "Forgive me, Catherine: but when I felt the hag's murderous hands busy about my head and neck, I felt such disgust and hatred that I must have said something or died. But I will be schooled to better havior, only see that thou let her not touch me."

"Now, God be praised!" said the Lady of Lochleven, withdrawing her head from the window, "the boat comes as fast as sail and oar can send wood through water. It brings the leech and a female—certainly, from the appearance, the very person I was in quest of. Were she but well out of this castle, with our honor safe, I would that she were on the top of the wildest mountain in Norway; or I would I had been there myself, ere I had undertaken this trust!"

While she thus expressed herself, standing apart at one window, Roland Græme, from the other, watched the boat bursting through the waters of the lake, which glided from its side in ripple and in foam. He, too, became sensible that at the stern was seated the medical chamberlain, clad in his black velvet cloak; and that his own relative, Magdalen Græme, in her assumed character of Mother Nicneven, stood in the bow, her hands clasped together, and pointed towards the castle, and her attitude, even at that distance, expressing enthusiastic eagerness to arrive at the landing-place. They arrived there accordingly; and while the supposed witch was detained in a room beneath, the physician was ushered to the Queen's apartment, which he entered with all due professional solemnity. Catherine had, in the meanwhile, fallen back from the Queen's bed, and taken an opportunity to whisper to Roland, "Methinks, from the information of the threadbare velvet cloak and the solemn beard, there would be little trouble in haltering yonder ass. But thy grandmother, Roland—thy grandmother's zeal will ruin us, if she get not a hint to dissemble."

Roland, without reply, glided towards the door of the apartment, crossed the parlor, and safely entered the ante-chamber; but when he attempted to pass farther, the word "Back! Back!" echoed from one to the other by two men armed with carabines, convinced him that the Lady of Lochleven's suspicions had not, even in the midst of her alarms, been so far lulled to sleep as to omit the precaution of stationing sentinels on her prisoners. He was compelled, therefore, to return to the parlor, or audience-chamber, in which he found the lady of the castle in conference with her learned leech.

"A truce with your cant phrase and your solemn foppery, Lundin," in such terms she accosted the man of art, "and let me know instantly, if thou canst tell, whether this lady hath swallowed aught that is less than wholesome."

"Nay, but good lady—honored patroness—to whom I am alike bondsman in my medical and official capacity, deal reasonably with me. If this, mine illustrious patient, will not a answer a question, saving with sighs and moans; if that other honorable lady will do nought but yawn in my face when I inquire after the diagnostics; and if that other young damsel, who I profess is a comely maiden——"

"Talk not to me of comeliness or of damsels," said the Lady of Lochleven; "I say, are they evil-disposed? In one word, man, have they taken poison—ay or no?"

"Poisons, madam," said the learned leech, "are of various sorts. There is your animal poison, as the *Lepus marinus*, as mentioned by Dioscorides and Galen; there are mineral and semi-mineral poisons, as those compounded of sublimate, regulus of antimony, vitriol, and the arsenical salts; there are your poisons from herbs and vegetables, as the aqua cymbalariæ, opium, aconitum, cantharides, and the like; there are also——"

"Now, out upon thee for a learned fool! And I myself am no better for expecting an oracle from such a log," said the lady.

"Nay, but if your ladyship will have patience. If I knew what food they have partaken of, or could see but the remnants of what they have last eaten; for as to the external and internal symptoms, I can discover nought like; for, as Galen saith in his second book *De Antidotis*——"

"Away, fool!" said the lady; "send me that hag hither; she shall avouch what it was that she hath given to the wretch Dryfesdale, or the pilniewinks and thumbikins shall wrench it out of her finger-joints!"

"Art hath no enemy unless the ignorant," said the morti

fied doctor; veiling, however, his remark under the Latin version, and stepping apart into a corner to watch the result.

In a minute or two Magdalen Græme entered the apartment, dressed as we have described her at the revel, but with her muffler thrown back, and all affectation of disguise. She was attended by two guards, of whose presence she did not seem even to be conscious, and who followed her with an air of embarrassment and timidity, which was probably owing to their belief in her supernatual power, coupled with the effect produced by her bold and undaunted demeanor. She confronted the Lady of Lochleven, who seemed to endure with high disdain the confidence of her air and manner.

"Wretched woman!" said the lady, after essaying for a moment to bear her down, before she addressed her, by the stately severity of her look, "what was that powder which thou didst give to a servant of this house, by name Jasper Dryfesdale, that he might work out with it some slow and secret vengeance? Confess its nature and properties, or, by the honor of Douglas, I give thee to fire and stake before the sun is lower!"

"Alas!" said Magdalen Græme in reply, "and when became a Douglas or a Douglas's man so unfurnished of his means of revenge that he should seek them at the hands of a poor and solitary woman? The towers in which your captives pine away into unpitied graves yet stand fast on their foundations; the crimes wrought in them have not yet burst their vaults asunder; your men have still their cross-bows, pistolets, and daggers; why need you seek to herbs or charms for the execution of your revenges?"

"Hear me, foul hag," said the Lady of Lochleven—"but what avails speaking to thee? Bring Dryfesdale hither, and let them be confronted together."

"You may spare your retainers the labor," replied Magdalen Græme. "I came not here to be confronted with a base groom, nor to answer the interrogatories of James's heretical leman. I came to speak with the Queen of Scotland. Give place there!"

And while the Lady of Lochleven stood confounded at her boldness, and at the reproach she had cast upon herself, Magdalen Græme strode past her into the bedchamber of the Queen, and, kneeling on the floor, made a salutation as if, in the Oriental fashion, she meant to touch the earth with her forehead.

"Hail, Princess!" she said—"hail, daughter of many a king, but graced above them all in that thou art called to suffer for the true faith!—hail to thee, the pure gold of whose crown has been tried in the seven-times-heated furnace of affliction—hear the comfort which God and Our Lady send thee by the mouth of thy unworthy servant. But first——" and stooping her head she crossed herself repeatedly, and, still upon her knees, appeared to be rapidly reciting some formula of devotion.

"Seize her and drag her to the massymore! To the deepest dungeon with the sorceress, whose master, the devil, could alone have inspired her with boldness enough to insult the mother of Douglas in his own castle!" Thus spoke the incensed Lady of Lochleven.

But the physician presumed to interpose. "I pray of you, honored madam, she be permitted to take her course without interruption. Peradventure we shall learn something concerning the nostrum she hath ventured, contrary to law and the rules of art, to adhibit to these ladies, through the medium of the steward Dryfesdale."

"For a fool," replied the Lady of Lochleven, "thou hast counseled wisely. I will bridle my resentment till their conference be over."

"God forbid, honored lady," said Doctor Lundin, "that you should suppress it longer—nothing may more endanger the frame of your honored body; and truly, if there be witchcraft in this matter, it is held by the vulgar, and even by solid authors on demonology, that three scruples of the ashes of the witch, when she hath been well and carefully burned at a stake, is a grand catholicon in such matter, even as they prescribe *crinis canis rabidi*—a hair of the dog that bit the patient—in cases of hydrophobia. I warrant neither treatment, being out of the regular practise of the schools; but, in the present case, there can be little harm in trying the conclusion upon this old necromancer and quacksalver: *fiat experimentum*, as we say, *in corpore vili*."

"Peace, fool!" said the lady, "she is about to speak."

At that moment Magdalen Græme arose from her knees, and turned her countenance on the Queen, at the same time advancing her foot, extending her arm, and assuming the mien and attitude of a sybil in frenzy. As her gray hair floated back from beneath her coif, and her eye gleamed fire from under its shaggy eyebrow, the effect of her expressive, though emaciated, features was heightened by an enthusiasm approaching to insanity, and her appearance struck with awe all who were present. Her eyes for a time glanced wildly around, as if seeking for something to aid her in collecting her powers of expression, and her lips had a nervous and quivering motion, as those of one who would fain speak, yet rejects as inadequate the words which present themselves. Mary herself caught the infection as if by a sort of magnetic influence, and raising herself from her bed, without being able to withdraw her eyes from those of Magdalen, waited as if for the oracle of a pythoness. She waited not long; for no sooner had the enthusiast collected herself than her gaze became intensely steady, her features assumed a determined energy, and when she began to speak, the words flowed from her with a profuse fluency which might have passed for inspiration, and which, perhaps, she herself mistook for such.

"Arise," she said, "Queen of France and of England! Arise, lioness of Scotland, and be not dismayed, though the nets of the hunters have encircled thee! Stoop not to feign with the false ones, whom thou shalt soon meet in the field. The issue of battle is with the God of armies, but by battle thy cause shall be tried. Lay aside, then, the arts of lower mortals, and assume those which become a queen! True defender of the only true faith, the armory of Heaven is open to thee! Faithful daughter of the church, take the keys of St. Peter, to bind and to loose! Royal Princess of the land, take the sword of St. Paul, to smite and to shear! There is darkness in thy destiny; but not in these towers, not under the rule of their haughty mistress, shall that destiny be closed. In other lands the lioness may crouch to the power of the tigress, but not in her own: not in Scotland shall the Queen of Scotland long remain captive; nor is the fate of the royal Stuart in the hands of the traitor Douglas. Let the Lady of Lochleven double her bolts and deepen her dungeons, they shall not retain thee. Each element shall give thee its assistance ere thou shalt continue captive: the land shall lend its earthquakes, the water its waves, the air its tempests, the fire its devouring flames, to desolate this house, rather than it shall continue the place of thy captivity. Hear this and tremble, all ye who fight against the light, for she says it to whom it hath been assured!"

She was silent, and the astonished physician said, "If there was ever an *energumene*, or possessed demoniac, in our days, there is a devil speaking with that woman's tongue!"

"Practise," said the Lady of Lochleven, recovering her surprise—"here is all practise and imposture. To the dungeon with her!"

"Lady of Lochleven," said Mary, arising from her bed, and coming forward with her wonted dignity, "ere you make arrest on any one in our presence, hear me but one word. I have done you some wrong: I believed you privy to the murderous purpose of your vassal, and I deceived you in suffering you to believe it had taken effect. I did you wrong, Lady of Lochleven, for I perceive your purpose to aid me was sincere. We tasted not of the liquid, nor are we now sick, save that we languish for our freedom."

"It is avowed like Mary of Scotland," said Magdalen Græme; "and know, besides, that had the Queen drained the draught to the dregs, it was harmless as the water from a sainted spring. Trow ye, proud woman," she added, addressing herself to the Lady of Lochleven, "that I—I—would have been the wretch to put poison in the hands of a servant or vassal of the house of Lochleven, knowing whom that house contained? as soon would I have furnished drug to slay my own daughter!"

"Am I thus bearded in mine own castle?" said the lady; "to the dungeon with her! She shall abye what is due to the vender of poisons and practiser of witchcrafts."

"Yet hear me for an instant, Lady of Lochleven," said Mary: "and do you," to Magdalen, "be silent at my command. Your steward, lady, has by confession attempted my life and those of my household, and this woman hath done her best to save them, by furnishing him with what was harmless, in place of the fatal drugs which he expected. Methinks I propose to you but a fair exchange when I say I forgive your vassal with all my heart, and leave vengeance to God and to his conscience, so that you also forgive the boldness of this woman in your presence; for we trust you do not hold it as a crime that she substituted an innocent beverage for the mortal poison which was to have drenched our cup!"

"Heaven forefend, madam," said the lady, "that I should account that a crime which saved the house of Douglas from a foul breach of honor and hospitality! We have written to our son touching our vassal's delict, and he must abide his doom, which will most likely be death. Touching this woman, her trade is damnable by Scripture, and is mortally punished by the wise laws of our ancestry: she also must abide her doom."

"And have I then," said the Queen, "no claim on the house of Lochleven for the wrong I have so nearly suffered within their walls? I ask but in requital the life of a frail and aged woman, whose brain, as yourself may judge, seems somewhat affected by years and suffering."

"If the Lady Mary," replied the inflexible Lady of Lochleven, "hath been menaced with wrong in the house of Douglas, it may be regarded as some compensation that her complots have cost that house the exile of a valued son."

"Plead no more for me, my gracious sovereign," said Magdalen Græme, "nor abase yourself to ask so much as a gray hair of my head at her hands. I knew the risk at which I served my church and my queen, and was ever prompt to pay my poor life as the ransom. It is a comfort to think that in slaying me, or in restraining my freedom, or even in injuring that single gray hair, the house whose honor she boasts so highly will have filled up the measure of their shame by the breach of their solemn written assurance of safety." And taking from her bosom a paper, she handed it to the Queen.

"It is a solemn assurance of safety in life and limb," said Queen Mary, "with space to come and go, under the hand and seal of the chamberlain of Kinross, granted to Magdalen Græme, commonly called Mother Nicneven, in consideration of her consenting to put herself, for the space of twenty-four hours, if required, within the iron gate of the Castle of Lochleven."

"Knave!" said the lady, turning to the chamberlain, "how dared you grant her such a protection?"

"It was by your ladyship's orders, transmitted by Randal, as he can bear witness," replied Doctor Lundin; "nay, I am only like the pharmacopolist, who compounds the drugs after the order of the mediciner."

"I remember—I remember," answered the lady; "but I meant the assurance only to be used in case, by residing in another jurisdiction, she could not have been apprehended under our warrant."

"Nevertheless," said the Queen, "the Lady of Lochleven is bound by the action of her deputy in granting the assurance."

"Madam," replied the lady, "the house of Douglas have never broken their safe-conduct, and never will: too deeply did they suffer by such a breach of trust, exercised on themselves, when your Grace's ancestor, the second James, in defiance of the rights of hospitality, and of his own written assurance of safety, poniarded the brave Earl of Douglas with his own hand, and within two yards of the social board at which he had just before sat the King of Scotland's honored guest."

"Methinks," said the Queen, carelessly, "in consideration of so very recent and enormous a tragedy, which I think only chanced some six-score years agone, the Douglasses should have shown themselves less tenacious of the company of their sovereigns than you, Lady of Lochleven, seem to be of mine."

"Let Randal," said the lady, "take the hag back to Kinross, and set her at full liberty, discharging her from our bounds in future, on peril of her head. And let your wisdom (to the chamberlain) keep her company. And fear not for your character, though I send you in such company; for, granting her to be a witch, it would be a waste of fagots to burn you for a wizard."

The crestfallen chamberlain was preparing to depart; but Magdalen Græme, collecting herself, was about to reply, when the Queen interposed, saying, "Good mother, we heartily thank you for your unfeigned zeal towards our person, and pray you, as our liege woman, that you abstain from whatever may lead you into personal danger; and, further, it is our will that you depart without a word of farther parley with any one in this castle. For thy present guerdon, take this small reliquary; it was given to us by our uncle the Cardinal, and hath had the benediction of the Holy Father himself; and now depart in peace and in silence. For you, learned sir," continued the Queen, advancing to the doctor, who made his reverence in a manner doubly embarrassed, by the awe of the Queen's presence, which made him fear to do too little, and by the apprehension of his lady's displeasure, in case he should chance to do too much—"for you, learned sir, as it was not your fault though surely our own good fortune, that we did not need your skill at this time, it would not become us, however circumstanced, to suffer our leech to leave us without such guerdon as we can offer."

With these words, and with the grace which never forsook her, though, in the present case, there might lurk under it a little gentle ridicule, she offered a small embroidered purse to the chamberlain, who, with extended hand and arched back, his learned face stooping until a physiognomist might have practised the metoposcopical science upon it, as seen from behind betwixt his gambadoes, was about to accept of the professional recompense offered by so fair as well as illustrious an hand. But the lady interposed, and, regarding the chamberlain, said aloud, "No servant of our house, without instantly relinquishing that character, and incurring withal our highest displeasure, shall dare receive any gratuity at the hand of the Lady Mary."

Sadly and slowly the chamberlain raised his depressed stature into the perpendicular attitude, and left the apartment dejectedly, followed by Magdalen Græme, after, with mute but expressive gesture, she had kissed the reliquary with which the Queen had presented her, and raising her clasped hands and uplifted eyes towards Heaven, had seemed to entreat a benediction upon the royal dame. As she left the castle, and went towards the quay where the boat lay, Roland Græme, anxious to communicate with her if possible, threw himself in her way, and might have succeeded in exchanging a few words with her, as she was guarded only by the dejected chamberlain and his halberdiers, but she seemed to have taken, in its most strict and literal acceptation, the command to be silent which she had received from the Queen; for, to the repeated signs of her grandson, she only replied by laying her finger on her lip.

Dr. Lundin was not so reserved. Regret for the handsome gratuity, and for the compulsory task of self-denial imposed on him, had grieved the spirit of that worthy officer and learned mediciner. "Even thus, my friend," said he, squeezing the page's hand as he bade him farewell, "is merit rewarded. I came to cure this unhappy lady; and I profess she well deserves the trouble, for, say what they will of her, she hath a most winning manner, a sweet voice, a gracious smile, and a most majestic wave of her hand. If she was not poisoned, say, my dear Master Roland, was that fault of mine, I being ready to cure her if she had? and now I am denied the permission to accept my well-earned honorarium. O Galen! O Hippocrates! is the graduate's cap and doctor's scarlet brought to this pass? *Frustra fatigamus remediis ægros!*"

He wiped his eyes, stepped on the gunwale, and the boat pushed off from the shore, and went merrily across the lake, which was dimpled by the summer wind.*

* See Supposed Conspiracy against the Life of Mary. Note 22.

CHAPTER XXXIII.

Death distant? No, alas! he's ever with us,
And shakes the dart at us in all our actings;
He lurks within our cup, while we're in health;
Sits by our sick-bed, mocks our medicines;
We cannot walk, or sit, or ride, or travel,
But Death is by to seize us when he lists.

The Spanish Father.

FROM the agitating scene in the Queen's presence-chamber, the Lady of Lochleven retreated to her own apartment, and ordered the steward to be called before her.

"Have they not disarmed thee, Dryfesdale?" she said, on seeing him enter, accoutered, as usual, with sword and dagger.

"No!" replied the old man; "how should they? Your ladyship, when you commanded me to ward, said nought of laying down my arms; "and, I think, none of your menials, without your order or your son's, dare approach Jasper Dryfesdale for such a purpose. Shall I now give up my sword to you? It is worth little now, for it has fought for your house till it is worn down to old iron, like the pantler's old chipping knife."

"You have attempted a deadly crime—poison under trust."

"Under trust—hem! I know not what your ladyship thinks of it, but the world without thinks the trust was given you even for that very end; and you would have been well off had it been so ended as I proposed, and you neither the worse nor the wiser."

"Wretch!" exclaimed the lady, "and fool as well as villain, who could not even execute the crime he had planned!"

"I bid as fair for it as man could," replied Dryfesdale. "I went to a woman—a witch and a Papist. If I found not poison, it was because it was otherwise predestined. I tried fair for it; but the half-done job may be clouted, if you will."

"Villain! I am even now about to send off an express messenger to my son, to take order how thou shouldst be disposed of. Prepare thyself for death, if thou canst."

"He that looks on death, lady," answered Dryfesdale, "as that which he may not shun, and which has its own fixed and certain hour, is ever prepared for it. He that is hanged in May will eat no flaunes in midsummer—so there is the moan made for the old serving-man. But whom, pray I, send you on so fair an errand?"

"There will be no lack of messengers," answered his mistress.

"By my hand, but there will," replied the old man: "your castle is but poorly manned, considering the watches that you must keep, having this charge. There is the warder and two others whom you discarded for tampering with Master George; then for the warder's tower, the bailie, the donjon—five men mount each guard, and the rest must sleep for the most part in their clothes. To send away another man were to harass the sentinels to death—unthrifty misuse for a household. To take in new soldiers were dangerous, the charge requiring tried men. I see but one thing for it: I will do your errand to Sir William Douglas myself."

"That were indeed a resource! And on what day within twenty years would it be done?" said the lady.

"Even with the speed of man and horse," said Dryfesdale; "for though I care not much about the latter days of an old serving-man's life, yet I would like to know as soon as may be whether my neck is mine own or the hangman's."

"Holdest thou thy own life so lightly?" said the lady.

"Else I had recked more of that of others," said the predestinarian. "What is death? it is but ceasing to live. And what is living? a weary return of light and darkness, sleeping and waking, being hungered and eating. Your dead man needs neither candle nor can, neither fire nor feather-bed; and the joiner's chest serves him for an eternal frieze jerkin."

"Wretched man! believest thou not that after death comes the judgment?"

"Lady," answered Dryfesdale, "as my mistress, I may not dispute your words; but, as spiritually speaking, you are still but a burner of bricks in Egypt, ignorant of the freedom of the saints; for, as was well shown to me by that gifted man, Nicolaus Schöfferbach, who was martyred by the bloody Bishop of Münster, he cannot sin who doth but execute that which is predestined, since——"

"Silence!" said the lady, interrupting him. "Answer me not with thy bold and presumptuous blasphemy, but hear me. Thou hast been long the servant of our house——"

"The born servant of the Douglas; they have had the best of me: I served them since I left Lockerbie. I was then ten years old, and you may soon add the threescore of it."

"Thy foul attempt has miscarried, so thou art guilty only in intention. It were a deserved deed to hang thee on the warder's tower; and yet, in thy present mind, it were but giving a soul to Satan. I take thine offer, then. Go hence; here is my packet; I will add to it but a line, to desire him to send me a faithful servant or two to complete the garrison. Let my son deal with you as he will. If thou art wise, thou wilt make for Lockerbie so soon as thy foot touches dry land, and let the packet find another bearer; at all rates, look it miscarries not."

"Nay, madam," replied he, "I was born, as I said, the Douglas's servant, and I will be no corbie-messenger in mine old age; your message to your son shall be done as truly by me as if it concerned another man's neck. I take my leave of your honor."

The lady issued her commands, and the old man was ferried over to the shore, to proceed on his extraordinary pilgrimage. It is necessary the reader should accompany him on his journey, which Providence had determined should not be of long duration.

On arriving at the village, the steward, although his disgrace had transpired, was readily accommodated with a horse, by the chamberlain's authority; and the roads being by no means esteemed safe, he associated himself with Auchtermuchty, the common carrier, in order to travel in his company to Edinburgh.

The worthy wagoner, according to the established custom of all carriers, stage-coachmen, and other persons in such public authority, from the earliest days to the present, never wanted good reasons for stopping upon the road as often as he would; and the place which had most captivation for him as a resting-place was a change-house, as it was termed, not very distant from a romantic dell, well known by the name of Keiry Craigs. Attractions of a kind very different from those which arrested the progress of John Auchtermuchty and his wains still continue to hover round this romantic spot, and none has visited its vicinity without a desire to remain long and to return soon.

Arrived near its favorite "howff," not all the authority of Dryfesdale, much diminished indeed by the rumors of his disgrace, could prevail on the carrier, obstinate as the brutes which he drove, to pass on without his accustomed halt, for which the distance he had traveled furnished little or no pretense. Old Keltie, the landlord, who had bestowed his name on a bridge in the neighborhood of his quondam dwelling, received the carrier with his usual festive cordiality, and adjourned with him into the house, under pretense of important business, which, I believe, consisted in their emptying together a muchkin stoup of usquebaugh. While the worthy host and his guest were thus employed, the discarded steward, with a double portion of moroseness in his gesture and look, walked discontentedly into the kitchen of the place, which was occupied but by one guest. The stranger was a slight figure, scarce above the age of boyhood, and in the dress of a page, but bearing an air of haughty aristocratic boldness, and even insolence, in his look and manner that might have made Dryfesdale conclude he had pretensions to superior rank, had not his experience taught him how frequently these airs of superiority were assumed by the domestics and military retainers of the Scottish nobility. "The pilgrim's morning to you, old sir," said the youth; "you come, as I think, from Lochleven Castle. What news of our bonny Queen? A fairer dove was never pent up in so wretched a dovecot!"

"They that speak of Lochleven, and of those whom its walls contain," answered Dryfesdale, "speak of what concerns the Douglas; and they who speak of what concerns the Douglas do it at their peril."

"Do you speak from fear of them, old man, or would you make a quarrel for them? I should have deemed your age might have cooled your blood."

"Never, while there are empty-pated coxcombs at each corner to keep it warm."

"The sight of thy gray hairs keeps mine cold," said the boy, who had risen up and now sat down again.

"It is well for thee, or I had cooled it with this holly rod," replied the steward. "I think thou be'st one of those swashbucklers, who brawl in ale-houses and taverns; and who, if words were pikes, and oaths were Andrew Ferraras, would soon place the religion of Babylon in the land once more, and the woman of Moab upon the throne."

"Now, by St. Bennet of Seyton," said the youth, "I will strike thee on the face, thou foul-mouthed old railing heretic!"

"St. Bennet of Seyton!" echoed the steward; "a proper warrant is St. Bennet's, and for a proper nest of wolf-birds like the Seytons! I will arrest thee as a traitor to King James and the good Regent. Ho! John Auchtermuchty, raise aid against the king's traitor!"

So saying, he laid his hand on the youth's collar, and drew his sword. John Auchtermuchty looked in, but, seeing the naked weapon, ran faster out than he entered. Keltie, the landlord, stood by and helped neither party, only exclaiming, "Gentlemen!—gentlemen! for the love of Heaven!" and so forth. A struggle ensued, in which the young man, chafed at Dryfesdale's boldness, and unable, with the ease he expected, to extricate himself from the old man's determined grasp, drew his dagger, and, with the speed of light, dealt him three wounds in the breast and body, the least of which was mortal. The old man sunk on the ground with a deep groan, and the host set up a piteous exclamation of surprise.

"Peace! ye bawling hound!" said the wounded steward; "are dagger-stabs and dying men such rarities in Scotland that you should cry as if the house were falling? Youth, I do not forgive thee, for there is nought betwixt us to forgive. Thou hast done what I have done to more than one; and I suffer what I have seen them suffer: it was all ordained to be thus and not otherwise. But if thou wouldst do me right, thou wilt send this packet safely to the hands of Sir William of Douglas; and see that my memory suffer not, as if I would have loitered on mine errand for fear of my life."

The youth, whose passion had subsided the instant he had done the deed, listened with sympathy and attention, when another person, muffled in his cloak, entered the apartment, and exclaimed—"Good God! Dryfesdale, and expiring!"

"Ay, and Dryfesdale would that he had been dead," answered the wounded man, "rather than that his ears had heard the words of the only Douglas that ever was false; but yet it is better as it is. Good my murderer, and the rest of you, stand back a little and let me speak with this unhappy apostate. Kneel down by me, Master George. You have heard that I failed in my attempt to take away that Moabitish stumbling-block and her retinue? I gave them that which I thought would have removed the temptation out of thy path; and this, though I had other reasons to show to thy mother and others, I did chiefly purpose for love of thee."

"For the love of me, base poisoner!" answered Douglas,

"wouldst thou have committed so horrible, so unprovoked a murder, and mentioned my name with it?"

"And wherefore not, George of Douglas?" answered Dryfesdale. "Breath is now scarce with me, but I would spend my last gasp on this argument. Hast thou not, despite the honor thou owest to thy parents, the faith that is due to thy religion, the truth that is due to thy king, been so carried away by the charms of this beautiful sorceress, that thou wouldst have helped her to escape from her prison-house, and lent her thine arm again to ascend the throne, which she had made a place of abomination? Nay, stir not from me—my hand, though fast stiffening, has yet force enough to hold thee. What dost thou aim at—to wed this witch of Scotland? I warrant thee, thou mayst succeed: her heart and hand have been oft won at a cheaper rate than thou, fool that thou art, would think thyself happy to pay. But, should a servant of thy father's house have seen thee embrace the fate of the idiot Darnley, or of the villain Bothwell—the fate of the murdered fool, or of the living pirate —while an ounce of ratsbane would have saved thee?"

"Think on God, Dryfesdale," said George Douglas, "and leave the utterance of those horrors. Repent if thou canst; if not, at least be silent. Seyton, aid me to support this dying wretch, that he may compose himself to better thoughts, if it be possible."

"Seyton!" answered the dying man—"Seyton! Is it by a Seyton's hand that I fall at last? There is something of retribution in that, since the house had nigh lost a sister by my deed.' Fixing his fading eyes on the youth, he added, "He hath her very features and presence! Stoop down, youth, and let me see thee closer: I would know thee when we meet in yonder world, for homicides will herd together there, and I have been one." He pulled Seyton's face, in spite of some resistance, closer to his own, looked at him fixedly, and added, "Thou hast begun young; thy career will be the briefer—ay, thou wilt be met with, and that anon: a young plant never throve that was watered with an old man's blood. Yet why blame I thee? Strange turns of fate," he muttered, ceasing to address Seyton, "I designed what I could not do, and he has done what he did not perchance design. Wondrous, that our will should ever oppose itself to the strong and uncontrollable tide of destiny—that we should strive with the stream when we might drift with the current! My brain will serve me to question it no farther. I would Schöfferbach were here. Yet why?

I am on a course which the vessel can hold without a pilot. Farewell, George of Douglas; I die true to thy father's house." He fell into convulsions at these words and shortly after expired.

Seyton and Douglas stood looking on the dying man, and when the scene was closed, the former was the first to speak. "As I live, Douglas, I meant not this, and am sorry; but he laid hands on me, and compelled me to defend my freedom, as I best might, with my dagger. If he were ten times thy friend and follower, I can but say that I am sorry."

"I blame thee not, Seyton," said Douglas, "though I lament the chance. There is an overruling destiny above us, though not in the sense in which it was viewed by that wretched man, who beguiled by some foreign mystagogues, used the awful word as the ready apology for whatever he chose to do. We must examine the packet."

They withdrew into an inner room, and remained deep in consultation, until they were disturbed by the entrance of Keltie, who, with an embarrassed countenance, asked Master George Douglas's pleasure respecting the disposal of the body. "Your honor knows," he added, "that I make my bread by living men, not by dead corpses; and old Mr. Dryfesdale, who was but a sorry customer while he was alive, occupies my public room now that he is deceased, and can neither call for ale nor brandy."

"Tie a stone round his neck," said Seyton, "and when the sun is down, have him to the Loch of Ore, heave him in, and let him alone for finding out the bottom."

"Under your favor, sir," said George Douglas, "it shall not be so. Keltie, thou art a true fellow to me, and thy having been so shall advantage thee. Send or take the body to the chapel at Scotland Well, or to the church of Ballingry, and tell what tale thou wilt of his having fallen in a brawl with some unruly guests to thine. Auchtermuchty knows not else, nor are the times so peaceful as to admit close looking into such accounts."

"Nay, let him tell the truth," said Seyton, "so as it harms out our scheme. Say that Henry Seyton met with him, my good fellow. I care not a brass boddle for the feud."

"A feud with the Douglas was ever to be feared, however," said George, displeasure mingling with his natural deep gravity of manner.

"Not when the best of the name is on my side," replied Seyton.

"Alas! Henry, if thou meanest me, I am but half a

Douglas in this emprize—half head, half heart, and half hand. But I will think on one who can never be forgotten, and be all or more than any of my ancestors was ever. Keltie, say it was Henry Seyton did the deed ; but beware, not a word of me ! Let Auchtermuchty carry this packet (which he had resealed with his own signet) to my father at Edinburgh ; and here is to pay for the funeral expenses and thy loss of custom."

"And the washing of the floor," said the landlord, "which will be an extraordinary job ; for blood, they say, will scarcely ever cleanse out."

"But as for your plan," said George of Douglas, addressing Seyton, as if in continuation of what they had been before treating of, "it has a good face ; but, under your favor, you are yourself too hot and too young, besides other reasons which are most against your playing the part you propose."

"We will consult the father abbot upon it," said the youth. "Do you ride to Kinross to-night ?"

"Ay, so I purpose," answered Douglas ; "the night will be dark, and suits a muffled man.* Keltie, I forgot, there should be a stone laid on that man's grave, according his name, and his only merit, which was being a faithful servant te the Douglas."

"What religion was the man of ?" said Seyton ; "he used words which made me fear I have sent Satan a subject before his time."

"I can tell you little of that," said George Douglas ; "he was noted for disliking both Rome and Geneva, and spoke of lights he had learned among the fierce sectaries of Lower Germany ; an evil doctrine it was, if we judge by the fruits. God keep us from presumptuously judging of Heaven's secrets !"

"Amen !" said the young Seyton, "and from meeting any encounter this evening."

"It is not thy wont to pray so," said George Douglas.

"No ! I leave that to you," replied the youth, "when you are seized with scruples of engaging with your father's vassals. But I would fain have this old man's blood off these hands of mine ere I shed more. I will confess to the abbot to-night, and I trust to have light penance for ridding the earth of such a miscreant. All I sorrow for is, that he was not a score of years younger. He drew steel first, however, that is one comfort."

* See Note 23.

CHAPTER XXXIV

> **Ay, Pedro.** Come you here with mask and lantern,
> Ladder of ropes and other moonshine tools?
> Why, youngster, thou mayst cheat the old duenna,
> Flatter the waiting-woman, bribe the valet;
> But know, that I her father play the gryphon,
> Tameless and sleepless, proof to fraud or bribe,
> And guard the hidden treasure of her beauty.
>
> *The Spanish Father.*

THE tenor of our tale carries us back to the Castle of Lochleven, where we take up the order of events on the same remarkable day on which Dryfesdale had been dismissed from the castle. It was past noon, the usual hour of dinner, yet no preparations seemed made for the Queen's entertainment. Mary herself had retired into her own apartment, where she was closely engaged in writing. Her attendants were together in the presence-chamber, and much disposed to speculate on the delay of the dinner; for it may be recollected that their breakfast had been interrupted. "I believe in my conscience," said the page, "that, having found the poisoning scheme miscarry, by having gone to the wrong merchant for their deadly wares, they are now about to try how famine will work upon us."

Lady Fleming was somewhat alarmed at this surmise, but comforted herself by observing, that the chimney of the kitchen had reeked that whole day in a manner which contradicted the supposition. Catherine Seyton presently exclaimed, "They were bearing the dishes across the court, marshaled by the Lady Lochleven herself, dressed out in her highest and stiffest rug, with her partlet and sleeves of cyprus, and her huge old-fashioned farthingale of crimson velvet."

"I believe, on my word," said the page, approaching the window also, "it was in that very farthingale that she captivated the heart of gentle King Jamie, which procured our poor Queen her precious bargain of a brother."

"That may hardly be, Master Roland," answered the Lady Fleming, who was a great recorder of the changes of fashion, "since the farthingales came first in when the Queen Regent went to St. Andrews, after the battle of Pinkie, and were then called *vertu-gardins*——"

She would have proceeded farther in this important discussion, but was interrupted by the entrance of the Lady of Lochleven, who preceded the servants bearing the dishes, and formally discharged the duty of tasting each of them. Lady Fleming regretted, in courtly phrase, that the Lady of Lochleven should have undertaken so troublesome an office.

"After the strange incident of this day, madam," said the lady, "it is necessary for my honor and that of my son that I partake whatever is offered to my involuntary guest. Please to inform the Lady Mary that I attend her commands."

"Her Majesty," replied Lady Fleming, with due emphasis on the word, "shall be informed that the Lady Lochleven waits."

Mary appeared instantly, and addressed her hostess with courtesy, which even approached to something more cordial. "This is nobly done, Lady Lochleven," she said; "for, though we ourselves apprehend no danger under your roof, our ladies have been much alarmed by this morning's chance, and our meal will be the more cheerful for your presence and assurance. Please you to sit down."

The Lady Lochleven obeyed the Queen's commands, and Roland performed the office of carver and attendant as usual. But, notwithstanding what the Queen had said, the meal was silent and unsocial; and every effort which Mary made to excite some conversation died away under the solemn and chill replies of the Lady of Lochleven. At length it became plain that the Queen, who had considered these advances as a condescension on her part, and who piqued herself justly on her powers of pleasing, became offended at the repulsive conduct of her hostess. After looking with a significant glance at Lady Fleming and Catherine, she slightly shrugged her shoulders and remained silent. A pause ensued, at the end of which the Lady Douglas spoke—"I perceive, madam, I am a check on the mirth of this fair company. I pray you to excuse me; I am a widow—alone here in a most perilous charge, deserted by my grandson, betrayed by my servant; I am little worthy of the grace you do me in offering me a seat at your table, where I am aware that wit and pastime are usually expected from the guests."

"If the Lady Lochleven is serious," said the Queen, "we wonder by what simplicity she expects our present meals to be seasoned with mirth. If she is a widow, she lives honored and uncontrolled at the head of her late husband's household. But I know at least of one widowed woman in the world before whom the words 'desertion' and 'betrayal' ought never to be mentioned, since no one has been made so bitterly acquainted with their import."

"I meant not, madam, to remind you of your misfortunes by the mention of mine," answered the Lady Lochleven, and there was again a deep silence.

Mary at length addressed Lady Fleming. "We can commit no deadly sins here, *ma bonne,* where we are so well warded and looked to; but if we could, this Carthusian silence might be useful as a kind of penance. If thou hast adjusted my wimple amiss, my Fleming, or if Catherine hath made a wry stitch in her broidery when she was thinking of something else than her work, or if Roland Græme hath missed a wild duck on the wing, and broke a quarrell-pane of glass in the turret window, as chanced to him a week since, now is the time to think on your sins and to repent of them."

"Madam, I speak with all reverence," said the Lady Lochleven; "but I am old, and claim the privilege of age. Methinks your followers might find fitter subjects for repentance than the trifles you mention, and so mention—once more, I crave your pardon—as if you jested with sin and repentance both."

"You have been our taster, Lady Lochleven," said the Queen, "I perceive you would eke out your duty with that of our father confessor; and since you choose that our conversation should be serious, may I ask you why the Regent's promise—since your son so styles himself—has not been kept to me in that respect? From time to time this promise has been renewed, and as constantly broken. Methinks those who pretend themselves to so much gravity and sanctity should not debar from others the religious succors which their consciences require."

"Madam, the Earl of Murray was indeed weak enough," said the Lady Lochleven, "to give so far way to your unhappy prejudices, and a religioner of the Pope presented himself on his part at our town of Kinross. But the Douglas is lord of his own castle, and will not permit his threshold to be darkened, no, not for a single moment, by an emissary belonging to the Bishop of Rome."

"Methinks it were well, then," said Mary, "that my Lord Regent would send me where there is less scruple and more charity."

"In this, madam," answered the Lady Lochleven, "you mistake the nature both of charity and of religion. Charity giveth to those who are in delirium the medicaments which may avail their health, but refuses those enticing cates and liquors which please the palate but augment the disease."

"This your charity, Lady Lochleven, is pure cruelty under the hypocritical disguise of friendly care. I am oppressed amongst you as if you meant the destruction both of my body and soul; but Heaven will not endure such iniquity forever, and they who are the most active agents in it may speedily expect their reward."

At this moment Randal entered the apartment, with a look so much perturbed that the Lady Fleming uttered a faint scream, the Queen was obviously startled, and the Lady of Lochleven, though too bold and proud to evince any marked signs of alarm, asked hastily what was the matter.

"Dryfesdale has beeu slain, madam," was the reply—"murdered as soon as he gained the dry land by young Master Henry Seyton,"

It was now Catherine's turn to start and grow pale. "Has the murderer of the Douglas's vassal escaped?" was the lady's hasty question.

"There was none to challenge him but old Keltie and the carrier Auchtermuchty," replied Randal, "unlikely men to stay one of the frackest youths in Scotland of his years, and who was sure to have friends and partakers at no great distance."

"Was the deed completed?" said the lady.

"Done, and done thoroughly," said Randal: "a Seyton seldom strikes twice. But the body was not despoiled, and your honor's packet goes forward to Edinburgh by Auchtermuchty, who leaves Keltie Bridge early to-morrow; marry, he has drunk two bottles of aquavitæ to put the fright out of his head, and now sleeps them off beside his cart-avers."

There was a pause when this fatal tale was told. The Queen and Lady Douglas looked on each other, as if each thought how she could best turn the incident to her own advantage in the coutroversy which was continually kept alive betwixt them. Catherine Seyton kept her kerchief at her eyes and wept.

"You see, madam, the bloody maxims and practise of the deluded Papists," said Lady Lochleven.

"Nay, madam," replied the Queen, "say rather you see the deserved judgment of Heaven upon a Calvinistical poisoner."

"Dryfesdale was not of the Church of Geneva or of Scotland," said the Lady Lochleven, hastily.

"He was a heretic, however," replied Mary. "There is but one true and unerring guide: the others lead alike into error."

"Well, madam, I trust it will reconcile you to your retreat that this deed shows the temper of those who might wish you at liberty. Bloodthirsty tyrants and cruel manquellers are they all, from the Clan Ranald and Clan Tosach in the north to the Ferniehurst and Buccleuch in the south, the murdering Seytons in the east, and——"

"Methinks, madam, you forget that I am a Seyton?" said Catherine, withdrawing her kerchief from her face, which was now colored with indignation.

"If I had forgot it, fair mistress, your forward bearing would have reminded me," said Lady Lochleven.

"If my brother has slain the villain that would have poisoned his sovereign and his sister," said Catherine, "I am only so far sorry that he should have spared the hangman his proper task. For aught further, had it been the best Douglas in the land, he would have been honored in falling by the Seyton's sword."

"Farewell, gay mistress," said the Lady of Lochleven, rising to withdraw; "it is such maidens as you who make giddy-fashioned revelers and deadly brawlers. Boys must needs rise, forsooth, in the grace of some sprightly damsel, who thinks to dance through life as through a French galliard." She then made her reverence to the Queen, and added, "To you also, madam, fare you well till curfew time, when I will make, perchance, more bold than welcome in attending upon your supper board. Come with me, Randal, and tell me more of this cruel fact."

"'Tis an extraordinary chance," said the Queen, when she had departed; "and, villain as he was, I would this man had been spared time for repentance. We will cause something to be done for his soul, if we ever attain our liberty, and the church will permit such grace to an heretic. But, tell me, Catherine, *ma mignonne*—this brother of thine, who is so 'frack,' as the fellow called him, bears he the same wonderful likeness to thee as formerly?"

"If your Grace means in temper, you know whether I am so frack as the serving-man spoke him."

"Nay, thou art prompt enough in all reasonable conscience," replied the Queen; "but thou art my own darling notwithstanding. But I meant, is this thy twin-brother as like thee in form and features as formerly? I remember thy dear mother alleged it as a reason for destining thee to the veil that, were ye both to go at large, thou wouldst surely get the credit of some of thy brother's mad pranks."

"I believe, madam," said Catherine, "there are some unusually simple people even yet who can hardly distinguish betwixt us, especially when, for diversion's sake, my brother hath taken a female dress," and, as she spoke, she gave a quick glance at Roland Græme, to whom this conversation conveyed a ray of light welcome as ever streamed into the dungeon of a captive through the door which opened to give him freedom.

"He must be a handsome cavalier this brother of thine, if he be so like you," replied Mary. "He was in France, I think, for these late years, so that I saw him not at Holyrood."

"His looks, madam, have never been much found fault with," answered Catherine Seyton; "but I would he had less of that angry and heady spirit which evil times have encouraged amongst our young nobles. God knows, I grudge not his life in your Grace's quarrel, and love him for the willingness with which he labors for your rescue. But wherefore should he brawl with an old ruffianly serving-man, and stain at once his name with such a broil and his hands with the blood of an old and ignoble wretch?"

"Nay, be patient, Catherine; I will not have thee traduce my gallant young knight. With Henry for my knight, and Roland Græme for my trusty squire, methinks I am like a princess of romance, who may shortly set at defiance the dungeons and the weapons of all wicked sorcerers. But my head aches with the agitation of the day. Take me *La Mer des Histoires*, and resume where we left off on Wednesday. Our Lady help thy head, girl, or rather may she help thy heart! I asked thee for the *Sea of Histoires*, and thou hast brought *La Cronique d'Amour*!"

Once embarked upon the *Sea of Histoires*, the Queen continued her labors with her needle, while Lady Fleming and Catherine read to her alternately for two hours.

As to Roland Græme, it is probable that he continued in secret intent upon the *Chronicle of Love*, notwithstanding the censure which the Queen seemed to pass upon that branch of study. He now remembered a thousand circumstances of voice and manner, which, had his own prepossession been less, must surely have discriminated the brother from the sister; and he felt ashamed that, having as it were by heart every particular of Catherine's gestures, words, and manners, he should have thought her, notwithstanding her spirits and levity, capable of assuming the bold step, loud tones, and forward assurance which accorded well enough with her brother's hasty and masculine character. He endeavored repeatedly to catch a glance of Catherine's eye, that he might judge how she was disposed to look upon him since he had made the discovery, but he was unsuccessful; for Catherine, when she was not reading herself, seemed to take so much interest in the exploits of the Teutonic Knights against the heathens of Esthonia and Livonia, that he could not surprise her eye even for a second. But when, closing the book, the Queen commanded their attendance in the garden, Mary, perhaps of set purpose (for Roland's anxiety could not escape so practised an observer), afforded him a favorable opportunity of accosting his mistress. The Queen commanded them to a little distance, while she engaged Lady Fleming in a particular and private conversation; the subject whereof, we learn from another authority, to have been the comparative excellence of the high standing ruff and the falling band. Roland must have been duller and more sheepish than ever was youthful lover if he had not endeavored to avail himself of this opportunity.

"I have been longing this whole evening to ask of you, fair Catherine," said the page, "how foolish and unapprehensive you must have thought me, in being capable to mistake betwixt your brother and you?"

"The circumstance does indeed little honor to my rustic manners," said Catherine, "since those of a wild young man were so readily mistaken for mine. But I shall grow wiser in time; and with that view I am determined not to think of your follies, but to correct my own."

"It will be the lighter subject of meditation of the two," said Roland.

"I know not that," said Catherine, very gravely; "I fear we have been both unpardonably foolish."

"I have been mad," said Roland—"unpardonably mad. But you, lovely Catherine——"

"I," said Catherine, in the same tone of unusual gravity, "have too long suffered you to use such expressions towards me. I fear I can permit it no longer, and I blame myself for the pain it may give you."

"And what can have happened so suddenly to change our relation to each other, or alter, with such sudden cruelty, your whole deportment to me?"

"I can hardly tell," replied Catherine, "unless it is that the events of the day have impressed on my mind the necessity of our observing more distance to each other. A chance similar to that which betrayed to you the existence of my brother may make known to Henry the terms you have used to me; and, alas! his whole conduct, as well as his deed this day, makes me too justly apprehensive of the consequences."

"Nay, fear nothing for that, fair Catherine," answered the page, "I am well able to protect myself against risks of that nature."

"That is to say," replied she, "that you would fight with my twin-brother to show your regard for his sister? I have heard the Queen say, in her sad hours, that men are, in love or in hate, the most selfish animals of creation; and your carelessness in this matter looks very like it. But be not so much abashed; you are no worse than others."

"You do me injustice, Catherine," replied the page, "I thought but of being threatened with a sword, and did not remember in whose hand your fancy had placed it. If your brother stood before me, with his drawn weapon in his hand, so like as he is to you in word, person, and favor, he might shed my life's blood ere I could find in my heart to resist him to his injury."

"Alas!" said she, "it is not my brother alone. But you remember only the singular circumstances in which we have met in equality, and I may say in intimacy. You think not that, whenever I re-enter my father's house, there is a gulf between us you may not pass but with the peril of your life. Your only known relative is of wild and singular habits, of a hostile and broken clan, the rest of your lineage unknown; forgive me that I speak what is the undeniable truth."

"Love, my beautiful Catherine, despises genealogies," answered Roland Græme.

"Love may, but so will not the Lord Seyton," rejoined the damsel.

"The Queen, thy mistress and mine, she will intercede. O! drive me not from you at the moment I thought myself most happy! And if I shall aid her deliverance, said not yourself that you and she would become my debtors?"

"All Scotland will become your debtors," said Catherine. "But for the active effects you might hope from our gratitude, you must remember I am wholly subjected to my father; and the poor Queen is, for a long time, more likely to be dependent on the pleasure of the nobles of her party than possessed of power to control them."

"Be it so," replied Roland; "my deeds shall control prejudice itself: it is a bustling world, and I will have my share.

The Knight of Avenel, high as he now stands, rose from as obscure an origin as mine."

"Ay," said Catherine, "there spoke the doughty knight of romance, that will cut his way to the imprisoned princess through fiends and fiery dragons!"

"But if I can set the princess at large, and procure her the freedom of her own choice," said the page, "where, dearest Catherine, will that choice alight?"

"Release the princess from duresse, and she will tell you," said the damsel; and, breaking off the conversation abruptly, she joined the Queen so suddenly that Mary exclaimed, half-aloud—'

"No more tidings of evil import—no dissension, I trust, in my limited household?" Then looking on Catherine's blushing cheek and Roland's expanded brow and glancing eye—"No—no," she said, "I see all is well. *Ma petite mignonne*, go to my apartment and fetch me down—let me see—ay, fetch my pomander box."

And having thus disposed of her attendant in the manner best qualified to hide her confusion, the Queen added, speaking apart to Roland, "I should at least have two grateful subjects of Catherine and you; for what sovereign but Mary would aid true love so willingly? Ay, you lay your hand on your sword—your *petite flamberge à rien* there. Well, short time will show if all the good be true that is protested to us. I hear them toll curfew from Kinross. To our chamber; this old dame hath promised to be with us again at our evening meal. Were it not for the hope of speedy deliverance, her presence would drive me distracted. But I will be patient."

"I profess," said Catherine, who just then entered, "I would I could be Henry, with all a man's privileges, for one moment: I long to throw my plate at that confect of pride, and formality, and ill-nature!"

The Lady Fleming reprimanded her young companion for this explosion of impatience, the Queen laughed, and they went to the presence-chamber, where almost immediately entered supper and the lady of the castle The Queen, strong in her prudent resolutions, endured her presence with great fortitude and equanimity, until her patience was disturbed by a new form, which had hitherto made no part of the ceremonial of the castle. When the other attendant had retired, Randal entered, bearing the keys of the castle fastened upon a chain, and, announcing that the watch was set and the gates locked, delivered the keys with all reverence to the Lady of Lochleven.

The Queen and her ladies exchanged with each other a look of disappointment, anger, and vexation; and Mary said aloud, "We cannot regret the smallness of our court, when we see our hostess discharge in person so many of its offices. In addition to her charges of principal steward of our household and grand almoner, she has to-night done duty as captain of our guard."

"And will continue to do so in future, madam," answered the Lady Lochleven, with much gravity; "the history of Scotland may teach me how ill the duty is performed which is done by an accredited deputy. We have heard, madam, of favorites of later date, and as little merit, as Oliver Sinclair."

"O, madam," replied the Queen, "my father had his female as well as his male favorites: there were the Ladies Sandilands and Olifaunt,* and some others, methinks; but their names cannot survive in the memory of so grave a person as you."

The Lady Lochleven looked as if she could have slain the Queen on the spot, but commanded her temper, and retired from the apartment, bearing in her hand the ponderous bunch of keys.

"Now God be praised for that woman's youthful frailty!" said the Queen. "Had she not that weak point in her character, I might waste my words on her in vain. But that stain is the very reverse of what is said of the witch's mark: I can make her feel there, though she is otherwise insensible all over. But how say you, girls—here is a new difficulty. How are these keys to be come by? There is no deceiving or bribing this dragon, I trow."

"May I crave to know," said Roland, "whether, if your Grace were beyond the walls of the castle, you could find means of conveyance to the firm land, and protection when you are there?"

"Trust us for that, Roland," said the Queen; "for to that point our scheme is indifferent well laid."

"Then, if your Grace will permit me to speak my mind, I think I could be of some use in this matter."

"As how, my good youth? Speak on," said the Queen, "and fearlessly."

"My patron, the Knight of Avenel, used to compel the youth educated in his household to learn the use of ax and hammer, and working in wood and iron; he used to speak

* The names of these ladies, and a third frail favorite of James, are preserved in an epigram too *gaillard* for quotation.

of old northern champions who forged their own weapons, and of the Highland captain, Donald nan Ord, or Donald of the Hammer, whom he himself knew, and who used to work at the anvil with a sledge-hammer in each hand. Some said he praised this art because he was himself of churl's blood. However, I gained some practise in it, as the Lady Catherine Seyton partly knows; for since we were here I wrought her a silver brooch."

"Ay," replied Catherine, "but you should tell her Grace that your workmanship was so indifferent that it broke to pieces next day, and I flung it away."

"Believe her not, Roland," said the Queen; "she wept when it was broken, and put the fragments into her bosom. But for your scheme—could your skill avail to forge a second set of keys?"

"No, madam, because I know not the wards. But I am convinced I could make a set so like that hateful bunch which the lady bore off even now, that, could they be exchanged against them by any means, she would never dream she was possessed of the wrong."

"And the good dame, thank Heaven, is somewhat blind," said the Queen; "but then for a forge, my boy, and the means of laboring unobserved?"

"The armorer's forge, at which I used sometimes to work with him, is the round vault at the bottom of the turret; he was dismissed with the warder for being supposed too much attached to George Douglas. The people are accustomed to see me busy there, and I warrant I shall find some excuse that will pass current with them for putting bellows and anvil to work."

"The scheme has a promising face," said the Queen; "about it, my lad, with all speed, and beware the nature of your work is not discovered."

"Nay, I will take the liberty to draw the bolt against chance visitors, so that I will have time to put away what I am working upon before I undo the door."

"Will not that of itself attract suspicion, in a place where it is so current already?" said Catherine.

"Not a whit," replied Roland; "Gregory the armorer, and every good hammerman, locks himself in when he is about some masterpiece of craft. Besides, something must be risked."

"Part we then to-night," said the Queen, "and God bless you, my children! If Mary's head ever rises above water, you shall all rise along with her."

CHAPTER XXXV

> It is a time of danger, not of revel;
> When churchmen turn to masquers.
>
> *Spanish Father.*

THE enterprise of Roland Græme appeared to prosper. A trinket or two, of which the work did not surpass the substance (for the materials were silver, supplied by the Queen), were judiciously presented to those most likely to be inquisitive into the labors of the forge and anvil, which they thus were induced to reckon profitable to others and harmless in itself. Openly, the page was seen working about such trifles. In private he forged a number of keys resembling so nearly in weight and in form those which were presented every evening to the Lady Lochleven, that, on a slight inspection, it would have been difficult to perceive the difference. He brought them to the dark rusty color by the use of salt and water; and, in the triumph of his art, presented them at length to Queen Mary in her presence-chamber, about an hour before the tolling of the curfew. She looked at them with pleasure, but at the same time with doubt. "I allow," she said, "that the Lady Lochleven's eyes, which are not of the clearest, may be well deceived, could we pass those keys on her in place of the real implements of her tyranny. But how is this to be done, and which of my little court dare attempt this *tour de jongleur* with any chance of success? Could we but engage her in some earnest matter of argument! but those which I hold with her always have been of a kind which make her grasp her keys the faster, as if she said to herself—'Here I hold what sets me above your taunts and reproaches.' And even for her liberty, Mary Stuart could not stoop to speak the proud heretic fair. What shall we do? Shall Lady Fleming try her eloquence in describing the last new head-tire from Paris? Alas! the good dame has not changed the fashion of her head-gear since Pinkie field, for aught that I know. Shall my *mignonne* Catherine sing to her one of those touching airs which draw the very souls out of me and Roland Græme? Alas! Dame Margaret Douglas would rather hear a Huguenot psalm of Clément Marot, sung to the tune of *Réveillez-vous, belle endormie.* Cousins and liege counselors, what is to be done, for our wits are really astray in this matter? Must our man-at-arms and the champion of our body, Roland Græme, manfully assault the old lady, and take the keys from her *par voie du fait?*"

"Nay! with your Grace's permission," said Roland, "I do not doubt being able to manage the matter with more discretion; for though, in your Grace's service, I do not fear——"

"A host of old women," interrupted Catherine, "each armed with rock and spindle; yet he has no fancy for pikes and partizans, which might rise at the cry of 'Help! a Douglas—a Douglas!'"

"They that do not fear fair ladies' tongues," continued the page, "need dread nothing else. But, gracious liege, I am wellnigh satisfied that I could pass the exchange of these keys on the Lady Lochleven; but I dread the sentinel who is now planted nightly in the garden, which, by necessity, we must traverse."

"Our last advices from our friend on the shore have promised us assistance in that matter," replied the Queen.

"And is your Grace well assured of the fidelity and watchfulness of those without?"

"For their fidelity I will answer with my life, and for their vigilance I will answer with my life. I will give thee instant proof, my faithful Roland, that they are ingenuous and trusty as thyself. Come hither. Nay, Catherine, attend us; we carry not so deft a page into our private chamber alone. Make fast the door of the parlor, Fleming, and warn us if you hear the least step—or stay, go thou to the door, Catherine (in a whisper), thy ears and thy wits are both sharper. Good Fleming, attend us thyself. (And again she whispered) Her reverend presence will be as safe a watch on Roland as thine can, so be not jealous, *mignonne.*"

Thus speaking, they were lighted by the Lady Fleming into the Queen's bedroom, a small apartment enlightened by a projecting window.

"Look from that window, Roland," she said; "see you amongst the several lights which begin to kindle, and to glimmer palely through the gray of the evening from the village of Kinross—seest thou, I say, one solitary spark apart from the others, and nearer it seems to the verge of the water? It is no brighter at this distance than the torch of the poor glow-worm, and yet, my good youth, that light is more dear to Mary Stuart than every star that twinkles in the blue vault of heaven. By that signal, I know that more than one true heart is plotting my deliverance; and without that consciousness, and the hope of freedom it gives me, I had long since stooped to my fate and died of a broken heart. Plan after plan has been formed and abandoned; but still the light glimmers, and while it glimmers my hope lives. O! how many evenings have I sat musing in despair over our ruined schemes, and scarce hoping that I should again see that blessed signal; when it has suddenly kindled, and, like the lights of St. Elmo in a tempest, brought hope and consolation where there was only dejection and despair!"

"If I mistake not," answered Roland, "the candle shines from the house of Blinkhoolie, the mail-gardener."

"Thou hast a good eye," said the Queen; "it is there where my trusty lieges—God and the saints pour blessings on them!—hold consultation for my deliverance. The voice of a wretched captive would die on these blue waters long ere it could mingle in their council, and yet I can hold communication—I will confide the whole to thee—I am about to ask those faithful friends if the moment for the great attempt is nigh. Place the lamp in the window, Fleming."

She obeyed, and immediately withdrew it. No sooner had she done so than the light in the cottage of the gardener disappeared.

"Now, count," said Queen Mary, "for my heart beats so thick that I cannot count myself."

The Lady Fleming began deliberately to count one, two, three, and when she had arrived at ten the light on the shore again showed its pale twinkle.

"Now, Our Lady be praised!" said the Queen; "it was but two nights since that the absence of the light remained while I could tell thirty. The hour of deliverance approaches. May God bless those who labor in it with such truth to me!—alas! with such hazard to themselves—and bless you too, my children! Come, we must to the audience-chamber again. Our absence might excite suspicion, should they serve supper."

They returned to the presence-chamber, and the evening concluded as usual.

The next noon, at dinner-time, an unusual incident occurred. While Lady Douglas of Lochleven performed her daily duty of assistant and taster at the Queen's table, she was told a man-at-arms had arrived, recommended by her son, but without any letter or other token than what he brought by word of month.

"Hath he given you that token?" demanded the lady.

"He reserved it, as I think, for your ladyship's ear," replied Randal.

"He doth well," said the lady; "tell him to wait in the hall. But no—with your permission, madam (to the Queen) —let him attend me here."

"Since you are pleased to receive your domestics in my presence," said the Queen, "I cannot choose——"

"My infirmities must plead my excuse, madam," replied the lady; "the life I must lead here ill suits with the years which have passed over my head, and compels me to waive ceremonial."

"O, my good lady," replied the Queen, "I would there were nought in this your castle more strongly compulsive than the cobweb chains of ceremony; but bolts and bars are harder matters to contend with."

As she spoke, the person announced by Randal entered the room, and Roland Græme at once recognized in him the Abbot Ambrosius.

"What is your name, good fellow?" said the lady.

"Edward Glendinning," answered the abbot, with a suitable reverence.

"Art thou of the blood of the Knight of Avenel?" said the Lady of Lochleven.

"Ay, madam, and that nearly," replied the pretended soldier.

"It is likely enough," said the lady, "for the knight is the son of his own good works, and has risen from obscure lineage to his present high rank in the estate. But he is of sure truth and approved worth, and his kinsman is welcome to us. You hold, unquestionably, the true faith?"

"Do not doubt of it, madam," said the disguised churchman.

"Hast thou a token to me from Sir William Douglas?" said the lady.

"I have, madam," replied he; "but it must be said in private."

"Thou art right," said the lady, moving towards the recess of a window; "say in what does it consist?"

"In the words of an old bard," replied the abbot.

"Repeat them," answered the lady; and he uttered, in a low tone, the lines from an old poem called *The Howlet* *—

See Note 24.

"O, Douglas! Douglas!
Tender and true."

"Trusty Sir John Holland!" said the Lady Douglas, apostrophizing the poet, "a kinder heart never inspired a rhyme, and the Douglas's honor was ever on thy harp-string! We receive you among our followers, Glendinning. But, Randal, see that he keep the outer ward only, till we shall hear more touching him from our son. Thou fearest not the night air, Glendinning?"

"In the cause of the lady before whom I stand, I fear nothing, madam," answered the disguised abbot.

"Our garrison, then, is stronger by one trustworthy soldier," said the matron. "Go to the buttery, and let them make much of thee."

When the Lady Lochleven had retired, the Queen said to Roland Græme, who was now almost constantly in her company, "I spy comfort in that stranger's countenance; I know not why it should be so, but I am well persuaded he is a friend."

"Your Grace's penetration does not deceive you," answered the page; and he informed her that the abbot of St. Mary's himself played the part of the newly-arrived soldier.

The Queen crossed herself, and looked upward. "Unworthy sinner that I am," she said, "that for my sake a man so holy, and so high in spiritual office, should wear the garb of a base sworder, and run the risk of dying the death of a traitor!"

"Heaven will protect its own servant, madam," said Catherine Seyton; "his aid would bring a blessing on our undertaking, were it not already blest for its own sake."

"What I admire in my spiritual father," said Roland, "was the steady front with which he looked on me, without giving the least sign of former acquaintance. I did not think the like was possible, since I have ceased to believe that Henry was the same person with Catherine."

"But marked you not how astuciously the good father," said the Queen, "eluded the questions of the woman Lochleven, telling her the very truth, which yet she received not as such?"

Roland thought in his heart that, when the truth was spoken for the purpose of deceiving, it was little better than a lie in disguise. But it was no time to agitate such questions of conscience.

"And now for the signal from the shore!" exclaimed Catherine; "my bosom tells me we shall see this night two lights instead of one gleam from that garden of Eden. And then, Roland, do you play your part manfully, and we will dance on the greensward like midnight fairies!"

Catherine's conjecture misgave not, nor deceived her. In the evening two beams twinkled from the cottage, instead of one; and the page heard, with beating heart, that the new retainer was ordered to stand sentinel on the outside of the castle. When he intimated this news to the Queen she held her hand out to him; he knelt, and when he raised it to his lips in all dutiful homage, he found it was damp and cold as marble. "For God's sake, madam, droop not now—sink not now!"

"Call upon Our Lady, my liege," said the Lady Fleming—"call upon your tutelar saint."

"Call the spirits of the hundred kings you are descended from!" exclaimed the page; "in this hour of need, the resolution of a monarch were worth the aid of a hundred saints."

"O! Roland Græme," said Mary, in a tone of deep despondency, "be true to me; many have been false to me. Alas! I have not always been true to myself. My mind misgives me that I shall die in bondage, and that this bold attempt will cost all our lives. It was foretold me by a soothsayer in France that I should die in prison, and by a violent death, and here comes the hour. O, would to God it found me prepared!"

"Madam," said Catherine Seyton, "remember you are a queen. Better we all died in bravely attempting to gain our freedom than remained here to be poisoned, as men rid them of the noxious vermin that haunt old houses."

"You are right, Catherine," said the Queen; "and Mary will bear her like herself. But, alas! your young and buoyant spirit can ill spell the causes which have broken mine. Forgive me, my children, and farewell for a while; I will prepare both mind and body for this awful venture."

They separated, till again called together by the tolling of the curfew. The Queen appeared grave, but firm and resolved; the Lady Fleming, with the art of an experienced courtier, knew perfectly how to disguise her inward tremors; Catherine's eye was fired, as if with the boldness of the project, and the half-smile which dwelt upon her beautiful mouth seemed to contemn all the risk and all the consequences of discovery; Roland, who felt how much success depended on his own address and boldness, summoned together his whole presence of mind, and if he found his spirits flag for a moment, cast his eye upon Catherine, whom he thought he had never seen look so beautiful. "I may be foiled," he thought, "but, with this reward in prospect, they must bring the devil to aid them ere they cross me." Thus resolved, he stood like a greyhound in the slips, with hand heart, and eye intent upon making and seizing opportunity for the execution of their project.

The keys had, with the wonted ceremonial, been presented to the Lady Lochleven. She stood with her back to the casement, which, like that of the Queen's apartment, commanded a view of Kinross, with the church, which stands at some distance from the town, and nearer to the lake, then connected with the town by straggling cottages. With her back to the casement, then, and her face to the table, on which the keys lay for an instant while she tasted the various dishes which were placed there, stood the Lady of Lochleven, more provokingly intent than usual—so at least it seemed to her prisoners—upon the huge and heavy bunch of iron, the implements of their restraint. Just when, having finished her ceremony as taster of the Queen's table, she was about to take up the keys, the page, who stood beside her, and had handed her the dishes in succession, looked sidewise to the churchyard, and exclaimed he saw corpse-candles in the vault. The Lady of Lochleven was not without a touch, though a slight one, of the superstitions of the time: the fate of her sons made her alive to omens, and a corpse-light, as it was called, in the family burial-place boded death. She turned her head towards the casement—saw a distant glimmering—forgot her charge for one second, and in that second were lost the whole fruits of her former vigilance. The page held the forged keys under his cloak, and with great dexterity exchanged them for the real ones. His utmost address could not prevent a slight clash as he took up the latter bunch. "Who touches the keys?" said the lady; and while the page answered that the sleeve of his cloak had stirred them, she looked round, possessed herself of the bunch which now occupied the place of the genuine keys, and again turned to gaze at the supposed corpse-candles.

"I hold these gleams," she said, after a moment's consideration, "to come, not from the churchyard, but from the hut of the old gardener Blinkhoolie. I wonder what thrift that churl drives, that of late he hath ever had light in his house till the night grew deep. I thought him an industrious, peaceful man. If he turns resetter of idle companions and night-walkers, the place must be rid of him."

"He may work his baskets, perchance," said the page, desirous to stop the train of her suspicion.

"Or nets, may he not?" answered the lady.

"Ay, madam," said Roland, "for trout and salmon."

"Or for fools and knaves," replied the lady; "but this shall be looked after to-morrow. I wish your Grace and your company a good evening. Randal, attend us." And Randal, who waited in the ante-chamber after having surrendered his bunch of keys, gave his escort to his mistress as usual, while, leaving the Queen's apartments, she retired to her own.

"To-morrow!" said the page, rubbing his hands with glee as he repeated the lady's last words; "fools look to-morrow, and wise folk use to-night. May I pray you, my gracious liege, to retire for one half-hour, until all the castle is composed to rest? I must go and rub with oil these blessed implements of our freedom. Courage and constancy, and all will go well, provided our friends on the shore fail not to send the boat you spoke of."

"Fear them not," said Catherine, "they are true as steel—if our dear mistress do but maintain her noble and royal courage." *

"Doubt not me, Catherine," replied the Queen; "a while since I was overborne, but I have recalled the spirit of my earlier and more sprightly days, when I used to accompany my armed nobles, and wish to be myself a man, to know what life it was to be in the fields with sword and buckler, jack and knapscap!"

"O, the lark lives not a gayer life, nor sings a lighter and gayer song, than the merry soldier," answered Catherine. "Your Grace shall be in the midst of them soon, and the look of such a liege sovereign will make each of your host worth three in the hour of need. But I must to my task."

"We have but brief time," said Queen Mary: "one of the two lights in the cottage is extinguished; that shows the boat is put off."

"They will row very slow," said the page, "or kent where depth permits, to avoid noise. To our several tasks. I will communicate with the good father."

At the dead hour of midnight, when all was silent in the castle, the page put the key into the lock of the wicket which opened into the garden, and which was at the bottom of a staircase that descended from the Queen's apartment. "Now, turn smooth and softly, thou good bolt," said he,

* See Demeanor of Queen Mary. Note 25.

"if ever oil softened rust!" and his precautions had been so effectual that the bolt revolved with little or no sound of resistance. He ventured not to cross the threshold, but exchanging a word with the disguised abbot, asked if the boat were ready.

"This half-hour," said the sentinel. "She lies beneath the wall, too close under the islet to be seen by the warder; but I fear she will hardly escape his notice in putting off again."

"The darkness," said the page, "and our profound silence, may take her off unobserved, as she came in. Hildebrand has the watch on the tower—a heavy-headed knave, who holds a can of ale to be the best head-piece upon a night-watch. He sleeps for a wager."

"Then bring the Queen," said the abbot, "and I will call Henry Seyton to assist them to the boat."

On tiptoe, with noiseless step and suppressed breath, trembling at every rustle of their own apparel, one after another the fair prisoners glided down the winding stair, under the guidance of Roland Græme, and were received at the wicket-gate by Henry Seyton and the churchman. The former seemed instantly to take upon himself the whole direction of the enterprise. "My lord abbot," he said, "give my sister your arm; I will conduct the Queen, and that youth will have the honor to guide Lady Fleming."

This was no time to dispute the arrangement, although it was not that which Roland Græme would have chosen. Catherine Seyton, who well knew the garden path, tripped on before like a sylph, rather leading the abbot than receiving assistance; the Queen, her native spirit prevailing over female fear and a thousand painful reflections, moved steadily forward, by the assistance of Henry Seyton; while the Lady Fleming encumbered with her fears and her helplessness Roland Græme, who followed in the rear, and who bore under the other arm a packet of necessaries belonging to the Queen. The door of the garden, which communicated with the shore of the islet, yielded to one of the keys of which Roland had possessed himself, although not until he had tried several—a moment of anxious terror and expectation. The ladies were then partly led, partly carried, to the side of the lake, where a boat with six rowers attended them, the men couched along the bottom to secure them from observation. Henry Seyton placed the Queen in the stern; the abbot offered to assist Catherine, but she was seated by the Queen's side before he could utter his proffer of help; and

Roland Græme was just lifting Lady Fleming over the boat-side when a thought suddenly occurred to him, and exclaiming, "Forgotten—forgotten! wait for me but one half minute," he replaced on the shore the helpless lady of the bed-chamber, threw the Queen's packet into the boat, and sped back through the garden with the noiseless speed of a bird on the wing.

"By Heaven, he is false at last!" said Seyton; "I ever feared it!"

"He is as true," said Catherine, "as Heaven itself, and that I will maintain."

"Be silent, minion," said her brother, "for shame, if not for fear. Fellows, put off, and row for your lives!"

"Help me—help me on board!" said the deserted Lady Fleming, and that louder than prudence warranted,

"Put off—put off!" cried Henry Seyton; "leave all behind, so the Queen is safe."

"Will you permit this, madam?" said Catherine, imploringly; "you leave your deliverer to death."

"I will not," said the Queen. "Seyton, I command you to stay at every risk."

"Pardon me, madam, if I disobey," said the intractable young man; and with one hand lifting in Lady Fleming, he began himself to push off the boat.

She was two fathoms' length from the shore, and the rowers were getting her head round, when Roland Græme, arriving, bounded from the beach, and attained the boat, overturning Seyton, on whom he lighted. The youth swore a deep but suppressed oath, and stopping Græme as he stepped towards the stern, said, "Your place is not with high-born dames; keep at the head and trim the vessel. Now give way—give way. Row, for God and the Queen!"

The rowers obeyed, and began to pull vigorously.

"Why did you not muffle the oars?" said Roland Græme; "the dash must awaken the sentinel. Row, lads, and get out of reach of shot; for had not old Hildebrand, the warder, supped upon poppy-porridge, this whispering must have waked him."

"It was all thine own delay," said Seyton; "thou shalt reckon with me hereafter for that and other matters."

But Roland's apprehension was verified too instantly to permit him to reply. The sentinel, whose slumbering had withstood the whispering, was alarmed by the dash of the oars. His challenge was instantly heard. "A boat—a boat! bring to, or I shoot!" And, as they continued to ply their oars, he called aloud, "Treason!—treason!" rung the bell of the castle, and discharged his harquebuss at the boat. The ladies crowded on each other like startled wild-fowl, at the flash and report of the piece, while the men urged the rowers to the utmost speed. They heard more than one ball whiz along the surface of the lake, at no great distance from their little bark; and from the lights, which glanced like meteors from window to window, it was evident the whole castle was alarmed, and their escape discovered.

"Pull!" again exclaimed Seyton; "stretch to your oars, or I will spur you to the task with my dagger; they will launch a boat immediately."

"That is cared for," said Roland; "I locked gate and wicket on them when I went back, and no boat will stir from the island this night, if doors of good oak and bolts of iron can keep men within stone walls. And now I resign my office of porter of Lochleven, and give the keys to the Kelpie's keeping."

As the heavy keys plunged in the lake, the abbot, who till then had been repeating his prayers, exclaimed, "Now, bless thee, my son! for thy ready prudence puts shame on us all." *

"I knew," said Mary, drawing her breath more freely, as they were now out of reach of the musketry—"I knew my squire's truth, promptitude, and sagacity. I must have him dear friends with my no less true knights, Douglas and Seyton; but where, then, is Douglas?"

"Here, madam," answered the deep and melancholy voice of the boatman who sat next her, and who acted as steersman.

"Alas! was it you who stretched your body before me," said the Queen, "when the balls were raining around us?"

"Believe you," said he, in a low tone, "that Douglas would have resigned to any one the chance of protecting his Queen's life with his own?"

The dialogue was here interrupted by a shot or two from one of those small pieces of artillery called falconets, then used in defending castles. The shot was too vague to have any effect, but the broader flash, the deeper sound, the louder return which was made by the midnight echoes of Bennarty terrified and imposed silence on the liberated prisoners. The boat was alongside of a rude quay or landing-place, running out from a garden of considerable extent, ere any of them again attempted to speak. They landed, and while the

* See Escape of Queen Mary from Lochleven. Note 26.

abbot returned thanks aloud to Heaven, which had thus far favored their enterprise, Douglas enjoyed the best reward of his desperate undertaking, in conducting the Queen to the house of the gardener. Yet, not unmindful of Roland Græme, even in that moment of terror and exhaustion, Mary expressly commanded Seyton to give his assistance to Fleming, while Catherine voluntarily, and without bidding, took the arm of the page. Seyton presently resigned Lady Fleming to the care of the abbot, alleging he must look after their horses; and his attendants, disencumbering themselves of their boat-cloaks, hastened to assist him.

While Mary spent in the gardener's cottage the few minutes which were necessary to prepare the steeds for their departure, she perceived in a corner the old man to whom the garden belonged, and called him to approach. He came as it were with reluctance.

"How, brother," said the abbot, "so slow to welcome thy royal Queen and mistress to liberty and to her kingdom!"

The old man, thus admonished, came forward, and, in good terms of speech, gave her Grace joy of her deliverance.

The Queen returned him thanks in the most gracious manner, and added, "It will remain to us to offer some immediate reward for your fidelity, for we wot well your house has been long the refuge in which our trusty servants have met to concert measures for our freedom." So saying, she offered gold, and added, "We will consider your services more fully hereafter."

"Kneel, brother," said the abbot—"kneel instantly, and thank her Grace's kindness."

"Good brother, that wert once a few steps under me, and art still very many years younger," replied the gardener, pettishly, "let me do mine acknowledgments in my own way. Queens have knelt to me ere now, and in truth my knees are too old and stiff to bend even to this lovely-faced lady. May it please your Grace, if your Grace's servants have occupied my house, so that I could not call it mine own; if they have trodden down my flowers in the zeal of their midnight comings and goings, and destroyed the hope of the fruit season by bringing their war-horses into my garden, I do but crave of your Grace in requital that you will choose your residence as far from me as possible. I am an old man, who would willingly creep to my grave as easily as I can, in peace, goodwill, and quiet labor."

"I promise you fairly, good man," said the Queen, "I will not make yonder castle my residence again, if I can help it.

But let me press on you this money; it will make some amends for the havoc we have made in your little garden and orchard."

"I thank your Grace, but it will make me not the least amends," said the old man. "The ruined labors of a whole year are not so easily replaced to him who has perchance but that one year to live; and, besides, they tell me I must leave this place, and become a wanderer in mine old age—I that have nothing on earth saving these fruit-trees, and a few old parchments and family secrets not worth knowing. As for gold, if I had loved it, I might have remained lord abbot of St. Mary's; and yet I wot not, for if Abbot Boniface be but the poor peasant Blinkhoolie, his successor, the Abbot Ambrosius, is still transmitted for the worse into the guise of a sword-and-buckler-man."

"Ha! Is this indeed the Abbot Boniface of whom I have heard?" said the Queen. "It is indeed I who should have bent the knee for your blessing, good father!"

"Bend no knee to me, lady! The blessing of an old man, who is no longer an abbot, go with you over dale and down. I hear the trampling of your horses."

"Farewell, father," said the Queen. "When we are once more seated at Holyrood, we will neither forget thee nor thine injured garden."

"Forget us both," said the Ex-Abbot Boniface, "and may God be with you!"

As they hurried out of the house, they heard the old man talking and muttering to himself, as he hastily drew bolt and bar behind them.

"The revenge of the Douglasses will reach the poor old man," said the Queen. "God help me, I ruin every one whom I approach!"

"His safety is cared for," said Seyton; "he must not remain here, but will be privately conducted to a place of greater security. But I would your Grace were in the saddle. To horse!—to horse!"

The party of Seyton and of Douglas were increased to about ten by those attendants who had remained with the horses. The Queen and her ladies, with all the rest who came from the boat, were instantly mounted; and holding aloof from the village, which was already alarmed by the firing from the castle, with Douglas acting as their guide, they soon reached the open ground, and began to ride as fast as was consistent with keeping together in good order.

CHAPTER XXXVI

He mounted himself on a coal-black steed,
  And her on a freckled gray,
With a bugelet horn hung down from his side,
  And roundly they rode away.

Old Ballad.

THE influence of the free air, the rushing of the horses over high and low, the ringing of the bridles, the excitation at once arising from a sense of freedom and of rapid motion, gradually dispelled the confused and dejected sort of stupefaction by which Queen Mary was at first overwhelmed. She could not at last conceal the change of her feelings to the person who rode at her rein, and who she doubted not was the Father Ambrosius; for Seyton, with all the heady impetuosity of a youth, proud, and justly so, of his first successful adventure, assumed all the bustle and importance of commander of the little party, which escorted, in the language of the time, the Fortune of Scotland. He now led the van, now checked his bounding steed till the rear had come up, exhorted the leaders to keep a steady, though rapid, pace, and commanded those who were hindmost of the party to use their spurs, and allow no interval to take place in their line of march; and anon he was beside the Queen or her ladies, inquiring how they brooked the hasty journey, and whether they had any commands for him. But while Seyton thus busied himself in the general cause with some advantage to the regular order of the march, and a good deal of personal ostentation, the horseman who rode beside the Queen gave her his full and undivided attention, as if he had been waiting upon some superior being. When the road was rugged and dangerous, he abandoned almost entirely the care of his own horse, and kept his hand constantly upon the Queen's bridle; if a river or larger brook traversed their course, his left arm retained her in the saddle, while his right held her palfrey's rein.

"I had not thought, reverend father," said the Queen, when they reached the other bank, "that the convent bred such good horsemen." The person she addressed sighed, but made no other answer. "I know not how it is," said Queen

Mary, "but either the sense of freedom, or the pleasure of my favorite exercise, from which I have been so long debarred, or both combined, seem to have given wings to me: no fish ever shot through the water, no bird through the air, with the hurried feeling of liberty and rapture with which I sweep through this night-wind, and over these wolds. Nay, such is the magic of feeling myself once more in the saddle, that I could almost swear I am at this moment mounted on my own favorite Rosabelle, who was never matched in Scotlond for swiftness, for ease of motion, and for sureness of foot."

"And if the horse which bears so dear a burden could speak," answered the deep voice of the melancholy George of Douglas, "would she not reply, who but Rosabelle ought at such an emergence as this to serve her beloved mistress, or who but Douglas ought to hold her bridle-rein?"

Queen Mary started; she foresaw at once all the evils like to arise to herself and him from the deep enthusiastic passion of this youth; but her feelings as a woman, grateful at once and compassionate, prevented her assuming the dignity of a Queen, and she endeavored to continue the conversation in an indifferent tone.

"Methought," she said, "I heard that, at the division of my spoils, Rosabelle had become the property of Lord Morton's paramour and lady-love, Alice."

"The noble palfrey had indeed been destined to so base a lot," answered Douglas. "She was kept under four keys, and under the charge of a numerous crew of grooms and domestics; but Queen Mary needed Rosabelle, and Rosabelle is here."

"And was it well, Douglas," said Queen Mary, "when such fearful risks of various kinds must needs be encountered, that you should augment their perils to yourself for a subject of so little momemt as a palfrey?"

"Do you call that of little moment," answered Douglas, "which has afforded you a moment's pleasure? Did you not start with joy when I first said you were mounted on Rosabelle? And to purchase you that pleasure, though it were to last no longer than the flash of lightning doth, would not Douglas have risked his life a thousand times?"

"O, peace, Douglas—peace," said the Queen, "this is unfitting language; and, besides, I would speak," said she, recollecting herself, "with the abbot of St. Mary's. Nay, Douglas, I will not let you quit my rein in displeasure."

"Displeasure, lady!" answered Douglas; "alas! sorrow

is all that I can feel for your well-warranted contempt. I should be as soon displeased with Heaven for refusing the wildest wish which mortal can form."

"Abide by my rein, however," said Mary, "there is room for my lord abbot on the other side; and, besides, I doubt if his assistance would be so useful to Rosabelle and me as yours has been, should the road again require it."

The abbot came up on the other side, and she immediately opened a conversation with him on the topic of the state of parties, and the plan fittest for her to pursue in consequence of her deliverance. In this conversation Douglas look little share, and never but when directly applied to by the Queen, while, as before, his attention seemed entirely engrossed by the care of Mary's personal safety. She learned, however, she had a new obligation to him, since, by his contrivance, the abbot, whom he had furnished with the family password, was introduced into the castle as one of the garrison.

Long before daybreak they ended their hasty and perilous journey before the gates of Niddrie, a castle in West Lothian, belonging to Lord Seyton. When the Queen was about to alight, Henry Seyton, preventing Douglas, received her in his arms, and, kneeling down, prayed her Majesty to enter the house of his father, her faithful servant.

"Your Grace," he added, "may repose yourself here in perfect safety: it is already garrisoned with good men for your protection; and I have sent a post to my father, whose instant arrival, at the head of five hundred men, may be looked for. Do not dismay yourself, therefore, should your sleep be broken by the trampling of horse; but only think that here are some scores more of the saucy Seytons come to attend you."

"And by better friends than the saucy Seytons a Scottish queen cannot be guarded," replied Mary. "Rosabelle went fleet as the summer breeze, and wellnigh as easy; but it is long since I have been a traveler, and I feel that repose will be welcome. Catherine, *ma mignone,* you must sleep in my apartment to-night, and bid me welcome to your noble father's castle. Thanks—thanks to all my kind deliverers; thanks, and a good-night is all I can now offer; but if I climb once more to the upper side of Fortune's wheel I will not have her bandage. Mary Stuart will keep her eyes open, and distinguish her friends. Seyton, I need scarcely recommend the venerable abbot, the Douglas, and my page to your honorable care and hospitality."

Henry Seyton bowed, and Catherine and Lady Fleming

attended the Queen to her apartment; where, acknowledging to them that she should have found it difficult in that moment to keep her promise of holding her eyes open, she resigned herself to repose, and awakened not till the morning was advanced.

Mary's first feeling when she awoke was the doubt of her freedom; and the impulse prompted her to start from bed, and hastily throwing her mantle over her shoulders, to look out at the casement of her apartment. O sight of joy! instead of the crystal sheet of Lochleven, unaltered save by the influence of the wind, a landscape of wood and moorland lay before her, and the park around the castle was occupied by the troops of her most faithful and most favorite nobles.

"Rise—rise, Catherine," cried the enraptured Princess—"arise and come hither! Here are swords and spears in true hands, and glittering armor on loyal breasts. Here are banners, my girl, floating in the wind, as lightly as summer cloud. Great God! what pleasure to my weary eyes to trace their devices—thine own brave father's—the princely Hamilton's — the faithful Fleming's. See—see—they have caught a glimpse of me, and throng towards the window!"

She flung the casement open, and with her bare head, from which the tresses flew back loose and disheveled, her fair arm, slenderly veiled by her mantle, returned by motion and sign the exulting shouts of the warriors, which echoed for many a furlong around. When the first burst of ecstatic joy was over she recollected how lightly she was dressed, and, putting her hands to her face, which was covered with blushes at the recollection, withdrew abruptly from the window. The cause of her retreat was easily conjectured, and increased the general enthusiasm for the princess who had forgotton her rank in her haste to acknowledge the services of her subjects. The unadorned beauties of the lovely woman, too, moved the military spectators more than the highest display of her regal state might; and what might have seemed too free in her mode of appearing before them was more than atoned for by the enthusiasm of the moment, and by the delicacy evinced in her hasty retreat. Often as the shouts died away, as often were they renewed, till wood and hill rung again; and many a deep oath was made that morning on the cross of the sword, that the hand should not part with the weapon till Mary Stuart was restored to her rights. But what are promises, what the hopes of mortals?

In ten days the gallant and devoted votaries were slain, were captives, or had fled.

Mary flung herself into the nearest seat, and still blushing, yet half-smiling, exclaimed, "*Ma mignonne,* what will they think of me?—to show myself to them with my bare feet hastily thrust into my slippers—only this loose mantle about me—my hair loose on my shoulders—my arms and neck so bare. O, the best they can suppose is, that her abode in yonder dungeon has turned their Queen's brain! But my rebel subjects saw me exposed when I was in the depth of affliction, why should I hold colder ceremony with these faithful and loyal men? Call Fleming, however; I trust she has not forgotten the little mail with my apparel. We must be as brave as we can, *mignonne.*"

"Nay, madam, our good Lady Fleming was in no case to remember anything."

"You jest, Catherine," said the Queen, somewhat offended; "it is not her nature, surely, to forget her duty so far as to leave us without a change of apparel?"

"Roland Græme, madam, took care of that," answered Catherine; "for he threw the mail with your Highness's clothes and jewels into the boat, ere he ran back to lock the gate. I never saw so awkward a page as that youth: the packet wellnigh fell on my head."

"He shall make thy heart amends, my girl," said Queen Mary, laughing, "for that and all other offenses given. But call Fleming, and let us put ourselves into apparel to meet our faithful lords."

Such had been the preparations, and such was the skill of Lady Fleming, that the Queen appeared before her assembled nobles in such attire as became, through it could not enchance, her natural dignity. With the most winning courtesy, she expressed to each individual her grateful thanks, and dignified not only every noble, but many of the lesser barons, by her peculiar attention.

"And whither now, my lords?" she said; "what way do your counsels determine for us?"

"To Draphane Castle," replied Lord Arbroath, "if your Majesty is so pleased, and thence to Dunbarton, to place your Grace's person in safety, after which we long to prove if these traitors will abide us in the field."

"And when do we journey?"

"We propose," said Lord Seyton, "if your Grace's fatigue will permit, to take horse after the morning's meal."

"Your pleasure, my lords, is mine," replied the Queen

"we will rule our journey by your wisdom now, and hope hereafter to have the advantage of governing by it our kingdom. You will permit my ladies and me, my good lords, to break our fast along with you; we must be half soldiers ourselves, and set state apart."

Low bowed many a helmeted head at this gracious proffer, when the Queen, glancing her eyes through the assembled leaders, missed both Douglas and Roland Græme, and inquired for them in a whisper to Catherine Seyton.

"They are in yonder oratory, madam, sad enough," replied Catherine, and the Queen observed that her favorite's eyes were red with weeping.

"This must not be," said the Queen. "Keep the company amused. I will seek them, and introduce them myself."

She went into the oratory, where the first she met was George Douglas, standing, or rather reclining, in the recess of a window, his back rested against the wall and his arms folded on his breast. At the sight of the Queen he started, and his countenance showed, for an instant, an expression of intense delight, which was instantly exchanged for his usual deep melancholy.

"What means this?" she said. "Douglas, why does the first deviser and bold executor of the happy scheme for our freedom shun the company of his fellow-nobles, and of the sovereign whom he has obliged?"

"Madam," replied Douglas, "those whom you grace with your presence bring followers to aid your cause, wealth to support your state—can offer you halls in which to feast, and impregnable castles for your defense. I am a houseless and landless man—disinherited by my [grand-] mother, and laid under her malediction—disowned by my name and kindred—who bring nothing to your standard but a single sword, and the poor life of its owner."

"Do you mean to upbraid me, Douglas," replied the Queen, "by showing what you have lost for my sake?"

"God forbid, madam!" interrupted the young man, eagerly; "were it to do again, and had I ten times as much rank and wealth, and twenty times as many friends to lose, my losses would be overpaid by the first step you made, as a free princess, upon the soil of your native kingdom."

"And what then ails you, that you will not rejoice with those who rejoice upon the same joyful occasion?" said the Queen.

"Madam," replied the youth, "though exheridated and disowned, I am yet a Douglas: with most of yonder nobles my family have been in feud for ages—a cold reception amongst them were an insult, and a kind one yet more humiliating."

"For shame, Douglas," replied the Queen, "shake off this unmanly gloom! I can make thee match for the best of them in title and fortune, and, believe me, I will. Go then amongst them, I command you."

"That word," said Douglas, "is enough. I go. This only let me say, that not for wealth or title would I have done that which I have done. Mary Stuart will not, and the Queen cannot, reward me."

So saying, he left the oratory, mingled with the nobles, and placed himself at the table. The Queen looked after him, and put her kerchief to her eyes.

"Now, Our Lady pity me," she said, "for no sooner are my prison cares ended than those which beset me as a woman and a queen again thicken around me. Happy Elizabeth! to whom political interest is everything, and whose heart never betrays thy head. And now must I seek this other boy, if I would prevent daggers-drawing betwixt him and the young Seyton."

Roland Græme was in the same oratory, but at such a distance from Douglas, that he could not overhear what passed betwixt the Queen and him. He also was moody and thoughtful, but cleared his brow at the Queen's question, "How now, Roland? you are negligent in your attendance this morning. Are you so much overcome with your night's ride?"

"Not so, gracious madam," answered Græme; "but I am told the page of Lochleven is not the page of Niddrie Castle; and so Master Henry Seyton hath in a manner been pleased to supersede my attendance."

"Now, Heaven forgive me," said the Queen, "how soon these cock-chickens begin to spar! With children and boys, at least, I may be a queen. I will have you friends. Some one send me Henry Seyton hither." As she spoke the last words aloud, the youth whom she had named entered the apartment. "Come hither," she said, "Henry Seyton. I will have you give your hand to this youth, who so well aided in the plan of my escape."

"Willingly, madam," answered Seyton, "so that the youth will grant me, as a boon, that he touch not the hand of another Seyton whom he knows of. My hand has passed current for hers with him before now; and to win my friendship, he must give up thoughts of my sister's love."

"Henry Seyton," said the Queen, "does it become you to add any condition to my command?"

"Madam," said Henry, "I am the servant of your Grace's throne, son to the most loyal man in Scotland. Our goods, our castles, our blood, are yours; our honor is in our own keeping. I could say more, but——"

"Nay, speak on, rude boy," said the Queen; "what avails it that I am released from Lochleven, if I am thus enthralled under the yoke of my pretended deliverers, and prevented from doing justice to one who has deserved as well of me as yourself?"

"Be not in this distemperature of me, sovereign lady," said Roland, "this young gentleman, being the faithful servant of your Grace, and the brother of Catherine Seyton, bears that about him which will charm down my passion at the hottest."

"I warn thee once more," said Henry Seyton, haughtily, "that you make no speech which may infer that the daughter of Lord Seyton can be aught to thee beyond what she is to every churl's blood in Scotland."

The Queen was again about to interfere, for Roland's complexion rose, and it became somewhat questionable how long his love for Catherine would suppress the natural fire of his temper. But the interposition of another person, hitherto unseen, prevented Mary's interference. There was in the oratory a separate shrine, inclosed with a high screen of pierced oak, within which was placed an image of St. Bennet, of peculiar sanctity. From this recess, in which she had been probably engaged in her devotions, issued suddenly Magdelen Græme, and addressed Henry Seyton in reply to his last offensive expression—"And of what clay, then, are they molded, these Seytons, that the blood of the Græmes may not aspire to mingle with theirs? Know, proud boy, that when I called this youth my daughter's child, I affirm his descent from Malise Earl of Strathern, called Malsie with the Bright Brand; and I trow the blood of your house springs from no higher source."

"Good mother," said Seyton, "methinks your sanctity should make you superior to these worldly vanities; and indeed it seems to have rendered you somewhat oblivious touching them, since, to be of gentle descent, the father's name and lineage must be as well qualified as the mother's."

"And if I say he comes of the blood of Avenel by the father's side," replied Magdalen Græme, "name I not blood as richly colored as thine own?"

"Of Avenel!" said the Queen; "is my page descended of Avenel?"

"Ay, gracious Princess, and the last male heir of that ancient house. Julian Avenel was his father, who fell in the battle against the Southron."

"I have heard the tale of sorrow," said the Queen; "it was thy daughter, then, who followed that unfortunate baron to the field, and died on his body? Alas! how many ways does woman's affection find to work out her own misery! The tale has oft been told and sung in hall and bower. And thou, Roland, art that child of misfortune, who was left among the dead and dying? Henry Seyton, he is thine equal in blood and birth."

"Scarcely so," said Henry Seyton, "even were he legitimate; but if the tale be told and sung aright, Julian Avenel was a false knight, and his leman a frail and credulous maiden."

"Now, by Heaven, thou liest!" said Roland Græme, and laid his hand on his sword. The entrance of Lord Seyton, however, prevented violence.

"Save me, my lord," said the Queen; "and separate these wild and untamed spirits."

"How, Henry!" said the baron, "are my castle and the Queen's presence no check on thy insolence and impetuosity? And with whom art thou brawling? Unless my eyes spell that token false, it is with the very youth who aided me so gallantly in the skirmish with the Leslies. Let me look, fair youth, at the medal which thou wearest in thy cap. By St. Bennet, it is the same! Henry, I command thee to forbear him, as thou lovest my blessing——"

"And as you honor my command," said the Queen; "good service hath he done me."

"Ay, madam," replied young Seyton, "as when he carried the billet, inclosed in the sword-sheath, to Lochleven. Marry, the good youth knew no more than a pack-horse what he was carrying."

"But I, who dedicated him to this great work," said Magdalen Græme—"I, by whose advice and agency this just heir hath been unloosed from her thraldom—I, who spared not the last remaining hope of a falling house in this great action—I, at least, knew and counseled; and what merit may be mine, let the reward, most gracious Queen, descend upon this youth. My ministry here is ended: you are free—a sovereign princess at the head of a gallant army, surrounded by valiant barons. My service could avail you no farther, but might well prejudice you; your fortune now rests upon men's hearts and men's swords. May they prove as trusty as the faith of women!"

"You will not leave us, mother," said the Queen—"you whose practises in our favor were so powerful, who dared so many dangers, and wore so many disguises, to blind our enemies and to confirm our friends—you will not leave us in the dawn of our reviving fortunes, ere we have time to know and to thank you?"

"You cannot know her," answered Magdalen Græme, "who knows not herself: there are times when, in this woman's frame of mine, there is the strength of him of Gath; in this overtoiled brain, the wisdom of the most sage counselor; and again the mist is on me, and my strength is weakness, my wisdom folly. I have spoken before princes and cardinals—ay, noble Princess, even before the princess of thine own house of Lorraine—and I know not whence the words of persuasion came which flowed from my lips, and were drunk in by their ears. And now, even when I most need words of persuasion, there is something which chokes my voice and robs me of utterance."

"If there be aught in my power to do thee pleasure," said the Queen, "the barely naming it shall avail as well as all thine eloquence."

"Sovereign lady," replied the enthusiast, "it shames me that at this high moment something of human frailty should cling to one whose vows the saints have heard, whose labors in the rightful cause Heaven has prospered. But it will be thus, while the living spirit is shrined in the clay of mortality. I will yield to the folly," she said, weeping as she spoke, "and it shall be the last." Then seizing Roland's hand, she led him to the Queen's feet, kneeling herself upon one knee, and causing him to kneel on both. "Mighty Princess," she said, "look on this flower—it was found by a kindly stranger on a bloody field of battle, and long it was ere my anxious eyes saw, and my arms pressed, all that was left of my only daughter. For your sake, and for that of the holy faith we both profess, I could leave this plant, while it was yet tender, to the nurture of strangers—ay, of enemies, by whom, perchance, his blood would have been poured forth as wine, had the heretic Glendinning known that he had in his house the heir of Julian Avenel. Since then I have seen him only in a few hours of doubt and dread, and now I part with the child of my love—forever—forever! O, for every weary step I have made in your rightful cause, in this and in foreign lands, give protection to the child whom I must no more call mine!"

"I swear to you, mother," said the Queen, deeply affected, "that, for your sake and his own, his happiness and fortune shall be our charge!"

"I thank you, daughter of princes," said Magdalen, and pressed her lips, first to the Queen's hand, then to the brow of her grandson. "And now," she said, drying her tears, and rising with dignity, "earth has had its own, and Heaven claims the rest. Lioness of Scotland, go forth and conquer! and if the prayers of a devoted votaress can avail thee, they will rise in many a land, and from many a distant shrine. I will glide like a ghost from land to land, from temple to temple; and where the very name of my country is unknown, the priests shall ask who is the queen of that distant northern clime, for whom the aged pilgrim was so fervent in prayer. Farewell! Honor be thine, and earthly prosperity, if it be the will of God; if not, may the penance thou shalt do here ensure thy happiness hereafter! Let no one speak or follow me—my resolution is taken—my vow cannot be canceled."

She glided from their presence as she spoke, and her last look was upon her beloved grandchild. He would have risen and followed, but the Queen and Lord Seyton interfered.

"Press not on her now," said Lord Seyton, "if you would not lose her forever. Many a time have we seen the sainted mother, and often at the most needful moment; but to press on her privacy, or to thwart her purpose, is a crime which she cannot pardon. I trust we shall yet see her at her need—a holy woman she is for certain, and dedicated wholly to prayer and penance; and hence the heretics hold her as one distracted, while true Catholics deem her a saint."

"Let me then hope," said the Queen, "that you, my lord, will aid me in the execution of her last request."

"What! in the protection of my young second?—cheerfully—that is, in all that your Majesty can think it fitting to ask of me. Henry, give thy hand upon the instant to Roland Avenel, for so I presume he must now be called."

"And shall be lord of the barony," said the Queen, "if God prosper our rightful arms."

"It can only be to restore it to my kind protectress, who now holds it," said young Avenel. "I would rather be landless all my life than she lost a rood of ground by me."

"Nay," said the Queen, looking to Lord Seyton, "his mind matches his birth. Henry, thou hast not yet given thy hand."

"It is his," said Henry, giving it with some appearance of courtesy, but whispering Roland at the same time, "For all this thou hast not my sister's."

"May it please your Grace," said Lord Seyton, "now that these passages are over, to honor our poor meal. Time it were that our banners were reflected in the Clyde. We must to horse with as little delay as may be."

CHAPTER XXXVII

Ay, sir—our ancient crown, in these wild times,
Oft stood upon a cast; the gamester's ducat,
So often staked, and lost, and then regain'd,
Scarce knew so many hazards.

The Spanish Father.

It is not our object to enter into the historical part of the reign of the ill-fated Mary, or to recount how, during the week which succeeded her flight from Lochleven, her partisans mustered around her with their followers, forming a gallant army, amounting to six thousand men. So much light has been lately thrown on the most minute details of the period by Mr. Chalmers, in his valuable *History of Queen Mary,* that the reader may be safely referred to it for the fullest information which ancient records afford concerning that interesting time. It is sufficient for our purpose to say, that while Mary's headquarters were at Hamilton, the Regent and his adherents had, in the King's name, assembled a host at Glasgow, inferior indeed to that of the Queen in numbers, but formidable from the military talents of Murray, Morton, the Laird of Grange, and others, who had been trained from their youth in foreign and domestic wars.

In these circumstances, it was the obvious policy of Queen Mary to avoid a conflict, secure that, were her person once in safety, the number of her adherents must daily increase; whereas, the forces of those opposed to her must, as had frequently happened in the previous history of her reign, have diminished, and their spirits become broken. And so evident was this to her counselors, that they resolved their first step should be to place the Queen in the strong castle of Dunbarton, there to await the course of events, the arrival of succors from France, and the levies which were made by her adherents in every province in Scotland. Accordingly, orders were given that all men should be on horseback or on foot, appareled in their armor, and ready to follow the Queen's standard in array of battle, the avowed determination being to escort her to the castle of Dunbarton in defiance of her enemies.

The muster was made upon Hamilton Moor, and the march

commenced in all the pomp of feudal times. Military music sounded, banners and pennons waved, armor glittered far and wide, and spears glanced and twinkled like stars in a frosty sky. The gallant spectacle of warlike parade was on this occasion dignified by the presence of the Queen herself, who, with a fair retinue of ladies and household attendants, and a special guard of gentlemen, amongst whom young Seyton and Roland were distinguished, gave grace at once and confidence to the army, which spread its ample files before, around, and behind her. Many churchmen also joined the cavalcade, most of whom did not scruple to assume arms, and declare their intention of wielding them in defense of Mary and the Catholic faith. Not so the abbot of St. Mary's. Roland had not seen this prelate since the night of their escape from Lochleven, and he now beheld him, robed in the dress of his order, assume his station near the Queen's person. Roland hastened to pull off his basnet, and beseech the abbot's blessing.

"Thou hast it, my son!" said the priest; "I see thee now under thy true name, and in thy rightful garb. The helmet with the holly-branch befits your brows well. I have long waited for the hour thou shouldest assume it."

"Then you knew of my descent, my good father?" said Roland.

"I did so, but it was under seal of confession from thy grandmother; nor was I at liberty to tell the secret till she herself should make it known."

"Her reason for such secrecy, my father?" said Roland Avenel.

"Fear, perchance, of my brother—a mistaken fear, for Halbert would not, to ensure himself a kingdom, have offered wrong to an orphan; besides that your title, in quiet times, even had your father done your mother that justice which I well hope he did, could not have competed with that of my brother's wife, the child of Julian's elder brother."

"They need fear no competition from me," said Avenel. "Scotland is wide enough, and there are many manors to win, without plundering my benefactor. But prove to me, my reverend father, that my father was just to my mother; show me that I may call myself a legitimate Avenel, and make me your bounden slave forever!"

"Ay," replied the abbot, "I hear the Seytons hold thee cheap for that stain on thy shield. Something, however, I have learnt from the late Abbot Boniface, which, if it prove sooth, may redeem that reproach."

"Tell me that blessed news," said Roland, "and the future service of my life——"

"Rash boy!" said the abbot, "I should but madden thine impatient temper by exciting hopes that may never be fulfilled, and is this a time for them? Think on what perilous march we are bound, and if thou hast a sin unconfessed, neglect not the only leisure which Heaven may perchance afford thee for confession and absolution."

"There will be time enough for both, I trust, when we reach Dunbarton," answered the page.

"Ay," said the abbot, "thou crowest as loudly as the rest; but we are not yet at Dunbarton, and there is a lion in the path."

"Mean you Murray, Morton, and the other rebels at Glasgow, my reverend father? Tush! they dare not look on the royal banner."

"Even so," replied the abbot, "speak many of those who are older, and should be wiser, than thou. I have returned from the southern shires, where I left many a chief of name arming in the Queen's interest. I left the lords here wise and considered men; I find them madmen on my return: they are willing, for mere pride and vainglory, to brave the enemy, and to carry the Queen, as it were in triumph, past the walls of Glasgow, and under the beards of the adverse army. Seldom does Heaven smile on such mistimed confidence. We shall be encountered, and that to the purpose."

"And so much the better," replied Roland; "the field of battle was my cradle."

"Beware it be not thy dying-bed," said the abbot. "But what avails it whispering to young wolves the dangers of the chase? You will know, perchance, ere this day is out, what yonder men are, whom you hold in rash contempt."

"Why, what are they?" said Henry Seyton, who now joined them. "Have they sinews of wire and flesh of iron? Will lead pierce and steel cut them? If so, reverend father, we have little to fear."

"They are evil men," said the abbot, "but the trade of war demands no saints. Murray and Morton are known to be the best generals in Scotland. No one ever saw Lindesay's or Ruthven's back. Kirkcaldy of Grange was named by the Constable Montmorency the first soldier in Europe. My brother, too good a name for such a cause, has been far and wide known for a leader."

"The better—the better!" said Seyton, triumphantly; "we shall have all these traitors of rank and name in a fair field before us. Our cause is the best, our numbers are the strongest, our hearts and limbs match theirs. St. Bennet, and set on!"

The abbot made no reply, but seemed lost in reflection; and his anxiety in some measure communicated itself to Roland Avenel, who ever, as their line of march led over a ridge or an eminence, cast an anxious look towards the towers of Glasgow, as if he expected to see symptoms of the enemy issuing forth. It was not that he feared the fight, but the issue was of such deep import to his country and to himself that the natural fire of his spirit burned with a less lively, though with a more intense, glow. Love, honor, fame, fortune, all seemed to depend on the issue of one field, rashly hazarded perhaps, but now likely to become unavoidable and decisive.

When, at length, their march came to be nearly parallel with the city of Glasgow, Roland became sensible that the high grounds before them were already in part occupied by a force, showing, like their own, the royal banner of Scotland, and on the point of being supported by columns of infantry and squadrons of horse, which the city gates had poured forth, and which hastily advanced to sustain those troops who already possessed the ground in front of the Queen's forces. Horseman after horseman galloped in from the advanced guard, with tidings that Murray had taken the field with his whole army; that his object was to intercept the Queen's march, and his purpose unquestionable to hazard a battle. It was now that the tempers of men were subjected to a sudden and a severe trial; and that those who had too presumptuously concluded that they should pass without combat were something disconcerted, when, at once, and with little time to deliberate, they found themselves placed in front of a resolute enemy. Their chiefs immediately assembled around the Queen, and held a hasty council of war. Mary's quivering lip confessed the fear which she endeavored to conceal under a bold and dignified demeanor. But her efforts were overcome by painful recollections of the disastrous issue of her last appearance in arms at Carberry Hill; and, when she meant to have asked them their advice for ordering the battle, she involuntarily inquired whether there were no means of escaping without an engagement?

"Escaping!" answered the Lord Seyton. "When I stand as one to ten of your Highness's enemies, I may think of escape, but never while I stand with three to two!"

"Battle!—battle!" exclaimed the assembled lords; "we

will drive the rebels from their vantage ground, as the hound turns the hare on the hillside."

"Methinks, my noble lords," said the abbot, "it were as well to prevent his gaining that advantage. Our road lies through yonder hamlet on the brow, and whichever party hath the luck to possess it, with its little gardens and inclosures, will attain a post of great defense."

"The reverend father is right," said the Queen. "O, haste thee, Seyton—haste, and get thither before them; they are marching like the wind."

Seyton bowed low, and turned his horse's head. "Your Highness honors me," he said; "I will instantly press forward and seize the pass."

"Not before me, my lord, whose charge is the command of the vanguard," said the Lord of Arbroath.

"Before you, or any Hamilton in Scotland," said the Seyton, "having the Queen's command. Follow me, gentlemen, my vassals and kinsmen. St. Bennet, and set on!"

"And follow me," said Arbroath, "my noble kinsmen and brave men-tenants; we will see which will first reach the post of danger. For God and Queen Mary!"

"Ill-omened haste and most unhappy strife," said the abbot, who saw them and their followers rush hastily and emulously to ascend the height, without waiting till their men were placed in order. "And you, gentlemen," he continued, addressing Roland and Seyton, who were each about to follow those who hastened thus disorderly to the conflict, "will you leave the Queen's person unguarded?"

"O, leave me not, gentlemen!" said the Queen—"Roland and Seyton, do not leave me; there are enough of arms to strike in this fell combat—withdraw not those to whom I trust for my safety!"

"We may not leave her Grace," said Roland, looking at Seyton, and turning his horse.

"I ever looked when thou wouldst find out that," rejoined the fiery youth.

Roland made no answer, but bit his lip till the blood came, and spurring his horse up to the side of Catherine Seyton's palfrey, he whispered in a low voice, "I never thought to have done aught to deserve you; but this day I have heard myself upbraided with cowardice, and my sword remained still sheathed, and all for the love of you."

"There is madness among us all," said the damsel: "my father, my brother, and you are all alike bereft of reason. Ye should think only of this poor Queen, and you are all inspired by your own absurd jealousies. The monk is the only soldier and man of sense amongst you all. My lord abbot," she cried aloud, "were it not better we should draw to the westward, and wait the event that God shall send us, instead of remaining here in the highway, endangering the Queen's person, and cumbering the troops in their advance?"

"You say well, my daughter," replied the abbot; "had we but one to guide us where the Queen's person may be in safety! Our nobles hurry to the conflict, without casting a thought on the very cause of the war."

"Follow me," said a knight, or man-at-arms, well mounted, and accoutred completely in black armor, but having the visor of his helmet closed, and bearing no crest on his helmet, or device upon his shield.

"We will follow no stranger," said the abbot, "without some warrant of his truth."

"I am a stranger and in your hands," said the horseman; "if you wish to know more of me, the Queen herself will be your warrant."

The Queen had remained fixed to the spot, as if disabled by fear, yet mechanically smiling, bowing, and waving her hand, as banners were lowered and spears depressed before her, while, emulating the strife betwixt Seyton and Arbroath, band on band pressed forward their march towards the enemy. Scarce, however, had the black rider whispered something in her ear, than she assented to what he said; and when he spoke aloud, and with an air of command, "Gentlemen, it is the Queen's pleasure that you should follow me," Mary uttered, with something like eagerness, the word "Yes."

All were in motion in an instant; for the black horseman, throwing off a sort of apathy of manner which his first appearance indicated, spurred his horse, to and fro, making him take such active bounds and short turns as showed the rider master of the animal; and getting the Queen's little retinue in some order for marching, he led them to the left, directing his course towards a castle, which, crowning a gentle yet commanding eminence, presented an extensive view over the country beneath, and, in particular, commanded a view of those heights which both armies hastened to occupy, and which it was now apparent must almost instantly be the scene of struggle and dispute.

"Yonder towers," said the abbot, questioning the sable horseman, "to whom do they belong? and are they now in the hands of friends?"

"They are untenanted," replied the stranger, "or, at least, they have no hostile inmates. But urge these youths, sir abbot, to make more haste; this is but an evil time to satisfy their idle curiosity, by peering out upon the battle in which they are to take no share."

"The worse luck mine," said Henry Seyton, who overheard him; "I would rather be under my father's banner at this moment than be made chamberlain of Holyrood, for this my present duty of peaceful ward well and patiently discharged."

"Your place under your father's banner will shortly be right dangerous," said Roland Avenel, who, pressing his horse towards the westward, had still his look reverted to the armies; "for I see yonder body of cavalry which presses from the eastward will reach the village ere Lord Seyton can gain it."

"They are but cavalry," said Seyton, looking attentively; "they cannot hold the village without shot of harquebuss."

"Look more closely," said Roland; "you will see that each of these horsemen who advance so rapidly from Glasgow carries a footman behind him."

"Now, by Heaven, he speaks well!" said the black cavalier; "one of you two must go carry the news to Lord Seyton and Lord Arbroath, that they hasten not their horsemen on before the foot, but advance more regularly."

"Be that my errand," said Roland, "for I first marked the stratagem of the enemy."

"But, by your leave," said Seyton, "yonder is my father's banner engaged, and it best becomes me to go to the rescue."

"I will stand by the Queen's decision," said Roland Avenel.

"What new appeal?—what new quarrel?" said Queen Mary. "Are there not in yonder dark host enemies enough to Mary Stuart, but must her very friends turn enemies to each other?"

"Nay, madam," said Roland, "the young Master of Seyton and I did but dispute who should leave your person to do a most needful message to the host. He thought his rank entitled him, and I deemed that the person of least consequence, being myself, were better periled——"

"Not so," said the Queen; "if one must leave me, be it Seyton."

Henry Seyton bowed till the white plumes on his helmet mixed with the flowing mane of his gallant war-horse, then placed himself firm in his saddle, shook his lance aloft with an air of triumph and determination, and striking his horse with the spurs, made towards his father's banner, which was still advancing up the hill, and dashed his steed over every obstacle that occurred in his headlong path.

"My brother! my father!" exclaimed Catherine, with an expression of agonized apprehension—"they are in the midst of peril, and I in safety!"

"Would to God," said Roland, "that I were with them, and could ransom every drop of their blood by two of mine!"

"Do I not know thou dost wish it?" said Catherine. "Can a woman say to a man what I have well-nigh said to thee, and yet think that he could harbor fear or faintness of heart? There is that in yon distant sound of approaching battle that pleases me even while it affrights me. I would I were a man, that I might feel that stern delight without the mixture of terror!"

"Ride up—ride up, Lady Catherine Seyton," cried the abbot, as they still swept on at a rapid pace, and were now close beneath the walls of the castle—"ride up, and aid Lady Fleming to support the Queen—she gives way more and more."

They halted and lifted Mary from the saddle, and were about to support her towards the castle, when she said faintly, "Not there—not there: these walls will I never enter more!"

"Be a queen, madam," said the abbot, "and forget that you are a woman."

"O, I must forget much—much more," answered the unfortunate Mary, in an undertone, "ere I can look with steady eyes on these well-known scenes! I must forget the days which I spent here as the bride of the lost—the murdered——"

"This is the castle of the Crookstone," said the Lady Fleming, "in which the Queen held her first court after she was married to Darnley."

"Heaven," said the abbot, "Thy hand is upon us! Bear yet up, madam; your foes are the foes of Holy Church, and God will this day decide whether Scotland shall be Catholic or heretic."

A heavy and continued fire of cannon and musketry bore a tremendous burden to his words, and seemed far more than they to recall the spirits of the Queen.

"To yonder tree," she said, pointing to a yew-tree which grew on a small mount close to the castle; "I know it well—from thence you may see a prospect wide as from the peaks of Schehallion."

And freeing herself from her assistants, she walked with a determined, yet somewhat wild, step up to the stem of the noble yew. The abbot, Catherine, and Roland Avenel followed her, while Lady Fleming kept back the inferior persons of her train. The black horseman also followed the Queen, waiting on her as closely as the shadow upon the light, but ever remaining at the distance of two or three yards; he folded his arms on his bosom, turned his back to the battle, and seemed solely occupied by gazing on Mary through the bars of his closed visor. The Queen regarded him not, but fixed her eyes upon the spreading yew.

"Ay, fair and stately tree," she said, as if at the sight of it she had been rapt away from the present scene, and had overcome the horror which had oppressed her at the first approach to Crookstone, "there thou standest, gay and goodly as ever, though thou hearest the sounds of war instead of the vows of love. All is gone since I last greeted thee—love and lover—vows and vower—king and kingdom. How goes the field, my lord abbot? with us, I trust; yet what but evil can Mary's eyes witness from this spot?"

Her attendants eagerly bent their eyes on the field of battle, but could discover nothing more than that it was obstinately contested. The small inclosures and cottage gardens in the village, of which they had a full and commanding view, and which shortly before lay, with their lines of sycamore and ash-trees, so still and quiet in the mild light of a May sun, were now each converted into a line of fire, canopied by smoke; and the sustained and constant report of the musketry and cannon, mingled with the shouts of the meeting combatants, showed that as yet neither party had given ground.

"Many a soul finds its final departure to heaven or hell in these awful thunders," said the abbot; "let those that believe in the Holy Church join me in orisons for victory in this dreadful combat."

"Not here—not here," said the unfortunate Queen—"pray not here, father, or pray in silence; my mind is too much torn between the past and the present to dare to approach the Heavenly throne. Or, if ye will pray, be it for one whose fondest affections have been her greatest crimes, and who has ceased to be a queen only because she was a deceived and a tender-hearted woman."

"Were it not well," said Roland, "that I rode somewhat nearer the hosts, and saw the fate of the day?"

"Do so, in the name of God," said the abbot, "for if our

friends are scattered, our flight must be hasty; but beware thou approach not too nigh the conflict: there is more than thine own life depends on thy safe return."

"O, go not too nigh," said Catherine; "but fail not to see how the Seytons fight, and how they bear themselves."

"Fear nothing, I will be on my guard," said Roland Avenel; and without waiting further answer, rode towards the scene of conflict, keeping, as he rode, the higher and uninclosed ground, and ever looking cautiously around him, for fear of involving himself in some hostile party. As he approached, the shots rung sharp and more sharply on his ear, the shouts came wilder and wilder, and he felt that thick beating of the heart, that mixture of natural apprehension, intense curiosity, and anxiety for the dubious event, which even the bravest experience when they approach alone to a scene of interest and of danger.

At length he drew so close that, from a bank, screened by bushes and underwood, he could distinctly see where the struggle was most keenly maintained. This was in a hollow way, leading to the village, up which the Queen's vanguard had marched, with more hasty courage than well-advised conduct, for the purpose of possessing themselves of that post of advantage. They found their scheme anticipated, and the hedges and inclosures already occupied by the enemy, led by the celebrated Kirkcaldy of Grange and the Earl of Morton; and not small was the loss which they sustained while struggling forward to come to close with the men-at-arms on the other side. But, as the Queen's followers were chiefly noblemen and barons, with their kinsmen and followers, they had pressed onward, contemning obstacles and danger, and had, when Roland arrived on the ground, met hand to hand at the gorge of the pass with the Regent's vanguard, and endeavored to bear them out of the village at the spear-point; while their foes, equally determined to keep the advantage which they had attained, struggled with the like obstinacy to drive back the assailants.

Both parties were on foot, and armed in proof; so that, when the long lances of the front ranks were fixed in each other's shields, corslets, and breastplates, the struggle resembled that of two bulls, who, fixing their frontlets hard against each other, remain in that posture for hours, until the superior strength or obstinacy of the one compels the other to take to flight, or bears him down to the earth. Thus locked together in the deadly struggle, which swayed slowly to and fro, as one or other party gained the advantage, those who fell were trampled on alike by friends and foes; those whose weapons were broken retired from the front ranks, and had their place supplied by others; while the rearward ranks, unable otherwise to take share in the combat, fired their pistols, and hurled their daggers, and the points and truncheons of the broken weapons, like javelins against the enemy.

"God and the Queen!" resounded from the one party; "God and the King!" thundered from the other; while, in the name of their sovereign, fellow-subjects on both sides shed each other's blood, and, in the name of their Creator, defaced His image. Amid the tumult was often heard the voices of the captains shouting their commands, of leaders and chiefs crying their gathering words, of groans and shrieks from the falling and the dying.

The strife had lasted nearly an hour. The strength of both parties seemed exhausted; but their rage was unabated, and their obstinacy unsubdued, when Roland, who turned eye and ear to all around him, saw a column of infantry, headed by a few horsemen, wheel round the base of the bank where he had stationed himself, and, leveling their long lances, attack the flank of the Queen's vanguard, closely engaged as they were in conflict on their front. The very first glance showed him that the leader who directed this movement was the Knight of Avenel, his ancient master; and the next convinced him that its effect would be decisive. The result of the attack of fresh and unbroken forces upon the flank of those already wearied with a long and obstinate struggle was, indeed, instantaneous.

The column of the assailants, which had hitherto shown one dark, dense, and united line of helmets, surmounted with plumage, was at once broken and hurled in confusion down the hill which they had so long endeavored to gain. In vain were the leaders heard calling upon their followers to stand to the combat, and seen personally resisting when all resistance was evidently vain. They were slain, or felled to the earth, or hurried backwards by the mingled tide of flight and pursuit. What were Roland's thoughts on beholding the rout, and feeling that all that remained for him was to turn bridle, and endeavor to insure the safety of the Queen's person! Yet, keen as his grief and shame might be, they were both forgotten when, almost close beneath the bank which he occupied, he saw Henry Seyton forced away from his own party in the tumult, covered with dust and blood, and defending himself desperately against several of the enemy who had gathered around him, attracted by his gay armor. Roland paused not a moment, but pushing his steed down the bank, leaped him amongst the hostile party, dealt three or four blows amongst them, which struck down two and made the rest stand aloof, then reaching Seyton his hand, he exhorted him to seize fast hold on his horse's mane.

"We live or die together this day," said he; "keep but fast hold till we are out of the press, and then my horse is yours."

Seyton heard, and exerted his remaining strength, and, by their joint efforts, Roland brought him out of danger, and behind the spot from whence he had witnessed the disastrous conclusion of the fight. But no sooner were they under shelter of the trees than Seyton let go his hold, and, in spite of Roland's efforts to support him, fell at length on the turf. "Trouble yourself no more with me," he said, "this is my first and my last battle, and I have already seen too much of it to wish to see the close. Hasten to save the Queen—and commend me to Catherine; she will never more be mistaken for me nor I for her—the last sword-stroke has made an eternal distinction."

"Let me aid you to mount my horse," said Roland, eagerly, "and you may yet be saved. I can find my own way on foot. Turn but my horse's head westward, and he will carry you fleet and easy as the wind."

"I will never mount steed more," said the youth; "farewell! I love thee better dying than ever I thought to have done while in life. I would that old man's blood were not on my hand! *Sancte Benedicte ora pro me!* Stand not to look on a dying man, but haste to save the Queen!"

These words were spoken with the last effort of his voice, and scarce were they uttered ere the speaker was no more. They recalled Roland to the sense of the duty which he had well-nigh forgotten, but they did not reach his ears only.

"The Queen—where is the Queen?" said Sir Halbert Glendinning, who, followed by two or three horsemen, appeared at this instant. Roland made no answer, but turning his horse, and confiding in his speed, gave him at once rein and spur, and rode over height and hollow towards the Castle of Crookstone. More heavily armed, and mounted upon a horse of less speed, Sir Halbert Glendinning followed with couched lance, calling out as he rode, "Sir with the holly-branch, halt, and show your right to bear that badge: fly not thus cowardly, nor dishonor the cognizance thou deservest not to wear! Halt, sir coward, or, by Heaven, I will strike thee with my lance on the back, and slay thee like a dastard. I am the Knight of Avenel—I am Sir Halbert Glendinning."

But Roland, who had no purpose of encountering his old master, and who, besides, knew the Queen's safety depended on his making the best speed he could, answered not a word to the defiances and reproaches which Sir Halbert continued to throw out against him; but making the best use of his spurs, rode yet harder than before, and had gained about a hundred yards upon his pursuer, when, coming near to the yew-tree where he had left the Queen, he saw them already getting to horse, and cried out as loud as he could, "Foes!—foes! Ride for it, fair ladies. Brave gentlemen, do your devoir to protect them!"

So saying, he wheeled his horse, and avoiding the shock of Sir Halbert Glendinning, charged one of that knight's followers, who was nearly on a line with him, so rudely with his lance that he overthrew horse and man. He then drew his sword and attacked the second, while the black man-at-arms, throwing himself in the way of Glendinning, they rushed on each other so fiercely that both horses were overthrown, and the riders lay rolling on the plain. Neither was able to arise, for the black horseman was pierced through with Glendinning's lance, and the Knight of Avenel, oppressed with the weight of his own horse, and sorely bruised besides, seemed in little better plight than he whom he had mortally wounded.

"Yield thee, Sir Knight of Avenel, rescue or no rescue," said Roland, who had put a second antagonist out of condition to combat, and hastened to prevent Glendinning from renewing the conflict.

"I may not choose but yield," said Sir Halbert, "since I can no longer fight; but it shames me to speak such a word to a coward like thee!"

"Call me not coward," said Roland, lifting his visor, and helping his prisoner to rise, "since but for old kindness at thy hand, and yet more at thy lady's, I had met thee as a brave man should."

"The favorite page of my wife!" said Sir Halbert, astonished. "Ah! wretched boy, I have heard of thy treason at Lochleven."

"Reproach him not, my brother," said the abbot, "he was but an agent in the hands of Heaven."

"To horse—to horse!" said Catherine Seyton; "mount

and be gone, or we are all lost. I see our gallant army flying for many a league. To horse, my lord abbot! To horse, Roland! My gracious liege, to horse! Ere this, we should have ridden a mile."

"Look on these features," said Mary, pointing to the dying knight, who had been unhelmed by some compassionate hand—"look there, and tell me if she who ruins all who love her ought to fly a foot farther to save her wretched life!"

The reader must have long anticipated the discovery which the Queen's feelings had made before her eyes confirmed it. It was the features of the unhappy George Douglas, on which death was stamping his mark.

"Look—look at him well," said the Queen, "thus has it been with all that loved Mary Stuart! The royalty of Francis, the wit of Chastelar, the power and gallantry of the gay Gordon, the melody of Rizzio, the portly form and youthful grace of Darnley, the bold address and courtly manners of Bothwell, and now the deep-devoted passion of the noble Douglas—naught could save them: they looked on the wretched Mary, and to have loved her was crime enough to deserve early death! No sooner had the victim formed a kind thought of me than the poisoned cup, the ax and block, the dagger, the mine were ready to punish them for casting away affection on such a wretch as I am! Importune me not: I will fly no farther. I can die but once, and I will die here."

While she spoke, her tears fell fast on the face of the dying man, who continued to fix his eyes on her with an eagerness of passion which death itself could hardly subdue. "Mourn not for me," he said faintly, "but care for your own safety. I die in mine armor as a Douglas should, and I die pitied by Mary Stuart!"

He expired with these words, and without withdrawing his eyes from her face; and the Queen, whose heart was of that soft and gentle mold which in domestic life, and with a more suitable partner than Darnley, might have made her happy, remained weeping by the dead man, until recalled to herself by the abbot, who found it necessary to use a style of unusual remonstrance. "We also, madam," he said—"we, your Grace's devoted followers, have friends and relatives to weep for. I leave a brother in imminent jeopardy—the husband of the Lady Fleming—the father and brother of the Lady Catherine, are all in yonder bloody field, slain, it is to be feared, or prisoners. We forget the fate of our own nearest and dearest to wait on our Queen, and she is too much occupied with her own sorrows to give one thought to ours."

"I deserve not your reproach, father," said the Queen, checking her tears; "but I am docile to it. Where must we go? what must we do?"

"We must fly, and that instantly," said the abbot; "whither is not so easily answered, but we may dispute it upon the road. Lift her to her saddle, and set forward."*

They set off accordingly. Roland lingered a moment to command the attendants of the Knight of Avenel to convey their master to the Castle of Crookstone, and to say that he demanded from him no other condition of liberty than his word that he and his followers would keep secret the direction in which the Queen fled. As he turned his rein to depart, the honest countenance of Adam Woodcock stared upon him with an expression of surprise which, at another time, would have excited his hearty mirth. He had been one of the followers who had experienced the weight of Roland's arm, and they now knew each other, Roland having put up his visor, and the good yeoman having thrown away his barret-cap, with the iron bars in front, that he might the more readily assist his master. Into this barret-cap, as it lay on the ground, Roland forgot not to drop a few gold pieces (fruits of the Queen's liberality), and with a signal of kind recollection and enduring friendship, he departed at full gallop to overtake the Queen, the dust raised by her train being already far down the hill.

"It is not fairy money," said honest Adam, weighing and handling the gold. "And it was Master Roland himself, that is a certain thing. The same open hand, and by Our Lady! (shrugging his shoulders) the same ready fist! My lady will hear of this gladly, for she mourns for him as if he were her son. And to see how gay he is! But these light lads are as sure to be uppermost as the froth to be on the top of the quart-pot. Your man of solid parts remains ever a falconer." So saying, he went to aid his comrades, who had now come up in greater numbers, to carry his master into the Castle of Crookstone.

* See Battle of Langside. Note 27.

CHAPTER XXXVIII

My native land, good-night!
BYRON.

MANY a bitter tear was shed during the hasty flight of Queen Mary, over fallen hopes, future prospects, and slaughtered friends. The deaths of the brave Douglas and of the fiery but gallant young Seyton seemed to affect the Queen as much as the fall from the throne, on which she had so nearly been again seated. Catherine Seyton devoured in secret her own grief, anxious to support the broken spirits of her mistress; and the abbot, bending his troubled thoughts upon futurity, endeavored in vain to form some plan which had a shadow of hope. The spirit of young Roland—for he also mingled in the hasty debates held by the companions of the Queen's flight—continued unchecked and unbroken.

"Your Majesty," he said, "has lost a battle. Your ancestor Bruce lost seven successively, ere he sat triumphant on the Scottish throne, and proclaimed with the voice of a victor, in the field of Bannockburn, the independence of his country. Are not these heaths, which we may traverse at will, better than the locked, guarded, and lake-moated Castle of Lochleven? We are free; in that one word there is comfort for all our losses."

He struck a bold note, but the heart of Mary made no response.

"Better," she said, "I had still been in Lochleven than seen the slaughter made by rebels among the subjects who offered themselves to death for my sake. Speak not to me of further efforts; they would only cost the lives of you, the friends who recommend them! I would not again undergo what I felt when I saw from yonder mount the swords of the fell horsemen of Morton raging among the faithful Seytons and Hamiltons, for their loyalty to their Queen; I would not again feel what I felt when Douglas's life-blood stained my mantle for his love to Mary Stuart—not to be empress of all that Britain's seas inclose. Find for me some place where I can hide my unhappy head, which brings destruction on all who love it ; it is the last favor that Mary asks of her faithful followers."

In this dejected mood, but still pursuing her flight with unabated rapidity, the unfortunate Mary, after having been joined by Lord Herries and a few followers, at length halted, for the first time, at the Abbey of Dundrennan, nearly sixty miles distant from the field of battle. In this remote corner of Galloway, the reformation not having yet been strictly enforced against the monks, a few still lingered in their cells unmolested ; and the prior, with tears and reverence, received the fugitive Queen at the gate of his convent.

"I bring you ruin, my good father," said the Queen, as she was lifted from her palfrey.

"It is welcome," said the prior, "if it comes in the train of duty."

Placed on the ground, and supported by her ladies, the Queen looked for an instant at her palfrey, which, jaded and drooping its head, seemed as if it mourned the distresses of its mistress.

"Good Roland," said the Queen, whispering, "let Rosabelle be cared for : ask thy heart, and it will tell thee why I make this trifling request even in this awful hour."

She was conducted to her apartment, and in the hurried consultation of her attendants the fatal resolution of the retreat to England was finally adopted. In the morning it received her approbation, and a messenger was despatched to the English warden, to pray him for safe conduct and hospitality, on the part of the Queen of Scotland. On the next day, the Abbot Ambrose walked in the garden of the abbey with Roland, to whom he expressed his disapprobation of the course pursued. "It is madness and ruin," he said : "better commit herself to the savage Highlanders or wild Bordermen than to the faith of Elizabeth. A woman to a rival woman a presumptive successor to the keeping of a jealous and —childless queen ! Roland, Herries is true and loyal, but his counsel has ruined his mistress."

"Ay, ruin follows us everywhere," said an old man, with a spade in his hand, and dressed like a lay-brother, of whose presence, in the vehemence of his exclamation, the abbot had not been aware. "Gaze not on me with such wonder ! I am he who was the Abbot Boniface at Kennaquhair, who was the gardener Blinkhoolie at Lochleven, hunted round to the place in which I served my noviciate, and now ye are come to rouse me up again ! A weary life I have had, for one to whom peace was ever the dearest blessing !"

"We will soon rid you of our company, good father," said the abbot; "and the Queen will, I fear, trouble your retreat no more."

"Nay, you said as much before," said the querulous old man, "and yet I was put forth from Kinross, and pillaged by troopers on the road. They took from me the certificate that you wot of—that of the baron; ay, he was a moss-trooper like themselves. You asked me of it, and I could never find it, but they found it; it showed the marriage of—of—my memory fails me. Now see how men differ! Father Nicolas would have told you an hundred tales of the Abbot Ingelram, on whose soul God have mercy! He was, I warrant you, fourscore and six, and I am not more than—let me see——"

"Was not 'Avenel' the name you seek, my good father?" said Roland, impatiently, yet moderating his tone for fear of alarming or offending the infirm old man.

"Ay, right—Avenel—Julian Avenel. You are perfect in the name. I kept all the special confessions, judging it held with my vow to do so. I could not find it when my successor, Ambrosius, spoke on't; but the troopers found it, and the knight who commanded the party struck his breast till his hauberk clattered like an empty watering-can."

"St. Mary!" said the abbot, "in whom could such a paper excite such interest? What was the appearance of the knight, his arms, his colors?"

"Ye distract me with your questions. I dared hardly look at him; they charged me with bearing letters for the Queen, and searched my mail. This was all along of your doings at Lochleven."

"I trust in God," said the abbot to Roland, who stood beside him, shivering and trembling with impatience, "the paper has fallen into the hands of my brother. I heard he had been with his followers on the scout betwixt Stirling and Glasgow. Bore not the knight a holly-bough in his helmet? Canst thou not remember?"

"O, remember—remember," said the old man, pettishly; "count as many years as I do, if your plots will let you, and see what, and how much, you remember. Why, I scarce remember the pearmains which I graffed here with my own hands some fifty years since."

At this moment a bugle sounded loudly from the beach.

"It is the death-blast to Queen Mary's royalty!" said Ambrosius: "the English warden's answer has been received—favorable, doubtless, for when was the door of the trap closed against the prey which it was set for? Droop not, Roland, this matter shall be shifted to the bottom; but we must not now leave the Queen. Follow me; let us do our duty, and trust the issue with God. Farewell, good father; I will visit thee again soon."

He was about to leave the garden, followed by Roland, with half-reluctant steps. The ex-abbot resumed his spade.

"I could be sorry for these men," he said, "ay, and for that poor queen, but what avail earthly sorrows to a man of fourscore? and it is a rare dropping morning for the early colewort."

"He is stricken with age," said Ambrosius, as he dragged Roland down to the sea-beach; "we must let him take his time to collect himself. Nothing now can be thought on but the fate of the Queen."

They soon arrived where she stood, surrounded by her little train, and by her side the sheriff of Cumberland, a gentleman of the house of Lowther, richly dressed, and accompanied by soldiers. The aspect of the Queen exhibited a singular mixture of alacrity and reluctance to depart. Her language and gestures spoke hope and consolation to her attendants, and she seemed desirous to persuade even herself that the step she adopted was secure, and that the assurance she had received of kind reception was altogether satisfactory; but her quivering lip and unsettled eye betrayed at once her anguish at departing from Scotland and her fears of confiding herself to the doubtful faith of England.

"Welcome, my lord abbot," she said, speaking to Ambrosius, "and you, Roland Avenel, we have joyful news for you: our loving sister's officer proffers us, in her name, a safe asylum from the rebels who have driven us from our own; only it grieves me we must here part from you for a short space."

"Part from us, madam!" said the abbot. "Is your welcome in England, then, to commence with the abridgement of your train and dismissal of your counselors?"

"Take it not thus, good father," said Mary; "the warden and the sheriff, faithful servants of our royal sister, deem it necessary to obey her instructions in the present case, even to the letter, and can only take upon them to admit me with my female attendants. An express will instantly be despatched from London, assigning me a place of residence; and I will speedily send to all of you whenever my court shall be formed."

"Your court formed in England! and while Elizabeth

lives and reigns?" said the abbot; "that will be when we shall see two suns in one heaven!"

"Do not think so," replied the Queen; "we are well assured of our sister's good faith. Elizabeth loves fame; and not all that she has won by her power and her wisdom will equal that which she will acquire by extending her hospitality to a distressed sister; not all that she may hereafter do of good, wise, and great, would blot out the reproach of abusing our confidence. Farewell, my page—now my knight—farewell for a brief season. I will dry the tears of Catherine, or I will weep with her till neither of us can weep longer." She held out her hand to Roland, who, flinging himself on his knees, kissed it with much emotion. He was about to render the same homage to Catherine, when the Queen, assuming an air of sprightliness, said, "Her lips thou foolish boy! and, Catherine, coy it not; these English gentlemen should see that, even in our cold clime, beauty knows how to reward bravery and fidelity!"

"We are not now to learn, the force of Scottish beauty, or the mettle of Scottish valor," said the sheriff of Cumberland, courteously. "I would it were in my power to bid these attendants upon her who is herself the mistress of Scottish beauty as welcome to England as my poor cares would make them. But our Queen's orders are positive in case of such an emergence, and they must not be disputed by her subject. May I remind your Majesty that the tide ebbs fast?"

The sheriff took the Queen's hand, and she had already placed her foot on the gangway by which she was to enter the skiff, when the abbot, starting from a trance of grief and astonishment at the words of the sheriff, rushed into the water, and seized upon her mantle.

"She foresaw it!—she foresaw it!" he exclaimed—"she foresaw your flight into her realm; and, foreseeing it, gave orders you should be thus received. Blinded, deceived, doomed princess! your fate is sealed when you quit this strand. Queen of Scotland thou shalt not leave thine heritage!" he continued, holding a still firmer grasp upon her mantle; "true men shall turn rebels to thy will, that they may save thee from captivity or death. Fear not the bills and bows whom that gay man has at his beck: we will withstand him by force. O, for the arm of my warlike brother! Roland Avenel, draw thy sword!"

The Queen stood irresolute and frightened—one foot upon the plank, the other on the sand of her native shore, which she was quitting forever.

"What needs this violence, sir priest?" said the sheriff of Cumberland. "I came hither at your Queen's command, to do her service; and I will depart at her least order, if she rejects such aid as I can offer. No marvel is it if our Queen's wisdom foresaw that such chance as this might happen amidst the turmoils of yon unsettled state; and, while willing to afford fair hospitality to her royal sister, deemed it wise to prohibit the entrance of a broken army of her followers into the English frontier."

"You hear," said Queen Mary, gently unloosing her robe from the abbot's grasp, "that we exercise full liberty of choice in leaving this shore; and, questionless, the choice will remain free to us in going to France, or returning to our own dominions, as we shall determine. Besides, it is too late. Your blessing, father, and God speed thee!"

"May He have mercy on thee, Princess, and speed thee also!" said the abbot, retreating. "But my soul tells me I look on thee for the last time!"

The sails were hoisted, the oars were plied, the vessel went freshly on her way through the firth, which divides the shores of Cumberland from those of Galloway; but not till the vessel diminished to the size of a child's frigate did the doubtful, and dejected, and dismissed followers of the Queen cease to linger on the sands; and long, long could they discern the kerchief of Mary, as she waved the oft-repeated signal of adieu to her faithful adherents and to the shores of Scotland.

If good tidings of a private nature could have consoled Roland for parting with his mistress, and for the distresses of his sovereign, he received such comfort some days subsequent to the Queen's leaving Dundrennan. A breathless post—no other than Adam Woodcock—brought despatches from Sir Halbert Glendinning to the abbot, whom he found with Roland, still residing at Dundrennan, and in vain torturing Boniface with fresh interrogations. The packet bore an earnest invitation to his brother to make Avenel Castle for a time his residence. "The clemency of the Regent," said the writer, "has extended pardon both to Roland and to you, upon condition of your remaining a time under my wardship. And I have that to communicate respecting the parentage of Roland which not only you will willingly listen to, but which will be also found to afford me, as the husband of his nearest relative, some interest in the future course of his life."

The abbot read this letter, and paused, as if considering what were best for him to do. Meanwhile, Woodcock took Roland aside, and addressed him as follows: "Now look, Master Roland, that you do not let any Papistrie nonsense lure either the priest or you from the right quarry. See you, you ever bore yourself as a bit of a gentleman. Read that, and thank God that threw old Abbot Boniface in our way, as two of the Seyton's men were conveying him towards Dundrennan here. We searched him for intelligence concerning that fair exploit of yours at Lochleven, that has cost many a man his life, and me a set of sore bones, and we found what is better for your purpose than ours."

The paper which he gave was, indeed, an attestation by Father Philip, subscribing himself unworthy sacristan and brother of the house of St. Mary's, stating, "That under a vow of secrecy he had united, in the holy sacrament of marriage, Julian Avenel and Catherine Græme; but that Julian having repented of his union, he, Father Philip, had been sinfully prevailed on by him to conceal and disguise the same according to a complot devised betwixt him and the said Julian Avenel, whereby the poor damsel was induced to believe that the ceremony had been performed by one not in holy orders, and having no authority to that effect; which sinful concealment the undersigned conceived to be the cause why he was abandoned to the misguiding of a water fiend, whereby he had been under a spell, which obliged him to answer every question, even touching the most solemn matters, with idle snatches of old songs, besides being sorely afflicted with rheumatic pains ever after. Wherefore he had deposited this testificate and confession, with the day and date of the said marriage, with his lawful superior, Boniface, abbot of St. Mary's, *sub sigillo confessionis*."

It appeared by a letter from Julian, folded carefully up with the certificate, that the Abbot Boniface had, in effect, bestirred himself in the affair, and obtained from the baron a promise to avow his marriage; but the death of both Julian and his injured bride, together with the abbot's resignation, his ignorance of the fate of their unhappy offspring, and, above all, the good father's listless and inactive disposition, had suffered the matter to become totally forgotten, until it was recalled by some accidental conversation with the Abbot Ambrosius concerning the fortunes of the Avenel family. At the request of his snccessor, the quondam abbot made search for it; but, as he would receive no assistance in looking among the few records of spiritual experiences and important confessions which he had conscientiously treasured, it might have remained forever hidden amongst them but for the more active researches of Sir Halbert Glendinning.

"So that you are like to be heir of Avenel at last, Master Roland, after my lord and lady have gone to their place," said Adam; "and as I have but one boon to ask, I trust you will not nick me with nay."

"Not if it be in my power to say 'yes,' my trusty friend."

"Why then, I must needs, if I live to see that day, keep on feeding the eyases with unwashed flesh," said Woodcock, sturdily, yet as if doubting the reception that his request might meet with.

"Thou shalt feed them with what you list for me," said Roland, laughing; "I am not many months older than when I left the castle, but I trust I have gathered wit enough to cross no man of skill in his own vocation."

"Then I would not change places with the King's falconer," said Adam Woodcock, "nor with the Queen's neither; but they say she will be mewed up, and never need one. I see it grieves you to think of it, and I could grieve for company; but what help for it? Fortune will fly her own flight, let a man halloo himself hoarse."

The abbot and Roland journeyed to Avenel, where the former was tenderly received by his brother, while the lady wept for joy to find that in her favorite orphan she had protected the sole surviving branch of her own family. Sir Halbert Glendinning and his household were not a little surprised at the change which a brief acquaintance with the world had produced in their former inmate, and rejoiced to find in the pettish, spoiled, and presuming page a modest and unassuming young man, too much acquainted with his own expectations and character to be hot or petulant in demanding the consideration which was readily and voluntarily yielded to him. The old major-domo Wingate was the first to sing his praises, to which Mrs. Lilias bore a loud echo, always hoping that God would teach him the true Gospel.

To the true Gospel the heart of Roland had secretly long inclined, and the departure of the good abbot for France, with the purpose of entering into some house of his order in that kingdom, removed his chief objection to renouncing the Cotholic faith. Another might have existed in the duty which he owed to Magdalen Græme, both by birth and from gratitude. But he learned, ere he had been long a resident in Avenel, that his grandmother had died at Cologne, in the performance of a penance too severe for her age, which she had taken upon herself in behalf of the Queen and Church of Scotland, so soon as she heard of the defeat at Langside. The zeal of the Abbot Ambrosius was more regulated; but he retired into the Scottish convent of——, and so lived there that the fraternity were inclined to claim for him the honors of canonisation. But he guessed their purpose, and prayed them on his death-bed to do no honors to the body of one as sinful as themselves; but to send his body and his heart to be buried in Avenel burial-aisle, in the Monastery of St. Mary's, that the last abbot of that celebrated house of devotion might sleep among its ruins.*

Long before that period arrived, Roland Avenel was wedded to Catherine Seyton, who, after two years' residence with her unhappy mistress, was dismissed, upon her being subjected to closer restraint than had been at first exercised. She returned to her father's house and as Roland was acknowledged for the successor and lawful heir of the ancient house of Avenel, greatly increased as the estate was by the providence of Sir Halbert Glendinning, there occurred no objections to the match on the part of her family. Her mother was recently dead when she first entered the convent; and her father, in the unsettled times which followed Queen Mary's flight to England, was not averse to an alliance with a youth who, himself loyal to Queen Mary, still held some influence, through means of Sir Halbert Glendinning, with the party in power.

Roland and Catherine, therefore, were united, spite of their differing faiths; and the White Lady, whose apparition had been infrequent when the house of Avenel seemed verging to extinction, was seen to sport by her haunted well, with a zone of gold around her bosom as broad as the baldrick of an earl.

*** See Burial of the Abbot's Heart in the Avenel Aisle. Note 28.**

NOTES TO THE ABBOT

Note 1.—Glendonwyne of Glendonwyne, p. 26

This was a house of ancient descent and superior consequence, including persons who fought at Bannockburn and Otterburn, and closely connected by alliance and friendship with the great Earls of Douglas. The knight in the story argues as most Scotsmen would do in his situation, for all of the same clan are popularly considered as descended from the same stock, and as having a right to the ancestral honor of the chief branch. This opinion, though sometimes ideal, is so strong, even at this day of innovation, that it may be observed as a national difference between my countrymen and the English. If you ask an Englishman of good birth whether a person of the same name be connected with him, he answers, if *in dubio*, "No, he is a mere namesake." Ask a similar question of a Scot—I mean a Scotsman—he replies, "He is one of our clan; I daresay there is a relationship, though I do not know how distant." The Englishman thinks of discountenancing a species of rivalry in Society; the Scotsman's answer is grounded on the ancient idea of strengthening the clan.

Note 2.—Bag for Hawks' Meat, p. 64

This same bag, like everything belonging to falconry, was esteemed an honorable distinction, and worn often by the nobility and gentry. One of the Somervilles of Camnethan was called Sir John with the Red Bag, because it was his wont to wear his hawking-pouch covered with satin of that color.

Note 3.—Cell of St. Cuthbert, p. 68

I may here observe, that this is entirely an ideal scene. St. Cuthbert, a person of established sanctity, had, no doubt, several places of worship on the Borders, where he flourished whilst living; but Tilmouth Chapel is the only one which bears some resemblance to the hermitage described in the text. It has, indeed, a well, famous for gratifying three wishes for every worshiper who shall quaff the fountain with sufficient belief in its efficacy. At this spot the saint is said to have landed in his stone coffin, in which he sailed down the Tweed from Melrose, and here the stone coffin long lay, in evidence of the fact. The late Sir Francis Blake Delaval is said to have taken the exact measure of the coffin, and to have ascertained, by hydrostatic principles, that it might have actually swum. A profane farmer in the neighborhood announced his intention of converting this last bed of the saint into a trough for his swine; but the profanation was rendered impossible, either by the saint or by some pious votary in his behalf, for on the following morning the stone sarcophagus was found broken in two fragments.

Tilmouth Chapel, with these points of resemblance, lies, however, in exactly the opposite direction as regards Melrose which the supposed cell of St. Cuthbert is said to have borne towards Kennaquhair.

Note 4.—Goss-hawk, p. 81

The comparison is taken from some beautiful verses in an old ballad, entitled "Fause Foodrage," published in the *Minstrelsy of the Scottish Border*. A deposed queen, to preserve her infant son from the traitors who have slain his father, exchanges him with the female offspring of a faithful friend, and goes on to direct the education of the children, and the private signals by which the parents are to hear news each of her own offspring.

And ye maun learn my gay goss-hawk
  Right weel to breast a steed;
And I sall learn your turtle dow,
  As weel to write and read.

And ye maun learn my gay goss-hawk
  To wield both bow and brand;
And I sall learn your turtle dow,
  To lay gowd wi' her hand.

At kirk and market when we meet,
  We'll dare make nae avowe,
But, "Dame, how does my gay goss-hawk?"
  "Madame, how does my dow?"

NOTE 5.—NUNNERY OF ST. BRIDGET, p. 101

This, like the cell of St. Cuthbert, is an imaginary scene; but I took one or two ideas of the desolation of the interior from a story told me by my father. In his youth—it may be near eighty years since, as he was born in 1729—he had occasion to visit an old lady who resided in a Border castle of considerable renown. Only one very limited portion of the extensive ruins sufficed for the accommodation of the inmates, and my father amused himself by wandering through the part that was untenanted. In a dining apartment, having a roof richly adorned with arches and drops, there was deposited a large stack of hay, to which calves were helping themselves from opposite sides. As my father was scaling a dark, ruinous turnpike staircase, his greyhound ran up before him, and probably was the means of saving his life, for the animal fell through a trap-door, or aperture in the stair, thus warning the owner of the danger of the ascent. As the dog continued howling from a great depth, my father got the old butler, who alone knew most of the localities about the castle, to unlock a sort of stable, in which Killbuck was found safe and sound, the place being filled with the same commodity which littered the stalls of Augeas, and which had rendered the dog's fall an easy one.

NOTE 6.—NUN OF KENT, p. 106

A fanatic nun, called the Holy Maid of Kent, who pretended to the gift of prophecy and power of miracles. Having denounced the doom of speedy death against Henry VIII. for his marriage with Anne Boleyn, the prophetess was attainted in Parliament, and executed, with her accomplices. Her imposture was for a time so successful that even Sir Thomas More was disposed to be a believer

NOTE 7.—HUNTING MASS, p. 114

In Catholic countries, in order to reconcile the pleasures of the great with the observances of religion, it was common, when a party was bent for the chase, to celebrate mass, abridged and maimed of its rites, called a hunting mass, the brevity of which was designed to correspond with the impatience of the audience.

NOTE 8.—ABBOT OF UNREASON, p. 116.

We learn, from no less authority than that of Napoleon Bonaparte, that there is but a single step between the sublime and ridiculous; and it is a transition from one extreme to another so very easy that the vulgar of every degree are peculiarly captivated with it. Thus the inclination to laugh becomes uncontrollable when the solemnity and gravity of time, place, and circumstances render it peculiarly improper. Some species of general license, like that which inspired the ancient Saturnalia, or the modern Carnival, has been commonly indulged to the people at all times, and in almost all countries. But it was, I think, peculiar to the Roman Catholic Church that, while they studied how to render their church rites imposing and magnificent, by all that pomp, music, architecture, and external display could add to them, they nevertheless connived, upon special occasions, at the frolics of the rude vulgar, who, in almost all Catholic countries, enjoyed, or at least assumed, the privilege of making some lord of the revels, who, under the name of the Abbot of Unreason, the Boy Bishop, or the President of Fools, occupied the churches, profaned the holy places by a mock imitation of the sacred rites, and sung indecent parodies on hymns of the church. The indifference of the clergy, even when their power was greatest, to the indecent exhibitions which they always tolerated, and sometimes encouraged, forms a strong contrast to the sensitiveness with which they regarded any serious attempt, by preaching or writing, to impeach any of the doctrines of the church. It could only be compared to the singular apathy with which they endured, and often admired, the gross novels which Chaucer, Dunbar, Boccaccio, Bandello, and others composed upon the bad morals of the clergy. It seems as if the churchmen in both instances had endeavored to compromise with the laity, and allowed them occasionallyto gratify their coarse humor by indecent satire, provided they would abstain from any grave question concerning the foundation of the doctrines on which was erected such an immense fabric of ecclesiastical power.

But the sports thus licensed assumed a very different appearance so soon as the Protestant doctrines began to prevail; and the license which their forefathers had exercised in mere gaiety of heart, and without the least intention of dishonoring religion by their frolics, was now persevered in by the common people as a mode of testifying their utter disregard for the Roman priesthood and its ceremonics.

I may observe, for example, the case of an apparitor sent to Borthwick from the Primate of St. Andrews, to cite the lord of that castle, who was opposed by an Abbot of Unreason, at whose command the officer of the spiritual court was appointed to be ducked in a mill-dam, and obliged to eat up his parchment citation.

The reader may be amused with the following whimsical details of this incident, which took place in the castle of Borthwick, in the year 1547. It appears that, in consequence of a process betwixt Master George Hay de Minzeane and the Lord Borthwick, letters of excommunication had passed against the latter, on account of the contumacy of certain witnesses. William Langlands, an apparitor or macer (*bacularius*) of the see of St. Andrews, presented these letters to the curate of the church of Borthwick, requiring him to publish the same at the service of high mass. It seems that the inhabitants of the castle were at this time engaged in the favorite sport of enacting the Abbot of Unreason, a species of high jinks, in which a mimic prelate was elected, who, like the Lord of Misrule in England, turned all sort of lawful authority, and particularly the church ritual, into ridicule. This frolicsome person, with his retinue, notwithstanding of the apparitor's character, entered the church, seized upon the Primate's officer without hesitation, and, dragging him to the mill-dam on the south side of the castle, compelled him to leap into the water. Not contented with this partial immersion, the Abbot of Unreason pronounced that Mr. William Langlands was not yet sufficiently bathed, and therefore caused his assistants to lay him on his back in the stream, and duck him in the most satisfactory and perfect manner. The unfortunate apparitor was then conducted back to the church, where, for his refreshment after his bath, the letters of excommunication were torn to pieces, and steeped in a bowl of wine; the mock abbot being probably of opinion that a tough parchment was but dry eating, Langlands was compelled to eat the letters and swallow the wine, and dismissed by the Abbot of Unreason, with the comfortable assurance that, if any more such letters should arrive during the continuance of his office, " they should a' gang the same gate," *i.e.* go the same road.

A similar scene occurs betwixt a sumner of the Bishop of Rochester and Harpool, the servant of Lord Cobham, in the old play of *Sir John Oldcastle*, when the former compels the church-officer to eat his citation. The dialogue contains most of the jests which may be supposed appropriate to such an extraordinary occasion.

Harpool. Marry, sir, is this process parchment?
Sumner. Yes, marry is it.
Harpool, And this seal wax?
Sumner. It is so.
Harpool. If this be parchment, and this be wax, eat you this parchment and wax, or I will make parchment of your skin, and beat your brains into wax. Sirrah Sumner, despatch—devour, sirrah, devour.
Sumner. I am my Lord of Rochester's sumner; I came to do my office, and thou shalt answer it.
Harpool. Sirrah, no railing, but betake thyself to thy teeth. Thou shalt eat no worse than thou bringest with thee. Thou bringest it for my lord; and wilt thou bring my lord worse than thou wilt eat thyself?
Sumner. Sir, I brought it not my lord to eat.
Harpool. O, do you Sir me now? All's one for that; I'll make you eat it for bringing it.
Sumner. I cannot eat it.
Harpool. Can you not? 'Sblood, I'll beat you till you have a stomach! [*Beats him.*]
Sumner. Oh, hold, hold, good Mr. Serving-man; I will eat it.

Harpool. Be champing, be chewing, sir, or I will chew you, you rogue. Tough wax is the purest of the honey.
Sumner. The purest of the honey! O Lord, sir! oh! oh!
Harpool. Feed, feed; 'tis wholesome, rogue—wholesome. Cannot you, like an honest sumner, walk with the devil your brother, to fetch in your bailiff's rents, but you must come to a nobleman's house with process? If the seal were as broad as the lead which covers Rochester Church, thou shouldst eat it.
Sumner. Oh, I am almost choked—I am almost choked!
Harpool. Who's within there? will you shame my lord? is there no beer in the house? Butler, I say.

Enter BUTLER.

Butler. Here—here.
Harpool. Give him beer. Tough old sheep-skin's but dry meat.

First Part of Sir John Oldcastle, Act ii. Scene 1.

NOTE 9.—THE HOBBY-HORSE, p. 117

This exhibition, the play-mare of Scotland, stood high among holyday gambols. It must be carefully separated from the wooden chargers which furnish out our nurseries. It gives rise to Hamlet's ejaculation—

But oh, but oh, the hobby-horse is forgot!

There is a very comic scene in Beaumont and Fletcher's play of *Women Pleased*, where Hope-on-high Bomby, a Puritan cobbler, refuses to dance with the hobby-horse. There was much difficulty and great variety in the motions which the hobby-horse was expected to exhibit.

The learned Mr. Douce, who has contributed so much to the illustration of our theatrical antiquities, has given us a full account of this pageant, and the burlesque horsemanship which it practised.

"The hobby-horse," says Mr. Douce, "was represented by a man equipped with as much pasteboard as was sufficient to form the head and hinder parts of a horse, the quadrupedal defects being concealed by a long mantle or foot-cloth that nearly touched the ground. The performer, on this occasion, exerted all his skill in burlesque horsemanship. In Sampson's play of the *Vow-breaker*, 1636, a miller personates the hobby-horse, and being angry that the mayor of the city is put in competition with him, exclaims, 'Let the major [mayor] play the hobby-horse among his brethren, an he will; I hope our town-lads cannot want a hobby-horse. Have I practised my reins, my careers, my pranckers, my ambles, my false trots, my smooth ambles, and Canterbury paces, and shall master major put me besides the hobby-horse? Have I borrowed the forehorse bells, his plumes, his braveries; nay, had his mane new shorn and frizzled, and shall the major put me besides the hobby-horse'"—Douce's *Illustrations*, vol. ii. p. 468.

NOTE 10.—REPRESENTATION OF ROBIN HOOD AND LITTLE JOHN, p. 118

The representation of Robin Hood was the darling May-game both in England and Scotland, and doubtless the favorite personification was often revived, when the Abbot of Unreason, or other pretenses of frolic, gave an unusual degree of license.

The Protestant clergy, who had formerly reaped advantage from the opportunities which these sports afforded them of directing their own satire and the ridicule of the lower orders against the Catholic Church, began to find that, when these purposes were served, their favorite pastimes deprived them of the wish to attend divine worship, and disturbed the frame of mind in which it can be attended to advantage. The celebrated Bishop Latimer gives a very naive account of the manner in which, bishop as he was, he found himself compelled to give place to Robin Hood and his followers.

"I came once myselfe to a place riding on a journey homeward from London, and I sent word over night into the towne that I would preach there in the morning, because it was holiday, and methought it was a holidayes worke. The church stood in my way, and I tooke my horse and my company and went thither (I thought I should have found a great company in the church), and when I came there the church doore was fast locked. I tarryed there halfe an houre and more. At last the key was found, and one of the parish comes to me, and says, 'Sir, this is a busie day with us, we cannot heare you; it is Robin Hood's day. The parish are gone abroad to gather for Robin Hood. I pray you let them not.' I was faine there to give place to Robin Hood. I thought my rochet should have been regarded though I was not but it would not serve, it was faine to give place to Robin Hood's men. It is no laughing matter, my friends; it is weeping matter, a heavy matter—a heavy matter. Under the pretense for gathering for Robin

Hood, a traytour and a theafe, to put out a preacher, to have his office lesse esteemed, to preferre Robin Hood before the ministration of God's Word; and all this hath come of unpreaching prelates. This realme hath been ill provided for, that it hath had such corrupt judgments in it, to preferre Robin Hood to God's Word."—*Bishop Latimer's Sixth Sermon before King Edward VI.*

While the English Protestants thus preferred the outlaw's pageant to the preaching of their excellent bishop, the Scottish Calvinistic clergy, with the celebrated John Knox at their head, and backed by the authority of the magistrates of Edinburgh, who had of late been chosen exclusively from this party, found it impossible to control the rage of the populace, when they attempted to deprive them of the privilege of presenting their pageant of Robin Hood.

(1561). "Vpon the xxi day of Julij Archibalde Dowglas of Kilspindie, Provest of Edr., David Symmer and Adame Fullartoun, bailies of the samyne, causit ane cordinare servant, callit James Gillioun [or Killone], takin of befoir, for playing in Edr. with Robene Hude, to wnderly the law, and put him to the knawlege of ane assyize, qlk yaij haid electit of yair favoraris, quha with schort deliberatioun condemnit him to be hangit for ye said cryme. And the deaconis of ye craftisman, fearing vproare, maid great solistatiouns at ye handis of ye said provest and baillies, and als requirit John Knox, minister, for eschewing of tumult, to superceid ye executioun of him, vnto ye tyme yai suld adverteis my Lord Duke yairof. And yan, if it wes his mynd and will yat he should be disponit vpoun, ye said deaconis and craftisman sould convey him yaire; quha answerit, yat yai culd na way stope ye executioun of justice. Quhan ye time of ye said pouer mans hanging approchit, and yat he hangman wes cum to ye jibbat with ye ledder, vpoune ye qlk ye said cordinare should have bene hangit, ane certaine and remanent craftischilder, quha wes put to ye horne with ye said Gillione, ffor ye said Robene Hiude's *playes*, and vyris yair assistaris and favoraris, past to wappinis, and yai brak down ye said jibbat, and yan chacit ye said provest, baillies, and Alexr. Guthrie, in ye said Alexander's writing-buith, and held yame yairin; and yairefter past to ye tolbuyt, and becaus the samyne was steiklt, and onnawayes culd get the keyes thairof, thai brake the said tolbuith dore with foure hamberis per force (the said provest and baillies luikand thairon), and not onlie put thar the said Gillone to fredome and libertie, and brocht him furth of the said tolbuit, bot alsua the remanent presonaris being thairintill. And this done, the said craftismen's servands, with the said condempnit cordonar, past doun to the Nethirbow, to have past furth thairit; bot becaus the samyne on thair coming thairto wes closit, thai past vp agane the Hie Streit of the said bourghe to the Castell hill, and in this menetyme the saidis provest and baillies and thair assistaris being in the writting-buith of the said Alexr. Guthrie, past and enterit in the said tolbuyt, and in the said servandis passage vp the Hie Streit, then schote furth thairof at thame ane dog, and hvrt ane servand of the said childer. This being done, thair wes nathing vthir but the one partie schuteand out and castand stanis furth of the said tolbuyt, and the vther pairtie schuteand hagbuttis in the same agane. And sua the craftismen's servandis, abone written, held and inclosit the said provest and baillies continewallie in the said tolbuyth, frae three houris efternone quhil aught houris at even, and na man of the said town prensit [sterit] to relieve thair said provest and bailles. And than thai send to the maisters of the Castell [craftismen], to caus tham if thai mycht stay the said servandis, quha maid ane maner to doe the same, bot thai could not bring the same to ane finall end, ffor the said servand wold on nowayes stay fra, quhill thai had revengit the hurting of ane of them; and thairefter the constable of the Castell come down thairfra, and he with the said maisters treatit betwix the said pties in this maner:—That the said provest and baillies sall reniit [discharge] to the said craftischilder all actioun, cryme, and offens that thai had committit aganes thame in any tyme bygane; and band oblast thame nevir to pussew them thairfor; and als commandit thair maisters to resaue them agane in thair services, as thai did befoir. And this being proclamit at the mercat crow, thai scalit, and the said provest and baillies come furth of the same tolbuyth," etc. etc. etc.

John Knox, who writes at large upon this tumult, informs us it was inflamed by the deacons of crafts, who, resenting the superiority assumed over them by the magistrates, would yield no assistance to put down the tumult. "They will be magistrates alone," said the recusant deacons, "e'en let them rule the populace alone"; and accordingly they passed quietly to take their "four-hours penny," and left the magistrates to help themselves as they could. Many persons were excommunicated for this outrage, and not admitted to church ordinances till they had made satisfaction.

Note 11.—"The Paip, that Pagan," p. 128

These rude rhymes are taken, with trifling alterations, from a ballad called "Trim-go-trix." It occurs in a singular collection, entitled *Ane Compendious*

Booke of Godly and Spirituall Songs, Collectit out of Sundrie Parts of the Scripture, with Sundrie of other Ballates Changed out of Prophaine Sanges, for Avoyding of Sinne and Harlotrie, with Augmentation of Sundrie Gude and Godly Ballates. Edinburgh, printed by Andro Hart. This curious collection has been reprinted in Mr. John Graham Dalyell's *Scottish Poems of the 16th Century.* Edin. 1801.

NOTE 12.—INABILITY OF EVIL SPIRITS TO ENTER A HOUSE UNINVITED, p. 144

There is a popular belief respecting evil spirits, that they cannot enter an inhabited house unless invited, nay, dragged over the threshold. There is an instance of the same superstition in the *Tales of the Genii*, where an enchanter is supposed to have intruded himself into the divan of the sultan.

"'Thus,' said the illustrious Misnar, 'let the enemies of Mahomet be dismayed! but inform me, O ye sages! under the semblance of which of your brethren did that foul enchanter gain admittance here?' 'May the lord of my heart,' answered Bahilu, the hermit of the faithful from Queda,' triumph over all his foes! As I travelled on the mountains from Queda, and saw neither the footsteps of beasts, nor the flights of birds, behold, I chanced to pass through a cavern, in whose hollow sides I found this accursed sage, to whom I unfolded the invitation of the Sultan of India, and we, joining, journeyed toward the divan; but ere we entered, he said unto me, 'Put thy hand forth, and pull me toward thee into the divan, calling on the name of Mahomet, for the evil spirits are on me, and vex me.'"

I have understood that many parts of these fine tales, and in particular that of the Sultan Misnar, were taken from genuine Oriental sources by the editor, Mr. James Ridley.

But the most picturesque use of this popular belief occurs in Coleridge's beautiful and tantalizing fragment of *Christabel.* Has not our own imaginative poet cause to fear that future ages will desire to summon him from his place of rest, as Milton longed

> To call up him, who left half told
> The story of Cambuscan bold?

The verses I refer to are when Christabel conducts into her father's castle a mysterious and malevolent being, under the guise of a distressed female stranger

> They cross'd the moat, and Christabel
> Took the key that fitted well;
> A little door she open'd straight,
> All in the middle of the gate;
> The gate that was iron'd within and without,
> Where an army in battle array had march'd out.
>
> The lady sank, belike thro' pain,
> And Christabel with might and main
> Lifted her up, a weary weight,
> Over the threshold of the gate:
> Then the lady rose again,
> And moved as she were not in pain.
>
> So free from danger, free from fear,
> They cross'd the court:—right glad they were,
> And Christabel devoutly cried
> To the lady by her side:
>
> "Praise we the Virgin, all divine,
> Who hath rescued thee from thy distress."
> "Alas, alas!" said Geraldine,
> "I cannot speak for weariness."
> So free from danger, free from fear,
> They cross'd the court:—right glad they were.

NOTE 13.—SEYTON, OR SETON, p. 161

George, fifth Lord Seyton, was immovably faithful to Queen Mary during all the mutabilities of her fortune. He was grand master of the household, in which capacity he had a picture painted of himself with his official baton, and the following motto:

> In adversitate patiens;
> In prosperitate benevolus.
> Hazard, yet forward.

On various parts of his castle he inscribed, as expressing his religious and political creed, the legend

UN DIEU, UN FOY, UN ROY, UN LOY.

He declined to be promoted to an earldom, which Queen Mary offered him at the same time when she advanced her natural brother to be Earl of Mar, and afterwards of Murray.

On his refusing this honor, Mary wrote, or caused to be written, the following lines in Latin and French :—

> Sunt comites; ducesque alii, sunt denique reges ;
> Sethoni dominum sit satis esse mihi.
>
> Il y a des comptes, des roys, des ducs ; ainsi
> C'est assez pour moy d'estre Seigneur de Seton.

Which may be thus rendered :—

> Earl ,duke, or king, be thou that list to be ;
> Seton, thy lordship is enough for me.

This distich reminds us of the "pride which aped humility" in the motto of the house of Couci :

> Je suis ni roy, ni prince aussi ;
> Je suis le Seigneur de Coucy.

After the battle of Langside, Lord Seton was obliged to retire abroad for safety, and was an exile for two years, during which he was reduced to the necessity of driving a wagon in Flanders for his subsistence. He rose to favor in James VI.'s reign, and resuming his paternal property, had himself painted in his wagoner's dress, and in the act of driving a wain with four horses, on the north end of a stately gallery at Seton Castle. He appears to have been fond of the arts ; for there exists a beautiful family-piece of him in the center of his family. Mr. Pinkerton, in his *Scottish Iconographia* [1797], published an engraving of this curious portrait. The original is the property of Lord Somerville, nearly connected with the Seton family, and is at present at his lordship's fishing-villa of the Pavilion, near Melrose.

NOTE 14.—FANFARONA, p. 162

A name given to the gold chains worn by the military men of the period. It is of Spanish origin ; for the fashion of wearing these costly ornaments was much followed amongst the conquerors of the New World.

NOTE 15.—MAIDEN OF MORTON, p. 167

A species of guillotine which the Regent Morton brought down from Halifax, certainly at a period considerably later than intimated in the tale. He was himself the first that suffered by the engine.—

This instrument, which is preserved in the Antiquarian Museum of Edinburgh, was brought to Scotland several years earlier than popular tradition assigns, and is said to have been used for the execution of criminals about twenty years before the Earl of Morton was beheaded, in 1582 (*Laing*).

NOTE 16.—THE RESIGNATION OF QUEEN MARY, p. 236

The details of this remarkable event are, as given in chapter xxii., imaginary ; but the outline of the events is historical. Sir Robert Lindesay [Melville], brother to the author of the *Memoirs*, was at first entrusted with the delicate commission of persuading the imprisoned Queen to resign her crown. As he flatly refused to interfere, they determined to send the Lord Lindesay, one of the rudest and most violent of their own faction, with instructions, first to use fair persuasions, and if these did not succeed, to enter into harder terms. Knox associates Lord Ruthven with Lindesay in this alarming commission. He was the son of that Lord Ruthven who was prime agent in the murder of Rizzio ; and little mercy was to be expected from his conjunction with Lindesay.

The employment of such rude tools argued a resolution on the part of those who had the Queen's person in their power to proceed to the utmost extremities, should they find Mary obstinate. To avoid this pressing danger, Sir Robert Melville was despatched by them to Lochleven, carrying with him, concealed in the scabbard of his sword, letters to the Queen from the Earl of Athole, Maitland of Lethington, and even from Throgmorton, the English ambassador, who was then favorable to the unfortunate Mary, conjuring her to yield to the necessity of the times, and to subscribe such deeds as Lindesay should lay before her, without being startled by their tenor; and assuring her that her doing so, in the state of captivity under which she was placed, would neither, in law, honor, or conscience, be binding upon her when she should obtain her liberty. Submitting, by the advice of one part of her subjects, to the menace of the others, and learning that Lindesay was arrived in a boasting, that is, threatening, humor, the Queen, "with some reluctancy, and with tears," saith Knox, subscribed one deed resigning her crown to her infant son, and another establishing the Earl of Murray regent. It seems agreed by historians that Lindesay behaved with great brutality on the occasion. The deeds were signed 24th July 1569.

NOTE 17.—GANELON, p. 258

Gan, Gano, or Ganelon of Mayence, is, in the romances on the subject of Charlemagne and his Paladins, always represented as the traitor by whom the Christian champions are betrayed.

NOTE 18.—SCOTTISH FAIRS, p. 271

At Scottish fairs, the bailie, or magistrate, deputed by the lord in whose name the meeting is held, attends the fair with his guard, decides trifling disputes, and punishes on the spot any petty delinquencies. His attendants are usually armed with halberds, and, sometimes at least, escorted by music. Thus, in the *Life and Death of Habbie Simpson*, we are told of that famous minstrel—

At fairs he play'd before the spear-men,
And gaily graithed in their gear-men;—
Steel bonnets, jacks, and swords shone clear then,
Like ony bead.
Now wha shall play before sic weir-men,
Since Habbie's dead!

NOTE 19.—KIERY CRAIGS, p. 273

Lord Chief-Commissioner Adam, in the year 1817, formed what was called a Blair-Adam Club, consisting of Sir Walter Scott and a few other friends, who assembled once a-year at Blair-Adam House, near the shores of Lochleven. In his *Reminiscences*, the Lord Chief-Commissioner, when referring to the anonymous publication of the Waverley Novels, records the following anecdote:—"What confirmed, and was certainly meant to disclose to me the author, was the mention of the Kiery Craigs, a picturesque piece of scenery in the grounds of Blair-Adam, as being in the vicinity of Kelty Bridge, the *howff* of Auchtermuchty, the Kinross carrier. It was only an intimate friend of the family . . . who could know anything of the Kiery Craigs or its name; and both the scenery and the name had attractions for Sir Walter.

"At our first meeting after the publication of the *Abbot*, when the party was assembled on the top of the rock, the Chief-Baron Shepherd, looking Sir Walter full in the face, and stamping his staff on the ground, said, 'Now, Sir Walter, I think we be upon the top of the Kiery Craigs.' Sir Walter preserved profound silence; but there was a conscious looking down, and a considerable elongation of his upper lip."—Blair-Adam *Tracts*, 1834, p, xxxv., and Lockhart's *Life of Scott*, vol. vi. p. 264 (*Laing*).

NOTE 20.—MOTHER NICNEVEN, p. 278

This was the name given to the grand Mother Witch, the very Hecate of Scottish popular superstition. Her name was bestowed, in one or two instances, upon sorceresses, who were held to resemble her by their superior skill in "Hell's black grammar."

NOTE 21.—DARK GREY MAN, p. 299

By an ancient, though improbable, tradition the Douglasses are said to have derived their name from a champion who had greatly distinguished himself in an action. When the king demanded by whom the battle had been won, the attendants are said to have answered, "Sholto Douglas, sir;" which is said to mean, "Yonder dark gray man." But the name is undoubtedly territorial, and taken from Douglas river and dale.

NOTE 22.—SUPPOSED CONSPIRACY AGAINST THE LIFE OF MARY, p. 353

A romancer, to use a Scottish phrase, wants but a hair to make a tether of. The whole detail of the steward's supposed conspiracy against the life of Mary is grounded upon an expression in one of her letters, which affirms that Jasper Dryfesdale [James Drysdale], one of the Laird of Lochleven's servants, had threatened to murder William Douglas (for his share in the Queen's escape), and averred that he would plant a dagger in Mary's own heart.—Chalmers's *Life of Queen Mary* [1822], vol. i. p. 278

NOTE 23.—MUFFLED MAN, p. 361

Generally a diguised man; originally one who wears his cloak or mantle muffled round the lower part of the face to conceal his countenance. I have on an ancient piece of iron the representation of a robber thus accoutred, endeavoring to make his way into a house, and opposed by a mastiff, to whom he in vain offers food. The motto is *Spernit dona fides*. It is part of a fire-grate said to have belonged to Archbishop Sharp.

NOTE 24.—*THE HOWLET*, p. 376

Sir John Holland's poem of *The Howlet* is known to collectors by the beautiful edition presented to the Bannatyne Club by Mr. David Laing.—

The preface contains remarks by Sir Walter Scott, who was president of the club. The poem was composed about the middle of the 15th century, and has generally been supposed to be a satire on James II. of Scotland (*Laing*).

NOTE 25.—DEMEANOR OF QUEEN MARY, p. 380

In the dangerous expedition to Aberdeenshire, Randolph, the English ambassador, gives Cecil the following account of Queen Mary's demeanor :—

"In all these garboiles, I assure you, I never saw her [the Queen] merrier, never dismayed; nor never thought that so much to be in her that I find. She repented nothing but, when the lords and others, at Inverness, came in the morning from the watch, that she was not a man to know what life it was to lie all night in the fields, or to walk on the causeway with a jack and a knapschalle, a Glasgow buckler, and a broadsword."—RANDOLPH *to* CECIL, *September* 18, 1562.

The writer of the above letter seems to have felt the same impression which Catherine Seyton, in the text, considered as proper to the Queen's presence among her armed subjects.

"Though we neither thought nor looked for other than on that day to have fought or never—what desperate blows would not have been given, when every man should have fought in the sight of so noble a queen, and so many fair ladies, our enemies to have taken them from us, and we to save our honors, not to be reft of them, your honor can easily judge!"—*The same to the same* [condensed], *September* 23, 1562.

NOTE 26.—ESCAPE OF QUEEN MARY FROM LOCHLEVEN, p. 383

It is well known that the escape of Queen Mary from Lochleven was effected by George Douglas, the youngest brother of Sir William Douglas, the lord of the castle; but the minute circumstances of the event have been a good deal confused, owing to two agents having been concerned in it who bore the same name. It has been always supposed that George Douglas was induced to abet Mary's escape by the ambitious hope that, by such service, he might merit her hand. But his purpose was discovered by his brother Sir William, and he was expelled from the castle. He continued, notwithstanding, to hover in the neighborhood, and maintain a correspondence with the royal prisoner and others in the fortress.

If we believe the English ambassador Drury, the Queen was grateful to George Douglas, and even proposed a marriage with him—a scheme which could hardly be serious, since she was still the wife of Bothwell, but which, if suggested at all, might be with a purpose of gratifying the Regent Murray's ambition, and propitiating his favor; since he was, it must be remembered, the brother uterine of George Douglas, for whom such high honor was said to be designed.

The proposal, if seriously made, was treated as inadmissible, and Mary again resumed her purpose of escape. Her failure in her first attempt has some picturesque particulars, which might have been advantageously introduced in fictitious narrative. Drury sends Cecil the following account of the matter :—

"But after, upon the 25th of the last (April 1567), she enterprised an escape, and was the rather nearer effect, through her accustomed long lying in bed all the morning. The manner of it was thus: there cometh in to her the laundress early as other times before she was wonted, and the Queen according to such a secret practise putteth on her the weed of the laundress, and so with the fardel of cloathes and her muffler upon her face, passeth out and entreth the boat to pass the loch; which, after some space, one of them that rowed said merrily, "Let us see what manner of dame this is," and therewith offered to pull down her muffler, which, to defend, she put up her hands, which they spied to be very fair and white; wherewith they entered into suspicion whom she was, beginning to wonder at her enterprise. Whereat she was little dismayed, but charged them, upon danger of their lives, to row her over to the shore, whch they nothing regarded, but eftsoons rowed her back again, promising her that it should be secreted, and especially from the lord of the house, under whose guard she lyeth. It seemeth she knew her refuge, and where to have found it if she had once landed; for there did, and yet do linger, at a little village called Kinross, hard at the loch side, the same George Douglas, one Sempil, and one Beton, the which two were sometime her trusty servants, and, as yet appeareth, they mind her no less affection."—Bishop Keith's *History of the Affairs of Church and State in Scotland*, p. 470.

Notwithstanding this disappointment, little spoke of by historians, Mary renewed her attempts to escape. There was in the Castle of Lochleven a lad named William Douglas, some relation probably of the baron, and about eighteen years old. This youth proved as accessible to Queen Mary's prayers and promises as was the brother of his patron, George Douglas, from whom this William must be carefully kept distinct. It was young William who played the part commonly assigned to his superior, George,—stealing the keys of the castle from the table on which they lay, while his lord was at supper. He let the Queen and a waiting-woman out of the apartment where they were secured, and out of the tower itself, embarked with them in a small skiff, and rowed them to the shore. To prevent instant pursuit, he, for precaution's sake, locked the iron grated door of the tower, and threw the keys into the lake. They found George Douglas and the Queen's servant, Beaton [Betoun], waiting for them, and Lord Seyton and James Hamilton of Orbieston in attendance, at the head of a party of faithful followers, with whom they fled to Niddrie Castle, and from thence to Hamilton.

In narrating this romantic story, both history and tradition confuse the two Douglasses together, and confer on George the successful execution of the escape from the castle, the merit of which belongs in reality to the boy called William, or, more frequently, the Little Douglas, either from his youth or his slight stature. The reader will observe, that in the romance the part of the Little Douglas has been assigned to Roland Græme. In another case, it would be tedious to point out in a work of amusement such minute points of historical fact; but the general interest taken in the fate of Queen Mary renders everything of consequence which connects itself with her misfortunes.

Note 27.—Battle of Langside, p. 412

I am informed in the most polite manner by D. MacVean, Esq., of Glasgow, that I have been incorrect in my locality, in giving an account of the battle of Langside. Crookstone Castle, he observes, lies four miles west from the field of battle, and rather in the rear of Murray's army. The real place from which Mary saw the rout of her last army was Cathcart Castle, which, being a mile and a half east from Langside, was situated in the rear of the Queen's own army. I was led astray in the present case by the authority of my deceased friend, James Grahame, the excellent and amiable author of the *Sabbath*, in his drama on the subject of Queen Mary; and by a traditionary report of Mary having seen the battle from the Castle of Crookstone, which seemed so much to increase the interest of the scene that I have been unwilling to make, in this particular instance, the fiction give way to the fact, which last is undoubtedly in favor of Mr. MacVean's system.

It is singular how tradition, which is sometimes a sure guide to truth, is, in other cases, prone to mislead us. In the celebrated field of battle at Killiecrankie, the traveler is struck with one of those rugged pillars of rough stone, which indicate the scenes of ancient conflict. A friend of the Author, well acquainted with the circumstances of the battle, was standing near this large stone, and looking on the scene around, when a Highland shepherd hurried down from the hill to offer his services as cicerone, and proceeded to inform him that Dundee was slain at that stone, which was raised to his memory. "Fie, Donald," answered my friend, "how can you tell such a story to a stranger? I am sure you know well enough that Dundee was killed at a considerable distance from this place, near the house of Fascally, and that this stone was here long before the battle, in 1688." "Oich!—oich!" said Donald, no way abashed, "and your honor's in the right, and I see you ken a' about it. And he wasna killed on the spot neither, but lived till the next morning; but a' the Saxon gentlemen like best to hear he was killed at the great stane." It is on the same principle of pleasing my readers that I retain Crookstone Castle instead of Cathcart.

If, however, the Author has taken a liberty in removing the actual field of battle somewhat to the eastward, he has been tolerably strict in adhering to the incidents of the engagement, as will appear from a comparison of events in the novel with the following account from an old writer.

"The Regent was out on foot and all his company, except the Laird of Grange, Alexander Hume of Manderston, and some Borderers to the number of two hundred. The Laird of Grange had already viewed the ground, and with all imaginable diligence caused every horseman to take behind him a footman of the Regent's, to guard behind them, and rode with speed to the head of the Langside Hill, and set down the sett footmen with their culverings at the head of a strait lane, where there were some cottage houses and yards of great advantage. Which soldiers with their continual shot killed divers of the vaunt-guard, led by the Hamiltouns, who, couragiously and fiercely ascending up the hill, were already out of breath, when the Regent's vaunt-guard joined with them. Where the worthy Lord Hume fought on foot with his pike in his hand very manfully, assisted by the Laird of Cesfoord, his brother-in-law, who helped him up again when he was strucken to the ground by many stroaks upon his face, by the throwing pistols at him after they had been discharged. He was also wounded with staves, and had many stroaks of spears through his legs; for he and Grange, at the joining, cried to let their adversaries first lay down their spears, to bear up theirs; which spears were so thick fixed in the others' jacks, that some of the pistols and great staves that were thrown by them which were behind, might be seen lying upon the spears.

"Upon the Queen's side the Earl of Arguile commanded the battle, and the Lord of Arbroth the vaunt-guard. But the Regent committed to the Laird of Grange the special care, as being an experimented captain, to oversee every danger, and to ride to every wing, to encourage and make help where greatest need was. He perceived, at the first joining, the right wing of the Regent's vaunt-guard put back, and like to fly, whereof the greatest part were commons of the barony of Renfrew; whereupon he rode to them, and told them that their enemy was already turning their backs, requesting them to stay and debate till he should bring them fresh men forth of the battle. Whither at full speed he did ride alone, and told the Regent that the enemy were shaken and flying away behind the little village, and desired a few number of fresh men to go with him. Where he found enough willing, as the Lord Lindesay, the Laird of Lochleven, Sir James Balfour, and all the Regent's servants, who followed him with diligence, and reinforced that wing which was beginning to fly; which fresh men with their loose weapons struck the enemies in their flanks and faces, which forced them incontinent to give place and turn back after long fighting and pushing others to and fro with their spears. There were not many horsemen to pursue after them, and the Regent cried to save and not to kill, and Grange was never cruel, so that there were few slain and taken. And the only slaughter was at the first rencounter by the shot of the soldiers, which Grange had planted at the lane-head behind some dikes."

It is remarkable that, while passing through the small town of Renfrew, some partizans, adherents of the house of Lennox, attempting to arrest Queen Mary and her attendants, were obliged to make way for her, not without slaughter.—The Castle of Rutherglen was demolished immediately after the battle by the Regent's party.

The suburban district of Glasgow towards the south, named Cathcart, takes its name from the old castle, and, owing to the growth of the city in this direction, the site of the battle of Langside is brought contiguous to the southeast side of the Queen's Park. On the west of this park the site of the Regent Murray's camp is commemorated by the "Camp Hill," and at the village of Langside there is a cottage which goes by the name of "Queen Mary's Cottage." The Queen's Park is in a direct line with Glasgow Bridge, from which it is three miles distant in a straight line (*Laing*).

NOTE 28.—BURIAL OF THE ABBOT'S HEART IN THE AVENEL AISLE, p. 421

This was not the explanation of the incident of searching for the heart, mentioned in the introduction to the tale, which the Author originally intended. It was designed to refer to the heart of Robert Bruce. It is generally known that that great monarch, being on his death-bed, bequeathed to the good Lord James of Douglas the task of carrying his heart to the Holy Land, to fulfil in a certain degree his own desire to perform a crusade. Upon Douglas's death, fighting against the Moors in Spain, a sort of military *hors d'œuvre* to which he could have pleaded no regular call of duty, his followers brought back the Bruce's heart, and deposited it in the abbey church of Melrose, the Kennaquhair of the tale.

This abbey had been always particularly favored by the Bruce. We have already seen his extreme anxiety that each of the reverend brethren should be daily supplied with a service of boiled almonds, rice and milk, pease, or the like, to be called the "king's mess," and that without the ordinary service of their table being either disturbed in quantity or quality. But this was not the only mark of the benignity of good King Robert towards the monks of Melrose, since, by a charter of the date 29th May 1326, he conferred on the Abbot of Melrose the sum of £2000 sterling, for rebuilding the Church of St. Mary's, ruined by the English; and there is little or no doubt that the principal part of the remains which now display such exquisite specimens of Gothic architecture, at its very purest period, had their origin in this munificent donation. The money was to be paid out of crown lands, estates forfeited to the King, and other property or demesnes of the crown.

A very curious letter, written to his son about three weeks before his death, has been pointed out to me by my friend Mr. Thomas Thomson, Deputy-Register for Scotland. It enlarges so much on the love of the royal writer to the community of Melrose, that it is well worthy of being inserted in a work connected in some degree with Scottish history.

Litera Domini Regis Roberti ad filium suum David

"Robertus dei gratia rex Scottorum, David precordialissimo filio suo, ac ceteris successoribus suis, Salutem, et sic ejus precepta tenere, ut cum sua benedictione possint regnare. Fili carissime, digne censeri videtur filius, qui, paternos in bonis mores imitans, piam ejus nititur exequi voluntatem, nec proprie sibi sumit nomen heredis, qui salubribus predecessoris affectibus non adherit; cupientes igitur, ut piam affectionem et scineram dilectionem, quam erga monasterium de Melros, ubi cor nostrum ex speciali devotione disposuimus tumulandum, et erga religiosos ibidem Deo servientes, ipsorum vita sanctissima nos ad hoc excitante, concepimus; tu ceterique successores mei pia scinceritate prosequamini, ut, ex vestre dilectionis affectu dictis religiosis nostri causa post mortem nostram ostenso, ipsi pro nobis ad orandum fervencius et forcius animentur. Vobis precipimus quantum possumus, instanter supplicamus, et ex toto corde injungimus, quatinus assignacionibus quas eisdem viris religiosis et fabrica ecclesie sue de novo fecimus ac eciam omnibus aliis donacionibus nostris, ipsos libere gaudere permittans, easdem potius si necesse fuerit augmentantes quam diminuentes, ipsorum peticiones auribus benevolis admittentes, ac ipsos contra suos invasores et emulos pia defensione protegentes. Hanc autem exhortacionem supplicacionem et preceptum tu, fili ceterique successores nostri, prestanti animo complere curetis, si nostram benedictionem habere velitis, una cum benedictione filii summi regis, qui filios docuit patrum voluntates in bono perficere, asserens in mundum se venisse non ut suam voluntatem faceret sed paternam. In testimonium autem nostre devotionis erga locum predictum sic a nobis dilectum et electum concepte, presentem literam religiosis predictis dimittimus, nostris successoribus in posterum ostendendam. Data apud Cardros, undecimo die Maij, anno regni nostri vicessimo quarto."

If this charter be altogether genuine, and there is no appearance of forgery, it gives rise to a curious doubt in Scottish history. The letter announces that the King had already destined his heart to be deposited at Melrose. The resolution to send it to Palestine, under the charge of Douglas, must have been adopted betwixt 11th May 1329, the date of the letter, and 7th June of the same year, when the Bruce died; or else we must suppose that the commission of Douglas extended not only to taking the Bruce's heart to Palestine, but to bring it safe back to its final place of deposit in the Abbey of Melrose.

It would not be worth inquiring by what caprice the Author was induced to throw the incident of the Bruce's heart entirely out of the story, save merely to say, that he found himself unable to fill up the canvas he had sketched, and indisposed to prosecute the management of the supernatural machinery with which his plan, when it was first rough-hewn, was concerted and combined.

GLOSSARY

OF

WORDS, PHRASES, AND ALLUSIONS

Aby, *abye*, to suffer, endure

Ad unguem, at the fingers' ends

Alexipharmics, antidotes to poisons, etc.

A moi! mes Français! Hither! my French guard

Anastasius, or Memoirs of a Greek written at the Close of the Eighteenth Century (1819), by Thomas Hope, a member of a wealthy Anglo-Dutch family

Andrea Ferrara, a Scottish broadsword

Anilities, old women's follies, acts of dotage

Aqua, etc. (p. 304), wonderful water! it has been proved

Argute, sharp, acute

Aristarch, a severe critic, after Aristarchus the most celebrated critic of antiquity, who lived at Alexandria before and after 200 B. C.

Arles, earnest money

Atrowling, a-rolling

Aver, a draught horse

Awmous, alms

Bacharac, or *Bacharach*, on the Rhine, in the wine-growing region. It is nearly 100 miles W. of Würzburg

Bachelor Samson Carrasco. *See Don Quixote*, Pt. II. chap. xiv.

Back-sword, sword with only one sharp edge

Bailie, or *Bailey*, the outer courtyard of a feudal castle

Banders, confederates

Bangsters, bullies, disorderly persons

Barnbougle, a ruined castle in Dalmeny Park, on the Firth of Forth, belonging to the Earl of Rosebery; it was rebuilt in 1880

Bayes's tragedy, *The Rehearsal* (1672), by George Villiers, Duke of Buckingham, Bayes being a character in the piece intended to satirize Dryden. The play (a comedy) concludes with a battle between soldiers and hobby-horses

Bears are you there with, a proverbial expression indicative of the repetition of an annoyance. A man, disliking a sermon on Elisha and the bears, went the next Sunday to a different church, but there the sermon was from the same text, and he exclaimed, "Are you there again with your bears?"

Beef-brewis, beef-broth

Bellona, the ancient Romans' goddess of war

Benedicite, bless you! a blessing

Benedicti, etc. (p. 84), Blessed are they who come in the name of the Lord

Benedictus, etc. (p. 290), Blessed be he who comes in the name of the Lord, condemned he who comes in the name of the enemy

Bield, shelter, refuge

Bilbo, *bilboa*, a sword made at Bilboa in North Spain

Birlit, made a whirring noise, spun away

Black-jack, a drinking-vessel or ale-pitcher made of waxed leather

Black Ormiston, concerned in the murder of Darnley

Bleeding heart, the badge of the Douglas family, from Good Earl James having carried Bruce's heart to Palestine

Bodle, a small copper coin = 1-6th of a penny English

Boll, or *bow*, a dry measure = 6 bushels

Bolt head, a hollow glass globe with a long neck, used in distillation

Border doom, hanging

Bow, *boll*, an old Scotch measure = 6 bushels

Bowton, *Hepburn of*, a relative of Bothwell, an agent in the murder of Darnley

Brag, proudly defy, challenge

Bran, the dog of Fingal in *Ossian's Poems*

Brancher, a young bird able to leave the nest and hop about on the branches

Brandy-wine, brandy

Branle, dance

Bravade, boast

Brent brow, smooth, high forehead

Broken clan, one that had no chief able to find security for their good behaviour, as the Græmes of the Debateable Land

Brownie, a gnome. *See* Elshe in the *Black Dwarf*

Bumbasted, or *bombasted*, stuffed with cotton-wool, etc.

Caleb Williams (1794), by William Godwin, father of Shelley's wife

Caliburn, the sword of King Arthur

Calipolis, wife of the Moorish prince in Peele's play *The Battle of Alcazar*

Callot's Temptations, the masterpiece of Jacques Callot, a 17th century

engraver of Nancy, whose plates witness to a most fantastic and grotesque imagination
Calm sough, a quiet tongue
Cambuscan, king of Sarra in Tartary, the model of kindly virtues, figures in Chaucer's *Squire's Tale* and in Spenser's *Faërie Queene*, Bk. iv.
Cantharides, Spanish flies, used to raise blisters—an animal not a vegetable poison
Cardinal (p. 352). *See* Uncle the Cardinal
Carrasco Bachelor Samson. See Bachelor Samson Carrasco
Carslogie, laird of, the head of the Clephane family; the house stands 1 1-2 miles from Cupar in Fife
Cates, delicacies, fancy confectionery
Catholicon, universal remedy
Celsus, a physician of the 1st century A. D., wrote in Latin a history of medicine as practised in ancient Alexandria
Change-house, alehouse
Chiragra, gout in the hand
Christian Majesty, Francis II., king of France; His Very Christian Majesty was the usual title-designate of the king of France
Churchill, a satiric poet of the 18th century. *See* Boswell's *Life of Johnson*, under the year 1763
Clout, a mark in the very middle of the target
Clouted, mended
Cock of the North, Earl of Huntly
Cog, to cheat, deceive, wheedle
Coif, woman's cap or covering for the head
Colewort, any kind of greens
Colman's drama, The Iron Chest, a three-act drama founded on Godwin's *Caleb Williams*, was written by George Colman, junior, and produced in 1796
Commendator, lay holder of a benefice
Conjuraverunt, etc. (p. 87), The princes have conspired among themselves, saying, Let us cast His cords from us
Corbie, raven; *corbie-messenger*, one that returns too late or not at all, an allusion to Noah's raven
Cordinare, cordwainer, shoemaker, leather-worker
Coronach, dirge
Couranto, a lively, rapid dance
Courcelles, French ambassador in Scotland, 1586-87
Crack-hemp, crack-halter, one fated to come to the gallows
Crafteschilder, servants, etc., of craftsmen, artizans
Crowd, a fiddle
Crown of the sun, old French gold coin of Louis XI. and Charles VIII., with the sun shown above the crown = 14s.
Cruizuedor, or *cruzade d'or*, a Portuguese gold coin worth about half-a-crown
Cubicular, groom of the bedchamber, chamberlain
Cuittle, to tickle, wheedle
Culpas meas, my sins
Curch, woman's cap
Cut, a gelding, a term of reproach
Cyprus, thin black stuff

Dalmatique, a loose, long ecclesiastical robe, with wide sleeves
Danske, Danish
Dark Grey Man (Douglas). *See* Note 21, p. 430
Darnaway (Castle), the seat of the Earl of Murray, near Forres in Elginshire
Debateable Land, between the rivers Sark and Esk, on the borders of Cumberland and Dumfries
Des Rodomontades Espagnolles, a collection of tales, anecdotes, etc., of Spanish boasting, taken from various authors by Jacques Gautier, or Gaultier (Rouen, 1612)
Diascordium, confection of scordium, the water germander
Dight your gabs, wipe your mouths, be silent
Dink, to deck, adorn
Discernit, etc. (p. 285), The wise man discriminates things which the fool confounds
Disponit upon, disposed of
Doom, judgment, verdict
Dortour, a dormitory
Douce, sober, sedate
Douglas lady of the house of (p. 342). Catherine Douglas endeavored to keep out the murderers of James I. of Scotland by thrusting her arm through the staple of the door (1437)
Do veniam, I give you leave
Dow, dove
Draphane, or *Draffan*, a castle belonging to the Hamiltons in Fifeshire; but Mary proceeded to Hamilton Park when she left Niddrie Castle
Drawncansir, a blustering braggart in *The Rehearsal* (1672), by G. Villiers Duke of Buckingham
Dreadour, dread, fear
Dudgeon-dagger, a small dagger with an ornamental wooden haft
Duenna, an old woman who watches that a younger observes the rules of decorum
Duke of Orkney, James Hepburn, Earl of Bothwell
Duncansbay Head, in the extreme north of Scotland

Earn, or erne, an eagle
Electuary, a medical confection or paste
En champ clos, in an inclosed field
Erne, or earn, eagle
Everiche, every
Exheridated, or *exheredated*, disinherited
Ex oribus parvulorum, Out of the mouths of babes

Facies hippocratica, hippocratic or sickly countenance
Farthingale, a hoop petticoat
Fash, trouble, concern
Fell, skin; cruel
Fiat experimentum, etc. (p. 348). Let the experiment be made upon a common body
Flaunes, or flams, pancakes
Fleech, to flatter, cajole
Foure-hammer, sledgehammer
Four-hours' penny, four o'clock meal—a phrase used by Knox

Fox, an old-fashioned broadsword
Frack, bold, prompt and resolute
French Paris, or Nicholas Hubert, a servant of Bothwell, sometime also of Mary, assisted in the murder of Darnley
Frounce, a distemper in hawks
Frustra, etc. (p. 353), In vain we vex the sick with remedies
Gaillard, wanton
Galliard, a lively dance; a gay youth
Galloway nag, a small strong breed of Galloway, the south-west extremity of Scotland
Galopin, scullion, cook's boy
Gambade, gambol, leap, spring
Gambadoes, gaiters, leggings
Garboiles, broils, confusions
Gazehound, a hound that pursues by sight, greyhound
Gear, matter, business
Gear-men, men in armor
Gestic lore, knowledge of dancing
Gled, a kite
Gleg, quick, sharp, keen
Gordon, Sir John, fourth son of the Earl of Huntly, and one of Queen Mary's lovers, was beheaded at Aberdeen for treason in 1562
Gospellers, Reformers
Gousty, dreary, desolate
Gowd, to lay, to embroider in gold
Graithed, equipped, decked
Graysteil, Sir Greysteil, a metrical romance in which are narrated the exploits of a brave knight, Sir Greysteil. To call a man by this title, as James V. did Archibald Douglas of Kilspindie, was esteemed a choice compliment. *See* Sir Eger
Guises, Mary's mother was of this powerful French (Lorraine) family
Guy of Warwick, the hero of a mediæval romance, slew a fierce Dun Cow on Dunsmore Heath, near Rugby

Hackit, or hawkit, white-faced
Hagg, or hag, a pit or break in a morass
Haggard, a wild hawk that has been tamed
Halidome, land held under a religious house
Harquebuss, an ancient firelock
Harry groat, a groat=4d., of Henry VIII.
Hawick to Hermitage Castle. Mary rode in one day from Jedburgh (not Hawick) to Hermitage Castle, near the Border, and back, a total distance of 40 miles, to visit the Earl of Bothwell, who had been wounded in a Border fight
Hay of Luncarty, the ancestor of three noble Scottish families—Errol, Tweeddale, and Kinnoul—was originally a peasant, who saved the Scottish army from defeat by the Danes shortly before the year 994
Hay of Talla, a Borderer, concerned in the murder of Darnley
Herling, young of the sea-trout
Heywood, Thomas, dramatist and actor of the first half of the 17th century
Hic jacet, etc. (p. 111), Here lies Abbot Eustace
Hob (Ormiston), uncle of the Black Laird of Ormiston, concerned in the murder of Darnley
Hobby, a strong, active nag
Hodden-grey, rough cloth, the natural color of the wool
Holyrood Palace was rebuilt in the reign of Charles II., not Charles I., namely, between 1671 and 1679
Hoodie, or hooded, crow, the carrion crow
Horn, put to. *See* Put to horn
Hors d'œuvre, digression
Hours, a Roman Catholic book of prayers for private devotions
Howff, a haunt, resort
Howlet, the owl

Ilk, the same; *ilka*, every
In adversitate, etc. (p. 428), Patient in adversity, benevolent in prosperity
In dubio, in doubt
Injeer, or ingere, to insinuate, force oneself in insidiously
"*In my school-days*," etc. (p. xii). *See Merchant of Venice*, Act i. sc. 1
Inter nos, between ourselves
Intrate, mei filii, Enter my sons

Jack-a-lent visages, long, serious faces, like penitents in Lent
Jeddart staff, a species of battle-axe formerly used by the men of Jedburgh or Jeddart
Jerking, a beating, whipping
Jesses, straps fastened round the legs of a hawk
Jester, celebrated, (p. 120). Howleglass, the German Till Eulenspiegel (*i.e.* Owl-Glass)
Je suis, etc. (p. 429), I am neither king nor prince; I am the Lord of Coucy
Jibbat, gibbet
Jiggeting, behaving in an affected manner, flaunting
Jouk, stoop, duck down; *jouk and let the jaw gang by*, stoop and let the wave pass
Jour de jeune, a fast-day
Julep, a sweet drink, cordial

Kail, colewort, cabbage
Kain-fowls, fowls paid as part of rent
Kelpie, a water-spirit
Kent, to propel a boat by pushing a long pole against the bottom of the lake
Kerrs, of Cessford and Ferniehurst, powerful Border chieftains, Catholics and supporters of Mary Queen of Scots
King Candaules, of ancient Lydia in Asia Minor, who exposed his wife to Gyges, in the 6th century B.C. The lady persuaded Gyges to slay her husband, and then married the slayer
Kirn-milk, butter-milk
Kittle, ticklish, difficult
Knapscap knapschalle, or knapscull, head-piece or helmet

Ladies Sandilands and Olifaunt. The third dame of the trio was named Weir. *See* Allan Ramsay's *Evergreen* (1724), vol. i.
La Mer des Histoires, a

universal history or chronicle, translated (1848) from the *Mare Historiarum* of John Colonna, Dominican, who in 1255 was made Archbishop of Messina, Sicily
Landward town, rural, inland farmstead
Lanercost, an ancient abbey in Cumberland, close beside the Roman Wall
Lavolta, a lively dance with a leaping step
Lawing, tavern-bill
Least penny, a worthless person
Lennox, a former county of Scotland, embracing Dumbarton and parts of Stirling, Perth, and Renfrew
Lennox, him of the, Henry Darnley, eldest son of the Earl of Lennox
Lenten-kail, broth made without meat
Let, retard, hinder
Licitum sit, It may be allowed
Lictor, an ancient Roman executive officer
Limbo lake, where unbaptized children and good heathens were believed by the Roman Catholic Church to spend their eternity
Ling, thin, long grass; heather
Lither, lazy
Loaning, lane, meadow
Lockeram, coarse linen
Lords of the Congregation, leaders of the Reformation in Scotland
Loretto, on the Italian coast of the Adriatic, 15 miles from Ancona; a church there contains the (reputed) house in which the Virgin Mary lived at Nazareth
Luath, the dog of Cuthullin, in *Ossian's Poems:* "Fingal"
Lunga roba corta scienzia, Long robe but little knowledge
Lunt, lighted match, torch
Lurdane, worthless fellow, blockhead

Mail, baggage
Mail-gardener, one who cultivates fruit, etc., on land for which he pays rent
Mair, more
Malvolio, the steward in Shakespeare's *Twelfth Night*
Ma mignonne, my darling
Maries, four, young ladies of noble birth, attendants of the Queen—Mary Livingstone, Mary Fleming, Mary Seatoun, and Mary Beatoun
Mark, a Scotch coin=1s. 1⅓d.; a Dutch coin=about 1s. 6d.
Marot, Clement, poet, translated the Psalms into French verse (1541), which were very popular at court, and usually sung to secular airs
Massymoore, a dungeon, a word of Moorish origin, introduced probably during the crusading era
Mazzard the head, skull
Medicamentum, medicine
Menzie, the entire establishment
Mercat crow, market cross
Messan, a small dog, lapdog; *messan-page*, cur of a page
Metoposcopical, physiognomical
Mew, to confine; cage for hawks
Mickle, great, big
Minion a favorite; pert, saucy woman
Mint, to aim at
Mirror of Knighthood, with fuller title, *The Mirror of Princely Deeds and Knighthood etc. translated out of the Spanish by Margaret Tyler and R. P.* (1585-1601)
Mithridate, an antidote to poison
More Scotico, in Scotch fashion
Morisco bells, used in a morris dance
Mumchance, an old game at cards or dice, in which silence was absolutely necessary
Mungo in the Padlock, a play (1768) by Isaac Bickerstaffe, the plot being based upon Cervantes's novel *The Jealous Husband*
Munster, Bishop of, suppressed with violence the fanatic and impious proceedings of the Anabaptists in Münster, the capital of Westphalia, in 1535
Mutchkin, a liquid measure=3-4 pint
My rebel subjects saw me, etc. (p. 390), an allusion to the condition in which Mary was led into Edinburgh after the battle of Carberry Hill, and the scenes that followed in the Provost's house
Mystagogue, interpreter of mysteries

Ne accesseris, etc. (p. 265), Go not into the council-chamber unless invited
Neighbored ill, agreed ill, disagreed
Nick with nay, disappoint by denying
Nicol Forest, a Border district of Cumberland

Oblast, obliged, engaged to
Over Heaven's forbode, Heaven forbid; *over God's forbode*, God forbid

Pairmain, a variety of apple
Pajon, Henri, a Parisian lawyer. *Prince Soly* was published in 1740
Palinurus, the steersman of Æneas. *See* Virgil's *Æneid*, v.
Pantler, keeper of pantry, one in charge of provisions
Pantoufle, slipper
Parcel poet, a bit of a poet, indifferent poet
Parent, relative
Partlet, a portion of dress, as a kerchief, for a lady's neck and shoulders
Par voie du fait, by violence, actual force
Pasche, Easter
Patch, paltry fellow, fool
Paven, or *pavan*, a slow, stately dance
Pearlin muffler, a lace veil
Peel-house, a small square tower of refuge
Pestis, the plague
Petite Flamberge à rien, useless little sword
Petronel, horseman's large pistol
Pickthank, an officious intermeddler, toady
Pie, magpie
Pilniewinks, instruments for torturing the fingers
Plack, a small copper coin = 1-3 of a penny English
Pleach, to interweave, plash
Poculum mane, etc. (p. 273), A cup drained in the morning restores exhausted nature

Podagra, gout in the foot
Pomander-box, a box of perfume
Popinjay, parrot
Portioner, one possessing or inheriting part of a property
Pottle, pottle-pot, a vessel holding 2 quarts, tankard
Prœmia cum, etc. (p. 275), The doctor is the devil when he asks for his fees
Prœtor, a Roman magistrate
Pragmatic, meddlesome, officious
Propale, to publish
Proud peat, a person of insufferable pride
Pudding-burn House, a stronghold of the Armstrongs in Liddesdale. *See* the circumstances alluded to in Scott's *Minstrelsy of the Scottish Border:* "Dick o' the Cow," vol. ii. pp. 63–75
Puir, poor
Put to horn, publicly call upon one to pay a debt under claim of being proclaimed guilty of treason
Pyet, magpie

Quarrel-pane, a diamond-shaped pane, formed like a quarrel, the head of the arrow of a cross-bow
Quean, wench
Queen Regent, Mary of Guise (or Lorraine), mother of Mary Queen of Scots
Quhele, wheel
Quhill, till
Quid dicis, mi fili, What dost thou say, my son?
Quousque Domine? how long, O Lord?

Raymond Lullius, a 13th century philosopher, a native of Majorca, who invented a system of mechanical logic with which he tried to convert the Mohammedans to Christianity
Redder's lick, the blow that so often falls on one who interferes in a quarrel
Redd up, tidy, put in order
Rede, to counsel, advise; advice
Regality, lord of, one holding territorial jurisdiction conferred by the king
Resetter, one who harbors loose characters and criminals
Réveillez-vous, etc. (p. 374), Awake, fair sleeper
Rifler, a hawk that catches its prey by the feathers only
Rive, to rend, tear
Rock, distaff
Roke, a rock
Roseberry Topping, a conspicuous hill in Cleveland, North Riding of Yorkshire
Rosewal and Lilian, a popular metrical romance that was still sung in the streets of Edinburgh as late as 1770. See Laing, *Early Metrical Tales* (1826)
Rowan-tree, in popular superstition a charm against witches
Ruffle, to play the bully, quarrel
Rung, club, cudgel

Sabœa, properly Sabra, daughter of Ptolemy, king of Egypt, the maiden who was rescued from the Dragon by St. George
St. James of Compostella, a celebrated resort of pilgrims, at Santiago, 30 miles from Corunna, in the north of Spain
St. Martin of Bullions, the St. Swithin or weeping saint of Scotland. If his festival (4th, *i.e.* 15th, July) prove wet, forty days of rain are expected
Salerno, school of, ranked as the first medical school in Europe during the early Middle Ages
Salve in nomine sancto, Hail in the holy name; *Salvete et vos*, Hail also to you
Sampson's VOW-BREAKER, or the Fair Maid of Clifton (1636), by William Sampson
Samyne, same
Sancte Benedicte, ora pro me, St. Benet, pray for me
Scalit, dispersed, separated
Scaur, a precipitous bank or rock
Scott, Michael, the magician, who figures in Scott's *Lay of the Last Minstrel*
Scrip, to mock, gibe
Sexton's pound, the grave
Sinclair, Oliver, an unworthy favorite of James V.
Sir Eger one of the heroes of the popular 16th century Scottish romance *Sir Eger, Sir Grahame, and Sir Greystil*, or *Sir Edgar and Sir Grime*
Sir Grime. *See* Sir Eger
Skeely, skilful, cunning in simples, etc.
Sniggling, smirking
Snood, a fillet with which a maiden binds her hair
Snottreth, bubbles
Snug the joiner, a character in *Midsummer Night's Dream*
Soltra Edge, or *Soutra Hill*, the westernmost ridge of the Lammermoor Hills in Lothian
Spae-wife, fortune-teller
Spernit dona fides, the faithful (dog) despises bribes
Springald, a stripling
Squab, short and thick, squat
Stammel, red linsey-woolsey
Staving and tailing, striking the bear with a staff and pulling the dog by the tail
Steikit, shut
Stentor, the Greek herald in the Trojan War, whose voice was equal to those of any fifty men
Stoop (of a falcon), swoop, darting down on its prey
Stoup, a vessel or measure for liquids
Sub sigillo confessionis, under the seal of confession
Subtriste, somewhat sad
Sub umbra vitis sui, under the shade of his own vine
Succory, chicory
Superceid, to suspend, postpone

Tace is Latin for a candle, silence is the word
Tale-Pyet, a tell-tale
Tent, attend, tend
Tercel gentle, a trained male falcon
Testificate, certificate
Testoon, or *teston*, a silver coin = 1s.
Theban, learned, a learned man—a Shakspearian

phrase (*Lear*, Act iii. sc. 4)
Thespis, the originator of the ancient Greek drama
Thumbikins, thumb-screws, instrument of torture
Tilbury, a gig
Tillyvalley, nonsense ! a fig for——!
To call up him, etc. (p. 428), from Milton's *Il Penseroso*
Tolbooth, jail
Totus mundus, etc. (p. 278), The whole world acts the player
Tour de jongleur, juggler's trick
Trangam, or *trangram*, a trinket, trumpery ornament
Tron, a church on the High Street of Edinburgh
Tussis, a cough
Tuto, cito, jucunde, safely, quickly, pleasantly
Two and a plack, two Scotch pennies and a plack = 1-2. English

Uncle the Cardinal. Charles of Guise, brother to Mary's mother, was the real ruler of France during the reign of Mary's first husband, the feeble Francis II.
Un Dieu, etc. (p. 429), one God, one faith, one king, one law
Usquebaugh, whisky

Vasquine, or *basquine*, gown or petticoat, worn by Basque and Spanish women
Vendisse, or *vendace*, a rare kind of white fish, whose flesh is accounted a great delicacy
Vertu-gardin, a hoop petticoat
Vin-de-pays, the common wine of the country
Vivers, victuals
Vix licitum, scarcely allowable

Wanion, with a, with a vengeance, the devil !
Wap, flap, stroke of a wing
Warlock, a wizard
Waur, worse
Weft, or *waft*, a waving, beckoning, signaling
Weird, fate, destiny
Weir-men, war-men, soldiers
Welted, furnished with a hem or border
Whaup, curlew
Whilly, to gull, wheedle
White-boy, petted favorite, darling
Wimple, a veil
Wine and bush. Vintners and tavern-keepers used in the Middle Ages to hang out a bush or bunch of ivy to indicate that their house was an inn ; hence the proverb, "Good wine needs no bush"
Witch of Berkley. *See* Southey's ballad *The Old Woman of Berkeley*
Wonot, will not
Wrath you not, do not get wroth
Wylie-coat, under vest

Yoldring, or *yorlin*, a yellow-hammer, bird

INDEX TO THE ABBOT

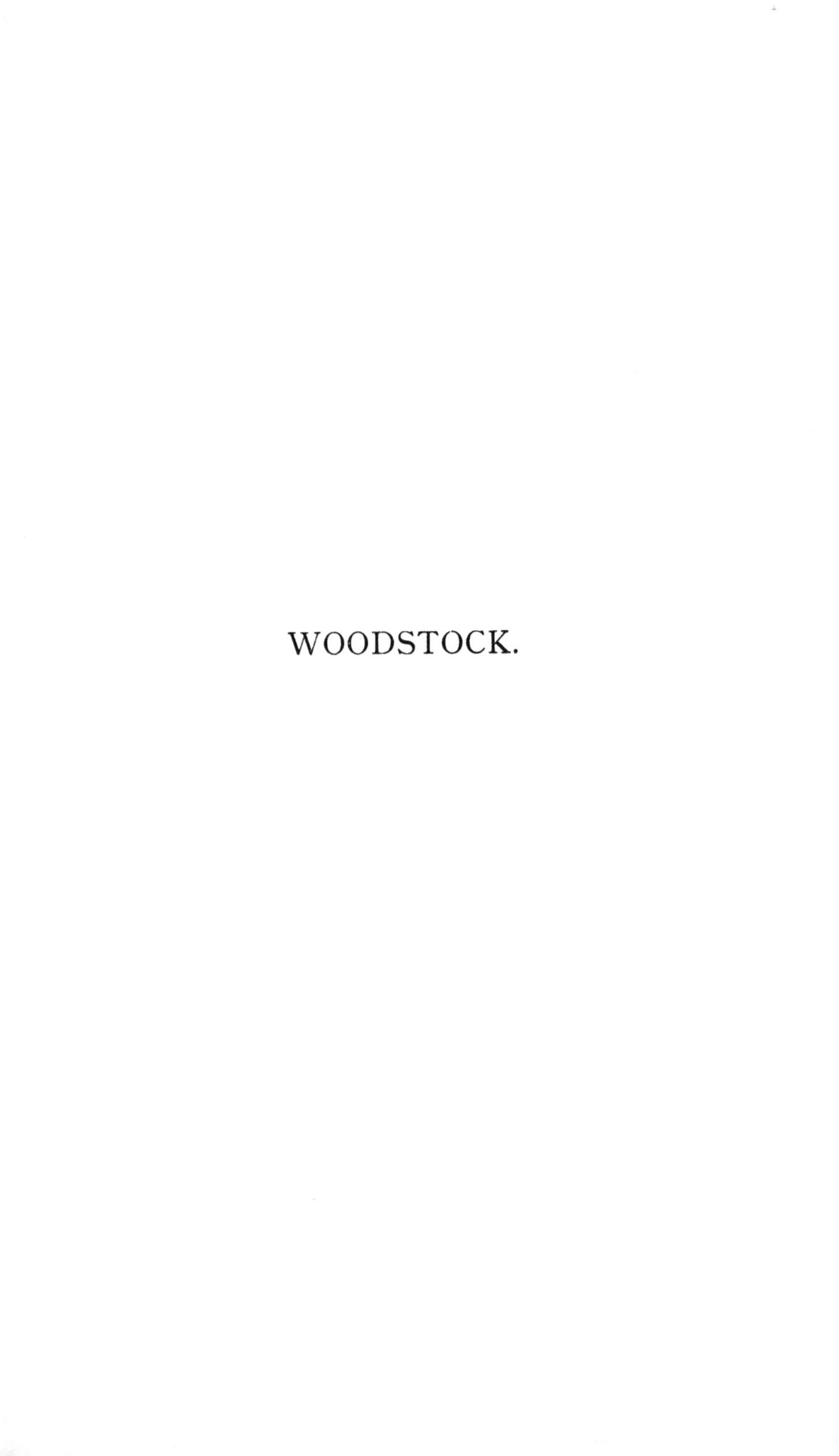

WOODSTOCK.

INTRODUCTION TO WOODSTOCK

THE busy period of the great Civil War was one in which the character and genius of different parties were most brilliantly displayed, and, accordingly, the incidents which took place on either side were of a striking and extraordinary character, and afforded ample foundation for fictitious composition. The author had in some measure attempted such in *Peveril of the Peak;* but the scene was in a remote part of the kingdom, and mingled with other national differences, which left him still at liberty to glean another harvest out of so ample a store.

In these circumstances, some wonderful adventures which happened at Woodstock in the year 1649 occurred to him as something he had long ago read of, although he was unable to tell where, and of which the hint appeared sufficient, although, doubtless, it might have been much better handled if the Author had not, in the lapse of time, lost everything like an accurate recollection of the real story.

It was not until about this period, namely, 1831, that the Author, being called upon to write this Introduction, obtained a general account of what really happened upon the marvelous occasion in question, in a work termed *The Every-day Book,* published by Mr. Hone, and full of curious antiquarian research, the object being to give a variety of original information concerning manners, illustrated by curious instances, rarely to be found elsewhere.* Among other matter, Mr. Hone quotes an article from the *British Magazine* for 1747, in the following words, and which is probably the document which the Author of *Woodstock* had formerly perused, although he was unable to refer to the source of his information. The tract is entitled, *The Genuine History of the Good Devil of Woodstock, Famous in the World in the Year* 1649, *and never accounted for, or at all understood to this Time.*

* Vol. ii. pp. 582–590, Lond. 1827 (*Laing*).

The teller of this *Genuine History* proceeds verbatim as follows:

Some original papers having lately fallen into my hands, under the name of *Authentic Memoirs of the Memorable Joseph Collins of Oxford, commonly known by the Name of Funny Joe, and now intended for the Press*, I was extremely delighted to find in them a circumstantial and unquestionable account of the most famous of all invisible agents, so well known in the year 1649, under the name of the Good Devil of Woodstock, and even adored by the people of that place, for the vexation and distress it occasioned some people they were not much pleased with. As this famous story, though related by a thousand people, and attested in all its circumstances, beyond all possibility of doubt, by people of rank, learning, and reputation, of Oxford and the adjacent towns, has never yet been accounted for, or at all understood, and is perfectly explained, in a manner that can admit of no doubt, in these papers, I could not refuse my readers their share of the pleasure it gave me in reading.

There is, therefore, no doubt that, in the year 1649, a number of incidents, supposed to be supernatural, took place at the king's palace of Woodstock, which the Commissioners of Parliament were then and there endeavoring to dilapidate and destroy. The account of this by the Commissioners themselves, or under their authority, was repeatedly published, and, in particular, is inserted as Relation Sixth of *Satan's Invisible World Discovered*,* by George Sinclair, Professor of Philosophy in Glasgow, an approved collector of such tales.

It was the object of neither of the great political parties of that day to discredit this narrative, which gave great satisfaction both to the Cavaliers and Roundheads; the former conceiving that the license given to the demons was in consequence of the impious desecration of the king's furniture and apartments, so that the citizens of Woodstock almost adored the supposed spirits, as avengers of the cause of royalty; while the friends of the Parliament, on the other hand, imputed to the malice of the fiend the obstruction of the pious work, as they judged that which they had in hand.

At the risk of prolonging a curious quotation, I include a page or two from Mr. Hone's *Every-day Book.*

"The honorable the Commissioners arrived at Woodstock manor house, October 13th, and took up their residence in the King's own

---

* Originally published at Edinburgh, 1685, 12mo (*Laing*).

rooms. His Majesty's bedchamber they made their kitchen, the council-hall their pantry, and the presence-chamber was the place where they sat for despatch of business. His Majesty's dining-room they made their wood-yard, and stowed it with no other wood but that of the famous Royal Oak from the High Park, which that nothing might be left with the name of the King about it, they had dug up by the roots, and bundled up into fagots for their firing.

"*October* 16.—This day they first sat for the despatch of business. In the midst of their first debate there entered a large black dog, as they thought, which made a terrible howling, overturned two or three of their chairs, and doing some other damage, went under the bed, and there gnawed the cords. The door this while continued constantly shut, when, after some two or three hours, Giles Sharp, their secretary, looking under the bed, perceived that the creature was vanished, and that a plate of meat which one of the servants had hid there was untouched, and showing them to their honors, they were all convinced there could be no real dog concerned in the case; the said Giles also deposed on oath, that, to his certain knowledge, there was not.

"*October* 17.—As they were this day sitting at dinner in a lower room, they heard plainly the noise of persons walking over their heads, though they well knew the doors were all locked, and there could be none there. Presently after they heard also all the wood of the King's Oak brought by parcels from the dining-room, and thrown with great violence into the presence-chamber, as also the chairs, stools, tables, and other furniture forcibly hurled about the room, their own papers of the minutes of their transactions torn, and the ink-glass broken. When all this had some time ceased, the said Giles proposed to enter first into these rooms, and, in presence of the commissioners, of whom he received the key, he opened the door, and entering, with their honors following him, he there found the wood strewed about the room, the chairs tossed about and broken, the papers torn, and the ink-glass broken over them all as they had heard, yet no footsteps appeared of any person whatever being there, nor had the doors ever been opened to admit or let out any persons since their honors were last there. It was therefore voted, *nem. con.*, that the person who did this mischief could have entered no other way than at the keyhole of the said doors.

"In the night following this same day, the said Giles, and two other of the Commissioners' servants, as they were in bed at [in] the same room with their honors, had their bed's feet lifted up so much higher than their heads, that they expected to have their necks broken, and then they were let fall at once with such violence as shook them up from the bed to a good distance; and this was repeated many times, their honors being amazed spectators. of it. In the morning the bedsteads were found cracked and broken, and the said Giles and his fellows declared they were sore to the bones with the tossing and jolting of the beds.

"*October* 19.—As they were all in bed together, the candles were blown out with a sulphurous smell, and instantly many trenchers of wood were hurled about the room; and one of them, putting his head above the clothes, had not less than six forcibly thrown at him, which wounded him very grievously. In the morning the trenchers were all found lying about the room, and were observed to be the same they had eaten on the day before, none being found remaining in the pantry.

"*October* 20.—This night the candles were put out as before; the curtains of the bed in which their honors lay were drawn to and fro many times with great violence; their honors received many cruel blows, and were much bruised beside, with eight great pewter dishes, and three dozen wooden trenchers, which were thrown on the bed, and afterwards heard rolling about the room.

"Many times also this night they heard the forcible falling of many fagots by their bedside, but in the morning no fagots were found there, no dishes or trenchers were there seen neither; and the aforesaid Giles attests that, by their different arranging in the pantry, they had assuredly been taken thence, and after put there again.

"*October* 21.—The keeper of their ordinary and his bitch lay with them. This night they had no disturbance.

"*October* 22.—Candles put out as before. They had the said bitch with them again, but were not by that protected: the bitch set up a very piteous cry; the clothes of their beds were all pulled off; and the bricks, without any wind, were thrown off the chimney-tops into the midst.

"*October* 24.—The candles put out as before. They thought all the wood of the King's Oak was violently thrown down by their bedsides; they counted sixty-four fagots that fell with great violence, and some hit and shook the bed; but in the morning none were found there, nor the door of the room opened in which the said fagots were.

"*October* 25.—The candles put out as before. The curtains of the bed in the drawing-room were many times forcibly drawn; the wood thrown out as before; a terrible crack like thunder was heard; and one of the servants, running to see if his masters were not killed, found at his return three dozen trenchers laid smoothly upon his bed under the quilt.

"*October* 26.—The beds were shaken as before; the windows seemed all broken to pieces, and glass fell in vast quantities all about the room. In the morning they found the windows all whole, but the floor strewed with broken glass, which they gathered and laid by.

"*October* 29.—At midnight candles went out as before; something walked majestically through the room, and opened and shut the window; great stones were thrown violently into the room, some whereof fell on the beds, others on the floor; and at about a quarter after one, a noise was heard as of forty cannon discharged together, and again repeated at about eight minutes' distance. This alarmed and raised all the neighborhood, who, coming into their honors' room, gathered up the great stones, fourscore in number, many of them like common pebbles and boulders, and laid them by, where they are to be seen to this day, at a corner of the adjoining field. This noise, like the discharge of cannon, was heard throughout the country for sixteen miles round. During these noises, which were heard in both rooms together, both the Commissioners and their servants gave one another over for lost, and cried out for help; and Giles Sharp, snatching up a sword, had well-nigh killed one of their honors, taking him for the spirit as he came in his shirt into the room. While they were together, the noise was continued, and part of the tiling of the house, and all the windows of an upper room, were taken away with it.

"*October* 30.—At midnight something walked into the chamber, treading like a bear; it walked many times about, then threw the warming-pan violently upon the floor, and so bruised it that it was spoiled. Vast quantities of glass were now thrown about the room, and vast numbers of great stones and horses' bones were thrown in; these were all found in the morning, and the floors, beds, and walls were all much damaged by the violence they were thrown in.

"*November* 1. Candles were placed in all parts of the room, and a great fire made. At midnight, the candles all yet burning, a noise like the burst of a cannon was heard in the room, and the burning billets were tossed all over the room and about the beds, that had not their honors called in Giles and his fellows, the house had been assuredly burned. An hour after the candles went out, as usual, the crack of many cannon was heard, and many pails full of green stinking water were thrown on their honors in bed; great stones were also thrown in as before, the bed-curtains and bedsteads torn and broken; the windows were now all really broken, and the whole neighborhood alarmed with the noises; nay, the very rabbit-stealers that were abroad that night in the warren were so frightened at the dismal thundering, that they fled for fear, and left their ferrits behind them.

"One of their honors this night spoke, and in the name of God asked what it was, and why it disturbed them so? No answer was given to this; but the noise ceased for a while, when the spirit came again, and, as they all agreed, brought with it seven devils worse than itself. One of the servants now lighted a large candle, and set it in the doorway between the two chambers, to see what passed; and as he * watched it, he plainly saw a hoof striking the candle and candlestick into the middle of the room, and afterwards making three scrapes over the snuff of the candle, to scrape it out. Upon this, the same person was so bold as to draw a sword; but he had scarce got it out, when he perceived another invisible hand had hold of it too, and pulled with him for it, and, at length prevailing, struck him so violently on the head with the pommel, that he fell down for dead with the blow. At this instant was heard another burst like the discharge of a broadside of a ship of war, and at about a minute or two's distance each, no less than nineteen more such; these shook the house so violently, that they expected every moment it would fall upon their heads. The neighbors on this were all alarmed, and, running to the house, they all joined in prayer and psalm-singing, during which the noise still continued in the other rooms, and the discharge of cannon without, though nobody was there."

Dr. Plot † concludes his relation of this memorable event ‡ with

---

* Probably this part was also played by Sharp, who was the regular ghost-seer of the party.

† [From this point to the end of the quotation the diction is slightly altered by Scott.]

‡ In his *Naturāl History of Oxfordshire.*

observing that, though tricks have often been played in affairs of this kind, many of these things are not reconcilable with juggling; such as, 1st, The loud noises beyond the power of man to make, without instruments which were not there; 2d, The tearing and breaking of the beds; 3d, The throwing about the fire; 4th, The hoof treading out the candle; and 5th, The striving for the sword, and the blow the man received from the pommel of it.

To show how great men are sometimes deceived, we may recur to the tract entitled *The Secret History of the Good Devil of Woodstock*, in which we find it, under the author's own hand, that he, Joseph Collins, commonly called Funny Joe, was himself this very devil; that, under the feigned name of Giles Sharp, he hired himself as a servant to the Commissioners; that, by the help of two friends—an unknown trap-door in the ceiling of the bedchamber, and a pound of common gunpowder—he played all these extraordinary tricks by himself; that his fellow-servants, whom he had introduced on purpose to assist him, had lifted up their own beds; and that the candles were contrived, by a common trick of gunpowder, to be extinguished at a certain time.

The dog who began the farce was, as Joe swore, no dog at all, but truly a bitch, who had shortly [the day] before whelped in that room, and made all this disturbance in seeking for her puppies; and which, when she had served his purpose, he (Joe Sharp, or Collins) let out, and then looked for. The story of the hoof and sword he himself bore witness to, and was never suspected as to the truth of them, though mere fictions. By the trap-door his friends let down stones, fagots, glass, water, etc., which they either left there or drew up again, as best suited his purpose; and by this way let themselves in and out, without opening the doors, or going through the keyholes; and all the noises described, he declares he made by placing quantities of white gunpowder over pieces of burning charcoal, on plates of tin, which, as they melted, exploded with a violent noise,

[One thing there was beyond all these, he tells us, which drove them from the house in reality, though they never owned it. This was, they had formed a reserve of part of the premises to themselves, and hid their mutual agreement, which they had drawn up in writing, under the earth in a pot, in a corner of the room in which they usually dined, in which an orange-tree grew. When in the midst of their dinner one day this earth of itself took fire, and burnt violently with a blue flame, filling the room with a strong sulphurous stench; and this he also professes was his own doing, by a secret mixture he had placed there the day before.]

I am very happy in having an opportunity of setting history right about these remarkable events, and would not have the reader disbelieve my author's account of them, from his naming either white gunpowder exploding when melted, or his making the earth about the pot take fire of its own accord; since, however improbable these accounts may appear to some readers, and whatever secrets they might be in Joe's time, they are now well known in chemistry. As to the last, there needs only to mix an equal quantity of iron filings, finely powdered, and powder of pure brimstone, and make them into a paste with fair water. This paste, when it hath lain together about twenty-six hours, will of itself take fire, and burn all the sulphur away with a blue flame and a bad smell. For the others, what he calls white gunpowder is plainly the thundering powder called by our chemists *pulvis fulminans*. It is composed of three parts of saltpetre, two parts of pearl ashes or salt of tartar, and one part of flour of brimstone, mixed together and beat to a fine powder; a small quantity of this held on the point of a knife over a candle will not go off till it melt, and then it gives a report like that of a pistol; and this he might easily dispose of in larger quantities, so as to make it explode of itself, while he, the said Joe, was with his masters.

Such is the explanation of the ghostly adventures of Woodstock, as transferred by Mr. Hone from the pages of the old tract termed the *Authentic Memoirs of the Memorable Joseph Collins of Oxford*, whose courage and loyalty were the only wizards which conjured up those strange and surprising apparitions and works of spirits which passed as so unquestionable in the eyes of the Parliamentary Commissioners, of Dr. Plot,, and other authors of credit. The *pulvis fulminans*, the secret principle he made use of, is now known to every apothecary's apprentice.

If my memory be not treacherous, the actor of these wonders made use of his skill in fireworks upon the following remarkable occasion. The Commissioners had not, in their zeal for the public service, overlooked their own private interests, and a deed was drawn up upon parchment, recording the share and nature of the advantages which they privately agreed to concede to each other; at the same time they were, it seems, loth to entrust to any one of their number the keeping of a document in which all were equally concerned. They hid the written agreement within a flower-pot, in which a shrub concealed it from the eyes of any chance spectator. But the rumor of the apparitions having gone abroad, curiosity drew many of the neighbors to Woodstock, and some in particular to whom the knowledge of this agreement would have afforded matter of scandal. As the Commissioners received these guests in the saloon where the flower-pot was placed, a match was suddenly set to some fireworks placed there by Sharp, the secretary. The flower-pot burst to pieces with the concussion, or was prepared so as to explode of itself, and the contract of the Commissioners, bearing testimony to their private roguery, was thrown into the midst of the visitors assembled. If I have recollected this incident accurately, for it is more than forty years since I perused the tract, it is probable that, in omitting it from the novel, I may also have passed over, from want of memory, other matters which might have made an essential addition to the story.

Nothing, indeed, is more certain than that incidents which are real preserve an infinite advantage in works of this nature over such as are fictitious. The tree, however, must remain where it has fallen.

Having occasion to be in London in October, 1831, I made some researches in the British Museum, and in that rich collection, with the kind assistance of the keepers, who manage it with so much credit to themselves and advantage to the public, I recovered two original pamphlets,* which contain a full account of the phenomena at Woodstock in 1649. The first is a satirical poem, published in that year, which plainly shows that the legend was current among the people in the very shape in which it was afterwards made public. I have not found the explanation of Joe Collins, which, as mentioned by Mr. Hone, resolves the whole into confederacy. It might, however, be recovered by a stricter search than I had leisure for. In the meantime, it may be observed, that neither the name of Joe Collins nor Sharp occurs among the *dramatis personæ* given in these tracts, published when he might have been endangered by anything which directed suspicion towards him, at least in 1649, and perhaps might have exposed him to danger even in 1660, from the malice of a powerful though defeated faction.*

1st *August*, 1832.

PREFACE TO FIRST EDITION.

It is not my purpose to inform my readers how the manuscripts of that eminent antiquary, the Rev. J. A. Rochecliffe, D.D., came into my possession. There are many ways in which such things happen, and it is enough to say they were rescued from an unworthy fate, and that they were honestly come by. As for the authenticity of the anecdotes which I have gleaned from the writings of this excellent person, and put together with my own unrivaled facility, the name of Dr. Rochecliffe will warrant accuracy, wherever that name happens to be known.

With his history the reading part of the world are well acquainted; and we might refer the tyro to honest Anthony

* See Appendix.

* [See Lockhart, *Life of Scott*, vol. viii. pp. 353–358.]

a Wood, who looked up to him as one of the pillars of High Church, and bestows on him an exemplary character in the *Athenæ Oxonienses*, although the Doctor was educated at Cambridge, England's other eye.

It is well known that Doctor Rochecliffe early obtained preferment in the church, on account of the spirited share which he took in the controversy with the Puritans; and that his work, entitled *Malleus Hæresis*, was considered as a knock-down blow by all except those who received it. It was that work which made him, at the early age of thirty, rector of Woodstock, and which afterwards secured him a place in the catalogue of the celebrated Century White; and, worse than being shown up by that fanatic, among the catalogues of scandalous and malignant priests admitted into benefices by the prelates, his opinions occasioned the loss of his living of Woodstock by the ascendency of presbytery. He was chaplain, during most part of the Civil War, to Sir Henry Lee's regiment, levied for the service of King Charles; and it was said he engaged more than once personally in the field. At least it is certain that Doctor Rochecliffe was repeatedly in great danger, as will appear from more passages than one in the following history, which speaks of his own exploits, like Cæsar, in the third person. I suspect, however, some Presbyterian commentator has been guilty of interpolating two or three passages. The manuscript was long in the possession of the Everards, a distinguished family of that persuasion.*

During the usurpation Doctor Rochecliffe was constantly engaged in one or other of the premature attempts at a restoration of monarchy; and was accounted, for his audacity, presence of mind, and depth of judgment, one of the greatest undertakers for the King in that busy time, with this trifling drawback, that the plots in which he busied himself were almost constantly detected. Nay, it was suspected that Cromwell himself sometimes contrived to suggest to him the intrigues in which he engaged, by which means the wily Protector made experiments on the fidelity of doubtful friends, and became well acquainted with the plots of declared enemies, which he thought it more easy to disconcert and disappoint than to punish severely.

Upon the Restoration, Doctor Rochecliffe regained his living of Woodstock, with other church preferment, and

* It is hardly necessary to say, unless to some readers of very literal capacity, that Doctor Rochecliffe and his manuscripts are alike apocryphal.

gave up polemics and political intrigues for philosophy. He was one of the constituent members of the Royal Society, and was the person through whom Charles required of that learned body solution of their curious problem, "Why, if a vessel is filled brimful of water, and a large live fish plunged into the water, nevertheless it shall not overflow the pitcher?" Doctor Rochecliffe's exposition of this phenomenon was the most ingenious and instructive of four that were given in; and it is certain the Doctor must have gained the honor of the day, but for the obstinacy of a plain, dull, country gentleman, who insisted that the experiment should be, in the first place, publicly tried. When this was done, the event showed it would have been rather rash to have adopted the facts exclusively on the royal authority; as the fish, however curiously inserted into his native element, splashed the water over the hall, and destroyed the credit of four ingenious essayists, besides a large Turkey carpet.

Doctor Rochecliffe, it would seem, died about 1685, leaving many papers behind him of various kinds, and, above all, many valuable anecdotes of secret history, from which the following Memoirs have been extracted, on which we intend to say only a few words by way of illustration.

The existence of Rosamond's Labyrinth, mentioned in these pages, is attested by Drayton in the reign of Queen Elizabeth.

> Rosamond's Labyrinth. whose ruins, together with her Well, being paved with square stone in the bottom, and also her Tower, from which the Labyrinth did run, are yet remaining . . . being vaults arched and walled with brick and stone, almost inextricably wound one with another, by which, if at any time her lodging were laid about by the Queen, she might easily avoid peril imminent, and, if need be, by secret issues take the air abroad, many furlongs about Woodstock, in Oxfordshire.*

It is highly probable that a singular piece of phantasmagoria, which was certainly played off upon the Commissioners of the Long Parliament, who were sent down to dispark and destroy Woodstock after the death of Charles I., was conducted by means of the secret passages and recesses in the ancient Labyrinth of Rosamond, round which successive monarchs had erected a hunting-seat or lodge.

There is a curious account of the disturbance given to those Honorable Commissioners, inserted by Dr. Plot in

* Drayton's *England's Heroical Epistles,* Note 1 on the Epistle, "Rosamond to King Henry."

his *Natural History of Oxfordshire*. But, as I have not the book at hand, I can only allude to the work of the celebrated Glanville, *Upon Witches*, who has extracted it as an highly-accredited narrative of supernatural dealings. The beds of the Commissioners and their servants were hoisted up till they were almost inverted, and then let down again so suddenly as to menace them with broken bones. Unusual and horrible noises disturbed those sacrilegious intromitters with royal property. The devil, on one occasion, brought them a warming-pan; on another, pelted them with stones and horses' bones. Tubs of water were emptied on them in their sleep; and so many other pranks of the same nature played at their expense, that they broke up housekeeping, and left their intended spoliation only half completed. The good sense of Doctor Plot suspected that these feats were wrought by conspiracy and confederation, which Glanville of course endeavors to refute with all his might; for it could scarce be expected that he, who believed in so convenient a solution as that of supernatural agency, would consent to relinquish the service of a key which will answer any lock, however intricate.

Nevertheless, it was afterwards discovered that Doctor Plot was perfectly right; and that the only demon who wrought all these marvels was a disguised Royalist—a fellow called Trusty Joe, or some such name, formerly in the service of the keeper of the park, but who engaged in that of the Commissioners on purpose to subject them to his persecution. I think I have seen some account of the real state of the transaction, and of the machinery by which the wizard worked his wonders; but whether in a book or a pamphlet, I am uncertain. I remember one passage particularly, to this purpose. The Commissioners having agreed to retain some articles out of the public account, in order to be divided among themselves, had entered into an indenture for ascertaining their share in the peculation, which they hid in a bow-pot for security. Now, when an assembly of divines, aided by the most strict religious characters in the neighborhood of Woodstock, were assembled to conjure down the supposed demon, Trusty Joe had contrived a firework, which he let off in the midst of the exorcism, and which destroyed the bow-pot; and, to the shame and confusion of the Commissioners, threw their secret indenture into the midst of the assembled ghost-seers, who became thus acquainted with their secret schemes of peculation.

It is, however, to little purpose for me to strain my memory about ancient and imperfect recollections concerning the particulars of these fantastic disturbances at Woodstock, since Doctor Rochecliffe's papers give such a much more accurate narrative than could be obtained from any account in existence before their publication. Indeed, I might have gone much more fully into this part of my subject, for the materials are ample; but, to tell the reader a secret, some friendly critics were of opinion they made the story hang on hand; and thus I was prevailed on to be more concise on the subject than I might otherwise have been.

The impatient reader, perhaps, is by this time accusing me of keeping the sun from him with a candle. Were the sunshine as bright, however, as it is likely to prove; and the flambeau, or link, a dozen of times as smoky, my friend must remain in the inferior atmosphere a minute longer, while I disclaim the idea of poaching on another's manor. Hawks, we say in Scotland, ought not to pick out hawks' eyes, or tire upon each other's quarry; and, therefore, if I had known that, in its date and its characters, this tale was likely to interfere with that recently published by a distinguished contemporary, I should unquestionably have left Doctor Rochecliffe's manuscript in peace for the present season. But before I was aware of this circumstance, this little book was half through the press; and I had only the alternative of avoiding any intentional imitation, by delaying a perusal of the contemporary work in question. Some accidental collision there must be, when works of a similar character are finished on the same general system of historical manners, and the same historical personages are introduced. Of course, if such have occurred, I shall be probably the sufferer. But my intentions have been at least innocent, since I look on it as one of the vantages attending the conclusion of *Woodstock*, that the finishing of my own task will permit me to have the pleasure of reading *Brambletye House*, from which I have hitherto conscientiously abstained.

WOODSTOCK.

CHAPTER I

Some were for gospel ministers,
And some for redcoat seculars,
As men most fit t' hold forth the word,
And wield the one and th' other sword.
BUTLER'S *Hudibras.*

THERE is a handsome parish church in the town of Woodstock—I am told so, at least, for I never saw it having scarce time, when at the place, to view the magnificence of Blenheim, its painted halls and tapestried bowers, and then return in due season to dine in hall with my learned friend, the provost of ——, being one of those occasions on which a man wrongs himself extremely if he lets his curiosity interfere with his punctuality. I had the church accurately described to me, with a view to this work; but, as I have some reason to doubt whether my informant had ever seen the inside of it himself, I shall be content to say that it is now a handsome edifice, most part of which was rebuilt forty or fifty years since, although it still contains some arches of the old chantry, founded, it is said, by King John. It is to this more ancient part of the building that my story refers.

On a morning in the end of September or beginning of October, in the year 1652 [1651], being a day appointed for a solemn thanksgiving for the decisive victory at Worcester, a respectable audience was assembled in the old chantry, or chapel, of King John.* The condition of the church and character of the audience both bore witness to the rage of civil war and the peculiar spirit of the times. The sacred edifice showed many marks of dilapidation. The windows, once filled with stained glass, had been dashed to pieces with pikes and muskets, as matters of and

*See John's Church, Woodstock. Note 1.

pertaining to idolatry. The carving on the reading-desk was damaged, and two fair screens of beautiful sculptured oak had been destroyed, for the same pithy and conclusive reason. The high altar had been removed, and the gilded railing which was once around it was broken down and carried off. The effigies of several tombs were mutilated, and now lay scattered about the church,

> Torn from their destined niche, unworthy meed
> Of knightly counsel or heroic deed!

The autumn wind piped through empty aisles, in which the remains of stakes and trevisses of rough-hewn timber, as well as a quantity of scattered hay and trampled straw, seemed to intimate that the hallowed precincts had been, upon some late emergency, made the quarters of a troop of horse.

The audience, like the building, was abated in splendor. None of the ancient and habitual worshipers during peaceful times were now to be seen in their carved galleries, with hands shadowing their brows, while composing their minds to pray where their fathers had prayed, and after the same mode of worship. The eye of the yeoman and peasant sought in vain the tall form of old Sir Henry Lee of Ditchley, as, wrapped in his laced cloak, and with beard and whiskers duly composed, he moved slowly through the aisles, followed by the faithful mastiff, or bloodhound, which in old time had saved his mater by his fidelity, and which regularly followed him to church. Bevis, indeed, fell under the proverb which avers, "He is a good dog which goes to church"; for, bating an occasional temptation to warble along with the accord, he behaved himself as decorously as any of the congregation, and returned as much edified, perhaps, as most of them. The damsels of Woodstock looked as vainly for the laced cloaks, jingling spurs, slashed boots, and tall plumes of the young cavaliers of this and other high-born houses, moving through the streets and the churchyard with the careless ease which indicates perhaps rather an overweening degree of self-confidence, yet shows graceful when mingled with good-humor and courtesy. The good old dames, too, in their white hoods and black velvet gowns, their daughters, "the cynosure of neighboring eyes,"—where were they all now, who, when they entered the church, use to divide men's thoughts between them and Heaven! "But, ah! Alice Lee—so sweet, so gentle, so condescending in thy loveliness," thus proceeds a contemporary annalist, whose manuscript we have deciphered; "why is my story to turn upon thy fallen fortunes? and why not rather to the period when, in the very dismounting from your palfrey, you attracted as many eyes as if an angel had descended, as many blessings as if the benignant being had come fraught with good tidings? No creature wert thou of an idle romancer's imagination, no being fantastically bedizened with inconsistent perfections: thy merits made me love thee well, and for thy faults—so well did they show amid thy good qualities, that I think they made me love thee better."

With the house of Lee had disappeared from the chantry of King John others of gentle blood and honored lineage—Freemantles, Winklecombes, Drycotts, etc.; for the air that blew over the towers of Oxford was unfavorable to the growth of Puritanism, which was more general in the neighboring counties. There were among the congregation, however, one or two that, by their habits and demeanor, seemed country gentlemen of consideration, and there were also present some of the notables of the town of Woodstock, cutlers or glovers chiefly, whose skill in steel or leather had raised them to a comfortable livelihood. These dignitaries wore long black cloaks, plaited close at the neck, and, like peaceful citizens, carried their Bibles and memorandum books at their girdles, instead of knife or sword.* This respectable, but least numerous, part of the audience were such decent persons as had adopted the Presbyterian form of faith, renouncing the liturgy and hierarchy of the Church of England, and living under the tuition of the Rev. Nehemiah Holdenough, much famed for the length and strength of his powers of predication. With these grave seniors sat their goodly dames in ruff and gorget, like the portraits which in catalogues of paintings are designed 'wife of a burgomaster', and their pretty daughters, whose study, like that of Chaucer's physician, was not always in the Bible, but who were, on the contrary, when a glance could escape the vigilance of their honored mothers, inattentive themselves and the cause of inattention in others.

But, besides these dignified persons, there were in the church a numerous collection of the lower orders, some brought thither by curiosity, but many of them unwashed

* This custom among the Puritans is mentioned often in old plays, and among others in the *Widow of Watling Street.*

artificers, bewildered in the theological discussions of the time, and of as many various sects as there are colors in the rainbow. The presumption of these learned Thebans being in exact proportion to their ignorance, the last was total and the first boundless. Their behavior in the church was anything but reverential or edifying. Most of them affected a cynical contempt for all that was only held sacred by human sanction: the church was to these men but a steeple-house, the clergyman an ordinary person, her ordinances dry bran and sapless pottage,* unfitted for the spiritualized palates of the saints, and the prayer and address to Heaven, to which each acceded or not, as in his too critical judgment he conceived fit.

The elder amongst them sat or lay on the benches, with their high steeple-crowned hats pulled over their severe and knitted brows, waiting for the Presbyterian parson, as mastiffs sit in dumb expectation of the bull that is to be brought to the stake. The younger mixed, some of them, a bolder license of manners with their heresies: they gazed round on the women, yawned, coughed, and whispered, eat apples, and cracked nuts, as if in the gallery of a theatre ere the piece commences.

Besides all these, the congregation contained a few soldiers, some in corslets and steel caps, some in buff, and others in red coats. These men of war had their bandoleers, with ammunition, slung round them, and rested on their pikes and muskets. They, too, had their peculiar doctrines on the most difficult points of religion, and united the extravagances of enthusiasm with the most determined courage and resolution in the field. The burghers of Woodstock looked on these military saints with no small degree of awe; for though not often sullied with deeds of plunder or cruelty, they had the power of both absolutely in their hands, and the peaceful citizens had no alternative, save submission to whatever the ill-regulated and enthusiastic imaginations of their martial guides might suggest.

After some time spent in waiting for him, Mr. Holdenough began to walk up the aisles of the chapel, not with the slow and dignified carriage with which the old rector was of yore wont to maintain the dignity of the surplice, but with a hasty step, like one who arrives too late at an appointment, and bustles forward to make the best use of

* See a curious vindication of this indecent simile here for the Common Prayer in Note 2, at end.

his time. He was a tall thin man, with an adust complexion, and the vivacity of his eye indicated some irascibility of temperament. His dress was brown, not black, and over his other vestments he wore, in honor of Calvin, a Geneva cloak of a blue color, which fell backwards from his shoulders as he posted on to the pulpit. His grizzled hair was cut as short as shears could perform the feat, and covered with a black silk skullcap, which stuck so close to his head, that the two ears expanded from under it as if they had been intended as handles by which to lift the whole person. Moreover, the worthy divine wore spectacles, and a long grizzled peaked beard, and he carried in his hand a small pocket Bible with silver clasps. Upon arriving at the pulpit, he paused a moment to take breath, then began to ascend the steps by two at a time.

But his course was arrested by a strong hand, which seized his cloak. It was that of one who had detached himself from the group of soldiery. He was a stout man of middle stature, with a quick eye, and a countenance which, though plain, had yet an expression that fixed the attention. His dress, though not strictly military, partook of that character. He wore large hose made of calves'-leather, and a tuck, as it was then called, or rapier, of tremendous length, balanced on the other side by a dagger. The belt was morocco, garnished with pistols.

The minister, thus intercepted in his duty, faced round upon the party who had seized him, and demanded, in no gentle tone, the meaning of the interruption.

"Friend," quoth the intruder, "is it thy purpose to hold forth to these good people?"

"Ay, marry is it," said the clergyman, "and such is my bounden duty. Woe to me if I preach not the Gospel. Prithee, friend, let me not in my labor——"

"Nay," said the man of warlike mien, "I am myself minded to hold forth; therefore, do thou desist, or if thou wilt do by mine advice, remain and fructify with those poor goslings, to whom I am presently about to shake forth the crumbs of comfortable doctrine."

"Give place, thou man of Satan," said the priest, waxing wroth; "respect mine order—my cloth."

"I see no more to respect in the cut of thy cloak, or in the cloth of which it is fashioned," said the other, "than thou didst in the bishop's rochets: they were black and white, thou art blue and brown. Sleeping dogs every one of you, lying down, loving to slumber—shepherds that starve the flock, but will not watch it, each looking to his own gain—hum."

Scenes of this indecent kind were so common at the time, that no one thought of interfering; the congregation looked on in silence, the better class scandalized, and the lower orders, some laughing, and others backing the soldier or minister, as their fancy dictated. Meantime the struggle waxed fiercer; Mr. Holdenough clamored for assistance.

"Master Mayor of Woodstock," he exclaimed, "wilt thou be among those wicked magistrates who bear the sword in vain? Citizens, will you not help your pastor? Worthy aldermen, will you see me strangled on the pulpit stairs by this man of buff and Belial? But lo, I will overcome him, and cast his cords from me."

As Holdenough spoke, he struggled to ascend the pulpit stairs, holding hard on the banisters. His tormentor held fast by the skirts of the cloak, which went nigh to the choking of the wearer, until, as he spoke the words last mentioned, in a half-strangled voice, Mr. Holdenough dexterously slipped the string which tied it round his neck, so that the garment suddenly gave way; the soldier fell backwards down the steps, and the liberated divine skipped into the pulpit and began to give forth a psalm of triumph over his prostrate adversary. But a great hubbub in the church marred his exultation, and although he and his faithful clerk continued to sing the hymn of victory, their notes were only heard by fits, like the whistle of a curlew during a gale of wind.

The cause of the tumult was as follows:—The Mayor was a zealous Presbyterian, and witnessed the intrusion of the soldier with great indignation from the very beginning, though he hesitated to interfere with an armed man while on his legs and capable of resistance. But no sooner did he behold the champion of Independency sprawling on his back, with the divine's Geneva cloak fluttering in his hands, than the magistrate rushed forward, exclaiming that such insolence was not to be endured, and ordered his constables to seize the prostrate champion, proclaiming, in the magnanimity of wrath, "I will commit every redcoat of them all—I will commit him were he Noll Cromwell himself!"

The worthy Mayor's indignation had overmastered his reason when he made this mistimed vaunt; for three soldiers, who had hitherto stood motionless like statues, made each a stride in advance, which placed them betwixt the municipal officers and the soldier, who was in the act of rising; then making at once the movement of resting arms according to the manual as then practised, their musket-butts rang on the church pavement within an inch of the gouty toes of Master Mayor. The energetic magistrate, whose efforts in favor of order were thus checked, cast one glance on his supporters, but that was enough to show him that force was not on his side. All had shrunk back on hearing that ominous clatter of stone and iron. He was obliged to descend to expostulation.

"What do you mean, my masters?" he said; "is it like a decent and God-fearing soldiery, who have wrought such things for the land as have never before been heard of, to brawl and riot in the church, or to aid, abet, and comfort a profane fellow, who hath, upon a solemn thanksgiving, excluded the minister from his own pulpit?"

"We have nought to do with thy church, as thou call'st it," said he who by a small feather in front of his morion, appeared to be the corporal of the party; "we see not why men of gifts should not be heard within these citadels of superstition, as well as the voice of the men of crape of old and the men of cloak now. Wherefore, we will pluck yon Jack Presbyter out of his wooden sentinel-box, and our own watchman shall relieve the guard, and mount thereon, and cry aloud and spare not."

"Nay, gentlemen," said the Mayor, "if such be your purpose, we have not the means to withstand you, being, as you see, peaceful and quiet men. But let me first speak with this worthy minister, Nehemiah Holdenough, to persuade him to yield up his place for the time without farther scandal."

The peacemaking Mayor then interrupted the quavering of Holdenough and the clerk, and prayed both to retire, else there would, he said, be certainly strife.

"Strife!" replied the Presbyterian divine, with scorn; "no fear of strife among men that dare not testify against this open profanation of the church and daring display of heresy. Would your neighbors of Banbury have brooked such an insult?"

"Come—come, Master Holdenough," said the Mayor, "put us not to mutiny and cry clubs. I tell you once more, we are not men of war or blood."

"Not more than may be drawn by the point of a needle," said the preacher, scornfully. "Ye tailors of Woodstock

—for what is a glover but a tailor working on kid-skin?—I forsake you, in scorn of your faint hearts and feeble hands, and will seek me elsewhere a flock which will not fly from their shepherd at the braying of the first wild ass which cometh from out the great desert."

So saying, the aggrieved divine departed from his pulpit, and shaking the dust from his shoes, left the church as hastily as he had entered it, though with a different reason for his speed. The citizens saw his retreat with sorrow, and not without a compunctious feeling, as if conscious that they were not playing the most courageous part in the world. The Mayor himself and several others left the church, to follow and appease him.

The Independent orator, late prostrate, was now triumphant, and inducting himself into the pulpit without farther ceremony, he pulled a Bible from his pocket, and selected his text from the forty-fifth Psalm—"Gird thy sword upon thy thigh, O most mighty, with thy glory and thy majesty: and in thy majesty ride prosperously." Upon this theme he commenced one of those wild declamations common at the period, in which men were accustomed to wrest and pervert the language of Scripture, by adapting it to modern events.* The language, which in its literal sense, was applied to King David, and typically referred to the coming of the Messiah, was, in the opinion of the military orator, most properly to be interpreted of Oliver Cromwell, the victorious general of the infant Commonwealth, which was never destined to come of age. "Gird on thy sword!" exclaimed the preacher, emphatically; "and was not that a pretty bit of steel as ever dangled from a corslet, or rung against a steel saddle? Ay, ye prick up your ears now, ye cutlers of Woodstock, as if ye should know something of a good fox broadsword. Did you forge it, I trow? Was the steel quenched with water from Rosamond's Well, or the blade blessed by the old cuckoldy priest of Godstow? You would have us think, I warrant me, that you wrought it and welded it, grinded and polished it, and all the while it never came on a Woodstock stithy! You were all too busy making whittles for the lazy crape-men of Oxford—bouncing priests, whose eyes were so closed up with fat, that they could not see destruction till she had them by the throat. But I can tell you where the sword was forged, and tempered, and welded, and grinded, and polished.

* See Vindication of the Book of Common Prayer. Note 2.

When you were, as I said before, making whittles for false priests, and daggers for dissolute G—d-d—n-me Cavaliers, to cut the people of England's throats with, it was forged at Long Marston Moor, where blows went faster than ever rung hammer on anvil; and it was tempered at Naseby, in the best blood of the Cavaliers; and it was welded in Ireland against the walls of Drogheda; and it was grinded on Scottish lives at Dunbar; and now of late it was polished in Worcester, till it shines as bright as the sun in the middle heaven, and there is no light in England that shall come nigh unto it."

Here the military part of the congregation raised a hum of approbation, which, being a sound like the "hear—hear" of the British House of Commons, was calculated to heighten the enthusiasm of the orator, by intimating the sympathy of the audience. "And then," resumed the preacher, rising in energy as he found that his audience partook in these feelings, "what sayeth the text? Ride on prosperously—do not stop—do not call a halt—do not quit the saddle—pursue the scattered fliers—sound the trumpet, not a levant or a flourish, but a point of war—sound, boot and saddle—to horse and away—a charge! Follow after the Young Man! What part have we in him? Slay, take, destroy, divide the spoil! Blessed art thou, Oliver, on account of thine honor; thy cause is clear, thy call is undoubted—never has defeat come near thy leading-staff, nor disaster attended thy banner. Ride on, flower of England's soldiers!—ride on, chosen leader of God's champions!—gird up the loins of thy resolution, and be steadfast to the mark of thy high calling!"

Another deep and stern hum, echoed by the ancient embowed arches of the old chantry, gave him an opportunity of an instant's repose; when the people of Woodstock heard him, and not without anxiety, turn the stream of his oratory into another channel.

"But wherefore, ye people of Woodstock, do I say these things to you, who claim no portion in our David, no interest in England's son of Jesse? You, who were fighting as well as your might could, and it was not very formidable, for the late Man, under that old bloodthirsty Papist Sir Jacob Aston, are you not now plotting, or ready to plot, for the restoring, as ye call it, of the Young Man—the unclean son of the slaughtered tyrant, the fugitive after whom the true hearts of England are now following, that they may take and slay him? 'Why should your rider turn his bridle our way?' Say you in your hearts; 'we will none of him; if we may help ourselves, we will rather turn us to wallow in the mire of monarchy, with the sow that was washed but newly.' Come, men of Woodstock, I will ask, and do you answer me. Hunger ye still after the flesh-pots of the monks of Godstow? and ye will say 'Nay'; but wherefore, except that the pots are cracked and broken, and the fire is extinguished wherewith thy oven used to boil? And again, I ask, drink ye still of the well of the fornications of the fair Rosamond? Ye will say "Nay"; but wherefore——?"

Here the orator, ere he could answer the question in his own way, was surprised by the following reply, very prettily pronounced by one of the congregation:—"Because you, and the like of you, have left us no brandy to mix with it."

All eyes turned to the audacious speaker, who stood beside one of the thick sturdy Saxon pillars, which he himself somewhat resembled, being short of stature, but very strongly made, a squat broad Little John sort of figure, leaning on a quarter-staff, and wearing a jerkin, which, though now sorely stained and discolored, had once been of the Lincoln green, and showed remnants of having been laced. There was an air of careless, good-humored audacity about the fellow; and, though under military restraint, there were some of the citizens who could not help crying out—"Well said, Joceline Joliffe!"

"Jolly Joceline, call ye him?" proceeded the preacher, without showing either confusion or displeasure at the interruption; "I will make him Joceline of the jail, if he interrupts me again. One of your park-keepers, I warrant, that can never forget they have borne C. R. upon their badges and bugle-horns, even as a dog bears his owner's name on his collar—a pretty emblem for Christian men! But the brute beast hath the better of him: the brute weareth his own coat, and the caitiff thrall wears his master's. I have seen such a wag make a rope's end wag ere now. Where was I? Oh, rebuking you for your backslidings, men of Woodstock. Yes, then ye will say ye have renounced Popery, and ye have renounced Prelacy, and then ye wipe your mouth like Pharisees as ye are; and who but you for purity of religion! But I tell you, ye are but like Jehu the son of Nimshi, who broke down the house of Baal, yet departed not from the sins of Jeroboam. Even so ye eat not fish on Friday with the blinded Papists, nor mince pies on the twenty-fifth day of December, like the slothful Prelatists; but ye will gorge on sack-posset each night in the year with your blind Presbyterian guide, and ye will speak evil of dignities, and revile the Commonwealth; and ye will glorify yourselves in your park of Woodstock, and say, 'Was it not walled in first of any other in England, and that by Henry, son of William called the Conqueror?' And ye have a princely lodge therein, and call the same a royal lodge; and ye have an oak which ye call the King's Oak; and ye steal and eat the venison of the park, and ye say, 'This is the king's venison, we will wash it down with a cup to the king's health: better we eat it than those Roundheaded Commonwealth knaves.' But listen unto me and take warning. For these things come we to controversy with you. And our name shall be a cannon-shot, before which your lodge, in the pleasantness whereof ye take pastime, shall be blown into ruins; and we will be as a wedge to split asunder the King's Oak into billets to heat a brown baker's oven; and we will dispark your park, and slay your deer, and eat them ourselves, neither shall you have any portion thereof, whether in neck or haunch. Ye shall not haft a tenpenny knife with the horns thereof, neither shall ye cut a pair of breeches out of the hide, for all ye be cutlers and glovers; and ye shall have no comfort or support neither from the sequestrated traitor Henry Lee, who called himself ranger of Woodstock, nor from any on his behalf; for they are coming hither who shall be called Maher-shalal-hash-baz, because he maketh haste to the spoil."

Here ended this wild effusion, the latter part of which fell heavy on the souls of the poor citizens of Woodstock, as tending to confirm a report of an unpleasing nature which had been lately circulated. The communication with London was indeed slow, and the news which it transmitted were uncertain; no less uncertain were the times themselves, and the rumors which were circulated, exaggerated by the hopes and fears of so many various factions. But the general stream of report, so far as Woodstock was concerned, had of late run uniformly in one direction. Day after day they had been informed that the fatal fiat of Parliament had gone out, for selling the park of Woodstock, destroying its lodge, disparking its forest, and erasing, as far as they could be erased, all traces of its ancient fame. Many of the citizens were likely to be sufferers on this occasion, as several of them enjoyed, either by sufferance or right, various convenient privileges of pasturage, cutting firewood, and the like, in the royal chase; and all the inhabitants of the little borough were hurt to think that the scenery of the place was to be destroyed, its edifices ruined, and its honors rent away. This is a patriotic sensation often found in such places, which ancient distinctions and long-cherished recollections of former days render so different from towns of recent date. The natives of Woodstock felt it in the fullest force. They had trembled at the anticipated calamity; but now, when it was announced by the appearance of those dark, stern, and at the same time omnipotent, soldiers—now that they heard it proclaimed by the mouth of one of their military preachers, they considered their fate as inevitable. The causes of disagreement among themselves were for the time forgotten, as the congregation, dismissed without psalmody or benediction, went slowly and mournfully homeward, each to his own place of abode.

CHAPTER II.

Come forth, old man. Thy daughter's side
  Is now the fitting place for thee;
When Time hath quell'd the oak's bold pride,
  The youthful tendril yet may hide
    The ruins of the parent tree.

WHEN the sermon was ended, the military orator wiped his brow; for, notwithstanding the coolness of the weather, he was heated with the vehemence of his speech and action. He then descended from the pulpit and spoke a word or two to the corporal who commanded the party of soldiers, who, replying by a sober nod of intelligence, drew his men together, and marched them in order to their quarters in the town.

The preacher himself, as if nothing extraordinary had happened, left the church and sauntered through the streets of Woodstock, with the air of a stranger who was viewing the town, without seeming to observe that he was himself in his turn anxiously surveyed by the citizens, whose furtive yet frequent glances seemed to regard him as something alike suspected and dreadful, yet on no account to be provoked. He heeded them not, but stalked on in the manner affected by the distinguished fanatics of the day—a stiff, solemn pace, a severe, and at the same time a contemplative, look, like that of a man discomposed at the interruption which earthly objects forced upon him, obliging him by their intrusion to withdraw his thoughts for an instant from celestial things. Innocent pleasures of what kind soever they held in suspicion and contempt, and innocent mirth they abominated. It was, however, a cast of mind that formed men for great and manly actions, as it adopted principle, and that of an unselfish character, for the ruling motive, instead of the gratification of passion. Some of these men were indeed hypocrites, using the cloak of religion only as a covering for their ambition; but many really possessed the devotional character and the severe republican virtue which others only affected. By far the greater number hovered between these extremes, felt to a certain extent the power of religion, and complied with the times in affecting a great deal.

The individual whose pretensions to sanctity, written as they were upon his brow and gait, have given rise to the above digression reached at length the extremity of the principal street, which terminates upon the park of Woodstock. A battlemented portal of Gothic appearance defended the entrance to the avenue. It was of mixed architecture, but on the whole, though composed of the styles of the different ages when it had received additions, had a striking and imposing effect. An immense gate composed of rails of hammered iron, with many a flourish and scroll, displaying as its uppermost ornament the ill-fated cipher of C. R., was now decayed, being partly wasted with rust, partly by violence.

The stranger paused, as if uncertain whether he should demand or assay entrance. He looked through the grating down an avenue skirted by majestic oaks, which led onward with a gentle curve, as if into the depths of some ample and ancient forest. The wicket of the large iron gate being left unwittingly open, the soldier was tempted to enter, yet with some hesitation, as he that intrudes upon ground which he conjectures may be prohibited; indeed his manner showed more reverence for the scene than could have been expected from his condition and character. He slackened his stately and consequential pace, and at length stood still and looked around him.

Not far from the gate, he saw rising from the trees one or two ancient and venerable turrets, bearing each its own vane of rare device glittering in the autumn sun. These indicated the ancient hunting-seat, or lodge, as it was called, which had, since the time of Henry II., been occasionally the residence of the English monarchs, when it pleased them to visit the woods of Oxford, which then so abounded in game that, according to old Fuller, huntsmen and falconers were nowhere better pleased. The situation which the lodge occupied was a piece of flat ground, now planted with sycamores, not far from the entrance to that magnificent spot where the spectator first stops to gaze upon Blenheim, to think of Marlborough's victories, and to applaud or criticise the cumbrous magnificence of Vanburgh's style.

There, too, paused our military preacher, but with other thoughts, and for other purpose, than to admire the scene around him. It was not long afterwards when he beheld two persons, a male and a female, approaching slowly, and so deeply engaged in their own conversation that they did not raise their eyes to observe that there stood a stranger in the path before them. The soldier took advantage of their state of abstraction, and, desirous at once to watch their motions and avoid their observation, he glided beneath one of the huge trees which skirted the path, and whose boughs, sweeping the ground on every side, ensured him against discovery, unless in case of an actual search.

In the meantime, the gentleman and lady continued to advance, directing their course to a rustic seat, which still enjoyed the sunbeams, and was placed adjacent to the tree where the stranger was concealed.

The man was elderly, yet seemed bent more by sorrow and infirmity than by the weight of years. He wore a mourning cloak, over a dress of the same melancholy color, cut in that picturesque form which Vandyck has rendered immortal. But although the dress was handsome, it was put on and worn with a carelessness which showed the mind of the wearer ill at ease. His aged, yet still handsome, countenance had the same air of consequence which distinguished his dress and his gait. A striking part of his appearance was a long white beard, which descended far over the breast of his slashed doublet, and looked singular from its contrast in color with his habit.

The young lady, by whom this venerable gentleman seemed to be in some degree supported as they walked arm in arm, was a slight and sylph-like form, with a person so delicately made, and so beautiful in countenance, that it seemed the earth on which she walked was too grossly massive a support for a creature so aerial. But mortal beauty must share human sorrows. The eyes of the beautiful being showed tokens of tears; her color was heightened as she listened to her aged companion; and it was plain, from his melancholy yet displeased look, that the conversation was as distressing to himself as to her. When they sat down on the bench we have mentioned, the gentleman's discourse could be distinctly overheard by the eavesdropping soldier, but the answers of the young lady reached his ear rather less distinctly.

"It is not to be endured!" said the old man, passionately; "it would stir up a paralytic wretch to start up a soldier. My people have been thinned, I grant you, or have fallen off from me in these times. I owe them no grudge for it, poor knaves; what should they do waiting on me, when the pantry has no bread and the buttery no ale? But we have still about us some rugged foresters of the old Woodstock breed—old as myself most of them. What of that? old wood seldom warps in the wetting. I will hold out the old house, and it will not be the first time that I have held it against ten times the strength that we hear of now."

"Alas! my dear father!" said the young lady, in a tone which seemed to intimate his proposal of defense to be altogether desperate.

"And why, alas?" said the gentleman, angrily; "is it because I shut my door against a score or two of these bloodthirsty hypocrites?"

"But their masters can as easily send a regiment or an army, if they will," replied the lady; "and what good would your present defense do, excepting to exasperate them to your utter destruction?"

"Be it so, Alice," replied her father; "I have lived my time, and beyond it. I have outlived the kindest and most prince-like of masters. What do I do on the earth since the dismal Thirtieth of January? The parricide of that day was a signal to all true servants of Charles Stuart to avenge his death, or die as soon after as they could find a worthy opportunity."

"Do not speak thus, sir, said Alice Lee: "it does not become your gravity and your worth to throw away that life which may yet be of service to your king and country. It will not and cannot always be thus. England will not long endure the rulers which these bad times have assigned her. In the meanwhile—(here a few words escaped the listener's ears)—and beware of that impatience which makes bad worse."

"Worse!" exclaimed the impatient old man. "*What* can be worse? Is it not at the worst already? Will not these people expel us from the only shelter we have left, dilapidate what remains of royal property under my charge, make the palace of princes into a den of thieves, and then wipe their mouths and thank God, as if they had done an alms-deed?"

"Still," said his daughter, "there is hope behind, and I trust the King is ere this out of their reach. We have reason to think well of my brother Albert's safety."

"Aye, Albert! there again," said the old man, in a tone of reproach; "had it not been for thy entreaties I had gone to Worcester myself; but I must needs lie here like a worthless hound when the hunt is up, when who knows what service I might have shown? An old man's head is sometimes useful when his arm is but little worth. But you and Albert were so desirous that he should go alone, and now who can say what has become of him?"

"Nay—nay, father," said Alice, "we have good hope that Albert escaped from that fatal day; young Abney saw him a mile from the field."

"Young Abney lied, I believe," said the father, in the same humor of contradiction. "Young Abney's tongue seems quicker than his hands, but far slower than his horse's heels when he leaves the Roundheads behind him. I would rather Albert's dead body were laid between Charles and Cromwell than hear he fled as early as young Abney."

"My dearest father," said the young lady, weeping as she spoke, "what can I say to comfort you?"

"Comfort me, say'st thou, girl? I am sick of comfort: an honorable death, with the ruins of Woodstock for my monument, were the only comfort to old Henry Lee. Yes, by the memory of my fathers! I will make good the lodge against these rebellious robbers."

"Yet be ruled, dearest father," said the maiden, "and submit to that which we cannot gainsay. My uncle Everard——"

Here the old man caught at her unfinished words. "Thy uncle Everard, wench! Well, get on. What of thy precious and loving uncle Everard?"

"Nothing, sir," she said, "if the subject displeases you."

"Displeases me!" he replied, "why should it displease me? or if it did, why shouldst thou, or any one, affect to care about it? What is it that hath happened of late years —what is it can be thought to happen that astrologer can guess at—which can give pleasure to us?"

"Fate," she replied, "may have in store the joyful restoration of our banished prince."

"Too late for my time, Alice," said the knight; "if there be such a white page in the heavenly book, it will not be turned until long after my day. But I see thou wouldst escape me. In a word, what of thy uncle Everard?"

"Nay, sir," said Alice, "God knows I would rather be silent forever than speak what might, as you would take it, add to your present distemperature."

"Distemperature!" said her father. "Oh, thou art a sweet-lipped physician, and wouldst, I warrant me, drop nought but sweet balm, and honey, and oil on my distemperature, if that is the phrase for an old man's aliment, when he is wellnigh heartbroken. Once more, what of thy uncle Everard?"

His last words were uttered in a high and peevish tone of voice; and Alice Lee answered her father in a trembling and submissive tone.

"I only meant to say, sir, that I am well assured that my uncle Everard, when we quit this place——"

"That is to say, when we are kicked out of it by crop-eared canting villains like himself. But on with thy bountiful uncle—what will he do? Will he give us the remains of his worshipful and economical housekeeping, the fragments of a thrice-sacked capon twice a-week, and a plentiful fast on the other five days? Will he give us beds beside his half-starved nags, and put them under a short allowance of straw, that his sister's husband—that I should have called my deceased angel by such a name!—and his sister's daughter, may not sleep on the stones? Or will he send us a noble each, with a warning to make it last, for he had never known the ready penny so hard to come by? Or what else will your uncle Everard do for us? Get us a furlough to beg? Why, I can do that without him."

"You misconstrue him much," answered Alice with more spirit than she had hitherto displayed; "and would you but question your own heart, you would acknowledge—I speak with reverence—that your tongue utters what your better judgment would disown. My uncle Everard is neither a miser nor a hypocrite—neither so fond of the goods of this world that he would not supply our distresses amply, nor so wedded to fanatical opinions as to exclude charity for other sects beside his own."

"Ay—ay, the Church of England is a *sect* with him, I doubt not, and perhaps with thee too, Alice," said the knight. "What is a Muggletonian, or a Ranter, or a Brownist, but a sectary? and thy phrase places them all, with Jack Presbyter himself, on the same footing with our learned prelates and religious clergy! Such is the cant of the day thou livest in, and why shouldst thou not talk like one of the wise virgins and psalm-singing sisters, since, though thou hast a profane old Cavalier for a father, thou art own niece to pious uncle Everard?"

"If you speak thus, my dear father," said Alice, "what can I answer you? Hear me but one patient word, and I shall have discharged my uncle Everard's commission?"

"Oh, it is a commission then? Surely, I suspected so

much from the beginning—nay, have some sharp guess touching the ambassador also. Come, madam the mediator, do your errand, and you shall have no reason to complain of my patience."

"Then, sir," replied his daughter, "my uncle Everard desires you would be courteous to the Commissioners who come here to sequestrate the parks and the property, or, at least, heedfully to abstain from giving them obstacle or opposition; it can, he says, do no good, even on your own principles, and it will give a pretext for proceeding against you as one in the worst degree of malignity, which he thinks may otherwise be prevented. Nay, he has good hope that if you follow his counsel, the committee may, through the interest he possesses, be inclined to remove the sequestration of your estate on a moderate fine. Thus says my uncle; and having communicated his advice, I have no occasion to urge your patience with farther argument."

"It is well thou dost not, Alice," answered Sir Henry Lee, in a tone of suppressed anger; "for, by the blessed Rood, thou hast well-nigh led me into the heresy of thinking thee no daughter of mine. Ah! my beloved companion, who art now far from the sorrows and cares of this weary world, couldst thou have thought that the daughter thou didst clasp to thy bosom would, like the wicked wife of Job, become a temptress to her father in the hour of affliction, and recommend to him to make his conscience truckle to his interest, and to beg back at the bloody hands of his master's, and perhaps his son's, murderers a wretched remnant of the royal property he has been robbed of? Why, wench, if I must beg, think'st thou I will sue to those who have made me a mendicant? No. I will never show my gray beard, worn in sorrow for my sovereign's death, to move the compassion of some proud sequestrator, who perhaps was one of the parricides. No; if Henry Lee must sue for food, it shall be of some sound loyalist like himself, who having but half a loaf remaining, will not nevertheless refuse to share it with him. For his daughter, she may wander her own way, which leads her to a refuge with her wealthy Roundhead kinsfolk; but let her no more call him father whose honest indigence she has refused to share."

"You do me injustice, sir," answered the young lady, with a voice animated, yet faltering—"cruel injustice. God knows, your way is my way, though it lead to ruin and beggary; and while you tread it, my arm shall support you while you will accept an aid so feeble."

"Thou word'st me, girl," answered the old Cavalier—"thou word'st me, as Will Shakspeare says: thou speakest of lending me thy arm; but thy secret thought is thyself to hang upon Markham Everard's."

"My father—my father," answered Alice, in a tone of deep grief, "what can thus have altered your clear judgment and kindly heart? Accursed be these civil commotions! not only do they destroy men's bodies, but they pervert their souls; and the brave, the noble, the generous become suspicious, harsh, and mean. Why upbraid me with Markham Everard? Have I seen or spoke to him since you forbid him my company, with terms less kind—I will speak it truly—than was due even to the relationship betwixt you? Why think I would sacrifice to that young man my duty to you? Know that, were I capable of such criminal weakness, Markham Everard were the first to despise me for it."

She put her handkerchief to her eyes, but she could not hide her sobs, nor conceal the distress they intimated.

The old man was moved. "I cannot tell," he said, "what to think of it. Thou seem'st sincere, and wert ever a good and kindly daughter—how thou hast let that rebel youth creep into thy heart I wot not; perhaps it is a punishment on me, who thought the loyalty of my house was like undefiled ermine. Yet here is a damned spot, and on the fairest gem of all—my own dear Alice. But do not weep—we have enough to vex us. Where is it that Shakspeare hath it—

> Gentle daughter,
> Give even way unto my rough affairs;
> Put you not on the temper of the times,
> Nor be, like them, to Percy troublesome?"

"I am glad," answered the young lady, "to hear you quote your favorite again, sir. Our little jars are ever well-nigh ended when Shakspeare comes in play."

"His book was the closet-companion of my blessed master," said Sir Henry Lee; "after the Bible—with reverence for naming them together!—he felt more comfort in it than in any other; and as I have shared his disease, why, it is natural I should take his medicine. Albeit, I pretend not to my master's art in explaining the dark passages; for I am but a rude man, and rustically brought up to arms and hunting."

"You have seen Shakspeare yourself, sir?" said the young lady.

"Silly wench," replied the knight, "he died when I was a mere child—thou hast heard me say so twenty times; but thou wouldst lead the old man away from the tender subject. Well, though I am not blind, I can shut my eyes and follow. Ben Jonson I knew, and could tell thee many a tale of our meetings at the Mermaid, where, if there was much wine, there was much wit also. We did not sit blowing tobacco in each other's faces, and turning up the whites of our eyes as we turned up the bottom of the wine-pot. Old Ben adopted me as one of his sons in the muses. I have shown you, have I not, the verses, 'To my much beloved son, the worshipful Sir Henry Lee of Ditchley, Knight and Baronet'?"

"I do not remember them at present, sir," replied Alice.

"I fear ye lie, wench," said her father; but no matter—thou canst not get any more fooling out of me just now. The Evil Spirit hath left Saul for the present. We are now to think what is to be done about leaving Woodstock—or defending it?"

"My dearest father," said Alice, "can you still nourish a moment's hope of making good the place?"

"I know not, wench," replied Sir Henry; "I would fain have a parting blow with them, 'tis certain, and who knows where a blessing may alight? But then, my poor knaves that must take part with me in so hopeless a quarrel—that thought hampers me, I confess."

"Oh, let it do so, sir," replied Alice, "there are soldiers in the town, and there are three regiments at Oxford."

"Ah, poor Oxford!" exclaimed Sir Henry, whose vacillating state of mind was turned by a word to any new subject that was suggested. "Seat of learning and loyalty! these rude soldiers are unfit inmates for thy learned halls and poetical bowers; but thy pure and brilliant lamp shall defy the foul breath of a thousand churls, were they to blow at it like Boreas. The burning bush shall not be consumed, even by the heat of this persecution."

"True, sir," said Alice, "and it may not be useless to recollect, that any stirring of the Royalists at this unpropitious moment will make them deal yet more harshly with the university, which they consider as being at the bottom of everything which moves for the King in these parts."

"It is true, wench," replied the knight; and small cause would make the villains sequestrate the poor remains which the civil wars have left to the colleges. That, and the risk of my poor fellows—— Well, thou hast disarmed me, girl. I will be as patient and calm as a martyr."

"Pray God you keep your word, sir!" replied his daughter; "but you are ever so much moved at the sight of any of these men, that——"

"Would you make a child of me, Alice?" said Sir Henry. "Why, know you not that I can look upon a viper, or a toad, or a bunch of engendering adders, without any worse feeling than a little disgust? and though a Roundhead, and especially a redcoat, are in my opinion more poisonous than vipers, more loathsome than toads, more hateful than knotted adders, yet can I overcome my nature so far, that, should one of them appear at this moment, thyself should see how civilly I woulden treat him."

As he spoke, the military preacher abandoned his leafy screen, and stalking forward, stood unexpectedly before the old Cavalier, who stared at him, as if he had thought his expressions had actually raised the devil.

"Who art thou?" at length said Sir Henry, in a raised and angry voice, while his daughter clung to his arm in terror, little confident that her father's pacific resolutions would abide the shock of this unwelcome apparition.

"I am one," replied the soldier, "who neither fear nor shame to call myself a poor day-laborer in the great work of England—umph! Ay, a simple and sincere upholder of the good old cause."

"And what the devil do you seek here?" said the old knight, fiercely.

"The welcome due to the steward of the Lords Commissioners," answered the soldier.

"Welcome art thou as salt would be to sore eyes," said the Cavalier. "But who be your Commissioners, man?"

The soldier with little courtesy held out a scroll, which Sir Henry took from him betwixt his finger and thumb, as if it were a letter from a pest-house; and held it at as much distance from his eyes as his purpose of reading it would permit. He then read aloud, and as he named the parties one by one, he added a short commentary on each name, addressed, indeed, to Alice, but in such a tone that showed he cared not for its being heard by the soldier.

"*Desborough*—the plowman Desborough—as groveling a clown as is in England—a fellow that would be best at home, like an ancient Scythian, under the tilt of a wagon; d—n him. *Harrison*, bloody-minded, a ranting enthusiast, who read the Bible to such purpose, that he never lacked a text to justify a murder; d—n him too. *Bletson*—a true-blue Commonwealth's man, one of Harrison's [Harrington's] Rota Club, with his noddle full of new-fangled notions about government, the clearest object of which is to establish the tail upon the head; a fellow who leaves you the statutes and law of old England, to prate of Rome and Greece—sees the Areopagus in Westminster Hall, and takes Old Noll for a Roman consul. Adad, he is like to prove a dictator amongst them instead. Never mind; d—n Bletson too."

"Friend," said the soldier, "I would willingly be civil, but it consists not with my duty to hear these godly men, in whose service I am, spoken of after this irreverent and unbecoming fashion. And albeit I know that you Malignants think you have a right to make free with that damnation which you seem to use as your own portion, yet it is superfluous to invoke it against others, who have better hopes in their thoughts and better words in their mouths."

"Thou art but a canting varlet," replied the knight; "and yet thou art right in some sense; for it is superfluous to curse men who already are damned as black as the smoke of hell itself."

"I prithee forbear," continued the soldier, "for manners' sake, if not for conscience: grisly oaths suit ill with gray beards."

"Nay, that is truth, if the devil spoke it," said the knight; "and I thank Heaven I can follow good counsel, though Old Nick gives it. And so, friend, touching these same Commissioners, bear them this message; that Sir Henry Lee is keeper of Woodstock Park, with right of waif and stray, vert and venison, as complete as any of them have to their estate—that is, if they possess any estate but what they have gained by plundering honest men—nevertheless, he will give place to those who have made their might their right, and will not expose the lives of good and true men, where the odds are so much against them. And he protests that he makes this surrender, neither as acknowledging of these so termed Commissioners, nor as for his own individual part fearing their force, but purely to avoid the loss of English blood, of which so much hath been spilt in these late times."

"It is well spoken," said the steward of the Commissioners; "and therefore, I pray you, let us walk together into the house, that thou mayest deliver up unto me the vessels, and gold and silver ornaments, belonging unto the Egyptian Pharaoh who committed them to thy keeping."

"What vessels?" exclaimed the fiery old knight; "and belonging to whom? Unbaptized dog, speak civil of the Martyr in my presence, or I will do a deed misbecoming of me on that caitiff corpse of thine!" And shaking his daughter from his right arm, the old man laid his hand on his rapier.

His antagonist, on the contrary, kept his temper completely, and waving his hand to add impression to his speech, he said, with a calmness which aggravated Sir Henry's wrath "Nay, good friend, I prithee be still, and brawl not: it becomes not gray hairs and feeble arms to rail and rant like drunkards. Put me not to use the carnal weapon in mine own defense, but listen to the voice of reason. Seest thou not that the Lord had decided this great controversy in favor of us and ours, against thee and thine? Wherefore render up thy stewardship peacefully, and deliver up to me the chattels of the Man, Charles Stuart."

"Patience is a good nag, but she will bolt," said the knight, unable longer to rein in his wrath. He plucked his sheathed rapier from his side, struck the soldier a severe blow with it, and instantly drawing it, and throwing the scabbard over the trees, placed himself in a posture of defense, with his sword's point within half a yard of the steward's body. The latter stepped back with activity, threw his long cloak from his shoulders, and drawing his long tuck, stood upon his guard. The swords clashed smartly together, while Alice, in her terror, screamed wildly for assistance. But the combat was of short duration. The old Cavalier had attacked a man as cunning of fence as he himself, or a little more so, and possessing all the strength and activity of which time had deprived Sir Henry, and the calmness which the other had lost in his passion. They had scarce exchanged three passes ere the sword of the knight flew up in the air, as if it had gone in search of the scabbard; and burning with shame and anger, Sir Henry stood disarmed, at the mercy of his antagonist. The republican showed no purpose of abusing his victory; nor did he, either during the combat or after the victory was won, in any respect alter the sour and grave composure which reigned upon his countenance: a combat of life and death seemed to him a thing as familiar, and as little to be feared, as an ordinary bout with foils.

"Thou art delivered into my hands," he said, "and by the law of arms I might smite thee under the fifth rib, even as Asahel was strcuck dead by Abner, the son of Ner, as he followed the chase on the hill of Ammah, that lieth before Giah, in the way of the wilderness of Gibeon; but far be it from me to spill thy remaining drops of blood. True it is, thou art the captive of my sword and of my spear; nevertheless, seeing that there may be a turning from thine evil ways, and a returning to those which are good, if the Lord enlarge thy date for repentance and amendment, wherefore should it be shortened by a poor sinful mortal, who is, speaking truly, but thy fellow-worm?"

Sir Henry Lee remained still confused and unable to answer, when there arrived a fourth person, whom the cries of Alice had summoned to the spot. This was Joceline Joliffe, one of the under-keepers of the walk, who, seeing how matters stood, brandished his quarterstaff, a weapon from which he never parted, and having made it describe the figure of eight in a flourish through the air, would have brought it down with a vengeance upon the head of the steward, had not Sir Henry interposed.

"We must trail bats now, Joceline, our time of shouldering them is past. It skills not striving against the stream: the devil rules the roast, and makes our slaves our tutors."

At this moment another auxiliary rushed out of the thicket to the knight's assistance. It was a large wolf-dog, in strength a mastiff, in form and almost in fleetness a greyhound. Bevis was the noblest of the kind which ever pulled down a stag, tawny-colored like a lion, with a black muzzle and black feet, just edged with a line of white round the toes. He was as tractable as he was strong and bold, Just as he was about to rush upon the soldier, the words, "Peace, Bevis!" from Sir Henry converted the lion into a lamb, and, instead of pulling the soldier down, he walked round and round, and snuffed, as if using all his sagacity to discover who the stranger could be towards whom, though of so questionable an appearance, he was enjoined forbearance. Apparently he was satisfied, for he laid aside his doubtful and threatening demonstrations, lowered his ears, smoothed down his bristles, and wagged his tail.

Sir Henry, who had great respect for the sagacity of his favorite, said in a low voice to Alice, "Bevis is of thy opinion, and counsels submission. There is the finger of Heaven in this to punish the pride ever the fault of our house. Friend," he continued, addressing the soldier, "thou hast given the finishing touch to a lesson which ten years of constant misfortune have been unable fully to teach me. Thou hast distinctly shown me the folly of thinking that a good cause can strengthen a weak arm. God forgive me for the thought, but I could almost turn infidel, and believe that Heaven's blessing goes ever with the longest sword. But it will not be always thus. God knows His time. Reach me my Toledo, Joceline, yonder it lies; and the scabbard, see where it hangs on the tree. Do not pull at my cloak, Alice, and look so miserably frightened: I shall be in no hurry to betake me to bright steel again, I promise thee. For thee, good fellow, I thank thee, and will make way for thy masters without farther dispute or ceremony. Joceline Joliffe is nearer thy degree than I am, and will make surrender to thee of the lodge and household stuff. Withhold nothing, Joliffe: let them have all. For me, I will never cross the threshold again. But where to rest for a night? I would trouble no one in Woodstock; hum—ay—it shall be so. Alice and I, Joceline, will go down to thy hut by Rosamond's Well: we will borrow the shelter of thy roof for one night at least; thou wilt give us welcome, wilt thou not? How now—a clouded brow?"

Joceline certainly looked embarrassed, directed first a glance to Alice, then looked to heaven, then to earth, and last to the four quarters of the horizon, and then murmured out, "Certainly—without question—might he but run down to put the house in order."

"Order enough—order enough, for those that may soon be glad of clean straw in a barn," said the knight. "But if thou hast an ill-will to harbor any obnoxious or malignant persons, as the phrase goes, never shame to speak it out, man. 'Tis true, I took thee up when thou wert but a ragged Robin,* made a keeper of thee, and so forth. What of that? Sailors think no longer of the wind than when it forwards them on the voyage: thy betters turn with the tide, why should not such a poor knave as thou?"

"God pardon your honor for your harsh judgment," said Joliffe. "The hut is yours, such as it is, and should be were it a king's palace, as I wish it were, even for your honor's sake and Mistress Alice's; only I could wish your honor would condescend to let me step down before, in case any neighbor be there—or—or—just to put matters some-

* The keeper's followers in the New Forest are called in popular language "ragged Robins."

thing into order for Mistress Alice and your honor—just to make things something seemly and shapely."

"Not a whit necessary," said the knight, while Alice had much trouble in concealing her agitation. "If thy matters are unseemly, they are fitter for a defeated knight; if they are unshapely, why, the liker to the rest of a world which is all unshaped. Go thou with that man. What is thy name, friend?"

"Joseph Tomkins is my name in the flesh," said the steward. "Men call me Honest Joe and Trusty Tomkins."

"If thou hast deserved such names, considering what trade thou hast driven, thou art a jewel indeed," said the knight; "yet if thou hast not, never blush for the matter, Joseph, for if thou art not in truth honest, thou hast all the better chance to keep the fame of it: the title and the thing itself have long walked separate ways. Farewell to thee—and farewell to fair Woodstock!"

So saying, the old knight turned round, and pulling his daughter's arm through his own, they walked onward into the forest, in the same manner in which they were introduced to the reader.

CHAPTER III

Now, ye wild blades, that make loose inns your stage,
To vapor forth the acts of this sad age,
Stout Edgehill fight, the Newberries and the West,
And northern clashes, where you still fought best,
Your strange escapes, your dangers void of fear,
When bullets flew between the head and ear,
Whether you fought by damme or the spirit,
Of you I speak.

Legend of Captain Jones.

JOSEPH TOMKINS and Joliffe the keeper remained for some time in silence, as they stood together looking along the path in which the figures of the knight of Ditchley and pretty Mistress Alice had disappeared behind the trees. They then gazed on each other in doubt, as men who scarce knew whether they stood on hostile or on friendly terms together, and were at a loss how to open a conversation. They heard the knight's whistle summon Bevis; but though the good hound turned his head and pricked his ears at the sound, yet he did not obey the call, but continued to snuff around Joseph Tomkins's cloak.

"Thou art a rare one, I fear me," said the keeper, looking to his new acquaintance. "I have heard of men who have charms to steal both dogs and deer."

"Trouble not thyself about my qualities, friend," said Joseph Tomkins, "but bethink thee of doing thy master's bidding."

Joceline did not immediately answer, but at length, as if in sign of truce, stuck the end of his quarterstaff upright in the ground, and leant upon it, as he said gruffly, "So, my tough old knight and you were at drawn bilbo, by way of afternoon service, sir preacher. Well for you I came not up till the blades were done jingling, or I had rung even-song upon your pate."

The Independent smiled grimly as he replied, "Nay, friend, it is well for thyself, for never should sexton have have been better paid for the knell he tolled. Nevertheless, why should there be war betwixt us, or my hand be against thine? Thou art but a poor knave, doing thy master's order, nor have I any desire that my own blood or thine should be shed touching this matter. Thou art, I understand, to give me peaceful possession of the Palace of Woodstock, so called; though there is now no palace in England, no, nor shall be in the days that come after, until we shall enter the palace of the New Jerusalem, and the reign of the saints shall commence on earth."

"Pretty well begun already, friend Tomkins," said the keeper: "you are little short of being kings already upon the matter as it now stands; and for your Jerusalem I wot not, but Woodstock is a pretty nest-egg to begin with. Well, will you shog—will you on—will you take sasine and livery? You heard my orders."

"Umph—I know not," said Tomkins. "I must beware of ambuscades, and I am alone here. Moreover, it is the High Thanksgiving appointed by Parliament, and owned to by the army; also the old man and the young woman may want to recover some of their clothes and personal property, and I would not that they were balked on my account. Wherefore, if thou wilt deliver me possession to-morrow morning, it shall be done in personal presence of my own followers, and of the Presbyterian man the Mayor, so that the transfer may be made before witnesses; whereas, were there none with us but thou to deliver and I to take possession, the men of Belial might say, 'Go to, Trusty Tomkins hath been an Edomite—Honest Joe hath been as an Ishmaelite, rising up early and dividing the spoil with them that served the Man—yea, they that wore beards and green jerkins, as in remembrance of the Man and of his government.'"

Joceline fixed his keen dark eyes upon the soldier as he spoke, as if in design to discover whether there was fair play in his mind or not. He then applied his five fingers to scratch a large shock head of hair, as if that operation was necessary to enable him to come to a conclusion. "This is all fair sounding, brother," said he; "but I tell you plainly, there are some silver mugs, and platters, and flagons, and so forth, in yonder house, which have survived the general sweep that sent all our plate to the smelting-pot, to put our knight's troop on horseback. Now, if thou takest not these off my hand, I may come to trouble, since it may be thought I have minished their numbers. Whereas, I being as honest a fellow——"

"As ever stole venison," said Tomkins; "nay, I do owe thee an interruption."

"Go to, then," replied the keeper; "if a stag may have come to mischance in my walk, it was no way in the course of dishonesty, but merely to keep my old dame's pan from rusting; but for silver porringers, tankards, and such-like, I would as soon have drunk the melted silver as stolen the vessel made out of it. So that I would not wish blame or suspicion fell on me in this matter. And therefore, if you will have the things rendered even now—why so; and if not, hold me blameless."

"Ay, truly?" said Tomkins; "and who is to hold me blameless, if they should see cause to think anything minished? Not the right worshipful Commissioners, to whom the property of the estate is as their own; therefore, as thou say'st, we must walk warily in the matter. To lock up the house and leave it were but the work of simple ones. What say'st thou to spend the night there, and then nothing can be touched without the knowledge of us both?"

"Why, concerning that," answered the keeper, "I should be at my hut to make matters somewhat conformable for the old knight and Mistress Alice, for my old dame Joan is something dunny, and will scarce know how to manage; and yet, to speak the truth, by the mass, I would rather not see Sir Henry to-night, since what has happened to-day hath roused his spleen, and it is peradventure he may have met something at the hut which will scarce tend to cool it."

"It is a pity," said Tomkins, "that, being a gentleman of such grave and goodly presence, he should be such a malignant Cavalier, and that he should, like the rest of that generation of vipers, have clothed himself with curses as with a garment."

"Which is as much as to say, the tough old knight hath a habit of swearing," said the keeper, grinning at a pun which has been repeated since his time; "but who can help it? it comes of use and wont. Were you now, in your bodily self, to light suddenly on a Maypole, with all the blythe morris-dancers prancing around it to the merry pipe and tabor, with bells jingling, ribbons fluttering, lads frisking and laughing, lasses leaping till you might see where the scarlet garter fastened the light-blue hose, I think some feeling, resembling either natural sociality, or old use and wont, would get the better, friend, even of thy gravity, and thou wouldst fling thy cuckoldy steeple-hat one way and that bloodthirsty long sword another, and trip like the noodles of Hogs-Norton when the pigs play on the organ."

The Independent turned fiercely round on the keeper, and replied, "How now, Mr. Green Jerkin, what language is this to one whose hand is at the plow? I advise thee to put curb on thy tongue, lest thy ribs pay the forfeit."

"Nay, do not take the high tone with me, brother," answered Joceline; "remember thou hast not the old knight of sixty-five to deal with, but a fellow as bitter and prompt as thyself—it may be a little more so—younger, at all events; and prithee, why shouldst thou take such umbrage at a Maypole? I would thou hadst known one Phil Hazeldine of these parts. He was the best morris-dancer betwixt Oxford and Burford."

"The more shame to him," answered the Independent; "and I trust he has seen the error of his ways, and made himself, as, if a man of action, he easily might, fit for better company than wood-hunters, deer-stealers, Maid Marions, swashbucklers, deboshed revelers, bloody brawlers, maskers and mummers, lewd men and light women, fools and fiddlers, and carnal self-pleasers of every description."

"Well," replied the keeper, "you are out of breath in time; for here we stand before the famous Maypole of Woodstock."

They paused in an open space of meadow-land, beautifully skirted by large oaks and sycamores, one of which, as king of the forest, stood a little detached from the rest, as if scorning the vicinity of any rival. It was scathed and gnarled in the branches, but the immense trunk still showed to what gigantic size the monarch of the forest can attain in the groves of Merry England.

"That is called the King's Oak," said Joceline; "the oldest men of Woodstock know not how old it is: they say Henry used to sit under it with fair Rosamond, and see the lasses dance, and the lads of the village run races, and wrestle for belts or bonnets."

"I nothing doubt it, friend," said Tomkins; "a tyrant and a harlot were fitting patron and patroness for such vanities."

"Thou mayst say thy say, friend," replied the keeper, "so thou lettest me say mine. There stands the Maypole, as thou seest, half a flight-shot from the King's Oak, in the midst of the meadow. The King gave ten shillings from the customs of Woodstock to make a new one yearly, besides a tree fitted for the purpose out of the forest. Now it is warped, and withered, and twisted, like a wasted brier-rod. The green, too, used to be close-shaved, and rolled till it was smooth as a velvet mantle ; now it is rough and overgrown."

"Well—well, friend Joceline," said the Independent, "but where was the edification of all this? What use of doctrine could be derived from a pipe and tabor; or was there ever aught like wisdom in a bagpipe?"

"You may ask better scholars that," said Joceline; "but methinks men cannot be always grave, and with the hat over their brow. A young maiden will laugh as a tender flower will blow—ay, and a lad will like her the better for it: just as the same blythe spring that makes the young birds whistle bids the blythe fawn skip. There have come worse days since the jolly old times have gone by. I tell thee, that in the holydays which you, Mr. Long-sword, have put down, I have seen this greensward alive with merry maidens and manly fellows. The good old rector himself thought it was no sin to come for a while and look on, and his goodly cassock and scarf kept us all in good order, and taught us to limit our mirth within the bounds of discretion. We might, it may be, crack a broad jest, or pledge a friendly cup a turn too often, but it was in mirth and good neighborhood. Ay, and if there was a bout at single-stick, or a bellyful of boxing, it was all for love and kindness; and better a few dry blows in drink than the bloody doings we have had in sober earnest, since the presbyter's cap got above the bishop's mitre, and we exchanged our goodly rectors and learned doctors, whose sermons were all bolstered up with as much Greek and Latin as might have confounded the devil himself, for weavers and cobblers, and such other pulpit volunteers as—as we heard this morning. It will out."

"Well, friend," said the Independent, with patience scarcely to have been expected, "I quarrel not with thee for nauseating my doctrine. If thine ear is so much tickled with tabor tunes and morris-tripping, truly it is not likely thou shouldst find pleasant savor in more wholesome and sober food. But let us to the lodge, that we may go about our business there before the sun sets."

"Troth, and that may be advisable for more reasons than one," said the keeper; "for there have been tales about the lodge which have made men afeard to harbor there after nightfall."

"Were not yon old knight and yonder damsel, his daughter, wont to dwell there?" said the Independent. "My information said so."

"Ay, truly did they," said Joceline; "and while they kept a jolly household, all went well enough; for nothing banishes fear like good ale. But after the best of our men went to the wars, and were slain at Naseby fight, they who were left found the lodge more lonesome, and the old knight has been much deserted of his servants: marry, it might be, that he has lacked silver of late to pay groom and lackey."

"A potential reason for the diminution of the household," said the soldier.

"Right, sir, even so," replied the keeper. "They spoke of steps in the great gallery, heard by dead of the night, and uoices that whispered at noon in the matted chambers; and the servants pretended that these things scared them away; but, in my poor judgment, when Martinmas and Whitsuntide came round without a penny-fee, the old blue-bottles of serving-men began to think of creeping elsewhere before the frost chilled them. No devil so frightful as that which dances in the pocket where there is no cross to keep him out."

"You were reduced, then, to a petty household?" said the Independent.

"Ay, marry, were we," said Joceline; "but we kept some half-score together, what with blue-bottles in the lodge, what with green caterpillars of the chase, like him who is yours to command: we stuck together till we found a call to take a morning's ride somewhere or other."

"To the town of Worcester," said the soldier, "where you were crushed like vermin and palmer-worms, as you are?"

"You may say your pleasure," replied the keeper: "I'll never contradict a man who has got my head under his belt. Our backs are at the wall, or you would not be here."

"Nay, friend," said the Independent, "thou riskest nothing by thy freedom and trust in me. I can be *bon camarado* to a good soldier, although I have striven with him even to the going down of the sun. But here we are in front of the lodge."

They stood accordingly in front of the old Gothic building, irregularly constructed, and at different times, as the humor of the English monarchs led them to taste the pleasures of Woodstock Chase, and to make such improvements for their own accommodation as the increasing luxury of each age required. The oldest part of the structure had been named by tradition Fair Rosamond's Tower; it was a small turret of great height, with narrow windows, and walls of massive thickness. The tower had no opening to the ground, or means of descending, a great part of the lower portion being solid mason-work. It was traditionally said to have been accessible only by a sort of small drawbridge, which might be dropped at pleasure from a little portal near the summit of the turret to the battlements of another tower of the same construction, but twenty feet lower, and containing only a winding staircase, called in Woodstock, Love's Ladder; because it is said that, by ascending this staircase to the top of the tower, and then making use of the drawbridge, Henry obtained access to the chamber of his paramour.

This tradition had been keenly impugned by Dr. Rochecliffe, the former rector of Woodstock, who insisted that what was called Rosamond's Tower was merely an interior keep, or citadel, to which the lord or warden of the castle might retreat when other points of safety failed him, and either protract his defense or, at the worst, stipulate for reasonable terms of surrender. The people of Woodstock, jealous of their ancient traditions, did not relish this new mode of explaining them away; and it is even said that the Mayor, whom we have already introduced, became Presbyterian in revenge of the doubts cast by the rector upon this important subject, rather choosing to give up the liturgy than his fixed belief in Rosamond's Tower and Love's Ladder.

The rest of the lodge was of considerable extent, and of different ages, comprehending a nest of little courts, surrounded by buildings which corresponded with each other, sometimes within doors, sometimes by crossing the courts, and frequently in both ways. The different heights of the buildings announced that they could only be connected by the usual variety of staircases, which exercised the limbs of our ancestors in the 16th and earlier centuries, and seem sometimes to have been contrived for no other purpose.

The varied and multiplied fronts of this irregular building were, as Dr. Rochecliffe was wont to say, an absolute banquet to the architectural antiquary, as they certainly contained specimens of every style which existed, from the pure Norman of Henry of Anjou down to the composite, half-Gothic, half-classical architecture of Elizabeth and her successor. Accordingly, the rector was himself as much enamored of Woodstock as ever was Henry of Fair Rosamond; and as his intimacy with Sir Henry Lee permitted him entrance at all times to the royal lodge, he used to spend whole days in wandering about the antique apartments, examining, measuring, studying, and finding out excellent reasons for architectural peculiarities, which probably only owed their existence to the freakish fancy of a Gothic artist. But the old antiquarian had been expelled from his living by the intolerance and troubles of the times, and his successor, Nehemiah Holdenough, would have considered an elaborate investigation of the profane sculpture and architecture of blinded and bloodthirsty Papists, together with the history of the dissolute amours of old Norman monarchs, as little better than a bowing down before the calves of Bethel, and a drinking of the cup of abominations.

We return to the course of our story.

"There is," said the Independent Tomkins, after he had carefully perused the front of the building, "many a rare monument of olden wickedness about this miscalled royal lodge; verily, I shall rejoice much to see the same destroyed, yea, burned to ashes, and the ashes thrown into the brook Kedron, or any other brook, that the land may be cleansed from the memory thereof, neither remember the iniquity with which their fathers have sinned."

The keeper heard him with secret indignation, and began to consider with himself whether, as they stood but one to one, and without chance of speedy interference, he was not called upon, by his official duty, to castigate the rebel who used language so defamatory. But he fortunately recollected that the strife must be a doubtful one, that the advantage of arms was against him, and that, in especial, even if he should succeed in the combat, it would be at the risk of severe retaliation. It must be owned, too, that there was something about the Independent so dark and mysterious, so grim and grave, that the more open spirit of the keeper felt oppressed, and, if not overawed, at least kept in doubt concerning him; and he thought it wisest, as well as safest, for his master and himself, to avoid all subjects of dispute, and know better with whom he was dealing before he made either friend or enemy of him.

The great gate of the lodge was strongly bolted, but the wicket opened on Joceline's raising the latch. There was a short passage of ten feet, which had been formerly closed by a portcullis at the inner end, while three loopholes opened on either side, through which any daring intruder might be annoyed, who, having surprised the first gate, must be thus exposed to a severe fire before he could force the second. But the machinery of the portcullis was damaged, and it now remained a fixture, brandishing its jaw, well furnished with iron fangs, but incapable of dropping it across the path of invasion.

The way, therefore, lay open to the great hall or outer vestibule of the lodge. One end of this long and dusky apartment was entirely occupied by a gallery, which had in ancient times served to accommodate the musicians and minstrels. There was a clumsy staircase at either side of it, composed of entire logs of a foot square; and in each angle of the ascent was placed, by way of sentinel, the figure of a Norman foot-soldier, having an open casque on his head, which displayed features as stern as the painter's genius could devise. Their arms were buff-jackets or shirts of mail, round bucklers, with spikes in the center, and buskins which adorned and defended the feet and ankles, but left the knees bare. These wooden warders held great swords, or maces, in their hands, like military guards on duty. Many an empty hook and brace, along the walls of the gloomy apartment, marked the spots from which arms, long preserved as trophies, had been, in the pressure of the war, once more taken down to do service in the field, like veterans whom extremity of danger recalls to battle. On other rusty fastenings were still displayed the hunting trophies of the monarchs to whom the lodge belonged, and of the silvan knights to whose care it had been from time to time confided.

At the nether end of the hall, a huge, heavy, stone-wrought chimney-piece projected itself ten feet from the wall, adorned with many a cipher and many a scutcheon of the royal house of England. In its present state, it yawned like the arched mouth of a funeral vault, or perhaps might be compared to the crater of an extinguished volcano. But the sable complexion of the massive stonework, and all around it, showed that the time had been when it sent its huge fires blazing up the huge chimney, besides puffing many a volume of smoke over the heads of the jovial guests, whose royalty or nobility did not render them sensitive enough to quarrel with such slight inconvenience. On these occasions, it was the tradition of the house, that two cart-loads of wood was the regular allowance for the fire between noon and curfew, and the andirons, or dogs, as they were termed, constructed for retaining the blazing firewood on the hearth, were wrought in the shape of lions of such gigantic size as might well warrant the legend. There were long seats of stone within the chimney, where, in despite of the tremendous heat, monarchs were sometimes said to have taken their station, and amused themselves with broiling the umbles, or dowsets, of the deer upon the glowing embers, with their own royal hands, when happy the courtier who was invited to taste the royal cookery. Tradition was here also ready with her record, to show what merry gibes, such as might be exchanged between prince and peer, had flown about at the jolly banquet which followed the Michaelmas hunt. She could tell, too, exactly, where King Stephen sat when he darned his own princely hose, and knew most of the old tricks he had put upon little Winkin, the tailor of Woodstock.

Most of this rude revelry belonged to the Plantagenet times. When the house of Tudor acceded to the throne, they were more chary of their royal presence, and feasted in halls and chambers far within, abandoning the outmost hall to the yeomen of the guard, who mounted their watch there, and passed away the night with wassail and mirth, exchanged sometimes for frightful tales of apparitions and sorceries, which made some of those grow pale in whose ears the trumpet of a French foeman would have sounded as jollily as a summons to the woodland chase.

Joceline pointed out the peculiarities of the place to his gloomy companion more briefly than we have detailed them to the reader.

The Independent seemed to listen with some interest at first, but, flinging it suddenly aside, he said, in a solemn tone, "Perish, Babylon, as thy master Nebuchadnezzar hath perished! He is a wanderer, and thou shalt be a waste place—yea, and a wilderness—yea, a desert of salt, in which there shall be thirst and famine."

"There is like to be enough of both to-night," said Joceline, "unless the good knight's larder be somewhat fuller than it is wont."

"We must care for the creature-comforts," said the Independent, "but in due season, when our duties are done. Whither lead these entrances?"

"That to the right," replied the keeper, "leads to what are called the state-apartments, not used since the year 1639, when his blessed Majesty——"

"How, sir!" interrupted the Independent, in a voice of thunder, "dost thou speak of Charles Stuart as blessing, or blessed? Beware the proclamation to that effect."

"I meant no harm," answered the keeper, suppressing his disposition to make a harsher reply. "My business is with bolts and bucks, not with titles and state affairs. But yet, whatever may have happed since, that poor king was followed with blessings enough from Woodstock; for he left a glove full of broad pieces for the poor of the place——"

"Peace, friend," said the Independent; "I will think thee else one of those besotted and blinded Papists who hold that bestowing of alms is an atonement and washing away of the wrongs and oppressions which have been wrought by the alms-giver. Thou sayest, then, these were the apartments of Charles Stuart?"

"And of his father, James, before him, and Elizabeth, before *him*, and bluff King Henry, who builded that wing, before them all."

"And there, I suppose, the knight and his daughter dwelt?"

"No," replied Joceline; "Sir Henry Lee had too much reverence for—for things which are now thought worth no reverence at all. Besides, the state-rooms are unaired and in indifferent order since of late years. The knight ranger's apartment lies by that passage to the left."

"And whither goes yonder stair, which seems both to lead upwards and downwards?"

"Upwards," replied the keeper, "it leads to many apartments, used for various purposes, of sleeping and other accommodation. Downwards, to the kitchen, offices, and vaults of the castle, which, at this time of the evening, you cannot see without lights."

"We will to the apartments of your knight, then," said the Independent. "Is there fitting accommodation there?"

"Such as has served a person of condition, whose lodging is now worse appointed," answered the honest keeper, his bile rising so fast that he added, in a muttering and inaudible tone, "So it may well serve a crop-eared knave like thee."

He acted as the usher, however, and led on towards the ranger's apartments.

This suite opened by a short passage from the hall, secured at time of need by two oaken doors, which could be fastened by large bars of the same, that were drawn out of the wall, and entered into square holes, contrived for their reception on the other side of the portal. At the end of this passage, a small anteroom received them, into which opened the sitting-apartment of the good knight, which, in the style of the times, might have been termed a fair summer parlor, lighted by two oriel windows, so placed as to command each of them a separate avenue, leading distant and deep into the forest. The principal ornament of the apartment, besides two or three family portraits of less interest, was a tall full-length picture that hung above the chimney-piece, which, like that in the hall, was of heavy stonework, ornamented with carved scutcheons, emblazoned with various devices. The portrait was that of a man about fifty years of age, in complete plate armor, and painted in the harsh and dry manner of Holbein, probably, indeed, the work of that artist, as the dates corresponded. The formal and marked angles, points, and projections of the armor were a good subject for the harsh pencil of that early school. The face of the knight was, from the fading of the colors, pale and dim, like that of some being from the other world, yet the lines expressed forcibly pride and exultation.

He pointed with his leading-staff, or truncheon, to the back ground, where, in such perspective as the artist possessed, were depicted the remains of a burning church, or monastery, and four or five soldiers, in red cassocks, bearing away in triumph what seemed a brazen font or laver. Above their heads might be traced in scroll, "*Lee Victor sic voluit.*" Right opposite to the picture hung, in a niche in the wall, a complete set of tilting armor, the black and gold colors and ornaments of which exactly corresponded with those exhibited in the portrait.

The picture was one of those which, from something marked in the features and expression, attract the observation even of those who are ignorant of art. The Independent looked at it until a smile passed transiently over his clouded brow. Whether he smiled to see the grim old cavalier employed in desecrating a religious house (an occupation much conforming to the practise of his own sect), whether he smiled in contempt of the old painter's harsh and dry mode of working, or whether the sight of this remarkable portrait revived some other ideas, the under-keeper could not decide.

The smile passed away in an instant, as the soldier looked to the oriel windows. The recesses within them were raised a step or two from the wall. In one was plaeed a walnut-tree reading-desk, and a huge stuffed arm-chair, covered with Spanish leather. A little cabinet stood beside, with some of its shuttles and drawers open, displaying hawks'-

bells, dog-whistles, instruments for trimming falcon's feathers, bridlebits of various constructions, and other trifles connected with silvan sport.

The other little recess was differently furnished. There lay some articles of needlework on a small table, besides a lute, with a book having some airs written down in it, and a frame for working embroidery. Some tapestry was displayed around the recess, with more attention to ornament than was visible in the rest of the apartment; the arrangement of a few bow-pots, with such flowers as the fading season afforded, showed also the superintendence of female taste.

Tomkins cast an eye of careless regard upon these subjects of female occupation, then stepped into the farther window, and began to turn the leaves of a folio which lay open on the reading-desk, apparently with some interest. Joceline, who had determined to watch his motions without interfering with them, was standing at some distance in dejected silence, when a door behind the tapestry suddenly opened, and a pretty village maid tripped out with a napkin in her hand, as if she had been about some household duty.

"How now, sir impudence," she said to Joceline, in a smart tone; "what do you here prowling about the apartments when the master is not at home?"

But, instead of the answer which perhaps she expected, Joceline Joliffe cast a mournful glance towards the soldier in the oriel window, as if to make what he said fully intelligible, and replied, with a dejected appearance and voice, "Alack, my pretty Phœbe, there come those here that have more right or might than any of us, and will use little ceremony in coming when they will, and staying while they please."

He darted another glance at Tomkins, who still seemed busy with the book before him, then sidled close to the astonished girl, who had continued looking alternately at the keeper and at the stranger, as if she had been unable to understand the words of the first, or to comprehend the meaning of the second being present.

"Go," whispered Joliffe, approaching his mouth so near her cheek that his breath waved the curls of her hair—"go, my dearest Phœbe, trip it as fast as a fawn down to my lodge. I will soon be there, and——"

"Your lodge, indeed!" said Phœbe; "you are very bold, for a poor kill-buck that never frightened anything before save a dun deer. *Your* lodge, indeed! I am like to go there, I think."

"Hush—hush! Phœbe: here is no time for jesting. Down to my hut, I say, like a deer, for the knight and Mrs. Alice are both there, and I fear will not return hither again. All's naught, girl, and our evil days are come at last with a vengeance: we are fairly at bay and fairly hunted down."

"Can this be, Joceline?" said the poor girl, turning to the keeper with an expression of fright in her countenance, which she had hitherto averted in rural coquetry.

"As sure, my dearest Phœbe, as——"

The rest of the asseveration was lost in Phœbe's ear, so closely did the keeper's lips approach it; and if they approached so very near as to touch her cheek, grief, like impatience, hath its privileges, and poor Phœbe had enough of serious alarm to prevent her from demurring upon such a trifle.

But no trifle was the approach of Joceline's lips to Phœbe's pretty though sunburnt cheek in the estimation of the Independent, who, a little before the object of Joceline's vigilance, had been more lately in his turn the observer of the keeper's demeanor, so soon as the interview betwixt Phœbe and him had become so interesting. And when he remarked the closeness of Joceline's argument, he raised his voice to a pitch of harshness that would have rivaled that of an ungreased and rusty saw, and which at once made Joceline and Phœbe spring six feet apart, each in contrary directions, and if Cupid was of the party, must have sent him out at the window like a wild duck flying from a culverin. Instantly throwing himself into the attitude of a preacher and a reprover of vice, "How now!" he exclaimed, "shameless and impudent as you are! What! chambering and wantoning in our very presence! How! would you play your pranks before the steward of the Commissioners of the High Court of Parliament, as ye would in a booth at the fulsome fair, or amidst the trappings and tracings of a profane dancing-school, where the scoundrel minstrels make their ungodly weapons to squeak, 'Kiss and be kind, the fiddler's blind?' But here," he said, dealing a perilous thump upon the volume—"here is the king and high priest of those vices and follies. Here is he, whom men of folly profanely call nature's miracle. Here is he, whom princes choose for their cabinet-keeper, and whom maids of honor take for their bedfellow. Here is the prime teacher of fine words, foppery, and folly. Here! (dealing another thump upon the volume; and oh! revered of the Roxburghe, it was the first folio—beloved of the Bannatyne, it was Hemminge and Condel—it was the *editio princeps*). On thee," he continued—"on thee, William Shakspeare, I charge whate'er of such lawless idleness and immodest folly hath defiled the land since thy day."

"By the mass, a heavy accusation," said Joceline, the bold recklessness of whose temper could not be long overawed. "Odds pitlikins, is our master's old favorite, Will of Stratford, to answer for every buss that has been snatched since James's time? A perilous reckoning truly! but I wonder who is sponsible for what lads and lasses did before his day?"

"Scoff not," said the soldier, "lest I, being called thereto by the voice within me, do deal with thee as a scorner. Verily I say, that since the devil fell from Heaven, he never lacked agents on earth; yet nowhere hath he met with a wizard having such infinite power over men's souls as this pestilent fellow Shakspeare. Seeks a wife a foul example for adultery, here she shall find it. Would a man know how to train his fellow to be a murderer, here shall he find tutoring. Would a lady marry a heathen negro, she shall have chronicled example for it. Would any one scorn at his Maker, he shall be furnished with a jest in this book. Would he defy his brother in the flesh, he shall be accommodated with a challenge. Would you be drunk, Shakspeare will cheer you with a cup. Would you plunge in sensual pleasures, he will soothe you to indulgence, as with the lascivious sounds of a lute. This, I say—this book is the wellhead and source of all those evils which have overrun the land like a torrent, making men scoffers, doubters, deniers, murderers, makebates, and lovers of the wine-pot, haunting unclean places, and sitting long at the evening wine. Away with him—away with him, men of England! to Tophet with his wicked book, and to the vale of Hinnom with his accursed bones! Verily, but that our march was hasty when we passed Stratford, in the year 1643, with Sir William Waller—but that our march was hasty——"

"Because Prince Rupert was after you with his Cavaliers," muttered the incorrigible Joceline.

"I say," continued the zealous trooper, raising his voice and extending his arm, "but that our march was by command hasty, and that we turned not aside in our riding, closing our ranks each one upon the other as becomes men of war, I had torn on that day the bones of that preceptor of vice and debauchery from the grave, and given them to the next dunghill. I would have made his memory a scoff and a hissing."

"That is the bitterest thing he has said yet," observed the keeper. "Poor Will would have liked the hissing worse than all the rest."

"Will the gentleman say any more ?" inquired Phœbe in a whisper. "Lack-a-day, he talks brave words, if one knew but what they meant. But it is a mercy our good knight did not see him ruffle the book at that rate. Mercy on us, there would certainly have been bloodshed. But oh the father—see how he is twisting his face about ! Is he ill of the colic, think'st thou, Joceline ? Or may I offer him a glass of strong waters ?"

"Hark thee hither, wench," said the keeper, "he is but loading his blunderbuss for another volley ; and while he turns up his eyes, and twists about his face, and clinches his fist, and shuffles and tramples with his feet in that fashion, he is bound to take no notice of anything. I would be sworn to cut his purse, if he had one, from his side, without his feeling it."

"La ! Joceline," said Phœbe, "and if he abides here in this turn of times, I daresay the gentleman will be easily served."

"Care not thou about that," said Joliffe ; "but tell me softly and hastily, what is in the pantry ?"

"Small housekeeping enough," said Phœbe ; "a cold capon and some comfits, and the great standing venison pasty, with plenty of spice—a manchet or two besides, and that is all."

"Well, it will serve for a pinch. Wrap thy cloak round thy comely body ; get a basket and a brace of trenchers and towels, they are heinously impoverished down yonder ; carry down the capon and the manchets ; the pasty must abide with this same soldier and me, and the pie-crust will serve us for bread."

"Rarely," said Phœbe, "I made the paste myself : it is as thick as the walls of Fair Rosamond's Tower."

"Which two pairs of jaws would be long in gnawing through, work hard as they might," said the keeper. "But what liquor is there ?"

"Only a bottle of Alicant and one of sack, with the stone jug of strong waters," answered Phœbe.

"Put the wine-flasks into thy basket," said Joceline, "the knight must not lack his evening draught ; and down with thee to the hut like a lapwing. There is enough for supper, and to-morrow is a new day. Ha! by Heaven I thought yonder man's eye watched us. No, he only rolled it round him in a brown study. Deep enough doubtless, as they all are! But d—n him, he must be bottomless if I cannot sound him before the night's out. Hie thee away, Phœbe."

But Phœbe was a rural coquette, and, aware that Joceline's situation gave him no advantage of avenging the challenge in a fitting way, she whispered in his ear, "Do you think our knight's friend, Shakspeare, really found out all these naughty devices the gentleman spoke of?"

Off she darted while she spoke, while Joliffe menaced future vengeance with his finger, as he muttered, "Go thy way, Phœbe Mayflower, the lightest-footed and lightest-hearted wench that ever tripped the sod in Woodstock Park! After her, Bevis, and bring her safe to our master at the hut!"

The large greyhound arose like a human servitor who had received an order, and followed Phœbe through the hall, first licking her hand to make her sensible of his presence, and then putting himself to a slow trot, so as best to accommodate himself to the light pace of her whom he convoyed, whom Joceline had not extolled for her activity without due reason. While Phœbe and her guardian thread the forest glades, we return to the lodge.

The Independent now seemed to start as if from a reverie. "Is the young woman gone?" said he.

"Ay, marry is she," said the keeper; "and if your worship hath farther commands, you must rest contented with male attendance."

"Commands—umph—I think the damsel might have tarried for another exhortation," said the soldier; "truly, I profess my mind was much inclined toward her for her edification."

"Oh, sir," replied Joliffe, "she will be at church next Sunday, and if your military reverence is pleased again to hold forth amongst us, she will have use of the doctrine with the rest. But young maidens of these parts hear no private homilies. And what is now your pleasure? Will you look at the other rooms, and at the few plate articles which have been left?"

"Umph—no," said the Independent; "it wears late, and gets dark. Thou hast the means of giving us beds, friend?"

"Better you never slept in," replied the keeper.

"And wood for a fire, and a light, and some small pittance of creature-comforts for refreshment of the outward man?" continued the soldier.

"Without doubt," replied the keeper, displaying a prudent anxiety to gratify this important personage.

In a few minutes a great standing candlestick was placed on an oaken table. The mighty venison pasty, adorned with parsley, was placed on the board on a clean napkin; the stone bottle of strong waters, with a black-jack full of ale, formed comfortable appendages; and to this meal sat down in social manner the soldier, occupying a great elbow-chair, and the keeper, at his invitation, using the more lowly accommodation of a stool, at the opposite side of the table. Thus agreeably employed, our history leaves them for the present.

CHAPTER IV

> Yon path of greensward
> Winds round by sparry grot and gay pavilion;
> There is no flint to gall thy tender foot,
> There's ready shelter from each breeze, or shower.
> But duty guides not that way: see her stand,
> With wand entwined with amaranth, near yon cliffs.
> Oft where she leads thy blood must mark thy footsteps,
> Oft where she leads thy head must bear the storm,
> And thy shrunk form endure heat, cold and hunger;
> But she will guide thee up to noble heights,
> Which he who gains seems native of the sky,
> While earthly things lie stretch'd beneath his feet,
> Diminish'd, shrunk, and valueless.
>
> *Anonymous.*

THE reader cannot have forgotten that, after his scuffle with the Commonwealth soldier, Sir Henry Lee, with his daughter Alice, had departed to take refuge in the hut of the stout keeper, Joceline Joliffe. They walked slow, as before, for the old knight was at once oppressed by perceiving these last vestiges of royalty fall into the hands of republicans and by the recollection of his recent defeat. At times he paused, and, with his arms folded on his bosom, recalled all the circumstances attending his expulsion from a house so long his home. It seemed to him that, like the champions of romance of whom he had sometimes read, he himself was retiring from the post which it was his duty to guard, defeated by a paynim knight, for whom the adventure had been reserved by fate. Alice had her own painful subjects of recollection, nor had the tenor of her last conversation with her father been so pleasant as to make her anxious to renew it until his temper should be more composed; for with an excellent disposition, and much love to his daughter, age and misfortunes, which of late came thicker and thicker, had given to the good knight' spassions a wayward irritability unknown to his better days. His daughter, and one or two attached servants who still followed his decayed fortunes, soothed his frailty as much as possible, and pitied him even while they suffered under its effects.

It was a long time ere he spoke, and then he referred to an incident already noticed. "It is strange," he said, "that Bevis should have followed Joceline and that fellow rather than me."

"Assure yourself, sir," replied Alice, "that his sagacity saw in this man a stranger, whom he thought himself obliged to watch circumspectly, and therefore he remained with Joceline."

"Not so, Alice," answered Sir Henry; "he leaves me because my fortunes have fled from me. There is a feeling in nature, affecting even the instinct, as it is called, of dumb animals, which teaches them to fly from misfortune. The very deer there will butt a sick or wounded buck from the herd; hurt a dog, and the whole kennel will fall on him and worry him; fishes devour their own kind when they are wounded with a spear; cut a crow's wing, or break its leg, the others will buffet it to death."

"That may be true of the more irrational kinds of animals among each other," said Alice, "for their whole life is well-nigh a warfare; but the dog leaves his own race to attach himself to ours—forsakes, for his master, the company, food, and pleasure of his own kind; and surely the fidelity of such a devoted and voluntary servant as Bevis hath been in particular ought not to be lightly suspected."

"I am not angry with the dog, Alice; I am only sorry," replied her father. "I have read in faithful chronicles that, when Richard II. and Henry of Bolingbroke were at Berkeley Castle, a dog of the same kind deserted the king, whom he had always attended upon, and attached himself to Henry, whom he then saw for the first time. Richard foretold, from the desertion of his favorite, his approaching deposition.* The dog was afterwards kept at Woodstock, and Bevis is said to be of his breed, which was heedfully kept up. What I might foretell of mischief from his desertion, I cannot guess, but my mind assures me it bodes no good."

There was a distant rustling among the withered leaves, a bouncing or galloping sound on the path, and the favorite dog instantly joined his master.

"Come into court, old knave," said Alice, cheerfully, "and defend thy character, which is well-nigh endangered by this absence." But the dog only paid her courtesy by gamboling around them, and instantly plunged back again, as fast as he could scamper.

"How now, knave," said the knight; "thou art too well

* The story occurs, I think, in Froissart's *Chronicles* [vol. iv. chap. 132 of Johnes's trans.]

trained, surely, to take up the chase without orders?" A minute more showed them Phœbe Mayflower approaching, her light pace so little impeded by the burden which she bore, that she joined her master and young mistress just as they arrived at the keeper's hut, which was the boundary of their journey. Bevis, who had shot a-head to pay his compliments to Sir Henry his master, had returned again to his immediate duty, the escorting Phœbe and her cargo of provisions. The whole party stood presently assembled before the door of the keeper's hut.

In better times, a substantial stone habitation, fit for the yeoman-keeper of a royal walk, had adorned this place. A fair spring gushed out near the spot, and once traversed yards and courts, attached to well-built and convenient knnels and mews. But in some of the skirmishes which were common during the civil wars, this little silvan dwelling had been attacked and defended, stormed and burned. A neighboring squire, of the Parliament side of the question, took advantage of Sir Henry Lee's absence, who was then in Charles's camp, and of the decay of the royal cause, and had, without scruple, carried off the hewn stones, and such building-materials as the fire left unconsumed, and repaired his own manor-house with them. The yeoman keeper, therefore, our friend Joceline, had constructed, for his own accommodation and that of the old woman he called his dame, a wattled hut, such as his own labor, with that of a neighbor or two, had erected in the course of a few days. The walls were plastered with clay, whitewashed, and covered with vines and other creeping plants; the roof was neatly thatched; and the whole, though merely a hut, had, by the neat-handed Joliffe, been so arranged as not to disgrace the condition of the dweller.

The knight advanced to the entrance; but the ingenuity of the architect, for want of a better lock to the door, which itself was but of wattles curiously twisted, had contrived a mode of securing the latch on the inside with a pin, which prevented it from rising; and in this manner it was at present fastened. Conceiving that this was some precaution of Joliffe's old housekeeper, of whose deafness they were all aware, Sir Henry raised his voice to demand admittance, but in vain. Irritated at this delay, he pressed the door at once with foot and hand, in a way which the frail barrier was unable to resist; it gave way accordingly, and the knight thus forcibly entered the kitchen, or outward apartment, of his servant. In the midst of the floor and with a posture which indicated embarrassment, stood a youthful stranger, in a riding-suit.

"This may be my last act of authority here," said the knight, seizing the stranger by the collar, "but I am still ranger of Woodstock for this night at least. Who or what art thou ?"

The stranger dropped the riding-mantle in which his face was muffled, and at the same time fell on one knee.

"Your poor kinsman, Markham Everard," he said, "who came hither for your sake, although he fears you will scarce make him welcome for his own."

Sir Henry started back, but recovered himself in an instant, as one who recollected that he had a part of dignity to perform. He stood erect, therefore, and replied, with considerable assumption of stately ceremony :

"Fair kinsman, it pleases me that you are come to Woodstock upon the very first night that, for many years which have past, is likely to promise you a worthy or a welcome reception."

"Now God grant it be so, that I rightly hear and duly understand you," said the young man ; while Alice, though she was silent, kept her looks fixed on her father's face, as if desirous to know whether his meaning was kind towards his nephew, which her knowledge of his character inclined her greatly to doubt.

The night meanwhile darted a sardonic look, first on his nephew, then on his daughter, and proceeded—"I need not, I presume, inform Mr. Markham Everard that it cannot be our purpose to entertain him, or even to offer him a seat, in this poor hut."

"I will attend you most willingly to the lodge," said the young gentleman. "I had, indeed, judged you were already there for the evening, and feared to intrude upon you. But if you would permit me, my dearest uncle, to escort my kinswoman and you back to the lodge, believe me, amongst all which you have so often done of good and kind, you never conferred benefit that will be so dearly prized."

"You mistake me greatly, Mr. Markham Everard," replied the knight. "It is not our purpose to return to the lodge to-night, nor, by Our Lady, to-morrow neither. I meant but to intimate to you in all courtesy, that at Woodstock Lodge you will find those for whom you are fitting society, and who, doubtless, will afford you a willing welcome, which I, sir, in this my present retreat, do not presume to offer to a person of your consequence."

"For heaven's sake," said the young man, turning to Alice, "tell me how I am to understand language so mysterious!"

Alice, to prevent his increasing the restrained anger of her father, compelled herself to answer, though it was with difficulty, "We are expelled from the lodge by soldiers."

"Expelled—by soldiers!" exclaimed Everard, in surprise; "there is no legal warrant for this."

"None at all," answered the knight, in the same tone of cutting irony which he had all along used, "and yet as lawful a warrant as for aught that has been wrought in England this twelvemonth and more. You are, I think, or were, an Inns-of-Court-man—marry, sir, your enjoyment of your profession is like that lease which a prodigal wishes to have of a wealthy widow. You have already survived the law which you studied, and its expiry doubtless has not been without a legacy—some decent pickings, some merciful increases, as the phrase goes. You have deserved it two ways: you wore buff and bandoleer, as well as wielded pen and ink—I have not heard if you held forth too?"

"Think of me and speak of me as harshly as you will, sir," said Everard, submissively. "I have but, in this evil time, guided myself by my conscience and my father's commands."

"O, an you talk of conscience," said the old knight, "I must have mine eye upon you, as Hamlet says. Never yet did Puritan cheat so grossly as when he was appealing to his conscience; and as for thy *father*——"

He was about to proceed in a tone of the same invective, when the young man interrupted him, by saying, in a firm tone, "Sir Henry Lee, you have ever been thought noble. Say of me what you will, but speak not of my father what the ear of a son should not endure, and which yet his arm cannot resent. To do me such wrong is to insult an unarmed man or to beat a captive."

Sir Henry paused, as if struck by the remark. "Thou hast spoken truth in that, Mark, wert thou the blackest Puritan whom hell ever vomited, to distract an unhappy country."

"Be that as you will to think it," replied Everard; "but let me not leave you to the shelter of this wretched hovel. The night is drawing to storm; let me but conduct you to the lodge, and expel those intruders, who can, as yet at least, have no warrant for what they do. I will not linger a moment behind them, save just to deliver my father's message. Grant me but this much, for the love you once bore me."

"Yes, Mark," answered his uncle, firmly, but sorrowfully, "thou speakest truth—I did love thee once. The bright-haired boy whom I taught to ride, to shoot, to hunt, whose hours of happiness were spent with me, wherever those of graver labors were employed—I did love that boy—ah, and I am weak enough to love even the memory of what he was. But he is gone, Mark—he is gone; and in his room I only behold an avowed and determined rebel to his religion and to his king—a rebel more detestable on account of his success, the more infamous through the plundered wealth with which he hopes to guild his villainy. But I am poor, thou think'st, and should hold my peace, lest men say, 'Speak, sirrah, when you should.' Know, however, that, indigent and plundered as I am, I feel myself dishonored in holding even but this much talk with the tool of usurping rebels. Go to the lodge if thou wilt, yonder lies the way; but think not that, to regain my dwelling there, or all the wealth I ever possessed in my wealthiest days, I would willingly accompany thee three steps on the greensward. If I must be thy companion, it shall be only when thy redcoats have tied my hands behind me, and bound my legs beneath my horse's belly. Thou mayst be my fellow-traveler then, I grant thee, if thou wilt, but not sooner."

Alice, who suffered cruelly during this dialogue, and was well aware that further argument would only kindle the knight's resentment still more highly, ventured at last, in her anxiety, to make a sign to her cousin to break off the interview and to retire, since her father commanded his absence in a manner so peremptory. Unhappily she was observed by Sir Henry, who, concluding that what he saw was evidence of a private understanding betwixt the cousins—his wrath acquired new fuel, and it required the utmost exertion of self-command, and recollection of all that was due to his own dignity, to enable him to veil his real fury under the same ironical manner which he had adopted at the beginning of this angry interview.

"If thou art afraid," he said, "to trace our forest glades by night, respected stranger, to whom I am perhaps bound to do honor as my successor in the charge of these walks, here seems to be a modest damsel who will be most willing to wait on thee, and be thy bower-bearer. Only, for her mother's sake, let there pass some slight form of marriage between you. Ye need no license or priest in these happy days, but may be buckled like beggars in a ditch, with a hedge for a church-roof and a tinker for a priest. I crave pardon of you for making such an officious and simple request: perhaps you are a Ranter, or one of the family of Love, or hold marriage rites as unnecessary as Knipperdoling or Jack of Leyden?"

"For mercy's sake, forbear such dreadful jesting, my father! and do you, Markham, begone, in God's name, and leave us to our fate. Your presence makes my father rave."

"Jesting!" said Sir Henry. "I was never more serious. Raving! I was never more composed. I could never brook that falsehood should approach me: I would no more bear by my side a dishonored daughter than a dishonored sword; and this unhappy day hath shown that both can fail."

"Sir Henry," said young Everard, "load not your soul with a heavy crime, which be assured you do, in treating your daughter thus unjustly. It is long now since you denied her to me, when we were poor and you were powerful. I acquiesced in your prohibition of all suit and intercourse. God knoweth what I suffered—but I acquiesced. Neither is it to renew my suit that I now come hither, and have, I do acknowledge, sought speech of her, not for her own sake only, but for yours also. Destruction hovers over you, ready to close her pinions to stoop and her talons to clutch. Yes, sir, look contemptuous as you will, such is the case; and it is to protect both you and her that I am here."

"You refuse then my free gift," said Sir Henry Lee; "or perhaps you think it loaded with too hard conditions?"

"Shame—shame on you, Sir Henry!" said Everard, waxing warm in his turn; "have your political prejudices so utterly warped every feeling of a father, that you can speak with bitter mockery and scorn of what concerns your own daughter's honor? Hold up your head, fair Alice, and tell your father he has forgotten nature in his fantastic spirit of loyalty. Know, Sir Henry, that, though I would prefer your daughter's hand to every blessing which Heaven could bestow on me, I would not accept it—my conscience would not permit me to do so—when I knew it must withdraw her from her duty to you."

"Your conscience is over-scrupulous, young man; carry it to some dissenting rabbi, and he who takes all that comes to net will teach thee it is sinning against our mercies to refuse any good thing that is freely offered to us."

"When it is freely offered, and kindly offered—not when the offer is made in irony and insult. Fare thee well, Alice; if aught could make me desire to profit by thy father's wild wish to cast thee from him in a moment of unworthy suspicion, it would be that, while indulging in such sentiments, Sir Henry Lee is tyrannically oppressing the creature who of all others in most dependent on his kindness, who of all others will most feel his severity, and whom of all others he is most bound to cherish and support."

"Do not fear for me, Mr. Everard," exclaimed Alice, aroused from her timidity by a dread of the consequences not unlikely to ensue, where civil war sets relations, as well as fellow-citizens, in opposition to each other. "Oh, begone, I conjure you—begone! Nothing stands betwixt me and my father's kindness but these unhappy family divisions —but your ill-timed presence here. For Heaven's sake, leave us!"

"Soh, mistress!" answered the hot old Cavalier, "you play lady paramount already, and who but you! You would dictate to our train, I warrant, like Goneril and Regan! But I tell thee, no man shall leave my house— and, humble as it is, *this* is now my house—while he has aught to say to me that is to be spoken, as this young man now speaks, with a bent brow and a lofty tone. Speak out, sir, and say your worst."

"Fear not my temper, Mrs. Alice," said Everard, with equal firmness and placidity of manner; "and you, Sir Henry, do not think that, if I speak firmly, I mean therefore to speak in anger, or officiously. You have taxed me with much, and, were I guided by the wild spirit of romantic chivalry, much which, even from so near a relative, I ought not, as being by birth and in the world's estimation a gentleman, to pass over without reply. Is it your pleasure to give me patient hearing?"

"If you stand on your defense," answered the stout old knight, "God forbid that you should not challenge a patient hearing—ay, though your pleading were two part disloyalty and one blasphemy. Only be brief; this has already lasted but too long."

"I will, Sir Henry," replied the young man; "yet it is hard to crowd into a few sentences the defense of a life which, though short, has been a busy one—too busy, your indignant gesture would assert. But I deny it: I have drawn my sword neither hastily nor without due consideration for a people whose rights have been trampled on and whose consciences have been oppressed. Frown not, sir—such is not your view of the contest, but such is mine. For my religious principles, at which you have scoffed, believe me that, though they depend not on set forms, they are no less sincere than your own, and thus far purer—excuse the word—that they are unmingled with the bloodthirsty dictates of a barbarous age, which you and others have called the code of chivalrous honor. Not my own natural disposition, but the better doctrine which my creed has taught, enables me to bear your harsh revilings without answering in a similar tone of wrath and reproach. You may carry insult to extremity against me at your pleasure, not on account of our relationship alone, but because I am bound in charity to endure it. This, Sir Henry, is much from one of our house. But, with forbearance far more than this requires, I can refuse at your hands the gift which, most of all things under Heaven, I should desire to obtain, because duty calls upon her to sustain and comfort you, and because it were sin to permit you, in your blindness, to spurn your comforter from your side. Farewell, Sir—not in anger, but in pity. We may meet in a better time, when your heart and your principles shall master the unhappy prejudices by which they are now overclouded. Farewell—farewell, Alice!"

The last words were repeated twice, and in a tone of feeling and passionate grief which differed utterly from the steady and almost severe tone in which he had addressed Sir Henry Lee. He turned and left the hut so soon as he had uttered these last words; and, as if ashamed of the tenderness which had mingled with his accents, the young Commonwealth's-man turned and walked sternly and resolvedly forth into the moonlight, which now was spreading its broad light and autumnal shadows over the woodland.

So soon as he departed, Alice, who had been during the whole scene in the utmost terror that her father might have been hurried, by his natural heat of temper, from violence of language into violence of action, sunk down upon a settle twisted out of willow-boughs, like most of Joceline's few movables, and endeavored to conceal the tears which accompanied the thanks she rendered in broken accents to Heaven, that, notwithstanding the near alliance and relationship of the parties, some fatal deed had not closed an interview so perilous and so angry. Phœbe Mayflower blubbered heartily for company, though she understood but little of what had passed; just, indeed, enough to enable her afterwards to report to some half-dozen particular friends that her old master, Sir Henry, had been perilous angry, and almost fought with young Master Everard, because he had well-nigh carried away her young mistress. "And what could he have done better," said Phœbe, "seeing the old man had nothing left either for Mrs. Alice or himself? and as for Mr. Mark Everard and our young lady, oh! they had spoken such loving things to each other as are not to be found in the history of Argalus and Parthenia,* who, as the story-book tells, were the truest pair of lovers in all Arcadia and Oxfordshire to boot."

Old Goody Jellicot had popped her scarlet hood into the kitchen more than once while the scene was proceeding; but, as the worthy dame was parcel blind and more than parcel deaf, knowledge was excluded by two principal entrances; and though she comprehended, by a sort of general instinct, that the gentlefolk were at high words, yet why they chose Joceline's hut for the scene of their dispute was as great a mystery as the subject of the quarrel.

But what was the state of the old Cavalier's mood, thus contradicted, as his most darling principles had been, by the last words of his departiug nephew? The truth is, that he was less thoroughly moved than his daughter expected; and in all probability his nephew's bold defense of his religious and political opinions rather pacified than aggravated his displeasure. Although sufficiently impatient of contradiction, still evasion and subterfuge were more alien to the blunt old ranger's nature than manly vindication and direct opposition; and he was wont to say, that he ever loved the buck best who stood boldest at bay. He graced his nephew's departure, however, with a quotation from Shakspeare, whom, as many others do, he was wont to quote from a sort of habit and respect, as a favorite of his unfortunate master, without having either much real taste for his works or great skill in applying the passages which he retained on his memory.

"Mark," he said—"mark this, Alice: the devil can quote Scripture for his purpose. Why, this young fanatic cousin of thine, with no more beard than I have seen on a clown playing Maid Marian on May-day, when the village barber had shaved him in too great a hurry, shall match any bearded Presbyterian or Independent of them all in laying down his doctrines and his uses, and bethumping us with

* *The Most Pleasant and Delightful History of Argalus and Parthenia* was a chap-book very popular in the 17th century (*Laing*).

his texts and his homilies. I would worthy and learned Doctor Rochecliffe had been here, with his battery ready mounted from the Vulgate, and the Septuagint, and what not: he would have battered the Presbyterian spirit out of him with a wanion. However, I am glad the young man is no sneaker; for, were a man of the devil's opinion in religion and of Old Noll's in politics, he were better open on it full cry than deceive you by hunting counter or running a false scent. Come, wipe thine eyes: the fray is over, and not like to be stirred again soon, I trust."

Encouraged by these words, Alice rose, and, bewildered as she was, endeavored to superintend the arrangements for their meal and their repose in their new habitation. But her tears fell so fast, they marred her counterfeited diligence; and it was well for her that Phœbe, though too ignorant and too simple to comprehend the extent of her distress, could afford her material assistance, in lack of mere sympathy.

With great readiness and address, the damsel set about everything that was requisite for preparing the supper and the beds; now screaming into Dame Jellicot's ear, now whispering into her mistress's, and artfully managing as if she was merely the agent under Alice's orders. When the cold viands were set forth, Sir Henry Lee kindly pressed his daughter to take refreshment, as if to make up, indirectly, for his previous harshness towards her; while he himself, like an experienced campaigner, showed that neither the mortifications nor brawls of the day, nor the thoughts of what was to come to-morrow, could diminish his appetite for supper, which was his favorite meal. He ate up two-thirds of the capon, and, devoting the first bumper to the happy restoration of Charles, second of the name, he finished a quart of wine; for he belonged to a school accustomed to feed the flame of their loyalty with copious brimmers. He even sang a verse of "The King shall enjoy his own again," in which Phœbe, half-sobbing, and Dame Jellicot, screaming against time and tune, were contented to lend their aid, to cover Mistress Alice's silence.

At length the jovial knight betook himself to his rest on the keeper's straw pallet, in a recess adjoining to the kitchen, and, unaffected by his change of dwelling, slept fast and deep. Alice had less quiet rest in old Goody Jellicot's wicker couch, in the inner apartment; while the dame and Phœbe slept on a mattress, stuffed with dry leaves, in the same chamber, soundly as those whose daily toil gains their daily bread, and whom morning calls up only to renew the toils of yesterday.

CHAPTER V

> My tongue pads slowly under this new language,
> And starts and stumbles at these uncouth phrases.
> They may be great in worth and weight, but hang
> Upon the native glibness of my speech
> Like Saul's plate-armor on the shepherd boy,
> Encumbering and not arming him.
>
> J. B.

As Markham Everard pursued his way towards the lodge, through one of the long sweeping glades which traversed the forest, varying in breadth, till the trees were now so close that the boughs made darkness over his head, then receding farther to let in glimpses of the moon, and anon opening yet wider into little meadows or savannahs, on which the moonbeams lay in silvery silence—as he thus proceeded on his lonely course, the various effects produced by that delicious light on the oaks, whose dark leaves, gnarled branches, and massive trunks it gilded more or less partially, might have drawn the attention of a poet or a painter.

But if Everard thought of anything saving the painful scene in which he had just played his part, and of which the result seemed the destruction of all his hopes, it was of the necessary guard to be observed in his night-walk. The times were dangerous and unsettled, the roads full of disbanded soldiers, and especially of Royalists, who made their political opinions a pretext for disturbing the country with marauding parties and robberies. Deer-stealers also, who are ever a desperate banditti, had of late infested Woodstock Chase. In short, the dangers of the place and period were such that Markham Everard wore his loaded pistols at his belt, and carried his drawn sword under his arm, that he might be prepared for whatever peril should cross his path.

He heard the bells of Woodstock church ring curfew, just as he was crossing one of the little meadows we have described, and they ceased as he entered an overshadowed and twilight part of the path beyond. It was there that he heard some one whistling; and, as the sound became clearer, it was plain the person was advancing towards him. This could hardly be a friend; for the party to which he belonged rejected, generally speaking, all music, unless psalmody. "If a man is merry, let him sing psalms," was a text which they were pleased to interpret as literally and to as little purpose as they did some others; yet it was too continued a sound to be a signal amongst night-walkers, and too light and cheerful to argue any purpose of concealment on the part of the traveler, who presently exchanged his whistling for singing, and trolled forth the following stanza to a jolly tune, with which the old Cavaliers were wont to wake the night owl—

"Hey for cavaliers! Ho for cavaliers!
Pray for cavaliers!
Rub a dub—rub a dub!
Have at old Beelzebub.
Oliver smokes for fear."

"I should know that voice," said Everard, uncocking the pistol which he had drawn from his belt, but continuing to hold it in his hand. Then came another fragment—

"Hash them, slash them,
All to pieces dash them."

"So ho!" cried Markham, "who goes there, and for whom?"

"For Church and King," answered a voice, which presently added, "No, d—n me, I mean *against* Church and King, and for the people that are uppermost, I forget which they are."

"Roger Wildrake, as I guess?" said Everard.

"The same gentleman, of Squattlesea Mere, in the moist county of Lincoln."

"Wildrake!" said Markham. "Wildgoose you should be called. You have been moistening your own throat to some purpose, and using it to gabble tunes very suitable to the times, to be sure."

"Faith, the tune's a pretty tune enough, Mark, only out of fashion a little, the more's the pity."

"What could I expect," said Everard, "but to meet some ranting, drunken Cavalier, as desperate and dangerous as night and sack usually make them? What if I had rewarded your melody by a ball in the gullet?"

"Why, there would have been a piper paid, that's all," said Wildrake. "But wherefore come you this way now? I was about to seek you at the hut."

"I have been obliged to leave it. I will tell you the cause hereafter," replied Markham.

"What! the old play-hunting Cavalier was cross, or Chloe was unkind?"

"Jest not, Wildrake; it is all over with me," said Everard.

"The devil it is," exclaimed Wildrake, "and you take it thus quietly! Zounds! let us back together. I'll plead your cause for you. I know how to tickle up an old knight and a pretty maiden. Let me alone for putting you *rectus in curia*, you canting rogue. "D—n me, Sir Henry Lee," says I, "your nephew is a piece of a Puritan, it won't deny; but I'll uphold him a gentleman and a pretty fellow, for all that." "Madam," says I, "you may think your cousin looks like a psalm-singing weaver, in that bare felt, and with that rascally brown cloak, that band, which looks like a baby's clout, and those loose boots, which have a whole calf skin in each of them; but let him wear on the one side of his head a castor, with a plume befitting his quality; give him a good Toledo by his side, with a broidered belt and an inlaid hilt, instead of the ton of iron contained in that basket-hilted black Andrew Ferrara; put a few smart words in his mouth, and, blood and wounds! madam," says I——"

"Prithee, truce with this nonsense, Wildrake," said Everard, "and tell me if you are sober enough to hear a few words of sober reason?"

"Pshaw! man, I did but crack a brace of quarts with yonder Puritanic Roundheaded soldiers up yonder at the town; and rat me but I passed myself for the best man of the party—twanged my nose and turned up my eyes as I took my can. Pah! the very wine tasted of hypocrisy. I think the rogue corporal smoked something at last; as for the common fellows, never stir, but *they* asked me to say grace over another quart!"

"This is just what I wished to speak with you about, Wildrake," said Markham. "You hold me, I am sure, for your friend?"

"True as steel. Chums at college and at Lincoln's Inn, we have been Nisus and Euryalus, Theseus and Pirithous, Orestes and Pylades, and, to sum up the whole with a Puritanic touch, David and Jonathan, all in one breath. Not even politics, the wedge that rends families and friendships asunder, as iron rives oak, have been able to split us."

"True," answered Markham; "and when you followed the King to Nottingham, and I enrolled under Essex, we swore, at our parting, that whichever side was victorious, he of us who adhered to it should protect his less fortunate comrade."

"Surely, man—surely; and have you not protected me accordingly? Did you not save me from hanging? and am I not indebted to you for the bread I eat?"

"I have but done that which, had the times been otherwise, you, my dear Wildrake, would, I am sure, have done for me. But, as I said, that is just what I wished to speak to you about. Why render the task of protecting you more difficult than it must necessarily be at any rate? Why thrust thyself into the company of soldiers, or such-like, where thou art sure to be warmed into betraying thyself? Why come hallooing and whooping out Cavalier ditties, like a drunken trooper of Prince Rupert, or one of Wilmot's swaggering body-guards?"

"Because I may have been both one and t'other in my day, for aught that you know," replied Wildrake "But, oddfish! is it necessary I should always be reminding you that our obligation of mutual protection, our league of offensive and defensive, as I may call it, was to be carried into effect without reference to the politics or religion of the party protected, or the least obligation on him to conform to those of his friend?"

"True," said Everard; "but with this most necessary qualification, that the party should submit to such outward conformity to the times as should make it more easy and safe for his friend to be of service to him. Now, you are perpetually breaking forth, to the hazard of your own safety and my credit."

"I tell you, Mark, and I would tell your namesake the apostle, that you are hard on me. You have practised sobriety and hypocrisy from your hanging sleeves till your Geneva cassock—from the cradle to this day—and it is a thing of nature to you; and you are surprised that a rough, rattling, honest fellow, accustomed to speak truth all his life, and especially when he found it at the bottom of a flask, cannot be so perfect a prig as thyself! Zooks! there is no equality betwixt us. A trained diver might as well, because he can retain his breath for ten minutes without inconvenience, upbraid a poor devil for being like to burst in twenty seconds, at the bottom of ten fathoms' water; and, after all, considering the guise so new to me, I think I bear myself indifferently well—try me!"

"Are there any more news from Worcester fight?" asked

Everard, in a tone so serious that it imposed on his companion, who replied in his genuine character—

"Worse! d—n me—worse an hundred times than reported—totally broken. Noll had certainly sold himself to the Devil, and his lease will have an end one day, that is all our present comfort."

"What! and would this be your answer to the first redcoat who asked the question?" said Everard. "Methinks you would find a speedy passport to the next *corps de garde.*"

"Nay—nay," answered Wildrake, "I thought you asked me in your own person. Lack-a-day! a great mercy—a glorifying mercy—a crowning mercy—a vouchsafing—an uplifting; I profess the Malignants are scattered from Dan to Beersheba, smitten, hip and thigh, even until the going down of the sun!"

"Hear you aught of Colonel Thornhaugh's wounds?"

"He is dead," answered Wildrake, "that's one comfort—the Roundheaded rascal! Nay, hold! it was but a trip of the tongue—I meant, the sweet, godly youth."

"And hear you aught of the young man, King of Scotland, as they call him?" said Everard.

"Nothing, but that he is hunted like a partridge on the mountains. May God deliver him and confound his enemies! Zoons, Mark Everard, I can fool it no longer. Do you not remember, that at the Lincoln's Inn gambols—though you did not mingle much in them, I think—I used always to play as well as any of them when it came to the action, but they could never get me to rehearse conformably. It's the same at this day. I hear your voice, and I answer to it in the true tone of my heart; but when I am in the company of your snuffling friends, you have seen me act my part indifferent well."

"But indifferent, indeed," replied Everard; "however, there is little call on you to do aught, save to be modest and silent. Speak little, and lay aside, if you can, your big oaths and swaggering looks—set your hat even on your brow."

"Ay, that is the curse! I have been always noted for the jaunty manner in which I wear my castor. Hard when a man's merits become his enemies!"

"You must remember you are my clerk."

"Secretary," answered Wildrake; "let it be secretary, if you love me."

"It must be clerk, and nothing else—plain clerk; and remember to be civil and obedient," replied Everard.

"But you should not lay on your commands with so much ostentatious superiority, Master Markham Everard. Remember I am your senior of three years' standing. Confound me, if I know how to take it!"

"Was ever such a fantastic wronghead! For my sake, if not for thine own, bend thy freakish folly to listen to reason. Think that I have incurred both risk and shame on thy account."

"Nay, thou art a right good fellow, Mark," replied the Cavalier, "and for thy sake I will do much; but remember to cough and cry hem! when thou seest me like to break bounds. And now tell me whither we are bound for the night?"

"To Woodstock Lodge, to look after my uncle's property," answered Markham Everard: "I am informed that soldiers have taken possession. Yet how could that be, if thou foundest the party drinking in Woodstock?"

"There was a kind of commissary or steward, or some such rogue, had gone down to the lodge," replied Wildrake; "I had a peep at him."

"Indeed!" replied Everard.

"Ay, verily," said Wildrake, "to speak your own language. Why, as I passed through the park in quest of you, scarce half an hour since, I saw a light in the lodge. Step this way, you will see it yourself."

"In the northwest angle?" returned Everard; "it is from a window in what they call Victor Lee's apartment."

"Well," resumed Wildrake, "I had been long one of Lunsford's lads, and well used to patroling duty—so, 'Rat me,' says I, 'if I leave a light in my rear without knowing what it means.' Besides, Mark, thou hadst said so much to me of thy pretty cousin, I thought I might as well have a peep, if I could."

"Thoughtless, incorrigible man! to what dangers do you expose yourself and your friends, in mere wantonness! But go on."

"By this fair moonshine, I believe thou art jealous, Mark Everard," replied his gay companion. "There is no occasion; for, in any case, I, who was to see the lady, was steeled by honor against the charms of my friend's Chloe. Then the lady was not to see me, so could make no comparisons to thy disadvantage, thou knowest. Lastly, as it fell out, neither of us saw the other at all."

"Of that I am well aware. Mrs. Alice left the lodge

long before sunset, and never returned. What *didst* thou see to introduce with such preface?"

"Nay, no great matter," replied Wildrake! "only, getting upon a sort of buttress—for I can climb like any cat that ever mewed in any gutter—and holding on by the vines and creepers which grew around, I obtained a station where I could see into the inside of that same parlor thou spokest of just now."

"And what saw'st thou there?" once more demanded Everard.

"Nay, no great matter, as I said before," replied the Cavalier; "for in these times it is no new thing to see churls carousing in royal or noble chambers. I saw two rascallions engaged in emptying a solemn stoup of strong waters, and despatching a huge venison pasty, which greasy mess, for their convenience, they had placed upon a lady's work-table. One of them was trying an air on a lute."

"The profane villain!" exclaimed Everard, "it was Alice's."

"Well said, comrade—I am glad your phlegm can be moved. I did but throw in these incidents of the lute and the table to try if it were possible to get a spark of human spirit out of you, be-sanctified as you are."

"What like were the men" said young Everard.

"The one a slouch-hatted, long-cloaked, sour-faced fanatic, like the rest of you, whom I took to be the steward or commissary I heard spoken of in the town; the other was a short sturdy fellow, with a wood-knife at his girdle, and a long quarter-staff lying beside him—a black-haired knave, with white teeth and a merry countenance—one of the under-rangers or bow-bearers of these walks, I fancy."

"They must have been Desborough's favorite, Trusty Tomkins," said Everard, "and Joceline Joliffe, the keeper. Tomkins is Desborough's right hand—an Independent, and hath pourings forth, as he calls them. Some think that his gifts have the better of his grace. I have heard of his abusing opportunities."

"They were improving them when I saw them," replied Wildrake, "and made the bottle smoke for it, when, as the devil would have it, a stone, which had been dislodged from the crumbling buttress, gave way under my weight. A clumsy fellow like thee would have been so long thinking what was to be done, that he must needs have followed it before he could make up his mind; but I, Mark—I hopped like a squirrel to an ivy twig, and stood fast, was well-nigh shot, though, for the noise alarmed them both. They looked to the oriel, and saw me on the outside ; the fanatic fellow took out a pistol—as they have always such texts in readiness hanging beside the little clasped Bible, thou know'st ; the keeper seized his hunting-pole. I treated them both to a roar and a grin—thou must know I can grimace like a baboon—I learned the trick from a French player, who could twist his jaws into a pair of nut-crackers—and therewithal I dropped myself sweetly on the grass, and ran off so trippingly, keeping the dark side of the wall as long as I could, that I am well-nigh persuaded they thought I was their kinsman, the devil, come among them uncalled. They were abominably startled."

"Thou art most fearfully rash, Wildrake," said his companion. "We are now bound for the house ; what if they should remember thee ?"

"Why, it is no treason, is it ? No one has paid for peeping since Tom of Coventry's days ; and if he came in for a reckoning, belike it was for a better treat than mine. But trust me, they will no more know me than a man who had only seen your friend Noll at a conventicle of saints would know the same Oliver on horseback ; and charging with his lobster-tailed squadron ; or the same Noll cracking a jest and a bottle with wicked Waller the poet."

"Hush ! not a word of Oliver, as thou dost value thyself and me. It is ill jesting with the rock you may split on. But here is the gate ; we will disturb these honest gentlemen's recreations."

As he spoke, he applied the large and ponderous knocker to the hall door.

"Rat-tat-tat-too !" said Wildrake ; "there is a fine alarm to you cuckolds and Roundheads !" He then half-mimicked, half-sung the march so called :

> "Cuckolds, come dig, cuckolds come, dig ;
> Round about cuckolds, come dance to my jig !"

"By Heaven ! this passes midsummer frenzy," said Everard, turning angrily on him.

"Not a bit—not a bit," replied Wildrake ; "it is but a slight expectoration, just like what one makes before beginning a long speech. I will be grave for an hour together, now I have got that point of war out of my head."

As he spoke, steps were heard in the hall, and the wicket of the great door was partly opened, but secured with a chain in case of accidents. The visage of Tomkins, and that of Joceline beneath it, appeared at the chink, illuminated by the lamp which the latter held in his hand, and Tomkins demanded the meaning of this alarm.

"I demand instant admittance," said Everard. "Joliffe, you know me well?"

"I do, sir," said Joceline, "and could admit you with all my heart; but, alas! sir, you see I am not key-keeper. Here is the gentleman whose warrant I must walk by. The Lord help me, seeing times are such as they be!"

"And when that gentleman, who I think may be Master Desborough's valet——"

"His Honor's unworthy secretary, an it please you," interposed Tomkins; while Wildrake whispered in Everard's ear, "I will be no longer secretary. Mark, thou wert quite right: the clerk must be the more gentlemanly calling."

"And if you are Master Desborough's secretary, I presume you know me and my condition well enough," said Everard, addressing the Independent, "not to hesitate to admit me and my attendant to a night's quarters in the lodge?"

"Surely not—surely not," said the Independent; "that is, if your worship thinks you would be better accommodated here than up at the house of entertainment in the town, which men unprofitably call St. George's Inn. There is but confined accommodation here, your honor, and we have been frayed out of our lives already by the visitation of Satan, albeit his fiery dart is now quenched."

"This may be all well in its place, sir secretary," said Everard, "and you may find a corner for it when you are next tempted to play the preacher. But I will take it for no apology for keeping me here in the cold harvest wind; and if not presently received, and suitably too, I will report you to your master for insolence in your office."

The secretary of Desborough did not dare offer farther opposition; for it is well known that Desborough himself only held his consequence as a kinsman of Cromwell, and the Lord General, who was well-nigh paramount already, was known to be strongly favorable both to the elder and younger Everard. It is true, they were Presbyterians and he an Independent; and that, though sharing those sentiments of correct morality and more devoted religious feeling by which, with a few exceptions, the Parliamentarian party were distinguished, the Everards were not disposed to carry these attributes to the extreme of enthusiasm practised by so many others at the time. Yet it was well known that, whatever might be Cromwell's own religious creed, he was not uniformly bounded by it in the choice of his favorites, but extended his countenance to those who could serve him, even although, according to the phrase of the time, they came out of the darkness of Egypt. The character of the elder Everard stood very high for wisdom and sagacity; besides, being of a good family and competent fortune, his adherence would lend a dignity to any side he might espouse. Then his son had been a distinguished and successful soldier, remarkable for the discipline he maintained among his men, the bravery which he showed in the time of action, and the humanity with which he was always ready to qualify the consequences of victory. Such men were not to be neglected, when many signs combined to show that the parties in the state who had successfully accomplished the deposition and death of the King were speedily to quarrel among themselves about the division of the spoils. The two Everards were therefore much courted by Cromwell, and their influence with him was supposed to be so great, that trusty Master Secretary Tomkins cared not to expose himself to risk, by contending with Colonel Everard for such a trifle as a night's lodging, or a greater thing.

Joceline was active on his side: more lights were obtained, more wood thrown on the fire, and the two newly-arrived strangers were introduced into Victor Lee's parlor, as it was called, from the picture over the chimney-piece, which we have already described. It was several minutes ere Colonel Everard could recover his general stoicism of deportment, so strongly was he impressed by finding himself in the apartment under whose roof he had passed so many of the happiest hours of his life. There was the cabinet which he had seen opened with such feelings of delight when Sir Henry Lee deigned to give him instructions in fishing, and to exhibit hooks and lines, together with all the materials for making the artificial fly, then little known. There hung the ancient family picture, which, from some old mysterious expressions of his uncle relating to it, had become to his boyhood, nay, his early youth, a subject of curiosity and of fear. He remembered how, when left alone in the apartment, the searching eye of the old warrior seemed always bent upon his, in whatever part of the room he placed himself, and how his childish imagination was perturbed at a phenomenon for which he could not account.

With these came a thousand dearer and warmer recollections of his early attachment to his pretty cousin Alice, when he assisted her at her lessons, brought water for her flowers, or accompanied her while she sung; and he remembered that, while her father looked at them with a good-humored and careless smile, he had once heard him mutter, "And if it should turn out so, why it might be best for both," and the theories of happiness he had reared on these words. All these visions had been dispelled by the trumpet of war, which called Sir Henry Lee and himself to opposite sides; and the transactions of this very day had shown that even Everard's success as a soldier and a statesman seemed absolutely to prohibit the chance of their being revived.

He was waked out of this unpleasing reverie by the approach of Joceline, who, being possibly a seasoned toper, had made the additional arrangements with more expedition and accuracy than could have been expected from a person engaged as he had been since nightfall.

He now wished to know the colonel's directions for the night.

"Would he eat anything?"

"No."

"Did his honor choose to accept Sir Henry Lee's bed, which was ready prepared?"

"Yes."

"That of Mistress Alice Lee should be prepared for the secretary."

"On pain of thine ears—no," replied Everard.

"Where then was the worthy secretary to be quartered?"

"In the dog-kennel, if you list," replied Colonel Everard; "but," added he, stepping to the sleeping-apartment of Alice, which opened from the parlor, locking it and taking out the key, "no one shall profane this chamber."

"Had his honor any other commands for the night?"

"None, save to clear the apartment of yonder man. My clerk will remain with me: I have orders which must be written out. Yet stay. Thou gavest my letter this morning to Mistress Alice?"

"I did."

"Tell me, good Joceline, what she said when she received it?"

"She seemed much concerned, sir; and indeed I think that she wept a little—but indeed she seemed very much distressed."

"And what message did she send to me?"

"None, may it please your honor. She began to say,

"Tell my cousin Everard that I will communicate my uncle's kind purpose to my father, if I can get fitting opportunity; but that I greatly fear——" and there checked herself, as it were, and said, "I will write to my cousin; and as it may be late ere I have an opportunity of speaking with my father, do thou come for my answer after service." So I went to church myself to while away the time; but when I returned to the chase, I found this man had summoned my master to surrender, and, right or wrong, I must put him in possession of the lodge. I would fain have given your honor a hint that the old knight and my young mistress were like to take you on the form, but I could not mend the matter."

"Thou hast done well, good fellow, and I will remember thee. And now, my masters," he said, advancing to the brace of clerks or secretaries, who had in the meanwhile sat quietly down beside the stone bottle, and made up acquaintance over a glass of its contents, "let me remind you that the night wears late."

"There is something cries tinkle, tinkle, in the bottle yet," said Wildrake, in reply.

"Hem! hem! hem!" coughed the colonel of the Parliament service; and if his lips did not curse his companion's imprudence, I will not answer for what arose in his heart. "Well!" he said, observing that Wildrake had filled his own glass and Tomkins's, "take that parting glass and begone."

"Would you not be pleased to hear first," said Wildrake, "how this honest gentleman saw the Devil to-night look through a pane of yonder window, and how he thinks he had a mighty strong resemblance to your worship's humble slave and varlet scribbler? Would you but hear this, sir, and just sip a glass of this very recommendable strong waters?"

"I will drink none, sir," said Colonel Everard, sternly; "and I have to tell *you* that you have drunken a glass too much already. Mr. Tomkins, sir, I wish you good-night."

"A word in season at parting," said Tomkins, standing up behind the long leathern back of a chair, hemming and snuffling as if preparing for an exhortation.

"Excuse me, sir," replied Markham Everard; "you are not now sufficiently yourself to guide the devotion of others."

"Woe be to them that reject——!" said the secretary of the Commissioners, stalking out of the room; the rest was lost in shutting the door, or suppressed for fear of offense.

"And now, fool Wildrake, begone to thy bed—yonder it lies," pointing to the knight's apartment.

"What, thou hast secured the lady's for thyself? I saw thee put the key in thy pocket."

"I would not, indeed I could not, sleep in that apartment. I can sleep nowhere; but I will watch in this arm-chair. I have made him place wood for repairing the fire. Good now, go to bed thyself, and sleep off thy liquor."

"Liquor! I laugh thee to scorn, Mark; thou art a milksop, and the son of a milksop, and know'st not what a good fellow can do in the way of crushing an honest cup."

"The whole vices of his faction are in this poor fellow individually," said the colonel to himself, eying his *protégé* askance, as the other retreated into the bedroom with no very steady pace. "He is reckless, intemperate, dissolute; and if I cannot get him safely shipped for France, he will certainly be both his own ruin and mine. Yet, withal, he is kind, brave, and generous, and would have kept the faith with me which he now expects from me; and in what consists the merit of our truth, if we observe not our plighted word when we have promised to our hurt? I will take the liberty, however, to secure myself against farther interruption on his part."

So saying, he locked the door of communication betwixt the sleeping-room, to which the Cavalier had retreated, and the parlor; and then, after pacing the floor thoughtfully, returned to his seat, trimmed the lamp, and drew out a number of letters. "I will read these over once more," he said, "that, if possible, the thought of public affairs may expel this keen sense of personal sorrow. Gracious Providence, where is this to end? We have sacrificed the peace of our families, the warmest wishes of our young hearts, to right the country in which we were born, and to free her from oppression; yet it appears that every step we have made towards liberty has but brought us in view of new and more terrific perils, as he who travels in a mountainous region is, by every step which elevates him higher, placed in a situation of more imminent hazard."

He read long and attentively various tedious and embarrassed letters, in which the writers, placing before him the glory of God, and the freedom and liberties of England, as their supreme ends, could not, by all the ambagitory expressions they made use of, prevent the shrewd eye of Markham Everard from seeing that self-interest and views of ambition were the principal moving-springs at the bottom of their plots.

CHAPTER VI

Sleep steals on us even like his brother Death.
We know not when it comes; we know it must come.
We may affect to scorn and to contemn it,
For 'tis the highest pride of human misery
To say it knows not of an opiate;
Yet the reft parent, the despairing lover,
Even the poor wretch who waits for execution,
Feels this oblivion, against which he thought
His woes had arm'd his senses, steal upon him,
And through the fenceless citadel, the body,
Surprise that haughty garrison, the mind.

HERBERT.

COLONEL EVERARD experienced the truth contained in the verses of the quaint old bard whom we have quoted above. Amid private grief, and anxiety for a country long a prey to civil war, and not likely to fall soon under any fixed or well established form of government, Everard and his father had, like many others, turned their eyes to General Cromwell, as the person whose valor had made him the darling of the army, whose strong sagacity had hitherto predominated over the high talents by which he had been assailed in Parliament, as well as over his enemies in the field, and who was alone in the situation to "settle the nation," as the phrase then went, or, in other words, to dictate the mode of government. The father and son were both reputed to stand high in the General's favor. But Markham Everard was conscious of some particulars which induced him to doubt whether Cromwell actually, and at heart, bore either to his father or to himself that good-will which was generally believed. He knew him for a profound politician, who could veil for any length of time his real sentiments of men and things, until they could be displayed without prejudice to his interest. And he, moreover, knew that the General was not likely to forget the opposition which the Presbyterian party had offered to what Oliver called the "great matter"—the trial, namely, and execution of the King. In this opposition his father and he had anxiously concurred, nor had the arguments, nor even the half-expressed threats, of Cromwell induced them to flinch from that course, far less to permit their names to be introduced into the commission nominated to sit in judgment on that memorable occasion.

This hesitation had occasioned some temporary coldness between the General and the Everards, father and son. But as the latter remained in the army, and bore arms under Cromwell both in Scotland and finally at Worcester, his services very frequently called forth the approbation of his commander. After the fight of Worcester, in particular, he was among the number of those officers on whom Oliver, rather considering the actual and practical extent of his own power than the name under which he exercised it, was with difficulty withheld from imposing the dignity of knights-bannerets at his own will and pleasure. It therefore seemed that all recollection of former disagreement was obliterated, and that the Everards had regained their former stronghold in the General's affections. There were, indeed, several who doubted this, and who endeavored to bring over this distinguished young officer to some other of the parties which divided the infant Commonwealth. But to these proposals he turned a deaf ear. Enough of blood, he said, had been spilled : it was time that the nation should have repose under a firmly established government, of strength sufficient to protect property, and of lenity enough to encourage the return of tranquillity. This, he thought, could only be accomplished by means of Cromwell; and the greater part of England was of the same opinion. It is true that, in thus submitting to the domination of a successful soldier, those who did so forgot the principles upon which they had drawn the sword against the late king; but in revolutions, stern and high principles are often obliged to give way to the current of existing circumstances; and in many a case, where wars have been waged for points of metaphysical right, they have been at last gladly terminated upon the mere hope of obtaining general tranquillity, as, after many a long siege, a garrison is often glad to submit on mere security for life and limb.

Colonel Everard, therefore, felt that the support which he afforded Cromwell was only under the idea that, amid a choice of evils, the least was likely to ensue from a man of the General's wisdom and valor being placed at the head of the state; and he was sensible that Oliver himself was likely to consider his attachment as lukewarm and imperfect, and measure his gratitude for it upon the same limited scale.

In the meanwhile, however, circumstances compelled him to make trial of the General's friendship. The sequestration of Woodstock, and the warrant to the Commissioners to dispose of it as national property, had been long granted, but the interest of the elder Everard had for weeks and months deferred its execution. The hour was now approaching when the blow could be no longer parried, especially as Sir Henry Lee, on his side, resisted every proposal of submitting himself to the existing government, and was therefore, now that his hour of grace was passed, enrolled in the list of stubborn and irreclaimable Malignants, with whom the Council of State was determined no longer to keep terms. The only mode of protecting the old knight and his daughter was to interest, if possible, the General himself in the matter; and revolving all the circumstances connected with their intercourse, Colonel Everard felt that a request which would so immediately interfere with the interests of Desborough, the brother-in-law of Cromwell, and one of the present Commissioners, was putting to a very severe trial the friendship of the latter. Yet no alternative remained.

With this view, and agreeably to a request from Cromwell, who at parting had been very urgent to have his written opinion upon public affairs, Colonel Everard passed the earlier part of the night in arranging his ideas upon the state of the Commonwealth, in a plan which he thought likely to be acceptable to Cromwell, as it exhorted him, under the aid of Providence, to become the saviour of the state, by convoking a free Parliament, and by their aid placing himself at the head of some form of liberal and established government, which might supersede the state of anarchy in which the nation was otherwise likely to be merged. Taking a general view of the totally broken condition of the Royalists, and of the various factions which now convulsed the state, he showed how this might be done without bloodshed or violence. From this topic he descended to the propriety of keeping up the becoming state of the executive government, in whose hands soever it should be lodged, and thus showed Cromwell, as the future Stadtholder, or Consul, or Lieutenant-General of Great Britain and Ireland, a prospect of demesne and residences becoming his dignity. Then he naturally passed to the disparking and destroying of the royal residences of England, made a woeful picture of the demolition which impended over Woodstock, and interceded for the preservation of that beautiful seat, as a matter of personal favor, in which he found himself deeply interested.

Colonel Everard, when he had finished his letter, did not find himself greatly risen in his own opinion. In the course of his political conduct, he had till this hour avoided mixing up personal motives with his public grounds of action, and yet he now felt himself making such a composition. But he comforted himself, or at least silenced this unpleasing recollection, with the consideration, that the weal of Britain, studied under the aspect of the times, absolutely required that Cromwell should be at the head of the government: and that the interest of Sir Henry Lee, or rather his safety and his existence, no less emphatically demanded the preservation of Woodstock, and his residence there. Was it a fault of his, that the same road should lead to both these ends, or that his private interest and that of the country should happen to mix in the same letter? He hardened himself, therefore, to the act, made up and addressed his packet to the Lord General, and then sealed it with his seal of arms. This done, he lay back in his chair, and, in spite of his expectations to the contrary, fell asleep in the course of his reflections, anxious and harassing as they were, and did not awaken until the cold gray light of dawn was peeping through the eastern oriel.

He started at first, rousing himself with the sensation of one who awakes in a place unknown to him; but the localities instantly forced themselves on his recollection. The lamp burning dimly in the socket, the wood-fire almost extinguished in its own white embers, the gloomy picture over the chimney-piece, the sealed packet on the table—all reminded him of the events of yesterday, and his deliberations of the succeeding night.

"There is no help for it," he said: "it must be Cromwell or anarchy. And probably the sense that his title, as head of the executive government, is derived merely from popular consent may check the too natural proneness of power to render itself arbitrary. If he govern by Parliaments, and with regard to the privileges of the subject, wherefore not Oliver as well as Charles? But I must take measures for having this conveyed safely to the hands of this future sovereign prince. It will be well to take the first word of influence with him, since there must be many who will not hesitate to recommend counsels more violent and precipitate."

He determined to entrust the impoatant packet to the

charge of Wildrake, whose rashness was never so distinguished as when by any chance he was left idle and unemployed; besides, even if his faith had not been otherwise unimpeachable, the obligations which he owed to his friend Everard must have rendered it such.

These conclusions passed through Colonel Everard's mind, as, collecting the remains of wood in the chimney, he gathered them into a hearty blaze, to remove the uncomfortable feeling of chilliness which pervaded his limbs; and by the time he was a little more warm, again sunk into a slumber, which was only dispelled by the beams of morning peeping into his apartment.

He arose, roused himself, walked up and down the room, and looked from the large oriel window on the nearest objects, which were the untrimmed hedges and neglected walks of a certain wilderness, as it is called in ancient treatises on gardening, which, kept of yore well ordered, and in all the pride of the topiary art, presented a succession of yew-trees cut into fantastic forms, of close alleys, and of open walks, filling about two or three acres of ground on that side of the lodge, and forming a boundary between its immediate precincts and the open park. Its inclosure was now broken down in many places, and the hinds with their fawns fed free and unstartled up to the very windows of the silvan palace.

This had been a favorite scene of Markham's sports when a boy. He could still distinguish, though now grown out of shape, the verdant battlements of a Gothic castle, all created by the gardener's shears, at which he was accustomed to shoot his arrows; or, stalking before it like the knight-errants of whom he read, was wont to blow his horn and bid defiance to the supposed giant or paynim knight by whom it was garrisoned. He remembered how he used to train his cousin, though several years younger than himself, to bear a part in those revels of his boyish fancy, and to play the character of an elfin page, or a fairy, or an enchanted princess. He remembered, too, many particulars of their later acquaintance, from which he had been almost necessarily led to the conclusion, that from an early period their parents had entertained some idea that there might be a well-fitted match betwixt his fair cousin and himself. A thousand visions, formed in so bright a prospect, had vanished along with it, but now returned like shadows, to remind him of all he had lost—and for what? "For the sake of England," his proud consciousness replied—"of England, in danger of becoming the prey at once of bigotry and tyranny." And he strengthened himself with the recollection, "If I have sacrificed my private happiness, it is that my country may enjoy liberty of conscience and personal freedom, which, under a weak prince and usurping statesman, she was but too likely to have lost."

But the busy fiend in his breast would not be repulsed by the bold answer. "Has thy resistance," it demanded, "availed thy country, Markham Everard? Lies not England, after so much bloodshed and so much misery, as low beneath the sword of a fortunate soldier as formerly under the scepter of an encroaching prince? Are Parliament, or what remains of them, fitted to contend with a leader, master of his soldiers' hearts, as bold and subtle as he is impenetrable in his designs? This General, who holds the army, and by that the fate of the nation, in his hand, will he lay down his power because philosophy would pronounce it his duty to become a subject?"

He dared not answer that his knowledge of Cromwell authorized him to expect any such act of self-denial. Yet still he considered that, in times of such infinite difficulty, that must be the best government, however little desirable in itself, which should most speedily restore peace to the land, and stop the wounds which the contending parties were daily inflicting on each other. He imagined that Cromwell was the only authority under which a steady government could be formed, and therefore had attached himself to his fortune, though not without considerable and recurring doubts, how far serving the views of this impenetrable and mysterious General was consistent with the principles under which he had assumed arms.

While these things passed in his mind, Everard looked upon the packet which lay on the table addressed to the Lord General, and which he had made up before sleep. He hesitated several times, when he remembered its purport, and in what degree he must stand committed with that personage, and bound to support his plans of aggrandizement, when once that communication was in Oliver Cromwell's possession.

"Yet it must be so," he said at last, with a deep sigh. "Among the contending parties, he is the strongest, the wisest and most moderate, and ambitious though he he, perhaps not the most dangerous. Some one must be trusted with power to preserve and enforce general order, and who can possess or wield such power like him that is head of the victorious armies of England? Come what will in future, peace and the restoration of law ought to be our first and most pressing object. This remnant of a parliament cannot keep their ground against the army, by mere appeal to the sanction of opinion. If they design to reduce the soldiery, it must be by actual warfare, and the land has been too long steeped in blood. But Cromwell may, and I trust will, make a moderate accommodation with them, on grounds by which peace may be preserved; and it is this to which we must look and trust for a settlement of the kingdom, alas! and for the chance of protecting my obstinate kinsman from the consequences of his honest though absurd pertinacity."

Silencing some internal feelings of doubt and reluctance by such reasoning as this, Markham Everard continued in his resolution to unite himself with Cromwell in the struggle which was evidently approaching betwixt the civil and military authorities, not as the course which, if at perfect liberty, he would have preferred adopting, but as the best choice between two dangerous extremities to which the times had reduced him. He could not help trembling, however, when he recollected that his father, though hitherto the admirer of Cromwell, as the implement by whom so many marvels had been wrought in England, might not be disposed to unite with his interest against that of the Long Parliament, of which he had been, till partly laid aside by continued indisposition, an active and leading member. This doubt also he was obliged to swallow, or strangle, as he might; but consoled himself with the ready argument, that it was impossible his father could see matters in another light than that in which they occurred to himself.

CHAPTER VII

DETERMINED at length to despatch his packet to the General without delay, Colonel Everard approached the door of the apartment in which, as was evident from the heavy breathing within, the prisoner Wildrake enjoyed a deep slumber. under the influence of liquor at once and of fatigue. In turning the key, the bolt, which was rather rusty, made a resistance so noisy as partly to attract the sleeper's attention, though not to awake him. Everard stood by his bedside, as he heard him mutter, "Is it morning already, jailer? Why, you dog, an you had but a cast of humanity in you, you would qualify your vile news with a cup of sack; hanging is sorry work, my masters, and sorrow's dry."

"Up, Wildrake—up, thou ill-omened dreamer!" said his friend, shaking him by the collar.

"Hands off!" answered the sleeper. "I can climb a ladder without help, I trow." He then sat up in the bed, and opening his eyes, stared around him, and exclaimed, "Zounds! Mark, is it only thou? I thought it was all over with me—fetters were struck from my legs—rope drawn round my gullet—irons knocked off my hands—all ready for a dance in the open element upon slight footing."

"Truce with thy folly, Wildrake! Sure the devil of drink, to whom thou hast, I think, sold thyself——"

"For a hogshead of sack," interrupted Wildrake; "the bargain was made in a cellar in the Vintry."

"I am as mad as thou art, to trust anything to thee," said Markham; "I scarce believe thou hast thy senses yet."

"What should ail me?" said Wildrake; "I trust I have not tasted liquor in my sleep, saving that I dreamed of drinking small-beer with Old Noll, of his own brewing. But do not look so glum, man: I am the same Roger Wildrake that I ever was—as wild as a mallard, but as true as a game-cock. I am thine own chum, man, bound to thee by thy kind deeds—*devinctus beneficio*—there is Latin for it; and where is the thing thou wilt charge me with that I will not, or dare not, execute, were it to pick the Devil's teeth with my rapier, after he had breakfasted upon Roundheads?"

"You will drive me mad," said Everard. "When I am about to entrust all I have most valuable on earth to your management, your conduct and language are those of a mere Bedlamite. Last night I made allowance for thy drunken fury; but who can endure thy morning madness? It is unsafe for thyself and me, Wildrake—it is unkind—I might say ungrateful."

"Nay, do not say *that*, my friend," said the Cavalier, with some show of feeling; "and do not judge of me with a severity that cannot apply to such as I am. We who have lost our all in these sad jars, who are compelled to shift for our living, not from day to day, but from meal to meal—we whose only hiding-place is the jail, whose prospect of final repose is the gallows, what canst thou expect from us, but to bear such a lot with a light heart, since we should break down under it with a heavy one?"

This was spoken in a tone of feeling which found a responding string in Everard's bosom. He took his friend's hand and pressed it kindly.

"Nay, if I seemed harsh to thee, Wildrake, I profess it was for thine own sake more than mine. I know thou hast at the bottom of thy levity as deep a principle of honor and feeling as ever governed a human heart. But thou art thoughtless, thou art rash; and I protest to thee, that wert thou to betray thyself in this matter in which I trust thee, the evil consequences to myself do not afflict me more than the thought of putting thee into such danger."

"Nay, if you take it on that tone, Mark," said the Cavalier, making an effort to laugh, evidently that he might conceal a tendency to a different emotion, "thou wilt make children of us both—babes and sucklings, by the hilt of this bilbo. Come, trust me; I can be cautious when time requires it: no man ever saw me drink when an alert was expected; and not one poor pint of wine will I taste until I have managed this matter for thee. Well, I am thy secretary—clerk, I had forgot—and carry thy despatches to Cromwell, taking good heed not to be surprised or choused out of my lump of loyalty (striking his finger on the packet), and I am to deliver it to the most loyal hands to which it is most humbly addressed. Adzooks, Mark, think of it a moment longer. Surely thou will not carry thy perverseness so far as to strike in with this bloody-minded rebel? Bid me give him three inches of my dudgeon-dagger, and I will do it much more willingly than present him with thy packet."

"Go to," replied Everard, "this is beyond our bargain. If you will help me, it is well; if not, let me lose no time in debating with thee, since I think every moment an age till the packet is in the General's possession. It is the only way left me to obtain some protection and a place of refuge for my uncle and his daughter."

"That being the case," said the Cavalier, "I will not spare the spur. My nag up yonder at the town will be ready for the road in a trice, and thou mayst reckon on my being with Old Noll—thy General, I mean—in as short time as man and horse may consume betwixt Woodstock and Windsor, where I think I shall for the present find thy friend keeping possession where he has slain."

"Hush, not a word of that. Since we parted last night, I have shaped thee a path which will suit thee better than to assume the decency of language and of outward manner of which thou hast so little. I have acquainted the General that thou hast been by bad example and bad education——"

"Which is to be interpreted by contraries, I hope," said Wildrake; "for sure I have been as well born and bred up as any lad of Leicestershire [Lincolnshire] might desire."

"Now, I prithee hush—thou hast, I say, by bad example, become at one time a Malignant, and mixed in the party of the late King. But seeing what things were wrought in the nation by the General, thou hast come to a clearness touching his calling to be a great implement in the settlement of these distracted kingdoms. This account of thee will not only lead him to pass over some of thy eccentricities, should they break out in spite of thee, but will also give thee an interest with him as being nore especially attached to his own person."

"Doubtless," said Wildrake, "as every fisher loves best the trouts that are of his own tickling."

"It is likely, I think, he will send thee hither with letters to me," said the colonel, "enabling me to put a stop to the proceedings of these sequestrators, and to give poor old Sir Henry Lee permission to linger out his days among the oaks he loves to look upon. I have made this my request to General Cromwell, and I think my father's friendship and my own may stretch so far on his regard without risk of cracking, especially standing matters as they now do—thou dost understand?"

"Entirely well," said the cavalier. "Stretch, quotha! I would rather stretch a rope than hold commerce with the old king-killing ruffian. But I have said I will be guided by thee, Markham, and rat me but I will."

"Be cautious then," said Everard: "mark well what he does and says—more especially what he does, for Oliver is one of those whose mind is better known by his actions than by his words; and stay—I warrant thee thou wert setting off without a cross in the purse?"

"Too true, Mark," said Wildrake, "the last noble melted last night among yonder blackguard troopers of yours."

"Well, Roger," replied the colonel, "that is easily mended." So saying, he slipped his purse into his friend's hand. "But art thou not an inconsiderate, weather-brained fellow, to set forth, as thou wert about to do, without anything to bear thy charges? What couldst thou have done?"

"Faith, I never thought of that. I must have cried "Stand," I suppose, to the first pursy townsman or greasy grazier that I met o' the heath; it is many a good fellow's shift in these bad times."

"Go to," said Everard; "be cautious—use none of your loose acquaintance—rule your tongue—beware of the wine-pot; for there is little danger if thou couldst only but keep thyself sober. Be moderate in speech, and forbear oaths or vaunting."

"In short metamorphose myself into such a prig as thou art, Mark? Well," said Wildrake, "so far as outside will go, I think I can make a Hope-on-High Bomby* as well as thou canst. Ah! those were merry days when we saw Mills present Bomby at the Fortune playhouse, Mark, ere I had lost my laced cloak and the jewel in my ear, or thou hadst gotten the wrinkle on thy brow and the Puritanic twist of thy mustachio."

"They were like most worldly pleasures, Wildrake," replied Everard, "sweet in the mouth and bitter in digestion. But away with thee; and when thou bring'st back my answer, thou wilt find me either here or at St. George's Inn, at the little borough. Good luck to thee. Be but cautious how thou bearest thyself."

The colonel remained in deep meditation. "I think," he said, "I have not pledged myself too far to the General. A breach between him and the Parliament seems inevitable, and would throw England back into civil war, of which all

*A Puritanic character in [*Women Pleased*] one of Beaumont and Fletcher's plays.

men are wearied. He may dislike my messenger; yet that I do not greatly fear. He knows I would choose such as I can myself depend on, and hath dealt enough with the stricter sort to be aware that there are among them, as well as elsewhere, men who can hide two faces under one hood."

CHAPTER VIII.

For there in lofty air was seen to stand
The stern Protector of the conquer'd land;
Drawn in that look with which he wept and swore,
Turn'd out the members, and made fast the door,
Ridding the House of every knave and drone,
Forced, though it grieved his soul, to rule alone.
CRABBE, *The Frank Courtship.*

LEAVING Colonel Everard to his meditations, we follow the jolly Cavalier, his companion, who, before mounting at the George, did not fail to treat himself to his morning draught of eggs and muscadine, to enable him to face the harvest wind.

Although he had suffered himself to be sunk in the extravagant license which was practised by the Cavaliers, as if to oppose their conduct in every point of the preciseness of their enemies, yet Wildrake, well born and well educated, and endowed with good natural parts, and a heart which even debauchery, and the wild life of a roaring Cavalier, had not been able entirely to corrupt, moved on his present embassy with a strange mixture of feelings, such as perhaps he had never in his life before experienced.

His feelings as a loyalist led him to detest Cromwell, whom in other circumstances he would scarce have wished to see, except in a field of battle, where he could have had the pleasure to exchange pistol-shots with him. But with this hatred there was mixed a certain degree of fear. Always victorious wherever he fought, the remarkable person whom Wildrake was now approaching had acquired that influence over the minds of his enemies which constant success is so apt to inspire: they dreaded while they hated him; and joined to these feelings was a restless, meddling curiosity, which made a particular feature in Wildrake's character, who, having long had little business of his own, and caring nothing about that which he had, was easily attracted by the desire of seeing whatever was curious or interesting around him.

"I should like to see the old rascal after all," he said, "were it but to say that I *had* seen him."

He reached Windsor in the afternoon, and felt on his arrival the strongest inclination to take up his residence at some of his old haunts, when he had occasionally frequented that fair town in gayer days. But resisting all temptations of this kind, he went courageously to the principal inn, from which its ancient emblem, the Garter, had long disappeared. The master, too, when Wildrake, experienced in his knowledge of landlords and hostelries, had remembered a dashing mine host of Queen Bess's school, had now sobered down to the temper of the times, shook his head when he spoke of the Parliament, wielded his spigot with the gravity of a priest conducting a sacrifice, wished England a happy issue out of all her afflictions, and greatly lauded his Excellency the Lord General. Wildrake also remarked that his wine was better than it was wont to be, the Puritans having an excellent gift of detecting every fallacy in that matter ; and that his measures were less and his charges larger—circumstances which he was induced to attend to, by mine host talking a good deal about his conscience.

He was told by this important personage that the Lord General received frankly all sorts of persons ; and that he might obtain access to him next morning, at eight o'clock, for the trouble of presenting himself at the castle gate, and announcing himself as the bearer of despatches to his Excellency.

To the castle the disguised Cavalier repaired at the hour appointed. Admittance was freely permitted to him by the red-coated soldier who, with austere looks, and his musket on his shoulder, mounted guard at the external gate of that noble building. Wildrake crossed through the under ward, or court, gazing as he passed upon the beautiful chapel which had but lately received, in darkness and silence, the unhonored remains of the slaughtered King of England. Rough as Wildrake was, the recollection of this circumstance affected him so strongly, that he had nearly turned back in a sort of horror, rather than face the dark and daring man to whom, amongst all the actors in that melancholy affair, its tragic conclusion was chiefly to be imputed. But he felt the necessity of subduing all sentiments of this nature, and compelled himself to proceed in a negotiation entrusted to his conduct by one to whom he was so much obliged as Colonel Everard. At the ascent which passed by the Round Tower, he looked to the ensign-staff, from which the banner of England was wont to float. It was gone, with all its rich emblazonry, its gorgeous quarterings, and splendid embroidery; and in its room waved that of the Commonwealth, the cross of St. George, in its colors of blue and red, not yet intersected by the diagonal cross of Scotland, which was soon after assumed, as if in evidence of England's conquest over her ancient enemy. This change of ensigns increased the train of his gloomy reflections, in which, although contrary to his wont, he became so deeply wrapped, that the first thing which recalled him to himself was the challenge from the sentinel, accompanied with a stroke of the butt of his musket on the pavement, with an emphasis which made Wildrake start.

"Whither away, and who are you?"

"The bearer of a packet," answered Wildrake, "to the worshipful the Lord General."

"Stand till I call the officer of the guard."

The corporal made his appearance, distinguished above those of his command by a double quantity of band round his neck, a double height of steeple-crowned hat, a larger allowance of cloak, and a treble proportion of sour gravity of aspect. It might be read on his countenance that he was one of those resolute enthusiasts to whom Oliver owed his conquests, whose religious zeal made them even more than a match for the high-spirited and high-born Cavaliers that exhausted their valor in vain defense of their sovereign's person and crown. He looked with grave solemnity at Wildrake, as if he was making in his own mind an inventory of his features and dress; and having fully perused them, he required "to know his business."

"My business," said Wildrake, as firmly as he could, for the close investigation of this man had given him some unpleasant nervous sensations—"my business is with your General."

"With his Excellency the Lord General, thou wouldst say?" replied the corporal. "Thy speech, my friend, savors too little of the reverence due to his Excellency."

"D—n his Excellency!" was at the lips of the Cavalier; but prudence kept guard, and permitted not the offensive words to escape the barrier. He only bowed, and was silent.

"Follow me," said the starched figure whom he addressed; and Wildrake followed him accordingly into the guard-house, which exhibited an interior characteristic of the times, and very different from what such military stations present at the present day.

By the fire sat two or three musketeers, listening to one who was expounding some religious mystery to them. He began half beneath his breath, but in tones of great volubility, which tones, as he approached the conclusion, became sharp and eager, as challenging either instant answer or silent acquiescence. The audience seemed to listen to the speaker with immovable features, only answering him with clouds of tobacco-smoke, which they rolled from under their thick mustachios. On a bench lay a soldier on his face; whether asleep or in a fit of contemplation it was impossible to decide. In the midst of the floor stood an officer, as he seemed by his embroidered shoulder-belt and scarf round his waist, otherwise very plainly attired, who was engaged in drilling a stout bumpkin, lately enlisted, to the manual, as it was then used. The motions and words of command were twenty at the very least; and until they were regnlarly brought to an end, the corporal did not permit Wildrake either to sit down or move forward beyond the threshold of the guard-house. So he had to listen in succession to—"Poise your musket—Rest your musket—Cock your musket—Handle your primers"—and many other forgotten words of discipline, until at length the words, "Order your musket," ended the drill for the time.

"Thy name, friend," said the officer to the recruit, when the lesson was over.

."Ephraim," answered the fellow, with an affected twang through the nose.

"And what besides Ephraim?"

"Ephraim Cobb, from the godly city of Glo'cester, where I have dwelt for seven years, serving apprentice to a praiseworthy cordwainer."

"It is a goodly craft," answered the officer; "but casting in thy lot with ours, doubt not that thou shalt be set beyond thine awl, and thy last to boot."

A grim smile of the speaker accompanied this poor attempt at a pun; and then turning round to the corporal, who stood two paces off, with the face of one who seemed desirous of speaking, said, "How now, corporal, what tidings?"

"Here is one with a packet, an [it] please your Excellency," said the corporal. "Surely my spirit doth not rejoice in him, seeing I esteem him as a wolf in sheep's clothing."

By these words, Wildrake learned that he was in the actual presence of the remarkable person to whom he was commissioned; and he paused to consider in what manner he ought to address him.

The figure of Oliver Cromwell was, as is generally known, in no way prepossessing. He was of middle stature, strong and coarsely made, with harsh and severe features, indicative, however, of much natural sagacity and depth of thought. His eyes were gray and piercing; his nose too large in proportion to his other features, and of a reddish hue. His manner of speaking, when he had the purpose to make himself distinctly understood, was energetic and forcible, though neither graceful nor eloquent. No man could on such occasions put his meaning into fewer and more decisive words. But when, as it often happened, he had a mind to play the orator, for the benefit of people's ears, without enlightening their understanding, Cromwell was wont to invest his meaning, or that which seemed to be his meaning, in such a mist of words, surrounding it with so many exclusions and exemptions, and fortifying it with such a labyrinth of parentheses, that though one of the most shrewd men in England, he was, perhaps, the most unintelligible speaker that ever perplexed an audience. It has been long since said by the historian, that a collection of the Protector's speeches would make, with a few exceptions, the most nonsensical book in the world; but he ought to have added, that nothing could be more nervous, concise, and intelligible than what he really intended should be understood.

It was also remarked of Cromwell, that, though born of a good family, both by father and mother, and although he had the usual opportunities of education and breeding connected with such an advantage, the fanatic democratic ruler could never acquire, or else disdained to practise, the courtesies usually exercised among the higher classes in their intercourse with each other. His demeanor was so blunt as sometimes might be termed clownish, yet there was in his language and manner a force and energy corresponding to his character, which impressed awe, if it did not impose respect; and there were even times when that dark and subtle spirit expanded itself, so as almost to conciliate affection. The turn for humor, which displayed itself by fits, was broad, and of a low, and sometimes practical, character. Something there was in his disposition congenial to that of his countrymen—a contempt of folly, a hatred of affectation, and a dislike of ceremony, which, joined to the strong intrinsic qualities of sense and courage, made him in many respects not an unfit representative of the democracy of England.

His religion must always be a subject of much doubt, and probably of doubt which he himself could hardly have cleared up. Unquestionably there was a time in his life when he was sincerely enthusiastic, and when his natural temper, slightly subject to hypochondria, was strongly agitated by the same fanaticism which influenced so many persons of the time. On the other hand, there were periods during his political career when we certainly do him no injustice in charging him with a hypocritical affectation. We shall probably judge him, and others of the same age, most truly, if we suppose that their religious professions were partly influential in their own breast, partly assumed in compliance with their own interest. And so ingenious is the human heart in deceiving itself as well as others, that it is probable neither Cromwell himself nor those making similar pretensions to distinguished piety could exactly have fixed the points at which their enthusiasm terminated and their hypocrisy commenced; or rather, it was a point not fixed in itself, but fluctuating with the state of health, with good or bad fortune, of high or low spirits, affecting the individual at the period.

Such was the celebrated person who, turning round on Wildrake, and scanning his countenance closely, seemed so little satisfied with what he beheld, that he instinctively hitched forward his belt, so as to bring the handle of his tuck-sword within his reach. But yet, folding his arms in his cloak, as if upon second thoughts laying aside suspicion, or thinking precaution beneath him, he asked the Cavalier what he was and whence he came.

"A poor gentleman, sir—that is, my lord," answered Wildrake, "last from Woodstock."

"And what may your tidings be, sir *gentleman?*" said Cromwell, with an emphasis. "Truly I have seen those most willing to take upon them that title bear themselves somewhat short of wise men, and good men, and true men, with all their gentility. Yet gentleman was a good title in Old England, when men remembered what it was construed to mean."

"You say truly, sir," replied Wildrake, suppressing, with difficulty, some of his usual wild expletives; "formerly gentlemen were found in gentlemen's places, but now the world is so changed, that you shall find the broidered belt has changed place with the under spur-leather."

"Say'st thou me?" said the General. "I profess thou art a bold companion, that can bandy words so wantonly:

thou ring'st somewhat too loud to be good metal, methinks. And, once again, what are thy tidings with me?"

"This packet," said Wildrake, "commended to your hands by Colonel Markham Everard."

"Alas, I must have mistaken thee," answered Cromwell, mollified at the mention of a man's name whom he had great desire to make his own; "forgive us, good friend, for such, we doubt not, thou art. Sit thee down, and commune with thyself as thou mayst, until we have examined the contents of thy packet. Let him be looked to, and have what he lacks." So saying, the General left the guard-house, where Wildrake took his seat in the corner, and awaited with patience the issue of his mission.

The soldiers now thought themselves obliged to treat him with more consideration, and offered him a pipe of Trinidado, and a black-jack filled with October. But the look of Cromwell, and the dangerous situation in which he might be placed by the least chance of detection, induced Wildrake to decline these hospitable offers, and stretching back in his chair and affecting slumber, he escaped notice or conversation, until a sort of aide-de-camp, or military officer, in attendance came to summon him to Cromwell's presence.

By this person he was guided to a postern-gate, through which he entered the body of the castle, and penetrating through many private passages and staircases, he at length was introduced into a small cabinet or parlor, in which was much rich furniture, some bearing the royal cipher displayed, but all confused and disarranged, together with several paintings in massive frames, having their faces turned towards the wall, as if they had been taken down for the purpose of being removed.

In this scene of disorder, the victorious General of the Commonwealth was seated in a large easy-chair, covered with damask, and deeply embroidered, the splendor of which made a strong contrast with the plain, and even homely, character of his apparel; although in look and action he seemed like one who felt that the seat which might have in former days held a prince was not too much distinguished for his own fortunes and ambition. Wildrake stood before him, nor did he ask him to sit down.

"Pearson," said Cromwell, addressing himself to the officer in attendance, "wait in the gallery, but be within call." Pearson bowed, and was retiring. "Who are in the gallery besides?"

"Worthy Mr. Gordon, the chaplain, was holding forth

but now to Colonel Overton and four captains of your Excellency's regiment."

"We would have it so," said the General: "we would not there were any corner in our dwelling where the hungry soul might not meet with manna. Was the good man carried onward in his discourse?"

"Mightily borne through," said Pearson; "and he was touching the rightful claims which the army, and especially your Excellency, hath acquired by becoming the instruments in the great work—not instruments to be broken asunder and cast away when the day of their service is over, but to be preserved and held precious, and prized for their honorable and faithful labors, for which they have fought and marched, and fasted and prayed, and suffered cold and sorrow; while others, who would now gladly see them disbanded, and broken, and cashiered, eat of the fat and drink of the strong."

"Ah, good man!" said Cromwell, "and did he touch upon this so feelingly? I could say something—but not now. Begone, Pearson, to the gallery. Let not our friends lay aside their swords, but watch as well as pray."

Pearson retired; and the General, holding the letter of Everard in his hand, looked again for a long while fixedly at Wildrake, as if considering in what strain he should address him.

When he did speak, it was, at first, in one of those ambiguous discourses which we have already described, and by which it was very difficult for any one to understand his meaning, if, indeed, he knew it himself. We shall be as concise in our statement as our desire to give the very words of a man so extraordinary will permit.

"This letter," he said, "you have brought us from your master, or patron, Markham Everard; truly an excellent and honorable gentleman as ever bore a sword upon his thigh, and one who hath ever distinguished himself in the great work of delivering these three poor and unhappy nations. Answer me not—I know what thou wouldst say. And this letter he hath sent to me by thee, his clerk, or secretary, in whom he hath confidence, and in whom he prays me to have trust, that there may be a careful messenger between us. And lastly, he hath sent thee to me—do not answer—I know what thou wouldst say—to me, who, albeit I am of that small consideration, that it would be too much honor for me even to bear a halberd in this great and victorious army of England, am nevertheless exalted to the rank of holding the guidance and the leading-staff thereof. Nay, do not answer, my friend—I know what thou wouldst say. Now, when communing thus together, our discourse taketh, in respect to what I have said, a threefold argument, or division: First, as it concerneth thy master; secondly, as it concerneth us and our office; thirdly and lastly, as it toucheth thyself. Now, as concerning this good and worthy gentleman, Colonel Markham Everard, truly he had played the man from the beginning of these unhappy buffetings, not turning to the right or to the left, but holding ever in his eye the mark at which he aimed. Ay, truly, a faithful, honorable gentleman, and one who may well call me friend; and truly I am pleased to think that he doth so. Nevertheless, in this vale of tears, we must be governed less by our private respects and partialities than by those higher principles and points of duty whereupon the good Colonel Markham Everard hath ever framed his purposes, as, truly, I have endeavored to form mine, that we may all act as becometh good Englishmen and worthy patriots. Then, as for Woodstock, it is a great thing which the good colonel asks, that it should be taken from the spoil of the godly, and left in keeping of the men of Moab, and especially of the Malignant, Henry Lee, whose hand hath been ever against us when he might find room to raise it—I say, he hath asked a great thing, both in respect of himself and me. For we of this poor but godly army of England are holden, by those of the Parliament, as men who should render in spoil for them, but be no sharer of it ourselves; even as the buck, which the hounds pull to earth, furnisheth no part of their own food, but they are lashed off from the carcass with whips, like those which require punishment for their forwardness, not reward for their services. Yet I speak not this so much in respect of this grant of Woodstock, in regard that, perhaps, their Lordships of the Council, and also the Committee-men of this Parliament, may graciously think they have given me a portion in the matter, in relation that my kinsman Desborough hath an interest allowed him therein; which interest, as he hath well deserved it for his true and faithful service to these unhappy and devoted countries, so it would ill become me to diminish the same to his prejudice, unless it were upon great and public respects. Thus thou seest how it stands with me, my honest friend, and in what mind I stand touching thy master's request to me; which yet I do not say that I can altogether, or unconditionally, grant or refuse, but only tell my simple thoughts with regard thereto. Thou understandest me, I doubt not?"

Now, Roger Wildrake, with all the attention he had been able to pay to the Lord General's speech, had got so much confused among the various clauses of the harangue, that his brain was bewildered, like that of a country clown when he chances to get himself involved among a crowd of carriages, and cannot stir a step to get out of the way of one of them, without being in danger of being ridden over by the others.

The General saw his look of perplexity, and began a new oration, to the same purpose as before: spoke of his love for his kind friend the colonel; his regard for his pious and godly kinsman, Master Desborough; the great importance of the palace and park of Woodstock; the determination of the Parliament that it should be confiscated, and the produce brought into the coffers of the state; his own deep veneration for the authority of Parliament, and his no less deep sense of the injustice done to the army; how it was his wish and will that all matters should be settled in an amicable and friendly manner, without self-seeking, debate, or strife, betwixt those who had been the hands acting and such as had been the heads governing in that great national cause; how he was willing, truly willing, to contribute to this work, by laying down, not his commission only, but his life also, if it were requested of him, or could be granted with safety to the poor soldiers, to whom, silly poor men, he was bound to be as a father, seeing that they had followed him with the duty and affection of children.

And here he arrived at another dead pause, leaving Wildrake as uncertain as before whether it was or was not his purpose to grant Colonel Everard the powers he had asked for the protection of Woodstock against the Parliamentary Commissioners. Internally he began to entertain hopes that the justice of Heaven, or the effects of remorse, had confounded the regicide's understanding. But no, he could see nothing but sagacity in that steady, stern eye, which, while the tongue poured forth its periphrastic language in such profusion, seemed to watch with severe accuracy the effect which his oratory produced on the listener.

"Egad," thought the Cavalier to himself, becoming a little familiar with the situation in which he was placed, and rather impatient of a conversation which led to no visible conclusion or termination, "if Noll were the devil himself, as he is the devil's darling, I will not be thus nose-led by him. I'll e'en brusque it a little, if he goes on at this rate, and try if I can bring him to a more intelligible mode of speaking."

Entertaining this bold purpose, but half afraid to execute it, Wildrake lay by for an opportunity of making the attempt, while Cromwell was apparently unable to express his own meaning. He was already beginning a third panegyric upon Colonel Everard, with sundry varied expressions of his own wish to oblige him, when Wildrake took the opportunity to strike in, on the General's making one of his oratorical pauses.

"So please you," he said, bluntly, "your worship has already spoken on two topics of your discourse, your own worthiness and that of my master, Colonel Everard. But, to enable me to do mine errand, it would be necessary to bestow a few words on the third head."

"The third!" said Cromwell.

"Ay," said Wildrake, "which, in your honor's subdivision of your discourse, touched on my unworthy self. What am I to do—what portion am I to have in this matter?"

Oliver started at once from the tone of voice he had hitherto used, and which somewhat resembled the purring of a domestic cat, into the growl of the tiger when about to spring. "*Thy* portion, jail-bird!" he exclaimed, "the gallows: thou shalt hang as high as Haman, if thou betray counsel! But," he added, softening his voice, "keep it like a true man, and my favor will be the making of thee. Come hither; thou art bold, I see, though somewhat saucy. Thou hast been a Malignant, so writes my worthy friend friend Colonel Everard; but thou hast now given up that falling cause. I tell thee, friend, not all that the Parliament or the army could do would have pulled down the Stuarts out of their high places, saving that Heaven had a controversy with them. Well, it is a sweet and comely thing to buckle on one's armor in behalf of Heaven's cause; otherwise truly, for mine own part, these men might have remained upon the throne even unto this day. Neither do I blame any for aiding them until these successive great judgments have overwhelmed them and their house. I am not a bloody man, having in me the feeling of human frailty; but, friend, whosoever putteth his hand to the plow, in the great actings which are now on foot in these nations, had best beware that he do not look back; for rely upon my simple word, that, if you fail me, I will not spare on you one foot's length of the gallows of Haman. Let me therefore know, at a word, if the leaven of thy malignancy is altogether drubbed out of thee?"

"Your honorable lordship," said the Cavalier, shrugging up his shoulders, "has done that for most of us, so far as cudgeling to some tune can perform it."

"Sayst thou?" said the General, with a grim smile on his lip, which seemed to intimate that he was not quite inaccessible to flattery; "yea, truly, thou dost not lie in that: we have been an instrument. Neither are we, as I have already hinted, so severely bent against those who have striven against us as Malignants as others may be. The Parliament-men best know their own interest and their own pleasure; but, to my poor thinking, it is full time to close these jars, and to allow men of all kinds the means of doing service to their country; and we think it will be thy fault if thou art not employed to good purpose for the state and thyself, on condition thou puttest away the old man entirely from thee, and givest thy earnest attention to what I have to tell thee."

"Your lordship need not doubt my attention," said the Cavalier.

And the republican General, after another pause, as one who gave his confidence not without hesitation, proceeded to explain his views with a distinctness which he seldom used, yet not without his being a little blessed now and then by his long habits of circumlocution, which indeed he never laid entirely aside, save in the field of battle.

"Thou seest," he said, "my friend, how things stand with me. The Parliament, I care not who knows it, love me not; still less do the Council of State, by whom they manage the executive government of the kingdom. I cannot tell why they nourish suspicion against me, unless it is because I will not deliver this poor innocent army, which has followed me in so many military actions, to be now pulled asunder, broken piece-meal and reduced, so that they who have protected the state at the expense of their blood will not have, perchance, the means of feeding themselves by their labor; which, methinks, were hard measure, since it is taking from Esau his birthright, even without giving him a poor mess of pottage."

"Esau is likely to help himself, I think," replied Wildrake.

"Truly, thou sayst wisely," replied the General: "it is ill starving an armed man, if there is food to be had for taking; nevertheless, far be it from me to encourage rebellion, or want of due subordination to these our rulers. I would only petition in a due and becoming, a sweet and harmonious, manner that they would listen to our conditions and consider our necessities. But, sir, looking on me, and estimating me so little as they do, you must think that it would be a provocation in me towards the Council of State, as well as the Parliament, if, simply to gratify your worthy master, I were to act contrary to their purposes or deny currrency to the commission under their authority, which is as yet the highest in the state—and long may it be so for me—to carry on the sequestration which they intend. And would it not also be said that I was lending myself to the Malignant interest, affording this den of the bloodthirsty and lascivious tyrants of yore to be in this our day a place of refuge to that old and inveterate Amalekite, Sir Henry Lee, to keep possession of the place in which he hath so long glorified himself? Truly it would be a perilous matter."

"Am I then to report," said Wildrake; "an it please you, that you cannot stead Colonel Everard in this matter?"

"Unconditionally, ay; but, taken conditionally, the answer may be otherwise," answered Cromwell. "I see thou art not able to fathom my purpose, and therefore I will partly unfold it to thee. But take notice that, should thy tongue betray my counsel, save in so far as carrying it to thy master, by all the blood which has been shed in these wild times, thou shalt die a thousand deaths in one!"

"Do not fear me, sir," said Wildrake, whose natural boldness and carelessness of character was for the present time borne down and quelled, like that of falcons in the presence of the eagle.

"Hear me, then," said Cromwell, "and let no syllable escape thee. Knowest thou not the young Lee whom they call Albert, a Malignant like his father, and one who went up with the Young Man to that last ruffle which we had with him at Worcester—may we be grateful for the victory!"

"I know there is such a young gentleman as Albert Lee," said Wildrake.

"And knowest thou not—I speak not by way of prying into the good colonel's secrets, but only as it behooves me to know something of the matter, that I may best judge how I am to serve him—knowest thou not that thy master, Markham Everard, is a suitor after the sister of this same

Malignant, a daughter of the old keeper, called Sir Henry Lee?"

"All this I have heard," said Wildrake, "nor can I deny that I believe in it."

"Well, then, go to. When the young man Charles Stuart fled from the field of Worcester, and was by sharp chase and pursuit compelled to separate himself from his followers, I know by sure intelligence that this Albert Lee was one of the last who remained with him, if not indeed the very last."

"It was devilish like him," said the Cavalier, without sufficiently weighing his expressions, considering in what presence they were to be uttered. "And I'll uphold him with my rapier to be a true chip of the old block."

"Ha, swearest thou?" said the General. "Is this thy reformation?"

"I never swear, so please you," replied Wildrake, recollecting himself, "except there is some mention of Malignants and Cavaliers in my hearing; and then the old habit returns, and I swear like one of Goring's troopers."

'Out upon thee," said the General; "what can it avail thee to practise a profanity so horrible to the ears of others, and which brings no emolument to him who uses it?"

"There are, doubtless, more profitable sins in the world than the barren and unprofitable vice of swearing," was the answer which rose to the lips of the Cavalier; but that was exchanged for a profession of regret for having given offense. The truth was, the discourse began to take a turn which rendered it more interesting than ever to Wildrake, who therefore determined not to lose the opportunity for obtaining possession of the secret that seemed to be suspended on Cromwell's lips; and that could only be through means of keeping guard upon his own.

"What sort of a house is Woodstock?" said the General, abruptly.

"An old mansion," said Wildrake, in reply; "and, so far as I could judge by a single night's lodgings, having abundance of back stairs, also subterranean passages, and all the communications under ground which are common in old raven-nests of the sort."

"And places for concealing priests, unquestionably," said Cromwell. "It is seldom that such ancient houses lack secret stalls wherein to mew up these calves of Bethel."

"Your Honor's Excellency," said Wildrake, "may swear to that."

"I swear not at all," replied the General, dryly. "But what think'st thou, good fellow? I will ask thee a blunt question—Where will those two Worcester fugitives that thou wottest of be more likely to take shelter—and that they must be sheltered somewhere I well know—than in this same old palace, with all the corners and concealments whereof young Albert hath been acquainted ever since his earliest infancy."

"Truly," said Wildrake, making an effort to answer the question with seeming indifference, while the possibility of such an event, and its consequences, flashed fearfully upon his mind—"truly, I should be of your honor's opinion, but that I think the company who, by the commission of Parliament, have occupied Woodstock are likely to fright them thence, as a cat scares doves from a pigeon-house. The neighborhood, with reverence, of Generals Desborough and Harrison will suit ill with fugitives from Worcester field."

"I thought as much, and so, indeed, would I have it." answered the General. "Long may it be ere our names shall be aught but a terror to our enemies! But in this matter, if thou art an active plotter for thy master's interest, thou mightst, I should think, work out something favorable to his present object."

"My brain is too poor to reach the depth of your honorable purpose," said Wildrake.

"Listen, then, and let it be to profit," said Cromwell. "Assuredly the conquest at Worcester was a great and crowning mercy; yet might we seem to be but small in our thankfulness for the same, did we not do what in us lies towards the ultimate improvement and final conclusion of the great work which has been thus prosperous in our hands, professing, in pure humility and singleness of heart, that we do not, in any way, deserve our instrumentality to be remembered, nay, would rather pray and entreat that our name and fortunes were forgotten than that the great work were in itself incomplete. Nevertheless, truly, placed as we now are, it concerns us more nearly than others—that is if so poor creatures should at all speak of themselves as concerned, whether more or less, with these changes which have been wrought around, not, I say, by ourselves, or our own power, but by the destiny to which we were called, fulfilling the same with all meekness and humility—I say, it concerns us nearly that all things should be done in conformity with the great work which hath been wrought, and is yet working, in these lands. Such is my plain and simple meaning. Nevertheless, it is much to be desired that this young man—this King of Scots, as he called himself—this Charles Stuart—should not escape forth from the nation, where his arrival has wrought so much disturbance and bloodshed."

"I have no doubt," said the Cavalier, looking down, "that your lordship's wisdom hath directed all things as they may best lead towards such a consummation; and I pray your pains may be paid as they deserve."

"I thank thee, friend," said Cromwell, with much humility; "doubtless we shall meet our reward, being in the hands of a good paymaster, who never passeth Saturday night. But understand me, friend—I desire no more than my own share in the good work. I would heartily do what poor kindness I can to your worthy master, and even to you in your degree—for such as I do not converse with ordinary men that our presence may be forgotten like an everyday's occurrence. We speak to men like thee for their reward or their punishment; and I trust it will be the former which thou in thine office wilt merit at my hand."

"Your honor," said Wildrake, "speaks like one accustomed to command."

"True; men's minds are linked to those of my degree by fear and reverence," said the General; "but enough of that, desiring, as I do, no other dependency on my special person than is alike to us all upon that which is above us. But I would desire to cast this golden ball into your master's lap. He hath served against this Charles Stuart and his father; but he is a kinsman near to the old knight, Lee, and stands well affected towards his daughter. *Thou* also wilt keep a watch, my friend—that ruffling look of thine will procure thee the confidence of every Malignant, and the prey cannot approach this cover, as though to shelter, like a cony in the rocks, but thou wilt be sensible of his presence."

"I make a shift to comprehend your Excellency," said the Cavalier; "and I thank you heartily for the good opinion you have put upon me, and which I pray I may have some handsome opportunity of deserving, that I may show my gratitude by the event. But still, with reverence, your Excellency's scheme seems unlikely while Woodstock remains in possession of the sequestrators. Both the old knight and his son, and far more such a fugitive as your honor hinted at, will take special care not to approach it till they are removed."

"It is for that I have been dealing with thee thus long,"

said the General. "I told thee that I was something unwilling, upon slight occasion, to dispossess the sequestrators by my own proper warrant, although having, perhaps, sufficient authority in the state both to do so and to despise the murmurs of those who blame me. In brief, I would be loth to tamper with my privileges, and make experiments between their strength and the powers of the commission granted by others, without pressing need, or at least great prospect of advantage. So, if thy colonel will undertake, for his love of the republic, to find the means of preventing its worst and nearest danger, which must needs occur from the escape of this Young Man, and will do his endeavor to stay him, in case his flight should lead him to Woodstock, which I hold very likely, I will give thee an order to these sequestrators to evacuate the palace instantly, and to the next troop of my regiment, which lies at Oxford, to turn them out by the shoulders, if they make any scruples,—ay, even, for example's sake, if they drag Desborough out foremost, though he be wedded to my sister."

"So please you, sir," said Wildrake, "and with your most powerful warrant, I trust I might expel the Commissioners, even without the aid of your most warlike and devout troopers."

"That is what I am least anxious about," replied the General: "I should like to see the best of them sit after I had nodded to them to begone—always excepting the worshipful House, in whose name our commissions run, but who, as some think, will be done with politics ere it be time to renew them. Therefore, what chiefly concerns me to know is, whether thy master will embrace a traffic which hath such a fair promise of profit with it. I am well convinced that, with a scout like thee, who hast been in the Cavaliers' quarters, and canst, I should guess, resume thy drinking, ruffianly, health-quaffing manners whenever thou hast a mind, he must discover where this Stuart hath ensconced himself. Either the young Lee will visit the old one in person, or he will write to him, or hold communication with him by letter. At all events, Markham Everard and thou must have an eye in every hair of your head." While he spoke, a flush passed over his brow, he rose from his chair, and paced the apartment in agitation. "Woe to you if you suffer the young adventurer to escape me! You had better be in the deepest dungeon in Europe than breathe the air of England, should you but dream of playing me false. I have spoken freely to thee, fellow—more freely than is my wont; the time required it. But, to share my confidence is like keeping a watch over a powder-magazine: the least and most insignificant spark blows thee to ashes. Tell your master what I have said, but not how I said it. Fie, that I should have been betrayed into this distemperature of passion! Begone, sirrah. Pearson shall bring thee sealed orders. Yet, stay—thou hast something to ask."

"I would know," said Wildrake, to whom the visible anxiety of the General gave some confidence, "what is the figure of this young gallant, in case I should find him?"

"A tall, rawboned, swarthy lad, they say he has shot up into. Here is his picture by a good hand, some time since." He turned round one of the portraits which stood with its face against the wall; but it proved not to be that of Charles the Second, but of his unhappy father.

The first motion of Cromwell indicated a purpose of hastily replacing the picture, and it seemed as if an effort was necessary to repress his disinclination to look upon it. But he did repress it, and, placing the picture against the wall, withdrew slowly and sternly, as if, in defiance of his own feelings, he was determined to gain a place from which to see it to advantage. It was well for Wildrake that his dangerous companion had not turned an eye on him, for *his* blood also kindled when he saw the portrait of his master in the hands of the chief author of his death. Being a fierce and desperate man, he commanded his passion with great difficulty; and if, on its first violence, he had been provided with a suitable weapon, it is possible Cromwell would never have mounted higher in his bold ascent towards supreme power.

But this natural and sudden flash of indignation, which rushed through the veins of an ordinary man like Wildrake, was presently subdued when confronted with the strong yet stifled emotion displayed by so powerful a character as Cromwell. As the Cavalier looked on his dark and bold countenance, agitated by inward and indescribable feelings, he found his own violence of spirit die away and lose itself in fear and wonder. So true it is that, as greater lights swallow up and extinguish the display of those which are less, so men of great, capacious, and overruling minds bear aside and subdue, in their climax of passion, the more feeble wills and passions of others: as, when a river joins a brook, the fiercer torrent shoulders aside the smaller stream.

Wildrake stood a silent, inactive, and almost a terrified spectator, while Cromwell, assuming a firm sternness of eye and manner, as one who compels himself to look on what some strong internal feeling renders painful and disgustful to him, proceeded, in brief and interrupted expressions, but yet with a firm voice, to comment on the portrait of the late king. His words seemed less addressed to Wildrake than to be the spontaneous unburdening of his own bosom, swelling under recollection of the past and anticipation of the future.

"That Flemish painter," he said—"that Antonio Vandyck, what a power he has! Steel may mutilate, warriors may waste and destroy, still the King stands uninjured by time; and our grandchildren, while they read his history, may look on his image, and compare the melancholy features with the woful tale. It was a stern necessity—it was an awful deed! The calm pride of that eye might have ruled worlds of crouching Frenchmen, or supple Italians, or formal Spaniards; but its glances only roused the native courage of the stern Englishman. Lay not on poor sinful man, whose breath is in his nostrils, the blame that he falls, when Heaven never gave him strength of nerves to stand. The weak rider is thrown by his unruly horse and trampled to death; the strongest man, the best cavalier, springs to the empty saddle, and uses bit and spur till the fiery steed knows its master. Who blames him who, mounted aloft, rides triumphantly amongst the people, for having succeeded where the unskilful and feeble fell and died? Verily he hath his reward. Then, what is that piece of painted canvas to me more than others? No; let him show to others the reproaches of that cold, calm face, that proud yet complaining eye. Those who have acted on higher respects have no cause to start at painted shadows. Not wealth nor power brought me from my obscurity; the oppressed consciences, the injured liberties of England, were the banner that I followed."

He raised his voice so high, as if pleading in his own defense before some tribunal, that Pearson, the officer in attendance, looked into the apartment; and observing his master, with his eyes kindling, his arm extended, his foot advanced, and his voice raised, like a general in the act of commanding the advance of his army, he instantly withdrew.

"It was other than selfish regards that drew me forth to action," continued Cromwell, "and I dare the world—ay, living or dead I challenge—to assert that I armed for a private cause, or as a means of enlarging my fortunes. Neither was there a trooper in the regiment who came there with less of personal evil will to yonder unhappy——"

Cromwell contemplating the portrait of Charles I., painted by Vandyke.

At this moment the door of the apartment opened, and a gentlewoman entered, who, from her resemblance to the General, although her features were soft and feminine, might be immediately recognized as his daughter. She walked up to Cromwell, gently but firmly passed her arm through his, and said to him in a persuasive tone, "Father, this is not well: you have promised me this should not happen."

The General hung down his head, like one who was either ashamed of the passion to which he had given way or of the influence which was exercised over him. He yielded, however, to the affectionate impulse, and left the apartment, without again turning his head towards the portrait which had so much affected him, or looking towards Wildrake, who remained fixed in astonishment.

CHAPTER IX.

Doctor. Go to, go to. You have known what you should not.
Macbeth.

WILDRAKE was left in the cabinet, as we have said, astonished and alone. It was often noised about that Cromwell, the deep and sagacious statesman, the calm and intrepid commander, he who had overcome such difficulties, and ascended to such heights, that he seemed already to bestride the land which he had conquered, had, like many other men of great genius, a constitutional taint of melancholy, which sometimes displayed itself both in words and actions, and had been first observed in that sudden and striking change, when, abandoning entirely the dissolute freaks of his youth, he embraced a very strict course of religious observances, which upon some occasions he seemed to consider as bringing him into more near and close contact with the spiritual world. This extraordinary man is said sometimes during that period of his life to have given way to spiritual delusions, or, as he himself conceived them, prophetic inspirations of approaching grandeur, and of strange, deep, and mysterious agencies, in which he was in future to be engaged, in the same manner as his younger years had been marked by fits of exuberant and excessive frolic and debaucheries. Something of this kind seemed to explain the ebullition of passion which he had now manifested.

With wonder at what he had witnessed, Wildrake felt some anxiety on his own account. Though not the most reflecting of mortals, he had sense enough to know that it is dangerous to be a witness of the infirmities of men high in power; and he was left so long by himself, as induced him to entertain some secret doubts whether the General might not be tempted to take means of confining or removing a witness who had seen him lowered, as it seemed, by the suggestions of his own conscience, beneath that lofty flight which, in general, he affected to sustain above the rest of the sublunary world.

In this, however, he wronged Cromwell, who was free either from an extreme degree of jealous suspicion or from anything which approached towards bloodthirstiness. Pearson appeared, after a lapse of about an hour, and, intimating to Wildrake that he was to follow, conducted him into a distant apartment, in which he found the General seated on a low couch. His daughter was in the apartment, but remained at some distance, apparently busied with some female needlework, and scarce turned her head as Pearson and Wildrake entered.

At a sign from the Lord General, Wildrake approached him as before. "Comrade," he said, "your old friends the Cavaliers look on me as their enemy, and conduct themselves towards me as if they desired to make me such. I profess they are laboring to their own prejudice; for I regard, and have ever regarded, them as honest and honorable fools, who were silly enough to run their necks into nooses, and their heads against stone walls, that a man called Stuart, and no other, should be king over them! Fools! are there no words made of letters that would sound as well as Charles Stuart with that magic title beside them? Why, the word king is like a lighted lamp, that throws the same bright gilding upon any combination of the alphabet, and yet you must shed your blood for a name! But thou, for thy part, shalt have no wrong from me. Here is an order, well warranted, to clear the lodge at Woodstock, and abandon it to thy master's keeping, or those whom he shall appoint. He will have his uncle and pretty cousin with him, doubtless. Fare thee well; think on what I told thee. They say beauty is a lodestone to yonder long lad thou dost wot of; but I reckon he has other stars at present to direct his course than bright eyes and fair hair. Be it as it may, thou knowest my purpose; peer out—peer out: keep a constant and careful lookout on every ragged patch that wanders by hedgerow or lane: these are days when a beggar's cloak may cover a king's ransom. There are some broad Portugal pieces for thee—something strange to thy pouch, I ween. Once more, think on what thou hast heard, and," he added, in a lower and more impressive tone of voice, "forget what thou hast seen. My service to thy master; and, yet once again, *remember*—and *forget*."

Wildrake made his obeisance, and, returning to his inn, left Windsor with all possible speed.

It was afternoon in the same day when the Cavalier rejoined his Roundhead friend, who was anxiously expecting him at the inn in Woodstock appointed for their rendezvous.

"Where hast thou been?—what hast thou seen?—what

strange uncertainty is in thy looks?—and why dost thou not answer me?"

"Because," said Wildrake, laying aside his riding-cloak and rapier, "you ask so many questions at once. A man has but one tongue to answer with, and mine is well-nigh glued to the roof of my mouth."

"Will drink unloosen it?" said the colonel; "though I daresay thou hast tried that spell at every alehouse on the road. Call for what thou wouldst have, man, only be quick."

"Colonel Everard," answered Wildrake, "I have not tasted so much as a cup of cold water this day."

"Then thou art out of humor for that reason," said the colonel; "salve thy sore with brandy, if thou wilt, but leave being so fantastic and unlike to thyself as thou showest in this silent mood."

"Colonel Everard," replied the Cavalier, very gravely, "I am an altered man."

"I think thou dost alter," said Everard, "every day in the year, and every hour of the day. Come, good now, tell me, hast thou seen the General, and got his warrant for clearing out the sequestrators from Woodstock?"

"I have seen the Devil," said Wildrake, "and have, as thou sayst, got a warrant from him."

"Give it me," said Everard, hastily catching at the packet.

"Forgive me, Mark," said Wildrake; "if thou knewest the purpose with which this deed is granted—if thou knewest—what it is not my purpose to tell thee—what manner of hopes are founded on thy accepting it, I have that opinion of thee, Mark Everard, that thou would'st as soon take a red-hot horseshoe from the anvil with thy bare hand as receive into it this slip of paper."

"Come—come," said Everard, "this comes of some of your exalted ideas of loyalty, which, excellent within certain bounds, drive us mad when encouraged up to some heights. Do not think, since I must needs speak plainly with thee, that I see without sorrow the downfall of our ancient monarchy, and the substitution of another form of government in its stead, but ought my regret for the past to prevent my acquiescing and aiding in such measures as are likely to settle the future? The royal cause is ruined, hadst thou and every Cavalier in England sworn the contrary—ruined, not to rise again, for many a day at least. The Parliament, so often draughted and drained of those who were courageous enough to maintain their own freedom of opinion, is now reduced to a handful of statesmen, who have lost the respect of the people, from the length of time during which they have held the supreme management of affairs. They cannot stand long unless they were to reduce the army; and the army, late servants, are now masters, and will refuse to be reduced. They know their strength, and that they may be an army subsisting on pay and free quarters throughout England as long as they will. I tell thee, Wildrake, unless we look to the only man who can rule and manage them, we may expect military law throughout the land; and I, for mine own part, look for any preservation of our privileges that may be vouchsafed to us only through the wisdom and forbearance of Cromwell. Now you have my secret. You are aware that I am not doing the best I would, but the best I can. I wish—not so ardently as thou, perhaps—yet I *do* wish that the King could have been restored on good terms of composition, safe for us and for himself. And now, good Wildrake, rebel as thou thinkest me, make me no worse a rebel than an unwilling one. God knows, I never laid aside love and reverence to the King, even in drawing my sword against his ill advisers."

"Ah, plague on you," said Wildrake, "that is the very cant of it—that's what you all say. All of you fought against the King in pure love and loyalty, and not otherwise. However, I see your drift, and I own that I like it better than I expected. The army is your bear now, and Old Noll is your bear-ward; and you are like a country constable, who makes interest with the bear-ward that he may prevent him from letting bruin loose. Well, there may come a day when the sun will shine on our side of the fence, and thereon shall you, and all the good fair-weather folks who love the stronger party, come and make common cause with us."

Without much attending to what his friend said, Colonel Everard carefully studied the warrant of Cromwell. "It is bolder and more peremptory than I expected," he said. "The General must feel himself strong, when he opposes his own authority so directly to that of the Council of State and the Parliament."

"You will not hesitate to act upon it?" said Wildrake.

"That I certainly will not," answered Everard; "but I must wait till I have the assistance of the Mayor, who, I think, will gladly see these fellows ejected from the lodge. I must not go altogether upon military authority, if possible." Then stepping to the door of the apartment, he despatched a servant of the house in quest of the chief magistrate, desiring he should be made acquainted that Colonel Everard desired to see him with as little loss of time as possible.

"You are sure he will come, like a dog at a whistle," said Wildrake. "The word captain or colonel makes the fat citizen trot in these days, when one sword is worth fifty corporation charters. But there are dragoons yonder, as well as the grim-faced knave whom I frightened the other evening when I showed my face in at the window. Think'st thou the knaves will show no rough play?"

"The General's warrant will weigh more with them than a dozen acts of Parliament," said Everard. "But it is time thou eatest, if thou hast in truth ridden from Windsor hither without baiting."

"I care not about it," said Wildrake: "I tell thee, your General gave me a breakfast which, I think, will serve me one while, if I am ever able to digest it. By the mass, it lay so heavy on my conscience, that I carried it to church to see if I could digest it there with my other sins. But not a whit."

"To church! To the door of the church, thou meanest," said Everard. "I know thy way: thou art ever wont to pull thy hat off reverently at the threshold, but for crossing it, that day seldom comes."

"Well," replied Wildrake, "and if I do pull off my castor and kneel, is it not seemly to show the same respects in a church which we offer in a palace? It is a dainty matter, is it not, to see your Anabaptists, and Brownists, and the rest of you, gather to a sermon with as little ceremony as hogs to a trough? But here comes food, and now for a grace, if I can remember one."

Everard was too much interested about the fate of his uncle and his fair cousin, and the prospect of restoring them to their quiet home, under the protection of that formidable truncheon which was already regarded as the leading-staff of England, to remark, that certainly a great alteration had taken place in the manners and outward behavior at least of his companion. His demeanor frequently evinced a sort of struggle betwixt old habits of indulgence and some newly-formed resolutions of abstinence; and it was almost ludicrous to see how often the hand of the neophyte directed itself naturally to a large black leathern jack, which contained two double flagons of strong ale, and how often, diverted from its purpose by the better reflections of the reformed toper, it seized, instead, upon a large ewer of salubrious and pure water.

It was not difficult to see that the task of sobriety was not yet become easy, and that, if it had the recommendation of the intellectual portion of the party who had resolved upon it, the outward man yielded a reluctant and restive compliance. But honest Wildrake had been dreadfully frightened at the course proposed to him by Cromwell, and, with a feeling not peculiar to the Catholic religion, had formed a solemn resolution within his own mind that, if he came off safe and with honor from this dangerous interview, he would show his sense of Heaven's favor by renouncing some of the sins which most easily beset him, and especially that of intemperance, to which, like many of his wild compeers, he was too much addicted.

This resolution, or vow, was partly prudential as well as religious; for it occurred to him as very possible that some matters of a difficult and delicate nature might be thrown into his hands at the present emergency, during the conduct of which it would be fitting for him to act by some better oracle than that of the Bottle, celebrated by Rabelais. In full compliance with this prudent determination, he touched neither the ale nor the brandy which were placed before him, and declined peremptorily the sack with which his friend would have garnished the board. Nevertheless, just as the boy removed the trenchers and napkins, together with the large black-jack which we have already mentioned and was one or two steps on his way to the door, the sinewy arm of the Cavalier, which seemed to elongate itself on purpose, as it extended far beyond the folds of the threadbare jacket, arrested the progress of the retiring Ganymede, and, seizing on the black-jack, conveyed it to the lips, which were gently breathing forth the aspiration, "D—n—I mean. Heaven forgive me! we are poor creatures of clay—one modest sip must be permitted to our frailty."

So murmuring, he glued the huge flagon to his lips, and as the head was slowly and gradually inclined backwards in proportion as the right hand elevated the bottom of the pitcher, Everard had great doubts whether the drinker and the cup were likely to part until the whole contents of the latter had been transferred to the person of the former. Roger Wildrake stinted, however, when, by a moderate computation, he had swallowed at one draught about a quart and a half.

He then replaced it on the salver, fetched a long breath to refresh his lungs, bade the boy get him gone with the rest of the liquors, in a tone which inferred some dread of his constancy, and then, turning to his friend Everard, he expatiated in praise of moderation, observing, that the mouthful which he had just taken had been of more service to him than if he had remained quaffing healths at table for four hours together.

His friend made no reply, but could not help being privately of opinion that Wildrake's temperance had done as much execution on the tankard in his single draught as some more moderate topers might have effected if they had sat sipping for an evening. But the subject was changed by the entrance of the landlord, who came to announce to his honor Colonel Everard that the worshipful Mayor of Woodstock, with the Rev. Master Holdenough, were come to wait upon him.

CHAPTER X

Here we have one head
Upon two bodies; your two-headed bullock
Is but an ass to such a prodigy.
These two have but one meaning, thought, and counsel;
And, when the single noddle has spoke out,
The four legs scraps assent to 't.

Old Play.

IN the goodly form of the honest Mayor there was a bustling mixture of importance and embarrassment, like the deportment of a man who was conscious that he had an important part to act, if he could but exactly discover what that part was. But both were mingled with much pleasure at seeing Everard, and he frequently repeated his welcomes and all-hails before he could be brought to attend to what that gentleman said in reply.

"Good, worthy colonel, you are indeed a desirable sight to Woodstock at all times, being, as I may say, almost our townsman, as you have dwelt so much and so long at the palace. Truly, the matter begins almost to pass my wit, though I have transacted the affairs of this borough for many a long day; and you are come to my assistance like—like——"

"*Tanquam deus ex machina*, as the ethnic poet hath it," said Master Holdenough, "although I do not often quote from such books. Indeed, Master Markham Everard—or worthy colonel, as I ought rather to say—you are simply the most welcome man who has come to Woodstock since the days of old King Harry."

"I had some business with you, my good friend," said the colonel, addressing the Mayor; "I shall be glad if it should so happen at the same time that I may find occasion to pleasure you or your worthy pastor."

"No question you can do so, good sir," interposed Master Holdenough: "you have the heart, sir, and you have the hand; and we are much in want of good counsel, and that from a man of action. I am aware, worthy colonel, that you and your worthy father have ever borne yourselves in these turmoils like men of a truly Christian and moderate spirit, striving to pour oil into the wounds of the land, which some would rub with vitriol and pepper; and we know you are faithful children of that church which we have reformed from its papistical and prelatical tenets."

"My good and reverend friend," said Everard, "I respect the piety and learning of many of your teachers; but I am also for liberty of conscience to all men. I neither side with sectaries nor do I desire to see them the object of suppression by violence."

"Sir—sir," said the Presbyterian, hastily, "all this hath a fair sound; but I would you should think what a fine country and church we are like to have of it, amidst the errors, blasphemies, and schisms which are daily introduced into the church and kingdom of England, so that worthy Master Edwards, in his *Gangræna*, declareth, that our native country is about to become the very sink and cesspool of all schisms, heresies, blasphemies, and confusions, as the army of Hannibal was said to be the refuse of all nations—*colluvies omnium gentium*. Believe me, worthy colonel, that they of the Honorable House view all this over-lightly, and with the winking connivance of old Eli. These instructors, the schismatics, shoulder the orthodox ministers out of their pulpits, thrust themselves into families, and break up the peace thereof, stealing away men's hearts from the established faith."

"My good Master Holdenough," replied the colonel, interrupting the zealous preacher, "there is ground of sorrow for all these unhappy discords; and I hold with you, that the fiery spirits of the present time have raised men's minds at once above sober-minded and sincere religion and above decorum and common sense. But there is no help save patience. Enthusiasm is a stream that may foam off in its own time, whereas it is sure to bear down every barrier which is directly opposed to it. But what are these schismatical proceedings to our present purpose?"

"Why, partly this, sir," said Holdenough, "although perhaps you may make less of it than I should have thought before we met. I was myself—I, Nehemiah Holdenough," he added, consequentially, "was forcibly expelled from my own pulpit, even as a man should have been thrust out of his own house, by an alien and an intruder, a wolf, who was not at the trouble even to put on sheep's clothing, but came in his native wolfish attire of buff and bandoleer, and held forth in my stead to the people, who are to me as a flock to the lawful shepherd. It is too true, sir. Master Mayor saw it, and strove to take such order to prevent it as a man might, though," turning to the Mayor, "I think still you might have striven a little more."

"Good now, good Master Holdenough, do not let us go back on that question," said the Mayor. "Guy of Warwick or Bevis of Hampton might do something with this generation; but truly, they are too many and too strong for the Mayor of Woodstock."

"I think Master Mayor speaks very good sense," said the colonel. "If the Independents are not allowed to preach, I fear me they will not fight; and then if you were to have another rising of Cavaliers?"

"There are worse folks may rise than Cavaliers," said Holdenough.

"How, sir!" replied Colonel Everard. "Let me remind you, Master Holdenough, that is no safe language in the present state of the nation."

"I say," said the Presbyterian, "there are worse folk may rise than Cavaliers; and I will prove what I say. The Devil is worse than the worst Cavalier that ever drank a health or swore an oath—and the Devil has arisen at Woodstock Lodge!"

"Ay, truly hath he," said the Mayor, "bodily and visibly, in figure and form. An awful time we live in!"

"Gentlemen, I really know not how I am to understand you," said Everard."

"Why, it was even about the Devil we came to speak with you," said the Mayor; "but the worthy minister is always so hot upon the sectaries——"

"Which are the Devil's brats, and nearly akin to him," said Master Holdenough. "But true it is, that the growth of these sects has brought up the Evil One even upon the face of the earth, to look after his own interest, where he finds it most thriving."

"Master Holdenough," said the colonel, "if you speak figuratively, I have already told you that I have neither the means nor the skill sufficient to temper these religious heats. But if you design to say that there has been an actual apparition of the Devil, I presume to think that you, with your doctrine and your learning, would be a fitter match for him than a soldier like me."

"True, sir; and I have that confidence in the commission which I hold, that I would take the field against the Foul Fiend without a moment's delay," said Holdenough; "but the place in which he hath of late appeared, being Woodstock, is filled with those dangerous and impious persons of whom I have been but now complaining; and though, confident in my own resources, I dare venture in disputation with their Great Master himself, yet without your protection, most worthy colonel, I see not that I may with prudence trust myself with the tossing and goring ox Desborough, or the bloody and devouring bear Harrison, or the cold and poisonous snake Bletson—all of whom are now at the lodge, doing license and taking spoil as they think meet; and, as all men say, the Devil has come to make a fourth with them."

"In good truth, worthy and noble sir," said the Mayor, "it is even as Master Holdenough says: our privileges are declared void, our cattle seized in the very pastures. They talk of cutting down and disparking the fair chase, which has been so long the pleasure of so many kings, and making Woodstock of as little note as any paltry village. I assure you we heard of your arrival with joy, and wondered at your keeping yourself so close in your lodgings. We know no one save your father or you that are like to stand the poor burgesses' friend in this extremity, since almost all the gentry around are Malignants, and under sequestration. We trust, therefore, you will make strong intercession in our behalf."

"Certainly, Master Mayor," said the colonel, who saw himself with pleasure anticipated; "it was my very purpose to have interfered in this matter, and I did but keep myself alone until I should be furnished with some authority from the Lord General."

"Powers from the Lord General!" said the Mayor, thrusting the clergyman with his elbow. "Dost thou hear that? What cock will fight that cock? We shall carry it now over their necks, and Woodstock shall be brave Woodstock still."

"Keep thine elbow from my side, friend," said Holdenough, annoyed by the action which the Mayor had suited to his words; "and may the Lord send that Cromwell prove not as sharp to the people of England as thy bones against my person! Yet I approve that we should use his authority to stop the course of these men's proceedings."

"Let us set out, then," said Colonel Everard; "and I trust we shall find the gentlemen reasonable and obedient."

The functionaries, lay and clerical, assented with much joy; and the colonel required and received Wildrake's assistance in putting on his cloak and rapier, as if he had been the dependant whose part he acted. The Cavalier contrived, however, while doing him these menial offices, to give his friend a shrewd pinch, in order to maintain the footing of secret equality betwixt them.

The colonel was saluted, as they passed through the streets, by many of the anxious inhabitants, who seemed to consider his intervention as affording the only chance of saving their fine park, and the rights of the corporation, as well as of individuals, from ruin and confiscation.

As they entered the park, the colonel asked his companions, "What is this you say of apparitions been seen amongst them ?"

"Why, colonel," said the clergyman, "you know yourself that Woodstock was always haunted ?"

"I have lived therein many a day," said the colonel, "and I know that I never saw the least sign of it, although idle people spoke of the house as they do of all old mansions, and gave the apartments ghosts and specters to fill up the places of as many of the deceased great as had ever dwelt there."

"Nay, but, good colonel," said the clergyman, "I trust you have not reached the prevailing sin of the times, and become indifferent to the testimony in favor of apparitions, which appears so conclusive to all but atheists and advocates for witches ?"

"I would not absolutely disbelieve what is so generally affirmed," said the colonel; "but my reason leads me to doubt most of the stories which I have heard of this sort, and my own experience never went to confirm any of them."

"Ay, but trust me," said Holdenough, "there was always a demon of one or the other species about this Woodstock. Not a man or woman in the town but has heard stories of apparitions in the forest or about the old castle. Sometimes it is a pack of hounds that sweep along, and the whoops and halloos of the huntsmen, and the winding of horns and the galloping of horse, which is heard as if first more distant, and then close around you ; and then anon it is a solitary huntsman, who asks if you can tell him which way the stag is gone. He is always dressed in green ; but the fashion of his clothes is some five hundred years old. This what we call Demon Meridianum—the noonday specter."

"My worthy and reverend sir," said the colonel, "I have lived at Woodstock many seasons, and have traversed the chase at all hours. Trust me, what you hear from the villagers is the growth of their idle folly and superstition."

"Colonel," replied Holdenough, "a negative proves nothing. What signifies, craving your pardon, that you have not seen anything, be it earthly or be it of the other world, to detract from the evidence of a score of people who have? And, besides, there is the Demon Nocturnum —the being that walketh by night. He has been among these Independents and schismatics last night. Ay, colonel, you may stare, but it is even so; they may try whether he will mend their gifts, as they profanely call them, of exposition and prayer. No, sir, I trow, to master the foul fiend there goeth some competent knowledge of theology, and an acquaintance of the humane letters, ay, and a regular clerical education and clerical calling."

"I do not in the least doubt," said the colonel, "the efficacy of your qualifications to lay the Devil; but still I think some odd mistake has occasioned this confusion amongst them, if there has any such in reality existed. Desborough is a blockhead, to be sure; and Harrison is fanatic enough to believe anything. But there is Bletson, on the other hand, who believes nothing. What do you know of this matter, good Master Mayor?"

"In sooth, and it was Master Bletson who gave the first alarm," replied the magistrate, "or, at least, the first distinct one. You see, sir, I was in bed with my wife, and no one else; and I was as fast asleep as a man can desire to be at two hours after midnight, when, behold you, they came knocking at my bedroom door, to tell me there was an alarm in Woodstock, and that the bell of the lodge was ringing at that dead hour of the night as hard as ever it rung when it called the court to dinner."

"Well, but the cause of this alarm?" said the colonel.

"You shall hear, worthy colonel—you shall hear," answered the Mayor, waving his hand with dignity; for he was one of those persons who will not be hurried out of their own pace. "So Mrs. Mayor would have persuaded me, in her love and affection, poor wretch, that to rise at such an hour out of my own warm bed was like to bring on my old complaint the lumbago, and that I should send the people to Alderman Dutton. 'Alderman Devil, Mrs. Mayor,' said I—I beg your reverence's pardon for using such a phrase—'Do you think I am going to lie a-bed when the town is on fire, and the Cavaliers up, and the devil to pay?" I beg pardon again, parson. But here we are before the gate of the palace; will it not please you to enter?"

"I would first hear the end of your story," said the

colonel; "that is, Master Mayor, if it happens to have an end."

"Everything hath an end," said the Mayor, "and that which we call a pudding hath two. Your worship will forgive me for being facetious. Where was I? O, I jumped out of bed, and put on my red plush breeches, with the blue nether stocks, for I always make a point of being dressed suitably to my dignity, night and day, summer or winter, Colonel Everard; and I took the constable along with me, in case the alarm should be raised by night-walkers or thieves, and called up worthy Master Holdenough out of his bed, in case it should turn out to be the Devil. And so I thought I was provided for the worst, and so away we came; and, by and by, the soldiers, who came to the town with Master Tomkins, who had been called to arms, came marching down to Woodstock as fast as their feet would carry them; so I gave our people the sign to let them pass us, and outmarch us, as it were, and this for a twofold reason."

"I will be satisfied," interrupted the colonel, "with one good reason. You desired the redcoats should have the *first* of the fray?"

"True, sir—very true; and also that they should have the *last* of it, in respect that fighting is their especial business. However, we came on at a slow pace, as men who are determined to do their duty without fear or favor, when suddenly we saw something white haste away up the avenue towards the town, when six of our constables and assistants fled at once, as conceiving it to be an apparition called the White Woman of Woodstock."

"Look you there, colonel," said Master Holdenough, "I told you there were demons of more kinds than one, which haunt the ancient scenes of royal debauchery and cruelty."

"I hope you stood your own ground, Master Mayor?" said the colonel.

"I—yes—most assuredly—that is, I did not, strictly speaking, keep my ground; but the town clerk and I retreated—retreated, colonel, and without confusion or dishonor, and took post behind worthy Master Holdenough, who, with the spirit of a lion, threw himself in the way of the supposed specter, and attacked it with such a siserary of Latin as might have scared the Devil himself, and thereby plainly discovered that it was no devil at all, nor white woman, neither woman of any color, but worshipful Master Bletson, a member of the House of Commons, and one of the commissioners sent hither upon this unhappy sequestration of the wood, chase, and lodge of Woodstock."

"And this was all you saw of the demon?" said the colonel.

"Truly, yes," answered the Mayor; "and I had no wish to see more. However, we conveyed Master Bletson, as in duty bound, back to the lodge, and he was ever maundering by the way how that he met a party of scarlet devils incarnate marching down to the lodge; but, to my poor thinking, it must have been the Independent dragoons who had just passed us."

"And more incarnate devils I would never wish to see," said Wildrake, who could remain silent no longer. His voice, so suddenly heard, showed how much the Mayor's nerves were still alarmed, for he started and jumped aside with an alacrity of which no one would at first sight suppose a man of his portly dignity to have been capable. Everard imposed silence on his intrusive attendant; and, desirous to hear the conclusion of this strange story, requested the Mayor to tell him how the matter ended, and whether they stopped the supposed specter.

"Truly, worthy sir," said the Mayor, "Master Holdenough was quite venturous upon confronting, as it were, the Devil, and compelling him to appear under the real form of Master Joshua Bletson, member of Parliament for the borough of Littlefaith."

"In sooth, Master Mayor," said the divine, "I were strangely ignorant of my own commission and its immunities if I were to value opposing myself to Satan, or any Independent in his likeness, all of whom, in the name of Him I serve, I do defy, spit at, and trample under my feet; and because Master Mayor is something tedious, I will briefly inform your honor that we saw little of the Enemy that night, save what Master Bletson said in the first feeling of his terrors, and save what we might collect from the disordered appearance of the Honorable Colonel Desborough and Major-General Harrison."

"And what plight were they in, I pray you?" demanded the colonel,

"Why, worthy sir, every one might see with half an eye that they had been engaged in a fight wherein they had not been honored with perfect victory; seeing that General Harrison was stalking up and down the parlor, with his drawn sword in his hand, talking to himself, his doublet unbuttoned, his points untrussed, his garters loose, and like to throw him down as he now and then trode on them, and gaping and grinning like a mad player. And yonder sat Desborough with a dry pottle of sack before him, which he had just emptied, and which, though the element in which he trusted, had not restored him sense enough to speak or courage enough to look over his shoulder. He had a Bible in his hand, forsooth, as if it would of itself make battle against the Evil One; but I peered over his shoulder, and, alas! the good gentleman held the bottom of the page uppermost. It was as if one of your musketeers, noble and valiant sir, were to present the butt of his piece at the enemy instead of the muzzle—ha, ha, ha! it was a sight to judge of schismatics by, both in point of head and in point of heart, in point of skill and in point of courage. Oh! colonel, then was the time to see the true character of an authorized pastor of souls over those unhappy men who leap into the fold without due and legal authority, and will, forsooth, preach, teach, and exhort, and blasphemously term the doctrine of the church saltless porridge and dry chips!"

"I have no doubt you were ready to meet the danger, reverend sir; but I would fain know of what nature it was, and from whence it was to be apprehended?"

"Was it for me to make such inquiry?" said the clergyman, triumphantly. "Is it for a brave soldier to number his enemies, or inquire from what quarter they are to come? No, sir, I was there with match lighted, bullet in my mouth, and my harquebuss shouldered, to encounter as many devils as Hell could pour in, were they countless as motes in the sunbeam, and although they came from all points of the compass. The Papists talk of the temptation of St. Anthony—pshaw! Let them double all the myriads which the brain of a crazy Dutch painter hath invented, and you will find a poor Presbyterian divine—I will answer for one at least—who, not in his own strength, but his Master's, will receive the assault in such sort that, far from returning against him as against yonder poor hound, day after day and night after night, he will at once pack them off as with a vengeance to the uttermost parts of Assyria."

"Still," said the colonel, "I pray to know whether you saw anything upon which to exercise your pious learning?"

"Saw," answered the divine; "no, truly," I saw nothing, nor did I look for anything. Thieves will not attack well-armed travelers, nor will devils or evil spirits come against one who bears in his bosom the Word of truth, in the very language in which it was first dictated. No, sir, they shun a divine who can understand the holy text, as a crow is said to keep wide of a gun loaded with hail-shot."

They had walked a little way back upon their road to give time for this conversation; and the colonel, perceiving it was about to lead to no satisfactory explanation of the real cause of alarm on the preceding night, turned round, and observing, it was time they should go the lodge, began to move in that direction with his three companions.

It had now become dark, and the towers of Woodstock arose high above the umbrageous shroud which the forest spread around the ancient and venerable mansion. From one of the highest turrets, which could still be distinguished as it rose against the clear blue sky, there gleamed a light like that of a candle within the building.

The Mayor stopped short, and catching fast hold of the divine and then of Colonel Everard, exclaimed, in a trembling and hasty, but suppressed, tone—"Do you see yonder light?"

"Ay," marry do I," said Colonel Everard; "and what does that matter? A light in a garret-room of such an old mansion as Woodstock is no subject for wonder, I trow."

"But a light from Rosamond's Tower is surely so?" said the Mayor.

"True," said the colonel, something surprised when, after a careful examination, he satisfied himself that the worthy magistrate's conjecture was right. "That is indeed Rosamond's Tower; and as the drawbridge by which it was accessible has been destroyed for centuries, it is hard to say what chance could have lighted a lamp in such an inaccessible place."

"That light burns with no earthly fuel," said the Mayor: "neither from whale nor olive oil, nor bees-wax, nor mutton-suet either. I dealt in these commodities, colonel, before I went into my present line; and I can assure you I could distinguish the sort of light they give, one from another, at a greater distance than yonder turret. Look you, that is no earthly flame. See you not something blue and reddish upon the edges? that bodes full well where it comes from. Colonel, in my opinion we had better go back to sup at the town, and leave the Devil and the redcoats to settle their matters together for to-night; and then when we come back the next morning, we will have a pull with the party that chances to keep a-field."

"You will do as you please, Master Mayor," said Everard,

"but my duty requires me that I should see the Commissioners to-night."

"And mine requires me to see the Foul Fiend," said Master Holdenough, "if he dare make himself visible to me. I wonder not that, knowing who is approaching, he betakes himself to the very citadel, the inner and the last defenses, of this ancient and haunted mansion. He is dainty, I warrant you, and must dwell where is a relish of luxury and murder about the walls of his chamber. In yonder turret sinned Rosamond, and in yonder turret she suffered; and there she sits, or more likely, the Enemy in her shape, as I have heard true men of Woodstock tell. I wait on you, good colonel; Master Mayor will do as he pleases. The strong man hath fortified himself in his dwelling-house, but, lo, there cometh another stronger than he."

"For me," said the Mayor, "who am as unlearned as I am unwarlike, I will not engage either with the powers of the Earth or the Prince of the Powers of the Air, and I would we were again at Woodstock; and harkye, good fellow," slapping Wildrake on the shoulder, "I will bestow on thee a shilling wet and a shilling dry if thou wilt go back with me."

"Gadzookers, Master Mayor," said Wildrake, neither flattered by the magistrate's familiarity of address nor captivated by his munificence, "I wonder who the devil made you and me fellows? And, besides, do you think I would go back to Woodstock with your worshipful cod's-head, when, by good management, I may get a peep of Fair Rosamond, and see whether she was that choice and incomparable piece of ware which the world has been told of by rhymers and ballad-makers?"

"Speak less lightly and wantonly, friend," said the divine; "we are to resist the Devil that he may flee from us, and not to tamper with him, or enter into his counsels, or traffic with the merchandise of his great Vanity Fair."

"Mind what the good man says, Wildrake," said the colonel; "and take heed another time how thou dost suffer thy wit to outrun discretion."

"I am beholden to the reverend gentleman for his advice," answered Wildrake, upon whose tongue it was difficult to impose any curb whatever, even when his own safety rendered it most desirable. "But, gadzookers, let him have had what experience he will in fighting with the Devil, he never saw one so black as I had a tussle with—not a hundred years ago."

"How, friend," said the clergyman, who understood everything literally when apparitions were mentioned, "have you had so late a visitation of Satan? Believe me, then, that I wonder why thou darest to entertain his name so often and so lightly as I see thou dost use it in thy ordinary discourse. But when and where didst thou see the Evil One?"

Everard hastily interposed, lest by something yet more strongly alluding to Cromwell his imprudent squire should, in mere wantonness, betray his interview with the General. "The young man raves," he said, "of a dream which he had the other night, when he and I slept together in Victor Lee's chamber, belonging to the ranger's apartments at the lodge."

"Thanks for help at a pinch, good patron," said Wildrake, whispering into Everard's ear, who in vain endeavored to shake him off, "a fib never failed a fanatic."

"You, also, spoke something too lightly of these matters, considering the work which we have in hand, worthy colonel," said the Presbyterian divine. "Believe me, the young man, thy servant, was more likely to see visions than to dream merely idle dreams in that apartment; for I have always heard that, next to Rosamond's Tower, in which, as I said, she played the wanton, and was afterwards poisoned by Queen Eleanor, Victor Lee's chamber was the place in the lodge of Woodstock more peculiarly the haunt of evil spirits. I pray you, young man, tell me this dream or vision of yours."

"With all my heart, sir," said Wildrake; then addressing his patron, who began to interfere, he said, "Tush, sir, you have had the discourse for an hour, and why should not I hold forth in my turn? By this darkness, if you keep me silent any longer, I will turn Independent preacher, and stand up in your despite for the freedom of private judgment. And so, reverend sir, I was dreaming of a carnal divertisement called a bull-baiting; and methought they were venturing dogs at head, as merrily as e'er I saw them at Tutbury bull-running; and methought I heard some one say, there was the Devil come to have a sight of the bull-ring. Well, I thought that, gadswoons, I would have a peep at his Infernal Majesty. So I looked, and there was a butcher in greasy woolen, with his steel by his side; but he was none of the Devil. And there was a drunken Cavalier, with his mouth full of oaths, and his stomach full of emptiness, and a gold-laced waistcoat in a very dilapidated condition, and a ragged hat, with a piece of a feather in it;

and he was none of the Devil neither. And there was a miller, his hands dusty with meal, and every atom of it stolen; and there was a vintner, his green apron stained with wine, and every drop of it sophisticated; but neither was the old gentleman I looked for to be detected among these artisans of iniquity. At length, sir, I saw a grave person with cropped hair, a pair of longish and projecting ears, a band as broad as a slobbering bib under his chin, a brown coat surmounted by a Geneva cloak, and I had Old Nicholas at once in his genuine paraphernalia, by ——!"

"Shame—shame!" said Colonel Everard. "What! behave thus to an old gentleman and a divine!"

"Nay, let him proceed," said the minister, with perfect equanimity; "if thy friend, or secretary, is gibing, I must have less patience than becomes my profession if I could not bear an idle jest, and forgive him who makes it. Or if, on the other hand, the Enemy has really presented himself to the young man in such a guise as he intimates, wherefore should we be surprised that he who can take upon him the form of an angel of light should be able to assume that of a frail and peccable mortal, whose spiritual calling and profession ought, indeed, to induce him to make his life an example to others, but whose conduct, nevertheless, such is the imperfection of our unassisted nature, sometimes rather presents us with a warning of what we should shun?"

"Now, by the mass, honest dominie—I mean, reverend sir—I crave you a thousand pardons," said Wildrake, penetrated by the quietness and patience of the Presbyter's rebuke. "By St. George, if quiet patience will do it, thou art fit to play a game at foils with the Devil himself and I would be contented to hold stakes."

As he concluded an apology which was certainly not uncalled for, and seemed to be received in perfectly good part, they approached so close to the exterior door of the lodge that they were challenged with the emphatic "Stand," by a sentinel who mounted guard there. Colonel Everard replied, "A friend"; and the sentinel repeating his command, "Stand, friend," proceeded to call the corporal of the guard. The corporal came forth, and at the same time turned out his guard. Colonel Everard gave his name and designation, as well as those of his companions, on which the corporal said, "He doubted not there would be orders for his instant admission; but, in the first place, Master Tomkins must be consulted, that he might learn their honors' mind."

"How, sir!" said the colonel, "do you, knowing who I am, presume to keep me on the outside of your post?"

"Not if your honor pleases to enter," said the corporal, "and undertakes to be my warranty; but such are the orders of my post."

"Nay, then, do your duty," said the colonel; "but are the Cavaliers up, or what is the matter, that you keep so close and strict a watch?"

The fellow gave no distinct answer, but muttered between his mustachios something about the enemy, and the roaring lion who goeth about seeking whom he may devour. Presently afterwards, Tomkins appeared, followed by two servants, bearing lights in great standing brass candlesticks. They marched before Colonel Everard and his party, keeping as close to each other as two cloves of the same orange: and starting from time to time, and shuddering, as they passed through sundry intricate passages, they led up a large and ample wooden staircase, the banisters, rail, and lining of which were executed in black oak, and finally into a long saloon, or parlor, where there was a prodigious fire, and about twelve candles of the largest size distributed in sconces against the wall. There were seated the Commissioners, who now held in their power the ancient mansion and royal domain of Woodstock.

CHAPTER XI.

> The bloody bear, an independent beast,
> Unlick'd to forms, in groans his hate express'd.
>
> . . . .
>
> Next him the buffoon ape, as atheists use,
> Mimick'd all sects, and had his own to choose.
>
> *Hind and Panther.*

THE strong light in the parlor which we have described served to enable Everard easily to recognize his acquaintances, Desborough, Harrison, and Bletson, who had assembled round an oak table of large dimensions, placed near the blazing chimney, on which were arranged wine, and ale, and materials for smoking, then the general indulgence of the time. There was a species of movable cupboard set betwixt the table and the door, calculated originally for a display of plate upon grand occasions, but at present only used as a screen; which purpose it served so effectually that, ere he had coasted around it, Everard heard the following fragment of what Desborough was saying, in his strong coarse voice: "Sent him to share with us, I'se warrant ye. It was always his Excellency my brother-in-law's way: if he made a treat for five friends, he would invite more than the table could hold. I have known him ask three men to eat two eggs."

"Hush—hush," said Bletson; and the servants making their appearance from behind the tall cupboard, announced Colonel Everard. It may not be uninteresting to the reader to have a description of the party into which he now entered.

Desborough was a stout, bull-necked man, of middle size, with heavy, vulgar features, grizzled, bushy eyebrows, and wall-eyes. The flourish of his powerful relative's fortunes had burst forth in the finery of his dress, which was much more ornamented than was usual among the Roundheads. There was embroidery on his cloak, and lace upon his band; his hat displayed a feather with a golden clasp; and all his habiliments were those of a Cavalier, or follower of the court, rather than the plain dress of a Parliamentarian officer. But, Heaven knows, there was little of courtlike grace or dignity in the person or demeanor of the individual, who became his fine suit as the hog on the sign-post does his gilded armor. It was not that he was positively deformed, or misshaped, for, taken in detail, the figure was well enough. But his limbs seemed to act upon different and contradictory principles. They were not, as the play says, in a concatenation accordingly: the right hand moved as if it were upon bad terms with the left, and the legs showed an inclination to foot it in different and opposite directions. In short, to use an extravagant comparison, the members of Colonel Desborough seemed rather to resemble the disputatious representatives of a federative congress than the well-ordered union of the orders of the state in a firm and well-compacted monarchy, where each holds his own place and all obey the dictates of a common head.

General Harrison, the second of the Commissioners, was a tall, thin, middle-aged man, who had risen into his high situation in the army, and his intimacy with Cromwell, by his dauntless courage in the field, and the popularity he had acquired by his exalted enthusiasm amongst the military saints, sectaries, and Independents who composed the strength of the existing army. Harrison was of mean extraction, and bred up to his father's employment of a butcher. Nevertheless, his appearance, though coarse, was not vulgar, like that of Desborough, who had so much the advantage of him in birth and education. He had a masculine height and strength of figure, was well made, and in his manner announced a rough military character, which might be feared, but could not easily become the object of contempt or ridicule. His aquiline nose and dark black eyes set off to some advantage a countenance otherwise irregular, and the wild enthusiasm that sometimes sparkled in them as he dilated on his opinions to others, and often seemed to slumber under his long dark eyelashes as he mused upon them himself, gave something strikingly wild, and even noble, to his aspect. He was one of the chief leaders of those who were called Fifth Monarchy men, who, going even beyond the general fanaticism of the age, presumptuously interpreted the Book of the Revelations after their own fancies, considered that the second advent of the Messiah, and the millennium, or reign of the saints upon earth, was close at hand, and that they themselves, illuminated, as they believed, with the power of foreseeing these approaching events, were the chosen instruments for the establishment of the New Reign, or

Fifth Monarchy, as it was called, and were fated also to win its honors, whether celestial or terrestrial.

When this spirit of enthusiasm, which operated like a partial insanity, was not immediately affecting Harrison's mind, he was a shrewd, worldly man and a good soldier, one who missed no opportunity of mending his fortune, and who, in expecting the exaltation of the Fifth Monarchy, was, in the meanwhile, a ready instrument for the establishment of the Lord General's supremacy. Whether it was owing to his early occupation, and habits of indifference to pain or bloodshed acquired in the shambles, to natural disposition and want of feeling, or, finally, to the awakened character of his enthusiasm, which made him look upon those who opposed him as opposing the Divine will, and therefore meriting no favor or mercy, is not easy to say; but all agreed that, after a victory or the successful storm a town, Harrison was one of the most cruel and pitiless men in Cromwell's army, always urging some misapplied text to authorize the continued execution of the fugitives, and sometimes even putting to death those who had surrendered themselves prisoners. It was said, that at times the recollection of some of those cruelties troubled his conscience, and disturbed the dreams of beatification in which his imagination indulged.

When Everard entered the apartment, this true representative of the fanatical soldiers of the day, who filled those ranks and regiments which Cromwell had politically kept on foot, while he procured the reduction of those in which the Presbyterian interest predominated, was seated a little apart from the others, his legs crossed and stretched out at length towards the fire, his head resting on his elbow, and turned upwards, as if studying, with the most profound gravity, the half-seen carving of the Gothic roof.

Bletson remains to be mentioned, who, in person and figure, was diametrically different from the other two. There was neither foppery nor slovenliness in his exterior, nor had he any marks of military service or rank about his person. A small walking rapier seemed merely worn as a badge of his rank as a gentleman, without his hand having the least purpose of becoming acquainted with the hilt, or his eye with the blade. His countenance was thin and acute, marked with lines which thought rather than age had traced upon it; and a habitual sneer on his countenance, even when he least wished to express contempt on his features, seemed to assure the individual addressed that in

Bletson he conversed with a person of intellect far superior to his own. This was a triumph of intellect only, however; for on all occasions of difference respecting speculative opinions, and indeed on all controversies whatsoever, Bletson avoided the ultimate *ratio* of blows and knocks.

Yet this peaceful gentleman had found himself obliged to serve personally in the Parliamentary army at the commencement of the Civil War, till, happening unluckily to come in contact with the fiery Prince Rupert, his retreat was judged so precipitate, that it required all the shelter his friends could afford to keep him free of an impeachment or a court-martial. But as Bletson spoke well, and with great effect, in the House of Commons, which was his natural sphere, and was on that aacount high in the estimation of his party, his behavior at Edgehill was passed over, and he continued to take an active share in all the political events of that bustling period, though he faced not again the actual front of war.

Bletson's theoretical politics had long inclined him to espouse the opinions of Harrington and others, who adopted the visionary idea of establishing a pure democratical republic in so extensive a country as Britain. This was a rash theory, where there is such an infinite difference betwixt ranks, habits, education, and morals; where there is such an immense disproportion betwixt the wealth of individuals; and where a large portion of the inhabitants consists of the inferior classes of the large towns and manufacturing districts—men unfitted to bear that share in the direction of a state which must be exercised by the members of a republic in the proper sense of the word. Accordingly, as soon as the experiment was made, it became obvious that no such form of government could be adopted with the smallest chance of stability; and the question came only to be, whether the remnant, or, as it was vulgarly called, the Rump, of the Long Parliament, now reduced by the seclusion of so many of the members to a few scores of persons, should continue, in spite of their unpopularity, to rule the affairs of Britain? Whether they should cast all loose by dissolving themselves, and issuing writs to convoke a new Parliament, the composition of which no one could answer for, any more than for the measures they might take when assembled? Or, lastly, whether Cromwell, as actually happened, was not to throw the sword into the balance, and boldly possess himself of that power which the remnant of the Parliament were unable to hold, and yet afraid to resign?

Such being the state of parties, the Council of State, in distributing the good things in their gift, endeavored to soothe and gratify the army, as a beggar flings crusts to a growling mastiff. In this view Desborough had been created a Commissioner in the Woodstock matter to gratify Cromwell, Harrison to soothe the fierce Fifth Monarchy men, and Bletson as a sincere republican, and one of their own leaven.

But if they supposed Bletson had the least intention of becoming a martyr to his republicanism, or submitting to any serious loss on account of it, they much mistook the man. He entertained their principles sincerely, and not the less that they were found impracticable ; for the miscarriage of his experiment no more converts the political speculator than the explosion of a retort undeceives an alchemist. But Bletson was quite prepared to submit to Cromwell, or any one else who might be possessed of the actual authority. He was a ready subject in practise to the powers existing, and made little difference betwixt various kinds of government, holding in theory all to be nearly equal in imperfection, so soon as they diverged from the model of Harrington's *Oceana.* Cromwell had already been tampering with him, like wax between his finger and thumb, and which he was ready shortly to seal with, smiling at the same time to himself when he beheld the Council of State giving rewards to Bletson as their faithful adherent, while he himself was secure of his allegiance, how soon soever the expected change of government should take place.

But Bletson was still more attached to his metaphysical than his political creed, and carried his doctrines of the perfectibility of mankind as far as he did those respecting the conceivable perfection of a model of government ; and as in the one case he declared against all power which did not emanate from the people themselves, so, in his moral speculations, he was unwilling to refer any of the phenomena of nature to a final cause. When pushed, indeed, very hard, Bletson was compelled to mutter some inarticulate and unintelligible doctrines concerning *Animus Mundi*, or Creative Power, in the works of nature, by which she originally called into existence, and still continues to preserve, her works. To this power, he said, some of the purest metaphysicians rendered a certain degree of homage ; nor was he himself inclined absolutely to censure those who, by the institution of holidays, choral dances, songs, and harmless feasts and libations, might be disposed to celebrate the great goddess

Nature; at least, dancing, singing, feasting, and sporting being comfortable things to both young and old, they might as well sport, dance, and feast in honor of such appointed holidays as under any other pretext. But then this moderate show of religion was to be practised under such exceptions as are admitted by the Highgate oath; and no one was to be compelled to dance, drink, sing, or feast whose taste did not happen to incline them to such divertisements, nor was any one to be obliged to worship the creative power, whether under the name of the *Animus Mundi* or any other whatsoever. The interference of the Deity in the affairs of mankind he entirely disowned, having proved to his own satisfaction that the idea originated entirely in priestcraft. In short, with the shadowy metaphysical exception aforesaid, Mr. Joshua Bletson of Darlington, member for Littlecreed [Littlefaith], came as near the predicament of an atheist as it is perhaps possible for a man to do. But we say this with the necessary salvo; for we have known many like Bletson, whose curtains have been shrewdly shaken by superstition, though their fears were unsanctioned by any religious faith. The devils, we are assured, believe and tremble; but on earth there are many who, in worse plight than even the natural children of perdition, tremble without believing, and fear even while they blaspheme.

It follows, of course, that nothing could be treated with more scorn by Mr. Bletson than the debates about Prelacy and Presbytery, about Presbytery and Independency, about Quakers and Anabaptists, Muggletonians and Brownists, and all the various sects with which the Civil War had commenced, and by which its dissensions were still continued. "It was," he said, "as if beasts of burden should quarrel amongst themselves about the fashion of their halters and pack-saddles, instead of embracing a favorable opportunity of throwing them aside." Other witty and pithy remarks he used to make when time and place suited; for instance, at the club called the Rota, frequented by St. John, and established by Harrington, for the free discussion of political and religious subjects.

But when Bletson was out of this academy or stronghold of philosophy, he was very cautious how he carried his contempt of the general prejudice in favor of religion and Christianity further than an implied objection or a sneer. If he had an opportunity of talking in private with an ingenuous and intelligent youth, he sometimes attempted to make a proselyte, and showed much address in bribing the vanity of inexperience, by suggesting that a mind like his ought to spurn the prejudices impressed upon it in childhood; and when assuming the *latus clavus* of reason, assuring him that such as he, laying aside the *bulla* of juvenile incapacity, as Bletson called it, should proceed to examine and decide for himself. It frequently happened that the youth was induced to adopt the doctrines in whole or in part of the sage who had seen his natural genius, and who had urged him to exert it in examining, detecting, and declaring for himself; and thus flattery gave proselytes to infidelity which could not have been gained by all the powerful eloquence or artful sophistry of the infidel.

These attempts to extend the influence of what was called freethinking and philosophy were carried on, as we have hinted, with a caution dictated by the timidity of the philosopher's disposition. He was conscious his doctrines were suspected, and his proceedings watched, by the two principal sects of Prelatists and Presbyterians, who, however inimical to each other, were still more hostile to one who was an opponent not only to a church establishment of any kind, but to every denomination of Christianity. He found it more easy to shroud himself among the Independents, whose demands were for a general liberty of conscience, or an unlimited toleration, and whose faith, differing in all respects and particulars, was by some pushed into such wild errors as to get totally beyond the bounds of every species of Christianity, and approach very near to infidelity itself, as extremes of each kind are said to approach each other. Bletson mixed a good deal among these sectaries; and such was his confidence in his own logic and address, that he is supposed to have entertained hopes of bringing to his opinions in time the enthusiastic Vane, as well as the no less enthusiastic Harrison, provided he could but get them to resign their visions of a Fifth Monarchy, and induce them to be contented with a reign of philosophers in England for the natural period of their lives, instead of the reign of the saints during the millennium.

Such was the singular group into which Everard was now introduced, showing, in their various opinions, upon how many devious coasts human nature may make shipwreck, when she has once let go her hold on the anchor which religion has given her to lean upon; the acute self-conceit and worldly learning of Bletson, the rash and ignorant conclusions of the fierce and under-bred Harrison, leading them into the opposite extremes of enthusiasm and infidelity, while Desborough, constitutionally stupid, thought nothing about religion at all; and while the others were active in making sail on different but equally erroneous courses, he might be said to perish like a vessel which springs a leak and founders in the roadstead. It was wonderful to behold what a strange variety of mistakes and errors, on the part of the King and his ministers, on the part of the Parliament and their leaders, on the part of the allied kingdoms of Scotland and England towards each other, had combined to rear up men of such dangerous opinions and interested characters among the arbiters of the destiny of Britain.

Those who argue for party's sake will see all the faults on the one side, without deigning to look at those on the other: those who study history for instruction will perceive that nothing but the want of concession on either side, and the deadly height to which the animosity of the King's and Parliament's parties had arisen, could have so totally overthrown the well-poised balance of the English constitution. But we hasten to quit political reflections, the rather that ours, we believe, will please neither Whig nor Tory.

CHAPTER XII

Three form a college; an you give us four,
Let him bring his share with him.
BEAUMONT AND FLETCHER.

MR. BLETSON arose and paid his respects to Colonel Everard with the ease and courtesy of a gentleman of the time, though on every account grieved at his intrusion, as a religious man who held his freethinking principles in detestation, and would effectually prevent his conversion of Harrison, and even of Desborough, if anything could be molded out of such a clod, to the worship of the *Animus Mundi*. Moreover, Bletson knew Everard to be a man of steady probity, and by no means disposed to close with a scheme on which he had successfully sounded the other two, and which was calculated to assure the Commissioners of some little private indemnification for the trouble they were to give themselves in the public business. The philosopher was yet less pleased when he saw the magistrate and the pastor who had met him in his flight of the preceding evening, when he had been seen, *parma non bene relicta*, with cloak and doublet left behind him.

The presence of Colonel Everard was as unpleasing to Desborough as to Bletson; but the former, having no philosophy in him, nor an idea that it was possible for any man to resist helping himself out of untold money, was chiefly embarrassed by the thought that the plunder which they might be able to achieve out of their trust might, by this unwelcome addition to their number, be divided into four parts instead of three; and this reflection added to the natural awkwardness with which he grumbled forth a sort of welcome, addressed to Everard.

As for Harrison, he remained like one on higher thoughts intent, his posture unmoved, his eyes fixed on the ceiling as before, and in no way indicating the least consciousness that the company had been more than doubled around him.

Meantime, Everard took his place at the table, as a man who assumed his own right, and pointed to his companions to sit down nearer the foot of the board. Wildrake so far misunderstood his signals as to sit down above the Mayor; but rallying his recollection at a look from his patron, he rose and took his place lower, whistling, however, as he went—a sound at which the company stared, as at a freedom highly unbecoming. To complete his indecorum, he seized upon a pipe, and filling it from a large tobacco-box, was soon immersed in a cloud of his own raising, from which a hand shortly after emerged, seized on the black-jack of ale, withdrew it within the vapory sanctuary, and, after a potential draught, replaced it upon the table, its owner beginning to renew the cloud which his intermitted exercise of the tube had almost allowed to subside.

Nobody made any observation on his conduct, out of respect, probably, to Colonel Everard, who bit his lip, but continued silent, aware that censure might extract some escapade more unequivocally characteristic of a Cavalier from his refractory companion. As silence seemed awkward, and the others made no advances to break it, beyond the ordinary salutation, Colonel Everard at length said, "I presume, gentlemen, that you are somewhat surprised at my arrival here, and thus intruding myself into your meeting?"

"Why the dickens should we be surprised, colonel?" said Desborough: "we know his Excellency my brother-in-law Noll's—I know my Lord Cromwell's—way of over-quartering his men in the towns he marches through. Thou hast obtained a share in our commission?"

"And in that," said Bletson, smiling and bowing, "the Lord General has given us the most acceptable colleague that could have been added to our number. No doubt your authority for joining with us must be under warrant of the Council of State?"

"Of that, gentlemen," said the colonel, "I will presently advise you." He took out his warrant accordingly, and was about to communicate the contents; but observing that there were three or four half-empty flasks upon the table, that Desborough looked more stupid than usual, and that the philosopher's eyes were reeling in his head, notwithstanding the temperance of Bletson's usual habits, he concluded that they had been fortifying themselves against the horrors of the haunted mansion, by laying in a store of what is called Dutch courage, and therefore prudently resolved to postpone his more important business with them till the cooler hour of morning. He, therefore, instead of presenting the General's warrant superseding their commission, contented himself with replying, "My business has, of course, some reference to your proceedings here. But here is—excuse my curiosity—a reverend gentleman," pointing to Holdenough, "who has told me that you are so strangely embarrassed here as to require both the civil and spiritual authority to enable you to keep possession of Woodstock."

"Before we go into that matter," said Bletson, blushing up to the eyes at the recollection of his own fears, so manifestly displayed, yet so inconsistent with his principles, "I should like to know who this other stranger is, who has come with the worthy magistrate and the no less worthy Presbyterian?"

"Meaning me?" said Wildrake, laying his pipe aside. "Gadzooks, the time hath been that I could have answered the question with a better title; but at present I am only his honor's poor clerk or secretary, whichever is the current phrase."

"'Fore George, my lively blade, thou art a frank fellow of thy tattle," said Desborough. "There is my* secretary Tomkins, whom men sillily enough call Fibbet, and the honorable Lieutenant-General Harrison's secretary, Bibbet, who are now at supper below stairs, that durst not for their ears speak a phrase above their breath in the presence of their betters, unless to answer a question."

"Yes, Colonel Everard," said the philosopher, with his quiet smile, glad, apparently, to divert the conversation from the topic of last night's alarm, and recollections which humbled his self-love and self-satisfaction—"yes, and when Master Fibbet and Master Bibbet *do* speak, their affirmations are as much in a common mold of mutual attestation as their names would accord in the verses of a poet. If Master Fibbet happens to tell a fiction, Master Bibbet swears it is truth. If master Bibbet chances to have gotten drunk in the fear of the Lord, Master Fibbet swears he is sober. I have called my own secretary Gibbet, though his name chances to be only Gibeon, a worthy Israelite at your service, but as pure a youth as ever picked a lamb-bone at Paschal. But I call him Gibbet, merely to make up the holy trefoil with another rhyme. This squire of thine, looks as though he might be worthy to be coupled with the rest of the fraternity."

"Not I, truly," said the Cavalier; "I'll be coupled with no Jew that was ever whelped, and no Jewess neither."

"Scorn not for that, young man," said the philosopher;

* [See page 159.]

"the Jews are, in point of religion, the elder brethren, you know."

"The Jews older than the Christians?" said Desborough; "'fore George, they will have thee before the General Assembly, Bletson, if thou venturest to say so."

Wildrake laughed without ceremony at the gross ignorance of Desborough, and was joined by a sniggling response from behind the cupboard, which, when inquired into, proved to be produced by the serving-men. These worthies, timorous as their betters, when they were supposed to have left the room, had only withdrawn to their present place of concealment.

"How now, ye rogues," said Bletson, angrily; "do you not know your duty better?"

"We beg your worthy honor's pardon," said one of the men, "but we dared not go downstairs without a light."

"A light, ye cowardly poltroons!" said the philosopher; "what—to show which of you looks palest when a rat squeaks? But take a candlestick and begone, you cowardly villains; the devils you are so much afraid of must be but paltry kites, if they hawk at such bats as you are."

The servants, without replying, took up one of the candlesticks and prepared to retreat, Trusty Tomkins at the head of the troop, when suddenly, as they arrived at the door of the parlor, which had been left half open, it was shut violently. The three terrified domestics tumbled back into the middle of the room, as if a shot had been discharged in their face, and all who were at the table started to their feet.

Colonel Everard was incapable of a moment's fear, even if anything frightful had been seen; but he remained stationary, to see what his companions would do, and to get at the bottom, if possible, of the cause of their alarm upon an occasion so trifling. The philosopher seemed to think that *he* was the person chiefly concerned to show manhood on the occasion.

He walked to the door accordingly, murmuring at the cowardice of the servants; but at such a snail's pace that it seemed he would most willingly have been anticipated by any one whom his reproaches had roused to exertion. "Cowardly blockheads!" he said at last, seizing hold of the handle of the door, but without turning it effectually round, "dare you not open a door? (still fumbling with the lock)—dare you not go down a staircase without a light? Here, bring me the candle, you cowardly villains! By Heaven, something sighs on the outside!"

As he spoke, he let go the handle of the parlor door, and stepped back a pace or two into the apartment, with cheeks as pale as the band he wore.

"*Deus adjutor meus!*" said the Presbyterian clergyman, rising from his seat. "Give place, sir," addressing Bletson; "it would seem I know more of this matter than thou, and I bless Heaven I am armed for the conflict."

Bold as a grenadier about to mount a breach, yet with the same belief in the existence of a great danger to be encountered, as well as the same reliance in the goodness of his cause, the worthy man stepped before the philosophical Bletson, and taking a light from a sconce in one hand, quietly opened the door with the other, and standing in the threshold, said, "Here is nothing."

"And who expected to see anything," said Bletson, "excepting those terrified oafs, who take fright at every puff of wind that whistles through the passages of this old dungeon?"

"Mark you, Master Tomkins," said one of the waiting-men in a whisper to the steward, "see how boldly the minister pressed forward before all of them. Ah! Master Tomkins, our parson is the real commissioned officer of the church; your lay-preachers are no better than a parcel of club-men and volunteers."

"Follow me those who list," said Master Holdenough, "or go before me those who choose, I will walk through the habitable places of this house before I leave it, and satisfy myself whether Satan hath really mingled himself among these dreary dens of ancient wickedness, or whether, like the wicked of whom holy David speaketh, we are afraid and flee when no one pursueth."

Harrison, who had heard these words, sprung from his seat, and drawing his sword, exclaimed, "Were there as many fiends in the house as there are hairs on my head, upon this cause I will charge them up to their very trenches."

So saying, he brandished his weapon, and pressed to the head of the column, where he moved side by side with the minister. The Mayor of Woodstock next joined the body, thinking himself safer perhaps in the company of his pastor; and the whole train moved forward in close order, accompanied by the servants bearing lights, to search the lodge for some cause of that panic with which they seemed to be suddenly seized.

"Nay, take me with you, my friends," said Colonel Everard, who had looked on in surprise, and was now about to follow the party, when Bletson laid hold on his cloak and begged him to remain.

"You see, my good colonel," he said, affecting a courage which his shaking voice belied, "here are only you and I, and honest Desborough, left behind in garrison, while all the others are absent on a sally. We must not hazard the whole troops on one sortie, that were unmilitary. Ha, ha, ha!"

"In the name of Heaven, what means all this?" said Everard, "I heard a foolish tale about apparitions as I came this way, and now I find you all half-mad with fear, and cannot get a word of sense among so many of you. Fie, Colonel Desborough—fie, Master Bletson; try to compose yourselves, and let me know, in Heaven's name, the cause of all this disturbance. One would be apt to think your brains were turned."

"And so mine well may," said Desborough, "ay, and overturned too, since my bed last night was turned upside down, and I was placed for ten minutes heels uppermost and head downmost, like a bullock going to be shot."

"What means this nonsense, Master Bletson? Desborough must have had the nightmare."

"No, faith, colonel; the goblins, or whatever else they were, had been favorable to honest Desborough, for they reposed the whole of his person on that part of his body which—hark, did you not hear something?—is the central point of gravity, namely, his head."

"Did you see anything to alarm you?" said the colonel.

"Nothing," said Bletson; "but we heard hellish noises, as all our people did, and I, believing little of ghosts and apparitions, concluded the Cavaliers were taking us at advantage, so, remembering Rainsborough's fate, I e'er jumped the window and ran to Woodstock, to call the soldiers to the rescue of Harrison and Desborough."

"And did you not first go to see what the danger was?"

"Ah, my good friend, you forget that I laid down my commission at the time of the self-denying ordinance. It would have been quite inconsistent with my duty as a Parliament-man to be brawling amidst a set of ruffians, without any military authority. No; when the Parliament commanded me to sheathe my sword, colonel, I have too much veneration for their authority to be found again with it drawn in my hand."

"But the Parliament," said Desborough, hastily, "did not command you to use your heels when your hands could have saved a man from choking. Ods dickens! you might have stopped when you saw my bed canted heels uppermost, and me half-stifled in the bedclothes—you might, I say, have stopped and lent a hand to put it to rights, instead of jumping out of the window, like a new-shorn sheep, so soon as you had run across my room."

"Nay, worshipful Master Desborough," said Bletson, winking on Everard, to show that he was playing on his thick-skulled colleague, "how could I tell your particular mode of reposing? There are many tastes: I have known men who slept by choice on a slope or angle of forty-five."

"Yes, but did ever a man sleep standing on his head, except by miracle?" said Desborough.

"Now, as to miracles," said the philosopher, confident in the presence of Everard, besides that an opportunity of scoffing at religion really in some degree diverted his fear, "I leave these out of the question, seeing that the evidence on such subjects seems as little qualified to carry conviction as a horsehair to land a leviathan."

A loud clap of thunder, or a noise as formidable, rang through the lodge as the scoffer had ended, which struck him pale and motionless, and made Desborough throw himself on his knees and repeat exclamations and prayers in much admired confusion.

"There must be contrivance here," exclaimed Everard; and snatching one of the candles from a sconce, he rushed out of the apartment, little heeding the entreaties of the philosopher, who, in the extremity of his distress, conjured him by the *Animus Mundi* to remain to the assistance of a distressed philosopher endangered by witches, and a Parliament-man assaulted by ruffians. As for Desborough, he only gaped like a clown in a pantomime; and, doubtful whether to follow or stop, his natural indolence prevailed, and he sat still.

When on the landing-place of the stairs, Everard paused a moment to consider which was the best course to take. He heard the voices of men talking fast and loud, like people who wish to drown their fears, in the lower story; and aware that nothing could be discovered by those whose inquiries were conducted in a manner so noisy, he resolved to proceed in a different direction, and examine the second floor, which he had now gained.

He had known every corner, both of the inhabited and uninhabited part of the mansion, and availed himself of the candle to traverse two or three intricate passages, which he was afraid he might not remember with sufficient accuracy. This movement conveyed him to a sort of *œil-de-bœuf*, an octagon vestibule, or small hall, from which various rooms opened. Amongst these doors, Everard selected that which led to a very long, narrow, and dilapidated gallery, built in the time of Henry VIII., and which, running along the whole south-west side of the building, communicated at different points with the rest of the mansion. This he thought was likely to be the post occupied by those who proposed to act the sprites upon the occasion; especially as its length and shape gave him some idea that it was a spot where the bold thunder might in many ways be imitated.

Determined to ascertain the truth, if possible, he placed his light on a table in the vestibule, and applied himself to open the door into the gallery. At this point he found himself strongly opposed, either by a bolt drawn, or, as he rather conceived, by somebody from within resisting his attempt. He was induced to believe the latter, because the resistance slackened and was renewed, like that of human strength, instead of presenting the permanent opposition of an inanimate obstacle. Though Everard was a strong and active young man, he exhausted his strength in the vain attempt to open the door; and having paused to take breath, was about to renew his efforts with foot and shoulder, and to call at the same time for assistance, when, to his surprise, on again attempting the door more gently, in order to ascertain if possible where the strength of the opposing obstacle was situated, he found it give way to a very slight impulse, some impediment fell broken to the ground, and the door flew wide open. The gust of wind occasioned by the sudden opening of the door blew out the candle, and Everard was left in darkness, save where the moonshine, which the long side-row of latticed windows dimmed, could imperfectly force its way into the gallery, which lay in ghostly length before him.

The melancholy and doubtful twilight was increased by a quantity of creeping plants on the outside, which, since all had been neglected in these ancient halls, now completely overgrown, had in some instances greatly diminished, and in others almost quite choked up, the space of the lattices, extending between the heavy stone shaft-work which divided the windows, both lengthways and across. On the other side there were no windows at all, and the gallery had been once hung round with paintings, chiefly portraits, by which that side of the apartment had been adorned. Most of the pictures had been removed, yet the empty frames of some, and the tattered remnants of others, were still visible along the extent of the waste gallery; the look of which was so desolate, and it appeared so well adapted for mischief, supposing there were enemies near him, that Everard could not help pausing at the entrance, and recommending himself to God, ere, drawing his sword, he advanced into the apartment, treading as lightly as possible, and keeping in the shadow as much as he could.

Markham Everard was by no means superstitious, but he had the usual credulity of the times; and though he did not yield easily to tales of supernatural visitations, yet he could not help thinking he was in the very situation where, if such things were ever permitted, they might be expected to take place, while his own stealthy and ill-assured pace, his drawn weapon and extended arms, being the very attitude and action of doubt and suspicion, tended to increase in his mind the gloomy feelings of which they are the usual indications, and with which they are constantly associated. Under such unpleasant impressions, and conscious of the neighborhood of something unfriendly, Colonel Everard had already advanced about half along the gallery, when he heard some one sigh very near him, and a low soft voice pronounce his name.

"Here I am," he replied, while his heart beat thick and short. "Who calls on Markham Everard?"

Another sigh was the only answer.

"Speak," said the colonel, "whoever or whatsoever you are, and tell me with what intent and purpose you are lurking in these apartments?"

"With a better intent than yours," returned the soft voice.

"Than mine!" answered Everard, in great surprise. "Who are you that dare judge of my intents?"

"What or who are you, Markham Everard, who wander by moonlight through these deserted halls of royalty, where none should be but those who mourn their downfall, or are sworn to avenge it?"

"It is—and yet it cannot be," said Everard; "yet it is, and must be. Alice Lee, the Devil or you speaks. Answer me, I conjure you. Speak openly—on what dangerous scheme are you engaged? where is your father? why are you here? wherefore do you run so deadly a venture? Speak, I conjure you, Alice Lee!"

"She whom you call on is at the distance of miles from

this spot. What if her genius speaks when she is absent? what if the soul of an ancestress of hers and yours were now addressing you? what if——"

"Nay, answered Everard, "but what if the dearest of human beings has caught a touch of her father's enthusiasm? what if she is exposing her person to danger, her reputation to scandal, by traversing in disguise and darkness a house filled with armed men? Speak to me, my fair cousin, in your own person. I am furnished with powers to protect my uncle, Sir Henry—to protect you too, dearest Alice, even against the consequences of this visionary and wild attempt. Speak—I see where you are, and, with all my respect, I cannot submit to be thus practised upon. Trust me—trust your cousin Markham with your hand, and believe that he will die or place you in honorable safety."

As he spoke, he exercised his eyes as keenly as possible to detect where the speaker stood; and it seemed to him that about three yards from him there was a shadowy form, of which he could not discern even the outline, placed as it was within the deep and prolonged shadow thrown by a space of wall intervening betwixt two windows upon that side of the room from which the light was admitted. He endeavored to calculate, as well as he could, the distance betwixt himself and the object which he watched, under the impression that, if, by even using a slight degree of compulsion, he could detach his beloved Alice from the confederacy into which he supposed her father's zeal for the cause of royalty had engaged her, he would be rendering them both the most essential favor. He could not indeed but conclude that, however successfully the plot which he conceived to be in agitation had preceeded against the timid Bletson, the stupid Desborough, and the crazy Harrison, there was little doubt that at length their artifices must necessarily bring shame and danger on those engaged in it.

It must also be remembered, that Everard's affection to his cousin, although of the most respectful and devoted character, partook less of the distant veneration which a lover of those days entertained for the lady whom he worshiped with humble diffidence, than of the fond and familiar feelings which a brother entertains towards a younger sister, whom he thinks himself entitled to guide, advise, and even in some degree to control. So kindly and intimate had been their intercourse, that he had little more hesitation in endeavoring to arrest her progress in the dangerous course in which she seemed to be engaged, even at the risk of giving her momentary offense, than he would have had in snatching her from a torrent of conflagration, at the chance of hurting her by the violence of his grasp. All this passed through his mind in the course of a single minute; and he resolved at all events to detain her on the spot, and compel, if possible, an explanation from her.

With this purpose, Everard again conjured his cousin, in the name of Heaven, to give up this idle and dangerous mummery; and lending an accurate ear to her answer, endeavored from the sound to calculate as nearly as possible the distance between them.

"I am not she for whom you take me," said the voice; "and dearer regards than aught connected with her life or death bid me warn you to keep aloof and leave this place."

"Not till I have convinced you of your childish folly," said the colonel, springing forward, and endeavoring to catch hold of her who spoke to him. But no female form was within his grasp. On the contrary, he was met by a shock which could come from no woman's arm, and which was rude enough to stretch him on his back on the floor. At the same time he felt the point of a sword at his throat, and his hands so completely mastered, that not the slightest defense remained to him.

"A cry for assistance," said a voice near him, but not that which he had hitherto heard, "will be stifled in your blood. No harm is meant you—be wise, and be silent."

The fear of death, which Everard had often braved in the field of battle, became more intense as he felt himself in the hands of unknown assassins, and totally devoid of all means of defense. The sharp point of the sword pricked his bare throat, and the foot of him who held it was upon his breast. He felt as if a single thrust would put an end to life, and all the feverish joys and sorrows which agitate us so strangely, and from which we are yet so reluctant to part. Large drops of perspiration stood upon his forehead: his heart throbbed, as if it would burst from its confinement in the bosom; he experienced the agony which fear imposes on the brave man, acute in proportion to that which pain inflicts when it subdues the robust and healthy.

"Cousin Alice," he attempted to speak, and the sword's point pressed his throat yet more closely—"cousin, let me not be murdered in a manner so fearful."

"I tell you," replied the voice, "that you speak to one who is not here; but your life is not aimed at, provided you swear on your faith as a Christian and your honor as a gentleman that you will conceal what has happened, whether from the people below or from any other person. On this condition you may rise; and if you seek her, you will find Alice Lee at Joceline's cottage in the forest."

"Since I may not help myself otherwise," said Everard, "I swear, as I have a sense of religion and honor, I will say nothing of this violence, nor make any search after those who are concerned in it."

"For that we care nothing," said the voice. "Thou hast an example how well thou mayst catch mischief on thy own part; but we are in case to defy thee. Rise and begone."

The foot, the sword's-point, were withdrawn, and Everard was about to start up hastily, when the voice, in the same softness of tone which distinguished it at first, said, "No haste—cold and bare steel is yet around thee. Now—now—now (the words dying away as at a distance)—thou art free. Be secret and be safe."

Markham Everard arose, and, in rising, embarrassed his feet with his own sword, which he dropped when springing forward, as he supposed, to lay hold of his fair cousin. He snatched it up in haste, and, as his hand clasped the hilt, his courage, which had given way under the apprehension of instant death, began to return; he considered, with almost his usual composure, what was to be done next. Deeply affronted at the disgrace which he had sustained, he questioned for an instant whether he ought to keep his extorted promise, or should not rather summon assistance, and make haste to discover and seize those who had been recently engaged in such violence on his person. But these persons, be they who they would, had had his life in their power; he had pledged his word in ransom of it; and what was more, he could not divest himself of the idea that his beloved Alice was a confidante, at least, if not an actor, in the confederacy which had thus baffled him. This prepossession determined his conduct; for, though angry at supposing she must have been an accessory to his personal ill-treatment, he could not in any event think of an instant search through the mansion, which might have compromised her safety, or that of his uncle. "But I will to the hut," he said—"I will instantly to the hut, ascertain her share in this wild and dangerous confederacy, and snatch her from ruin, if it be possible."

As, under the influence of the resolution which he had formed, Everard groped his way through the gallery, and regained the vestibule, he heard his name called by the well-known voice of Wildrake. "What—ho!—halloo!—Colonel Everard—Mark Everard—it is dark as the Devil's mouth—speak—where are you? The witches are keeping their hellish sabbath here, as I think. Where are you?"

"Here—here!" answered Everard. "Cease your bawling. Turn to the left, and you will meet me."

Guided by his voice, Wildrake soon appeared, with a light in one hand and his drawn sword in the other. "Where have you been?" he said—"what has detained you? Here are Bletson and the brute Desborough terrified out of their lives, and Harrison raving mad, because the Devil will not be civil enough to rise to fight him in single *duello*."

"Saw or heard you nothing as you came along?" said Everard.

"Nothing," said his friend, "excepting that, when I first entered this cursed ruinous labyrinth the light was struck out of my hand, as if by a switch, which obliged me to return for another."

"I must come by a horse instantly, Wildrake, and another for thyself, if it be possible."

"We can take two of those belonging to the troopers," answered Wildrake. "But for what purpose should we run away, like rats, at this time in the evening? Is the house falling?"

"I cannot answer you," said the colonel, pushing forward into a room where there were some remains of furniture.

Here the Cavalier took a more strict view of his person, and exclaimed in wonder, "What the devil have you been fighting with, Markham, that has bedizened you after this sorry fashion?"

"Fighting!" exclaimed Everard.

"Yes," replied his trusty attendant, "I say fighting. Look at yourself in the mirror."

He did, and saw he was covered with dust and blood. The latter proceeded from a scratch which he received in the throat, as he struggled to extricate himself. With unaffected alarm, Wildrake undid his friend's collar, and with eager haste proceeded to examine the wound, his hands trembling, and his eyes glistening with apprehension for his benefactor's life. When, in spite of Everard's opposition, he had examined the hurt, and found it trifling, he resumed the natural wildness of his character, perhaps the more readily that he had felt shame in departing from it into one which expressed more of feeling than he would be thought to possess.

"If that be the Devil's work, Mark," said he, "the Foul Fiend's claws are not nigh so formidable as they are represented; but no one shall say that your blood has been shed unrevenged, while Rodger Wildrake was by your side. Where left you this same imp? I will back to the field of fight, confront him with my rapier, and were his nails tenpenny nails, and his teeth as long as those of a harrow, he shall render me reason for the injury he has done you."

"Madness—madness!" exclaimed Everard; "I had this trifling hurt by a fall; a basin and towel will wipe it away. Meanwhile, if you will ever do me kindness, get the troop-horses: command them for the service of the public, in the name of his Excellency the General. I will but wash, and join you in an instant before the gate."

"Well, I will serve you, Everard, as a mute serves the Grand Signior, without knowing why or wherefore. But will you go without seeing these people below?"

"Without seeing any one," said Everard; "lose no time, for God's sake."

He found out the non-commissioned officer, and demanded the horses in a tone of authority, to which the corporal yielded undisputed obedience, as one well aware of Colonel Everard's military rank and consequence. So all was in a minute or two ready for the expedition.

CHAPTER XIII

She kneeled, and saintlike
Cast her eyes to heaven, and prayed devoutly.
King Henry VIII.

COLONEL EVERARD's departure at the late hour, for so it was then thought, of seven in the evening excited much speculation. There was a gathering of menials and dependants in the outer chamber, or hall, for no one doubted that his sudden departure was owing to his having, as they expressed it, "seen something," and all desired to know how a man of such acknowledged courage as Everard looked under the awe of a recent apparition. But he gave them no time to make comments; for, striding through the hall wrapped in his riding suit, he threw himself on horseback, and rode furiously through the chase, towards the hut of the keeper Joliffe.

It was the disposition of Markham Everard to be hot, keen, earnest, impatient, and decisive to a degree of precipitation. The acquired habits which education had taught, and which the strong moral and religious discipline of his sect had greatly strengthened, were such as to enable him to conceal, as well as to check, this constitutional violence, and to place him upon his guard against indulging it. But when in the high tide of violent excitation, the natural impetuosity of the young soldier's temper was sometimes apt to overcome these artificial obstacles, and then, like a torrent foaming over a wear, it became more furious as if in revenge for the constrained calm which it had been for some time obliged to assume. In these instances he was accustomed to see only that point to which his thoughts were bent, and to move straight towards it, whether a moral object or the storming or a breach, without either calculating or even appearing to see the difficulties which were before him.

At present, his ruling and impelling motive was to detach his beloved cousin, if possible from the dangerous and discreditable machinations in which he suspected her to have engaged, or, on the other hand, to discover that she really had no concern with these stratagems. He should know how to judge of that in some measure, he thought, by finding her present or absent at the hut, towards which he was now galloping. He had read, indeed, in some ballad or minstrel's tale, of a singular deception practised on a jealous old man by means of a subterranean communication between his house and that of a neighbor, which the lady in question made use of to present herself in the two places alternately with such speed and so much address that, after repeated experiments, the dotard was deceived into the opinion that his wife and the lady who was so very like her, and to whom his neighbor paid so much attention, were two different persons. But in the present case there was no room for such a deception ; the distance was too great, and as he took by much the nearest way from the castle, and rode full speed, it would be impossible, he knew, for his cousin, who was a timorous horsewoman even by daylight, to have got home before him.

Her father might indeed be displeased at his interference ; but what title had he to be so ? Was not Alice Lee the near relation of his blood, the dearest object of his heart, and would he now abstain from an effort to save her from the consequences of a silly and wild conspiracy, because the old knight's spleen might be awakened by Everard's making his appearance at their present dwelling contrary to his commands ? No. He would endure the old man's harsh language, as he endured the blast of the autumn wind, which was howling around him, and swinging the crashing branches of the trees under which he passed, but could not oppose, or even retard, his journey.

If he found not Alice, as he had reason to believe she would be absent, to Sir Henry Lee himself he would explain what he had witnessed. However she might have become accessory to the juggling tricks performed at Woodstock, he could not but think it was without her father's knowledge, so severe a judge was the old knight of female propriety, and so strict an assertor of female decorum. He would take the same opportunity, he thought, of stating to him the well-grounded hopes he entertained that his dwelling at the lodge might be prolonged, and the sequestrators removed from the royal mansion and domains, by other means than those of the absurd species of intimidation which seemed to be resorted to, to scare them from thence.

All this seemed to be so much within the line of his duty

as a relative, that it was not until he halted at the door of of the ranger's hut, and threw his bridle into Wildrake's hand, that Everard recollected the fiery, high, and unbending character of Sir Henry Lee, and felt, even when his fingers were on the latch, a reluctance to intrude himself upon the presence of the irritable old knight.

But there was no time for hesitation. Bevis, who had already bayed more than once from within the lodge [hut], was growing impatient, and Everard had but just time to bid Wildrake hold the horses until he should send Joceline to his assistance, when old Joan unpinned the door, to demand who was without at that time of the night. To have attempted anything like an explanation with poor Dame Joan would have been quite hopeless: the colonel therefore put her gently aside, and shaking himself loose from the hold she had laid on his cloak, entered the kitchen of Joceline's dwelling. Bevis, who had advanced to support Joan in her opposition, humbled his lion port, with that wonderful instinct which makes his race remember so long those with whom they have been familiar, and acknolwedged his master's relative by doing homage in his fashion with his head and tail.

Colonel Everard, more uncertain in his purpose every moment as the necessity of its execution drew near, stole over the floor like one who treads in a sick-chamber, and opening the door of the interior apartment with a slow and trembling hand, as he would have withdrawn the curtains of a dying friend, he saw within the scene which we are about to describe.

Sir Henry Lee sat in a wicker arm-chair by the fire. He was wrapped in a cloak, and his limbs extended on a stool, as if he were suffering from gout or indisposition. His long white beard, flowing over the dark-colored garment, gave him more the appearance of a hermit than of an aged soldier or man of quality; and that character was increased by the deep and devout attention with which he listened to by a respectable old man, whose dilapidated dress showed still something of the clerical habit, and who, with a low, but full and deep, voice, was reading the Evening Service according to the Church of England. Alice Lee kneeled at the feet of her father, and made the responses with a voice that might have suited the choir of angels, and a modest and serious devotion which suited the melody of her tone. The face of the officiating clergyman would have been good-looking had it not been disfigured with a black patch which covered the left eye and a part of his face, and had not the features which were visible been marked with traces of care and suffering.

When Colonel Everard entered, the clergyman raised his finger, as cautioning him to forbear disturbing the divine service of the evening, and pointed to a seat; to which, struck deeply with the scene he had witnessed, the intruder stole with as light a step as possible, and knelt devoutly down as one of the little congregation.

Everard had been bred by his father what was called a Puritan—a member of a sect who, in the primitive sense of the word, were persons that did not except against the doctrines of the Church of England, or even in all respects against its hierarchy, but chiefly dissented from it on the subject of certain ceremonies, habits, and forms of ritual, which were insisted upon by the celebrated and unfortunate Laud with ill-timed tenacity. But even if, from the habits of his father's house, Everard's opinions had been diametrically opposed to the doctrines of the English Church, he must have been reconciled to them by the regularity with which the service was performed in his uncle's family at Woodstock, who, during the blossom of his fortunes, generally had a chaplain residing in the lodge for that special purpose.

Yet, deep as was the habitual veneration with which he heard the impressive service of the church, Everard's eyes could not help straying toward's Alice and his thoughts wandering to the purpose of his presence there. She seemed to have recognized him at once, for there was a deeper glow than usual upon her cheek, her fingers trembled as they turned the leaves of her prayer-book, and her voice, lately as firm as it was melodious, faltered when she repeated the responses. It appeared to Everard, as far as he could collect by the stolen glances which he directed towards her, that the character of her beauty, as well as of her outward appearance, had changed with her fortunes.

The beautiful and high-born young lady had now approached as nearly as possible to the brown stuff dress of an ordinary village maiden; but what she had lost in gaiety of appearance, she had gained as it seemed in dignity. Her beautiful light-brown tresses, now folded around her head, and only curled where nature had so arranged them, gave her an air of simplicity which did not exist when her head-dress showed the skill of a curious tirewoman. A light, joyous air, with something of a humorous expression, which

Everard surprises Sir Henry and his daughter at their evening prayers

seemed to be looking for amusement, had vanished before the touch of affliction, and a calm melancholy supplied its place, which seemed on the watch to administer comfort to others. Perhaps the former arch, though innocent, expression of countenance was uppermost in her lover's recollection when he concluded that Alice had acted a part in the disturbances which had taken place at the lodge. It is certain that, when he now looked upon her, it was with shame for having nourished such a suspicion, and the resolution to believe rather that the Devil had imitated her voice than that a creature who seemed so much above the feelings of this world, and so nearly allied to the purity of the next, should have had the indelicacy to mingle in such maneuvers as he himself and others had been subjected to.

These thoughts shot through his mind, in spite of the impropriety of indulging them at such a moment. The service now approached the close; and, a good deal to Colonel Everard's surprise as well as confusion, the officiating priest, in firm and audible tone, and with every attribute of dignity, prayed to the Almighty to bless and preserve "Our Sovereign Lord, King Charles, the lawful and undoubted king of these realms." The petition (in those days most dangerous) was pronounced with a full, raised, and distinct articulation, as if the priest challenged all who heard him to dissent if they dared. If the republican officer did not assent to the petition, he thought at least it was no time to protest against it.

The service was concluded in the usual manner, and the little congregation arose. It now included Wildrake, who had entered during the latter prayer, and was the first of the party to speak, running up to the priest and shaking him by the hand most heartily, swearing at the same time that he truly rejoiced to see him. The good clergyman returned the pressure with a smile, observing, he should have believed his asseveration without an oath. In the meanwhile, Colonel Everard, approaching his uncle's seat, made a deep inclination of respect, first to Sir Henry Lee and then to Alice, whose color now spread from her cheek to her brow and bosom.

"I have to crave your excuse," said the colonel with hesitation, "for having chosen for my visit, which I dare not hope would be very agreeable at any time, a season most peculiarly unsuitable."

"So far from it, nephew," answered Sir Henry, with much more mildness of manner than Everard had dared to expect, "that your visits at other times would be much more welcome had we the fortune to see you often at our hours of worship."

"I hope the time will soon come, sir, when Englishmen of all sects and denominations," replied Everard, "will be free in conscience to worship in common the great Father, whom they all after their manner call by that affectionate name."

"I hope so too, nephew," said the old man in the same unaltered tone; "and we will not at present dispute whether you would have the Church of England coalesce with the Conventicle or the Conventicle conform to the Church. It was, I ween, not to settle jarring creeds that you have honored our poor dwelling, where, to say the truth, we dared scarce have expected to see you again, so coarse was our last welcome."

"I should be happy to believe," said Colonel Everard, hesitating, "that—that—in short, my presence was not now so unwelcome here as on that occasion."

"Nephew," said Sir Henry, "I will be frank with you. When you were last here, I thought you had stolen from me a precious pearl, which at one time it would have been my pride and happiness to have bestowed on you; but which, being such as you have been of late, I would bury in the depths of the earth rather than give to your keeping. This somewhat chafed, as honest Will says, 'the rash humor which my mother gave me.' I thought I was robbed, and I thought I saw the robber before me. I am mistaken: I am not robbed; and the attempt without the deed I can pardon."

"I would not willingly seek offense in your words, sir," said Colonel Everard, "when their general purport sounds kind; but I can protest before Heaven that my views and wishes towards you and your family are as void of selfish hopes and selfish ends as they are fraught with love to you and to yours."

"Let us hear them, man; we are not much accustomed to good wishes nowadays, and their very rarity will make them welcome."

"I would willingly, Sir Henry, since you might not choose me to give you a more affectionate name, convert those wishes into something effectual for your comfort. Your fate, as the world now stands, is bad, and, I fear, like to be worse."

"Worse than I expect it cannot be. Nephew, I do not

shrink before my changes of fortune. I shall wear coarser clothes, I shall feed on more ordinary food; men will not doff their cap to me as they were wont, when I was the great and the wealthy. What of that? Old Harry Lee loved his honor better than his title, his faith better than his land and lordship. Have I not seen the Thirtieth of January? I am neither philomath nor astrologer; but old Will teaches me that when green leaves fall winter is at hand, and that darkness will come when the sun sets."

"Bethink you, sir," said Colonel Everard, "if, without any submission asked, any oath taken, any engagement imposed, express or tacit, excepting that you are not to excite disturbances in the public peace, you can be restored to your residence in the lodge, and your usual fortunes and perquisites there—I have great reason to hope this may be permitted, if not expressly, at least on sufferance."

"Yes, I understand you. I am to be treated like the royal coin, marked with the ensign of the Rump, to make it pass current, although I am too old to have the royal insignia grinded off from me. Kinsman, I will have none of this. I have lived at the lodge too long; and let me tell you, I have left it in scorn long since, but for the orders of one whom I may yet live to do service to. I will take nothing from the usurpers, be their name Rump or Cromwell—be they one devil or legion: I will not take from them an old cap to cover my gray hairs, a cast cloak to protect my frail limbs from the cold. They shall not say they have, by their unwilling bounty, made Abraham rich. I will live, as I will die, the Loyal Lee."

"May I hope you will think of it, sir; and that you will, perhaps, considering what slight submission is asked, give me a better answer?"

"Sir, if I retract my opinion, which is not my wont, you shall hear of it. And now, cousin, have you more to say? We keep that worthy clergyman in the outer room."

"Something I had to say—something touching my cousin Alice," said Everard, with embarrassment; "but I fear that the prejudices of both are so strong against me——"

"Sir, I dare turn my daughter loose to you. I will go join the good doctor in Dame Joan's apartment. I am not unwilling that you should know that the girl hath, in all reasonable sort, the exercise of her free will."

He withdrew, and left the cousins together.

Colonel Everard advanced to Alice, and was about to take her hand. She drew back, took the seat which her father had occupied, and pointed out to him one at some distance.

"Are we then so much estranged, my dearest Alice?" he said.

"We will speak of that presently," she replied. "In the first place, let me ask the cause of your visit here at so late an hour."

"You heard," said Everard, "what I stated to your father?"

"I did; but that seems to have been only a part of your errand; something there seemed to be which applied particularly to me."

"It was a fancy—a strange mistake," answered Everard. "May I ask if you have been abroad this evening?"

"Certainly not," she replied. "I have small temptation to wander from my present home, poor as it is; and whilst here I have important duties to discharge. But why does Colonel Everard ask so strange a question?"

"Tell me in turn why your cousin Markham has lost the name of friendship and kindred, and even of some nearer feeling, and then I will answer you, Alice."

"It is soon answered," she said. "When you drew your sword against my father's cause, almost against his person, I studied, more than I should have done, to find excuse for you. I knew—that is, I thought I knew—your high feelings of public duty. I knew the opinions in which you had been bred up; and I said, 'I will not, even for this, cast him off: he opposes his King because he is loyal to his country.' You endeavored to avert the great and concluding tragedy of the Thirteenth of January, and it confirmed me in my opinion that Markham Everard might be misled, but could not be base or selfish."

"And what has changed your opinion, Alice? or who dare," said Everard, reddening, "attach such epithets to the name of Markham Everard?"

"I am no subject," she said, "for exercising your valor, Colonel Everard, nor do I mean to offend. But you will find enough of others who will avow that Colonel Everard is truckling to the usurper Cromwell, and that all his fair pretexts for forwarding his country's liberties are but a screen for driving a bargain with the successful encroacher, and obtaining the best terms he can for himself and his family."

"For myself—never!"

"But for your family you have. Yes, I am well assured that you have pointed out to the military tyrant the way in which he and his satraps may master the government. Do you think my father or I would accept an asylum purchased at the price of England's liberty and your honor?"

"Gracious Heaven, Alice, what is this? You accuse me of pursuing the very course which so lately had your approbation."

"When you spoke with authority of your father, and recommended our submission to the existing government, such as it was, I own I thought—that my father's gray head might, without dishonor, have remained under the roof where it had so long been sheltered. But did your father sanction your becoming the adviser of yonder ambitious soldier to a new course of innovation, and his abettor in the establishment of a new species of tyranny? It is one thing to submit to oppression, another to be the agent of tyrants. And O, Markham—their bloodhound!"

"How! bloodhound? What mean you? I own it is true I could see with content the wounds of this bleeding country stanched, even at the expense of beholding Cromwell, after his matchless rise, take a yet further step to power—but to be his bloodhound! What is your meaning?"

"It is false, then? Ah, I thought I could swear it had been false!"

"What, in the name of God, is it you ask?"

"It is false that you are engaged to betray the young King of Scotland?"

"Betray him! *I* betray him, or any fugitive! Never! I would he were well out of England. I would lend him my aid to escape, were he in the house at this instant, and think in acting so I did his enemies good service, by preventing their soiling themselves with his blood; but betray him, never!"

"I knew it—I was sure it was impossible. Oh, be yet more honest; disengage yourself from yonder gloomy and ambitious soldier! Shun him and his schemes, which are formed in injustice, and can only be realized in yet more blood."

"Believe me," replied Everard, "that I choose the line of policy best fitting the times."

"Choose that," she said, "which best befits duty, Markham—which best befits truth and honor. Do your duty, and let Providence decide the rest. Farewell, we tempt my father's patience too far; you know his temper—farewell, Markham."

She extended her hand, which he pressed to his lips, and

left the apartment. A silent bow to his uncle, and a sign to Wildrake, whom he found in the kitchen of the cabin, were the only tokens of recognition exhibited, and leaving the hut, he was soon mounted, and, with his companion, advanced on his return to the lodge.

CHAPTER XIV.

Deeds are done on earth
Which have their punishment ere the earth closes
Upon the perpetrators. Be it the working
Of the remorse-stirred fancy, or the vision,
Distinct and real, of unearthly being,
All ages witness, that beside the couch
Of the fell homicide oft stalks the ghost
Of him he slew, and shows the shadowy wound.
Old Play.

EVERARD had come to Joceline's hut as fast as horse could bear him, and with the same impetuosity of purpose and of speed. He saw no choice in the course to be pursued, and felt in his own imagination the strongest right to direct, and even reprove, his cousin, beloved as she was, on account of the dangerous machinations with which she appeared to have connected herself. He returned slowly, and in a very different mood.

Not only had Alice, prudent as beautiful, appeared completely free from the weakness of conduct which seemed to give him some authority over her, but her views of policy, if less practicable, were so much more direct and noble than his own, as led him to question whether he had not compromised himself too rashly with Cromwell, even although the state of the country was so greatly divided and torn by faction, that the promotion of the General to the possession of the executive government seemed the only chance of escaping a renewal of the Civil War. The more exalted and purer sentiments of Alice lowered him in his own eyes; and though unshaken in his opinion, that it were better the vessel should be steered by a pilot having no good title to the office than that she should run upon the breakers, he felt that he was not espousing the most direct, manly, and disinterested side of the question.

As he rode on, immersed in these unpleasant contemplations, and considerably lessened in his own esteem by what had happened, Wildrake, who rode by his side, and was no friend to long silence, began to enter into conversation. "I have been thinking, Mark," said he, "that if you and I had been called to the bar—as, by the by, has been in danger of happening to me in more senses than one—I say, had we become barristers, I would have had the better-oiled tongue of the two—the fairer art of persuasion."

"Perhaps so," replied Everard, "though I never heard thee use any, save to induce an usurer to lend thee money or a taverner to abate a reckoning."

"And yet this day, or rather night, I could have, as I think, made a conquest which baffled you."

"Indeed?" said the colonel, becoming attentive.

"Why, look you," said Wildrake, "it was a main object with you to induce Mistress Alice Lee—by Heaven, she is an exquisite creature, I approve of your taste, Mark—I say, you desire to persuade her, and the stout old Trojan her father, to consent to return to the lodge, and live there quietly, and under connivance, like gentlefolk, instead of lodging in a hut hardly fit to harbor a Tom of Bedlam."

"Thou art right: such, indeed, was a great part of my object in this visit," answered Everard.

"But, perhaps, you also expected to visit there yourself, and so keep watch over pretty Mistress Lee—eh?"

"I never entertained so selfish a thought," said Everard; "and if this nocturnal disturbance at the mansion were explained and ended, I would instantly take my departure."

"Your friend Noll would expect something more from you," said Wildrake: "he would expect, in case the knight's reputation for loyalty should draw any of our poor exiles and wanderers about the lodge, that you should be on the watch and ready to snap them. In a word, as far as I can understand his long-winded speeches, he would have Woodstock a trap, your uncle and his pretty daughter the bait of toasted cheese—craving your Chloe's pardon for the comparison—you the spring-fall which should bar their escape, his lordship himself being the great grimalkin to whom they are to be given over to be devoured."

"Dared Cromwell mention this to thee in express terms?" said Everard, pulling up his horse and stopping in the midst of the road.

"Nay, not in express terms, which I do not believe he ever used in his life, you might as well expect a drunken man to go straight forward; but he insinuated as much to me, and indicated that you might deserve well of him—gadzo, the damnable proposal sticks in my throat—by betraying our noble and rightful King (here he pulled off his hat), whom God grant in health and wealth long to reign, as the worthy clergyman says, though I fear just now his Majesty is both sick and sorry, and never a penny in his pouch to boot."

"This tallies with what Alice hinted," said Everard; "but how could she know it? Didst thou give her any hint of such a thing?"

"I!" replied the Cavalier—"I, who never saw Mistress Alice in my life till to-night, and then only for an instant—zooks, man, how is that possible?"

"True," replied Everard, and seemed lost in thought. At length he spoke—"I should call Cromwell to account for his bad opinion of me; for, even though not seriously expressed, but, as I am convinced, it was, with the sole view of proving you, and perhaps myself, it was, nevertheless, a misconstruction to be resented."

"I'll carry a cartel for you, with all my heart and soul," said Wildrake; "and turn out with his godliness's second with as good will as I ever drank a glass of sack."

"Pshaw!" replied Everard, "those in his high place fight no single combats. But tell me, Roger Wildrake, didst thou thyself think me capable of the falsehood and treachery implied in such a message?"

"I!" exclaimed Wildrake, "Markham Everard, you have been my early friend, my constant benefactor. When Colchester was reduced, you saved me from the gallows, and since that thou hast twenty times saved me from starving. But, by Heaven, if I thought you capable of such villainy as your General recommended, by yonder blue sky, and all the works of creation which it bends over, I would stab you with my own hand."

"Death," replied Everard, "I should indeed deserve, but not from you, perhaps; but fortunately I cannot, if I would, be guilty of the treachery you would punish. Know, that I had this day secret notice, and from Cromwell himself, that the Young Man has escaped by sea from Bristol."

"Now, God Almighty be blessed, who protected him through so many dangers!" exclaimed Wildrake. "Huzza! Up hearts, Cavaliers! Hey for Cavaliers! God bless King Charles! Moon and stars catch my hat!" and he threw it up as high as he could into the air. The celestial bodies which he invoked did not receive the present despatched to them; but, as in the case of Sir Henry Lee's scabbard, an old gnarled oak became a second time the receptacle of a waif and stray of loyal enthusiasm. Wildrake looked rather foolish at the circumstance, and his friend took the opportunity of admonishing him.

"Art thou not ashamed to bear thee so like a schoolboy?"

"Why," said Wildrake, "I have but sent a Puritan's hat upon a loyal errand. I laugh to think how many of the schoolboys thou talk'st of will be cheated into climbing the pollard next year, expecting to find the nest of some unknown bird in yonder unmeasured margin of felt."

"Hush, now, for God's sake, and let us speak calmly," said Everard. "Charles has escaped, and I am glad of it. I would willingly have seen him on his father's throne by composition, but not by the force of the Scottish army and the incensed and vengeful Royalists——"

"Master Markham Everard——" began the Cavalier, interrupting him.

"Nay, hush, dear Wildrake," said Everard; "let us not dispute a point on which we cannot agree, and give me leave to go on. I say, since the young man has escaped, Cromwell's offensive and injurious stipulation falls to the ground; and I see not why my uncle and his family should not again enter their own house, under the same terms of connivance as many other Royalists. What may be incumbent on me is different, nor can I determine my course, until I have an interview with the General, which, as I think, will end in his confessing that he threw in this offensive proposal to sound us both. It is much in his manner; for he is blunt, and never sees or feels the punctilious honor which the gallants of the day stretch to such delicacy."

"I'll acquit him of having any punctilio about him," said Wildrake, "either touching honor or honesty. Now, to come back to where we started. Supposing you were not to reside in person at the lodge, and to forbear even visiting there, unless on invitation, when such a thing can be brought about, I tell you frankly, I think your uncle and his daughter might be induced to come back to the lodge, and reside there as usual. At least the clergyman, that worthy old cock, gave me to hope as much."

"He had been hasty in bestowing his confidence," said Everard.

"True," replied Wildrake; "he confided in me at once, for he instantly saw my regard for the church. I thank Heaven I never passed a clergyman in his canonicals without pulling my hat off; and thou knowest, the most desperate duel I ever fought was with young Grayless of the Inner Temple, for taking the wall of the Rev. Dr. Bunce. Ah, I can gain a chaplain's ear instantly. Gadzooks, they know whom they have to trust to in such a one as I."

"Dost thou think, then," said Colonel Everard, "or rather does this clergyman think, that, if they were secure of intrusion from me, the family would return to the lodge, supposing the intruding Commissioners gone, and this noctural disturbance explained and ended?"

"The old knight," answered Wildrake, "may be wrought upon by the doctor to return, if he is secure against intrusion. As for disturbances, the stout old boy, so far as I can learn in two minutes' conversation, laughs at all this turmoil as the work of mere imagination, the consequence of the remorse of their own evil consciences, and says that goblin or devil was never heard of at Woodstock until it became the residence of such men as they who have now usurped the possession."

"There is more than imagination in it," said Everard. "I have personal reason to know there is some conspiracy carrying on, to render the house untenable by the Commissioners. I acquit my uncle of accession to such a silly trick; but I must see it ended ere I can agree to his and my cousin's residing where such a confederacy exists; for they are likely to be considered as the contrivers of such pranks, be the actual agent who he may."

"With reverence to your better acquaintance with the gentleman, Everard, I should rather suspect the old father of Puritans—I beg your pardon again—has something to do with the business; and if so, Lucifer will never look near the true old knight's beard, nor abide a glance of yonder maiden's innocent blue eyes. I will uphold them as safe as pure gold in a miser's chest."

"Sawest thou aught thyself, which makes thee think thus?"

"Not a quill of the Devil's pinion saw I," replied Wildrake. "He supposes himself too secure of an old Cavalier who must steal, hang, or drown in the long-run, so he gives himself no trouble to look after the assured booty. But I heard the serving-fellows prate of what they had seen and heard; and though their tales were confused enough, yet if there was any truth among them at all, I should say the Devil must have been in the dance. But, halloo! here comes some one upon us. Stand, friend, who art thou?"

"A poor day-laborer in the great work of England—

Joseph Tomkins by name—secretary to a godly and well-endowed leader in this poor Christian army of England, called General Harrison."

"What news, Master Tomkins?" said Everard; "and why are you on the road at this late hour?"

"I speak to the worthy Colonel Everard, as I judge?" said Tomkins; "and truly I am glad of meeting your honor. Heaven knows, I need such assistance as yours. Oh, worthy Master Everard, here has been a sounding of trumpets, and a breaking of vials, and a pouring forth, and——!"

"Prithee, tell me, in brief, what is the matter—whree is thy master—and, in a word, what has happened?"

"My master is close by, parading it in the little meadow, beside the hugeous oak which is called by the name of the late Man; ride but two steps forward, and you may see him walking swiftly to and fro, advancing all the while the naked weapon."

Upon proceeding as directed, but with as little noise as possible, they descried a man, whom of course they concluded must be Harrison, walking to and fro beneath the King's Oak, as a sentinel under arms, but with more wildness of demeanor. The tramp of the horses did not escape his ear; and they heard him call out, as if at the head of the brigade—"Lower pikes against cavalry; here comes Prince Rupert. Stand fast, and you shall turn them aside, as a bull would toss a cur-dog. Lower your pikes still, my hearts, the end secured against your foot—down on your right knee, front rank—spare not for the spoiling of your blue aprons. Ha—Zerobabel—ay, that is the word!"

"In the name of Heaven, about whom or what is he talking?" said Everard; "wherefore does he go about with his weapon drawn?"

"Truly, sir, when aught disturbs my master, General Harrison,* he is something rapt in the spirit, and conceives that he is commanding a reserve of pikes at the great battle of Armageddon; and for his weapon, alack, worthy sir, wherefore should he keep Sheffield steel in calves' leather, when there are fiends to be combated—incarnate fiends on earth, and raging infernal fiends under the earth?"

"This is intolerable," said Everard. "Listen to me, Tomkins. Thou art not now in the pulpit, and I desire none of thy preaching language. I know thou canst speak intelligibly when thou art so minded. Remember, I may

* [Compare p. 133.]

serve or harm thee; and as you hope or fear anything on my part, answer straightforward. What has happened to drive out thy master to the wild wood at this time of night?"

"Forsooth, worthy and honored sir, I will speak with the precision I may. True it is, and of verity, that the breath of man, which is in his nostrils, goeth forth and returneth——"

"Hark you, sir," said Colonel Everard, "take care where you ramble in your correspondence with me. You have heard how, at the great battle of Dunbar in Scotland, the General himself held a pistol to the head of Lieutenant Hewcreed, threatening to shoot him through the brain if he did not give up holding forth and put his squadron in line to the front. Take care, sir."

"Verily, the lieutenant then charged with an even and unbroken order," said Tomkins, "and bore a thousand plaids and bonnets over the beach before him into the sea. Neither shall I pretermit or postpone your honor's commands, but speedily obey them, and that without delay."

"Go to, fellow; thou knowest what I would have," said Evarard; "speak at once—I know thou canst if thou wilt. Trusty Tompkins is better known than he thinks for."

"Worthy sir," said Tompkins, in a much less periphrastic style, "I will obey your worship as far as the spirit will permit. Truly, it was not an hour since, when my worshipful master being at table with Master Bibbet and myself, not to mention the worshipful Master Bletson and Colonel Desborough, and behold there was a violent knocking at the gate, as of one in haste. Now, of a certainty, so much had our household been harrassed with witches and spirits, and other objects of sound and sight, that the sentinels could not be brought to abide upon their posts without doors, and it was only by provision of beef and strong liquors that we were able to maintain a guard of three men in the hall, who nevertheless ventured not to open the door, lest they should be surprised with some of the goblins wherewith their imaginations were overwhelmed. And they heard the knocking, which increased until it seemed that the door was wellnigh about to be beaten down. Worthy Master Bibbet was a little overcome with liquor, as is his fashion, good man, about this time of the evening, not that he is in the least given to ebriety, but simply, that since the Scottish campaign he hath had a perpetual ague, which obliges him so to nourish his frame against the damps of the night; wherefore, as it is well known to your honor that I discharge the office of a faithful servant, as well to Major-General Harrison and the other Commissioners, as to my just and lawful master, Colonel Desborough——"

"I know all that. And now that thou art trusted by both, I pray to Heaven thou mayst merit the trust," said Colonel Everard.

"And devoutly do I pray," said Tomkins, "that your worshipful prayers may be answered with favor; for certainly to be, and to be called and entitled, Honest Joe and Trusty Tomkins is to me more than ever would be an earl's title, were such things to be granted anew in this regenerated government."

"Well, go on—go on; or if thou dalliest much longer, I will make bold to dispute the article of your honesty. I like short tales, sir, and doubt what is told with a long unnecessary train of words."

"Well, good sir, be not hasty. As I said before, the doors rattled till you would have thought the knocking was reiterated in every room of the palace. The bell rung out for company, though we could not find that any one tolled the clapper, and the guards left off their firelocks merely because they knew not what better to do. So, Master Bibbet being, as I said, unsusceptible of his duty, I went down with my poor rapier to the door, and demanded who was there; and I was answered in a voice which, I must say, was much like another voice, that it was one wanting Major-General Harrison. So, as it was then late, I answered mildly that General Harrison was betaking himself to his rest, and that any who wished to speak to him must return on the morrow morning, for that, after nightfall, the door of the palace, being in the room of a garrison, would be opened to no one. So the voice replied, and bid me open directly, without which he would blow the folding-leaves of the door into the middle of the hall. And therewithal the noise recommenced, that we thought the house would have fallen; and I was in some measure constrained to open the door, even like a besieged garrison which can hold out no longer."

"By my honor, and it was stoutly done of you, I must say," said Wildrake, who had been listening with much interest. "I am a bold daredevil enough, yet when I had two inches of oak plank between the actual fiend and me, hang him that would demolish the barrier between us, say I. I would as soon, when aboard, bore a hole in the ship and let in the waves ; for you know we always compare the Devil to the deep sea.'

"Prithee, peace, Wildrake," said Everard, "and let him go on with his history. Well, and what saw'st thou when the door was opened? The great Devil with his horns and claws thou wilt say, no doubt?"

"No, sir, I will say nothing but what is true. When I undid the door, one man stood there, and he, too, seeming a man of no extraordinary appearance. He was wrapped in a taffeta cloak, of a scarlet color, and with a red lining. He seemed as if he might have been in his time a very handsome man, but there was something of paleness and sorrow in his face ; a long love-lock and long hair he wore, even after the abomination of the Cavaliers, and the unloveliness, as learned Master Prynne well termed it, of love-locks ; a jewel in his ear ; a blue scarf over his shoulder, like a military commander for the King ; and a hat with a white plume, bearing a peculiar hatband."

"Some unhappy officer of Cavaliers, of whom so many are in hiding, and seeking shelter through the country," briefly replied Everard.

"True, worthy sir—right as a judicious ex-position. But there was something about this man, if he was a man, whom I, for one could not look upon without trembling ; nor the musketeers who were in the hall, without betraying much alarm, and swallowing, as they themselves will aver, the very bullets which they had in their mouths for loading their carbines and muskets. Nay, the wolf and deer-dogs, that are the fiercest of their kind, fled from this visitor, and crept into holes and corners, moaning and wailing in a low and broken tone. He came into the middle of the hall, and still he seemed no more than an ordinary man, only somewhat fantastically dressed, in a doublet of black velvet pinked upon scarlet satin under his cloak, a jewel in his ear, with large roses in his shoes, and a kerchief in his hand, which he sometimes pressed against his left side."

"Gracious Heaven!" said Wildrake, coming close up to Everard, and whispering in his ear, with accents which terror rendered tremulous (a mood of mind most unusual to the daring man who seemed now overcome by it), "it must have been poor Dick Robison the player, in the very dress in which I have seen him play Philaster—ay, and drunk a jolly bottle with him after it at the Mermaid! I remember how many frolics we had together, and all his little fantastic fashions. He served for his old master, Charles, in Mohun's troop, and was murdered by this butcher's dog, as I have heard, after surrender, at the battle of Naseby field."

"Hush! I have heard of the deed!" said Everard; "for God's sake hear the man to an end. Did this visitor speak to thee, my friend?"

"Yes, sir, in a pleasing tone of voice, but somewhat fanciful in the articulation, and like one who is speaking to an audience as from a bar or a pulpit, more than in the voice of ordinary men or ordinary matters. He desired to see Major-General Harrison."

"He did! and you," said Everard, infected by the spirit of the time, which, as is well known, leaned to credulity upon all matters of supernatural agency—"what did you do?"

"I went up to the parlor and related that such a person inquired for him. He started when I told him, and eagerly desired to know the man's dress; but no sooner did I mention his dress, and the jewel in his ear, than he said, "Begone!" tell him I will not admit him to speech of me. Say that I defy him, and will make my defiance good at the great battle in the valley of Armageddon, when the voice of the angel shall call all fowls which fly under the face of heaven to feed on the flesh of the captain and the soldier, the war-horse and his rider. Say to the Evil One, I have power to appeal our conflict even till that day, and that in the front of that fearful day he will again meet with Harrison." I went back with this answer to the stranger, and his face was writhed into such a deadly frown as a mere human brow hath seldom worn. "Return to him," he said, "and say it is MY HOUR; and that if he come not instantly down to speak with me, I will mount the stairs to him. Say that I COMMAND him to descend, by the token, that on the field of Naseby, *he did not the work negligently*."

"I have heard," whispered Wildrake, who felt more and more strongly the contagion of superstition, "that these words were blasphemously used by Harrison when he shot my poor friend Dick."

"What happened next?" said Everard. "See that thou speakest the truth!"

"As gospel unexpounded by a steeple-man," said the Independent; "yet truly it is but little I have to say. I saw my master come down, with a blank yet resolved air; and when he entered the hall and saw the stranger, he made a pause. The other waved on him as if to follow, and walked out at the portal. My worthy patron seemed as if he were about to follow, yet again paused, when this visitant, be he man or fiend, re-entered and said, "Obey thy doom."

" 'By pathless march, by greenwood tree,
It is thy weird to follow me—
To follow me through the ghastly moonlight—
To follow me through the shadows of night—
To follow me, comrade, still art thou bound.
I conjure thee by the unstanched wound—
I conjure thee by the last words I spoke,
When the body slept and the spirit awoke,
In the very last pangs of the deadly stroke.' "

So saying, he stalked out, and my master followed him into the wood. I followed also at a distance, But when I came up, my master was alone, and bearing himself as you now behold him."

"Thou hast had a wonderful memory, friend," said the colonel, coldly, "to remember these rhymes in a single recitation: there seems something of practise in all this."

"A single recitation, my honored sir!" exclaimed the Independent. "Alack, the rhyme is seldom out of my poor master's mouth, when, as sometimes haps, he is less triumphant in his wrestles with Satan. But it was the first time I ever heard it uttered by another; and, to say the truth, he ever seems to repeat it unwillingly, as a child after his pedagogue, and as it was not indited by his own head, as the Psalmist saith."

"It is singular," said Everard. "I have heard and read that the spirits of the slaughtered have a strange power over the slayer; but I am astonished to have it insisted upon that there may be truth in such tales. Roger Wildrake—what art thou afraid of man? why dost thou shift thy place thus?"

"Fear! it is not fear—it is hate, deadly hate. I see the murderer of poor Dick before me, and—see, he throws himself into a posture of fence. Sa—sa—say'st thou, brood of a butcher's mastiff? thou shalt not want an antagonist."

Ere any one could stop him, Wildrake threw aside his cloak, drew his sword, and almost with a single bound cleared the distance betwixt him and Harrison, and crossed swords with the latter, as he stood brandishing his weapon, as if in immediate expectation of an assailant. Accordingly, the republican general was not for an instant taken at unawares, but the moment the swords clashed, he shouted, "Ha! I feel thee now, thou hast come in body at last.

Welcome—welcome! The sword of the Lord and of Gideon!"

"Part them—part them," cried Everard, as he and Tomkins, at first astonished at the suddenness of the affray, hastened to interfere. Everard, seizing on the Cavalier, drew him forcibly backwards, and Tomkins contrived, with risk and difficulty, to master Harrison's sword, while the general exclaimed, "Ha! two to one—two to one! thus fight demons."

Wildrake, on his side, swore a dreadful oath, and added, "Markham, you have canceled every obligation I owed you: they are all out of sight—gone, d—n me!"

"You have indeed acquitted these obligations rarely," said Everard. "Who knows how this affair shall be explained and answered?"

"I will answer it with my life," said Wildrake.

"Good now, be silent," said Tomkins, "and let me manage. It shall be so ordered that the good general shall never know that he hath encountered with a mortal man; only let that man of Moab put his sword into the scabbard's rest and be still."

"Wildrake, let me entreat thee to sheathe thy sword," said Everard, "else, on my life, thou must turn it against me."

"No, 'fore George, not so mad as that neither; but I'll have another day with him."

"Thou, another day!" exclaimed Harrison, whose eye had still remained fixed on the spot where he found such palpable resistance. "Yes, I know thee well; day by day, week by week, thou makest the same idle request, for thou knowest that my heart quivers at thy voice. But my hand trembles not when opposed to thine: the spirit is willing to the combat, if the flesh be weak when opposed to that which is not of the flesh."

"Now, peace all, for Heaven's sake," said the steward Tomkins: then added, addressing his master, "There is no one here, if it please your Excellency, but Tomkins and the worthy Colonel Everard."

General Harrison, as sometimes happens in cases of partial insanity (that is, supposing his to have been a case of mental delusion), though firmly and entirely persuaded of the truth of his own visions, yet was not willing to speak on the subject to those who, he knew, would regard them as imaginary. Upon this occasion, he assumed the appearance of perfect ease and composure, after the violent agitatation he had just manifested, in a manner which showed how anxious he was to disguise his real feelings from Everard, whom he considered as unlikely to participate them.

He saluted the colonel with profound ceremony, and talked of the fineness of the evening, which had summoned him forth of the lodge, to take a turn in the park and enjoy the favorable weather. He then took Everard by the arm, and walked back with him towards the lodge, Wildrake and Tomkins following close behind and leading the horses. Everard, desirous to gain some light on these mysterious incidents, endeavored to come on the subject more than once, by a mode of interrogation which Harrison (for madmen are very often unwilling to enter on the subject of their mental delusion) parried with some skill, or addressed himself for aid to his steward Tomkins, who was in the habit of being voucher for his master upon all occasions, which led to Desborough's ingenious nickname of Fibbet.

"And wherefore had you your sword drawn, my worthy general," said Everard, "when you were only on an evening walk of pleasure?"

"Truly, excellent colonel, these are times when men must watch with their loins girded, and their lights burning, and their weapons drawn. The day draweth nigh, believe me or not as you will, that men must watch least they be found naked and unarmed, when the seven trumpets shall sound, 'Boot and saddle'; and the pipes of Jezer shall strike up, 'Horse and away.'"

"True, good general; but methought I saw you making passes even now as if you were fighting?" said Everard.

"I am of a strange fantasy, friend Everard," answered Harrison; "and when I walk alone, and happen, as but now, to have my weapon drawn, I sometimes, for exercise' sake, will practise a thrust against such a tree as that. It is a silly pride men have in the use of weapons. I have been accounted a master of fence, and have fought prizes when I was unregenerated, and before I was called to do my part in the great work, entering as a trooper into our victorious general's first regiment of horse."

"But, methought," said Everard, "I heard a weapon clash with yours?'

"How! a weapon clash with my sword? How could that be, Tomkins?"

"Truly, sir," said Tomkins, "it must have been a bough of the tree; they have them of all kinds here, and your honor may have pushed against one of them which the

Brazilians call iron-wood, a block of which, being struck with a hammer, saith Purchas in his *Pilgrimage,* ringeth like an anvil."

"Truly, it may be so," said Harrison; "for those rulers who are gone assembled in this their abode of pleasure many strange trees and plants, though they gathered not of the fruit of that tree which beareth twelve manner of fruits, or of those leaves which are for the healing of the nations."

Everard pursued his investigation; for he was struck with the manner in which Harrison evaded his question, and the dexterity with which he threw his transcendental and fanatical notions, like a sort of veil, over the darker visions excited by remorse and conscious guilt.

"But," said he, "if I may trust my eyes and ears I cannot but still think that you had a real antagonist. Nay, I am sure I saw a fellow, in a dark-colored jerkin, retreat though the wood."

"Did you?" said Harrison, with a tone of surprise, while his voice faltered in spite of him. "Who could he be? Tomkins, did you see the fellow Colonel Everard talks of with the napkin in his hand—the bloody napkin which he always pressed to his side?"

This last expression, in which Harrison gave a mark different from that which Everard had assigned, but corresponding to Tomkins' original description of the supposed specter, had more effect on Everard in confirming the steward's story than anything he had witnessed or heard. The voucher answered the draft upon him as promptly as usual, that he had seen such a fellow glide past them into the thicket; that he dared to say he was some deer-stealer, for he had heard they were become very audacious.

"Look ye there now, Master Everard," said Harrison, hurrying from the subject. "Is it not time now that we should lay aside our controversies, and join hand in hand to repairing the breaches of our Zion? Happy and contented were I, my excellent friend, to be a treader of mortar, or a bearer of a hod, upon this occasion, under our great leader, with whom Providence has gone forth in this great national controversy; and truly, so devoutly do I hold by our excellent and victorious General Oliver—whom Heaven long preserve!—that were he to command me, I should not scruple to pluck forth of his high place the man whom they call Speaker, even as I lent a poor hand to pluck down the man whom they called King. Wherefore, as I know your judgment holdeth with mine on this matter, let me urge unto you lovingly, that we may act as brethren, and build up the breaches and re-establish the bulwarks of our English Zion, whereby we shall be doubtless chosen as pillars and buttresses, under our excellent Lord General, for supporting and sustaining the same, and endowed with proper revenues and incomes, both "spiritual and temporal, to serve as a pedestal on which we may stand, seeing that otherwise our foundation will be on the loose sand. Nevertheless," continued he, his mind again diverging from his views of temporal ambition into his visions of the Fifth Monarchy, "these things are but vanity in respect of the opening of the book which is sealed; for all things approach speedily towards lightning and thundering, and unloosing of the great dragon from the bottomless pit, wherein he is claimed."

With this mingled strain of earthly politics and fanatical prediction, Harrison so overpowered Colonel Everard as to leave him no time to urge him farther on the particular circumstances of his nocturnal skirmish, concerning which it is plain he had no desire to be interrogated. They now reached the lodge of Woodstock.

CHAPTER XV

Now the wasted brands do glow,
  While the screech-owl, sounding loud,
Puts the wretch that lies in woe
  In remembrance of a shroud.
Now it is the time of night
  That the graves, all gaping wide,
Every one lets out its sprite,
  In the church-way paths to glide.
Midsummer Night's Dream.

BEFORE the gate of the palace the guards were now doubled. Everard demanded the reason of this from the corporal, whom he found in the hall with his soldiers, sitting or sleeping around a great fire, maintained at the expense of the carved chairs and benches, with fragments of which it was furnished.

"Why, verily," answered the man, "the *corps de garde*, as your worship says, will be harassed to pieces by such duty; nevertheless, fear hath gone abroad among us, and no man will mount guard alone. We have drawn in, however, one or two of our outposts from Banbury and elsewhere, and we are to have a relief from Oxford to-morrow."

Everard continued minute inquiries concerning the sentinels that were posted within as well as without the lodge; and found that, as they had been stationed under the eye of Harrison himself, the rules of prudent discipline had been exactly observed in the distribution of the poste. There remained nothing, therefore, for Colonel Everard to do but, remembering his own adventure of the evening, to recommend that an additional sentinel should be placed, with a companion, if judged indispensable, in that vestibule, or ante-room, from which the long gallery where he had met with the rencontre and other suits of apartments diverge. The corporal respectfully promised all obedience to his. orders. The serving-men, being called, appeared also in double force. Everard demanded to know whether the Commissioners had gone to bed, or whether he could get speech with them.

"They are in their bedroom, forsooth," replied one of the fellows; "but I think they be not yet undressed."

"What!" said Everard, "are Colonel Desborough and Master Bletson both in the same sleeping apartment?"

"Their honors have so chosen it," said the man; "and their honors' secretaries remain upon guard all night."

"It is the fashion to double guards all over the house," said Wildrake. "Had I a glimpse of a tolerably good-looking housemaid now, I should know how to fall into the fashion."

"Peace, fool!" said Everard. "And where are the Mayor and Master Holdenough."

"The Mayor has returned to the borough on horseback, behind the trooper who goes to Oxford for the reinforcement; and the man at the steeple-house hath quartered himself in the chamber which Colonel Desborough had last night, being that in which he is most likely to meet the —— your honor understands. The lord pity us, we are a harrassed family."

"And where be General Harrison's knaves," said Tomkins, "that they do not marshal him to his apartment?"

"Here—here—here, Master Tomkins," said three fellows, pressing forward, with the same consternation on their faces which seemed to pervade the whole inhabitants of Woodstock.

"Away with you, then," said Tomkins. "Speak not to his worship; you see he is not in the humor."

"Indeed," observed Colonel Everard, "he looks singularly wan; his features seem writhen as by a palsy stroke; and though he was talking so fast while we came along, he hath not opened his mouth since we came to the light."

"It is his manner after such visitations," said Tomkins. "Give his honor your arms, Zedekiah and Jonathan, to lead him off. I will follow instantly. You, Nicodemus, tarry to wait upon me: it is not well walking alone in this mansion."

"Master Tomkins," said Everard, "I have heard of you often as a sharp, intelligent man; tell me fairly, are you in earnest afraid of anything supernatural haunting this house?"

"I would be loth to run the chance, sir," said Tomkins, very gravely; "by looking on my worshipful master, you may form a guess how the living look after they have spoken with the dead." He bowed low, and took his leave.

Everard proceeded to the chamber which the two remaining Commissioners had, for comfort's sake, chosen to inhabit in company. They were preparing for bed as he went into their apartment. Both started as the door opened; both rejoiced when they saw it was only Everard who entered.

"Harkye hither," said Bletson, pulling him aside, "sawest thou ever ass equal to Desborough? The fellow is as big as an ox and as timorous as a sheep; he has insisted on my sleeping here to protect him. Shall we have a merry night on't, ha? We will, if thou will take the third bed, which was prepared for Harrison; but he is gone out, like a mooncalf, to look for the valley of Armageddon in the park of Woodstock."

"General Harrison has returned with me but now," said Everard.

"Nay but, as I shall live, he comes not into our apartment," said Desborough, overhearing his answer. "No man that has been supping, for aught I know, with the Devil has a right to sleep among Christian folk."

"He does not propose to," said Everard; "he sleeps, as I understand, apart—and alone."

"Not quite alone, I daresay," said Desborough, "for Harrison hath a sort of attraction for goblins: they fly round him like moths about a candle. But, I prithee, good Everard, do thou stay with us. I know not how it is, but although thou hast not thy religion always in thy mouth, nor speakest many hard words about it, like Harrison, nor makest long preachments, like a certain most honorable relation of mine who shall be nameless, yet somehow I feel myself safer in thy company than with any of them. As for this Bletson, he is such a mere blasphemer, that I fear the Devil will carry him away ere morning."

"Did you ever hear such a paltry coward?" said Bletson apart to Everard. "Do tarry, however, mine honored colonel. I know your zeal to assist the distressed, and you see Desborough is in that predicament, that he will require near him more than one good example to prevent him thinking of ghosts and fiends."

"I am sorry I cannot oblige you, gentlemen," said Everard; "but I have settled my mind to sleep in Victor Lee's apartment, so I wish you good-night; and if you would repose without disturbance, I would advise that you commend yourselves, during the watches of the night, to Him unto whom night is even as mid-day. I had intended to have spoken with you this evening on the subject of my being here; but I will defer the conference till to-morrow, when, I think, I will be able to show you excellent reasons for leaving Woodstock."

"We have seen plenty such already," said Desborough. "For one, I came here to serve the estate, with some moderate advantage doubtless to myself for my trouble; but if I am set upon my head again to-night, as I was the night before, I would not stay longer to gain a king's crown, for I am sure my neck would be unfitted to bear the weight of it."

"Good-night," exclaimed Everard, and was about to go, when Bletson again pressed close, and whispered to him, "Hark thee, colonel, you know my friendship for thee—I do implore thee to leave the door of thy apartment open, that, if thou meetest with any disturbance, I may hear thee call, and be with thee upon the very instant. Do this, dear Everard—my fears for thee will keep me awake else; for I know that, notwithstanding your excellent sense, you entertain some of those superstitious ideas which we suck in with our mother's milk, and which constitute the ground of our fears in situations like the present; therefore, leave thy door open, if you love me, that you may have ready assistance from me in case of need."

"My master," said Wildrake, "trusts, first, in his Bible, sir, and then in his good sword. He has no idea that the Devil can be baffled by the charm of two men lying in one room, still less that the Foul Fiend can be argued out of existence by the nullifidians of the Rota."

Everard seized his imprudent friend by the collar and dragged him off as he was speaking, keeping fast hold of him till they were both in the chamber of Victor Lee, where they had slept on a former occasion. Even then he continued to hold Wildrake, until the servant had arranged the lights and was dismissed from the room; then letting him go, addressed him with the upbraiding question, "Art thou not a prudent and sagacious person, who in times like these seek'st every opportunity to argue yourself into a broil, or embroil yourself in an argument? Out on you!"

"Ay, out on me, indeed," said the Cavalier—"out on me for a poor tame-spirited creature, that submits to be bandied about in this manner by a man who is neither better born nor better bred than myself. I tell thee, Mark, you make an unfair use of your advantages over me. Why will you not let me go from you and live and die after my own fashion?"

"Because, before we had been a week separate, I should hear of your dying after the fashion of a dog. Come, my good friend, what madness was it in thee to fall foul on

Harrison, and then to enter into useless argument with Bletson?"

"Why, we are in the Devil's house, I think, and I would willingly give the landlord his due wherever I travel. To have sent him Harrison, or Bletson now, just as a lunch to stop his appetite, till Crom——"

"Hush! stone walls have ears," said Everard, looking around him. "Here stands thy night-drink. Look to thy arms, for we must be as careful as if the Avenger of Blood were behind us. Yonder is thy bed; and I, as thou seest, have one prepared in the parlor. The door only divides us."

"Which I will leave open, in case thou shouldst halloo for assistance, as yonder nullifidian hath it. But how hast thou got all this so well put in order, good patron?"

"I gave the steward Tomkins notice of my purpose to sleep here."

"A strange fellow that," said Wildrake, "and, as I judge, has taken measure of every one's foot: all seems to pass through his hands."

"He is, I have understood," replied Everard, "one of the men formed by the times—has a ready gift of preaching and expounding, which keeps him in high terms with the Independents, and recommends himself to the more moderate people by his intelligence and activity."

"Has his sincerity ever been doubted?" said Wildrake.

"Never that I heard of," said the colonel; "on the contrary, he has been familiarly called Honest Joe and Trusty Tomkins. For my part, I believe his sincerity has always kept pace with his interest. But come, finish thy cup, and to bed. What, all emptied at one draught?"

"Adzookers, yes—my vow forbids me to make two on't; but, never fear, the nightcap will only warm my brain, not clog it. So, man or devil, give me notice if you are disturbed, and rely on me in a twinkling." So saying, the Cavalier retreated into his separate apartment; and Colonel Everard, taking off the most cumbrous part of his dress, lay down in his hose and doublet, and composed himself to rest.

He was awakened from sleep by a slow and solemn strain of music, which died away as at a distance. He started up and felt for his arms, which he found close beside him. His temporary bed being without curtains, he could look around him without difficulty; but as there remained in the chimney only a few red embers of the fire, which he had arranged before he went asleep, it was impossible he could discern anything. He felt, therefore, in spite of his natural courage, that undefined and thrilling species of tremor which attends a sense that danger is near, and an uncertainty concerning its cause and character. Reluctant as he was to yield belief to supernatural occurrences, we have already said he was not absolutely incredulous; as perhaps, even in this more sceptical age, there are many fewer complete and absolute infidels on this particular than give themselves out for such. Uncertain whether he had not dreamed of these sounds which seemed yet in his ears, he was unwilling to risk the raillery of his friend by summoning him to his assistance. He sat up, therefore, in his bed, not without experiencing that nervous agitation to which brave men as well as cowards are subject; with this difference, that the one sinks under it like the vine under the hailstorm, and the other collects his energies to shake it off, as the cedar of Lebanon is said to elevate its boughs to disperse the snow which accumulates upon them.

The story of Harrison, in his own absolute despite, and notwithstanding a secret suspicion which he had of trick or connivance, returned on his mind at this dead and solitary hour. Harrison, he remembered, had described the vision by a circumstance of its appearance different from that which his own remark had been calculated to suggest to the mind of the visionary: that bloody napkin, always pressed to the side, was then a circumstance present either to his bodily eye or to that of his agitated imagination. Did, then, the murdered revisit the living haunts of those who had forced them from the stage with all their sins unaccounted for? And if they did, might not the same permission authorize other visitations of a similar nature—to warn, to instruct, to punish? "Rash are they," was his conclusion, "and credulous, who receive as truth every tale of the kind; but no less rash may it be to limit the power of the Creator over the works which He has made, and to suppose that, by the permission of the Author of nature, the laws of nature may not, in peculiar cases and for high purposes, be temporarily suspended."

While these thoughts passed through Everard's mind, feelings unknown to him, even when he stood first on the rough and perilous edge of battle, gained ground upon him. He feared he knew not what; and where an open and discernible peril would have drawn out his courage, the absolute uncertainty of his situation increased his sense of the danger. He felt an almost irresistible desire to spring from his bed and heap fuel on the dying embers, expecting by the blaze to see some strange sight in his chamber. He was also strongly tempted to awaken Wildrake; but shame, stronger than fear itself, checked these impulses. What! should it be thought that Markham Everard, held one of the best soldiers who had drawn a sword in this sad war—Markham Everard, who had obtained such distinguished rank in the army of the Parliament, though so young in years, was afraid of remaining by himself in a twilight-room at midnight? It never should be said.

This was, however, no charm for his unpleasant current of thought. There rushed on his mind the various traditions of Victor Lee's chamber, which, though he had often despised them as vague, unauthenticated, and inconsistent rumors, engendered by ancient superstition and transmitted from generation to generation by loquacious credulity, had yet something in them which did not tend to allay the present unpleasant state of his nerves. Then, when he recollected the events of that very afternoon—the weapon pressed against his throat, and the strong arm which threw him backward on the floor—if the remembrance served to contradict the idea of flitting phantoms and unreal daggers, it certainly induced him to believe that there was in some part of this extensive mansion a party of Cavaliers, or Malignants, harbored, who might arise in the night, overpower the guards, and execute upon them all, but on Harrison in particular, as one of the regicide judges, that vengeance which was so eagerly thirsted for by the attached followers of the slaughtered monarch.

He endeavored to console himself on this subject by the number and position of the guards, yet still was dissatisfied with himself for not having taken yet more exact precautions, and for keeping an extorted promise of silence which might consign so many of his party to the danger of assassination. These thoughts, connected with his military duties, awakened another train of reflections. He bethought himself, that all he could now do was to visit the sentries and ascertain that they were awake, alert, on the watch, and so situated that in time of need they might be ready to support each other. "This better befits me," he thought, "than to lie here like a child, frightening myself with the old woman's legend which I have laughed at when a boy. What although old Victor Lee was a sacrilegious man, as common report goes, and brewed ale in the font which he brought from the ancient palace of Holyrood, while church and building were in flames? And what although his eldest son was when a child scalded to death in the same vessel? How many churches have been demolished since his time? How many fonts desecrated? So many, indeed, that, were the vengeance of Heaven to visit such aggressions in a supernatural manner, no corner in England, no, not the most petty parish church, but would have its apparition. Tush, these are idle fancies, unworthy, especially, to be entertained by those educated to believe that sancitity resides in the intention and the act, not in the buildings or fonts, or the form of worship,"

As thus he called together the articles of his Calvinistic creed, the bell of the great clock (a token seldom silent in such narratives) tolled three, and was immediately followed by the hoarse call of the sentinels through vault and gallery, upstairs and beneath, challenging and answering each other with the usual watchword, "All's well." Their voices mingled with the deep boom of the bell, yet ceased before that was silent, and when they had died away, the tingling echo of the prolonged knell was scarcely audible. Ere yet that last distant tingling had finally subsided into silence, it seemed as if it again was awakened; and Everard could hardly judge at first whether a new echo had taken up the falling cadence, or whether some other and separate sound was disturbing anew the silence to which the deep knell had, as its voice ceased, consigned the ancient mansion and the woods around it.

But the doubt was soon cleared up. The musical tones, which had mingled with the dying echoes of the knell, seemed at first to prolong, and afterwards to survive, them. A wild strain of melody, beginning at a distance, and growing louder as it advanced, seemed to pass from room to room, from cabinet to gallery, from hall to bower, through the deserted and dishonored ruins of the ancient residence of so many sovereigns; and, as it approached, no soldier gave alarm, nor did any of the numerous guests of various degrees who spent an unpleasant and terrified night in that ancient mansion seem to dare to announce to each other the inexplicable cause of apprehension.

Everard's excited state of mind did not permit him to be so passive. The sounds approached so nigh, that it seemed they were performing in the very next apartment a solemn service for the dead, when he gave the alarm, by calling loudly to his trusty attendant and friend Wildrake, who slumbered in the next chamber with only a door betwixt them, and even that ajar.

"Wildrake—Wildrake! Up—up! Dost thou not hear the alarm?"

There was no answer from Wildrake, though the musical sounds, which now rung through the apartment as if the performers had actually been within its precincts, would have been sufficient to awaken a sleeping person, even without the shout of his comrade and patron.

"Alarm, Roger Wildrake—alarm!" again called Everard, getting out of bed and grasping his weapons. "Get a light, and cry alarm!"

There was no answer. His voice died away as the sound of the music seemed also to die; and the same soft sweet voice, which still to his thinking resembled that of Alice Lee, was heard in his apartment, and, as he thought, at no distance from him.

"Your comrade will not answer," said the low soft voice. "Those only hear the alarm whose consciences feel the call."

"Again this mummery!" said Everard. "I am better armed than I was of late; and but for the sound of that voice, the speaker had bought his trifling dear."

It was singular, we may observe in passing, that the instant the distinct sounds of the human voice were heard by Everard, all idea of supernatural interference was at an end, and the charm by which he had been formerly fettered appeared to be broken; so much is the influence of imaginary or superstitious terror dependent, so far as respects strong judgments at least, upon what is vague or ambiguous; and so readily do distinct tones and express ideas bring such judgments back to the current of ordinary life.

The voice returned answer, as addressing his thoughts as well as his words. "We laugh at the weapons thou thinkest should terrify us. Over the guardians of Woodstock they have no power. Fire, if thou wilt, and try the effect of thy weapons. But know, it is not our purpose to harm thee: thou art of a falcon breed, and noble in thy disposition, though, unreclaimed and ill nurtured, thou hauntest with kites and carrion crows. Wing thy flight from hence on the morrow, for, if thou tarriest with the bats, owls, vultures and ravens which have thought to nestle here, thou wilt inevitably share their fate. Away, then, that these halls may be swept and garnished for the reception of those who have a better right to inhabit them."

Everard answered in a raised voice. "Once more I

warn you, think not to defy me in vain. I am no child to be frightened by goblins' tales, and no coward, armed as I am, to be alarmed at the threats of banditti. If I give you a moment's indulgence, it is for the sake of dear and misguided friends, who may be concerned with this dangerous gambol. Know, I can bring a troop of soldiers round the castle, who will search its most inward recesses for the author of this audacious frolic; and if that search should fail, it will cost but a few barrels of gunpowder to make the mansion a heap of ruins, and bury under them the authors of such an ill-judged pastime."

"You speak proudly, sir colonel," said another voice, similar to that harsher and stronger tone by which he had been addressed in the gallery; "try your courage in this direction."

"You should not dare me twice," said Colonel Everard, "had I a glimpse of light to take aim by."

As he spoke, a sudden gleam of light was thrown with a brilliancy which almost dazzled the speaker, showing distinctly a form somewhat resembling that of Victor Lee, as represented in his picture, holding in one hand a lady completely veiled, and in the other his leading staff or truncheon. Both figures were animated, and, as it appeared, standing within six feet of him.

"Were it not for the woman," said Everard, "I would not be thus mortally dared."

"Spare not for the female form, but do your worst," replied the same voice. "I defy you."

"Repeat your defiance when I have counted thrice," said Everard, "and take the punishment of your insolence. Once—I have cocked my pistol. Twice—I never missed my aim. By all that is sacred, I fire if you do not withdraw. When I pronounce the next number, I will shoot you dead where you stand. I am yet unwilling to shed blood: I give you another chance of flight, once—twice—THRICE!"

Everard aimed at the bosom, and discharged his pistol. The figure waved its arm in an attitude of scorn; and a loud laugh arose, during which the light, as gradually growing weaker, glanced and glimmered upon the apparition of the aged knight, and then disappeared. Everard's life-blood ran cold to his heart. "Had he been of human mold," he thought, "the bullet must have pierced him, but I have neither will nor power to fight with supernatural beings."

The feeling of oppression was now so strong as to be actually sickening. He groped his way, however, to the fireside, and flung on the embers, which were yet gleaming, a handful of dry fuel. It presently blazed, and afforded him light to see the room in every direction. He looked cautiously, almost timidly, around, and half expected some horrible phantom to become visible. But he saw nothing save the old furniture, the reading desk, and other articles, which had been left in the same state as when Sir Henry Lee departed. He felt an uncontrollable desire, mingled with much repugnance, to look at the portrait of the ancient knight, which the form he had seen so strongly resembled. He hesitated betwixt the opposing feelings, but at length snatched, with desperate resolution, the taper which he had extinguished, and relighted it, ere the blaze of the fuel had again died away. He held it up to the ancient portrait of Victor Lee, and gazed on it with eager curiosity, not unmingled with fear. Almost the childish terror of his early days returned, and he thought the severe pale eye of the ancient warrior followed his, and menaced him with its displeasure. And although he quickly argued himself out of such an absurd belief, yet the mixed feelings of his mind were expressed in words that seemed half addressed to the ancient portrait.

"Soul of my mother's ancestor," he said, "be it for weal or for woe, by designing men or by supernatural beings, that these ancient halls are disturbed, I am resolved to leave them on the morrow."

"I rejoice to hear it, with all my soul," said a voice behind him.

He turned, saw a tall figure in white, with a sort of turban upon its head, and dropping the candle in the exertion, instantly grappled with it.

"*Thou* at least are palpable," he said.

"Palpable!" answered he whom he grasped so strongly. "'Sdeath, methinks you might know that without the risk of choking me; and if you loose me not, I'll show you that two can play at the game of wrestling."

"Roger Wildrake!" said Everard, letting the Cavalier loose, and stepping back.

"Roger Wildrake? ay, truly. Did you take me for Roger Bacon, come to help you to raise the Devil, for the place smells of sulphur consumedly?"

"It is the pistol I fired. Did you not hear it?"

"Why, yes, it was the first thing waked me, for that nightcap which I pulled on made me sleep like a dormouse. Pshaw, I feel my brains giddy with it yet."

"And wherefore came you not on the instant? I never needed help more."

"I come as fast as I could," answered Wildrake; "but it was some time ere I got my senses collected, for I was dreaming of that cursed field at Naseby; and then the door of my room was shut, and hard to open, till I played the locksmith with my foot."

"How! it was open when I went to bed," said Everard.

"It was locked when I came out of bed, though," said Wildrake, "and I marvel you heard me not when I forced it open."

"My mind was occupied otherwise," said Everard.

"Well," said Wildrake, "but what has happened? Here am I bolt upright, and ready to fight, if this yawning fit will give me leave. Mother Redcap's mightiest is weaker than I drank last night, by a bushel to a barleycorn. I have quaffed the very elixir of malt. Ha—yaw."

"And some opiate besides, I should think," said Everard.

"Very like—very like; less than the pistol-shot would not wake me—even me, who with but an ordinary grace-cup sleep as lightly as a maiden on the first of May, when she watches for the earliest beam to go to gather dew. But what are you about to do next?"

"Nothing," answered Everard.

"Nothing?" said Wildrake, in surprise.

"I speak it," said Colonel Everard, "less for your information than for that of others who may hear me, that I will leave the lodge this morning, and, if it is possible, remove the Commissioners."

"Hark," said Wildrake, "do you not hear some noise, like the distant sound of the applause of a theater? The goblins of the place rejoice in your departure."

"I shall leave Woodstock," said Everard, "to the occupation of my uncle Sir Henry Lee, and his family, if they choose to resume it; not that I am frightened into this as a concession to the series of artifices which have been played off on this occasion, but solely because such was my intention from the beginning. But let me warn," he added, raising his voice—"let me warn the parties concerned in this combination that, though it may pass off successfully on a fool like Desborough, a visionary like Harrison, a coward like Bletson——"

Here a voice distinctly spoke, as standing near them—"Or a wise, moderate, and resolute person like Colonel Everard."

"By Heaven, the voice came from the picture," said Wildrake, drawing his sword; "I will pink his plated armor for him."

"Offer no violence," said Everard, startled at the interruption, but resuming with firmness what he was saying. "Let those engaged be aware that, however this string of artifices may be immediately successful, it must, when closely looked into, be attended with the punishment of all concerned, the total demolition of Woodstock, and the irredeemable downfall of the family of Lee. Let all concerned think of this, and desist in time."

He paused, and almost expected a reply, but none such came.

"It is a very odd thing," said Wildrake; "but—yaw-ha—my brain cannot compass it just now: it whirls round like a toast in a bowl of muscadine. I must sit down—ha-yaw—and discuss it at leisure. Grammercy, good elbow-chair."

So saying, he threw himself, or rather sank gradually, down on a large easy-chair, which had been often pressed by the weight of stout Sir Henry Lee, and in an instant was sound asleep. Everard was far from feeling the same inclination for slumber, yet his mind was relieved of the apprehension of any farther visitation that night; for he considered his treaty to evacuate Woodstock as made known to, and accepted in all probability by, those whom the intrusion of the Commissioners had induced to take such singular measures for expelling them. His opinion, which had for a time bent towards a belief in something supernatural in the disturbances, had now returned to the more rational mode of accounting for them by dexterous combination, for which such a mansion as Woodstock afforded as many facilities.

He heaped the hearth with fuel, lighted the candle, and examining poor Wildrake's situation, adjusted him as easily in the chair as he could, the Cavalier stirring his limbs no more than an infant. His situation went far, in his patron's opinion, to infer trick and confederacy, for ghosts have no occasion to drug men's possets. He threw himself on the bed, and while he thought these strange circumstances over, a sweet and low strain of music stole through the chamber, the words "Good-night—good-night—good-night," thrice repeated, each time in a softer and more distant tone, seeming to assure him that the goblins and he were at truce, if not at peace, and that he had no more disturbance to expect that night. He had scarcely the courage to call out a "good-night"; for, after all his conviction of the existence of a trick, it was so well performed as to bring with it a feeling of fear, just like what an audience experience during the performance of a tragic scene, which they knew to be unreal, and which yet effects their passions by its near approach to nature. Sleep overtook him at last, and left him not till broad daylight on the ensuing morning.

CHAPTER XVI

And yonder shines Aurora's harbinger
At whose approach ghosts, wandering here and there,
Troop home to churchyard.

Midsummer Night's Dream.

WITH the fresh air, and the rising of morning, every feeling of the preceding night had passed away from Colonel Everard's mind, excepting wonder how the effects which he had witnessed could be produced. He examined the whole room, sounding both floor and wainscot with his knuckles and cane, but was unable to discern any secret passages; while the door, secured by a strong cross-bolt, and the lock besides, remained as firm as when he had fastened it on the preceding evening. The apparition resembling Victor Lee next called his attention. Ridiculous stories had been often circulated of this figure, or one exactly resembling it, having been met with by night among the waste apartments and corridors of the old palace; and Markham Everard had often heard such in his childhood. He was angry to recollect his own deficiency of courage, and the thrill which he felt on the preceding night when, by confederacy doubtless, such an object was placed before her eyes.

"Surely," he said, "this fit of childish folly could not make me miss my aim: more likely that the bullet had been withdrawn clandestinely from my pistol."

He examined that which was undischarged; he found the bullet in it. He investigated the apartment opposite to the point at which he had fired, and at five feet from the floor, in a direct line between the bedside and the place where the appearances had been seen, a pistol-ball had recently buried itself in the wainscot. He had little doubt, therefore, that he had fired in a just direction; and indeed, to have arrived at the place where it was lodged, the bullet must have passed through the appearance at which he aimed, and proceeded point-blank to the wall beyond. This was mysterious, and induced him to doubt whether the art of witchcraft or conjuration had not been called in to assist the machinations of those daring conspirators, who being themselves mortal, might nevertheless, according to the universal creed of the times, have invoked and obtained assistance from the inhabitants of another world.

His next investigation respected the picture of Victor Lee itself. He examined it minutely as he stood on the floor before it, and compared its pale, shadowy, faintly-traced outlines, its faded colors, the stern repose of the eye, and deathlike pallidness of the countenance with its different aspect on the preceding night, when illuminated by the artificial light which fell upon it, while it left every other part of the room in comparative darkness. The features seemed then to have an unnatural glow, while the rising and falling of the flame in the chimney gave the head and limbs something which resembled the appearance of actual motion. Now, seen by day, it was a mere picture of the hard and ancient school of Holbein; last night, it seemed for the moment something more. Determined to get to the bottom of this contrivance if possible, Everard, by the assistance of a table and chair, examined the portrait still more closely, and endeavored to ascertain the existence of any private spring by which it might be slipped aside—a contrivance not unfrequent in ancient buildings, which usually abounded with means of access and escape, communicated to none but the lords of the castle, or their immediate confidants. But the panel on which Victor Lee was painted was firmly fixed in the wainscoting of the apartment, of which it made a part, and the colonel satisfied himself that it could not have been used for the purprse which he had suspected.

He next aroused his faithful squire Wildrake, who, notwithstanding his deep share of the "blessedness of sleep," had scarce even yet got rid of the effects of the grace-cup of the preceding evening. "It was the reward," according to his own view of the matter, "of his temperance, one single draught having made him sleep more late and more sound than a matter of half a dozen, or from thence to a dozen, pulls would have done, when he was guilty of the enormity of rere-suppers,* and of drinking deep after them."

"Had your temperate draught," said Everard, "been but a thought more strongly seasoned, Wildrake, thou hadst slept so sound that the last trump only could have waked thee."

"And then," answered Wildrake, "I should have waked

* See Note 3.

with a headache, Mark; for I see my modest sip has not exempted me from that epilogue. But let us go forth, and see how the night, which we have passed so strangely, has been spent by the rest of them. I suspect they are all right willing to evacuate Woodstock, unless they have either rested better than we or at least been more lucky in lodgings."

"In that case, I will despatch thee down to Joceline's hut, to negotiate the re-entrance of Sir Henry Lee and his family into their old apartments, where, my interest with the General being joined with the indifferent repute of the place itself, I think they have little chance of being disturbed either by the present or by any new Commissioners."

"But how are they to defend themselves against the fiends, my gallant colonel?" said Wildrake. "Methinks, had I an interest in yonder pretty girl such as thou dost boast, I should be loth to expose her to the terrors of a residence at Woodstock, where these devils—I beg their pardon, for I suppose they hear every word we say—these merry goblins make such gay work from twilight till morning."

"My dear Wildrake," said the colonel, "I, as well as you, believe it possible that our speech may be overheard; but I care not, and will speak my mind plainly. I trust Sir Henry and Alice are not engaged in this silly plot: I cannot reconcile it with the pride of the one, the modesty of the other, or the good sense of both, that any motive could engage them in so strange a conjunction. But the fiends are all of your own political persuasion, Wildrake, all true-blue Cavaliers; and I am convinced that Sir Henry and Alice Lee, though they be unconnected with them, have not the slightest cause to be apprehensive of their goblin machinations. Besides, Sir Henry and Joceline must know every corner about the place: it will be far more difficult to play off any ghostly machinery upon him than upon strangers. But let us to our toilet, and when water and brush have done their work, we will inquire what is next to be done."

"Nay, that wretched Puritan's garb of mine is hardly worth brushing," said Wildrake; "and but for this hundred-weight of rusty iron, with which thou hast bedizened me, I look more like a bankrupt Quaker than anything else. But I'll make *you* as spruce as ever was a canting rogue of your party."

So saying, and humming at the same time the Cavalier tune—

"Though for a time we see Whitehall
With cobwebs hung around the wall,
Yet Heaven shall make amends for all,
When the King shall enjoy his own again."

"Thou forgettest who are without," said Colonel Everard.

"No, I remember who are within," replied his friend. "I only sing to my merry goblins, who will like me all the better for it. Tush, man, the devils are my *bonos socios*, and when I see them, I will warrant they prove such roaring boys as I knew when I served under Lunsford and Goring—fellows with long nails that nothing escaped, bottomless stomachs that nothing filled, mad for pillaging, ranting, drinking, and fighting, sleeping rough on the trenches, and dying stubbornly in their boots. Ah! those merry days are gone! Well, it is the fashion to make a grave face on't among Cavaliers, and specially the parsons that have lost their tithe-pigs; but I was fitted for the element of the time, and never did or can desire merrier days than I had during that same barbarous, bloody, and unnatural rebellion."

"Thou wert ever a wild sea-bird, Roger, even according to your name, liking the gale better than the calm, the boisterous ocean better than the smooth lake, and your rough, wild struggle against the wind than daily food, ease, and quiet."

"Pshaw! a fig for your smooth lake, and your old woman to feed me with brewer's grains, and the poor drake obliged to come swattering whenever she whistles! Everard, I like to feel the wind rustle against my pinions—now diving, now on the crest of the wave, now in ocean, now in sky; that is the wildrake's joy, my grave one. And in the Civil War so it went with us—down in one county, up in another, beaten to-day, victorious to-morrow, now starving in some barren leaguer, now reveling in a Presbyterian's pantry—his cellars, his plate-chest, his old judicial thumb-ring, his pretty serving-wench, all at command!"

"Hush, friend," said Everard; "remember I hold that persuasion."

"More the pity, Mark—more the pity," said Wildrake; "but, as you say, it is needless talking of it. Let us e'en go and see how your Presbyterian pastor, Mr. Holdenough, has fared, and whether he has proved more able to foil the Foul Fiend than have you his disciple and auditor."

They left the apartment accordingly, and were overwhelmed with the various incoherent accounts of sentinels and others, all of whom had seen or heard something extraordinary in the course of the night. It is needless to describe particularly the various rumors which each contributed to the common stock, with the greater alacrity that in such cases there seems always to be a sort of disgrace in not having seen or suffered as much as others.

The most moderate of the narrators only talked of sounds like the mewing of a cat, or the growling of a dog, especially the squeaking of a pig. They heard also as if it had been nails driven and saws used, and the clashing of fetters, and the rustling of silk gowns, and the notes of music, and in short all sorts of sounds which have nothing to do with each other. Others swore they had smelt savors of various kinds, chiefly bituminous, indicating a Satanic derivation; others did not indeed swear, but protested, to visions of men in armor, horses without heads, asses with horns, and cows with six legs, not to mention black figures, whose cloven hoofs gave plain information what realm they belonged to.

But these strongly-attested cases of nocturnal disturbances among the sentinels had been so general as to prevent alarm and succor on any particular point, so that those who were on duty called in vain on the *corps de garde*, who were trembling on their own post; and an alert enemy might have done complete execution on the whole garrison. But amid this general *alerté*, no violence appeared to be meant and annoyance, not injury, seemed to have been the goblins' object, excepting in the case of one poor fellow, a trooper, who had followed Harrison in half his battles, and now was sentinel in that very vestibule upon which Everard had recommended them to mount a guard. He had presented his carabine at something which came suddenly upon him, when it was wrested out of his hands, and he himself knocked down with the butt end of it. His broken head and the drenched bedding of Desborough, upon whom a tub of ditch-water had been emptied during his sleep, were the only pieces of real evidence to attest the disturbances of the night.

The reports from Harrison's apartment were, as delivered by the grave Master Tomkins, that truly the general had passed the night undisturbed, though there was still upon him a deep sleep, and a folding of the hands to slumber; from which Everard argued that the machinators had esteemed Harrison's part of the reckoning sufficiently paid off on the preceding evening.

He then proceeded to the apartment doubly garrisoned by the worshipful Desborough and the philosophical Bletson.

They were both up and dressing themselves, the former open-mouthed in his feeling of fear and suffering. Indeed, no sooner had Everard entered than the ducked and dismayed colonel made a dismal complaint of the way he had spent the night, and murmured not a little against his worshipful kinsman for imposing a task upon him which inferred so much annoyance.

"Could not his Excellency my kinsman Noll," he said, "have given his poor relative and brother-in-law a sop somewhere else than out of this Woodstock, which seems to be the Devil's own porridge-pot? I cannot sup broth with the Devil: I have no long spoon—not I. Could he not have quartered me in some quiet corner, and given this haunted place to some of his preachers and prayers, who know the Bible as well as the muster-roll? whereas I know the four hoofs of a clean-going nag, or the points of a team of oxen, better than all the books of Moses. But I will give it over, at once and forever: hopes of earthly gain shall never make me run the risk of being carried away bodily by the Devil, besides being set upon my head one whole night, and soused with ditch-water the next. No—no; I am too wise for that."

Master Bletson had a different part to act. He complained of no personal annoyances; on the contrary, he declared "he should have slept as well as ever he did in his life, but for the abominable disturbances around him, of men calling to arms every half hour, when so much as a cat trotted by one of their posts. He would rather," he said, "have slept among a whole sabaoth of witches, if such creatures could be found."

"Then you think there is no such thing as apparitions, Master Bletson?" said Everard. "I used to be sceptical on the subject; but, on my life, to-night has been a strange one."

"Dreams—dreams—dreams, my simple colonel," said Bletson, though his pale face and shaking limbs belied the assumed courage with which he spoke. "Old Chaucer, sir, hath told us the real moral on't. He was an old frequenter of the forest of Woodstock, here——"

"Chaser!" said Desborough; "some huntsman belike, by his name. Does he walk, like Hearne at Windsor?"

"Chaucer," said Bletson, "my dear Desborough, is one of those wonderful fellows, as Colonel Everard knows, who live many a hundred years after they are buried, and whose words haunt our ears after their bones are long moldered in the dust."

"Ay—ay! well," answered Desborough, to whom this description of the old poet was unintelligible, "I for one desire his room rather than his company—one of your conjures, I warrant him. But what says he to the matter?"

"Only a slight spell, which I will take the freedom to repeat to Colonel Everard," said Bletson; "but which would be as bad as Greek to thee, Desborough. Old Geoffrey lays the whole blame of our nocturnal disturbance on superfluity of humors,

> Which causen folke to dread in their dreams
> Of arrowes, and of fire with red gleams,
> Right as the humor of melancholy
> Causeth many a man in sleep to cry
> For fear of great bulls and bears black,
> And others that black devils will them take."

While he was thus declaiming, Everard observed a book sticking out from beneath the pillow of the bed lately occupied by the honorable member.

"Is that Chaucer?" he said, making to the volume. "I would like to look at the passage——"

"Chaucer!" said Bletson, hastening to interfere; "no, that is Lucretius—my darling Lucretius. I cannot let you see it: I have some private marks."

But by this time Everard had the book in his hand. "Lucretius!" he said. "No, Master Bletson, this is not Lucretius, but a fitter comforter in dread or in danger. Why should you be ashamed of it? Only, Bletson, instead of resting your head, if you can but anchor your heart upon this volume, it may serve you in better stead than Lucretius or Chaucer either."

"Why, what book is it?" said Bletson, his pale cheek coloring with the shame of detection. "Oh, the Bible!" throwing it down contemptuously; "some book of my fellow Gibeon's: these Jews have been always superstitious, ever since Juvenal's time, thou knowest—

> Qualiacunque voles Judæi somnia vendunt.

He left me the old book for a spell, I warrant you, for 'tis a well-meaning fool."

"He would scarce have left the New Testament as well as the Old," said Everard. "Come, my dear Bletson, do not be ashamed of the wisest thing you ever did in your life, supposing you took your Bible in an hour of apprehension, with a view to profit by the contents."

Bletson's vanity was so much galled that it overcame his constitutional cowardice. His little thin fingers quivered for eagerness, his neck and cheeks were as red as scarlet, and his articulation was as thick and vehement as—in short, as if he had been no philosopher.

"Master Everard," he said, "you are a man of the sword, sir; and, sir, you seem to suppose yourself entitled to say whatever comes into your mind with respect to civilians, sir. But I would have you remember, sir, that there are bounds beyond which human patience may be urged sir, and jests which no man of honor will endure, sir; and, therefore, I expect an apology for your present language, Colonel Everard, and this unmannerly jesting, sir, or you may chance to hear from me in a way that will not please you."

Everard could not help smiling at this explosion of valor, engendered by irritated self-love.

"Look you, Master Bletson," he said, "I have been a soldier, that is true, but I was never a bloody-minded one; and as a Christian, I am unwilling to enlarge the kingdom of darkness by sending a new vassel thither before his time. If Heaven gives you time to repent, I see no reason why my hand should deprive you of it, which, were we to have a rencontre, would be your fate in the thrust of a sword or the pulling of a trigger. I therefore prefer to apologize; and I call Desborough, if he has recovered his wits, to bear evidence that I *do* apologize for having suspected you, who are completely the slave of your own vanity, of any tendency, however slight, towards grace or good sense. And I farther apologize for the time that I have wasted in endeavoring to wash an Ethiopian white, or in recommending rational inquiry to a self-willed atheist."

Bletson, overjoyed at the turn the matter had taken—for the defiance was scarce out of his mouth ere he began to tremble for the consequences—answered with great eagerness and servility of manner—"Nay, dearest colonel, say no more of it, an apology is all that is necessary among men of honor; it neither leaves dishonor with him who asks it nor infers degradation on him who makes it."

"Not such an apology as I have made, I trust," said the colonel.

"No, no—not in the least," answered Bletson; "one apology serves me just as well as another, and Desborough will bear witness you have made one, and that is all there can be said on the subject."

"Master Desborough and you," rejoined the colonel,

"will take care how the matter is reported, I daresay, and I only recommend to both that, if mentioned at all, it may be told correctly."

"Nay—nay, we will not mention it at all," said Bletson: "we will forget it from this moment. Only, never suppose me capable of superstitious weakness. Had I been afraid of an apparent and real danger—why, such fear is natural to man, and I will not deny that the mood of mind may have happened to me as well as to others. But to be thought capable of resorting to spells, and sleeping with books under my pillow to secure myself against ghosts—on my word, it was enough to provoke one to quarrel, for the moment, with his very best friend. And now, colonel, what is to be done, and how is our duty to be executed at this accursed place? If I should get such a wetting as Desborough's, why I should die of catarrh, though you see it hurts him no more than a bucket of water thrown over a post-horse. You are, I presume, a brother in our commission; how are you of opinion we should proceed?"

"Why, in good time here comes Harrison," said Everard, "and I will lay my commission from the Lord General before you all, which, as you see, Colonel Desborough, commands you to desist from acting on your present authority, and intimates his pleasure accordingly, that you withdraw from this place."

Desborough took the paper and examined the signature. "It is Noll's signature sure enough," said he, dropping his under jaw; "only, every time of late he has made the "Oliver" as large as a giant, while the "Cromwell" creeps after like a dwarf, as if the surname were like to disappear one of these days altogether. But is his Excellency our kinsman, Noll Cromwell, since he has the surname yet, so unreasonable as to think his relations and friends are to be set upon their heads till they have the crick in their neck, drenched as if they had been plunged in a horse-pond, frightened, day and night, by all sorts of devils, witches, and fairies, and get not a penny of smart money? Adzooks—forgive me for swearing—if that's the case, I had better home to my farm, and mind team and herd, than dangle after such a thankless person, though I *have* wived his sister. She was poor enough when I took her, for as high as Noll holds his head now."

"It is not my purpose," said Bletson, "to stir debate in this honorable meeting; and no one will doubt the veneration and attachment which I bear to our noble General, whom the current of events, and his own matchless qualities of courage and constancy, have raised so high in these deplorable days. If I were to term him a direct and immediate emanation of the *Animus Mundi* itself—something which nature had produced in her proudest hour, while exerting herself, as is her law, for the preservation of the creatures to whom she has given existence—I should scarce exhaust the ideas which I entertain of him; always protesting, that I am by no means to be held as admitting, but merely as granting for the sake of argument, the possible existence of that species of emanation or exhalation from the *Animus Mundi* of which I have made mention. I appeal to you, Colonel Desborough, who are his Excellency's relation—to you, Colonel Everard, who hold the dearer title of his friend, whether I have overrated my zeal in his behalf?"

Everard bowed at this pause, but Desborough gave a more complete authentication. "Nay, I can bear witness to that. I have seen when you were willing to tie his points or brush his cloak, or the like; and to be treated thus ungratefully, and gudgeoned of the opportunities which had been given you——"

"It is not for that," said Bletson, waving his hand gracefully. "You do me wrong, Master Desborough—you do, indeed, kind sir, although I know you meant it not. No, sir—no partial consideration of private interest prevailed on me to undertake this charge. It was conferred on me by the Parliament of England, in whose name this war commenced, and by the Council of State, who are the conservators of England's liberty. And the chance and serene hope of serving the country, the confidence that I—and you, Master Desborough, and you, worthy General Harrison—superior, as I am, to all selfish considerations—to which I am sure you also, good Colonel Everard, would be superior, had you been named in this commission, as I would to Heaven you had—I say the hope of serving the country, with the aid of such respectable associates, one and all of them—as well as you, Colonel Everard, supposing you to have been of the number—induced me to accept of this opportunity, whereby I might, gratuitously, with your assistance, render so much advantage to our dear mother the Commonwealth of England. Such was my hope, my trust, my confidence. And now comes my Lord General's warrant to dissolve the authority by which we are entitled to act. Gentlemen, I ask this honorable meeting—with all respect to his Excellency—whether his commission be paramount to that from which he himself directly holds *his* commission? No one will say so. I ask whether he has climbed into the seat from which the late Man descended, or hath a great seal, or means to proceed by prerogative in such a case? I cannot see reason to believe it, and therefore I must resist such doctrine. I am in your judgment, my brave and honorable colleagues; but, touching my own poor opinion, I feel myself under the unhappy necessity of proceeding in our commission, as if the interruption had not taken place; with this addition, that the Board of Sequestrators should sit by day at this same lodge of Woodstock, but that, to reconcile the minds of weak brethren, who may be afflicted by superstitious rumors, as well as to avoid any practise on our persons by the Malignants, who, I am convinced, are busy in this neighborhood, we should remove our sittings after sunset to the George Inn, in the neighboring borough.

"Good Master Bletson," replied Colonel Everard, "it is not for me to reply to you; but you may know in what characters this army of England and their General write their authority. I fear me the annotation on this precept of the General will be expressed by the march of a troop of horse from Oxford to see it executed. I believe there are orders out for that effect; and you know by late experience that the soldier will obey his General equally against King and Parliament."

"That obedience is conditional," said Harrison, starting fiercely up. "Know'st thou not, Markham Everard, that I have followed the man Cromwell as close as the bull-dog follows his master? and so I will yet; but I am no spaniel, either to be beaten or to have the food I have earned snatched from me, as if I were a vile cur, whose wages are a whipping and free leave to wear my own skin. I looked, amongst the three of us, that we might honestly and piously, and with advantage to the Commonwealth, have gained out of this commission three, or it may be five, thousand pounds. And does Cromwell imagine I will part with it for a rough word? No man goeth a warfare on his own charges. He that serves the altar must live by the altar, and the saints must have means to provide them with good harness and fresh horses against the unsealing and the pouring forth. Does Cromwell think I am so much of a tame tiger as to permit him to rend from me at pleasure the miserable dole he hath thrown me? Of a surety I will resist; and the men who are here, being chiefly of my own regiment—men who wait, and who expect, with lamps burning and loins girded, and each one his weapon bound upon his thigh—will aid me to make this house good against every assault—ay, even against Cromwell himself, until the latter coming. Selah—Selah!"

"And I," said Desborough, "will levy troops and protect your out-quarters, not choosing at present to close myself up in garrison——"

"And I," said Bletson, "will do my part, and hie me to town and lay the matter before Parliament, arising in my place for that effect."

Everard was little moved by all these little threats. The only formidable one, indeed, was that of Harrison, whose enthusiasm, joined with his courage, and obstinacy, and character among the fanatics of his own principles, made him a dangerous enemy. Before trying any arguments with the refractory major-general, Everard endeavored to moderate his feelings, and threw something in about the late disturbances.

"Talk not to me of supernatural disturbances, young man—talk not to me of enemies in the body or out of the body. Am I not the champion chosen and commissioned to encounter and to conquer the great Dragon, and the Beast which cometh out of the sea? Am I not to command the left wing and two regiments of the center, when the saints shall encounter with the countless legions of Gog and Magog? I tell thee that my name is written on the sea of glass mingled with fire, and that I will keep this place of Woodstock against all mortal men, and against all devils, whether in field or chamber, in the forest or in the meadow, even till the saints reign in the fulness of their glory!"

Everard saw it was then time to produce two or three lines under Cromwell's hand, which he had received from the General subsequently to the communication through Wildrake. The information they contained was calculated to allay the disappointment of the Commissioners. This document assigned as the reason of superseding the Woodstock Commission, that he should probably propose to the Parliament to require the assistance of General Harrison, Colonel Desborough, and Master Bletson, the honorable member for Littlefaith, in a much greater matter, namely, the disposing of the royal property, and disparking of the king's forest, at Windsor. So soon as this idea was started, all parties pricked up their ears; and their drooping, and gloomy and vindictive, looks began to give place to courteous smiles, and to a cheerfulness which laughed in their eyes and turned their mustachios upward.

Colonel Desborough acquitted his right honorable and excellent cousin and kinsman of all species of unkindness; Master Bletson discovered that the interest of the state was trebly concerned in the good administration of Windsor more than in that of Woodstock; as for Harrison, he exclaimed, without disguise or hesitation, that the gleaning of the grapes of Windsor was better than the vintage of Woodstock. Thus speaking, the glance of his dark eye expressed as much triumph in the proposed earthly advantage as if it had not been, according to his vain persuasion, to be shortly exchanged for his share in the general reign of the millennium. His delight, in short, resembled the joy of an eagle, who preys upon a lamb in the evening with not the less relish because she descries in the distant landscape an hundred thousand men about to join battle with daybreak, and to give her an endless feast on the hearts and life-blood of the valiant.

Yet, though all agreed that they would be obedient to the General's pleasure in this matter, Bletson proposed, as a precautionary measure, in which all agreed, that they should take up their abode for some time in the town of Woodstock, to wait for their new commissions respecting Windsor; and this upon the prudential consideration, that it was best not to slip one knot until another was first tied.

Each commissioner, therefore, wrote to Oliver individually, stating, in his own way, the depth and height, length and breadth, of his attachment to him. Each expressed himself resolved to obey the General's injunctions to the uttermost; but with the same scrupulous devotion to the Parliament, each found himself at a loss how to lay down the commission entrusted to them by that body, and therefore felt bound in conscience to take up his residence at the borough of Woodstock, that he might not seem to abandon the charge committed to them until they should be called to administrate the weightier matter of Windsor, to which they expressed their willingness instantly to devote themselves, according to his Excellency's pleasure.

This was the general style of their letters, varied by the characteristic flourishes of the writers. Desborough, for example, said something about the religious duty of providing for one's own household only he blundered the text; Bletson wrote long and big words about the political obligation incumbent on every member of the community, on every person, to sacrifice his time and talents to the service of his country; while Harrison talked of the littleness of present affairs, in comparison of the approaching tremendous change of all things beneath the sun. But although the garnishing of the various epistles was different, the result came to the same, that they were determined at least to keep sight of Woodstock until they were well assured of some better and more profitable commission.

Everard also wrote a letter in the most grateful terms to Cromwell, which would probably have been less warm had he known more distinctly than his follower chose to tell him the expectation under which the wily General had granted his request. He acquainted his Excellency with his purpose of continuing at Woodstock, partly to assure himself of the motions of the three Commissioners, and to watch whether they did not again enter upon the execution of the trust which they had for the present renounced; and partly to see that some extraordinary circumstances which had taken place in the lodge, and which would doubtless transpire, were not followed by any explosion to the disturbance of the public peace. He knew, as he expressed himself, that his Excellency was so much the friend of order, that he would rather disturbances or insurrections were prevented than punished; and he conjured the General to repose confidence in his exertions for the public service by every mode within his power, not aware, it will be observed, in what peculiar sense his general pledge might be interpreted.

These letters, being made up into a packet, were forwarded to Windsor by a trooper, detached on that errand.

CHAPTER XVII

> We do that in our zeal
> Our calmer moments are afraid to answer.
>
> *Anonymous.*

WHILE the Commissioners were preparing to remove themselves from the lodge to the inn at the borough of Woodstock, with all that state and bustle which attend the movements of great persons, and especially of such to whom greatness is not entirely familiar, Everard held some colloquy with the Presbyterian clergyman, Master Holdenough, who had issued from the apartment which he had occupied, as it were in defiance of the spirits by whom the mansion was supposed to be disturbed, and whose pale cheek and pensive brow gave token that he had not passed the night more comfortably than the other inmates of the lodge of Woodstock. Colonel Everard having offered to procure the reverend gentleman some refreshment, received this reply: "This day shall I not taste food, saving that which we are assured of as sufficient for our sustenance, where it is promised that our bread shall be given us and our water shall be sure. Not that I fast in the Papistical opinion that it adds to those merits which are but an accumulation of filthy rags; but because I hold it needful that no grosser sustenance should this day cloud my understanding, or render less pure and vivid the thanks I owe to Heaven for a most wonderful preservation."

"Master Holdenough," said Everard, "you are, I know, both a good man and a bold one, and I saw you last night courageously go upon your sacred duty, when soldiers, and tried ones, seemed considerably alarmed."

"Too courageous—too venturous," was Master Holdenough's reply, the boldness of whose aspect seemed completely to have died away. "We are frail creatures, Master Everard, and frailest when we think ourselves strongest. Oh, Colonel Everard," he added, after a pause, and as if the confidence was partly involuntary, "I have seen that which I shall never survive!"

"You surprise me, reverend sir," said Everard; "may I request you will speak more plainly? I have heard some stories of this wild night, nay, have witnessed strange things myself; but, methinks, I would be much interested in knowing the nature of your disturbance."

"Sir," said the clergyman, "you are a discreet gentleman; and though I would not willingly that these heretics, schismatics, Brownists, Muggletonians, Anabaptists, and so forth, had such an opportunity of triumph as my defeat in this matter would have afforded them, yet with you, who have been ever a faithful follower of our church, and are pledged to the good cause by the great National League and Covenant, surely I would be more open. Sit we down, therefore, and let me call for a glass of pure water, for as yet I feel some bodily faltering; though, I thank Heaven, I am in mind resolute and composed as a merely mortal man may after such a vision. They say, worthy colonel, that looking on such things foretells, or causes, speedy death. I know not if it be true; but if so, I only depart like the tired sentinel when his officer releases him from his post; and glad shall I be to close these wearied eyes against the sight, and shut these harassed ears against the croaking, as of frogs, of Antinomians, and Pelagians, and Socinians, and Arminians, and Arians, and Nullifidians, which have come up into our England like those filthy reptiles into the house of Pharaoh."

Here one of the servants who had been summoned entered with a cup of water, gazing at the same time in the face of the clergyman, as if his stupid gray eyes were endeavoring to read what tragic tale was written on his brow; and shaking his empty skull as he left the room, with the air of one who was proud of having discovered that all was not exactly right, though he could not so well guess what was wrong.

Colonel Everard invited the good man to take some refreshment more genial than the pure element, but he declined. "I am in some sort a champion," he said; "and though I have been foiled in the late controversy with the enemy, still I have my trumpet to give the alarm, and my sharp sword to smite withal; therefore, like the Nazarites of old, I will eat nothing that cometh of the vine, neither drink wine nor strong drink, until these my days of combat shall have passed away."

Kindly and respectfully the colonel anew pressed Master Holdenough to communicate the events that had befallen him on the preceding night; and the good clergyman proceeded as follows, with that little characteristical touch of vanity in his narrative which naturally arose out of the part he had played in the world, and the influence which he had exercised over the minds of others. "I was a young man at the University of Cambridge," he said, "when I was particularly bound in friendship to a fellow-student, perhaps because we were esteemed, though it is vain to mention it, the most hopeful scholars at our college, and so equally advanced, that it was difficult, perhaps, to say which was the greater proficient in his studies. Only our tutor, Master Purefoy, used to say that, if my comrade had the advantage of me in gifts, I had the better of him in grace; for he was attached to the profane learning of the classics, always unprofitable, often impious and impure, and I had light enough to turn my studies into the sacred tongues. Also we differed in our opinions touching the Church of England, for he held Arminian opinions, with Laud, and those who would connect our ecclesiastical establishment with the civil, and make the church dependent on the breath of an earthly man. In fine, he favored Prelacy both in essentials and ceremonial; and although we parted with tears and embraces, it was to follow very different courses. He obtained a living, and became a great controversial writer in behalf of the bishops and of the court. I also, as is well known to you, to the best of my poor abilities, sharpened my pen in the cause of the poor oppressed people, whose tender consciences rejected the rites and ceremonies more befitting a Papistical than a Reformed church, and which, according to the blinded policy of the court, were enforced by pains and penalties. Then came the Civil War, and I—called thereunto by my conscience, and nothing fearing or suspecting what miserable consequences have chanced, through the rise of these Independents—consented to lend my countenance and labor to the great work, by becoming chaplain to Colonel Harrison's regiment. Not that I mingled with carnal weapons in the field—which Heaven forbid that a minister of the altar should—but I preached, exhorted, and, in time of need, was a surgeon, as well to the wounds of the body as of the soul. Now, it fell, towards the end of the war, that a party of Malignants had seized on a strong house in the shire of Shrewsbury, situated on a small island, advanced into a lake, and accessible only by a small and narrow causeway. From thence they made excursions, and vexed the country; and high time it was to suppress them, so that a part of our regiment went to reduce them; and I was requested to go, for they were few in number to take in so strong a place, and the colonel judged that my exhortations would make them do valiantly. And so, contrary to my wont, I went forth with them, even to the field, where there was valiant fighting on both sides. Nevertheless, the Malignants, shooting their wall-pieces at us, had so much the advantage, that, after bursting their gates with a salvo of our cannon, Colonel Harrison ordered his men to advance on the causeway, and try to carry the place by storm. Natheless, although our men did valiantly, advancing in good order, yet being galled on every side by the fire, they at length fell into disorder, and were retreating with much loss, Harrison himself valiantly bringing up the rear, and defending them as he could against the enemy, who sallied forth in pursuit of them, to smite them hip and thigh. Now, Colonel Everard, I am a man of a quick and vehement temper by nature, though better teaching than the old law hath made me mild and patient as you now see me. I could not bear to see our Israelites flying before the Philistines, so I rushed upon the causeway, with the Bible in one hand and a halberd, which I had caught up, in the other, and turned back the foremost fugitives by threatening to strike them down, pointing out to them at the same time a priest in his cassock, as they call it, who was among the Malignants, and asking them whether they would not do as much for a true servant of Heaven as the uncircumcised would for a priest of Baal. My words and strokes prevailed: they turned at once, and shouting out, 'Down with Baal and his worshipers!' they charged the Malignants so unexpectedly home, that they not only drove them back into their house of garrison, but entered it with them, as the phrase is, pell-mell. I also was there, partly hurried on by the crowd, partly to prevail on our enraged soldiers to give quarter; for it grieved my heart to see Christians and Englishmen hashed down with swords and gunstocks, like curs in the street when there is an alarm of mad dogs. In this way, the soldiers fighting and slaughtering, and I calling to them to stay their hand, we gained the very roof of the building, which was in part leaded, and to which, as a last tower of refuge, those of the Cavaliers who yet escaped had retired. I was myself, I may say, forced up the narrow winding staircase by our soldiers, who rushed on like dogs of chase upon their prey; and when extricated from the passage, I found myself in the midst of a horrid scene. The scattered defenders were, some resisting with the fury of despair, some on their knees, imploring for compassion in words and tones to break a man's heart when he thinks on them; some were calling on God for mercy—and it was time, for man had none. They were stricken down, thrust through, flung from the battlements into the lake; and the wild cries of the victors, mingled with the groans, shrieks, and clamors of the vanquished, made a sound so horrible, that only death can erase it from my memory. And the men who butchered their fellow-creatures thus were neither pagans from distant savage lands, nor ruffians, the refuse and offscourings of our own people. They were in calm blood reasonable, nay, religious, men, maintaining a fair repute both heavenward and earthward. Oh, Master Everard, your trade of war should be feared and avoided, since it converts such men into wolves towards their fellow-creatures!"

"It is a stern necessity," said Everard, looking down, "and as such alone is justifiable. But proceed, reverend sir; I see not how this storm, an incident but e'en too frequent on both sides during the late war, connects with the affair of last night."

"You shall hear anon," said Mr. Holdenough; then paused, as one who makes an effort to compose himself before continuing a relation the tenor of which agitated him with much violence. "In this infernal tumult," he resumed—"for surely nothing on earth could so much resemble Hell as when men go thus loose in mortal malice on their fellow-creatures—I saw the same priest whom I had distinguished on the causeway, with one or two other Malignants, pressed into a corner by the assailants, and defending themselves to the last, as those who had no hope. I saw him—I knew him—oh, Colonel Everard!"

He grasped Everard's hand with his own left hand, and pressed the palm of his right to his face and forehead, sobbing aloud.

"It was your college companion?" said Everard, anticipating the catastrophe.

"Mine ancient—mine only friend, with whom I had spent the happy days of youth! I rushed forward—I struggled—I entreated. But my eagerness left me neither voice nor language: all was drowned in the wretched cry which I had myself raised. 'Down with the priest of Baal. Slay Mattan—slay him were he between the altars!' Forced over the battlements, but struggling for life, I could see him cling to one of those projections which were formed to carry the water from the leads; but they hacked at his arms and hands. I heard the heavy fall into the bottomless abyss below. Excuse me; I cannot go on!"

"He may have escaped?"

"Oh! no—no—no, the tower was four stories in height. Even those who threw themselves into the lake from the lower windows, to escape by swimming, had no safety; for mounted troopers on the shore caught the same bloodthirsty humor which had seized the storming party, galloped around the margin of the lake, and shot those who were struggling for life in the water, or cut them down as they strove to get to land. They were all cut off and destroyed. Oh! may the blood shed on that day remain silent! Oh! that the earth may receive it in her recesses! Oh! that it may be mingled forever with the dark waters of that lake, so that it may never cry for vengeance against those whose anger was fierce, and who slaughtered in their wrath! And, oh! may the erring man be forgiven who came into their assembly, and lent his voice to encourage their cruelty! Oh! Albany, my brother—my brother, I have lamented for thee even as David for Jonathan!"*

The good man sobbed aloud, and so much did Colonel Everard sympathize with his emotions, that he forbore to press him upon the subject of his own curiosity until the full tide of remorseful passion had for the time abated. It was, however, fierce and agitating, the more so, perhaps, that indulgence in strong mental feeling of any kind was foreign to the severe and ascetic character of the man, and was therefore the more overpowering when it had at once surmounted all restraints. Large tears flowed down the trembling features of his thin, and usually stern, or at least austere, countenance; he eagerly returned the compression of Everard's hand, as if thankful for the sympathy which the caress implied.

Presently after, Master Holdenough wiped his eyes, withdrew his hand gently from that of Everard, shaking it kindly as they parted, and proceeded with more composure: "Forgive me this burst of passionate feeling, worthy colonel. I am conscious it little becomes a man of my cloth, who should be the bearer of consolation to others, to give way in mine own person to an extremity of grief, weak at least, if indeed it is not sinful; for what are we, that we should weep and murmur touching that which is permitted? But Albany was to me as a brother. The happiest days of my life, ere my call to mingle myself in the strife of the land had awakened me to my duties, were spent in his company. I—but I will make the rest of my story short." Here he

* See Dr. Michael Hudson. Note 4.

drew his chair close to that of Everard, and spoke in a solemn and mysterious tone of voice, almost lowered to a whisper—"I saw him last night."

"Saw *him*—saw whom?" said Everard. "Can you mean the person whom——"

"Whom I saw so ruthlessly slaughtered," said the clergyman—"my ancient college friend, Joseph Albany."

"Master Holdenough, your cloth and your character alike must prevent your jesting on such a subject as this."

"Jesting!" answered Holdenough; "I would as soon jest on my death-bed—as soon jest upon the Bible."

"But you must have been deceived," answered Everard, hastily; "this tragical story necessarily often returns to your mind, and in moments when the imagination overcomes the evidence of the outward senses, your fancy must have presented to you an unreal appearance. Nothing more likely, when the mind is on the stretch after something supernatural, than that the imagination should supply the place with a chimera, while the over-excited feelings render it difficult to dispel the delusion."

"Colonel Everard," replied Holdenough, with austerity, "in discharge of my duty I must not fear the face of man; and, therefore, I tell you plainly, as I have done before with more observance, that when you bring your carnal learning and judgment, as it is but too much your nature to do, to investigate the hidden things of another world, you might as well measure with the palm of your hand the waters of the Isis. Indeed, good sir, you err in this, and give men too much pretense to confound your honorable name with witch advocates, freethinkers, and atheists, even with such as this man Bletson, who, if the discipline of the church had its hands strengthened, as it was in the beginning of the great conflict, would have been long ere now cast out of the pale, and delivered over to the punishment of the flesh, that his spirit might, if possible, be yet saved."

"You mistake, Master Holdenough," said Colonel Everard: "I do not deny the existence of such preternatural visitations, because I cannot, and dare not, raise the voice of my own opinion against the testimony of ages, supported by such learned men as yourself. Nevertheless, though I grant the possibility of such things, I have scarce yet heard of an instance in my days so well fortified by evidence that I could at once and distinctly say, 'This must have happened by supernatural agency, and not otherwise.'

"Hear, then, what I have to tell," said the divine, "on

the faith of a man, a Christian, and, what is more, a servant of our Holy Church; and therefore, though unworthy, an elder and a teacher among Christians. I had taken my post yester evening in the half-furnished apartment wherein hangs a huge mirror, which might have served Goliath of Gath to have admired himself in, when clothed from head to foot in his brazen armor. I the rather chose this place, because they informed me it was the nearest habitable room to the gallery in which they say you had been yourself assailed that evening by the Evil One. Was it so, I pray you?"

"By some one with no good intentions I was assailed in that apartment. So far," said Colonel Everard, "you were correctly informed."

"Well, I chose my post as well as I might, even as a resolved general approaches his camp, and casts up his mound as nearly as he can to the besieged city. And, of a truth, Colonel Everard, if I felt some sensation of bodily fear—for even Elias and the prophets, who commanded the elements, had a portion in our frail nature, much more such a poor sinful being as myself—yet was my hope and my courage high; and I thought of the texts which I might use, not in the wicked sense of periapts, or spells, as the blinded Papists employ them, together with the sign of the cross and other fruitless forms, but as nourishing and supporting that true trust and confidence in the blessed promises, being the true shield of faith wherewith the fiery darts of Satan may be withstood and quenched. And thus armed and prepared, I sat me down to read, at the same time to write, that I might compel my mind to attend to those subjects which became the situation in which I was placed, as preventing any unlicensed excursions of the fancy, and leaving no room for my imagination to brood over idle fears. So I methodized, and wrote down what I thought meet for the time, and peradventure some hungry souls may yet profit by the food which I then prepared."

"It was wisely and worthily done, good and reverend sir," replied Colonel Everard; "I pray you to proceed."

"While I was thus employed, sir, and had been upon the matter for about three hours, not yielding to weariness, a strange thrilling came over my senses, and the large and old-fashioned apartment seemed to wax larger, more gloomy, and more cavernous, while the air of the night grew more cold and chill: I know not if it was that the fire began to decay, or whether there cometh before such things as were then about to happen a breath and atmosphere, as it were, of terror, as Job saith in a well-known passage, "Fear came upon me, and trembling, which made my bones to shake;" and there was a tingling noise in my ears, and a dizziness in my brain, so that I felt like those who call for aid when there is no danger, and was even prompted to flee, when I saw no one to pursue. It was then that something seemed to pass behind me, casting a reflection on the great mirror before which I had placed my writing-table, and which I saw by assistance of the large standing light which was then in front of the glass. And I looked up, and I saw in the glass distinctly the appearance of a man; as sure as these words issue from my mouth, it was no other than the same Joseph Albany—the companion of my youth—he whom I had seen precipitated down the battlements of Clidesthrough Castle into the deep lake below!"

"What did you do?"

"It suddenly rushed on my mind," said the divine, "that the stoical philosopher Athenodorus had eluded the horrors of such a vision by patiently pursuing his studies; and it shot at the same time across my mind that I, a Christian divine, and a steward of the mysteries, had less reason to fear evil, and better matter on which to employ my thoughts, than was possessed by a heathen, who was blinded even by his own wisdom. So, instead of betraying any alarm, or even turning my head around, I pursued my writing, but with a beating heart, I admit, and with a throbbing hand."

"If you could write at all," said the colonel, "with such an impression on your mind, you may take the head of the English army for dauntless resolution."

"Our courage is not our own, colonel," said the divine, "and not as ours should it be vaunted of. And again, when you speak of this strange vision as an impression on my fancy and not a reality obvious to my senses, let me tell you once more, your worldly wisdom is but foolishness touching the things that are not worldly."

"Did you not look again upon the mirror?" said the colonel.

"I did, when I had copied out the comfortable text, 'Thou shalt tread down Satan under thy feet.'"

"And what did you then see?"

"The reflection of the same Joseph Albany," said Holdenough, "passing slowly as from behind my chair, the same in member and lineament that I had known him in his youth, excepting that his cheek had the marks of the more advanced age at which he died, and was very pale."

"What did you then?"

"I turned from the glass, and plainly saw the figure which had made the reflection in the mirror retreating towards the door, not fast nor slow, but with a gliding, steady pace. It turned again when near the door, and again showed me its pale, ghastly countenance, before it disappeared. But how it left the room, whether by the door or otherwise, my spirits were too much hurried to remark exactly; nor have I been able, by any effort of recollection, distinctly to remember."

"This is a strange, and as coming from you, a most excellently well-attested apparition," answered Everard. "And yet, Master Holdenough, if the other world has been actually displayed, as you apprehend, and I will not dispute the possibility, assure yourself there are also wicked men concerned in these machinations. I myself have undergone some recontres with visitants who possessed bodily strength, and wore, I am sure, earthly weapons."

"Oh! doubtless—doubtless," replied Master Holdenough: "Beelzebub loves to charge with horse and foot mingled, as was the fashion of the old Scottish general, Davie Leslie. He has his devils in the body as well as his devils disembodied, and uses the one to support and back the other."

"It may be as you say, reverend sir," answered the colonel. "But what do you advise in this case?"

"For that I must consult with my brethren," said the divine; "and if there be but left in our borders five ministers of the true kirk, we will charge Satan in full body, and you shall see whether we have not power over him to resist till he shall flee from us. But failing that ghostly armament against these strange and unearthly enemies, truly I would recommend that, as a house of witchcraft and abomination, this polluted den of ancient tyranny and prostitution should be totally consumed by fire, lest Satan, establishing his headquarters so much to his mind, should find a garrison and a fastness from which he might sally forth to infest the whole neighborhood. Certain it is, that I would recommend to no Christian soul to inhabit the mansion; and, if deserted, it would become a place for wizards to play their pranks, and witches to establish their Sabbath, and those who, like Demas, go about after the wealth of this world, seeking for gold and silver, to practise spells and charms to the prejudice of the souls of the covetous. Trust me, therefore, it were better that it were spoiled and broken down, not leaving one stone upon another."

"I say nay to that, my good friend," said the colonel; "for the Lord General hath permitted, by his license, my mother's brother, Sir Henry Lee, and his family, to return into the house of his fathers, being indeed the only roof under which he hath any chance of obtaining shelter for his gray hairs."

"And was this done by your advice, Markham Everard?" said the divine, austerely.

"Certainly it was," returned the colonel. "And wherefore should I not exert mine influence to obtain a place of refuge for the brother of my mother?"

"Now as sure as thy soul liveth," answered the Presbyter, "I had believed this from no tongue but thine own. Tell me, was it not this very Sir Henry Lee, who by the force of his buff-coats and his green jerkins, enforced the Papist Laud's order to remove the altar to the eastern end of the church at Woodstock? and did not he swear by his beard, that he would hang in the very street of Woodstock whoever should deny to drink the King's health? and is not his hand red with the blood of the saints? and hath there been a ruffler in the field for Prelacy and high prerogative more unmitigable or fiercer?"

"All this may have been as you say, good Master Holdenough," answered the colonel; "but my uncle is now old and feeble, and hath scarce a single follower remaining, and his daughter is a being whom to look upon would make the sternest weep for pity—a being who——"

"Who is dearer to Everard," said Holdenough, "than his good name, his faith to his friends, his duty to his religion. This is no time to speak with sugared lips. The paths in which you tread are dangerous. You are striving to raise the Papistical candlestick which Heaven in its justice removed out of its place—to bring back to this hall of sorceries those very sinners who are bewitched with them. I will not permit the land to be abused by their witchcrafts. They shall not come hither."

He spoke this with vehemence, and striking his stick against the ground; and the colonel, very much dissatisfied, began to express himself haughtily in return. "You had better consider your power to accomplish your threats, Master Holdenough," he said, "before you urge them so peremptorily."

"And have I not the power to bind and to loose?" said the clergyman.

"It is a power little available, save over those of your own church," said Everard, with a tone something contemptuous.

"Take heed—take heed," said the divine, who, though an excellent, was, as we have elsewhere seen, an irritable, man. "Do not insult me; but think honorably of the messenger, for the sake of Him whose commission he carries. Do not, I say, defy me; I am bound to discharge my duty, were it to the displeasing of my twin brother."

"I can see nought your office has to do in the matter," said Colonel Everard; "and I, on my side, give you warning not to attempt to meddle beyond your commission."

"Right—you hold me already to be as submissive as one of your grenadiers," replied the clergyman, his acute features trembling with a sense of indignity, so as even to agitate his gray hair; "but beware, sir, I am not so powerless as you suppose. I will invoke every true Christian in Woodstock to gird up his loins, and resist the restoration of Prelacy, oppression, and Malignancy within our borders. I will stir up the wrath of the righteous against the oppressor—the Ishmaelite—the Edomite—and against his race, and against those who support him and encourage him to rear up his horn. I will call aloud, and spare not, and arouse the many whose love hath waxed cold, and the multitude who care for none of these things. There shall be a remnant to listen to me; and I will take the stick of Joseph, which was in the hand of Ephraim, and go down to cleanse this place of witches and sorcerers, and of enchantments, and will cry and exhort, saying, 'Will you plead for Baal? will you serve him? Nay, take the prophets of Baal; let not a man escape.'"

"Master Holdenough—Master Holdenough," said Colonel Everard, with much impatience, "by the tale yourself told me, you have exhorted upon that text once too often already."

The old man struck his palm forcibly against his forehead and fell back into a chair as these words were uttered, as suddenly, and as much without power of resistance, as if the colonel had fired a pistol through his head. Instantly regretting the reproach which he had suffered to escape him in his impatience, Everard hastened to apologize, and to offer every conciliatory excuse, however inconsistent, which occurred to him on the moment. But the old man was too deeply affected; he rejected his hand, lent no ear to what he said, and finally started up, saying sternly, "You have abused my confidence, sir—abused it vilely, to turn it into my own reproach; had I been a man of the sword, you dared not. But enjoy your triumph, sir, over an old man, and your father's friend; strike at the wound his imprudent confidence showed you."

"Nay, my worthy and excellent friend——" said the colonel.

"Friend!" answered the old man, vehemently. "We are foes, sir—foes now, and forever."

So saying, and starting from the seat into which he had rather fallen than thrown himself, he ran out of the room with a precipitation of step which he was apt to use upon occasions of irritable feeling, and which was certainly more eager than dignified, especially as he muttered while he ran, and seemed as if he were keeping up his own passion by recounting over and over the offence which he had received.

"Soh!" said Colonel Everard, "and there was not strife enough between mine uncle and the people of Woodstock already, but I must needs increase it, by chafing this irritable and quick-tempered old man, eager as I knew him to be in his ideas of church-government, and stiff in his prejudices respecting all who dissent from him! The mob of Woodstock will rise; for though he would not get a score of them to stand by him in any honest or intelligible purpose, yet let him cry 'havoc and destruction,' and I will warrant he has followers enow. And my uncle is equally wild and unpersuadable. For the value of all the estate he ever had, he would not allow a score of troopers to be quartered in the house for defense; and if he be alone, or has but Joceline to stand by him, he will be as sure to fire upon those who come to attack the lodge as if he had a hundred men in garrison; and then what can chance but danger and bloodshed."

This progress of melancholy anticipation was interrupted by the return of Master Holdenough, who, hurrying into the room with the same precipitate pace at which he had left it, ran straight up to the colonel, and said, "Take my hand, Markham—take my hand hastily; for the old Adam is whispering at my heart that it is a disgrace to hold it extended so long."

"Most heartily do I receive your hand, my venerable friend," said Everard, "and I trust in sign of renewed amity."

"Surely—surely," said the divine, shaking his hand kindly; "thou hast, it is true, spoken bitterly, but thou hast spoken truth in good time, and I think, though your words were severe, with a good and kindly purpose. Verily, and of a truth, it were sinful in me again to be hasty in provoking violence, remembering that which you have upbraided me with——"

"Forgive me, good Master Holdenough," said Colonel Everard, "it was a hasty word: I meant not in serious earnest to *upbraid.*"

"Peace, I pray you—peace," said the divine; "I say, the allusion to that which you have *most justly* upbraided me with—though the charge aroused the gall of the old man within me, the inward tempter being ever on the watch to bring us to his lure—ought, instead of being resented, to have been acknowledged by me as a favor, for so are the wounds of a friend termed faithful. And surely I, who have by one unhappy exhortation to battle and strife sent the living to the dead, and, I fear, brought back even the dead among the living, should now study peace and good-will, and reconciliation of difference, leaving punishment to the Great Being whose laws are broken, and vengeance to Him who hath said, 'I will repay it.'"

The old man's mortified features lighted up with a humble confidence as he made this acknowledgment; and Colonel Everard, who knew the constitutional infirmities and the early prejudices of professional consequence and exclusive party opinion which he must have subdued ere arriving at such a tone of candor, hastened to express his admiration of his Christian charity, mingled with reproaches on himself for having so deeply injured his feelings.

"Think not of it—think not of it, excellent young man," said Holdenough; "we have both erred—I in suffering my zeal to outrun my charity; you, perhaps, in pressing hard on an old and peevish man, who had so lately poured out his sufferings into your friendly bosom. Be it all forgotten. Let your friends, if they are not deterred by what has happened at this manor of Woodstock, resume their habitation as soon as they will. If they can protect themselves against the powers of the air, believe me that, if I can prevent it by aught in my power, they shall have no annoyance from earthly neighbors; and assure yourself, good sir, that my voice is still worth something with the worthy mayor, and the good aldermen, and the better sort of housekeepers up yonder in the town, although the lower classes are blown about with every wind of doctrine. And yet farther, be assured, colonel, that, should your mother's brother, or any of his family, learn that they have taken up a rash bargain in returning to this unhappy and unhallowed house, or should they find any qualms in their own hearts and consciences which require a ghostly comforter, Nehemiah Holdenough will be as much at their command by night or day as if they had been bred up within the holy pale of the church in which he is an unworthy minister ; and neither the awe of what is fearful to be seen within these walls, nor his knowledge of their blinded and carnal state, as bred up under a prelatic dispensation, shall prevent him doing what lies in his poor abilities for their protection and edification."

"I feel all the force of your kindness, reverend sir," said Colonel Everard, "but I do not think it likely that my uncle will give you trouble on either score. He is a man much accustomed to be his own protector in temporal danger, and in spiritual doubts to trust to his own prayers and those of his church."

"I trust I have not been superfluous in offering mine assistance," said the old man, something jealous that his proffered spiritual aid had been held rather intrusive. "I ask pardon if that is the case—I humbly ask pardon; I would not willingly be superfluous."

The colonel hastened to appease this new alarm of the watchful jealousy of his consequence, which, joined with a natural heat of temper which he could not always subdue, were the good man's only faults.

They had regained their former friendly footing, when Roger Wildrake returned from the hut of Joceline, and whispered his master that his embassy had been successful. The colonel then addressed the divine, and informed him that, as the Commissioners had already given up Woodstock, and as his uncle, Sir Henry Lee, proposed to return to the lodge about noon, he would, if his reverence pleased, attend him up to the borough.

"Will you not tarry," said the reverend man, with something like inquisitive apprehension in his voice, "to welcome your relatives upon their return to this their house ?"

"No, my good friend," said Colonel Everard ; "the part which I have taken in these unhappy broils, perhaps also the mode of worship in which I have been educated, have so prejudiced me in mine uncle's opinion, that I must be for some time a stranger to his house and family."

"Indeed ! I rejoice to hear it, with all my heart and soul," said the divine. "Excuse my frankness—I do indeed rejoice ; I had thought—no matter what I had thought, I would not again give offence. But truly, though the maiden hath a pleasant feature, and he, as all men say, is in human things unexceptionable, yet—but I give you pain—in sooth, I will say no more unless you ask my sincere and unprejudiced advice, which you shall command, but which I will not press on you superfluously. Wend we to the borough together; the pleasant solitude of the forest may dispose us to open our hearts to each other."

They did walk up to the little town in company, and, somewhat to Master Holdenough's surprise, the colonel, though they talked on various subjects, did not request of him any ghostly advice on the subject of his love to his fair cousin, while, greatly beyond the expectation of the soldier, the clergyman kept his word, and, in his own phrase, was not so superfluous as to offer upon so delicate a point his unasked counsel.

CHAPTER XVIII

> Then are the harpies gone. Yet ere we perch
> Where such foul birds have roosted, let us cleanse
> The foul obscenity they've left behind them.
>
> *Agamemnon.*

THE embassy of Wildrake had been successful, chiefly through the mediation of the Episcopal divine, whom we formerly found acting in the character of a chaplain to the family, and whose voice had great influence on many accounts with its master.

A little before high-noon, Sir Henry Lee, with his small household, were again in unchallenged possession of their old apartments at the lodge of Woodstock; and the combined exertions of Joceline Joliffe, of Phœbe, and of old Joan were employed in putting to rights what the late intruders had left in great disorder.

Sir Henry Lee had, like all persons of quality of that period, a love of order amounting to precision, and felt, like a fine lady whose dress has been disordered in a crowd, insulted and humiliated by the rude confusion into which his household goods had been thrown, and impatient till his mansion was purified from all marks of intrusion. In his anger he uttered more orders than the limited number of his domestics were likely to find time or hands to execute. "The villains have left such sulphurous steams behind them, too," said the old knight, "as if old Davie Leslie and the whole Scottish army had quartered among them."

"It may be near as bad," said Joceline, "for men may say, for certain, it was the Devil came down bodily among them and made them troop off."

"Then," said the knight, "is the Prince of Darkness a gentleman, as old Will Shakspeare says. He never interferes with those of his own coat, for the Lees have been here, father and son, these five hundred years, without disquiet; and no sooner came these misbegotten churls than he plays his own part among them."

"Well, one thing he and they have left us," said Joliffe, "which we may thank them for; and that is, such a well-filled larder and buttery as has been seldom seen in Woodstock Lodge this many a day—carcasses of mutton, large rounds of beef, barrels of confectioners' ware, pipes and runlets of sack, muscadine, ale, and what not. We shall have a royal time on't through half the winter; and Joan must get to salting and pickling presently."

"Out, villain!" said the knight; "are we to feed on the fragments of such scum of the earth as these? Cast them forth instantly. Nay," checking himself, "that were a sin; but give them to the poor, or see them sent to the owners. And, hark ye, I will none of their strong liquors. I would rather drink like a hermit all my life than seem to pledge such scoundrels as these in their leavings, like a miserable drawer, who drains off the ends of the bottles after the guests have paid their reckoning and gone off. And, harkye, I will taste no water from the cistern out of which these slaves have been serving themselves; fetch me down a pitcher from Rosamond's spring."

Alice heard this injunction, and well guessing there was enough for the other members of the family to do, she quietly took a small pitcher, and, flinging a cloak around her, walked out in person to procure Sir Henry the water which he desired. Meantime, Joceline said, with some hesitation, "that a man still remained, belonging to the party of these strangers, who was directing about the removal of some trunks and mails which belonged to the Commissioners, and who could receive his honor's commands about the provisions."

"Let him come hither." The dialogue was held in the hall. "Why do you hesitate and drumble in that manner?"

"Only, sir," said Joceline—"only perhaps your honor might not wish to see him, being the same who, not long since——" He paused.

"Sent my rapier a-hawking through the firmament, thou wouldst say? Why, when did I take spleen at a man for standing his ground against me? Roundhead as he is, man, I like him the better of that, not the worse. I hunger and thirst to have another turn with him. I have thought on his passado ever since, and I believe, were it to try again, I know a feat would control it. Fetch him directly."

Trusty Tomkins was presently ushered in, bearing himself with an iron gravity which neither the terrors of the preceding night nor the dignified demeanor of the high-born personage before whom he stood were able for an instant to overcome.

"How now, good fellow?" said Sir Henry; "I would fain see something more of thy fence, which baffled me the other evening; but truly, I think the light was somewhat too faint for my old eyes. Take a foil, man—I walk here in the hall, as Hamlet says, and 'tis the breathing-time of day with me—take a foil, then, in thy hand."

"Since it is your worship's desire," said the steward, letting fall his long cloak, and taking the foil in his hand.

"Now," said the knight, "if your fitness speaks, mine is ready. Methinks the very stepping on this same old pavement hath charmed away the gout which threatened me. Sa—sa—I tread as firm as a game-cock!"

They began the play with great spirit; and whether the old knight really fought more coolly with the blunt than with the sharp weapon, or whether the steward gave him some grains of advantage in this merely sportive encounter, it is certain Sir Henry had the better in the assault. His success put him into excellent humor.

"There," said he, "I found your trick—nay, you cheat me not twice the same way. There was a very palpable hit. Why, had I had but light enough the other night—— But it skills not speaking of it. Here we leave off. I must not fight, as we unwise Cavaliers did with you Roundhead rascals, beating you so often that we taught you to beat us at last. And good now, tell me why you are leaving your larder so full here? Do you think I or my family can use broken victuals? What, have you no better employment for your rounds of sequestrated beef than to leave them behind you when you shift your quarters?"

"So please your honor," said Tomkins, "it may be that you desire not the flesh of beeves, of rams, or of goats. Nevertheless, when you know that the provisions were provided and paid for out of your own rents and stock at Ditchley, sequestrated to the use of the state more than a year since, it may be you will have less scruple to use them for your own behoof."

"Rest assured that I shall," said Sir Henry; "and glad you have helped me to a share of mine own. Certainly I was an ass to suspect your masters of subsisting, save at honest men's expense.

"And as for the rumps of beeves," continued Tomkins, with the same solemnity, "there is a rump at Westminster which will stand us of the army much hacking and hewing yet ere it is discussed to our mind."

Sir Henry paused, as if to consider what was the meaning of this innuendo; for he was not a person of very quick apprehension. But having at length caught the meaning of it, he burst into an explosion of louder laughter than Joceline had seen him indulge in for a good while.

"Right, knave," he said, "I taste thy jest. It is the very moral of the puppet-show. Faustus raised the Devil, as the Parliament raised the army; and then, as the Devil flies away with Faustus, so will the army fly away with the Parliament—or the rump, as I call'st it, or sitting part of the so-called Parliament. And then, look you, friend, the very Devil of all hath my willing consent to fly away with the army in its turn, from the highest general down to the lowest drum-boy. Nay, never look fierce for the matter; remember there is daylight enough now for a game at sharps."

Trusty Tomkins appeared to think it best to suppress his displeasure; and observing that the wains were ready to transport the Commissioners' property to the borough, took a grave leave of Sir Henry Lee.

Meantime the old man continued to pace his recovered hall, rubbing his hands, and evincing greater signs of glee than he had shown since the fatal Thirtieth of January.

"Here we are again in the old frank, Joliffe—well victualled too. How the knave solved my point of conscience! The dullest of them is a special casuist where the question concerns profit. Look out if there are not some of our own ragged regiment lurking about, to whom a bellyful would be a godsend, Joceline. Then his fence, Joceline! though the fellow foins well—very sufficient well. But thou saw'st how I dealt with him when I had fitting light, Joceline?"

"Ay, and so your honor did," said Joceline. "You taught him to know the Duke of Norfolk from Saunders Gardner. I'll warrant him he will not wish to come under your honor's thumb again."

"Why, I am waxing old," said Sir Henry; "but skill will not rust through age, though sinews must stiffen. But my age is like a lusty winter, as old Will says—frosty but kindly. And what if, old as we are, we live to see better days yet! I promise thee, Joceline, I love this jarring betwixt the rogues of the board and the rogues of the sword. When thieves quarrel, true men have a chance of coming by their own."

Thus triumphed the old Cavalier, in the treble glory of having recovered his dwelling, regained, as he thought, his character as a man of fence, and finally discovered some prospect of a change of times, in which he was not without hopes that something might turn up for the Royal interest.

Meanwhile, Alice, with a prouder and a lighter heart than had danced in her bosom for several days, went forth with a gaiety to which she of late had been a stranger, to contribute her assistance to the regulation and supply of the household, by bringing the fresh water wanted from Fair Rosamond's Well.

Perhaps she remembered that, when she was but a girl, her cousin Markham used, among others, to make her perform that duty, as presenting the character of some captive Trojan princess, condemned by her situation to draw the waters from some Grecian spring, for the use of the proud victor. At any rate, she certainly joyed to see her father reinstated in his ancient habitation; and the joy was not the less sincere, that she knew their return to Woodstock had been procured by means of her cousin, and that, even in her father's prejudiced eyes, Everard had been in some degree exculpated of the accusations the old knight had brought against him; and that, if a reconciliation had not yet taken place, the preliminaries had been established on which such a desirable conclusion might easily be founded. It was like the commencement of a bridge: when the foundation is securely laid, and the piers raised above the influence of the torrent, the throwing of the arches may be accomplished in a subsequent season.

The doubtful fate of her only brother might have clouded even this momentary gleam of sunshine; but Alice had been bred up during the close and frequent contests of civil war, and had acquired the habit of hoping in behalf of those dear to her until hope was lost. In the present case, all reports seemed to assure her of her brother's safety.

Besides these causes for gaiety, Alice Lee had the pleasing feeling that she was restored to the habitation and the haunts of her childhood, from which she had not departed without much pain, the more felt, perhaps, because suppressed, in order to avoid irritating her father's sense of his misfortune. Finally, she enjoyed for the instant the gleam of self satisfaction by which we see the young and well-disposed so often animated, when they can be, in common phrase, helpful to those whom they love, and perform at the moment of need some of those little domestic tasks which age receives with so much pleasure from the dutiful hands of youth. So that, altogether, as she hasted through the remains and vestiges of a wilderness already mentioned, and from thence about a bow-shot into the park, to bring a pitcher of water from Rosamond's spring, Alice Lee, her features enlivened and her complexion a little raised by the exercise, had, for the moment, regained the gay and brilliant vivacity of expression which had been the characteristic of her beauty in her earlier and happier days.

This fountain of old memory had been once adorned with architectural ornaments in the style of the 16th century, chiefly relating to ancient mythology. All these were now wasted and overthrown, and existed only as moss-covered ruins, while the living spring continued to furnish its daily treasures, unrivaled in purity, though the quantity was small, gushing out amid disjointed stones, and bubbling through fragments of ancient sculpture.

With a light step and laughing brow the young lady of Lee was approaching the fountain usually so solitary, when she paused on beholding some one seated beside it. She proceeded, however, with confidence, though with a step something less gay, when she observed that the person was a female : some menial, perhaps, from the town, whom a fanciful mistress occasionally despatched for the water of a spring supposed to be peculiarly pure, or some aged woman, who made a little trade by carrying it to the better sort of families, and selling it for a trifle. There was no cause, therefore, for apprehension.

Yet the terrors of the times were so great, that Alice did not see a stranger even of her own sex without some apprehension. Denaturalized women had as usual followed the camps of both armies during the Civil War, who, on the one side with open profligacy and profanity, on the other with the fraudful tone of fanaticism or hypocrisy, exercised nearly in like degree their talents for murder or plunder. But it was broad daylight, the distance from the lodge was but trifling and though a little alarmed at seeing a stranger where she expected deep solitude, the daughter of the haughty old knight had too much of the lion about her to fear without some determined and decided cause.

Alice walked, therefore, gravely on towards the fount, and composed her looks as she took a hasty glance of the female who was seated there, and addressed herself to her task of filling her pitcher.

The woman whose presence had surprised and somewhat startled Alice Lee was a person of the lower rank, whose red cloak, russet kirtle, handkerchief trimmed with Coventry blue, and a coarse steeple hat, could not indicate at best anything higher than the wife of a small farmer, or, perhaps, the helpmate of a bailiff or hind. It was well if she proved nothing worse. Her clothes, indeed, were of good materials; but, what the female eye discerns with half a glance, they were indifferently adjusted and put on. This looked as if they did not belong to the person by whom they were worn, but were articles of which she had become the mistress by some accident, if not by some successful robbery. Her size, too, as did not escape Alice, even in the short perusal she afforded the stranger, was unusual, her features swarthy and singularly harsh, and her manner altogether unpropitious. The young lady almost wished, as she stooped to fill her pitcher, that she had rather turned back and sent Joceline on the errand; but repentance was too late now, and she had only to disguise as well as she could her unpleasant feelings.

"The blessings of this bright day to one as bright as it is!" said the stranger, with no unfriendly though a harsh, voice.

"I thank you," said Alice in reply; and continued to fill her pitcher busily, by assistance of an iron bowl which remained still chained to one of the stones beside the fountain.

"Perhaps, my pretty maiden, if you would accept my help, your work would be sooner done," said the stranger.

"I thank you," said Alice; "but had I needed assistance, I could have brought those with me who had rendered it."

"I do not doubt of that, my pretty maiden," answered the female; "there are too many lads in Woodstock with eyes in their heads. No doubt you could have brought with you any one of them who looked on you, if you had listed?"

Alice replied not a syllable, for she did not like the freedom used by the speaker, and was desirous to break off the conversation.

"Are you offended, my pretty mistress?" said the stranger. "That was far from my purpose. I will put my question otherwise. Are the good dames of Woodstock so careless of their pretty daughters as to let the flower of them all wander about the wild chase without a mother, or a somebody to prevent the fox from running away with the lamb? That carelessness, methinks, shows small kindness."

"Content yourself, good woman, I am not far from protection and assistance," said Alice, who liked less and less the effrontery of her new acquaintance.

"Alas! my pretty maiden," said the stranger, patting with her large and hard hand the head which Alice had kept bended down towards the water which she was laving, "it would be difficult to hear such a pipe as yours at the town of Woodstock, scream as loud as you would."

Alice shook the woman's hand angrily off, took up her pitcher, though not above half full, and, as she saw the stranger rise at the same time, said, not without fear doubtless, but with a natural feeling of resentment and dignity, "I have no reason to make my cries heard as far as Woodstock; were there occasion for my crying for help at all, it is nearer at hand."

She spoke not without a warrant; for, at the moment, broke through the bushes and stood by her side the noble hound Bevis, fixing on the stranger his eyes that glanced fire, raising every hair on his gallant mane as upright as the bristles of a wild boar when hard pressed, grinning till a case of teeth, which would have matched those of any wolf in Russia, were displayed in full array, and, without either barking or springing, seeming by his low determined growl, to await but the signal for dashing at the female, whom he plainly considered as a suspicious person.

But the stranger was undaunted. "My pretty maiden," she said, "you have indeed a formidable guardian there, where cockneys or bumpkins are concerned; but we who have been at the wars know spells for taming such furious dragons; and therefore let not your-footed protector go loose on me, for he is a noble animal, and nothing but self-defense would induce me to do him injury." So saying, she drew a pistol from her bosom and cocked it, pointing it towards the dog, as if apprehensive that he would spring upon her.

"Hold, woman—hold!" said Alice Lee; "the dog will not do you harm. Down, Bevis—couch down. And ere you attempt to hurt him, know he is the favorite hound of Sir Henry Lee of Ditchley, the keeper of Woodstock Park, who would severely revenge any injury offered to him."

"And you, pretty one, are the old knight's housekeeper, doubtless? I have often heard the Lees have good taste."

"I am his daughter, good woman."

"His daughter! I was blind; but yet it is true, nothing less perfect could answer the description which all the world has given of Mistress Alice Lee. I trust that my folly has given my young mistress no offence, and that she will allow me, in token of reconciliation, to fill her pitcher and carry it as far as she will permit."

"As you will, good mother; but I am about to return instantly to the lodge, to which, in these times, I cannot admit strangers. You can follow me no farther than the verge of the wilderness, and I am already too long from home: I will send some one to meet and relieve you of the pitcher." So saying, she turned her back, with a feeling of terror which she could hardly account for, and began to walk quickly towards the lodge, thinking thus to get rid of her troublesome acquaintance.

But she reckoned without her host, for in a moment her new companion was by her side, not running, indeed, but walking with prodigious, long, unwomanly strides, which soon brought her up with the hurried and timid steps of the frightened maiden. But her manner was more respectful than formerly, though her voice sounded remarkably harsh and disagreeable, and her whole appearance suggested an undefined yet irresistible feeling of apprehension.

"Pardon a stranger, lovely Mistress Alice," said her persecutor, "that was not capable of distinguishing between a lady of your high quality and a peasant wench, and who spoke to you with a degree of freedom ill befitting your rank, certainly, and condition, and which, I fear, has given you offence."

"No offence whatever," replied Alice; "but, good woman, I am near home, and can excuse your farther company. You are unknown to me."

"But it follows not," said the stranger, "that *your* fortunes may not be known to *me*, fair Mistress Alice. Look on my swarthy brow; England breeds none such, and in the lands from which I come the sun, which blackens our complexion, pours, to make amends, rays of knowledge into our brains which are denied to those of your lukewarm climate. Let me look upon your pretty hand (attempting to possess herself of it), and I promise you you shall hear what will please you."

"I hear what does *not* please me," said Alice, with dignity; "you must carry your tricks of fortune-telling and palmistry to the women of the village. We of the gentry hold them to be either imposture or unlawful knowledge."

"Yet you would fain hear of a certain colonel, I warrant you, whom certain unhappy circumstances have separated from his family; you would give better than silver if I could assure you that you see him in a day or two—ay, perhaps sooner."

"I know nothing of what you speak, good woman; if you want alms, there is a piece of silver, it is all I have in my purse."

"It were pity that I should take it," said the female; "and yet give it me, for the princess in the fairy tale must ever deserve, by her generosity, the bounty of the benevolent fairy, before she is rewarded by her protection."

"Take it—take it; give me my pitcher," said Alice, "And begone; yonder comes one of my father's servants. What, ho! Joceline—Joceline!"

The old fortune-teller hastily dropped something into the pitcher as she restored it to Alice Lee, and, plying her long limbs, disappeared speedily under cover of the wood.

Bevis turned, and barked, and showed some inclination to harass the retreat of this suspicious person, yet, as if uncertain, ran towards Joliffe, and fawned on him, as to demand his advice and encouragement. Joceline pacified the animal, and coming up to his young lady, asked her, with surprise, what was the matter, and whether she had been frightened? Alice made light of her alarm, for which, indeed, she could not have assigned any very competent reason, for the manners of the woman, though bold and intrusive, were not menacing. She only said she had met a fortune-teller by Rosamond's Well, and had had some difficulty in shaking her off.

"Ah, the gipsy thief," said Joceline, "how well she scented there was food in the pantry! They have noses like ravens, these strollers. Look you, Mistress Alice, you shall not see a raven or a carrion-crow in all the blue sky for a mile around you; but let a sheep drop suddenly down on the greensward, and before the poor creature's dead you shall see a dozen of such guests croaking, as if inviting each other to the banquet. Just so it is with these sturdy beggars. You will see few enough of them when there's nothing to give, but when hough's in the pot, they will have share on't."

"You are so proud of your fresh supply of provender," said Alice, "that you suspect all of a design on't. I do not think this woman will venture near your kitchen, Joceline."

"It will be best for her health," said Joceline, "lest I

give her a ducking for digestion. But give me the pitcher, Mistress Alice, meeter I bear it than you. How now! what jingles at the bottom? Have you lifted the pebbles as well as the water?

"I think the woman dropped something into the pitcher," said Alice.

"Nay, we must look to that, for it is like to be a charm, and we have enough of the Devil's ware about Woodstock already; we will not spare for the water—I can run back and fill the pitcher". He poured out the water upon the grass, and at the bottom of the pitcher was found a gold ring, in which was set a ruby, apparently of some value.

"Nay, if this be not enchantment, I know not what is," said Joceline. "Truly, Mistress Alice, I think you had better throw away this grimcrack. Such gifts from such hands are a kind of press-money which the Devil uses for enlisting his regiment of witches; and if they take but so much as a bean from him, they become his bond slaves for life. Ay, you look at the gewgaw, but to-morrow you will find a lead ring and a common pebble in its stead."

"Nay, Joceline, I think it will be better to find out that dark-complexioned woman, and return to her what seems of some value. So, cause inquiry to be made, and be sure you return her ring. It seems too valuable to be destroyed."

"Umph! that is always the way with women," murmured Joceline. "You will never get the best of them, but she is willing to save a bit of finery. Well, Mistress Alice, I trust that you are too young and too pretty to be enlisted in a regiment of witches."

"I shall not be afraid of it till you turn conjurer," said Alice; "so hasten to the well, where you are like still to find the woman, and let her know that Alice Lee desires none of her gifts, any more than she did of her society."

So saying, the young lady pursued her way to the lodge, while Joceline went down to Rosamond's Well to execute her commission. But the fortune-teller, or whoever she might be, was nowhere to be found neither, finding that to be the case, did Joceline give himself much trouble in tracking her farther.

"If this ring, which I daresay the jade stole somewhere," said the under-keeper to himself, "be worth a few nobles, it is better in honest hands than in those of vagabonds. My master has a right to all waifs and strays, and certainly such a ring, in possession of a gypsy, must be a waif So I shall confiscate it without scruple, and apply the produce to the support of Sir Henry's household, which is like to be poor enough. Thank Heaven, my military experience has taught me how to carry hooks at my finger-ends—that is trooper's law. Yet, hang it, after all, I had best take it to Mark Everard and ask his advice. I hold him now to be your learned counsellor in law where Mistress Alice's affairs are concerned, and my learned doctor, who shall be nameless, for such as concern church and state and Sir Henry Lee. And I'll give them leave to give mine umbles to the kites and ravens if they find me conferring my confidence where it is not safe."

CHAPTER XIX

> **Being skilless in these parts, which, to a stranger,
> Unguided and unfriended, often prove
> Rough and inhospitable.**
>
> *Twelfth Night.*

THERE was a little attempt at preparation, now that the dinner-hour was arrived, which showed that, in the opinion of his few but faithful domestics, the good knight had returned in triumph to his home.

The great tankard, exhibiting in bas-relief the figure of Michael subduing the arch enemy, was placed on the table, and Joceline and Phœbe dutifully attended—the one behind the chair of Sir Henry, the other to wait upon her young mistress, and both to make out, by formal and regular observance, the want of a more numerous train.

"A health to King Charles!" said the old knight, handing the massive tankard to his daughter; "drink it, my love, though it be rebel ale which they have left us. I will pledge thee: for the toast will excuse the liquor, had Noll himself brewed it."

The young lady touched the goblet with her lip, and returned it to her father, who took a copious draught.

"I will not say blessing on their hearts," said he; "though I must own they drank good ale."

"No wonder, sir; they come lightly by the malt, and need not spare it," said Joceline.

"Say'st thou?" said the knight; "thou shalt finish the tankard thyself for that very jest's sake." Nor was his follower slow in doing reason to the Royal pledge. He bowed and replaced the tankard, saying, after a triumphant glance at the sculpture, "I had a gibe with that same redcoat about the St. Michael just now."

"Redcoat—ha! what redcoat?" said the hasty old man. "Do any of these knaves still lurk about Woodstock? Quoit him downstairs instantly, Joceline. Know we not Galloway nags?"

"So please you, he is in some charge here, and will speedily be gone. It is he—he who had a rencontre with your honor in the wood."

"Ay, but I paid him off for it in the hall, as you yourself saw. I was never in better fence in my life, Joceline. That same steward fellow is not so utterly black-hearted a rogue as the most of them, Joceline. He fences well—excellent well. I will have thee try a bout in the hall with him to-morrow, though I think he will be too hard for thee. I know thy strength to an inch."

He might say this with some truth; for it was Joceline's fashion, when called on, as sometimes happened, to fence with his patron, just to put forth as much of his strength and skill as obliged the knight to contend hard for the victory, which, in the long run, he always contrived to yield up to him, like a discreet serving-man.

"And what said this Roundheaded steward of our great St. Michael's standing-cup?"

"Marry, he scoffed at our good saint, and said he was little better than one of the golden calves of Bethel. But I told him he should not talk so, until one of their own Roundheaded saints had given the Devil as complete a cross-buttock as St. Michael had given him, as 'tis carved upon the cup there. I trow that made him silent enough. And then he would know whether your honor and Mistress Alice, not to mention old Joan and myself, since it is your honor's pleasure I should take my bed here, were not afraid to sleep in a house that had been so much disturbed. But I told him we feared no fiends or goblins, having the prayers of the church read every evening."

"Joceline," said Alice, interrupting him, "wert thou mad? You know at what risk to ourselves and the good doctor the performance of that duty takes place."

"Oh, Mistress Alice," said Joceline, a little abashed, "you may be sure I spoke not a word of the Doctor. No—no, I did not let him into the secret that we had such a reverend chaplain. I think I know the length of this man's foot. We have had a jollification or so together. He is hand and glove with me, for as great a fanatic as he is."

"Trust him not too far," said the knight. "Nay, I fear thou hast been imprudent already, and that it will be unsafe for the good man to come here after nightfall, as is proposed. These Independents have noses like blood-hounds, and can smell out a loyalist under any disguise."

"If your honor thinks so," said Joceline, "I'll watch for the Doctor with good-will, and bring him into the lodge by the old condemned postern, and so up to this apartment; and sure this man Tomkins would never presume to come hither; and the Doctor may have a bed in Woodstock Lodge, and he never the wiser; or, if your honor does not think that safe, I can cut his throat for you, and I would not mind it a pin."

"God forbid!" said the knight. "He is under our roof, and a guest, though not an invited one. Go, Joceline; it shall be thy penance, for having given thy tongue too much license, to watch for the good doctor, and to take care of his safety while he continues with us. An October night or two in the forest would finish the good man."

"He is more like to finish our October than our October is to finish him," said the keeper; and withdrew under the encouraging smile of his patron.

He whistled Bevis along with him to share in his watch; and having received exact information where the clergyman was most likely to be found, assured his master that he would give the most pointed attention to his safety.

When the attendants had withdrawn, having previously removed the remains of the meal, the old knight, leaning back in his chair, encouraged pleasanter visions than had of late passed through his imagination, until by degrees he was surprised by actual slumber; while his daughter, not venturing to move but on tiptoe, took some needlework, and, bringing it close by the old man's side, employed her fingers on this task, bending her eyes from time to time on her parent with the affectionate zeal, if not the effective power, of a guardian angel. At length, as the light faded away and night came on, she was about to order candles to be brought. But, remembering how indifferent a couch Joceline's cottage had afforded, she could not think of interrupting the first sound and refreshing sleep which her father had enjoyed, in all probability, for the last two nights and days.

She herself had no other amusement, as she sat facing one of the great oriel windows, the same by which Wildrake had on a former occasion looked in upon Tompkins and Joceline while at their compotations, than watching the clouds which a lazy wind sometimes chased from the broad disk of the harvest-moon, sometimes permitted to accumulate and exclude her brightness. There is, I know not why, something peculiarly pleasing to the imagination in contemplating the Queen of Night when she is "wading," as the expression is, among the vapors which she has not power to dispel, and which on their side are unable entirely to quench her luster. It is the striking image of patient virtue calmly pursuing her path through good report and bad report, having that excellence in herself which ought to command all admiration, but bedimmed in the eyes of the world by suffering, by misfortune, by calumny."

As some such reflections, perhaps, were passing through Alice's imagination, she became sensible, to her surprise and alarm, that some one had clambered up upon the window, and was looking into the room. The idea of supernatural fear did not in the slightest degree agitate Alice. She was too much accustomed to the place and situation; for folk do not see specters in the scenes with which they have been familiar from infancy. But danger from marauders in a disturbed country was a more formidable subject of apprehension, and the thought armed Alice, who was naturally high-spirited, with such desperate courage, that she snatched a pistol from the wall, on which some firearms hung, and while she screamed to her father to awake, had the presence of mind to present it at the intruder. She did so the more readily, because she imagined she recognized in the visage, which she partially saw, the features of the woman whom she had met with at Rosamond's Well, and which had appeared to her peculiarly harsh and suspicious. Her father at the same time seized his sword and came forward, while the person at the window, alarmed at these demonstrations, and endeavoring to descend, missed footing, as had Cavaliero Wildrake before, and went down to the earth with no small noise. Nor was the reception on the bosom of our common mother either soft or safe; for, by a most terrific bark and growl, they heard that Bevis had come up and seized on the party, ere he or she could gain their feet.

"Hold fast, but worry not," said the old knight. "Alice, thou art the queen of wenches! Stand fast here till I run down and secure the rascal."

"For God's sake, no, my dearest father!" Alice exclaimed. "Joceline will be up immediately. Hark! I hear him."

There was indeed a bustle below, and more than one light danced to and fro in confusion, while those who bore them called to each other, yet suppressing their voices as they spoke, as men who would only be heard by those they addressed. The individual who had fallen under the power of Bevis was most impatient in his situation, and called with least precaution—"Here, Lee—Forester—take the dog off, else I must shoot him!"

"If thou dost," said Sir Henry from the window, "I blow thy brains out on the spot. Thieves, Joceline—thieves! come up and secure this ruffian. Bevis, hold on!"

"Back, Bevis—down, sir," cried Joceline. "I am coming—I am coming, Sir Henry. St. Michael, I shall go distracted!"

A terrible thought suddenly occurred to Alice: could Joceline have become unfaithful, that he was calling Bevis off the villain, instead of encouraging the trusty dog to secure him? Her father, meantime, moved perhaps by some suspicion of the same kind, hastily stepped aside out of the moonlight, and pulled Alice close to him, so as to be invisible from without, yet so placed as to hear what should pass. The scuffle between Bevis and his prisoner seemed to be ended by Joceline's interference, and there was close whispering for an instant, as of people in consultation.

"All is quiet now," said one voice; I will up and prepare the way for you." And immediately a form presented itself on the outside of the window, pushed open the lattice, and sprung into the parlor. But almost ere his step was upon the floor, certainly before he had obtained any secure footing, the old knight, who stood ready with his rapier drawn, made a desperate pass, which bore the intruder to the ground. Joceline, who clambered up next with a dark lantern in his hand, uttered a dreadful exclamation when he saw what had happened, crying out, "Lord in Heaven, he has slain his own son!"

"No—no—I tell you no," said the fallen young man, who was indeed young Albert Lee, the only son of the old knight. "I am not hurt. No noise, on your lives; get lights instantly." At the same time, he started from the floor as quickly as he could, under the embarrassment of a cloak and doubtlet skewered as it were together by the rapier of the old knight, whose pass, most fortunately, had been diverted from the body of Albert by the interruption of his cloak, the blade passing right across his back, piercing the clothes, while the hilt coming against his side with the whole force of the lounge had borne him to the ground.

Joceline all the while enjoined silence to every one, under the strictest conjurations. "Silence, as you would long live on earth—silence, as you would have a place in Heaven—be but silent for a few minutes; all our lives depend on it."

Meanwhile he procured lights with inexpressible despatch, and they then beheld that Sir Henry, on hearing the fatal words, had sunk back on one of the large chairs, without either motion, color, or sign of life.

"Oh, brother, how could you come in this manner?" said Alice.

"Ask no questions. Good God! for what am I reserved?" He gazed on his father as he spoke, who, with clay-cold features rigidly fixed, and his arms extended in the most absolute helplessness, looked rather the image of death upon a monument than a being in whom existence was only suspended. "Was my life spared," said Albert, raising his hands with a wild gesture to Heaven, "only to witness such a sight as this?"

"We suffer what Heaven permits, young man—we endure our lives while Heaven continues them. Let me approach." The same clergyman who had read the prayers at Joceline's hut now came forward. "Get water," he said, "instantly." And the helpful hand and light foot of Alice, with the ready-witted tenderness which never stagnates in vain lamentations while there is any room for hope, provided with incredible celerity all that the clergyman called for.

"It is but a swoon," he said, on feeling Sir Henry's palm—"a swoon produced from the instant and unexpected shock. Rouse thee up, Albert; I promise thee it will be nothing save a syncope. A cup, my dearest Alice, and a ribbon, or a bandage—I must take some blood—some aromatics, too, if they can be had, my good Alice."

But while Alice procured the cup and bandage, stripped her father's sleeve, and seemed by intuition even to anticipate every direction of the reverend doctor, her brother, hearing no word and seeing no sign of comfort, stood with both hands clasped and elevated into the air, a monument of speechless despair. Every feature in his face seemed to express the thought, "Here lies my father's corpse, and it is I whose rashness has slain him!"

"But when a few drops of blood began to follow the lancet; at first falling singly, and then trickling in a freer stream; when, in consequence of the application of cold water to the temples, and aromatics to the nostrils, the old man sighed feebly, and made an effort to move his limbs, Albert Lee changed his posture, at once to throw himself at the feet of the clergyman and kiss, if he would have permitted him, his shoes and the hem of his raiment.

"Rise, foolish youth," said the good man, with a reproving tone; "must it be always thus with you? Kneel to Heaven, not to the feeblest of its agents. You have been saved once again from great danger; would you deserve Heaven's bounty, remember you have been preserved for other purposes than you now think on. Begone you and Joceline, you have a duty to discharge; and be assured it will go better with your father's recovery that he see you not for a few minutes. Down—down to the wilderness, and bring in your attendant."

"Thanks—thanks—a thousand thanks," answered Albert Lee; and springing through the lattice, he disappeared as unexpectedly as he had entered. At the same time Joceline followed him, and by the same road.

Alice, whose fears of her father were now something abated upon this new movement among the persons of the scene, could not resist appealing to her venerable assistant. "Good Doctor, answer me but one question; was my brother Albert here just now, or have I dreamed all that has happened for these ten minutes past? Methinks, but for your presence, I could suppose the whole had passed in my sleep—that horrible thrust, that death-like, corpse-like old man, that soldier in mute despair—I must indeed have dreamed."

"If you have dreamed, my sweet Alice," said the Doctor, "I wish every sick-nurse had your property, since you have been attending to our patient better during your sleep than most of these old dormice can do when they are most awake. But your dream came through the gate of horn, my pretty darling, which you must remind me to explain to you at leisure. Albert has really been here, and will be here again."

"Albert!" repeated Sir Henry, "who names my son?"

"It is I, my kind patron," said the Doctor; "permit me to bind up your arm."

"My wound! with all my heart, Doctor," said Sir Henry, raising himself, and gathering his recollection by degrees. "I knew of old thou wert body-curer as well as soul-curer, and served my regiment for surgeon as well as chaplain. But where is the rascal I killed? I never made a fairer *stramacon* in my life. The shell of my rapier struck against his ribs. So dead he must be, or my right hand has forgot its cunning."

"Nobody was slain," said the Doctor; "we must thank God for that, since there were none but friends to slay. Here is a good cloak and doublet, though, wounded in a fashion which will require some skill in tailor-craft to cure. But I was your last antagonist, and took a little blood from you, merely to prepare you for the pleasure and surprise of seeing your son, who, though hunted pretty close, as you may believe, hath made his way from Worcester hither, where, with Joceline's assistance, we will care well enough for his safety. It was even for this reason that I pressed you to accept of your nephew's proposal to return to the old lodge, where a hundred men might be concealed, though a thousand were making search to discover them. Never such a place for hide-and-seek, as I shall make good when I can find means to publish my *Wonders of Woodstock.*"

"But, my son—my dear son," said the knight, "shall I not then instantly see him? and wherefore did you not forewarn me of this joyful event?"

"Because I was uncertain of his motions," said the Doctor, "and rather thought he was bound for the sea-side, and that it would be best to tell you of his fate when he was safe on board and in full sail for France. We had appointed to let you know all when I came hither to-night to join you. But there is a redcoat in the house whom we care not to trust farther than we could not help. We dared not, therefore, venture in by the hall; and so, prowling round the building, Albert informed us that an old prank of his, when a boy, consisted of entering by this window. A lad who was with us would needs make the experiment, as there seemed to be no light in the chamber, and the moonlight without made us liable to be detected. His foot slipped, and our friend Bevis came upon us."

"In good truth, you acted simply," said Sir Henry, "to attack a garrison without a summons. But all this is nothing to my son Albert. Where is he? Let me see him."

"But, Sir Henry, wait," said the Doctor, "till your restored strength——"

"A plague of my restored strength, man!" answered the knight, as his old spirit began to awaken within him. "Dost not remember that I lay on Edgehill field all night, bleeding like a bullock from five several wounds, and wore my armor within six weeks, and you talk to me of the few drops of blood that follow such a scratch as a cat's claw might have made?"

"Nay, if you feel so courageous," said the Doctor, "I will fetch your son; he is not far distant." So saying, he left the apartment, making a sign to Alice to remain, in case any symptoms of her father's weakness should return.

It was fortunate, perhaps, that Sir Henry never seemed to recollect the precise nature of the alarm which had at once, and effectually as the shock of the thunderbolt, for the moment suspended his faculties. Something he said more than once of being certain he had done mischief with that *stramaçon*, as he called it; but his mind not recur to that danger as having been incurred by his son. Alice, glad to see that her father appeared to have forgotten a circumstance so fearful, as men often forget the blow or other sudden cause which has thrown them into a swoon, readily excused herself from throwing much light on the matter, by pleading the general confusion. And in a few minutes, Albert cut off all farther inquiry by entering the room, followed by the Doctor, and throwing himself alternately into the arms of his father and of his sister.

CHAPTER XX

> The boy is—hark ye, sirrah, what's your name?
> Oh, Jacob—ay, I recollect—the same.
>
> CRABBE.

THE affectionate relatives were united as those who, meeting under great adversity, feel still the happiness of sharing it in common. They embraced again and again, and gave way to those expansions of the heart which at once express and relieve the pressure of mental agitation. At length the tide of emotion began to subside; and Sir Henry, still holding his recovered son by the hand, resumed the command of his feelings which he usually practised.

"So you have seen the last of our battles, Albert," he said, "and the King's colors have fallen forever before the rebels?"

"It is but even so," said the young man: "the last cast of the die was thrown, and, alas! lost, at Worcester; and Cromwell's fortune carried it there, as it has wherever he has shown himself."

"Well, it can but be for a time—it can but be for a time," answered his father: "the Devil is potent, they say, in raising and gratifying favorites, but he can grant but short leases. And the King—the King, Albert—the King—in my ear—close—close!"

"Our last news were confident that he had escaped from Bristol."

"Thank God for that—thank God for that!" said the knight. "Where didst thou leave him?"

"Our men were almost all cut to pieces at the bridge," Albert replied; "but I followed his Majesty, with about five hundred other officers and gentlemen, who were resolved to die around him, until, as our numbers and appearance drew the whole pursuit after us, it pleased his Majesty to dismiss us, with many thanks and words of comfort to us in general, and some kind expressions to most of us in especial. He sent his royal greeting to you, sir, in particular, and said more than becomes me to repeat."

"Nay, I will hear it every word, boy," said Sir Henry;

"is not the certainty that thou hast discharged thy duty, and that King Charles owns it, enough to console me for all we have lost and suffered, and wouldst thou stint me of it from a false shamefacedness? I will have it out of thee, were it drawn from thee with cords."

"It shall need no such compulsion," said the young man. "It was his Majesty's pleasure to bid me tell Sir Henry Lee, in his name, that if his son could not go before his father in the race of loyalty, he was at least following him closely, and would soon move side by side."

"Said he so?" answered the knight. "Old Victor Lee will look down with pride on thee, Albert! But I forget—you must be weary and hungry."

"Even so, sir," said Albert; "but these are things which of late I have been in the habit of enduring for safety's sake."

"Joceline!—what ho, Joceline!"

The under-keeper entered, and received orders to get supper prepared directly.

"My son and Dr. Rochecliffe are half starving," said the knight.

"And there is a lad, too, below," said Joceline, "a page, he says, of Colonel Albert's, whose belly rings cupboard too, and that to no common tune; for I think he could eat a horse, as the Yorkshireman says, behind the saddle. He had better eat at the sideboard; for he has devoured a whole loaf of bread and butter, as fast as Phœbe could cut it, and it has not staid his stomach for a minute; and truly I think you had better keep him under your own eyes, for the steward beneath might ask him troublesome questions if he went below. And then he is impatient, as all your gentlemen pages are, and is saucy among the women."

"Whom is it he talks of? What page hast thou got, Albert, that bears himself so ill?" said Sir Henry.

"The son of a dear friend, a noble lord of Scotland, who followed the great Montrose's banner, afterwards joined the King in Scotland, and came with him as far as Worcester. He was wounded the day before the battle, and conjured me to take this youth under my charge, which I did, something unwillingly; but I could not refuse a father, perhaps on his death-bed, pleading for the safety of an only son."

"Thou hadst preserved an halter, hadst thou hesitated," said Sir Henry; "the smallest tree can always give some shelter, and it pleases me to think the old stock of Lee is not so totally prostrate, but it may yet be a refuge for the distressed. Fetch the youth in; he is of noble blood, and these are no times of ceremony, he shall sit with us at the same table, page though he be; and if you have not schooled him handsomely in his manners, he may not be the worse of some lessons from me."

"You will excuse his national drawling accent, sir?" said Albert, "though I know you like it not."

"I have, small cause, Albert," answered the knight—"small cause. Who stirred up these disunions? The Scots. Who strengthened the hands of Parliament, when their cause was well-nigh ruined? The Scots again. Who delivered up the King, their countryman, who had flung himself upon their protection? The Scots again. But this lad's father, you say, has fought on the part of the noble Montrose; and such a man as the great Marquis may make amends for the degeneracy of a whole nation."

"Nay, father," said Albert, "and I must add that, though this lad is uncouth and wayward, and, as you will see, something wilful, yet the King has not a more zealous friend in England; and, when occasion offered, he fought stoutly, too, in his defense. I marvel he comes not."

"He hath taken the bath," said Joceline, "and nothing less would serve than that he should have it immediately; the supper, he said, might be got ready in the mean time; and he commands all about him as if he were in his father's old castle, where he might have called long enough, I warrant, without any one to hear him."

"Indeed?" said Sir Henry, "this must be a forward chick of the game to crow so early. What is his name?"

"His name! It escapes me every hour, it is so hard a one," said Albert. "Kerneguy is his name—Louis Kerneguy; his father was Lord Killstewers, of Kincardineshire."

"Kerneguy and Killstewers, and Kin—what d'ye call it? Truly," said the knight, "these Northern men's names and titles smack of their origin: they sound like a northwest wind, rumbling and roaring among heather and rocks."

"It is but the asperities of the Celtic and Saxon dialects," said Dr. Rochecliffe, "which, according to Verstegan, still linger in those northern parts of the island. But peace—here comes supper, and Master Louis Kerneguy."

Supper entered accordingly, borne in by Joceline and Phœbe, and after it, leaning on a huge knotty stick, and having his nose in the air like a questing hound, for his attention was apparently more fixed on the good provisions that went before him than anything else, came Master Kerneguy, and seated himself, without much ceremony, at the lower end of the table.

He was a tall, rawboned lad, with a shock head of hair, fiery red, like many of his country, while the harshness of his national features was increased by the contrast of his complexion, turned almost black by the exposure to all sorts of weather, which, in that skulking and rambling mode of life, the fugitive Royalists had been obliged to encounter. His address was by no means prepossessing, being a mixture of awkwardness and forwardness, and showing, in a remarkable degree, how a want of easy address may be consistent with an admirable stock of assurance. His face intimated having received some recent scratches, and the care of Dr. Rochecliffe had decorated it with a number of patches, which even enhanced its natural plainness. Yet the eyes were brilliant and expressive, and, amid his ugliness—for it amounted to that degree of irregularity—the face was not deficient in some lines which expressed both sagacity and resolution.

The dress of Albert himself was far beneath his quality as the son of Sir Henry Lee, and commander of a regiment in the Royal service; but that of his page was still more dilapidated. A disastrous green jerkin, which had been changed to a hundred hues by sun and rain, so that the original could scarce be discovered, huge clouterly shoes, leathern breeches—such as were worn by hedgers—coarse gray worsted stockings, were the attire of the honorable youth, whose limping gait, while it added to the ungainliness of his manner, showed, at the same time, the extent of his sufferings. His appearance bordered so much upon what is vulgarly called the queer, that even with Alice it would have excited some sense of ridicule, had not compassion been predominant.

The grace was said; and the young squire of Ditchley, as well as Dr. Rochecliffe, made an excellent figure at a meal the like of which, in quality and abundance, did not seem to have lately fallen to their share. But their feats were child's play to those of the Scottish youth. Far from betraying any symptoms of the bread and butter with which he had attempted to close the orifice of his stomach, his appetite appeared to have been sharpened by a nine days' fast; and the knight was disposed to think that the very genius of famine himself, come forth from his native regions of the North, was in the act of honoring him with a visit, while, as if afraid of losing a moment's exertion, Master Kerneguy never looked either to right or left, or spoke a single word to any at table.

"I am glad to see that you have brought a good appetite for our country fare, young gentleman," said Sir Henry.

"Bread of Gude! sir," said the page, "and ye'll find flesh, I'se find appetite conforming, ony day o' the year. But the truth is, sir, that the appeteezement has been coming on for three days or four, and the meat in this southland of yours has been scarce, and hard to come by; so, sir, I'm making up for lost time, as the piper of Sligo said, when he eat a hail side o' mutton."

"You have been country-bred, young man," said the knight, who, like others of his time, held the reins of discipline rather tight over the rising generation; "at least, to judge from the youths of Scotland whom I have seen at his late Majesty's court in former days: they had less appetite, and more—more——" As he sought the qualifying phrase which might supply the place of "good manners," his guest closed the sentence in his own way—"And more meat, it may be—the better luck theirs."

Sir Henry stared and was silent. His son seemed to think it time to interpose. "My dear father," he said, "think how many years have run since the Thirty-eighth, when the Scottish troubles first began, and I am sure that you will not wonder that, while the barons of Scotland have been, for one cause or other, perpetually in the field, the education of their children at home must have been much neglected, and that young men of my friend's age know better how to use a broadsword or to toss a pike than the decent ceremonials of society."

"The reason is a sufficient one," said the knight, "and, since thou sayest thy follower Kernigo can fight, we'll not let him lack victuals, a God's name. See, he looks angrily still at yonder cold loin of mutton; for God's sake put it all on his plate."

"I can bide the bit and the buffet," said the Honorable Master Kerneguy: "a hungry tike ne'er minds a blaud with a rough bane."

"Now, God ha'e mercy, Albert, but if this be the son of a Scots peer," said Sir Henry to his son, in a low tone of voice, "I would not be the English plowman who would change manners with him, for his ancient blood, and his nobility, and his estate to boot, an he has one. He has eaten, as I am a Christian, near four pounds of solid butcher's meat, and with the grace of a wolf tugging at the carcass of a dead horse. Oh, he is about to drink at last. Soh! He wipes his mouth, though, and dips his fingers in the ewer, and dries them, I profess, with the napkin! There is some grace in him, after all."

"Here is wussing all your vera gude healths!" said the youth of quality, and took a draught in proportion to the solids which he had sent before: he then flung his knife and fork awkwardly on the trencher, which he pushed back towards the center of the table, extended his feet beneath it till they rested on their heels, folded his arms on his well-replenished stomach, and, lolling back in his chair, looked much as if he was about to whistle himself asleep.

"Soh!" said the knight, "the Honorable Master Kernigo hath laid down his arms. Withdraw these things, and give us our glasses. Fill them around, Joceline; and if the Devil or the whole Parliament were within hearing, let them hear Henry Lee of Ditchley drink a health to King Charles, and confusion to his enemies!"

"Amen!" said a voice from behind the door.

All the company looked at each other in astonishment, at a response so little expected. It was followed by a solemn and peculiar tap, such as a kind of freemasonry had introduced among Royalists, and by which they were accustomed to make themselves and their principles known to each other when they met by accident.

"There is no danger," said Albert, knowing the sign—"it is a friend; yet I wish he had been at a greater distance just now."

"And why, my son, should you wish the absence of one true man, who may, perhaps, wish to share our abundance, on one of those rare occasions when we have superfluity at our disposal? Go, Joceline, see who knocks; and, if a safe man, admit him."

"And if otherwise," said Joceline, "methinks I shall be able to prevent his troubling the good company."

"No violence, Joceline, on your life," said Albert Lee; and Alice echoed, "For God's sake, no violence!"

"No unnecessary violence at least," said the good knight; "for, if the time demands it, I will have it seen that I am master of my own house."

Joceline Joliffe nodded assent to all parties, and went on tiptoe to exchange one or two other mysterious symbols and knocks ere he opened the door.

It may be here remarked that this species of secret association, with its signals of union, existed among the more dissolute and desperate class of Cavaliers—men habituated to the dissipated life which they had been accustomed to in an ill-disciplined army, where everything like order and regularity was too apt to be accounted a badge of Puritanism. These were the "roaring boys" who met in hedge alehouses, and, when they had by any chance obtained a little money or a little credit, determined to create a counter-revolution by declaring their sittings permanent, and proclaimed in the words of one of their choicest ditties—

> "We'll drink till we bring
> In triumph back the king."

The leaders and gentry, of a higher description and more regular morals, did not indeed partake such excesses, but they still kept their eye upon a class of persons who, from courage and desperation, were capable of serving on an advantageous occasion the fallen cause of Royalty; and recorded the lodges and blind taverns at which they met, as wholesale merchants know the houses of call of the mechanics whom they may have occasion to employ, and can tell where they may find them when need requires. It is scarce necessary to add, that among the lower class, and sometimes even among the higher, there were men found capable of betraying the projects and conspiracies of their associates, whether well or indifferently combined, to the governors of the state. Cromwell, in particular, had gained some correspondents of this kind of the highest rank and of the most undoubted character among the Royalists, who, if they made scruple of impeaching or betraying individuals who confided in them, had no hesitation in giving the government such general information as served to enable him to disappoint the purposes of any plot or conspiracy.

To return to our story. In much shorter time than we have spent in reminding the reader of these historical particulars, Joliffe had made his mystic communication; and being duly answered as by one of the initiated, he undid the door, and there entered our old friend Roger Wildrake, Round-head in dress, as his safety and his dependence on Colonel Everard compelled him to be, but that dress worn in a most Cavalier like manner, and forming a stronger contrast than usual with the demeanor and language of the wearer, to which it was never very congenial.

His Puritanic hat, the emblem of that of Ralpho in the prints to *Hudibras*, or, as he called it, his felt umbrella, was set most knowingly on one side of the head, as if it had been a Spanish hat and feather; his straight, square-caped, sad-colored cloak was flung gaily upon one shoulder, as if it had been of three-piled taffeta, lined with crimson silk; and he paraded his huge calf-skin boots, as if they had been silken hose and Spanish leather shoes, with roses on the instep. In short, the airs which he gave himself, of a most thorough-paced wild gallant and Cavalier, joined to a glistening of self-satisfaction in his eye and an inimitable swagger in his gait, which completely announced his thoughtless, conceited, and reckless character, formed a most ridiculous contrast to his gravity of attire.

It could not, on the other hand, be denied that, in spite of the touch of ridicule which attached to his character, and the loose morality which he had learned in the dissipation of town pleasures, and afterwards in the disorderly life of a soldier, Wildrake had points about him both to make him feared and respected. He was handsome, even in spite of his air of debauched effrontery; a man of the most decided courage, though his vaunting rendered it sometimes doubtful; and entertained a sincere sense of his political principles, such as they were, though he was often so imprudent in asserting and boasting of them as, joined with his dependence on Colonel Everard, induced prudent men to doubt his sincerity.

Such as he was, however, he entered the parlor of Victor Lee, where his presence was anything but desirable to the parties present, with a jaunty step, and a consciousness of deserving the best possible reception. This assurance was greatly aided by circumstances which rendered it obvious that, if the jocund Cavalier had limited himself to one draught of liquor that evening, in terms of his vow of temperance, it must have been a very deep and long one.

"Save ye, gentlemen—save ye. Save you, good Sir Henry Lee, though I have scarce the honor to be known to you. Save you, worthy Doctor, and a speedy resurrection to the fallen Church of England."

"You are welcome, sir," said Sir Henry Lee, whose feelings of hospitality, and of the fraternal reception due to a Royalist sufferer, induced him to tolerate this intrusion more than he might have done otherwise. "If you have fought or suffered for the King, sir, it is an excuse for joining us, and commanding our services in anything in our power, although at present we are a family-party. But I think I saw you in waiting upon Master Markham Everard, who calls himself Colonel Everard. If your message is from him, you may wish to see me in private?"

"Not at all, Sir Henry—not at all. It is true, as my ill hap will have it, that, being on the stormy side of the hedge, like all honest men—you understand me, Sir Henry—I am glad, as it were, to gain something from my old friend and comrade's countenance, not by truckling or disowning my principles, sir—I defy such practises—but, in short, by doing him any kindness in my power when he is pleased to call on me. So I came down here with a message from him to the old Roundheaded son of a —— I beg the young lady's pardon, from the crown of her head down to the very toes of her slipper. And so, sir, chancing as I was stumbling out in the dark, I heard you give a toast, sir, which warmed my heart, sir, and ever will, sir, till death chills it; and so I made bold to let you know there was an honest man within hearing."

Such was the self-introduction of Master Wildrake, to which the knight replied, by asking him to sit down and take a glass of sack to his Majesty's glorious restoration. Wildrake, at this hint, squeezed in without ceremony beside the young Scotsman, and not only pledged his landlord's toast, but seconded its import, by volunteering a verse or two of his favorite loyal ditty, "The King shall enjoy his own again." The heartiness which he threw into his song opened still farther the heart of the old knight, though Albert and Alice looked at each other with looks resentful of the intrusion, and desirous to put an end to it. The Honourable Master Kerneguy either possessed that happy indifference of temper which does not deign to notice such circumstances, or he was able to assume the appearance of it to perfection, as he sat sipping sack and cracking walnuts, without testifying the least sense that an addition had been made to the party. Wildrake, who liked the liquor and the company, showed no unwillingness to repay his landlord, by being at the expense of the conversation.

"You talk of fighting and suffering, Sir Henry Lee—Lord help us, we have had all our share. All the world knows what Sir Henry Lee has done from Edge [hill] Field downwards, wherever a loyal sword was drawn or a loyal flag fluttered. Ah, God help us! I have done something too. My name is Roger Wildrake of Squattlesea Mere, Lincoln; not that you are ever like to have heard it before, but I was captain in Lunsford's light horse, and afterwards with Goring. I was a child-eater, sir—a babe-bolter."

"I have heard of your regiment's exploits, sir; and perhaps you may find I have seen some of them, if we should spend ten minutes together. And I think I have heard of your name too. I beg to drink your health, Captain Wildrake of Squattlesea Mere, Lincolnshire."

"Sir Henry, I drink yours in this pint bumper, and upon my knee; and I would do as much for that young gentleman (looking at Albert), and the squire of the green cassock too, holding it for green, as the colors are not to my eyes altogether clear and distinguishable."

It was a remarkable part of what is called by theatrical folk the by-play of this scene, that Albert was conversing apart with Doctor Rochecliffe in whispers, even more than the divine seemed desirous of encouraging, yet to whatever their private conversation referred, it did not deprive the young colonel of the power of listening to what was going forward in the party at large, and interfering from time to time, like a watch-dog who can distinguish the slightest alarm even when employed in the engrossing process of taking his food.

"Captain Wildrake," said Albert, "we have no objection —I mean my friend and I—to be communicative on proper occasions; but you, sir, who are so old a sufferer, must needs know, that at such casual meetings as this men do not mention their names unless they are specially wanted. It is a point of conscience, sir, to be able to say, if your principal, Captain Everard, or Colonel Everard, if he be a colonel, should examine you upon oath, 'I did not know who the persons were whom I heard drink such and such toasts.'"

"Faith, I have a better way of it, worthy sir," answered Wildrake: "I never can, for the life of me, remember that there were any such and such toasts drunk at all. It's a strange gift of forgetfulness I have."

"Well, sir," replied the younger Lee; "but we, who have unhappily more tenacious memories, would willingly abide by the more general rule."

"Oh, sir," answered Wildrake, "with all my heart. I intrude on no man's confidence, d—n me, and I only spoke for civility's sake, having the purpose of drinking your health in a good fashion." Then he broke forth into melody:

"Then let the health go round, a-round, a-round, a-round,
Then let the health go round.
For though your stocking be of silk,
Your knee shall kiss the ground, a-ground, a-ground, a-ground,
Your knee shall kiss the ground."

"Urge it no farther," said Sir Henry, addressing his son. "Master Wildrake is one of the old school—one of the tantivy boys; and we must bear a little, for if they drink hard, they fought well. I will never forget how a party came up and rescued us clerks of Oxford, as they called the regiment I belonged to, out of a cursed embroglio during the attack on Brentford. I tell you, we were inclosed with the cockneys' pikes both front and rear, and we should have come off but ill, had not Lunsford's light horse, the babe-eaters, as they called them, charged up to the pike's point and brought us off."

"I am glad you thought on that, Sir Henry," said Wildrake; "and do you remember what the officer of Lunsford's said?"

"I think I do," said Sir Henry, smiling.

"Well, then, did not he call out, when the women were coming down, howling like sirens as they were, 'Have none of you a plump child that you could give us, to break our fast upon?'"

"Truth itself!" said the knight; "and a great fat woman stepped forward with a baby, and offered it to the supposed cannibal."

All at the table, Master Kerneguy excepted, who seemed to think that good food of any kind required no apology, held up their hands in token of amazement.

"Ay," said Wildrake, "the——a-hem!—I crave the lady's pardon again, from tip of top-knot to hem of farthingale—but the cursed creature proved to be a parish nurse, who had been paid for the child half a year in advance. Gad, I took the baby out of the bitch-wolf's hand; and I have contrived, though God knows I have lived in a skeldering sort of way myself, to breed up bold Breakfast, as I call him, ever since. It was paying dear for a jest though."

"Sir, I honor you for your humanity," said the old knight. "Sir, I thank you for your courage. Sir, I am glad to see you here," said the good knight, his eyes watering almost to overflowing. "So you were the wild officer who cut us out of the toils? Oh, sir, had you but stopped when I called on you, and allowed us to clear the streets of Brentford with our musketeers, we would have been at London Stone that day! But your good-will was the same."

"Ay, truly was it," said Wildrake, who now sat triumphant and glorious in his easy-chair. "And here is to all the brave hearts, sir, that fought and fell in that same storm of Brentford. We drove all before us like chaff, till the shops, where they sold strong waters and other temptations, brought us up. Gad, sir, we, the babe-eaters, had too many acquaintances in Brentford, and our stout Prince Rupert was ever better at making way than drawing off. Gad, sir, for my own poor share, I did but go into the house of a poor widow lady, who maintained a charge of daughters, and whom I had known of old, to get my horse fed, a morsel of meat, and so forth, when these cockney pikes of the artillery ground, as you very well call them, rallied, and came in with their armed heads, as boldly as so many Cotswold rams. I sprang downstairs—got to my horse; but, egad, I fancy all my troop had widows and orphan maidens to comfort as well as I, for only five of us got together. We cut our way through successfully; and gad, gentlemen, I carried my little Breakfast on the pommel before me; and there was such a hallooing and screeching, as if the whole town thought I was to kill, roast, and eat the poor child so soon as I got to quarters. But devil a cockney charged up to my bonny bay, poor lass, to rescue little cake-bread; they only cried 'Haro,' and 'Out upon me.'"

"Alas! alas!" said the knight, "we made ourselves seem worse than we were; and we were too bad to deserve God's blessing even in a good cause. But it is needless to look back; we did not deserve victories when God gave them, for we never improved them like good soldiers, or like Christian men; and so we gave these canting scoundrels the advantage of us, for they assumed, out of mere hypocrisy, the discipline and orderly behavior which we, who drew our swords in a better cause, ought to have practised out of true principle. But here is my hand, captain. I have often wished to see the honest fellow who charged up so smartly in our behalf, and I reverence you for the care you took of the poor child. I am glad this dilapidated place has still some hospitality to offer you, although we cannot treat you to roasted babes or stewed sucklings—eh, captain?"

"Troth, Sir Henry, the scandal was sore against us on that score. I remember Lacy, who was an old play-actor, and a lieutenant in ours, made drollery on it in a play which was sometimes acted at Oxford when our hearts were something up, called, I think, *The Old Troop*." *

So saying, and feeling more familiar as his merits were known, he hitched his chair up against that of the Scottish lad, who was seated next him, and who, in shifting his

* See Cannibalism imputed to the Cavaliers. Note 5.

place, was awkward enough to disturb, in his turn, Alice Lee, who sat opposite, and, a little offended, or at least embarrassed, drew her chair away from the table.

"I crave pardon," said the Honorable Master Kerneguy; "but, sir," to Master Wildrake, "ye hae e'en garr'd me hurt the young lady's shank."

"I crave your pardon, sir, and much more that of the fair lady, as is reasonable; though, rat me, sir, if it was I set your chair a-trundling in that way. Zooks, sir, I have brought with me no plague nor pestilence, nor other infectious disorder, that ye should have started away as if I had been a leper, and discomposed the lady, which I would have prevented with my life, sir. Sir, if ye be Northern-born, as your tongue bespeaks, egad, it was I ran the risk in drawing near you; so there was small reason for you to bolt."

"Master Wildrake," said Albert, interfering, "this young gentleman is a stranger as well as you, under protection of Sir Henry's hospitality, and it cannot be agreeable for my father to see disputes arise among his guests. You may mistake the young gentleman's quality from his present appearance: this is the Honorable Master Louis Kerneguy, sir, son of my Lord Killstewers of Kincardineshire, one who has fought for the King, young as he is."

"No dispute shall rise through me, sir—none through me," said Wildrake; "your exposition sufficeth, sir. Master Louis Girnigo, son of my Lord Kilsteer, in Gringardenshire, I am your humble slave, sir, and drink your health, in token that I honor you, and all true Scots who draw their Andrew Ferraras on the right side, sir."

"I'se beholden to you, and thank you, sir," said the young man, with some haughtiness of manner, which hardly corresponded with his rusticity; "and I wuss your health in a ceevil way."

Most judicious persons would have here dropped the conversation; but it was one of Wildrake's marked peculiarities that he could never let matters stand when they were well. He continued to plague the shy, proud, and awkward lad with his observations. "You speak your national dialect pretty strongly, Master Girnigo," said he, "but I think not quite the language of the gallants that I have known among the Scottish Cavaliers. I knew, for example, some of the Gordons, and others of good repute, who always put an *f* for the *wh*, as *faat* for *what*, *fan* for *when*, and the like."

Albert Lee here interposed, and said that the provinces

of Scotland, like those of England, had their different modes of pronunciation.

"You are very right, sir," said Wildrake. "I reckon myself, now, a pretty good speaker of their cursed jargon—no offense, young gentleman; and yet, when I took a turn with some of Montrose's folk, in the South Hielands, as they call their beastly wildernesses—no offense again—I chanced to be by myself, and to lose my way, when I said to a shepherd fellow, making my mouth as wide and my voice as broad as I could, 'Whore am I ganging till?' confound me if the fellow could answer me, unless indeed he was sulky, as the bumpkins will be now and then to the gentlemen of the sword."

This was familiarly spoken, and though partly addressed to Albert, was still more directed to his immediate neighbor, the young Scotsman, who seemed, from bashfulness, or some other reason, rather shy of his intimacy. To one or two personal touches from Wildrake's elbow, administered during his last speech, by way of a practical appeal to him in particular, he only answered, "Misunderstandings were to be expected when men converse in national deealects."

Wildrake, now considerably drunker than he ought to have been in civil company, caught up the phrase and repeated it. "Misunderstanding, sir—misunderstanding, sir! I do not know how I am to construe that, sir; but, to judge from the information of these scratches on your honorable visnomy, I should augur that you had been of late at misunderstanding with the cat, sir."

"You are mistaken, then, friend, for it was with the dowg," answered the Scotsman, dryly, and cast a look towards Albert.

"We had some trouble with the watch-dogs in entering so late in the evening," said Albert, in explanation, "and this youth had a fall among some rubbish, by which he came by these scratches."

"And now, dear Sir Henry," said Dr. Rochecliffe, "allow us to remind you of your gout, and our long journey. I do it the rather that my good friend your son has been, during the whole time of supper, putting questions to me aside, which had much better be reserved till to-morrow. May we therefore ask permission to retire to our night's rest?"

"These private committees in a merry meeting," said Wildrake, "are a solecism in breeding. They always put me in mind of the cursed committees at Westminster. But shall we to roost before we rouse the night-owl with a catch?"

"Aha, canst thou quote Shakspeare?" said Sir Henry, pleased at discovering a new good quality in his acquaintance, whose military services were otherwise but just able to counterbalance the intrusive freedom of his conversation. "In the name of merry Will," he continued—"whom I never saw, though I have seen many of his comrades, as Alleyn, Hemminge, and so on, we will have a single catch, and one rouse about, and then to bed."

After the usual discussion about the choice of the song, and the parts which each was to bear, they united their voices in trolling a loyal glee, which was popular among the party at the time, and in fact believed to be composed by no less a person than Doctor Rochecliffe himself.

Glee for King Charles

Bring the bowl which you boast,
  Fill it up to the brim;
'Tis to him we love most,
  And to all who love him.
Brave gallants, stand up,
  And avaunt, ye base carles!
Were there death in the cup,
  Here's a health to King Charles!

Though he wanders through dangers,
  Unaided, unknown,
Dependent on strangers,
  Estranged from his own;
Though 'tis under our breath,
  Amidst forfeits and perils,
Here's to honor and faith,
  And a health to King Charles!

Let such honors abound
  As the time can afford,
The knee on the ground
  And the hand on the sword;
But the time shall come round,
  When, 'mid lords, dukes, and earls,
The loud trumpets shall sound
  Here's a health to King Charles!

After this display of loyalty, and a final libation, the party took leave of each other for the night. Sir Henry offered his old acquaintance Wildrake a bed for the evening, who weighed the matter somewhat in this fashion: "Why, to speak truth, my patron will expect me at the borough; but then he is used to my staying out of doors a-nights. Then there's the Devil, that they say haunts

Woodstock; but with the blessing of this reverend doctor, I defy him and all his works. I saw him not when I slept here twice before, and I am sure if he was absent then, he has not come back with Sir Henry Lee and his family. So I accept your courtesy, Sir Henry, and I thank you, as a Cavalier of Lumsford should thank one of the fighting clerks of Oxon. God bless the King! I care not who hears it, and confusion to Noll and his red nose!" Off he went accordingly with a bottle-swagger, guided by Joceline, to whom Albert, in the mean time, had whispered, to be sure to quarter him far enough from the rest of the family.

Young Lee then saluted his sister, and, with the formality of those times, asked and received his father's blessing with an affectionate embrace. His page seemed desirous to imitate one part of his example, but was repelled by Alice, who only replied to his offered salute with a courtesy. He next bowed his head in an awkward fashion to her father, who wished him a good night. "I am glad to see, young man," he said, "that you have at least learned the reverence due to age. It should always be paid, sir; because in doing so you render that honor to others which you will expect yourself to receive when you approach the close of your life. More will I speak with you at leisure, on your duties as a page, which office in former days used to be the very school of chivalry; whereas of late, by the disorderly times, it has become little better than a school of wild and disordered license, which made rare Ben Jonson exclaim——"

"Nay, father," said Albert, interposing, "you must consider this day's fatigue, and the poor lad is almost asleep on his legs; to-morrow, he will listen with more profit to your kind admonitions. And you, Louis, remember at least one part of your duty: take the candles and light us—here Joceline comes to show us the way. Once more, good-night, good Doctor Rochecliffe—good night, all."

CHAPTER XXI.

Groom. Hail noble prince!
King Richard. Thanks, noble peer!
The cheapest of us is a groat too dear.

Richard II.

ALBERT and his page were ushered by Joceline to what was called the Spanish Chamber, a huge old scrambling bedroom, rather in a dilapidated condition, but furnished with a large standing-bed for the master and a truckle-bed for the domestic, as was common at a much later period in old English houses, where the gentleman often required the assistance of a groom of the chambers to help him to bed, if the hospitality had been exuberant. The walls were covered with hangings of cordovan leather, stamped with gold, and representing fights between the Spaniards and Moriscoes, bull-feats, and other sports peculiar to the Peninsula, from which it took its name of the Spanish Chamber. These hangings were in some places entirely torn down, in others defaced and hanging in tatters. But Albert stopped not to make observations, anxious, it seemed, to get Joceline out of the room; which he achieved by hastily answering his offers of fresh fuel, and more liquor, in the negative, and returning, with equal conciseness, the under-keeper's good wishes for the evening. He at length retired, somewhat unwillingly, and as if he thought that his young master might have bestowed a few more words upon a faithful old retainer after so long absence.

Joliffe was no sooner gone than, before a single word was spoken between Albert Lee and his page, the former hastened to the door, examined lock, latch, and bolt, and made them fast, with the most scrupulous attention. He superadded to these precautions that of a long screw-bolt, which he brought out of his pocket, and which screwed on to the staple in such a manner as to render it impossible to withdraw it, or open the door, unless by breaking it down. The page held a light to him during the operation, which his master went through with much exactness and dexterity. But when Albert arose from his knee, on which he had rested during the accomplishment of this task, the manner of the companions was on the sudden entirely changed towards each other. The Honorable Master Kerneguy, from a cubbish lout of a raw Scotsman, seemed to have acquired at once all the grace and ease of motion and manner which could be given by an acquaintance of the earliest and most familiar kind with the best company of the time.

He gave the light he held to Albert with the easy indifference of a superior, who rather graces than troubles his dependant by giving him some slight service to perform. Albert, with the greatest appearance of deference, assumed in his turn the character of torch-bearer, and lighted his page across the chamber, without turning his back upon him as he did so. He then set the light on a table by the bedside, and, approaching the young man with deep reverence, received from him the solid green jacket with the same profound respect as if he had been a first lord of the bedchamber, or other officer of the household of the highest distinction, disrobing his sovereign of the Mantle of the Garter. The person to whom this ceremony was addressed endured it for a minute or two with profound gravity, and then bursting out a-laughing, exclaimed to Albert, "What a devil means all this formality? thou complimentest with these miserable rags as if they were silks and sables, and with poor Louis Kerneguy as if he were the King of Great Britain?"

"And if your Majesty's commands, and the circumstances of the time, have made me for a moment seem to forget that you are my sovereign, surely I may be permitted to render my homage as such while you are in your own royal palace of Woodstock?"

"Truly," replied the disguised monarch, "the sovereign and the palace are not ill matched: "these tattered hangings and my ragged jerkin suit each other admirably. *This* Woodstock!—*this* the bower where the royal Norman revelled with the fair Rosamond Clifford! Why, it is a place of assignation for owls!" Then, suddenly recollecting himself, with his natural courtesy, he added, as if fearing he might have hurt Albert's feeling—"But the more obscure and retired, it is the fitter for our purpose, Lee; and if it does seem to be a roost for owls, as there is no denying, why, we know it has nevertheless brought up eagles."

He threw himself as he spoke upon a chair, and indolently, but gracefully, received the kind offices of Albert, who undid the coarse buttonings of the leathern gamashes which defended his legs, and spoke to him the whilst. "What a fine specimen of the olden time is your father, Sir Henry. It is strange I should not have seen him before; but I heard my father often speak of him as being among the flower of our real old English gentry. By the mode in which he began to school me, I can guess you had a tight taskmaster of him, Albert. I warrant you never wore hat in his presence, eh?"

"I never cocked it at least in his presence, please your Majesty, as I have seen some youngsters do," answered Albert; "indeed, if I had, it must have been a stout beaver to have saved me from a broken head."

"Oh, I doubt it not," replied the King; "a fine old gentleman, but with that, methinks, in his countenance that assures you he would not hate the child in sparing the rod. Harkye, Albert. Suppose the same glorious Restoration come round, which, if drinking to its arrival can hasten it, should not be far distant, for in that particular our adherents never neglect their duty—suppose it come, therefore, and that thy father, as must be, of course, becomes an earl and one of the privy council, odds-fish, man, I shall be as much afraid of him as ever was my grandfather Henry Quatre of old Sully. Imagine there were such a trinket now about the court as the Fair Rosamond, or La Belle Gabrielle, what a work there would be of pages and grooms of the chamber to get the pretty rogue clandestinely shuffled out by the back-stairs, like a prohibited commodity, when the step of the Earl of Woodstock was heard in the ante-chamber."

"I am glad to see your Majesty so merry after your fatiguing journey."

"The fatigue was nothing, man," said Charles; "a kind welcome and a good meal made amends for all that. But they must have suspected thee of bringing a wolf from the braes of Badenoch along with you, instead of a two-legged being, with no more than the usual allowance of mortal stowage for provisions. I was really ashamed of my appetite; but thou knowest I had eat nothing for twenty-four hours, save the raw egg you stole for me from the old woman's hen-roost. I tell thee, I blush to show myself so ravenous before that high-bred and respectable old gentleman your father, and the very pretty girl your sister—or cousin, is she?"

"She is my sister," said Albert Lee, dryly, and added, in the same breath, "Your Majesty's appetite suited well enough with the character of a raw Northern lad. Would your Majesty now please to retire to rest?"

"Not for a minute or two," said the King, retaining his

seat. "Why, man, I have scarce had my tongue unchained to-day; and to talk with that Northern twang, and besides, the fatigue of being obliged to speak every word in character —gad, it's like walking as the galley-slaves do on the Continent, with a twenty-four pound shot chained to their legs: they may drag it along, but they cannot move with comfort. And, by the way, thou art slack in paying me my well-deserved tribute of compliments on my counterfeiting. Did I not play Louis Kerneguy as round as a ring?"

"If your Majesty asks my serious opinion, perhaps I may be forgiven if I say your dialect was somewhat too coarse for a Scottish youth of high birth, and your behavior perhaps a little too churlish. I thought too, though I pretend not to be skilful, that some of your Scottish sounded as if it were not genuine."

"Not genuine! There is no pleasing thee, Albert. Why, who should speak genuine Scottish but myself? Was I not their king for a matter of ten months? and if I did not get knowledge of their language, I wonder what else I got by it. Did not east country, and south country, and west country, and Highlands caw, croak, and shriek about me, as the deep guttural, the broad drawl, and the high sharp yelp predominated by turns? Odds-fish, man, have I not been speeched at by their orators, addressed by their senators, rebuked by their kirkmen? Have I not set on the cutty-stool, mon (again assuming the Northern dialect), and thought it grace of worthy Mas John Gillespie, that I was permitted to do penance in mine own privy chamber, instead of the face of the congregation, and wilt thou tell me, after all, that I cannot speak Scottish enough to baffle an Oxon knight and his family?"

'May it please your Majesty, I began by saying I was no judge of the Scottish language."

"Pshaw, it is mere envy; just so you said at Norton's, that I was too courteous and civil for a young page—now you think me too rude."

"And there is a medium, if one could find it," said Albert, defending his opinion in the same tone in which the King attacked him; "so this morning, when you were in the woman's dress, you raised your petticoats rather unbecomingly high, as you waded through the first little stream; and when I told you of it, to mend the matter, you draggled through the next without raising them at all."

"O, the devil take the woman's dress!" said Charles; "I hope I shall never be driven to that disguise again. Why, my ugly face was enough to put gowns, caps, and kirtles out of fashion forever: the very dogs fled from me. Had I passed any hamlet that had but five huts in it, I could not have escaped the cucking-stool. I was a libel on womanhood. These leathern conveniences are none of the gayest, but they are *propria quæ maribus;* and right glad am I to be repossessed of them. I can tell you too, my friend, I shall resume all my masculine privileges with my proper habiliments; and as you say I have been too coarse to-night, I will behave myself like a courtier to Mistress Alice to-morrow. I made a sort of acquaintance with her already, when I seemed to be of the same sex with herself, and found out there are other colonels in the wind besides you, Colonel Albert Lee."

"May it please your Majesty," said Albert, and then stopped short, from the difficulty of finding words to express the unpleasant nature of his feelings.

They could not escape Charles; but he proceeded without scruple, "I pique myself on seeing as far into the hearts of young ladies as most folk, though God knows they are sometimes too deep for the wisest of us. But I mentioned to your sister in my character of fortune-teller—thinking, poor simple man, that a country girl must have no one but her brother to dream about—that she was anxious about a certain colonel. I had hit the theme, but not the person; for I alluded to you, Albert, and I presume the blush was too deep ever to be given to a brother. So up she got, and away she flew from me like a lapwing. I can excuse her; for, looking at myself in the well, I think if I had met such a creature as I seemed I should have called fire and fagot against it. Now, what think you, Albert—who can this colonel be, that more than rivals you in your sister's affection?"

Albert, who well knew that the King's mode of thinking, where the fair sex was concerned, was far more gay than delicate, endeavored to put a stop to the present topic by a grave answer.

"His sister," he said, "had been in some measure educated with the son of her maternal uncle, Markham Everard; but as his father and he himself had adopted the cause of the Roundheads, the families had in consequence been at variance; and any projects which might have been formerly entertained were of course long since dismissed on all sides."

"You are wrong, Albert—you are wrong," said the King,

pitilessly pursuing his jest. "You colonels, whether you wear blue or orange sashes, are too pretty fellows to be dismissed so easily, when once you have acquired an interest. But Mistress Alice, so pretty, and who wishes the restoration of the King with such a look and accent, as if she were an angel whose prayers must needs bring it down, must not be allowed to retain any thoughts of a canting Roundhead. What say you—will you give me leave to take her to task about it? After all, I am the party most concerned in maintaining true allegiance among my subjects; and if I gain the pretty maiden's good-will, that of the sweetheart will soon follow. This was jolly King Edward's way—Edward the Fourth, you know. The king-making Earl of Warwick, the Cromwell of his day, dethroned him more than once; but he had the hearts of the merry dames of London, and the purses and veins of the cockneys bled freely, till they brought him home again. How say you? shall I shake off my Northern slough, and speak with Alice in my own character, showing what education and manners have done for me, to make the best amends they can for an ugly face?"

"May it please your Majesty," said Albert, in an altered and embarrassed tone, "I did not expect——"

Here he stopped, not able to find words adequate at the same time to express his sentiments and respectful enough to the King, while in his father's house and under his own protection.

"And what is it that Master Lee does not expect?" said Charles, with marked gravity on his part.

Again Albert attempted a reply, but advanced no farther than, "I would hope, if it please your Majesty——" when he again stopped short, his deep and hereditary respect for his sovereign, and his sense of the hospitality due to his misfortunes, preventing his giving utterance to his irritated feeling.

"And what does Colonel Albert Lee hope?" said Charles, in the same dry and cold manner in which he had before spoken. "No answer! Now *I hope* that Colonel Lee does not see in a silly jest anything offensive to the honor of his family, since methinks that were an indifferent compliment to his sister, his father, and himself, not to mention Charles Stuart, whom he calls his king; and *I expect* that I shall not be so hardly construed as to be supposed capable of forgetting that Mistress Alice Lee is the daughter of my faithful subject and host, and the sister of my guide and preserver. Come—come, Albert," he added, changing at once to his naturally frank and unceremonious manner, "you forget how long I have been abroad, where men, women, and children talk gallantry morning, noon, and night, with no more serious thought than just to pass away the time, and I forget too, that you are of the old-fashioned English school, a son after Sir Henry's own heart, and don't understand raillery upon such subjects. But I ask your pardon, Albert, sincerely, if I have really hurt you."

So saying, he extended his hand to Colonel Lee, who, feeling he had been rather too hasty in construing the King's jest in an unpleasant sense, kissed it with reverence, and attempted an apology.

"Not a word—not a word," said the good-natured prince, raising his penitent adherent as he attempted to kneel; "we understand each other. You are somewhat afraid of the gay reputation which I acquired in Scotland; but I assure you, I will be as stupid as you or your cousin colonel could desire in presence of Mrs. Alice Lee, and only bestow my gallantry, should I have any to throw away, upon the pretty little waiting-maid who attended at supper—unless you should have monpolized her ear for your own benefit, Colonel Albert."

"It is monopolized, sure enough, though not by me, if it please your Majesty, but by Joceline Joliffe, the under-keeper, whom we must not disoblige, as we have trusted him so far already, and may have occasion to repose even entire confidence in him. I half think he suspects who Louis Kerneguy may in reality be."

"You are an engrossing set, you wooers of Woodstock," said the King, laughing. "Now, if I had a fancy, as a Frenchman would not fail to have in such a case, to make pretty speeches to the deaf old woman I saw in the kitchen, as a *pis-aller*, I daresay I should be told that *her* ear was engrossed for Dr. Rochecliffe's sole use?"

"I marvel at your Majesty's good spirits," said Albert, "that, after a day of danger, fatigue, and accidents, you should feel the power of amusing yourself thus."

"That is to say, the groom of the chambers wishes his Majesty would go to sleep? Well, one word or two on more serious business, and I have done. I have been completely directed by you and Rochecliffe: I have changed my disguise from female to male upon the instant, and altered my destination from Hampshire to take shelter here. Do you still hold it the wiser course?"

"I have great confidence in Dr. Rochecliffe," replied

Albert, "whose acquaintance with the scattered Royalists enables him to gain the most accurate intelligence. His pride in the extent of his correspondence, and the complication of his plots and schemes for your Majesty's service, is indeed the very food he lives upon; but his sagacity is equal to his vanity. I repose, besides, the utmost faith in Joliffe. Of my father and sister I would say nothing: yet I would not, without reason, extend the knowledge of your Majesty's person farther than it is indispensably necessary."

"Is it handsome in me," said Charles, pausing, "to withhold my full confidence from Sir Henry Lee?"

"Your Majesty heard of his almost death-swoon of last night: what would agitate him most deeply must not be hastily communicated."

"True; but are we safe from a visit of the redcoats: they have them in Woodstock as well as in Oxford?" said Charles.

"Dr. Rochecliffe says, not unwisely," answered Lee, "that it is best sitting near the fire when the chimney smokes; and that Woodstock, so lately in possession of the sequestrators, and still in the vicinity of the soldiers, will be less suspected, and more carelessly searched, than more distant corners, which might seem to promise more safety. Besides," he added, "Rochecliffe is in possession of curious and important news concerning the state of matters at Woodstock, highly favorable to your Majesty's being concealed in the palace for two or three days, till shipping is provided. The Parliament, or usurping Council of State, had sent down sequestrators, whom their own evil consciences, assisted, perhaps, by the tricks of some daring Cavaliers, had frightened out of the lodge, without much desire to come back again. Then the more formidable usurper, Cromwell, had granted a warrant of possession to Colonel Everard, who had only used it for the purpose of repossessing his uncle in the lodge, and who kept watch in person at the little borough, to see that Sir Henry was not disturbed."

"What! Mistress Alice's colonel?" said the King. "That sounds alarming; for, grant that he keeps the other fellows at bay, think you not, Master Albert, he will have an hundred errands a-day to bring him here in person?"

"Dr. Rochecliffe says," answered Lee, "the treaty between Sir Henry and his nephew binds the latter not to approach the lodge unless invited; indeed, it was not without great difficulty, and strongly arguing the good consequences it might produce to your Majesty's cause, that my father could be prevailed on to occupy Woodstock at all; but be assured he will be in no hurry to send an invitation to the colonel."

"And be you assured that the colonel will come without waiting for one," said Charles. "Folk cannot judge rightly where sisters are concerned: they are too familiar with the magnet to judge of its powers of attraction. Everard will be here, as if drawn by cart-ropes; fetters, not to talk of promises, will not hold him; and then, methinks, we are in some danger."

"I hope not," said Albert. "In the first place, I know Markham is a slave to his word; besides, were any chance to bring him here, I think I could pass your Majesty upon him without difficulty as Louis Kerneguy. Then, although my cousin and I have not been on good terms for these some years, I believe him incapable of betraying your Majesty; and lastly, if I saw the least danger of it, I would, were he ten times the son of my mother's sister [brother], run my sword through his body ere he had time to execute his purpose."

"There is but another question," said Charles, "and I will release you, Albert. You seem to think yourself secure from search. It may be so; but, in any other country, this tale of goblins which is flying about would bring down priests and ministers of justice to examine the reality of the story, and mobs of idle people to satisfy their curiosity."

"Respecting the first, sir, we hope and understand that Colonel Everard's influence will prevent any immediate inquiry, for the sake of preserving undisturbed the peace of his uncle's family; and as for any one coming without some sort of authority, the whole neighbors have so much love and fear of my father, and are, besides, so horribly alarmed about the goblins of Woodstock, that fear will silence curiosity."

"On the whole, then," said Charles, "the chances of safety seem to be in favor of the plan we have adopted, which is all I can hope for in a condition where absolute safety is out of the question. The bishop recommended Dr. Rochecliffe as one of the most ingenious, boldest, and most loyal sons of the Church of England; you, Albert Lee, have marked your fidelity by a hundred proofs. To you and your local knowledge I submit myself. And now, prepare our arms; alive I will not be taken, yet I will not believe that a son of the King of England, and heir of her throne, could be destined to danger in his own palace, and under the guard of the loyal Lees."

Albert Lee laid pistols and swords in readiness by the King's bed and his own; and Charles, after some slight apology, took his place in the larger and better bed, with a sigh of pleasure, as from one who had not lately enjoyed such an indulgence. He bid good-night to his faithful attendant, who deposited himself on his truckle; and both monarch and subject were soon fast asleep.

CHAPTER XXII

Give Sir Nicholas Threlkeld praise;
Here it, good man, old in days,
Thou tree of succor and of rest
To this young bird that was distress'd;
Beneath thy branches he did stay;
And he was free to sport and play,
When falcons were abroad for prey.

WORDSWORTH.

THE fugitive prince slept, in spite of danger, with the profound repose which youth and fatigue inspire. But the young Cavalier, his guide and guard, spent a more restless night, starting from time to time and listening; anxious, not withstanding Doctor Rochecliffe's assurances, to procure yet more particular knowledge concerning the state of things around them than he had been yet able to collect.

He rose early after daybreak; but although he moved with as little noise as was possible, the slumbers of the hunted prince were easily disturbed. He started up in his bed, and asked if there was any alarm.

"None, please your Majesty," replied Lee; "only, thinking on the questions your Majesty was asking last night, and the various chances there are of your Majesty's safety being endangered from unforeseen accidents, I thought of going thus early, both to communicate with Doctor Rochecliffe and to keep such a lookout as befits the place where are lodged for the time the fortunes of England. I fear I must request of your Majesty, for your own gracious security, that you have the goodness to condescend to secure the door with your own hand after I go out."

"Oh, talk not to Majesty, for Heaven's sake, dear Albert!" answered the poor King, endeavoring in vain to put on a part of his clothes in order to traverse the room. "When a king's doublet and hose are so ragged that he can no more find his way into them than he could have traveled through the Forest of Dean without a guide, good faith, there should be an end of Majesty, until it chances to be better accommodated. Besides, there is the chance of these big words bolting out at unawares, when there are ears to hear them whom we might think dangerous."

"Your commands shall be obeyed," said Lee, who had now succeeded in opening the door, from which he took his departure, leaving the King, who had hustled along the floor for that purpose, with his dress wofully ill arranged, to make it fast again behind him, and begging him in no case to open to any one, unless he or Rochecliffe were of the party who summoned him.

Albert then set out in quest of Doctor Rochecliffe's apartment, which was only known to himself and the faithful Joliffe, and had at different times accommodated that sturdy churchman with a place of concealment when, from his bold and busy temper, which led him into the most extensive and hazardous machinations on the King's behalf, he had been strictly sought after by the opposite party. Of late, the inquest after him had died entirely away, as he had prudently withdrawn himself from the scene of his intrigues. Since the loss of the battle of Worcester, he had been afloat again, and more active than ever; and had, by friends and correspondents, and especially the Bishop of ——, been the means of directing the King's flight towards Woodstock, although it was not until the very day of his arrival that he could promise him a safe reception at that ancient mansion.

Albert Lee, though he revered both the undaunted spirit and ready resources of the bustling and intriguing churchman, felt he had not been enabled by him to answer some of Charles's questions yesternight in a way so distinct as one trusted with the King's safety ought to have done; and it was now his object to make himself personally acquainted, if possible, with the various bearings of so weighty a matter, as became a man on whom so much of the responsibility was likely to descend.

Even his local knowledge was scarce adequate to find the Doctor's secret apartment, had he not traced his way after a genial flavor of roasted game through divers blind passages, and up and down through certain very useless stairs, through cupboards and hatchways, and so forth, to a species of *sanctum sanctorum*, where Joceline Joliffe was ministering to the good Doctor a solemn breakfast of wild-fowl, with a cup of small beer stirred with a sprig of rosemary, which Doctor Rochecliffe preferred to all strong potations. Beside him sat Bevis on his tail, slobbering and looking amiable, moved by the rare smell of the breakfast, which had quite overcome his native dignity of disposition.

The chamber in which the Doctor had established himself

was a little octangular room, with walls of great thickness, within which were fabricated various issues, leading in different directions, and communicating with different parts of the building. Around him were packages with arms, and near him one small barrel, as it seemed, of gunpowder; many papers in different parcels, and several keys for correspondence in cipher; two or three scrolls covered with hieroglyphics were also beside him, which Albert took for plans of nativity; and various models of machinery, in which Doctor Rochecliffe was an adept. There were also tools of various kinds, masks, cloaks, and a dark lantern, and a number of other indescribable trinkets belonging to the trade of a daring plotter in dangerous times. Last, there was a casket with gold and silver coin of different countries, which was left carelessly open, as if it were the least of Doctor Rochecliffe's concern, although his habits in general announced narrow circumstances, if not actual poverty. Close by the divine's plate lay a Bible and Prayer Book, with some proof-sheets, as they are technically called, seemingly fresh from the press. There were also within the reach of his hand a dirk, or Scottish poniard, a powder-horn, and a musketoon, or blunderbuss, with a pair of handsome pocket-pistols. In the midst of this miscellaneous collection, the Doctor sat eating his breakfast with great appetite, as little dismayed by the various implements of danger around him as a workman is when accustomed to the perils of a gunpowder manufactory.

"Soh, young gentleman," he said, getting up and extending his hand, "are you come to breakfast with me in good fellowship, or to spoil my meal this morning, as you did my supper last night, by asking untimely questions?"

"I will pick a bone with you with all my heart," said Albert; "and if you please, Doctor, I would ask some questions which seem not quite untimely."

So saying he sat down and assisted the Doctor in giving a very satisfactory account of a brace of wild ducks and a leash of teal. Bevis, who maintained his place with great patience and insinuation, had his share of a collop, which was also placed on the well-furnished board; for, like most high-bred dogs, he declined eating waterfowl.

"Come hither, then, Albert Lee," said the Doctor, laying down his knife and fork, and plucking the towel from his throat, so soon as Joceline was withdrawn; "thou art still the same lad thou wert when I was thy tutor—never satisfied with having got a grammar rule, but always persecuting me with questions why the rule stood so, and not otherwise—over-curious after information which thou couldst not comprehend, as Bevis slobbered and whined for the duck-wing, which he could not eat."

"I hope you will find me more reasonable, Doctor," answered Albert; "and at the same time, that you will recollect I am not now *sub ferula*, but am placed in circumstances where I am not at liberty to act upon the *ipse dixit* of any man, unless my own judgment be convinced. I shall deserve richly to be hanged, drawn and quartered should any misfortune happen by my misgovernment in this business."

"And it is therefore, Albert, that I would have thee trust the whole to me, without interfering. Thou sayst, forsooth, thou art not *sub ferula;* but recollect that, while you have been fighting in the field, I have been plotting in the study; that I know all the combinations of the King's friends, ays and all the motions of his enemies, as well as a spider knows, every mesh of his web. Think of my experience, man. Not a Cavalier in the land but has heard of Rochecliffe the Plotter I have been a main limb in everything that has been attempted since forty-two—penned declarations, conducted correspondence, communicated with chiefs, recruited followers, commissioned arms, levied money, appointed rendezvouses. I was in the Western Rising; and before that, in the City Petition, and in Sir John Owen's stir in Wales; in short, almost in every plot for the King, since Tomkins and Challoner's matter."

"But were not all these plots unsuccessful?" said Albert; "and were not Tomkins and Challoner hanged, Doctor?"

"Yes, my young friend," answered the Doctor, gravely, "as many others have been with whom I have acted; but only because they did not follow my advice implicitly. You never heard that I was hanged myself."

"The time may come, Doctor, said Albert. "The pitcher goes oft to the well——. The proverb, as my father would say, is somewhat musty. But I, too, have some confidence in my own judgment; and, much as I honor the church, I cannot altogether subscribe to passive obedience. I will tell you in one word what points I must have explanation on; and it will remain with you to give it, or to return a message to the King that you will not explain your plan; in which case, if he acts by my advice, he will leave Woodstock, and resume his purpose of getting to the coast without delay."

"Well, then," said the Doctor, "thou suspicious monster, make thy demands, and if they be such as I can answer without betraying confidence, I will reply to them."

"In the first place, then, what is all this story about ghosts, and witchcrafts, and apparitions; and do you consider it as safe for his Majesty to stay in a house subject to such visitations, real or pretended?"

"You must be satisfied with my answer *in verbo sacerdotis:* the circumstances you allude to will not give the least annoyance to Woodstock during the King's residence. I cannot explain farther; but for this I will be bound, at the risk of my neck."

"Then," said Lee, "we must take Doctor Rochecliffe's bail that the Devil will keep the peace towards our Sovereign Lord the King—good. Now there lurked about this house the greater part of yesterday, and perhaps slept here, a fellow called Tomkins—a bitter Independent, and a secretary, or clerk, or something or other, to the regicide dog Desborough. The man is well known—a wild ranter in religious opinions, but in private affairs far-sighted, cunning, and interested even as any rogue of them all."

"Be assured we will avail ourselves of his crazy fanaticism to mislead his wicked cunning: a child may lead a hog if it has wit to fasten a cord to the ring in its nose," replied the Doctor.

"You may be deceived," said Albert; "the age has many such as this fellow, whose views of the spiritual and temporal world are so different, that they resemble the eyes of a squinting man—one of which, oblique and distorted, sees nothing but the end of his nose, while the other, instead of partaking the same defect, views strongly, sharply, and acutely whatever is subjected to its scrutiny."

"But we will put a patch on the better eye," said the Doctor, "and he shall only be allowed to speculate with the imperfect optic. You must know, this fellow has always seen the greatest number and the most hideous apparitions: he has not the courage of a cat in such matters, though stout enough when he hath temporal antagonists before him. I have placed him under the charge of Joceline Joliffe, who, betwixt plying him with sack and ghost-stories, would make him incapable of knowing what was done if you were to proclaim the King in his presence."

"But why keep such a fellow here at all?"

"Oh, sir, content you; he lies leaguer, as a sort of ambassador for his worthy masters, and we are secure from any intrusion so long as they get all the news of Woodstock from Trusty Hawkins."

"I know Joceline's honesty well, said Albert; "and if he can assure me that he will keep a watch over this fellow, I will so far trust in him. He does not know the depth of the stake, 'tis true, but that my life is concerned will be quite enough to keep him vigilant. Well, then, I proceed. What if Markham Everard comes down on us?"

"We have his word to the contrary," answered Rochecliffe—"his word of honor transmitted by his friend. Do you think it likely he will break it?"

"I hold him incapable of doing so," answered Albert; "and, besides, I think Markham would make no bad use of anything which might come to his knowledge. Yet God forbid we should be under the necessity of trusting any who ever wore the Parliament's colors in a matter of such dear concernment!"

"Amen!" said the Doctor. "Are your doubts silenced now?"

"I still have an objection," said Albert, "to yonder impudent rakehelly fellow, styling himself a Cavalier, who pushed himself on our company last night, and gained my father's heart by a story of the storm of Brentford, which I daresay the rogue never saw."

"You mistake him, dear Albert," replied Rochecliffe: "Roger Wildrake, although till of late I only knew him by name, is a gentleman, was bred at the Inns of Court, and spent his estate in the King's service."

"Or rather in the devil's service," said Albert. "It is such fellows as he, who, sunk from the license of their military habits into idle debauched ruffians, infest the land with riots and robberies, brawl in hedge alehouses and cellars where strong waters are sold at midnight, and, with their deep oaths, their hot loyalty, and their drunken valor, make decent men abominate the very name of Cavalier."

"Alas!" said the Doctor, "it is but too true; but what can you expect? When the higher and more qualified classes are broken down and mingled undistinguishably with the lower orders, they are apt to lose the most valuable marks of their quality in the general confusion of morals and manners, just as a handful of silver medals will become defaced and discolored if jumbled about among the vulgar copper coin. Even the prime medal of all, which we Royalists would so willingly wear next our very hearts, has not, perhaps, entirely escaped some deterioration. But let other tongues than mine speak on that subject."

Albert Lee paused deeply after having heard these communications on the part of Rochecliffe. "Doctor," he said, "it is generally agreed, even by some who think you may occasionally have been a little over-busy in putting men upon dangerous actions——"

"May God forgive them who entertain so false an opinion of me!" said the Doctor.

—"That, nevertheless, you have done and suffered more in the King's behalf than any man of your function."

"They do me but justice there," said Doctor Rochecliffe —"absolute justice."

"I am therefore disposed to abide by your opinion, if, all things considered, you think it safe that we should remain at Woodstock."

"That is not the question," answered the divine.

"And what is the question, then?" replied the young soldier.

"Whether any safer course can be pointed out. I grieve to say that the question must be comparative as to the point of option. Absolute safety is—alas the while!—out of the question on all sides. Now, I say Woodstock is, fenced and guarded as at present, by far the most preferable place of concealment."

"Enough," replied Albert, "I give up to you the question, as to a person whose knowledge of such important affairs, not to mention your age and experience, is more intimate and extensive than mine can be."

"You do well," answered Rochecliffe; "and if others had acted with the like distrust of their own knowledge, and confidence in competent persons, it had been better for the age. This makes understanding bar himself up within his fortalice, and wit betake himself to his high tower. (Here he looked around his cell with an air of self-complacence.) The wise man foreseeth the tempest, and hideth himself."

"Doctor," said Albert, "let our foresight serve others far more precious than either of us. Let me ask you, if you have well considered whether our precious charge should remain in society with the family, or betake himself to some of the more hidden corners of the house?"

"Hum!" said the Doctor, with an air of deep reflection, "I think he will be safest as Louis Kerneguy, keeping himself close beside you——"

"I fear it will be necessary," added Albert, "that I scout

abroad a little, and show myself in some distant part of the country, lest, coming here in quest of me, they should find higher game."

"Pray do not interrupt me. Keeping himself close beside you or your father, in or near to Victor Lee's apartment, from which, you are aware, he can make a ready escape, should danger approach. This occurs to me as best for the present; I hope to hear of the vessel to-day—to-morrow at farthest."

Albert Lee bid the active but opinionated man good-morrow; admiring how this species of intrigue had become a sort of element in which the Doctor seemed to enjoy himself, notwithstanding all that the poet has said concerning the horrors which intervene betwixt the conception and execution of a conspiracy.

In returning from Doctor Rochecliffe's sanctuary, he met with Joceline, who was anxiously seeking him. "The young Scotch gentleman," he said, in a mysterious manner, "has arisen from bed, and, hearing me pass, he called me into his apartment."

"Well," replied Albert, "I will see him presently."

"And he asked me for fresh linen and clothes. Now, sir, he is like a man who is quite accustomed to be obeyed, so I gave him a suit which happened to be in a wardrobe in the west tower, and some of your linen to conform; and when he was dressed, he commanded me to show him to the presence of Sir Henry Lee and my young lady. I would have said something, sir, about waiting till you come back, but he pulled me good-naturedly by the hair—as, indeed, he has a rare humor of his own—and told me, he was guest to Master Albert Lee, and not his prisoner; so, sir, though I thought you might be displeased with me for giving him the means of stirring abroad, and perhaps being seen by those who should not see him, what could I say?"

"You are a sensible fellow, Joceline, and comprehend always what is recommended to you. This youth will not be controlled, I fear, by either of us; but we must look the closer after his safety. You keep your watch over that drying fellow the steward?"

"Trust him to my care: on that side have no fear. But, ah, sir! I would we had the young Scot in his old clothes again, for the riding-suit of yours which he now wears hath set him off in other-guess fashion."

From the manner in which the faithful dependant expressed himself, Albert saw that he suspected who the Scottish page in reality was: yet he did not think it proper to acknowledge to him a fact of such importance, secure as he was equally of his fidelity whether explicitly trusted to the full extent or left to his own conjectures. Full of anxious thought, he went to the apartment of Victor Lee, in which Joliffe told him he would find the party assembled. The sound of laughter, as he laid his hand on the lock of the door, almost made him start, so singularly did it jar with the doubtful and melancholy reflections which engaged his own mind. He entered, and found his father in high good-humor, laughing and conversing freely with his young charge, whose appearance was, indeed, so much changed to the better in externals, that it seemed scarce possible a night's rest, a toilet, and a suit of decent clothes could have done so much in his favor in so short a time. It could not, however, be imputed to the mere alteration of dress, although that, no doubt, had its effect. There was nothing splendid in that which Louis Kerneguy (we continue to call him by his assumed name) now wore. It was merely a riding-suit of gray cloth, with some silver lace, in the fashion of a country gentleman of the time. But it happened to fit him very well, and to become his very dark complexion, especially as he now held up his head, and used the manners, not only of a well-behaved, but of a highly accomplished, gentleman. When he moved, his clumsy and awkward limp was exchanged for a sort of shuffle, which, as it might be the consequence of a wound in those perilous times, had rather an interesting than an ungainly effect. A least it was as genteel an expression that the party had been over-hard traveled as the most polite pedestrian could propose to himself.

The features of the wanderer were harsh as ever, but his red shock peruke, for such it proved, was laid aside, his sable elf-locks were trained, by a little of Joceline's assistance, into curls, and his fine black eyes shone from among the shade of these curls, and corresponded with the animated, though not handsome, character of the whole head. In his conversation, he had laid aside all the coarseness of dialect which he had so strongly affected on the preceding evening; and although he continued to speak a little Scotch, for the support of his character as a young gentleman of that nation, yet it was not in a degree which rendered his speech either uncouth or unintelligible, but merely afforded a certain Doric tinge essential to the personage he represented. No person on earth could better understand the society in which he moved; exile had made him acquainted with life in all its shades and varieties; his spirits, if not uniform, were elastic; he had that species of epicurean philosophy which, even in the most extreme difficulties and dangers, can in an interval of ease, however brief, avail itself of the enjoyments of the moment; he was, in short, in youth and misfortune, as afterwards in his regal condition, a good-humored but hard-hearted voluptuary—wise, save where his passions intervened; beneficent, save when prodigality had deprived him of the means, or prejudice of the wish, to confer benefits his faults such as might often have drawn down hatred, but that they were mingled with so much urbanity that the injured person felt it impossible to retain the full sense of his wrongs.

Albert Lee found the party, consisting of his father, sister, and the supposed page, seated by the breakfast-table, at which he also took his place. He was a pensive and an anxious beholder of what passed, while the page, who had already completely gained the heart of the good old Cavalier by mimicking the manner in which the Scottish divines preached in favor of "Ma gude Lord Marquis of Argyle and the Solemn League and Covenant," was now endeavoring to interest the fair Alice by such anecdotes, partly of warlike and perilous adventure, as possessed the same degree of interest for the female ear which they have had ever since Desdemona's days. But it was not only of dangers by land and sea that the disguised page spoke; but much more, and much oftener, on foreign revels, banquets, balls, where the pride of France, of Spain, or of the Low Countries was exhibited in the eyes of their most eminent beauties. Alice being a very young girl, who, in consequence of the Civil War, had been almost entirely educated in the country, and often in great seclusion, it was certainly no wonder that she should listen with willing ears and a ready smile to what the young gentleman, their guest, and her brother's *protégé*, told with so much gaiety, and mingled with such a shade of dangerous adventure, and occasionally of serious reflection, as prevented the discourse from being regarded as merely light and frivolous.

In a word, Sir Henry Lee laughed, Alice smiled from time to time, and all were satisfied but Albert, who would himself, however, have been scarce able to allege a sufficient reason for his depression of spirits.

The materials of breakfast were at last removed, under the active superintendence of the neat-handed Phœbe, who looked over her shoulder, and lingered more than once, to listen to the fluent discourse of their new guest, whom, on the preceding evening, she had, while in attendance at supper, accounted one of the most stupid inmates to whom the gates of Woodstock had been opened since the times of Fair Rosamond.

Louis Kerneguy, then, when they were left only four in the chamber, without the interruption of domestics, and the successive bustle occasioned by the discussion and removal of the morning meal, became apparently sensible that his friend and ostensible patron Albert ought not altogether to be suffered to drop to leeward in the conversation, while he was himself successfully engaging the attention of those members of his family to whom he had become so recently known. He went behind his chair, therefore, and, leaning on the back, said with a good-humored tone, which made his purpose entirely intelligible:

"Either my good friend, guide, and patron has heard worse news this morning than he cares to tell us, or he must have stumbled over my tattered jerkin and leathern hose, and acquired, by contact, the whole mass of stupidity which I threw off last night with those most dolorous garments. Cheer up, my dear Colonel Albert, if your affectionate page may presume to say so: you are in company with those whose society, dear to strangers, must be doubly so to you. Odds-fish, man, cheer up! I have seen you gay on a biscuit and a mouthful of water-cresses; don't let your heart fail you on Rhenish wine and venison."

"Dear Louis," said Albert, rousing himself into exertion, and somewhat ashamed of his own silence, "I have slept worse, and been astir earlier than you."

"Be it so," said his father; "yet I hold it no good excuse for your sullen silence. Albert, you have met your sister and me, so long separated from you, so anxious on your behalf, almost like mere strangers, and yet you are returned safe to us, and you find us well."

"Returned indeed—but for safety, my dear father, that word must be a stranger to us Worcester folk for some time. However, it is not my own safety about which I am anxious."

"About whose, then, should you be anxious? All accounts agree that the King is safe out of the dogs's jaws."

"Not without some danger, though," muttered Louis, thinking of his encounter with Bevis on the preceding evening.

"No, not without danger, indeed," echoed the knight; "but, as old Will says—

> There's such divinity doth hedge a king.
> That treason dares not peep at what it would.

No—no, thank God, that's cared for: our hope and fortune is escaped, so all news affirm—escaped from Bristol; if I thought otherwise, Albert, I should be as sad as you are. For the rest of it, I have lurked a month in this house when discovery would have been death, and that is no longer since than after Lord Holland and the Duke of Buckingham's rising at Kingston; and hang me, if I thought once of twisting my brow into such a tragic fold as yours, but cocked my hat at misfortune as a Cavalier should."

"If I might put in a word," said Louis, "it would be to assure Colonel Albert Lee that I verily believe the king would think his own hap, wherever he may be, much the worse that his best subjects were seized with dejection on his account."

"You answer boldly on the King's part, young man," said Sir Henry.

"Oh, my father was meikle about the King's hand," answered Louis, recollecting his present character.

"No wonder, then," said Sir Henry, "that you have so soon recovered your good spirits and good breeding, when you heard of his Majesty's escape. Why, you are no more like the lad we saw last night than the best hunter I ever had was like a drayhorse."

"Oh, there is much in rest, and food, and grooming," answered Louis. "You would hardly know the tired jade you dismounted from last night, when she is brought out prancing and neighing the next morning, rested, refreshed, and ready to start again, especially if the brute hath some good blood, for such pick up unco fast."

"Well, then, but since thy father was a courtier, and thou hast learned, I think, something of the trade, tell us a little, Master Kerneguy, about him we love most to hear about—the King; we are all safe and secret, you need not be afraid. He was a hopeful youth; I trust his flourishing blossom now gives promise of fruit?"

As the knight spoke, Louis bent his eyes on the ground, and seemed at first uncertain what to answer. But, admirable at extricating himself from such dilemmas, he replied, "That he really could not presume to speak on such a subject in the presence of his patron, Colonel Albert Lee, who must be a much better judge of the character of King Charles than he could pretend to be."

Albert was accordingly next assailed by the Knight, seconded by Alice, for some account of his Majesty's character.

"I will speak but according to facts," said Albert; "and then I must be acquitted of partiality. If the King had not possessed enterprise and military skill, he never would have attempted the expedition to Worcester; had he not had personal courage, he had not so long disputed the battle that Cromwell almost judged it lost. That he possesses prudence and patience must be argued from the circumstances attending his flight; and that he has the love of his subjects is evident, since, necessarily known to many, he has been betrayed by none."

"For shame, Albert!" replied his sister; "is that the way a good Cavalier doles out the character of his prince, applying an instance at every concession, like a pedler measuring linen with his rod? Out upon you! no wonder you were beaten, if you fought as coldly for your King as you now talk for him."

"I did my best to trace a likeness from what I have seen and known of the original, sister Alice," replied her brother. "If you would have a fancy portrait, you must get an artist of more imagination than I have to draw it for you."

"I will be that artist myself," said Alice, "and, in *my* portrait our monarch shall show all that he ought to be, having such high pretensions; all that he must be, being so loftily descended; all that I am sure he is, and that every loyal heart in the kingdom ought to believe him."

"Well said, Alice," quoth the old knight. "Look thou upon this picture, and on this! Here is our young friend shall judge. I wager my best nag—that is, I would wager him had I one left—that Alice proves the better painter of the two. My son's brain is still misty, I think, since his defeat: he has not got the smoke of Worcester out of it. Plague on thee! a young man, and cast down for one beating! Had you been banged twenty times like me, it had been time to look grave. But come, Alice, forward; the colors are mixed on your palette—forward with something that shall show like one of Vandyck's living portraits, placed beside the dull dry presentation there of our ancestor Victor Lee."

Alice, it must be observed, had been educated by her father in the notions of high, and even exaggerated, loyalty which characterized the Cavaliers, and she was really an enthusiast in the Royal cause. But besides, she was in good spirits at her brother's happy return, and wished to prolong the gay humor in which her father had of late scarcely ever indulged.

"Well, then," she said, "though I am no Apelles, I will try to paint an Alexander, such as I hope, and am determined to believe, exists in the person of our exiled sovereign, soon I trust to be restored. And I will not go farther than his own family. He shall have all the chivalrous courage, all the warlike skill, of Henry of France, his grandfather, in order to place him on the throne; all his benevolence, love of his people, patience even of unpleasing advice, sacrifice of his own wishes and pleasures to the commonweal, that, seated there, he may be blest while living, and so long remembered when dead, that for ages after it shall be thought sacrilege to breathe an aspersion against the throne which he has occupied. Long after he is dead, while there remains an old man who has seen him, were the condition of that survivor no higher than a groom or a menial, his age shall be provided for at the public charge, and his gray hairs regarded with more distinction than an earl's coronet, because he remembers the second Charles, the monarch of every heart in England."

While Alice spoke, she was hardly conscious of the presence of any one save her father and brother; for the page withdrew himself somewhat from the circle, and there was nothing to remind her of him. She gave the reins, therefore, to her enthusiasm, and as the tears glittered in her eye, and her beautiful features became animated, she seemed like a descended cherub proclaiming the virtues of a patriot monarch. The person chiefly interested in her description held himself back, as we have said, and concealed his own features, yet so as to preserve a full view of the beautiful speaker.

Albert Lee, conscious in whose presence this eulogium was pronounced, was much embarrassed; but his father, all whose feelings were flattered by the panegyric, was in rapture.

"So much for the *king*, Alice," he said; "and now for the *man*."

"For the man," replied Alice, in the same tone, "need I wish him more than the paternal virtues of his unhappy father, of whom his worst enemies have recorded that, if moral virtues and religious faith were to be selected as the qualities which merited a crown, no man could plead the possession of them in a higher or more indisputable degree. Temperate, wise, and frugal, yet munificent in rewarding merit—a friend to letters and the muses, but a severe discourager of the misuse of such gifts—a worthy gentleman—a kind master—the best friend, the best father, the best Christian——" Her voice began to falter, and her father's handkerchief was already at his eyes.

"He was, girl—he was!" exclaimed Sir Henry; "but no more on't, I charge ye—no more on't—enough; let his son but possess his virtues, with better advisers, and better fortunes, and he will be all that England, in her warmest wishes, could desire."

There was a pause after this; for Alice felt as if she had spoken too frankly and too zealously for her sex and youth; Sir Henry was occupied in melancholy recollections on the fate of his late sovereign; while Kerneguy and his supposed patron felt embarrassed, perhaps from a consciousness that the real Charles fell far short of his ideal character, as designed in such glowing colors. In some cases, exaggerated or unappropriate praise becomes the most severe satire.

But such reflections were not of a nature to be long willingly cherished by the person to whom they might have been of great advantage. He assumed a tone of raillery, which is, perhaps, the readiest mode of escaping from the feelings of self-reproof. "Every Cavalier," he said, "should bend his knee to thank Mistress Alice Lee for having made such a flattering portrait of the King their master, by laying under contribution for his benefit the virtues of all his ancestors; only there was one point he would not have expected a female painter to have passed over in silence. When she made him, in right of his grandfather and father, a muster of royal and individual excellencies, why could she not have endowed him at the same time with his mother's personal charms? Why should not the son of Henrietta Maria, the finest woman of her day, add the recommendations of a handsome face and figure to his internal qualities? He had the same hereditary title to good looks as to mental qualifications; and the picture, with such an addition, would be perfect in its way, and God send it might be a resemblance!"

"I understand you, Master Kerneguy," said Alice, "but I am no fairy, to bestow, as those do in the nursery tales, gifts which Providence has denied. I am woman enough to have made inquiries on the subject, and I know the general report is that the King, to have been the son of such handsome parents, is unusually hard-favored."

"Good God, sister!" said Albert, starting impatiently from his seat.

"Why, you yourself told me so," said Alice, surprised at the emotion he testified; "and you said——"

"This is intolerable," muttered Albert; "I must out to speak with Joceline without delay. Louis (with an imploring look to Kerneguy), you will surely come with me?"

"I would with all my heart," said Kerneguy, smiling maliciously; "but you see how I suffer still from lameness. Nay—nay, Albert," he whispered, resisting young Lee's attempts to prevail on him to leave the room, "can you suppose I am fool enough to be hurt by this? On the contrary, I have a desire of profiting by it."

"May God grant it!" said Lee to himself, as he left the room, "it will be the first lecture you ever profited by; and the Devil confound the plots and plotters who made me bring you to this place!" So saying, he carried his discontent forth into the park.

CHAPTER XXIII

For there, they say, he daily doth frequent
With unrestrained loose companions;
While he, young, wanton, and effeminate boy,
Takes on the point of honor, to support
So dissolute a crew.

Richard II

THE conversation which Albert had in vain endeavored to interrupt flowed on in the same course after he had left the room. It entertained Louis Kerneguy; for personal vanity, or an over-sensitiveness to deserved reproof, were not among the faults of his character, and were indeed incompatible with an understanding which, combined with more strength of principle, steadiness of exertion, and self-denial, might have placed Charles high on the list of English monarchs. On the other hand, Sir Henry listened with natural delight to the noble sentiments uttered by a being so beloved as his daughter. His own parts were rather steady than brilliant; and he had that species of imagination which is not easily excited without the action of another, as the electrical globe only scintillates when rubbed against its cushion. He was well pleased, therefore, when Kerneguy pursued the conversation, by observing that Mistress Alice Lee had not explained how the same good fairy that conferred moral qualities could not also remove corporeal blemishes.

"You mistake, sir," said Alice, "I confer nothing. I do but attempt to paint our King such as I *hope* he is, such as I am sure he *may* be, should he himself desire to be so. The same general report, which speaks of his countenance as unprepossessing, describes his talents as being of the first order. He has, therefore, the means of arriving at excellence, should he cultivate them sedulously and employ them usefully—should he rule his passions and be guided by his understanding. Every good man cannot be wise; but it is in the power of every wise man, if he pleases, to be as eminent for virtue as for talent."

Young Kerneguy rose briskly and took a turn through the room; and ere the knight could make any observation on the singular vivacity in which he had indulged, he threw himself again into his chair, and said in rather an altered tone of voice—"It seems, then, Mistress Alice Lee, that the good friends who have described this poor king to you have been as unfavorable in their account of his morals as of his person?"

"The truth must be better known to you, sir," said Alice, "than it can be to me. Some rumors there have been which accuse him of a license which, whatever allowance flatterers make for it, does not, to say the least, become the son of the Martyr; I shall be happy to have these contradicted on good authority."

"I am surprised at your folly," said Sir Henry Lee, "in hinting at such things, Alice; a pack of scandal, invented by the rascals who have usurped the government—a thing devised by the enemy."

"Nay, sir," said Kerneguy, laughing, "we must not let our zeal charge the enemy with more scandal than they actually deserve. Mistress Alice has put the question to me. I can only answer, that no one can be more devotedly attached to the King than I myself; that I am very partial to his merits and blind to his defects; and that, in short, I would be the last man in the world to give up his cause where it was tenable. Nevertheless, I must confess that, if all his grandfather of Navarre's morals have not descended to him, this poor king has somehow inherited a share of the specks that were thought to dim the luster of that great prince—that Charles is a little soft-hearted or so, where beauty is concerned. Do not blame him too severely, pretty Mistress Alice; when a man's hard fate has driven him among thorns, it were surely hard to prevent him from trifling with the few roses he may find among them?"

Alice, who probably thought the conversation had gone far enough, rose while Master Kerneguy was speaking, and was leaving the room before he had finished, without apparently hearing the interrogation with which he concluded. Her father approved of her departure, not thinking the turn which Kerneguy had given to the discourse altogether fit for her presence; and, desirous civilly to break off the conversation—"I see," he said, "this is about the time when, as Will says, the household affairs call my daughter hence; I will therefore challenge you, young gentleman to stretch your limbs in a little exercise with me, either at single rapier, or rapier and poniard, backsword, spadroon, or your national weapons of broadsword and target; for all or any of which I think we shall find implements in the hall."

"It would be too high a distinction," Master Kerneguy said, "for a poor page to be permitted to try a passage of arms with a knight so renowned as Sir Henry Lee, and he hoped to enjoy so great an honor before he left Woodstock, but at the present moment his lameness continued to give him so much pain, that he should shame himself in the attempt."

Sir Henry then offered to read him a play of Shakspeare, and for this purpose turned up *King Richard II.* But hardly had he commenced with

"Old John of Grant, time-honored Lancaster,"

when the young gentleman was seized with such an incontrollable fit of the cramp as could only be relieved by immediate exercise. He therefore begged permission to be allowed to saunter abroad for a little while, if Sir Henry Lee considered he might venture without danger.

"I can answer for the two or three of our people that are still left about the place," said Sir Henry; "and I know my son has disposed them so as to be constantly on the watch. If you hear the bell toll at the lodge, I advise you to come straight home by the way of the King's Oak, which you see in yonder glade towering above the rest of the trees. We will have some one stationed there to introduce you secretly into the house."

The page listened to these cautions with the impatience of a schoolboy, who, desirous of enjoying his holiday, hears without marking the advice of tutor or parent about taking care not to catch cold and so forth.

The absence of Alice Lee had removed all which had rendered the interior of the lodge agreeable and the mercurial young page fled with precipitation from the exercise and amusement which Sir Henry had proposed. He girded on his rapier, and threw his cloak, or rather that which belonged to his borrowed suit, about him, bringing up the lower part so as to muffle the face and show only the eyes over it, which was a common way of wearing them in those days, both in streets, in the country, and in public places, when men had a mind to be private, and to avoid interruption from salutations and greetings in the market-place. He hurried across the open space which divided the front of the lodge from the wood, with the haste of a bird escaped from the cage, which, though joyful at its liberation, is at the same time sensible of its need of protection and shelter.

The wood seemed to afford these to the human fugitive, as it might have done to the bird in question.

When under the shadow of the branches, and within the verge of the forest, covered from observation, yet with the power of surveying the front of the lodge and all the open ground before it, the supposed Louis Kerneguy meditated on his escape.

"What an infliction—to fence with a gouty old man, who knows not, I daresay, a trick of the sword which was not familiar in the days of old Vincent Saviolo! Or, as a change of misery, to hear him read one of those wildernesses of scenes which the English call a play, from prologue to epilogue—from Enter the first to the final *Exeunt omnes*—an unparalleled horror—a penance which would have made a dungeon darker, and added dulness even to Woodstock!"

Here he stopped and looked around, then continued his meditations—"So, then, it was here that the gay old Norman secluded his pretty mistress. I warrant, without having seen her, that Rosamond Clifford was never half so handsome as that lovely Alice Lee. And what a soul there is in the girl's eye! with what abandonment of all respects, save that expressing the interest of the moment, she poured forth her tide of enthusiasm! Were I to be long here, in spite of prudence and half a dozen very venerable obstacles besides, I should be tempted to try to reconcile her to the indifferent visage of this same hard-favored prince. Hard-favored! it is a kind of treason for one who pretends to so much loyalty to say so of the King's features, and in my mind deserves punishment. Ah, pretty Mistress Alice! many a Mistress Alice before you has made dreadful exclamations on the irregularities of mankind and the wickedness of the age, and ended by being glad to look out for apologies for their own share in them. But then her father—the stout old Cavalier—my father's old friend—should such a thing befall, it would break his heart. Break a pudding's end—he has more sense. If I give his grandson a title to quarter the arms of England, what matter if a bar sinister is drawn across them? Pshaw! far from an abatement, it is a point of addition: the heralds in their next visitation will place him higher in the roll for it. Then, if he did wince a little at first, does not the old traitor deserve it—first, for his disloyal intention of punching mine anointed body black and blue with his vile foils; and secondly, his atrocious complot with Will Shakspeare, a fellow as much out of date as himself, to read me to death with five acts of a historical play, or chronicle, 'being the piteous Life and Death of Richard the Second?' Odds-fish, my own life is piteous enough, as I think; and my death may match it, for aught I see coming yet. Ah, but then the brother— my friend, my guide, my guard! So far as this little proposed intrigue concerns him, such practising would be thought not quite fair. But your bouncing, swaggering, revengeful brothers exist only on the theatre. Your dire revenge, with which a brother persecuted a poor fellow who had seduced his sister, or been seduced by her, as the case might be, as relentlessly as if he had trodden on his toes without making an apology, is entirely out of fashion, since Dorset killed the Lord Bruce many a long year since.* Pshaw! when a king is the offender, the bravest man sacrifices nothing by pocketing a little wrong which he cannot personally resent. And in France there is not a noble house where each individual would not cock his hat an inch higher if they could boast of such a left-handed alliance with the Grand Monarque."

Such were the thoughts which rushed throught the mind of Charles at his first quitting the lodge of Woodstock and plunging into the forest that surrounded it. His profligate logic, however, was not the result of his natural disposition, nor received without scruple by his sound understanding. It was a train of reasoning which he had been led to adopt from his too close intimacy with the witty and profligate youth of quality by whom he had been surrounded. It arose from the evil communication with Villiers, Wilmot, Sedley, and others, whose genius was destined to corrupt that age, and the monarch on whom its character afterwards come so much to depend. Such men, bred amidst the license of civil war, and without experiencing that curb which in ordinary times the authority of parents and relations imposes upon the headlong passions of youth, were practised in every species of vice, and could recommend it as well by precept as by example, turning into pitiless ridicule all those nobler feelings which withhold men from gratifying lawless passion. The events of the King's life had also favored his reception of this epicurean doctrine. He saw himself, with, the highest claims to sympathy and assistance, coldly regarded by the courts which he visited, rather as a permitted

* This melancholy story may be found in *The Guardian* [Nos. 129 and 133]. An intrigue of Lord Sackville, afterwards Earl of Dorset, was the cause of the fatal duel.

suppliant than an exiled monarch. He beheld his own rights and claims treated with scorn and indifference ; and, in the same proportion, he was reconciled to the hard-hearted and selfish courts of dissipation which promised him immediate indulgence. If this was obtained at the expense of the happiness of others, should he of all men be scrupulous upon the subject since he treated others only as the world treated him?

But although the foundations of this unhappy system had been laid, the prince was not at this early period so fully devoted to it as he was fouud to have become when a door was unexpectedly opened for his restoration. On the contrary, though the train of gay reasoning which we have above stated, as if it had found vent in uttered language, did certainly arise in his mind, as that which would have been suggested by his favorite counselors on such occasions, he recollected that what might be passed over as a peccadillo in France or the Netherlands, or turned into a diverting novel or pasquinade by the wits of his own wandering court, was likely to have the aspect of horrid ingratitude and infamous treachery among the English gentry, and would inflict a deep, perhaps an incurable, wound upon his interest among the more aged and respectable part of his adherents. Then it occurred to him—for his own interest did not escape him, even in this mode of considering the subject—that he was in the power of the Lees, father and son, who were always understood to be at least sufficiently punctilious on the score of honor; and if they should suspect such an affront as his imagination had conceived, they could be at no loss to find means of the most ample revenge, either by their own hands or by those of the ruling faction.

"The risk of re-opening the fatal window at Whitehall and renewing the tragedy of the man in the mask were a worse penalty," was his final reflection, "than the old stool of the Scottish penance ; and lovely though Alice Lee is, I cannot afford to intrigue at such a hazard. So, farewell, pretty maiden ! unless, as sometimes has happened, thou hast a humor to throw thyself at thy King's feet, and when I am too magnanimous to refuse thee my protection. Yet, when I think of the pale clay-cold figure of the old man, as he lay last night extended before me, * and inagine the fury of Albert Lee raging with impatience, his hand on a sword which only his loyalty prevents him from plunging into his sovereign's heart—nay, the picture is too horrible ! Charles must

* [Compare pp. 299 and 234-236.]

forever change his name to Joseph, even if he were strongly tempted, which may fortune in mercy prohibit!"

To speak the truth of a prince more unfortunate in his early companions, and the callousness which he acquired by his juvenile adventures and irregular mode of life, than in his natural disposition, Charles came the more readily to this wise conclusion, because he was by no means subject to those violent and engrossing passions to gratify which the world has been thought well lost. His amours, like many of the present day, were rather matters of habit and fashion than of passion and affection; and, in comparing himself in this respect to his grandfather Henry IV., he did neither his ancestor nor himself perfect justice. He was, to parody the words of a bard, himself actuated by the stormy passions which an intriguer often only simulates—

None of those who loved so kindly,
None of those who loved so blindly.

An amour was with him a matter of amusement, a regular consequence, as it seemed to him, of the ordinary course of things in society. He was not at the trouble to practise seductive arts, because he had seldom found occasion to make use of them, his high rank, and the profligacy of part of the female society with which he had mingled, rendering them unnecessary. Added to this, he had, for the same reason, seldom been crossed by the obstinate interference of relations, or even of husbands, who had generally seemed not unwilling to suffer such matters to take their course. So that, notwithstanding his total looseness of principle, and systematic disbelief in the virtue of women and the honor of men as connected with the character of their female relatives, Charles was not a person to have studiously introduced disgrace into a family where a conquest might have been violently disputed, attained with difficulty, and accompanied with general distress, not to mention the excitation of all fiercer passions against the author of the scandal.

But the danger of the King's society consisted in his being much of an unbeliever in the existence of such cases as were likely to be embittered by remorse on the part of the principal victim, or rendered perilous by the violent resentment of her connections or relatives. He had even already found such things treated on the continent as matters of ordinary occurrence, subject, in all cases where a man of high influence was concerned, to an easy arrangement; and he was really, generally speaking, skeptical on the subject of severe virtue in either sex, and apt to consider it as a veil assumed by prudery in women and hypocrisy in men, to extort a higher reward for their compliance.

While we are discussing the character of his disposition to gallantry, the wanderer was conducted, by the walk he had chosen, through several whimsical turns, until at last it brought him under the windows of Victor Lee's apartment, where he descried Alice watering and arranging some flowers placed on the oriel window, which was easily accessible by daylight, although at night he had found it a dangerous attempt to scale it. But not Alice only, her father also showed himself near the window, and beckoned him up. The family party seemed now more promising than before, and the fugitive prince was weary of playing battledore and shuttlecock with his conscience, and much disposed to let matters go as chance should determine.

He climbed lightly up the broken ascent, and was readily welcomed by the old knight, who held activity in high honor. Alice also seemed glad to see the lively and interesting young man; and by her presence, and the unaffected mirth with which she enjoyed his sallies, he was animated to display those qualities of wit and humor which nobody possessed in a higher degree.

His satire delighted the old gentleman, who laughed till his eyes ran over as he heard the youth, whose claims to his respect he little dreamed of, amusing him with successive imitations of the Scottish Presbyterian clergyman, of the proud and poor hidalgo of the North, of the fierce and overweening pride and Celtic dialect of the mountain chief, of the slow and more pedantic Lowlander, with all of which his residence in Scotland had made him familiar. Alice also laughed and applauded, amused herself and delighted to see that her father was so; and the whole party were in the highest glee when Albert Lee entered, eager to find Louis Kerneguy and to lead him away to a private colloquy with Doctor Rochecliffe, whose zeal, assiduity, and wonderful possession of information had constituted him their master-pilot in those difficult times.

It is unnecessary to introduce the reader to the minute particulars of their conference. The information obtained was so far favorable, that the enemy seemed to have had no intelligence of the King's route towards the south, and remained persuaded that he had made his escape from Bristol, as had been reported, and as had indeed been proposed; but the master of the vessel prepared for the King's passage had taken the alarm, and sailed without his royal freight. His departure, however, and the suspicion of the service in which he was engaged, served to make the belief general that the King had gone off along with him.

But, though this was cheering, the Doctor had more unpleasant tidings from the sea-coast, alleging great difficulties in securing a vessel to which it might be fit to commit a charge so precious; and, above all, requesting his Majesty might on no account venture to approach the shore until he should receive advice that all the previous arrangements had been completely settled.

No one was able to suggest a safer place of residence than that which he at present occupied. Colonel Everard was deemed certainly not personally unfriendly to the King; and Cromwell, as was supposed, reposed in Everard an unbounded confidence. The interior presented numberless hiding-places and secret modes of exit, known to no one but the ancient residents of the lodge—nay, far better to Rochecliffe than to any of them, as, when rector at the neighboring town, his prying disposition as an antiquary had induced him to make very many researches among the old ruins, the results of which he was believed, in some instances, to have kept to himself.

To balance these conveniences, it was no doubt true that the Parliamentary Commissioners were still at no great distance, and would be ready to resume their authority upon the first opportunity. But no one supposed such an opportunity was likely to occur; and all believed, as the influence of Cromwell and the army grew more and more predominant, that the disappointed Commissioners would attempt nothing in contradiction to his pleasure, but wait with patience an indemnification in some other quarter for their vacated commissions. Report, through the voice of Master Joseph Tomkins, stated that they had determined, in the first place, to retire to Oxford, and were making preparations accordingly. This promised still farther to ensure the security of Woodstock. It was therefore settled that the King, under the character of Louis Kerneguy, should remain an inmate of the lodge until a vessel should be procured for his escape, at the port which might be esteemed the safest and most convenient.

CHAPTER XXIV

> The deadliest snakes are those which, twined 'mongst flowers,
> Blend their bright coloring with the varied blossoms,
> Their fierce eyes glittering like the spangled dewdrop;
> In all so like what nature has most harmless,
> That sportive innocence, which dreads no danger,
> Is poison'd unawares.
>
> *Old Play.*

CHARLES (we must now give him his own name) was easily reconciled to the circumstances which rendered his residence at Woodstock advisable. No doubt he would much rather have secured his safety by making an immediate escape out of England; but he had been condemned already to many uncomfortable lurking-places, and more disagreeable disguises, as well as to long and difficult journeys, during which, between pragmatical officers of justice belonging to the prevailing party, and parties of soldiers whose officers usually took on them to act on their own warrant, risk of discovery had more than once become very imminent. He was glad, therefore, of comparative repose and of comparative safety.

Then it must be considered that Charles had been entirely reconciled to the society at Woodstock, since he had become better acquainted with it. He had seen that, to interest the beautiful Alice, and procure a great deal of her company, nothing more was necessary than to submit to the humors, and cultivate the intimacy, of the old Cavalier her father. A few bouts at fencing, in which Charles took care not to put out his more perfect skill and full youthful strength and activity; the endurance of a few scenes from Shakspeare, which the knight read with more zeal than taste; a little skill in music, in which the old man had been a proficient; the deference paid to a few old-fashioned opinions, at which Charles laughed in his sleeve—were all-sufficient to gain for the disguised prince an interest in Sir Henry Lee, and to conciliate in an equal degree the good-will of his lovely daughter.

Never were there two young persons who could be said to commence this species of intimacy with such unequal advantages. Charles was a libertine, who, if he did not in cold blood resolve upon prosecuting his passion for Alice to a dishonorable conclusion, was at every moment liable to be provoked to attempt the strength of a virtue in which he was no believer. Then Alice, on her part, hardly knew even what was implied by the word libertine or seducer. Her mother had died early in the commencement of the Civil War, and she had been bred up chiefly with her brother and cousin; so that she had an unfearing and unsuspicious frankness of manner, upon which Charles was not unwilling or unlikely to put a construction favorable to his own views. Even Alice's love for her cousin—the first sensation which awakens the most innocent and simple mind to feelings of shyness and restraint towards the male sex in general—had failed to excite such an alarm in *her* bosom. They were nearly related; and Everard, though young, was several years her elder, and had, from her infancy, been an object of her respect as well as of her affection. When this early and childish intimacy ripened into youthful love, confessed and returned, still it differed in some shades from the passion existing between lovers originally strangers to each other, until their affections have been united in the ordinary course of courtship. Their love was fonder, more familiar, more perfectly confidential, purer too, perhaps, and more free from starts of passionate violence or apprehensive jealousy.

The possibility that any one could have attempted to rival Everard in her affection was a circumstance which never occurred to Alice; and that this singular Scottish lad, whom she laughed with on account of his humor, and laughed at for his peculiarities, should be an object of danger or of caution never once entered her imagination. The sort of intimacy to which she admitted Kerneguy was the same to which she would have received a companion of her own sex, whose manners she did not always approve, but whose society she found always amusing.

It was natural that the freedom of Alice Lee's conduct, which arose from the most perfect indifference, should pass for something approaching to encouragement in the royal gallant's apprehension, and that any resolutions he had formed against being tempted to violate the hospitality of Woodstock should begin to totter, as opportunities for doing so became more frequent.

These opportunities were favored by Albert's departure from Woodstock the very day after his arrival. It had been agreed in full council with Charles and Rochecliffe that he should go to visit his uncle Everard in the county of Kent, and, by showing himself there, obviate any cause of suspicion which might arise from his residence at Woodstock, and remove any pretext for disturbing his father's family on account of their harboring one who had been so lately in arms. He had also undertaken, at his own great personal risk, to visit different points on the sea-coast, and ascertain the security of different places for providing shipping for the King's leaving England.

These circumstances were alike calculated to procure the King's safety and facilitate his escape. But Alice was thereby deprived of the presence of her brother, who would have been her most watchful guardian, but who had set down the King's light talk upon a former occasion to the gaiety of his humor, and would have thought he had done his sovereign great injustice had he seriously suspected him of such a breach of hospitality as a dishonorable pursuit of Alice would have implied.

There were, however, two of the household at Woodstock who appeared not so entirely reconciled with Louis Kerneguy or his purposes. The one was Bevis, who seemed from their first unfriendly rencontre, to have kept up a pique against their new guest, which no advances on the part of Charles were able to soften. If the page was by chance left alone with his young mistress, Bevis chose always to be of the party, came close by Alice's chair and growled audibly when the gallant drew near her. "It is a pity," said the disguised prince, "that your Bevis is not a bull-dog, that we might dub him a Roundhead at once. He is too handsome, too noble, too aristocratic to nourish those inhospitable prejudices against a poor houseless Cavalier. I am convinced the spirit of Pym or Hampden has transmigrated into the rogue, and continues to demonstrate his hatred against royalty and all its adherents."

Alice would then reply, that Bevis was loyal in word and deed, and only partook her father's prejudices against the Scots, which, she could not but acknowledge, were tolerably strong,

"Nay, then," said the supposed Louis, "I must find some other reason, for I cannot allow Sir Bevis's resentment to rest upon national antipathy. So we will suppose that some gallant Cavalier, who wended to the wars and never returned, has adopted this shape to look back upon the haunts he left so unwillingly, and is jealous at seeing even poor Louis

Kerneguy drawing near to the lady of his lost affections." He approached her chair as he spoke, and Bevis gave one of his deep growls.

"In that case, you had best keep your distance," said Alice, laughing, "for the bite of a dog possessed by the ghost of a jealous lover cannot be very safe." And the King carried on the dialogue in the same strain, which, while it led Alice to apprehend nothing more serious than the apish gallantry of a fantastic boy, certainly induced the supposed Louis Kerneguy to think that he had made one of those conquests which often and easily fall to the share of sovereigns. Notwithstanding the acuteness of his apprehension, he was not sufficiently aware that the royal road to female favor is only open to monarchs when they travel in grand costume, and that when they woo incognito their path of courtship is liable to the same windings and obstacles which obstruct the course of private individuals.

There was, besides Bevis, another member of the family who kept a lookout upon Louis Kerneguy, and with no friendly eye. Phœbe Mayflower, though her experience extended not beyond the sphere of the village, yet knew the world much better than her mistress, and besides she was five years older. More knowing, she was more suspicious. She thought that odd-looking Scotch boy made more up to her young mistress than was proper for his condition of life; and, moreover, that Alice gave him a little more encouragement than Parthenia would have afforded to any such Jack-a-dandy in the absence of Argalus; for the volume treating of the loves of these celebrated Arcadians was then the favorite study of swains and damsels throughout merry England. Entertaining such suspicions, Phœbe was at a loss how to conduct herself on the occasion, and yet resolved she would not see the slightest chance of the course of Colonel Everard's true love being obstructed without attempting a remedy. She had a peculiar favor for Markham herself; and, morever, he was, according to her phrase, as handsome and personable a young man as was in Oxfordshire; and this Scottish scarecrow was no more to be compared to him than chalk was to cheese. And yet she allowed that Master Girnigy had a wonderfully well-oiled tongue, and that such gallants were not to be despised. What was to be done? She had no facts to offer, only vague suspicion; and was afraid to speak to her mistress, whose kindness, great as it was, did not, nevertheless, encourage familiarity.

She sounded Joceline; but he was, she knew not why, so

deeply interested about this unlucky lad, and held his importance so high, that she could make no impression on him. To speak to the old knight would have been to raise a general tempest. The worthy chaplain, who was at Woodstock grand referee on all disputed matters, would have been the damsel's most natural resource, for he was peaceful as well as moral by profession, and politic by practise. But it happened he had given Phœbe unintentional offense by speaking of her under the classical epithet of *Rustica Fidele*, the which epithet, as she understood it not, she held herself bound to resent as contumelious, and declaring she was not fonder of a *fiddle* than other folk, had ever since shunned all intercourse with Doctor Rochecliffe which she could easily avoid.

Master Tomkins was always coming and going about the house under various pretexts; but he was a Roundhead, and she was too true to the Cavaliers to introduce any of the enemy as parties to their internal discords; besides, he had talked to Phœbe herself in a manner which induced her to decline everything in the shape of familiarity with him. Lastly, Cavaliero Wildrake might have been consulted; but Phœbe had her own reasons for saying, as she did with some emphasis, that Cavaliero Wildrake was an impudent London rake. At length she resolved to communicate her suspicions to the party having most interest in verifying or confuting them.

"I'll let Master Markham Everard know that there is a wasp buzzing about his honeycomb," said Phœbe; "and, moreover, that I know that this young Scotch scapegrace shifted himself out of a woman's into a man's dress at Goody Green's, and gave Goody Green's Dolly a gold piece to say nothing about it; and no more she did to any one but me, and she knows best herself whether she gave change for the gold or not; but Master Louis is a saucy jackanapes, and like enough to ask it."

Three or four days elapsed while matters continued in this condition, the disguised prince sometimes thinking on the intrigue which Fortune seemed to have thrown in his way for his amusement, and taking advantage of such opportunities as occurred to increase his intimacy with Alice Lee; but much oftener harassing Doctor Rochecliffe with questions about the possibility of escape, which the good man, finding himself unable to answer, secured his leisure against royal importunity by retreating into the various unexplored recesses of the lodge, known perhaps only to himself, who had been for nearly a score of years employed in writing the *Wonders of Woodstock.*

It chanced on the fourth day that some trifling circumstance had called the knight abroad ; and he had left the young Scotsman, now familiar in the family, along with Alice in the parlor of Victor Lee. Thus situated, he thought the time not unpropitious for entering upon a strain of gallantry of a kind which might be called experimental, such as is practised by the Croats in skirmishing, when they keep bridle in hand, ready to attack the enemy or canter off without coming to close quarters, as circumstances may recommend. After using for nearly ten minutes a sort of metaphysical jargon, which might, according to Alice's pleasure, have been interpreted either into gallantry, or the language of serious pretension, and when he supposed her engaged in fathoming his meaning, he had the mortification to find, by a single and brief question, that he had been totally unattended to, and that Alice was thinking on anything at the moment rather than the sense of what he had been saying. She asked him if he could tell what it was o'clock, and this with an air of real curiosity concerning the lapse of time which put coquetry entirely out of the question.

"I will go look at the sun-dial, Mistress Alice," said the gallant, rising and coloring, through a sense of the contempt with which he thought himself treated.

"You will do me a pleasure, Master Kerneguy," said Alice, without the least consciousness of the indignation she had excited.

Master Louis Kerneguy left the room accordingly, not however, to procure the information required, but to vent his anger and mortification, and to swear, with more serious purpose than he had dared to do before, that Alice should rue her insolence. Good-natured as he was, he was still a prince, unaccustomed to contradiction, far less to contempt, and his self-pride felt, for the moment, wounded to the quick. With a hasty step he plunged into the chase, only remembering his own safety so far as to choose the deeper and sequestered avenues, where, walking on with the speedy and active step which his recovery from fatigue now permitted him to exercise according to his wont, he solaced his angry purposes, by devising schemes of revenge on the insolent country coquette, from which no consideration of hospitality was in future to have weight enough to save her.

The irritated gallant passed

The dial-stone, aged and green,

without deigning to ask it a single question; nor could it have satisfied his curiosity if he had, for no sun happened to shine at the moment. He then hastened forward, muffling himself in his cloak, and assuming a stooping and slouching gait, which diminished his apparent height. He was soon involved in the deep and dim alleys of the wood, into which he had insensibly plunged himself, and was traversing it at a great rate, without having any distinct idea in what direction he was going, when suddenly his course was arrested, first by a loud halloo, and then by a summons to stand, accompanied by what seemed still more startling and extraordinary, the touch of a cane upon his shoulder, imposed in a good-humored but somewhat imperious manner.

There were few symptoms of recognition which would have been welcome at this moment; but the appearance of the person who had thus arrested his course was least of all that he could have anticipated as timely or agreeable. When he turned, on receiving the signal, he beheld himself close to a young man nearly six feet in height, well made in joint and limb, but the gravity of whose apparel, although handsome and gentlemanlike, and a sort of precision in his habit, from the cleanness and stiffness of his band to the unsullied purity of his Spanish-leather shoes, bespoke a love of order which was foreign to the impoverished and vanquished Cavaliers, and proper to the habits of those of the victorious party, who could afford to dress themselves handsomely, and whose rule—that is, such as regarded the higher and more respectable classes—enjoined decency and sobriety of garb and deportment. There was yet another weight against the prince in the scale, and one still more characteristic of the inequality in the comparison under which he seemed to labor. There was strength in the muscular form of the stranger who had brought him to this involuntary parley, authority and determination in his brow, a long rapier on the left, and a poniard or dagger on the right side of his belt, and a pair of pistols stuck into it, which would have been sufficient to give the unknown the advantage (Louis Kerneguy having no weapon but his sword), even had his personal strength approached nearer than it did to that of the person by whom he was thus suddenly stopped.

Bitterly regretting the thoughtless fit of passion that brought him into his present situation, but especially the want of the pistols he had left behind, and which do so much to place bodily strength and weakness upon an equal footing, Charles yet availed himself of the courage and presence of mind in which few of his unfortunate family had for centuries been deficient. He stood firm and without motion, his cloak still wrapped round the lower part of his face, to give time for explanation, in case he was mistaken for some other person.

This coolness produced its effect; for the other party said, with doubt and surprise on his part, "Joceline Joliffe, is it not? If I know not Joceline Joliffe, I should at least know my own cloak."

"I am not Joceline Joliffe, as you may see, sir," said Kerneguy, calmly, drawing himself erect to show the difference of size, and dropping the cloak from his face and person.

"Indeed!" replied the stranger, in surprise, "then, sir unknown, I have to express my regret at having used my cane in intimating that I wished you to stop. From that dress, which I certainly recognize for my own, I concluded you must be Joceline, in whose custody I had left my habit at the lodge."

"If it had been Joceline, sir," replied the supposed Kerneguy, with perfect composure, "methinks you should not have struck so hard."

The other party was obviously confused by the steady calmness with which he was encountered. The sense of politeness dictated, in the first place, an apology for a mistake, when he thought he had been tolerably certain of the person. Master Kerneguy was not in a situation to be punctilious: he bowed gravely, as indicating his acceptance of the excuse offered, then turned, and walked, as he conceived, towards the lodge, though he had traversed the woods, which were cut with various alleys in different directions, too hastily to be certain of the real course which he wished to pursue.

He was much embarrassed to find that this did not get him rid of the companion whom he had thus involuntarily acquired. Walked he slow, walked he fast, his friend in the genteel but Puritanic habit, strong in person, and well armed, as we have described him, seemed determined to keep him company, and, without attempting to join or enter into conversation, never suffered him to outstrip his surveillance for more than two or three yards. The wanderer mended his pace; but although he was then, in his youth, as afterwards in his riper age, one of the best walkers in Britain, the stranger, without advancing his pace to a run, kept fully equal to him, and his persecution became so close, and constant, and inevitable, that the pride and fear of Charles were both alarmed, and he began to think that, whatever the danger might be of a single-handed renconter, he would nevertheless have a better bargain of this tall satellite if they settled the debate betwixt them in the forest than if they drew near any place of habitation, where the man in authority was likely to find friends and concurrence.

Betwixt anxiety, therefore, vexation, and anger, Charles faced suddenly round on his pursuer as they reached a small, narrow glade which led to the little meadow over which presided the King's Oak, the ragged and scathed branches and gigantic trunk of which formed a vista to the little wild avenue.

"Sir," said he to his pursuer, "you have already been guilty of one piece of impertinence towards me. You have apologized; and knowing no reason why you should distinguish me as an object of incivility, I have accepted your excuse without scruple. Is there anything remains to be settled betwixt us, which causes you to follow me in this manner? If so, I shall be glad to make it a subject of explanation or satisfaction, as the case may admit of. I think you can owe me no malice, for I never saw you before to my knowledge. If you can give any good reason for asking it, I am willing to render you personal satisfaction. If your purpose is merely impertinent curiosity, I let you know that I will not suffer myself to be dogged in my private walks by any one."

"When I recognize my own cloak on another man's shoulders," replied the stranger, drily, "methinks I have a natural right to follow, and see what becomes of it; for know, sir, though I have been mistaken as to the wearer, yet I am confident I had as good a right to stretch my cane across the cloak you are muffled in as ever had any one to brush his own garments. If, therefore, we are to be friends, I must ask, for instance, how you came by that cloak, and where you are going with it? I shall otherwise make bold to stop you, as one who has sufficient commission to do so."

"Oh, unhappy cloak," thought the wanderer, "ay, and thrice unhappy the idle fancy that sent me here with it wrapped around my nose, to pick quarrels and attract observation, when quiet and secrecy were peculiarly essential to my safety!"

"If you will allow me to guess, sir," continued the stranger, who was no other than Markham Everard, "I will convince you that you are better known than you think for."

"Now, Heaven forbid!" prayed the party addressed, in silence, but with as much devotion as ever he applied to a prayer in his life. Yet, even in this moment of extreme urgency, his courage and composure did not fail; and he recollected it was of the utmost importance not to seem startled, and to answer so as, if possible, to lead the dangerous companion with whom he had met to confess the extent of his actual knowledge or suspicions concerning him.

"If you know me, sir," he said, "and are a gentleman, as your appearance promises, you cannot be at a loss to discover to what accident you must attribute my wearing these clothes, which you say are yours."

"Oh, sir," replied Colonel Everard, his wrath in no sort turned away by the mildness of the stranger's answer, "we have learned our Ovid's *Metamorphoses*, and we know for what purposes young men of quality travel in disguise; we know that even female attire is resorted to on certain occasions; we have heard of Vertumnus and Pomona."

The monarch, as he weighed those words, again uttered a devout prayer that this ill-looking affair might have no deeper root than the jealousy of some admirer of Alice Lee, promising to himself that, devotee as he was to the fair sex, he would make no scruple of renouncing the fairest of Eve's daughters in order to get out of the present dilemma.

"Sir," he said, "you seem to be a gentleman. I have no objection to tell you, as such, that I also am of that class."

"Or somewhat higher, perhaps?" said Everard.

"A gentleman," replied Charles, "is a term which comprehends all ranks entitled to armorial bearings. A duke, a lord, a prince is no more than a gentleman; and if in misfortune, as I am, he may be glad if that general term of courtesy is allowed him."

"Sir," replied Everard, "I have no purpose to entrap you to any acknowledgment fatal to your own safety. Nor do I hold it my business to be active in the arrest of private individuals, whose perverted sense of national duty may have led them into errors rather to be pitied than punished by candid men. But if those who have brought civil war and disturbance into their native country proceed to carry dishonor and disgrace into the bosom of families, if they attempt to carry on their private debaucheries to the injury of the hospitable roofs which afford them refuge from the consequences of their public crimes, do you think, my lord, that we shall bear it with patience?"

"If it is your purpose to quarrel with me," said the prince, "speak it out at once like a gentleman. You have the advantage, no doubt, of arms, but it is not that odds which will induce me to fly from a single man. If, on the other hand, you are disposed to hear reason, I tell you in calm words, that I neither suspect the offense to which you allude nor comprehend why you give me the title of my lord."

"You deny, then, being the Lord Wilmot?" said Everard.

"I may do so most safely," said the prince.

"Perhaps you rather style yourself Earl of Rochester? We heard that the issuing of some such patent by the King of Scots was a step which your ambition proposed."

"Neither lord nor earl am I, as sure as I have a Christian soul to be saved. My name is——"

"Do not degrade yourself by unnecessary falsehood, my lord, and that to a single man, who I promise you, will not invoke public justice to assist his own good sword should he see cause to use it. Can you look at that ring and deny that you are Lord Wilmot?"

He handed to the disguised prince a ring which he took from his purse, and his opponent instantly knew it for the same he had dropped into Alice's pitcher at the fountain, obeying only, though imprudently, the gallantry of the moment, in giving a pretty gem to a handsome girl, whom he had accidentally frightened.

"I know the ring," he said; "it has been in my possession. How it should prove me to be Lord Wilmot, I cannot conceive; and beg to say, it bears false witness against me."

"You shall see the evidence," answered Everard; and resuming the ring, he pressed a spring ingeniously contrived in the collet of the setting, on which the stone flew back and showed within it the cipher of Lord Wilmot beautifully engraved in miniature, with a coronet. "What say you now, sir?"

"That probabilities are no proofs," said the prince: "there is nothing here save what can be easily accounted for. I am the son of a Scottish nobleman, who was mortally wounded and made prisoner at Worcester fight. When he took leave, and bid me fly, he gave me the few valuables he possessed, and that among others. I have heard him talk of having changed rings with Lord Wilmot, on some occasion in Scotland, but I never knew the trick of the gem which you have shown me."

In this, it may be necessary to say, Charles spoke very truly; nor would he have parted with it in the way he did, had he suspected it would be easily recognized. He proceeded after a minute's pause: "Once more, sir—I have told you much that concerns my safety; if you are generous, you will let me pass, and I may do you on some future day as good service. If you mean to arrest me, you must do so here, and at your own peril, for I will neither walk farther your way nor permit you to dog me on mine. If you let me pass, I will thank you; if not, take to your weapon."

"Young gentleman," said Colonel Everard, "whether you be actually the gay young nobleman for whom I took you, you have made me uncertain; but, intimate as you say your family has been with him, I have little doubt that you are proficient in the school of debauchery of which Wilmot and Villiers are professors, and their hopeful master a graduated student. Your conduct at Woodstock, where you have rewarded the hospitality of the family by meditating the most deadly wound to their honor, has proved you too apt a scholar in such an academy. I intended only to warn you on this subject; it will be your own fault if I add chastisement to admonition."

"Warn me, sir!" said the prince, indignantly, "and chastisement! This is presuming more on my patience than is consistent with your own safety. Draw, sir." So saying, he laid his hand on his sword.

"My religion," said Everard, "forbids me to be rash in shedding blood. Go home, sir—be wise—consult the dictates of honor as well as prudence. Respect the honor of the house of Lee, and know there is one nearly allied to it by whom your motions will be called to severe account."

"Aha!" said the prince, with a bitter laugh, "I see the whole matter now: we have our Roundheaded colonel, our Puritan cousin, before us—the man of texts and morals, whom Alice Lee laughs at so heartily. If your religion, sir, prevents you from giving satisfaction, it should prevent you from offering insult to a person of honor."

The passions of both were now fully up; they drew mutually, and began to fight, the colonel relinquishing the advantage he could have obtained by the use of his firearms. A thrust of the arm or a slip of the foot might, at the moment, have changed the destinies of Britain, when the arrival of a third party broke off the combat.

CHAPTER XXV

Stay, for the king has thrown his warder down.
Richard II.

THE combatants whom we left engaged at the end of the last chapter made mutual passes at each other with apparently equal skill and courage. Charles had been too often in action, and too long a party as well as a victim to civil war, to find anything new or surprising in being obliged to defend himself with his own hands; and Everard had been distinguished as well for his personal bravery as for the other properties of a commander. But the arrival of a third party prevented the tragic conclusion of a combat in which the success of either party must have given him much cause for regretting his victory.

It was the old knight himself who arrived, mounted upon a forest pony, for the war and sequestration had left him no steed of a more dignified description. He thrust himself between the combatants, and commanded them on their lives to hold. So soon as a glance from one to the other had ascertained to him whom he had to deal with, he demanded, "Whether the devils of Woodstock whom folk talked about had got possession of them both, that they were tilting at each other within the verge of the royal liberties? Let me tell both of you," he said, "that, while old Henry Lee is at Woodstock, the immunities of the park shall be maintained as much as if the King were still on the throne. None shall fight duellos here, excepting the stags in their season. Put up, both of you, or I shall lug out as thirdsman, and prove, perhaps the worst devil of the three. As Will says—

I'll so maul you and your toasting-irons,
That you shall think the Devil has come from Hell."

The combatants desisted from their encounter, but stood looking at each other sullenly, as men do in such a situation, each unwilling to seem to desire peace more than the other, and averse therefore to be the first to sheathe his sword.

"Return your weapons, gentlemen, upon the spot," said

the knight yet more peremptorily, "one and both of you, or you will have something to do with me, I promise you. You may be thankful times are changed. I have known them such, that your insolence might have cost each of you your right hand, if not redeemed with a round sum of money. Nephew, if you do not mean to alienate me forever, I command you to put up. Master Kerneguy, you are my guest. I request of you not to do me the insult of remaining with your sword drawn, where it is my duty to see peace observed."

"I obey you, Sir Henry," said the King, sheathing his rapier. "I hardly indeed know wherefore I was assaulted by this gentleman. I assure you, none respects the King's person or privileges more than myself, though the devotion is somewhat out of fashion."

"We may find a place to meet, sir," replied Everard, "where neither the royal person nor privileges can be offended."

"Faith, very hardly, sir," said Charles, unable to suppress the rising jest—"I mean the King has so few followers, that the loss of the least of them might be some small damage to him; but, risking all that, I will meet you wherever there is fair field for a poor Cavalier to get off in safety, if he has the luck in fight."

Sir Henry Lee's first idea had been fixed upon the insult offered to the royal demesne; he now began to turn his thoughts towards the safety of his kinsman, and of the young Royalist, as he deemed him. "Gentlemen," he said, "I must insist on this business being put to a final end. Nephew Markham, is this your return for my condescension in coming back to Woodstock on your warrant, that you should take an opportunity to cut the throat of my guest?"

"If you knew his purpose as well as I do——" said Markham, and then paused, conscious that he might only incense his uncle without convincing him, as anything he might say of Kerneguy's addresses to Alice was likely to be imputed to his own jealous suspicions; he looked on the ground, therefore, and was silent.

"And you, Master Kerneguy," said Sir Henry, "can you give me any reason why you seek to take the life of this young man, in whom, though unhappily forgetful of his loyalty and duty, I must yet take some interest as my nephew by affinity?"

"I was not aware the gentleman enjoyed that honor, which certainly would have protected him from my sword," answered Kerneguy. "But the quarrel is his; nor can I tell any reason why he fixed it upon me, unless it were the difference of our political opinions."

"You know the contrary," said Everard: "you know that I told you you were safe from me as a fugitive Royalist; and your last words showed you were at no loss to guess my connection with Sir Henry. That, indeed, is of little consequence. I should debase myself did I use the relationship as a means of protection from you or any one."

As they thus disputed, neither choosing to approach the real cause of quarrel, Sir Henry looked from the one to the other with a peacemaking countenance, exclaiming—

> "Why, what an intricate impeach is this?
> I think you both have drunk of Circe's cup.

Come, my young masters, allow an old man to mediate between you. I am not short-sighted in such matters. The mother of mischief is no bigger than a gnat's wing; and I have known fifty instances in my own day, when, as Will says—

> Gallants have been confronted hardly,
> In single opposition, hand to hand,

in which, after the field was fought, no one could remember the cause of quarrel. Tush! a small thing will do it—the taking of the wall, or the gentle rub of the shoulder in passing each other, or a hasty word, or a misconceived gesture. Come, forget your cause of quarrel, be what it will; you have had your breathing, and though you put up your rapiers unbloodied, that was no default of yours, but by command of your elder, and one who had right to use authority. In Malta, where the duello is punctiliously well understood, the persons engaged in a single combat are bound to halt on the command of a knight, or priest, or lady, and the quarrel so interrupted is held as honorably terminated, and may not be revived. Nephew, it is, I think, impossible that you can nourish spleen against this young gentleman for having fought for his king. Hear my honest proposal, Markham. You know I bear no malice, though I have some reason to be offended with you. Give the young man your hand in friendship, and we will back to the lodge, all three together, and drink a cup of sack in token of reconciliation."

Markham Everard found himself unable to resist this approach towards kindness on his uncle's part. He suspected, indeed, what was partly the truth, that it was not entirely from reviving good-will, but also, that his uncle thought, by such attention, to secure his neutrality at least, if not his assistance, for the safety of the fugitive Royalist. He was sensible that he was placed in an awkward predicament; and that he might incur the suspicions of his own party, for holding intercourse even with a near relation who harbored such guests. But, on the other hand, he thought his services to the Commonwealth had been of sufficient importance to outweigh whatever envy might urge on that topic. Indeed, although the Civil War had divided families much, and in many various ways, yet, when it seemed ended by the triumph of the republicans, the rage of political hatred began to relent, and the ancient ties of kindred and friendship regained at least a part of their former influence. Many reunions were formed; and those who, like Everard, adhered to the conquering party, often exerted themselves for the protection of their deserted relatives.

As these things rushed through his mind, accompanied with the prospect of a renewed intercourse with Alice Lee, by means of which he might be at hand to protect her against every chance either of injury or insult, he held out his hand to the supposed Scottish page, saying at the same time, "That, for his part, he was very ready to forget the cause of quarrel, or rather, to consider it as arising out of a misapprehension, and to offer Master Kerneguy such friendship as might exist between honorable men who had embraced different sides in politics."

Unable to overcome the feeling of personal dignity, which prudence recommended to him to forget, Louis Kerneguy in return bowed low, but without accepting Everard's proffered hand.

"He had no occasion," he said, "to make any exertions to forget the cause of quarrel, for he had never been able to comprehend it; but, as he had not shunned the gentleman's resentment, so he was now willing to embrace and return any degree of his favor with which he might be pleased to honor him."

Everard withdrew his hand with a smile, and bowed in return to the salutation of the page, whose stiff reception of his advances he imputed to the proud, pettish disposition of a Scotch boy, trained up in extravagant ideas of family consequence and personal importance, which his acquaintance with the world had not yet been sufficient to dispel.

Sir Henry Lee, delighted with the termination of the quarrel, which he supposed to be in deep deference to his own authority, and not displeased with the opportunity of renewing some acquaintance with his nephew, who had, notwithstanding his political demerits, a warmer interest in his affections than he was, perhaps, himself aware of, said, in a tone of consolation, "Never be mortified, young gentleman. I protest it went to my heart to part you, when I saw you stretching yourselves so handsomely, and in fair love of honor, without any malicious or bloodthirsty thoughts. I promise you, had it not been for my duty as ranger here, and sworn to the office, I would rather have been your umpire than your hindrance. But a finished quarrel is a forgotten quarrel; and your tilting should have no further consequence excepting the appetite it may have given you."

So saying, he urged forward his pony, and moved in triumph towards the lodge by the nearest alley. His feet almost touching the ground, the ball of his toe just resting in the stirrup, the forepart of the thigh brought round to the saddle, the heels turned outwards, and sunk as much as possible, his body precisely erect, the reins properly and systematically divided in his left hand, his right holding a riding-rod diagonally pointed towards the horse's left ear, he seemed a champion of the menage, fit to have reined Bucephalus himself. His youthful companions, who attended on either hand like equerries, could scarce suppress a smile at the completely adjusted and systematic posture of the rider, contrasted with the wild and diminutive appearance of the pony, with its shaggy coat, and long tail and mane, and its keen eyes sparkling like red coals from amongst the mass of hair which fell over its small countenance. If the reader has the Duke of Newcastle's book on horsemanship (*splendida moles!*) he may have some idea of the figure of the good knight, if he can conceive such a figure as one of cavaliers there represented, seated, in all the graces of his art, on a Welsh or Exmoor pony, in its native savage state, without grooming or discipline of any kind, the ridicule being greatly enhanced by the disproportion of size betwixt the animal and its rider,

Perhaps the knight saw their wonder, for the first words he said after they left the ground were, "Pixie, though small, is mettlesome, gentlemen (here he contrived that Pixie should himself corroborate the assertion, by executing a gambade)—he is diminutive, but full of spirit; indeed, save that I am somewhat too large for an elfin horseman (the knight was upwards of six feet high), I should remind myself, when I mount him, of the Fairy King, as described by Mike Drayton :

Himself he on an earwig set,
Yet scarce upon his back could get,
So oft and high he did curvet,
Ere he himself did settle.
He made him stop, and turn, and bound,
To gallop, and to trot the round,
He scarce could stand on any ground,
He was so full of mettle."

"My old friend, Pixie!" said Everard, stroking the pony's neck, "I am glad that he has survived all these bustling days. Pixie must be above twenty years old, Sir Henry?"

"Above twenty years, certainly. Yes, nephew Markham, war is a whirlwind in a plantation, which only spares what is least worth leaving. Old Pixie and his old master have survived many a tall fellow and many a great horse, neither of them good for much themselves. Yet, as Will says, an old man can do somewhat. So Pixie and I still survive."

So saying, he again contrived that Pixie should show some remnants of activity.

"Still survive!" said the young Scot, completing the sentence which the good knight had left unfinished—"ay, still survive,

To witch the world with noble horsemanship."

Everard colored, for he felt the irony; but not so his uncle, whose simple vanity never permitted him to doubt the sincerity of the compliment.

"Are you avised of that?" he said. "In King James's time, indeed, I have appeared in the tilt-yard, and there you might have said—

You saw young Harry with his beaver up.

As to seeing old Harry, why——" Here the knight paused, and looked as a bashful man in labor of a pun. "As to old Harry—why, you might as well see the *Devil*. You take me, Master Kerneguy: the Devil, you know, is my namesake—ha—ha—ha! Cousin Everard, I hope your precision is not startled by an innocent jest?"

He was so delighted with the applause of both his companions, that he recited the whole of the celebrated passage referred to, and concluded with defying the present age, bundle all its wits, Donne, Cowley, Waller, and the rest of them together, to produce a poet of a tenth part of the genius of old Will.

"Why, we are said to have one of his descendants among us—Sir William D'Avenant," said Louis Kerneguy; "and many think him as clever a fellow."

"What!" exclaimed Sir Henry. "Will D'Avenant, whom I knew in the north, an officer under Newcastle, when the Marquis lay before Hull? Why, he was an honest Cavalier, and wrote good doggerel enough; but how came he akin to Will Shakspeare, I trow?"

"Why," replied the young Scot, "by the surer side of the house, and after the old fashion, if D'Avenant speaks truth. It seems that his mother was a good-looking, laughing, buxom mistress of an inn between Stratford and London, at which Will Shakspeare often quartered as he went down to his native town, and that, out of friendship and gossipred, as we say in Scotland, Will Shakspeare became god-father to Will D'Avenant; and not contented with this spiritual affinity, the younger Will is for establishing some claim to a natural one, alleging that his mother was a great admirer of wit, and there were no bounds to her complaisance for men of genius." *

"Out upon the hound!" said Colonel Everard; "would he purchase the reputation of descending from poet, or from prince, at the expense of his mother's good fame? his nose ought to be slit."

"That would be difficult," answered the disguised prince, recollecting the peculiarity of the bard's countenance. †

"Will D'Avenant the son of Will Shakspeare!" said the knight, who had not yet recovered his surprise at the enormity of the pretension; "why, it reminds me of a verse in the puppet-show of *Phaeton,* where the hero complains to his mother—

> Besides, by all the village boys, I'm sham'd;
> You the Sun's son, you rascal, you be d—d! ‡

I never heard such unblushing assurance in my life! Will D'Avenant the son of the brightest and best poet that ever

* See Will D'Avenant and Shakspeare. Note 6.

† D'Avenant actually wanted the nose, the foundation of many a jest of the day.

‡ See Note 7.

was, is, or will be! But I crave your pardon, nephew. You, I believe, love no stage-plays."

"Nay, I am not altogether so precise as you would make me, uncle. I have loved them perhaps too well in my time, and now I condemn them not altogether, or in gross, though I approve not their excesses and extravagances. I cannot, even in Shakspeare, but see many things both scandalous to decency and prejudicial to good manners—many things which tend to ridicule virtue, or to recommend vice, at least to mitigate the hideousness of its features. I cannot think these fine poems are an useful study, and especially for the youth of either sex, in which bloodshed is pointed out as the chief occupation of the men, and intrigue as the sole employment of the women."

In making these observations, Everard was simple enough to think that he was only giving his uncle an opportunity of defending a favorite opinion, without offending him by a contradiction which was so limited and mitigated. But here, as on other occasions, he forgot how obstinate his uncle was in his views, whether of religion, policy, or taste, and that it would be as easy to convert him to the Presbyterian form of government, or engage him to take the abjuration oath, as to shake his belief in Shakspeare. There was another peculiarity in the good knight's mode of arguing, which Everard, being himself of a plain and downright character, and one whose religious tenets were in some degree unfavorable to the suppressions and simulations often used in society, could never perfectly understand. Sir Henry, sensible of his natural heat of temper, was wont scrupulously to guard against it, and would for some time, when in fact much offended, conduct a debate with all the external appearance of composure, till the violence of his feelings would rise so high as to overcome and bear away the artificial barriers opposed to it, and rush down upon the adversary with accumulating wrath. It thus frequently happened that, like a wily old general, he retreated in the face of his disputant in good order and by degrees, with so moderate a degree of resistance as to draw on his antagonist's pursuit to the spot where, at length, making a sudden and unexpected attack, with horse, foot, and artillery at once, he seldom failed to confound the enemy, though he might not overthrow him.

It was on this principle, therefore, that, hearing Everard's last observation, he disguised his angry feelings, and answered, with a tone where politeness was called in to keep guard upon passion, "That undoubtedly the Presbyterian gentry had given, through the whole of these unhappy times, such proofs of an humble, unaspiring, and unambitious desire of the public good as entitled them to general credit for the sincerity of those very strong scruples which they entertained against works in which the noblest sentiments of religion and virtue—sentiments which might convert hardened sinners, and be placed with propriety in the mouths of dying saints and martyrs—happened, from the rudeness and coarse taste of the times, to be mixed with some broad jests and similar matter, which lay not much in the way, excepting of those who painfully sought such stuff out, that they might use it in vilifying what was in itself deserving of the highest applause. But what he wished especially to know from his nephew was, whether any of those gifted men who had expelled the learned scholars and deep divines of the Church of England from the pulpit, and now flourished in their stead, received any inspiration from the muses, if he might use so profane a term without offense to Colonel Everard, or whether they were not as sottishly and brutally averse from elegant letters as they were from humanity and common sense?"

Colonel Everard might have guessed, by the ironical tone in which this speech was delivered, what storm was mustering within his uncle's bosom—nay, he might have conjectured the state of the old knight's feelings from his emphasis on the word "colonel," by which epithet, as that which most connected his nephew with the party he hated, he never distinguished Everard unless when his wrath was rising; while, on the contrary, when disposed to be on good terms with him, he usually called him Kinsman, or Nephew Markham. Indeed, it was under a partial sense that this was the case, and in the hope to see his cousin Alice, that the colonel forbore making any answer to the harangue of his uncle, which had concluded just as the old knight had alighted at the door of the lodge, and was entering the hall, followed by his two attendants.

Phœbe at the same time made her appearance in the hall, and received orders to bring some "beverage" for the gentlemen. The Hebe of Woodstock failed not to recognize and welcome Everard by an almost imperceptible courtesy; but she did not serve her interest, as she designed, when she asked the knight, as a question of course, whether he commanded the attendance of Mistress Alice. A stern "No," was the decided reply: and the ill-timed interference seemed to increase his previous irritation against Everard for his depreciation of Shakspeare. "I would insist," said Sir Henry, resuming the obnoxious subject, "were it fit for a poor disbanded Cavalier to use such a phrase towards a commander of the conquering army, upon knowing whether the convulsion which has sent us saints and prophets without end has not also afforded us a poet with enough both of gifts and grace to outshine poor old Will, the oracle and idol of us blinded and carnal Cavaliers?"

"Surely, sir," replied Colonel Everard, "I know verses written by a friend of the Commonwealth, and those, too, of a dramatic character, which, weighed in an impartial scale, might equal even the poetry of Shakspeare, and which are free from the fustian and indelicacy with which that great bard was sometimes content to feed the coarse appetites of his barbarous audience."

"Indeed!" said the knight, keeping down his wrath with difficulty. "I should like to be acquainted with this masterpiece of poetry! May we ask the name of this distinguished person?"

"It must be Vicars or Withers at least," said the feigned page.

"No, sir," replied Everard, "nor Drummond of Hawthornden, nor Lord Stirling neither. And yet the verses will vindicate what I say, if you will make allowance for indifferent recitation, for I am better accustomed to speak to a battalion than to those who love the muses. The speaker is a lady benighted, who, having lost her way in a pathless forest, at first expresses herself agitated by the supernatural fears to which her situation gave rise."

"A play, too, and written by a Roundhead author!" said Sir Henry in surprise.

"A dramatic production at least," replied his nephew; and began to recite simply, but with feeling, the lines now so well known, but which had then obtained no celebrity, the fame of the author resting upon the basis rather of his polemical and political publications than on the poetry doomed in after days to support the eternal structure of his immortality.

> "These thoughts may startle, but will not astound
> The virtuous mind, that ever walks attended
> By a strong siding champion, Conscience."

"My own opinion, nephew Markham—my own opinion," said Sir Henry, with a burst of admiration—"better expressed, but just what I said when the scoundrelly Roundheads pretended to see ghosts at Woodstock. Go on, I prithee."

Everard proceeded:

> "O welcome, pure-eyed Faith, white-handed Hope,
> Thou hovering angel, girt with golden wings,
> And thou unblemish'd form of Chastity!
> I see ye visibly, and now believe
> That he the Supreme Good, to whom all things ill
> Are but as slavish officers of vengeance,
> Would send a glistering guardian, if need were,
> To keep my life and honor unassail'd.
> Was I deceived, or did a sable cloud
> Turn forth her silver lining on the night?

The rest has escaped me," said the reciter; "and I marvel I have been able to remember so much."

Sir Henry Lee, who had expected some effusion very different from those classical and beautiful lines, soon changed the scornful expression of his countenance, relaxed his contorted upper lip, and, stroking down his beard with his left hand, rested the forefinger of the right upon his eyebrow, in sign of profound attention. After Everard had ceased speaking, the old man sighed as at the end of a strain of sweet music. He then spoke in a gentler manner than formerly.

"Cousin Markham," he said, "these verses flow sweetly, and sound in my ears like the well-touched warbling of a lute. But thou knowest I am something slow of apprehending the full meaning of that which I hear for the first time. Repeat me these verses again, slowly and deliberately; for I always love to hear poetry twice, the first time for sound, and the latter time for sense."

Thus encouraged, Everard recited again the lines, with more hardihood and better effect; the knight distinctly understanding, and, from his looks and motions, highly applauding them.

"Yes," he broke out, when Everard was again silent—"yes, I *do* call that poetry, though it were even written by a Presbyterian, or an Anabaptist either. Ay, there were good and righteous people to be found even amongst the offending towns which were destroyed by fire. And certainly I have heard, though with little credence—begging your pardon, cousin Everard—that there are men among you who have seen the error of their ways in rebelling against the best and kindest of masters, and bringing it to that pass that he was murdered by a gang yet fiercer than themselves. Ay, doubtless the gentleness of spirit and the purity of mind which dictated those beautiful lines has long ago taught a man so amiable to say, 'I have sinned—I have sinned.' Yes, I doubt not so sweet a harp has been broken, even in remorse, for the crimes he was witness to; and now he sits drooping for the shame and sorrow of England, all his noble rhymes, as Will says,

Like sweet bells jangled, but of tune and harsh.

Dost thou not think so, Master Kerneguy?"

"Not I, Sir Henry," answered the page, somewhat maliciously.

"What, dost not believe the author of these lines must needs be of the better file, and leaning to our persuasion?"

"I think, Sir Henry, that the poetry qualifies the author to write a play on the subject of Dame Potiphar and her recusant lover; and as for his calling—that last metaphor of the cloud in a black coat or cloak, with silver lining, would have dubbed him a tailor with me, only that I happen to know that he is a schoolmaster by profession, and by political opinions qualified to be Poet Laureate to Cromwell; for what Colonel Everard has repeated with such unction is the production of no less celebrated a person than John Milton."

"John Milton!" exclaimed Sir Henry, in astonishment. "What! John Milton, the blasphemous and bloody-minded author of the *Defensio Populi Anglicani!*—the advocate of the infernal High Court of Fiends!—the creature and parasite of that grand impostor, that loathsome hypocrite, that detestable monster, that prodigy of the universe, that disgrace of mankind, that landscape of iniquity, that sink of sin, and that compendium of baseness, Oliver Cromwell?"

"Even the same John Milton," answered Charles—"schoolmaster to little boys, and tailor to the clouds, which he furnishes with suits of black, lined with silver, at no other expense than that of common sense."

"Markham Everard," said the old knight, "I will never forgive thee—never—never. Thou hast made me speak words of praise respecting one whose offal should fatten the region-kites. Speak not to me, sir, but begone. Am I, your kinsman and benefactor, a fit person to be juggled out of my commendation and eulogy, and brought to bedaub such a whitened sepulcher as the sophist Milton?"

"I profess," said Everard, "this is hard measure, Sir

Henry. You pressed me—you defied me, to produce poetry as good as Shakspeare's. I only thought of the verses, not of the politics of Milton."

"Oh yes, sir," replied Sir Henry, "we well know your power of making distinctions: you could make war against the King's prerogative, without having the least design against his person. Oh Heaven forbid! But Heaven will hear and judge you. Set down the beverage, Phœbe (this was added by way of parenthesis to Phœbe, who entered with refreshment), Colonel Everard is not thirsty. You have wiped your mouths, and said you have done no evil. But though you have deceived man, yet God you cannot deceive. And you shall wipe no lips in Woodstock, either after meat or drink, I promise you."

Charged thus at once with the faults imputed to his whole religious sect and political party, Everard felt too late of what imprudence he had been guilty in giving the opening, by disputing his uncle's taste in dramatic poetry. He endeavored to explain, to apologize.

"I mistook your purpose, honored sir, and thought you really desired to know something of our literature; and in repeating what you deemed not unworthy your hearing, I profess I thought I was doing you pleasure, instead of stirring your indignation."

"O ay!" returned the knight, with unmitigated rigor of resentment—"profess—profess. Ay, that is the new phrase of asseveration, instead of the profane adjuration of courtiers and Cavaliers. Oh, sir, *profess* less and *practise* more, and so good-day to you. Master Kerneguy, you will find beverage in my apartment."

While Phœbe stood gaping in admiration at the sudden quarrel which had arisen, Colonel Everard's vexation and resentment was not a little increased by the nonchalance of the young Scotsman, who, with his hands thrust into his pockets with a courtly affectation of the time, had thrown himself into one of the antique chairs, and though habitually too polite to laugh aloud, and possessing that art of internal laughter by which men of the world learn to indulge their mirth without incurring quarrels or giving direct offense, was at no particular trouble to conceal that he was exceedingly amused by the result of the colonel's visit to Woodstock. Colonel Everard's patience, however, had reached bounds which it was very likely to surpass; for, though differing widely in politics, there was a resemblance betwixt the temper of the uncle and nephew.

"Damnation!" exclaimed the colonel, in a tone which became a Puritan as little as did the exclamation itself.

"Amen!" said Louis Kerneguy, but in a tone so soft and gentle, that the ejaculation seemed rather to escape him than to be designedly uttered.

"Sir!" said Everard, striding towards him in that sort of humor when a man, full of resentment, would not unwillingly find an object on which to discharge it.

"*Plait-il?*" said the page in the most equable tone, looking up in his face with the most unconscious innocence.

"I wish to know, sir," retorted Everard, "the meaning of that which you said just now?"

"Only a pouring out of the spirit, worthy sir," returned Kerneguy—"a small skiff despatched to Heaven on my own account, to keep company with your holy petition just now expressed."

"Sir, I have known a merry gentleman's bones broke for such a smile as you wear just now," replied Everard.

"There, look you now!" answered the malicious page, who could not weigh even the thoughts of his safety against the enjoyment of his jest. "If you had stuck to your *professions*, worthy sir, you must have choked by this time; but your round execration bolted like a cork from a bottle of cider, and now allows your wrath to come foaming out after it, in the honest unbaptized language of common ruffians."

"For Heaven's sake, Master Girnigy," said Phœbe, "forbear giving the colonel these bitter words! And do you, good Colonel Markham, scorn to take offense at his hands—he is but a boy."

"If the Colonel or you choose, Mistress Phœbe, you shall find me a man; I think the gentleman can say something to the purpose already. Probably he may recommend to you the part of the Lady in *Comus;* and I only hope his own admiration of John Milton will not induce him to undertake the part of Samson Agonistes, and blow up this old house with execrations, or pull it down in wrath about our ears."

"Young man," said the colonel, still in towering passion, "if you respect my principles for nothing else, be grateful for the protection which, but for them, you would not easily attain."

"Nay, then," said the attendant, "I must fetch those who have more influence with you than I have," and away tripped Phœbe; while Kerneguy answered Everard in the same provoking tone of calm indifference—

"Before you menace me with a thing so formidable as your

resentment, you ought to be certain whether I may not be compelled by circumstances to deny you the opportunity you seem to point at."

At this moment Alice, summoned no doubt by her attendant, entered the hall hastily.

"Master Kerneguy," she said, "my father requests to see you in Victor Lee's apartment."

Kerneguy arose and bowed, but seemed determined to remain till Everard's departure, so as to prevent any explanation betwixt the cousins.

"Markham," said Alice, hurriedly—"cousin Everard—I have but a moment to remain here—for God's sake, do you instantly begone! Be cautious and patient—but do not tarry here—my father is fearfully incensed."

"I have had my uncle's word for that, madam," replied Everard, "as well as his injunction to depart, which I will obey without delay. I was not aware that you would have seconded so harsh an order quite so willingly; but I go, madam, sensible I leave those behind whose company is more agreeable."

"Unjust—ungenerous—ungrateful!" said Alice; but fearful her words might reach ears for which they were not designed, she spoke them in a voice so feeble, that her cousin, for whom they were intended, lost the consolation they were calculated to convey.

He bowed coldly to Alice, as taking leave, and said, with an air of that constrained courtesy which sometimes covers among men of condition the most deadly hatred, "I believe, Master Kerneguy, that I must make it convenient at present to suppress my own peculiar opinions on the matter which we have hinted at in our conversation, in which case I will send a gentleman who, I hope, may be able to conquer yours."

The supposed Scotsman made him a stately, and at the same time a condescending, bow, said he should expect the honor of his commands, offered his hand to Mistress Alice, to conduct her back to her father's apartment, and took a triumphant leave of his rival.

Everard, on the other hand, stung beyond his patience, and, from the grace and composed assurance of the youth's carriage, still conceiving him to be either Wilmot or some of his compeers in rank and profligacy, returned to the town of Woodstock, determined not to be outbearded, even though he should seek redress by means which his principles forbade him to consider as justifiable."

CHAPTER XXVI

> Boundless intemperance
> In nature is a tyranny; it hath been
> The untimely emptying of many a throne,
> And fall of many kings.
>
> *Macbeth.*

WHILE Colonel Everard retreated in high indignation from the little refection which Sir Henry Lee had in his good-humor offered, and withdrawn under the circumstances of provocation which we have detailed, the good old knight, scarce recovered from his fit of passion, partook of it with his daughter and guest, and shortly after, recollecting some silvan task (for, though to little efficient purpose, he still regularly attended to his duties as ranger), he called Bevis, and went out, leaving the two young people together.

"Now," said the amorous prince to himself, "that Alice is left without her lion, it remains to see whether she is herself of a tigress breed. So, Sir Bevis has left his charge," he said aloud; "I thought the knights of old, those stern guardians of which he is so fit a representative, were more rigorous in maintaining a vigilant guard."

"Bevis," said Alice, "knows that his attendance on me is totally needless; and, moreover, he has other duties to perform, which every true knight prefers to dangling the whole morning by a lady's sleeve."

"You speak treason against all true affection," said the gallant: "a lady's lightest wish should to a true knight be more binding than aught excepting the summons of his sovereign. I wish, Mistress Alice, you would but intimate your slightest desire to me, and you should see how I have practised obedience."

"You never brought me word what o'clock it was this morning," replied the young lady, "and there I sat questioning of the wings of Time, when I should have remembered that gentlemen's gallantry can be quite as fugitive as Time himself. How do you know what your disobedience may have cost me and others? Pudding and pastry may have been burned to a cinder, for, sir, I practise the old domestic rule of visiting the kitchen; or I may have missed prayers, or I may have been too late for an appointment, simply by the negligence of Master Louis Kerneguy failing to let me know the hour of the day."

"O," replied Kerneguy, "I am one of those lovers who cannot endure absence. I must be eternally at the feet of my fair enemy—such, I think, is the title with which romances teach us to grace the fair and cruel to whom we devote our hearts and lives. Speak for me, good lute," he added, taking up the instrument, "and show whether I know not my duty."

He sung, but with more taste than execution, the air of a French *rondelai,* to which some of the wits or sonnetteers in his gay and roving train had adapted English verses.

"An hour with thee! When earliest day
Dapples with gold the eastern gray,
Oh, what can frame my mind to bear
The toil and turmoil, cark and care,
New griefs which coming hours unfold,
And sad remembrance of the old?
One hour with thee.

One hour with thee! When burning June
Waves his red flag at pitch of noon;
What shall repay the faithful swain
His labor on the sultry plain,
And more than cave or sheltering bough,
Cool feverish blood, and throbbing brow?
One hour with thee.

One hour with thee! When sun is set,
O, what can teach me to forget
The thankless labors of the day,
The hopes, the wishes, flung away,
The increasing wants, and lessening gains,
The master's pride, who scorns my pains?
One hour with thee.

Truly, there is another verse," said the songster; "but I sing it not to you, Mistress Alice, because some of the prudes of the court liked it not."

"I thank you, Master Louis," answered the young lady, "both for your discretion in singing what has given me pleasure and in forbearing what might offend me. Though a country girl, I pretend to be so far of the court mode as to receive nothing which does not pass current among the better class there."

"I would," answered Louis, "that you were so well confirmed in their creed as to let all pass with you to which court ladies would give currency."

"'Speak for me, good lute,' said Louis Kerneguy, taking up the instrument."

"And what would be the consequence?" said Alice, with perfect composure.

"In that case," said Louis, embarrassed like a general who finds that his preparations for attack do not seem to strike either fear or confusion into the enemy—"in that case you would forgive me, fair Alice, if I spoke to you in a warmer language than that of mere gallantry—if I told you how much my heart was interested in what you consider as idle jesting—if I seriously owned it was in your power to make me the happiest or the most miserable of human beings."

"Master Kerneguy," said Alice, with the same unshaken nonchalance, "let us understand each other. I am little acquainted with high-bred manners, and I am unwilling, I tell you plainly, to be accounted a silly country girl, who, either from ignorance or conceit, is startled at every word of gallantry addressed to her by a young man, who for the present, has nothing better to do than coin and circulate such false compliments. But I must not let this fear of seeming rustic and awkwardly timorous carry me too far; and being ignorant of the exact limits, I will take care to stop within them."

"I trust, madam," said Kerneguy, "that however severely you may be disposed to judge of me, your justice will not punish me too severely for an offense of which your charms are alone the occasion?"

"Hear me out, sir, if you please," resumed Alice. "I have listened to you when you spoke *en berger*—nay, my complaisance has been so great as to answer you en *bergere*—for I do not think anything except ridicule can come of dialogues between Lindor and Jeanneton; and the principal fault of the style is its extreme and tiresome silliness and affectation. But when you begin to kneel, offer to take my hand, and speak with a more serious tone, I must remind you of our real characters. I am the daughter of Sir Henry Lee, sir; and you are, or profess to be, Master Louis Kerneguy, my brother's page, and a fugitive for shelter under my father's roof, who incurs danger by the harbor he affords you, and whose household, therefore, ought not to be disturbed by your unpleasing importunities."

"I would to Heaven, fair Alice," said the King, "that your objections to the suit which I am urging, not in jest but most seriously, as that on which my happiness depends, rested only on the low and precarious station of Louis Kerneguy! Alice, thou hast the soul of thy family, and must needs love honor. I am no more the needy Scottish page whom I have, for my own purposes, personated than I am the awkward lout whose manners I adopted on the first night of our acquaintance. This hand, poor as I seem, can confer a coronet."

"Keep it," said Alice, "for some more ambitious damsel, my lord—for such I conclude is your title, if this romance be true—I would not accept your hand could you confer a duchy."

"In one sense, lovely Alice, you have neither overrated my power nor my affection. It is your king—it is Charles Stuart who speaks to you! He can confer duchies, and if beauty can merit them, it is that of Alice Lee. Nay—nay, rise—do not kneel; it is for your sovereign to kneel to thee, Alice, to whom he is a thousand times more devoted than the wanderer Louis dared venture to profess himself. My Alice has, I know, been trained up in those principles of love and obedience to her sovereign, that she cannot, in conscience or in mercy, inflict on him such a wound as would be implied in the rejection of his suit."

In spite of all Charles's attempts to prevent her, Alice had persevered in kneeling on one knee, until she had touched with her lip the hand with which he attempted to raise her. But this salutation ended, she stood upright, with her arms folded on her bosom, her looks humble, but composed, keen and watchful, and so possessed of herself, so little flattered by the communication which the King had supposed would have been overpowering, that he scarce knew in what terms next to urge his solicitation.

"Thou art silent—thou art silent," he said, "my pretty Alice. Has the king no more influence with thee than the poor Scottish page?"

"In one sense, every influence," said Alice; "for he commands my best thoughts, my best wishes, my earnest prayers, my devoted loyalty, which, as the men of the house of Lee have been ever ready to testify with the sword, so are the women bound to seal, if necessary, with thir blood. But beyond the duties of a true and devoted subject, the king is even less to Alice Lee than poor Louis Kerneguy. The page could have tendered an honorable union; the monarch can but offer a contaminated coronet."

"You mistake, Alice—you mistake," said the King, eagerly. "Sit down and let me speak to you—sit down. What is't you fear?"

"I fear nothing, my liege," answered Alice. "What *can* I fear from the king of Britain—I, the daughter of his loyal subject, and under my father's roof? But I remember the distance betwixt us, and though I might trifle and jest with mine equal, to my king I must only appear in the dutiful posture of a subject, unless where his safety may seem to require that I do not acknowledge his dignity."

Charles, though young, being no novice in such scenes, was surprised to encounter resistance of a kind which had not been opposed to him in similar pursuits, even in cases where he had been unsuccessful. There was neither anger, nor injured pride, nor disorder, nor disdain, real or affected, in the manners and conduct of Alice. She stood, as it seemed, calmly prepared to argue on the subject which is generally decided by passion—showed no inclination to escape from the apartment, but appeared determined to hear with patience the suit of the lover, while her countenance and manner intimated that she had this complaisance only in deference tc the commands of the king.

"She is ambitious," thought Charles: "it is by dazzling her love of glory, not by mere passionate entreaties, that I must hope to be successful. I pray you be seated, my fair Alice," he said, "the lover entreats—the king commands you."

"The king," said Alice, "may permit the relaxation of the ceremonies due to royalty, but he cannot abrogate the subject's duty, even by express command. I stand here while it is your Majesty's pleasure to address me, a patient listener, as in duty bound."

"Know then, simple girl," said the King, "that, in accepting my proffered affection and protection, you break through no law, either of virtue or morality. Those who are born to royalty are deprived of many of the comforts of private life—chiefly that which is, perhaps, the dearest and most precious, the power of chosing their own mates for life. Their formal weddings are guided upon principles of political expedience only, and those to whom they are wedded are frequently, in temper, person, and disposition, the most unlikely to make them happy. Society has commiseration, therefore, towards us, and binds our unwilling and often unhappy wedlocks with chains of a lighter and more easy character than those which fetter other men, whose marriage ties, as more voluntarily assumed, ought, in proportion, to be more strictly binding. And, therefore, ever since the time that old Henry built these walls, priests and prelates, as well as nobles and statesmen, have been accustomed to see a Fair Rosamond rule the heart of an affectionate monarch, and console him for the few hours of constraint and state which he must bestow upon some angry and jealous Eleanor. To such a connection the world attaches no blame: they rush to the festival to admire the beauty of the lovely Esther, while the imperious Vashti is left to queen it in solitude; they throng the palace to ask her protection, whose influence is more in the state an hundred times than that of the proud consort; her offspring rank with the nobles of the land, and vindicate by their courage, like the celebrated Longsword, Earl of Salisbury, their descent from royalty and from love. From such connections our richest ranks of nobles are recruited; and the mother lives, in the greatness of her posterity, honored and blessed, as she died lamented and wept in the arms of love and friendship."

"Did Rosamond so die, my lord?" said Alice. "Our records say she was poisoned by the injured queen—poisoned, without time allowed to call to God for the pardon of her many faults. Did her memory so live? I have heard that, when the bishop purified the church at Godstowe, her monument was broken open by his orders, and her bones thrown out into unconsecrated ground."

"Those were rude old days, sweet Alice," answered Charles: "queens are not now so jealous, nor bishops so rigorous. And know, besides, that, in the lands to which I would lead the loveliest of her sex, other laws obtain, which remove from such ties even the slightest show of scandal. There is a mode of matrimony which, fulfilling all the rights of the church, leaves no stain on the conscience; yet, investing the bride with none of the privileges peculiar to her husband's condition, infringes not upon the duties which the king owes to his subjects. So that Alice Lee may, in all respects, become the real and lawful wife of Charles Stuart, except that their private union gives her no title to be Queen of England."

"My ambition," said Alice, "will be sufficiently gratified to see Charles king, without aiming to share either his dignity in public or his wealth and regal luxury in private."

"I understand thee, Alice," said the King, hurt but not displeased. "You ridicule me, being a fugitive, for speaking like a king. It is a habit, I admit, which I have learned, and of which even misfortune cannot cure me. But my case is not so desperate as you may suppose. My friends are still many in these kingdoms; my allies abroad are bound, by regard to their own interest, to espouse my cause.

I have hopes given me from Spain, from France, and from other nations; and I have confidence that my father's blood has not been poured forth in vain, nor is doomed to dry up without due vengeance. My trust is in Him from whom princes derive their title, and, think what thou wilt of my present condition, I have perfect confidence that I shall one day sit on the throne of England."

"May God grant it!" said Alice; "and that He *may* grant it, noble prince, deign to consider whether you now pursue a conduct likely to conciliate His favor. Think of the course you recommend to a motherless maiden, who has no better defense against your sophistry than what a sense of morality, together with the natural feeling of female dignity, inspires. Whether the death of her father, which would be the consequence of her imprudence, whether the despair of her brother, whose life has been so often in peril to save that of your Majesty, whether the dishonor of the roof which has sheltered you, will read well in your annals, or are events likely to propitiate God, whose controversy with your house has been but too visible, or recover the affections of the people of England, in whose eyes such actions are an abomination, I leave to your own royal mind to consider."

Charles paused, struck with a turn to the conversation which placed his own interest more in collision with the gratification of his present passion than he had supposed.

"If your Majesty," said Alice, courtesying deeply, "has no farther commands for my attendance, may I be permitted to withdraw?"

"Stay yet a little, strange and impracticable girl," said the King, "and answer me but one question. Is it the lowness of my present fortunes that makes my suit contemptible?"

"I have nothing to conceal, my liege," she said, "and my answer shall be as plain and direct as the question you have asked. If I could have been moved to an act of ignominious, insane, and ungrateful folly, it could only arise from my being blinded by that passion which I believe is pleaded as an excuse for folly and for crime much more often than it has a real existence. I must, in short, have been in love, as it is called; and that might have been with my equal, but surely never with my sovereign, whether such only in title or in possession of his kingdom."

"Yet loyalty was ever the pride, almost the ruling passion, of your family, Alice," said the King.

"And could I reconcile that loyalty," said Alice, "with

indulging my sovereign, by permitting him to prosecute a suit dishonorable to himself as to me? Ought I, as a faithful subject, to join him in a folly which might throw yet another stumbling-block in the path to his restoration, and could only serve to diminish his security, even if he were seated upon his throne?"

"At this rate," said Charles, discontentedly, "I had better have retained my character of the page than assumed that of a sovereign, which it seems is still more irreconcilable with my wishes."

"My candor shall go still farther," said Alice. "I could have felt as little for Louis Kerneguy as for the heir of Britain; for such love as I have to bestow—and it is not such as I read of in romance, or hear poured forth in song—has been already conferred on another object. This gives your Majesty pain; I am sorry for it, but the wholesomest medicines are aften bitter,"

"Yes," answered the King, with some asperity, "and physicians are reasonable enough to expect their patients to swallow them as if they were honeycomb. It is true, then, that whispered tale of the cousin colonel; and the daughter of the loyal Lee has set her heart upon a rebellious fanatic?"

"My love was given ere I knew what these words 'fanatic' and 'rebel' meant. I recalled it not, for I am satisfied that, amidst the great distractions which divide the kingdom, the person to whom you allude has chosen his part, erroneously perhaps, but conscientiously; he, therefore, has still the highest place in my affection and esteem. More he cannot have, and will not ask, until some happy turn shall reconcile these public differences, and my father be once more reconciled to him. Devoutly do I pray that such an event may occur by your Majesty's speedy and unanimous restoration!"

"You have found out a reason," said the King, pettishly, "to make me detest the thought of such a change; nor have you, Alice, any sincere interest to pray for it. On the contrary, do you not see that your lover, walking side by side with Cromwell, may, or rather must, share his power? nay, if Lambert does not anticipate him, he may trip up Oliver's heels and reign in his stead. And think you not he will find means to overcome the pride of the loyal Lees, and achieve an union for which things are better prepared than that which Cromwell is said to meditate betwixt one of his brats and the no less loyal heir of Fauconberg?"

"Your Majesty," said Alice, "has found a way at length

to avenge yourself—if what I have said deserves vengeance."

"I could point out a yet shorter read to your union," said Charles, without minding her distress, or perhaps enjoying the pleasure of retaliation. "Suppose that you sent your colonel word that there was one Charles Stuart here, who had come to disturb the saints in their peaceful government, which they had acquired by prayer and preaching, pike and gun; and suppose he had the art to bring down a half-score of troopers—quite enough, as times go, to decide the fate of this heir of royalty—think you not the possession of such a prize as this might obtain from the Rumpers, or from Cromwell, such a reward as might overcome your father's objections to a Roundhead's alliance, and place the fair Alice and her cousin colonel in full possession of their wishes?"

"My liege," said Alice, her cheeks glowing and her eyes sparkling, for she too had her share of the hereditary temperament of her family, "this passes my patience. I have heard, without expressing anger, the most ignominious persuasions addressed to myself, and I have vindicated myself for refusing to be the paramour of a fugitive prince, as if I had been excusing myself from accepting a share of an actual crown. But do you think I can hear all who are dear to me slandered without emotion or reply? I will not, sir; and were you seated with all the terrors of your father's Star Chamber around you, you should hear me defend the absent and the innocent. Of my father I will say nothing, but that, if he is now without wealth, without state, almost without a sheltering home and needful food, it is because he spent all in the service of the King. He needed not to commit anv act of treachery or villainy to obtain wealth: he had an ample competence in his own possessions. For Markham Everard—he knows no such thing as selfishness: he would not for broad England, had she the treasures of Peru in her bosom, and a paradise on her surface, do a deed that would disgrace his own name or injure the feelings of another. Kings, my liege, may take a lesson from him. My liege, for the present I take my leave."

"Alice—Alice, stay!" exclaimed the King. "She is gone. This must be virtue—real, disinterested, overawing virtue—or there is no such thing on earth. Yet Wilmot and Villiers will not believe a word of it, but add the tale to the other wonders of Woodstock. 'Tis a rare wench! and I profess, to use the colonel's obtestation, that I know not whether to forgive and be friends with her or study a dire revenge. If it were not for that accursed cousin—that Puritan colonel, I could forgive everything else to so noble a wench. But a Roundheaded rebel preferred to me, the preference avowed to my face, and justified with the assertion that a King might take a lesson from him—it is gall and wormwood. If the old man had not come up this morning as he did, the King should have taken or given a lesson, and a severe one. It was a mad rencontre to venture upon with my rank and responsiblility: and yet this wench has made me so angry with her, and so envious of him, that, if an opportunity offered, I should scarce be able to forbear him. Ha! whom have we here!"

The interjection at the conclusion of this royal soliloquy was occasioned by the unexpected entrance of another personage of the drama.

CHAPTER XXVII

> *Benedick.* Shall I speak a word in your ear?
> *Claudio.* God bless me from a challenge!
> *Much Ado about Nothing.*

As Charles was about to leave the apartment, he was prevented by the appearance of Wildrake, who entered with an unusual degree of swagger in his gait, and of fantastic importance on his brow. "I crave your pardon, fair sir," he said; "but, as they say in my country, when doors are open dogs enter. I have knocked and called in the hall to no purpose; so, knowing the way to this parlor, sir—for I am a light partisan, and the road I once travel I never forget—I ventured to present myself unannounced."

"Sir Henry Lee is abroad, sir, I believe, in the chase," said Charles, coldly, for the appearance of this somewhat vulgar debauchee was not agreeable to him at the moment, "and Master Albert Lee has left the lodge for two or three days."

"I am aware of it, sir," said Wildrake; "but I have no business at present with either."

"And with whom is your business?" said Charles; "that is, if I may be permitted to ask, since I think it cannot in possibility be with me."

"Pardon me in turn, sir," answered the Cavalier; "in no possibility can it be imparted to any other but yourself, if you be, as I think you are, though in something better habit, Master Louis Girnigo, the Scottish gentleman who waits upon Master Albert Lee."

"I am all you are like to find for him," answered Charles.

"In truth," said the Cavalier, "I do perceive a difference, but rest and better clothing will do much; and I am glad of it, since I would be sorry to have brought a message such as I am charged with to a tatterdemalion."

"Let us get to the business, sir, if you please," said the King; "you have a message for me, you say?"

"True, sir," replied Wildrake; "I am the friend of Colonel Markham Everard, sir, a tall man, and a worthy person in the field, although I could wish him a better cause.

A message I have to you, it is certain, in a slight note, which I take the liberty of presenting with the usual formalities." So saying, he drew his sword, put the billet he mentioned upon the point, and making a profound bow, presented it to Charles.

The disguised monarch accepted of it with a grave return of the salute, and said, as he was about to open the letter, "I am not, I presume, to expect friendly contents in an epistle presented in so hostile a manner?"

"A-hem, sir," replied the ambassador, clearing his voice, while he arranged a suitable answer, in which the mild strain of diplomacy might be properly maintained; "not utterly hostile, I suppose, sir, is the invitation, though it be such as must be construed in the commencement rather bellicose and pugnacious. I trust, sir, we shall find that a few thrusts will make a handsome conclusion of the business; and so, as my old master used to say, *Pax nascitur ex bello.* For my own poor share, I am truly glad to have been graced by my friend Mark Everard in this matter, the rather as I feared the Puritan principles with which he is imbued—I will confess the truth to you, worthy sir—might have rendered him unwilling, from certain scruples, to have taken the gentlemanlike and honorable mode of righting himself in such a case as the present. And as I render a friend's duty to my friend, so I humbly hope, Master Louis Girnigo, that I do no injustice to you, in preparing the way for the proposed meeting, where, give me leave to say, I trust that, if no fatal accident occur, we shall be all better friends when the skirmish is over than we were before it began."

"I should suppose so, sir, in any case," said Charles, looking at the letter; "worse than mortal enemies we can scarce be, and it is that footing upon which this billet places us."

'You say true, sir," said Wildrake; "it is, sir, a cartel introducing to a single combat, for the pacific object of restoring a perfect good understanding betwixt the survivors—in case that fortunately that word can be used in the plural after the event of the meeting."

"In short, we only fight, I suppose," replied the King, "that we may come to a perfectly good and amicable understanding?"

"You are right again, sir; and I thank you for the clearness of your apprehension," said Wildrake. "Ah, sir, it is easy to do with a person of honor and of intellect in such a case as this. And I beseech you, sir, as a personal kindness to myself, that, as the morning is like to be frosty, and myself am in some sort rheumatic, as war will leave its scars behind, sir—I say, I will entreat of you to bring with you some gentleman of honor, who will not disdain to take part of what is going forward—a sort of pot-luck, sir—with a poor old soldier like myself, that we may take no harm by standing unoccupied during such cold weather."

"I understand, sir," replied Charles; "if this matter goes forward, be assured I will endeavor to provide you with a suitable opponent."

"I shall remain greatly indebted to you, sir," said Wildrake; "and I am by no means curious about the quality of my antagonist. It is true I write myself esquire and gentleman, and should account myself especially honored by crossing my sword with that of Sir Henry or Master Albert Lee; but should that not be convenient, I will not refuse to present my poor person in opposition to any gentleman who has served the King, which I always hold as a sort of letters of nobility in itself, and, therefore, would on no account decline the duello with such a person."

"The King is much obliged to you, sir," said the disguised prince, "for the honor you do his faithful subjects."

"Oh, sir, I am scrupulous on that point—very scrupulous. When there is a Roundhead in question, I consult the herald's books, to see that he is entitled to bear arms, as is Master Markham Everard, without which, I promise you, I had borne none of his cartel. But a Cavalier is with me a gentleman of course. Be his birth ever so low, his loyalty has ennobled his condition."

"It is well, sir," said the King. "This paper requests me to meet Master Everard at six to-morrow morning, at the tree called the King's Oak, I object neither to the place nor time. He proffers the sword, at which, he says, we possess some equality. I do not decline the weapon. For company, two gentlemen. I shall endeavor to procure myself an associate and a suitable partner for you, sir, if you incline to join in the dance."

"I kiss your hand, sir, and rest yours, under a sense of obligation," answered the envoy.

"I thank you, sir," continued the King; "I will therefore be ready at place and time, and suitably furnished; and I will either give your friend such satisfaction with my sword as he requires, or will render him such cause for not doing so as he will be contented with."

"You will excuse me, sir," said Wildrake, "if my mind is too dull, under the circumstances, to conceive any alternative that can remain betwixt two men of honor in such a case, excepting—sa—sa——!" He threw himself into a fencing position, and made a pass with his sheathed rapier, but not directed towards the person of the King, whom he addressed.

"Excuse me, sir," said Charles, "if I do not trouble your intellects with the consideration of a case which may not occur. But, for example, I may plead urgent employment on the part of the public," This he spoke in a low and mysterious tone of voice, which Wildrake appeared perfectly to comprehend; for he laid his forefinger on his nose with what he meant for a very intelligent and apprehensive nod.

"Sir," said he, "if you be engaged in any affair for the King, my friend shall have every reasonable degree of patience. Nay, I will fight him myself in your stead, merely to stay his stomach, rather than you should be interrupted. And, sir, if you can find room in your enterprise for a poor gentleman that has followed Lunsford and Goring, you have but to name day, time, and place of rendezvous; for truly, sir, I am tired of the scald hat, cropped hair, and undertaker's cloak with which my friend has bedizened me, and would willingly ruffle it out once more in the King's cause, when whether I be banged or hanged I care not."

"I shall remember what you say, sir, should an opportunity occur," said the King; "and I wish his Majesty had many such subjects. I presume our business is now settled?"

"When you shall have been pleased, sir, to give me a trifling scrap of writing, to serve for my credentials; for such, you know, is the custom: your written cartel hath its written answer."

"That, sir, will I presently do," said Charles, "and in good time; here are the materials."

"And, sir," continued the envoy—"ahi!—ahem!—if you have interest in the household for a cup of sack. I am a man of few words, and am somewhat hoarse with much speaking; moreover, a serious business of this kind always makes one thirsty. Besides, sir, to part with dry lips argues malice, which God forbid should exist in such an honorable conjuncture,"

"I do not boast much influence in the house, sir," said the King; "but if you would have the condescension to accept of this broad piece towards quenching your thirst at the George——"

"Sir," said the Cavalier, for the times admitted of this strange species of courtesy, nor was Wildrake a man of such peculiar delicacy as keenly to dispute the matter, "I am once again beholden to you. But I see not how it consists with my honor to accept of such accommodation, unless you were to accompany and partake?"

"Pardon me, sir," replied Charles, "my safety recommends that I remain rather private at present."

"Enough said," Wildrake observed; "poor Cavaliers must not stand on ceremony. I see, sir, you understand cutter's law: when one tall fellow has coin, another must not be thirsty. I wish you, sir, a continuance of health and happiness until to-morrow, at the King's Oak, at six o'clock."

"Farewell, sir," said the King; and added, as Wildrake went down the stair whistling "Hey for cavaliers," to which air his long rapier, jarring against the steps and banisters, bore no unsuitable burden—"Farewell, thou too just emblem of the state to which war, and defeat, and despair have reduced many a gallant gentleman."

During the rest of the day there occurred nothing peculiarly deserving of notice. Alice sedulously avoided showing towards the disguised prince any degree of estrangement or shyness, which could be discovered by her father or by any one else. To all appearance, the two young persons continued on the same footing in every respect. Yet she made the gallant himself sensible than this apparent intimacy was assumed merely to save appearances, and in no way designed as retracting from the severity with which she had rejected his suit. The sense that this was the case, joined to his injured self-love and his enmity against a successful rival, induced Charles early to withdraw himself to a solitary walk in the wilderness, where, like Hercules in the Emblem of Cebes, divided betwixt the personifications of virtue and of pleasure, he listened alternately to the voice of wisdom and of passionate folly.

Prudence urged to him the importance of his own life to the future prosecution of the great object in which he had for the present miscarried—the restoration of monarchy in England, the rebuilding of the throne, the regaining the crown of his father, the avenging his death, and restoring to their fortunes and their country the numerous exiles who were suffering poverty and banishment on account of their attachment to his cause. Pride too, or rather a just and natural sense of dignity, displayed the unworthiness of a prince descending to actual personal conflict with a subject of any degree, and the ridicule which would be thrown on his memory, should he lose his life for an obscure intrigue by the hand of a private gentleman. What would his sage counsellors, Nicholas and Hyde, what would his kind and wise governor, the Marquis of Hertford, say to such an act of rashness and folly? Would it not be likely to shake the allegiance of the staid and prudent persons of the Royalist party, since wherefore should they expose their lives and estates to raise to the government of a kingdom a young man who could not command his own temper? To this was to be added the consideration that even his success would add double difficulties, to his escape, which already seemed sufficiently precarious. If, stopping short of death, he merely had the better of his antagonist, how did he know that he might not seek revenge by delivering up to government the Malignant Louis Kerneguy, whose real character could not in that case fail to be discovered?

These considerations strongly recommended to Charles that he should clear himself of the challenge without fighting; and the reservation under which he had accepted it afforded him some opportunity of doing so.

But Passion also had her arguments, which she addressed to a temper rendered irritable by recent distress and mortification. In the first place, if he was a prince, he was also a gentleman, entitled to resent as such, and obliged to give or claim the satisfaction expected on occasion of differences among gentlemen. With Englishmen, she urged, he could never lose interest by showing himself ready, instead of sheltering himself under his royal birth and pretensions, to come frankly forward, and maintain what he had done or said on his own responsibility. In a free nation, it seemed as if he would rather gain than lose in the public estimation by a conduct which could not but seem gallant and generous. Then a character for courage was far more necessary to support his pretensions than any other kind of reputation; and the lying under a challenge, without replying to it, might bring his spirit into question. What would Villiers and Wilmot say of an intrigue in which he had allowed himself to be shamefully baffled by a country girl, and had failed to revenge himself on his rival? The pasquinades which they would compose, the witty sarcasms which they would circulate, on the occasion, would be harder to endure than the grave rebukes of Hertford, Hyde, and Nicholas. This reflection, added to the stings of youthful and awakened courage, at length fixed his resolution, and he returned to Woodstock determined to keep his appointment, come of it what might.

Perhaps there mingled with his resolution a secret belief that such a rencontre would not prove fatal. He was in the flower of his youth, active in all his exercises, and no way inferior to Colonel Everard, as far as the morning's cxperiment had gone, in that of self-defense. At least such recollection might pass through his royal mind, as he hummed to himself a well-known ditty, which he had picked up during his residence in Scotland—

"A man may drink and not be drunk;
A man may fight and not be slain;
A man may kiss a bonnie lass,
And yet be welcome back again."

Meanwhile the busy and all-directing Doctor Rochecliffe had contrived to intimate to Alice that she must give him a private audience, and she found him by appointment in what was called the study, once filled with ancient books, which, long since converted into cartridges, had made more noise in the world at their final exit than during the space which had intervened betwixt that their first publication. The Doctor seated himself in a high-backed leathern easy-chair, and signed to Alice to fetch a stool and sit down beside him.

"Alice," said the old man, taking her hand affectionately, "thou art a good girl, a wise girl, a virtuous girl, one of those whose price is above rubies—not that 'rubies' is the proper translation—but remind me to tell you of that another time. Alice, thou knowest who this Louis Kerneguy is; nay, hesitate not to me, I know everything—I am well aware of the whole matter. Thou knowest this honored house holds the Fortunes of England." Alice was about to answer. "Nay, speak not, but listen to me, Alice. How does he bear himself towards you?"

Alice colored with the deepest crimson. "I am a country-bred girl," she said, "and his manners are too courtlike for me."

"Enough said—I know it all. Alice, he is exposed to a great danger to-morrow, and you must be the happy means to prevent him."

"I prevent him!—how, and in what manner?" said Alice, in surprise. "It is my duty, as a subject, to do anything—anything that may become my father's daughter——"

Here she stopped, considerably embarrassed.

"Yes," continued the Doctor, "to-morrow he hath made an appointment—an appointment with Markham Everard; the hour and place are set—six in the morning, by the King's Oak. If they meet, one will probably fall."

"Now, may God forefend they should meet," said Alice, turning as suddenly pale as she had previously reddened. "But harm cannot come of it: Everard will never lift his sword against the King."

"For that," said Doctor Rochecliffe, "I would not warrant. But if that unhappy young gentleman shall have still some reserve of the loyalty which his general conduct entirely disavows, it would not serve us here; for he knows not the King, but considers him merely as a Cavalier, from whom he has received injury."

"Let him know the truth, Doctor Rochecliffe, let him know it instantly," said Alice. "*He* lift hand against the King, a fugitive and defenseless! He is incapable of it. My life on the issue, he becomes most active in his preservation."

"That is the thought of a maiden, Alice," answered the Doctor; "and, as I fear, of a maiden whose wisdom is misled by her affections. It were worse than treason to admit a rebel officer, the friend of the arch-traitor Cromwell, into so great a secret. I dare not answer for such rashness. Hammond was trusted by his father, and you know what came of it."

"Then let my father know. He will meet Markham, or send to him, representing the indignity done to him by attacking his guest."

"We dare not let your father into the secret who Louis Kerneguy really is. I did but hint the possibility of Charles taking refuge at Woodstock, and the rapture into which Sir Henry broke out, the preparations for accommodation and defense which he began to talk of, plainly showed that the mere enthusiasm of his loyalty would have led to a risk of discovery. It is you, Alice, who must save the hopes of every true Royalist."

"I!" answered Alice; "it is impossible. Why cannot my father be induced to interfere, as in behalf of his friend and guest, though he know him as no other than Louis Kerneguy?"

"You have forgot your father's character, my young friend," said the Doctor: "an excellent man, and the best of Christians, till there is a clashing of swords, and then he starts up the complete martialist, as deaf to every pacific reasoning as if he were a game-cock."

"You forget, Doctor Rochecliffe," said Alice, "that this very morning, if I understand the thing aright, my father prevented them from fighting."

"Ay," answered the Doctor, "because he deemed himself bound to keep the peace in the Royal Park; but it was done with such regret, Alice, that, should he find them at it again, I am clear to fore tell he will only so far postpone the combat as to conduct them to some unprivileged ground, and there bid them tilt and welcome, while he regaled his eyes with a scene so pleasing. No, Alice, it is you, and you only, who can help us in this extremity."

"I see no possibility," said she, again coloring, "how I can be of the least use."

"You must send a note," answered Doctor Rochecliffe, "to the King—a note such as all women know how to write better than any man can teach them—to meet you at the precise hour of the rendezvous. He will not fail you, for I know his unhappy foible."

"Dr. Rochecliffe," said Alice, gravely, "you have known me from infancy. What have you seen in me to induce you to believe that I should ever follow such unbecoming counsel?"

"And if you have known *me* from infancy," retorted the Doctor, "what have you seen of *me* that you should suspect me of giving counsel to my friend's daughter which it would be misbecoming in her to follow? You cannot be fool enough, I think, to suppose that I mean you should carry your complaisance farther than to keep him in discourse for an hour or two, till I have all in readiness for his leaving this place, from which I can frighten him by the terrors of an alleged search? So, C. S. mounts his horse and rides off, and Mistress Alice Lee has the honor of saving him."

"Yes, at the expense of her own reputation," said Alice, "and the risk of an eternal stain on my family. You say you know all. What can the King think of my appointing an assignation with him after what has passed, and how will it be possible to disabuse him respecting the purpose of my doing so?"

"I will disabuse him, Alice—I will explain the whole."

"Dr. Rochecliffe," said Alice, "you propose what is impossible. You can do much by your ready wit and great wisdom; but if new-fallen snow were once sullied, not all your art could wash it white again; and it is altogether the same with a maiden's reputation."

"Alice, my dearest child," said the Doctor, "bethink you that, if I recommend this means of saving the life of the King, at least rescuing him from instant peril, it is because I see no other of which to avail myself. If I bid you assume, even for a moment, the semblance of what is wrong, it is but in the last extremity, and under circumstances which cannot return. I will take the surest means to prevent all evil report which can arise from what I recommend."

"Say not so, Doctor," said Alice: "better undertake to turn back the Isis than to stop the course of calumny. The King will make boast to his whole licentious court of the ease with which, but for a sudden alarm, he could have brought off Alice Lee as a paramour: the mouth which confers honor on others will then be the means to deprive me of mine. Take a fitter course, one more becoming your own character and profession. Do not lead him to fail in an engagement of honor, by holding out the prospect of another engagement equally dishonorable, whether false or true. Go to the King himself, speak to him, as the servants of God have a right to speak, even to earthly sovereigns. Point out to him the folly and the wickedness of the course he is about to pursue; urge upon him that he fear the sword, since wrath bringeth the punishment of the sword. Tell him, that the friends who died for him in the field at Worcester, on the scaffolds, and on the gibbets, since that bloody day, that the remnants who are in prison, scattered, fled, and ruined on his account, deserve better of him and his father's race than that he should throw away his life in an idle brawl. Tell him, that it is dishonest to venture that which is not his own, dishonorable to betray the trust which brave men have reposed in his virtue and in his courage."

Dr. Rochecliffe looked on her with a melancholy smile, his eyes glistening as he said, "Alas, Alice, even I could not plead that just cause to him so eloquently or so impressively as thou dost. But, alack! Charles would listen to neither. It is not from priests or women, he would say, that men should receive counsel in affairs of honor."

"Then, hear me, Doctor Rochecliffe—I will appear at the place of rendezvous, and I will prevent the combat—do not fear that I can do what I say—at a sacrifice, indeed, but not that of my reputation. My heart may be broken (she endeavored to stifle her sobs with difficulty) for the consequence; but not in the imagination of a man, and far less that man her sovereign, shall a thought of Alice Lee be associated with dishonor." She hid her face in her handkerchief, and burst out into unrestrained tears.

"What means this hysterical passion?" said Doctor Rochecliffe, surprised and somewhat alarmed by the vehemence of her grief. "Maiden, I must have no concealments—I must know."

"Exert your ingenuity, then, and discover it," said Alice, for a moment put out of temper at the Doctor's pertinacious self-importance. "Guess my purpose, as you can guess at everything else. It is enough to have to go through my task, I will not endure the distress of telling it over, and that to one who—forgive me, dear Doctor—might not think my agitation on this occasion fully warranted."

"Nay, then, my young mistress, you must be ruled," said Rochecliffe; "and if I cannot make you explain yourself, I must see whether your father can gain so far on you." So saying, he arose somewhat displeased, and walked towards the door.

"You forget what you yourself told me, Doctor Rochecliffe," said Alice, "of the risk of communicating this great secret to my father."

"It is too true," he said, stopping short and turning round; "and I think, wench, thou art too smart for me, and I have not met many such. But thou art a good girl, and wilt tell me thy device of free-will; it concerns my character and influence with the King, that I should be fully acquainted with whatever is *actum atque tractatum,* done and treated of in this matter."

"Trust your character to me, good Doctor," said Alice, attempting to smile; "it is of firmer stuff than those of women, and will be safer in my custody than mine could have been in yours. And thus much I condescend: you shall see the whole scene—you shall go with me yourself, and much will I feel emboldened and heartened by your company."

"That is something," said the Doctor, though not altogether satisfied with this limited confidence. "Thou wert ever a clever wench, and I will trust thee—indeed, trust thee I find I must, whether voluntarily or no."

"Meet me, then," said Alice, "in the wilderness to-morrow. But first tell me, are you well assured of time and place? a mistake were fatal."

"Assure yourself my information is entirely accurate," said the Doctor, resuming his air of consequence, which had been a little diminished during the latter part of their conference.

"May I ask," said Alice, "through what channel you acquired such important information?"

"You may ask, unquestionably," he answered, now completely restored to his supremacy; "but whether I will answer or not is a very different question. I conceive neither your reputation nor my own is interested in your remaining in ignorance on that subject. So I have my secrets as well as you, mistress; and some of them, I fancy, are a good deal more worth knowing."

"Be it so," said Alice, quietly; "if you will meet me in the wilderness by the broken dial at half-past five exactly, we will go together to-morrow, and watch them as they come to the rendezvous. I will on the way get the better of my present timidity, and explain to you the means I design to employ to prevent mischief. You can perhaps think of making some effort which may render my interference, unbecoming and painful as it must be, altogether unnecessary."

"Nay, my child," said the Doctor, "if you place yourself in my hands, you will be the first that ever had reason to complain of my want of conduct, and you may well judge you are the very last—one excepted—whom I would see suffer for want of counsel. At half-past five, then, at the dial in the wilderness, and God bless our undertaking!"

Here their interview was interrupted by the sonorous voice of Sir Henry Lee, which shouted their names, "Daughter Alice—Doctor Rochecliffe," through passage and gallery.

"What do you here," said he entering, "sitting like two crows in a mist, when we have such rare sport below? Here is this wild crackbrained boy Louis Kerneguy, now making me laugh till my sides are fit to split, and now playing on his guitar sweetly enough to win a lark from the heavens. Come away with you—come away. It is hard work to laugh alone."

CHAPTER XXVIII

> This is the place, the center of the grove;
> Here stands the oak, the monarch of the wood.
>
> JOHN HOME.

THE sun had risen on the broad boughs of the forest, but without the power of penetrating into its recesses, which hung rich with heavy dewdrops, and were beginning on some of the trees to exhibit the varied tints of autumn; it being the season when nature, like a prodigal whose race is well-nigh run, seems desirous to make up in profuse gaiety and variety of colors for the short space which her splendor has then to endure. The birds were silent; and even Robin Redbreast, whose chirruping song was heard among the bushes near the lodge, emboldened by the largesses with which the good old knight always encouraged his familiarity, did not venture into the recesses of the wood, where he encountered the sparrow-hawk and other enemies of a similar description, preferring the vicinity of the dwellings of man, from whom he, almost solely among the feathered tribes, seems to experience disinterested protection.

The scene was therefore at once lovely and silent, when the good Doctor Rochecliffe, wrapped in a scarlet roquelaure, which had seen service in its day, muffling his face more from habit than necessity, and supporting Alice on his arm, she also defended by a cloak against the cold and damp of the autumn morning, glided through the tangled and long grass of the darkest alleys, almost ankle-deep in dew, towards the place appointed for the intended duel. Both so eagerly maintained the consultation in which they were engaged, that they were alike insensible of the roughness and discomforts of the road, though often obliged to force their way through brushwood and coppice, which poured down on them all the liquid pearls with which they were loaded, till the mantles tbey were wrapped in hung lank by their sides, and clung to their shoulders heavily charged with moisture. They stopped when they had attained a station under the coppice, and shrouded by it, from which they could see all that passed on the little esplanade before the

King's Oak, whose broad and scathed form, contorted and shattered limbs, and frowning brows made it appear like some ancient war-worn champion, well selected to be the umpire of a field of single combat.

The first person who appeared at the rendezvous was the gay Cavalier Roger Wildrake. He also was wrapped in his cloak, but had discarded his Puritanic beaver, and wore in its stead a Spanish hat, with a feather and gilt hat-band, all of which had encountered bad weather and hard service; but to make amends for the appearance of poverty by the show of pretension, the castor was accurately adjusted after what was rather profanely called the d— me cut, used among the more desperate Cavaliers. He advanced hastily, and exclaimed aloud, "First in the field after all, by Jove, though I bilked Everard in order to have my morning draught. It has done me much good," he added, smacking his lips. "Well, I suppose I should search the ground ere my principal comes up, whose Presbyterian watch trudges as slow as his Presbyterian step."

He took his rapier from under his cloak, and seemed about to search the thickets around.

"I will prevent him," whispered the Doctor to Alice. "I will keep faith with you: you shall not come on the scene, *nisi dignus vindice nodus;* I'll explain that another time. *Vindex* is feminine as well as masculine, so the quotation is defensible. Keep you close."

So saying, he stepped forward on the esplanade, and bowed to Wildrake.

"Master Louis Kerneguy," said Wildrake, pulling off his hat; but instantly discovering his error, he added, "But no—I beg your pardon, sir—fatter, shorter, older. Mr. Kerneguy's friend, I suppose, with whom I hope to have a turn by and by. And why not now, sir, before our principals come up? just a snack to stay the orifice of the stomach, till the dinner is served, sir. What say you?"

"To open the orifice of the stomach more likely, or to give it a new one," said the Doctor.

"True, sir," said Roger, who seemed now in his element, "you say well—that is as thereafter may be. But come, sir, you wear your face muffled. I grant you, it is honest men's fashion at this unhappy time; the more is the pity. But we do all above board: we have no traitors here. I'll get into my gears first, to encourage you, and show you that you have to deal with a gentleman, who honors the King, and is a match fit to fight with any who follow him, as doubtless you do, sir, since you are the friend of Master Louis Kerneguy."

All this while, Wildrake was busied undoing the clasps of his square-caped cloak.

"Off—off, ye lendings," he said; "borrowings I should more properly call you—

Via the curtain which shadow'd Borgia!"

So saying, he threw the cloak from him and appeared *in cuerpo*, in a most Cavalier-like doublet, of greasy crimson satin, pinked and slashed with what had been once white tiffany; breeches of the same; and nether-stocks, or, as we now call them, stockings, darned in many places, and which, like those of Poins, had been once peach-colored. A pair of pumps, ill-calculated for a walk through the dew, and a broad shoulder-belt of tarnished embroidery, completed his equipment.

"Come, sir," he exclaimed, "make haste, off with your slough. Here I stand tight and true, as loyal a lad as ever stuck rapier through a Roundhead. Come, sir, to your tools!" he continued; "we may have half a dozen thrusts before they come yet, and shame them for their tardiness. Pshaw!" he exclaimed, in a most disappointed tone, when the Doctor, unfolding his cloak, showed his clerical dress. "Tush! it's but the parson after all."

Wildrake's respect for the church, however, and his desire to remove one who might possibly interrupt a scene to which he looked forward with peculiar satisfaction, induced him presently to assume another tone.

"I beg pardon," he said, "my dear Doctor. I kiss the hem of your cassock—I do, by the thundering Jove—I beg your pardon again. But I am happy I have met with you: they are raving for your presence at the lodge—to marry, or christen, or bury, or confess, or something very urgent. For Heaven's sake, make haste!"

"At the lodge?" said the Doctor. "Why, I left the lodge this instant—I was there later, I am sure, than you could be, who came the Woodstock road."

"Well," replied Wildrake, "it is at Woodstock they want you. Rat it, did I say the lodge? No, no—Woodstock. Mine host cannot be hanged—his daughter married—his bastard christened—or his wife buried, without the assistance of a *real* clergyman. Your Holdenoughs won't do for them. He's a true man, mine host; so, as you value your function, make haste."

"You will pardon me, Master Wildrake," said the Doctor: "I wait for Master Louis Kerneguy."

"The devil you do!" exclaimed Wildrake. "Why, I always knew the Scots could do nothing without their minister; but, d—n it, I never thought they put them to this use neither. But I have known jolly customers in orders, who understood to handle the sword as well as their Prayer Book. You know the purpose of our meeting, Doctor. Do you come only as a ghostly comforter—or as a surgeon, perhaps—or do you ever take bilboa in hand? Sa—sa!"

Here he made a fencing demonstration with his sheathed rapier.

"I have done so, sir, on necessary occasion," said Doctor Rochecliffe.

"Good, sir, let this stand for a necessary one," said Wildrake. "You know my devotion for the church. If a divine of your skill would do me the honor to exchange but three passes with me, I should think myself happy forever."

"Sir," said Rochecliffe, smiling, "were there no other objection to what you propose, I have not the means: I have no weapon."

"What! you want the *de quoi?* that is unlucky indeed. But you have a stout cane in your hand; what hinders our trying a pass, my rapier being sheathed, of course, until our principals come up? My pumps are full of this frost-dew; and I shall be a toe or two out of pocket if I am to stand still all the time they are stretching themselves; for I fancy, Doctor, you are of my opinion, that the matter will not be a fight of cock-sparrows."

"My business here is to make it, if possible, be no fight at all," said the divine.

"Now, rat me, Doctor, but that is too spiteful," said Wildrake; "and were it not for my respect for the church, I could turn Presbyterian, to be revenged."

"Stand back a little, if you please, sir," said the Doctor: "do not press forward in that direction. For Wildrake, in the agitation of his movements, induced by his disappointment, approached the spot where Alice remained still concealed.

"And wherefore not, I pray you, Doctor?" said the Cavalier.

But on advancing a step, he suddenly stopped short and muttered to himself, with a round oath of astonishment, "A petticoat in the coppice, by all that is reverend, and at this hour in the morning—whew-ew-ew!" He gave vent to his surprise in a long, low, interjectional whistle; then turning to the Doctor, with his finger on the side of his nose, "You're sly, Doctor, d—d sly! But why not give me a hint of your—your commodity there—your contraband goods? Gad, sir, I am not a man to expose the eccentricities of the church."

"Sir," said Doctor Rochecliffe, "you are impertinent; and if time served, and it were worth my while, I would chastise you."

And the Doctor, who had served long enough in the wars to have added some of the qualities of a captain of horse to those of a divine, actually raised his cane, to the infinite delight of the rake, whose respect for the church was by no means able to subdue his love of mischief.

"Nay, Doctor," said he, "if you wield your weapon back-sword fashion in that way, and raise it as high as your head, I shall be through you in a twinkling." So saying, he made a pass with his sheathed rapier, not precisely at the Doctor's person, but in that direction; when Rochecliffe, changing the direction of his cane from the broadsword guard to that of the rapier, made the Cavalier's sword spring ten yards out of his hand, with all the dexterity of my friend Francalanza.*

At this moment both the principal parties appeared on the field.

Everard exclaimed angrily to Wildrake, "Is this your friendship? In Heaven's name, what make you in that fool's jacket, and playing the pranks of a jack-pudding?" while his worthy second, somewhat crestfallen, held down his head, like a boy caught in roguery, and went to pick up his weapon, stretching his head, as he passed, into the coppice, to obtain another glimpse, if possible, of the concealed object of his curiosity.

Charles, in the mean time, still more surprised at what he beheld, called out on his part—"What! Doctor Rochecliffe become literally one of the church militant, and tilting with my friend Cavalier Wildrake? May I use the freedom to ask him to withdraw, as Colonel Everard and I have some private business to settle?"

It was Doctor Rochecliffe's cue, on this important occasion, to have armed himself with the authority of his sacred office, and used a tone of interference which might have overawed even a monarch, and make him feel that his monitor spoke by a warrant higher than his own. But the

* A fencing-master in Edinburgh—1826 (*Laing*).

indiscreet latitude he had just given to his own passion, and the levity in which he had been detected, were very unfavorable to his assuming that superiority to which so uncontrollable a spirit as that of Charles, wilful as a prince and capricious as a wit, was at all likely to submit. The Doctor did, however, endeavor to rally his dignity, and replied, with the gravest, and at the same time the most respectful tone he could assume, that he also had business of the most urgent nature, which prevented him from complying with Master Kerneguy's wishes and leaving that spot.

"Excuse this untimely interruption," said Charles, taking off his hat and bowing to Colonel Everard, "which I will immediately put an end to."

Everard gravely returned his salute, and was silent.

"Are you mad, Doctor Rochecliffe?" said Charles; "or are you deaf? or have you forgotten your mother-tongue. I desired you to leave this place."

"I am not mad," said the divine, rousing up his resolution, and regaining the natural firmness of his voice; "I would prevent others from being so. I am not deaf; I would pray others to hear the voice of reason and religion. I have not forgotten my mother-tongue; but I have come hither to speak the language of the Master of kings and princes."

"To fence with broomsticks, I should rather suppose," said the King. "Come, Doctor Rochecliffe, this sudden fit of assumed importance befits you as little as your late frolic. You are not, I apprehend, either a Catholic priest or a Scotch Mas John, to claim devoted obedience from your hearers, but a Church of England man, subject to the rules of that communion—and to its HEAD." In speaking the last words the King sunk his voice to a low and impressive whisper. Everard observing this drew back, the natural generosity of his temper directing him to avoid overhearing private discourse in which the safety of the speakers might be deeply concerned. They continued, however, to observe great caution in their forms of expression.

"Master Kerneguy," said the clergyman, "it is not I who assume authority or control over your wishes—God forbid: I do but tell you what reason, Scripture, religion, and morality alike prescribe for your rule of conduct."

"And I, Doctor," said the King, smiling, and pointing to the unlucky cane, "will take your example rather than your precept. If a reverend clergyman will himself fight a bout at single-stick, what right can he have to interfere in gentlemen's quarrels? Come, sir, remove yourself, and do not let your present obstinacy cancel former obligations."

"Bethink yourself," said the divine, "I can say one word which will prevent all this."

"Do it," replied the King, "and in doing so belie the whole tenor and actions of an honorable life: abandon the principles of your church, and become a perjured traitor and an apostate, to prevent another person from discharging his duty as a gentleman. This were indeed killing your friend to prevent the risk of his running himself into danger. Let the passive obedience which is so often in your mouth, and no doubt in your head, put your feet for once into motion, and step aside for ten minutes. Within that space your assistance may be needed, either as body-curer or soul-curer."

"Nay, then," said Doctor Rochecliffe, "I have but one argument left."

While this conversation was carried on apart, Everard had almost forcibly detained by his own side his follower Wildrake, whose greater curiosity and lesser delicacy would otherwise have thrust him forward, to get, if possible, into the secret. But when he saw the Doctor turn into the coppice, he whispered eagerly to Everard—"A gold Carolus to a Commonwealth farthing, the Doctor has not only come to preach a peace, but has brought the principal conditions along with him."

Everard made no answer; he had already unsheathed his sword, and Charles hardly saw Rochecliffe's back fairly turned than he lost no time in following his example. But, ere they had done more than salute each other with the usual courteous flourish of their weapons, Doctor Rochecliffe again stood between them, leading in his hand Alice Lee, her garments dank with dew, and her long hair heavy with moisture and totally uncurled. Her face was extremely pale, but it was the paleness of desperate resolution, not of fear. There was a dead pause of astonishment: the combatants rested on their swords, and even the forwardness of Wildrake only vented itself in half-suppressed ejaculations, as, "Well done, Doctor—this beats the 'parson among the pease.' No less than your patron's daughter. And Mistress Alice, whom I thought a very snowdrop, turned out a dog-violet after all—a Lindabrides, by Heavens, and altogether one of ourselves!"

Excepting these unheeded mutterings, Alice was the first to speak.

"Master Everard," she said—"Master Kerneguy, you are surprised to see me here. Yet, why should I not tell the reason at once? Convinced that I am, however guiltlessly, the unhappy cause of your misunderstanding, I am too much interested to prevent fatal consequences to pause upon any step which may end it. Master Kerneguy, have my wishes, my entreaties, my prayers—have your noble thoughts, the recollections of your own high duties, no weight with you in this matter? Let me entreat you to consult reason, religion, and common sense, and return your weapon."

"I am obedient as an Eastern slave, madam," answered Charles, sheathing his sword; "but I assure you, the matter about which you distress yourself is a mere trifle, which will be much better settled betwixt Colonel Everard and myself in five minutes than with the assistance of the whole convocation of the church, with a female parliament to assist their reverend deliberations. Mr. Everard, will you oblige me by walking a little farther? We must change ground, it seems."

"I am ready to attend you, sir," said Everard, who had sheathed his sword as soon as his antagonist did so.

"I have then no interest with you, sir," said Alice, continuing to address the King. "Do you not fear I should use the secret in my power to prevent this affair going to extremity. Think you this gentleman, who raises his hand against you, if he knew——"

"If he knew that I were Lord Wilmot, madam, you would say? Accident has given him proof to that effect, with which he is already satisfied, and I think you would find it difficult to induce him to embrace a different opinion."

Alice paused, and looked on the King with great indignation, the following words dropping from her mouth by intervals, as if they burst forth one by one in spite of feelings that would have restrained them—"Cold—selfish—ungrateful—unkind! Woe to the land which——" here she paused with marked emphasis, then added—"which shall number thee, or such as thee, among her nobles and rulers!"

"Nay, fair Alice," said Charles, whose good-nature could not but feel the severity of this reproach, though too slightly to make all the desired impression, "you are too unjust to me—too partial to a happier man. Do not call me unkind: I am but here to answer Mr. Everard's summons. I could neither decline attending nor withdraw now I am here without loss of honor; and my loss of honor would be a disgrace which must extend to many. I cannot fly from Mr. Everard: it would be too shameful. If he abides by his message, it must be decided as such affairs usually are. If he retreats or yields it up, I will, for your sake, wave punctilio. I will not even ask an apology for the trouble it has afforded me, but let all pass as if it were the consequence of some unhappy mistake, the grounds of which shall remain, on my part uninquired into. This I will do for your sake, and it is much for a man of honor to condescend so far. You *know* that the condescension from me in particular is great indeed. Then do not call me ungenerous, or ungrateful, or unkind, since I am ready to do all which, as a man, I can do, and more perhaps than as a man of honor I ought to do."

"Do you hear this, Markham Everard?" exclaimed Alice—do you hear this? The dreadful option is left entirely at your disposal. You were wont to be temperate in passion, religious, forgiving; will you, for a mere punctilio, drive on this private and unchristian broil to a murderous extremity? Believe me, if you *now*, contrary to all the better principles of your life, give the reins to your passions, the consequences may be such as you will rue for your lifetime, and even, if Heaven have not mercy, rue after your life is finished."

Markham Everard remained for a moment gloomily silent, with his eyes fixed on the ground. At length he looked up and answered her. "Alice, you are a soldier's daughter, a soldier's sister. All your relations, even including one whom you then entertained some regard for, have been made soldiers by these unhappy discords. Yet you have seen them take the field, in some instances on contrary sides, to do their duty where their principles called them, without manifesting this extreme degree of interest. Answer me—and your answer shall decide my conduct—Is this youth, so short while known, already of more value to you than those dear connections, father, brother, and kinsman, whose departure to battle you saw with comparative indifference? Say *this*, and it shall be enough: I leave the ground, never to see you or this country again."

"Stay, Markham—stay; and believe me when I say that, if I answer your question in the affirmative, it is because Master Kerneguy's safety comprehends more—much more than that of any of those you have mentioned."

"Indeed! I did not know a coronet had been so superior in value to the crest of a private gentleman," said Everard; "yet I have heard that many women think so."

"You apprehend me amiss," said Alice, perplexed between the difficulty of so expressing herself as to prevent immediate mischief, and at the same time anxious to combat the jealousy and disarm the resentment which she saw arising in the bosom of her lover. But she found no words fine enough to draw the distinction, without leading to a discovery of the King's actual character, and perhaps, in consequence, to his destruction. "Markham," she said, "have compassion on me. Press me not at this moment; believe me, the honor and happiness of my father, of my brother, and of my whole family are interested in Master Kerneguy's safety—are inextricably concerned in this matter resting where it now does."

"Oh, ay, I doubt not," said Everard: "the house of Lee ever looked up to nobility, and valued in their connections the fantastic loyalty of a courtier beyond the sterling and honest patriotism of a plain country gentleman. For them the thing is in course. But on your part—you, Alice—O! on your part, whom I have loved so dearly, who has suffered me to think that my affection was not unrepaid—can the attractions of an empty title, the idle court compliments of a mere man of quality, during only a few hours, lead you to prefer a libertine lord to such a heart as mine?"

"No—no—believe me, no," said Alice, in the extremity of distress.

"Put your answer, which seems so painful, in one word, and say for *whose* safety it is you are thus deeply interested?"

"For both—for both," said Alice.

"That answer will not serve, Alice," answered Everard; "here is no room for equality, I must and will know to what I have to trust. I understand not the paltering which makes a maiden unwilling to decide betwixt two suitors; nor would I willingly impute to *you* the vanity that cannot remain contented with one lover at once."

The vehemence of Everard's displeasure, when he supposed his own long and sincere devotion lightly forgotten amid the addresses of a profligate courtier, awakened the spirit of Alice Lee, who, as we elsewhere said, had a portion in her temper of the lion humor that was characteristic of her family.

"If I am thus misinterpreted," she said—"if I am not judged worthy of the least confidence or candid construction, hear my declaration, and my assurance that, strange as my words may seem, they are, when truly interpreted, such as do you no wrong. I tell you—I tell all present, and I tell this gentleman himself, who well knows the sense in which I speak, that his life and safety are, or ought to be, of more value to me than those of any other man in the kingdom—nay, in the world, be that other who he will."

These words she spoke in a tone so firm and decided as admitted no farther discussion. Charles bowed low and with gravity, but remained silent. Everard, his features agitated by the emotions which his pride barely enabled him to suppress, advanced to his antagonist, and said, in a tone which he vainly endeavored to make a firm one, "Sir, you heard the lady's declaration, with such feelings, doubtless, of gratitude as the case eminently demands. As her poor kinsman, and an unworthy suitor, sir, I presume to yield my interest in her to you; and, as I will never be the means of giving her pain, I trust you will not think I act unworthily in retracting the letter which gave you the trouble of attending this place at this hour. Alice," he said, turning his head towards her—"farewell, Alice, at once and for ever!"

The poor young lady, whose adventitious spirit had almost deserted her, attempted, to repeat the word "farewell," but, failing in the attempt, only accomplished a broken and imperfect sound, and would have sunk to the earth, but for Doctor Rochecliffe, who caught her as she fell. Roger Wildrake, also, who had twice or thrice put to his eyes what remained of a kerchief, interested by the lady's evident distress, though unable to comprehend the mysterious cause, hastened to assist the divine in supporting so fair a burden.

Meanwhile, the disguised prince had beheld the whole in silence, but with an agitation to which he was unwonted, and which his swarthy features, and still more his motions, began to betray. His posture was at first absolutely stationary, with his arms folded on his bosom, as one who waits to be guided by the current of events; presently after, he shifted his position, advanced and retired his foot, clenched and opened his hand, and otherwise showed symptoms that he was strongly agitated by contending feelings, was on the point, too, of forming some sudden resolution and yet still in uncertainty what course he should pursue. But when he saw Markham Everard, after one look of unspeakable anguish towards Alice, turning his back to depart, he broke out into his familiar ejaculation, "Odds-fish! this must not be." In three strides he overtook the slowly-retiring Everard, tapped him smartly on the shoulder, and, as he turned round, said, with an air of command, which he well knew how to adopt at pleasure, "One word with you, sir."

"At your pleasure, sir," replied Everard, and naturally conjecturing the purpose of his antagonist to be hostile, took hold of his rapier with the left hand, and laid the right on the hilt, not displeased at the supposed call; for anger is at least as much akin to disappointment as pity is said to be to love.

"Pshaw!" answered the King, "that cannot be *now*. Colonel Everard, I am Charles Stuart!"

Everard recoiled in the greatest surprise, and next exclaimed, "Impossible—it cannot be! The King of Scots has escaped from Bristol. My Lord Wilmot, your talents for intrigue are well known, but this will not pass upon me."

"The King of Scots, Master Everard," replied Charles, "since you are so pleased to limit his sovereignty—at any rate, the eldest son of the late sovereign of Britain—is now before you; therefore it is impossible he could have escaped from Bristol. Doctor Rochecliffe shall be my voucher, and will tell you, moreover, that Wilmot is of a fair complexion and light hair; mine, you may see, is swart as a raven."

Rochecliffe, seeing what was passing, abandoned Alice to the care of Wildrake, whose extreme delicacy in the attempts he made to bring her back to life formed an amiable contrast to his usual wildness, and occupied him so much, that he remained for the moment ignorant of the disclosure in which he would have been so much interested. As for Doctor Rochecliffe, he came forward, wringing his hands in all the demonstration of extreme anxiety, and with the usual exclamations attending such a state.

"Peace, Doctor Rochecliffe!" said the King, with such complete self-possession as indeed became a prince. "We are in the hands, I am satisfied, of a man of honor. Master Everard must be pleased in finding only a fugitive prince in the person in whom he thought he had discovered a successful rival. He cannot but be aware of the feelings which prevented me from taking advantage of the cover which this young lady's devoted loyalty afforded me, at the

King Charles II.

risk of her own happiness. He is the party who is to profit by my candor; and certainly I have a right to expect that my condition, already indifferent enough, shall not be rendered worse by his becoming privy to it, under such circumstances. At any rate, the avowal is made; and it is for Colonel Everard to consider how he is to conduct himself."

"Oh, your Majesty!—my Liege!—my King!—my royal Prince!" exclaimed Wildrake, who, at length, discovering what was passing, had crawled on his knees, and seizing the King's hand, was kissing it, more like a child mumbling gingerbread, or like a lover devouring the yielded hand of his mistress, than in the manner in which such salutations pass at court. "If my dear friend Mark Everard should prove a dog on this occasion, rely on me I will cut his throat on the spot, were I to do the same for myself the moment afterwards."

"Hush—hush, my good friend and loyal subject," said the King, "and compose yourself; for though I am obliged to put on the prince for a moment, we have not privacy or safety to receive our subjects in King Cambyses's vein."

Everard, who had stood for a time utterly confounded, awoke at length like a man from a dream.

"Sire," he said, bowing low and with profound deference, "if I do not offer you the homage of a subject with knee and sword, it is because God, by whom kings reign, has denied you for the present the power of ascending your throne without rekindling civil war. For your safety being endangered by me, let not such an imagination for an instant cross your mind. Had I not respected your person, were I not bound to you for the candor with which your noble avowal has prevented the misery of my future life, your misfortunes would have rendered your person as sacred, so far as I can protect it, as it could be esteemed by the most devoted Royalist in the kingdom. If your plans are soundly considered and securely laid, think that all which is now passed is but a dream. If they are in such a state that I can aid them, saving my duty to the Commonwealth, which will permit me to be privy to no schemes of actual violence, your Majesty may command my services."

"It may be I may be troublesome to you, sir," said the King, "for my fortunes are not such as to permit me to reject even the most limited offers of assistance; but if I can, I will dispense with applying to you: I would not willingly put any man's compassion at war with his sense of duty on my account. Doctor, I think there will be no farther tilting to-day, either with sword or cane ; so we may as well return to the lodge, and leave these (looking at Alice and Everard), who may have more to say in explanation."

"No—no !" exclaimed Alice, who was now perfectly come to herself, and, partly by her own observation and partly from the report of Dr. Rochecliffe, comprehended all that had taken place. "My cousin Everard and I have nothing to explain : he will forgive me for having riddled with him when I dare not speak plainly ; and I forgive him for having read my riddle wrong. But my father has my promise, we must not correspond or converse for the present ; I return instantly to the lodge and he to Woodstock, unless you, sire," bowing to the King, "command his duty otherwise. Instant to the town, cousin Markham ; and if danger should approach, give us warning."

Everard would have delayed her departure, would have excused himself for his unjust suspicion, would have said a thousand things ; but she would not listen to him, saying, for all other answer, "Farewell, Markham, till God send better days !"

"She is an angel of truth and beauty," said Roger Wildrake ; "and, I like a blasphemous heretic, called her a Lindabrides ! But has your Majesty—craving your pardon —no commands for poor Hodge Wildrake, who will blow out his own or any other man's brains in England to do your Grace a pleasure ?"

"We entreat our good friend Wildrake to do nothing hastily," said Charles, smiling : "such brains as his are rare, and should not be rashly dispersed, as the like may not be easily collected. We recommend him to be silent and prudent, to tilt no more with loyal clergymen of the church of England, and to get himself a new jacket with all convenient speed, to which we beg to contribute our royal aid. When fit time comes, we hope to find other service for him."

As he spoke, he slid ten pieces into the hand of poor Wildrake, who, confounded with the excess of his loyal gratitude, blubbered like a child, and would have followed the King, had not Doctor Rochecliffe, in few words, but peremptory, insisted that he should return with his patron, promising him he should certainly be employed in assisting the King's escape, could an opportunity be found of using his services

"Be so generous, reverend sir, and you bind me to you forever," said the Cavalier; "and I conjure you not to keep malice against me on account of the foolery you wot of."

"I have no occasion, Captain Wildrake," said the Doctor, "for I think I had the best of it."

"Well, then, Doctor, I forgive you on my part; and I pray you, for Christian charity, let me have a finger in this good service; for as I live in hope of it, rely that I shall die of disappointment."

While the Doctor and soldier thus spoke together, Charles took leave of Everard (who remained uncovered while he spoke to him) with his usual grace. "I need not bid you no longer be jealous of me,,' said the King; "for I presume you will scarce think of a match betwixt Alice and me, which would be too losing a one on her side. For other thoughts, the wildest libertine could not entertain them towards so high-minded a creature; and believe me, that my sense of her merit did not need this last distinguished proof of her truth and loyalty. I saw enough of her from her answers to some idle sallies of gallantry, to know with what a lofty character she is endowed. Mr. Everard, her happiness, I see, depends on you, and I trust you will be the careful guardian of it. If we can take any obstacle out of the way of your joint happiness, be assured we will use our influence. Farewell, sir; if we cannot be better friends, do not at least let us entertain harder or worse thoughts of each other than we have now."

There was something in the manner of Charles that was extremely affecting; something, too, in his condition as a fugitive in the kingdom which was his own by inheritance, that made a direct appeal to Everard's bosom, though in contradiction to the dictates of that policy which he judged it his duty to pursue in the distracted circumstances of the country. He remained, as we have said, uncovered; and in his manner testified the highest expression of reverence, up to the point when such might seem a symbol of allegiance. He bowed so low as almost to approach his lips to the hand of Charles, but he did not kiss it. "I would rescue your person, sir," he said, "with the purchase of my own life. More——" He stopped short, and the King took up his sentence where it broke off—"More you cannot do," said Charles, "to maintain an honorable consistency; but what you have said is enough. You cannot render homage to my proffered hand as that of a sovereign, but you will not prevent my taking yours as a friend, if you allow me to call myself so—I am sure, as a well-wisher at least."

The generous soul of Everard was touched. He took the King's hand and pressed it to his lips.

"Oh!" he said, "were better times to come——"

"Bind yourself to nothing, dear Everard," said the good-natured prince, partaking his emotion. "We reason ill while our feelings are moved. I will recruit no man to his loss, nor will I have my fallen fortunes involve those of others, because they have humanity enough to pity my present condition. If better times come, why, we will meet again, and I hope to our mutual satisfaction. If not, as your future father-in-law would say (a benevolent smile came over his face, and accorded not unmeetly with his glistening eye)—if not, this parting was well made."

Everard turned away with a deep bow, almost choking under contending feelings, the uppermost of which was a sense of the generosity with which Charles, at his own imminent risk, had cleared away the darkness that seemed about to overwhelm his prospects of happiness for life, mixed with a deep sense of the perils by which he was environed. He returned to the little town, followed by his attendant Wildrake, who turned back so often, with weeping eyes and hands clasped and uplifted as supplicating Heaven, that Everard was obliged to remind him that his gestures might be observed by some one, and occasion suspicion.

The generous conduct of the King during the closing part of this remarkable scene had not escaped Alice's notice; and, erasing at once from her mind all resentment of Charles's former conduct, and all the suspicions they had deservedly excited, awakened in her bosom a sense of the natural goodness of his disposition, which permitted her to unite regard for his person with that reverence for his high office in which she had been educated as a portion of her creed. She felt convinced, and delighted with the conviction, that his virtues were his own, his libertinism the fault of education, or rather want of education, and the corrupting advice of sycophants and flatterers. She could not know, or perhaps did not in that moment consider, that, in a soil where no care is taken to eradicate tares, they will outgrow and smother the wholesome seed, even if the last is more natural to the soil. For, as Doctor Rochecliffe informed her afterwards for her edification—promising, as was his custom, to explain the precise words on some future occasion, if she would put him in mind—*Virtus rectorem ducemque desiderat; vitia sine magistro discuntur.**

There was no room for such reflections at present. Conscious of mutual sincerity, by a sort of intellectual communication, through which individuals are led to understand each other better, perhaps, in delicate circumstances than by words, reserve and stimulation appeared to be now banished from the intercourse between the King and Alice. With manly frankness, and, at the same time, with princely condescension, he requested her, exhausted as she was, to accept of his arm on the way homeward, instead of that of Doctor Rochecliffe; and Alice accepted of his support with modest humility, but without a shadow of mistrust or fear. It seemed as if the last half hour had satisfied them perfectly with the character of each other, and that each had full conviction of the purity and sincerity of the other's intentions.

Doctor Rochecliffe, in the mean time, had fallen some four or five paces behind; for, less light and active than Alice (who had, besides, the assistance of the King's support), he was unable, without effort and difficulty, to keep up with the pace of Charles, who then was, as we have elsewhere noticed, one of the best walkers in England, and was sometimes apt to forget (as great men will) that others were inferior to him in activity.

"Dear Alice," said the King, but as if the epithet were entirely fraternal, "I like your Everard much. I would to God he were of our determination; but since that cannot be, I am sure he will prove a generous enemy."

"May it please you, sire," said Alice, modestly, but with some firmness, "my cousin will never be your Majesty's personal enemy; and he is one of the few on whose slightest word you may rely more than on the oath of those who profess more strongly and formally. He is utterly incapable of abusing your Majesty's most generous and voluntary confidence."

"On my honor, I believe so, Alice," replied the King. "But, odds-fish! my girl, let Majesty sleep for the present: it concerns my safety, as I told your brother lately. Call me 'sir,' then, which belongs alike to king, peer, knight, and gentleman, or rather let me be wild Louis Kerneguy again."

Alice looked down and shook her head. "That cannot be, please your Majesty."

* See Dr. Rochecliffe's Quotations. Note 8.

"What! Louis was a saucy companion—a naughty, presuming boy—and you cannot abide him? Well, perhaps you are right. But we will wait for Doctor Rochecliffe," he said, desirous, with good-natured delicacy, to make Alice aware that he had no purpose of engaging her in any discussion which could recall painful ideas. They paused accordingly, and again she felt relieved and grateful.

"I cannot persuade our fair friend, Mistress Alice, Doctor," said the King, "that she must, in prudence, forbear using titles of respect to me while there are such very slender means of sustaining them."

"It is a reproach to earth and to fortune," answered the divine, as fast as his recovered breath would permit him, "that your most sacred Majesty's present condition should not accord with the rendering of those honors which are your own by birth, and which, with God's blessing on the efforts of your loyal subjects, I hope to see rendered to you as your hereditary right by the universal voice of the three kingdoms."

"True, Doctor," replied the King; "but, in the mean while, can you expound to Mistress Alice Lee two lines of Horace, which I have carried in my thick head several years, till now they have come pat to my purpose. As my canny subjects of Scotland say, If you keep a thing seven years, you are sure to find a use for it at last. *Telephus*—ay, so it begins—

> Telephus et Peleus, cum pauper et exul uterque,
> Projicit ampullas et sesquipedalia verba."

"I will explain the passage to Mistress Alice," said the Doctor, "when she reminds me of it; or rather," he added, recollecting that his ordinary dilatory answer on such occasions ought not to be returned when the order for exposition emanated from his sovereign, "I will repeat a poor couplet from my own translation of the poem—

> Heroes and kings, in exile forced to roam,
> Leave swelling phrase and seven-leagued words at home."

"A most admirable version, Doctor," said Charles. "I feel all its force, and particularly the beautiful rendering of *sesquipedalia verba* into seven-leagued boots—words, I mean: it reminds me, like half the things I meet with in this world, of the *Contes de Commère l'Oye*." *

* *Tales of Mother Goose.*

Thus conversing, they reached the lodge; and as the King went to his chamber to prepare for the breakfast summons, now impending, the idea crossed his mind, "Wilmot, and Villiers, and Killigrew would laugh at me, did they hear of a campaign in which neither man nor woman had been conquered. But, odds-fish! let them laugh as they will, there is something at my heart which tells me that for once in my life I have acted well."

That day and the next were spent in tranquillity, the King waiting impatiently for the intelligence which was to announce to him that a vessel was prepared somewhere on the coast. None such was yet in readiness; but he learned that the indefatigable Albert Lee was, at great personal risk, traversing the sea-coast from town to village, and endeavoring to find means of embarkation among the friends of the Royal cause and the correspondents of Doctor Rochecliffe.

CHAPTER XXIX

Ruffian, let go that rude uncivil touch.
Two Gentlemen of Verona.

It is time we should give some account of the other actors in our drama, the interest due to the principal personages having for some time engrossed our attention exclusively.

We are, therefore, to inform the reader that the lingering longings of the Commissioners, who had been driven forth of their proposed paradise of Woodstock, not by a cherub indeed, but, as they thought, by spirits of another sort, still detained them in the vicinity. They had, indeed, left the little borough under pretence of indifferent accommodation The more palpable reasons were, that they entertained some resentment against Everard, as the means of their disappointment, and had no mind to reside where their proceedings could be overlooked by him, although they took leave in terms of the utmost respect. They went, however, no farther than Oxford, and remained there, as ravens, who are accustomed to witness the chase, sit upon a tree or crag, at a little distance, and watch the disembowelling of the deer, expecting the relics which fall to their share. Meantime, the university and city, but especially the former, supplied them with some means of employing their various faculties to advantage, until the expected moment when as they hoped, they should either be summoned to Windsor or Woodstock should once more be abandoned to their discretion.

Bletson, to pass the time, vexed the souls of such learned and pious divines and scholars as he could intrude his hateful presence upon, by sophistry, atheistical discourse, and challenges to them to impugn the most scandalous theses. Desborough, one of the most brutally ignorant men of the period, got himself nominated the head of a college, and lost no time in cutting down trees and plundering plate, As for Harrison, he preached in full uniform in St Mary's Church, wearing his buff-coat, boots, and spurs, as if he were about to take the field for the fight at Armageddon. And it was hard to say whether that seat of learning, religion, and loyalty, as it is called by Clarendon, was more vexed by the rapine of Desborough, the cold scepticism of Bletson, or the frantic enthusiasm of the Fifth Monarchy champion.

Ever and anon, soldiers, under pretense of relieving guard, or otherwise, went and came betwixt Woodstock and Oxford, and maintained, it may be supposed, a correspondence with Trusty Tomkins, who, though he chiefly resided in the town of Woodstock, visited the lodge occasionally, and to whom, therefore, they doubtless trusted for information concerning the proceedings there.

Indeed, this man Tomkins seemed by some secret means to have gained the confidence in part, if not in whole, of almost every one connected with these intrigues. All closeted him, all conversed with him in private; those who had the means propitiated him with gifts, those who had not were liberal of promises. When he chanced to appear at Woodstock, which always seemed as it were by accident, if he passed through the hall, the knight was sure to ask him to take the foils and was equally certain to be, after less or more resistance, victorious in the encounter; so, in consideration of so many triumphs, the good Sir Henry almost forgave him the sins of rebellion and Puritanism. Then, if his slow and formal step was heard in the passages approaching the gallery, Doctor Rochecliffe, though he never introduced him to his peculiar boudoir, was sure to meet Master Tomkins in some neutral apartment, and to engage him in long conversations, which apparently had great interest for both.

Neither was the Independent's reception below-stairs less gracious than above. Joceline failed not to welcome him with the most cordial frankness; the pasty and the flagon were put in immediate requisition, and good cheer was the general word. The means for this, it may be observed, had grown more plenty at Woodstock since the arrival of Doctor Rochecliffe, who, in quality of agent for several Royalists, had various sums of money at his disposal. By these funds it is likely that Trusty Tomkins also derived his own full advantage.

In his occasional indulgence in what he called a fleshly frailty (and for which he said he had a privilege), which was in truth an attachment to strong liquors, and that in no moderate degree, his language, at other times remarkably decorous and reserved, became wild and animated. He sometimes talked with all the unction of an old debauchee of former exploits, such as deer-stealing, orchard-robbing, drunken gambols, and desperate affrays in which he had been engaged in the earlier part of his life, sung bacchanalian and amorous ditties, dwelt sometimes upon adventures which drove Phœbe Mayflower from the company, and penetrated even the deaf ears of Dame Jellicot, so as to make the buttery in which he held his carousals no proper place for the poor old woman.

In the middle of these wild rants, Tomkins twice or thrice suddenly ran into religious topics, and spoke mysteriously, but with great animation and a rich eloquence, on the happy and preeminent saints, who were saints, as he termed them, indeed—men who had stormed the inner treasure-house of Heaven, and possessed themselves of its choicest jewels. All other sects he treated with the utmost contempt, as merely quarreling, as he expressed it, like hogs over a trough, about husks and acorns; under which derogatory terms he included alike the usual rites and ceremonies of public devotion, the ordinances of the established churches of Christianity, and the observances, nay, the forbearances, enjoined by every class of Christians. Scarcely hearing, and not at all understanding, him, Joceline, who seemed his most frequent confidant on such occasions, generally led him back into some strain of rude mirth, or old recollection of follies before the Civil Wars, without caring about or endeavoring to analyze the opinion of this saint of an evil fashion, but fully sensible of the protection which his presence afforded at Woodstock, and confident in the honest meaning of so freespoken a fellow, to whom ale and brandy, when better liquor was not to be come by, seemed to be principal objects of life, and who drank a health to the King, or any one else, whenever required, provided the cup in which he was to perform the libation were but a brimmer.

These peculiar doctrines, which were entertained by a sect sometimes termed the Family of Love, but more commonly Ranters,* had made some progress in times when such variety of religious opinions were prevalent, that men pushed the jarring heresies to the verge of absolute and most impious insanity. Secrecy had been enjoined on these frantic believers in a most blasphemous doctrine, by the fear of consequences, should they come to be generally announced; and it was the care of Mr. Tomkins to conceal the spiritual freedom which he pretended to have acquired from all whose resentment would have been stirred by his public avowal of it. This was not difficult; for their pro-

* See the Famalists. Note 9.

fession of faith permitted, nay, required, their occasional conformity with the sectaries or professors of any creed which chanced to be uppermost.

Tomkins had accordingly the art to pass himself on Dr. Rochecliffe as still a zealous member of the Church of England, though serving under the enemy's colors, as a spy in their camp; and as he had on several occasions given him true and valuable intelligence, this active intriguer was the more easily induced to believe his professions.

Nevertheless, lest this person's occasional presence at the lodge, which there were perhaps no means to prevent without exciting suspicion, should infer danger to the King's person, Rochecliffe, whatever confidence he otherwise reposed in him, recommended that, if possible, the King should keep always out of his sight, and when accidentally discovered, that he should only appear in the character of Louis Kerneguy. Joseph Tomkins, he said, was, he really believed, Honest Joe; but honesty was a horse which might be overburdened, and there was no use in leading our neighbor into temptation.

It seemed as if Tomkins himself had acquiesced in this limitation of confidence exercised towards him, or that he wished to seem blinder than he really was to the presence of this stranger in the family. It occurred to Joceline, who was a very shrewd fellow, that once or twice, when by inevitable accident Tomkins had met Kerneguy, he seemed less interested in the circumstance than he would have expected from the man's disposition, which was naturally prying and inquisitive. "He asked no questions about the young stranger," said Joceline. "God avert that he knows or suspects too much!" But his suspicions were removed when, in the course of their subsequent conversation, Joseph Tomkins mentioned the King's escape from Bristol as a thing positively certain, and named both the vessel in which he said he had gone off and the master who commanded her, seeming so convinced of the truth of the report, that Joceline judged it impossible he could have the slightest suspicion of the reality.

Yet, notwithstanding this persuasion, and the comradeship which had been established between them, the faithful under-keeper resolved to maintain a strict watch over his gossip Tomkins, and be in readiness to give the alarm should occasion arise. True, he thought, he had reason to believe that his said friend, notwithstanding his drunken and enthusiastic rants, was as trustworthy as he was esteemed by Dr. Rochecliffe; yet still he was an adventurer, the outside and lining of whose cloak were of different colors, and a high reward, and pardon for past acts of malignancy, might tempt him once more to turn his tippet. For these reasons Joceline kept a strict, though unostentatious, watch over Trusty Tomkins.

We have said that the discreet seneschal was universally well received at Woodstock, whether in the borough or at the lodge, and that even Joceline Joliffe was anxious to conceal any suspicions which he could not altogether repress under a great show of cordial hospitality. There were, however, two individuals who, for very different reasons, nourished personal dislike against the individual so generally acceptable.

One was Nehemiah Holdenough, who remembered with great bitterness of spirit the Independent's violent intrusion into his pulpit, and who ever spoke of him in private as a lying missionary, into whom Satan had put a spirit of delusion; and preached, besides, a solemn sermon on the subject of the false prophet, out of whose mouth came frogs. The discourse was highly prized by the Mayor and most of the better class, who conceived that their minister had struck a heavy blow at the very root of Independency. On the other hand, those of the private spirit contended, that Joseph Tomkins had made a successful and triumphant rally, in an exhortation on the evening of the same day, in which he proved, to the conviction of many handicraftsmen, that the passage in Jeremiah, "The prophets prophesy falsely, and the priests bear rule by their means," was directly applicable to the Presbyterian system of church government. The clergyman despatched an account of his adversary's conduct to the Reverend Master Edwards to be inserted in the next edition of *Gangræna,* as a pestilent heretic; and Tomkins recommended the parson to his master, Desborough, as a good subject on whom to impose a round fine, for vexing the private spirit; assuring him, at the same time, that, though the minister might seem poor, yet, if a few troopers were quartered on him till the fine was paid, every rich shopkeeper's wife in the borough would rob the till, rather than go without the mammon of unrighteousness with which to redeem their priest from sufferance, holding, according to his expression, with Laban, "You have taken from me my gods, and what have I more?" There was, of course, little cordiality between the polemical disputants, when religious debate took so worldly a turn.

But Joe Tomkins was much more concerned at the evil opinion which seemed to be entertained against him by one whose good graces he was greatly more desirous to obtain than those of Nehemiah Holdenough. This was no other than pretty Mistress Phœbe Mayflower, for whose conversion he had felt a strong vocation ever since his lecture upon Shakespeare on their first meeting at the lodge. He seemed desirous, however, to carry on this more serious work in private, and especially to conceal his labors from his friend Joceline Joliffe, lest, perchance, he had been addicted to jealousy. But it was in vain that he plied the faithful damsel, sometimes with verses from the Canticles, sometimes with quotations from Green's *Arcadia*, or pithy passages from *Venus and Adonis*, and doctrines of a nature yet more abstruse, from the popular work entitled *Aristotle's Masterpiece*. Unto no wooing of his, sacred or profane, metaphysical or physical, would Phœbe Mayflower seriously incline.

The maiden loved Joceline Joliffe, on the one hand; and, on the other, if she disliked Joseph Tomkins when she first saw him, as a rebellious Puritan, she had not been at all reconciled by finding reason to regard him as a hypocritical libertine. She hated him in both capacities, never endured his conversation when she could escape from it, and when obliged to remain, listened to him only because she knew he had been so deeply trusted, that to offend him might endanger the security of the family in the service of which she had been born and bred up, and to whose interest she was devoted. For reasons somewhat similar, she did not suffer her dislike of the steward to become manifest before Joceline Joliffe, whose spirit, as a forester and a soldier, might have been likely to bring matters to an arbitrament, in which the *couteau de chasse* and quarter-staff of her favorite would have been too unequally matched with the long rapier and pistols which his dangerous rival always carried about his person. But it is difficult to blind jealousy when there is any cause of doubt; and perhaps the sharp watch maintained by Joceline on his comrade was prompted not only by his zeal for the King's safety, but by some vague suspicion that Tomkins was not ill-disposed to poach upon his own fair manor.

Phœbe, in the mean while, like a prudent girl, sheltered herself as much as possible, by the presence of Goody Jellicot. Then, indeed, it is true, the Independent, or whatever he was, used to follow her with his addresses to very little purpose; for Phœbe seemed as deaf, through wilfulness, as the old matron by natural infirmity. This indifference highly incensed her new lover, and induced him anxiously to watch for a time and place in which he might plead his suit with an energy that should command attention. Fortune, that malicious goddess, who so often ruins us by granting the very object of our vows, did at length procure him such an opportunity as he had long coveted.

It was about sunset, or shortly after, when Phœbe, upon whose activity much of the domestic arrangements depended, went as far as Fair Rosamond's spring to obtain water for the evening meal, or rather to gratify the prejudice of the old knight, who believed that celebrated fountain afforded the choicest supplies of the necessary element. Such was the respect in which he was held by his whole family, that to neglect any of his wishes that could be gratified, though with inconvenience to themselves, would, in their estimation, have been almost equal to a breach of religious duty.

To fill the pitcher had, we know, been of late a troublesome task; but Joceline's ingenuity had so far rendered it easy, by repairing rudely a part of the ruined front of the ancient fountain, that the water was collected, and, trickling along a wooden spout, dropped from a height of about two feet. A damsel was thereby enabled to place her pitcher under the slowly dropping supply, and without toil to herself might wait till her vessel was filled.

Phœbe Mayflower, on the evening we allude to, saw, for the first time, this little improvement; and, justly considering it as a piece of gallantry of her silvan admirer, designed to save her the trouble of performing her task in a more inconvenient manner, she gratefully employed the minutes of ease which the contrivance procured her, in reflecting on the good-nature and ingenuity of the obliging engineer, and perhaps in thinking he might have done as wisely to have waited till she came to the fountain, that he might have secured personal thanks for the trouble he had taken. But then she knew he was detained in the buttery with that odious Tomkins, and rather than have seen the Independent along with him, she would have renounced the thought of meeting Joceline.

As she was thus reflecting, Fortune was malicious enough to send Tomkins to the fountain, and without Joceline. When she saw his figure darken the path up which he came, an anxious reflection came over the poor maiden's breast, that she was alone, and within the verge of the forest, where in general persons were prohibited to come during the twilight, for disturbing the deer settling to their repose. She encouraged herself, however, and resolved to show no sense of fear, although, as the steward approached, there was something in the man's look and eye no way calculated to allay her apprehensions.

"The blessings of the evening upon you, my pretty maiden," he said. "I meet you even as the chief servant of Abraham, who was a steward like myself, met Rebecca, the daughter of Bethuel, the son of Milcah, at the well of the city of Nahor, in Mesopotamia. Shall I not, therefore, say to you, 'Set down thy pitcher that I may drink?'"

"The pitcher is at your service, Master Tomkins," she replied, "and you may drink as much as you will; but you have, I warrant, drank better liquor, and that not long since."

It was, indeed, obvious that the steward had risen from a revel, for his features were somewhat flushed, though he had stopped far short of intoxication. But Phœbe's alarm at his first appearance was rather increased when she observed how he had been lately employed.

"I do but use my privilege, my pretty Rebecca: the earth is given to the saints, and the fulness thereof. They shall occupy and enjoy it, both the riches of the mine and the treasures of the vine; and they shall rejoice, and their hearts be merry within them. Thou hast yet to learn the privileges of the saints, my Rebecca."

"My name is Phœbe," said the maiden, in order to sober the enthusiastic rapture which he either felt or affected.

"Phœbe after the flesh," he said, "but Rebecca being spiritualized; for art thou not a wandering and stray sheep, and am I not sent to fetch thee within the fold? Wherefore else was it said, 'Thou shalt find her seated by the well, in the wood which is called after the ancient harlot, Rosamond?'"

"You have found me sitting here sure enough," said Phœbe; "but if you wish to keep me company, you must walk to the lodge with me; and you shall carry my pitcher for me, if you will be so kind. I will hear all the good things you have to say to me as we go along. But Sir Henry calls for his glass of water regularly before prayers."

"What!" exclaimed Tomkins, "hath the old man of bloody hand and perverse heart sent thee hither to do the work of a bondswoman? Verily thou shalt return enfranchised; and for the water thou hast drawn for him, it shall be poured forth, even as David caused to be poured forth the water of the well of Bethlehem."

So saying, he emptied the water-pitcher, in spite of Phœbe's exclamations and entreaties. He then replaced the vessel beneath the little conduit, and continued—"Know that this shall be a token to thee. The filling of that pitcher shall be like the running of a sand-glass; and if, within the time which shall pass ere it rises to the brim, thou shalt listen to the words which I shall say to thee, then it shall be well with thee, and thy place shall be high among those who, forsaking the instruction which is as milk for babes and sucklings, eat the strong food which nourishes manhood. But if the pitcher shall overbrim with water ere thy ear shall hear and understand, thou shalt then be given as a prey, and as a bondsmaiden, unto those who shall possess the fat and the fair of the earth."

"You frighten me, Master Tomkins," said Phœbe, "though I am sure you do not mean to do so. I wonder how you dare speak words so like the goods words in the Bible, when you know how you laughed at your own master, and all the rest of them, when you helped to play the hobgoblins at the lodge."

"Think'st thou, then, thou simple fool, that in putting that deceit upon Harrison and the rest, I exceeded my privileges? Nay, verily. Listen to me, foolish girl. When in former days I lived the most wild, malignant rakehell in Oxfordshire, frequenting wakes and fairs, dancing around Maypoles, and showing my lustihood at football and cudgel-playing—yea, when I was called, in the language of the uncircumcised, Philip Hazeldine, and was one of the singers in the choir, and one of the ringers in the steeple, and served the priest yonder, by name Rochecliffe—I was not farther from the straight road than when, after long reading, I at length found one blind guide after another all burners of bricks in Egypt. I left them one by one, the poor tool Harrison being the last; and by my own unassisted strength I have struggled forward to the broad and blessed light whereof thou too, Phœbe, shalt be partaker."

"I thank you, Master Tomkins," said Phœbe, suppressing some fear under an appearance of indifference; "but I shall have light enough to carry home my pitcher, would you but let me take it, and that is all the want of light I shall have this evening."

So saying, she stooped to take the pitcher from the fountain; but he snatched hold of her by the arm, and prevented her from accomplishing her purpose. Phœbe, however, was the daughter of a bold forester, prompt at thoughts of self-defense; and though she missed getting hold of the pitcher, she caught up instead a large pebble, which she kept concealed in her right hand.

"Stand up, foolish maiden, and listen," said the Independent, sternly; "and know, in one word, that sin, for which the spirit of man is punished with the vengeance of Heaven, lieth not in the corporal act, but in the thought of the sinner. Believe, lovely Phœbe, that to the pure all acts are pure, and that sin is in our thought, not in our actions, even as the radiance of the day is dark to a blind man, but seen and enjoyed by him whose eyes receive it. To him who is but a novice in the things of the spirit, much is enjoined, much is prohibited, and he is fed with milk fit for babes; for him are ordinances, prohibitions, and commands. But the saint is above these ordinances and restraints. To him, as to the chosen child of the house, is given the pass-key to open all locks which withhold him from the enjoyment of his heart's desire. Into such pleasant paths will I guide thee, lovely Phœbe, as shall unite in joy, in innocent freedom, pleasures which, to the unprivileged, are sinful and prohibited."

"I really wish, Master Tomkins, you would let me go home," said Phœbe, not comprehending the nature of his doctrine, but disliking at once his words and his manner. He went on, however, with the accused and blasphemous doctrines which, in common with others of the pretended saints, he had adopted, after having long shifted from one sect to another, until he settled in the vile belief that sin, being of a character exclusively spiritual, only existed in the thoughts, and that the worst actions were permitted to those who had attained to the pitch of believing themselves above ordinance. "Thus, my Phœbe," he continued, endeavoring to draw her towards him, "I can offer thee more than ever was held out to woman since Adam first took his bride by the hand. It shall be for others to stand dry-lipped, doing penance, like Papists, by abstinence, when the vessel of pleasure pours forth its delights. Dost thou love money? I have it, and can procure more—am at liberty to procure it on every hand and by every means: the earth is mine and its fulness. Do you desire power? Which of these poor cheated commissioner fellows' estates dost thou covet, I will work it out for thee; for I deal with a mightier spirit than any of them. And it is not without warrant that I have aided the Malignant Rochecliffe and the clown Joliffe to frighten and baffle them in the guise they did. Ask what thou wilt, Phœbe, I can give, or I can procure it for thee. Then enter with me into a life of delight in this world, which shall prove but an anticipation of the joys of Paradise hereafter!"

Again the fanatical voluptuary endeavored to pull the poor girl towards him, while she, alarmed, but not scared out of her presence of mind, endeavored, by fair entreaty, to prevail on him to release her. But his features, in themselves not marked, had acquired a frightful expression, and he exclaimed, "No, Phœbe, do not think to escape: thou art given to me as a captive; thou hast neglected the hour of grace, and it has glided past. See, the water trickles over thy pitcher, which was to be a sign between us. Therefore I will urge thee no more with words, of which thou art not worthy, but treat thee as a recusant of offered grace."

"Master Tomkins," said Phœbe, in an imploring tone, "consider, for God's sake, I am a fatherless child; do me no injury, it would be a shame to your strength and your manhood. I cannot understand your fine words—I will think on them till to-morrow." Then, in rising resentment, she added more vehemently, "I will not be used rudely; stand off, or I will do you a mischief." But, as he pressed upon her with a violence of which the object could not be mistaken, and endeavored to secure her right hand, she exclaimed, "Take it, then, with a wanion to you!" and struck him an almost stunning blow on the face with the pebble which she held ready for such an extremity.

The fanatic let her go, and staggered backward, half stupefied; while Phœbe instantly betook herself to flight, screaming for help as she ran, but still grasping the victorious pebble. Irritated to frenzy by the severe blow which he had received, Tomkins pursued, with every black passion in his soul and in his face, mingled with fear lest his villainy should be discovered. He called on Phœbe loudly to stop, and had the brutality to menace her with one of his pistols if she continued to fly. Yet she slacked not her pace for his threats, and he must either have executed them, or seen her escape to carry the tale to the lodge, had she not unhappily stumbled over the projecting root of a fir-tree.

But, as he rushed upon his prey, rescue interposed in

the person of Joceline Joliffe, with his quarter-staff on his shoulder. "How now! what means this?" he said, stepping between Phœbe and her pursuer. Tomkins, already roused to fury, made no other answer than by discharging at Joceline the pistol which he held in his hand. The ball gazed the under-keeper's face, who, in requital of the assault, and saying, "Aha! let ash answer iron." applied his quater-staff with so much force to the Independent's head, that, lighting on the left temple, the blow proved almost instantly mortal.

A few convulsive struggles were accompanied with these broken words, "Joceline—I am gone—but I forgive thee. Doctor Rochecliffe—I wish I had minded more—— Oh! the clergyman—the funeral service——" As he uttered these words, indicative, it may be, of his return to a creed which perhaps he had never abjured so thoroughly as he had persuaded himself, his voice was lost in a groan, which, rattling in the throat, seemed unable to find its way to the air. These were the last symptoms of life: the clenched hands presently relaxed, the closed eyes opened and stared on the heaven's a lifeless jelly, the limbs extended themselves and stiffened. The body, which was lately animated with life, was now a lump of senseless clay; the soul, dismissed from its earthly tenement in a moment so unhallowed, was gone before the judgment-seat.

"Oh, what have you done—what have done, Joceline?" exclaimed Phœbe; "you have killed the man!"

"Better than he should have killed me," answered Joceline; "for he was none of the blinkers that miss their mark twice running. And yet I am sorry for him. Many a merry bout have we had together when he was wild Philip Hazeldine, and then he was bad enough; but since he daubed over his vices with hypocrisy, he seems to have proved worse devil than ever."

"Oh, Joceline, come away," said poor Phœbe, "and do not stand gazing on him thus"; for the woodman, resting on his fatal weapon, stood looking down on the corpse with the appearance of a man half-stunned at the event.

"This comes of the ale-pitcher," she continued, in the true style of female consolation, "as I have often told you. For Heaven's sake, come to the lodge, and let us consult what is to be done."

"Stay first, girl, and let me drag him out of the path: we must not have him lie here in all men's sight. Will you not help me, wench?"

"I cannot, Joceline. I would not touch a lock on him for all Woodstock."

"I must to this gear myself, then," said Joceline, who, a soldier as well as a woodsman, still had great reluctance to the necessary task. Something in the face and broken words of the dying man had made a deep and terrific impression on nerves not easily shaken. He accomplished it, however, so far as to drag the late steward out of the open path, and bestow his body amongst the undergrowth of brambles and briers, so as not to be visible unless particularly looked after. He then returned to Phœbe, who had sat speechless all the while beneath the tree over whose roots she had stumbled.

"Come away, wench," he said—"come away to the lodge, and let us study how this is to be answered for; the mishap of his being killed will strangely increase our danger. What had he sought of thee, wench, when you ran from him like a madwoman? But I can guess: Phil was always a devil among the girls, and I think, as Doctor Rochecliffe says, that, since he turned saint, he took to himself seven devils worse than himself. Here is the very place where I saw him with his sword in his hand raised against the old knight, and he a child of the parish. It was high treason at least; but, by my faith, he hath paid for it at last."

"But, oh, Joceline," said Phœbe, "how could you take so wicked a man into your councils, and join him in all his plots about scaring the Roundhead gentlemen?"

"Why, look thee, wench, I thought I knew him at the first meeting, especially when Bevis, who was bred here when he was a dog-leader, would not fly at him; and when we made up our old acquaintance at the lodge, I found he kept up a close correspondence with Dr. Rochecliffe, who was persuaded that he was a good king's-man, and held consequently good intelligence with him. The Doctor boasts to have learned much through his means; I wish to Heaven he may not have been as communicative in turn."

"Oh, Joceline," said the waiting-woman, "you should never have let him within the gate of the lodge!"

"No more I would, if I had known how to keep him out; but when he went so frankly into our scheme, and told me how I was to dress myself like Robison the player, whose ghost haunted Harrison—I wish no ghost may haunt me! when he taught me how to bear myself to terrify his lawful master, what could I think, wench? I only trust the Doctor has kept the great secret of all from his knowledge. But here we are at the lodge. Go to thy chamber, wench, and compose thyself. I must seek out Doctor Rochecliffe. He is ever talking of his quick and ready invention; here come times, I think, that will demand it all."

Phœbe went to her chamber accordingly; but the strength arising from the pressure of danger giving way when the danger was removed, she quickly fell into a succession of hysterical fits, which required the constant attention of Dame Jellicot, and the less alarmed, but more judicious, care of Mrs. Alice, before they even abated in their rapid recurrence.

The under-keeper carried his news to the politic Doctor, who was extremely disconcerted, alarmed, nay, angry with Joceline for having slain a person on whose communications he had accustomed himself to rely. Yet his looks declared his suspicion whether his confidence had not been too rashly conferred—a suspicion which pressed him the more anxiously, that he was unwilling to avow it, as a derogation from his character for shrewdness on which he valued himself.

Doctor Rochecliffe's reliance, however, on the fidelity of Tomkins had apparently good grounds. Before the Civil Wars, as may be partly collected from what has been already hinted at, Tomkins, under his true name of Hazeldine, had been under the protection of the rector of Woodstock, occasionally acted as his clerk, was a distinguished member of his choir, and, being a handy and ingenious fellow, was employed in assisting the antiquarian researches of Dr. Rochecliffe through the interior of Woodstock. When he engaged on the opposite side in the Civil Wars, he still kept up his intelligence with the divine, to whom he had afforded what seemed valuable information from time to time. His assistance had latterly been eminently useful in aiding the Doctor, with the assistance of Joceline and Phœbe, in contriving and executing the various devices by which the Parliamentary Commissioners had been expelled from Woodstock. Indeed, his services in this respect had been thought worthy of no less a reward than a present of what plate remained at the lodge, which had been promised to the Independent accordingly. The Doctor, therefore, while admitting he might be a bad man, regretted him as a useful one, whose death, if inquired after, was likely to bring additional danger on a house which danger already surrounded, and which contained a pledge so precious.

CHAPTER XXX

> *Cassio.* That thrust had been my enemy indeed,
> But that my coat is better than thou know'st.
>
> *Othello.*

On the dark October night succeeding the evening on which Tomkins was slain, Colonel Everard, besides his constant attendant Roger Wildrake, had Master Nehemiah Holdenough with him as a guest at supper. The devotions of the evening having been performed according to the Presbyterian fashion, a light entertainment, and a double quart of burnt claret, were placed before his friends at nine o'clock, an hour unusually late. Master Holdenough soon engaged himself in a polemical discourse against sectaries and Independents, without being aware that his eloquence was not very interesting to his principal hearer, whose ideas in the meanwhile wandered to Woodstock and all which it contained—the Prince, who lay concealed there, his uncle, above all, Alice Lee. As for Wildrake, after bestowing a mental curse both on sectaries and Presbyterians, as being, in his opinion, never a barrel the better herring, he stretched out his limbs, and would probably have composed himself to rest, but that he as well as his patron had thoughts which murdered sleep.

The party were waited upon by a little gipsy-looking boy, in an orange-tawny doublet, much decayed, and garnished with blue worsted lace. The rogue looked somewhat stinted in size, but active both in intelligence and in limb, as his black eyes seemed to promise by their vivacity. He was an attendant of Wildrake's choice, who had conferred on him the *nom de guerre* of Spitfire, and had promised him promotion so soon as his young *protégé*, Breakfast, was fit to succeed him in his present office. It need scarce be said, that the menage was maintained entirely at the expense of Colonel Everard, who allowed Wildrake to arrange the household very much according to his pleasure. The page did not omit, in offering the company wine from time to time, to accommodate Wildrake with about twice the number of opportunities of refreshing himself which he considered it necessary to afford to the colonel or his reverend guest.

While they were thus engaged, the good divine lost in his own argument and the hearers in their private thoughts, their attention was about half-past ten arrested by a knocking at the door of the house. To those who have anxious hearts, trifles give cause of alarm. Even a thing so simple as a knock at the door may have a character which excites apprehension. This was no quiet, gentle tap, intimating a modest intruder; no redoubled rattle, as the pompous annunciation of some vain person; neither did it resemble the formal summons to formal business, nor the cheerful visit of some welcome friend. It was a single blow, solemn and stern, if not actually menacing, in the sound.

The door was opened by some of the persons of the house; a heavy foot ascended the stair, a stout man entered the room, and, drawing the cloak from his face, said, "Markham Everard, I greet thee in God's name."

It was General Cromwell.

Everard, surprised and taken at unawares, endeavored in vain to find words to express his astonishment. A bustle occurred in receiving the General, assisting him to uncloak himself, and offering in dumb show the civilities of reception.

The General cast his keen eye around the apartment, and fixing it first on the divine, addressed Everard as follows:—

"A reverend man I see is with thee. Thou art not one of those, good Markham, who let the time unnoted and unimproved pass away. Casting aside the things of this world, pressing forward to those of the next, it is by thus using our time in this poor seat of terrestrial sin and care that we may, as it were—— But how is this?" he continued, suddenly changing his tone, and speaking briefly, sharply, and anxiously—"one hath left the room since I entered?"

Wildrake had, indeed, been absent for a minute or two, but had now returned, and stepped forward from a bay window, as if he had been out of sight only, not out of the apartment. "Not so, sir, I stood but in the background out of respect. Noble General, I hope all is well with the estate, that your Excellency makes us so late a visit? Would not your Excellency choose some——"

"Ah!" said Oliver, looking sternly and fixedly at him, "our trusty go-between—our faithful confidant. No, sir; at present, I desire nothing more than a kind reception, which, methinks, my friend Markham Everard is in no hurry to give me."

"You bring your own welcome, my lord," said Everard, compelling himself to speak. "I can only trust it was no bad news that made your Excellency a late traveler, and ask, like my follower, what refreshment I shall command for your accommodation."

"The state is sound and healthy, Colonel Everard," said the General; "and yet the less so, that many of its members, who have been hitherto workers together, and propounders of good counsel, and advancers of the public weal, have now waxed cold in their love and in their affection for the good cause, for which we should be ready, in our various degrees, to act and do, so soon as we are called to act that whereunto we are appointed, neither rashly nor over-slothfully, neither lukewarmly nor over-violently, but with such a frame and disposition in which zeal and charity may, as it were, meet and kiss each other in our streets. Howbeit, because we look back after we have put our hand to the plow, therefore is our force waxed dim."

"Pardon me, sir," said Nehemiah Holdenough, who, listening with some impatience, began to guess in whose company he stood—"pardon me, for unto this I have a warrant to speak."

"Ah! ah!" said Cromwell. "Surely, most worthy sir, we grieve the Spirit when we restrain those pourings forth, which, like water from a rock——"

"Nay, therein I differ from you, sir," said Holdenough; "for, as there is the mouth to transmit the food, and the profit to digest what Heaven hath sent, so is the preacher ordained to teach, and the people to hear, the shepherd to gather the flock into the sheepfold, the sheep to profit by the care of the shepherd."

"Ah! my worthy sir," said Cromwell, with much unction, "methinks you verge upon the great mistake which supposes that churches are tall, large houses built by masons, and hearers are men—wealthy men, who pay tithes, the larger as well as the less; and that the priests, men in black gowns or gray cloaks, who receive the same are in guerdon the only distributors of Christian blessings. Whereas, in my apprehension, there is more of Christian liberty in leaving it to the discretion of the hungry soul to seek his edification where it can be found, whether from the mouth of a lay teacher, who claimeth his warrant from Heaven alone, or at the dispensation of those who take ordination and degrees from synods and universities, at best but associations of poor sinful creatures like themselves."

"You speak you know not what, sir," replied Holdenough, impatiently. "Can light come out of darkness, sense out of ignorance, or knowledge of the mysteries of religion from such ignorant mediciners as give poisons instead of wholesome medicaments, and cram with filth the stomachs of such as seek to them for food ?"

This, which the Presbyterian divine uttered rather warmly, the General answered with the utmost mildness.

"Lack-a-day—lack-a-day! a learned man, but intemperate: over-zeal hath eaten him up. A well-a-day, sir, you may talk of your regular gospel meals, but a word spoken in season by one whose heart is with your heart, just perhaps when you are riding on to encounter an enemy, or are about to mount a breach, is to the poor spirit like a rasher on the coals, which the hungry shall find preferable to a great banquet, at such times when the full soul loatheth the honeycomb. Nevertheless, although I speak thus in my poor judgment, I would not put force on the conscience of any man, leaving to the learned to follow the learned, and the wise to be instructed by the wise, while poor, simple, wretched souls are not to be denied a drink from the stream which runneth by the way. Ay, verily, it would be a comely sight in England when men shall go on as in a better world, bearing with each other's infirmities, joining in each other's comforts. Ay, truly, the rich drink out of silver flagons and goblets of silver, the poor out of paltry bowls of wood; and even so let it be, since they both drink the same element."

Here an officer opened the door and looked in, to whom Cromwell, exchanging the canting drawl, in which it seemed he might have gone on interminably, for the short brief tone of action, called out, "Pearson, is he come ?"

"No, sir," replied Pearson; "we have inquired for him at the place you noted, and also at other haunts of his about the town."

"The knave!" said Cromwell, with bitter emphasis; "can he have proved false? No—no, his interest is too deeply engaged. We shall find him by and by. Hark thee hither."

While this conversation was going forward, the reader must imagine the alarm of Everard. He was certain that the personal attendance of Cromwell must be on some most important account, and he could not but strongly suspect that the General had some information respecting Charles's lurking-place. If taken, a renewal of the tragedy of the

Thirtieth of January was instantly to be apprehended, and the ruin of the whole family of Lee, with himself probably included, must be the necessary consequence.

He looked eagerly for consolation at Wildrake, whose countenance expressed much alarm, which he endeavored to bear out with his usual look of confidence. But the weight within was too great: he shuffled with his feet, rolled his eyes, and twisted his hands, like an unassured witness before an acute and not to be deceived judge.

Oliver, meanwhile, left his company not a minute's leisure to take counsel together. Even while his perplexed eloquence flowed on in a stream so mazy that no one could discover which way its course was tending, his sharp, watchful eye rendered all attempts of Everard to hold communication with Wildrake, even by signs, altogether vain. Everard, indeed, looked for an instant at the window, then glanced at Wildrake, as if to hint there might be a possibility to escape that way. But the Cavalier had replied with a disconsolate shake of the head, so slight as to be almost imperceptible. Everard, therefore, lost all hope, and the melancholy feeling of approaching an inevitable evil was only varied by anxiety concerning the shape and manner in which it was about to make its approach.

But Wildrake had a spark of hope left. The very instant Cromwell entered he had got out of the room and down to the door of the house. "Back—back!" repeated by two armed sentinels, convinced him that, as his fears had anticipated, the General had come neither unattended nor unprepared. He turned on his heel, ran up stairs, and meeting on the landing-place the boy whom he called Spitfire, hurried him into the small apartment which he occupied as his own. Wildrake had been shooting that morning, and game lay on the table. He pulled a feather from a woodcock's wing, and saying hastily, "For thy life, Spitfire, mind my orders. I will put thee safe out at the window into the court; the yard wall is not high, and there will be no sentry there. Fly to the lodge, as thou wouldst win Heaven, and give this feather to Mistress Alice Lee, if possible; if not, to Joceline Joliffe; say I have won the wager of the young lady. Dost mark me, boy?"

The sharp-witted youth clapped his hand in his master's, and only replied, "Done, and done."

Wildrake opened the window, and, though the height was considerable, he contrived to let the boy down safely by holding his cloak. A heap of straw on which Spitfire lighted rendered the descent perfectly safe, and Wildrake saw him scramble over the wall of the courtyard, at the angle which bore on a back lane; and so rapidly was this accomplished, that the Cavalier had just re-entered the room when, the bustle attending Cromwell's arrival subsiding, his own absence began to be noticed.

He remained, during Cromwell's lecture on the vanity of creeds, anxious in mind whether he might not have done better to send an explicit verbal message, since there was no time to write. But the chance of the boy being stopped, or becoming confused with feeling himself the messenger of a hurried and important communication, made him, on the whole, glad that he had preferred a more enigmatical way of conveying the intelligence. He had, therefore, the advantage of his patron, for he was conscious still of a spark of hope.

Pearson had scarce shut the door, when Holdenough, as ready in arms against the future Dictator as he had been prompt to encounter the supposed phantoms and fiends of Woodstock, resumed his attack upon the schismatics, whom he undertook to prove to be at once soul-slayers, false brethren, and false messengers; and was proceeding to allege texts in behalf of his proposition, when Cromwell, apparently tired of the discussion, and desirous to introduce a discourse more accordant with his real feelings, interrupted him, though very civilly, and took the discourse into his own hands.

"Lack-a-day," he said, "the good man speaks truth according to his knowledge and to his lights—ay, bitter truths, and hard to be digested, while we see as men see, and not with the eyes of angels. False messengers, said the reverend man? Ay, truly, the world is full of such. You shall see them who will carry your secret message to the house of your mortal foe, and will say to him, 'Lo! my master is going forth with a small train, by such and such desolate places; be you speedy, therefore, that you may arise and slay him.' And another, who knoweth where the foe of your house and enemy of your person lies hidden, shall, instead of telling his master thereof, carry tidings to the enemy even where he lurketh, saying, 'Lo! my master knoweth of your secret abode; up, now, and fly, lest he come on thee like a lion on his prey.' But shall this go without punishment?" looking at Wildrake with a withering glance. "Now, as my soul liveth, and as He liveth who hath made me a ruler in Israel, such false messengers shall be knitted to gibbets on the wayside and their right hands shall be nailed above their heads, in an extended position, as if pointing out to others the road from which they themselves have strayed."

"Surely," said Master Holdenough, "it is right to cut off such offenders."

"Thank ye, Mas John," muttered Wildrake; "when did the Presbyterian fail to lend the Devil a shove?"

"But, I say," continued Holdenough, "that the matter is estranged from our present purpose, for the false brethren of whom I spoke are——"

"Right, excellent sir, they be those of our own house," answered Cromwell: "the good man is right once more. Ay, of whom can we now say that he is a true brother, although he has lain in the same womb with us? Although we have struggled in the same cause, eat at the same table, fought in the same battle, worshiped at the same throne, there shall be no truth in him. Ah, Markham Everard—Markham Everard!"

He paused at this ejaculation; and Everard, desirous at once of knowing how far he stood committed, replied, "Your Excellency seems to have something in your mind in which I am concerned. May I request you will speak it out, that I may know what I am accused of?"

"Ah, Mark—Mark!" replied the General, "there needeth no accuser speak when the still small voice speaks within us. Is there not moisture on thy brow, Mark Everard? Is there not trouble in thine eye? Is there not a failure in thy frame? And who ever saw such things in noble and stout Markham Everard, whose brow was only moist after having worn the helmet for a summer's day, whose hand only shook when it had wielded for hours the weighty falchion? But go to, man! thou doubtest overmuch. Hast thou not been to me as a brother, and shall I not forgive thee even the seventy-seventh time? The knave hath tarried somewhere, who should have done by this time an office of much import. Take advantage of his absence, Mark: it is a grace that God gives thee beyond expectance. I do not say, fall at my feet; but speak to me as a friend to his friend."

"I have never said anything to your Excellency that was in the least undeserving the title you have assigned to me," said Colonel Everard, proudly.

"Nay—nay, Markham," answered Cromwell; "I say not you have. But—but you ought to have remembered the message I sent you by that person (pointing to Wildrake); and you must reconcile it with your conscience, how, having such a message, guarded with such reasons, you could think yourself at liberty to expel my friends from Woodstock, being determined to disappoint my object, whilst you availed yourself of the boon on condition of which my warrant was issued."

Everard was about to reply, when, to his astonishment, Wildrake stepped forward; and with a voice and look very different from his ordinary manner, and approaching a good deal to real dignity of mind, said, boldly and calmly, "You are mistaken, Master Cromwell, and address yourself to the wrong party here."

The speech was so sudden and intrepid, that Cromwell stepped a pace back, and motioned with his right hand towards his weapon, as if he had expected that an address of a nature so unusually bold was to be followed by some act of violence. He instantly resumed his indifferent posture; and irritated at a smile which he observed on Wildrake's countenance, he said, with the dignity of one long accustomed to see all tremble before him, "This to me, fellow! Know you to whom you speak?"

"Fellow!" echoed Wildrake, whose reckless humor was now completely set afloat. "No fellow of yours, Master Oliver. I have known the day when Roger Wildrake of Squattlesea Mere, Lincoln, a handsome young gallant, with a good estate, would have been thought no fellow of the bankrupt brewer of Huntingdon."

"Be silent," said Everard—"be silent, Wildrake, if you love your life!"

"I care not a maravedi for my life," said Wildrake. "Zounds, if he dislikes what I say, let him take to his tools! I know, after all, he hath good blood in his veins; and I will indulge him with a turn in the court yonder, had he been ten times a brewer."

"Such ribaldry, friend," said Oliver, "I treat with the contempt it deserves. But if thou hast anything to say touching the matter in question, speak out like a man, though thou look'st more like a beast."

"All I have to say is," replied Wildrake, "that, whereas you blame Everard for acting on your warrant, as you call it, I can tell you, he knew not a word of the rascally conditions you talk of. I took care of that; and you may take the vengeance on me, if you list."

"Slave! dare you tell this to *me?*" said Cromwell, still

heedfully restraining his passion, which he felt was about to discharge itself upon an unworthy object.

"Ay, you will make every Englishman a slave, if you have your own way," said Wildrake, not a whit abashed; for the awe which had formerly overcome him when alone with this remarkable man had vanished, now that they were engaged in an altercation before witnesses. "But do your worst, Master Oliver; I tell you beforehand, the bird has escaped you."

"You dare not say so! Escaped! So, ho! Pearson, tell the soldiers to mount instantly. Thou art a lying fool! Escaped! Where, or from whence?"

"Ay, that is the question," said Wildrake; "for look you, sir, that men do go from hence is certain; but how they go, or to what quarter——"

Cromwell stood attentive, expecting some useful hint, from the careless impetuosity of the Cavalier, upon the route which the King might have taken.

—"Or to what quarter, as I said before, why, your Excellency, Master Oliver, may e'en find that out yourself."

As he uttered the last words, he unsheathed his rapier, and made a full pass at the General's body. Had his sword met no other impediment than the buff jerkin, Cromwell's course had ended on the spot. But, fearful of such attempts, the General wore under his military dress a shirt of the finest mail, made of rings of the best steel, and so light and flexible that it was little or no encumbrance to the motions of the wearer. It proved his safety on this occasion, for the rapier sprung in shivers; while the owner, now held back by Everard and Holdenough, flung the hilt with passion on the ground, exclaiming, "Be damned the hand that forged thee! To serve me so long, and fail me when thy true service would have honored us both forever! But no good could come of thee, since thou wert pointed, even in jest, at a learned divine of the Church of England."

In the first instant of alarm, and perhaps suspecting Wildrake might be supported by others, Cromwell half drew from his bosom a concealed pistol, which he hastily returned, observing that both Everard and the clergyman were withholding the Cavalier from another attempt.

Pearson and a soldier or two rushed in. "Secure that fellow," said the General, in the indifferent tone of one to whom imminent danger was too familiar to cause irritation. "Bind him, but not so hard, Pearson;" for the men, to show their zeal, were drawing their belts, which they used for want of cords, brutally tight round Wildrake's limbs. "He would have assassinated me, but I would reserve him for his fit doom."

"Assassinated! I scorn your words, Master Oliver," said Wildrake; "I proffered you a fair duello."

"Shall we shoot him in the street, for an example?" said Pearson to Cromwell; while Everard endeavored to stop Wildrake from giving further offense.

"On your life, harm him not; but let him be kept in safe ward, and well looked after," said Cromwell; while the prisoner exclaimed to Everard, "I prithee let me alone. I am now neither thy follower nor any man's, and I am as willing to die as ever I was to take a cup of liquor. And harkye, speaking of that, Master Oliver, you were once a jolly fellow, prithee let one of thy lobsters here advance yonder tankard to my lips, and your Excellency shall hear a toast, a song, and a—secret."

"Unloose his head, and hand the debauched beast the tankard," said Oliver; "while yet he exists, it were shame to refuse him the element he lives in."

"Blessings on your head for once!" said Wildrake, whose object in continuing this wild discourse was, if possible, to gain a little delay, when every moment was precious. "Thou hast brewed good ale, and that's warrant for a blessing. For my toast and my song, here they go together—

Son of a witch,
Mayst thou die in a ditch,
  With the butchers who back thy quarrels;
Aud rot above ground,
While the world shall resound
  A welcome to Royal King Charles!

And now for my secret, that you may not say I had your liquor for nothing—I fancy my song will scarce pass current for much. My secret is, Master Cromwell, that the bird is flown, and your red nose will be as white as your winding-sheet before you can smell out which way.'

"Pshaw, rascal," answered Cromwell, contemptuously, "keep your scurril jests for the gibbet foot."

"I shall look on the gibbet more boldly," replied Wildrake, "than I have seen you look on the Royal Martyr's picture."

This reproach touched Cromwell to the very quick.

"Villain!" he exclaimed; "drag him hence, draw out a party, and—— But hold, not now—to prison with him; let him be close watched, and gagged if he attempts to speak to the sentinels. Nay, hold—I mean, put a bottle of brandy into his cell, and he will gag himself in his own way, I warrant you. When day comes, that men can see the example, he shall be gagged after my fashion."

During the various breaks in his orders, the General was evidently getting command of his temper; and though he began in fury, he ended with the contemptuous sneer of one who overlooks the abusive language of an inferior. Something remained on his mind notwithstanding, for he continued stationary, as if fixed to the same spot in the apartment, his eyes bent on the ground, and with closed hand pressed against his lips, like a man who is musing deeply. Pearson, who was about to speak to him, drew back, and made a sign to those in the room to be silent.

Master Holdenough did not mark, or, at least, did not obey, it. Approaching the General, he said, in a respectful but firm tone, "Did I understand it to be your Excellency's purpose that this poor man shall die next morning?"

"Hah!" exclaimed Cromwell, starting from his reverie, "what say'st thou?"

"I took leave to ask if it was your will that this unhappy man should die to-morrow?"

"Whom saidst thou?" demanded Cromwell. "Markham Everard—shall he die, saidst thou?"

"God forbid!" replied Holdenough, stepping back. "I asked whether this blinded creature, Wildrake, was to be so suddenly cut off?"

"Ay, marry is he," said Cromwell, "were the whole General Assembly of Divines at Westminster, the whole Sanhedrim of Presbytery, to offer bail for him."

"If you will not think better of it, sir," said Holdenough, "at least give not the poor man the means of destroying his senses. Let me go to him as a divine, to watch with him, in case he may yet be admitted into the vineyard at the latest hour—yet brought into the sheepfold, though he has neglected the call of the pastor till time is well-nigh closed upon him."

"For God's sake," said Everard, who had hitherto kept silence, because he knew Cromwell's temper on such occasions, "think better of what you do!"

"Is it for thee to teach me?" replied Cromwell. "Think thou of thine own matters, and believe me it will require all thy wit. And for you, reverend sir, I will have no father-confessors attend my prisoners—no tales out of school. If the fellow thirsts after ghostly comfort, as he is much more like to thirst after a quartern of brandy, there is Corporal Humgudgeon, who commands the *corps de garde*, will preach and pray as well as the best of ye. But this delay is intolerable; comes not this fellow yet?"

"No, sir," replied Pearson. "Had we not better go down to the lodge? The news of our coming hither may else get there before us."

"True," said Cromwell, speaking aside to his officer, "but you know Tomkins warned us against doing so, alleging there were so many postern-doors, and sally-ports, and concealed entrances in the old house, that it was like a rabbit-warren, and that an escape might be easily made under our very noses, unless he were with us, to point out all the ports which should be guarded. He hinted, too, that he might be delayed a few minutes after his time of appointment; but we have now waited half an hour."

"Does your Excellency think Tomkins is certainly to be depended upon?" said Pearson.

"As far as his interest goes, unquestionably," replied the General. "He has ever been the pump by which I have sucked the marrow out of many a plot, in special those of the conceited fool Rochecliffe, who is goose enough to believe that such a fellow as Tomkins would value anything beyond the offer of the best bidder. And yet it groweth late—I fear we must to the lodge without him. Yet, all things well considered, I will tarry here till midnight. Ah! Everard, thou mightest put this gear to rights if thou wilt! Shall some foolish principle of fantastic punctilio have more weight with thee, man, than have the pacification and welfare of England, the keeping of faith to thy friend and benefactor, and who will be yet more so, and the fortune and security of thy relations? Are these, I say, lighter in the balance than the cause of a worthless boy, who with his father and his father's house have troubled Israel for fifty years?"

"I do not understand your Excellency, nor at what service you point, which I can honestly render," replied Everard. "That which is dishonest I should be loth that you proposed."

"Then this at least might suit your honesty, or scrupulous humor, call it which thou wilt," said Cromwell. "Thou knowest, surely, all the passages about Jezebel's palace down yonder? Let me know how they may be guarded against the escape of any from within."

"I cannot pretend to aid you in this matter," said Everard: "I know not all the entrances and posterns about Woodstock, and if I did, I am not free in conscience to communicate with you on this occasion."

"We shall do without you, sir," replied Cromwell, haughtily; "and if aught is found which may criminate you, remember you have lost right to my protection."

"I shall be sorry," said Everard, "to have lost your friendship, General; but I trust my quality as an Englishman may dispense with the necessity of protection from any man. I know no law which obliges me to be spy or informer, even if I were in the way of having opportunity to do service in either honorable capacity."

"Well, sir," said Cromwell, "for all your privileges and qualities, I will make bold to take you down to the lodge at Woodstock to-night, to inquire into affairs in which the state is concerned. Come hither, Pearson." He took a paper from his pocket containing a rough sketch or ground-plan of Woodstock Lodge, with the avenues leading to it. "Look here," he said, "we must move in two bodies on foot, and with all possible silence; thou must march to the rear of the old house of iniquity with twenty file of men, and dispose them around it the wisest thou canst. Take the reverend man there along with you. He must be secured at any rate, and may serve as a guide. I myself will occupy the front of the lodge, and thus having stopped all the earths, thou wilt come to me for farther orders; silence and despatch is all. But for the dog Tomkins, who broke appointment with me, he had need render a good excuse, or woe to his father's son! Reverend sir, be pleased to accompany that officer. Colonel Everard, you are to follow me; but first give your sword to Captain Pearson, and consider yourself as under arrest."

Everard gave his sword to Pearson without any comment, and with the most anxious presage of evil followed the Republican General, in obedience to commands which it would have been useless to dispute.

CHAPTER XXXI

> "Were my son William here but now,
> He wadna fail the pledge."
> Wi' that in at the door there ran
> A ghastly-looking page—
> "I saw them, master, O! I saw,
> Beneath the thornie brae,
> Of black-mail'd warriors many a rank."
> "Revenge!" he cried, "and gae!"
>
> HENRY MACKENZIE.

THE little party at the lodge were assembled at supper, at the early hour of eight o'clock. Sir Henry Lee, neglecting the food that was placed on the table, stood by a lamp on the chimney-piece, and read a letter with mournful attention.

"Does my son write to you more particularly than to me, Doctor Rochecliffe?" said the knight. "He only says here that he will return probably this night; and that Master Kerneguy must be ready to set off with him instantly. What can this haste mean? Have you heard of any new search after our suffering party? I wish they would permit me to enjoy my son's company in quiet but for a day."

"The quiet which depends on the wicked ceasing from troubling," said Dr. Rochecliffe, "is connected, not by days and hours, but by minutes. Their glut of blood at Worcester had satiated them for a moment, but their appetite, I fancy, has revived."

"You have news, then, to that purpose?" said Sir Henry.

"Your son," replied the Doctor, "wrote to me by the same messenger; he seldom fails to do so, being aware of what importance it is that I should know everything that passes. Means of escape are provided on the coast, and Master Kerneguy must be ready to start with your son the instant he appears."

"It is strange," said the knight; "for forty years I have dwelt in this house, man and boy, and the point only was how to make the day pass over our heads; for if I did not scheme out some hunting-match or hawking, or the like, I might have sat here on my arm-chair, as undisturbed as a sleeping dormouse, from one end of the year to the other; and now I am more like a hare on her form, that dare not sleep unless with her eyes open, and scuds off when the wind rustles among the fern."

"It is strange," said Alice, looking at Doctor Rochecliffe, "that the Roundhead steward has told you nothing of this. He is usually communicative enough of the motions of his party; and I saw you close together this morning."

"I must be closer with him this evening," said the Doctor gloomily; "but he will not blab."

"I wish you may not trust him too much," said Alice in reply. "To me, that man's face, with all its shrewdness, evinces such a dark expression, that methinks I read treason in his very eye."

"Be assured, that matter is looked to," answered the Doctor, in the same ominous tone as before. No one replied, and there was a chilling and anxious feeling of apprehension which seemed to sink down on the company at once, like those sensations which make such constitutions as are particularly subject to the electrical influence conscious of an approaching thunderstorm.

The disguised monarch, apprised that day to be prepared on short notice to quit his temporary asylum, felt his own share of the gloom which involved the little society. But he was the first also to shake it off, as what neither suited his character nor his situation. Gaiety was the leading distinction of the former, and presence of mind, not depression of spirits, was required by the latter.

"We make the hour heavier," he said, "by being melancholy about it. Had you not better join me, Mistress Alice, in Patrick Carey's jovial farewell? Ah, you do not know Pat Carey,* a younger brother of Lord Falkland's?"

"A brother of the immortal Lord Falkland's, and write songs!" said the Doctor.

"Oh, Doctor, the Muses take tithe as well as the church," said Charles, "and have their share in every family of distinction. You do not know the words, Mistress Alice, but you can aid me notwithstanding, in the burden at least—

Come, now that we're parting, and 'tis one to ten
If the towers of sweet Woodstock I e'er see agen,
Let us e'en have a frolic, and drink like tall men,
While the goblet goes merrily round." †

* See Note 10.

† The original song of Carey bears Wykeham, instead of Wood-

The song arose, but not with spirit. It was one of those efforts at forced mirth by which, above all other modes of expressing it, the absence of real cheerfulness is most distinctly intimated. Charles stopt the song, and upbraided the choristers.

"You sing, my dear Mistress Alice, as if you were chanting one of the seven penitential psalms; and you, good Doctor, as if you recited the funeral service."

The Doctor rose hastily from the table, and turned to the window; for the expression connected singularly with the task which he was that evening to discharge. Charles looked at him with some surprise; for the peril in which he lived made him watchful of the slightest motions of those around him, then turned to Sir Henry, and said, "My honored host, can you tell any reason for this moody fit, which has so strangely crept upon us all?"

"Not I, my dear Louis," replied the knight: "I have no skill in these nice quillets of philosophy. I could as soon undertake to tell you the reason why Bevis turns round three times before he lies down. I can only say for myself, that, if age and sorrow and uncertainty be enough to break a jovial spirit, or at least to bend it now and then, I have my share of them all; so that I, for one, cannot say that I am sad merely because I am not merry. I have but too good cause for sadness. I would I saw my son, were it but for a minute!"

Fortune seemed for once disposed to gratify the old man; for Albert Lee entered at that moment. He was dressed in a riding-suit, and appeared to have traveled hard. He cast his eye hastily around as he entered. It rested for a second on that of the disguised prince, and, satisfied with the glance which he received in lieu, he hastened, after the fashion of the olden day, to kneel down to his father and request his blessing.

"It is thine, my boy," said the old man, a tear springing to his eyes as he laid his hand on the long locks which distinguished the young Cavalier's rank and principles, and which, usually combed and curled with some care, now hung wild and disheveled about his shoulders. They remained an instant in this posture, when the old man suddenly started from it, as if ashamed of the emotion which he had expressed before so many witnesses, and passing the back

stock, for the locality. The verses are full of the bacchanalian spirit of the time.

of his hand hastily across his eyes, bid Albert get up and mind his supper, "since I daresay you have ridden fast and far since you last baited. And we'll send round a cup to his health, if Doctor Rochecliffe and the good company pleases. Joceline, thou knave, skink about; thou look'st as if thou hadst seen a ghost."

"Joceline," said Alice, "is sick for sympathy. One of the stags ran at Phœbe Mayflower to-day, and she was fain to have Joceline's assistance to drive the creature off; the girl has been in fits since she came home."

"Silly slut," said the old knight. "She a woodman's daughter! But, Joceline, if the deer gets dangerous, you must send a broad arrow through him."

"It will not need, Sir Henry," said Joceline, speaking with great difficulty of utterance: "he is quiet enough now, he will not offend in that sort again."

"See it be so," replied the knight; "remember Mistress Alice often walks in the chase. And now fill round, and fill, too, a cup to thyself to over-red thy fear, as mad Will has it. Tush, man, Phœbe will do well enough: she only screamed and ran, that thou mightest have the pleasure to help her. Mind what thou dost, and do not go spilling the wine after that fashion. Come, here is a health to our wanderer, who has come to us again."

"None will pledge it more willingly than I," said the disguised prince, unconsciously assuming an importance which the character he personated scarce warranted; but Sir Henry, who had become fond of the supposed page, with all his peculiarities, imposed only a moderate rebuke upon his petulance. "Thou art a merry, good-humored youth, Louis," he said; "but it is a world to see how the forwardness of the present generation hath gone beyond the gravity and reverence which in my youth was so regularly observed towards those of higher rank and station. I dared no more have given my own tongue the rein, when there was a doctor of divinity in company, than I would have dared to have spoken in church in service-time."

"True, sir," said Albert, hastily interfering; "but Master Kerneguy had the better right to speak at present, that I have been absent on his business as well as my own, have seen several of his friends, and bring him important intelligence."

Charles was about to rise and beckon Albert aside, naturally impatient to know what news he had procured, or what scheme of safe escape was now decreed for him. But

Dr. Rochecliffe twitched his cloak, as a hint to him to sit still, and not show any extraordinary motive for anxiety, since, in case of a sudden discovery of his real quality, the violence of Sir Henry Lee's feelings might have been likely to attract too much attention.

Charles, therefore, only replied, as to the knight's stricture, that he had a particular title to be sudden and unceremonious in expressing his thanks to Colonel Lee, that gratitude was apt to be unmannerly; finally, that he was much obliged to Sir Henry for his admonition, and that, quit Woodstock when he would, "he was sure to leave it a better man than he came there."

His speech was of course ostensibly directed towards the father; but a glance at Alice assured her that she had a full share in the compliment.

"I fear," he concluded, addressing Albert, "that you come to tell us our stay here must be very short."

"A few hours only," said Albert, "just enough for needful rest for ourselves and our horses. I have procured two which are good and tried. But Doctor Rochecliffe broke faith with me. I expected to have met some one down at Joceline's hut, where I left the horses; and finding no person, I was delayed an hour in littering them down myself, that they might be ready for to-morrow's work, for we must be off before day."

"I—I—intended to have sent Tomkins; but—but——" hesitated the Doctor—"I——"

"The Roundhead rascal was drunk, or out of the way, I presume," said Albert. "I am glad of it, you may easily trust him too far."

"Hitherto he has been faithful," said the Doctor, "and I scarce think he will fail me now. But Joceline will go down and have the horses in readiness in the morning."

Joceline's countenance was usually that of alacrity itself in a case extraordinary. Now, however, he seemed to hesitate.

"You will go with me a little way, Doctor?" he said, as he edged himself closely to Rochecliffe.

"How! puppy, fool, and blockhead," said the knight, "wouldst thou ask Doctor Rochecliffe to bear thee company at this hour? Out, hound! get down to the kennel yonder instantly, or I will break the knave's pate of thee."

Joceline looked with an eye of agony at the divine, as if entreating him to interfere in his behalf; but just as he was about to speak, a most melancholy howling arose at the hall-door, and a dog was heard scratching for admittance.

"What ails Bevis next?" said the old knight. "I think this must be All Fools Day, and that everything around me is going mad!"

The same sound startled Albert and Charles from a private conference in which they had engaged, and Albert ran to the hall-door to examine personally into the cause of the noise.

"It is no alarm," said the old knight to Kerneguy, "for in such cases the dog's bark is short, sharp, and furious. These long howls are said to be ominous. It was even so Bevis's grandsire bayed the whole livelong night on which my poor father died. If it comes now as a presage, God send it regard the old and useless, not the young, and those who may yet serve king and country!"

The dog had pushed passed Colonel Lee, who stood a little while at the hall-door to listen if there were anything stirring without, while Bevis advanced into the room where the company were assembled, bearing something in his mouth, and exhibiting, in an unusual degree, that sense of duty and interest which a dog seems to show when he thinks he has the charge of something important. He entered, therefore, drooping his long tail, slouching his head and ears, and walking with the stately yet melancholy dignity of a war-horse at his master's funeral. In this manner he paced through the room, went straight up to Joceline, who had been regarding him with astonishment, and uttering a short and melancholy howl, laid at his feet the object which he bore in his mouth. Joceline stooped, and took from the floor a man's glove, of the fashion worn by the troopers, having something like the old-fashioned gauntlet projections of thick leather arising from the wrist, which go half-way up to the elbow, and secure the arm against a cut with a sword. But Joceline had no sooner looked at what in itself was so common an object than he dropped it from his hand, staggered backward, uttered a groan, and nearly fell to the ground.

"Now, the coward's curse be upon thee for an idiot!" said the knight, who had picked up the glove and was looking at it; "thou shouldst be sent back to school, and flogged till the craven's blood was switched out of thee. What dost thou look at but a glove, thou base poltroon, and a very dirty glove too? Stay, here is writing. Joseph Tomkins! Why, that is the Roundheaded fellow. I wish he hath not come to some mischief; for this is not dirt on the cheveron, but blood. Bevis may have bit the fellow, and yet the dog seemed to love him well too; or the stag may have hurt him. Out, Joceline, instantly, and see where he is; wind your bugle."

"I cannot go," said Joliffe, "unless——" and again he looked piteously at Doctor Rochecliffe, who saw no time was to be lost in appeasing the ranger's terrors, as his ministry was most needful in the present circumstances. "Get spade and mattock," he whispered to him, "and a dark lantern, and meet me in the wilderness."

Joceline left the room; and the Doctor, before following him, had a few words of explanation with Colonel Lee. His own spirit, far from being dismayed on the occasion, rather rose higher, like one whose natural element was intrigue and danger. "Here hath been wild work," he said, "since you parted. Tomkins was rude to the wench Phœbe, Joceline and he had a brawl together, and Tomkins is lying dead in the thicket not far from Rosamond's Well. It will be necessary that Joceline and I go directly to bury the body; for, besides that some one might stumble upon it and raise an alarm, this fellow Joceline will never be fit for any active purpose till it is under ground. Though as stout as a lion, the under-keeper has his own weak side, and is more afraid of a dead body than a living one. When do you propose to start to-morrow?"

"By daybreak, or earlier," said Colonel Lee; "but we will meet again. A vessel is provided, and I have relays in more places than one; we go off from the coast of Sussex, and I am to get a letter at ——, acquainting me precisely with the spot."

"Wherefore not go off instantly?" inquired the Doctor.

"The horses would fail us," replied Albert: "they have been hard ridden to-day."

"Adieu," said Rochecliffe, "I must to my task. Do you take rest and repose for yours. To conceal a slaughtered body, and convey on the same night a king from danger and captivity, are two feats which have fallen to few folks save myself; but let me not, while putting on my harness, boast myself as if I were taking it off after a victory." So saying, he left the apartment, and, muffling himself in his cloak, went out into what was called the wilderness.

The weather was a raw frost. The mist lay in partial wreaths upon the lower grounds; but the night, considering that the heavenly bodies were in a great measure hidden by the haze, was not extremely dark. Doctor Rochecliffe could not, however, distinguish the under-keeper, until he had hemmed once or twice, when Joceline answered the signal by showing a glimpse of light from the dark lantern which he carried. Guided by this intimation of his presence, the divine found him leaning against a buttress which had once supported a terrace, now ruinous. He had a pickax and shovel, together with a deer's hide hanging over his shoulder.

"What do you want with the hide, Joceline?" said Dr. Rochecliffe, "that you lumber it about with you on such an errand?"

"Why, look you, Doctor," he answered, "it is as well to tell you all about it. The man and I—he there—you know whom I mean—had many years since a quarrel about this deer. For, though we were great friends, and Philip was sometimes allowed by my master's permission to help me in mine office, yet I knew, for all that, Philip Hazeldine was sometimes a trespasser. The deer-stealers were very bold at that time, it being just before the breaking out of the war, when men were becoming unsettled. And so it chanced that one day, in the chase, I found two fellows, with their faces blacked, and shirts over their clothes, carrying as prime a buck between them as any was in the park. I was upon them in the instant; one escaped, but I got hold of the other fellow, and who should it prove to be but trusty Phil Hazeldine! Well, I don't know whether it was right or wrong, but he was my old friend and pot-companion, and I took his word for amendment in future; and he helped me to hang up the deer on a tree, and I came back with a horse to carry him to the lodge, and tell the knight the story, all but Phil's name. But the rogues had been too clever for me; for they had flayed and dressed the deer, and quartered him, and carried him off, and left the hide and horns, with a chime, saying

The haunch to thee,
The breast to me,
The hide and the horns for the keeper's fee.

And this I knew for one of Phil's mad pranks, that he would play in those days with any lad in the country. But I was so nettled, that I made the deer's hide be curried and dressed by a tanner, and swore that it should be his winding-sheet or mine; and though I had long repented my rash oath, yet now, Doctor, you see what it has come to: though I forgot it, the Devil did not."

"It was a very wrong thing to make a vow so sinful," said Rochecliffe; "but it would have been greatly worse had you endeavored to keep it. Therefore, I bid you cheer up," said the good divine; "for in this unhappy case I could not have wished, after what I have heard from Phœbe and yourself, that you should have kept your hand still, though I may regret that the blow has proved fatal. Nevertheless, thou hast done even that which was done by the great and inspired legislator when he beheld an Egyptian tyrannizing over a Hebrew, saving that, in the case present, it was a female, when, says the Septuagint, ***Percussum Egyptium** abscondit sabulo,* the meaning whereof I will explain to you another time. Wherefore, I exhort you not to grieve beyond measure; for, although this circumstance is unhappy in time and place, yet, from what Phœbe hath informed me of yonder wretch's opinions, it is much to be regretted that his brains had not been beaten out in his cradle, rather than that he had grown up to be one of those Grindletonians, or Muggletonians, in whom is the perfection of every foul and blasphemous heresy, united with such an universal practise of hypocritical assentation as would deceive their master, even Satan himself."

"Nevertheless, sir," said the forester, "I hope you will bestow some of the service of the church on this poor man, as it was his last wish, naming you, sir, at the same time; and unless this were done, I should scarce dare to walk out in the dark again, for my whole life."

"Thou art a silly fellow; but if," continued the Doctor, "he named me as he departed, and desired the last rites of the church, there was, it may be, a turning from evil and a seeking to good even in his last moments; and if Heaven granted him grace to form a prayer so fitting, wherefore should man refuse it? All I fear is the briefness of time."

"Nay, your reverence may cut the service somewhat short," said Joceline; "assuredly he does not deserve the whole of it; only if something were not to be done, I believe I should flee the country. They were his last words; and methinks he sent Bevis with his glove to put me in mind of them."

"Out, fool! Do you think," said the Doctor, "dead men send gauntlets to the living, like knights in a romance; or, if so, would they choose dogs to carry their challenges? I tell thee, fool, the cause was natural enough. Bevis, questing about, found the body, and brought the glove to you to intimate where it was lying, and to require assistance; for such is the high instinct of these animals towards one in peril."

"Nay, if you think so, Doctor," said Joceline; "and, doubtless, I must say, Bevis took an interest in the man—if indeed it was not something worse in the shape of Bevis, for methought his eyes looked wild and fiery, as if he would have spoken."

As he talked thus, Joceline rather hung back, and in doing so displeased the Doctor, who exclaimed, "Come along, thou lazy laggard. Art thou a soldier, and a brave one, and so much afraid of a dead man? Thou hast killed men in battle and in chase, I warrant thee."

"Ay, but their backs were to me," said Joceline: "I never saw one of them cast back his head and glare at me as yonder fellow did, his eye retaining a glance of hatred, mixed with terror and reproach, till it became fixed like a jelly. And were you not with me, and my master's concerns, and something else, very deeply at stake, I promise you I would not again look at him for all Woodstock."

"You must, though," said the Doctor, suddenly pausing, "for here is the place where he lies. Come hither deep into the copse; take care of stumbling. Here is a place just fitting, and we will draw the briers over the grave afterwards."

As the Doctor thus issued his directions, he assisted also in the execution of them; and while his attendant labored to dig a shallow and misshapen grave, a task which the state of the soil, perplexed with roots and hardened by the influence of the frost, rendered very difficult, the divine read a few passages out of the funeral service, partly in order to appease the superstitious terrors of Joceline, and partly because he held it matter of conscience not to deny the church's rites to one who had requested their aid in extremity.

CHAPTER XXXII

Case ye, case ye, on with your vizards.
Henry IV.

THE company whom we had left in Victor Lee's parlor were about to separate for the night, and had risen to take a formal leave of each other, when atapwas heard at the hall-door. Albert, the vidette of the party, hastened to open it, enjoining, as he left the room, the rest to remain quiet until he had ascertained the cause of the knocking. When he gained the portal, he called to know who was there, and what they wanted at so late an hour.

"It is only me," answered a treble voice.

"And what is your name, my little fellow?" said Albert.

"Spitfire, sir," replied the voice without.

"Spitfire?" said Albert.

"Yes, sir," replied the voice; "all the world calls me so, and Colonel Everard himself. But my name is Spittal for all that."

"Colonel Everard! arrive you from him?" demanded young Lee.

"No, sir; I come, sir, from Roger Wildrake, Esquire, of Squattlesea Mere, if it like you," said the boy; "and I have brought a token to Mistress Lee, which I am to give into her own hands, if you would but open the door, sir, and let me in; but I can do nothing with a three-inch board between us."

"It is some freak of that drunken rakehell," said Albert, in a low voice to his sister, who had crept out after him on tiptoe.

"Yet, let us not be hasty in concluding so," said the young lady; "at this moment the least trifle may be of consequence. What token has Master Wildrake sent me, my little boy?"

"Nay, nothing very valuable neither," replied the boy; "but he was so anxious you should get it, that he put me out of the window as one would chuck out a kitten, that I might not be stopped by the soldiers."

"Hear you?" said Alice to her brother. "Undo the gate, for God's sake."

Her brother, to whom her feelings of suspicion were now sufficiently communicated, opened the gate in haste, and admitted the boy, whose appearance, not much dissimilar to that of a skinned rabbit in a livery, or a monkey at a fair, would at another time have furnished them with amusement. The urchin messenger entered the hall, making several odd bows and congés, and delivered the woodcock's feather * with much ceremony to the young lady, assuring her it was the prize she had won upon a wager about hawking.

"I prithee, my little man," said Albert, "was your master drunk or sober when he sent thee all this way with a feather at this time of night?"

"With reverence, sir," said the boy, "he was what *he* calls sober, and what I would call concerned in liquor for any other person."

"Curse on the drunken coxcomb!" said Albert. "There is a tester for thee, boy, and tell thy master to break his jests on suitable persons and at fitting times."

"Stay yet a minute," exclaimed Alice; "we must not go too fast, this craves wary walking."

"A feather," said Albert—"all this work about a feather! Why, Dr. Rochecliffe, who can suck intelligence out of every trifle as a magpie would suck an egg, could make nothing of this."

"Let us try what we can do without him then," said Alice. Then addressing herself to the boy—"So there are strangers at your master's?"

"At Colonel Everard's, madam, which is the same thing," said Spitfire.

"And what manner of strangers," said Alice, "guests, I suppose?"

"Ay, mistress," said the boy—"a sort of guests that make themselves welcome wherever they come, if they meet not a welcome from their landlord—soldiers, madam."

"The men that have been long lying at Woodstock?" said Albert.

"No, sir," said Spitfire, "newcomers with gallant buff-coats and steel breastplates; and their commander—your honor and your ladyship never saw such a man!—at least I am sure Bill Spitfire never did."

"Was he tall or short?" said Albert, now much alarmed.

"Neither one nor other," said the boy: "stout made, with slouching shoulders, a nose large, and a face one would

* See Signal of Danger. Note 11.

not like to say 'No' to. He had several officers with him. I saw him but for a moment, but I shall never forget him while I live."

"You are right," said Albert Lee to his sister, pulling her to one side—"quite right: the Archfiend himself is upon us!"

"And the feather," said Alice, whom fear had rendered apprehensive of slight tokens, "means flight, and a woodcock is a bird of passage."

"You have hit it," said her brother; "but the time has taken us cruelly short. Give the boy a trifle more—nothing that can excite suspicion—and dismiss him. I must summon Rochecliffe and Joceline."

He went accordingly, but, unable to find those he sought, he returned with hasty steps to the parlor, where, in his character of Louis, the page was exerting himself to detain the old knight, who, while laughing at the tales he told him, was anxious to go to see what was passing in the hall.

"What is the matter, Albert?" said the old man; "who calls at the lodge at so undue an hour, and wherefore is the hall-door opened to them? I will not have my rules, and the regulations laid down for keeping this house, broken through because I am old and poor. Why answer you not? why keep a-chattering with Louis Kerneguy, and neither of you all the while minding what I say? Daughter Alice, have you sense and civility enough to tell me what or who it is that is admitted here contrary to my general orders?"

"No one, sir," replied Alice; "a boy brought a message, which I fear is an alarming one."

"There is only fear, sir," said Albert, stepping forward, "that, whereas we thought to have stayed with you till to-morrow, we must now take farewell of you to-night."

"Not so, brother," said Alice, "you must stay and aid the defense here; if you and Master Kerneguy are both missed, the pursuit will be instant, and probably successful; but if you stay, the hiding-places about this house will take some time to search. You can change coats with Kerneguy too."

"Right, noble wench," said Albert—"most excellent. Yes—Louis, I remain as Kerneguy, you fly as young Master Lee."

"I cannot see the justice of that," said Charles.

"Nor I neither," said the knight, interfering. "Men come and go, lay schemes, and alter them, in my house, without deigning to consult me! And who is Master Kerneguy, or what is he to me, that my son must stay and take the chance of mischief, and this your Scotch page is to escape in his dress? I will have no such contrivance carried into effect, though it were the finest cobweb that was ever woven in Doctor Rochecliffe's brains. I wish you no ill, Louis, thou art a lively boy; but I have been somewhat too lightly treated in this, man."

"I am fully of your opinion, Sir Henry," replied the person whom he addressed. "You have been, indeed, repaid for your hospitality by want of that confidence which could never have been so justly reposed. But the moment is come when I must say, in a word, I am that unfortunate Charles Stuart whose lot it has been to become the cause of ruin to his best friends, and whose present residence in your family threatens to bring destruction to you and all around you."

"Master Louis Kerneguy," said the knight, very angrily, "I will teach you to choose the subjects of your mirth better when you address them to me; and, moreover, very little provocation would make me desire to have an ounce or two of that malapert blood from you."

"Be still, sir, for Godsake!" said Albert to his father. "This is indeed the KING; and such is the danger of his person, that every moment we waste may bring round a fatal catastrophe."

"Good God!" said the father, clasping his hands together, and about to drop on his knees, "has my earnest wish been accomplished, and is it in such a manner as to make me pray it had never taken place?"

He then attempted to bend his knee to the King, kissed his hand, while large tears trickled from his eyes, then said, "Pardon, my Lord—your Majesty, I mean—permit me to sit in your presence but one instant till my blood beats more freely, and then——"

Charles raised his ancient and faithful subject from the ground; and even in that moment of fear, and anxiety, and danger insisted on leading him to his seat, upon which he sunk in apparent exhaustion, his head drooping upon his long white beard, and big unconscious tears mingling with its silver hairs. Alice and Albert remained with the King, arguing and urging his instant departure.

"The horses are at the under-keeper's hut," said Albert, "and the relays only eighteen or twenty miles off. If the horses can but carry you so far——"

"Will you not rather," interrupted Alice, "trust to the concealments of this place, so numerous and so well tried—

Rochecliffe's apartments, and the yet farther places of secrecy ?"

"Alas !" said Albert, "I know them only by name. My father was sworn to confide them to but one man, and he had chosen Rochecliffe."

"I prefer taking the field to any hiding-hole in England," said the King. "Could I but find my way to this hut where the horses are, I would try what arguments whip and spur could use to get them to the rendezvous, where I am to meet Sir Thomas Acland and fresh cattle. Come with me, Colonel Lee, and let us run for it. The Roundheads have beat us in battle ; but if it come to a walk or a race, I think I can show which has the best mettle."

"But then," said Albert, "we lose all the time which may otherwise be gained by the defense of this house—leaving none here but my poor father, incapable from his state of doing anything ; and you will be instantly pursued by fresh horses, while ours are unfit for the road. Oh, where is the villain Joceline ?"

"What can have become of Doctor Rochecliffe ?" said Alice—"he that is so ready with advice. Where can they be gone ? Oh, if my father could but rouse himself !"

"Your father *is* roused," said Sir Henry, rising and stepping up to them with all the energy of full manhood in his countenance and motions. "I did but gather my thoughts, for when did there fail a Lee when his king needed counsel or aid ?" He then began to speak, with the ready and distinct utterance of a general at the head of an army, ordering every motion for attack and defense, unmoved himself, and his own energy compelling obedience, and that cheerful obedience, from all who heard him. "Daughter," he said, "beat up Dame Jellicot. Let Phœbe rise, if she were dying, and secure doors and windows."

"That hath been done regularly since—we have been thus far honored," said his daughter, looking at the King ; "yet, let them go through the chambers once more." And Alice retired to give the orders, and presently returned.

The old knight proceeded, in the same decided tone of promptitude and despatch—"Which is your first stage ?"

"Gray's—Rothebury, by Henley, where Sir Thomas Acland and young Knolles are to have horses in readiness," said Albert ; "but how to get there with our weary cattle?"

"Trust me for that," said the knight ; and proceeding with the same tone of authority—"Your Majesty must instantly to Joceline's lodge," he said, "there are your horses and your means of flight. The secret places of this house, well managed, will keep the rebel dogs in play two or three hours good. Rochecliffe is, I fear, kidnapped, and his Independent hath betrayed him. Would I had judged the villain better! I would have struck him through at one of our trials of fence, with an unbated weapon, as Will says. But for your guide when on horseback, half a bowshot from Joceline's hut is that of old Martin the verdurer; he is a score of years older than I, but as fresh as an old oak; beat up his quarters, and let him ride with you for death and life. He will guide you to your relay, for no fox that ever earthed in the chase knows the country so well for seven leagues around."

"Excellent, my dearest father—excellent," said Albert; "I had forgot Martin the verdurer."

"Young men forget all," answered the knight. "Alas, that the limbs should fail, when the head which can best direct them—is come perhaps to its wisest!"

"But the tired horses," said the King; "could we not get fresh cattle?"

"Impossible at this time of night," answered Sir Henry; "but tired horses may do much with care and looking to.' He went hastily to the cabinet which stood in one of the oriel windows, and searched for something in the drawers, pulling out one after another.

"We lose time, father," said Albert, afraid that the intelligence and energy which the old man displayed had been but a temporary flash of the lamp, which was about to relapse into evening twilight.

"Go to, sir boy," said his father, sharply; "is it for thee to tax me in this presence? Know, that were the whole Roundheads that are out of Hell in present assemblage round Woodstock, I could send away the royal hope of England by a way that the wisest of them could never guess. Alice, my love, ask no questions, but speed to the kitchen, and fetch a slice or two of beef, or better of venison; cut them long, and thin, d'ye mark me——"

"This is wandering of the mind," said Albert, apart to the King. "We do him wrong, and your Majesty harm, to listen to him."

"I think otherwise," said Alice, "and I know my father better than you." So saying, she left the room, to fulfil her father's orders.

"I think so, too," said Charles. "In Scotland, the Presbyterian ministers, when thundering in their pulpits on my own sins and those of my house, took the freedom to call me to my face Jeroboam, or Rehoboam, or some such name, for following the advice of young counselors; odds-fish, I will take that of the graybeard for once, for never saw I more sharpness and decision than in the countenance of that noble old man."

By this time Sir Henry had found what he was seeking. "In this tin box," he said, "are six balls prepared of the most cordial spices, mixed with medicaments of the choicest and most invigorating quality. Given from hour to hour, wrapped in a covering of good beef or venison, a horse of spirit will not flag for five hours, at the speed of fifteen miles an hour; and, please God, the fourth of the time places your Majesty in safety; what remains may be useful on some future occasion. Martin knows how to administer them; and Albert's weary cattle shall be ready, if walked gently for ten minutes, in running to devour the way, as old Will says. Nay, waste not time in speech; your Majesty does me but too much honor in using what is your own. Now, see if the coast is clear, Albert, and let his Majesty set off instantly. We will play our parts but ill, if any take the chase after him for these two hours that are between night and day. Change dresses, as you proposed, in yonder sleeping-apartment; something may be made of that, too."

"But, good Sir Henry," said the King, "your zeal overlooks a principal point. I have, indeed, come from the under-keeper's hut you mention to this place, but it was by daylight, and under guidance: I shall never find my way thither in utter darkness and without a guide; I fear you must let the colonel go with me. And I entreat and command, you will put yourself to no trouble or risk to defend the house; only make what delay you can in showing its secret recesses."

"Rely on me, my royal and liege sovereign," said Sir Henry; "but Albert *must* remain here, and Alice shall guide your Majesty to Joceline's hut in his stead."

"Alice!" said Charles, stepping back in surprise; "why, it is dark night—and—and—and——" He glanced his eye towards Alice, who had by this time returned to the apartment, and saw doubt and apprehension in her look—and intimation that the reserve under which he had placed his disposition for gallantry, since the morning of the proposed duel, had not altogether effaced the recollection of his previous conduct. He hastened to put a strong negative upon a proposal which appeared so much to embarrass her.

"It is impossible for me, indeed, Sir Henry, to use Alice's services: I must walk as if bloodhounds were at my heels!"

"Alice shall trip it," said the knight, "with any wench in Oxfordshire; and what would your Majesty's best speed avail, if you knew not the way to go?"

"Nay—nay, Sir Henry," continued the King, "the night is too dark—we stay too long—I will find it myself."

"Lose no time in exchanging your dress with Albert," said Sir Henry; "leave me to take care of the rest."

Charles still inclined to expostulate, withdrew, however, into the apartment where young Lee and he were to exchange clothes; while Sir Henry said to his daughter, "Get thee a cloak, wench, and put on thy thickest shoes. Thou mightst have ridden Pixie, but he is something spirited, and thou art a timid horsewoman, and ever wert so—the only weakness I have known of thee."

"But, my father," said Alice, fixing her eyes very earnestly on Sir Henry's face, "must I really go alone with the King? Might not Phœbe or Dame Jellicot go with us?"

"No—no—no," answered Sir Henry. "Phœbe, the silly slut, has, as you well know, been in fits to-night, and, I take it, such a walk as you must take is no charm for hysterics. Dame Jellicot hobbles as slow as a broken-winded mare; besides her deafness, were there occasion to speak to her. No—no, you shall go alone, and entitle yourself to have it written on your tomb, 'Here lies she who saved the King!' And, hark you, do not think of returning to-night, but stay at the verdurer's with his niece. The park and chase will shortly be filled with our enemies, and whatever chances here you will learn early enough in the morning."

"And what is it I may then learn?" said Alice. "Alas, who can tell? O, dearest father, let me stay and share your fate! I will pull off the timorous woman, and fight for the King, if it be necessary. But—I cannot think of becoming his only attendant in the dark night, and through a road so lonely."

"How!" said the knight, raising his voice; "do you bring ceremonious and silly scruples forward, when the King's safety, nay, his life, is at stake? By this mark of loyalty," stroking his gray beard as he spoke, "could I think thou wert other than becomes a daughter of the house of Lee, I would——"

At this moment the King and Albert interrupted him by entering the apartment, having exchanged dresses, and, from their stature, bearing some resemblance to each other, though Charles was evidently a plain and Lee a handsome young man. Their complexions were different; but the difference could not be immediately noticed, Albert having adopted a black peruke and darkened his eyebrows.

Albert Lee walked out to the front of the mansion, to give one turn around the lodge, in order to discover in what direction any enemies might be approaching, that they might judge of the road which it was safest for the royal fugitive to adopt. Meanwhile the King, who was first in entering the apartment, had heard a part of the angry answer which the old knight made to his daughter, and was at no loss to guess the subject of his resentment. He walked up to him with the dignity which he perfectly knew to assume when he chose it.

"Sir Henry," he said, "it is our pleasure, nay, our command, that you forbear all exertion of paternal authority in this matter. Mistress Alice, I am sure, must have good and strong reasons for what she wishes; and I should never pardon myself were she placed in an unpleasant situation on my account. I am too well acquainted with woods and wildernesses to fear losing my way among my native oaks of Woodstock."

"Your Majesty shall not incur the danger," said Alice, her temporary hesitation entirely removed by the calm, clear, and candid manner in which Charles uttered these last words. "You shall run no risk that I can prevent; and the unhappy chances of the times in which I have lived have from experience made the forest as well known to me by night as by day. So, if you scorn not my company, let us away instantly."

"If your company is given with good-will, I accept it with gratitude," replied the monarch.

"Willingly," she said—"most willingly. Let me be one of the first to show that zeal and that confidence which I trust all England will one day emulously display in behalf of your majesty."

"She uttered these words with an alacrity of spirit, and made the trifling change of habit with a speed and dexterity, which showed that all her fears were gone, and that her heart was entirely in the mission on which her father had despatched her.

"All is safe around," said Albert Lee, showing himself;

"you may take which passage you will—the most private is the best."

Charles went gracefully up to Sir Henry Lee ere his departure, and took him by the hand. "I am too proud to make professions," he said, "which I may be too poor ever to realize. But while Charles Stuart lives, he lives the obliged and indebted debtor of Sir Henry Lee."

"Say not so, please your Majesty—say not so," exclaimed the old man, struggling with the hysterical sobs which rose to his throat. "He who might claim all cannot become indebted by accepting some small part."

"Farewell, good friend—farewell!" said the King; "think of me as a son, a brother to Albert and to Alice, who are, I see, already impatient. Give me a father's blessing, and let me be gone."

"The God through whom kings reign bless your Majesty,' said Sir Henry, kneeling and turning his reverend face and clasped hands up to Heaven—"the Lord of Hosts bless you, and save your Majesty from your present dangers, and bring you in His own good time to the safe possession of the crown that is your due!"

Charles received his blessing like that of a father, and Alice and he departed on their journey.

As they left the apartment, the old knight let his hands sink gently as he concluded this fervent ejaculation, his head sinking at the same time. His son dared not disturb his meditation, yet feared the strength of his feelings might overcome that of his constitution, and that he might fall into a swoon. At length, he ventured to approach and gradually touch him. The old knight started to his feet, and was at once the same alert, active-minded, forecasting director which he had shown himself a little before.

"You are right, boy," he said, "we must be up and doing. They lie, the Roundheaded traitors, that call him dissolute and worthless! He hath feelings worthy the son of the blessed Martyr. You saw, even in the extremity of danger, he would have perilled his safety rather than take Alice's guidance, when the silly wench seemed in doubt about going. Profligacy is intensely selfish, and thinks not of the feelings of others. But hast thou drawn bolt and bar after them? I vow I scarce saw when they left the hall."

"I let them out at the little postern," said the colonel; "and when I returned, I was afraid I had found you ill."

"Joy—joy—only joy, Albert. I cannot allow a thought of doubt to cross my breast. God will not desert the descendant of an hundred kings: the rightful heir will not be given up to the ruffians. There was a tear in his eye as he took leave of me, I am sure of it. Wouldst not die for him, boy?"

"If I lay my life down for him to-night," said Albert, "I would only regret it because I should not hear of his escape to-morrow."

"Well, let us to this gear," said the knight; "think'st thou that thou know'st enough of his manner, clad as thou art in his dress, to induce the women to believe thee to be the page, Kerneguy."

"Umph," replied Albert, "it is not easy to bear out a personification of the King when women are in the case. But there is only a very little light below, and I can try."

"Do so instantly," said his father; "the knaves will be here presently."

Albert accordingly left the apartment, while the knight continued—"If the women be actually persuaded that Kerneguy is still here, it will add strength to my plot: the beagles will open on a false scent, and the royal stag be safe in cover ere they regain the slot of him. Then to draw them on from hiding-place to hiding-place! Why, the east will be gray before they have sought the half of them. Yes, I will play at bob-cherry with them, hold the bait to their nose which they are never to gorge upon. I will drag a trail for them which will take them some time to puzzle out. But at what cost do I do this?" continued the old knight interrupting his own joyous soliloquy. "Oh, Absalom—Absalom, my son—my son! But let him go; he can but die as his fathers have died, and in the cause for which they lived. But he comes. Hush! Albert, hast thou succeeded? hast thou taken royalty upon thee so as to pass current?"

"I have, sir," replied Albert; "the women will swear that Louis Kerneguy was in the house this very last minute."

"Right, for they are good and faithful creatures," said the knight, "and would swear what for his Majesty's safety at any rate; yet they will do it with more nature and effect, if they believe they are swearing truth. How didst thou impress the deceit upon them?"

"By a trifling adoption of the royal manner, sir, not worth mentioning."

"Out, rogue!" replied the knight. "I fear the King's character will suffer under your mummery."

"Umph," said Albert, muttering what he dared not utter aloud, "were I to follow the example close up, I know whose character would be in the greatest danger."

"Well, now we must adjust the defense of the outworks, the signals, etc., betwixt us both, and the best way to baffle the enemy for the longest time possible." He then again had recourse to the secret drawers of his cabinet, and pulled out a piece of parchment, on which was a plan. "This," said he, "is a scheme of the citadel, as I call it, which may hold out long enough after you have been forced to evacuate the places of retreat you are already acquainted with. The ranger was always sworn to keep this plan secret, save from one person only, in case of sudden death. Let us sit down and study it together."

They accordingly adjusted their measures in a manner which will better show itself from what afterwards took place than were we to state the various schemes which they proposed, and provisions made against events that did not arrive.

At length young Lee, armed and provided with some food and liquor, took leave of his father, and went and shut himself up in Victor Lee's apartment, from which was an opening to the labyrinth of private apartments, or hiding-places, that had served the associates so well in the fantastic tricks which they had played off at the expense of the Commissioners of the Commonwealth.

"I trust," said Sir Henry, sitting down by his desk, after having taken a tender farewell of his son, "that Rochecliffe has not blabbed out the secret of the plot to yonder fellow Tomkins, who was not unlikely to prate it out of school. But here am I seated, perhaps for the last time, with my Bible on the one hand and old Will on the other, prepared, thank God to die as I have lived. I marvel they come not yet," he said, after waiting for some time: "I always thought the devil had a smarter spur to give his agents, when they were upon his own special service."

CHAPTER XXXIII

But, see, his face is black, and full of blood;
His eyeballs further out than when he lived,
Staring full ghastly like a strangled man;
His hair uprear'd, his nostrils stretch'd with struggling;
His hands abroad display'd, as one who grasp'd
And tugg'd for life, but was by strength subdued.
Henry VI., Part II.

HAD those whose unpleasant visit Sir Henry expected come straight to the lodge, instead of staying for three hours at Woodstock, they would have secured their prey. But the Familist, partly to prevent the King's escape, partly to render himself of more importance in the affair, had represented the party at the lodge as being constantly on the alert, and had therefore inculcated upon Cromwell the necessity of his remaining quiet until he (Tomkins) should appear to give him notice that the household were retired to rest. On this condition he undertook, not only to discover the apartment in which the unfortunate Charles slept, but, if possible, to find some mode of fastening the door on the outside, so as to render flight impossible. He had also promised to secure the key of a postern, by which the soldiers might be admitted into the house without exciting alarm. Nay, the matter might, by means of his local knowledge, be managed, as he represented it, with such security, that he would undertake to place his Excellency, or whomsoever he might appoint for the service, by the side of Charles Stuart's bed, ere he had slept off the last night's claret. Above all, he had stated that, from the style of the old house, there were many passages and posterns which must be carefully guarded, before the least alarm was caught by those within, otherwise the success of the whole enterprise might be endangered. He had therefore besought Cromwell to wait for him at the village, if he found him not there on his arrival; and assured him that the marching and countermarching of soldiers was at present so common, that, even if any news were carried to the lodge that fresh troops had arrived in the borough, so ordinary a circumstance would not give them the least alarm. He recommended that the soldiers chosen for this service should be such as could be depended upon—no fainters in spirit—none who turn back from Mount Gilead for fear of the Amalekites, but men of war, accustomed to strike with the sword, and to need no second blow. Finally, he represented that it would be wisely done if the General should put Pearson, or any other officer whom he could completely trust, into the command of the detachment, and keep his own person, if he should think it proper to attend, secret even from the soldiers.

All this man's counsels Cromwell had punctually followed. He had traveled in the van of this detachment of one hundred picked soldiers whom he had selected for the service—men of dauntless resolution, bred in a thousand dangers, and who were steeled against all feelings of hesitation and compassion by the deep and gloomy fanaticism which was their chief principle of action—men to whom, as their general, and no less as the chief among the elect, the commands of Oliver were like a commission from the Deity.

Great and deep was the General's mortification at the unexpected absence of the personage on whose agency he so confidently reckoned, and many conjectures he formed as to the cause of such mysterious conduct. Sometimes he thought Tomkins had been overcome by liquor, a frailty to which Cromwell knew him to be addicted; and when he held this opinion, he discharged his wrath in maledictions, which, of a different kind from the wild oaths and curses of the Cavaliers, had yet in them as much blasphemy, and more determined malevolence. At other times he thought some unexpected alarm, or perhaps some drunken Cavalier revel, had caused the family of Woodstock Lodge to make later hours than usual. To this conjecture, which appeared the most probable of any, his mind often recurred; and it was the hope that Tomkins would still appear at the rendezvous which induced him to remain at the borough, anxious to receive communication from his emissary, and afraid of endangering the success of the enterprise by any premature exertion on his own part.

In the meantime, Cromwell, finding it no longer possible to conceal his personal presence, disposed of everything so as to be ready at a minute's notice. Half his soldiers he caused to dismount, and had the horses put into quarters; the other half were directed to keep their horses saddled, and themselves ready to mount at an instant's warning. The men were brought into the house by turns, and had some refreshment, leaving a sufficient guard on the horses, which was changed from time to time.

Thus Cromwell waited with no little uncertainty, often casting an anxious eye upon Colonel Everard, who, he suspected, could, if he chose it, well supply the place of his absent confidant. Everard endured this calmly, with unaltered countenance, and brow neither ruffled nor dejected.

Midnight at length tolled, and it became necessary to take some decisive step. Tomkins might have been treacherous; or, a suspicion which approached more near to the reality, his intrigue might have been discovered, and he himself murdered, or kidnapped, by the vengeful Royalists. In a word, if any use was to be made of the chance which fortune afforded of securing the most formidible claimant of the supreme power, which he already aimed at, no farther time was to be lost. He at length gave orders to Pearson to get the men under arms; he directed him concerning the mode of forming them, and that they should march with the utmost possible silence; or, as it was given out in the orders, "Even as Gideon marched in silence, when he went down against the camp of the Midianites, with only Phurah his servant. Peradventure," continued this strange document, "we too may learn of what yonder Midianites have dreamed."

A single patrol, followed by a corporal and five steady, experienced soldiers, formed the advanced guard of the party; then followed the main body. A rear-guard of ten men guarded Everard and the minister. Cromwell required the attendance of the former, as it might be necessary to examine him, or confront him with others; and he carried Master Holdenough with him, because he might escape if left behind, and perhaps raise some tumult in the village. The Presbyterians, though they not only concurred with, but led the way in, the civil war, were at its conclusion highly dissatisfied with the ascendency of the military sectaries, and not to be trusted as cordial agents in anything where their interest was concerned. The infantry, being disposed of as we have noticed, marched off from the left of their line, Cromwell and Pearson, both on foot, keeping at the head of the center or main body of the detachment. They were all armed with petronels, short guns similar to the modern carabine, and, like them, used by horsemen. They marched in the most profound silence and with the utmost regularity, the whole body moving like one man.

About one hundred yards behind the rearmost of the

dismounted party came the troopers who remained on horseback, and it seemed as if even the irrational animals were sensible to Cromwell's orders, for the horses did not neigh, and even appeared to place their feet on the earth cautiously, and with less noise than usual.

Their leader, full of anxious thoughts, never spoke, save to enforce by whispers his caution respecting silence, while the men, surprised and delighted to find themselves under the command of their renowned General, and destined, doubtless, for some secret service of high import, used the utmost precaution in attending to his reiterated orders.

They marched down the street of the little borough in the order we have mentioned. Few of the townsmen were abroad; and one or two who had protracted the orgies of the evening to that unusual hour were too happy to escape the notice of a strong party of soldiers, who often acted in the character of police, to inquire about their purpose for being under arms so late, or the route which they were pursuing.

The external gate of the chase had, ever since the party had arrived at Woodstock, been strictly guarded by three file of troopers, to cut off all communication between the lodge and the town. Spitfire, Wildrake's emissary, who had often been a-birdnesting, or on similar mischievous excursions, in the forest, had evaded these men's vigilance by climbing over a breach, with which he was well acquainted, in a different part of the wall.

Between this party and the advanced guard of Cromwell's detachment a whispered challenge was exchanged, according to the rules of discipline. The infantry entered the park, and were followed by the cavalry, who were directed to avoid the hard road, and ride as much as possible upon the turf, which bordered on the avenue. Here, too, an additional precaution was used, a file or two of foot soldiers being detached to search the woods on either hand, and make prisoner, or, in the event of resistance, put to death, any whom they might find lurking there, under what pretense soever.

Meanwhile the weather began to show itself as propitious to Cromwell as he had found most incidents in the course of his successful career. The gray mist, which had hitherto obscured everything, and rendered marching in the wood embarrassing and difficult, had now given way to the moon, which, after many efforts, at length forced her way through the vapor, and hung her dim dull cresset in the heavens, which she enlightened, as the dying lamp of an anchorite does the cell in which he reposes. The party were in sight of the front of the palace, when Holdenough whispered to Everard, as they walked near each other—"See ye not—yonder flutters the mysterious light in the turret of the incontinent Rosamond? This night will try whether the devil of the sectaries or the devil of the Malignants shall prove the stronger. O, sing jubilee, for the kingdom of Satan is divided against itself!"

Here the divine was interrupted by a non-commissioned officer, who came hastily, yet with noiseless steps, to say, in a low stern whisper—"Silence, prisoner in the rear—silence, on pain of death."

A moment afterwards the whole party stopped their march, the word "halt" being passed from one to another, and instantly obeyed.

The cause of this interruption was the hasty return of one of the flanking party to the main body, bringing news to Cromwell that they had seen a light in the wood at some distance on the left.

"What can it be?" said Cromwell, his low stern voice, even in a whisper, making itself distinctly heard. "Does it move, or is it stationary?"

"So far as we can judge, it moveth not," answered the trooper. "Strange—there is no cottage near the spot where it is seen."

"So please your Excellency, it may be a device of Sathan," said Corporal Humgudgeon, snuffling through his nose; "he is mighty powerful in these parts of late."

"So please your idiocy, thou art an ass," said Cromwell; but, instantly recollecting that the corporal had been one of the adjutators or tribunes of the common soldiers, and was therefore to be treated with suitable respect, he said, "Nevertheless, if it be the device of Satan, please it the Lord we will resist him, and the foul slave shall fly from us. Pearson," he said, resuming his soldier-like brevity, "take four file, and see what is yonder. No—the knaves may shrink from thee. Go thou straight to the lodge; invest it in the way we agree, so that a bird shall not escape out of it; form an outer and an inward ring of sentinels, but give no alarm until I come. Snould any attempt to escape, KILL them." He spoke that command with terrible emphasis. "Kill them on the spot," he repeated, "be they who or what they will. Better so than trouble the Commonwealth with prisoners."

Pearson heard, and proceeded to obey his commander's orders.

Meanwhile, the future Protector disposed the small force which remained with him in such a manner that they should approach from different points at once the light which excited his suspicions, and gave them orders to creep as near to it as they could, taking care not to lose each other's support, and to be ready to rush in at the same moment when he should give the sign, which was to be a loud whistle. Anxious to ascertain the truth with his own eyes, Cromwell, who had by instinct all the habits of military foresight which, in others, are the result of professional education and long experience, advanced upon the object of his curiosity. He skulked from tree to tree with the light step and prowling sagacity of an Indian bush-fighter; and before any of his men had approached so near as to descry them, he saw, by the lantern which was placed on the ground, two men, who had been engaged in digging what seemed to be an ill-made grave. Near them lay extended something wrapped in a deer's hide, which greatly resembled the dead body of a man. They spoke together in a low voice, yet so that their dangerous auditor could perfectly overhear what they said.

"It is done at last," said one—"the worst and hardest labor I ever did in my life. I believe there is no luck about me left. My very arms feel as if they did not belong to me; and, strange to tell, toil as hard as I would, I could not gather warmth in my limbs."

"I have warmed me enough," said Rochecliffe, breathing short with fatigue.

"But the cold lies at my heart," said Joceline; "I scarce hope ever to be warm again. It is strange, and a charm seems to be on us. Here have we been nigh two hours in doing what Diggen the sexton would have done to better purpose in half a one."

"We are wretched spademen enough," answered Doctor Rochecliffe. "Every man to his tools—thou to thy bugle-horn, and I to my papers in cipher. But do not be discouraged; it is the frost on the ground, and the number of roots which rendered our task difficult. And now, all due rites done to this unhappy man, and having read over him the service of the church, *valeat quantum*, let us lay him decently in this place of last repose; there will be small lack of him above ground. So cheer up thy head, man, like a soldier as thou art; we have read the service over his body, and should times permit it, we will have him removed to consecrated ground, though he is all unworthy of such favor. Here, help me to lay him on the earth ; we will drag briers and thorns over the spot when we have shoveled dust upon dust and do thou think of this chance more manfully ; and remember, thy secret is in thine own keeping."

"I cannot answer for that," said Joceline. "Methinks the very night winds among the leaves will tell of what we have been doing ; methinks the trees themselves will say, 'There is a dead corpse lies among our roots.' Witnesses are soon found when blood hath been spilled."

"They are so, and that right early," exclaimed Cromwell, starting from the thicket, laying hold on Joceline, and putting a pistol to his head. At any other period of his life, the forester would, even against the odds of numbers, have made a desperate resistance ; but the horror he had felt at the slaughter of an old companion, although in defense of his own life, together with fatigue and surprise, had altogether unmanned him, and he was seized as easily as a sheep is secured by the butcher. Doctor Rochecliffe offered some resistance, but was presently secured by the soldiers who pressed around him.

"Look, some of you," said Cromwell, "what corpse this is upon whom these lewd sons of Belial have done a murder. Corporal Grace-be-here Humgudgeon, see if thou knowest the face."

"I profess I do, even as I should do mine own in a mirror," snuffled the corporal, after looking on the countenance of the dead man by the help of the lantern. "Of a verity it is our trusty brother in the faith, Joseph Tomkins."

"Tomkins !" exclaimed Cromwell, springing forward and satisfying himself with a glance at the features of the corpse —"Tomkins ! and murdered, as the fracture of the temple intimates ! Dogs that ye are, confess the truth. You have murdered him because you have discovered his treachery—I should say his true spirit towards the Commonwealth of England, and his hatred of those complots in which you would have engaged his honest simplicity."

"Ay," said Grace-be-here Hungudgeon, "and then to misuse his dead body with your Papistical doctrines, as if you had crammed cold porridge into its cold mouth. I pray thee, General, let these men's bonds be made strong."

"Forbear, corporal," said Cromwell ; "our time presses. Friend, to you, whom I believe to be Doctor Anthony

[Albany] Rochecliffe by name and surname, I have to give the choice of being hanged at daybreak to-morrow, or making atonement for the murder of one of the Lord's people by telling what thou knowest of the secrets which are in yonder house."

"Truly, sir," replied Rocheliffe, "you found me but in my duty as a clergyman interring the dead; and respecting answering your questions, I am determined myself, and do advise my fellow-sufferer on this occasion——"

"Remove him," said Cromwell; "I know his stiffneckedness of old, though I have made him plow in my furrow, when he thought he was turning up his own swathe. Remove him to the rear, and bring hither the other fellow. Come thou here—this way—closer—closer. Corporal Grace-be-here, do thou keep thy hand upon the belt with which he is bound. We must take care of our life for the sake of this distracted country, though, lack-a-day, for its own proper worth we could peril it for a pin's point. Now, mark me, fellow, choose betwixt buying thy life by a full confession or being tucked presently up to one of these old oaks. How likest thou that?"

"Truly, master," answered the under-keeper, affecting more rusticity than was natural to him, for his frequent intercourse with Sir Henry Lee had partly softened and polished his manners, "I think the oak is like to bear a lusty acorn, that is all."

"Dally not with me, friend," continued Oliver; "I profess to thee in sincerity I am no trifler. What guests have you seen at yonder house called the lodge?"

"Many a brave guest in my day, I'se warrant ye, master," said Joceline. "Ah, to see how the chimneys used to smoke some twelve years back! Ah, sir, a sniff of it would have dined a poor man."

"Out, rascal!" said the General, "dost thou jeer me? Tell me at once what guests have been of late in the lodge; and look thee, friend, be assured that, in rendering me this satisfaction, thou shalt not only rescue thy neck from the halter, but render also an acceptable service to the state, and one which I will see fittingly rewarded. For, truly, I am not of those who would have the rain fall only on the proud and stately plants, but rather would, so far as my poor wishes and prayers are concerned, that it should also fall upon the lowly and humble grass and corn, that the heart of the husbandman may be rejoiced, and that, as the cedar of Lebanon waxes in its height, in its boughs, and in its roots, so may the humble and lowly hyssop that groweth upon the walls flourish, and—and, truly—— Understand'st thou me, knave?"

"Not entirely, if it please your honor," said Joceline; "but it sounds as if you were preaching a sermon, and has a marvelous twang of doctrine with it."

"Then, in one word, thou knowest there is one Louis Kerneguy, or Carnego, or some such name, in hiding at the lodge yonder?"

"Nay, sir," replied the under-keeper, "there have been many coming and going since Worcester field; and how should I know who they are? My service is out of doors, I trow."

"A thousand pounds," said Cromwell, "do I tell down to thee, if thou canst place that boy in my power."

"A thousand pounds is a marvelous matter, sir," said Joceline; "but I have more blood on my hand than I like already. I know not how the price of life may thrive; and, 'scape or hang, I have no mind to try."

"Away with him to the rear," said the General; and let him not speak with his yoke-fellow yonder. Fool that I am, to waste time in expecting to get milk from mules. Move on towards the lodge."

They moved with the same silence as formerly, notwithstanding the difficulties which they encountered from being unacquainted with the road and its various intricacies. At length they were challenged, in a low voice, by one of their own sentinels, two concentric circles of whom had been placed around the lodge, so close to each other as to preclude the possibility of an individual escaping from within. The outer guard was maintained partly by horse upon the roads and open lawn, and where the ground was broken and bushy by infantry. The inner circle was guarded by foot soldiers only. The whole were in the highest degree alert, expecting some interesting and important consequences from the unusual expedition on which they were engaged.

"Any news, Pearson?" said the General to his aid-de-camp, who came instantly to report to his superior.

He received for answer, "None."

Cromwell led his officer forward just opposite to the door of the lodge, and there paused betwixt the circles of guards, so that their conversation could not be overheard.

He then pursued his inquiry, demanding—"Were there any lights, any appearance of stirring—any attempt at sally—any preparation for defense?"

"All as silent as the valley of the shadow of death, even as the vale of Jehosaphat."

"Pshaw! tell me not of Jehosaphat, Pearson," said Cromwell. "These words are good for others, but not for thee. Speak plainly, and like a blunt soldier as thou art. Each man hath his own mode of speech; and bluntness, not sanctity, is thine."

"Well, then, nothing has been stirring," said Pearson. "Yet peradventure——"

"Peradventure not me," said Cromwell, "or thou wilt tempt me to knock thy teeth out. I ever distrust a man when he speaks after another fashion from his own."

"Zounds! let me speak to an end," answered Pearson, "and I will speak in what language your Excellency will."

"Thy 'zounds,' friend," said Oliver, "showed little of grace, but much of sincerity. Go to, then—thou knowest I love and trust thee. Hast thou kept close watch? It behoves us to know that, before giving the alarm."

"On my soul," said Pearson, "I have watched as closely as a cat at a mouse-hole. It is beyond possibility that anything could have eluded our vigilance, or even stirred within the house, without our being aware of it."

"'Tis well," said Cromwell; "thy services shall not be forgotten, Pearson. Thou canst not preach and pray, but thou canst obey thine orders, Gilbert Pearson, and that may make amends."

"I thank your Excellency," replied Pearson; but I beg leave to chime in with the humors of the times. A poor fellow hath no right to hold himself singular."

He paused, expecting Cromwell's orders what next was to be done, and, indeed, not a little surprised that the General's active and prompt spirit had suffered him, during a moment so critical, to cast away a thought upon a circumstance so trivial as his officer's peculiar mode of expressing himself. He wondered still more when, by a brighter gleam of moonshine than he had yet enjoyed he observed that Cromwell was standing motionless, his hands supported upon his sword, which he had taken out of the belt, and his stern brows bent on the ground. He waited for some time impatiently, yet afraid to interfere, lest he should awaken this unwonted fit of ill-timed melancholy into anger and impatience. He listened to the muttering sounds which escaped from the half-opening lips of his principal, in which the words "hard necessity," which occurred more than once, were all of which the sense could be distinguished. "My Lord General," at length he said, "time flies."

"Peace, busy fiend, and urge me not!" said Cromwell. "Think'st thou like other fools, that I have made a paction with the Devil for success, and am bound to do my work within an appointed hour, lest the spell should lose its force?"

"I only think, my Lord General," said Pearson, "that Fortune has put into your offer what you have long desired to make prize of, and that you hesitate."

Cromwell sighed deeply as he answered, "Ah, Pearson, in this troubled world a man who is called, like me, to work great things in Israel had need to be, as the poets feign, a thing made of hardened metal, immovable to feelings of human charities, impassible, resistless. Pearson, the world will hereafter, perchance, think of me as being such a one as I have described, 'an iron man, and made of iron mold.' Yet they will wrong my memory: my heart is flesh, and my blood is mild as that of others. When I was a sportsman, I have wept for the gallant heron that was struck down by my hawk, and sorrowed for the hare which lay screaming under the jaws of my greyhound; and canst thou think it a light thing to me that, the blood of this lad's father lying in some measure upon my head, I should now put in peril that of the son? They are of the kindly race of English sovereigns, and, doubtless, are adored like to demigods by those of their own party. I am called 'parricide,' 'bloodthirsty usurper,' already for shedding the blood of one man, that the plague might be stayed; or as Achan was slain that Israel might thereafter stand against the face of their enemies. Nevertheless, who has spoke unto me graciously since that high deed? Those who acted in the matter with me are willing that I should be the scapegoat of atonement; those who looked on and helped not bear themselves now as if they had been born down by violence; and while I looked that they should shout applause on me, because of the victory of Worcester, whereof the Lord had made me the poor instrument, they look aside and say, 'Ha! ha! the king-killer, the parricide—soon shall his place be made desolate.' Truly it is a great thing, Gilbert Pearson, to be lifted above the multitude; but when one feeleth that his exaltation is rather hailed with hate and scorn than with love and reverence, in sooth, it is still a hard matter for a mild, tender-conscienced, infirm spirit to bear; and God be my witness that, rather than do this new deed, I would shed my own best heart's-blood in a pitched-field, twenty against one." Here he fell into a flood of tears, which he sometimes was wont to do. This extremity of emotion was of a singular character. It was not actually the result of penitence, and far less that of absolute hypocrisy, but arose merely from the temperature of that remarkable man, whose deep policy and ardent enthusiasm were intermingled with a strain of hypochondriacal passion, which often led him to exhibit scenes of this sort, though seldom, as now, when he was called to the execution of great undertakings.

Pearson, well acquainted as he was with the peculiarities of his General, was baffled and confounded by this fit of hesitation and contrition, by which his enterprising spirit appeared to be so suddenly paralyzed. After a moment's silence he said, with some dryness of manner, "If this be the case, its a pity your Excellency came hither. Corporal Humgudgeon and I, the greatest saint and greatest sinner in your army, had done the deed and divided the guilt and the honor betwixt us."

"Ha!" said Cromwell, as if touched to the quick, "wouldst thou take the prey from the lion?"

"If the lion behaves like a village cur," said Pearson, boldly, "who now barks and seems as if he would tear all to pieces, and now flies from a raised stick or a stone, I know not why I should fear him. If Lambert had been here, there had been less speaking and more action."

"Lambert! What of Lambert?" said Cromwell, very sharply.

"Only," said Pearson, "that I long since hesitated whether I should follow your Eacellency or him, and I begin to be uncertain whether I have made the best choice, that's all."

"Lambert!" exclaimed Cromwell, impatiently, yet softening his voice lest he should be overheard descanting on the character of his rival. "What is Lambert? a tulip-fancying fellow, whom nature intended for a Dutch gardener at Delft or Rotterdam. Ungrateful as thou art, what could Lambert have done for thee?"

"He would not," answered Pearson, "have stood here hesitating before a locked door, when Fortune presented the means of securing, by one blow, his own fortune and that of all who followed him."

"Thou art right, Gilbert Pearson," said Cromwell, grasping his officer's hand and strongly pressing it. "Be the half of this bold accompt thine, whether the reckoning be on earth or heaven."

"Be the whole of it mine hereafter," said Pearson, hardily, "so your Excellency have the advantage of it upon earth. Step back to the rear till I force the door: there may be danger, if despair induce them to make a desperate sally."

"And if they do sally, is there one of my Ironsides who fears fire or steel less than myself?" said the General. "Let ten of the most determined men follow us, two with halberds, two with petronels, the others with pistols. Let all their arms be loaded, and fire without hesitation, if there is any attempt to resist or to sally forth. Let Corporal Humgudgeon be with them, and do thou remain here, and watch against escape, as thou wouldst watch for thy salvation."

The General then struck at the door with the hilt of his sword—at first with a single blow or two, then with a reverberation of strokes that made the ancient building ring again. This noisy summons was repeated once or twice without producing the least effect.

"What can this mean?" said Cromwell; "they cannot surely have fled, and left the house empty?"

"No," replied Pearson, "I will ensure you against that; but your Excellency strikes so fiercely, you allow no time for an answer. Hark! I hear the baying of a hound, and the voice of a man who is quieting him. Shall we break in at once or hold parley?"

"I will speak to them first," said Cromwell. "Halloo! who is within there?"

"Who is it inquires?" answered Sir Henry Lee from the interior; "or what want you here at this dead hour?"

"We come by warrant of the Commonwealth of England," said the General.

"I must see your warrant ere I undo either bolt or latch," replied the knight, "we are enough of us to make good the castle; neither I nor my fellows will deliver it up but upon good quarter and conditions, and we will not treat for these save in fair daylight."

"Since you will not yield to our right, you must try our might," replied Cromwell. "Look to yourselves within, the door will be in the midst of you in five minutes."

"Look to yourselves without," replied the stout-hearted Sir Henry; "we will pour our shot upon you if you attempt the least violence."

But, alas! while he assumed this bold language, his whole garrison consisted of two poor terrified women; for his son, in conformity with the plan which they had fixed upon, had withdrawn from the hall into the secret recesses of the palace.

"What can they be doing now, sir?" said Phœbe, hearing a noise as it were of a carpenter turning, screw-nails, mixed with a low buzz of men talking,

"They are fixing a petard," said the knight, with great composure. "I have noted thee for a clever wench, Phœbe, and I will explain it to thee: 'tis a metal pot, shaped much like one of the roguish knaves' own sugar-loaf hats, supposing it had narrower brims; it is charged with some few pounds of fine gunpowder. Then——"

"Gracious! we shall be all blown up!" exclaimed Phœbe, the word "gunpowder" being the only one which she understood in the knight's description.

"Not a bit, foolish girl. Pack old Dame Jellicot into the embrasure of yonder window," said the knight, "on that side of the door, and we will ensconce ourselves on this, and we shall have time to finish my explanatiion, for they have bungling engineers. We had a clever French fellow at Newark would have done the job in the firing of a pistol."

They had scarce got into the place of security when the knight proceeded with his description. "The petard being formed, as I tell you, is secured with a thick and strong piece of plank, termed the madrier, and the whole being suspended, or rather secured, against the gate to be forced—— But thou mindest me not?"

"How can I, Sir Henry," she said, "within reach of such a thing as you speak of? O Lord! I shall go mad with very terror; we shall be crushed—blown up—in a few minutes!"

"We are secure from the explosion," replied the knight, gravely, "which will operate chiefly in a forward direction into the middle of the chamber; and from any fragments that may fly laterally, we are sufficiently secured by this deep embrasure."

"But they will slay us when they enter," said Phœbe.

"They will give thee fair quarter, wench," said Sir Henry; "and if I do not bestow a brace of balls on that rogue engineer, it is because I would not incur the penalty inflicted by martial law, which condemns to the edge of the sword all persons who attempt to defend an untenable post. Not that I think the rigor of the law could reach Dame Jellicot or thyself, Phœbe, considering that you carry no arms. If Alice had been here she might indeed have done somewhat, for she can use a birding-piece."

Phœbe might have appealed to her own deeds of the day, as more allied to feats of *mêlée* and battle than any which her young lady ever acted; but she was in an agony of inexpressible terror, expecting, from the knight's account of the petard, some dreadful catastrophe, of what nature she did not justly understand, notwithstanding his liberal communication on the subject.

"They are strangely awkward at it," said Sir Henry: "little Boutirlin would have blown the house up before now. Ah! he is a fellow would take the earth like a rabbit; if he had been here, never may I stir but he would have countermined them ere now, and

> 'Tis sport to have the engineer
> Hoist with his own petard,

as our immortal Shakspeare has it."

"Oh, lord, the poor mad old gentleman," thought Phœbe. "Oh, sir, had you not better leave alone play-books, and think of your end?" uttered she aloud, in sheer terror and vexation of spirit.

"If I had not made up my mind to that many days since," answered the knight, "I had not now met this hour with a free bosom.

> As gentle and as jocund as to rest,
> Go I to death: truth hath a quiet breast."

As he spoke, a broad glare of light flashed from without through the windows of the hall, and betwixt the strong iron stanchions with which they were secured—a broad discolored light it was, which shed a red dusky illumination on the old armor and weapons, as if it had been the reflection of a conflagration. Phœbe screamed aloud, and, forgetful of reverence in the moment of passion, clung close to the knight's cloak and arm, while Dame Jellicot, from her solitary niche, having the use of her eyes, though bereft of her hearing, yelled like an owl when the moon breaks out suddenly.

"Take care, good Phœbe," said the knight; "you will prevent my using my weapon if you hang upon me thus. The bungling fools cannot fix their petard without the use of torches! Now let me take the advantage of this interval. Remember what I told thee, and how to put off time."

"Oh, Lord—ay, sir," said Phœbe, "I will say anything. Oh, Lord, that it were but over! Ah! ah! (two prolonged screams)—I hear something hissing like a serpent."

"It is the fusee, as we martialists call it," replied the knight; "that is, Phœbe, the match which fires the petard, and which is longer or shorter, according to the distance——"

Here the knight's discourse was cut short by a dreadful explosion, which, as he had foretold, shattered the door, strong as it was, to pieces, and brought down the glass clattering from the windows, with all the painted heroes and heroines who had been recorded on that fragile place of memory for centuries. The women shrieked incessantly, and were answered by the bellowing of Bevis, though shut up at a distance from the scene of action. The knight, shaking Phœbe from him with difficulty, advanced into the hall to meet those who rushed in, with torches lighted and weapons prepared.

"Death to all who resist—life to those who surrender!" exclaimed Cromwell, stamping with his foot. "Who commands this garrison?"

"Sir Henry Lee of Ditchley," answered the old knight, stepping forward, "who, having no other garrison than two weak women, is compelled to submit to what he would willingly have resisted.',

"Disarm the inveterate and malignant rebel," cried Oliver. "Art thou not ashamed, sir, to detain me before the door of a house which you had no force to defend? Wearest thou so white a beard, and knowest thou not that to refuse surrendering an indefensible post, by the martial law, deserves hanging?"

"My beard and I," said Sir Henry, "have settled that matter between us, and agree right cordially. It is better to run the risk of being hanged like honest men than to give up our trust like cowards and traitors."

"Ha! say'st thou?" said Cromwell; "thou hast powerful motives, I doubt not, for running thy head into a noose. But I will speak with thee by and by. Ho! Pearson—Gilbert Pearson, take this scroll. Take the elder woman with thee—let her guide you to the various places therein mentioned. Search every room therein set down, and arrest, or slay upon the slightest resistance, whomsoever you find there. Then note those places marked as commanding points for cutting off interconrse through the mansion, the landing places of the great staircase, the great gallery, and so forth. Use the woman civilly. The plan annexed to the scroll will point out the posts, even if she prove stupid or refractory. Meanwhile, the corporal, with a party, will bring the old man and the girl there to some apartment—the parlor, I think, called Victor Lee's, will do as well as another. We will then be out of this stifling smell of gunpowder."

So saying, and without requiring any farther assistance or guidance, he walked towards the apartment he had named. Sir Henry had his own feelings when he saw the unhesitating decision with which the General led the way, and which seemed to intimate a more complete acquaintance with the various localities of Woodstock than was consistent with his own present design, to engage the Commonwealth party in a fruitless search through the intricacies of the lodge.

"I will now ask thee a few questions, old man," said the General, when they had arrived in the room; "and I warn thee, that hope of pardon for thy many and persevering efforts against the Commonwealth can be no otherwise merited than by the most direct answers to the questiour I am about to ask."

Sir Henry bowed. He would have spoken, but he felt his temper rising high, and became afraid it might be exhausted before the part he had settled to play, in order to afford the King time for his escape, should be brought to an end.

"What household have you had here, Sir Henry Lee, within these few days—what guests—what visitors? We know that your means of housekeeping are not so profuse as usual, so the catalogue cannot be burdensome to your memory."

"Far from it," replied the knight, with unusual command of temper; "my daughter, and latterly my son, have been my guests; and I have had these females, and one Joceline Joliffe, to attend upon us."

"I do not ask after the regular members of your household, but after those who have been within your gates, either as guests or as Malignant fugitives taking shelter."

"There may have been more of both kinds, sir, than I, if it please your valor, am able to answer for," replied the knight. "I remember my kinsman Everard was here one morning; also, I bethink me, a follower of his, called Wildrake."

"Did you not also receive a young Cavalier called Louis Garnegey ?" said Comwell.

"I remember no such name, where I to hang for it," said the knight.

"Kerneguy, or some such word," said the General; "we will not quarrel for a sound."

"A Scotch lad, called Louis Kerneguy, was a guest of mine," said Sir Henry; "and left me this morning for Dorsetshire.

"So late !" exclaimed Cromwell, stamping with his foot. "How fate contrives to baffle us, even when she seems most favorable! What direction did he take, old man?" continued Cromwell—"what horse did he ride—who went with him?"

"My son went with him," replied the knight; "he brought him here as the son of a Scottish lord. I pray you, sir, to be finished with these questions; for although I owe thee, as Will Shakspeare says

> Respect for thy great place, and let the devil
> Be sometimes honor'd for his burning throne,

yet I feel my patience wearing thin."

Cromwell here whispered to the corporal, who in turn uttered orders to two soldiers, who left the room. "Place the knight aside; we will now examine the servant damsel," said the General. "Dost thou know," said he to Phœbe, "of the presence of one Louis Kerneguy, calling himself a Scotch page, who came here a few days since?"

"Surely, sir," she replied, "I cannot easily forget him; and I warrant no well-looking wench that comes in his way will be like to forget him either."

"Aha," said Cromwell, "sayst thou so? truly I believe the woman will prove the truer witness. When did he leave this house?"

"Nay, I know nothing of his movements, not I," said Phœbe: "I am only glad to keep out of his way. But if he have actually gone hence, I am sure he was here some two hours since, for he crossed me in the lower passage, between the hall and the kitchen."

"How did you know it was he?" demanded Cromwell.

"By a rude enough token," said Phœbe, "La, sir, you do ask such questions!" she added, hanging down her head,

Humgudgeon here interfered, taking upon himself the freedom of a coadjutor. "Verily," he said, "if what the damsel is called to speak upon hath aught unseemly, I crave your Excellency's permission to withdraw, not desiring that my nightly meditations may be disturbed with tales of such a nature."

"Nay, your honor," said Phœbe, "I scorn the old man's words, in the way of seemliness or unseemliness either. Master Louis did but snatch a kiss, that is the truth of it, if it must be told."

Here Humgudgeon groaned deeply, while his Excellency avoided laughing with some difficulty. "Thou hast given excellent tokens, Phœbe," he said; "and if they be true, as I think they seem to be, thou shalt not lack thy reward. And here comes our spy from the stables."

"There are not the least signs," said the trooper, "that horses have been in the stables for a month: there is no litter in the stalls, no hay in the racks, the corn-binns are empty, and the mangers are full of cobwebs."

"Ay—ay," said the old knight, "I have seen when I kept twenty good horses in these stalls, with many a groom and stable-boy to attend them."

"In the meanwhile," said Cromwell, "their present state tells little for the truth of your own story, that there were horses to-day, on which this Kerneguy and your son fled from justice."

"I did not say that the horses were kept there," said the knight. "I have horses and stables elsewhere."

"Fie—fie, for shame—for shame!" said the General; "can a white-bearded man, I ask it once more, be a false witness?"

"Faith, sir," said Sir Henry Lee, "it is a thriving trade, and I wonder not that you who live on it are so severe in prosecuting interlopers. But it is the times, and those who rule the times, that make graybeards deceivers."

"Thou art facetious, friend, as well as daring, in thy malignancy," said Cromwell; "but credit me, I will cry quittance with you ere I am done. Whereunto lead these doors?"

"To bedrooms," answered the knight.

"Bedrooms! only to bedrooms?" said the republican general, in a voice which indicated, such was the internal occupation of his thoughts, that he had not fully understood the answer.

"Lord, sir," said the knight, "why should you make it

so strange? I say these doors lead to bedrooms—to places where honest men sleep and rogues lie awake."

"You are running up a farther account, Sir Henry," said the General; "but we will balance it once and for all."

During the whole of the scene, Cromwell, whatever might be the internal uncertainty of his mind, maintained the most strict temperance in language and manner, just as if he had no farther interest in what was passing than as a military man employed in discharging the duty enjoined him by his superiors. But the restraint upon his passion was but

The torrent's smoothness ere it dash below.*

The course of his resolution was hurried on even more forcibly because no violence of expression attended or announced its current. He threw himself into a chair, with a countenance that indicated no indecision of mind, but a determination which awaited only the signal for action. Meanwhile the knight, as if resolved in nothing to forego the privileges of his rank and place, sat himself down in turn, and putting on his hat, which lay on a table, regarded the General with a calm look of fearless indifference. The soldiers stood around, some holding the torches, which illuminated the apartment with a lurid and somber glare of light, the others resting upon their weapons. Phœbe, with her hands folded, her eyes turned upwards till the pupils were scarce visible, and every shade of color banished from her ruddy cheek, stood like one in immediate apprehension of the sentence of death being pronounced and instant execution commanded.

Heavy steps were at last heard, and Pearson and some of the soldiers returned. This seemed to be what Cromwell waited for. He started up, and asked hastily, "Any news, Pearson? any prisoners—any Malignants slain in thy defense?"

"None, so please your Excellency," answered the officer.

"And are thy sentinels all carefully placed, as Tomkins's scroll gave direction, and with fitting orders?"

"With the most deliberate care," said Pearson.

"Art thou very sure," said Cromwell, pulling him a little to one side, "that this is all well and duly cared for? Bethink thee that, when we engage ourselves in the private

* But mortal pleasure, what art thou in truth?
The torrent's smoothness ere it dash below.
CAMPBELL'S *Gertrude of Wyoming.*

communications, all will be lost should the party we look for have the means of dodging us by an escape into the more open rooms, and from thence perhaps into the forest."

"My Lord General," answered Pearson, "if placing the guards on the places pointed out in this scroll be sufficient, with the strictest orders to stop, and, if necessary, to stab or shoot, whoever crosses their post, such orders are given to men who will not fail to execute them. If more is necessary, your Excellency has only to speak."

"No—no—no, Pearson," said the General, thou hast done well. This night over, and let it end but as we hope, thy reward shall not be awanting. And now to business. Sir Henry Lee, undo me the secret spring of yonder picture of your ancestor. Nay, spare yourself the trouble and guilt of falsehood or equivocation, and, I say, undo me that spring presently."

"When I acknowledge you for my master, and wear your livery, I may obey your commands," answered the knight; "even then I would need first to understand them."

"Wench," said Cromwell, addressing Phœbe, "go thou undo the spring; you could do it fast enough when you aided at the gambols of the demons of Woodstock, and terrified even Mark Everard, who, I judged, had more sense."

"Oh, Lord, sir, what shall I do?" said Phœbe, looking to the knight; "they konw all about it. What shall I do?"

"For thy life, hold out to the last, wench! Every minute is worth a million."

"Ha! heard you that, Pearson?" said Cromwell to the officer; then, stamping with his foot, he added, "Undo the spring, or I will else use levers and wrenching-irons. Or, ha! another petard were well bestowed. Call the engineer."

"Oh, Lord, sir," cried Phœbe, "I shall never live another peter: I will open the spring."

"Do as thou wilt," said Sir Henry; "it shall profit them but little."

Whether from real agitation or from a desire to gain time, Phœbe was some minutes ere she could get the spring to open; it was indeed secured with art, and the machinery on which it acted was concealed in the frame of the portrait. The whole, when fastened, appeared quite motionless, and betrayed, as when examined by Colonel Everard, no external mark of its being possible to remove it. It was now withdrawn, however, and showed a narrow recess, with steps which ascended on one side into the thickness of the wall.

Cromwell was now like a greyhound slipped from the leash with the prey in full view. "Up," he cried, "Pearson, thou art swifter than I. Up thou next, corporal." With more agility than could have been expected from his person or years, which were past the meridian of life, and exclaiming, "Before, those with the torches!" he followed the party, like an eager huntsman in the rear of his hounds, to encourage at once and direct them, as they penetrated into the labyrinth described by Doctor Rochecliffe in the *Wonders of Woodstock.*

CHAPTER XXXIV

The king, therefore, for his defense
  Against the furious queen,
At Woodstock builded such a bower
  As never yet was seen.
Most curiously that bower was built,
  Of stone and timber strong;
An hundred and fifty doors
  Did to this bower belong:
And they so cunningly contrived,
  With turnings around about,
That none but with a clew of thread
  Could enter in or out.

Ballad of Fair Rosamond.

THE tradition of the country, as well as some historical evidence, confirmed the opinion that there existed, within the old royal lodge at Woodstock, a labyrinth, or connected series of subterranean passages, built chiefly by Henry II. for the security of his mistress, Rosamond Clifford, from the jealousy of his queen, the celebrated Eleanor. Doctor Rochecliffe, indeed, in one of those fits of contradiction with which antiquaries are sometimes seized, was bold enough to dispute the alleged purpose of the perplexed maze of rooms and passages with which the walls of the ancient palace were perforated; but the fact was undeniable, that in raising the fabric some Norman architect had exerted the utmost of the complicated art which they have often shown elsewhere, in creating secret passages and chambers of retreat and concealment. There were stairs which were ascended merely, as it seemed, for the purpose of descending again; passages which, after turning and winding for a considerable way, returned to the place where they set out; there were trap-doors and hatchways, panels and portcullises. Although Oliver was assisted by a sort of ground-plan, made out and transmitted by Joseph Tomkins, whose former employment in Doctor Rochecliffe's service had made him fully acquainted with the place, it was found imperfect; and, moreover, the most serious obstacles to their progress occurred in the shape of strong doors, party-walls, and iron gates; so that the party blundered on in the dark, uncertain whether they were not going farther from, rather than approaching, the extremity of the labyrinth. They were obliged to send for mechanics, with sledge-hammers and other instruments, to force one or two of those doors, which resisted all other means of undoing them. Laboring along in these dusky passages, where, from time to time, they were like to be choked by the dust which their acts of violence excited, the soldiers were obliged to be relieved oftener than once, and the bulky Corporal Grace-be-here himself puffed and blew like a grampus that has got into shoal water. Cromwell alone continued, with unabated zeal, to push on his researches; to encourage the soldiers, by the exhortations which they best understood, against fainting for lack of faith; and to secure, by sentinels at proper places, possession of the ground which they had already explored. His acute and observing eye detected, with a sneering smile, the cordage and machinery by which the bed of poor Desborough had been inverted, and several remains of the various disguises, as well as private modes of access, by which Desborough, Bletson, and Harrison had been previously imposed upon. He pointed them out to Pearson, with no farther comment than was implied in the exclamation, "The simple fools!"

But his assistants began to lose heart and be discouraged, and required all his spirit to raise theirs. He then called their attention to voices which they seemed to hear before them, and urged these as evidence that they were moving on the track of some enemy of the Commonwealth, who, for the execution of his Malignant plots, had retreated into these extraordinary fastnesses.

The spirits of the men became at last downcast notwithstanding all this encouragement. They spoke to each other in whispers of the devils of Woodstock, who might be all the while decoying them forward to a room said to exist in the palace, where the floor, revolving on an axis, precipitated those who entered into a bottomless abyss. Humgudgeon hinted, that he had consulted the Scriptnre that morning by way of lot, and his fortune had been to alight on the passage, "Eutychus fell down from the third loft." The energy and authority of Cromwell, however, and the refreshment of some food and strong waters, reconciled them to pursuing their task.

Nevertheless, with all their unwearied exertions, morning dawned on the search before they had reached Doctor Rochecliffe's sitting-apartment, into which, after all, they obtained entrance by a mode much more difficult than that which the Doctor himself employed. But here their ingenuity was long at fault. From the miscellaneous articles that were strewed around, and the preparations made for food and lodging, it seemed they had gained the very citadel of the labyrinth; but though various passages opened from it, they all terminated in places with which they were already acquainted, or communicated with the other parts of the house, where their own sentinels assured them none had passed. Cromwell remained long in deep uncertainty. Meantime he directed Pearson to take charge of the ciphers and more important papers which lay on the table. "Though there is little there," he said, "that I have not already known, by means of Trusty Tomkins. Honest Joseph, for an artful and thorough-paced agent, the like of thee is not left in England."

After a considerable pause, during which he sounded with the pommel of his sword almost every stone in the building and every plank in the floor, the General gave orders to bring the old knight and Doctor Rochecliffe to the spot, trusting that he might work out of them some explanation of the secrets of this apartment.

"So please your Excellency to let me to deal with them," said Pearson, who was a true soldier of fortune, and had been a buccaneer in the West Indies, "I think that, by a whipcord twitched tight round their forehead, and twisted about with a pistol-butt, I could make either the truth start from their lips or the eyes from their heads."

"Out upon thee, Pearson!" said Cromwell, with abhorrence; "we have no warrant for such cruelty, neither as Englishmen nor Christians. We may slay Malignants as we crush noxious animals, but to torture them is a deadly sin; for it is written, 'He made them to be pitied of those who carried them captive.' Nay, I recall the order even for their examination, trusting that wisdom will be granted us without it, to discover their most secret devices."

There was a pause accordingly, during which an idea seized upon Cromwell's imagination. "Bring me hither," he said, "yonder stool"; and placing it beneath one of the windows, of which there were two so high in the wall as not to be accessible from the floor, he clambered up into the entrance of the window, which was six or seven feet deep, corresponding with the thickness of the wall. "Come up hither, Pearson," said the General; "but ere thou comest, double the guard at the foot of the turret called

Love's Ladder, and bid them bring up the other petard. So now, come thou hither."

The inferior officer, however brave in the field, was one of those whom a great height strikes with giddiness and sickness. He shrunk back from the view of the precipice, on the verge of which Cromwell was standing with complete indifference, till the General, catching the hand of his follower, pulled him forward as far as he would advance. "I think," said the General, "I have found the clue, but by this light it is no easy one. See you, we stand in the portal near the top of Rosamond's Tower; and yon turret which rises opposite to our feet is that which is called Love's Ladder, from which the drawbridge reached that admitted the profligate Norman tyrant to the bower of his mistress."

"True, my lord, but the drawbridge is gone," said Pearson.

"Ay, Pearson," replied the General; "but an active man might spring from the spot we stand upon to the battlements of yonder turret."

"I do not think so, my lord," said Pearson.

"What!" said Cromwell; "not if the avenger of blood were behind you, with his slaughter-weapon in his hand?"

"The fear of instant death might do much," answered Pearson; "but when I look at that sheer depth on either side, and at the empty chasm between us and yonder turret, which is, I warrant you, twelve feet distant, I confess the truth, nothing short of the most imminent danger should induce me to try. Pah, the thought makes my head grow giddy! I tremble to see your Highness stand there, balancing yourself as if you meditated a spring into the empty air. I repeat, I would scarce stand so near the verge as does your Highness, for the rescue of my life."

"Ah, base and degenerate spirit!" said the General—"soul of mud and clay, wouldst thou not do it, and much more, for the possession of empire? That is, peradventure," continued he, changing his tone as one who has said too much, "shouldst thou be called on to do this, that thereby becoming a great man in the tribes of Israel, thou mightest redeem the captivity of Jerusalem—ay, and it may be, work some great work for the afflicted people of this land?"

"Your Highness may feel such calls," said the officer; "but they are not for poor Gilbert Pearson, your faithful follower. You made a jest of me yesterday when I tried to speak your language; and I am no more able to fufil your designs than to use your mode of speech."

"But, Pearson," said Cromwell, "thou hast thrice, yea, four times, called me 'your Highness.'"

"Did I, my lord? I was not sensible of it. I crave your pardon," said the officer.

"Nay," said Oliver, "there was no offence. I do indeed stand high, and I may perchance stand higher, though, alas! it were fitter for a simple soul like me to return to my plow and my husbandry. Nevertheless, I will not wrestle against the Supreme will, should I be called on to do yet more in that worthy cause. For surely He who hath been to our British Israel as a shield of help and a sword of excellency, making her enemies be found liars unto her, will not give over the flock to those foolish shepherds of Westminster, who shear the sheep and feed them not, and who are in very deed hirelings, not shepherds."

"I trust to see your lordship quoit them all downstairs," answered Pearson. "But may I ask why we pursue this discourse even now, until we have secured the common enemy?"

"I will tarry no jot of time," said the General; "fence the communication of Love's Ladder, as it is called, below, as I take it for almost certain that the party whom we have driven from fastness to fastness during the night has at length sprung to the top of yonder battlements from the place where we now stand. Finding the turret is guarded below, the place he has chosen for his security will prove a rat-trap, from whence there is no returning."

"There is a cask of gunpowder in this cabinet," said Pearson; "were it not better, my lord, to mine the tower, if he will not render himself, and send the whole turret with its contents one hundred feet into the air?"

"Ah, silly man," said Cromwell, striking him familiarly on the shoulder, "if thou hadst done this without telling me, it had been good service. But we will first summon the turret, and then think whether the petard will serve our turn: it is but mining at last. Blow a summons there, down below."

The trumpets rang at his bidding, till the old walls echoed from every recess and vaulted archway. Cromwell, as if he cared not to look upon the person whom he expected to appear, drew back, like a necromancer afraid of the specter which he has evoked.

"He has come to the battlement," said Pearson to his General.

"In what dress or appearance?" answered Cromwell from within the chamber.

"A gray riding-suit, passmented with silver, russet walking-boots, a cut band, a gray hat and plume, black hair."

"It is he—it is he," said Cromwell, "and another crowning mercy is vouchsafed."

Meantime, Pearson and young Lee exchanged defiance from their respective posts.

"Surrender," said the former, "or we blow you up in your fastness."

"I am come of too high a race to surrender to rebels," said Albert, assuming the air with which, in such a condition, a king might have spoken.

"I bear you to witness," cried Cromwell, exultingly, "he hath refused quarter. Of a surety, his blood be on his head. One of you bring down the barrel of powder. As he loves to soar high, we will add what can be taken from the soldiers' bandoleers. Come with me, Pearson; thou understandst this gear. Corporal Grace-be-here, stand thou fast on the platform of the window, where Captain Pearson and I stood but even now, and bend the point of thy partizan against any who shall attempt to pass. Thou art as strong as a bull, and I will back thee against despair itself."

"But," said the corporal, mounting reluctantly, "the place is as the pinnacle of the Temple; and it is written, that Eutychus fell down from the third loft and was taken up dead."

"Because he slept upon his post," answered Cromwell, readily. "Beware thou of carelessness, and thus thy feet shall be kept from stumbling. You four soldiers, remain here to support the corporal, if it be necessary; and you, as well as the corporal, will draw into the vaulted passage the minute the trumpets sound a retreat. It is as strong as a casemate, and you may lie there safe from the effects of the mine. Thou, Zerubbabel Robins, I know, wilt be their lance-prisade."

Robins bowed, and the General departed to join those who were without.

As he reached the door of the hall, the petard was heard to explode, and he saw that it had succeeded; for the solders rushed, brandishing their swords and pistols, in at the postern of the turret, whose gate had been successfully forced. A thrill of exultation, but not unmingled with horror, shot across the veins of the ambitious soldier.

"Now—now," he cried, "they are dealing with him!" His expectations were deceived. Pearson and the others returned disappointed, and reported they had been stopped by a strong trap-door of grated iron, extended over the narrow stair; and they could see there was an obstacle of the same kind some ten feet higher. To remove it by force, while a desperate and well-armed man had the advantage of the steps above them, might cost many lives. "Which, lack-a-day," said the General, "it is our duty to be tender of. What dost thou advise, Gilbert Pearson?"

"We must use powder, my lord," answered Pearson, who saw his master was too modest to reserve to himself the whole merit of the proceeding: "there may be a chamber easily and conveniently formed under the foot of the stair. We have a sausage, by good luck, to form the train, and so——"

"Ah!" said Cromwell, "I know thou canst manage such gear well. But, Gilbert, I go to visit the posts, and give them orders to retire to a safe distance when the retreat is sounded. You will allow them five minutes for this purpose."

"Three is enough for any knave of them all," said Pearson. "They will be lame indeed, that require more on such a service. I ask but one, though I fire the train myself."

"Take heed," said Cromwell, "that the poor soul be listened to, if he asks quarter. It may be, he may repent him of his hardheartedness, and call for mercy."

"And mercy he shall have," answered Pearson, "provided he calls loud enough to make me hear him; for the explosion of that damned petard has made me as deaf as the devil's dam."

"Hush, Gilbert—hush!" said Cromwell; "you offend in your language."

"Zooks, sir, I must speak either in your way or in my own," said Pearson, "unless I am to be dumb as well as deaf. Away with you, my lord, to visit the posts; and you will presently hear me make some noise in the world."

Cromwell smiled gently at his aide-de-camp's petulance, patted him on the shoulder, and called him a mad fellow, walked a little way, then turned back to whisper, "What thou dost, do quickly"; then returned again towards the outer circle of guards, turning his head from time to time, as if to assure himself that the corporal, to whom he had entrusted the duty, still kept guard with his advanced weapon upon the terrific chasm between Rosamond's Tower and the corresponding turret. Seeing him standing on his post, the General muttered between his mustachios, 'The fellow hath the strength and courage of a bear; and yonder is a post where one shall do more to keep back than an hundred in making way." He cast a last look on the gigantic figure, who stood in that airy position like some Gothic statue, the weapon half-leveled against the opposite turret, with the butt rested against his right foot, his steel cap and burnished corslet glittering in the rising sun.

Cromwell then passed on to give the necessary orders, that such sentinels as might be endangered at their present posts by the effect of the mine should withdraw at the sound of the trumpet to the places which he pointed out to them. Never, on any occasion of his life, did he display more calmness and presence of mind. He was kind, nay, facetious, with the soldiers, who adored him; and yet he resembled a volcano before the eruption commences—all peaceful and quiet without, while an hundred contradictory passions were raging in his bosom.

Corporal Humgudgeon, meanwhile, remained steady upon his post; yet, though as determined a soldier as ever fought among the redoubted regiment of Ironsides, and possessed of no small share of that exalted fanaticism which lent so keen an edge to the natural courage of those stern religionists, the veteran felt his present situation to be highly uncomfortable. Within a pike's length of him arose a turret, which was about to be dispersed in massive fragments through the air; and he felt small confidence in the length of time which might be allowed for his escape from such a dangerous vicinity. The duty of constant vigilance upon his post was partly divided by this natural feeling, which induced him from time to time to bend his eyes on the miners below, instead of keeping them riveted on the opposite turret.

At length the interest of the scene arose to the uttermost. After entering and returning from the turret, and coming out again more than once, in the course of about twenty minutes, Pearson issued, as it might be supposed, for the last time, carrying in his hand, and uncoiling as he went along, the sausage, or linen bag (so called from its appearance), which, strongly sewed together and crammed with gunpowder, was to serve as a train betwixt the mine to be sprung and the point occupied by the engineer who was to give fire. He was in the act of finally adjusting it, when the attention of the corporal on the tower became irresistibly and exclusively riveted upon the preparations for the explosion. But, while he watched the aide-de-camp drawing his pistol to give fire, and the trumpeter handling his instrument, as waiting the order to sound the retreat, fate rushed on the unhappy sentinel in a way he least expected.

Young, active, bold, and completely possessed of his presence of mind, Albert Lee, who had been from the loopholes a watchful observer of every measure which had been taken by his besiegers, had resolved to make one desperate effort for self-preservation. While the head of the sentinel on the opposite platform was turned from him, and bent rather downwards, he suddenly sprang across the chasm, though the space on which he lighted was scarce wide enough for two persons, threw the surprised soldier from his precarious stand, and jumped himself down into the chamber. The gigantic trooper went sheer down twenty feet, struck against a projecting battlement, which launched the wretched man outwards, and then fell on the earth with such tremendous force, that the head, which first touched the ground, dinted a hole in the soil of six inches in depth, and was crushed like an egg-shell. Scarce knowing what had happened, yet startled and confounded at the descent of this heavy body, which fell at no great distance from him, Pearson snapped his pistol at the train, no previous warning given, the powder caught, and the mine exploded. Had it been strongly charged with powder, many of those without might have suffered; but the explosion was only powerful enough to blow out, in a lateral direction, a part of the wall just above the foundation, sufficient, however, to destroy the equipoise of the building. Then, amid a cloud of smoke, which began gradually to encircle the turret like a shroud, arising slowly from its base to its summit, it was seen to stagger and shake by all who had courage to look steadily at a sight so dreadful. Slowly, at first, the building inclined outwards, then rushed precipitately to its base, and fell to the ground in huge fragments, the strength of its resistance showing the excellence of the mason-work. The engineer, so soon as he had fired the train, fled in such alarm that he wellnigh ran against his General, who was advancing towards him, while a huge stone from the summit of the building, flying farther than the rest, lighted within a yard of them.

"Thou hast been over-hasty, Pearson," said Cromwell, with the greatest composure possible; "hath no one fallen in that same tower of Siloe?"

"Some one fell," said Pearson, still in great agitation, "and yonder lies his body half buried in the rubbish."

With a quick and resolute step, Cromwell approached the spot, and exclaimed, "Pearson thou hast ruined me: the Young Man hath escaped. This is our own sentinel, plague on the idiot! Let him rot beneath the ruins which crushed him!"

A cry now resounded from the platform of Rosamond's Tower, which appeared yet taller than formerly, deprived of the neighboring turret, which emulated though it did not attain to its height—"A prisoner, noble General—a prisoner! The fox whom we have chased all night is now in the snare: the Lord hath delivered him into the hand of His servants."

"Look you keep him in safe custody," exclaimed Cromwell, "and bring him presently down to the apartment from which the secret passages have their principal entrance."

"Your Excellency shall be obeyed."

The proceedings of Albert Lee, to which these exclamations related, had been unfortunate. He had dashed from the platform, as we have related, the gigantic strength of the soldier opposed to him, and had instantly jumped down into Rochecliffe's chamber. But the soldiers stationed there threw themselves upon him, and after a struggle, which was hopelessly maintained against such advantage of numbers, had thrown the young Cavalier to the ground, two of them, drawn down by his strenuous exertions, falling across him. At the same moment a sharp and severe report was heard, which, like a clap of thunder in the immediate vicinity, shook all around them, till the strong and solid tower tottered like the mast of a stately vessel when about to part by the board. In a few seconds, this was followed by another sullen sound, at first low and deep, but augmenting like the roar of a cararact, as it descends, reeling, bellowing, and rushing, as if to astound both heaven and earth. So awful, indeed, was the sound of the neighbor tower as it fell, that both the captive and those who struggled with him continued for a minute or two passive in each other's grasp.

Albert was the first who recovered consciousness and activity. He shook off those who lay above him, and made a desperate effort to gain his feet, in which he partly succeeded. But as he had to deal with men accustomed to every species of danger, and whose energies was recovered nearly as soon as his own, he was completely secured, and his arms held down. Loyal and faithful to his trust, and resolved to sustain to the last the character which he had assumed, he exclaimed, as his struggles were finally overpowered, "Rebel villains! would you slay your king?"

"Ha, heard you that?" cried one of the soldiers to the lance-prisade, who commanded the party. "Shall I not strike this son of a wicked father under the fifth rib, even as the tyrant of Moab was smitten by Ehud with a dagger of a cubit's length?"

But Robins answered, "Be it far from us, Merciful Strickalthrow, to slay in cold blood the captive of our bow and of our spear. Methinks, since the storm of Tredah* we have shed enough of blood; therefore, on your lives do him no evil, but take from him his arms, and let us bring him before the chosen instrument, even our General, that he may do with him what is meet in his eyes."

By this time the soldier whose exultation had made him the first to communicate the intelligence from the battlements to Cromwell returned, and brought commands corresponding to the orders of their temporary officer; and Albert Lee, disarmed and bound, was conducted as a captive into the apartment which derived its name from the victories of his ancestor, and placed in the presence of General Cromwell.

Running over in his mind the time which had elapsed since the departure of Charles till the siege, if it may be termed so, had terminated in his own capture, Albert had every reason to hope that his royal master must have had time to accomplish his escape. Yet he determined to maintain to the last a deceit which might for a time ensure the King's safety. The difference betwixt them could not, he thought, be instantly discovered, begrimed as he was with dust and smoke, and with blood issuing from some scratches received in the scuffle.

In this evil plight, but bearing himself with such dignity as was adapted to the princely character, Albert was ushered into the apartment of Victor Lee, where, in his father's own chair, reclined the triumphant enemy of the cause to which the house of Lee had been hereditarily faithful.

* See Note 12.

CHAPTER XXXV

> **A barren title hast thou bought too dear:**
> **Why didst thou tell me that thou wert a king?**
> *Henry IV.* **Part I.**

OLIVER CROMWELL arose from his seat as the two veteran soldiers, Zerubbabel Robins and Merciful Strickalthrow, introduced into the apartment the prisoner, whom they held by the arms, and fixed his stern hazel eye on Albert long before he could give vent to the ideas which were swelling in his bosom. Exultation was the most predominant.

"Art not thou," he at length said, "that Egyptian which, before these days, madest an uproar, and leddest out into the wilderness many thousand men, who were murderers? Ha, youth! I have hunted thee from Sterling to Worcester, from Worcester to Woodstock, and we have met at last."

"I would," replied Albert, speaking in the character which he had assumed, "that we had met where I could have shown thee the difference betwixt a rightful king and an ambitious usurper!"

"Go to, young man," said Cromwell; "say rather the difference between a judge raised up for the redemption of England and the son of those kings whom the Lord in His anger permitted to reign over her. But we will not waste useless words. God knows that it is not of our will that we are called to such high matters, being as humble in our thoughts as we are of ourselves, and in our unassisted nature frail and foolish, and unable to render a reason but for the better spirit within us, which is not of us. Thou art weary, young man, and thy nature requires rest and refection, being doubtless dealt with delicately, as one who hath fed on the fat and drank of the sweet, and who hath been clothed in purple and fine linen."

Here the General suddenly stopped, and then abruptly exclaimed—"But is this—— Ah! whom have we here? These are not the locks of the swarthy lad Charles Stuart. A cheat—a cheat!"

Albert hastily cast his eyes on a mirror which stood in the room, and perceived that a dark peruke, found among Doctor Rochecliffe's miscellaneous wardrobe, had been disordered in the scuffle with the soldiery, and that his own light brown hair was escaping from beneath it.

"Who is this?" said Cromwell, stamping with fury. "Pluck the disguise from him!"

The soldiers did so; and bringing him at the same time towards the light, the deception could not be maintained for a moment longer, with any possibility of success. Cromwell came up to him with his teeth set, and grinding against each other as he spoke, his hands clenched, and trembling with emotion, and speaking with a voice low-pitched, bitterly and deeply emphatic, such as might have preceded a stab with his dagger.

"Thy name, young man?"

He was answered calmly and firmly, while the countenance of the speaker wore a cast of triumph, and even contempt—

"Albert Lee of Ditchley, a faithful subject of King Charles."

"I might have guessed it," said Cromwell. "Ay, and to King Charles shalt thou go, as soon as it is noon on the dial. Pearson," he continued, "let him be carried to the others; and let them be executed at twelve exactly."

"All, sir?" said Pearson, surprised; for Cromwell, though he at times made formidable examples, was, in general, by no means sanguinary.

"*All*," repeated Cromwell, fixing his eye on young Lee. "Yes, young sir, your conduct has devoted to death thy father, thy kinsman, and the stranger that was in thine household. Such wreck hast thou brought on thy father's house."

"My father, too—my aged father!" said Albert, looking upward, and endeavoring to raise his hands in the same direction, which was prevented by his bonds. "The Lord's will be done!"

"All this havoc can be saved, if," said the General, "thou wilt answer one question—Where is the young Charles Stuart, who was called King of Scotland?"

"Under Heaven's protection, and safe from thy power," was the firm and unhesitating answer of the young Royalist.

"Away with him to prison!" said Cromwell; "and from thence to execution with the rest of them, as Malignants taken in the fact. Let a court-martial sit on them presently."

"One word," said young Lee, as they led him from the room.

"Stop—stop," said Cromwell, with the agitation of renewed hope; "let him be heard."

"You love texts of Scripture," said Albert. "Let this be the subject of your next homily. 'Had Zimri peace, who slew his master?'"

"Away with him," said the General; "let him die the death! I have said it."

As Cromwell spoke these words, his aide-de-camp observed that he became unwontedly pale.

"Your Excellency is overtoiled in the public service," said Pearson: "a course of the stag in the evening will refresh you. The old knight hath a noble hound here, if we can but get him to hunt without his master, which may be hard, as he is faithful, and——"

"Hang him up!" said Cromwell.

"What—whom—hang the noble dog? Your Excellency was wont to love a good hound."

"It matters not," said Cromwell; "let him be killed. Is it not written, that they slew in the valley of Achor, not only the accursed Achan, with his sons and his daughters, but also his oxen and his asses, and his sheep, and every live thing belonging unto him? And even thus shall we do to the Malignant family of Lee, who have aided Sisera in his flight, when Israel might have been delivered of his trouble forever. But send out couriers and patrols. Follow, pursue, watch in every direction. Let my horse be ready at the door in five minutes, or bring me the first thou canst find."

It seemed to Pearson that this was something wildly spoken, and that the cold perspiration was standing upon the General's brow as he said it. He therefore again pressed the necessity of repose; and it would appear that nature seconded strongly the representation. Cromwell arose and made a step or two towards the door of the apartment; but stopped, staggered, and, after a pause, sat down in a chair. "Truly, friend Pearson," he said, "this weary carcass of our is an impediment to us, even in our most necessary business, and I am fitter to sleep than to watch, which is not my wont. Place guards, therefore, till we repose ourselves for an hour or two. Send out in every direction, and spare not for horses' flesh. Wake me if the court-martial should require instruction, and forget not to see the sentence punctually executed on the Lees and those who were arrested with them."

As Cromwell spoke thus, he arose and half-opened a bedroom door, when Pearson again craved pardon for asking if he had rightly understood his Excellency, that all the prisoners were to be executed.

"Have I not said it?" answered Cromwell, displeasedly. "Is it because thou art a man of blood, and hast ever been, that thou dost affect these scruples, to show thyself tender-hearted at my expense? I tell thee that, if there lack one in the full tale of execution, thine own life shall pay the forfeit."

So saying, he entered the apartment, followed by the groom of his chamber, who attended upon Pearson's summons.

When his General had retired, Pearson remained in great perplexity what he ought to do; and that from no scruples of conscience, but from uncertainty whether he might not err either in postponing or in too hastily and too literally executing the instructions he had received.

In the mean time, Strickalthrow and Robins had returned, after lodging Albert in prison, to the room where Pearson was still musing on his General's commands. Both these men were adjutators in their army, and old soldiers, whom Cromwell was accustomed to treat with great familiarity; so that Robins had no hesitation to ask Captain Pearson "Whether he meant to execute the commands of the General, even to the letter?"

Pearson shook his head with an air of doubt, but added, "There was no choice left."

"Be assured," said the old man, "that, if thou dost this folly, thou wilt cause Israel to sin, and that the General will not be pleased with your service. Thou knowest, and none better than thou, that Oliver, although he be like unto David the son of Jesse in faith, and wisdom, and courage, yet there are times when the evil spirit cometh upon him as it did upon Saul, and he uttereth commands which he will not thank any one for executing."

Pearson was too good a politician to assent directly to a proposition which he could not deny: he only shook his head once more, and said that it was easy for those to talk who were not responsible, but the soldier's duty was to obey his orders, and not to judge of them.

"Very righteous truth," said Merciful Strickalthrow, a grim old Scotchman: "I marvel where our brother Zerubbabel caught up this softness of heart?"

"Why, I do but wish," said Zerubbabel, "that four or five human creatures may draw the breath of God's air for a few hours more ; there can be small harm done by delaying the execution, and the General will have some time for reflection."

"Ay," said Captain Pearson, "but I in my service must be more pointedly obsequious than thou in thy plainness art bound to be, friend Zerubbabel."

"Then shall the coarse frieze cassock of the private soldier help the golden gaberdine of the captain to bear out the blast," said Zerubbabel. "Ay, indeed, I can show you warrant why we be aidful to each other in doing acts of kindness and long-suffering, seeing the best of us are poor, sinful creatures, who might suffer, being called to a brief accounting."

"Of a verity you surprise me, brother Zerubbabel," said Strickalthrow, "that thou, being an old and experienced soldier, whose head hath grown gray in battle, shouldst give such advice to a young officer. Is not the General's commission to take away the wicked from the land, and to root out the Amalekite, and the Jebusite, and the Perizzite, and the Hittite, and the Girgashite, and the Amorite ? and are not these men justly to be compared to the five kings who took shelter in the cave of Makkedah, who were delivered into the hands of Joshua the son of Nun ? and he caused his captains and his soldiers to come near and tread on their necks, and then he smote them, and he slew them, and then he hanged them on five trees, even till evening. And thou, Gilbert Pearson by name, be not withheld from the duty which is appointed to thee, but do even as has been commanded by him who is raised up to judge and to deliver Israel ; for it is written, 'Cursed is he who holdeth back his sword from the slaughter.'"

Thus wrangled the two military theologians, while Pearson, much more solicitous to anticipate the wishes of Oliver than to know the will of Heaven, listened to them with great indecision and perplexity.

CHAPTER XXXVI

But let us now, like soldiers on the watch,
Put the soul's armor on, alike prepared
For all a soldier's warfare brings.

JOANNA BAILLIE.

THE reader will recollect that, when Rochecliffe and Joceline were made prisoners, the party which escorted them had two other captives in their train—Colonel Everard, namely, and the Rev. Nehemiah Holdenough. When Cromwell had obtained entrance into Woodstock, and commenced his search after the fugitive prince, the prisoners were placed in what had been an old guard-room, and which was by its strength well calculated to serve for a prison, and a guard was placed over them by Pearson. No light was allowed, save that of a glimmering fire of charcoal. The prisoners remained separated from each other, Colonel Everard conversing with Nehemiah Holdenough at a distance from Doctor Rochecliffe, Sir Henry Lee, and Joceline. The party was soon after augmented by Wildrake, who was brought down to the lodge, and thrust in with so little ceremony that, his arms being bound, he had very nearly fallen on his nose in the middle of the prison.

"I thank you, my good friends," he said, looking back to the door, which they who had pushed him were securing. "*Point de cérémonie*—no apology for stumbling, so we light in good company. Save ye, save ye, gentlemen all. What *à la mort*, and nothing stirring to keep the spirits up, and make a night on't? the last we shall have, I take it: for a make to a million but we trine to the nubbing cheat tomorrow. Patron—noble patron, how goes it? This was but a scurvy trick of Noll, so far as you were concerned; as for me, why, I might have deserved something of the kind at his hand."

"Prithee, Wildrake, sit down," said Everard; "thou art drunk—disturb us not."

"Drunk—I drunk!" cried Wildrake. "I have been splicing the main-brace, as Jack says at Wapping—have been tasting Noll's brandy in a bumper to the King's health, and another to his Excellency's confusion, and another to the d——n of Farliament, and it may be one or two more, but all to devilish good toasts. But I'm not drunk."

"Prithee, friend, be not profane," said Nehemiah Holdenough.

"What, my little Presbyterion parson, my slender Mas John! Thou shalt say amen to this world instantly," said Wildrake. "I have had a weary time in't for one. Ha, noble Sir Henry, I kiss your hand. I tell thee, knight, the point of my Toledo was near Cromwell's heart last night, as ever a button on the breast of his doublet. Rat him, he wears secret armor. He a soldier! Had it not been for a cursed steel shirt, I would have spitted him like a lark. Ha, Doctor Rochecliffe! thou knowest I can wield my weapon,"

"Yes," replied the Doctor, "and you know I can use mine."

"I prithee be quiet, Master Wildrake," said Sir Henry.

"Nay, good knight," answered Wildrake, "be somewhat more cordial with a comrade in distress. This is a different scene from the Brentford storming-party. The jade Fortune has been a very step-mother to me. I will sing you a song I made on my own ill-luck."

"At this moment, Captain Wildrake, we are not in a fitting mood for singing," said Sir Henry, civilly and gravely.

"Nay, it will aid your devotions. Egad, it sounds like a penitential psalm :

When I was a young lad,
My fortune was bad.
If e'er I do well 'tis a wonder.
I spent all my means
Amid sharpers and queans,
Then I got a commission to plunder.
I have stockings, 'tis true,
But the devil a shoe,
I am forced to wear boots in all weather;
Be d—d the boot sole,
Curse on the spur-roll,
Confounded be the upper-leather." *

The door opened as Wildrake finished this stanza at the top of his voice, and in rushed a sentinel, who, greeting him by the title of a "blasphemous bellowing bull of Bashan," bestowed a severe blow with his ramrod on the shoulders of

* Such a song, or something very like it, may be found in Ramsay's *Tea-table Miscellany*, among the wild slips of minstrelsy which are there collected.

the songster, whose bonds permitted him no means of returning the compliment.

"Your humble servant again, sir," said Wildrake, shrugging his shoulders; "sorry I have no means of showing my gratitude. I am bound ever to keep the peace, like Captain Bobadil. Ha, knight, did you hear my bones clatter? That blow came twangingly off: the fellow might inflict the bastinado, were it in presence of the Grand Seignior; he has no taste for music, knight—is no way moved by the 'concord of sweet sounds.' I will warrant him fit for treason, stratagem, and spoil. Eh—all down in the mouth? Well, I'll go to sleep to-night on a bench, as I've done many a night, and I will be ready to be hanged decently in the morning, which never happened to me before in all my life.

> When I was a young lad,
> My fortune was bad—

Pshaw! This is not the tune it goes to." Here he fell fast asleep, and sooner or later all his companions in misfortune followed his example.

The benches intended for the repose of the soldiers of the guard afforded the prisoners convenience enough to lie down though their slumbers, it may be believed, were neither sound nor undisturbed. But, when daylight was but a little while broken, the explosion of gunpowder which took place, and the subsequent fall of the turret to which the mine was applied, would have awakened the Seven Sleepers, or Morpheus himself. The smoke, penetrating through the windows, left them at no loss for the cause of the din.

"There went my gunpowder," said Rochecliffe, "which has, I trust, blown up as many rebel villains as it might have been the means of destroying otherwise in a fair field. It must have caught fire by chance."

"By chance! no," said Sir Henry; "depend on it, my bold Albert has fired the train, and that in yonder blast Cromwell was flying towards the heaven whose battlements he will never reach. Ah, my brave boy! and perhaps thou art thyself sacrificed, like a youthful Samson among the rebellious Philistines! Bnt I will not be long behind thee, Albert."

Everard hastened to the door, hoping to obtain from the guard, to whom his name and rank might be known, some explanation of the noise, which seemed to announce some dreadful catastrophe.

But Nehemiah Holdenough, whose rest had been broken by the trumpet which gave signal for the explosion, appeared in the very acme of horror. "It is the trumpet of the Archangel!" he cried—"it is the crushing of this world of elements—it is the summons to the judgment-seat! The dead are obeying the call—they are with us—they are amongst us—they arise in their bodily frames—they come to summon us!"

As he spoke, his eyes were riveted upon Doctor Rochecliffe, who stood directly opposite to him. In rising hastily, the cap which he commonly wore, according to a custom then usual both among clergymen and gownmen of a civil profession, had escaped from his head, and carried with it the large silk patch which he probably wore for the purpose of disguise; for the cheek which was disclosed was unscarred, and the eye as good as that which was usually uncovered.

Colonel Everard, returning from the door, endeavored in vain to make Master Holdenough comprehend what he learned from the guard without, that the explosion had involved only the death of one of Cromwell's soldiers. The Presbyterian divine continued to stare wildly at him of the Episcopal persuasion.

But Doctor Rochecliffe heard and understood the news brought by Colonel Everard, and, relieved from the instant anxiety which had kept him stationary, he advanced towards the retiring Calvinist, extending his hand in the most friendly manner.

"Avoid thee—avoid thee!" said Holdenough, "the living may not join hands with the dead."

"But I," said Rochecliffe, "am as much alive as you are."

"Thou alive!—thou! Joseph Albany, whom my own eyes saw precipitated from the battlements of Clidesthrough Castle?"

"Ay," answered the Doctor, "but you did not see me swim ashore on a marsh covered with sedges—*fugit ad salices*—after a manner which I will explain to you another time."

Holdenough touched his hand with doubt and uncertainty. "Thou art indeed warm and alive," he said, "and yet after so many blows, and a fall so tremendous, thou canst not be *my* Joseph Albany."

"I am Joseph Albany Rochecliffe," said the Doctor, "become so in virtue of my mother's little estate, which fines and confiscations have made an end of."

"And is it so indeed?" said Holdenough, "and have I recovered mine old chum?"

"Even so," replied Rochecliffe, "by the same token I appeared to you in the Mirror Chamber. Thou wert so bold, Nehemiah, that our whole scheme would have been shipwrecked, had I not appeared to thee in the shape of a departed friend. Yet, believe me, it went against my heart to do it."

"Ah, fie on thee—fie on thee," said Holdenough, throwing himself into his arms, and clasping him to his bosom, "thou wert ever a naughty wag. How couldst thou play me such a trick? Ah, Albany, dost thou remember Dr. Purefoy and Caius College?"

"Marry, do I," said the Doctor, thrusting his arm through the Presbyterian divine's, and guiding him to a seat apart from the other prisoners, who witnessed this scene with much surprise. "Remember Caius College!" said Rochecliffe, "ay, and the good ale we drank, and our parties to Mother Huffcap's."

"Vanity of vanities," said Holdenough, smiling kindly at the same time, and still holding his recovered friend's arm inclosed and handlocked in his.

"But the breaking the principal's orchard, so cleanly done," said the Doctor; "it was the first plot I ever framed, and much work I had to prevail on thee to go into it."

"Oh, name not that iniquity," said Nehemiah, "since I may well say, as the pious Master Baxter, that these boyish offenses have had their punishment in later years, inasmuch as that inordinate appetite for fruit hath produced stomachic affections under which I yet labor."

"True—true, dear Nehemiah," said Rochecliffe; "but care not for them—a dram of brandy will correct it all. Mr. Baxter was"—he was about to say, "an ass," but checked himself, and only filled np the sentence with "a good man, I daresay, but over-scrupulous."

So they sat down together the best of friends, and for half an hour talked with mutual delight over old college stories. By degrees they got on the politics of the day; and though then they unclasped their hands, and there occurred between them such expressions as "Nay, my dear brother," and "There I must needs differ," and "On this point I crave leave to think"; yet a hue and cry against the Independents and other sectarists being started, they followed like brethren in full halloo, and it was hard to guess which was most forward. Unhappily, in the course of this amicable intercourse, something was mentioned about the bishopric of Titus, which at once involved them in the doctrinal question of church government. Then, alas! the floodgates were opened, and they showered on each other Greek and Hebrew texts, while their eyes kindled, their cheeks glowed, their hands became clenched, and they looked more like fierce polemics about to rend each other's eyes out than Christian divines.

Roger Wildrake, by making himself an auditor of the debate, contrived to augment its violence. He took, of course, a most decided part in a question the merits of which were totally unknown to him. Somewhat overawed by Holdenough's ready oratory and learning, the Cavalier watched with a face of anxiety the countenance of Doctor Rochecliffe; but when he saw the proud eye and steady bearing of the Episcopal champion, and heard him answer Greek with Greek, and Hebrew with Hebrew, Wildrake backed his arguments as he closed them with a stout rap upon the bench, and an exulting laugh in the face of the antagonist. It was with some difficulty that Sir Henry and Colonel Everard, having at length and reluctantly interfered, prevailed on the two alienated friends to adjourn their dispute, removing at the same time to a distance, and regarding each other with looks in which old friendship appeared to have totally given way to mutual animosity.

But while they sat lowering on each other, and longing to renew a contest in which each claimed the victory, Pearson entered the prison, and, in a low and troubled voice, desired the persons whom it contained to prepare for instant death.

Sir Henry Lee received the doom with the stern composure which he had hitherto displayed. Colonel Everard attempted the interposition of a strong and resentful appeal to the Parliament against the judgment of the court-martial and the General. But Pearson declined to receive or transmit any such remonstrance, and, with a dejected look and mien of melancholy presage, renewed his exhortation to them to prepare for the hour of noon, and withdrew from the prison.

The operation of this intelligence on the two clerical disputants was more remarkable. They gazed for a moment on each other with eyes in which repentant kindness and a feeling of generous shame quenched every lingering feeling of resentment, and joining in the mutual exclamation—"My brother—my brother, I have sinned—I have sinned in offending thee!" they rushed into each other's arms, shed tears as they demanded each other's forgiveness, and, like two warriors who sacrifice a personal quarrel to discharge their duty against the common enemy, they recalled nobler ideas of their sacred character, and, assuming the part which best became them on an occasion so melancholy, began to exhort those around them to meet the doom that had been announced with the firmness and dignity which Christianity alone can give.

CHAPTER XXXVII

Most gracious prince, good Cannyng cried,
  Leave vengeance to our God,
And lay the iron rule aside:
  Be thine the olive rod.
Ballad of Sir Charles Bawdin.

THE hour appointed for execution had been long past, and it was about five in the evening when the Protector summoned Pearson to his presence. He went with fear and reluctance, uncertain how he might be received. After reremaining about a quarter of an hour, the aide-de-camp returned to Victor Lee's parlor, where he found the old soldier, Zerubabbel Robins, in attendance for his return.

"How is Oliver?" said the old man, anxiously.

"Why, well," answered Pearson, "and hath asked no questions of the execution, but many concerning the reports we have been able to make regarding the flight of the Young Man, and is much moved at thinking he must now be beyond pursuit. Also I gave him certain papers belonging to the Malignant Dr. Rochecliffe."

"Then will I venture upon him," said the adjutator; "so give me a napkin that I may look like a sewer, and fetch up the food which I directed should be in readiness."

Two troopers attended accordingly with a ration of beef, such as was distributed to the private soldiers, and dressed after their fashion, a pewter pot of ale,a trencher with salt, black pepper, and a loaf of ammunition bread. "Come with me," he said to Pearson, "and fear not—Noll loves an innocent jest." He boldly entered the General's sleeping apartment, and said aloud, "Arise, thou that art called to be a judge in Israel; let there be no more folding of the hands to sleep. Lo, I come as a sign to thee; wherefore rise, eat, drink, and let thy heart be glad within thee, for thou shalt eat with joy the food of him that laboreth in the trenches, seeing that, since thou wert commander over the host, the poor sentinel hath had such provisions as I have now placed for thine own refreshment."

"Truly, brother Zerubbabel," said Cromwell, accustomed

to such starts of enthusiasm among his followers, "we would wish that it were so, neither is it our desire to sleep soft nor feed more highly than the meanest that ranks under our banners. Verily, thou hast chosen well for my refreshment, and the smell of the food is savory to my nostrils."

He arose from the bed on which he had lain down half dressed, and wrapping his cloak around him, sat down by the bedside, and partook heartily of the plain food which was prepared for him. While he was eating, Cromwell commanded Pearson to finish his report—"You need not desist for the presence of a worthy soldier, whose spirit is as my spirit."

"Nay, but," interrupted Robbins, "you are to know that Gilbert Pearson hath not fully executed thy commands touching a part of those Malignants, all of whom should have died at noon."

"What execution—what Malignants?" said Cromwell, laying down his knife and fork.

"Those in the prison here at Woodstock." answered Zerubbabel, "whom your Excellency commanded should be executed at noon, as taken in the fact of rebellion against the Commonwealth."

"Wretch!" said Cromwell, starting up and addressing Pearson, "thou hast not touched Mark Everard, in whom there was no guilt, for he was deceived by him who passed between us, neither hast thou put forth thy hand on the pragmatic Presbyterian minister, to have all those of their classes cry sacrilege, and alienate them from us forever."

"If your Excellency wish them to live, they live: their life and death are in the power of a word," said Pearson.

"Enfranchise them: I must gain the Presbyterian interest over to us if I can."

"Rochecliffe, the arch-plotter." said Pearson, "I thought to have executed, but——"

"Barbarous man," said Cromwell, "alike ungrateful and impolitic, wouldst thou have destroyed our decoy-duck? This doctor is but like a well, a shallow one indeed, but something deeper than the springs which discharge their secret tribute into his keeping; then come I with a pump and suck it all up to the open air. Enlarge him, and let him have money if he wants it. I know his haunts: he can go nowhere but our eye will be upon him. But you look at each other darkly, as if you had more to say than you durst. I trust you have not done to death Sir Henry Lee?"

"No. Yet the man," replied Pearson, "is a confirmed Malignant, and——"

"Ay, but he is also a noble relic of the ancient English gentleman," said the General. "I would I knew how to win the favor of that race! But we, Pearson, whose royal robes are the armor which we wear on our bodies, and whose leading-staves are our scepters, are too newly set up to draw the respect of the proud Malignants, who cannot brook to submit to less than royal lineage. Yet what can they see in the longest kingly line in Europe save that it runs back to a successful soldier? I grudge that one man should be honored and followed, because he is the descendant of a victorious commander, while less honor and allegiance is paid to another, who, in personal qualities and in success, might emulate the founder of his rival's dynasty. Well, Sir Henry Lee lives, and shall live for me, His son, indeed, hath deserved the death which he has doubtless sustained."

"My lord," stammered Pearson, "since your Excellency has found I am right in suspending your order in so many instances I trust you will not blame me in this also. I thought it best to await more special orders."

"Thou art in a mighty merciful humor this morning, Pearson," said Cromwell, not entirely satisfied.

"If your Excellency please, the halter is ready, and so is the provost-marshal."

"Nay, if such a bloody fellow as thou hast spared him, it would ill become me to destroy him," said the General, "But then here is among Rochecliffe's papers the engagement of twenty desperadoes to take us off; some example ought to be made."

"My lord," said Zerubbabel, "consider now how often this young man, Albert Lee, hath been near you, nay, probably quite close to your Excellency, in these dark passages, which he knew and we did not. Had he been of an assassin's nature, it would have cost him but a pistol-shot, and the light of Israel was extinguished. Nay, in the unavoidable confusion which must have ensued, the sentinels quitting their posts, he might have had a fair chance of escape."

"Enough Zerubbabel—he lives," said the General. "He shall remain in custody for some time, however, and be then banished from England. The other two are safe, of course; for you would not dream of considering such paltry fellows as fit victims for my revenge."

"One fellow, the under-keeper, called Joliffe, deserves death, however," said Pearson, "since he has frankly admitted that he slew honest Joseph Tomkins."

"He deserves a reward for saving us a labor," said Cromwell: "that Tomkins was a most double-hearted villain. I have found evidence among these papers here, that, if we had lost the fight at Worcester, we should have had reason to regret that we had ever trusted Master Tomkins: it was only our success which anticipated his treachery. Write us down debtor, not creditor, to Joceline, an you call him so, and to his quarter-staff."

"There remains the sacrilegious and graceless Cavalier who attempted your Excellency's life last night," said Pearson.

"Nay," said the General, "that were stooping too low for revenge. His sword had no more power than had he thrusted with a tobacco-pipe. Eagles stoop not at mallards, or wild drakes either."

"Yet, sir," said Pearson, "the fellow should be punished as a libeller. The quantity of foul and pestilential abuse which we found in his pockets makes me loth he should go altogether free. Please to look at them, sir."

"A most vile hand," said Oliver, as he looked at a sheet or two of our friend Wildrake's poetical miscellanies. "The very handwriting seems to be drunk, and the very poetry not sober. What have we here?

"When I was a young lad,
"My fortune was bad;
If e'er I do well, 'tis a wonder."

Why, what trash is this? and then again—

"Now a plague on the poll
Of old politic Noll!
We will drink till we bring
In triumph back the King."

In truth, if it could be done that way, this poet would be a stout champion. Give the poor knave five pieces, Pearson, and bid him go sell his ballads. If he come within twenty miles of our person, though, we will have him flogged till the blood runs down to his heels."

"There remains only one sentenced person," said Pearson—"a noble wolf-hound, finer than any your Excellency saw in Ireland. He belongs to the old knight, Sir Henry

Lee. Should your Excellency not desire to keep the fine creature yourself, might I presume to beg that I might have leave?"

"No, Pearson," said Cromwell; "the old man, so faithful himself, shall not be deprived of his faithful dog. I would *I* had any creature, were it but a dog, that followed me because it loved me, not for what it could make of me."

"Your Excellency is unjust to your faithful soldiers," said Zerubbabel, bluntly, "who follow you like dogs, fight for you like dogs, and have the grave of a dog on the spot where they happen to fall."

"How now, old grumbler," said the General, "what means this change of note?"

"Corporal Humgudgeon's remains are left to molder under the ruins of yonder tower, and Tomkins is thrust into a hole in a thicket like a beast."

"True—true," said Cromwell; "they shall be removed to the churchyard, and every soldier shall attend with cockades of sea-green and blue ribbon. Every one of the non-commissioned officers and adjutators shall have a mourning scarf; we ourselves will lead the procession, and there shall be a proper dole of wine, burnt brandy, and rosemary. See that it is done, Pearson. After the funeral, Woodstock shall be dismantled and destroyed, that its recesses may not again afford shelter to rebels and Malignants."

The commands of the General were punctually obeyed, and when the other prisoners were dismissed, Albert Lee remained for some time in custody. He went abroad after his liberation, entered in King Charles's guards, where he was promoted by that monarch. But his fate, as we shall see hereafter, only allowed him a short though bright career.

We return to the liberation of the other prisoners from Woodstock. The two divines, completely reconciled to each other, retreated arm-in-arm to the parsonage-house, formerly the residence of Doctor Rochecliffe, but which he now visited as the guest of his successor, Nehemiah Holdenough. The Presbyterian had no sooner installed his friend under his roof than he urged upon him an offer to partake it, and the income annexed to it, as his own. Dr. Rochecliffe was much affected, but wisely rejected the generous offer, considering the difference of their tenets on church government, which each entertained as religiously as his creed. Another debate, though a light one, on the subject of the office of bishops in the primitive church, confirmed him in his resolution. They parted the next day, and their friendship remained undisturbed by controversy till Mr. Holdenough's death, in 1658—a harmony which might be in some degree owing to their never meeting again after their imprisonment. Doctor Rochecliffe was restored to his living after the Restoration, and ascended from thence to high clerical preferment.

The inferior personages of the grand jail-delivery at Woodstock Lodge easily found themselves temporary accommodations in the town among old acquaintance; but no one ventured to entertain the old knight, understood to be so much under the displeasure of the ruling powers; and even the innkeeper of the George, who had been one of his tenants, scarce dared to admit him to the common privileges of a traveler, who has food and lodging for his money. Everard attended him unrequested, unpermitted, but also unforbidden. The heart of the old man had been turned once more towards him when he learned how he had behaved at the memorable rencontre at the King's Oak, and saw that he was an object of the enmity, rather than the favor, of Cromwell. But there was another secret feeling which tended to reconcile him to his nephew—the consciousness that Everard shared with him the deep anxiety which he experienced on account of his daughter, who had not yet returned from her doubtful and perilous expedition. He felt that he himself would perhaps be unable to discover where Alice had taken refuge during the late events, or to obtain her deliverance if she was taken into custody. He wished Everard to offer him his service in making a search for her, but shame prevented his preferring the request; and Everard, who could not suspect the altered state of his uncle's mind, was afraid to make the proposal of assistance, or even to name the name of Alice.

The sun had already set, they sat looking each other in the face in silence, when the trampling of horses was heard, there was knocking at the door, there was a light step on the stair, and Alice, the subject of their anxiety, stood before them. She threw herself joyfully into her father's arms, who glanced his eye heedfully round the room, as he said in a whisper, "Is all safe?"

"Safe and out of danger, as I trust," replied Alice: "I have a token for you."

Her eye then rested on Everard, she blushed, was embarrassed, and silent.

"You need not fear your Presbyterian cousin," said the

knight, with a good-humored smile, "he has himself proved a confessor at least for loyalty, and ran the risk of being a martyr."

She pulled from her bosom the royal rescript, written on a small and soiled piece of paper, and tied round with a worsted thread instead of a seal. Such as it was, Sir Henry ere he opened it pressed the little packet with Oriental veneration to his lips, to his heart, to his forehead; and it was not before a tear had dropt on it that he found courage to open and read the billet. It was in these words:—

"LOYAL OUR MUCH-ESTEEMED FRIEND AND OUR TRUSTY SUBJECT,

"It having become known to us that a purpose of marriage has been entertained betwixt Mrs. Alice Lee, your only daughter, and Markham Everard, Esq., of Eversly Chase, her kinsman, and by affiancy your nephew, and being assured that this match would be highly agreeable to you, had it not been for certain respects to our service, which induced you to refuse your consent thereto—we do therefore acquaint you that, far from our affairs suffering by such an alliance, we do exhort and, so far as we may, require you to consent to the same, as you would wish to do us good pleasure, and greatly to advance our affairs. Leaving to you, nevertheless, as becometh a Christian king, the full exercise of your own discretion concerning other obstacles to such an alliance which may exist independent of those connected with our service. Witness our hand, together with our thankful recollections of your good services to our late royal father as well as ourselves, C. R."

Long and steadily did Sir Henry gaze on the letter, so that it might almost seem as if he were getting it by heart. He then placed it carefully in his pocket-book, and asked Alice the account of her adventures of the preceding night. They were briefly told. Their midnight walk through the chase had been speedily and safely accomplished. Nor had the King once made the slightest relapse into the naughty Louis Kerneguy. When she had seen Charles and his attendant set off, she had taken some repose in the cottage where they parted. With the morning came news that Woodstock was occupied by soldiers, so that return thither might have led to danger, suspicion, and inquiry. Alice therefore did not attempr it, but went to a house in the neighborhood, inhabited by a lady of established loyalty, whose husband had been major of Sir Henry Lee's regiment, and had fallen at the battle of Naseby. Mrs. Aylmer was a sensible woman, and indeed the necessities of the singular times had sharpened every one's faculties for stratagem and intrigue. She sent a faithful servant to scout about the mansion at Woodstock, who no sooner saw the prisoners dismissed and in safety, and ascertained the knight's destination for the evening, than he carried the news to his mistress, and by her orders attended Alice on horseback to join her father.

There was seldom, perhaps, an evening meal made in such absolute silence as by this embarrassed party, each occupied with their own thoughts, and at a loss how to fathom those of the others. At length the hour came when Alice felt herself at liberty to retire to repose after a day so fatiguing. Everard handed her to the door of her apartment, and was then himself about to take leave, when, to his surprise, his uncle asked him to return, pointed to a chair, and, giving him the King's letter to read, fixed his looks on him steadily, during the perusal, determined that, if he could discover aught short of the utmost delight in the reading, the commands of the King himself should be disobeyed, rather than Alice should be sacrificed to one who received not her hand as the greatest blessing earth had to bestow. But the features of Everard indicated joyful hope, even beyond what the father could have anticipated, yet mingled with surprise; and when he raised his eye to the knight's with timidity and doubt, a smile was on Sir Henry's countenance as he broke silence. "The King," he said, "had he no other subject in England, should dispose at will of those of the house of Lee. But methinks, the family of Everard have not been so devoted of late to the crown as to comply with a mandate inviting its heir to marry the daughter of a beggar."

"The daughter of Sir Henry Lee," said Everard, kneeling to this uncle, and perforce kissing his hand, "would grace he house of a duke."

"The girl is well enough," said the knight proudly; "for myself, my poverty shall neither shame nor encroach on my friends. Some few pieces I have by Doctor Rochecliffe's kindness, and Joceline and I will strike out something."

"Nay, my dear uncle, you are richer than you think for," said Everard. "That part of your estate which my father redeemed for payment of a moderate composition is still your own, and held by trustees in your name, myself being one of them. You are only our debtor for an advance of moneys, for which, if it will content you, we will count with you like usurers. My father is incapable of profiting by making a bargain on his own account for the estate of a distressed friend; and all this you would have learned long since, but that you would not—I mean, time did not serve for explanation—I mean——"

"You mean I was too hot to hear reason, Mark, and I believe it is very true. But I think we understand each other *now*. To-morrow I go with my family to Kingston, where is an old house I may still call mine. Come thither at thy leisure, Mark,—or thy best speed, as thou wilt—but come with thy father's consent."

"With my father in person," said Everard, "if you will permit."

"Be that," answered the knight, "as he and you will. I think Joceline will scarce shut the door in thy face, or Bevis growl as he did after poor Louis Kerneguy. Nay, no more raptures, but good night, Mark—good night; and if thou art not tired with the fatigue of yesterday—why, if you appear here at seven in the morning, I think we must bear with your company on the Kingston road."

Once more Everard pressed the knight's hand, caressed Bevis, who received his kindness graciously, and went home to dreams of happiness, which were realized, as far as this motley world permits, within a few months afterwards.

CHAPTER XXXVIII

My life was of a piece,
Spent in your service—dying at your feet.
Don Sebastian.

YEARS rush by us like the wind. We see not whence the eddy comes, nor whitherward it is tending, and we seem ourselves to witness their flight without a sense that we are changed; and yet Time is beguiling man of his strength, as the winds rob the woods of their foliage.

After the marriage of Alice and Markham Everard, the old knight resided near them, in an ancient manor-house, belonging to the redeemed portion of his estate, where Joceline and Phœbe, now man and wife, with one or two domestics, regulated the affairs of his household. When he tired of Shakspeare and solitude, he was ever a welcome guest at his son-in-law's, where he went the more frequently that Markham had given up all concern in public affairs, disapproving of the forcible dismissal of the Parliament, and submitting to Cromwell's subsequent domination rather as that which was the lesser evil than as to a government which he regarded as legal. Cromwell seemed ever willing to show himself his friend; but Everard, resenting highly the proposal to deliver up the King, which he considered as an insult to his honor, never answered such advances, and became, on the contrary, of the opinion, which was now generally prevalent in the nation, that a settled government could not be obtained without the recall of the banished family. There is no doubt that the personal kindness which he had received from Charles rendered him the more readily disposed to such a measure. He was peremptory, however, in declining all engagements during Oliver's life, whose power he considered as too firmly fixed to be shaken by any plots which could be formed against it.

Meantime Wildrake continued to be Everard's protected dependant as before, though sometimes the connection tended not a little to his inconvenience. That respectable person, indeed, while he remained stationary in his patron's house or that of the old knight, discharged many little duties in the family, and won Alice's heart by his attention to the children, teaching the boys, of whom they had three, to ride, fence, toss the pike, and many similar exercsies ; and, above all, filling up a great blank in her father's existence, with whom he played at chess and backgammon, or read Shakspeare, or was clerk to prayers when any sequestrated divine ventured to read the service of the church; or he found game for him while the old gentleman continued to go a-sporting ; and, especially, he talked over the storming of Brentford, and the battles of Edgehill, Banbury, Roundway Down, and others—themes which the aged Cavalier delighted in, but which he could not so well enter upon with Colonel Everard, who had gained his laurels in the Parliament service.

The assistance which he received from Wildrake's society became more necessary after Sir Henry was deprived of his gallant and only son, who was slain in the fatal battle of Dunkirk, where, unhappily, English colors were displayed on both the contending sides, the French then being allied with Oliver, who sent to their aid a body of auxiliaries, and the troops of the banished king fighting in behalf of the Spaniards. Sir Henry received the melancholy news like an old man—that is, with more external composure than could have been anticipated. He dwelt for weeks and months on the lines forwarded by the indefatigable Dr. Rochecliffe, superscribed in small letters "C. R.," and subscribed "Louis Kerneguy," in which the writer conjured him to endure his inestimable loss with the greater firmness that he had still left one son (intimating himself), who would always regard him as a father.

But in spite of this balsam, sorrow, acting inperceptibly, and sucking the blood like a vampire, seemed gradually drying up the springs of life; and, without any formed illness or outward complaint, the old man's strength and vigor gradually abated, and the ministry of Wildrake proved daily more indispensable.

It was not, however, always to be had. The Cavalier was one of those happy persons whom a strong constitution, an unreflecting mind, and exuberant spirits enable to play through their whole lives the part of a schoolboy—happy for the moment and careless of consequences. Once or twice every year, when he had collected a few pieces, the Cavaliero Wildrake made a start to London, where, as he described it, he went on the ramble, drank as much wine as he could come by, and led a "skeldering" life, to use his own phrase, among roystering Cavaliers like himself, till by some rash speech or wild action he got into the Marshalsea, the Fleet, or some other prison, from which he was to be delivered at the expense of interest, money, and sometimes a little reputation.

At length Cromwell died, his son resigned the government, and the various changes which followed induced Everard, as well as many others, to adopt more active measures in the King's behalf. Everard even remitted considerable sums for his service, but with the utmost caution, and corresponding with no intermediate agent, but with the Chancellor himself, to whom he communicated much useful information upon public affairs. With all his prudence, he was very nearly engaged in the ineffectual rising of Booth and Middleton in the west, and with great difficulty escaped from the fatal consequences of that ill-timed attempt. After this, although the estate of the kingdom was trebly unsettled, yet no card seemed to turn up favorable to the Royal, cause, until the movement of General Monk from Scotland. Even then, it was when at the point of complete success that the fortunes of Charles seemed at a lower ebb than ever, especially when intelligence had arrived at the little court which he then kept in Brussels that Monk, on arriving in London, had put himself under the orders of the Parliament.

It was at this time, and in the evening, while the King, Buckingham, Wilmot, and some other gallants of his wandering court were engaged in a convivial party, that the Chancellor (Clarendon) suddenly craved audience, and, entering with less ceremony than he would have done at another time, announced extraordinary news. For the messenger, he said, he could say nothing, saving that he appeared to have drunk much and slept little; but that he had brought a sure token of credence from a man for whose faith he would venture his life.

The King demanded to see the messenger himself.

A man entered, with something the manners of a gentleman, and more those of a rakehelly debauchee—his eyes swelled and inflamed, his gait disordered and stumbling, partly through lack of sleep, partly through the means he had taken to support his fatigue. He staggered without ceremony to the head of the table, seized the King's hand, which he mumbled like a piece of gingerbread; while Charles, who began to recollect him from his mode of salutation, was not very much pleased that their meeting should have taken place before so many witnesses.

"I bring good news," said the uncouth messenger—"glorious news! The King shall enjoy his own again! My feet are beautiful on the mountains. Gad, I have lived with Presbyterians till I have caught their language; but we are all one man's children now—all your Majesty's poor babes. The Rump is all ruined in London. Bonfires flaming, music playing, rumps roasting, healths drinking, London in a blaze of light from the Strand to Rotherhithe, tankards clattering——"

"We can guess at that," said the Duke of Buckingham.

"My old friend Mark Everard sent me off with the news—I'm a villain if I've slept since. Your Majesty recollects me, I am sure. Your Majesty remembers sa—sa—at the King's Oak at Woodstock?

O, we'll dance and sing and play,
For 'twill be a joyous day
When the King shall enjoy his own again."

"Master Wildrake, I remember you well," said the King. "I trust the good news is certain?"

"Certain! your Majesty; did I not hear the bells? did I not see the bonfires? did I not drink your Majesty's health so often that my legs would scarce carry me to the wharf? It is as certain as that I am poor Roger Wildrake of Squattlesea Mere, Lincoln."

The Duke of Buckingham here whispered to the King," "I have always suspected your Majesty kept odd company during the escape from Worcester, but this seems a rare sample."

"Why, pretty much like yourself and other company I have kept here so many years—as stout a heart, as empty a head," said Charles, "as much lace, though somewhat tarnished, as much brass on the brow, and nearly as much copper in the pocket."

"I would your Majesty would entrust this messenger of good news with me, to get the truth out of him," said Buckingham.

"Thank your Grace," replied the King; "but he has a will as well as yourself, and such seldom agree. My Lord Chancellor hath wisdom, and to that we must trust ourselves. Master Wildrake, you will go with my Lord Chancellor, who will bring us a report of your tidings; meantime, I assure you that you shall be no loser for being the first messenger of good news." So saying, he gave a signal to the Chancellor to take away Wildrake, whom he judged, in his present humor, to be not unlikely to communicate some former passages at Woodstock which might rather entertain than edify the wits of his court.

Corroboration of the joyful intelligence soon arrived, and Wildrake was presented with a handsome gratuity and small pension, which, by the King's special desire, had no duty whatever attached to it.

Shortly afterwards, all England was engaged in chorusing his favorite ditty—

> "O, the twenty-ninth of May,
> It was a glorious day,
> When the King did enjoy his own again."

On that memorable day, the King prepared to make his progress from Rochester to London, with a reception on the part of his subjects so unanimously cordial as made him say gaily, "It must have been his own fault to stay so long away from a country where his arrival gave so much joy." On horseback, betwixt his brothers, the Dukes of York and Gloucester, the restored monarch trode slowly over roads strewn with flowers, by conduits running wine, under triumphal arches, and through streets hung with tapestry. There were the citizens in various bands, some arrayed in coats of black velvet, with gold chains, some in military suits of cloth of gold, or cloth of silver, followed by all those craftsmen who, having hooted the father from Whitehall, had now come to shout the son into possession of his ancestral palace.

On his progress through Blackheath he passed that army which, so long formidable to England herself, as well as to Europe, had been the means of restoring the monarchy which their own hands had destroyed. As the King passed the last files of this formidable host, he came to an open part of the heath, where many persons of quality, with others of inferior rank, had stationed themselves to gratulate him as he passed towards the capital.

There was one group, however, which attracted peculiar attention from those around, on account of the respect shown to the party by the soldiers who kept the ground, and who, whether Cavaliers or Roundheads, seemed to contest emulously which should contribute most to their accommodation; for both the elder and younger gentlemen of the party had been distinguished in the Civil War. It was a family group, of which the principal figure was an old man seated in a chair, having a complacent smile on his face and a tear swelling to his eye, as he saw the banners wave on in interminable succession, and heard the multitude shouting the long-silenced acclamation, "God save King Charles!" His cheek was ashy pale and his long beard bleached like the thistle-down; his blue eye was cloudless, yet it was obvious that its vision was failing. His motions were feeble, and he spoke little, except when he answered the prattle of his grandchildren or asked a question of his daughter, who sat beside him, matured in matronly beauty, or of Colonel Everard, who stood behind. There, too, the stout yeoman, Joceline Joliffe, still in his silvan dress, leaned, like a second Benaiah, on the quarter-staff that had done the King good service in its day, and his wife, a buxom matron as she had been a pretty maiden, laughed at her own consequence, and ever and anon joined her shrill notes to the stentorian halloo which her husband added to the general exclamation.

Three fine boys and two pretty girls prattled around their grandfather, who made them such answers as suited their age, and repeatedly passed his withered hand over the fair locks of the little darlings, while Alice, assisted by Wildrake blazing in a splendid dress, and his eyes washed with only a single cup of canary, took off the children's attention from time to time, lest they should weary their grandfather. We must not omit one other remarkable figure in the group—a gigantic dog, which bore the signs of being at the extremity of canine life, being perhaps fifteen or sixteen years old. But, though exhibiting the ruin only of his former appearance, his eyes dim, his joints stiff, his head slouched down, and his gallant carriage and graceful motions exchanged for a stiff, rheumatic, hobbling gait, the noble hound had lost none of his instinctive fondness for his master. To lie by Sir Henry's feet in the summer or by the fire in winter, to raise his head to look on him, to lick his withered hand or his shrivelled cheek from time to time, seemed now all that Bevis lived for.

Three or four livery-servants attended to protect this group from the thronging multitude; but it needed not. The high respectability and unpretending simplicity of their appearance gave them, even in the eyes of the coarsest of the people, an air of patriarchal dignity which commanded general regard; and they sat upon the bank which they had chosen for their station by the wayside as undisturbed as if they had been in their own park.

And now the distant clarions announced the royal presence. Onward came pursuivant and trumpet, onward came plumes and cloth of gold, and waving standards, I displayed, and sword gleaming to the sun; and at length, heading a group of the noblest in England, and supported by his royal brothers on either side, onward came King Charles. He had already halted more than once, in kindness perhaps as well as policy, to exchange a word with persons whom he recognized among the spectators, and the shouts of the bystanders applauded a courtesy which seemed so well timed. But when he had gazed an instant on the party we have described, it was impossible, if even Alice had been too much changed to be recognized, not instantly to know Bevis and his venerable master. The monarch sprung from his horse, and walked instantly up to the old knight, amid thundering acclamations which rose from the multitudes around, when they saw Charles with his own hand oppose the feeble attempts of the old man to rise to do him homage. Gently replacing him on his seat,

"Bless," he said, "father—bless your son, who has returned in safety, as you blessed him when he departed in danger."

"May God bless—and preserve——" muttered the old man, overcome by his feelings. And the King, to give him a few moments' repose, turned to Alice. "And you," he said, "my fair guide, how have you been employed since our perilous night-walk? But I need not ask," glancing round—"in the service of king and kingdom, bringing up subjects as loyal as their ancestors. A fair lineage, by my faith, and a beautiful sight to the eye of an English King! Colonel Everard, we shall see you, I trust, at Whitehall?" Here he nodded to Wildrake.

"And thou, Joceline, thou canst hold thy quarter-staff with one hand, sure? Thrust forward the other palm."

Looking down in sheer bashfulness, Joceline, like a bull about to push, extended to the King, over his lady's shoulder, a hand as broad and hard as a wooden trencher, which the King filled with gold coins. "Buy a head-gear for my friend Phœbe with some of these," said Charles; "she too has been doing her duty to old England."

The King then turned once more to the knight, who

seemed making an effort to speak. He took his aged hand in both his own, and stooped his head toward him to catch his accents, while the old man, detaining him with the other hand, said something faltering, of which Charles could only cacth the quotation :—

> "Unthread the rude eye of rebellion,
> And welcome home again discarded faith."

Extricating himself, therefore, as gently as possible, from a scene which began to grow painfully embarrassing, the good-natured King said, speaking with unusual distinctness to ensure the old man's comprehending him, "This is something too public a place for all we have to say. But if you come not soon to see King Charles at Whitehall, he will send down Louis Kerneguy to visit you, that you may see how rational that mischievous lad is become since his travels."

So saying, he once more pressed affectionately the old man's hand, bowed to Alice and all around, and withdrew, Sir Henry Lee listening with a smile, which showed he comprehended the gracious tendency of what had been said. The old man leaned back on his seat and muttered the *Nunc dimittis.*

"Excuse me for having made you wait, my lords," said the King, as he mounted his horse. "Indeed, had it not been for these good folks, you might have waited for me long enough to little purpose. Move on, sirs."

The array moved on accordingly; the sounds of trumpets and drums again rose amid the acclamation, which had been silent while the King stopped; while the effect of the whole procession resuming its motion was so spendidly dazzling that even Alice's anxiety about her father's health was for a moment suspended, while her eye followed the long line of varied brilliancy that proceeded over the heath. When she looked again at Sir Henry, she was startled to see that his cheek, which had gained some color during his conversation with the King, had relapsed into earthy paleness: that his eyes were closed, and opened not again; and that his features expressed, amid their quietude, a rigidity which is not that of sleep. They ran to his assistance, but it was to late. The light that burned so low in the socket had leaped up and expired in one exhilarating flash.

The rest must be conceived. I have only to add, that

* See Note 13.

his faithful dog did not survive him many days; and that the image of Bevis * lies carved at his master's feet, on the tomb which was erected to the memory of Sir Henry Lee of Ditchley.

* See Note 13.

APPENDICES TO INTRODUCTION

No. I

THE WOODSTOCK SCUFFLE

OR

MOST DREADFULL APARITIONS THAT WERE LATELY SEENE IN THE MANNORHOUSE OF WOODSTOCH, NEERE OXFORD, TO THE GREAT TERROR AND WONDERFULL AMASEMENT OF ALL THERE THAT DID BEHOLD THEM.

[Printed in the yeere 1649. 4to.]

It were a wonder if one writes,
And not of wonders and strange sights;
For ev'ry where such things affrights
Poore people,

That men are ev'n at their wits' end.
God judgments ev'ry where doth send,
And yet we don't our lives amend,
But tipple,

And sweare, and lie, and cheat, and ——,
Because the world shall drown no more,
As if no judgments were in store
But water.

But by the stories which I tell,
You'll heare of terrors come from hell,
And fires, and shapes most terrible
For matter.

It is not long since that a child
Spake from the ground in a large field,
And made the people almost wild
That heard it,

Of which there is a printed book,
Wherein each man the truth may look;
If children speak, the matter's took
For verdict.

But this is stranger than that voice,
The wonder's greater, and the noyse;
And things appeare to men, not boyes,
At Woodstock;

Where Rosamond had once a bower,
To keep her from Queen Elinour,
And had escap'd her poys'nous power
By good luck.

But fate had otherwise decreed,
And Woodstock mannor saw a deed,
Which is in Hollinshed or Speed
Chro-nicled;

But neither Hollinshed nor Stow,
Nor no historians such things shew
Though in them wonders we well know
Are pickled;

For nothing else is history
But pickle of antiquity,
Where things are kept in memory
From stincking,

Which otherwaies would have lain dead,
As in oblivion buried
Which now you may call into head
With thinking.

The dreadfull story, which is true,
And now committed unto view,
By better pen, had it its due,
Should see light;

But I, contented, doe indite,
Not things of wit, but things of right;
You can't expect that things that fright
Should delight.

O hearken, therefore, harke and shake!
My very pen and hand doth quake,
While I the true relation make
O' th' wonder,

Which hath long time, and still appeares
Unto the state's Commissioners,
And puts them in their beds to feares
From under.

They came, good men, imploi'd by th' state,
To sell the lands of Charles the late,
And there they lay, and long did waite
For chapmen.

You may have easy pen'worths, woods,
Lands, ven'son, householdstuf, and goods;
They little thought of dogs that wou'd
There snap men.

But when they'd sup'd, and fully fed,
They set up remnants and to bed,
Where scarce they had laid down a head
To slumber,

But that their beds were heav'd on high;
They thought some dog under did lie,
And meant i' th' chamber (fie, fie, fie)
To scumber.

Some thought the cunning cur did mean
To eat their mutton (which was lean)
Reserv'd for breakfast, for the men
Were thrifty;

And up one rises in his shirt,
Intending the slie cur to hurt,
And forty thrusts made at him for't,
Or fifty.

But empty came his sword again,
He found hee thrust but all in vain;
The mutton safe, hee went amain
To's fellow.

And now (assured all was well)
The bed again began to swell,
The men were frighted, and did smell
O' th' yellow.

From heaving, now the cloaths it pluckt;
The men, for feare, together stuck,
And in their sweat each other duck't.
They wished

A thousand times that it were day,
"'Tis sure the divell! Let us pray."
They pray'd amain; and, as they say,
So * *

Aproach of day did cleere the doubt,
For all devotions were run out,
They now waxt strong and something stout.
One peaked

Under the bed, but nought was there;
Hee view'd the chamber ev'ry where,
Nothing apear'd but what, for feare,
They leaked.

Their stomachs then return'd apace,
They found the mutton in the place,
And fell unto it with a grace.
They laughed

Each at the other's pannick feare,
And each his bedfellow did jeere,
And having sent for ale and beere,
They quaffed.

And then abroad the summons went,
Who'll buy king's-land o' th' Parli'ment?
A paper-book contein'd the rent,
Which lay there;

That did contein the severall farmes,
Quit-rents, knight services, and armes;
But that they came not in by swarmes
To pay there.

Night doth invite to bed again.
The grand Commissioners were lain;
But then the thing did heave amain.
It busled,

And with great clamor filled their eares.
The noyse was doubled, and their feares;
Nothing was standing but their haires;
They nuzled.

Oft were the blankets pul'd, the sheete
Was closely twin'd betwixt their feete;
It seems the spirit was discreete
And civill;

Which makes the poore Commissioners
Feare they shall get but small arreares
And that there's yet for cavaliers
One divell.

They cast about what best to doe;
Next day they would to wise men goe,
To neighb'ring towns some cours to know.
For schollars

Come not to Woodstock, as before,
And Allen's dead as a nayle-doore,
And so's old John, eclep'd the poore,
His follower.

Rake Oxford o're, there's not a man
That rayse or lay a spirit can,
Or use the circle, or the wand,
Or conjure,

Or can say boh! unto a divell,
Or to a goose that is uncivill,
Nor where Keimbolton purg'd out evill
'Tis sin sure.

There were two villages hard by,
With teachers of presbytery,
Whe knew the house was hidiously
Be-pestred.

But 'lasse! their new divinity
Is not so deep, or not so high;
Their witts doe (as their meanes did) lie
Sequestred.

But Master Joffman was the wight
Which was to exorcise the spright;
Hee'll preach and pray you day and night
At pleasure.

And by that painfull gainfull trade,
He hath himselfe full wealthy made;
Great store of guilt he hath 'tis said,
And treasure.

But no intreaty of his friends
Could get him to the house of fiends,
Hee came not over for such ends
From Dutch-land;

But worse divinity hee brought,
And hath us reformation taught,
And, with our money, he hath bought
Him much land.

Had the old parsons preached still,
The dlv'l should nev'r have had his wil;
But those that had or art or skill
Are outed,

And those to whom the pow'r was giv'n
Of driving spirits are out-driv'n;
Their colledges dispos'd, and livings,
To groutheads.

There was a justice who did boast,
Hee had as great a gift almost,
Who did desire him to accost
This evill;

But hee would not employ his gifts,
But found out many sleights and shifts;
Hee had no prayers, nor no snifts,
For th' divell.

Some other way they cast about,
These brought him in, they throw not out;
A woman, great with child, will do't;
They got one.

And she i' th' room that night must lie;
But when the thing about did flie,
And broke the windows furiously,
And hot one

Of the contractors o're the head,
Who lay securely in his bed,
The woman, shee-affrighted, fled,
While they *

And now they lay the cause on her,
That e're that night the thing did stir,
Because her selfe and grandfather
Were Papists;

They must be barnes-regenerate
(*A Hans en kelder* of the state,
Which was in reformation gatt),
They said, which

Doth make the divell stand in awe,
Pull in his hornes, his hoof, his claw;
But having none, they did in draw
A spay'd bitch.

But in the night there was such worke,
The spirit swaggered like a Turke;
The bitch had spi'd where it did lurke,
And howled

In such a wofull manner, that
Their very hearts went pit a pat;
The pore spay'd bitch did not know what,
And fouled

The stately rooms, where kings once lay;
But the contractors shew'd the way.
But mark what now I tell you, pray
'Tis worth it.

That book I told you of before,
Wherein were tenants written store,
A register for many more
Not forth yet;

That very book, as it did lie,
Took of a flame, no mortall eye
Seeing one jot of fire thereby,
Or taper;

For all the candles about flew,
And those that burned, burned blew,
Never kept soldiers such a doe
Or vaper.

The book thus burnt and none knew how,
The poore contractors made a vow
To worke no more; this spoil'd their plow
In that place.

Some other part o' th' house they'll find
To which the devill hath no mind,
But hee, it seems, is not inclin'd
With that grace;

But other prancks it plaid elsewhere.
An oake there was stood many a yeere,
Of goodly growth as any where,
Was hewn down.

Which into fewell-wood was cut,
And some into a wood-pile put,
But it was hurled all about
And thrown down.

In sundry formes it doth appeare:
Now like a grasping claw to teare,
Now like a dog, anon a beare,
It tumbles;

And all the windowes batter'd are,
No man the quarter enter dare;
All men (except the glasier)
Doe grumble.

Once in the likenesse of a woman,
Of stature much above the common,
'Twas seene, but spak a word to no man,
And vanish'd.

'Tis thought the ghost of some good wife
Whose husband was depriv'd of life,
Her children cheated, land in strife
Shee banist.

No man can tell the cause of these
So wondrous dreadfull outrages;
Yet if upon your sinne you please
To discant.

You'le find our actions out-doe hell's.
O wring your hands and cease the bells,
Repentance must, or nothing else
Appease can't.

No. II

THE JUST DEVIL OF WOODSTOCK

OR

A TRUE NARRATIVE OF THE SEVERAL APPARITIONS, THE FRIGHTS AND PUNISHMENTS, INFLICTED UPON THE RUMPISH COMMISSIONERS SENT THITHER TO SURVEY THE MANNORS AND HOUSES BELONGING TO HIS MAJESTIE.

[London, printed in the year 1660. 4to.]

The names of the persons in the ensuing Narrative mentioned, with others:—

Captain Cockaine.	Mr. Crook, the Lawyer.
Captain Hart.	Mr. Browne, the Surveyor.
Captain Crook.	Their three Servants.
Captain Carlesse.	Their Ordinary-keeper, and others.
Captain Roe.	The Gatekeeper, with the Wife and Servants.

Besides many more, who each night heard the noise, as Sir Gerard Fleetwood and his lady, with his family; Mr. Hyans, with his family; and several others, who lodged in the outer courts; and during the three last nights, the inhabitants of Woodstock town and other neighbor villages.

And there were many more, both divines and others, who came out of the country, and from Oxford, to see the glass and stones and other stuffe the devil had brought, wherewith to beat out the Commissioners; the marks upon some walls remain, and many, this to testifie.

THE PREFACE TO THE ENSUING NARRATIVE

Since it hath pleased the Almighty God, out of His infinite mercy, so to make us happy, by restoring of our native king to us, and us unto our native liberty through him, that now the good may say, *magna temporum felicitas ubi sentire quæ velis, et dicere licet quæ sentias*, we cannot but esteem ourselves engaged, in the highest of degrees, to render unto Him the highest thanks we can express, although, surpris'd with joy, we become as lost in the performance, when gladness and admiration strikes us silent, as we look back upon the precipice of our late condition, and those miraculous deliverances beyond expression, freed from the slavery and those desperate perils we dayly lived in fear of, during the tyrannicall times of that detestable usurper, Oliver Cromwel; he who had raked up such judges as would wrest the most innocent language into high treason, when he had the cruel conscience to take away our lives, upon no other ground of justice or reason (the stones of London streets would rise to witness it, if all their citizens were silent); and with these judges had such councillors as could advise him unto worse, which will less want of witness. For should the many auditors be silent, the press, as God would have it, hath given it us in print, where one of them, and his conscience-keeper, too, speaks out, "What shall we do with these men?" saith he: *Æger intemperans crudelem facit medicum, et immedicabile vulnus ense recidendum.* Who these men are that should be brought to such Sicilian Vespers, the former page sets forth—those which conceit *utopias*, and have their day-dreams of the return of I know not what golden age, with the old line. What usage, when such a privy councillor had power, could he expect, who then had published this narrative?* This, which so plainly shews the devil himself dislikt their doings (so much more bad were they then he would have them be), severer sure then was the devil to their Commissioners at Woodstock; for he warned them, with dreadful noises, to drive them from their work. This councellor, without more ado, would have all who retain'd conceits of allegiance to their soveraign to be absolutely cut off by the usurper's sword. A sad sentence

* *Mr. Nathaniel Fines* [Fiennes], *his Speech before Oliver Cromwel and his two Houses of Parliament, the* 20 *of January* 1657, *he being Cromwel's Seal-keeper.*

for a loyal party to a lawfull king. But Heaven is always just; the party is repriv'd, and do acknowledge the hand of God in it, as is rightly applyed, and as justly sensible of their deliverance, in that the foundation, which this councellor saith was already so well laid, is now turned up, and what he calls day-dreams are come to pass. That old line, which (as with him) there seemed *aliquid divine* to the contrary, is now restored. And that rock which, as he saith, the prelates and all their adherents, nay, and their master and supporter, too, with all his posterity, have split themselves upon, is nowhere to be heard of. And that posterity are safely arrived in their ports, and masters of that mighty navy, their enemies so much encreased to keep them out with. The eldest sits upon the throne, his place by birthright and descent,

Pacatumque regit patriis virtutibus orbem;

upon which throne long may he sit, and reign in peace, that by his just government the enemies of ours, the true Protestant Church, of that glorious martyr, our late soveraign, and of his royal posterity, may be either absolutely converted or utterly confounded.

If any shall now ask the why this narrative was not sooner published, as neerer to the times wherein the things were acted, he hath the reason for it in the former lines; which will the more cleerly appear unto his apprehension, if he shall perpend how much cruelty is requisite to the maintenance of rebellion, and how great care is necessary in the supporters, to obviate and divert the smallest things that tend to the unblinding of the people; so that it needs will follow that they must have accounted this amongst the great obstructions to their sales of his Majestie's lands, the devil not joyning with them in the security; and greater to the pulling down the royal pallaces, when their chapmen should conceit the devil would haunt them in their houses, for building with so ill got materials; as no doubt but that he hath, so numerous and confident are the relations made of the same, though scarce any so totally remarkeable as this (if it be not that others have been more conceald), in regard of the strange circumstances as long continuances, but especially the number of the persons together, to whom all things were so visibly both seen and done, so that surely it exceeds any other; for the devils thus manifesting themselves, it appears evidently that there are such things as devils to persecute the wicked in this world as in the next.

Now, if to these were added the diverse reall phantasms seen at Whitehall in Cromwell's times, which caused him to keep such nightly guards in and about his bedchamber, and yet so oft to change his lodgings; if those things done at St. James, where the devil so joal'd the centinels against the sides of the queen's chappell doors, that some of them fell sick upon it, and, others not taking warning by it, kild one outright, whom they buried in the place, and all other such dreadful things, those that inhabited the royal houses have been affrighted with; and if to these were likewise added a relation of all those regicides and their abettors the devil hath entred into, as he did the Gadarenes' swine, with so many more of them who hath fallen mad and dyed in hydeous forms of such distractions *—that which hath been of this within these 12 last years in England (should all of this nature our chronicles do tell, with all the superstitious monks have writ, be put together would make the greater volume, and of more strange occurrents.

And now as to the penman of this narrative, know that he was a divine, and at the time of those things acted, which are here related, the minister and schoolmaster of Woodstock; a person learned and discreet, not byassed with factious humours, his name Widows, who each day put in writing what he heard from their mouthes, and such things as they told to have befallen them the night before, therein keeping to their own words; and, never thinking that what he had writ should happen to be made publick, gave it no better dress to set it forth. And because to do it now shall not be construed to change the story, the reader hath it here accordingly exposed.

THE JUST DEVILL OF WOODSTOCK

The 16 day of *October*, in the year of our Lord 1649, the Commissioners for surveying and valuing his Majestie's mannor house, parks, woods, deer, demesnes, and all things thereunto belonging, by name Captain Crook, Captain Hart, Captain Cockaine, Captain Carelesse, and Captain Roe, their messenger, with Mr. Brown, their secretary, and two or three servants, went from Woodstock town, where they had lain some nights before, and took up their lodgings in his Majestie's house after this manner:—The bed-chamber and withdrawing-room they both lodged in and made their kitchin, the presence-chamber their room for

* St. Matt. viii. 28 and St. Luke viii. 26.

dispatch of their business with all commers, of the council-hall their brew-house, as of the dining-room their wood-house where they laid in the clefts of that antient standard in the High Park, for many ages beyond memory known by the name of the King's Oak, which they had chosen out, and caused to be dug up by the roots.

October 17.—About the middle of the night, these new guests were first awaked by a knocking at the presence-chamber door, which they also conceived did open, and something to enter, which came through the room, and also walkt through the withdrawing-room into the bedchamber, and there walkt about that room with a heavy step during half an hour, then crept under the bed where Captain Hart and Captain Carelesse lay, where it did seem (as it were) to bite and gnaw the mat and bed-coards, as if it would tear and rend the feather beds; which having done a while, then would heave a while, and rest; then heave them up again in the bed more high than it did before, sometime on the one side, sometime on the other, as if it had tried which captain was heaviest. Thus having heaved some half an hour, from thence it walkt out and went under the servants' bed, and did the like to them; thence it walkt into a withdrawing-room, and there did the same to all who lodged there. Thus, having welcomed them for more than two hours' space, it walkt out as it came in, and shut the outer door again, but with a clap of some mightie force. These guests were in a sweat all this while, but out of it falling into a sleep again, it became morning first before they spake their minds; then would they have it to be a dog, yet they described it more to the likeness of a great bear: so fell to the examining under the beds, where, finding only the mats scracht, but the bed-coards whole, and the quarter of beef which lay on the floor untoucht, they entertained other thoughts.

October 18.—They were all awaked as the night before, and now conceived that they heard all the great clefts of the King's Oak brought into the presence-chamber, and there thumpt down, and after roul about the room; they could hear their chairs and stools tost from one side of the room unto the other, and then (as it were) altogether josled. Thus having done an hour together, it walkt into the withdrawing-room, where lodged the two captains, the secretary, and two servants; here stopt the thing a while, as if it did take breath, but raised a hideous one, then walkt into the bed-chamber, where lay those as before, and under the bed it went, where it did heave and heave again, that now they in bed were put to catch hold upon [the] bed-posts, and sometimes one of the other, to prevent their being tumbled out upon the ground; then coming out as from under the bed, and taking hold upon the bed-posts, it would shake the whole bed, almost as if a cradle rocked. Thus having done here for half an hour, it went into the withdrawing-room, where first it came and stood at the bed's feet, and heaving up the bed's feet, flopt down again a while, until at last it heaved the feet so high that those in bed thought to have been set upon their heads; and having thus for two hours entertained them, went out as in the night before, but with a great noise.

October 19.—This night they awaked not until the midst of the night; they perceived the room to shake with something that walkt about the bedchamber, which having done so a while, it walkt into a withdrawing-room, where it took up a brasse warming-pan, and returning with it into the bedchamber, therein made so loud a noise, in these captains' own words, it was as loud and scurvie as a ring of fine untuned bells rung backward; but the captains, not to seem afraid, next day made mirth of what had past, and jested at the devil in the pan.

October 20.—These captains and their company, still lodging as before, were awakened in this night, with some things flying about the rooms, and out of one room into the other, as thrown with some great force. Captain Hart, being in a slumber, was taken by the shoulder and shaked until he did sit up in his bed, thinking that it had been one of his fellows, when suddenly he was taken on the pate with a trencher, that it made him shrink down into the bed-clothes, and all of them in both rooms kept their heads at least within their sheets, so fiercely did three dozen of trenchers fly about the rooms; yet Captain Hart ventured again to peep out to see what was the matter, and what it was that threw, but then the trenchers came so fast and neer about his ears, that he was fain quickly to couch again. In the morning they found all their trenchers, pots, and spits upon and about their beds, and all such things as were of common use scattered about the rooms. This night there was also, in several parts of the room and outer rooms, such noises of beating at doors and on the walls, as if that several smiths had been at work; and yet our captain [s] shrunk not from their work, but went on in that, and lodged as they had done before.

October 21st.—About midnight they heard great knocking at every door; after a while the doors flew open, and into the withdrawing-room entred something as of a mighty proportion, the figure of it they knew not how to describe. This walkt awhile about the room shaking the floor at every step, then came it up close to the bedside where lay Captain[s] Crook and Carelesse; and after a little pause, as it were, the bed-curtains, both at sides and feet, were drawn up and down slowly, then faster again for a quarter of an hour, then from end to end as fast as imagination can fancie the running of the rings, then shaked it the beds, as if the joints thereof had crackt; then walkt the thing into the bedchamber, and so plaied with those beds there; then took up eight peuter dishes, and bouled them about the room and over the servants in the truckle-beds; then sometimes were the dishes taken up and thrown crosse the high beds and against the walls, and so much battered; but there were more dishes wherein was meat in the same room, that were not at all removed. During this, in the presence-chamber there was stranger noise of weightie things thrown down, and, as they supposed, the clefts of the King's Oak did roul about the room, yet at the wonted hour went away, and left them to take rest such as they could.

October 22.—Hath mist of being set down; the officers, imployed in their work farther off, came not that day to Woodstock.

October 23.—Those that lodged in the withdrawing-room, in the midst of the night were awakened with the cracking of fire, as if it had been with thorns and sparks of fire burning, whereupon they supposed that the bedchamber had taken fire, and listning to it farther, they heard their fellows in bed sadly groan, which gave them to suppose they might be suffocated; wherefore they called upon their servants to make all possible haste to help them. When the two servants were come in, they found all asleep, and so brought back word, but that there were no bedclothes upon them; wherefore they were sent back to cover them, and to stir up and mend the fire. When the servants had covered them and were come to the chimney, in the corners they found their wearing-apparrel, boots, and stockings, but they had no sooner toucht the embers, when the fire-brands flew about their ears so fast, that away ran they into the other room for the shelter of their coverlids; then after them walkt something that stampt about the room as if it had been exceeding angry, and likewise threw about the trenchers, platters, and all such things in the room; after two hours went out, yet stampt again over their heads.

October 24.—They lodged all abroad.

October 25.—This afternoon was come unto them Mr. Richard Crook the lawyer, brother to Captain Crook, and now deputy-steward of the mannor unto Captain Parsons and Major Butler, who had put out Mr. Hyans, his Majestie's officer. To entertain this new guest, the Commissioners caused a very great fire to be made, of neer the chimney-full of wood of the King's Oak, and he was lodged in the withdrawing-room with his brother, and his servant in the same room. About the midst of the night a wonderful knocking was heard, and into the room something did rush, which, coming to the chimney-side, dasht out the fire as with the stampt of some prodigious foot, then threw down such weighty stuffe, what ere it was (they took it to be the residue of the clefts and roots of the King's Oak), close by the bedside, that the house and bed shook with it. Captain Cockaine and his fellow arose, and took their swords to go unto the Crooks. The noise ceased at their rising, so that they came to the door and called. The two brothers, though fully awaked, and heard them call, were so amazed, that they made no answer until Captain Cockaine had recovered the boldness to call very loud, and came unto their bedside; then faintly first, after some more assurance, they came to understand one another, and comforted the lawyer. Whilst this was thus, no noise was heard, which made them think the time was past of that night's troubles, so that, after some little conference, they applied themselves to take some rest. When Captain Cockaine was come to his own bed, which he had left open, he found it closely covered, which he much wondered at; but turning the clothes down, and opening it to get in, he found the lower sheet strewed over with trenchers. Their whole three dozens of trenchers were orderly disposed between the sheets, which he and his fellow endeavoring to cast out, such noise arose about the room, that they were glad to get into bed with some of the trenchers. The noise lasted a full half-hour after this. This entertainment so ill did like the lawyer, and being not so well studied in the point as to resolve this the devil's law case, that he next day resolved to be gone; but having not dispatcht all that he came for, profit and perswasions prevailed with him to stay the other hearing, so that he lodged as he did the night before.

October 26.—This night each room was better furnished with fire and candle than before; yet about twelve at night came something in that dasht all out, then did walk about the room, making a noise, not to be set forth by the comparison with any other thing; sometimes came it to the bedsides and drew the curtains to and fro, then twerle them, then walk about again, and return to the bed-posts, shake them with all the bed, so that they in bed were put to hold one upon the other, then walk about the room again, and come to the servants' bed, and gnaw and [scratch] the wainscot head, and shake altogether in that room; at the time of this being in doing, they in the bed-chamber heard such strange dropping down from the roof of the room, that they supposed 'twas like the fall of money by the sound. Captain Cockaine, not frighted with so small a noise (and lying near the chimney), stept out and made shift to light a candle, by the light of which he perceived the room strewed over with broken glass, green, and some as it were pieces of broken bottles; he had not long been considering what it was, when suddainly his candle was hit out, and glass flew about the room, that he made haste to the protection of the coverlets; the noise of thundering rose more hideous then at any time before; yet, at a certain time, all vanisht into calmness. The morning after was the glass about the room, which the maid that was to make clean the rooms swept up into a corner, and many came to see it. But Mr. Richard Crook would stay no longer, yet as he stopt, going through Woodstock town, he was there heard to say, that he would not lodge amongst them another night for a fee of £500.

October 27.—The Commissiners had not yet done their work, wherefore they must stay; and being all men of the sword, they must not seem afraid to encounter with anything, though it be the devil; therefore, with pistols charged, and drawn swords laied by their bedsides, they applied themselves to take some rest, when something in the midst of night so opened and shut the window casements with such claps, that it awakened all that slept; some of them peeping out to look what was the matter with the windows, stones flew about the rooms as if hurled with many hands; some hit the walls, and some the beds' heads close above the pillows, the dints of which were then, and yet (it is conceived) are to be seen, thus sometime throwing stones, and sometime making thundering noise, for two hours space. It ceast, and all was quiet till the morn. After their rising, and the maid come in to make the fire, they looked about the rooms; they found fourscore stones brought in that night, and going to lay them together in the corner where the glass (before mentioned, had been swept up, they found that every piece of glass had been carried away that night. Many people came next day to see the stones, and all observed that they were not of such kind of stones as are naturall in the countrey thereabout; with these were noise like claps of thunder, or report of cannon planted against the rooms, heard by all that lodged in the outer courts, to their astonishment and at Woodstock town, taken to be thunder.

October 28.—This night, both strange and differing noise from the former first wakened Captain Hart, who lodged in the bedchamber, who, hearing Roe and Brown to groan, called out to Cockaine and Cocka [Crook] to come and help them, for Hart could not now stir himself; Cockaine would faine have answered, but he could not, or look about; something, he thought, stopt both his breath and held down his eyelids. Amazed thus, he struggles and kickt about, till he had awaked Captain Crook, who, half asleep, grew very angry at his kicks, and multiplied words. It grew to an appointment in the field; but this fully recovered Cockaine to remember that Captain Hart had called for help, wherefore to them he ran in the other room, whom he found sadly groaning, where, scraping in the chimney, he both found a candle and fire to light it; but had not gone two steps, when something blew the candle out, and threw him in the chair by the bedside, when presently cried out Captain Careless, with a most pittiful voice, "Come hither—O come hither, brother Cockaine, the thing's gone of me." Cockaine, scarce yet himself, helpt to set him up in his bed, and after Captain Hart, and having scarce done that to them, and also to the other two, they heard Captain Crook crying out, as if something had been killing him. Cockaine snatcht up the sword that lay by their bed, and ran into the room to save Crook, but was in much more likelyhood to kill him, for at his coming, the thing that pressed Crook went of him, at which Crook started out of his bed, whom Cockaine thought a spirit, made at him, at which Crook cried out, "Lord help—Lord save me." Cockaine let fall his hand, and Crook, embracing Cockaine, desired his reconcilement, giving him many thanks for his deliverance. Then rose they all and came together, discoursed sometimes godly and sometimes praied, for all this while was there such stamping over the roof of the house, as if 1000 horse had there been trotting; this night all the stones brought in the night before, and laid up in the withdrawing-room, were all carried again away by that which brought them in, which at the wonted time left of, and, as it were, went out, and so away.

October 29.—Their businesse having now received so much forwardnesse as to be neer dispatcht, they encouraged one the other, and resolved to try further; therefore, they provided more lights and fires, and further, for their assistance, prevailed with their ordinary-keeper to lodge amongst them, and bring his mastive bitch; and it was so this night with them, that they had no disturbance at all.

October 30.—So well they had past the night before, that this night they went to bed confident and carelesse; untill about twelve of the clock, something knockt at the door as with a smith's great hammer, but with such force as if it had cleft the door; then ent'red something like a bear, but seem'd to swell more big, and walkt about the room, and out of one room into the other, treading so heavily, as the floare had not been strong enough to bear it. When it came into the bedchamber, it dasht against the beds' heads some kind of glass vessell, that broke in sundry pieces, and sometimes would take up those pieces and hurle them about the room, and into the other room; and when it did not hurle the glasse at their heads, it did strike upon the tables, as if many smiths, with their greatest hammers, had been laying on as upon an anvill; sometimes it thumpt against the walls as if it would beat a hole through; then upon their heads, such stamping, as if the roof of the house were beating down upon their heads; and having done thus, during the space (as was conjectured) of two hours, it ceased and vanished, but with a more fierce shutting of the doors then at any time before. In the morning they found the pieces of glass about the room, and observed that it was much differing from that glasse brought in three nights before, this being of a much thicker substance, which severall persons which came in carried away some pieces of. The Commissioners were in debate of lodging there no more; but all their businesse was not done, and some of them were so conceited as to believe, and to attribute the rest they enjoyed, the night before this last, unto the mastive bitch; wherefore, they resolved to get more company, and the mastive bitch, and try another night.

October 31. This night, the fires and lights prepared, the ordinary-keeper and his bitch, with another man perswaded by him, they all took their beds and fell asleep. But about twelve at night, such rapping was on all sides of them, that it wakened all of them; as the doors did seem to open, the mastive bitch fell fearfully a-yelling, and presently ran fiercely into the bed to them in the truckle-bed; as the thing came by the table, it struck so fierce a blow on that, as that it made the frame to crack, then took the warming-pan from off the table, and stroke it against the walls with so much force as that it was beat flat together, lid and bottom. Now were they hit as they lay covered over head and ears within the bedclothes. Captain Careless was taken a sound blow on the head with the shoulder-blade bone of a dead horse before they had been but thrown at, when they peept, up and mist); Brown had a shrewed blow on the leg with the backbone, and another on the head; and every one of them felt severall blows of bones and stones through the bedclothes, for now these things were thrown as from an angry hand that meant further mischief; the stones flew in at window as shot out of a gun, nor was the bursts lesse (as from without) then of a cannon, and all the windows broken down. Now as the hurling of the things did cease, and the thing walkt up and down, Captain Cockaine and Hart cried out, "In the name of the Father, Son, and Holy Ghost, what are you? What would you have? What have we done that you disturb us thus?" No voice replied, as the captains said, yet some of their servants have said otherwise, and the noise ceast. Hereupon Captain Hart and Cockain rose, who lay in the bedchamber, renewed the fire and lights, and one great candle, in a candlestick, they placed in the door, that might be seen by them in both the rooms. No sooner were they got to bed, but the noise arose on all sides more loud and hideous then at any time before, insomuch as (to use the captains' own words) it returned and brought seven devils worse then itself; and presently they saw the candle and candlestick in the passage of the door dasht up to the roof of the room by a kick of the hinder parts of a horse, and after with the hoof trode out the snuffe, and so dasht out the fire in the chimnies. As this was done, there fell, as from the sieling, upon them in the truckle-beds, such quantities of water, as if it had been poured out of buckets, which stunk worse than any earthly stink could make; and as this was in doing, something crept under the high beds, tost them up to the roof of the house, with the Commissioners in them, until the testers of the beds were beaten down upon them, and the bedsted-frames broke under them; and here some pause being made, they all, as if with one consent, started up, and ran down the stairs until they came into the Councel Hall, where two sate up a-brewing, but now were fallen asleep; those they scared much with wakening of them, having been much perplext before with the strange noise, which commonly was taken by them abroad for thunder, sometimes for rumbling wind. Here the Captains and their company got fire and candle, and every one carrying something of either, they returned into the presence chamber, where some applied themselves to make the fire, whilst others fell to prayers, and having got some clothes about them, they spent the residue of the night in singing psalms and prayers; during which, no noise was in that room, but most hideously round about, as at some distance.

It should have been told before, how that, when Captain Hart first rose this night (who lay in the bedchamber next the fire), he found their book of valuations crosse the embers smoaking, which he snacht up and cast upon the table there, which the night before was left upon the table in the presence amongst their other papers. This book was in the morning found a handful burnt, and had burnt the table where it lay; Brown, the clerk, said, he would not for a £100 and a £100 that it had been burnt a handful further.

This night it happened that there were six cony-stealers, who were come with their nets and ferrets to the cony-burrows by Rosamond's Well; but with the noise this night from the manor-house, they were so terrified, that like men distracted away they ran, and left their haies all ready pitched, ready up, and the ferrets in the cony-burrows.

Now the Commissioners, more sensible of their danger, considered more seriously of their safety, and agreed to go and confer with Mr. Hoffman, the minister of Wotton (a man not of the meanest note for life or learning, by some esteemed more high), to desire his advice, together with his company and prayers. Mr. Hoffman held it too high a point to resolve on suddenly and by himself, wherefore desired time to consider upon it, which being agreed unto, he forthwith rode to Mr. Jenkinson and Mr. Wheat, the two next justices of peace, to try what warrant they could give him for it. They both (as 'tis said from themselves) encouraged him to be assisting to the Commissioners, according to his calling.

But certain it is that, when they came to fetch him to go with them, Mr. Hoffman answered, that he would not lodge there one night for £500, and being asked to pray with them, he held up his hands and said, that he would not meddle upon any terms.*

Mr. Hoffman refusing to undertake the quarrel, the Commissioners held it not safe to lodge where they had been thus entertained any longer, but caused all things to be removed into the chambers over the gatehouse, where they staied but one night, and what rest they enjoyed there, we have but an uncertain relation of, for they went away early the next morning. But if it may be held fit to set down what hath been delivered by the report of others, they were also the same night much affrighted with dreadful apparitions, but observing that these passages spread much in discourse, to be also in particulars taken notice of, and that the nature of it made not for their cause, they agreed to the concealing of things for the future; yet this is well-known and certain, that the gate- keeper's wife was in so strange an agony in her bed, and in her bedchamber such noise (whilst her husband was above with the commissioners), that two maids in the next room to her durst not venture to assist her, but affrighted ran out to call company, and their master, and found the woman (at their coming in) gasping for breath; and the next day said, that she saw and suffered that which for all the world she would not be hired to again.

From Woodstock the Commissioners removed unto Euelme, and some of them returned to Woodstock the Sunday se'nnight after (the book of valuations wanting something that was for haste left imperfect), but lodged not in any of those rooms where they had lain before, and yet were not unvisited (as they confess themselves) by the devill, whom they called their nightly guest. Captain Crook came not untill Tuesday night, and how he sped that night the gate-keeper's wife can tell if she dareth, but what she hath whispered to her gossips shall not be made a part of this our narrative, nor many more particulars which have fallen from the Commissioners themselves and their servants to other persons. They are all or most of them alive, and may add to it when they please, and surely have not a better way to be revenged of him who troubled them, then according to the proverb, tell truth and shame the devil.

There remains this observation to be added, that on a Wednesday morning all these officers went away; and that since them diverse persons of severall qualities have lodged often and sometimes long in the same rooms, both in the presence, withdrawing-room, and bedchamber belonging unto his sacred Majesty; yet none have had the least disturbance, or heard the smallest noise, for which the cause was not as ordinary as apparent, except the Commissioners and their company, who came in order to the alienating and pulling down the house, which is well-nigh performed.

A SHORT SURVEY OF WOODSTOCK, NOT TAKEN BY ANY OF THE BEFORE-MENTIONED COMMISSIONERS.*

The noble seat called Woodstock is one of the ancient honors belonging to the crown. Severall mannors owe suite and service to the place; but the custom of the countrey giving it but the title of a mannor, we shall erre with them to be the better understood.

The mannor-house hath been a large fabrick, and accounted amongst his Majestie's standing houses, because there was alwaies kept a standing furniture. This great house was built by King Henry the First, but amplyfied with the gatehouse and outsides of the outer court by King Henry the Seventh, the stables by King James.

About a bow-shoot from the gate southwest remain foundation signs of that structure erected by King Henry the Second for the security of Lady Rosamond, daughter of Walter Lord Clifford, which some poets have compared to the Deda-

* By which is to be noted, that a Presbyterian minister dares not encounter an Independent devil. *Original marginal note.*

† This survey of Woodstock is appended to the preceding pamphlet.

lian labyrinth, but the form and circuit both of the place and ruins shew it to have been a house and of one pile, perhaps of strength, according to the fashion of those times, and probably was fitted with secret places of recess, and avenews to hide or convey away such persons as were not willing to be found if narrowly sought after. About the midst of the place ariseth a spring, called at present Rosamond's Well; it is but shallow, and shews to have been paved and walled about, likely contrived for the use of them within the house, when it should be of danger to go out.

A quarter of a mile distant from the king's house is seated Woodstock town, new and old. This new Woodstock did arise by some buildings which Henry the Second gave leave to be erected (as received by tradition) at the suite of the Lady Rosamond, for the use of out-servants upon the wastes of the mannor of Bladon, where is the mother church; this is a hamlet belonging to it, though encreased to a market-town by the advantage of the court residing sometime near, which of late years they have been sensible of the want of; this town was made a corporation in the 11 year of Henry the Sixth, by charter, with power to send two burgesses to parliament or not, as they will themselves.

Old Woodstock is seated on the west side of the brook named Glyme, which also runneth through the park; the town consists not of above four or five houses, but it is to be conceived that it hath been much larger, but very anciently so, for in some old law historians there is mention of the assize at Woodstock, for a law made in a micelgemote (the name of parliaments before the coming of the Norman) in the days of King Ethelred.

And in like manner, that thereabout was a king's house, if not in the same place where Henry the First built the late standing pile before his; for in such days those great councels were commonly held in the king's pallaces. Some of those lands have belonged to the orders of the Knights Templers, there being records which call them *terras quas rex excambiavit cum Templariis.*

But now this late large mannor-house is in a manner almost turned into heaps of rubbish; some seven or eight rooms left for the accommodation of a tenant that should rent the king's medows (of those who had no power to let them), with several high uncovered walls standing, the prodigious spectacles of malice unto monarchy, which ruines still bear semblance of their state, and yet aspire, in spight of envy or of weather, to shew, what kings do build, subjects may sometimes shake, but utterly can never overthrow.

That part of the park called the High Park hath been lately subdivided by Sir Arthur Haselrig, to make pastures for his breed of colts, and other parts plowed up. Of the whole saith Roffus Warwicensis, in MS. *Hen. I.*, p. 122, *Fecit iste rex parcum de Woodstock, cum palatio infra pradictum parcum, qui parcus erat primus parcus Angliæ, et continet in circuitu septum miliaria; constructus erat anno* 14 *hujus regis, aut parum post.* Without the park the king's demesn woods were, it cannot well be said now are, the timber being all sold off, and underwoods so cropt and spoiled by that beast the Lord Munson, and other greedy cattel, that they are hardly recoverable. Beyond which lieth Stonefield, and other mannors that hold of Woodstock, with other woods, that have been aliened by former kings, but with reservation of liberty for his Majestie's deer, and other beasts of forrest, to harbour in at pleasure, as in due place is to be shewed.

No. III.

[The following extract from a letter is docketed by the Author "to be inserted as an illustration of *Woodstock.*" It does not seem to have been included in any of the editions previous to that of 1871; but has been invariably printed since.]

Oxford, *Sept.* 3.

Having got sight of a letter concerning the sickness and death of old Mr. Lenthal from a person of known worth and integrity, I could not conceal it from you, being, as I conceive, of publick concern, which letter was as followeth:—

Sir—When I came to his presence he told me "he was very glad to see me, for he had two great works to do, and I must assist him in both: to fit his body for the earth, and his soul for heaven," to which purpose he desired me to pray with him. I told him the Church had appointed an office at the visitation of the sick, and I must use that. He said, "Yes, he chiefly desired the prayers of the Church," wherein he joined with a great fervency and devotion. After prayers he desired absolution. I told him I was very ready and willing to pronounce it, but he must first come to Christian contrition for the sins and failings of his life. "Well, sir," said he, "then instruct me to my duty."

I desired him to examine his life by the ten commandments, and wherein he found his failings to fly to the gospel for mercy. Then I read the ten commandments in order to him, mentioning the principal sins against each commandment. To pass by other things (under the seal of this office), when I came to the fifth commandment, and remembered him that disobedience, rebellion, and schism were the great sins against this commandment—"Yes, sir," he said, "there's my trouble, my disobedience, not against my natural parents, but against the *pater patriæ*, our deceased sovereign. I confess with Saul [Paul] I held their clothes whilst they murthered him, but herein I was not so criminal as Saul was, for God thou knowest I never consented to his death. I ever prayed and endeavoured what I could against it, but I did too much, Almighty God forgive me."

I then desired him to deal freely and openly in that business, and if he knew any of those villains that plotted or contrived that horrid murder which were not yet detected, now to discover 'em. He answered, "He was a stranger to that business, his soul never entered into that secret, but what concerns myself," said he, "I will confess freely. Three things are especially laid to my charge, wherein I am indeed too guilty: that I went from the Parliament to the army, that I proposed the bloody question for trying the King, and that I sat after the King's death. To the first I may give this in answer, that Cromwell and his agents deceived a wiser man than myself, that excellent King, and then might well deceive me also, and so they did. I knew the Presbyterians would never restore the King to his just rights; these men swore they would.

"For the second no excuse can be made; but I have the King's pardon, and I hope Almighty God will grant me His mercy also. Yet, sir," said he, "even then, when I put the question, I hoped the very putting the question would have cleared him, because I believed four for one were against it; but they deceived me also.

"To the third I make this candid confession, that 'twas my own baseness, and cowardice and unworthy fear to submit my life and estate to the mercy of those men that murthered the King, that hurried me on against my own conscience to act with them. Yet then I thought I might do some good and hinder some ill. Something I did for the church and universities, something for the King when I broke the oath of abjuration, as that Sir O—— B—— and yourself knows, something also for his return, as my L. G., and Mr. J—— T——, and yourself know, but the ill I did overweighed the little good I would have done. God forgive me for this also."

After this I remembered him that the Fathers of the Church also had been barbarously murthered and ruined, and asked whether he had any hand or gave any consent therein. He answered, "None; for he always did believe that was the primitive and best government of the church," and said he died a dutiful son of the Church of England as it was established before these times; for he had not yet seen the alteration of the liturgy.

After this office, wherein he indeed showed himself a very hearty penitent, he again desired the absolution of the church, which I then pronounced, and which he received with much content and satisfaction; for, says he, "Now—now indeed do I feel the joy and benefit of that office which Christ hath left in His church." Then praying for the King, that he might long and happily reign over us, and for the peace of the church, he again desired prayers. The next day he received the sacrament, and after that work I desired him to express himself to Dr. Dickenson, a learned physician, Fellow of Merton College, who received the sacrament with him, concerning the King's death, because he had only done it to me in confession; which he did to the same effect as he had spake to me. The rest of his time was spent in devotion and penitential meditations to his last.

'Twere vain to add one word to this letter, yet who can but observe that September the 3d, the day of renowned Montrose's banishment, of the battles of Dunbar and Worcester, and of that monster Oliver Cromwell's death, was also the day when Master Lenthal, Speaker of that long and fatal Parliament, ended his life; the candour and manner of whose departure such as were members (if yet there be any rumps of that rump) will do well to imitate.

NOTES TO WOODSTOCK

NOTE 1.—JOHN'S CHURCH, WOODSTOCK, p. 1

LITTLE remains now of this ancient church, it being rebuilt in 1785, except on the southern side, where a portion of the old structure, with a Norman doorway, is still preserved (*Laing*).

NOTE 2.—*VINDICATION OF THE BOOK OF COMMON PRAYER*, p. 8

The author of this singular and rare tract indulges in the allegorical style, till he fairly hunts down the allegory.

But as for what you call porridge, who hatched the name I know not, neither is it worth the inquiring after, for I hold porridge good food. It is better to a sick man than meat, for a sick man will sooner eat pottage than meat. Pottage will digest with him when meat will not: pottage will nourish the blood, fill the veins, run into every part of a man, make him warmer; so will these prayers do, set our soul and body in a heat, warm our devotion, work fervency in us, lift up our soul to God. For there be herbs of God's own planting in our pottage as you call it—the Ten Commandments, dainty herbs to season any pottage in the world: there is the Lord's Prayer, and that is a most sweet pot-herb cannot be denied; then there is also David's herbs, his prayers and psalms, helps to make our pottage relish well; the psalm of the blessed Virgin, a good pot-herb. Though they be, as some term them, *cock-crowd* pottage, yet they are as sweet, as good, as dainty, and as fresh as they were at the first. The sun hath not made them sour with its heat, neither hath the cold water taken away their vigor and strength. Compare them with the Scriptures, and see if they be not as well seasoned and crumbed. If you find anything in them that is either too salt, too fresh, or too bitter, that herb shall be taken out and better put in, if it can be got, or none. And as in kitchen pottage there are many good herbs, so there is likewise in this church pottage, as you call it. For first, there is in kitchen pottage good water to make them; so, on the contrary, in the other pottage there is the water of life. 2. There is salt to season them; so in the other is a prayer of grace to season their hearts. 3. There is oatmeal to nourish the body; in the other is the bread of life. 4. There is thyme in them to relish them, and it is very wholesome; in the other is the wholesome exhortation not to harden our heart while it is called to-day. This relisheth well. 5. There is a small onion to give a taste; in the other is a good herb, called Lord have mercy on us. These and many other holy herbs are contained in it, all boiling in the heart of man, will make as good pottage as the world can afford, especially if you use these herbs for digestion—the herb repentance, the herb grace, the herb faith, the herb love, the herb hope, the herb good works, the herb piety, the herb zeal, the herb fervency, the herb ardency, the herb constancy, with many more of this nature, most excellent for digestion.

Ohe! jam satis. In this manner the learned divine hunts his metaphor at a very cold scent, through a pamphlet of six mortal quarto pages.

NOTE 3.—RERE-SUPPERS, p. 185

Rere-suppers (*quasi arrière*) belonged to a species of luxury introduced in the jolly days of King James's extravagance, and continued through the subsequent reign. The supper took place at an early hour, six or seven o'clock at latest; the rere-supper was a postliminary banquet—a *hors d'œuvre*, which made its appearance at ten or eleven, and served as an apology for prolonging the entertainment till midnight.

NOTE 4.—DR. MICHAEL HUDSON, p. 203

Michael Hudson, the 'plain-dealing' chaplain of King Charles I., resembled, in his loyalty to that unfortunate monarch, the fictitious character of Doctor

Rochecliffe ; and the circumstances of his death were copied in the narrative of the Presbyterian's account of the slaughter of his schoolfellow. He was chosen by Charles I., along with John Ashburnham. as his guide and attendant, when he adopted the ill-advised resolution of surrendering his person to the Scots army.

He was taken prisoner by the Parliament, remained long in their custody, and was treated with great severity. He made his escape for about a year [two months] in 1647, was retaken, and again escaped in 1648; and, heading an insurrection of Cavaliers, seized on a strong moated house in Lincolnshire [Northamptonshire], called Woodford [Woodcroft] House. He gained the place without resistance; and there are among Peck's *Desiderata Curiosa* several accounts of his death, among which we shall transcribe that of Bishop Kenneth, as the most correct and concise:

"I have been on the spot," saith his lordship, "and made all possible inquiries, and find that the relation given by Mr. Wood may be a little rectified and supplied.

"Mr. Hudson and his beaten party did not fly to Woodcroft, but had quietly taken possession of it, and held it for a garrison, with a good party of horse, who made a stout defense, and frequent sallies, against a party of the Parliament at Stanford, till the colonel commanding there sent a stronger detachment, under a captain, his own kinsman, who was shot from the house, upon which the colonel himself came up to renew the attack and demand surrendry, and brought them to capitulate upon terms of safe quarter. But the colonel, in base revenge, commanded they should not spare that rogue Hudson. Upon which Hudson fought his way up to the leads; and when he saw they were pushing in upon him, threw himself over the battlements [another account says he caught hold of a spout or outstone], and hung by the hands as intending to fall into the moat beneath, till they cut off his wrists and let him drop, and then ran down to hunt him in the water, where they found him paddling with his stumps, and barbarously knocked him on the head.'—Peck's *Desiderata Curiosa*, Book ix.

Other accounts mention he was refused the poor charity of coming to die on land, by one Egborough, servant to Mr. Spinks, the intruder into the parsonage A man called Walker, a chandler or grocer, cut out the tongue of the unfortunate divine, and showed it as a trophy through the country. But it was remarked, with vindictive satisfaction, that Egborough was killed by the bursting of his own gun ; and that Walker, obliged to abandon his trade through poverty, became a scorned mendicant.

For some time a grave was not vouchsafed to the remains of this brave and loyal divine, till one of the other party said, "Since he is dead, let him be buried."

NOTE 5.—CANNIBALISM IMPUTED TO THE CAVALIERS, p. 246

The terrors preceding the civil wars, which agitated the public mind, rendered the grossest and most exaggerated falsehoods current among the people. When Charles I. appointed Sir Thomas Lunsford to the situation of Lord Lieutenant of the Tower, the celebrated John Lillburn takes to himself the credit of exciting the public hatred against this officer and Lord Digby, as pitiless bravoes of the most bloody-minded description, from whom the people were to expect nothing but bloodshed and massacre. Of Sir Thomas Lunsford, in particular, it was reported that his favorite food was the flesh of children, and he was painted like an ogre in the act of cutting a child into steaks and broiling them. The colonel fell at the siege of Bristol in 1643, but the same calumny pursued his remains, and the credulous multitude were told,

> The post who came from Coventry,
> Riding in a red rocket,
> Did tidings tell how Lunsford fell,
> A child's hand in his pocket.

Many allusions to this report, as well as to the credulity of those who believed it, may be found in the satires and lampoons of the time, although, says Dr. Grey, Lunsford was a man of great sobriety, industry, and courage. Butler says, that the preachers

> Made children with their lives to run for't,
> As bad as Bloodybones or Lunsford.

But this extraordinary report is chiefly insisted upon in a comedy called *The Old Troop*, written by John Lacy, the comedian. The scene is laid during the civil wars of England, and the persons of the drama are chiefly those who were in arms for the King. They are represented as plundering the country without mercy, which Lacy might draw from the life, having, in fact, begun his career as a lieutenant of cavalry, in the service of Charles I. The troopers find the peasants loth to surrender to them their provisions, on which, in order to compel them, they pretend to be in earnest in the purpose of eating the children. A scene of coarse but humorous comedy is then introduced, which Dean Swift had not, perhaps, forgotten, when he recommended the eating of the children of the poor as a mode of relieving the distresses of their parents.

Lieutenant. Second me, and I'll make them bring out all they have, I warrant you. Do but talk as if we used to eat children. . . . Why, look you, good woman, we do believe you are poor, so we'll make a shift with our old diet; you have children in the town?

Woman. Why do you ask, sir?

Lieutenant. Only have two or three to supper. Flea-flint, you have the best way of cooking children.

Flea-flint. I can powder them to make you taste your liquor. I am never without a dried child's tongue or ham.

Woman. O! bless me!

Flea-flint. Mine's but the ordinary way; but Ferret-farm is the man; he makes you the savoriest pie of a child chaldron that ever was eat.

Lieutenant. A plague! all the world cannot cook a child like Mr. Raggou [a French cook or messman to the troop, and the buffoon of the piece].

Raggou. Begar me tink so; for vat was me bred in de King of Mogul's kitchen for? Tere ve kill twenty shild of a day. Take you one shild by both his two heels, and put his head between your two leg, den take your great a knife and slice off all de buttock,—so fashion; begar, that make a de best Scots collop in de varle.

Lieutenant. Ah, he makes the best pottage of a child's head and purtenance; but you must boil it with bacon. Woman, you must get bacon.

Ford. And then it must be very young.

Lieutenant. Yes, yes. Good woman, it must be a fine squab child, of half a year old—a man child, dost hear?

Woman. O Lord—yes, sir!—*The Old Troop*, Act iii.

After a good deal more to this purpose, the villagers determine to carry forth their sheep, poultry, etc., to save their children. In the mean time, the Cavaliers are in some danger of being cross-bit, as they then called it; that is, caught in their own snare. A woman enters, who announces herself thus:—

Nurse. By your leaves, your good worships, I have made bold to bring you in some provisions.

Ferret. Provisions! where, where is thy provisions?

Nurse. Here, an 't please you, I have brought you a couple of fine fleshy children

Cornet. Was ever such a horrid woman! what shall we do?

Nurse. Truly, gentlemen, they are fine squab children: shall I turn them up? They have the bravest brawny buttocks.

Lieutenant. No, no; but, woman, art thou not troubled to part with thy children?

Nurse. Alas, they are none of mine, sir, they are but nurse children. . . .

Lieutenant. What a beast is this!—whose children are they?

Nurse. A Londoner's that owes me for a year's nursing; I hope they'll prove excellent meat; they are twins too.

Raggou. Aha, but! but begar we never eat no twin shild, de law forbid that.—
—(Act iv.)

In this manner the Cavaliers escape from the embarrassing consequences of their own stratagem, which, as the reader will perceive, has been made use of in chapter xx.

Note 6.—Will D'Avenant and Shakspeare, p. 304

This gossiping tale is to be found in the Variorum Shakspeare. D'Avenant did not much mind throwing out hints in which he sacrificed his mother's character to his desire of being held a descendant from the admirable Shakspeare.

Note 7.—"Besides, by all the village boys," p. 304

We observe this couplet in Fielding's farce of *Tumble-down-Dick*, founded on the same classical story. As it was current in the time of the Commonwealth, it must have reached the author of *Tom Jones* by tradition; for no one will suspect the present author of making the anachronism.

NOTE 8.—DR. ROCHECLIFFE'S QUOTATIONS, p. 351

The quotations of the learned doctor and antiquary were often left uninterpreted, though seldom uncommunicated, owing to his contempt for those who did not understand the learned languages, and his dislike to the labor of translation, for the benefit of ladies and of country gentlemen. That fair readers and rural thanes may not on this occasion burst in ignorance, we add the meaning of the passage in the text—"Virtue requires the aid of a governor and a director; vices are learned without a teacher."

NOTE 9.—THE FAMILISTS, p. 356

The Familists were originally founded by David George of Delft, an enthusiast, who believed himself the Messiah. They branched off into various sects of Grindletonians, Familists of the Mountains, of the Valleys, Familists of Cape Order, etc. etc., of the Scattered Flock, etc. etc. Among doctrines too wild and foul to be quoted, they held the lawfulness of occasional conformity with any predominant sect when it suited their convenience, of complying with the order of any magistrate, or superior power, however sinful. They disowned the principal doctrines of Christianity, as a law which had been superseded by the advent of David George; nay, obeyed the wildest and loosest dictates of evil passions, and are said to have practised among themselves the grossest libertinism. See Edwards's *Gangrœna*, Pagitt's *Heresiography*, and a very curious work written by Ludovic Claxton, one of the leaders of the sect, called the *Lost Sheep Found*, small quarto, London, 1660.

NOTE 10.—PATRICK CAREY, p. 382

"You do not know Patrick Carey," says King Charles in the novel; and, what is more singular, Patrick Carey has had two editors, each unknown alike to the other, except by name only. In 1771, Mr. John Murray published Carey's *Poems*, from a collection said to be in the hands of the Rev. Mr. Pierrepoint Crimp [Cromp]. A very probable conjecture is stated, that the author was only known to private friendship. As late as 1819, the Author of *Waverley*, ignorant of the edition of 1771, published a second quarto from an elaborate manuscript, though in bad order, apparently the autograph of the poet. Of Carey, the second editor, like the first, only knew the name and the spirit of the verses. He has since been enabled to ascertain that the poetic Cavalier was a younger brother of the celebrated Henry Lord Carey, who fell at the battle of Newbury, and escaped the researches of Horace Walpole, to whose list of noble authors he would have been an important addition. So completely has the fame of the great Lord Falkland eclipsed that of his brothers, that this brother Patrick has been overlooked even by genealogists.

NOTE 11.—SIGNAL OF DANGER, p. 392

On a particular occasion, a lady, suspecting, by the passage of a body of guards through her estate, that the arrest of her neighbor, Patrick Home of Polwarth, afterwards first Earl of Marchmont, was designed, sent him a feather by a shepherd boy, whom she dared not trust with a more explicit message. Danger sharpens the intellect, and this hint was the commencement of those romantic adventures which gave Grizzel Lady Murray the materials from which she compiled her account of her grandfather's escape, published by Mr. Thomas Thomson, Deputy-Register of Scotland. The anecdote of the feather does not occur there, but the Author has often heard it from the late Lady Diana Scott, the lineal descendant and representative of Patrick Earl of Marchmont.

NOTE 12.—TREDAGH, p. 435

Tredagh, or Drogheda, was taken by Cromwell in 1649, by storm, and the governor and whole garrison put to the sword.

NOTE 13.—BEVIS, p. 465

It may interest some readers to know, that Bevis, the gallant hound, one of the handsomest and most active of the ancient Highland deer-hounds, had his prototype in a dog called Maida, the gift of the late Chief of Glengarry to the Author. A beautiful sketch of him was made by Edwin Landseer, and afterwards engraved. I cannot suppress the avowal of some personal vanity when I mention, that a friend, going through Munich, picked up a common snuff-box, such as are sold for one franc, on which was displayed the form of this veteran favorite, simply marked as "Der Lieblingshund von Walter Scott." Mr. Landseer's painting is at Blair-Adam, the property of my venerable friend, the Right Honorable Lord Chief Commissioner Adam.

GLOSSARY

OF

WORDS, PHRASES, AND ALLUSIONS

Accord, harmony
Achor, valley of (p. 438). See Joshua vii.
Actum atque tractatum, done and treated of
Adjutator, a misconception for *agitator*, a soldier of the Parliamentary forces chosen by his comrades to look after their common interests
Adust, looking as if burned or scorched
Æger intemperans, etc. (p. 470), an intractable patient makes the doctor cruel, and a wound that will not heal must be cut out with the knife
Ail, to prevent, hinder
A la mort, all melancholy, despondent
Alert, alerte, an, an alarm, surprise, sudden attack
Alicant, a strong, sweet Spanish wine, made at Alicante
Aliquid divini, something of the divine about it
Allen Thomas, mathematician (1542-1632), regarded by the vulgar as a magician
Alleyn Edward, actor (1566-1626), and founder of Dulwich College, London
Ambagitory, circumlocutory
Andrew Ferrara, a Scottish broadsword
Apelles, a famous painter of ancient Greece (Asia Minor)
Areopagus, a court of ancient Athens, which safeguarded the purity of religious faith
Argalus. See footnote on p. 55 above
"*As gentle and as jocund*," etc. (p. 417), from *Richard II.*, Act i. sc. 3
Aston, Sir Jacob, more probably it should be Sir Arthur Aston (d. 1649), the only general officer of the Catholic religion in the Royalist army
Athenæ Oxonienses. See Wood, Anthony à
Athenodorus, a Stoic philosopher, a native of Tarsus, who possessed some influence with the Roman Emperor Augustus

Badenoch, a wild district in the southeast of Inverness-shire
Ballads, bid him go sell his. See Bid him go, etc.
Bannatyne, an Edinburgh literary club, founded in 1823 by Sir Walter Scott and others, for printing rare works illustrating Scottish history, topography, literature, etc. It was dissolved in 1861
Bastinado, a mode of punishment by beating the soles of the feet, in Turkey and Persia
Baxter, Master, the celebrated Presbyterian divine (1615-1691), author of *The Saints' Everlasting Rest*
Bedlam, Tom of. See Tom of Bedlam
Bevis of Hampton or *Southampton*, hero of a mediæval romance of chivalry
Bide the bit and the buffet, endure a good meal as well as a blow
Bid him go sell his ballads (p. 451). The origin of this saying is probably the anecdote recorded (*Biog. Brit.*, p. 631) of General Lesley, when the Cavalier poet, John Cleveland, was brought before him with nothing in his pockets except political ballads
Bilbo, or *Bilboa*, a sword, made at Bilboa in Spain
Bilked, tricked, deceived
Black-jack, a beer-jug, made of waxed leather
Blaud, a rough blow
Blenheim, the seat presented to the great Duke of Marlborough by the English nation, planned by Sir John Vanburgh (*q. v.*)
Bobadil, Captain, a character in Ben Jonson's *Every Man in his Humor*
Bon camarado, a good comrade
Bonos socios, good comrades
Booth and Middleton, rising of, at Chester in August 1659, the leaders being George Booth and Sir Thomas Middleton
Bottle, oracle of. The search for Bacbuc, the oracular bottle that was to give an answer to the question, "Shall Panurge marry or not?" is described in Rabelais's *Pantagruel*, Books iv. and v.
Boulter, boulder, large stone
Bow-pot, or *bough-pot*, a pot or vase for holding boughs or flowers
Brambletye House, "or *Cavaliers and Roundheads*," a historical novel (1826), by Horace Smith
Bread of Gude, God's bread, an oath
Brentford, attack on. There in 1642 the Royalists defeated the Parliamentary troops
Brown baker, a baker of brown bread
Brownist, an adherent of Robert Brown (1550-1630), who dissented from the Church of England

form of church government

Bucephalus, the favorite war-horse of Alexander the Great

Buckingham, Duke of (rising of), in Surrey in 1648

Bulla, an ornament worn by young Romans round the neck, but laid aside on attaining manhood

Busled, bustled

Butler (p. 480). *See Hudibras*, Part III. canto ii. lines 1112, 1113

Cambyses's vein. See King Cambyses's vein

Canted, tilted, turned in a slanting position

Carolus, a gold coin struck in the reign of Charles (Lat. *Carolus*) I., and worth 20s. or a little more

Cebes, Emblem of (p. 327), a table exhibiting the dangers and temptations of human life, described in a little book by Cebes, a philosopher of Thebes, and a pupil and friend of Socrates

Century White. See Peveril of the Peak, Note 1

Chaldron, or *chaudron*, entrails

Cheat, nubbing. See Trine to the nubbing cheat

Cheveron, or *chevron*, a glove

Choused, cheated, defrauded

City Petition, craving the abolition of Episcopacy, presented by Alderman Pennington on 11th Dec. 1641, and said to have been signed by 20,000 citizens of London

Clarendon, Edward Hyde, Earl of, minister of Charles II. after the Restoration, and historian.

Clefts, split wood for fuel

Clouterly, clumsy, awkward

Cock-crowed, that the cock has crowed over of a morning, *i.e.* no longer fresh, stale

Colchester was reduced, by Fairfax in August 1648; two of the Royalist defenders, Sir Charles Lucas and Sir George Lisle, were executed by the victors. *See* Defoe, *Tour in the Eastern Counties* (1724)

Collet, the edge round the setting of a precious stone

Colluvies omnium gentium, refuse, off-scourings of all nations

Comus, a poem (1634), by Milton

Concatenation accordingly, in a (p. 124). This phrase is put by Goldsmith into the mouth of one of Tony Lumpkin's boon companions in *She Stoops to Conquer*, Act i. sc. 2

Conformable, suitable, becoming to one's rank or condition

Conspiracy, horrors of (p. 268), an allusion to Shakespeare, *Julius Cæsar*, Act ii. sc. 1

Cordovan, made at Cordoba or Cordova in Spain

Corps de garde, the guard or sentinel detachment

Couteau de chasse, a hanger, hunting-knife

Cowley, Abraham, poet (1618–1667), famous for his ingenuity and versatility of mind

C. R. (p. 10), *Carolus Rex*, *i.e.* King Charles

Croats, a Slav people dwelling between the Adriatic and Hungary, who furnished excellent light cavalry to the Imperial armies during the Thirty Years, Seven Years, and other wars

Cross (in purse), money stamped or marked with a cross

Culverin, an early form of cannon, very long in shape

Cutter's law, that those who have something shall share with those who have nothing; "cutter" means a ruffian, bravo

Dean, Forest of. See Forest of Dean

Dedalian labyrinth, constructed in the island of Crete, to keep the Minotaur, by an Athenian inventor named Dædalos

Defensio Populi Anglicani, by Milton, was written (1651) to justify the execution of Charles I., in reply to the Dutch scholar Salmasius

Demas. See Second Epistle to Timothy iv. 10

De quoi, the wherewithall, the essential thing

Der Lieblingshund von Walter Scott, Walter Scott's favorite dog

Deus adjutor meus, the Lord is my helper

Devinctus beneficio, bound by kindness

Digby, Lord, first Earl of Bristol (1580–1654), statesman of Charles I., proposed Lunsford for the post of lieutenant of the Tower

Divertisement, amusement, pastime

Dog, story of desertion by (p. 47), is told in Froissart's *Chronicles*, trans. Johnes, vol. iv. chap. cxxxii.

Dorset killed the Lord Bruce. See The Guardian, Nos. 129, 133. The duel was fought at Bergen-op-Zoom in Holland in 1613

Doune, John, poet (1573–1631), famous for his wit and his handsome person

Dowsets, or *doucets*, testicles of the deer

Drayton, Mike, poet (1563–1631), author of the geographical account of Great Britain entitled *Polyolbion*, and the dainty piece of fancy, the poem *Nymphidia*

Drumble, to be confused, mumble

Drummond of Hawthornden, Scottish poet (1585–1649) a fervent admirer of Charles I.

Dudgeon-dagger, a small dagger, with an ornamental wooden haft

Dunkirk, was taken by the forces of Cromwell in 1658

Dunny, deaf, dull of apprehension

Dutch-land, or *Deutschland*, Germany

Edwards, Master, Thomas Edwards, a fanatical Puritan divine, author of *Gangræna, or a Catalogue of Many of the Errors, Blasphemies, and Pernicious Practices of the Sectaries of this Time* (1646)

Ehud (p. 435). *See* Judges iii.

En berger, en bergère, after the manner of the

swains and shepherdesses in pastoral poetry
Ethnic, heathen, non-Christian
Euelme, or *Ewelme*, a village 3 miles from Wallingford in Oxfordshire
Euryalus. *See* Nisus

Falkland, Lord, Lucius Cary, a gallant adherent of Charles I., who fell at Newbury, 20th September 1643
Family of Love. *See* Love, Family of
Fauconberg, Thomas Belasyse, Earl, son and grandson of Royalists, went over to Cromwell, and in 1667 married his daughter Mary
Faustus, Dr. Faust of the well-known German legend
Fecit iste Rex, etc. (p. 477). This king made the park of Woodstock, and the palace there; this was the first park in England, and measured seven miles in circumference; it was laid out in the fourteenth year of this king, or a little later
Fielding's "*TUMBLE-DOWN-DICK*." *See* Tumble-down-Dick
Foin, to thrust in fencing
Forest of Dean, an ancient forest in Gloucestershire
Fortune playhouse, in Aldersgate, London, opened in 1600
Fox (broadsword), an old slang expression for a sword
Frank, a pen, pig-sty, used jocularly
Frayed, frightened, terrified
Fugit ad salices, fled (for refuge) to the willows (or osiers)
Fuller, Thomas, the shrewd and kindly divine of the Church of England (1630–61)

Galloway nag, a horse of small breed, under fourteen hands high
Gamashes, leggings
Gambade, a curvet, gambol
Gardner, Saunders. *See* Know (to) Duke of Norfolk, etc.
Garr'd, made, caused, forced
Gate of horn (p. 232). According to the ancients, dreams come to us through two gates—one of ivory, these are illusory; the other of horn, which alone prove true
Gear, business, affair
"*Gentle daughter*," etc. (p. 20), from *Henry IV.*, Part II. Act ii. sc. 3
Glanville, Joseph, Church of England clergyman, who, though something of a rationalizer, defended the belief in *Witches and Witchcraft* (1666)
Goring, Lord George, Royalist cavalry general in the Civil War
Gossipred, friendship, good-fellowship
Grandfather of Navarre, Henry of Navarre, afterwards Henry IV. of France
Grand Monarque, Louis XIV. of France (1643–1715)
Grand Seignior, or *Signior*, the sultan of the Turks
Green's "*ARCADIA*," or *Menaphon* (1599), by Robert Greene, author of *Friar Bacon and Friar Bungay*
Grey, Dr. Zachary, edited an edition of *Hudibras* (1744), with copious notes
Grouthead, or *growthead*, a lout, blockhead
Guardian, The, a periodical issued by Steele in 1713 as successor to *The Spectator*
Gudgeoned, cheated, imposed on
Guy of Warwick, hero of a medieval romance of chivalry

Haie, or *hay*, a snare or net for catching rabbits and other animals
Hail, whole
Hammond, Robert, a Parliamentary officer, upon whose protection Charles I. threw himself after his escape from Hampton Court in November 1647, and from whom he was torn by the Army in the November following
Hampden, John, champion of liberty, a leader of the Long Parliament, and an opponent of Charles I.
Hans en kelder (p. 469), Jack in the cellar, a favorite Dutch toast to an expected "little stranger," drunk in a peculiar cup, out of which, when the wine was poured in, the figure of a tiny infant rose to the surface
Haro, or *harrow*, a cry for help, of indignation, lamentation
Harrington's "*OCEANA*," a book, written partly as a romance, partly as a philosophical treatise, by James Harrington, to demonstrate the ideally best form of government
Harrison's Rota Club, more correctly *James Harrington's*, formed in November 1659 to discuss the political theories laid down in his *Oceana* (1656). *See* Harrington's *Oceana* above
Hearne at Windsor, a spectral hunter. *See Merry Wives of Windsor*, Act iv. sc. 4
Hebe, in ancient Greek mythology, cupbearer to the Gods in Olympus
Hemminge, or *Heming, John*, fellow-actor (d. 1630) of Shakespeare, and editor (with Condell) of the first folio edition of Shakespeare's plays
Henry of Bolingbroke and the dog. *See* Dog, etc.
Henry of France, his grandfather. Charles I. of England married Henrietta Maria, daughter of Henry IV. of France
Henry Quatre, Henry IV. of France
Hertford, Marquis of, William Seymour, appointed tutor or governor to Charles (II.) in 1642
Highgate oath, said to have been formerly exacted from travelers passing over Highgate Hill, on the north side of London, that they would never eat brown bread when they could get white, etc., but with the proviso, "unless they preferred it"
"*Himself he on an earwig set*," etc. (p. 303), from Drayton's *Nymphidia, the Court of Fairy* (1627)
Hogs-Norton, noodles of. *See* Noodles, etc.
Holland, Lord (rising of), in Surrey in 1648

Hollinshed, or *Holinshed Richard*, English chronicler of the 16th century,

Holyrood, palace of, in flames (p. 176). The abbey and palace of Holyrood were burned by the English under the Earl of Hertford (Protector Somerset) in 1544

Horn, gate of. See Gate of horn

Hors d'œuvre, an extra dish, meal

Hot, hit, struck

Hough, hock-joint

Hudibras, the poem (1662–78) by Samuel Butler, satirizing the Puritans

Hudson, Dr. Michael, escaped in November 1647, and was recaptured in January 1648 (to correct Note 4, p. 479)

Hunt counter, to go away from the game, back along the track

Hyde. See Clarendon, Earl of

"*I'll so maul you*," etc. (p. 298), from *King John*, Act iv. sc. 3

In cuerpo, without upper cloak, with body exposed

In verbo sacerdotis, on the word of a priest

Ipse dixit, the mere statement, simple assertion

Isis, the name given to the Thames above Oxford

Jack of Leyden. See Leyden, Jack of

January, Thirtieth, date of the beheading of Charles I.

J. B. (motto to chap. v. p. 57), James Ballantyne, the printer. "Where is this from?" asked Ballantyne on the proofsheet. "The Devil," wrote Scott; but crossing that out, he substituted "J. B."

Jeanneton, the typical simpleton of the French pastoral romances

Joal'd, or *jowled*, dashed with violence

Juvenal, a Roman satirical poet of the 1st century A. D.

Keimbolton, or *Kimbolton, Lord*, earlier title of the Parliamentary general, the Earl of Manchester

Killigrew, Thomas, groom of the bedchamber to Charles II., a witty reprobate and manager of the king's players

Kiug Cambyses's vein, an allusion to the chief character, a blustering, noisy, ranting fellow, in *Cambyses, King of Persia*, a play by Thomas Preston

Knipperdoling, or *Knipperdolling, Bernhard*, an Anabaptist leader at Münster in 1534–35. *See further* Leyden, Jack of

Know (to) Duke of Norfolk from Saunders Gardner (p. 217). A proverbial expression. "I believe the genuine reading is to teach a man to know the Lord his God from Tam Frazer" (Scott's marginal note on proof-sheet)

Laban, "*You have*," etc. (p. 358). *See* Genesis xxxi. 30

La Belle Gabrielle, Gabrielle d'Estrées, mistress of Henry IV. of France

Lacy, John. See Note 5, p. 480

Lambert, John, republican soldier of the Fifth Monarchy type, and long a supporter of Cromwell

Lance-prisade, or *lancepesade*, a sort of temporary corporal

Latus clavus, the broad stripe placed on a young Roman noble's tunic when he became a senator

Laving, lifting up water and pouring it into a utensil, lading out

Leaguer, a fortified camp

Leaked, voided urine

Lee Victor sic voluit, such was the will of Victor Lee

Leslie, David, a soldier under Gustavus Augustus of Sweden, and later under Alexander Leslie, Earl of Leven, whom Cromwell defeated at Dunbar in 1650

Levant, a signal with a trumpet

Leyden, Jack of, or *Johann Bockhold*, who had himself crowned "king of the New Zion" that the Anabaptists established at Münster, in Westphalia, in 1534–35, where they indulged in the wildest excesses

"*Like sweet bells jangled*," etc. (p. 309), *Hamlet*, from Act iii. sc. 1

Lillburn, or *Lilburne-John*, a Leveller or ultra-republican, a turbulent agitator of the time of Charles I. and Cromwell

Lindabrides (p. 341), a woman of easy virtue, the name is borrowed from the heroine of *The Mirror of Knighthood*, a 16th-century translation of a Spanish romance of chivalry

Lindor, the literary type of the love-sick swain in Spanish literature

Lobster, nickname for a soldier, because of his red coat

Longsword, Earl of Salisbury, son of Henry II. and (according to untenable tradition) Rosamond Clifford

Love, Family of, or *Familists*, a division of the Anabaptists, traced to the Dutchman, David Joris or George; they made some stir in England in the times of Elizabeth and James I. *See* Note 9, p. 482

Lucretius, a Roman poet, of the 1st century B. C., a professed disbeliever in religious influences

Lunsford, Sir Thomas, a Royalist commander. *See further* Note 5, p. 480

"*Made children*," etc. (p. 481), from *Hudibras*, Part III. canto ii. lines 1112, 1113

Madrier, the plank on which a petard was fixed or mounted

Magna Temporum, etc. (p. 470), happy are the times in which you are allowed to think what you like, and say what you think

Maher-shalal-hash-baz, the son of Isaiah the prophet; the name signifies "The spoil speedeth, the prey hasteth," and points to the plundering of Damascus and Samaria shortly to take place by the king of Assyria. *See* Isaiah viii. 1-4

Make, or *maik*, a halfpenny

Makebate, one who stirs up quarrels and dissensions

Makkedah, cave of (p. 440). *See* Joshua x.

Mallard, the wild drake, male of the common wild duck

Malleus hæresis, the hammer of heresy
Manchet, a small loaf of fine white bread
Maravedi, an old Spanish copper coin worth less than a farthing
Mas John, any Presbyterian divine (p. 254). The General Assembly ordained, just previous to the battle of Dunbar, that the King should do public penance for the sins of the crown
Mask, man in the (p. 282), the public executioner, who was masked when he performed his gruesome functions
Mattan, slay (p. 202). *See* 2 Kings xi. 18
Meikle, much, a good deal
Mermaid, a tavern in Cheapside, a favorite haunt of Ben Jonson and other wits in the 17th century
Micelgemote, great council of the kingdom, national assembly
Moab, tyrant of (p. 435). *See* Judges iii.
Mogul, King of, the Great Mogul or Emperor of Delhi in India
Mohun, an actor, was a major in the Royalist army
Moriscoes, the descendants of the Moors settled in Spain
Mother Redcap. *Compare Fortunes of Nigel*, Glossary
Muggletonian, a follower of Lodowick Muggleton (1607-97) and John Reeve, who claimed to be prophets and taught peculiar doctrines
Muscadine, a sweet, strong wine made in Italy and France

Navarre, grandfather of. *See* Grandfather of Navarre
Newcastle, Duke of, his book (p. 302), entitled *La Méthode et Invention Nouvelle de dresser les Chevaux* (1657), and adorned with very fine engravings, was written by the Duke of Newcastle, Charles I.'s general, who took great delight in training horses
Nicholas, Sir Edward, Secretary of State to Charles II. after the Restoration
Nisi dignus vindice nodus, unless the difficulty call for such a deliverer
Nisus and Euryalus, devoted friends, Nisus being a companion of Æneas. *See* Virgil's *Æneid*, Bk. ix.
Noble, a gold coin=6s. 8d.
Nom de guerre, pseudonym, nickname
Noodles of Hogs-Norton, an old English proverb, pointing to boorishness and stupidity
Norfolk, Duke of. *See* Know (to) Duke of Norfolk, etc.
Nullifidian, one who believes nothing, an unbeliever
Nunc Dimittis, the well-known canticle of the Prayer Book
Nuzled, or nuzzled, hid the nose under the bedclothes

Odds pitlikins, or Ods pitikins, a corruption of God's pity! a kind of oath
Œil de bœuf, an oval window, small octagonal hall
Ohe, jam satis, Ah! enough, enough!
Orestes and Pylades, cousins and devoted friends; Orestes was the son of Agamemnon and Clytæmnestra
Other-guess, other-gates, or *other-guise*, another sort or fashion
Over-red, to cover over with red coloring matter, to summon up courage against (*Macbeth*, Act v. sc. 3)
Owen, Sir John, attempted in 1648 to stir up North Wales for the King

Pacatumque regit, etc. (p. 471), he rules over a world at peace through the virtues of his forefathers
Pagitt, Ephraim, a London clergyman, author of *Heresiography, or Description of the Hereticks and Sectaries of these Latter Times* (1645)
Parcel, partly, to some extent
Parma non bene relicta, his shield being ingloriously left behind him
Parthenia. *See* footnote on p. 55 above
Paschal, Easter
Passado, a forward thrust in fencing
Passmented, laced
Pater patriæ, the father of his country
Pax nascitur ex bello, peace grows out of war
Peaked, or peeked, peeped, looked in a prying manner
Penny-fee, wages paid in money
Percustum Egyptium, etc. (p. 389), he hid in the sand the Egyptian that he had killed
Periapt, a charm, amulet
Petronal, a horseman's pistol or small carbine
Philaster, a character in a play (1620) with that title by Beaumont and Fletcher
Philomath, lover of learning
Pirithous. *See* Theseus
Pis-aller, the last resource
Plait-il? Your pleasure?
Poins, a character in Shakespeare's *Henry IV*.
Point de cérémonie, make no ceremony
Point of war, a signal by beat of drum or by trumpet
Portugal piece, a silver coin=8 reals=4s., sometimes called a piece of eight
Pottle, a measure of wine, a large tankard
Prophet and frogs (p. 358), an allusion to Revelation xvi. 13
Prophets prophesy fasely, etc. (p. 358), from Jeremiah v. 31
Propria quæ maribus, the right thing for men
Prynne, Master, an intemperate pamphleteer, and a bitter opponent of Laud, published in 1627 *The Unlovelinesse of Lovelockes*, an attack upon the Cavaliers
Pulvis fulminans, fulminating powder
Purchas, Samuel, author of *Purchas, his Pilgrimage; or Relations of the World and the Religions observed in all Ages* (1613)
Pylades. *See* Orestes
Pym, John, a champion of liberty and opponent of Charles I., who impeached Buckingham, Strafford, and Laud

"*Qualiacunque voles,*" etc. (p. 190). The Jews will sell you whatever dreams you wish for; from Juvenal's *Satires*, vi. 547

Quasi arrière, as it were *arrière*, *i. e.* behind, later

Quean, wench, woman of light reputation

Questing Hound, one that gives tongue when in pursuit of game

Quillet, a subtlety, nicety, quibble

Quoit down, to throw, hurl down

Rainsborough, one of Cromwell's officers, was killed, whilst resisting capture, by a party of Royalists sent from Pontefract, in an inn at Doncaster, on 29th October 1648

Ralpho, the Independent squire of Hudibras (*q. v.*)

Ranter, or Familist. See Note 9, p. 482

"*Rash Humor,*" etc. (p. 150), from *Julius Cæsar*, Act iv. sc. 3

Ratio, reason, conclusion

Rectus in curia, right with the court, of good character before the court

"*Respect for thy great place,*" etc. (p. 420), from *Measure for Measure*, Act v. sc. 1

Richard II., deserted by his dog. See Dog, etc.

Rocket, or rochet, a short cloak

Rondelai, a peculiar form of French verse

Rood, cross

Roquelaure, a short cloak worn by both men and women

Rota. See Harrison's Rota Club

Rouse, a bumper

Roxburghe, a book club, instituted in London in 1812, for printing old and rare books

Rustica Fidele, more correctly *Phidyle*, to whom Horace addressed the 23d Ode of the Third Book of his *Odes*

Sack-posset, a drink made of Canary wine, milk, etc.

St. John, Oliver (*circa* 1598–1673), lawyer, advised Hampden in the Ship Money affair, and was a partisan of Cromwell, whose cousin he married

Salvo, reservation

Sanctum sanctorum, holy of holies, most private apartment

Sanhedrim, the national council of the Jews

Sasine and livery, in English law, livery with seisin, an old form of conveying land

Saviolo, Vincent, an Italian fencing-master, author of *V. Saviolo, his Practice* (1595), a work on the management of the weapons in a duel

Scald, or scalled, scurvy, paltry, contemptible

Scumber, to dung

Sedley, Sir Charles, a profligate wit and poet of the court of Charles II.

Selah, a word occurring at the end of certain verses in the Psalms and elsewhere in the Old Testament, apparently a musical term, but of unknown meaning

Seven Sleepers, noble youths of Ephesus, who were shut up in a cave during the persecution of the Christians by the Roman Emperor Decius, about 250; there they slept until the year 447, when they awakened for a short space, and then fell back into their last long sleep

Sicilian Vespers, the massacre of their French oppressors by the people of Sicily, on 30th March 1282

Siloe, or Siloam tower of, an allusion to St. Luke xiii. 4

Sinning against our mercies, being ungrateful for the favors of Providence—a Scotch phrase

Siserary, a telling blow, vehement attack

Skeldering, living by begging, tricking, etc.

Skink, to pour out wine

Slie, sly

Slot, the track, footmarks

Snift, a snivel

Spadroon, a large two-handed sword

Spay'd, castrated

Splendida moles, a grand work

Squab, an unfledged bird, very young animal

Stirling, Lord, William Alexander, Earl of Stirling, Scottish poet (died 1640)

Stow, John, English chronicler (1525–1605)

Stramacon, or stramazone, a wrist-stroke in fencing

Sub ferula, under the master's rod, under tutelage

Sully, Maximilian de Béthune, Duke of, minister to Henry IV. of France, and personally a man of surly and imperious temper

Swattering, moving rapidly and noisily in water

Tanquam deus ex machina, like the personal interference of a deity

Tantivy boys, roystering fellows, strictly the High Church Tories of James II.'s time

"*Telephus et Peleus,*" etc. (p. 352), from Horace, *Ars Poetica*, 96, 97

Terras quas Rex, etc. (p. 477), lands which the king exchanged with the Templars

Tester, an old silver coin =6d.

Thebans, in ancient Greece, were twitted with being stupid

"*The post who came,*" etc. (p. 480), altered from John Cleveland's poem, "Rupertismus" (*Works*, 1677)

"*There's such divinity,*" etc. (p. 272), from *Hamlet*, Act iv. sc. 5

"*These thoughts may startle,*" etc. (p. 307), from Milton's *Comus* (1634)

Theseus and Pirithous, devoted friends; Theseus being an Athenian hero and Pirithous one of the Lapithæ. *See* Homer's *Iliad*, Bk. ii.

Thirtieth, January, the date of the beheading of Charles I.

Tiffany, a kind of gauze or thin silk

Tike, or tyke, a dog, cur

Tire upon, to seize and tear the quarry

"'*Tis sport to have the engineer,*" etc. (p. 417), from *Hamlet*, Act iii. sc. 4

Titus, bishopric of (p. 446). Titus the companion of St. Paul, was the first

bishop of Gortyna (Crete)
Toledo, a sword made at Toledo in Spain
Tompkin's and Challoner's matter. In 1643 these gentlemen, with Waller and others, tried to form a party amongst the Londoners to mediate between the King and Parliament. Charles countenanced the movement. Challoner and Tomkins were executed by order of the House of Commons
Tom of Bedlam, crazy pauper, an inmate of Bethlehem Hospital (for the Insane) in London
Topiary art, landscape-gardening
"*To witch the world*," etc. (p. 303), from *Henry IV.*, Part I. Act iv. sc. 1
Trevisses, divisions between the stalls in a stable
Trine to the nubbing cheat, to hang on the gallows
Trinidado, Trinidad tobacco
Tuck, a long, narrow sword, rapier
Tumble-down-Dick, or Phœton in Suds, by Henry Fielding, was acted at the Haymarket, London, in 1737
Tutbury bull-running. Under a charter granted by John of Gaunt in 1381, the minstrels in the honor of Tutbury, Staffordshire, held a court there every 16th August, and were allowed to chase a maddened bull, which, if they caught it before sunset, they were permitted to keep

Umbles, or humbles, entrails of the deer
Unbated (weapon), unblunted, having no button on the point
Unco, unusually, uncommonly
Utopia, an ideal state with an ideal society and an ideal government

Valeat quantum, so far as is requisite
Vanburgh, more correctly *Vanbrugh, Sir John*, dramatist and architect of the reigns of William III. and Anne
Vane, Sir Henry, a leader of the Independents and a bitter opponent of the Church of England
Venus and Adonis, Shakespeare's poem
Verdurer, an officer who has charge of the trees and underwood in a forest
Verstegan, Richard, an English antiquary, who died in 1635
Vert and venison, the forest trees and the game amongst them
Vertumnus and Pomona, The former, an Etruscan and Roman divinity, assumed various disguises in order to gain access to Pomona, goddess of fruit-trees
Vicars, John, a Presbyterian zealot (1582-1652), who wrote a few poems
Villiers, George, second Duke of Buckingham, a fickle but brilliant courtier of Charles II.
Vindex, deliverer, liberator
Vintry, a portion of Thames Street, London, between London and Blackfriars Bridges, where the wine-merchants unshipped their wines

Waller, Edmund, poet, who praised both Cromwell and Charles I.
Wanion, with a, with a vengeance, mischief be to him (it)
Watling Street, an old Roman Road, running from Dover, through London (where was a street of this name) and York, to the North of England
Weird, destiny, fate
Western Rising. In 1645 the Royalists organized the Western Association of Cornwall, Devon, Somerset, and Dorset, as a counterpoise to the Parliamentary Association of the Eastern counties
Whittle, a large knife, usually carried at the girdle
Who but you, a peculiar form of emphasis, laying stress upon the person indicated
"*Why, what an intricate impeach*," etc. (p. 300), from *Comedy of Errors*, Act v. sc. 1
Widow of Watling Street, an old English *ballad*
Will, honest old, Shakespeare
Wilmot (p. 60), Henry Earl of Rochester, father of John, second Earl of Rochester, the witty reprobate of Charles II.'s reign
Wilmot (p. 281), John Earl of Rochester
Withers, or Wither, George, poet and satirist (1588–1667)
Wood, Anthony a, antiquary and historian of Oxford, whose *Athenœ Oxonienses* (1691) gives a history of all Oxford's scholars and writers between 1500 and 1690
Woodford House, Lincolnshire (p. 480), should read Woodcroft House, Northamptonshire
Word'st me, girl, a reminiscence of *Antony and Cleopatra*, Act v. sc. 2
Wussing, wishing

Young Man (p. 9), Prince Charles, afterwards Charles II., was at the time of the opening of this novel a fugitive in England, seeking to escape to the Continent
"*You saw young Harry*," etc. (p. 303), from *Henry IV.*, Part I. Act iv. sc. 1

INDEX

INDEX

www.ingramcontent.com/pod-product-compliance
Lightning Source LLC
Chambersburg PA
CBHW022013120726
47902CB00012B/2

* 9 7 8 1 4 3 4 4 1 3 3 5 2 *